ALSO BY CHIMAMANDA NGOZI ADICHIE
FROM CLIPPER LARGE PRINT

Half of a Yellow Sun
The Thing Around Your Neck

Americanah

Chimamanda Ngozi Adichie

W F HOWES LTD

This large print edition published in 2013 by
W F Howes Ltd
Unit 4, Rearsby Business Park, Gaddesby Lane,
Rearsby, Leicester LE7 4YH

1 3 5 7 9 10 8 6 4 2

First published in the United Kingdom in 2013
by Fourth Estate

A CIP catalogue record for this book is available
from the British Library

ISBN 978 1 47124 111 6

Typeset by Palimpsest Book Production Limited,
Falkirk, Stirlingshire
Printed and bound by
CPI Group (UK), Ltd, Croydon, CR0 4YY

This book is for our next generation, *ndi na-abia n'iru*: Toks, Chisom, Amaka, Chinedum, Kamsiyonna and Arinze.

For my wonderful father in this, his eightieth year.

And, as always, for Ivara.

PART I

CHAPTER 1

Princeton, in the summer, smelled of nothing, and although Ifemelu liked the tranquil greenness of the many trees, the clean streets and stately homes, the delicately overpriced shops and the quiet, abiding air of earned grace, it was this, the lack of a smell, that most appealed to her, perhaps because the other American cities she knew well had all smelled distinctly. Philadelphia had the musty scent of history. New Haven smelled of neglect. Baltimore smelled of brine, and Brooklyn of sun-warmed garbage. But Princeton had no smell. She liked taking deep breaths here. She liked watching the locals who drove with pointed courtesy and parked their latest-model cars outside the organic grocery store on Nassau Street or outside the sushi restaurants or outside the ice cream shop that had fifty different flavours including red pepper or outside the post office where effusive staff bounded out to greet them at the entrance. She liked the campus, grave with knowledge, the Gothic buildings with their vine-laced walls, and the way everything transformed, in the half-light of night, into a ghostly scene. She liked, most of all, that in this place of affluent ease, she could pretend to be someone else, someone specially admitted into a hallowed American club, someone adorned with certainty.

But she did not like that she had to go to Trenton to braid her hair. It was unreasonable to expect a braiding salon in Princeton – the few black locals she had seen were so light-skinned and lank-haired she could not imagine them wearing braids – and yet as she waited at Princeton Junction station for the train, on an afternoon ablaze with heat, she wondered why there *was* no place where she could braid her hair. The chocolate bar in her handbag had melted. A few other people were waiting on the platform, all of them white and lean, in short, flimsy clothes. The man standing closest to her was eating an ice cream cone; she had always found it a little irresponsible, the eating of ice cream cones by grown-up American men, especially the eating of ice cream cones by grown-up American men in public. He turned to her and said, 'About time,' when the train finally creaked in, with the familiarity strangers adopt with each other after sharing in the disappointment of a public service. She smiled at him. The greying hair on the back of his head was swept forward, a comical arrangement to disguise his bald spot. He had to be an academic, but not in the humanities or he would be more self-conscious. A firm science like chemistry, maybe. Before, she would have said, 'I know,' that peculiar American expression that professed

4

agreement rather than knowledge, and then she would have started a conversation with him, to see if he would say something she could use in her blog. People were flattered to be asked about themselves and if she said nothing after they spoke, it made them say more. They were conditioned to fill silences. If they asked what she did, she would say vaguely, 'I write a lifestyle blog,' because saying 'I write an anonymous blog called *Raceteenth or Various Observations About American Blacks (Those Formerly Known as Negroes) by a Non-American Black*' would make them uncomfortable. She had said it, though, a few times. Once to a dreadlocked white man who sat next to her on the train, his hair like old twine ropes that ended in a blond fuzz, his tattered shirt worn with enough piety to convince her that he was a social warrior and might make a good guest blogger. 'Race is totally over-hyped these days, black people need to get over themselves, it's all about class now, the haves and the have-nots,' he told her evenly, and she used it as the opening sentence of a post titled 'Not All Dreadlocked White American Guys Are Down'. Then there was the man from Ohio, who was squeezed next to her on a flight. A middle manager, she was sure, from his boxy suit and contrast collar. He wanted to know what she meant by 'lifestyle blog', and she told him, expecting him to become reserved, or to end the conversation by saying something defensively bland like 'The only race that matters is the human race.' But he said, 'Ever

5

write about adoption? Nobody wants black babies in this country, and I don't mean biracial, I mean black. Even the black families don't want them.'

He told her that he and his wife had adopted a black child and their neighbours looked at them as though they had chosen to become martyrs for a dubious cause. Her blog post about him, 'Badly-Dressed White Middle Managers from Ohio Are Not Always What You Think', had received the highest number of comments for that month. She still wondered if he had read it. She hoped so. Often, she would sit in cafés, or airports, or train stations, watching strangers, imagining their lives, and wondering which of them were likely to have read her blog. Now her ex-blog. She had written the final post only days ago, trailed by two hundred and seventy-four comments so far. All those readers, growing month by month, linking and cross-posting, knowing so much more than she did; they had always frightened and exhilarated her. SapphicDerrida, one of the most frequent posters, wrote: *I'm a bit surprised by how personally I am taking this. Good luck as you pursue the unnamed 'life change' but please come back to the blogosphere soon. You've used your irreverent, hectoring, funny and thought-provoking voice to create a space for real conversations about an important subject.* Readers like SapphicDerrida, who reeled off statistics and used words like 'reify' in their comments, made Ifemelu nervous, eager to be fresh and to impress, so that she began, over time, to feel like a vulture hacking into the carcasses of people's stories for something she could use. Sometimes making fragile links to race. Sometimes not believing herself. The more she wrote, the less sure she became. Each post scraped off yet one more scale of self until she felt naked and false.

The ice-cream-eating man sat beside her on the train and, to discourage conversation, she stared fixedly at a brown stain near her feet, a spilled frozen Frappuccino, until they arrived at Trenton. The platform was crowded with black people, many of them fat, in short, flimsy clothes. It still startled her, what a difference a few minutes of train travel made. During her first year in America, when she took New Jersey Transit to Penn Station and then the subway to visit Aunty Uju in Flatlands, she was struck by how mostly slim white people got off at the stops in Manhattan and, as the train went further into Brooklyn, the people left were mostly black and fat. She had not thought of them as 'fat', though. She had thought of them as 'big', because one of the first things her friend Ginika told her was that 'fat' in America was a bad word, heaving with moral judgement like 'stupid' or 'bastard', and not a mere description like 'short' or 'tall'. So she had banished 'fat' from her vocabulary. But 'fat' came back to her last winter, after almost thirteen years, when a man in line behind her at the supermarket muttered, 'Fat people don't need to be eating that shit,' as she paid for her giant bag of Tostitos. She glanced at him, surprised, mildly offended, and thought it a perfect blog post, how this stranger had decided she was fat. She would file the post under the tag 'race, gender and body size'. But back home, as she stood and faced the mirror's truth, she realized that she had ignored, for too long, the new tightness of her clothes, the rubbing together of her inner thighs, the softer, rounder parts of her that shook when she moved. She *was* fat.

She said the word 'fat' slowly, funnelling it back and forward, and thought about all the other things she had learned not to say aloud in America. She was fat. She was not curvy or big-boned; she was fat, it was the only word that felt true. And she had ignored, too, the cement in her soul. Her blog was doing well, with thousands of unique visitors each month, and she was earning good speaking fees, and she had a fellowship at Princeton and a relationship with Blaine – 'You are the absolute love of my life,' he'd written in her last birthday card – and yet there was cement in her soul. It had been there for a while, an early morning disease of fatigue, a bleakness and borderlessness. It brought with it amorphous longings, shapeless desires, brief imaginary glints of other lives she could be living, that over the months melded into a piercing home-sickness. She scoured Nigerian websites, Nigerian profiles on Facebook, Nigerian blogs, and each click brought yet another story of a young person who had recently moved back home, clothed in American or British degrees, to start an investment company, a music production business, a fashion label, a magazine, a fast-food franchise. She looked at photographs of these men and women and felt the dull ache of loss, as though they had prised open her hand and taken something of hers. They were living her life. Nigeria became where she was supposed to be, the only place she could sink her roots in without the constant urge to tug them out and shake off the soil. And, of course, there was also Obinze. Her first love, her first lover, the only person with whom she had never felt the need to explain herself. He was now a husband and father, and they had not been in touch in years, yet she could not pretend that he was not a part of her homesickness, or that she did not often think of him, sifting through their past, looking for portents of what she could not name.

The rude stranger in the supermarket – who knew what problems *he* was wrestling with, haggard and thin-lipped as he was – had intended to offend her but had instead prodded her awake.

She began to plan and to dream, to apply for jobs in Lagos. She did not tell Blaine at first, because she wanted to finish her fellowship at Princeton, and then after her fellowship ended, she did not tell him because she wanted to give herself time to be sure. But as the weeks passed, she knew she would never be sure. So she told him that she was moving back home, and she added, 'I have to,' knowing he would hear in her words the sound of an ending.

'Why?' Blaine asked, almost automatically, stunned by her announcement. There they were, in his living room in New Haven, awash in soft jazz and daylight, and she looked at him, her good, bewildered man, and felt the day take on a sad, epic quality. They had lived together for three years, three years free of crease, like a smoothly ironed sheet, until their only fight, months ago, when Blaine's eyes froze with blame and he refused to speak to her. But they had survived that fight, mostly because of Barack Obama, bonding anew over their shared passion. On election night, before Blaine kissed her, his face wet with tears, he held her tightly as though Obama's victory was also their personal victory. And now here she was telling him it was over. 'Why?' he asked. He taught ideas of nuance and complexity in his classes and yet he was asking her for a single reason, the *cause*. But she had not had a bold epiphany and there was no cause; it was simply that layer after layer of discontent had settled in her, and formed a mass that now propelled her. She did not tell him this, because it would hurt him to know she had felt that way for a while, that her relationship with him was like being content in a house but always sitting by the window and looking out.

'Take the plant,' he said to her, on the last day she saw him, when she was packing the clothes she kept in his apartment. He looked defeated, standing slump-shouldered in the kitchen. It was his houseplant, hopeful green leaves rising from three bamboo stems, and when she took it, a sudden crushing loneliness lanced through her and stayed with her for weeks. Sometimes, she still felt it. How was it possible to miss something you no longer wanted? Blaine needed what she was unable to give and she needed what he was unable to give, and she grieved this, the loss of what could have been.

So here she was, on a day filled with the opulence of summer, about to braid her hair for the journey home. Sticky heat sat on her skin. There were people thrice her size on the Trenton platform and she looked admiringly at one of them, a woman in a very short skirt. She thought nothing of slender legs shown off in miniskirts – it was safe and easy, after all, to display legs of which the world approved – but the fat woman's act was about the quiet conviction that one shared only with oneself, a sense of rightness that others failed to see. Her decision to move back was similar; whenever she felt besieged by doubts, she would think of herself as standing valiantly alone, as almost heroic, so as to squash her uncertainty. The fat woman was co-coordinating a group of teen-agers who looked sixteen and seventeen years old. They crowded around, a summer programme advertised on the front and back of their yellow T-shirts, laughing and talking. They reminded Ifemelu of her cousin Dike. One of the boys, dark and tall, with the leanly muscled build of an athlete, looked just like Dike. Not that Dike would ever wear those shoes that looked like espadrilles. Weak kicks, he would call them. It was a new one; he first used it a few days ago when he told her about going shopping with Aunty Uju. 'Mom wanted to buy me these crazy shoes. Come on, Coz, you know I can't wear weak kicks!'

Ifemelu joined the taxi line outside the station. She hoped her driver would not be a Nigerian, because he, once he heard her accent, would either be aggressively eager to tell her that he had a master's degree, the taxi was a second job and his daughter was on the dean's list at Rutgers; or he would drive in sullen silence, giving her change and ignoring her 'thank you', all the time nursing humiliation, that this fellow Nigerian, a small girl at that, who perhaps was a nurse or an accountant or even a doctor, was looking down on him. Nigerian taxi drivers in America were all convinced that they really were not taxi drivers. She was next in line. Her taxi driver was black and middle-aged. She opened the door and glanced at the back of the driver's seat. *Mervin Smith*. Not Nigerian, but you could never be too sure. Nigerians took on all sorts of names here. Even she had once been somebody else.

'How you doing?' the man asked.

She could tell right away, with relief, that his accent was Caribbean.

'I'm very well. Thank you.' She gave him the address of Mariama African Hair Braiding. It was her first time at this salon – her regular one was closed because the owner had gone back to Côte d'Ivoire to get married – but it would look, she was sure, like all the other African hair braiding salons she had known: they were in the part of the city that had graffiti, dank buildings and no white people, they displayed bright signboards with names like Aisha and Fatima African Hair Braiding, they had radiators that were too hot in the winter and air conditioners that did not cool in the summer, and they were full of Francophone West African women braiders, one of whom would be the owner and speak the best English and answer the phone and be deferred to by the others. Often, there was a baby tied to someone's back with a piece of cloth. Or a toddler asleep on a wrapper spread over a battered sofa. Sometimes, older children stopped by. The conversations were loud and swift, in French or Wolof or Malinke, and when they spoke English to customers, it was broken, curious, as though they had not quite eased into the language itself before taking on a slangy Americanism. Words came out half-completed. Once a Guinean braider in Philadelphia had told Ifemelu, 'Amma like, Oh Gad, Az someh.' It took many repetitions for Ifemelu to understand that the woman was saying, 'I'm like, Oh God, I was so mad.'

Mervin Smith was upbeat and chatty. He talked, as he drove, about how hot it was, how rolling blackouts were sure to come.

'This is the kind of heat that kills old folks. If

they don't have air conditioning, they have to go to the mall, you know. The mall is free air conditioning. But sometimes there's nobody to take them. People have to take care of the old folks,' he said, his jolly mood unfazed by Ifemelu's silence.

'Here we are!' he said, parking in front of a shabby block. The salon was in the middle, between a Chinese restaurant called Happy Joy and a convenience store that sold lottery tickets. Inside, the room was thick with disregard, the paint peeling, the walls plastered with large posters of braided hairstyles and smaller posters that said QUICK TAX REFUND. Three women, all in T-shirts and knee-length shorts, were working on the hair of seated customers. A small TV mounted on a corner of the wall, the volume a little too loud, was showing a Nigerian film: a man beating his wife, the wife cowering and shouting, the poor audio quality jarring.

'Hi!' Ifemelu said.

They all turned to look at her but only one, who had to be the eponymous Mariama, said, 'Hi. Welcome.'

'I'd like to get braids.'

'What kind of braids you want?'

Ifemelu said she wanted a medium kinky twist and asked how much it was.

'Two hundred,' Mariama said.

'I paid one sixty last month.' She had last braided her hair three months ago.

Mariama said nothing for a while, her eyes back on the hair she was braiding.

'So one sixty?' Ifemelu asked.

Mariama shrugged and smiled. 'Okay, but you have to come back next time. Sit down. Wait for Aisha. She will finish soon.' Mariama pointed at the smallest of the braiders, who had a skin condition, pinkish-cream whorls of discoloration on her arms and neck that looked worryingly infectious.

'Hi, Aisha,' Ifemelu said.

Aisha glanced at Ifemelu, nodding ever so slightly, her face blank, almost forbidding in its expressionlessness. There was something strange about her.

Ifemelu sat close to the door; the fan on the chipped table was turned on high but did little for the stuffiness in the room. Next to the fan were combs, packets of hair attachments, magazines bulky with loose pages, piles of colourful DVDs. A broom was propped in one corner, near the candy dispenser and the rusty hair dryer that had not been used in a hundred years. On the TV screen, a father was beating two children, wooden punches that hit the air above their heads.

'No! Bad father! Bad man!' the other braider said, staring at the TV and flinching.

'You from Nigeria?' Mariama asked.

'Yes,' Ifemelu said. 'Where are you from?'

'Me and my sister Halima are from Mali. Aisha is from Senegal,' Mariama said.

Aisha did not look up, but Halima smiled at

15

Ifemelu, a smile that, in its warm knowingness, said welcome to a fellow African; she would not smile at an American in the same way. She was severely cross-eyed, pupils darting in opposite directions, so that Ifemelu felt thrown off-balance, not sure which of Halima's eyes was on her.

Ifemelu fanned herself with a magazine. 'It's so hot,' she said. At least, these women would not say to her 'You're hot? But you're from Africa!'

'This heat wave is very bad. Sorry the air conditioner broke yesterday,' Mariama said.

Ifemelu knew the air conditioner had not broken yesterday, it had been broken for much longer, perhaps it had always been broken; still she nodded and said that perhaps it had packed up from overuse. The phone rang. Mariama picked it up and after a minute said 'Come now,' the very words that had made Ifemelu stop making appointments with African hair braiding salons. Come now, they always said, and then you arrived to find two people waiting to get micro braids and still the owner would tell you 'Wait, my sister is coming to help.' The phone rang again and Mariama spoke in French, her voice rising, and she stopped braiding to gesture with her hand as she shouted into the phone. Then she unfolded a yellow Western Union form from her pocket and began reading out the numbers. 'Trois! Cinq! Non, non, cinq!'

The woman whose hair she was braiding in tiny, painful-looking cornrows said sharply, 'Come on! I'm not spending the whole day here!'

'Sorry, sorry,' Mariama said. Still, she finished repeating the Western Union numbers before she continued braiding, the phone lodged between her shoulder and ear.

Ifemelu opened her novel, Jean Toomer's *Cane*, and skimmed a few pages. She had been meaning to read it for a while now, and imagined she would like it since Blaine did not. A precious performance, Blaine had called it, in that gently forbearing tone he used when they talked about novels, as though he was sure that she, with a little more time and a little more wisdom, would come to accept that the novels he liked were superior, novels written by young and youngish men and packed with *things*, a fascinating, confounding accumulation of brands and music and comic books and icons, with emotions skimmed over, and each sentence stylishly aware of its own stylishness. She had read many of them, because he recommended them, but they were like cotton candy that so easily evaporated from her tongue's memory.

She closed the novel; it was too hot to concentrate. She ate some melted chocolate, sent Dike a text to call her when he was finished with basketball practice, and fanned herself. She read the signs on the opposite wall – NO ADJUSTMENTS TO BRAIDS AFTER ONE WEEK. NO PERSONAL CHECKS. NO REFUNDS – but she carefully avoided looking at the corners of the room because she knew that clumps of mouldy newspapers would be stuffed beneath pipes and grime and things long rotten.

Finally, Aisha finished with her customer and asked what colour Ifemelu wanted for her hair attachments.

'Colour four.'

'Not good colour,' Aisha said promptly.

'That's what I use.'

'It look dirty. You don't want colour one?'

'Colour one is too black, it looks fake,' Ifemelu said, loosening her headwrap. 'Sometimes I use colour two, but colour four is closest to my natural colour.'

Aisha shrugged, a haughty shrug, as though it was not her problem if her customer did not have good taste. She reached into a cupboard, brought out two packets of attachments, checked to make sure they were both the same colour.

She touched Ifemelu's hair. 'Why you don't have relaxer?'

'I like my hair the way God made it.'

'But how you comb it? Hard to comb,' Aisha said.

Ifemelu had brought her own comb. She gently combed her hair, dense, soft and tightly coiled, until it framed her head like a halo. 'It's not hard to comb if you moisturize it properly,' she said, slipping into the coaxing tone of the proselytizer that she used whenever she was trying to convince other black women about the merits of wearing their hair natural. Aisha snorted; she clearly could not understand why anybody would choose to suffer through combing natural hair, instead of simply relaxing it.

She sectioned out Ifemelu's hair, plucked a little attachment from the pile on the table and began deftly to twist.

'It's too tight,' Ifemelu said. 'Don't make it tight.' Because Aisha kept twisting to the end, Ifemelu thought that perhaps she had not understood, and so Ifemelu touched the offending braid and said, 'Tight, tight.'

Aisha pushed her hand away. 'No. No. Leave it. It good.'

'It's tight!' Ifemelu said. 'Please loosen it.'

Mariama was watching them. A flow of French came from her. Aisha loosened the braid.

'Sorry,' Mariama said. 'She doesn't understand very well.'

But Ifemelu could see, from Aisha's face, that she understood very well. Aisha was simply a true market woman, immune to the cosmetic niceties of American customer service. Ifemelu imagined her working in a market in Dakar, like the braiders in Lagos who would blow their noses and wipe their hands on their wrappers, roughly jerk their customers' heads to position them better, complain about how full or how hard or how short the hair was, shout out to passing women, while all the time conversing too loudly and braiding too tightly.

'You know her?' Aisha asked, glancing at the television screen.

'What?'

Aisha repeated herself, and pointed at the actress on the screen.

'No,' Ifemelu said.

'But you Nigerian.'

'Yes, but I don't know her.'

Aisha gestured to the pile of DVDs on the table. 'Before, too much voodoo. Very bad. Now Nigeria film is very good. Big nice house!'

Ifemelu thought little of Nollywood films, with their exaggerated histrionics and their improbable plots, but she nodded in agreement because to hear 'Nigeria' and 'good' in the same sentence was a luxury, even coming from this strange Senegalese woman, and she chose to see in this an augury of her return home.

Everyone she had told she was moving back seemed surprised, expecting an explanation, and when she said she was doing it because she wanted to, puzzled lines would appear on foreheads.

'You are closing your blog and selling your condo to go back to Lagos and work for a magazine that doesn't pay that well,' Aunty Uju had said and then repeated herself, as though to make Ifemelu see the gravity of her own foolishness. Only her old friend in Lagos, Ranyinudo, had made her return seem normal. 'Lagos is now full of American returnees, so you better come back and join them. Every day you see them carrying a bottle of water as if they will die of heat if they are not drinking water every minute,' Ranyinudo said. They had kept in touch, she and Ranyinudo, throughout the years. At first, they wrote infrequent letters, but as cybercafés opened, cell phones spread and

Facebook flourished, they communicated more often. It was Ranyinudo who had told her, some years ago, that Obinze was getting married. 'Meanwhile o, he has serious money now. See what you missed!' Ranyinudo had said. Ifemelu feigned indifference to this news. She had cut off contact with Obinze, after all, and so much time had passed, and she was newly in a relationship with Blaine, and happily easing herself into a shared life. But after she hung up, she thought endlessly of Obinze. Imagining him at his wedding left her with a feeling like sorrow, a faded sorrow. But she was pleased for him, she told herself, and to prove to herself that she was pleased for him, she decided to write to him. She was not sure if he still used his old address and she sent the e-mail half expecting that he would not reply, but he did. She did not write again, because she by then had acknowledged her own small, still-burning light. It was best to leave things alone. Last December, when Ranyinudo told her she had run into him at the Palms mall, with his baby daughter (and Ifemelu still could not picture this new sprawling, modern mall in Lagos; all that came to mind when she tried to was the cramped Mega Plaza she remembered) – 'He was looking so *clean*, and his daughter is so fine,' Ranyinudo said – Ifemelu felt a pang at all the changes that had happened in his life.

'Nigeria film very good now,' Aisha said again.
'Yes,' Ifemelu said enthusiastically. This was what

21

she had become, a seeker of signs. Nigerian films were good, therefore her move back home would be good.

'You from Yoruba in Nigeria,' Aisha said.

'No. I am Igbo.'

'You Igbo?' For the first time, a smile appeared on Aisha's face, a smile that showed as much of her small teeth as her dark gums. 'I think you Yoruba because you dark and Igbo fair. I have two Igbo men. Very good. Igbo men take care of women real good.'

Aisha was almost whispering, a sexual suggestion in her tone, and in the mirror, the discoloration on her arms and neck became ghastly sores. Ifemelu imagined some bursting and oozing, others flaking. She looked away.

'Igbo men take care of women real good,' Aisha repeated. 'I want marry. They love me but they say the family want Igbo woman. Because Igbo marry Igbo always.'

Ifemelu swallowed the urge to laugh. 'You want to marry both of them?'

'No.' Aisha made an impatient gesture. 'I want marry one. But this thing is true? Igbo marry Igbo always?'

'Igbo people marry all kinds of people. My cousin's husband is Yoruba. My uncle's wife is from Scotland.'

Aisha paused in her twisting, watching Ifemelu in the mirror, as though deciding whether to believe her.

'My sister say it is true. Igbo marry Igbo always,' she said.

'How does your sister know?'

'She know many Igbo people in Africa. She sell cloth.'

'Where is she?'

'In Africa.'

'Where? In Senegal?'

'Benin.'

'Why do you say Africa instead of just saying the country you mean?' Ifemelu asked.

Aisha clucked. 'You don't know America. You say Senegal and American people, they say, Where is that? My friend from Burkina Faso, they ask her, your country in Latin America?' Aisha resumed twisting, a sly smile on her face, and then asked, as if Ifemelu could not possibly understand how things were done here, 'How long you in America?'

Ifemelu decided then that she did not like Aisha at all. She wanted to curtail the conversation now, so that they would say only what they needed to say during the six hours it would take to braid her hair, and so she pretended not to have heard and instead brought out her phone. Dike had still not replied to her text. He always replied within minutes, or maybe he was still at basketball practice, or with his friends, watching some silly video on YouTube. She called him and left a long message, raising her voice, going on and on about his basketball practice and was it as hot up in Massachusetts and was he still taking Page to see the movie today.

23

Then, feeling reckless, she composed an e-mail to Obinze and, without permitting herself to reread it, she sent it off. She had written that she was moving back to Nigeria and, even though she had a job waiting for her, even though her car was already on a ship bound for Lagos, it suddenly felt true for the first time. *I recently decided to move back to Nigeria.*

Aisha was not discouraged. Once Ifemelu looked up from her phone, Aisha asked again, 'How long you in America?'

Ifemelu took her time putting her phone back into her bag. Years ago, she had been asked a similar question, at a wedding of one of Aunty Uju's friends, and she had said two years, which was the truth, but the jeer on the Nigerian's face had taught her that, to earn the prize of being taken seriously among Nigerians in America, among Africans in America, indeed among immigrants in America, she needed more years. Six years, she began to say when it was just three and a half. Eight years, she said when it was five. Now that it was thirteen years, lying seemed unnecessary but she lied anyway.

'Fifteen years,' she said.

'Fifteen? That long time.' A new respect slipped into Aisha's eyes. 'You live here in Trenton?'

'I live in Princeton.'

'Princeton.' Aisha paused. 'You student?'

'I've just finished a fellowship,' she said, knowing that Aisha would not understand what a fellowship was, and in the rare moment that Aisha looked intimidated, Ifemelu felt a perverse pleasure. Yes, Princeton. Yes, the sort of place that Aisha could only imagine, the sort of place that would never have signs that said QUICK TAX REFUND; people in Princeton did not need quick tax refunds.

'But I'm going back home to Nigeria,' Ifemelu added, suddenly remorseful. 'I'm going next week.'

'To see the family.'

'No. I'm moving back. To live in Nigeria.'

'Why?'

'What do you mean, why? Why not?'

'Better you send money back. Unless your father is big man? You have connections?'

'I've found a job there,' she said.

'You stay in America fifteen years and you just go back to work?' Aisha smirked. 'You can stay there?'

Aisha reminded her of what Aunty Uju had said, when she finally accepted that Ifemelu was serious about moving back – *Will you be able to cope?* – and the suggestion, that she was somehow irrevocably altered by America, had grown thorns on her skin. Her parents, too, seemed to think that she might not be able to 'cope' with Nigeria. 'At least you are now an American citizen, so you can always return to America,' her father had said. Both of them had asked if Blaine would be coming with her, their question heavy with hope. It amused her how often they asked about Blaine now, since it had taken them a while to make peace with the

25

idea of her black American boyfriend. She imagined them nursing quiet plans for her wedding; her mother would think of a caterer and colours, and her father would think of a distinguished friend he could ask to be the sponsor. Reluctant to flatten their hope, because it took so little to keep them hoping, which in turn kept them happy, she told her father, 'We decided I will come back first and then Blaine will come after a few weeks.'

'Splendid,' her father said, and she said nothing else because it was best if things were simply left at splendid.

Aisha tugged a little too hard at her hair. 'Fifteen years in America very long time,' Aisha said, as though she had been pondering this. 'You have boyfriend? You marry?'

'I'm also going back to Nigeria to see my man,' Ifemelu said, surprising herself. *My man.* How easy it was to lie to strangers, to create with strangers the versions of our lives that we have imagined.

'Oh! Okay!' Aisha said, excited; Ifemelu had finally given her a comprehensible reason for wanting to move back. 'You will marry?'

'Maybe. We'll see.'

'Oh!' Aisha stopped twisting and stared at her in the mirror, a dead stare, and Ifemelu feared, for a moment, that the woman had clairvoyant powers and could tell she was lying.

'I want you see my men. I call them. They come and you see them. First I call Chijioke. He work

26

cab driver. Then Emeka. He work security. You see them.'

'You don't have to call them just to meet me.'

'No. I call them. You tell them Igbo can marry not Igbo. They listen to you.'

'No, really. I can't do that.'

Aisha kept speaking as if she hadn't heard. 'You tell them. They listen to you because you their Igbo sister. Any one is okay. I want marry.'

Ifemelu looked at Aisha, a small, ordinary-faced Senegalese woman with patchwork skin who had two Igbo boyfriends, implausible as it seemed, and who was now insistent that Ifemelu should meet them and urge them to marry her. It would have made for a good blog post: 'A Peculiar Case of a Non-American Black, or How the Pressures of Immigrant Life Can Make You Act Crazy.'

CHAPTER 2

When Obinze first saw her e-mail, he was sitting in the back of his Range Rover in still Lagos traffic, his jacket slung over the front seat, a rusty-haired child beggar glued outside his window, a hawker pressing colourful CDs against the other window, the radio turned on low to the Pidgin English news on Wazobia FM, and the grey gloom of imminent rain all around. He stared at his BlackBerry, his body suddenly rigid. First, he skimmed the e-mail, instinctively wishing it were longer. *Ceiling, kedu? Hope all is well with work and family. Ranyinudo said she ran into you some time ago and that you now have a child! Proud Papa. Congratulations. I recently decided to move back to Nigeria. Should be in Lagos in a week. Would love to keep in touch. Take care. Ifemelu.*

He read it again slowly and felt the urge to smooth something, his trousers, his shaved-bald head. She had called him Ceiling. In the last e-mail from her, sent just before he got married, she had called him Obinze, apologized for her silence over the years, wished him happiness in sunny sentences and mentioned the black American she was living

28

with. A gracious e-mail. He had hated it. He had hated it so much that he Googled the black American – and why should she give him the man's full name if not because she wanted him Googled? – a lecturer at Yale, and found it infuriating that she lived with a man who referred on his blog to friends as 'cats', but it was the photo of the black American, oozing intellectual cool in distressed jeans and black-framed glasses, that had tipped Obinze over, made him send her a cold reply. *Thank you for the good wishes, I have never been happier in my life,* he'd written. He hoped she would write something mocking back – it was so unlike her, not to have been even vaguely tart in that first e-mail – but she did not write at all and when he e-mailed her again, after his honeymoon in Morocco, to say he wanted to keep in touch and wanted to talk sometime, she did not reply.

The traffic was moving. A light rain was falling. The child beggar ran along, his doe-eyed expression more theatrical, his motions frantic: bringing his hand to his mouth, again and again, fingertips pursed together. Obinze rolled down the window and held out a hundred-naira note. From the rear-view mirror, his driver, Gabriel, watched with grave disapproval.

'God bless you, oga!' the child beggar said.

'Don't be giving money to these beggars, sir,' Gabriel said. 'They are all rich. They are using begging to make big money. I heard about one that built a block of six flats in Ikeja!'

'So why are you working as a driver instead of a beggar, Gabriel?' Obinze asked, and laughed, a little too heartily. He wanted to tell Gabriel that his girlfriend from university had just e-mailed him, actually his girlfriend from university *and* secondary school. The first time she let him take off her bra, she lay on her back moaning softly, her fingers splayed on his head, and afterwards she said, 'My eyes were open but I did not see the ceiling. This never happened before.' Other girls would have pretended that they had never let another boy touch them, but not her, never her. There was a vivid honesty about her. She began to call what they did together *ceiling*, their warm entanglements on his bed when his mother was out, wearing only underwear, touching and kissing and sucking, hips moving in simulation. *I'm longing for ceiling*, she once wrote on the back of his geography notebook, and for a long time afterwards he could not look at that notebook without a gathering frisson, a sense of secret excitement. In university, when they finally stopped simulating, she began to call *him* Ceiling, in a playful way, in a suggestive way – but when they fought or when she retreated into moodiness, she called him Obinze. She had never called him The Zed, as his friends did. 'Why do you call him Ceiling anyway?' his friend Okwudiba once asked her, on one of those languorous days after first semester exams. She had joined a group of his friends sitting around a filthy plastic table in a beer parlour off campus.

She drank from her bottle of Maltina, swallowed, glanced at Obinze and said, 'Because he is so tall his head touches the ceiling, can't you see?' Her deliberate slowness, the small smile that stretched her lips, made it clear that she wanted them to know that this was not why she called him Ceiling. And he was not tall. She kicked him under the table and he kicked her back, watching his laughing friends; they were all a little afraid of her and a little in love with her. Did she see the ceiling when the black American touched her? Had she used 'ceiling' with other men? It upset him now to think that she might have. His phone rang and for a confused moment he thought it was Ifemelu calling from America.

'Darling, *kedu ebe I no*?' His wife, Kosi, always began her calls to him with those words: Where are you? He never asked where she was when he called her, but she would tell him, anyway: I'm just getting to the salon. I'm on Third Mainland Bridge. It was as if she needed the reassurance of their physicality when they were not together. She had a high, girlish voice. They were supposed to be at Chief's house for the party at seven-thirty and it was already past six.

He told her he was in traffic. 'But it's moving, and we've just turned into Ozumba Mbadiwe. I'm coming.'

On Lekki Expressway, the traffic moved swiftly in the waning rain and soon Gabriel was pressing the horn in front of the high black gates of his

31

home. Mohammed, the gateman, wiry in his dirty white caftan, flung open the gates and raised a hand in greeting. Obinze looked at the tan colonnaded house. Inside was his furniture imported from Italy, his wife, his two-year-old daughter, Buchi, the nanny Christiana, his wife's sister Chioma, who was on a forced holiday because university lecturers were on strike yet again, and the new housegirl, Marie, who had been brought from Benin Republic after his wife decided that Nigerian housegirls were unsuitable. The rooms would all be cool, air-conditioner vents swaying quietly, and the kitchen would be fragrant with curry and thyme, and CNN would be on downstairs, while the television upstairs would be turned to Cartoon Network, and pervading it all would be the undisturbed air of well-being. He climbed out of the car. His gait was stiff, his legs difficult to lift. He had begun, in the past months, to feel bloated from all he had acquired – the family, the houses, the cars, the bank accounts – and would, from time to time, be overcome by the urge to prick everything with a pin, to deflate it all, to be free. He was no longer sure, he had in fact never been sure, whether he liked his life because he really did or whether he liked it because he was supposed to.

'Darling,' Kosi said, opening the door before he got to it. She was all made-up, her complexion glowing, and he thought, as he often did, what a beautiful woman she was, eyes perfectly almond-shaped, a startling symmetry to her features. Her crushed-silk dress was cinched tightly at the waist and made her figure look very hourglassy. He hugged her, carefully avoiding her lips, painted pink and lined in a darker pink.

'Sunshine in the evening! *Asa! Ugo!*' he said. 'Chief doesn't need to put on any lights at the party, once you arrive.'

She laughed. The same way she laughed, with an open, accepting enjoyment of her own looks, when people asked her 'Is your mother white? Are you a half-caste?' because she was so fair-skinned. It had always discomfited him, the pleasure she took in being mistaken for mixed-race.

'Daddy-daddy!' Buchi said, running to him in the slightly off-balance manner of toddlers. She was fresh from her evening bath, wearing her flowered pyjamas and smelling sweetly of baby lotion.

'Buch-buch! Daddy's Buch!' He swung her up, kissed her, nuzzled her neck and, because it always made her laugh, pretended to throw her down on the floor.

'Will you bathe or just change?' Kosi asked, following him upstairs, where she had laid out a blue caftan on his bed. He would have preferred a dress shirt or a simpler caftan instead of this, with its overly decorative embroidery, which Kosi had bought for an outrageous sum from one of those new pretentious fashion designers on The Island. But he would wear it to please her.

'I'll just change,' he said.

'How was work?' she asked, in the vague, pleasant way that she always asked. He told her he was thinking about the new block of flats he had just completed in Parkview. He hoped Shell would rent it because the oil companies were always the best renters, never complaining about abrupt hikes, paying easily in American dollars so that nobody had to deal with the fluctuating naira.

'Don't worry,' she said, and touched his shoulder. 'God will bring Shell. We will be okay, darling.'

The flats were in fact already rented by an oil company but he sometimes told her senseless lies such as this, because a part of him hoped she would ask a question or challenge him, though he knew she would not, because all she wanted was to make sure the conditions of their life remained the same, and how he made that happen she left entirely to him.

Chief's party would bore him, as usual, but he went because he went to all of Chief's parties, and each time he parked in front of Chief's large compound, he remembered the first time he had come there, with his cousin Nneoma. He was newly back from England, had been in Lagos for only a week, but Nneoma was already grumbling about how he could not just lie around in her flat reading and moping.

'Ahn ahn! *O gini?* Are you the first person to have this problem? You have to get up and hustle.

Everybody is hustling, Lagos is about hustling,'
Nneoma said. She had thick-palmed, capable
hands and many business interests; she travelled
to Dubai to buy gold, to China to buy women's
clothing, and lately, she had become a distributor
for a frozen chicken company. 'I would have said
you should come and help me in my business but
no, you are too soft, you speak too much English.
I need somebody with gra-gra,' she said.

Obinze was still reeling from what had happened
to him in England, still insulated in layers of his
own self-pity, and to hear Nneoma's dismissive
question – 'Are you the first person to have this
problem?' – upset him. She had no idea, this cousin
who had grown up in the village, who looked at
the world with stark and insensitive eyes. But
slowly, he realized she was right; he was not the
first and he would not be the last. He began
applying for jobs listed in newspapers, but nobody
called him for an interview, and his friends from
school, who were now working at banks and
mobile phone companies, began to avoid him,
worried that he would thrust yet another CV into
their hands.

One day, Nneoma said, 'I know this very rich
man, Chief. The man chased and chased me, eh,
but I refused. He has a serious problem with
women, and he can give somebody AIDS. But you
know these men, the one woman that says no to
them is the one that they don't forget. So from
time to time, he will call me and sometimes I go

and greet him. He even helped me with capital to start over my business after those children of Satan stole my money last year. He still thinks that one day I will agree for him. Ha, *o di egwu*, for where? I will take you to him. Once he is in a good mood, the man can be very generous. He knows everybody in this country. Maybe he will give us a note for a managing director somewhere.'

A steward let them in; Chief was sitting on a gilded chair that looked like a throne, sipping cognac and surrounded by guests. He sprang up, a smallish man, high-spirited and ebullient. 'Nneoma! Is this you? So you remember me today!' he said. He hugged Nneoma, moved back to look boldly at her hips outlined in her fitted skirt, her long weave falling to her shoulders. 'You want to give me heart attack, eh?'

'How can I give you heart attack? What will I do without you?' Nneoma said playfully.

'You know what to do,' Chief said, and his guests laughed, three guffawing, knowing men.

'Chief, this is my cousin, Obinze. His mother is my father's sister, the professor,' Nneoma said. 'She is the one that paid my school fees from beginning to end. If not for her, I don't know where I would be today.'

'Wonderful, wonderful!' Chief said, looking at Obinze as though he was somehow responsible for this generosity.

'Good evening, sir,' Obinze said. It surprised him that Chief was something of a fop, with his air of fussy grooming: nails manicured and shiny, black velvet slippers at his feet, a diamond cross around his neck. He had expected a larger man and a rougher exterior.

'Sit down. What can I offer you?'

Big Men and Big Women, Obinze would later learn, did not talk to people, they instead talked at people, and that evening Chief had talked and talked, pontificating about politics, while his guests crowed, 'Exactly! You are correct, Chief! Thank you!' They were wearing the uniform of the Lagos youngish and wealthyish – leather slippers, jeans and open-neck tight shirts, all with familiar designer logos – but there was, in their manner, the ploughing eagerness of men in need.

After his guests left, Chief turned to Nneoma. 'Do you know that song "No One Knows Tomorrow"?' Then he proceeded to sing the song with childish gusto. *No one knows tomorrow! To-mor-row! No one knows tomorrow!* Another generous splash of cognac in his glass. 'That is the one principle that this country is based on. The major principle. No one knows tomorrow. Remember those big bankers during Abacha's government? They thought they owned this country, and the next thing they knew, they were in prison. Look at that pauper who could not pay his rent before, then Babangida gave him an oil well, and now he has a private jet!' Chief spoke with a triumphant tone, mundane observations delivered as grand discoveries, while Nneoma listened and

37

smiled and agreed. Her animation was exaggerated, as though a bigger smile and a quicker laugh, each ego-burnish shinier than the last, would ensure that Chief would help them. Obinze was amused by how obvious it seemed, how frank she was in her flirtations. But Chief merely gave them a case of red wine as a gift, and said vaguely to Obinze, 'Come and see me next week.'

Obinze visited Chief the next week and then the next; Nneoma told him to just keep hanging around until Chief did something for him. Chief's steward always served fresh pepper soup, deeply flavourful pieces of fish in a broth that made Obinze's nose run, cleared his head and somehow unclogged the future and filled him with hope, so that he sat contentedly, listening to Chief and his guests. They fascinated him, the unsubtle cowering of the almost rich in the presence of the rich, and the rich in the presence of the very rich; to have money, it seemed, was to be consumed by money. Obinze felt repulsion and longing; he pitied them, but he also imagined being like them. One day, Chief drank more cognac than usual, and talked haphazardly about people stabbing you in the back and small boys growing tails and ungrateful fools suddenly thinking they were sharp. Obinze was not sure what exactly had happened, but somebody had upset Chief, a gap had opened, and as soon as they were alone, he said, 'Chief, if there is something I can help you do, please tell me. You can depend on me.' His own words surprised him. He had stepped out of himself. He was high on pepper soup. This was what it meant to hustle. He was in Lagos and he had to hustle.

Chief looked at him, a long, shrewd look. 'We need more people like you in this country. People from good families, with good home training. You are a gentleman, I see it in your eyes. And your mother is a professor. It is not easy.'

Obinze half smiled, to seem humble in the face of this odd praise.

'You are hungry and honest, that is very rare in this country. Is that not so?' Chief asked.

'Yes,' Obinze said, even though he was not sure whether he was agreeing about his having this quality or about the rarity of this quality. But it did not matter, because Chief sounded certain.

'Everybody is hungry in this country, even the rich men are hungry, but nobody is honest.'

Obinze nodded, and Chief gave him another long look, before silently turning back to his cognac. On his next visit, Chief was his usual garrulous self.

'I was Babangida's friend. I was Abacha's friend. Now that the military has gone, Obasanjo is my friend,' he said. 'Do you know why? Is it because I am stupid?'

'Of course not, Chief,' Obinze said.

'They said the National Farm Support Corporation is bankrupt and they're going to privatize it. Do you know this? No. How do I know this? Because I have friends. By the time you know it, I would have taken a position and I would have benefited from the arbitrage. That is our free market!' Chief laughed. 'The corporation was set up in the sixties and it owns property everywhere. The houses are all rotten and termites are eating the roofs. But they are selling them. I'm going to buy seven properties for five million each. You know what they are listed for in the books? One million. You know what the real worth is? Fifty million.' Chief paused to stare at one of his ringing mobile phones – four were placed on the table next to him – and then ignored it and leaned back on the sofa. 'I need somebody to front this deal.'

'Yes, sir, I can do that,' Obinze said.

Later, Nneoma sat on her bed, excited for him, giving him advice while smacking her head from time to time; her scalp was itchy beneath her weave and this was the closest she could come to scratching.

'This is your opportunity! The Zed, shine your eyes! They call it a big-big name, evaluation consulting, but it is not difficult. You undervalue the properties and make sure it looks as if you are following due process. You acquire the property, sell off half to pay your purchase price and you are in business! You'll register your own company. Next thing, you'll build a house in Lekki and buy some cars and ask our hometown to give you some titles and your friends to put congratulatory messages in the newspapers for you and before you know, any bank you walk into, they will want to package a loan immediately and give it to you, because they think you no longer need the money! And after you register your own company, you must find a white man. Find one of your white friends in England. Tell everybody he is your General Manager. You will see how doors will open for you because you have an oyinbo General Manager. Even Chief has some white men that he brings in for show when he needs them. That is how Nigeria works. I'm telling you.'

And it was, indeed, how it worked and still worked for Obinze. The ease of it had dazed him. The first time he took his offer letter to the bank, he had felt surreal saying 'fifty' and 'fifty-five' and leaving out the 'million' because there was no need to state the obvious. It had startled him, too, how easy many other things became, how even just the semblance of wealth oiled his paths. He had only to drive to a gate in his BMW and the gatemen would salute and open it for him, without asking questions. Even the American embassy was different. He had been refused a visa years ago, when he was newly graduated and drunk with American ambitions, but with his new bank statements, he easily got a visa. On his first trip, at the airport in Atlanta, the immigration officer was chatty and warm, asking him, 'So how much cash you got?' When Obinze said he didn't have much, the man looked surprised. 'I see Nigerians like you declaring thousands and thousands of dollars all the time.'

This was what he now was, the kind of Nigerian

expected to declare a lot of cash at the airport. It brought to him a disorienting strangeness, because his mind had not changed at the same pace as his life, and he felt a hollow space between himself and the person he was supposed to be.

He still did not understand why Chief had decided to help him, to use him while overlooking, even encouraging, the astonishing collateral benefits. There was, after all, a trail of prostrating visitors to Chief's house, relatives and friends bringing other relatives and friends, their pockets full of requests and appeals. He sometimes wondered if Chief would one day ask something of him, the hungry and honest boy he had made big, and in his more melodramatic moments, he imagined Chief asking him to organize an assassination.

As soon as they arrived at Chief's party, Kosi led the way around the room, hugging men and women she barely knew, calling the older ones 'ma' and 'sir' with exaggerated respect, basking in the attention her face drew but flattening her personality so that her beauty did not threaten. She praised a woman's hair, another's dress, a man's tie. She said 'We thank God' often. When one woman asked her, in an accusing tone, 'What cream do you use on your face? How can one person have this kind of perfect skin?' Kosi laughed graciously and promised to send the woman a text message with details of her skin-care routine.

Obinze had always been struck by how important

it was to her to be a wholesomely agreeable person, to have no sharp angles sticking out. On Sundays, she would invite his relatives for pounded yam and onugbu soup and then watch over to make sure everyone was suitably overfed. *Uncle, you must eat o! There is more meat in the kitchen! Let me bring you another Guinness!* The first time he took her to his mother's house in Nsukka, just before they got married, she leaped up to help with serving the food, and when his mother made to clean up afterwards, she got up, offended, and said, 'Mummy, how can I be here and you will be cleaning?' She ended every sentence she spoke to his uncles with 'sir'. She put ribbons in the hair of his cousins' daughters. There was something immodest about her modesty: it announced itself.

Now she was curtsying and greeting Mrs Akin-Cole, a famously old woman from a famously old family, who had the supercilious expression, eyebrows always raised, of a person used to receiving homage; Obinze often imagined her belching champagne bubbles.

'How is your child? Has she started school?' Mrs Akin-Cole asked. 'You must send her to the French school. They are very good, very rigorous. Of course they teach in French but it can only be good for the child to learn another civilized language, since she already learns English at home.'

'Okay, ma. I'll look at the French school,' Kosi said.

'The French school is not bad, but I prefer Sidcot

Hall. They teach the complete British curriculum,' said another woman, whose name Obinze had forgotten. He knew she had made a lot of money during General Abacha's government. She had been a pimp, as the story went, providing young girls for the army officers who, in turn, gave her inflated supply contracts. Now, in her tight sequined dress that outlined the swell of her lower belly, she had become a certain kind of middle-aged Lagos woman, dried up by disappointments, blighted by bitterness, the sprinkle of pimples on her forehead smothered in heavy foundation.

'Oh, yes, Sidcot Hall,' Kosi said. 'It's already on top of my list because I know they teach the British curriculum.'

Obinze would ordinarily not have said anything at all, just watched and listened, but today, for some reason, he said, 'Didn't we all go to primary schools that taught the Nigerian curriculum?'

The women looked at him; their puzzled expressions implied that he could not possibly be serious. And in some ways, he was not. Of course he, too, wanted the best for his daughter. Sometimes, like now, he felt like an intruder in his new circle, of people who believed that the latest schools, the latest curriculums, would ensure the wholeness of their children. He did not share their certainties. He spent too much time mourning what could have been and questioning what should be.

When he was younger, he had admired people with moneyed childhoods and foreign accents, but he had come to sense an unvoiced yearning in them, a sad search for something they could never find. He did not want a well-educated child enmeshed in insecurities. Buchi would not go to the French school, of that he was sure.

'If you decide to disadvantage your child by sending her to one of these schools with half-baked Nigerian teachers, then you only have yourself to blame,' Mrs Akin-Cole said. She spoke with the unplaceable foreign accent, British and American and something else all at once, of the wealthy Nigerian who did not want the world to forget how worldly she was, how her British Airways executive card was choking with miles.

'One of my friends, her son goes to a school on the mainland and do you know, they have only five computers in the whole school. Only five!' the other woman said. Obinze remembered her name now. Adamma.

Mrs Akin-Cole said, 'Things have changed.'

'I agree,' Kosi said. 'But I also see what Obinze is saying.'

She was taking two sides at once, to please everyone; she always chose peace over truth, was always eager to conform. Watching her now as she talked to Mrs Akin-Cole, the gold shadow on her eyelids shimmering, he felt guilty about his thoughts. She was such a devoted woman, such a well-meaning, devoted woman. He reached out and held her hand.

'We'll go to Sidcot Hall and the French school,

and also look at some Nigerian schools like Crown Day,' Kosi said, and looked at him with a plea.

'Yes,' he said, squeezing her hand. She would know it was an apology, and later, he would apologize properly. He should have kept quiet, left her conversation unruffled. She often told him that her friends envied her, and said he behaved like a foreign husband, the way he made her breakfast on weekends and stayed home every night. And, in the pride in her eyes, he saw a shinier, better version of himself. He was about to say something to Mrs Akin-Cole, something meaningless and mollifying, when he heard Chief's raised voice behind him: 'But you know that as we speak, oil is flowing through illegal pipes and they sell it in bottles in Cotonou! Yes! Yes!'

Chief was upon them.

'My beautiful princess!' Chief said to Kosi, and hugged her, pressing her close; Obinze wondered if Chief had ever propositioned her. It would not surprise him. He had once been at Chief's house when a man brought his girlfriend to visit, and when she left the room to go to the toilet, Obinze heard Chief tell the man, 'I like that girl. Give her to me and I will give you a nice plot of land in Ikeja.'

'You look so well, Chief,' Kosi said. 'Ever young!'

'Ah, my dear, I try, I try.' Chief jokingly tugged at the satin lapels of his black jacket. He did look well, spare and upright, unlike many of his peers who looked like pregnant men.

'My boy!' he said to Obinze.

'Good evening, Chief.' Obinze shook his hand with both hands, bowing slightly. He watched the other men at the party bow, too, clustering around Chief, jostling to out-laugh one another when Chief made a joke.

The party was more crowded. Obinze looked up and saw Ferdinand, a stocky acquaintance of Chief's who had run for governor in the last elections, had lost and, as all losing politicians did, had gone to court to challenge the results. Ferdinand had a steely, amoral face; if one examined his hands, the blood of his enemies might be found crusted under his fingernails. Ferdinand's eyes met his and Obinze looked away. He was worried that Ferdinand would come over to talk about the shady land deal he had mentioned the last time they ran into each other, and so he mumbled that he was going to the toilet and slipped away from the group.

At the buffet table, he saw a young man looking with sad disappointment at the cold cuts and pastas. Obinze was drawn to his gaucheness; in the young man's clothes, and in the way that he stood, was an outsiderness he could not shield even if he had wanted to.

'There's another table on the other side with Nigerian food,' Obinze told him, and the young man looked at him and laughed in gratitude. His name was Yemi and he was a newspaper journalist. Not surprising; pictures from Chief's parties were always splattered in the weekend papers.

Yemi had studied English at university and Obinze asked him what books he liked, keen to talk about something interesting at last, but he soon realized that, for Yemi, a book did not qualify as literature unless it had polysyllabic words and incomprehensible passages.

'The problem is that the novel is too simple, the man does not even use any big words,' Yemi said.

It saddened Obinze that Yemi was so poorly educated and did not know that he was poorly educated. It made him want to be a teacher. He imagined himself standing in front of a class full of Yemis, teaching. It would suit him, the teaching life, as it had suited his mother. He often imagined other things he could have done, or that he could still do: teach in a university, edit a newspaper, coach professional table tennis.

'I don't know what your line of business is, sir, but I am always looking for a better job. I'm completing my master's now,' Yemi said, in the manner of the true Lagosian who was always hustling, eyes eternally alert to the brighter and the better; Obinze gave him his card before going back to find Kosi.

'I was wondering where you were,' she said.

'Sorry, I ran into somebody,' Obinze said. He reached into his pocket to touch his BlackBerry. Kosi was asking if he wanted more food. He didn't. He wanted to go home. A rash eagerness had overcome him, to go into his study and reply to Ifemelu's e-mail, something he had unconsciously been composing in his mind. If she was considering coming back to Nigeria, then it meant she was no longer with the black American. But she might be bringing him with her; she was after all the kind of woman who would make a man easily uproot his life, the kind who, because she did not expect or ask for certainty, made a certain kind of sureness become possible. When she held his hand during their campus days, she would squeeze until both palms became slick with sweat, and she would say, teasing, 'Just in case this is the last time we hold hands, let's really hold hands. Because a motorcycle or a car can kill us now, or I might see the real man of my dreams down the street and leave you or you might see the real woman of your dreams and leave me.' Perhaps the black American would come back to Nigeria, too, clinging on to her. Still, he sensed, from the e-mail, that she was single. He brought out his BlackBerry to calculate the American time when it had been sent. Early afternoon. Her sentences had a hasty quality; he wondered what she had been doing then. And he wondered what else Ranyinudo had told her about him.

On the Saturday in December when he ran into Ranyinudo at the Palms mall, he was carrying Buchi in one arm, waiting at the entrance for Gabriel to bring the car around, and holding a bag with Buchi's biscuits in the other hand. 'The Zed!' Ranyinudo called out. In secondary school she had been the bubbly tomboy, very tall and skinny and straightforward, not armed with the mysteriousness of girls. The boys had all liked her but never chased her, and they fondly called her Leave Me in Peace, because of how often she would say, whenever asked about her unusual name, 'Yes, it is an Igbo name and it means "leave us in peace", so you leave me in peace!' He was surprised at how chic she looked now, and how different, with her short spiky hair and tight jeans, her body full and curvy.

'The Zed – The Zed! Longest time! You don't ask about us again. Is this your daughter? Oh, bless! The other day I was with one of my friends, Dele. You know Dele from Hale Bank? He said you own that building near the Ace office in Banana Island? Congratulations. You've really done well o. And Dele said you are so humble.'

He had been uncomfortable, with her overdone fussing, the deference that seeped subtly from her pores. He was, in her eyes, no longer The Zed from secondary school, and the stories of his wealth made her assume he had changed more than he possibly could have. People often told him how humble he was, but they did not mean real humility, it was merely that he did not flaunt his membership in the wealthy club, did not exercise the rights it brought – to be rude, to be inconsiderate, to be greeted rather than to greet – and because so many others like him exercised those rights, his choices were interpreted as humility. He did not boast, either, or speak about the things he owned, which made people assume he owned much more than he did. Even his closest friend Okwudiba often told him how humble he was, and it irked him slightly, because he wished Okwudiba would see that to call him humble was to make rudeness normal. Besides, humility had always seemed to him a specious thing, invented for the comfort of others; you were praised for humility by people because you did not make them feel any more lacking than they already did. It was honesty that he valued; he had always wished himself to be truly honest, and always feared that he was not.

In the car on the way home from Chief's party, Kosi said, 'Darling, you must be hungry. You ate only that spring roll?'

'And suya.'

'You need to eat. Thank God I asked Marie to cook,' she said, and added, giggling, 'Me, I should have respected myself and left those snails alone! I think I ate up to ten. They were so nice and peppery.'

Obinze laughed, vaguely bored, but happy that she was happy.

Marie was slight, and Obinze was not sure whether she was timid or whether her halting English made her seem so. She had been with them only a month. The last housegirl, brought by a relative of Gabriel's, was thickset and had arrived clutching a duffel bag. He was not there when Kosi looked through it – she did that routinely with all domestic help because she wanted to know what was being brought into her home – but he came out when he heard Kosi shouting, in that impatient, shrill manner she put on with domestic help to command authority, to ward off disrespect. The girl's bag was on the floor, open, clothing fluffing out. Kosi stood beside it, holding up, at the tips of her fingers, a packet of condoms.

'What is this for? Eh? You came to my house to be a prostitute?'

The girl looked down at first, silent, then she looked Kosi in the face and said quietly, 'In my last job, my madam's husband was always forcing me.'

Kosi's eyes bulged. She moved forward for a moment, as though to attack the girl in some way, and then stopped.

'Please carry your bag and go now-now,' she said.

The girl shifted, looking a little surprised, and then she picked up her bag and turned to the door. After she left, Kosi said, 'Can you believe the nonsense, darling? She came here with condoms and she actually opened her mouth to say that rubbish. Can you believe it?'

'Her former employer raped her so she decided to protect herself this time,' Obinze said.

Kosi stared at him. 'You feel sorry for her. You don't know these housegirls. How can you feel sorry for her?'

He wanted to ask, *How can you not?* But the tentative fear in her eyes silenced him. Her insecurity, so great and so ordinary, silenced him. She was worried about a housegirl whom it would never even occur to him to seduce. Lagos could do this to a woman married to a young and wealthy man; he knew how easy it was to slip into paranoia about housegirls, about secretaries, about *Lagos Girls*, those sophisticated monsters of glamour who swallowed husbands whole, slithering them down their jewelled throats. Still, he wished Kosi feared less, conformed less.

Some years ago, he had told her about an attractive banker who had come to his office to talk to him about opening an account, a young woman wearing a fitted shirt with an extra button undone, trying to hide the desperation in her eyes. 'Darling, your secretary should not let any of these bank marketing girls come into your office!' Kosi had said, as though she seemed no longer to see him, Obinze, and instead saw blurred figures, classic types: a wealthy man, a female banker who had been given a target deposit amount, an easy exchange. Kosi expected him to cheat, and her concern was to minimize the possibilities he might have. 'Kosi, nothing can happen unless I want it to. I will never want it to,' he had said, in what was both a reassurance and a rebuke.

She had, in the years since they got married, grown an intemperate dislike of single women and an intemperate love of God. Before they got

53

married, she went to service once a week at the Anglican church on the Marina, a Sunday tick-the-box routine that she did because she had been brought up that way, but after their wedding, she switched to the House of David because, as she told him, it was a Bible-believing church. Later, when he found out that the House of David had a special prayer service for Keeping Your Husband, he had felt unsettled. Just as he had when he once asked why her best friend from university, Elohor, hardly visited them, and Kosi said, 'She's still single,' as though that was a self-evident reason.

Marie knocked on his study door and came in with a tray of rice and fried plantains. He ate slowly. He put in a Fela CD and then started to write the e-mail on his computer; his BlackBerry keyboard would cramp his fingers and his mind. He had introduced Ifemelu to Fela at university. She had, before then, thought of Fela as the mad weed-smoker who wore underwear at his concerts, but she had come to love the Afrobeat sound and they would lie on his mattress in Nsukka and listen to it and then she would leap up and make swift, vulgar movements with her hips when the run-run-run chorus came on. He wondered if she remembered that. He wondered if she remembered how his cousin had sent mix tapes from abroad, and how he made copies for her at the famous electronics shop in the market where music blared all day long, ringing in your ears even after you had left. He had wanted her to have the music he had. She had never really been interested in Biggie and Warren G and Dr Dre and Snoop Dogg, but Fela was different. On Fela, they had agreed.

He wrote and rewrote the e-mail, not mentioning his wife or using the first person plural, trying for a balance between earnest and funny. He did not want to alienate her. He wanted to make sure she would reply this time. He clicked Send and then minutes later checked to see if she had replied. He was tired. It was not a physical fatigue – he went to the gym regularly and felt better than he had in years – but a draining lassitude that numbed the margins of his mind. He got up and went out to the verandah; the sudden hot air, the roar of his neighbour's generator, the smell of diesel exhaust fumes brought a lightness to his head. Frantic winged insects flitted around the electric bulb. He felt, looking out at the muggy darkness farther away, as if he could float, and all he needed to do was to let himself go.

PART II

CHAPTER 3

Mariama finished her customer's hair, sprayed it with sheen, and, after the customer left, she said, 'I'm going to get Chinese.'

Aisha and Halima told her what they wanted – General Tso's Chicken Very Spicy, Chicken Wings, Orange Chicken – with the quick ease of people saying what they said every day.

'You want anything?' Mariama asked Ifemelu.

'No, thanks,' Ifemelu said.

'Your hair take long. You need food,' Aisha said.

'I'm fine. I have a granola bar,' Ifemelu said. She had some baby carrots in a Ziploc, too, although all she had snacked on so far was her melted chocolate.

'What bar?' Aisha asked.

Ifemelu showed her the bar, organic, one hundred per cent whole grain with real fruit.

'That not food!' Halima scoffed, looking away from the television.

'She here fifteen years, Halima,' Aisha said, as if the length of years in America explained Ifemelu's eating of a granola bar.

'Fifteen? Long time,' Halima said.

Aisha waited until Mariama left before pulling out her cell phone from her pocket. 'Sorry, I make quick call,' she said, and stepped outside. Her face had brightened when she came back; there was a smiling, even-featured prettiness, drawn out by that phone call, that Ifemelu had not earlier seen.

'Emeka work late today. So only Chijioke come to see you, before we finish,' she said, as if she and Ifemelu had planned it all together.

'Look, you don't have to ask them to come. I won't even know what to tell them,' Ifemelu said.

'Tell Chijioke Igbo can marry not Igbo.'

'Aisha, I can't tell him to marry you. He will marry you if he wants to.'

'They want marry me. But I am not Igbo!' Aisha's eyes glittered; the woman had to be a little mentally unstable.

'Is that what they told you?' Ifemelu asked.

'Emeka say his mother tell him if he marry American, she kill herself,' Aisha said.

'That's not good.'

'But me, I am African.'

'So maybe she won't kill herself if he marries you.'

Aisha looked blankly at her. 'Your boyfriend mother want him to marry you?'

Ifemelu thought first of Blaine then she realized that Aisha, of course, meant her make-believe boyfriend.

'Yes. She keeps asking us when we will get married.' She was amazed by her own fluidness, it was as if she had convinced even herself that she was not living on memories mildewed by thirteen years. But it could have been true; Obinze's mother had liked her, after all.

'Ah!' Aisha said, in well-meaning envy.

A man with dry, greying skin and a mop of white hair came in with a plastic tray of herbal potions for sale.

'No, no, no,' Aisha said to him, palm raised as though to ward him off. The man retreated. Ifemelu felt sorry for him, hungry-looking in his worn dashiki, and wondered how much he could possibly make from his sales. She should have bought something.

'You talk Igbo to Chijioke. He listen to you,' Aisha said. 'You talk Igbo?'

'Of course I speak Igbo,' Ifemelu said, defensive, wondering if Aisha was again suggesting that America had changed her. 'Take it easy!' she added, because Aisha had pulled a tiny-toothed comb through a section of her hair.

'Your hair hard,' Aisha said.

'It is not hard,' Ifemelu said firmly. 'You are using the wrong comb.' And she pulled the comb from Aisha's hand and put it down on the table.

Ifemelu had grown up in the shadow of her mother's hair. It was black-black, so thick it drank two containers of relaxer at the salon, so full it took hours under the hooded dryer, and, when finally released from pink plastic rollers, sprang free and

61

full, flowing down her back like a celebration. Her father called it a crown of glory. 'Is it your real hair?' strangers would ask, and then reach out to touch it reverently. Others would say 'Are you from Jamaica?' as though only foreign blood could explain such bounteous hair that did not thin at the temples. Through the years of childhood, Ifemelu would often look in the mirror and pull at her own hair, separate the coils, will it to become like her mother's, but it remained bristly and grew reluctantly; braiders said it cut them like a knife.

One day, the year Ifemelu turned ten, her mother came home from work looking different. Her clothes were the same, a brown dress belted at the waist, but her face was flushed, her eyes unfocused. 'Where is the big scissors?' she asked, and when Ifemelu brought it to her, she raised it to her head and, handful by handful, chopped off all her hair. Ifemelu stared, stunned. The hair lay on the floor like dead grass. 'Bring me a big bag,' her mother said. Ifemelu obeyed, feeling herself in a trance, with things happening that she did not understand. She watched her mother walk around their flat, collecting all the Catholic objects, the crucifixes hung on walls, the rosaries nested in drawers, the missals propped on shelves. Her mother put them all in the polythene bag, which she carried to the backyard, her steps quick, her faraway look un-wavering. She made a fire near the rubbish dump, at the same spot where she burned her used sani-tary pads, and first she threw in her hair, wrapped in old newspaper, and then, one after the other, the objects of faith. Dark grey smoke curled up into the air. From the verandah, Ifemelu began to cry because she sensed that something had happened, and the woman standing by the fire, splashing in more kerosene as it dimmed and stepping back as it flared, the woman who was bald and blank, was not her mother, could not be her mother.

When her mother came back inside, Ifemelu backed away, but her mother hugged her close.

'I am saved,' she said. 'Mrs Ojo ministered to me this afternoon during the children's break and I received Christ. Old things have passed away and all things have become new. Praise God. On Sunday we will start going to Revival Saints. It is a Bible-believing church and a living church, not like St Dominic's.' Her mother's words were not hers. She spoke them too rigidly, with a demeanour that belonged to someone else. Even her voice, usually high-pitched and feminine, had deepened and curdled. That afternoon, Ifemelu watched her mother's essence take flight. Before, her mother said the rosary once in a while, crossed herself before she ate, wore pretty images of saints around her neck, sang Latin songs and laughed when Ifemelu's father teased her about her terrible pronunciation. She laughed, too, whenever he said, 'I am an agnostic respecter of religion,' and she would tell him how lucky he was to be married to her, because even though he went to church only for weddings and funerals, he would get into heaven on the wings of her faith. But, after that afternoon, her God changed. He became exacting. Relaxed hair offended Him. Dancing offended Him. She bartered with Him, offering starvation in exchange for prosperity, for a job promotion, for good health. She fasted herself bone-thin: dry fasts on weekends, and on weekdays, only water until evening. Ifemelu's father followed her with anxious eyes, urging her to eat a little more, to fast a little less, and he always spoke carefully, so that she would not call him the devil's agent and ignore him, as she had done with a cousin who was staying with them. 'I am fasting for your father's conversion,' she told Ifemelu often. For months, the air in their flat was like cracked glass. Everyone tiptoed around her mother, who had become a stranger, thin and knuckly and severe. Ifemelu worried that she would, one day, simply snap into two and die.

Then, on Easter Saturday, a dour day, the first quiet Easter Saturday in Ifemelu's life, her mother ran out of the kitchen and said, 'I saw an angel!' Before, there would have been cooking and bustling, many pots in the kitchen and many relatives in the flat, and Ifemelu and her mother would have gone to night mass, and held up lit candles, singing in a sea of flickering flames, and then come home to continue cooking the big Easter lunch. But the flat was silent. Their relatives had kept away and lunch would be the usual rice and stew.

Ifemelu was in the living room with her father, and when her mother said 'I saw an angel!' Ifemelu saw exasperation in his eyes, a brief glimpse before it disappeared.

'What happened?' he asked, in the placating tone used for a child, as if humouring his wife's madness would make it go away quickly.

Her mother told them of a vision she had just had, a blazing appearance near the gas cooker of an angel holding a book trimmed in red thread, telling her to leave Revival Saints because the pastor was a wizard who attended nightly demonic meetings under the sea.

'You should listen to the angel,' her father said.

And so her mother left the church and began to let her hair grow again, but stopped wearing necklaces and earrings because jewellery, according to the pastor at Miracle Spring, was ungodly, unbefitting a woman of virtue. Shortly afterwards, on the same day as the failed coup, while the traders who lived downstairs were crying because the coup would have saved Nigeria and market women would have been given cabinet positions, her mother saw another vision. This time, the angel appeared in her bedroom, above the wardrobe, and told her to leave Miracle Spring and join Guiding Assembly. Halfway through the first service Ifemelu attended with her mother, in a marble-floored convention hall, surrounded by perfumed people and the ricochet of rich voices, Ifemelu looked at her mother and saw that she was crying and laughing at the same time. In this church of surging hope, of thumping and clapping, where Ifemelu imagined a swirl of affluent angels above, her mother's spirit had found a home. It was a church full of the newly wealthy; her mother's small car, in the parking lot, was the oldest, with its dull paint and many scratches. If she worshipped with the prosperous, she said, then God would bless her as He had blessed them. She began to wear jewellery again, to drink her Guinness stout; she fasted only once a week and often said '*My* God tells me' and '*My* Bible says,' as though other people's were not just different but misguided. Her response to a 'Good morning' or a 'Good afternoon' was a cheerful 'God bless you!' Her God became genial and did not mind being commanded. Every morning, she woke the household up for prayers, and they would kneel on the scratchy carpet of the living room, singing, clapping, covering the day ahead with the blood of Jesus, and her mother's words would pierce the stillness of dawn: 'God, my heavenly father, I command you to fill this day with blessings and prove to me that you are God! Lord, I am waiting on you for my prosperity! Do not let the evil one win, do not let my enemies triumph over me!' Ifemelu's father once said the prayers were delusional battles with imaginary traducers, yet he insisted that Ifemelu always wake up early to pray. 'It keeps your mother happy,' he told her.

In church, at testimony time, her mother was

first to hurry to the altar. 'I had catarrh this morning,' she would start. 'But as Pastor Gideon started to pray, it cleared. Now it is gone. Praise God!' The congregation would shout 'Alleluia!' and other testimonies would follow. *I did not study because I was sick and yet I passed my exams with flying colours! I had malaria and prayed over it and was cured! My cough disappeared as Pastor started praying!* But always her mother went first, gliding and smiling, enclosed in salvation's glow. Later in the service, when Pastor Gideon would leap out in his sharp-shouldered suit and pointy shoes, and say, 'Our God is not a poor God, amen? It is our portion to prosper, amen?' Ifemelu's mother would raise her arm high, heavenward, as she said, 'Amen, Father Lord, amen.'

Ifemelu did not think that God had given Pastor Gideon the big house and all those cars, he had of course bought them with money from the three collections at each service, and she did not think that God would do for all as He had done for Pastor Gideon, because it was impossible, but she liked that her mother ate regularly now. The warmth in her mother's eyes was back, and there was a new joy in her bearing, and she once again lingered at the dining table with her father after meals, and sang loudly while taking a bath. Her new church absorbed her but did not destroy her. It made her predictable and easy to lie to. 'I am going to Bible study' and 'I am going to Fellowship' were the easiest ways for Ifemelu to go out unquestioned during her teenage years. Ifemelu was uninterested in church, indifferent about making any religious effort, perhaps because her mother already made so much. Yet her mother's faith comforted her; it was, in her mind, a white cloud that moved benignly above her as she moved. Until The General came into their lives.

Every morning, Ifemelu's mother prayed for The General. She would say, 'Heavenly father, I command you to bless Uju's mentor. May his enemies never triumph over him!' Or she would say, 'We cover Uju's mentor with the precious blood of Jesus!' And Ifemelu would mumble something nonsensical instead of saying 'Amen.' Her mother said the word 'mentor' defiantly, a thickness in her tone, as though the force of her delivery would truly turn The General into a mentor, and also remake the world into a place where young doctors could afford Aunty Uju's new Mazda, that green, glossy, intimidatingly streamlined car.

Chetachi, who lived upstairs, asked Ifemelu, 'Your mum said Aunty Uju's mentor also gave her a loan for the car?'

'Yes.'

'Eh! Aunty Uju is lucky o!' Chetachi said.

Ifemelu did not miss the knowing smirk on her face. Chetachi and her mother must have already gossiped about the car; they were envious, chattering people who visited only to see what others had, to size up new furniture or new electronics.

'God should bless the man o. Me I hope I will also meet a mentor when I graduate,' Chetachi said. Ifemelu bristled at Chetachi's goading. Still, it was her mother's fault, to so eagerly tell the neighbours her mentor story. She should not have; it was nobody's business what Aunty Uju did. Ifemelu had overheard her telling somebody in the backyard, 'You see, The General wanted to be a doctor when he was young, and so now he helps young doctors, God is really using him in people's lives.' And she sounded sincere, cheerful, convincing. She believed her own words. Ifemelu could not understand this, her mother's ability to tell herself stories about her reality that did not even resemble her reality. When Aunty Uju first told them about her new job – 'The hospital has no doctor vacancy but The General made them create one for me' were her words – Ifemelu's mother promptly said, 'This is a miracle!'

Aunty Uju smiled, a quiet smile that held its peace; she did not, of course, think it was a miracle, but would not say so. Or maybe there *was* something of a miracle in her new job as consultant at the military hospital in Victoria Island, and her new house in Dolphin Estate, the cluster of duplexes that wore a fresh foreignness, some painted pink, others the blue of a warm sky, hemmed by a park with grass lush as a new rug and benches where people could sit – a rarity even on The Island. Only weeks before, she had been a new graduate and all her classmates were talking about going abroad to

69

take the American medical exams or the British exams, because the other choice was to tumble into a parched wasteland of joblessness. The country was starved of hope, cars stuck for days in long, sweaty petrol lines, pensioners raising wilting placards demanding their pay, lecturers gathering to announce yet one more strike. But Aunty Uju did not want to leave; she had, for as long as Ifemelu could remember, dreamed of owning a private clinic, and she held that dream in a tight clasp.

'Nigeria will not be like this forever, I'm sure I will find part-time work and it will be tough, yes, but one day I will start my clinic, and on The Island!' Aunty Uju had told Ifemelu. Then she went to a friend's wedding. The bride's father was an air vice marshal, it was rumoured that the Head of State might attend, and Aunty Uju joked about asking him to make her medical officer at Aso Rock. He did not attend, but many of his generals did, and one of them asked his ADC to call Aunty Uju, to ask her to come to his car in the parking lot after the reception, and when she went to the dark Peugeot with a small flag flying from its front, and said, 'Good afternoon, sir,' to the man in the back, he told her, 'I like you. I want to take care of you.' Maybe there was a kind of miracle in those words, *I like you, I want to take care of you*, Ifemelu thought, but not in the way her mother meant it. 'A miracle! God is faithful!' her mother said that day, eyes liquid with faith.

★ ★ ★

She said, in a similar tone, 'The devil is a liar. He wants to start blocking our blessing, he will not succeed,' when Ifemelu's father lost his job at the federal agency. He was fired for refusing to call his new boss Mummy. He came home earlier than usual, wracked with bitter disbelief, his termination letter in his hand, complaining about the absurdity of a grown man calling a grown woman Mummy because she had decided it was the best way to show her respect. 'Twelve years of dedicated labour. It is unconscionable,' he said. Her mother patted his back, told him God would provide another job and, until then, they would manage on her vice-principal salary. He went out job hunting every morning, teeth clenched and tie firmly knotted, and Ifemelu wondered if he just walked into random companies to try his luck, but soon he began to stay at home in a wrapper and singlet, lounging on the shabby sofa near the stereo. 'You have not had a morning bath?' her mother asked him one afternoon, when she came back from work looking drained, clutching files to her chest, wet patches under her armpits. Then she added irritably, 'If you have to call somebody Mummy to get your salary, you should have done so!'

He said nothing; for a moment, he seemed lost, shrunken and lost. Ifemelu felt sorry for him. She asked him about the book placed face down on his lap, a familiar-looking book that she knew he had read before. She hoped he would give her one of his long talks about something like the history

71

of China, and she would half listen as always, while cheering him up. But he was in no mood for talk. He shrugged as though to say she could look at the book if she wanted to. Her mother's words too easily wounded him; he was too alert to her, his ears always pricked up at her voice, his eyes always rested on her. Recently, before he was fired, he had told Ifemelu, 'Once I attain my promotion, I will buy your mother something truly memorable,' and when she asked him what, he smiled and said, mysteriously, 'It will unveil itself.'

Looking at him as he sat mute on the sofa, she thought how much he looked like what he was, a man full of blanched longings, a middle-brow civil servant who wanted a life different from what he had, who had longed for more education than he was able to get. He talked often of how he could not go to university because he had to find a job to support his siblings, and how people he was cleverer than in secondary school now had doctorates. His was a formal, elevated English. Their house helps hardly understood him but were nevertheless very impressed. Once, their former house help, Jecinta, had come into the kitchen and started clapping quietly, and told Ifemelu, 'You should have heard your father's big word now! *O di egwu!*' Sometimes Ifemelu imagined him in a classroom in the fifties, an overzealous colonial subject wearing an ill-fitting school uniform of cheap cotton, jostling to impress his missionary teachers. Even his handwriting was mannered, all curves and

72

flourishes, with a uniform elegance that looked like something printed. He had scolded Ifemelu as a child for being recalcitrant, mutinous, intransigent, words that made her little actions seem epic and almost prideworthy. But his mannered English bothered her as she got older, because it was costume, his shield against insecurity. He was haunted by what he did not have – a postgraduate degree, an upper-middle-class life – and so his affected words became his armour. She preferred it when he spoke Igbo; it was the only time he seemed unconscious of his own anxieties.

Losing his job made him quieter, and a thin wall grew between him and the world. He no longer muttered 'nation of intractable sycophancy' when the nightly news started on NTA, no longer held long monologues about how Babangida's government had reduced Nigerians to imprudent idiots, no longer teased her mother. And, most of all, he began to join in the morning prayers. He had never joined before; her mother had once insisted that he do so, before leaving to visit their hometown. 'Let us pray and cover the roads with the blood of Jesus,' she had said, and he replied that the roads would be safer, less slippery, if not covered with blood. Which had made her mother frown and Ifemelu laugh and laugh.

At least he still did not go to church. Ifemelu used to come home from church with her mother and find him sitting on the floor in the living room, sifting through his pile of LPs, and singing along to a song on the stereo. He always looked fresh, rested, as though being alone with his music had replenished him. But he hardly played music after he lost his job. They came home to find him at the dining table, bent over loose sheets of paper, writing letters to newspapers and magazines. And Ifemelu knew that, if given another chance, he would call his boss Mummy.

It was a Sunday morning, early, and somebody was banging on the front door. Ifemelu liked Sunday mornings, the slow shifting of time, when she, dressed for church, would sit in the living room with her father while her mother got ready. Sometimes they talked, she and her father, and other times they were silent, a shared and satisfying silence, as they were that morning. From the kitchen, the hum of the refrigerator was the only sound to be heard, until the banging on the door. A rude interruption. Ifemelu opened it and saw the landlord standing there, a round man with bulging, reddened eyes who was said to start his day with a glass of harsh gin. He looked past Ifemelu at her father, and shouted, 'It is now three months! I am still waiting for my money!' His voice was familiar to Ifemelu, the brassy shouting that always came from the flats of their neighbours, from somewhere else. But now he was here in their flat, and the scene jarred her, the land-lord shouting at *their* door, and her father turning a steely, silent face to him. They had never owed rent before. They had lived in this flat all her life; it was cramped, the kitchen walls blackened by kerosene fumes, and she was embarrassed when her school friends came to visit, but they had never owed rent.

'A braggart of a man,' her father said after the landlord left, and then he said nothing else. There was nothing else to say. They owed rent.

Her mother appeared, singing and heavily perfumed, her face dry and bright with powder that was one shade too light. She extended a wrist towards Ifemelu's father, her thin gold bracelet hung unclasped.

'Uju is coming after church to take us to see the house in Dolphin Estate,' her mother said. 'Will you follow us?'

'No,' he said shortly, as though Aunty Uju's new life was a subject he would rather avoid.

'You should come,' she said, but he did not respond, as he carefully snapped the bracelet around her wrist, and told her he had checked the water in her car.

'God is faithful. Look at Uju, to afford a house on The Island!' her mother said happily.

'Mummy, but you know Aunty Uju is not paying one kobo to live there,' Ifemelu said.

Her mother glanced at her. 'Did you iron that dress?'

'It doesn't need ironing.'

'It is rumpled. *Ngwa,* go and iron it. At least there is light. Or change into something else.'

Ifemelu got up reluctantly. 'This dress is not rumpled.'

'Go and iron it. There is no need to show the world that things are hard for us. Ours is not the worst case. Today is Sunday Work with Sister Ibinabo, so hurry up and let's go.'

Sister Ibinabo was powerful, and because she pretended to wear her power lightly, it only made her more so. The pastor, it was said, did whatever she asked him. It was not clear why; some said she had started the church with him, others that she knew a terrible secret from his past, still others that she simply had more spiritual power than he did but could not be pastor because she was a woman. She could prevent pastoral approval of a marriage, if she wanted to. She knew everyone and everything and she seemed to be everywhere at the same time, with her weather-beaten air, as though life had tossed her around for a long time. It was difficult to tell how old she was, whether fifty or sixty, her body wiry, her face closed like a shell. She never laughed but often smiled the thin smile of the pious. The mothers were in reverent awe of her; they brought her small presents, they eagerly handed their daughters to her for Sunday Work. Sister Ibinabo, the saviour of young females. She was asked to talk to troubled and troublesome girls. Some mothers asked if their daughters could live with her, in the flat behind the church. But Ifemelu had always sensed, in Sister Ibinabo, a deep-sown, simmering hostility to young girls. Sister Ibinabo did not like them, she merely watched them and warned them, as though offended by what in them was still fresh and in her was long dried up.

'I saw you wearing tight trousers last Saturday,' Sister Ibinabo said to a girl, Christie, in an exaggerated whisper, low enough to pretend it was a whisper but high enough for everyone to hear. 'Everything is permissible but not everything is beneficial. Any girl that wears tight trousers wants to commit the sin of temptation. It is best to avoid it.'

Christie nodded, humble, gracious, carrying her shame.

In the church back room, the two tiny windows did not let in much light, and so the electric bulb was always turned on during the day. Fund-raising envelopes were piled on the table, and next to them was a stack of coloured tissue, like fragile cloth. The girls began to organize themselves. Soon, some of them were writing on the envelopes, and others were cutting and curling pieces of tissue, gluing them into flower shapes, and stringing them together to form fluffy garlands. Next Sunday, at a special Thanksgiving service, the garlands would hang around the thick neck of Chief Omenka and the smaller necks of his family members. He had donated two new vans to the church.

'Join that group, Ifemelu,' Sister Ibinabo said.

Ifemelu folded her arms, and as often happened when she was about to say something she knew was better unsaid, the words rushed up her throat. 'Why should I make decorations for a thief?'

Sister Ibinabo stared in astonishment. A silence fell. The other girls looked on expectantly.

'What did you say?' Sister Ibinabo asked quietly, offering a chance for Ifemelu to apologize, to put the words back in her mouth. But Ifemelu felt herself unable to stop, her heart thumping, hurtling on a fast-moving path.

'Chief Omenka is a 419 and everybody knows it,' she said. 'This church is full of 419 men. Why should we pretend that this hall was not built with dirty money?'

'It is God's work,' Sister Ibinabo said quietly. 'If you cannot do God's work, then you should go. Go.'

Ifemelu hurried out of the room, past the gate and towards the bus station, knowing that in minutes the story would reach her mother inside the main church building. She had ruined the day. They would have gone to see Aunty Uju's house and had a nice lunch. Now, her mother would be testy and prickly. She wished she had said nothing. She had, after all, joined in making garlands for other 419 men in the past, men who had special seats in the front row, men who donated cars with the ease of people giving away chewing gum. She had happily attended their receptions, she had eaten rice and meat and coleslaw, food tainted by fraud, and she had eaten knowing this and had not choked, and had not even considered choking. Yet something had been different today. When Sister Ibinabo was talking to Christie, with that poisonous spite she claimed was religious

78

guidance, Ifemelu had looked at her and suddenly seen something of her own mother. Her mother was a kinder and simpler person, but like Sister Ibinabo, she was a person who denied that things were as they were. A person who had to spread the cloak of religion over her own petty desires. Suddenly, the last thing Ifemelu wanted was to be in that small room full of shadows. It had all seemed benign before, her mother's faith, all drenched in grace, and suddenly it no longer was. She wished, fleetingly, that her mother was not her mother, and for this she felt not guilt and sadness but a single emotion, a blend of guilt and sadness.

The bus stop was eerily empty, and she imagined all the people who would have been crowded here, now in churches, singing and praying. She waited for the bus, wondering whether to go home or somewhere else to wait for a while. It was best to go home, and face whatever she had to face.

Her mother pulled her ear, an almost-gentle tug, as though reluctant to cause real pain. She had done that since Ifemelu was a child. 'I will beat you!' she would say, when Ifemelu did something wrong, but there was never any beating, only the limp ear pull. Now, she pulled it twice, once and then again to emphasize her words. 'The devil is using you. You have to pray about this. Do not judge. Leave the judging to God!'

Her father said, 'You must refrain from your

natural proclivity towards provocation, Ifemelu. You have singled yourself out at school where you are known for insubordination and I have told you that it has already sullied your singular academic record. There is no need to create a similar pattern in church.'

'Yes, Daddy.'

When Aunty Uju arrived, Ifemelu's mother told her what had happened. 'Go and give that Ifemelu a talking-to. You are the only person she will listen to. Ask her what I did to her that makes her want to embarrass me in the church like this. She insulted Sister Ibinabo! It is like insulting Pastor! Why must this girl be a troublemaker? I have been saying it since, that it would be better if she was a boy, behaving like this.'

'Sister, you know her problem is that she doesn't always know when to keep her mouth shut. Don't worry, I will talk to her,' Aunty Uju said, playing her role of pacifier, soothing her cousin's wife. She had always got along with Ifemelu's mother, the easy relationship between two people who carefully avoided conversations of any depth. Perhaps Aunty Uju felt gratitude to Ifemelu's mother for embracing her, accepting her status as the special resident relative. Growing up, Ifemelu did not feel like an only child because of the cousins, aunts and uncles who lived with them. There were always suitcases and bags in the flat; sometimes a relative or two would sleep on the floor of the living room for weeks. Most were her father's family, brought to Lagos to learn

80

a trade or go to school or look for a job, so that the people back in the village would not mutter about their brother with only one child who did not want to help raise others. Her father felt an obligation to them, he insisted that everyone be home before eight p.m., made sure there was enough food to go around, and locked his bedroom door even when he went to the bathroom, because any of them could wander in and steal something. But Aunty Uju was different. Too clever to waste away in that backwater, he said. He called her his youngest sister although she was the child of his father's brother, and he had been more protective, less distant, with her. Whenever he came across Ifemelu and Aunty Uju curled up in bed talking, he would fondly say 'You two.' After Aunty Uju left to go to university in Ibadan, he told Ifemelu, almost wistfully, 'Uju exerted a calming influence on you.' He seemed to see, in their closeness, proof of his own good choice, as though he had knowingly brought a gift to his family, a buffer between his wife and daughter.

And so, in the bedroom, Aunty Uju told Ifemelu, 'You should have just made the garland. I've told you that you don't have to say everything. You have to learn that. You don't have to *say* everything.'

'Why can't Mummy like the things you get from The General without pretending they are from God?'

'Who says they are not from God?' Aunty Uju asked, and made a face, pulling her lips down at the sides. Ifemelu laughed.

According to the family legend, Ifemelu had been a surly three-year-old who screamed if a stranger came close, but the first time she saw Aunty Uju, thirteen and pimply faced, Ifemelu walked over and climbed into her lap and stayed there. She did not know if this had happened, or had merely become true from being told over and over again, a charmed tale of the beginning of their closeness. It was Aunty Uju who sewed Ifemelu's little-girl dresses and, as Ifemelu got older, they would pore over fashion magazines, choosing styles together. Aunty Uju taught her to mash an avocado and spread it on her face, to dissolve Robb in hot water and place her face over the steam, to dry a pimple with toothpaste. Aunty Uju brought her James Hadley Chase novels wrapped in newspaper to hide the near-naked women on the cover, hot-stretched her hair when she got lice from the neighbours, talked her through her first menstrual period, supplementing her mother's lecture that was full of biblical quotes about virtue but lacked useful details about cramps and pads. When Ifemelu met Obinze, she told Aunty Uju that she had met the love of her life, and Aunty Uju told her to let him kiss and touch but not to let him put it inside.

CHAPTER 4

The gods, the hovering deities who gave and took teenage loves, had decided that Obinze would go out with Ginika. Obinze was the new boy, a fine boy even if he was short. He had transferred from the university secondary school in Nsukka, and only days after, everyone knew of the swirling rumours about his mother. She had fought with a man, another professor at Nsukka, a real fight, punching and hitting, and she had won, too, even tearing his clothes, and so she was suspended for two years and had moved to Lagos until she could go back. It was an unusual story; market women fought, mad women fought, but not women who were professors. Obinze, with his air of calm and inwardness, made it even more intriguing. He was quickly admitted into the clan of swaggering, carelessly cool males, the Big Guys; he lounged in the corridors with them, stood with them at the back of the hall during assembly. None of them tucked in their shirts, and for this they always got into trouble, glamorous trouble, with the teachers, but Obinze came to school every day with his shirt neatly tucked in and soon all the

Big Guys tucked in, too, even Kayode DaSilva, the coolest of them all.

Kayode spent every vacation in his parents' house in England, which looked large and forbidding in the photos Ifemelu had seen. His girlfriend, Yinka, was like him – she, too, went to England often and lived in Ikoyi and spoke with a British accent. She was the most popular girl in their form, her school bag made of thick monogrammed leather, her sandals always different from what anybody else had. The second most popular girl was Ginika, Ifemelu's close friend. Ginika did not go abroad often, and so did not have the air of *away* as Yinka did, but she had caramel skin and wavy hair that, when unbraided, fell down to her neck instead of standing Afro-like. Each year, she was voted Prettiest Girl in their form, and she would wryly say, 'It's just because I'm a half-caste. How can I be finer than Zainab?'

And so it was the natural order of things, that the gods should match Obinze and Ginika. Kayode was throwing a hasty party in their guest quarters while his parents were away in London. He told Ginika, 'I'm going to introduce you to my guy Zed at the party.'

'He's not bad,' Ginika said, smiling.

'I hope he did not get his mother's fighting genes o,' Ifemelu teased. It was nice to see Ginika interested in a boy; almost all the Big Guys in school had tried with her and none had lasted long; Obinze seemed quiet, a good match.

Ifemelu and Ginika arrived together, the party still at its dawn, the dance floor bare, boys running around with cassette tapes, shyness and awkwardness still undissolved. Each time Ifemelu came to Kayode's house, she imagined what it was like to live here, in Ikoyi, in a gracious and gravelled compound, with servants who wore white.

'See Kayode with the new guy,' Ifemelu said.

'I don't want to look,' Ginika said. 'Are they coming?'

'Yes.'

'My shoes are so tight.'

'You can dance in tight shoes,' Ifemelu said.

The boys were before them. Obinze looked overdressed, in a thick corduroy jacket, while Kayode wore a T-shirt and jeans.

'Hey, babes!' Kayode said. He was tall and rangy, with the easy manner of the entitled. 'Ginika, meet my friend Obinze, Zed, this is Ginika, the queen God made for you if you are ready to work for it!' He was smirking, already a little drunk, the golden boy making a golden match.

'Hi,' Obinze said to Ginika.

'This is Ifemelu,' Kayode said. 'Otherwise known as Ifemsco. She's Ginika's right-hand man. If you misbehave, she will flog you.'

They all laughed on cue.

'Hi,' Obinze said. His eyes met Ifemelu's and held, and lingered.

Kayode was making small talk, telling Obinze that Ginika's parents were also university

85

professors. 'So both of you are book people,' Kayode said. Obinze should have taken over and begun talking to Ginika, and Kayode would have left, and Ifemelu would have followed, and the will of the gods would have been fulfilled. But Obinze said little, and Kayode was left to carry the conversation, his voice getting boisterous, and from time to time he glanced at Obinze, as though to urge him on. Ifemelu was not sure when something happened, but in those moments, as Kayode talked, something strange happened. A quickening inside her, a dawning. She realized, quite suddenly, that she wanted to breathe the same air as Obinze. She became, also, acutely aware of the present, the now, Toni Braxton's voice from the cassette player, *be it fast or slow, it doesn't let go, or shake me,* the smell of Kayode's father's brandy, which had been sneaked out of the main house, and the tight white shirt that chafed at her armpits. Aunty Uju had made her tie it, in a loose bow, at her navel and she wondered now if it was truly stylish or if she looked silly.

The music stopped abruptly. Kayode said, 'I'm coming,' and left to find out what was wrong, and in the new silence, Ginika fiddled with the metal bangle that encircled her wrist.

Obinze's eyes met Ifemelu's again.

'Aren't you hot in that jacket?' Ifemelu asked. The question came out before she could restrain herself, so used was she to sharpening her words, to watching for terror in the eyes of boys. But he was smiling. He looked amused. He was not afraid of her.

'Very hot,' he said. 'But I'm a country bumpkin and this is my first city party so you have to forgive me.' Slowly, he took his jacket off, green and padded at the elbows, under which he wore a long-sleeved shirt. 'Now I'll have to carry a jacket around with me.'

'I can hold it for you,' Ginika offered. 'And don't mind Ifem, the jacket is fine.'

'Thanks, but don't worry. I should hold it, as punishment for wearing it in the first place.' He looked at Ifemelu, eyes twinkling.

'I didn't mean it like that,' Ifemelu said. 'It's just that this room is so hot and that jacket looks heavy.'

'I like your voice,' he said, almost cutting her short.

And she, who was never at a loss, croaked, 'My voice?'

'Yes.'

The music had begun. 'Let's dance?' he asked. She nodded.

He took her hand and then smiled at Ginika, as though to a nice chaperone whose job was now done. Ifemelu thought Mills and Boon romances were silly, she and her friends sometimes enacted the stories, Ifemelu or Ranyinudo would play the man and Ginika or Priye would play the woman – the man would grab the woman, the woman would fight weakly, then collapse against him with shrill moans – and they would all burst out laughing. But in the filling-up dance floor of Kayode's party, she was jolted by a small truth in those romances. It was indeed true that because of a male, your stomach could tighten up and refuse to unknot itself, your body's joints could unhinge, your limbs fail to move to music, and all effortless things suddenly become leaden. As she moved stiffly, she saw Ginika in her side vision, watching them, her expression puzzled, mouth slightly slack, as though she did not quite believe what had happened.

'You actually said "country bumpkin",' Ifemelu said, her voice high above the music.

'What?'

'Nobody says "country bumpkin". It's the kind of thing you read in a book.'

'You have to tell me what books you read,' he said.

He was teasing her, and she did not quite get the joke, but she laughed anyway. Later, she wished that she remembered every word they said to each other as they danced. She remembered, instead, feeling adrift. When the lights were turned off, and the blues dancing started, she wanted to be in his arms in a dark corner, but he said, 'Let's go outside and talk.'

They sat on cement blocks behind the guest-house, next to what looked like the gateman's bathroom, a narrow stall which, when the wind blew, brought a stale smell. They talked and talked, hungry to know each other. He told her that his father had died when he was seven, and how clearly he remembered his father teaching him to ride a tricycle on a tree-lined street near their campus home, but sometimes he would discover, in panic, that he could not remember his father's face and a sense of betrayal would overwhelm him and he would hurry to examine the framed photo on their living room wall.

'Your mother never wanted to remarry?'

'Even if she wanted to, I don't think she would, because of me. I want her to be happy, but I don't want her to remarry.'

'I would feel the same way. Did she really fight with another professor?'

'So you heard that story.'

'They said it's why she had to leave Nsukka University.'

'No, she didn't fight. She was on a committee and they discovered that this professor had misused funds and my mother accused him publicly and he got angry and slapped her and said he could not take a woman talking to him like that. So my mother got up and locked the door of the conference room and put the key in her bra. She told him she could not slap him back because he was stronger than her, but he would have to apologize to her publicly, in front of all the people who had seen him slap her. So he did. But she knew he didn't mean it. She said he did it in a kind of "okay sorry if that's what you want to hear and just bring out the key" way. She came home that day really angry, and she kept talking about how things had changed and what did it mean that now somebody could just slap another person. She wrote circulars and articles about it, and the student union got involved. People were saying, Oh, why did he slap her when she's a widow, and that annoyed her even more. She said she should not have been slapped because she is a full human being, not because she doesn't have a husband to speak for her. So some of her female students went and printed Full Human Being on T-shirts. I guess it made her well-known. She's usually very quiet and doesn't have many friends.'

'Is that why she came to Lagos?'

'No. She's been scheduled to do this sabbatical for a while. I remember the first time she told me we would go away for her two-year sabbatical, and I was excited because I thought it would be in America, one of my friend's dads had just gone to America, and then she said it was Lagos, and I asked her what was the point? We might as well just stay in Nsukka.'

Ifemelu laughed. 'But at least you can still get on a plane to come to Lagos.'

'Yes, but we came by road,' Obinze said, laughing. 'But now I'm happy it was Lagos or I would not have met you.'

'Or met Ginika,' she teased.

'Stop it.'

'Your guys will kill you. You're supposed to be chasing her.'

'I'm chasing you.'

She would always remember this moment, those words. *I'm chasing you.*

'I saw you in school some time ago. I even asked Kay about you,' he said.

'Are you serious?'

'I saw you holding a James Hadley Chase, near the lab. And I said, Ah, correct, there is hope. She reads.'

'I think I've read them all.'

'Me too. What's your favourite?'

'Miss Shumway Waves a Wand.'

'Mine is *Want to Stay Alive?* I stayed up one night to finish it.'

'Yes, I like that too.'

'What about other books? Which of the classics do you like?'

'Classics, *kwa*? I just like crime and thrillers. Sheldon, Ludlum, Archer.'

'But you also have to read proper books.'

She looked at him, amused by his earnestness. 'Aje-butter! University boy! That must be what your professor mother taught you.'

'No, seriously.' He paused. 'I'll give you some to try. I love the American ones.'

'You have to read proper books,' she mimicked.

'What about poetry?'

'What's that last one we did in class, "Ancient Mariner"? So boring.'

Obinze laughed, and Ifemelu, uninterested in pursuing the subject of poetry, asked, 'So what did Kayode say about me?'

'Nothing bad. He likes you.'

'You don't want to tell me what he said.'

'He said, "Ifemelu is a fine babe but she is too much trouble. She can argue. She can talk. She never agrees. But Ginika is just a sweet girl."' He paused, then added, 'He didn't know that was exactly what I hoped to hear. I'm not interested in girls that are too nice.'

'Ahn-ahn! Are you insulting me?' She nudged him, in mock anger. She had always liked this image of herself as too much trouble, as different, and she sometimes thought of it as a carapace that kept her safe.

'You know I'm not insulting you.' He put an arm around her shoulders and pulled her to him gently; it was the first time their bodies had met and she felt herself stiffen. 'I thought you were so fine, but not just that. You looked like the kind of person who will do something because you want to, and not because everyone else is doing it.'

She rested her head against his and felt, for the first time, what she would often feel with him: a self-affection. He made her like herself. With him, she was at ease; her skin felt as though it was her right size. She told him how she very much wanted God to exist but feared He did not, how she worried that she should know what she wanted to do with her life but did not even know what she wanted to study at university. It seemed so natural, to talk to him about odd things. She had never done that before. The trust, so sudden and yet so complete, and the intimacy, frightened her. They had known nothing of each other only hours ago, and yet, there had been a knowledge shared between them in those moments before they danced, and now she could think only of all the things she yet wanted to tell him, wanted to do with him. The similarities in their lives became good omens: that they were both only children, their birthdays two days apart, and their home-towns in Anambra State. He was from Abba and she was from Umunnachi and the towns were minutes away from each other.

'Ahn-ahn! One of my uncles goes to your village all the time!' he told her. 'I've been a few times with him. You people have terrible roads.'

'I know Abba. The roads are worse.'

'How often do you go to your village?'

'Every Christmas.'

'Just once a year! I go very often with my mother, at least five times a year.'

'But I bet I speak Igbo better than you.'

'Impossible,' he said, and switched to Igbo. '*Ama m atu inu*. I even know proverbs.'

'Yes. The basic one everybody knows. A frog does not run in the afternoon for nothing.'

'No. I know serious proverbs. *Akota ife ka ubi, e lee oba*. If something bigger than the farm is dug up, the barn is sold.'

'Ah, you want to try me?' she asked, laughing. '*Acho afu adi ako n'akpa dibia*. The medicine man's bag has all kinds of things.'

93

'Not bad,' he said. '*E gbuo dike n'ogu uno, e luo na ogu agu, e lote ya.* If you kill a warrior in a local fight, you'll remember him when fighting enemies.'

They traded proverbs. She could say only two more before she gave up, with him still raring to go.

'How do you know all that?' she asked, impressed. 'Many guys won't even speak Igbo, not to mention knowing proverbs.'

'I just listen when my uncles talk. I think my dad would have liked that.'

They were silent. Cigarette smoke wafted up from the entrance of the guesthouse, where some boys had gathered. Party noises hung in the air: loud music, the raised voices and high laughter of boys and girls, all of them looser and freer than they would be the next day.

'Aren't we going to kiss?' she asked.

He seemed startled. 'Where did that come from?'

'I'm just asking. We've been sitting here for so long.'

'I don't want you to think that is all I want.'

'What about what I want?'

'What do you want?'

'What do you think I want?'

'My jacket?'

She laughed. 'Yes, your famous jacket.'

'You make me shy,' he said.

'Are you serious? Because *you* make *me* shy.'

'I don't believe anything makes you shy,' he said.

They kissed, pressed their foreheads together,

held hands. His kiss was enjoyable, almost heady; it was nothing like her ex-boyfriend Mofe, whose kisses she had thought too salivary.

When she told Obinze this some weeks later – she said, 'So where did you learn to kiss? Because it's nothing like my ex-boyfriend's salivary fumbling' – he laughed and repeated 'salivary fumbling!' and then told her that it was not technique, but emotion. He had done what her ex-boyfriend had done but the difference, in this case, was love.

'You know it was love at first sight for both of us,' he said.

'For both of us? Is it by force? Why are you speaking for me?'

'I'm just stating a fact. Stop struggling.'

They were sitting side by side on a desk in the back of his almost empty classroom. The end-of-break bell began to ring, jangling and discordant.

'Yes, it's a fact,' she said.

'What?'

'I love you.' How easily the words came out, how loudly. She wanted him to hear and she wanted the boy sitting in front, bespectacled and studious, to hear and she wanted the girls gathered in the corridor outside to hear.

'Fact,' Obinze said, with a grin.

Because of her, he had joined the debate club, and after she spoke, he clapped the loudest and longest, until her friends said, 'Obinze, please, it is enough.' Because of him, she joined the sports club and watched him play football, sitting by the touchline and holding his bottle of water. But it was table tennis that he loved, sweating and shouting as he played, glistening with energy, smashing the small white ball, and she marvelled at his skill, how he seemed to stand too far away from the table and yet managed to get the ball. He was already the undefeated school champion, as he had been, he told her, in his former school. When she played with him, he would laugh and say, 'You don't win by hitting the ball with anger o!' Because of her, his friends called him 'woman wrapper'. Once, as he and his friends talked about meeting after school to play football, one of them asked, 'Has Ifemelu given you permission to come?' And Obinze swiftly replied, 'Yes, but she said I have only an hour.' She liked that he wore their relationship so boldly, like a brightly coloured shirt. Sometimes she worried that she was too happy. She would sink into moodiness, and snap at Obinze, or be distant. And her joy would become a restless thing, flapping its wings inside her, as though looking for an opening to fly away.

CHAPTER 5

After Kayode's party, Ginika was stilted; an alien awkwardness grew between them.

'You know I didn't think it would happen that way,' Ifemelu told her.

'Ifem, he was looking at you from the beginning,' Ginika said, and then, to show that she was fine with it all, she teased Ifemelu about stealing her guy without even trying. Her breeziness was forced, laid on thickly, and Ifemelu felt burdened with guilt, and with a desire to overcompensate. It seemed wrong, that her close friend Ginika, pretty, pleasant, popular Ginika with whom she had never quarrelled, was reduced to pretending that she did not care, even though a wistfulness underlined her tone whenever she talked about Obinze. 'Ifem, will you have time for us today or is it Obinze all the way?' she would ask.

And so when Ginika came to school one morning, her eyes red and shadowed, and told Ifemelu, 'My popsie said we are going to America next month,' Ifemelu felt almost relieved. She would miss her friend, but Ginika's leaving forced them both to wring out their friendship and lay it out newly fresh to dry, to return to where they used to be. Ginika's parents had been talking for a while about resigning from the university and starting over in America. Once, while visiting, Ifemelu had heard Ginika's father say, 'We are not sheep. This regime is treating us like sheep and we are starting to behave as if we are sheep. I have not been able to do any real research in years, because every day I am organizing strikes and talking about unpaid salary and there is no chalk in the classrooms.' He was a small, dark man, smaller-looking and darker-looking beside Ginika's large, ash-haired mother, with an undecided air about him, as though he was always dithering between choices. When Ifemelu told her own parents that Ginika's family was finally leaving, her father sighed and said, 'At least they are fortunate to have that option,' and her mother said, 'They are blessed.'

But Ginika complained and cried, painting images of a sad, friendless life in a strange America. 'I wish I could live with you people while they go,' she told Ifemelu. They had gathered at Ginika's house, Ifemelu, Ranyinudo, Priye and Tochi, and were in her bedroom, picking through the clothes she would not be taking with her.

'Ginika, just make sure you can still talk to us when you come back,' Priye said.

'She'll come back and be a serious Americanah like Bisi,' Ranyinudo said.

They roared with laughter, at that word 'Americanah', wreathed in glee, the fourth syllable extended, and at the thought of Bisi, a girl in the form below them, who had come back from a short trip to America with odd affectations, pretending she no longer understood Yoruba, adding a slurred *r* to every English word she spoke.

'But, Ginika, seriously, I would give anything to be you right now,' Priye said. 'I don't understand why you don't want to go. You can always come back.'

At school, friends gathered around Ginika. They all wanted to take her out to the tuck shop, and to see her after school, as though her impending departure had made her even more desirable. Ifemelu and Ginika were lounging in the corridor, during short break, when the Big Guys joined them: Kayode, Obinze, Ahmed, Emenike and Osahon.

'Ginika, where in America are you going?' Emenike asked. He was awed by people who went abroad. After Kayode came back from a trip to Switzerland with his parents, Emenike had bent down to caress Kayode's shoes, saying 'I want to touch them because they have touched snow.'

'Missouri,' Ginika said. 'My dad got a teaching job there.'

'Your mother is an American, *abi*? So you have an American passport?' Emenike asked.

'Yes. But we haven't travelled since I was in primary three.'

'American passport is the coolest thing,' Kayode

said. 'I would exchange my British passport tomorrow.'

'Me too,' Yinka said.

'I very nearly had one o,' Obinze said. 'I was eight months old when my parents took me to America. I keep telling my mum that she should have gone earlier and had me there!'

'Bad luck, man,' Kayode said.

'I don't have a passport. Last time we travelled, I was on my mum's passport,' Ahmed said.

'I was on my mum's until primary three, then my dad said we needed to get our own passports,' Osahon said.

'I've never gone abroad but my father has promised that I will go for university. I wish I could just apply for my visa now instead of waiting to finish school,' Emenike said. After he spoke, a hushed silence followed.

'Don't leave us now, wait until you finish,' Yinka finally said, and she and Kayode burst out laughing. The others laughed, too, even Emenike himself, but there was, underneath their laughter, a barbed echo. They knew he was lying, Emenike who made up stories of rich parents that everyone knew he didn't have, so immersed in his need to invent a life that was not his. The conversation ebbed, changed to the mathematics teacher who did not know how to solve simultaneous equations. Obinze took Ifemelu's hand and they drifted away. They did that often, slowly detaching themselves from their friends, to sit in a corner by the library or take a walk on the green behind the laboratories. As they walked, she wanted to tell Obinze that she didn't know what it meant to 'be on your mother's passport', that her mother didn't even have a passport. But she said nothing, walking beside him in silence. He fitted here, in this school, much more than she did. She was popular, always on every party list, and always announced, during assembly, as one of the 'first three' in her class, yet she felt sheathed in a translucent haze of difference. She would not be here if she had not done so well on the entrance examination, if her father had not been determined that she would go to 'a school that builds both character and career'. Her primary school had been different, full of children like her, whose parents were teachers and civil servants, who took the bus and did not have drivers. She remembered the surprise on Obinze's face, a surprise he had quickly shielded, when he asked, 'What's your phone number?' and she replied, 'We don't have a phone.'

He was holding her hand now, squeezing gently. He admired her for being outspoken and different, but he did not seem able to see beneath that. To be here, among people who had gone abroad, was natural for him. He was fluent in the knowledge of foreign things, especially of American things. Everybody watched American films and exchanged faded American magazines, but he knew details about American presidents from a hundred years ago. Everybody watched American shows, but he knew about Lisa Bonet leaving *The Cosby Show* to go and do *Angel Heart* and Will Smith's huge debts before he was signed to do *The Fresh Prince of Bel Air.* 'You look like a black American' was his ultimate compliment, which he told her when she wore a nice dress, or when her hair was done in large braids. Manhattan was his zenith. He often said 'It's not as if this is Manhattan' or 'Go to Manhattan and see how things are.' He gave her a copy of *Huckleberry Finn*, the pages creased from his thumbing, and she started reading it on the bus home but stopped after a few chapters. The next morning, she put it down on his desk with a decided thump. 'Unreadable nonsense,' she said.

'It's written in different American dialects,' Obinze said.

'And so what? I still don't understand it.'

'You have to be patient, Ifem. If you really get into it, it's very interesting and you won't want to stop reading.'

'I've already stopped reading. Please keep your proper books and leave me with the books I like. And by the way, I still win when we play Scrabble, Mr Read Proper Books.'

Now, she slipped her hand from his as they walked back to class. Whenever she felt this way, panic would slice into her at the slightest thing, and mundane events would become arbiters of doom. This time, Ginika was the trigger; she was standing near the staircase, her backpack on her shoulder, her face gold-streaked in the sunlight, and suddenly

Ifemelu thought how much Ginika and Obinze had in common. Ginika's house at the University of Lagos, the quiet bungalow, the yard crowned by bougainvillea hedges, was perhaps like Obinze's house in Nsukka, and she imagined Obinze realizing how better suited Ginika was for him, and then this joy, this fragile, glimmering thing between them, would disappear.

Obinze told her, one morning after assembly, that his mother wanted her to visit.

'Your mother?' she asked him, agape.

'I think she wants to meet her future daughter-in-law.'

'Obinze, be serious!'

'I remember in primary six, I took this girl to the send-off party and my mum dropped both of us off and gave the girl a handkerchief. She said, "A lady always needs a handkerchief." My mother can be strange, *sha*. Maybe she wants to give you a handkerchief.'

'Obinze Maduewesi!'

'She's never done this before but then I've never had a serious girlfriend before. I think she just wants to see you. She said you should come to lunch.'

Ifemelu stared at him. What sort of mother in her right mind asked her son's girlfriend to visit? It was odd. Even the expression 'come to lunch' was something people said in books. If you were Boyfriend and Girlfriend, you did not visit each other's homes; you registered for after-school lessons, for French Club, for anything that could mean seeing each other outside school. Her parents did not, of course, know about Obinze. Obinze's mother's invitation frightened and excited her; for days, she worried about what to wear.

'Just be yourself,' Aunty Uju told her and Ifemelu replied, 'How can I just be myself? What does that even mean?'

On the afternoon she visited, she stood outside the door of their flat for a while before she pressed the bell, suddenly and wildly hoping that they had gone out. Obinze opened the door.

'Hi. My mum just came back from work.'

The living room was airy, the walls free of photographs except for a turquoise painting of a long-necked woman in a turban.

'That's the only thing that is ours. Everything else came with the flat,' Obinze said.

'It's nice,' she mumbled.

'Don't be nervous. Remember, she wants you here,' Obinze whispered, just before his mother appeared. She looked like Onyeka Onwenu, the resemblance was astounding: a full-nosed, full-lipped beauty, her round face framed by a low Afro, her faultless complexion the deep brown of cocoa. Onyeka Onwenu's music had been one of the luminous joys of Ifemelu's childhood, and had remained undimmed in the aftermath of childhood. She would always remember the day her father came home with the new album *In the Morning Light*; Onyeka Onwenu's face on it was a revelation, and for a long time she traced that photo with her finger. The songs, each time her father played them, made their flat festive, turned him into a looser person who sang along with songs steeped in femaleness, and Ifemelu would guiltily fantasize about him being married to Onyeka Onwenu instead of to her mother. When she greeted Obinze's mother with a 'Good afternoon, ma,' she almost expected her, in response, to break into song in a voice as peerless as Onyeka Onwenu's. But she had a low, murmuring voice.

'What a beautiful name you have. Ifemelunamma,' she said.

Ifemelu stood tongue-tied for seconds. 'Thank you, ma.'

'Translate it,' she said.

'Translate?'

'Yes, how would you translate your name? Did Obinze tell you I do some translation? From the French. I am a lecturer in literature, not English literature, mind you, but literatures in English, and my translating is something I do as a hobby. Now translating your name from Igbo to English might be Made-in-Good-Times or Beautifully Made, or what do you think?'

Ifemelu could not think. There was something about the woman that made her want to say intelligent things, but her mind was blank.

'Mummy, she came to greet you, not to translate her name,' Obinze said, with a playful exasperation.

'Do we have a soft drink to offer our guest? Did you bring out the soup from the freezer? Let's go to the kitchen,' his mother said. She reached out and picked off a piece of lint from his hair, and then hit his head lightly. Their fluid, bantering rapport made Ifemelu uncomfortable. It was free of restraint, free of the fear of consequences; it did not take the familiar shape of a relationship with a parent. They cooked together, his mother stirring the soup, Obinze making the garri, while Ifemelu stood by drinking a Coke. She had offered to help, but his mother had said, 'No, my dear, maybe next time,' as though she did not just let anyone help in her kitchen. She was pleasant and direct, even warm, but there was a privacy about her, a reluctance to bare herself completely to the world, the same quality as Obinze. She had taught her son the ability to be, even in the middle of a crowd, somehow comfortably inside himself.

'What are your favourite novels, Ifemelunamma?' his mother asked. 'You know Obinze will only read American books? I hope you're not that foolish.'

'Mummy, you're just trying to force me to like this book.' He gestured to the book on the kitchen table, Graham Greene's *The Heart of the Matter*. 'My mother reads this book twice a year. I don't know why,' he said to Ifemelu.

'It is a wise book. The human stories that matter

106

are those that endure. The American books you read are lightweights.' She turned to Ifemelu. 'This boy is too besotted with America.'

'I read American books because America is the future, Mummy. And remember that your husband was educated there.'

'That was when only dullards went to school in America. American universities were considered to be at the same level as British secondary schools then. I did a lot of brushing-up on that man after I married him.'

'Even though you left your things in his flat so that his other girlfriends would stay away?'

'I've told you not to pay any attention to your uncle's false stories.'

Ifemelu stood there mesmerized. Obinze's mother, her beautiful face, her air of sophistication, her wearing a white apron in the kitchen, was not like any other mother Ifemelu knew. Here, her father would seem crass, with his unnecessary big words, and her mother provincial and small.

'You can wash your hands at the sink,' Obinze's mother told her. 'I think the water is still running.'

They sat at the dining table, eating garri and soup, Ifemelu trying hard to be, as Aunty Uju had said, 'herself', although she was no longer sure what 'herself' was. She felt undeserving, unable to sink with Obinze and his mother into their atmosphere.

'The soup is very sweet, ma,' she said politely.

'Oh, Obinze cooked it,' his mother said. 'Didn't he tell you that he cooks?'

'Yes, but I didn't think he could make soup, ma,' Ifemelu said.

Obinze was smirking.

'Do you cook at home?' his mother asked.

Ifemelu wanted to lie, to say that she cooked and loved cooking, but she remembered Aunty Uju's words. 'No, ma,' she said. 'I don't like cooking. I can eat Indomie noodles day and night.'

His mother laughed, as though charmed by the honesty, and when she laughed, she looked like a softer-faced Obinze. Ifemelu ate her food slowly, thinking how much she wanted to remain there with them, in their rapture, forever.

Their flat smelled of vanilla on weekends, when Obinze's mother baked. Slices of mango glistening on a pie, small brown cakes swelling with raisins. Ifemelu stirred the batter and peeled the fruit; her own mother did not bake, their oven housed cockroaches.

'Obinze just said "trunk", ma. He said it's in the trunk of your car,' she said. In their America–Britain jousting, she always sided with his mother.

'Trunk is a part of a tree and not a part of a car, my dear son,' his mother said. When Obinze pronounced 'schedule' with the *k* sound, his mother said, 'Ifemelunamma, please tell my son I don't speak American. Could he say that in English?'

On weekends, they watched films on video. They

sat in the living room, eyes on the screen, and Obinze said, 'Mummy, *chelu*, let's hear,' when his mother, from time to time, gave her commentary on the plausibility of a scene, or the foreshadowing, or whether an actor was wearing a wig. One Sunday, midway into a film, his mother left for the pharmacy, to buy her allergy medicine. 'I'd forgotten they close early today,' she said. As soon as her car engine started, a dull revving, Ifemelu and Obinze hurried to his bedroom and sank onto his bed, kissing and touching, their clothing rolled up, shifted aside, pulled halfway. Their skin warm against each other. They left the door and the window louvres open, both of them alert to the sound of his mother's car. In a sluice of seconds, they were dressed, back in the living room, Play pressed on the video recorder.

Obinze's mother walked in and glanced at the TV. 'You were watching this scene when I left,' she said quietly. A frozen silence fell, even from the film. Then the sing-song cries of a beans hawker floated in through the window.

'Ifemelunamma, please come,' his mother said, turning to go inside.

Obinze got up, but Ifemelu stopped him. 'No, she called me.'

His mother asked her to come inside her bedroom, asked her to sit on the bed.

'If anything happens between you and Obinze, you are both responsible. But Nature is unfair to women. An act is done by two people but if there are any consequences, one person carries it alone. Do you understand me?'

'Yes.' Ifemelu kept her eyes averted from Obinze's mother, firmly fixed on the black-and-white linoleum on the floor.

'Have you done anything serious with Obinze?'

'No.'

'I was once young. I know what it is like to love while young. I want to advise you. I am aware that, in the end, you will do what you want. My advice is that you wait. You can love without making love. It is a beautiful way of showing your feelings but it brings responsibility, great responsibility, and there is no rush. I will advise you to wait until you are at least in the university, wait until you own yourself a little more. Do you understand?'

'Yes,' Ifemelu said. She did not know what 'own yourself a little more' meant.

'I know you are a clever girl. Women are more sensible than men, and you will have to be the sensible one. Convince him. Both of you should agree to wait so that there is no pressure.'

Obinze's mother paused and Ifemelu wondered if she had finished. The silence rang in her head.

'Thank you, ma,' Ifemelu said.

'And when you want to start, I want you to come and see me. I want to know that you are being responsible.'

Ifemelu nodded. She was sitting on Obinze's mother's bed, in the woman's bedroom, nodding and agreeing to tell her when she started having sex with her son. Yet she felt the absence of shame. Perhaps it was Obinze's mother's tone, the evenness of it, the normalness of it.

'Thank you, ma,' Ifemelu said again, now looking at Obinze's mother's face, which was open, no different from what it usually was. 'I will.'

She went back to the living room. Obinze seemed nervous, perched on the edge of the centre table. 'I'm so sorry. I'm going to talk to her about this when you leave. If she wants to talk to anybody, it should be me.'

'She said I should never come here again. That I am misleading her son.'

Obinze blinked. 'What?'

Ifemelu laughed. Later, when she told him what his mother had said, he shook his head. 'We have to tell her when we start? What kind of rubbish is that? Does she want to buy condoms for us? What is wrong with that woman?'

'But who told you we are ever going to start anything?'

CHAPTER 6

During the week, Aunty Uju hurried home to shower and wait for The General and, on weekends, she lounged in her nightdress, reading or cooking or watching television, because The General was in Abuja with his wife and children. She avoided the sun and used creams in elegant bottles, so that her complexion, already naturally light, became lighter, brighter, and took on a sheen. Sometimes, as she gave instructions to her driver, Sola, or her gardener, Baba Flower, or her two house helps, Inyang who cleaned and Chikodili who cooked, Ifemelu would remember Aunty Uju, the village girl brought to Lagos so many years ago, who Ifemelu's mother mildly complained was so parochial she kept touching the walls, and what was it with all those village people who could not stand on their feet without reaching out to smear their palm on a wall? Ifemelu wondered if Aunty Uju ever looked at herself with the eyes of the girl she used to be. Perhaps not. Aunty Uju had steadied herself into her new life with a lightness of touch, more consumed by The General himself than by her new wealth.

112

The first time Ifemelu saw Aunty Uju's house in Dolphin Estate, she did not want to leave. The bathroom fascinated her, with its hot water tap, its gushing shower, its pink tiles. The bedroom curtains were made of raw silk, and she told Aunty Uju, 'Ahn-ahn, it's a waste to use this material as a curtain! Let's sew a dress with it.' The living room had glass doors that slid noiselessly open and noiselessly shut. Even the kitchen was air-conditioned. She wanted to live there. It would impress her friends; she imagined them sitting in the small room just off the living room, which Aunty Uju called the TV room, watching programmes on satellite. And so she asked her parents if she could stay with Aunty Uju during the week. 'It's closer to school, I won't need to take two buses. I can go on Mondays and come home on Fridays,' Ifemelu said. 'I can also help Aunty Uju in the house.'

'My understanding is that Uju has sufficient help,' her father said.

'It is a good idea,' her mother said to her father. 'She can study well there, at least there will be light every day. No need for her to study with kerosene lamps.'

'She can visit Uju after school and on weekends. But she is not going to live there,' her father said.

Her mother paused, taken aback by his firmness. 'Okay,' she said, with a helpless glance at Ifemelu.

For days, Ifemelu sulked. Her father often indulged her, giving in to what she wanted, but this time he ignored her pouts, her deliberate

113

silences at the dinner table. He pretended not to notice when Aunty Uju brought them a new television. He settled back in his well-worn sofa, reading his well-worn book, while Aunty Uju's driver put down the brown Sony carton. Ifemelu's mother began to sing a church song – 'the Lord has given me victory, I will lift him higher' – which was often sung at collection time.

'The General bought more than I needed in the house. There was nowhere to put this one,' Aunty Uju said, a general statement made to nobody in particular, a way of shrugging off thanks. Ifemelu's mother opened the carton, gently stripped away the Styrofoam packaging.

'Our old one doesn't even show anything any more,' she said, although they all knew that it still did.

'Look at how slim it is!' she added. 'Look!'

Her father raised his eyes from the book. 'Yes, it is,' he said, and then lowered his gaze.

The landlord came again. He barged past Ifemelu into the flat, into the kitchen, and reached up to the electric meter, yanking off the fuse, cutting off what little electricity they had.

After he left, Ifemelu's father said, 'What ignominy. To ask us for two years' rent. We have been paying one year.'

'But even that one year, we have not paid,' her mother said, and in her tone was the slightest of accusations.

'I've spoken to Akunne about a loan,' her father said. He disliked Akunne, his almost-cousin, the prosperous man from their hometown to whom everyone took their problems. He called Akunne a lurid illiterate, a money-miss-road.

'What did he say?'

'He said I should come and see him next Friday.' His fingers were unsteady; he was struggling, it seemed, to suppress emotions. Ifemelu hastily looked away, hoping he had not seen her watching him, and asked him if he could explain a difficult question in her homework. To distract him, to make it seem that life could happen again.

Her father would not ask Aunty Uju for help, but if Aunty Uju presented him with the money, he would not refuse. It was better than being indebted to Akunne. Ifemelu told Aunty Uju how the landlord banged on their door, a loud, unnecessary banging for the benefit of the neighbours, while hurling insults at her father. 'Are you not a real man? Pay me my money. I will throw you out of this flat if I don't get that rent by next week!'

As Ifemelu mimicked the landlord, a wan sadness crossed Aunty Uju's face. 'How can that useless landlord embarrass Brother like this? I'll ask Oga to give me the money.'

Ifemelu stopped. 'You don't have money?'

'My account is almost empty. But Oga will give it to me. And do you know I have not been paid a salary since I started work? Every day, there is a new story from the accounts people. The trouble started with my position that does not officially exist, even though I see patients every day.'

'But doctors are on strike,' Ifemelu said.

'The military hospitals still pay. Not that my pay will be enough for the rent, *sha*.'

'You don't have money?' Ifemelu asked again, slowly, to clarify, to be sure. 'Ahn-ahn, Aunty, but how can you not have money?'

'Oga never gives me big money. He pays all the bills and he wants me to ask for everything I need. Some men are like that.'

Ifemelu stared. Aunty Uju, in her big pink house with the wide satellite dish blooming from its roof, her generator brimming with diesel, her freezer stocked with meat, and she did not have money in her bank account.

'Ifem, don't look as if somebody died!' Aunty Uju laughed, her wry laugh. She looked suddenly small and bewildered among the detritus of her new life, the fawn-coloured jewel case on the dressing table, the silk robe thrown across the bed, and Ifemelu felt frightened for her.

'He even gave me a little more than I asked for,' Aunty Uju told Ifemelu the next weekend, with a small smile, as though amused by what The General had done. 'We'll go to the house from the salon so I can give it to Brother.'

It startled Ifemelu, how much a relaxer retouching cost at Aunty Uju's hair salon; the haughty hairdressers sized up each customer, eyes swinging from head to shoes, to decide how much attention she was worth. With Aunty Uju, they hovered and grovelled, curtsying deeply as they greeted her, overpraising her handbag and shoes. Ifemelu watched, fascinated. It was here, at a Lagos salon, that the different ranks of imperial femaleness were best understood.

'Those girls, I was waiting for them to bring out their hands and beg you to shit so they could worship that too,' Ifemelu said, as they left the salon.

Aunty Uju laughed and patted the silky hair extensions that fell to her shoulders: Chinese weave-on, the latest version, shiny and straight as straight could be; it never tangled.

'You know, we live in an ass-licking economy. The biggest problem in this country is not corruption. The problem is that there are many qualified people who are not where they are supposed to be because they won't lick anybody's ass, or they don't know which ass to lick or they don't even know how to lick an ass. I'm lucky to be licking the right ass.' She smiled. 'It's just luck. Oga said I was well brought up, that I was not like all the Lagos girls who sleep with him on the first night and the next morning give him a list of what they want him to buy. I slept with him on the first night but I did not ask for anything, which was stupid of me now that I think of it, but I did not sleep with him because I wanted something. Ah, this

thing called power. I was attracted to him even
with his teeth like Dracula. I was attracted to his
power.'

Aunty Uju liked to talk about The General,
different versions of the same stories repeated and
savoured. Her driver had told her – she swayed
his loyalty by arranging his wife's prenatal visits
and his baby's immunizations – that The General
asked for details of where she went and how long
she stayed, and each time Aunty Uju told Ifemelu
the story, she would end with a sigh, 'Does he
think I can't see another man without him knowing,
if I wanted to? But I don't want to.'

They were in the cold interior of the Mazda. As
the driver backed out of the gates of the salon
compound, Aunty Uju gestured to the gateman,
rolled down her window and gave him some
money.

'Thank you, madam!' he said, and saluted.

She had slipped naira notes to all the salon
workers, to the security men outside, to the
policemen at the road junction.

'They're not paid enough to afford school fees
for even one child,' Aunty Uju said.

'That small money you gave him will not help
him pay any school fees,' Ifemelu said.

'But he can buy a little extra something and he
will be in a better mood and he won't beat his
wife this night,' Aunty Uju said. She looked out
of the window and said, 'Slow down, Sola,' so that
she could get a good look at an accident on

Osborne Road; a bus had hit a car, the front of the bus and the back of the car were now mangled metal, and both drivers were shouting in each other's faces, buffered by a gathering crowd. 'Where do they come from? These people that appear once there is an accident?' Aunty Uju leaned back in her seat. 'Do you know I have forgotten what it feels like to be in a bus? It is so easy to get used to all this.'

'You can just go to Falomo now and get on a bus,' Ifemelu said.

'But it won't be the same. It's never the same when you have other choices.' Aunty Uju looked at her. 'Ifem, stop worrying about me.'

'I'm not worrying.'

'You've been worrying since I told you about my account.'

'If somebody else was doing this, you would say she was stupid.'

'I would not even advise you to do what I'm doing.' Aunty Uju turned back to the window. 'He'll change. I'll make him change. I just need to go slowly.'

At the flat, Aunty Uju handed Ifemelu's father a plastic bag swollen with cash. 'It's rent for two years, Brother,' she said, with an embarrassed casualness, and then made a joke about the hole in his singlet. She did not look him in the face as she spoke and he did not look her in the face as he thanked her.

★   ★   ★

119

The general had yellowed eyes, which suggested to Ifemelu a malnourished childhood. His solid, thickset body spoke of fights that he had started and won, and the buck-teeth that gaped through his lips made him seem vaguely dangerous. Ifemelu was surprised by the gleeful coarseness of him. 'I'm a village man!' he said happily, as though to explain the drops of soup that landed on his shirt and on the table while he ate, or his loud burping afterwards. He arrived in the evenings, in his green uniform, holding a gossip magazine or two, while his ADC, at an obsequious pace behind him, brought his briefcase and put it on the dining table. He rarely left with the gossip magazines; copies of *Vintage People* and *Prime People* and *Lagos Life* littered Aunty Uju's house, with their blurry photos and garish headlines.

'If I tell you what these people do, eh,' Aunty Uju would say to Ifemelu, tapping at a magazine photo with her French-manicured nail. 'Their real stories are not even in the magazines. Oga has the real gist.' Then she would talk about the man who had sex with a top general to get an oil bloc, the military administrator whose children were fathered by somebody else, the foreign prostitutes flown in weekly for the Head of State. She repeated the stories with affectionate amusement, as though she thought The General's keenness on raunchy gossip was a charming and forgivable indulgence. 'Do you know he is afraid of injections? A whole General Officer Commanding and if he sees a needle, he is afraid!' Aunty Uju said, in the same tone. It was, to her, an endearing detail. Ifemelu could not think of The General as endearing, with his loud, boorish manner, the way he reached out to slap Aunty Uju's backside as they went upstairs, saying, 'All this for me? All this for me?' and the way he talked and talked, never acknowledging an interruption, until he finished a story. One of his favourites, which he often told Ifemelu while drinking Star beer after dinner, was the story of how Aunty Uju was different. He told it with a self-congratulatory tone, as if her difference reflected his own good taste. 'The first time I told her I was going to London and asked what she wanted, she gave me a list. Before I looked at it, I said I already know what she wants. Is it not perfume, shoes, bag, watch and clothes? I know Lagos girls. But you know what was in it? One perfume and four books! I was shocked. *Chai.* I spent one good hour in that bookshop in Piccadilly. I bought her twenty books! Which Lagos babe do you know that will be asking for books?'

Aunty Uju would laugh, suddenly girlish and pliant. Ifemelu would smile dutifully. She thought it undignified and irresponsible, this old married man telling her stories; it was like showing her his unclean underwear. She tried to see him through Aunty Uju's eyes, a man of wonders, a man of worldly excitements, but she could not. She recognized the lightness of being, the joyfulness that Aunty Uju had on weekdays; it was how she felt

121

when she was looking forward to seeing Obinze after school. But it seemed wrong, a waste, that Aunty Uju should feel this for The General. Aunty Uju's ex-boyfriend, Olujimi, was different, nice-looking and smooth-voiced; he glistened with a quiet polish. They had been together for most of university and when you saw them, you saw why they were together. 'I outgrew him,' Aunty Uju said.

'Don't you outgrow and move on to something better?' Ifemelu asked. And Aunty Uju laughed as though it was really a joke.

On the day of the coup, a close friend of The General's called Aunty Uju to ask if she was with him. There was tension; some army officers had already been arrested. Aunty Uju was not with The General, did not know where he was, and she paced upstairs and then downstairs, worried, making phone calls that yielded nothing. Soon she began to heave, struggling to breathe. Her panic had turned into an asthma attack. She was gasping, shaking, piercing her arm with a needle, trying to inject herself with medicine, drops of blood staining the bedcovers, until Ifemelu ran down the street to bang on the door of a neighbour whose sister was also a doctor. Finally, The General called to say that he was fine, the coup had failed and all was well with the Head of State; Aunty Uju's trembling stopped.

On a Muslim holiday, one of those two-day holidays when non-Muslims in Lagos said 'Happy

122

Sallah' to whoever they assumed to be a Muslim, often gatemen from the north, and NTA showed footage after footage of men slaughtering rams, The General promised to visit; it would be the first time he spent a public holiday with Aunty Uju. She was in the kitchen the entire morning supervising Chikodili, singing loudly from time to time, being a little too familiar with Chikodili, a little too quick to laugh with her. Finally, the cooking done and the house smelling of spices and sauces, Aunty Uju went upstairs to shower.

'Ifem, please come and help me trim my hair down there. Oga said it disturbs him!' Aunty Uju said, laughing, and then lay on her back, legs spread and held high, an old gossip magazine beneath her, while Ifemelu worked with a shaving stick. Ifemelu had finished and Aunty Uju was coating an exfoliating mask on her face when The General called to say he could no longer come. Aunty Uju, her face ghoulish, covered in chalk-white paste except for the circles of skin around her eyes, hung up and walked into the kitchen and began to put the food in plastic containers for the freezer. Chikodili looked on in confusion. Aunty Uju worked feverishly, jerking the freezer compartment, slamming the cupboard, and as she pushed back the pot of jollof rice, the pot of egusi soup fell off the cooker. Aunty Uju stared at the yellowish-green sauce spreading across the kitchen floor as though she did not know how it had happened. She turned to Chikodili and screamed,

123

'Why are you looking like a mumu? Come on, clean it up!'

Ifemelu was watching from the kitchen entrance. 'Aunty, the person you should be shouting at is The General.'

Aunty Uju stopped, her eyes bulging and enraged. 'Is it me you are talking to like that? Am I your agemate?'

Aunty Uju charged at her. Ifemelu had not expected Aunty Uju to hit her, yet when the slap landed on the side of her face, making a sound that seemed to her to come from far away, finger-shaped welts rising on her cheek, she was not surprised. They stared at each other. Aunty Uju opened her mouth as though to say something and then she closed it and turned and walked upstairs, both of them aware that something between them was now different. Aunty Uju did not come downstairs until evening, when Adesuwa and Uche came to visit. She called them 'my friends in quotes'. 'I'm going to the salon with my friends in quotes,' she would say, a wan laughter in her eyes. She knew they were her friends only because she was The General's mistress. But they amused her. They visited her insistently, comparing notes on shopping and travel, asking her to go to parties with them. It was strange what she knew and did not know about them, she once told Ifemelu. She knew that Adesuwa owned land in Abuja, given to her when she dated the Head of State, and that a famously wealthy Hausa man had bought Uche's boutique in Surulere, but she did not know how many siblings either of them had or where their parents lived or whether they had gone to university.

Chikodili let them in. They wore embroidered caftans and spicy perfume, their Chinese weaves hanging down to their backs, their conversation lined with a hard-edged worldliness, their laughter short and scornful. *I told him he must buy it in my name o. Ah, I knew he would not bring the money unless I said somebody was sick. No now, he doesn't know I opened the account.* They were going to a Sallah party in Victoria Island and had come to take Aunty Uju.

'I don't feel like going,' Aunty Uju told them, while Chikodili served orange juice, a carton on a tray, two glasses placed beside it.

'Ahn-ahn. Why now?' Uche asked.

'Serious big men are coming,' Adesuwa said. 'You never know if you will meet somebody.'

'I don't want to meet anybody,' Aunty Uju said, and there was quiet, as though each of them had to catch their breath, Aunty Uju's words a gale that tore through their assumptions. She was supposed to want to meet men, to keep her eyes open; she was supposed to see The General as an option that could be bettered. Finally, one of them, Adesuwa or Uche, said, 'This your orange juice is the cheap brand o! You don't buy Just Juice any more?' A lukewarm joke, but they laughed to ease the moment away.

After they left, Aunty Uju came over to the dining table, where Ifemelu sat reading.

'Ifem, I don't know what got into me. *Ndo.*' She held Ifemelu's wrist, then ran her hand, almost meditatively, over the embossed title of Ifemelu's Sidney Sheldon novel. 'I must be mad. He has a beer belly and Dracula teeth and a wife and children and he's old.'

For the first time, Ifemelu felt older than Aunty Uju, wiser and stronger than Aunty Uju, and she wished that she could wrest Aunty Uju away, shake her into a clear-eyed self, who would not lay her hopes on The General, slaving and shaving for him, always eager to fade his flaws. It was not as it should be. Ifemelu felt a small gratification to hear, later, Aunty Uju shouting on the phone. 'Nonsense! You knew you were going to Abuja from the beginning so why let me waste my time preparing for you!'

The cake a driver delivered the next morning, with 'I'm sorry my love' written on it in blue frosting, had a bitter aftertaste but Aunty Uju kept it in the freezer for months.

Aunty Uju's pregnancy came like a sudden sound in a still night. She arrived at the flat wearing a sequined bou-bou that caught the light, glistening like a flowing celestial presence, and said that she wanted to tell Ifemelu's parents about it before they heard the gossip. '*Adi m ime,*' she said simply.

Ifemelu's mother burst into tears, loud dramatic

cries, looking around, as though she could see, lying around her, the splintered pieces of her own story. 'My God, why have you forsaken me?'

'I did not plan this, it happened,' Aunty Uju said. 'I fell pregnant for Olujimi in university. I had an abortion and I am not doing it again.' The word 'abortion', blunt as it was, scarred the room, because they all knew that what Ifemelu's mother did not say was that surely there were ways to take care of this. Ifemelu's father put his book down and picked it up again. He cleared his throat. He soothed his wife.

'Well, I cannot ask about the man's intentions,' he said finally to Aunty Uju. 'So I should ask what your own intentions are.'

'I will have the baby.'

He waited to hear more, but Aunty Uju said nothing else, and so he sat back, assailed. 'You are an adult. This is not what I hoped for you, Obianuju, but you are an adult.'

Aunty Uju went over and sat on the arm of his sofa. She spoke in a low, pacifying voice, stranger for being formal, but saved from falseness by the soberness of her face. 'Brother, this is not what I hoped for myself either, but it has happened. I am sorry to disappoint you, after everything you have done for me, and I beg you to forgive me. But I will make the best of this situation. The General is a responsible man. He will take care of his child.'

Ifemelu's father shrugged wordlessly. Aunty Uju

put an arm around him, as though it were he who needed comforting.

Later, Ifemelu would think of the pregnancy as symbolic. It marked the beginning of the end and made everything else seem rapid, the months rushing past, time hurtling forward. There was Aunty Uju, dimpled with exuberance, her face aglow, her mind busy with plans as her belly curved outwards. Every few days, she came up with a new girl's name for the baby. 'Oga is happy,' she said. 'He is happy to know that he can still score a goal at his age, old man like him!' The General came more often, even on some weekends, bringing her hot water bottles, herbal pills, things he had heard were good for pregnancy.

He told her, 'Of course you will deliver abroad,' and asked which she preferred, America or England. He wanted England, so that he could travel with her; the Americans had barred entry to high-ranking members of the military government. But Aunty Uju chose America, because her baby could still have automatic citizenship there. The plans were made, a hospital picked, a furnished condo rented in Atlanta. 'What is a condo, anyway?' Ifemelu asked. And Aunty Uju shrugged and said, 'Who knows what Americans mean? You should ask Obinze, he will know. At least it is a place to live. And Oga has people there who will help me.' Aunty Uju was dampened only when her driver told her that The General's wife had heard about

128

the pregnancy and was furious; there had, apparently, been a tense family meeting with his relatives and hers. The General hardly spoke about his wife but Aunty Uju knew enough: a lawyer who had given up working to raise their four children in Abuja, a woman who looked portly and pleasant in newspaper photographs. 'I wonder what she is thinking,' Aunty Uju said sadly, musingly. While she was in America, The General had one of the bedrooms repainted a brilliant white. He bought a cot, its legs like delicate candles. He bought stuffed toys, and too many teddy bears. Inyang propped them in the cot, lined some up on a shelf and, perhaps because she thought nobody would notice, she took one teddy bear to her room in the back. Aunty Uju had a boy. She sounded high and elated over the phone. 'Ifem, he has so much hair! Can you imagine? What a waste!'

She called him Dike, after her father, and gave him her surname, which left Ifemelu's mother agitated and sour.

'The baby should have his father's name, or is the man planning to deny his child?' Ifemelu's mother asked, as they sat in their living room, still digesting the news of the birth.

'Aunty Uju said it was just easier to give him her name,' Ifemelu said. 'And is he behaving like a man that will deny his child? Aunty told me he's even talking about coming to pay her bride price.'

'God forbid,' Ifemelu's mother said, almost spitting the words out, and Ifemelu thought of all those fervent prayers for Aunty Uju's mentor. Her mother, when Aunty Uju came back, stayed in Dolphin Estate for a while, bathing and feeding the gurgling, smooth-skinned baby, but she faced The General with a cold officiousness. She answered him in monosyllables, as though he had betrayed her by breaking the rules of her pretence. A relationship with Aunty Uju was acceptable, but such flagrant proof of the relationship was not. The house smelled of baby powder. Aunty Uju was happy. The General held Dike often, suggesting that perhaps he needed to be fed again or that a doctor needed to see the rash on his neck.

For Dike's first birthday party, The General brought a live band. They set up in the front garden, near the generator house, and stayed until the last guests left, all of them slow and sated, taking food wrapped in foil. Aunty Uju's friends came, and The General's friends came, too, their expressions determined, as though to say that no matter the circumstances, their friend's child was their friend's child. Dike, newly walking, tottered around in a suit and red bow tie, while Aunty Uju followed him, trying to get him to be still for a few moments with the photographer. Finally, tired, he began to cry, yanking at his bow tie, and The General picked him up and carried him around. It was the image of The General that would endure in Ifemelu's mind, Dike's arms around his neck, his face lit up, his front teeth jutting out as he

130

smiled, saying, 'He looks like me o, but thank God he took his mother's teeth.'

The General died the next week, in a military plane crash. 'On the same day, the very same day, that the photographer brought the pictures from Dike's birthday,' Aunty Uju would often say, in telling the story, as though this held some particular significance.

It was a Saturday afternoon, Obinze and Ifemelu were in the TV room, Inyang was upstairs with Dike, Aunty Uju was in the kitchen with Chikodili when the phone rang. Ifemelu picked it up. The voice on the other end, The General's ADC, crackled through a bad connection, but was still clear enough to give her details: the crash happened a few miles outside Jos, the bodies were charred, there were already rumours that the Head of State had engineered it to get rid of officers who he feared were planning a coup. Ifemelu held the phone too tightly, stunned. Obinze went with her to the kitchen, and stood by Aunty Uju as Ifemelu repeated the ADC's words.

'You are lying,' Aunty Uju said. 'It is a lie.'

She marched towards the phone, as though to challenge it, too, and then she slid to the floor, a boneless, bereft sliding, and began to weep. Ifemelu held her, cradled her, all of them unsure of what to do, and the silence in between her sobs seemed too silent. Inyang brought Dike downstairs.

'Mama?' Dike said, looking puzzled.

'Take Dike upstairs,' Obinze told Inyang.

There was banging on the gate. Two men and three women, relatives of The General, had bullied Adamu to open the gate, and now stood at the front door, shouting. 'Uju! Pack your things and get out now! Give us the car keys!' One of the women was skeletal, agitated and red-eyed, and as she shouted – 'Common harlot! God forbid that you will touch our brother's property! Prostitute! You will never live in peace in this Lagos!' – she pulled her headscarf from her head and tied it tightly around her waist, in preparation for a fight. At first, Aunty Uju said nothing, staring at them, standing still at the door. Then she asked them to leave in a voice hoarse from tears, but the relatives' shouting intensified, and so Aunty Uju turned to go back indoors. 'Okay, don't go,' she said. 'Just stay there. Stay there while I go and call my boys from the army barracks.'

Only then did they leave, telling her, 'We are coming back with our own boys.' Only then did Aunty Uju begin to sob again. 'I have nothing. Everything is in his name. Where will I take my son to now?'

She picked up the phone from its cradle and then stared at it, uncertain whom to call.

'Call Uche and Adesuwa,' Ifemelu said. *They* would know what to do.

Aunty Uju did, pressing the speaker button, and then leaned against the wall.

'You have to leave immediately. Make sure you clear the house, take everything,' Uche said. 'Do it fast-fast before his people come back. Arrange a tow van and take the generator. Make sure you take the generator.'

'I don't know where to find a van,' Aunty Uju mumbled, with a helplessness foreign to her.

'We're going to arrange one for you, fast-fast. You have to take that generator. That is what will pay for your life until you gather yourself. You have to go somewhere for a while, so that they don't give you trouble. Go to London or America. Do you have American visa?'

'Yes.'

Ifemelu would remember the final moments in a blur, Adamu saying there was a journalist from *City People* at the gate, Ifemelu and Chikodili stuffing clothes in suitcases, Obinze carrying things out to the van, Dike stumbling around and chortling. The rooms upstairs had grown unbearably hot; the air conditioners had suddenly stopped working, as though they had decided, in unison, to pay tribute to the end.

CHAPTER 7

Obinze wanted to go to the University of Ibadan because of a poem.

He read the poem to her, J. P. Clark's 'Ibadan', and he lingered on the words 'running splash of rust and gold'.

'Are you serious?' she asked him. 'Because of this poem?'

'It's so beautiful.'

Ifemelu shook her head, in mocking, exaggerated incredulity. But she, too, wanted to go to Ibadan, because Aunty Uju had gone there. They filled out their JAMB forms together, sitting at the dining table while his mother hovered around, saying, 'Are you using the right pencil? Cross-check everything. I have heard of the most unlikely mistakes that you will not believe.'

Obinze said, 'Mummy, we are more likely to fill it out without mistakes if you stop talking.'

'At least you should make Nsukka your second choice,' his mother said. But Obinze did not want to go to Nsukka, he wanted to escape the life he had always had, and Nsukka, to Ifemelu, seemed remote and dusty. And so they both agreed to make the University of Lagos their second choice.

The next day, Obinze's mother collapsed in the library. A student found her spread on the floor like a rag, a small bump on her head, and Obinze told Ifemelu, 'Thank God we haven't submitted our JAMB forms.'

'What do you mean?'

'My mum is returning to Nsukka at the end of this session. I have to be near her. The doctor said this thing will keep happening.' He paused. 'We can see each other during long weekends. I will come to Ibadan and you come to Nsukka.'

'You're a joker,' she told him. '*Biko*, I'm changing to Nsukka as well.'

The change pleased her father. It was heartening, he said, that she would go to university in Igboland, since she had lived her whole life in the west. Her mother was downcast. Ibadan was only an hour away, but Nsukka meant a day's journey on the bus.

'It's not a day, Mummy, just seven hours,' Ifemelu said.

'And what is the difference between that and a day?' her mother asked.

Ifemelu was looking forward to being away from home, to the independence of owning her own time, and she felt comforted that Ranyinudo and Tochi were going to Nsukka too. So was Emenike, who asked Obinze if they could be room-mates, in the boys' quarters of Obinze's house. Obinze said yes. Ifemelu wished he had not. 'There's just something about Emenike,' she said. 'But anyway, as long as he goes away when we are busy with ceiling.'

Later, Obinze would ask, half seriously, if Ifemelu thought his mother's fainting had been deliberate, a plot to keep him close. For a long time, he spoke wistfully of Ibadan, until he visited the campus, for a table tennis tournament, and returned to tell her, sheepishly, 'Ibadan reminded me of Nsukka.'

To go to Nsukka was to finally see Obinze's home, a bungalow resting in a compound filled with flowers. Ifemelu imagined him growing up, riding his bicycle down the sloping street, returning home from primary school with his bag and water bottle. Still, Nsukka disoriented her. She thought it too slow, the dust too red, the people too satisfied with the smallness of their lives. But she would come to love it, a hesitant love at first. From the window of her hostel room, where four beds were squashed into a space for two, she could look out to the entrance of Bello Hall. Tall gmelina trees swayed in the wind, and underneath them were hawkers, guarding trays of bananas and groundnuts, and okadas all parked close to each other, the motor-cyclists talking and laughing, but each of them alert to customers. She put up bright blue wall-paper in her corner and because she had heard stories of room-mate squabbles – one final-year student, it was said, had poured kerosene into the drawer of the first-year student for being what was called 'saucy' – she felt fortunate about her room-mates. They were easy-going and soon she was sharing with them and borrowing from them the things that easily ran out, toothpaste and powdered milk and Indomie noodles and hair pomade. Most mornings, she woke up to the rumbling murmur of voices in the corridor, the Catholic students saying the rosary, and she would hurry to the bathroom, to collect water in her bucket before the tap stopped, to squat over the toilet before it became unbearably full. Sometimes, when she was too late, and the toilets already swirled with maggots, she would go to Obinze's house, even if he was not there, and once the house help Augustina opened the front door, she would say, 'Tina-Tina, how now? I came to use the toilet.'

She often ate lunch in Obinze's house, or they would go to town, to Onyekaozulu, and sit on wooden benches in the dimness of the restaurant, eating, on enamel plates, the tenderest of meats and the tastiest of stews. She spent some nights in Obinze's boys' quarters, lounging on his mattress on the floor, listening to music. Sometimes she would dance in her underwear, wiggling her hips, while he teased her about having a small bottom: 'I was going to say shake it, but there's nothing to shake.'

University was bigger and baggier, there was room to hide, so much room; she did not feel as though she did not belong because there were many options for belonging. Obinze teased her about how popular she already was, her room busy during the first-year rush, final-year boys dropping by, eager to try their luck, even though a large photo of Obinze hung above her pillow. The boys amused her. They came and sat on her bed and solemnly offered to 'show her around campus', and she imagined them saying the same words in the same tone to the first-year girl in the next room. One of them, though, was different. His name was Odein. He came to her room, not as part of the first-year rush but to talk to her room-mates about the students' union, and after that, he would come by to visit her, to say hello, some-times bringing a pack of suya, hot and spicy, wrapped in oil-stained newspaper. His activism surprised Ifemelu – he seemed a little too urbane, a little too cool, to be in the students' union government – but also impressed her. He had thick, perfectly shaped lips, the lower the same size as the upper, lips that were both thoughtful and sensual, and as he spoke – 'If the students are not united, nobody will listen to us' – Ifemelu imagined kissing him, in a way that she imagined doing something she knew she never would. It was because of him that she joined the demonstration, and convinced Obinze to join, too. They chanted 'No Light! No Water!' and 'VC is a Goat!' and found themselves carried along with the roaring crowd that settled, finally, in front of the vice chancellor's house. Bottles were broken, a car was set on fire, and then the vice chancellor came out, diminutive, encased between security men, and spoke in pastel tones.

Later, Obinze's mother said, 'I understand the students' grievances, but we are not the enemy. The military is the enemy. They have not paid our salary in months. How can we teach if we cannot eat?' And, still later, the news spread around campus of a strike by lecturers, and students gathered in the hostel foyer, bristling with the known and the unknown. It was true, the hall rep confirmed the news, and they all sighed, contemplating this sudden unwanted break, and returned to their rooms to pack; the hostel would be closed the next day. Ifemelu heard a girl close by say, 'I don't have ten kobo for transport to go home.'

The strike lasted too long. The weeks crawled past. Ifemelu was restless, antsy; every day she listened to the news, hoping to hear that the strike was over. Obinze called her at Ranyinudo's house; she would arrive minutes before he was due to call and sit by the grey rotary phone, waiting for it to ring. She felt cut away from him, each of them living and breathing in separate spheres, he bored and spiritless in Nsukka, she bored and spiritless in Lagos, and everything curdled in lethargy. Life had become a turgid and suspended film. Her mother asked if she wanted to join the sewing class at church, to keep her occupied, and her father said that this, the unending university strike, was why young people became armed robbers. The strike was nationwide, and all her friends were home, even Kayode was home, back on holiday from his American university. She visited friends and went to parties, wishing Obinze lived in Lagos. Sometimes Odein, who had a car, would pick her up and take her where she needed to go. 'That your boyfriend is lucky,' he told her, and she laughed, flirting with him. She still imagined kissing him, sloe-eyed and thick-lipped Odein.

One weekend, Obinze visited and stayed with Kayode.

'What is going on with this Odein?' Obinze asked her.

'What?'

'Kayode said he took you home after Osahon's party. You didn't tell me.'

'I forgot.'

'You forgot.'

'I told you he picked me up the other day, didn't I?'

'Ifem, what is going on?'

She sighed. 'Ceiling, it's nothing. I'm just curious about him. Nothing is ever going to happen. But I am curious. You get curious about other girls, don't you?'

He was looking at her, his eyes fearful. 'No,' he said coldly. 'I don't.'

'Be honest.'

'I am being honest. The problem is you think

everyone is like you. You think you're the norm but you're not.'

'What do you mean?'

'Nothing. Just forget it.'

He did not want to talk about it any further, but the air between them was marred, and remained disturbed for days, even after he went back home, so that when the strike ended ('The lecturers have called it off! Praise God!' Chetachi shouted from their flat one morning) and Ifemelu returned to Nsukka, they were tentative with each other for the first few days, their conversations on tiptoe, their hugs abridged.

It surprised Ifemelu, how much she had missed Nsukka itself, the routines of unhurried pace, friends gathered in her room until past midnight, the inconsequential gossip told and retold, the stairs climbed slowly up and down as though in a gradual awakening, and each morning whitened by the harmattan. In Lagos, the harmattan was a mere veil of haze, but in Nsukka, it was a raging, mercurial presence; the mornings were crisp, the afternoons ashen with heat and the nights unknown. Dust whirls would start in the far distance, very pretty to look at as long as they were far away, and swirl until they coated everything brown. Even eyelashes. Everywhere, moisture would be greedily sucked up; the wood laminate on tables would peel off and curl, pages of exercise books would crackle, clothes would dry minutes after being hung out, lips would crack and bleed, and Robb

141

and Mentholatum kept within reach, in pockets and handbags. Skin would be shined with Vaseline, while the forgotten bits – between the fingers or at the elbows – turned a dull ash. The tree branches would be stark and, with their leaves fallen, wear a kind of proud desolation. The church bazaars would leave the air redolent, smoky from mass cooking. Some nights, the heat lay thick like a towel. Other nights, a sharp cold wind would descend, and Ifemelu would abandon her hostel room and, snuggled next to Obinze on his mattress, listen to the whistling pines howling outside, in a world suddenly fragile and breakable.

Obinze's muscles were aching. He lay on his belly, and Ifemelu straddled him, massaging his back and neck and thighs with her fingers, her knuckles, her elbows. He was painfully taut. She stood on him, placed one foot gingerly on the back of a thigh, and then the other. 'Does it feel okay?'

'Yes.' He groaned in pleasure-pain. She pressed down slowly, his skin warm under the soles of her feet, his tense muscles unknotting. She steadied herself with a hand on the wall, and dug her heels deeper, moving inch by inch while he grunted, 'Ah! Ifem, yes, just there. Ah!'

'You should stretch after playing ball, mister man,' she said, and then she was lying on his back, tickling his underarms and kissing his neck.

'I have a suggestion for a better kind of massage,' he said. When he undressed her, he did not stop, as usual, at her underwear. He pulled it down and she raised her legs to aid him.

'Ceiling,' she said, half-certain. She did not want him to stop, but she had imagined this differently, assumed they would make a carefully planned ceremony of it.

'I'll come out,' he said.

'You know it doesn't always work.'

'If it doesn't work, then we'll welcome Junior.'

'Stop it.'

He looked up. 'But, Ifem, we're going to get married anyway.'

'Look at you. I might meet a rich handsome man and leave you.'

'Impossible. We'll go to America when we graduate and raise our fine children.'

'You'll say anything now because your brain is between your legs.'

'But my brain is always there!'

They were both laughing, and then the laughter stilled, gave way to a new, strange graveness, a slippery joining. It felt, to Ifemelu, like a weak copy, a floundering imitation of what she had imagined it would be. After he pulled away, jerking and gasping and holding himself, a discomfort nagged at her. She had been tense through it all, unable to relax. She had imagined his mother watching them; the image had forced itself onto her mind, and it had, even more oddly, been a double image, of his mother and Onyeka Onwenu, both watching them with unblinking eyes. She knew she could not possibly tell Obinze's mother what had happened, even though she had promised to, and had believed then that she would. But now she could not see how. What would she say? What words would she use? Would Obinze's mother expect details? She and Obinze should have planned it better; that way, she would know how to tell his mother. The unplannedness of it all had left her a little shaken, and also a little disappointed. It seemed somehow as though it had not been worth it after all.

When, a week or so later, she woke up in pain, a sharp stinging on her side and a great, sickening nausea pervading her body, she panicked. Then she vomited and her panic grew.

'It's happened,' she told Obinze. 'I'm pregnant.' They had met, as usual, in front of the Ekpo refectory after their morning lecture. Students milled around. A group of boys were smoking and laughing close by and for a moment, their laughter seemed directed at her.

Obinze's brows wrinkled. He did not seem to understand what she was saying. 'But, Ifem, it can't be. It's too early. Besides, I came out.'

'I told you it doesn't work!' she said. He suddenly seemed young, a confused small boy looking helplessly at her. Her panic grew. On an impulse, she hailed a passing okada and jumped on the back and told the motorcyclist that she was going to town.

'Ifem, what are you doing?' Obinze asked. 'Where are you going?'

'To call Aunty Uju,' she said.

Obinze got on the next okada and was soon speeding behind her, past the university gates and to the NITEL office, where Ifemelu gave the man behind the peeling counter a piece of paper with Aunty Uju's American number. On the phone, she spoke in code, making it up as she went along, because of the people standing there, some waiting to make their own calls, others merely loitering, but all listening, with unabashed and open interest, to the conversations of others.

'Aunty, I think what happened to you before Dike came has happened to me,' Ifemelu said. 'We ate the food a week ago.'

'Just last week? How many times?'

'Once.'

'Ifem, calm down. I don't think you're pregnant. But you need to do a test. Don't go to the campus medical centre. Go to town, where nobody will know you. But calm down first. It will be okay, *inugo*?'

Later, Ifemelu sat on a rickety chair in the waiting room of the lab, stony and silent, ignoring Obinze. She was angry with him. It was unfair, she knew, but she was angry with him. As she went into the dirty toilet with a small container the lab girl had given her, he had asked, already getting up, 'Should I come with you?' and she snapped, 'Come with me for what?' And she wanted to slap the lab girl. A yellow-faced beanpole of a girl who sneered and shook her head when Ifemelu

145

first said, 'Pregnancy test,' as though she could not believe she was encountering one more case of immorality. Now, she was watching them, smirking and humming insouciantly.

'I have the result,' she said after a while, holding the unsealed paper, her expression disappointed because it was negative. Ifemelu was too stunned, at first, to be relieved, and then she needed to urinate again.

'People should respect themselves and live like Christians to avoid trouble,' the lab girl said as they left.

That evening, Ifemelu vomited again. She was in Obinze's room, lying down and reading, still frosty towards him, when a rush of salty saliva filled her mouth and she leaped up and ran to the toilet.

'It must be something I ate,' she said. 'That yam pottage I bought from Mama Owerre.'

Obinze went inside the main house and came back to say his mother was taking her to the doctor's. It was late evening, his mother did not like the young doctor who was on call at the medical centre in the evenings, and so she drove to Dr Achufusi's house. As they passed the primary school with its trimmed hedges of whistling pine, Ifemelu suddenly imagined that she was indeed pregnant, and the girl had used expired test chemicals in that dingy lab. She blurted out, 'We had sex, Aunty. Once.' She felt Obinze tense. His mother looked at her in the rear-view mirror. 'Let us see the doctor first,' she said. Dr Achufusi, an avuncular and pleasant man, pressed at Ifemelu's side and announced, 'It's your appendix, very inflamed. We should get it out quickly.' He turned to Obinze's mother. 'I can schedule her for tomorrow afternoon.'

'Thank you so much, Doctor,' Obinze's mother said.

In the car, Ifemelu said, 'I've never had surgery, Aunty.'

'It's nothing,' Obinze's mother said briskly. 'Our doctors here are very good. Get in touch with your parents and tell them not to worry. We will take care of you. After they discharge you, you can stay in the house until you feel strong.'

Ifemelu called her mother's colleague, Aunty Bunmi, and gave her a message, as well as Obinze's home phone number, to pass on to her mother. That evening, her mother called; she sounded short of breath.

'God is in control, my precious,' her mother said. 'Thank God for this your friend. God will bless her and her mother.'

'It's him. A boy.'

'Oh.' Her mother paused. 'Please thank them. God bless them. We will take the first bus tomorrow morning to Nsukka.'

Ifemelu remembered a nurse cheerfully shaving her pubic hair, the rough scratch of the razor blade, the smell of antiseptic. Then there was a blankness, an erasure of her mind, and when she emerged from it, groggy and still swaying on the edge of memory, she heard her parents talking to Obinze's mother. Her mother was holding her hand. Later, Obinze's mother would ask them to stay in her house, there was no point wasting money on a hotel. 'Ifemelu is like a daughter to me,' she said.

Before they returned to Lagos, her father said, with that intimidated awe he had in the face of the well-educated, 'She has BA London First Class.' And her mother said, 'Very respectful boy, that Obinze. He has good home training. And their hometown is not far from us.'

Obinze's mother waited a few days, perhaps for Ifemelu to regain her strength, before she called them and asked them to sit down and turn the TV off.

'Obinze and Ifemelu, people make mistakes, but some mistakes can be avoided.'

Obinze remained silent. Ifemelu said, 'Yes, Aunty.'

'You must always use a condom. If you want to be irresponsible, then wait until you are no longer in my care.' Her tone had hardened, become censorious. 'If you make the choice to be sexually active, then you must make the choice to protect yourself. Obinze, you should take your pocket money and buy condoms. Ifemelu, you too. It is not my concern if you are embarrassed. You should go into the pharmacy and buy them. You should never ever let the boy be in charge of your own protection. If he does not want to use it, then he does not care enough about you and you should not be there. Obinze, you may not be the person who will get pregnant but if it happens it will change your entire life and you cannot undo it. And please, both of you, keep it between both of you. Diseases are everywhere. AIDS is real.'

They were silent.

'Did you hear me?' Obinze's mother asked.

'Yes, Aunty,' Ifemelu said.

'Obinze?' his mother said.

'Mummy, I've heard you,' Obinze said, adding, sharply, 'I'm not a small boy!' Then he got up and stalked out of the room.

CHAPTER 8

Strikes now were common. In the newspapers, university lecturers listed their complaints, the agreements that were trampled in the dust by government men whose own children were schooling abroad. Campuses were emptied, classrooms drained of life. Students hoped for short strikes, because they could not hope to have no strike at all. Everyone was talking about leaving. Even Emenike had left for England. Nobody knew how he managed to get a visa. 'So he didn't even tell you?' Ifemelu asked Obinze, and Obinze said, 'You know how Emenike is.' Ranyinudo, who had a cousin in America, applied for a visa but was rejected at the embassy by a black American who she said had a cold and was more interested in blowing his nose than in looking at her documents. Sister Ibinabo started the Student Visa Miracle Vigil on Fridays, a gathering of young people, each one holding out an envelope with a visa application form, on which Sister Ibinabo laid a hand of blessing. One girl, already in her final year at the University of Ife, got an American visa the first time she tried, and gave a tearful, excited testimony in church. 'Even if I have to start from the beginning in America, at least I know when I will graduate,' she said.

One day, Aunty Uju called. She no longer called frequently; before, she would call Ranyinudo's house if Ifemelu was in Lagos, or Obinze's house if Ifemelu was at school. But her calls had dried up. She was working three jobs, not yet qualified to practise medicine in America. She talked about the exams she had to take, various steps meaning various things that Ifemelu did not understand. Whenever Ifemelu's mother suggested asking Aunty Uju to send them something from America – multivitamins, shoes – Ifemelu's father would say no, they had to let Uju find her feet first, and her mother would say, a hint of slyness in her smile, that four years was long enough to find one's feet.

'Ifem, *kedu*?' Aunty Uju asked. 'I thought you would be in Nsukka. I just called Obinze's house.'

'We're on strike.'

'Ahn-ahn! The strike hasn't ended?'

'No, that last one ended, we went back to school and then they started another one.'

'What is this kind of nonsense?' Aunty Uju said. 'Honestly, you should come and study here, I am sure you can easily get a scholarship. And you can help me take care of Dike. I'm telling you, the small money I make is all going to his babysitter. And by God's grace, by the time you come, I will have passed all my exams and started my residency.' Aunty Uju sounded enthusiastic but vague; until she voiced it, she had not given the idea much thought.

Ifemelu might have left it at that, a formless idea floated but allowed to sink again, if not for Obinze. 'You should do it, Ifem,' he said. 'You have nothing to lose. Take the SATs and try for a scholarship. Ginika can help you apply to schools. Aunty Uju is there, so at least you have a foundation to start with. I wish I could do the same but I can't just get up and go. It's better for me to finish my first degree and then come to America for graduate school. International students can get funding and financial aid for graduate school.'

Ifemelu did not quite grasp what it all meant, but it sounded correct because it came from him, the America expert, who so easily said 'graduate school' instead of 'postgraduate school'. And so she began to dream. She saw herself in a house from *The Cosby Show*, in a school with students holding notebooks miraculously free of wear and crease. She took the SATs at a Lagos centre, packed with thousands of people, all bristling with their own American ambitions. Ginika, who had just graduated from college, applied to schools on her behalf, calling to say, 'I just wanted you to know I'm focusing on the Philadelphia area because I went here,' as though Ifemelu knew where Philadelphia was. To her, America was America.

The strike ended. Ifemelu returned to Nsukka,

eased back into campus life, and from time to time, she dreamed of America. When Aunty Uju called to say that there were acceptance letters and a scholarship offer, she stopped dreaming. She was too afraid to hope, now that it seemed possible.

'Make small-small braids that will last long, it's very expensive to make hair here,' Aunty Uju told her.

'Aunty, let me get the visa first!' Ifemelu said.

She applied for a visa, convinced that a rude American would reject her application, it was what happened so often, after all, but the grey-haired woman wearing a St Vincent de Paul pin on her lapel smiled at her and said, 'Pick up your visa in two days. Good luck with your studies.'

On the afternoon that she picked up her passport, the pale-toned visa on the second page, she organized that triumphant ritual that signalled the start of a new life overseas: the division of personal property among friends. Ranyinudo, Priye and Tochi were in her bedroom, drinking Coke, her clothes in a pile on the bed, and the first thing they all reached for was her orange dress, her favourite dress, a gift from Aunty Uju; the A-line flair and neck-to-hem zipper had always made her feel both glamorous and dangerous. It makes things easy for me, Obinze would say, before he slowly began to unzip it. She wanted to keep the dress, but Ranyinudo said, 'Ifem, you know you'll have any kind of dress you want in America and next time we see you, you will be a serious Americanah.'

Her mother said Jesus told her in a dream that Ifemelu would prosper in America. Her father pressed a slender envelope into her hand, saying, 'I wish I had more,' and she realized, with sadness, that he must have borrowed it. In the face of the enthusiasm of others, she suddenly felt flaccid and afraid.

'Maybe I should stay and finish here,' she told Obinze.

'Ifem, no, you should go. Besides, you don't even like geology. You can study something else in America.'

'But the scholarship is partial. Where will I find the money to pay the balance? I can't work with a student visa.'

'You can do work-study at school. You'll find a way. Seventy-five per cent off your tuition is a big deal.'

She nodded, riding the wave of his faith. She visited his mother to say goodbye.

'Nigeria is chasing away its best resources,' Obinze's mother said resignedly, hugging her.

'Aunty, I will miss you. Thank you so much for everything.'

'Stay well, my dear, and do well. Write to us. Make sure you keep in touch.'

Ifemelu nodded, tearful. As she left, already parting the curtain at the front door, Obinze's mother said, 'And make sure you and Obinze have a plan. Have a plan.' Her words, so unexpected and so right, lifted Ifemelu's spirits. Their plan became this: he would come to America the minute he graduated. He would find a way to get a visa. Perhaps, by then, she would be able to help with his visa.

In the following years, even after she was no longer in touch with him, she would sometimes remember his mother's words – *make sure you and Obinze have a plan* – and feel comforted.

CHAPTER 9

Mariama returned carrying oil-stained brown paper bags from the Chinese restaurant, trailing the smells of grease and spice into the stuffy salon.

'The film finished?' She glanced at the blank TV screen, and then flipped through the pile of DVDs to select another.

'Excuse me, please, to eat,' Aisha said to Ifemelu. She perched on a chair at the back and ate fried chicken wings with her fingers, her eyes on the TV screen. The new film began with trailers, jaggedly cut scenes interspersed with flashes of light. Each ended with a male Nigerian voice, theatrical and loud, saying 'Grab your copy now!' Mariama ate standing up. She said something to Halima.

'I finish first and eat,' Halima replied in English.

'You can go ahead and eat if you want to,' Halima's customer said, a young woman with a high voice and a pleasant manner.

'No, I finish. Just small more,' Halima said. Her customer's head had only a tuft of hair left in front, sticking up like animal fur, while the rest was done in neat micro braids that fell to her neck.

'I have a hour before I have to go pick up my daughters,' the customer said.

'How many you have?' Halima asked.

'Two,' the customer said. She looked about seventeen. 'Two beautiful girls.'

The new film had started. The grinning face of a middle-aged actress filled the screen.

'Oh-oh, yes! I like her!' Halima said. 'Patience! She don't take any nonsense!'

'You know her?' Mariama asked Ifemelu, pointing at the TV screen.

'No,' Ifemelu said. Why did they insist on asking if she knew Nollywood actors? The entire room smelled too strongly of food. It made the stuffy air rank with oiliness, and yet it also made her slightly hungry. She ate some of her carrots. Halima's customer tilted her head this way and that in front of the mirror and said, 'Thank you so much, it's gorgeous!'

After she left, Mariama said, 'Very small girl and already she has two children.'

'Oh oh oh, these people,' Halima said. 'When a girl is thirteen already she knows all the positions. Never in Afrique!'

'Never!' Mariama agreed.

They looked at Ifemelu for her agreement, her approval. They expected it, in this shared space of their Africanness, but Ifemelu said nothing and turned a page of her novel. They would, she was sure, talk about her after she left. That Nigerian girl, she feels very important because of Princeton.

Look at her food bar, she does not eat real food any more. They would laugh with derision, but only a mild derision, because she was still their African sister, even if she had briefly lost her way. A new smell of oiliness flooded the room when Halima opened her plastic container of food. She was eating and talking to the television screen. 'Oh, stupid man! She will take your money!'

Ifemelu brushed away at some sticky hair on her neck. The room was seething with heat. 'Can we leave the door open?' she asked.

Mariama opened the door, propped it with a chair. 'This heat is really bad.'

Each heat wave reminded Ifemelu of her first, the summer she arrived. It was summer in America, she knew this, but all her life she had thought of 'overseas' as a cold place of wool coats and snow, and because America was 'overseas', and her illusions so strong they could not be fended off by reason, she bought the thickest sweater she could find in Tejuosho market for her trip. She wore it for the journey, zipping it all the way up in the humming interior of the plane and then unzipping it as she left the airport building with Aunty Uju. The sweltering heat alarmed her, as did Aunty Uju's old Toyota hatchback, with a patch of rust on its side and peeling fabric on the seats. She stared at buildings and cars and signboards, all of them matt, disappointingly matt; in the landscape of her imagination, the mundane things in America were covered in a high-shine gloss. She was startled, most of all, by the teenage boy in a baseball cap standing near a brick wall, face down, body leaning forward, hands between his legs. She turned to look again.

'See that boy!' she said. 'I didn't know people do things like this in America.'

'You didn't know people pee in America?' Aunty Uju asked, barely glancing at the boy before turning back to a traffic light.

'Ahn-ahn, Aunty! I mean that they do it outside. Like that.'

'They don't. It's not like back home where everybody does it. He can get arrested for that, but this is not a good neighbourhood anyway,' Aunty Uju said shortly. There was something different about her. Ifemelu had noticed it right away at the airport, her roughly braided hair, her ears bereft of earrings, her quick casual hug, as if it had been weeks rather than years since they had last seen each other.

'I'm supposed to be with my books now,' Aunty Uju said, eyes focused on the road. 'You know my exam is coming.'

Ifemelu had not known that there was yet another exam; she had thought Aunty Uju was waiting for a result. But she said, 'Yes, I know.'

Their silence was full of stones. Ifemelu felt like apologizing, although she was not quite sure what she would be apologizing for. Perhaps Aunty Uju regretted her presence, now that she was here, in Aunty Uju's wheezing car.

Aunty Uju's cell phone rang. 'Yes, this is Uju.' She pronounced it *you-joo* instead of *oo-joo*.

'Is that how you pronounce your name now?' Ifemelu asked afterwards.

'It's what they call me.'

Ifemelu swallowed the words 'Well, that isn't your name.' Instead she said in Igbo, 'I did not know it would be so hot here.'

'We have a heat wave, the first one this summer,' Aunty Uju said, as though *heat wave* was something Ifemelu was supposed to understand. She had never felt a heat quite so *hot*. An enveloping, uncompassionate heat. Aunty Uju's door handle, when they arrived at her one-bedroom apartment, was warm to the touch. Dike sprang up from the carpeted floor of the living room, scattered with toy cars and action figures, and hugged her as though he remembered her. 'Alma, this is my cousin!' he said to his babysitter, a pale-skinned, tired-faced woman with black hair held in a greasy ponytail. If Ifemelu had met Alma in Lagos, she would have thought of her as white, but she would learn that Alma was Hispanic, an American category that was, confusingly, both an ethnicity and a race, and she would remember Alma when, years later, she wrote a blog post titled 'Understanding America for the Non-American Black: What Hispanic Means'.

Hispanic means the frequent companions of American blacks in poverty rankings,

Hispanic means a slight step above American blacks in the American race ladder, Hispanic means the chocolate-skinned woman from Peru, Hispanic means the indigenous people of Mexico. Hispanic means the biracial-looking folks from the Dominican Republic. Hispanic means the paler folks from Puerto Rico. Hispanic also means the blond, blue-eyed guy from Argentina. All you need to be is Spanish-speaking but not from Spain and voilà, you're a race called Hispanic.

But that afternoon, she hardly noticed Alma, or the living room furnished only with a couch and a TV, or the bicycle lodged in a corner, because she was absorbed by Dike. The last time she saw him, on the day of Aunty Uju's hasty departure from Lagos, he had been a one-year-old, crying unendingly at the airport as though he understood the upheaval his life had just undergone, and now here he was, a first grader with a seamless American accent and a hyper-happiness about him; the kind of child who could never stay still and who never seemed sad.

'Why do you have a sweater? It's too hot for a sweater!' he said, chortling, still holding on to her in a drawn-out hug. She laughed. He was so small, so innocent, and yet there was a precociousness about him, but it was a sunny one; he did not nurse dark intentions about the adults in his world.

161

That night, after he and Aunty Uju got into bed and Ifemelu settled on a blanket on the floor, he said, 'How come she has to sleep on the floor, Mom? We can all fit in,' as though he could sense how Ifemelu felt. There was nothing *wrong* with the arrangement – she had, after all, slept on mats when she visited her grandmother in the village – but this was America at last, glorious America at last, and she had not expected to bed on the floor.

'I'm fine, Dike,' she said.

He got up and brought her his pillow. 'Here. It's soft and comfy.'

Aunty Uju said, 'Dike, come and lie down. Let your aunty sleep.'

Ifemelu could not sleep, her mind too alert to the newness of things, and she waited to hear Aunty Uju's snoring before she slipped out of the room and turned on the kitchen light. A fat cockroach was perched on the wall near the cabinets, moving slightly up and down as though breathing heavily. If she had been in their Lagos kitchen, she would have found a broom and killed it, but she left the American cockroach alone and went and stood by the living room window. Flatlands, Aunty Uju said this section of Brooklyn was called. The street below was poorly lit, bordered not by leafy trees but by closely parked cars, nothing like the pretty street on *The Cosby Show*. Ifemelu stood there for a long time, her body unsure of itself, overwhelmed by a sense of newness. But she felt, also, a frisson of expectation, an eagerness to discover America.

'I think it's better if you take care of Dike for the summer and save me babysitting money and then start looking for a job when you get to Philadelphia,' Aunty Uju said the next morning. She had woken Ifemelu up, giving brisk instructions about Dike, saying she would go to the library to study after work. Her words tumbled out. Ifemelu wished she would slow down a little.

'You can't work with your student visa, and work-study is rubbish, it pays nothing, and you have to be able to cover your rent and the balance of your tuition. Me, you can see I am working three jobs and yet it's not easy. I talked to one of my friends, I don't know if you remember Ngozi Okonkwo? She's now an American citizen and she has gone back to Nigeria for a while, to start a business. I begged her and she agreed to let you work with her Social Security card.'

'How? I'll use her name?' Ifemelu asked.

'Of course you'll use her name,' Aunty Uju said, eyebrows raised, as though she had barely stopped herself from asking if Ifemelu was stupid. There was a small white blob of face cream on her hair, caught at the root of a braid, and Ifemelu was going to tell her to wipe it off but she changed her mind, saying nothing, and watched Aunty Uju hurry to the door. She felt singed by Aunty Uju's reproach. It was as if, between them, an old

163

intimacy had quite suddenly lapsed. Aunty Uju's impatience, that new prickliness in her, made Ifemelu feel that there were things she should already know but, through some personal failing of hers, did not know. 'There's corned beef so you can make sandwiches for lunch,' Aunty Uju had said, as though those words were perfectly normal and did not require a humorous preamble about how Americans ate bread for lunch. But Dike didn't want a sandwich. After he had shown her all his toys, and they had watched some episodes of *Tom and Jerry*, with him laughing, thrilled, because she had watched them all before in Nigeria and so told him what would happen before it did, he opened the refrigerator and pointed at what he wanted her to make him. 'Hot dogs.' Ifemelu examined the curiously long sausages and then began to open cupboards to look for some oil.

'Mommy says I have to call you Aunty Ifem. But you're not my aunt. You're my cousin.'

'So call me Cousin.'

'Okay, Coz,' Dike said, and laughed. His laughter was so warm, so open. She had found the vegetable oil.

'You don't need oil,' Dike said. 'You just cook the hot dog in water.'

'Water? How can a sausage be cooked in water?'

'It's a hot dog, not a sausage.'

Of course it was a sausage, whether or not they called it the ludicrous name of 'hot dog', and so she fried two in a little oil as she was used to doing with

Satis sausages. Dike looked on in horror. She turned the stove off. He backed away and said 'Ugh.' They stood looking at each other, between them a plate with a bun and two shrivelled hot dogs. She knew then that she should have listened to him.

'Can I have a peanut butter and jelly sandwich instead?' Dike asked. She followed his instructions for the sandwich, cutting off the bread crusts, layering on the peanut butter first, stifling her laughter at how closely he watched her, as though she just might decide to fry the sandwich.

When, that evening, Ifemelu told Aunty Uju about the hot dog incident, Aunty Uju said with none of the amusement Ifemelu had expected, 'They are not sausages, they are hot dogs.'

'It's like saying that a bikini is not the same thing as underwear. Would a visitor from space know the difference?'

Aunty Uju shrugged; she was sitting at the dining table, a medical textbook open in front of her, eating a hamburger from a rumpled paper bag. Her skin dry, her eyes shadowed, her spirit bleached of colour. She seemed to be staring at, rather than reading, the book.

At the grocery store, Aunty Uju never bought what she needed; instead she bought what was on sale and made herself need it. She would take the colourful flyer at the entrance of Key Food, and go looking for the sale items, aisle after aisle, while Ifemelu wheeled the cart and Dike walked along.

'Mommy, I don't like that. Get the blue one,' Dike said, as Aunty Uju put cartons of cereal in the cart.

'It's buy one, get one free,' Aunty Uju said.

'It doesn't taste good.'

'It tastes just like your regular cereal, Dike.'

'No.' Dike took a blue carton from the shelf and hurried ahead to the checkout counter.

'Hi, little guy!' The cashier was large and cheerful, her cheeks reddened and peeling from sunburn. 'Helping Mommy out?'

'Dike, put it back,' Aunty Uju said, with the nasal, sliding accent she put on when she spoke to white Americans, in the presence of white Americans, in the hearing of white Americans. *Pooh-reet-back.* And with the accent emerged a new persona, apologetic and self-abasing. She was over-eager with the cashier. 'Sorry, sorry,' she said as she fumbled to get her debit card from her wallet. Because the cashier was watching, Aunty Uju let Dike keep the cereal but in the car she grabbed his left ear and twisted it, yanked it.

'I have told you, do not ever take anything in the grocery! Do you hear me? Or do you want me to slap you before you hear?'

Dike pressed his palm to his ear.

Aunty Uju turned to Ifemelu. 'This is how children like to misbehave in this country. Jane was even telling me that her daughter threatens to call the police when she beats her. Imagine. I don't blame the girl, she has come to America and learned about calling the police.'

Ifemelu rubbed Dike's knee. He did not look at her. Aunty Uju was driving a little too fast.

Dike called out from the bathroom, where he had been sent to brush his teeth before bed.

'Dike, *I mechago*?' Ifemelu asked.

'Please don't speak Igbo to him,' Aunty Uju said. 'Two languages will confuse him.'

'What are you talking about, Aunty? We spoke two languages growing up.'

'This is America. It's different.'

Ifemelu held her tongue. Aunty Uju closed her medical book and stared ahead at nothing. The television was off and the sound of water running came from the bathroom.

'Aunty, what is it?' Ifemelu asked. 'What is wrong?'

'What do you mean? Nothing is wrong.' Aunty Uju sighed. 'I failed my last exam. I got the result just before you came.'

'Oh.' Ifemelu was watching her.

'I've never failed an exam in my life. But they weren't testing actual knowledge, they were testing our ability to answer tricky multiple-choice questions that have nothing to do with real medical knowledge.' She stood up and went to the kitchen. 'I'm tired. I am so tired. I thought by now things would be better for me and Dike. It's not as if anybody was helping me and I just could not believe how quickly money went. I was studying and working three jobs. I was doing retail at the mall, and a research assistantship, and I even did some hours at Burger King.'

'It will get better,' Ifemelu said, helplessly. She knew how hollow she sounded. Nothing was familiar. She was unable to comfort Aunty Uju because she did not know how. When Aunty Uju spoke about her friends who had come to America earlier and passed their exams – Nkechi in Maryland had sent her the dining set, Kemi in Indiana bought her the bed, Ozavisa had sent crockery and clothes from Hartford – Ifemelu said, 'God bless them,' and the words felt bulky and useless in her mouth.

She had assumed, from Aunty Uju's calls home, that things were not too bad, although she realized now that Aunty Uju had always been vague, mentioning 'work' and 'exam' without details. Or perhaps it was because she had not asked for details, had not expected to understand details. And she thought, watching her, how the old Aunty Uju would never have worn her hair in such scruffy braids. She would never have tolerated the ingrown hair that grew like raisins on her chin, or worn trousers that gathered bulkily between her legs. America had subdued her.

CHAPTER 10

That first summer was Ifemelu's summer of waiting; the real America, she felt, was just around the next corner she would turn. Even the days, sliding one into the other, languorous and limpid, the sun lingering until very late, seemed to be waiting. There was a stripped-down quality to her life, a kindling starkness, without parents and friends and home, the familiar landmarks that made her who she was. And so she waited, writing Obinze long, detailed letters, calling him once in a while – calls kept brief because Aunty Uju said she could not waste the phone card – and spending time with Dike. He was a mere child, but she felt, with him, a kinship close to friendship; they watched his favourite cartoon shows together, *Rugrats* and *Franklin*, and they read books together, and she took him out to play with Jane's children. Jane lived in the next apartment. She and her husband, Marlon, were from Grenada and spoke in a lyrical accent as though just about to break into song. 'They are like us; he has a good job and he has ambition and they spank their children,' Aunty Uju had said approvingly.

Ifemelu and Jane laughed when they discovered how similar their childhoods in Grenada and Nigeria had been, with Enid Blyton books and Anglophile teachers and fathers who worshipped the BBC World Service. She was only a few years older than Ifemelu. 'I married very young. Everybody wanted Marlon, so how could I say no?' she said, half teasing. They would sit together on the front steps of the building and watch Dike and Jane's children, Elizabeth and Junior, ride their bicycles to the end of the street and then back, Ifemelu often calling out to Dike not to go any farther, the children shouting, the concrete sidewalks gleaming in the hot sun, and the summer lull disrupted by the occasional rise and fall of loud music from passing cars.

'Things must still be very strange for you,' Jane said.

Ifemelu nodded. 'Yes.'

An ice cream van drove into the street, and with it a tinkling melody.

'You know, this is my tenth year here and I feel as if I'm still settling in,' Jane said. 'The hardest thing is raising my kids. Look at Elizabeth, I have to be very careful with her. If you are not careful in this country, your children become what you don't know. It's different back home because you can control them. Here, no.' Jane wore an air of harmlessness, with her plain face and jiggly arms, but there was, beneath her ready smile, an icy watchfulness.

'How old is she? Ten?' Ifemelu asked.

'Nine and already trying to be a drama queen. We pay good money for her to go to private school because the public schools here are useless. Marlon says we'll move to the suburbs soon so they can go to better schools. Otherwise she will start behaving like these black Americans.'

'What do you mean?'

'Don't worry, you will understand with time,' Jane said, and got up to get some money for the children's ice cream.

Ifemelu looked forward to sitting outside with Jane, until the evening Marlon came back from work and told Ifemelu in a hasty whisper, after Jane went in to get some lemonade for the children, 'I've been thinking about you. I want to talk to you.' She did not tell Jane. Jane would never hold Marlon responsible for anything, her light-skinned, hazel-eyed Marlon whom everyone wanted, and so Ifemelu began to avoid both of them, to design elaborate board games that she and Dike could play indoors.

Once, she asked Dike what he had done in school before summer, and he said, 'Circles.' They would sit on the floor in a circle and share their favourite things.

She was appalled. 'Can you do division?'

He looked at her strangely. 'I'm only in first grade, Coz.'

'When I was your age I could do simple division.'

The conviction lodged in her head that American children learned nothing in elementary school, and it hardened when he told her that his teacher sometimes gave out homework coupons; if you got a homework coupon, then you could skip one day of homework. Circles, homework coupons, what foolishness would she next hear? And so she began to teach him mathematics – she called it 'maths' and he called it 'math' and so they agreed not to shorten the word. She could not think, now, of that summer without thinking of long division, of Dike's brows furrowed in confusion as they sat side by side at the dining table, of her swings from bribing him to shouting at him. Okay, try it one more time and you can have ice cream. You're not going to play unless you get them all right. Later, when he was older, he would say that he found mathematics easy because of her summer of torturing him. 'You must mean summer of tutoring,' she would say in what became a familiar joke that, like comfort food, they would reach for from time to time.

It was, also, her summer of eating. She enjoyed the unfamiliar – the McDonald's hamburgers with the brief tart crunch of pickles, a new taste that she liked on one day and disliked on the next, the wraps Aunty Uju brought home, wet with piquant dressing, and the bologna and pepperoni that left a film of salt in her mouth. She was disoriented by the blandness of fruits, as though Nature had forgotten to sprinkle some seasoning on the oranges and the bananas, but she liked to look at them, and to touch them; because bananas were so big, so evenly yellow, she forgave them their tastelessness. Once, Dike said, 'Why are you doing that? Eating a banana with peanuts?'

'That's what we do in Nigeria. Do you want to try?'

'No,' he said firmly. 'I don't think I like Nigeria, Coz.'

Ice cream was, fortunately, a taste unchanged. She scooped straight from the buy-one-get-one-free giant tubs in the freezer, globs of vanilla and chocolate, while staring at the television. She followed shows she had watched in Nigeria – *The Fresh Prince of Bel Air*, *A Different World* – and discovered new shows she had not known – *Friends*, *The Simpsons* – but it was the commercials that captivated her. She ached for the lives they showed, lives full of bliss, where all problems had sparkling solutions in shampoos and cars and packaged foods, and in her mind they became the real America, the America she would only see when she moved to school in the autumn. At first, the evening news puzzled her, a litany of fires and shootings, because she was used to NTA news, where self-important army officers cut ribbons or gave speeches. But as she watched day after day, images of men being hauled off in handcuffs, distraught families in front of charred, smouldering houses, the wreckage of cars crashed in police chases, blurred videos of armed robberies in shops, her puzzlement ripened to worry. She panicked when there was a sound by the window, when Dike went too far down the street on his bicycle. She stopped taking out the trash after dark, because a man with a gun might be lurking outside. Aunty Uju said, laughing shortly, 'If you keep watching television, you will think these things happen all the time. Do you know how much crime happens in Nigeria? Is it because we don't report it like they do here?'

CHAPTER 11

Aunty Uju came home dry-faced and tense, the streets dark and Dike already in bed, to ask 'Do I have mail? Do I have mail?' the question always repeated, her entire being at a perilous edge, about to tip over. Some nights, she would talk on the phone for a long time, her voice hushed, as though she were protecting something from the world's prying gaze. Finally, she told Ifemelu about Bartholomew. 'He is an accountant, divorced, and he is looking to settle down. He is from Eziowelle, very near us.'

Ifemelu, floored by Aunty Uju's words, could only say, 'Oh, okay,' and nothing else. 'What does he do?' and 'Where is he from?' were the questions her own mother would ask, but when had it started to matter to Aunty Uju that a man was from a hometown close to theirs?

One Saturday, Bartholomew visited from Massachusetts. Aunty Uju cooked peppered gizzards, powdered her face and stood by the living room window, waiting to see his car pull in. Dike watched her, playing half-heartedly with his action figures, confused but also excited because he could

175

sense her expectation. When the doorbell rang, she told Dike, urgently, 'Behave well!'

Bartholomew wore khaki trousers pulled up high on his belly, and spoke with an American accent filled with holes, mangling words until they were impossible to understand. Ifemelu sensed, from his demeanour, a deprived rural upbringing that he tried to compensate for with his American affectation, his gonnas and wannas.

He glanced at Dike, and said, almost indifferently, 'Oh, yes, your boy. How are you doing?'

'Good,' Dike mumbled.

It irked Ifemelu that Bartholomew was not interested in the son of the woman he was courting, and did not bother to pretend that he was. He was jarringly unsuited for, and unworthy of, Aunty Uju. A more intelligent man would have realized this and tempered himself, but not Bartholomew. He behaved grandiosely, like a special prize that Aunty Uju was fortunate to have, and Aunty Uju humoured him. Before he tasted the gizzards, he said, 'Let me see if this is any good.'

Aunty Uju laughed and in her laughter was a certain assent, because his words 'Let me see if this is any good' were about her being a good cook, and therefore a good wife. She had slipped into the rituals, smiling a smile that promised to be demure to him but not to the world, lunging to pick up his fork when it slipped from his hand, serving him more beer. Quietly, Dike watched from the dining table, his toys untouched.

176

Bartholomew ate gizzards and drank beer. He talked about Nigerian politics with the fervid enthusiasm of a person who followed it from afar, who read and reread articles on the Internet. 'Kudirat's death will not be in vain, it will only galvanize the democratic movement in a way that even her life did not! I just wrote an article about this issue online in *Nigerian Village*.' Aunty Uju nodded while he talked, agreeing with everything he said. Often, silence gaped between them. They watched television, a drama, predictable and filled with brightly shot scenes, one of which featured a young girl in a short dress.

'A girl in Nigeria will never wear that kind of dress,' Bartholomew said. 'Look at that. This country has no moral compass.'

Ifemelu should not have spoken, but there was something about Bartholomew that made silence impossible, the exaggerated caricature that he was, with his back-shaft haircut unchanged since he came to America thirty years ago and his false, overheated moralities. He was one of those people who, in his village back home, would be called 'lost'. *He went to America and got lost,* his people would say. *He went to America and refused to come back.*

'Girls in Nigeria wear dresses much shorter than that o,' Ifemelu said. 'In secondary school, some of us changed in our friends' houses so our parents wouldn't know.'

Aunty Uju turned to her, eyes narrow with warning.

Bartholomew looked at her and shrugged, as though she was not worth responding to. Dislike simmered between them. For the rest of the afternoon, he ignored her. He would, in the future, often ignore her. Later, she read his online posts on *Nigerian Village*, all of them sour-toned and strident, under the moniker 'Igbo Massachusetts Accountant', and it surprised her how profusely he wrote, how actively he pursued airless arguments.

He had not been back to Nigeria in years and perhaps he needed the consolation of those online groups, where small observations flared and blazed into attacks, personal insults flung back and forth. Ifemelu imagined the writers, Nigerians in bleak houses in America, their lives deadened by work, nursing their careful savings throughout the year so that they could visit home in December for a week, when they would arrive bearing suitcases of shoes and clothes and cheap watches, and see, in the eyes of their relatives, brightly burnished images of themselves. Afterwards they would return to America to fight on the Internet over their mythologies of home, because home was now a blurred place between here and there, and at least online they could ignore the awareness of how inconsequential they had become.

Nigerian women came to America and became wild, Igbo Massachusetts Accountant wrote in one post; it was an unpleasant truth but one that had to be said. What else accounted for the high divorce rates among Nigerians in America and the low rates among Nigerians in Nigeria? Delta Mermaid replied that women simply had laws protecting them in America and the divorce rates would be just as high if those laws were in Nigeria. Igbo Massachusetts Accountant's rejoinder: *You have been brainwashed by the West. You should be ashamed to call yourself a Nigerian.* In response to Eze Houston, who wrote that Nigerian men were cynical when they went back to Nigeria looking for nurses and doctors to marry, only so that the new wives would earn money for them back in America, Igbo Massachusetts Accountant wrote, *What is wrong with a man wanting financial security from his wife? Don't women want the same thing?*

After he left that Saturday, Aunty Uju asked Ifemelu, 'What did you think?'

'He uses bleaching creams.'

'What?'

'Couldn't you see? His face is a funny colour. He must be using the cheap ones with no sunscreen. What kind of man bleaches his skin, *biko*?'

Aunty Uju shrugged, as though she had not noticed the greenish-yellow tone of the man's face, worse at his temples.

'He's not bad. He has a good job.' She paused. 'I'm not getting any younger. I want Dike to have a brother or a sister.'

'In Nigeria, a man like him would not even have the courage to talk to you.'

'We are not in Nigeria, Ifem.'

Before Aunty Uju went into the bedroom, tottering under her many anxieties, she said, 'Please just pray that it will work.'

Ifemelu did not pray, but even if she did, she could not bear praying for Aunty Uju to be with Bartholomew. It saddened her that Aunty Uju had settled merely for what was familiar.

Because of obinze, Manhattan intimidated Ifemelu. The first time she took the subway from Brooklyn to Manhattan, her palms sweaty, she walked the streets, watching, absorbing. A sylphlike woman running in high heels, her short dress floating behind her, until she tripped and almost fell, a pudgy man coughing and spitting on the kerb, a girl dressed all in black raising a hand for the taxis that sliced past. The endless skyscrapers taunted the sky, but there was dirt on the building windows. The dazzling imperfection of it all calmed her. 'It's wonderful but it's not heaven,' she told Obinze. She could not wait until he, too, saw Manhattan. She imagined them both walking hand in hand, like the American couples she saw, lingering at a shop window, pausing to read menus taped on restaurant doors, stopping at a food cart to buy cold bottles of iced tea. 'Soon,' he said in his letter. They said 'soon' to each other often, and 'soon' gave their plan the weight of something real.

Finally, Aunty Uju's result came. Ifemelu brought in the envelope from the mailbox, so slight, so ordinary, *United States Medical Licensing Examination* printed on it in even script, and held it in her hand for a long time, willing it to be good news. She raised it up as soon as Aunty Uju walked indoors. Aunty Uju gasped. 'Is it thick? Is it thick?' she asked.

'What? *Gini*?' Ifemelu asked.

'Is it thick?' Aunty Uju asked again, letting her handbag slip to the floor and moving forward, her hand outstretched, her face savage with hope. She took the envelope and shouted, 'I made it!' and then opened it to make sure, peering at the thin sheet of paper. 'If you fail, they send you a thick envelope so that you can reregister.'

'Aunty! I knew it! Congratulations!' Ifemelu said.

Aunty Uju hugged her, both of them leaning into each other, hearing each other's breathing, and it brought to Ifemelu a warm memory of Lagos.

'Where's Dike?' Aunty Uju asked, as though he was not already in bed when she came home from her second job. She went into the kitchen, stood under the bright ceiling light and looked, again, at the result, her eyes wet. 'So I will be a family physician in this America,' she said, almost in a whisper. She opened a can of Coke and left it undrunk.

Later, she said, 'I have to take my braids out for my interviews and relax my hair. Kemi told me that I shouldn't wear braids to the interview. If you have braids, they will think you are unprofessional.'

181

'So there are no doctors with braided hair in America?' Ifemelu asked.

'I have told you what they told me. You are in a country that is not your own. You do what you have to do if you want to succeed.'

There it was again, the strange naïveté with which Aunty Uju had covered herself like a blanket. Sometimes, while having a conversation, it would occur to Ifemelu that Aunty Uju had deliberately left behind something of herself, something essential, in a distant and forgotten place. Obinze said it was the exaggerated gratitude that came with immigrant insecurity. Obinze, so like him to have an explanation. Obinze, who anchored her through that summer of waiting – his steady voice over the phone, his long letters in blue airmail envelopes – and who understood, as summer was ending, the new gnawing in her stomach. She wanted to start school, to find the real America, and yet there was that gnawing in her stomach, an anxiety, and a new, aching nostalgia for the Brooklyn summer that had become familiar: children on bicycles, sinewy black men in tight white tank tops, ice cream vans tinkling, loud music from roofless cars, sun shining into night, and things rotting and smelling in the humid heat. She did not want to leave Dike – the mere thought brought a sense of treasure already lost – and yet she wanted to leave Aunty Uju's apartment, and begin a life in which she alone determined the margins.

Dike had once told her, wistfully, about his

friend who had gone to Coney Island and come back with a picture taken on a steep, sliding ride, and so she surprised him on the weekend before she left, saying 'We're going to Coney Island!' Jane had told her what train to take, what to do, how much it would cost. Aunty Uju said it was a good idea, but gave her no money to add to what she had. As she watched Dike on the rides, screaming, terrified and thrilled, a little boy entirely open to the world, she did not mind what she had spent. They ate hot dogs and milkshakes and cotton candy. 'I can't wait until I don't have to come with you to the girls' bathroom,' he told her, and she laughed and laughed. On the train back, he was tired and sleepy. 'Coz, this was the bestest day ever with you,' he said, resting against her.

The bittersweet glow of an ending limbo overcame her days later when she kissed Dike goodbye – once then twice and three times, while he cried, a child so unused to crying, and she bit back her own tears and Aunty Uju said over and over that Philadelphia was not very far away. Ifemelu rolled her suitcase to the subway, took it to the Forty-second Street terminal and got on a bus to Philadelphia. She sat by the window – somebody had stuck a blob of chewed gum on the pane – and spent long minutes looking again at the Social Security card and driver's licence that belonged to Ngozi Okonkwo. Ngozi Okonkwo was at least ten years older than she was, with a narrow face, eyebrows that started as little balls before loping into arcs, and a jaw shaped like the letter *V*.

'I don't even look like her at all,' Ifemelu had said when Aunty Uju gave her the card.

'All of us look alike to white people,' Aunty Uju said.

'Ahn-ahn, Aunty!'

'I'm not joking. Amara's cousin came last year and she doesn't have her papers yet, so she has been working with Amara's ID. You remember Amara? Her cousin is very fair and slim. They do not look alike at all. Nobody noticed. She works as a home health aide in Virginia. Just make sure you always remember your new name. I have a friend who forgot and one of her co-workers called her and called her and she was blank. Then they became suspicious and reported her to immigration.'

CHAPTER 12

There was Ginika, standing in the small, crowded bus terminal, wearing a miniskirt and a tube top that covered her chest but not her midriff, and waiting to scoop Ifemelu up and into the real America. Ginika was much thinner, half her old size, and her head looked bigger, balanced on a long neck that brought to mind a vague, exotic animal. She extended her arms, as though urging a child into an embrace, laughing, calling out, 'Ifemsco! Ifemsco!' and Ifemelu was taken back, for a moment, to secondary school: an image of gossiping girls in their blue-and-white uniforms, felt berets perched on their heads, crowded in the school corridor. She hugged Ginika. The theatrics of their holding each other close, disengaging and then holding each other close again, made her eyes fill, to her mild surprise, with tears.

'Look at you!' Ginika said, gesturing, jangling the many silver bangles around her wrist. 'Is it really you?'

'When did *you* stop eating and start looking like a dried stockfish?' Ifemelu asked.

Ginika laughed, took the suitcase and turned to the door. 'Come on, let's go. I'm parked illegally.'

The green Volvo was at the corner of a narrow street. An unsmiling woman in uniform, ticket booklet in hand, was stumping towards them when Ginika jumped in and started the car. 'Close!' she said, laughing. A homeless man in a grubby T-shirt, pushing a trolley filled with bundles, had stopped just by the car, as though to rest briefly, staring ahead at nothing, and Ginika glanced at him as she eased the car into the street. They drove with the windows down. Philadelphia was the smell of the summer sun, of burnt asphalt, of sizzling meat from food carts tucked into street corners, foreign brown men and women hunched inside. Ifemelu would come to like the gyros from those carts, flatbread and lamb and dripping sauces, as she would come to love Philadelphia itself. It did not raise the spectre of intimidation as Manhattan did; it was intimate but not provincial, a city that might yet be kind to you. Ifemelu saw women on the sidewalks going to lunch from work, wearing sneakers, proof of their American preference for comfort over elegance, and she saw young couples clutching each other, kissing from time to time as if they feared that, if they unclasped their hands, their love would dissolve, melt into nothingness.

'I borrowed my landlord's car. I didn't want to come get you in my shit-ass car. I can't believe it, Ifemsco. You're in America!' Ginika said. There was a metallic, unfamiliar glamour in her gauntness, her olive skin, her short skirt that had risen up, barely covering her crotch, her straight-straight hair that she kept tucking behind her ears, blonde streaks shiny in the sunlight.

'We're entering University City, and that's where Wellson campus is, shay you know? We can go for you to see the school first and then we can go to my place, out in the suburbs, and after we can go to my friend's place in the evening. She's doing a get-together.' Ginika had lapsed into Nigerian English, a dated, overcooked version, eager to prove how unchanged she was. She had, with a strenuous loyalty, kept in touch through the years: calling and writing letters and sending books and shapeless trousers she called slacks. And now she was saying 'shay you know' and Ifemelu did not have the heart to tell her that nobody said 'shay' any more.

Ginika recounted anecdotes about her own early experiences in America, as though they were all filled with subtle wisdom that Ifemelu would need.

'If you see how they laughed at me in high school when I said that somebody was boning for me. Because boning here means to have sex! So I had to keep explaining that in Nigeria it means carrying face. And can you imagine "half-caste" is a bad word here? In freshman year, I was telling a bunch of my friends about how I was voted prettiest girl in school back home. Remember? I should never have won. Zainab should have won. It was just because I was a half-caste. There's even more of that here. There's some shit you'll get from white people in this country that I won't get. But anyway, I was telling them about back home and how all the boys were chasing me because I was a half-caste, and they said I was dissing myself. So now I say biracial, and I'm supposed to be offended when somebody says half-caste. I've met a lot of people here with white mothers and they are so full of issues, eh. I didn't know I was even supposed to *have* issues until I came to America. Honestly, if anybody wants to raise biracial kids, do it in Nigeria.'

'Of course. Where all the boys chase the half-caste girls.'

'Not *all* the boys, by the way.' Ginika made a face. 'Obinze had better hurry up and come to the US, before somebody will carry you away. You know you have the kind of body they like here.'

'What?'

'You're thin with big breasts.'

'Please, I'm not thin. I'm slim.'

'Americans say "thin". Here "thin" is a good word.'

'Is that why you stopped eating? All your bum has gone. I always wished I had a bum like yours,' Ifemelu said.

'Do you know I started losing weight almost as soon as I came? I was even close to anorexia. The kids at my high school called me Pork. You know at home when somebody tells you that you lost weight, it means something bad. But here somebody tells you that you lost weight and you say thank you. It's just different here,' Ginika said, a little wistfully, as though she, too, were new to America.

Later, Ifemelu watched Ginika at her friend Stephanie's apartment, a bottle of beer poised at her lips, her American-accented words sailing out of her mouth, and was struck by how like her American friends Ginika had become. Jessica, the Japanese American, beautiful and animated, playing with the emblemed key of her Mercedes. Pale-skinned Teresa, who had a loud laugh and wore diamond studs and shabby, worn-out shoes. Stephanie, the Chinese American, her hair a perfect swingy bob that curved inwards at her chin, who from time to time reached into her monogrammed bag to get her cigarettes and step out for a smoke. Hari, coffee-skinned and black-haired and wearing a tight T-shirt, who said, 'I am Indian, not Indian American,' when Ginika introduced Ifemelu. They all laughed at the same things and said 'Gross!' about the same things; they were well choreographed. Stephanie announced that she had home-made beer in her fridge and everyone chanted 'Cool!' Then Teresa said, 'Can I have the regular beer, Steph?' in the small voice of a person afraid to offend. Ifemelu sat on a lone armchair at the end of the room, drinking orange juice, listening to them talk. *That company is so evil. Oh my God, I can't believe there's so much sugar in this stuff. The Internet is totally going to change the world.* She heard Ginika ask, 'Did you know they use something from animal bones to make that breath mint?' and the others groaned. There were codes Ginika knew, ways of being that she had mastered. Unlike Aunty Uju, Ginika had come to America with the flexibility and fluidness of youth, the cultural cues had seeped into her skin, and now she went bowling, and knew what Tobey Maguire was about, and found double-dipping gross. Bottles and cans of beer were piling up. They all lounged in glamorous lassitude on the sofa, and on the rug, while heavy rock, which Ifemelu thought was unharmonious noise, played on the CD player. Teresa drank the fastest, rolling each empty can of beer on the wood floor, while the others laughed with an enthusiasm that puzzled Ifemelu because it really was not that funny. How did they know when to laugh, what to laugh about?

Ginika was buying a dress for a dinner party, hosted by the lawyers she was interning with.

'You should get some things, Ifem.'

'I'm not spending ten kobo of my money unless I have to.'

'Ten cents.'

'Ten cents.'

'I'll give you a jacket and bedding stuff, but at least you need tights. The cold is coming.'

'I'll manage,' Ifemelu said. And she would. If

she needed to, she would wear all her clothes at the same time, in layers, until she found a job. She was terrified to spend money.

'Ifem, I'll pay for you.'

'It's not as if you are earning much.'

'At least I am earning some,' Ginika quipped.

'I really hope I find a job soon.'

'You will, don't worry.'

'I don't understand how anybody will believe I'm Ngozi Okonkwo.'

'Don't show them the licence when you go to an interview. Just show the Social Security card. Maybe they won't even ask. Sometimes they don't for small jobs like that.'

Ginika led the way into a clothing store, which Ifemelu thought too fevered; it reminded her of a nightclub, disco music playing loudly, the interior shadowy, and the salespeople, two thin-armed young women in all black, moving up and down too swiftly. One was chocolate-skinned, her long black weave highlighted with auburn, the other was white, inky hair floating behind her as she came up to them.

'Hi, ladies, how are you? Is there anything I can help you with?' she asked in a tinkly, sing-song voice. She pulled clothes off hangers and unfurled them from shelves to show Ginika. Ifemelu was looking at the price tags, converting them to naira, exclaiming, 'Ahn-ahn! How can this thing cost this much?' She picked up and carefully examined some of the clothes, to find out what each was,

191

underwear or blouse, shirt or dress, and sometimes she was still not certain.

'This literally just came in,' the salesperson said of a sparkly dress, as though divulging a big secret, and Ginika said, 'Oh my God, really?' with a great excitement. Under the too-bright lighting of the fitting room, Ginika tried on the dress, walking on tiptoe. 'I love it.'

'But it's shapeless,' Ifemelu said. It looked, to her, like a boxy sack on which a bored person had haphazardly stuck sequins.

'It's postmodern,' Ginika said.

Watching Ginika preen in front of the mirror, Ifemelu wondered whether she, too, would come to share Ginika's taste for shapeless dresses, whether this was what America did to you.

At the checkout, the blonde cashier asked, 'Did anybody help you?'

'Yes,' Ginika said.

'Chelcy or Jennifer?'

'I'm sorry, I don't remember her name.' Ginika looked around, to point at her helper, but both young women had disappeared into the fitting rooms at the back.

'Was it the one with long hair?' the cashier asked.

'Well, both of them had long hair.'

'The one with dark hair?'

Both of them had dark hair.

Ginika smiled and looked at the cashier and the cashier smiled and looked at her computer screen, and two damp seconds crawled past before she cheerfully said, 'It's okay, I'll figure it out later and make sure she gets her commission.'

As they walked out of the store, Ifemelu said, 'I was waiting for her to ask "Was it the one with two eyes or the one with two legs?" Why didn't she just ask "Was it the black girl or the white girl?"'

Ginika laughed. 'Because this is America. You're supposed to pretend that you don't notice certain things.'

Ginika asked Ifemelu to stay with her, to save on rent, but her apartment was too far away, at the end of the Main Line, and the commuter train, taken every day into Philadelphia, would cost too much. They looked at apartments together in West Philadelphia, Ifemelu surprised by the rotting cabinets in the kitchen, the mouse that dashed past an empty bedroom.

'My hostel in Nsukka was dirty but there were no rats o.'

'It's a mouse,' Ginika said.

Ifemelu was about to sign a lease – if saving money meant living with mice, then so be it – when Ginika's friend told them of a room for rent, a great deal, as college life went. It was in a four-bedroom apartment with mouldy carpeting, above a pizza store on Powelton Avenue, on the corner where drug addicts sometimes dropped crack pipes, miserable pieces of twisted metal that glinted in the sun. Ifemelu's room was the cheapest, the smallest, facing the scuffed brick walls of the next building. Dog hair floated around. Her room-mates, Jackie, Elena and Allison, looked almost interchangeable, all small-boned and slim-hipped, their chestnut hair ironed straight, their lacrosse sticks piled in the narrow hallway. Elena's dog ambled about, large and black, like a shaggy donkey; once in a while, a mound of dog shit appeared at the bottom of the stairs and Elena would scream 'You're in big trouble now, buddy!' as though performing for the room-mates, playing a role whose lines everyone knew. Ifemelu wished the dog were kept outside, which was where dogs belonged. When Elena asked why Ifemelu had not petted her dog, or scratched his head in the week since she moved in, she said, 'I don't like dogs.'

'Is that like a cultural thing?'

'What do you mean?'

'I mean like I know in China they eat cat meat and dog meat.'

'My boyfriend back home loves dogs. I just don't.'

'Oh,' Elena said, and looked at her, brows furrowed, as Jackie and Allison had earlier looked at her when she said she had never gone bowling, as though wondering how she could have turned out a normal human being without ever having gone bowling. She was standing at the periphery of her own life, sharing a fridge and a toilet, a shallow intimacy, with people she did not know at all. People who lived in exclamation points.

'Great!' they said often. 'That's great!' People who did not scrub in the shower; their shampoos and conditioners and gels were cluttered in the bathroom, but there was not a single sponge, and this, the absence of a sponge, made them seem unreachably alien to her. (One of her earliest memories was of her mother, a bucket of water between them in the bathroom, saying to her, '*Ngwa*, scrub between your legs very well, very well . . . ,' and Ifemelu had applied a little too much vigour with the loofah, to show her mother just how clean she could get herself, and for a few days afterwards had hobbled around with her legs spread wide.) There was something unquestioning about her room-mates' lives, an assumption of certainty that fascinated her, so that they often said, 'Let's go get some,' about whatever it was they needed – more beer, pizza, buffalo wings, liquor – as though this getting was not an act that required money. She was used, at home, to people first asking 'Do you have money?' before they made such plans. They left pizza boxes on the kitchen table, and the kitchen itself in casual disarray for days, and on weekends their friends gathered in the living room, with packs of beer stacked in the refrigerator and streaks of dried urine on the toilet seat.

'We're going to a party. Come with us, it'll be fun!' Jackie said, and Ifemelu pulled on her slim-fitting trousers and a halter-neck blouse borrowed from Ginika.

'Won't you get dressed?' she asked her room-mates before they left, all of them wearing slouchy jeans, and Jackie said, 'We *are* dressed. What are you talking about?' with a laugh that suggested yet another foreign pathology had emerged. They went to a fraternity house on Chestnut Street, where everyone stood around drinking vodka-rich punch from plastic cups, until Ifemelu accepted that there would be no dancing; to party here was to stand around and drink. They were all a jumble of frayed fabric and slack collars, the students at the party, all their clothes looked determinedly worn. (Years later, a blog post would read: *When it comes to dressing well, American culture is so self-fulfilled that it has not only disregarded this courtesy of self-presentation, but has turned that disregard into a virtue. 'We are too superior/busy/cool/not-uptight to bother about how we look to other people, and so we can wear pajamas to school and underwear to the mall.'*) As they got drunker and drunker, some lay limp on the floor and others took felt-tipped pens and began to write on the exposed skin of the fallen. *Suck me off. Go Sixers.*

'Jackie said you're from Africa?' a boy in a baseball cap asked her.

'Yes.'

'That's really cool!' he said, and Ifemelu imagined telling Obinze about this, the way she would mimic the boy. Obinze pulled every strand of story from her, going over details, asking questions, and some-times he would laugh, the sound echoing down the line. She had told him how Allison had said, 'Hey, we're getting a bite to eat. Come with us!' and she thought it was an invitation and that, as with invitations back home, Allison or one of the others would buy her meal. But when the waitress brought the bill, Allison carefully began to untangle how many drinks each person had ordered and who had the calamari appetizer, to make sure nobody paid for anybody else. Obinze had found this very funny, finally saying, 'That's America for you!'

It was, to her, funny only in retrospect. She had struggled to hide her bafflement at the boundaries of hospitality, and also at this business of tipping – paying an extra fifteen or twenty per cent of your bill to the waitress – which was suspiciously like bribing, a forced and efficient bribing system.

CHAPTER 13

At first, Ifemelu forgot that she was someone else. In an apartment in South Philadelphia, a tired-faced woman opened the door and led her into a strong stench of urine. The living room was dark, unaired, and she imagined the whole building steeped in months, even years, of accumulated urine, and herself working every day in this urine cloud. From inside the apartment, a man was groaning, deep and eerie sounds; they were the groans of a person for whom groaning was the only choice left, and they frightened her.

'That's my dad,' the woman said, looking at her with keen assessing eyes. 'Are you strong?'

The advertisement in the *City Paper* had stressed strong. *Strong Home Health Aide. Pays cash.*

'I'm strong enough to do the job,' Ifemelu said, and fought the urge to back out of the apartment and run and run.

'That's a pretty accent. Where are you from?'

'Nigeria.'

'Nigeria. Isn't there a war going on there?'

'No.'

'Can I see your ID?' the woman asked, and then,

glancing at the licence, added, 'How do you pronounce your name again?'

'Ifemelu.'

'What?'

Ifemelu almost choked. 'Ngozi. You hum the *N*.'

'Really.' The woman, with her air of unending exhaustion, seemed too tired to question the two different pronunciations. 'Can you live in?'

'Live in?'

'Yes. Live here with my dad. There's a spare bedroom. You would do three nights a week. You'd need to clean him up in the morning.' The woman paused. 'You *are* pretty slight. Look, I've two more people to interview and I'll get back to you.'

'Okay. Thank you.' Ifemelu knew she would not get the job and for this she was grateful.

She repeated 'I'm Ngozi Okonkwo' in front of the mirror before her next interview, at the Seaview restaurant. 'Can I call you Goz?' the manager asked after they shook hands, and she said yes, but before she said yes, she paused, the slightest and shortest of pauses, but still a pause. And she wondered if that was why she did not get the job.

Later Ginika said, 'You could have just said Ngozi is your tribal name and Ifemelu is your jungle name and throw in one more as your spiritual name. They'll believe all kinds of shit about Africa.'

Ginika laughed, a sure throaty laugh. Ifemelu laughed, too, although she did not fully understand the joke. And she had the sudden sensation of fogginess, of a milky web through which she tried to claw. Her autumn of half blindness had begun, the autumn of puzzlements, of experiences she had knowing there were slippery layers of meaning that eluded her.

The world was wrapped in gauze; she could see the shapes of things but not clearly enough, never enough. She told Obinze that there were things she should know how to do but didn't, details she should have corralled into her space but hadn't. And he reminded her of how quickly she was adapting, his tone always calm, always consoling. She applied to be a waitress, hostess, bartender, cashier, and then waited for job offers that never came, and for this she blamed herself. It had to be that she was not doing something right; and yet she did not know what it might be. Autumn had come, wet and grey-skied. Her meagre bank account was leaking money. The cheapest sweaters from Ross still startled with their high cost, bus and train tickets added up, and groceries punctured holes in her bank balance, even though she stood guard at the checkout, watching the electronic display and saying, 'Please stop. I won't be taking the rest,' when it got to thirty dollars. Each day, there seemed to be a letter for her on the kitchen table, and inside the envelope was a tuition bill, and words printed in capital letters: *YOUR RECORDS WILL BE FROZEN UNLESS PAYMENT IS*

RECEIVED BY THE DATE AT THE BOTTOM OF THIS NOTICE.

It was the boldness of the capital letters more than the words that frightened her. She worried about the possible consequences, a vague but constant worry. She did not imagine a police arrest for not paying her school fees, but what did happen if you did not pay your school fees in America? Obinze told her nothing would happen, suggested she speak to the bursar about getting on a payment plan so that she would at least have taken some action. She called Obinze often, with cheap phone cards she bought from the crowded store of a gas station on Lancaster Avenue, and just scratching off the metallic dust, to reveal the numbers printed beneath, flooded her with anticipation: to hear Obinze's voice again. He calmed her. With him, she could feel whatever she felt, and she did not have to force some cheer into her voice, as she did with her parents, telling them she was very fine, very hopeful to get a waitress job, settling down very well with her classes.

The highlight of her days was talking to Dike. His voice, higher-pitched on the phone, warmed her as he told her what had happened on his TV show, how he had just beaten a new level on Game Boy. 'When are you coming to visit, Coz?' he asked often. 'I wish you were taking care of me. I don't like going to Miss Brown's. Her bathroom is stinky.'

She missed him. Sometimes she told him things

she knew he would not understand, but she told him anyway. She told him about her professor who sat on the grass at lunch to eat a sandwich, the one who asked her to call him by his first name, Al, the one who wore a studded leather jacket and had a motorcycle. On the day she got her first piece of junk mail, she told him, 'Guess what? I got a letter today.' That credit card preapproval, with her name correctly spelled and elegantly italicized, had roused her spirits, made her a little less invisible, a little more present. Somebody knew her.

CHAPTER 14

And then there was Cristina Tomas. Cristina Tomas with her rinsed-out look, her washy blue eyes, faded hair and pallid skin, Cristina Tomas seated at the front desk with a smile, Cristina Tomas wearing whitish tights that made her legs look like death. It was a warm day, Ifemelu had walked past students sprawled on green lawns; cheery balloons were clustered below a WELCOME FRESHMEN sign.

'Good afternoon. Is this the right place for registration?' Ifemelu asked Cristina Tomas, whose name she did not then know.

'Yes. Now. Are. You. An. International. Student?'

'Yes.'

'You. Will. First. Need. To. Get. A. Letter. From. The. International. Students. Office.'

Ifemelu half smiled in sympathy, because Cristina Tomas had to have some sort of illness that made her speak so slowly, lips scrunching and puckering, as she gave directions to the international students office. But when Ifemelu returned with the letter, Cristina Tomas said, 'I. Need. You. To. Fill. Out. A. Couple. Of. Forms. Do. You. Understand. How.

To. Fill. These. Out?' and she realized that Cristina Tomas was speaking like that because of *her*, her foreign accent, and she felt for a moment like a small child, lazy-limbed and drooling.

'I speak English,' she said.

'I bet you do,' Cristina Tomas said. 'I just don't know how *well*.'

Ifemelu shrank. In that strained, still second when her eyes met Cristina Tomas's before she took the forms, she shrank. She shrank like a dried leaf. She had spoken English all her life, led the debating society in secondary school, and always thought the American twang inchoate; she should not have cowered and shrunk, but she did. And in the following weeks, as autumn's coolness descended, she began to practise an American accent.

School in america was easy, assignments sent in by e-mail, classrooms air-conditioned, professors willing to give make-up tests. But she was uncomfortable with what the professors called 'participation', and did not see why it should be part of the final grade; it merely made students talk and talk, class time wasted on obvious words, hollow words, sometimes meaningless words. It had to be that Americans were taught, from elementary school, to always *say something* in class, no matter what. And so she sat stiff-tongued, surrounded by students who were all folded easily on their seats, all flush with knowledge, not of the subject of the classes, but of how to *be* in the classes. They never said 'I don't know.' They said, instead, 'I'm not sure,' which did not give any information but still suggested the possibility of knowledge. And they ambled, these Americans, they walked without rhythm. They avoided giving direct instructions: they did not say 'Ask somebody upstairs'; they said 'You might want to ask somebody upstairs.' When you tripped and fell, when you choked, when misfortune befell you, they did not say 'Sorry.' They said 'Are you okay?' when it was obvious that you were not. And when you said 'Sorry' to them when they choked or tripped or encountered misfortune, they replied, eyes wide with surprise, 'Oh, it's not your fault.' And they overused the word 'excited', a professor excited about a new book, a student excited about a class, a politician on TV excited about a law; it was altogether too much excitement. Some of the expressions she heard every day astonished her, jarred her, and she wondered what Obinze's mother would make of them. *You shouldn't of done that. There is three things. I had a apple. A couple days. I want to lay down.* 'These Americans cannot speak English o,' she told Obinze. On her first day at school, she had visited the health centre, and had stared a little too long at the bin filled with free condoms in the corner. After her physical, the receptionist told her, 'You're all set!' and she, blank, wondered what 'You're all set' meant until she assumed it had to mean that she had done all she needed to.

She woke up every day worrying about money. If she bought all the textbooks she needed, she would not have enough to pay her rent, and so she borrowed textbooks during class and made feverish notes which, reading them later, sometimes confused her. Her new class friend, Samantha, a thin woman who avoided the sun, often saying 'I burn easily,' would, from time to time, let her take a textbook home. 'Keep it until tomorrow and make notes if you need to,' she would say. 'I know how tough things can be, that's why I dropped out of college years ago to work.' Samantha was older, and a relief to befriend, because she was not a slack-jawed eighteen-year-old as so many others in her communications major were. Still, Ifemelu never kept the books for more than a day, and sometimes refused to take them home. It stung her, to have to beg. Sometimes after classes, she would sit on a bench in the quad and watch the students walking past the large grey sculpture in the middle; they all seemed to have their lives in the shape that they wanted, they could have jobs if they wanted to have jobs, and above them, small flags fluttered serenely from lampposts.

She hungered to understand everything about America, to wear a new, knowing skin right away: to support a team at the Super Bowl, understand what a Twinkie was and what sports 'lockouts' meant, measure in ounces and square feet, order a 'muffin' without thinking that it really was a

206

cake, and say 'I "scored" a deal' without feeling silly.

Obinze suggested she read American books, novels and histories and biographies. In his first e-mail to her – a cybercafé had just opened in Nsukka – he gave her a list of books. *The Fire Next Time* was the first. She stood by the library shelf and skimmed the opening chapter, braced for boredom, but slowly she moved to a couch and sat down and kept reading until three-quarters of the book was gone, then she stopped and took down every James Baldwin title on the shelf. She spent her free hours in the library, so wondrously well lit; the sweep of computers, the large, clean, airy reading spaces, the welcoming brightness of it all, seemed like a sinful decadence. She was used, after all, to reading books with pages missing, fallen off while passing through too many hands. And now to be in a cavalcade of books with healthy spines. She wrote to Obinze about the books she read, careful, sumptuous letters that opened, between them, a new intimacy; she had begun, finally, to grasp the power books had over him. His longing for Ibadan because of 'Ibadan' had puzzled her; how could a string of words make a person ache for a place he did not know? But in those weeks when she discovered the rows and rows of books with their leathery smell and their promise of pleasures unknown, when she sat, knees tucked underneath her, on an armchair in the lower level or at a table upstairs with the fluorescent light reflecting off the book's pages, she finally understood. She read the books on Obinze's list but also, randomly, pulled out book after book, reading a chapter before deciding which she would speed-read in the library and which she would check out. And as she read, America's mythologies began to take on meaning, America's tribalisms – race, ideology and region – became clear. And she was consoled by her new knowledge.

'You know you said "excited"?' Obinze asked her one day, his voice amused. 'You said you were excited about your media class.'

'I did?'

New words were falling out of her mouth. Columns of mist were dispersing. Back home, she would wash her underwear every night and hang it in a discreet corner of the bathroom. Now that she piled them up in a basket and threw them into the washing machine on Friday evenings, she had come to see this, the heaping of dirty underwear, as normal. She spoke up in class, buoyed by the books she read, thrilled that she could disagree with professors and get, in return, not a scolding about being disrespectful but an encouraging nod.

'We watch films in class,' she told Obinze. 'They talk about films here as if films are as important as books. So we watch films and then we write a response paper and almost everybody gets an A. Can you imagine? These Americans are not serious o.'

In her honours history seminar, Professor Moore, a tiny, tentative woman with the emotionally malnourished look of someone who did not have friends, showed some scenes from *Roots*, the images bright on the board of the darkened classroom. When she turned off the projector, a ghostly white patch hovered on the wall for a moment before disappearing. Ifemelu had first watched *Roots* on video with Obinze and his mother, sunk into sofas in their living room in Nsukka. As Kunta Kinte was being flogged into accepting his slave name, Obinze's mother got up abruptly, so abruptly she almost tripped on a leather pouffe, and left the room, but not before Ifemelu saw her reddened eyes. It startled her, that Obinze's mother, fully hemmed into her self-containment, her intense privacy, could cry watching a film. Now, as the window blinds were raised and the classroom once again plunged into light, Ifemelu remembered that Saturday afternoon, and how she had felt lacking, watching Obinze's mother, and wishing that she, too, could cry.

'Let's talk about historical representation in film,' Professor Moore said.

A firm, female voice from the back of the class, with a non-American accent, asked, 'Why was "nigger" bleeped out?'

And a collective sigh, like a small wind, swept through the class.

'Well, this was a recording from network television and one of the things I wanted us to talk

209

about is how we represent history in popular culture and the use of the N-word is certainly an important part of that,' Professor Moore said.

'It makes no sense to me,' the firm voice said. Ifemelu turned. The speaker's natural hair was cut as low as a boy's and her pretty face, wide-foreheaded and fleshless, reminded Ifemelu of the East Africans who always won long-distance races on television.

'I mean, "nigger" is a word that exists. People use it. It is part of America. It has caused a lot of pain to people and I think it is insulting to bleep it out.'

'Well,' Professor Moore said, looking around, as though for help.

It came from a gravelly voice in the middle of the class. 'Well, it's because of the pain that word has caused that you *shouldn't* use it!' *Shouldn't* sailed astringently into the air, the speaker an African American girl wearing bamboo hoop earrings.

'Thing is, each time you say it, the word hurts African Americans,' a pale, shaggy-haired boy in front said.

Ifemelu raised her hand; Faulkner's *Light in August*, which she had just read, was on her mind. 'I don't think it's always hurtful. I think it depends on the intent and also on who is using it.'

A girl next to her, face flushing bright red, burst out, 'No! The word is the same for whoever says it.'

'That is nonsense.' The firm voice again. A voice unafraid. 'If my mother hits me with a stick and a stranger hits me with a stick, it's not the same thing.'

Ifemelu looked at Professor Moore to see how the word 'nonsense' had been received. She did not seem to have noticed; instead, a vague terror was freezing her features into a smirk-smile.

'I agree it's different when African Americans say it, but I don't think it should be used in films, because that way people who shouldn't use it can use it and hurt other people's feelings,' a light-skinned African American girl said, the last of the four black people in class, her sweater an unsettling shade of fuchsia.

'But it's like being in denial. If it was used like that, then it should be represented like that. Hiding it doesn't make it go away.' The firm voice.

'Well, if you all hadn't sold us, we wouldn't be talking about any of this,' the gravelly-voiced African American girl said, in a lowered tone that was, nonetheless, audible.

The classroom was wrapped in silence. Then rose that voice again. 'Sorry, but even if no Africans had been sold by other Africans, the transatlantic slave trade would still have happened. It was a European enterprise. It was about Europeans looking for labour for their plantations.'

Professor Moore interrupted in a small voice. 'Okay, now let's talk about the ways in which history can be sacrificed for entertainment.'

After class, Ifemelu and the firm voice drifted towards each other.

'Hi. I'm Wambui. I'm from Kenya. You're Nigerian, right?' She had a formidable air; a person who went about setting everyone and everything right in the world.

'Yes. I'm Ifemelu.'

They shook hands. They would, in the next weeks, ease into a lasting friendship. Wambui was the president of the African Students Association.

'You don't know about ASA? You must come to the next meeting on Thursday,' she said.

The meetings were held in the basement of Wharton Hall, a harshly lit, windowless room, paper plates, pizza cartons and soda bottles piled on a metal table, folding chairs arranged in a limp semi-circle. Nigerians, Ugandans, Kenyans, Ghanaians, South Africans, Tanzanians, Zimbabweans, one Congolese and one Guinean sat around eating, talking, fuelling spirits, and their different accents formed meshes of solacing sounds. They mimicked what Americans told them: *You speak such good English. How bad is AIDS in your country? It's so sad that people live on less than a dollar a day in Africa.* And they themselves mocked Africa, trading stories of absurdity, of stupidity, and they felt safe to mock, because it was mockery born of longing, and of the heartbroken desire to see a place made whole again. Here, Ifemelu felt a gentle, swaying sense of renewal. Here, she did not have to explain herself.

★　　★　　★

212

Wambui had told everyone that Ifemelu was looking for a job. Dorothy, the girly Ugandan with long braids who worked as a waitress in Center City, said her restaurant was hiring. But first, Mwombeki, the Tanzanian double major in engineering and political science, looked over Ifemelu's résumé and asked her to delete the three years of university in Nigeria: American employers did not like lower-level employees to be too educated. Mwombeki reminded her of Obinze, that ease about him, that quiet strength. At meetings, he made everyone laugh. 'I got a good primary education because of Nyerere's socialism,' Mwombeki said often. 'Otherwise I would be in Dar right now, carving ugly giraffes for tourists.' When two new students came for the first time, one from Ghana and the other from Nigeria, Mwombeki gave them what he called the welcome talk.

'Please do not go to Kmart and buy twenty pairs of jeans because each costs five dollars. The jeans are not running away. They will be there tomorrow at an even more reduced price. You are now in America: do not expect to have hot food for lunch. That African taste must be abolished. When you visit the home of an American with some money, they will offer to show you their house. Forget that in your house back home, your father would throw a fit if anyone came close to his bedroom. We all know that the living room was where it stopped and, if absolutely necessary, then the toilet. But please smile and follow the American and see the house and make sure you say you like everything. And do not be shocked by the indiscriminate touching of American couples. Standing in line at the cafeteria, the girl will touch the boy's arm and the boy will put his arm around her shoulder and they will rub shoulders and back and rub rub rub but please do not imitate this behaviour.'

They were all laughing. Wambui shouted something in Swahili.

'Very soon you will start to adopt an American accent, because you don't want customer service people on the phone to keep asking you "What? What?" You will start to admire Africans who have perfect American accents, like our brother here, Kofi. Kofi's parents came from Ghana when he was two years old, but do not be fooled by the way he sounds. If you go to their house, they eat kenkey every day. His father slapped him when he got a C in a class. There's no American nonsense in that house. He goes back to Ghana every year. We call people like Kofi American African, not African American, which is what we call our brothers and sisters whose ancestors were slaves.'

'It was a B minus, not a C,' Kofi quipped.

'Try and make friends with our African American brothers and sisters in a spirit of true pan-Africanism. But make sure you remain friends with fellow Africans, as this will help you keep your perspective. Always attend African Students Association meetings, but if you must, you can also try the Black Student Union. Please note that in general, African

Americans go to the Black Student Union and Africans go to the African Students Association. Sometimes it overlaps but not a lot. The Africans who go to BSU are those with no confidence who are quick to tell you "I am *originally* from Kenya" even though Kenya just pops out the minute they open their mouths. The African Americans who come to our meetings are the ones who write poems about Mother Africa and think every African is a Nubian queen. If an African American calls you a Mandingo or a booty scratcher, he is insulting you for being African. Some will ask you annoying questions about Africa, but others will connect with you. You will also find that you might make friends more easily with other internationals, Koreans, Indians, Brazilians, whatever, than with Americans both black and white. Many of the internationals understand the trauma of trying to get an American visa and that is a good place to start a friendship.'

There was more laughter, Mwombeki himself laughing loudly, as though he had not heard his own jokes before.

Later, as Ifemelu left the meeting, she thought of Dike, wondered which he would go to in college, ASA or BSU, and what he would be considered, American African or African American. He would have to choose what he was, or rather, what he was would be chosen for him.

Ifemelu thought the interview at the restaurant where Dorothy worked had gone well. It was for a hostess position, and she wore her nice shirt, smiled warmly, shook hands firmly. The manager, a chortling woman full of a seemingly uncontrollable happiness, told her, 'Great! Wonderful to talk to you! You'll hear from me soon!' And so when, that evening, her phone rang, she snatched it up, hoping it was a job offer.

'Ifem, *kedu*?' Aunty Uju said.

Aunty Uju called too often to ask if she had found a job. 'Aunty, you will be the first person I will call when I do,' Ifemelu had said during the last call, only yesterday, and now Aunty Uju was calling again.

'Fine,' Ifemelu said, and was about to add, 'I have not found anything yet,' when Aunty Uju said, 'Something happened with Dike.'

'What?' Ifemelu asked.

'Miss Brown told me that she saw him in a closet with a girl. The girl is in third grade. Apparently they were showing each other their private parts.'

There was a pause.

'Is that all?' Ifemelu asked.

'What do you mean, is that all? He is not yet seven years old! What type of thing is this? Is this what I came to America for?'

'We actually read something about this in one of my classes the other day. It's normal. Children are curious about things like that at an early age, but they don't really understand it.'

'Normal *kwa*? It's not normal at all.'

'Aunty, we were all curious as children.'

'Not at seven years old! Tufiakwa! Where did he learn that from? It is that day care he goes to. Since Alma left and he started going to Miss Brown, he has changed. All those wild children with no home training, he is learning rubbish from them. I've decided to move to Massachusetts at the end of this term.'

'Ahn-ahn!'

'I'll finish my residency there and Dike will go to a better school and better day care. Bartholomew is moving from Boston to a small town, Warrington, to start his business, so it will be a new beginning for both of us. The elementary school there is very good. And the local doctor is looking for a partner because his practice is growing. I've spoken to him and he is interested in my joining him when I finish.'

'You're leaving New York to go to a village in Massachusetts? Can you just leave residency like that?'

'Of course. My friend Olga, the one from Russia? She is leaving, too, but she will have to repeat a year in her new programme. She wants to practise dermatology and most of our patients here are black and she said skin diseases look different on black skin and she knows she will not end up practising in a black area, so she wants to go where the patients will be white. I don't blame her. It's true my programme is higher ranked, but sometimes job opportunities are better in smaller places. Besides, I don't want Bartholomew to think I am not serious. I'm not getting any younger. I want to start trying.'

'You're really going to marry him.'

Aunty Uju said with mock exasperation, 'Ifem, I thought we had passed that stage. Once I move, we'll go to court and get married, so that he can act as Dike's legal parent.'

Ifemelu heard the beep-beep of an incoming call. 'Aunty, let me call you back,' she said, and switched over without waiting for Aunty Uju's response. It was the restaurant manager.

'I'm sorry, Ngozi,' she said, 'but we decided to hire a more qualified person. Good luck!'

Ifemelu put the phone down and thought of her mother, how she often blamed the devil. *The devil is a liar. The devil wants to block us.* She stared at the phone, and then at the bills on her table, a tight, suffocating pressure rising inside her chest.

CHAPTER 15

The man was short, his body a glut of muscles, his hair thinning and sun-bleached. When he opened the door, he looked her over, mercilessly sizing her up, and then he smiled and said, 'Come on in. My office is in the basement.' Her skin prickled, an unease settling over her. There was something venal about his thin-lipped face; he had the air of a man to whom corruption was familiar.

'I'm a pretty busy guy,' he said, gesturing to a chair in his cramped home office that smelled slightly of damp.

'I assumed so from the advertisement,' Ifemelu said. *Female personal assistant for busy sports coach in Ardmore, communication and interpersonal skills required.* She sat on the chair, perched really, suddenly thinking that, from reading a *City Paper* ad, she was now alone with a strange man in the basement of a strange house in America. Hands thrust deep in his jeans pockets, he walked back and forth with short quick steps, talking about how much in demand he was as a tennis coach, and Ifemelu thought he might trip on the stacks

219

of sports magazines on the floor. She felt dizzy just watching him. He spoke as quickly as he moved, his expression uncannily alert; his eyes stayed wide and unblinking for too long.

'So here's the deal. There are two positions, one for office work and the other for help relaxing. The office position has already been filled. She started yesterday, she goes to Bryn Mawr, and she'll spend the whole week just clearing up my backlog of stuff. I bet I have some unopened cheques in there somewhere.' He withdrew a hand to gesture towards his messy desk. 'Now what I need is help to relax. If you want the job you have it. I'd pay you a hundred dollars a day, with the possibility of a raise, and you'd work as needed, no set schedule.'

A hundred dollars, almost enough for her monthly rent. She shifted on the chair. 'What exactly do you mean by "help to relax"?'

She was watching him, waiting for his explanation. It began to bother her, thinking of how much she had paid for the suburban train ticket.

'Look, you're not a kid,' he said. 'I work so hard I can't sleep. I can't relax. I don't do drugs, so I figured I need help to relax. You can give me a massage, help me relax, you know. I had somebody doing it before, but she's just moved to Pittsburgh. It's a great gig, at least she thought so. Helped her with a lot of her college debt.' He had said this to many other women, she could tell, from the measured pace with which the words came out.

He was not a kind man. She did not know exactly what he meant, but whatever it was, she regretted that she had come.

She stood up. 'Can I think about this and give you a call?'

'Of course.' He shrugged, shoulders thick with sudden irritability, as though he could not believe she did not recognize her good fortune. As he let her out, he shut the door quickly, not responding to her final 'Thank you.' She walked back to the station, mourning the train fare. The trees were awash with colour, red and yellow leaves tinted the air golden, and she thought of the words she had recently read somewhere: *Nature's first green is gold.* The crisp air, fragrant and dry, reminded her of Nsukka during the harmattan season, and brought with it a sudden stab of homesickness, so sharp and so abrupt that it filled her eyes with tears.

Each time she went to a job interview, or made a phone call about a job, she told herself that this would, finally, be her day; this time, the waitress, hostess, babysitter position would be hers, but even as she wished herself well, there was already a gathering gloom in a far corner of her mind. 'What am I doing wrong?' she asked Ginika, and Ginika told her to be patient, to have hope. She typed and retyped her résumé, invented past waitressing experience in Lagos, wrote Ginika's name as an employer whose children she had babysat, gave the name of Wambui's landlady as a reference, and, at each interview, she smiled warmly and shook hands firmly, all the things that were suggested in a book she had read about interviewing for American jobs. Yet there was no job. Was it her foreign accent? Her lack of experience? But her African friends all had jobs, and college students got jobs all the time with no experience. Once, she went to a gas station near Chestnut Street and a large Mexican man said, with his eyes on her chest, 'You're here for the attendant position? You can work for me in another way.' Then, with a smile, the leer never leaving his eyes, he told her the job was taken. She began to think more about her mother's devil, to imagine how the devil might have a hand here. She added and subtracted endlessly, determining what she would need and not need, cooking rice and beans each week, and heating up small portions in the microwave for lunch and dinner. Obinze offered to send her some money. His cousin had visited from London and given him some pounds. He would change it to dollars in Enugu.

'How can you be sending me money from Nigeria? It should be the other way around,' she said. But he sent it to her anyway, a little over a hundred dollars carefully sealed in a card.

Ginika was busy, working long hours at her internship and studying for her law school exams, but she called often to check up on Ifemelu's job searching, and always with that upbeat voice, as though to urge Ifemelu towards hope. 'This woman I did an internship with her charity, Kimberly, called me to say her babysitter is leaving and she's looking. I told her about you and she'd like to meet you. If she hires you, she'll pay cash under the table so you won't have to use that fake name. When do you finish tomorrow? I can come and take you to her for an interview.'

'If I get this job, I will give you my first month's salary,' Ifemelu said, and Ginika laughed.

Ginika parked in the circular driveway of a house that announced its wealth, the stone exterior solid and overbearing, four white pillars rising portentously at the entrance. Kimberly opened the front door. She was slim and straight, and raised both hands to push her thick golden hair away from her face, as though one hand could not possibly tame all that hair.

'How nice to meet you,' she said to Ifemelu, smiling, as they shook hands, her hand small, bony-fingered, fragile. In her gold sweater belted at an impossibly tiny waist, with her gold hair, in gold flats, she looked improbable, like sunlight.

'This is my sister Laura, who's visiting. Well, we visit each other almost every day! Laura practically lives next door. The kids are in the Poconos until tomorrow, with my mother. I thought it would be best to do this when they're not here anyway.'

'Hi,' Laura said. She was as thin and straight and blonde as Kimberly. Ifemelu, describing them to Obinze, would say that Kimberly gave the impression of a tiny bird with fine bones, easily crushed, while Laura brought to mind a hawk, sharp-beaked and dark-minded.

'Hello, I'm Ifemelu.'

'What a beautiful name,' Kimberly said. 'Does it mean anything? I love multicultural names because they have such wonderful meanings, from wonderful rich cultures.' Kimberly was smiling the kindly smile of people who thought 'culture' the unfamiliar colourful reserve of colourful people, a word that always had to be qualified with 'rich'. She would not think Norway had a 'rich culture'.

'I don't know what it means,' Ifemelu said, and sensed rather than saw a small amusement on Ginika's face.

'Would you like some tea?' Kimberly asked, leading the way into a kitchen of shiny chrome and granite and affluent empty space. 'We're tea drinkers, but of course there are other choices.'

'Tea is great,' Ginika said.

'And you, Ifemelu?' Kimberly asked. 'I know I'm mauling your name but it really is such a beautiful name. Really beautiful.'

'No, you said it properly. I'd like some water or orange juice, please.' Ifemelu would come to realize later that Kimberly used 'beautiful' in a peculiar way. 'I'm meeting my beautiful friend from graduate school,' Kimberly would say, or 'We're working with this beautiful woman on the inner-city project,' and always, the women she referred to would turn out to be quite ordinary-looking, but always black. One day, late that winter, when she was with Kimberly at the huge kitchen table, drinking tea and waiting for the children to be brought back from an outing with their grandmother, Kimberly said, 'Oh, look at this beautiful woman,' and pointed at a plain model in a magazine whose only distinguishing feature was her very dark skin. 'Isn't she just stunning?'

'No, she isn't.' Ifemelu paused. 'You know, you can just say "black". Not every black person is beautiful.'

Kimberly was taken aback, something wordless spread on her face and then she smiled, and Ifemelu would think of it as the moment they became, truly, friends. But on that first day, she liked Kimberly, her breakable beauty, her purplish eyes full of the expression Obinze often used to describe the people he liked: *obi ocha*. A clean heart. Kimberly asked Ifemelu questions about her experience with children, listening carefully as though what she wanted to hear was what might be left unsaid.

'She doesn't have CPR certification, Kim,' Laura said. She turned to Ifemelu. 'Are you willing to take the course? It's very important if you are going to have children in your care.'

'I'm willing to.'

'Ginika said you left Nigeria because college professors are always on strike there?' Kimberly asked.

'Yes.'

Laura nodded knowingly. 'Horrible, what's going on in African countries.'

'How are you finding the US so far?' Kimberly asked.

Ifemelu told her about the vertigo she had felt the first time she went to the supermarket; in the cereal aisle, she had wanted to get cornflakes, which she was used to eating back home, but suddenly confronted by a hundred different cereal boxes, in a swirl of colours and images, she had fought dizziness. She told this story because she thought it was funny; it appealed harmlessly to the American ego.

Laura laughed. 'I can see how you'd be dizzy!'

'Yes, we're really about excess in this country,' Kimberly said. 'I'm sure back home you ate a lot of wonderful organic food and vegetables, but you're going to see it's different here.'

'Kim, if she was eating all of this wonderful organic food in Nigeria, why would she come to the US?' Laura asked. As children, Laura must have played the role of the big sister who exposed the stupidity of the little sister, always with kindness and good cheer, and preferably in the company of adult relatives.

'Well, even if they had very little food, I'm just saying it was probably all organic vegetables, none of the Frankenfood we have here,' Kimberly said. Ifemelu sensed, between them, the presence of spiky thorns floating in the air.

'You haven't told her about television,' Laura said. She turned to Ifemelu. 'Kim's kids do supervised TV, only PBS. So if she hired you, you would need to be completely present and monitor what goes on, especially with Morgan.'

'Okay.'

'I don't have a babysitter,' Laura said, her 'I' glowing with righteous emphasis. 'I'm a full-time, hands-on mom. I thought I would return to work when Athena turned two, but I just couldn't bear to let her go. Kim is really hands-on, too, but she's busy sometimes, she does wonderful work with her charity, and so I'm always worried about the babysitters. The last one, Martha, was wonderful, but we did wonder whether the one before her, what was her name again, let Morgan watch inappropriate shows. I don't do any television at all with my daughter. I think there's too much violence. I might let her do a few cartoons when she's a little older.'

'But there's violence in cartoons, too,' Ifemelu said.

Laura looked annoyed. 'It's cartoon. Kids are traumatized by the real thing.'

Ginika glanced at Ifemelu, a knitted-brow look that said: Just leave it alone. In primary school, Ifemelu had watched the firing squad that killed Lawrence Anini, fascinated by the mythologies around his armed robberies, how he wrote warning letters to newspapers, fed the poor with what he stole, turned himself into air when the police came.

Her mother had said, 'Go inside, this is not for children,' but half-heartedly, after Ifemelu had already seen most of the shooting anyway, Anini's body roughly tied to a pole, jerking as the bullets hit him, before slumping against the criss-cross of rope. She thought about this now, how haunting and yet how ordinary it had seemed.

'Let me show you the house, Ifemelu,' Kimberly said. 'Did I say it right?'

They walked from room to room – the daughter's room with pink walls and a frilly bedcover, the son's room with a set of drums, the den with a piano, its polished wooden top crowded with family photographs.

'We took that in India,' Kimberly said. They were standing by an empty rickshaw, wearing T-shirts, Kimberly with her golden hair tied back, her tall and lean husband, her small blond son and older red-haired daughter, all holding water bottles and smiling. They were always smiling in the photos they took, while sailing and hiking and visiting tourist spots, holding each other, all easy limbs and white teeth. They reminded Ifemelu of television commercials, of people whose lives were lived always in flattering light, whose messes were still aesthetically pleasing.

'Some of the people we met had nothing, absolutely nothing, but they were so happy,' Kimberly said. She extracted a photograph from the crowded back of the piano, of her daughter with two Indian women, their skin dark and weathered, their smiles

228

showing missing teeth. 'These women were so wonderful,' she said.

Ifemelu would also come to learn that, for Kimberly, the poor were blameless. Poverty was a gleaming thing; she could not conceive of poor people being vicious or nasty, because their poverty had canonized them, and the greatest saints were the foreign poor.

'Morgan loves that, it's Native American. But Taylor says it's scary!' Kimberly pointed to a small piece of sculpture amid the photographs.

'Oh.' Ifemelu suddenly did not remember which was the boy and which the girl; both names, Morgan and Taylor, sounded to her like surnames.

Kimberly's husband came home just before Ifemelu left.

'Hello! Hello!' he said, gliding into the kitchen, tall and tanned and tactical. Ifemelu could tell, from the longish length, the near-perfect waves that grazed his collar, that he took fastidious care of his hair.

'You must be Ginika's friend from Nigeria,' he said, smiling, brimming with his awareness of his own charm. He looked people in the eye not because he was interested in them but because he knew it made them feel that he was interested in them.

With his appearance, Kimberly became slightly breathless. Her voice changed; she spoke now in the high-pitched voice of the self-consciously female. 'Don, honey, you're early,' she said as they kissed.

Don looked into Ifemelu's eyes and told her how he had nearly visited Nigeria, just after Shagari was elected, when he worked as a consultant to an international development agency, but the trip fell through at the last minute and he had felt bad because he had been hoping to go to the shrine and see Fela perform. He mentioned Fela casually, intimately, as though it was something they had in common, a secret they shared. There was, in his storytelling, an expectation of successful seduction. Ifemelu stared at him, saying little, refusing to be ensnared, and feeling strangely sorry for Kimberly. To be saddled with a sister like Laura and a husband like this.

'Don and I are involved with a really good charity in Malawi, actually Don is much more involved than I am.' Kimberly looked at Don, who made a wry face and said, 'Well, we do our best but we know very well that we're not messiahs.'

'We really should plan a trip to visit. It's an orphanage. We've never been to Africa. I would love to do something with my charity in Africa.'

Kimberly's face had softened, her eyes misted over, and for a moment Ifemelu was sorry to have come from Africa, to be the reason that this beautiful woman, with her bleached teeth and bounteous hair, would have to dig deep to feel such pity, such hopelessness. She smiled brightly, hoping to make Kimberly feel better.

'I'm interviewing one more person and then I'll let you know, but I really think you're a great fit for us,' Kimberly said, leading Ifemelu and Ginika to the front door.

'Thank you,' Ifemelu said. 'I would love to work for you.'

The next day, Ginika called and left a message, her tone low. 'Ifem, I'm so sorry. Kimberly hired somebody else but she said she'll keep you in mind. Something will work out soon, don't worry too much. I'll call later.'

Ifemelu wanted to fling the phone away. *Keep her in mind.* Why would Ginika even repeat such an empty expression, 'keep her in mind'?

It was late autumn, the trees had grown antlers, dried leaves were sometimes trailed into the apartment, and the rent was due. Her room-mates' cheques were on the kitchen table, one on top of the other, all of them pink and bordered by flowers. She thought it unnecessarily decorative, to have flowered cheques in America; it almost took away from the seriousness of a cheque. Beside the cheques was a note, in Jackie's childish writing: *Ifemelu, we're almost a week late for rent.* Writing a cheque would leave her account empty. Her mother had given her a small jar of Mentholatum the day before she left Lagos, saying, 'Put this in your bag, for when you will be cold.' She rummaged now in her suitcase for it, opened and sniffed it, rubbing some under her nose. The scent made her want to weep. The answering machine was blinking but she did not check it because it would be yet another variation of Aunty Uju's message. 'Has anyone called you back? Have you tried the nearby McDonald's and Burger King? They don't always advertise but they might be hiring. I can't send you anything until next month. My own account is empty, honestly to be a resident doctor is slave labour.'

Newspapers were strewn on the floor, job listings circled in ink. She picked one up and flipped through, looking at advertisements she had already seen. ESCORTS caught her eye again. Ginika had said to her, 'Forget that escort thing. They say it isn't prostitution but it is, and the worst thing is that you get maybe a quarter of what you earn because the agency takes the rest. I know this girl who did it in freshman year.' Ifemelu read the advertisement and thought, again, of calling, but she didn't, because she was hoping that the last interview she went for, a waitress position in a little restaurant that didn't pay a salary, only tips, would come through. They had said they would call her by the end of the day if she got the job; she waited until very late but they did not call.

And then Elena's dog ate her bacon. She had heated up a slice of bacon on a paper towel, put it on the table and turned to open the fridge. The dog swallowed the bacon and the paper towel. She stared at the empty space where her bacon had been, and then she stared at the dog, its expression smug, and all the frustrations of her life boiled up in her head. A dog eating her bacon, a dog eating her bacon while she was jobless.

'Your dog just ate my bacon,' she told Elena, who was slicing a banana at the other end of the kitchen, the pieces falling into her cereal bowl.

'You just hate my dog.'

'You should train him better. He shouldn't eat people's food from the kitchen table.'

'You better not kill my dog with voodoo.'

'What?'

'Just kidding!' Elena said. Elena was smirking, her dog's tail wagging, and Ifemelu felt acid in her veins; she moved towards Elena, hand raised and ready to explode on Elena's face, before she caught herself with a jolt, stopped and turned and went upstairs. She sat on her bed and hugged her knees to her chest, shaken by her own reaction, how quickly her fury had risen. Downstairs, Elena was screaming on the phone: 'I swear to God, bitch just tried to hit me!' Ifemelu had wanted to slap her dissolute room-mate not because a slobbering dog had eaten her bacon but because she was at war with the world, and woke up each day feeling bruised, imagining a horde of faceless people who were all against her. It terrified her, to be unable to visualize tomorrow. When her parents called and left a voice message, she saved it, unsure if that would be the last time she would hear their voices. To be here, living abroad, not knowing when she could go home again, was to watch love become anxiety. If she called her mother's friend

Aunty Bunmi and the phone rang to the end, with no answer, she panicked, worried that perhaps her father had died and Aunty Bunmi did not know how to tell her.

Later, Allison knocked on her door. 'Ifemelu? Just wanted to remind you, your rent cheque isn't on the table. We're already really late.'

'I know. I'm writing it.' She lay face up on her bed. She didn't want to be the room-mate who had rent problems. She hated that Ginika had bought her groceries last week. She could hear Jackie's raised voice from downstairs. 'What are we supposed to do? We're not her fucking parents.'

She brought out her chequebook. Before she wrote the cheque, she called Aunty Uju to speak to Dike. Then, refreshed by his innocence, she called the tennis coach in Ardmore.

'When can I start working?' she asked.

'Want to come over right now?'

'Okay,' she said.

She shaved her underarms, dug out the lipstick she had not worn since the day she left Lagos, most of it left smeared on Obinze's neck at the airport. What would happen with the tennis coach? He had said 'massage', but his manner, his tone, had dripped suggestion. Perhaps he was one of those white men she had read about, with strange tastes, who wanted women to drag a feather over their back or urinate on them. She could certainly do that, urinate on a man for a hundred dollars.

The thought amused her, and she smiled a small wry smile. Whatever happened, she would approach it looking her best, she would make it clear to him that there were boundaries she would not cross. She would say, from the beginning, 'If you expect sex, then I can't help you.' Or perhaps she would say it more delicately, more suggestively. 'I'm not comfortable going too far.' She might be imagining too much; he might just want a massage.

When she arrived at his house, his manner was brusque. 'Come on up,' he said, and led the way to his bedroom, bare but for a bed and a large painting of a tomato soup can on the wall. He offered her something to drink, in a perfunctory way that suggested he expected her to say no, and then he took off his shirt and lay on the bed. Was there no preface? She wished he had done things a little more slowly. Her own words had deserted her.

'Come over here,' he said. 'I need to be warm.'

She should leave now. The power balance was tilted in his favour, had been tilted in his favour since she walked into his house. She should leave. She stood up.

'I can't have sex,' she said. Her voice felt squeaky, unsure of itself. 'I can't have sex with you,' she repeated.

'Oh no, I don't expect you to,' he said, too quickly.

She moved slowly towards the door, wondering if it was locked, if he had locked it, and then she wondered if he had a gun.

'Just come here and lie down,' he said. 'Keep me warm. I'll touch you a little bit, nothing you'll be uncomfortable with. I just need some human contact to relax.'

There was, in his expression and tone, a complete assuredness; she felt defeated. How sordid it all was, that she was here with a stranger who already knew she would stay. He knew she would stay because she had come. She was already here, already tainted. She took off her shoes and climbed into his bed. She did not want to be here, did not want his active finger between her legs, did not want his sigh-moans in her ear, and yet she felt her body rousing to a sickening wetness. Afterwards, she lay still, coiled and deadened. He had not forced her. She had come here on her own. She had lain on his bed, and when he placed her hand between his legs, she had curled and moved her fingers. Now, even after she had washed her hands, holding the crisp, slender hundred-dollar bill he had given her, her fingers still felt sticky; they no longer belonged to her.

'Can you do twice a week? I'll cover your train fare,' he said, stretching and dismissive; he wanted her to leave.

She said nothing.

'Shut the door,' he said, and turned his back to her.

She walked to the train, feeling heavy and slow, her mind choked with mud, and, seated by the window, she began to cry. She felt like a small ball, adrift and alone. The world was a big, big place and she was so tiny, so insignificant, rattling around emptily. Back in her apartment, she washed her hands with water so hot that it scalded her fingers, and a small soft welt flowered on her thumb. She took off all her clothes and squashed them into a rumpled ball that she threw at a corner, staring at it for a while. She would never again wear those clothes, never even touch them. She sat naked on her bed and looked at her life, in this tiny room with the mouldy carpet, the hundred-dollar bill on the table, her body rising with loathing. She should never have gone there. She should have walked away. She wanted to shower, to scrub herself, but she could not bear the thought of touching her own body, and so she put on her nightdress, gingerly, to touch as little of herself as possible. She imagined packing her things, somehow buying a ticket and going back to Lagos. She curled on her bed and cried, wishing she could reach into herself and yank out the memory of what had just happened. Her voicemail light was blinking. It was probably Obinze. She could not bear to think of him now. She thought of calling Ginika. Finally, she called Aunty Uju.

'I went to work for a man in the suburbs today. He paid me a hundred dollars.'

'Ehn? That's very good. But you have to keep looking for something permanent. I've just realized I have to buy health insurance for Dike because the one this new hospital in Massachusetts offers is nonsense, it does not cover him. I am still in shock by how much I have to pay.'

'Won't you ask me what I did, Aunty? Won't you ask me what I did before the man paid me a hundred dollars?' Ifemelu asked, a new anger sweeping over her, treading itself through her fingers so that they shook.

'What did you do?' Aunty Uju asked flatly.

Ifemelu hung up. She pressed New on her machine. The first message was from her mother, speaking quickly to reduce the cost of the call: 'Ifem, how are you? We are calling to see how you are. We have not heard from you in a while. Please send a message. We are well. God bless you.'

Then Obinze's voice, his words floating into the air, into her head. 'I love you, Ifem,' he said, at the end, in that voice that seemed suddenly so far away, part of another time and place. She lay rigid on her bed. She could not sleep, she could not distract herself. She began to think about killing the tennis coach. She would hit him on the head over and over with an axe. She would plunge a knife into his muscled chest. He lived alone, he probably had other women coming to his room to spread their legs for his stubby finger with its bitten-back nail. Nobody would know which of them had done it. She would leave the knife sunk in his chest and then search his drawers for his bundle of one-hundred-dollar bills, so that she could pay her rent and her tuition.

That night, it snowed, her first snow, and in the

morning, she watched the world outside her window, the parked cars made lumpy, misshapen, by layered snow. She was bloodless, detached, floating in a world where darkness descended too soon and everyone walked around burdened by coats, and flattened by the absence of light. The days drained into one another, crisp air turning to freezing air, painful to inhale. Obinze called many times but she did not pick up her phone. She deleted his voice messages unheard and his e-mails unread, and she felt herself sinking, sinking quickly, and unable to pull herself up.

She woke up torpid each morning, slowed by sadness, frightened by the endless stretch of day that lay ahead. Everything had thickened. She was swallowed, lost in a viscous haze, shrouded in a soup of nothingness. Between her and what she should feel, there was a gap. She cared about nothing. She wanted to care, but she no longer knew how; it had slipped from her memory, the ability to care. Sometimes she woke up flailing and helpless, and she saw, in front of her and behind her and all around her, an utter hopelessness. She knew there was no point in being here, in being alive, but she had no energy to think concretely of how she could kill herself. She lay in bed and read books and thought of nothing. Sometimes she forgot to eat and other times she waited until midnight, her room-mates in their rooms, before heating up her food, and she left the dirty plates under her bed, until greenish mould fluffed up around the oily remnants of rice and beans. Often, in the middle of eating or reading, she would feel a crushing urge to cry and the tears would come, the sobs hurting her throat. She had turned off the ringer of her phone. She no longer went to class. Her days were stilled by silence and snow.

Allison was banging on her door again. 'Are you there? Phone call! She says it's an emergency, for God's sake! I know you're there, I heard you flush the toilet a minute ago!'

The flat, dulled banging, as though Allison was hitting the door with an open palm rather than a knuckle, unnerved Ifemelu. 'She's not opening,' she heard Allison say, and then, just when she thought Allison had left, the banging resumed. She got up from her bed, where she had been lying and taking turns reading two novels chapter by chapter, and with leaden feet moved to the door. She wanted to walk quickly, normally, but she could not. Her feet had turned into snails. She unlocked the door. With a glare, Allison thrust the phone in her hand.

'Thanks,' she said, limply, and added, in a lower mumble, 'Sorry.' Even talking, making words rise up her throat and out of her mouth, exhausted her.

'Hello?' she said into the phone.

'Ifem! What's going on? What's happening to you?' Ginika asked.

'Nothing,' she said.

'I've been so worried about you. Thank God I found your roommate's number! Obinze has been calling me. He's worried out of his mind,' Ginika said. 'Even Aunty Uju called to ask if I had seen you.'

'I've been busy,' Ifemelu said vaguely.

There was a pause. Ginika's tone softened. 'Ifem, I'm here, you know that, right?'

Ifemelu wanted to hang up and return to her bed. 'Yes.'

'I have good news. Kimberly called me to ask for your phone number. The babysitter she hired just left. She wants to hire you. She wants you to start on Monday. She said she wanted you from the beginning but Laura talked her into hiring the other person. So, Ifem, you have a job! Cash! Under the table! Ifemsco, this is great. She'll pay you two-fifty a week, more than the old babysitter. And pure cash under the table! Kimberly is a really great person. I'm coming tomorrow to take you over there to see her.'

Ifemelu said nothing, struggling to understand. Words took so long to form meaning.

The next day, Ginika knocked and knocked on her door before Ifemelu finally opened, and saw Allison standing on the landing at the back, watching curiously.

'We're late already, get dressed,' Ginika said, firmly, authoritatively, with no room for dissent. Ifemelu pulled on a pair of jeans. She felt Ginika watching her. In the car, Ginika's rock music filled the silence between them. They were on Lancaster Avenue, just about to cross over from West Philadelphia, with boarded-up buildings and hamburger wrappers strewn around, and into the spotless, tree-filled suburbs of the Main Line, when Ginika said, 'I think you're suffering from depression.'

Ifemelu shook her head and turned to the window. Depression was what happened to Americans, with their self-absolving need to turn everything into an illness. She was not suffering from depression; she was merely a little tired and a little slow. 'I don't have depression,' she said. Years later, she would blog about this: 'On the Subject of Non-American Blacks Suffering from Illnesses Whose Names They Refuse to Know.' A Congolese woman wrote a long comment in response: She had moved to Virginia from Kinshasa and, months into her first semester of college, begun to feel dizzy in the morning, her heart pounding as though in flight from her, her stomach fraught with nausea, her fingers tingling. She went to see a doctor. And even though she checked 'yes' to all the symptoms on the card the doctor gave her, she refused to accept the diagnosis of panic attacks because panic attacks happened only to Americans. Nobody in Kinshasa had panic attacks. It was not even that it was called by another name, it was simply not called at all. Did things begin to exist only when they were named?

'Ifem, this is something a lot of people go through, and I know it's not been easy for you adjusting to a new place and still not having a job. We don't talk about things like depression in Nigeria but it's real. You should see somebody at the health centre. There's always therapists.'

Ifemelu kept her face to the window. She felt, again, that crushing desire to cry, and she took a deep breath, hoping it would pass. She wished she had told Ginika about the tennis coach, taken the train to Ginika's apartment on that day, but now it was too late, her self-loathing had hardened inside her. She would never be able to form the sentences to tell her story.

'Ginika,' she said. 'Thank you.' Her voice was hoarse. The tears had come, she could not control them. Ginika stopped at a gas station, gave her a tissue and waited for her sobs to die down before she started the car and drove to Kimberly's house.

CHAPTER 16

Kimberly called it a signing bonus. 'Ginika told me you've had some challenges,' Kimberly said. 'Please don't refuse.'

It would not have occurred to Ifemelu to refuse the cheque; now she could pay some bills, send something home to her parents. Her mother liked the shoes she sent, tasselled and tapering, the kind she could wear to church. 'Thank you,' her mother said, and then sighing heavily over the phone line, she added, 'Obinze came to see me.'

Ifemelu was silent.

'Whatever problem you have, please discuss it with him,' her mother said.

Ifemelu said, 'Okay,' and began to talk about something else. When her mother said there had been no light for two weeks, it seemed suddenly foreign to her, and home itself a distant place. She could no longer remember what it felt like to spend an evening in candlelight. She no longer read the news on Nigeria.com because each headline, even the most unlikely ones, somehow reminded her of Obinze.

At first, she gave herself a month. A month to let her self-loathing seep away, then she would call

Obinze. But a month passed and still she kept Obinze sealed in silence, gagged her own mind so that she would think of him as little as possible. She still deleted his e-mails unread. Many times she started to write to him, she crafted e-mails, and then stopped and discarded them. She would have to tell him what happened, and she could not bear the thought of telling him what happened. She felt shamed; she had failed. Ginika kept asking what was wrong, why she had shut out Obinze, and she said it was nothing, she just wanted some space, and Ginika gaped at her in disbelief. *You just want some space?*

Early in the spring, a letter arrived from Obinze. Deleting his e-mails took a click, and after the first click, the others were easier because she could not imagine reading the second if she had not read the first. But a letter was different. It brought to her the greatest sorrow she had ever felt. She sank to her bed, holding the envelope in her hand; she smelled it, stared at his familiar handwriting. She imagined him at his desk in his boys' quarters, near his small humming refrigerator, writing in that calm manner of his. She wanted to read the letter, but she could not get herself to open it. She put it on her table. She would read it in a week; she needed a week to gather her strength. She would reply, too, she told herself. She would tell him everything. But a week later, the letter still lay there. She placed a book on top of it, then another book, and one day it was swallowed beneath files and books. She would never read it.

★   ★   ★

245

Taylor was easy, a childish child, the playful one who was sometimes so naïve that Ifemelu guiltily thought him stupid. But Morgan, only three years older, already wore the mourning demeanour of a teenager. She read many grades above her level, was steeped in enrichment classes and watched adults with a hooded gaze, as though privy to the darkness that lurked in their lives. At first, Ifemelu disliked Morgan, responding to what she thought was Morgan's own disturbingly full-grown dislike. She was cool, sometimes even cold, to Morgan during her first weeks with them, determined not to indulge this spoilt silken child with a dusting of burgundy freckles on her nose, but she had come, with the passing months, to care for Morgan, an emotion she was careful not to show to Morgan. Instead she was firm and neutral, staring back when Morgan stared. Perhaps it was why Morgan did what Ifemelu asked. She would do it coldly, indifferently, grudgingly, but she would do it. She routinely ignored her mother. And with her father, her brooding watchfulness sharpened into poison. Don would come home and sweep into the den, expecting that everything would stop because of him. And everything did stop, except for whatever Morgan was doing. Kimberly, fluttery and ardent, would ask how his day was, scrambling to please, as though she could not quite believe that he had again come home to her. Taylor would hurl himself into Don's arms. And Morgan would look up from the TV or a book or a game to watch him, as though she saw through him, while Don pretended not to squirm under her piercing eyes. Sometimes Ifemelu wondered. Was it Don? Was he cheating and had Morgan found out? Cheating was the first thing anyone would think of with a man like Don, with that lubricious aura of his. But he might be satisfied with suggestiveness alone; he would flirt outrageously but not do more, because an affair would require some effort and he was the kind of man who took but did not give.

Ifemelu thought often of that afternoon early in her babysitting: Kimberly was out, Taylor was playing and Morgan reading in the den. Suddenly, Morgan put down her book, calmly walked upstairs and ripped off the wallpaper in her room, pushed down her dresser, yanked off her bedcovers, tore down the curtains, and was on her knees pulling and pulling and pulling at the strongly glued carpet when Ifemelu ran in and stopped her. Morgan was like a small, steel robot, writhing to be let free, with a strength that frightened Ifemelu. Perhaps the child would end up being a serial murderer, like those women on television crime documentaries, standing half-naked on dark roads to lure truck drivers and then strangle them. When finally Ifemelu let go, slowly loosening her grip on a quietened Morgan, Morgan went back downstairs to her book.

Later, Kimberly, in tears, asked her, 'Honey, please tell me what's wrong.'

And Morgan said, 'I'm too old for all that pink stuff in my room.'

Now, Kimberly took Morgan twice a week to a therapist in Bala Cynwyd. Both she and Don were more tentative towards her, more cowering under her denouncing stare.

When Morgan won an essay contest at school, Don came home with a present for her. Kimberly anxiously stood at the bottom of the stairs while Don went up to present the gift, wrapped in sparkly paper. He came down moments later.

'She wouldn't even look at it. She just got up and went into the bathroom and stayed there,' he said. 'I left it on the bed.'

'It's okay, honey, she'll come around,' Kimberly said, hugging him, rubbing his back.

Later, Kimberly, sotto voce, told Ifemelu, 'Morgan's really hard on him. He tries so hard and she won't let him in. She just won't.'

'Morgan doesn't let anyone in,' Ifemelu said. Don needed to remember that Morgan, and not he, was the child.

'She listens to you,' Kimberly said, a little sadly.

Ifemelu wanted to say, 'I don't give her too many choices,' because she wished Kimberly would not be so sheer in her yieldingness; perhaps Morgan just needed to feel that her mother could push back. Instead she said, 'That's because I'm not her family. She doesn't love me and so she doesn't feel all these complicated things for me. I'm just a nuisance at best.'

'I don't know what I'm doing wrong,' Kimberly said.

'It's a phase. It will pass, you'll see.' She felt protective of Kimberly, she wanted to shield Kimberly.

'The only person she really cares about is my cousin Curt. She adores him. If we have family gatherings, she'll brood unless Curt is there. I'll see if he can come visit and talk to her.'

Laura had brought a magazine.

'Look at this, Ifemelu,' she said. 'It isn't Nigeria, but it's close. I know celebrities can be flighty but she seems to be doing good work.'

Ifemelu and Kimberly looked at the page together: a thin white woman, smiling at the camera, holding a dark-skinned African baby in her arms, and all around her, little dark-skinned African children were spread out like a rug. Kimberly made a sound, a hmmm, as though she was unsure how to feel.

'She's stunning too,' Laura said.

'Yes, she is,' Ifemelu said. 'And she's just as skinny as the kids, only that her skinniness is by choice and theirs is not by choice.'

A pop of loud laughter burst out from Laura. 'You *are* funny! I love how sassy you are!'

Kimberly did not laugh. Later, alone with Ifemelu, she said, 'I'm sorry Laura said that. I've never liked that word "sassy". It's the kind of word that's used for certain people and not for others.' Ifemelu shrugged and smiled and changed the subject. She did not understand why Laura looked

249

up so much information about Nigeria, asking her about 419 scams, telling her how much money Nigerians in America sent back home every year. It was an aggressive, unaffectionate interest; strange indeed, to pay so much attention to something you did not like. Perhaps it was really about Kimberly, and Laura was in some distorted way aiming at her sister by saying things that would make Kimberly launch into apologies. It seemed too much work for too little gain, though. At first, Ifemelu thought Kimberly's apologizing sweet, even if unnecessary, but she had begun to feel a flash of impatience, because Kimberly's repeated apologies were tinged with self-indulgence, as though she believed that she could, with apologies, smooth all the scalloped surfaces of the world.

A few months into her babysitting, Kimberly asked her, 'Would you consider living in? The basement is really a one-bedroom apartment with a private entrance. It would be rent-free, of course.'
Ifemelu was already looking for a studio apartment, eager to leave her room-mates now that she could afford to, and she did not want to be further enmeshed in the lives of the Turners, yet she considered saying yes, because she heard a plea in Kimberly's voice. In the end, she decided she could not live with them. When she said no, Kimberly offered her the use of their spare car. 'It'll make it much easier for you to get here after your classes. It's an old thing. We were going to

give it away. I hope it doesn't stop you on the road,' she said, as if the Honda, only a few years old, its body unmarked, could possibly stop on the road.

'You really shouldn't trust me to take your car home. What if I don't come back one day?' Ifemelu said.

Kimberly laughed. 'It's not worth very much.'

'You do have an American licence?' Laura asked. 'I mean, you can drive legally in this country?'

'Of course she can, Laura,' Kimberly said. 'Why would she accept the car if she couldn't?'

'I'm just checking,' Laura said, as though Kimberly could not be depended upon to ask the necessary tough questions of non-American citizens. Ifemelu watched them, so alike in their looks, and both unhappy people. But Kimberly's unhappiness was inward, unacknowledged, shielded by her desire for things to be as they should, and also by hope: she believed in other people's happiness because it meant that she, too, might one day have it. Laura's unhappiness was different, spiky, she wished that everyone around her were unhappy because she had convinced herself that she would always be.

'Yes, I have an American licence,' Ifemelu said, and then she began to talk about the safe-driving course she had taken in Brooklyn, before she got her licence, and how the instructor, a thin white man with matted hair the colour of straw, had cheated. In the dark basement room full of

251

foreigners, the entrance of which was an even darker flight of narrow stairs, the instructor had collected all the cash payments before he showed the safe-driving film on the wall projector. From time to time, he made jokes that nobody understood and chuckled to himself. Ifemelu was a little suspicious of the film: how could a car driving so slowly have caused that amount of damage in an accident, leaving the driver's neck broken? Afterwards, he gave out the test questions. Ifemelu found them easy, quickly shading in the answers in pencil. A small South Asian man beside her, perhaps fifty years old, kept glancing over at her, his eyes pleading, while she pretended not to understand that he wanted her help. The instructor collected the papers, brought out a clay-coloured eraser and began to wipe out some of the answers and to shade in others. Everybody passed. Many of them shook his hand, said 'Thank you, thank you' in a wide range of accents before they shuffled out. Now they could apply for American driver's licences. Ifemelu told the story with a false openness, as though it was merely a curiosity for her, and not something she had chosen to goad Laura.

'It was a strange moment for me, because until then I thought nobody in America cheated,' Ifemelu said.

Kimberly said, 'Oh my goodness.'

'This happened in Brooklyn?' Laura asked.

'Yes.'

Laura shrugged, as though to say that it would, of course, happen in Brooklyn but not in the America in which she lived.

At issue was an orange. A round, flame-coloured orange that Ifemelu had brought with her lunch, peeled and quartered and enclosed in a Ziploc bag. She ate it at the kitchen table, while Taylor sat nearby writing in his homework sheet.

'Would you like some, Taylor?' she asked, and offered him a piece.

'Thanks,' he said. He put it into his mouth. His face crumpled. 'It's bad! It's got stuff in it!'

'Those are the seeds,' she said, looking at what he had spat into his hand.

'The seeds?'

'Yes, the orange seeds.'

'Oranges don't have stuff in them.'

'Yes, they do. Throw that in the trash, Taylor. I'm going to put the learning video in for you.'

'Oranges don't have stuff in them,' he repeated.

All his life, he had eaten oranges without seeds, oranges grown to look perfectly orange and to have faultless skin and no seeds, so at eight years old he did not know that there was such a thing as an orange with seeds. He ran into the den to tell Morgan about it. She looked up from her book, raised a slow, bored hand and tucked her red hair behind her ear.

'Of course oranges have seeds. Mom just buys the seedless variety. Ifemelu didn't get the right kind.' She gave Ifemelu one of her accusatory glares.

'The orange is the right one for me, Morgan. I grew up eating oranges with seeds,' Ifemelu said, turning on the video.

'Okay.' Morgan shrugged. With Kimberly she would have said nothing, only glowered.

The doorbell rang. It had to be the carpet cleaner. Kimberly and Don were hosting a cocktail party fund-raiser the next day, for a friend of theirs about whom Don had said, 'It's just an ego trip for him running for Congress, he won't even come close,' and Ifemelu was surprised that he seemed to recognize the ego of others, while blinded in the fog of his own. She went to the door. A burly, red-faced man stood there, carrying cleaning equipment, something slung over his shoulder, something else that looked like a lawn mower propped at his feet.

He stiffened when he saw her. First surprise flitted over his features, then it ossified to hostility.

'You need a carpet cleaned?' he asked, as if he did not care, as if she could change her mind, as if he wanted her to change her mind. She looked at him, a taunt in her eyes, prolonging a moment loaded with assumptions: he thought she was a homeowner, and she was not what he had expected to see in this grand stone house with the white pillars.

'Yes,' she said finally, suddenly tired. 'Mrs Turner told me you were coming.'

It was like a conjuror's trick, the swift disappearance of his hostility. His face sank into a grin. She, too, was the help. The universe was once again arranged as it should be.

'How are you doing? Know where she wants me to start?' he asked.

'Upstairs,' she said, letting him in, wondering how all that cheeriness could have existed earlier in his body. She would never forget him, bits of dried skin stuck to his chapped, peeling lips, and she would begin the blog post 'Sometimes in America, Race Is Class' with the story of his dramatic change, and end with: *It didn't matter to him how much money I had. As far as he was concerned I did not fit as the owner of that stately house because of the way I looked. In America's public discourse, 'Blacks' as a whole are often lumped with 'Poor Whites.' Not Poor Blacks and Poor Whites. But Blacks and Poor Whites. A curious thing indeed.*

Taylor was excited. 'Can I help? Can I help?' he asked the carpet cleaner.

'No thanks, buddy,' the man said. 'I got it.'

'I hope he doesn't start in my room,' Morgan said.

'Why?' Ifemelu asked.

'I just don't want him to.'

Ifemelu wanted to tell Kimberly about the carpet cleaner, but Kimberly might become flustered and apologize for what was not her fault as she often, too often, apologized for Laura.

It was discomfiting to observe how Kimberly lurched, keen to do the right thing and not knowing what the right thing was. If she told Kimberly about the carpet cleaner, there was no telling how she would respond – laugh, apologize, snatch up the phone to call the company and complain.

And so, instead, she told Kimberly about Taylor and the orange.

'He really thought seeds meant it was bad? How funny.'

'Morgan of course promptly set him right,' Ifemelu said.

'Oh, she would.'

'When I was a little girl my mother used to tell me that an orange would grow on my head if I swallowed a seed. I had many anxious mornings of going to look in the mirror. At least Taylor won't have that childhood trauma.'

Kimberly laughed.

'Hello!' It was Laura, coming in through the back door with Athena, a tiny wisp of a child with hair so thin that her pale scalp gaped through. A waif. Perhaps Laura's blended vegetables and strict diet rules had left the child malnourished.

Laura put a vase on the table. 'This will look terrific tomorrow.'

'It's lovely,' Kimberly said, bending to kiss Athena's head. 'That's the caterer's menu. Don thinks the hors d'oeuvre selection is too simple. I'm not sure.'

'He wants you to add more?' Laura said, scanning the menu.

'He just thought it was a little simple, he was very sweet about it.'

In the den, Athena began to cry. Laura went to her and, soon enough, a string of negotiations followed: 'Do you want this one, sweetheart? The yellow or the blue or the red? Which do you want?'

Just give her one, Ifemelu thought. To overwhelm a child of four with choices, to lay on her the burden of making a decision, was to deprive her of the bliss of childhood. Adulthood, after all, already loomed, where she would have to make grimmer and grimmer decisions.

'She's been grumpy today,' Laura said, coming back into the kitchen, Athena's crying quelled. 'I took her to her follow-up from the ear infection and she's been an absolute bear all day. Oh, and I met the most charming Nigerian man today. We get there and it turns out a new doctor has just joined the practice and he's Nigerian and he came by and said hello to us. He reminded me of you, Ifemelu. I read on the Internet that Nigerians are the most educated immigrant group in this country. Of course, it says nothing about the millions who live on less than a dollar a day back in your country, but when I met the doctor I thought of that article and of you and other privileged Africans who are here in this country.' Laura paused and Ifemelu, as she often did, felt that Laura had more to say but was holding back. It felt strange, to be called privileged. Privileged was people like Kayode DaSilva, whose passport sagged with the weight of visa stamps, who went to London for summer and to Ikoyi Club to swim, who could casually get up and say 'We're going to Frenchies for ice cream.'

'I've never been called privileged in my life!' Ifemelu said. 'It feels good.'

'I think I'll switch and have him be Athena's doctor. He was wonderful, so well-groomed and well-spoken. I haven't been very satisfied with Dr Bingham since Dr Hoffman left, anyway.' Laura picked up the menu again. 'In graduate school I knew a woman from Africa who was just like this doctor, I think she was from Uganda. She was wonderful, and she didn't get along with the African American woman in our class at all. She didn't have all those issues.'

'Maybe when the African American's father was not allowed to vote because he was black, the Ugandan's father was running for parliament or studying at Oxford,' Ifemelu said.

Laura stared at her, made a mocking confused face. 'Wait, did I miss something?'

'I just think it's a simplistic comparison to make. You need to understand a bit more history,' Ifemelu said.

Laura's lips sagged. She staggered, collected herself.

'Well, I'll get my daughter and then go find some history books from the library, if I can figure out what they look like!' Laura said, and marched out.

Ifemelu could almost hear Kimberly's heart beating wildly.

'I'm sorry,' Ifemelu said.

Kimberly shook her head and murmured, 'I know Laura can be challenging,' her eyes on the salad she was mixing.

Ifemelu hurried upstairs to Laura.

'I'm sorry. I was rude just now and I apologize.' But she was sorry only because of Kimberly, the way she had begun to mix the salad as though to reduce it to a pulp.

'It's fine,' Laura sniffed, smoothing her daughter's hair, and Ifemelu knew that for a long time afterwards, she would not unwrap from herself the pashmina of the wounded.

Apart from a stiff 'Hi', Laura did not speak to her at the party the next day. The house filled with the gentle murmur of voices, guests raising wineglasses to their lips. They were similar, all of them, their clothes nice and safe, their sense of humour nice and safe, and, like other upper-middle-class Americans, they used the word 'wonderful' too often. 'You'll come and help out with the party, won't you, please?' Kimberly had asked Ifemelu, as she always did of their gatherings. Ifemelu was not sure how she helped out, since the events were catered and the children went to bed early, but she sensed, beneath the lightness of Kimberly's invitation, something close to a need. In some small way that she did not entirely understand, her presence seemed to steady Kimberly. If Kimberly wanted her there, then she would be there.

'This is Ifemelu, our babysitter and my friend,' Kimberly introduced her to guests.

'You're so beautiful,' a man told her, smiling, his teeth jarringly white. 'African women are gorgeous, especially Ethiopians.'

A couple spoke about their safari in Tanzania. 'We had a wonderful tour guide and we're now paying for his first daughter's education.' Two women spoke about their donations to a wonderful charity in Malawi that built wells, a wonderful orphanage in Botswana, a wonderful microfinance cooperative in Kenya. Ifemelu gazed at them. There was a certain luxury to charity that she could not identify with and did not have. To take 'charity' for granted, to revel in this charity towards people whom one did not know – perhaps it came from having had yesterday and having today and expecting to have tomorrow. She envied them this.

A petite woman in a severe pink jacket said, 'I'm chair of the board of a charity in Ghana. We work with rural women. We're always interested in African staff, we don't want to be the NGO that won't use local labour. So if you're ever looking for a job after graduation and want to go back and work in Africa, give me a call.'

'Thank you.' Ifemelu wanted, suddenly and desperately, to be from the country of people who gave and not those who received, to be one of those who had and could therefore bask in the grace of having given, to be among those who could afford copious pity and empathy. She went out to the deck in search of fresh air. Over the hedge, she could see the Jamaican nanny of the neighbours' children, walking down the driveway, the one who always evaded Ifemelu's eyes, and did not like to say hello. Then she noticed a movement on the other end of the deck. It was Don. There was something furtive about him and she felt rather than saw that he had just ended a cell phone conversation.

'Great party,' he told her. 'It's just an excuse for Kim and me to have friends over. Roger is totally out of his league and I've told him that, no chance in hell . . .'

Don kept talking, his voice too larded in bonhomie, her dislike clawing at her throat. She and Don did not talk like this. It was too much information, too much talk. She wanted to tell him that she had heard nothing of his phone conversation, if there had been anything at all to hear, that she knew nothing and that she did not want to know.

'They must be wondering where you are,' she said.

'Yes, we must go back,' he said, as though they had come out together. Back inside, Ifemelu saw Kimberly standing in the middle of the den, slightly apart from her circle of friends; she had been looking around for Don and when she saw him, her eyes rested on him, and her face became soft, and shorn of worry.

Ifemelu left the party early; she wanted to speak to Dike before his bedtime. Aunty Uju picked up the phone.

'Has Dike slept?' Ifemelu asked.

'He's brushing his teeth,' she said, and then in a lower voice, she added, 'He was asking me about his name again.'

'What did you tell him?'

'The same thing. You know, he never asked me this kind of thing before we moved here.'

'Maybe it's having Bartholomew in the picture, and the new environment. He's used to having you to himself.'

'This time he didn't ask why he has my name, he asked if he has my name because his father did not love him.'

'Aunty, maybe it's time to tell him you were not a second wife,' Ifemelu said.

'I was practically a second wife.' Aunty Uju sounded defiant, even petulant, clenching her fist tightly around her own story. She had told Dike that his father was in the military government, that she was his second wife, and that they had given him her surname to protect him, because some people in the government, not his father, had done some bad things.

'Okay, here's Dike,' Aunty Uju said, in a normal tone.

'Hey, Coz! You should have seen my soccer game today!' Dike said.

'How come you score all the great goals when I'm not there? Are these goals in your dreams?' Ifemelu asked.

He laughed. He still laughed easily, his sense of

humour whole, but since the move to Massachusetts, he was no longer transparent. Something had filmed itself around him, making him difficult to read, his head perennially bent towards his Game Boy, looking up once in a while to view his mother, and the world, with a weariness too heavy for a child. His grades were falling. Aunty Uju threatened him more often. The last time Ifemelu visited, Aunty Uju told him, 'I will send you back to Nigeria if you do that again!' speaking Igbo as she did to him only when she was angry, and Ifemelu worried that it would become for him the language of strife.

Aunty Uju, too, had changed. At first, she had sounded curious, expectant about her new life. 'This place is so *white*,' she said. 'Do you know I went to the drugstore to quickly buy lipstick, because the mall is thirty minutes away, and all the shades were too pale! But they can't carry what they can't sell! At least this place is quiet and restful, and I feel safe drinking the tap water, something I will never even try in Brooklyn.'

Slowly, over the months, her tone soured.

'Dike's teacher said he is aggressive,' she told Ifemelu one day, after she had been called to come in and see the principal. 'Aggressive, of all things. She wants him to go to what they call special ed, where they will put him in a class alone and bring somebody who is trained to deal with mental children to teach him. I told the woman that it is not my son, it is her father who is aggressive. Look at him, just because he looks different, when he does what other little boys do, it becomes aggression. Then the principal told me, "Dike is just like one of us, we don't see him as different at all." What kind of pretending is that? I told him to look at my son. There are only two of them in the whole school. The other child is a half-caste, and so fair that if you look from afar you will not even know that he is black. My son sticks out, so how can you tell me that you don't see any difference? I refused completely that they should put him in a special class. He is brighter than all of them combined. They want to start now to mark him. Kemi warned me about this. She said they tried to do it to her son in Indiana.'

Later, Aunty Uju's complaints turned to her residency programme, how slow and small it was, medical records still handwritten and kept in dusty files, and then when she finished her residency, she complained about the patients who thought they were doing her a favour by seeing her. She hardly mentioned Bartholomew; it was as though she lived only with Dike in the Massachusetts house by the lake.

CHAPTER 17

Ifemelu decided to stop faking an American accent on a sunlit day in July, the same day she met Blaine. It was convincing, the accent. She had perfected, from careful watching of friends and newscasters, the blurring of the *t*, the creamy roll of the *r*, the sentences starting with 'So', and the sliding response of 'Oh really', but the accent creaked with consciousness, it was an act of will. It took an effort, the twisting of lip, the curling of tongue. If she were in a panic, or terrified, or jerked awake during a fire, she would not remember how to produce those American sounds. And so she resolved to stop, on that summer day, the weekend of Dike's birthday. Her decision was prompted by a telemarketer's call. She was in her apartment on Spring Garden Street, the first that was truly hers in America, hers alone, a studio with a leaky faucet and a noisy heater. In the weeks since she moved in, she had felt light-footed, cloaked in well-being, because she opened the fridge knowing that everything in it was hers and she cleaned the bathtub knowing she would not find tufts of disconcertingly foreign room-mate hair in the drain. 'Officially two

265

blocks away from the real hood' was how the apartment super, Jamal, had put it, when he told her to expect to hear gunshots from time to time, but although she had opened her window every evening, straining and listening, all she heard were the sounds of late summer, music from passing cars, the high-spirited laughter of playing children, the shouting of their mothers.

On that July morning, her weekend bag already packed for Massachusetts, she was making scrambled eggs when the phone rang. The caller ID showed 'unknown' and she thought it might be a call from her parents in Nigeria. But it was a telemarketer, a young, male American who was offering better long-distance and international phone rates. She always hung up on telemarketers, but there was something about his voice that made her turn down the stove and hold on to the receiver, something poignantly young, untried, untested, the slightest of tremors, an aggressive customer-service friendliness that was not aggressive at all; it was as though he was saying what he had been trained to say but was mortally worried about offending her.

He asked how she was, how the weather was in her city, and told her it was pretty hot in Phoenix. Perhaps it was his first day on the job, his telephone piece poking uncomfortably in his ear while he half hoped that the people he was calling would not be home to pick up. Because she felt strangely sorry for him, she asked whether he had rates better than fifty-seven cents a minute to Nigeria.

'Hold on while I look up Nigeria,' he said, and she went back to stirring her eggs.

He came back and said his rates were the same, but wasn't there another country that she called? Mexico? Canada?

'Well, I call London sometimes,' she said. Ginika was there for the summer.

'Okay, hold on while I look up France,' he said.

She burst out laughing.

'Something funny over there?' he asked.

She laughed harder. She had opened her mouth to tell him, bluntly, that what was funny was that he was selling international telephone rates and did not know where London was, but something held her back, an image of him, perhaps eighteen or nineteen, overweight, pink-faced, awkward around girls, keen on video games, and with no knowledge of the roiling contradictions that were the world. So she said, 'There's a hilarious old comedy on TV.'

'Oh, really?' he said, and he laughed too. It broke her heart, his greenness, and when he came back on to tell her the France rates, she thanked him and said they were better than the rates she already had and that she would think about switching carriers.

'When is a good time to call you back? If that's okay . . .' he said. She wondered whether they were paid on commission. Would his pay cheque be bigger if she did switch her phone company? Because she would, as long as it cost her nothing.

'Evenings,' she said.

'May I ask who I'm talking to?'

'My name is Ifemelu.'

He repeated her name with exaggerated care. 'Is it a French name?'

'No. Nigerian.'

'That where your family came from?'

'Yes.' She scooped the eggs onto a plate. 'I grew up there.'

'Oh, really? How long have you been in the US?'

'Three years.'

'Wow. Cool. You sound totally American.'

'Thank you.'

Only after she hung up did she begin to feel the stain of a burgeoning shame spreading all over her, for thanking him, for crafting his words 'You sound American' into a garland that she hung around her own neck. Why was it a compliment, an accomplishment, to sound American? She had won; Cristina Tomas, pallid-faced Cristina Tomas under whose gaze she had shrunk like a small, defeated animal, would speak to her normally now. She had won, indeed, but her triumph was full of air. Her fleeting victory had left in its wake a vast, echoing space, because she had taken on, for too long, a pitch of voice and a way of being that was not hers. And so she finished eating her eggs and resolved to stop faking the American accent. She first spoke without the American accent that afternoon at Thirtieth Street Station, leaning towards the woman behind the Amtrak counter.

'Could I have a round-trip to Haverhill, please? Returning Sunday afternoon. I have a Student Advantage card,' she said, and felt a rush of pleasure from giving the *t* its full due in 'advantage', from not rolling her *r* in 'Haverhill'. This was truly her; this was the voice with which she would speak if she were woken up from a deep sleep during an earthquake. Still, she resolved that if the Amtrak woman responded to her accent by speaking too slowly as though to an idiot, then she would put on her Mr Agbo Voice, the mannered, overcareful pronunciations she had learned during debate meetings in secondary school when the bearded Mr Agbo, tugging at his frayed tie, played BBC recordings on his cassette player and then made all the students pronounce words over and over until he beamed and cried 'Correct!' She would also affect, with the Mr Agbo Voice, a slight raising of her eyebrows in what she imagined was a haughty foreigner pose. But there was no need to do any of these because the Amtrak woman spoke normally. 'Can I see an ID, miss?'

And so she did not use her Mr Agbo Voice until she met Blaine.

The train was crowded. The seat next to Blaine was the only empty one in that car, as far as she could see, and the newspaper and bottle of juice placed on it seemed to be his. She stopped, gesturing towards the seat, but he kept his gaze levelly ahead. Behind her, a woman was pulling along a heavy suitcase and the conductor was announcing that all personal belongings had to be moved from free seats and Blaine saw her standing there – how could he possibly not see her? – and still he did nothing. So her Mr Agbo Voice emerged. 'Excuse me. Are these yours? Could you possibly move them?'

She placed her bag on the overhead rack and settled onto the seat, stiffly, holding her magazine, her body aligned towards the aisle and away from him. The train had begun to move when he said, 'I'm really sorry I didn't see you standing there.'

His apologizing surprised her, his expression so earnest and sincere that it seemed as though he had done something more offensive. 'It's okay,' she said, and smiled.

'How are you?' he asked.

She had learned to say 'Good-how-are-you?' in that sing-song American way, but now she said, 'I'm well, thank you.'

'My name's Blaine,' he said, and extended his hand.

He looked tall. A man with skin the colour of gingerbread and the kind of lean, proportioned body that was perfect for a uniform, any uniform. She knew right away that he was African American, not Caribbean, not African, not a child of immigrants from either place. She had not always been able to tell. Once she had asked a taxi driver, 'So where are you from?' in a knowing, familiar tone, certain that he was from Ghana, and he said 'Detroit' with a shrug. But the longer she spent in America, the better she had become at distinguishing, sometimes from looks and gait, but mostly from bearing and demeanour, that fine-grained mark that culture stamps on people. She felt confident about Blaine: he was a descendant of the black men and women who had been in America for hundreds of years.

'I'm Ifemelu, it's nice to meet you,' she said.

'Are you Nigerian?'

'I am, yes.'

'Bourgie Nigerian,' he said, and smiled. There was a surprising and immediate intimacy to his teasing her, calling her privileged.

'Just as bourgie as you,' she said. They were on firm flirting territory now. She looked him over quietly, his light-coloured khakis and navy shirt, the kind of outfit that was selected with the right amount of thought; a man who looked at himself in the mirror but did not look for too long. He knew about Nigerians, he told her, he was an assistant professor at Yale, and although his interest was mostly in southern Africa, how could he not know about Nigerians when they were everywhere?

'What is it, one in every five Africans is Nigerian?' he asked, still smiling. There was something both ironic and gentle about him. It was as if he believed that they shared a series of intrinsic jokes that did not need to be verbalized.

'Yes, we Nigerians get around. We have to. There are too many of us and not enough space,' she said, and it struck her how close to each other they were, separated only by the single armrest. He spoke the kind of American English that she had just given up, the kind that made race pollsters on the telephone assume that you were white and educated.

'So is southern Africa your discipline?' she asked.

'No. Comparative politics. You can't do just Africa in political science graduate programmes in this country. You can compare Africa to Poland or Israel, but focusing on Africa itself? They don't let you do that.'

His use of 'they' suggested an 'us', which would be the both of them. His nails were clean. He was not wearing a wedding band. She began to imagine a relationship, both of them waking up in the winter, cuddling in the stark whiteness of the morning light, drinking English Breakfast tea; she hoped he was one of those Americans who liked tea. His juice, the bottle stuffed in the pouch in front of him, was organic pomegranate. A plain brown bottle with a plain brown label, both stylish and salutary. No chemicals in the juice and no ink wasted on decorative labels. Where had he bought it? It was not the sort of thing that was sold at the train station. Perhaps he was vegan and distrusted large corporations and shopped only at farmers' markets and brought his own organic juice from home. She had little patience for Ginika's friends, most of whom were like that, their righteousness made her feel both irritated and lacking, but she was prepared to forgive Blaine's pieties. He was holding a hardcover library book whose title she could not see and had stuffed his *New York Times* next to the juice bottle. When he glanced at her magazine, she wished she had brought out the Esiaba Irobi book of poems that she planned to read on the train back. He would think that she read only shallow fashion magazines. She felt the sudden and unreasonable urge to tell him how much she loved the poetry of Yusef Komunyakaa, to redeem herself. First, she shielded, with her palm, the bright red lipstick on the cover model's face. Then, she reached forward and pushed the magazine into the pouch in front of her and said, with a slight sniff, that it was absurd how women's magazines forced images of small-boned, small-breasted white women on the rest of the multi-boned, multi-ethnic world of women to emulate.

'But I keep reading them,' she said. 'It's like smoking, it's bad for you but you do it anyway.'

'Multi-boned and multi-ethnic,' he said, amused, his eyes warm with unabashed interest; it charmed her that he was not the kind of man who, when he was interested in a woman, cultivated a certain cool, pretended indifference.

'Are you a grad student?' he asked.

'I'm a junior at Wellson.'

Did she imagine it or did his face fall, in disappointment, in surprise? 'Really? You seem more mature.'

'I am. I'd done some college in Nigeria before

273

I left to come here.' She shifted on her seat, determined to get back on firm flirting ground. 'You, on the other hand, look too young to be a professor. Your students must be confused about who the professor is.'

'I think they're probably confused about a lot of stuff. This is my second year of teaching.' He paused. 'Are you thinking of graduate school?'

'Yes, but I'm worried I will leave grad school and no longer be able to speak English. I know this woman in grad school, a friend of a friend, and just listening to her talk is scary. The semiotic dialectics of intertextual modernity. Which makes no sense at all. Sometimes I feel that they live in a parallel universe of academia speaking academese instead of English and they don't really know what's happening in the real world.'

'That's a pretty strong opinion.'

'I don't know how to have any other kind.'

He laughed, and it pleased her to have made him laugh.

'But I hear you,' he said. 'My research interests include social movements, the political economy of dictatorships, American voting rights and representation, race and ethnicity in politics, and campaign finance. That's my classic spiel. Much of which is bullshit anyway. I teach my classes and I wonder if any of it matters to the kids.'

'Oh, I'm sure it does. I'd love to take one of your classes.' She had spoken too eagerly. It had not come out as she wanted. She had cast herself, without meaning to, in the role of a potential student. He seemed keen to change the direction of the conversation; perhaps he did not want to be her teacher either. He told her he was going back to New Haven after visiting friends in Washington, DC. 'So where are you headed?' he asked.

'Warrington. A bit of a drive from Boston. My aunt lives there.'

'So do you ever come up to Connecticut?'

'Not much. I've never been to New Haven. But I've gone to the malls in Stamford and Clinton.'

'Oh, yes, malls.' His lips turned down slightly at the sides.

'You don't like malls?'

'Apart from being soulless and bland? They're perfectly fine.'

She had never understood the quarrel with malls, with the notion of finding exactly the same shops in all of them; she found malls quite comforting in their sameness. And with his carefully chosen clothes, surely he had to shop somewhere?

'So do you grow your own cotton and make your own clothes?' she asked.

He laughed, and she laughed too. She imagined both of them, hand in hand, going to the mall in Stamford, she teasing him, reminding him of this conversation on the day they met, and raising her face to kiss him. It was not in her nature to talk to strangers on public transportation – she would do it more often when she started her blog a few years later – but she talked and talked, perhaps because of the newness of her own voice. The more they talked, the more she told herself that this was no coincidence; there was a significance to her meeting this man on the day that she returned her voice to herself. She told him, with the suppressed laughter of a person impatient for the punchline of her own joke, about the telemarketer who thought that London was in France. He did not laugh, but instead shook his head.

'They don't train these telemarketer folks well at all. I bet he's a temp with no health insurance and no benefits.'

'Yes,' she said, chastened. 'I felt kind of sorry for him.'

'So my department moved buildings a few weeks ago. Yale hired professional movers and told them to make sure to put everything from each person's old office in the exact same spot in the new office. And they did. All my books were shelved in the right position. But you know what I noticed later? Many of the books had their spines upside down.' He was looking at her, as though to experience a shared revelation, and for a blank moment, she was not sure what the story was about.

'Oh. The movers couldn't read,' she said finally.

He nodded. 'There was just something about it that totally killed me . . .' He let his voice trail away.

She began to imagine what he would be like in bed: he would be a kind, attentive lover for whom emotional fulfilment was just as important as ejaculation, he would not judge her slack flesh, he would wake up even-tempered every morning. She hastily looked away, afraid that he might have read her mind, so startlingly clear were the images there.

'Would you like a beer?' he asked.

'A beer?'

'Yes. The café car serves beers. You want one? I'm going to get one.'

'Yes. Thank you.'

She stood up, self-consciously, to let him pass and hoped she would smell something on him, but she didn't. He did not wear cologne. Perhaps he had boycotted cologne because the makers of cologne did not treat their employees well. She watched him walk up the aisle, knowing that he knew that she was watching him. The beer offer had pleased her. She had worried that all he drank was organic pomegranate juice, but now the thought of organic pomegranate juice was pleasant if he drank beer as well. When he came back with the beers and plastic cups, he poured hers with a flourish that, to her, was thick with romance. She had never liked beer. Growing up, it had been male alcohol, gruff and inelegant. Now, sitting next to Blaine, laughing as he told her about the first time he got truly drunk in his freshman year, she realized that she could like beer. The grainy fullness of beer.

He talked about his undergraduate years: the stupidity of eating a semen sandwich during his fraternity initiation, constantly being called Michael Jordan in China the summer of his junior year when he travelled through Asia, his mother's death from cancer the week after he graduated.

'A semen sandwich?'

'They masturbated into a piece of pita bread and you had to take a bite, but you didn't have to swallow.'

'Oh God.'

'Well, hopefully you do stupid things when you're young so you don't do them when you're older,' he said.

When the conductor announced that the next stop was New Haven, Ifemelu felt a stab of loss. She tore out a page from her magazine and wrote her phone number. 'Do you have a card?' she asked.

He touched his pockets. 'I don't have any with me.'

There was silence while he gathered his things. Then the screeching of the train brakes. She sensed, and hoped she was wrong, that he did not want to give her his number.

'Well, will you write your number then, if you remember it?' she asked. A lame joke. The beer had pushed those words out of her mouth.

He wrote his number on her magazine. 'You take care,' he said. He touched her shoulder lightly as he left and there was something in his eyes, something both tender and sad, that made her tell herself that she had been wrong to sense reluctance from him. He already missed her. She moved to his seat, revelling in the warmth his body had left in its wake, and watched through the window as he walked along the platform.

When she arrived at Aunty Uju's house, the first thing she wanted to do was call him. But she thought it was best to wait a few hours. After an hour, she said fuck it and called. He did not answer. She left a message. She called back later. No answer. She called and called and called. No answer. She called at midnight. She did not leave messages. The whole weekend she called and called and he never picked up the phone.

Warrington was a somnolent town, a town contented with itself; winding roads cut through thick woods – even the main road, which the residents did not want widened for fear that it would bring in foreigners from the city, was winding and narrow – sleepy homes were shielded by trees, and on weekends the blue lake was stippled with boats. From the dining room window of Aunty Uju's house, the lake shimmered, a blueness so tranquil that it held the gaze. Ifemelu stood by the window while Aunty Uju sat at the table drinking orange juice and airing her grievances like jewels. It had become a routine of Ifemelu's visits: Aunty Uju collected all her dissatisfactions in a silk purse, nursing them, polishing them, and then on the Saturday of Ifemelu's visit, while Bartholomew was out and Dike upstairs, she would spill them out on the table, and turn each one this way and that, to catch the light.

Sometimes she told the same story twice. How she had gone to the public library the other day, had forgotten to bring out the unreturned book from her handbag, and the guard told her, 'You people never do anything right.' How she walked into an examining room and a patient asked 'Is the doctor coming?' and when she said she was the doctor the patient's face changed to fired clay.

'Do you know, that afternoon she called to transfer her file to another doctor's office! Can you imagine?'

'What does Bartholomew think about all this?' Ifemelu gestured to take in the room, the view of the lake, the town.

'That one is too busy chasing business. He leaves early and comes home late every day. Sometimes Dike doesn't even set eyes on him for a whole week.'

'I'm surprised you're still here, Aunty,' Ifemelu said quietly, and by 'here' they both knew that she did not merely mean Warrington.

'I want another child. We've been trying.' Aunty Uju came and stood beside her, by the window.

There was the clatter of footsteps on the wooden stairs, and Dike came into the kitchen, in a faded T-shirt and shorts, holding his Game Boy. Each time Ifemelu saw him, he seemed to her to have grown taller and to have become more reserved.

'Are you wearing that shirt to camp?' Aunty Uju asked him.

'Yes, Mom,' he said, his eyes on the flickering screen in his hand.

Aunty Uju got up to check the oven. She had agreed this morning, his first of summer camp, to make him chicken nuggets for breakfast.

'Coz, we're still playing soccer later, right?' Dike asked.

'Yes,' Ifemelu said. She took a chicken nugget from his plate and put it in her mouth. 'Chicken nuggets for breakfast is strange enough, but is this chicken or just plastic?'

'Spicy plastic,' he said.

She walked him to the bus and watched him get on, the pale faces of the other children at the window, the bus driver waving to her too cheerfully. She was standing there waiting when the bus brought him back that afternoon. There was a guardedness on his face, something close to sadness.

'What's wrong?' she asked, her arm around his shoulder.

'Nothing,' he said. 'Can we play soccer now?'

'After you tell me what happened.'

'Nothing happened.'

'I think you need some sugar. You'll probably have too much tomorrow, with your birthday cake. But let's get a cookie.'

'Do you bribe the kids you babysit with sugar? Man, they're lucky.'

She laughed. She brought out the packet of Oreos from the fridge.

'Do you play soccer with the kids you babysit?' he asked.

'No,' she said, even though she played once in a while with Taylor, kicking the ball back and forth in their oversized, wooded backyard. Sometimes, when Dike asked her about the children she cared for, she indulged his childish interest, telling him about their toys and their lives, but she was careful not to make them seem important to her.

'So how was camp?'

'Good.' A pause. 'My group leader, Haley? She gave sunscreen to everyone but she wouldn't give me any. She said I didn't need it.'

She looked at his face, which was almost expressionless, eerily so. She did not know what to say.

'She thought that because you're dark you don't need sunscreen. But you do. Many people don't know that dark people also need sunscreen. I'll get you some, don't worry.' She was speaking too fast, not sure that she was saying the right thing, or what the right thing to say was, and worried because this had upset him enough that she had seen it on his face.

'It's okay,' he said. 'It was kind of funny. My friend Danny was laughing about it.'

'Why did your friend think it was funny?'

'Because it was!'

'You wanted her to give you the sunscreen, too, right?'

'I guess so,' he said with a shrug. 'I just want to be regular.'

She hugged him. Later, she went to the store and bought him a big bottle of sunscreen, and the next time she visited, she saw it lying on his dresser, forgotten and unused.

Understanding America for the Non-American Black: American Tribalism

In America, tribalism is alive and well. There are four kinds – class, ideology, region, and race. First, class. Pretty easy. Rich folk and poor folk.

Second, ideology. Liberals and conservatives. They don't merely disagree on political issues, each side believes the other is evil. Intermarriage is discouraged and on the rare occasion that it happens, is considered remarkable. Third, region. The North and the South. The two sides fought a civil war and tough stains from that war remain. The North looks down on the South while the South resents the North. Finally, race. There's a ladder of racial hierarchy in America. White is always on top, specifically White Anglo-Saxon Protestant, otherwise known as WASP, and American Black is always on the bottom, and what's in the middle depends on time and place. (Or as that marvelous rhyme goes: if you're white, you're all right; if you're brown, stick around; if you're black, get back!) Americans assume that everyone will get their tribalism. But it takes a while to figure it all out. So in undergrad, we had a visiting speaker and a classmate whispers to another, 'Oh my God, he looks so Jewish,' with a shudder, an actual shudder. Like Jewish was a bad thing. I didn't get it. As far as I could see, the man was white, not much different from the classmate herself. Jewish to me was something vague, something biblical. But I learned quickly. You see, in America's ladder of races, Jewish is white but also some rungs below white. A bit confusing, because I knew this straw-haired, freckled girl who said she was Jewish. How can Americans tell who is Jewish? How did the classmate know the guy was Jewish? I read somewhere how American colleges used to ask applicants for their mother's surnames, to make sure they weren't Jewish because they wouldn't admit Jewish people. So maybe that's how to tell? From people's names? The longer you are here, the more you start to get it.

CHAPTER 18

Mariama's new customer was wearing jeans shorts, the denim glued to her backside, and sneakers the same bright pink shade as her top. Large hoop earrings grazed her face. She stood in front of the mirror, describing the kind of cornrows she wanted.

'Like a zigzag with a parting at the side right here, but you don't add the hair at the beginning, you add it when you get to the ponytail,' she said, speaking slowly, over-enunciating. 'You understand me?' she added, already convinced, it seemed, that Mariama did not.

'I understand,' Mariama said quietly. 'You want to see a photo? I have that style in my album.'

The album was flipped through and, finally, the customer was satisfied and seated, frayed plastic hoisted around her neck, her chair height adjusted, and Mariama all the time smiling a smile full of things restrained.

'This other braider I went to the last time,' the customer said. 'She was African, too, and she wanted to burn my damned hair! She brought out this lighter and I'm going, Shontay White, don't let that woman bring that thing close to your hair. So I ask her, What's that for? She says, I want to clean your braids, and I go, What? Then she tries to show me, she tries to run the lighter over one braid and I went all crazy on her.'

Mariama shook her head. 'Oh, that's bad. Burning is not good. We don't do that.'

A customer came in, her hair covered in a bright yellow headwrap.

'Hi,' she said. 'I'd like to get braids.'

'What kind of braids you want?' Mariama asked.

'Just regular box braids, medium size.'

'You want it long?' Mariama asked.

'Not too long, maybe shoulder length?'

'Okay. Please sit down. She will do it for you,' Mariama said, gesturing to Halima, who was sitting at the back, her eyes on the television. Halima stood up and stretched, for a little too long, as though to register her reluctance.

The woman sat down and gestured to the pile of DVDs. 'You sell Nigerian films?' she asked Mariama.

'I used to but my supplier went out of business. You want to buy?'

'No. You just seem to have a lot of them.'

'Some of them are real nice,' Mariama said.

'I can't watch that stuff. I guess I'm biased. In my country, South Africa, Nigerians are known for stealing credit cards and doing drugs and all kinds of crazy stuff. I guess the films are kind of like that too.'

'You're from South Africa? You don't have accent!' Mariama exclaimed.

The woman shrugged. 'I've been here a long time. It doesn't make much of a difference.'

'No,' Halima said, suddenly animated, standing behind the woman. 'When I come here with my son they beat him in school because of African accent. In Newark. If you see my son face? Purple like onion. They beat, beat, beat him. Black boys beat him like this. Now accent go and no problems.'

'I'm sorry to hear that,' the woman said.

'Thank you.' Halima smiled, enamoured of the woman because of this extraordinary feat, an American accent. 'Yes, Nigeria very corrupt. Worst corrupt country in Africa. Me, I watch the film but no, I don't go to Nigeria!' She half waved her palm in the air.

'I cannot marry a Nigerian and I won't let anybody in my family marry a Nigerian,' Mariama said, and darted Ifemelu an apologetic glance. 'Not all but many of them do bad things. Even killing for money.'

'Well, I don't know about that,' the customer said, in a half-heartedly moderate tone.

Aisha looked on, sly and quiet. Later, she whispered to Ifemelu, her expression suspicious, 'You here fifteen years, but you don't have American accent. Why?'

Ifemelu ignored her and, once again, opened Jean Toomer's *Cane*. She stared at the words and wished

287

suddenly that she could turn back time and post-pone this move back home. Perhaps she had been hasty. She should not have sold her condo. She should have accepted *Letterly* magazine's offer to buy her blog and keep her on as a paid blogger. What if she got back to Lagos and realized what a mistake it was to move back? Even the thought that she could always return to America did not comfort her as much as she wished it to.

The film had ended, and in the new noiseless-ness of the room, Mariama's customer said, 'This one's rough,' touching one of the thin cornrows that zigzagged over her scalp, her voice louder than it needed to be.

'No problem. I will do it again,' Mariama said. She was agreeable, and smooth-tongued, but Ifemelu could tell that she thought her customer was a troublemaker, and there was nothing wrong with the cornrow, but this was a part of her new American self, this fervour of customer service, this shiny falseness of surfaces, and she had accepted it, embraced it. When the customer left, she might shrug out of that self and say something to Halima and to Aisha about Americans, how spoilt and childish and entitled they were, but when the next customer came, she would become, again, a faultless version of her American self.

Her customer said, 'It's cute,' as she paid Mariama, and shortly after she left, a young white woman came in, soft-bodied and tanned, her hair held back in a loose ponytail.

'Hi!' she said.

Mariama said 'Hi,' and then waited, wiping her hands over and over the front of her shorts.

'I wanted to get my hair braided? You can braid my hair, right?'

Mariama smiled an overly eager smile. 'Yes. We do every kind of hair. Do you want braids or cornrows?' She was furiously cleaning the chair now. 'Please sit.'

The woman sat down and said she wanted cornrows. 'Kind of like Bo Derek in the movie? You know that movie *10*?'

'Yes, I know,' Mariama said. Ifemelu doubted that she did.

'I'm Kelsey,' the woman announced as though to the whole room. She was aggressively friendly. She asked where Mariama was from, how long she had been in America, if she had children, how her business was doing.

'Business is up and down but we try,' Mariama said.

'But you couldn't even have this business back in your country, right? Isn't it wonderful that you get to come to the US and now your kids can have a better life?'

Mariama looked surprised. 'Yes.'

'Are women allowed to vote in your country?' Kelsey asked.

A longer pause from Mariama. 'Yes.'

'What are you reading?' Kelsey turned to Ifemelu. Ifemelu showed her the cover of the novel. She did not want to start a conversation. Especially not with Kelsey. She recognized in Kelsey the nationalism of liberal Americans who copiously criticized America but did not like you to do so; they expected you to be silent and grateful, and always reminded you of how much better than wherever you had come from America was.

'Is it good?'

'Yes.'

'It's a novel, right? What's it about?'

Why did people ask 'What is it about?' as if a novel had to be about only one thing. Ifemelu disliked the question; she would have disliked it even if she did not feel, in addition to her depressed uncertainty, the beginning of a headache. 'It may not be the kind of book you would like if you have particular tastes. He mixes prose and verse.'

'You have a great accent. Where are you from?'

'Nigeria.'

'Oh. Cool.' Kelsey had slender fingers; they would be perfect for advertising rings. 'I'm going to Africa in the fall. Congo and Kenya and I'm going to try and see Tanzania too.'

'That's nice.'

'I've been reading books to get ready. Everybody recommended *Things Fall Apart*, which I read in high school. It's very good but sort of quaint, right? I mean like it didn't help me understand modern Africa. I've just read this great book, *A Bend in the River*. It made me truly understand how modern Africa works.'

Ifemelu made a sound, halfway between a snort and a hum, but said nothing.

'It's just so honest, the most honest book I've read about Africa,' Kelsey said.

Ifemelu shifted. Kelsey's knowing tone grated. Her headache was getting worse. She did not think the novel was about Africa at all. It was about Europe, or the longing for Europe, about the battered self-image of an Indian man born in Africa, who felt so wounded, so diminished, by not having been born European, a member of a race which he had elevated for their ability to create, that he turned his imagined personal insufficiencies into an impatient contempt for Africa; in his knowing haughty attitude to the African, he could become, even if only fleetingly, a European. She leaned back on her seat and said this in measured tones. Kelsey looked startled; she had not expected a mini-lecture. Then, she said kindly, 'Oh, well, I see why you would read the novel like that.'

'And I see why *you* would read it like you did,' Ifemelu said.

Kelsey raised her eyebrows, as though Ifemelu was one of those slightly unbalanced people who were best avoided. Ifemelu closed her eyes. She had the sensation of clouds gathering over her head. She felt faint. Perhaps it was the heat. She had ended a relationship in which she was not unhappy, closed a blog she enjoyed, and now she was chasing something she could not articulate clearly, even to herself. She could have blogged about Kelsey, too, this girl who somehow believed that she was miraculously neutral in how she read books, while other people read emotionally.

'You want to use hair?' Mariama asked Kelsey. 'Hair?'

Mariama held up a pack of the attachments in a see-through plastic wrapping. Kelsey's eyes widened, and she glanced quickly around, at the pack from which Aisha took small sections for each braid, at the pack that Halima was only just unwrapping.

'Oh my God. So that's how it's done. I used to think African American women with braided hair had such full hair!'

'No, we use attachments,' Mariama said, smiling.

'Maybe next time. I think I'll just do my own hair today,' Kelsey said.

Her hair did not take long, seven cornrows, the too-fine hair already slackening in the plaits. 'It's great!' she said afterwards.

'Thank you,' Mariama said. 'Please come back again. I can do another style for you next time.'

'Great!'

Ifemelu watched Mariama in the mirror, thinking of her own new American selves. It was with Curt that she had first looked in the mirror and, with a flush of accomplishment, seen someone else.

Curt liked to say that it was love at first laugh. Whenever people asked how they met, even people they hardly knew, he would tell the story of how Kimberly had introduced them, he the cousin visiting from Maryland, she the Nigerian babysitter whom Kimberly talked so much about, and how taken he was by her deep voice, by the braid that had escaped from her rubber band. But it was when Taylor dashed into the den, wearing a blue cape and underwear, shouting, 'I am Captain Underpants!' and she threw back her head and laughed, that he had fallen in love. Her laugh was so vibrant, shoulders shaking, chest heaving; it was the laugh of a woman who, when she laughed, really laughed. Sometimes when they were alone and she laughed, he would say teasingly, 'That's what got me. And you know what I thought? If she laughs like that, I wonder how she does *other things*.' He told her, too, that she had known he was smitten – how could she not know? – but pretended not to because she didn't want a white man. In truth, she did not notice his interest. She had always been able to sense the desire of men, but not Curt's, not at first. She still thought of Blaine, saw him walking along the platform at the New Haven train station, an apparition that filled her with a doomed yearning. She had not merely been attracted to Blaine, she had been arrested by Blaine, and in her mind he had become the perfect American partner that she would never have. Still, she had had other crushes since then, minor compared to that strike on the train, and had only just emerged from a crush on Abe in her ethics class, Abe who was white, Abe who liked her well enough, who thought her smart and funny, even attractive, but who did not see her as female. She was curious about Abe, interested in Abe, but all the flirting she did was, to him, merely niceness: Abe would hook her up with his black friend, if he had a black friend. She was invisible to Abe. This crushed her crush, and perhaps also made her overlook Curt. Until one afternoon when she was playing catch with Taylor, who threw the ball high, too high, and it fell into the thicket near the neighbour's cherry tree.

'I think we've lost that one,' Ifemelu said. The week before, a Frisbee had disappeared in there. Curt rose from the patio chair (he had been watching her every move, he told her later) and bounded into the bush, almost diving, as though into a pool, and emerged with the yellow ball.

'Yay! Uncle Curt!' Taylor said. But Curt did not give Taylor the ball; instead he held it out to Ifemelu. She saw in his eyes what he wanted her to see. She smiled and said, 'Thank you.' Later in the kitchen, after she had put in a video for Taylor and was drinking a glass of water, he said, 'This is where I ask you to dinner, but at this point, I'll take anything I can get. May I buy you a drink, an ice cream, a meal, a movie ticket? This evening? This weekend before I go back to Maryland?'

He was looking at her with wonder, his head slightly lowered, and she felt an unfurling inside her. How glorious it was, to be so wanted, and by this man with the rakish metal band around his wrist and the cleft-chinned handsomeness of models in department store catalogues. She began to like him because he liked her. 'You eat so delicately,' he told her on their first date, at an Italian restaurant in Old City. There was nothing particularly delicate about her raising a fork to her mouth but she liked that he thought that there was.

'So, I'm a rich white guy from Potomac, but I'm not nearly as much of an asshole as I'm supposed to be,' he said, in a way that made her feel he had said that before, and that it had been received well when he did. 'Laura always says my mom is richer than God, but I'm not sure she is.'

He talked about himself with such gusto, as though determined to tell her everything there was to know, and all at once. His family had been hoteliers for a hundred years. He went to college in California to escape them. He graduated and travelled through Latin America and Asia. Something began to pull him homewards, perhaps his father's death, perhaps his unhappiness with a relationship. So he moved, a year ago, back to Maryland, started a software business just so that he would not be in the family business, bought an apartment in Baltimore, and went down to Potomac every Sunday to have brunch with his mother. He talked about himself with an uncluttered simplicity, assuming that she enjoyed his stories simply because he enjoyed them himself. His boyish enthusiasm fascinated her. His body was firm as they hugged good night in front of her apartment.

'I'm about to move in for a kiss in exactly three seconds,' he said. 'A real kiss that can take us places, so if you don't want that to happen, you might want to back off right now.'

She did not back off. The kiss was arousing in the way that unknown things are arousing. Afterwards he said, with urgency, 'We have to tell Kimberly.'

'Tell Kimberly what?'

'That we're dating.'

'We are?'

He laughed, and she laughed, too, although she had not been joking. He was open and gushing; cynicism did not occur to him. She felt charmed and almost helpless in the face of this, carried along by him; perhaps they were indeed dating after one kiss since he was so sure that they were.

Kimberly's greeting to her the next day was 'Hello there, lovebird.'

'So you'll forgive your cousin for asking out the help?' Ifemelu asked.

Kimberly laughed and then, in an act that both surprised and moved Ifemelu, Kimberly hugged her. They moved apart awkwardly. Oprah was on the TV in the den and she heard the audience erupt in applause.

'Well,' Kimberly said, looking a little startled by the hug herself. 'I just wanted to say I'm really . . . happy for you both.'

'Thank you. But it's only been one date and there has been no consummation.'

Kimberly giggled and for a moment it felt as though they were high school girlfriends gossiping about boys. Ifemelu sometimes sensed, underneath the well-oiled sequences of Kimberly's life, a flash of regret not only for things she longed for in the present but for things she had longed for in the past.

'You should have seen Curt this morning,' Kimberly said. 'I've never seen him like this! He's really excited.'

'About what?' Morgan asked. She was standing by the kitchen entrance, her prepubescent body stiff with hostility. Behind her, Taylor was trying to straighten the legs of a small plastic robot.

'Well, honey, you're going to have to ask Uncle Curt.'

Curt came into the kitchen, smiling shyly, his hair slightly wet, wearing a fresh, light cologne. 'Hey,' he said. He had called her at night to say he couldn't sleep. 'This is really corny but I am so full of you, it's like I'm *breathing* you, you know?' he had said, and she thought that the romance novelists were wrong and it was men, not women, who were the true romantics.

'Morgan is asking why you seem so excited,' Kimberly said.

'Well, Morg, I'm excited because I have a new girlfriend, somebody really special who you might know.'

Ifemelu wished Curt would remove the arm he had thrown around her shoulder; they were not announcing their engagement, for goodness' sake. Morgan was staring at them. Ifemelu saw Curt through her eyes: the dashing uncle who travelled the world and told all the really funny jokes at Thanksgiving dinner, the cool one young enough to get her, but old enough to try and make her mother get her.

'Ifemelu is your girlfriend?' Morgan asked.

'Yes,' Curt said.

'That's disgusting,' Morgan said, looking genuinely disgusted.

'Morgan!' Kimberly said.

Morgan turned and stalked off upstairs.

'She has a crush on Uncle Curt, and now the babysitter steps onto her turf. It can't be easy,' Ifemelu said.

Taylor, who seemed happy both with the news and with having straightened out the robot's legs, said, 'Are you and Ifemelu going to get married and have a baby, Uncle Curt?'

'Well, buddy, right now we are just going to be spending a lot of time together, to get to know each other.'

'Oh, okay,' Taylor said, slightly dampened, but when Don came home, Taylor ran into his arms and said, 'Ifemelu and Uncle Curt are going to get married and have a baby!'

'Oh,' Don said.

His surprise reminded Ifemelu of Abe in her

298

ethics class: Don thought she was attractive and interesting, and thought Curt was attractive and interesting, but it did not occur to him to think of both of them, together, entangled in the delicate threads of romance.

Curt had never been with a black woman; he told her this after their first time, in his penthouse apartment in Baltimore, with a self-mocking toss of his head, as if this were something he should have done long ago but had somehow neglected.

'Here's to a milestone, then,' she said, pretending to raise a glass.

Wambui once said, after Dorothy introduced them to her new Dutch boyfriend at an ASA meeting, 'I can't do a white man, I'd be scared to see him naked, all that paleness. Unless maybe an Italian with a serious tan. Or a Jewish guy, dark Jewish.' Ifemelu looked at Curt's pale hair and pale skin, the rust-coloured moles on his back, the fine sprinkle of golden chest hair, and thought how strongly, at this moment, she disagreed with Wambui.

'You are so sexy,' she said.

'You are *sexier*.'

He told her he had never been so attracted to a woman before, had never seen a body so beautiful, her perfect breasts, her perfect butt. It amused her, that he considered a perfect butt what Obinze called a flat ass, and she thought her breasts were ordinary big breasts, already with a downward slope. But his words pleased her, like an unnecessary lavish gift. He wanted to suck her finger, to lick honey from her nipple, to smear ice cream on her belly, as though it was not enough simply to lie bare skin to bare skin.

Later, when he wanted to do impersonations – 'How about you be Foxy Brown,' he said – she thought it endearing, his ability to act, to lose himself so completely in character, and she played along, humouring him, pleased by his pleasure, although it puzzled her that this could be so exciting to him. Often, naked beside him, she found herself thinking of Obinze. She struggled not to compare Curt's touch to his. She had told Curt about her secondary school boyfriend Mofe, but she said nothing about Obinze. It felt a sacrilege to discuss Obinze, to refer to him as an 'ex', that flippant word that said nothing and meant nothing. With each month of silence that passed between them, she felt the silence itself calcify, and become a hard and hulking statue, impossible to defeat. She still, often, began to write to him, but always she stopped, always she decided not to send the e-mails.

With Curt, she became, in her mind, a woman free of knots and cares, a woman running in the rain with the taste of sun-warmed strawberries in her mouth. 'A drink' became a part of the architecture of her life, mojitos and martinis, dry whites and fruity reds. She went hiking with him, kayaking, camping near his family's vacation home, all things she would never have imagined herself doing before. She was lighter and leaner; she was Curt's Girlfriend, a role she slipped into as into a favourite, flattering dress. She laughed more because he laughed so much. His optimism blinded her. He was full of plans. 'I have an idea!' he said often. She imagined him as a child surrounded by too many brightly coloured toys, always being encouraged to carry out 'projects', always being told that his mundane ideas were wonderful.

'Let's go to Paris tomorrow!' he said one weekend. 'I know it's totally unoriginal but you've never been and I love that I get to show you Paris!'

'I just can't get up and go to Paris. I have a Nigerian passport. I need to apply for a visa, with bank statements and health insurance and all sorts of proof that I won't stay and become a burden to Europe.'

'Yeah, I forgot about that. Okay, we'll go next weekend. We'll get the visa stuff done this week. I'll get a copy of my bank statement tomorrow.'

'Curtis,' she said, a little sternly, to make him be reasonable, but standing there looking down at the city from so high up, she was already caught in the whirl of his excitement. He was upbeat, relentlessly so, in a way that only an American of his kind could be, and there was an infantile quality to this that she found admirable and repulsive. One day, they took a walk on South Street, because she had never seen what he told her was the best part of Philadelphia, and he slipped his hand into hers as they wandered past tattoo parlours and groups of boys with pink hair. Near Condom Kingdom, he ducked into a tiny tarot shop, pulling her along. A woman in a black veil told them, 'I see light and long-term happiness ahead for you two,' and Curt said, 'So do we!' and gave her an extra ten dollars. Later, when his ebullience became a temptation to Ifemelu, an unrelieved sunniness that made her want to strike at it, to crush it, this would be one of her best memories of Curt, as he was in the tarot shop on South Street on a day filled with the promise of summer: so handsome, so happy, a true believer. He believed in good omens and positive thoughts and happy endings to films, a trouble-free belief, because he had not considered them deeply before choosing to believe; he just simply believed.

CHAPTER 19

Curt's mother had a bloodless elegance, her hair shiny, her complexion well-preserved, her tasteful and expensive clothes made to look tasteful and expensive; she seemed like the kind of wealthy person who did not tip well. Curt called her 'Mother', which had a certain formality, an archaic ring. On Sundays, they had brunch with her. Ifemelu enjoyed the Sunday ritual of those meals in the ornate hotel dining room, full of nicely dressed people, silver-haired couples with their grandchildren, middle-aged women with brooches pinned on their lapels. The only other black person was a stiffly dressed waiter. She ate fluffy eggs and thinly sliced salmon and crescents of fresh melon, watching Curt and his mother, both blindingly golden-haired. Curt talked, while his mother listened, rapt. She adored her son – the child born late in life when she wasn't sure she could still have children, the charmer, the one whose manipulations she always gave in to. He was her adventurer who would bring back exotic species – he had dated a Japanese girl, a Venezuelan girl – but would, with time, settle down properly. She would tolerate anybody he liked, but she felt no obligation for affection.

'I'm Republican, our whole family is. We are very anti-welfare but we did very much support civil rights. I just want you to know the kind of Republicans we are,' she told Ifemelu when they first met, as though it was the most important thing to get out of the way.

'And would you like to know what kind of Republican I am?' Ifemelu asked.

His mother first looked surprised, and then her face stretched into a tight smile. 'You're funny,' she said.

Once, his mother told Ifemelu, 'Your lashes are pretty,' abrupt, unexpected words, and then sipped her Bellini, as though she had not heard Ifemelu's surprised 'Thank you.'

On the drive back to Baltimore, Ifemelu said, 'Lashes? She must have really tried hard to find something to compliment!'

Curt laughed. 'Laura says my mother doesn't like beautiful women.'

One weekend, Morgan visited.

Kimberly and Don wanted to take the children to Florida, but Morgan refused to go. So Curt asked her to spend the weekend in Baltimore. He planned a boating trip, and Ifemelu thought he should have some time alone with Morgan. 'You're not coming, Ifemelu?' Morgan asked, looking deflated. 'I thought we were all going *together*.' The word 'together' said with more animation than Ifemelu had ever heard from Morgan. 'Of course I'm coming,' she said. As she put on mascara and lip gloss, Morgan watched.

'Come here, Morg,' she said, and she ran the lip gloss over Morgan's lips. 'Smack your lips. Good. Now why are you so pretty, Miss Morgan?' Morgan laughed. On the pier, Ifemelu and Curt walked along, each holding Morgan's hand, Morgan happy to have her hands held, and Ifemelu thought, as she sometimes fleetingly did, of being married to Curt, their life engraved in comfort, he getting along with her family and friends and she with his, except for his mother. They joked about marriage. Since she first told him about bride price ceremonies, that Igbo people did them before the wine-carrying and church wedding, he joked about going to Nigeria to pay her bride price, arriving at her ancestral home, sitting with her father and uncles, and insisting he get her for free. And she joked, in return, about walking down the aisle in a church in Virginia, to the tune of 'Here Comes the Bride', while his relatives stared in horror and asked one another, in whispers, why the help was wearing the bride's dress.

They were curled up on the couch, she reading a novel, he watching sports. She found it endearing, how absorbed he was in his games, eyes small and still in concentration. During commercial breaks, she teased him: Why did American football have no inherent logic, just overweight men jumping on top of one another? And why did baseball players spend so much time spitting and then making sudden incomprehensible runs? He laughed and tried to explain, yet again, the meaning of home runs and touchdowns, but she was uninterested, because understanding meant she could no longer tease him, and so she glanced back at her novel, ready to tease him again at the next break.

The couch was soft. Her skin was glowing. At school, she took extra credits and raised her GPA. Outside the tall living room windows, the Inner Harbor spread out below, water gleaming and lights twinkling. A sense of contentment overwhelmed her. That was what Curt had given her, this gift of contentment, of ease. How quickly she had become used to their life, her passport filled with visa stamps, the solicitousness of flight attendants in first-class cabins, the feathery bed linen in the hotels they stayed in and the little things she hoarded: jars of preserves from the breakfast tray, little vials of conditioner, woven slippers, even face towels if they were especially soft. She had slipped out of her old skin. She almost liked winter, the glittering coat of frosted ice on the tops of cars, the lush warmth of the cashmere sweaters Curt bought her. In stores, he did not look first at the prices of things. He bought her groceries and textbooks, sent her gift certificates for department stores, took her shopping himself. He asked her to give up babysitting; they could spend more time together if she didn't have to work every day. But she refused. 'I have to have a job,' she said.

She saved money, sent more home. She wanted her parents to move to a new flat. There had been an armed robbery in the block of flats next to theirs.

'Something bigger in a better neighbourhood,' she said.

'We are okay here,' her mother said. 'It is not too bad. They built a new gate in the street and banned okadas after six p.m., so it is safe.'

'A gate?'

'Yes, near the kiosk.'

'Which kiosk?'

'You don't remember the kiosk?' her mother asked. Ifemelu paused. A sepia tone to her memories. She could not remember the kiosk.

Her father had, finally, found a job, as the deputy director of human resources in one of the new banks. He bought a mobile phone. He bought new tyres for her mother's car. Slowly, he was easing back into his monologues about Nigeria.

'One could not describe Obasanjo as a good man, but it must be conceded that he has done some good things in the country; there is a flourishing spirit of entrepreneurship,' he said.

It felt strange to call them directly, to hear her father's 'Hello?' after the second ring, and when he heard her voice, he raised his, almost shouting, as he always did with international calls. Her mother liked to take the phone out to the verandah, to make sure the neighbours overheard: *'Ifem, how is the weather in America?'*

Her mother asked breezy questions and accepted breezy replies. 'Everything is going well?' and Ifemelu had no choice but to say yes. Her father remembered classes she'd mentioned, and asked about specifics. She chose her words, careful not to say anything about Curt. It was easier not to tell them about Curt.

'What are your employment prospects?' her father asked. Her graduation was approaching, her student visa expiring.

'I have been assigned to a career counsellor, and I'm meeting her next week,' she said.

'All graduating students have a counsellor assigned to them?'

'Yes.'

Her father made a sound, of admiring respect. 'America is an organized place, and job opportunities are rife there.'

'Yes. They have placed many students in good jobs,' Ifemelu said. It was untrue, but it was what her father expected to hear. The career services office, an airless space, piles of files sitting forlornly on desks, was known to be full of counsellors who reviewed résumés and asked you to change the font or format and gave you outdated contact information for people who never called you back. The first time Ifemelu went there, her counsellor, Ruth, a caramel-skinned African American woman, asked, 'What do you really want to do?'

'I want a job.'

'Yes, but what kind?' Ruth asked, slightly incredulous.

Ifemelu looked at her résumé on the table. 'I'm a communications major, so anything in communications, the media.'

'Do you have a passion, a dream job?'

Ifemelu shook her head. She felt weak, for not having a passion, not being sure what she wanted to do. Her interests were vague and varied, magazine publishing, fashion, politics, television; none of them had a firm shape. She attended the school career fair, where students wore awkward suits and serious expressions, and tried to look like adults worthy of real jobs. The recruiters, themselves not long out of college, the young who had been sent out to catch the young, told her about 'opportunity for growth' and 'good fit' and 'benefits', but they all became noncommittal when they realized she was not an American citizen, that they would, if they hired her, have to descend into the dark tunnel of immigration paperwork. 'I should have majored in engineering or something,' she told Curt. 'Communications majors are a dime a dozen.'

'I know some people my dad did business with, they might be able to help,' Curt said. And, not long afterwards, he told her she had an interview at an office in downtown Baltimore, for a position in public relations. 'All you need to do is ace the interview and it's yours,' he said. 'So I know folks in this other bigger place, but the good thing about this one is they'll get you a work visa *and* start your green card process.'

'What? How did you do it?'

He shrugged. 'Made some calls.'

'Curt. Really. I don't know how to thank you.'

'I have some ideas,' he said, boyishly pleased.

It was good news, and yet a soberness wrapped itself around her. Wambui was working three jobs under the table to raise the five thousand dollars she would need to pay an African American man for a green-card marriage, Mwombeki was desperately trying to find a company that would hire him on his temporary visa, and here she was, a pink balloon, weightless, floating to the top, propelled by things outside of herself. She felt, in the midst of her gratitude, a small resentment: that Curt could, with a few calls, rearrange the world, have things slide into the spaces that he wanted them to.

When she told Ruth about the interview in Baltimore, Ruth said, 'My only advice? Lose the braids and straighten your hair. Nobody says this kind of stuff but it matters. We want you to get that job.'

Aunty Uju had said something similar in the past, and she had laughed then. Now, she knew enough not to laugh. 'Thank you,' she said to Ruth.

Since she came to America, she had always braided her hair with long extensions, always alarmed at how much it cost. She wore each style for three months, even four months, until her scalp itched unbearably and the braids sprouted fuzzily from a bed of new growth. And so it was a new adventure, relaxing her hair. She removed her braids, careful to leave her scalp unscratched, to leave undisturbed the dirt that would protect it. Relaxers had grown in their range, boxes and boxes in the 'ethnic hair' section of the drugstore, faces of smiling black women with impossibly straight and shiny hair, beside words like 'botanical' and 'aloe' that promised gentleness. She bought one in a green carton. In her bathroom, she carefully smeared the protective gel around her hairline before she began to slather the creamy relaxer on her hair, section by section, her fingers in plastic gloves. The smell reminded her of chemistry lab in secondary school, and so she forced open the bathroom window, which was often jammed. She timed the process carefully, washing off the relaxer in exactly twenty minutes, but her hair remained kinky, its denseness unchanged. The relaxer did not take. That was the word – 'take' – that the hairdresser in West Philadelphia used. 'Girl, you need a professional,' the hairdresser said as she reapplied another relaxer. 'People think they're saving money by doing it at home but they're really not.'

Ifemelu felt only a slight burning, at first, but as the hairdresser rinsed out the relaxer, Ifemelu's head bent backwards against a plastic sink, needles of stinging pain shot up from different parts of her scalp, down to different parts of her body, back up to her head.

'Just a little burn,' the hairdresser said. 'But look how pretty it is. Wow, girl, you've got the white-girl swing!'

Her hair was hanging down rather than standing up, straight and sleek, parted at the side and curving to a slight bob at her chin. The verve was gone. She did not recognize herself. She left the salon almost mournfully; while the hairdresser had flat-ironed the ends, the smell of burning, of something organic dying which should not have died, had made her feel a sense of loss. Curt looked uncertain when he saw her.

'Do you like it, babe?' he asked.

'I can see you don't,' she said.

He said nothing. He reached out to stroke her hair, as though doing so might make him like it.

She pushed him away. 'Ouch. Careful. I have a bit of relaxer burn.'

'What?'

'It's not too bad. I used to get it all the time in Nigeria. Look at this.'

She showed him a keloid behind her ear, a small enraged swelling of skin, which she got after Aunty Uju straightened her hair with a hot comb in secondary school. 'Pull back your ear,' Aunty Uju often said, and Ifemelu would hold her ear, tense and unbreathing, terrified that the red-hot comb fresh from the stove would burn her but also

312

excited by the prospect of straight, swingy hair. And one day it did burn her, as she moved slightly and Aunty Uju's hand moved slightly and the hot metal singed the skin behind her ear.

'Oh my God,' Curt said, his eyes wide. He insisted on gently looking at her scalp to see how much she had been hurt. 'Oh my God.'

His horror made her more concerned than she would ordinarily have been. She had never felt so close to him as she did then, sitting still on the bed, her face sunk in his shirt, the scent of fabric softener in her nose, while he gently parted her newly straightened hair.

'Why do you have to do this? Your hair was gorgeous braided. And when you took out the braids the last time and just kind of let it be? It was even more gorgeous, so full and cool.'

'My full and cool hair would work if I were interviewing to be a backup singer in a jazz band, but I need to look professional for this interview, and professional means straight is best but if it's going to be curly then it has to be the white kind of curly, loose curls or, at worst, spiral curls but never kinky.'

'It's so fucking *wrong* that you have to do this.'

At night, she struggled to find a comfortable position on her pillow. Two days later, there were scabs on her scalp. Three days later, they oozed pus. Curt wanted her to see a doctor and she laughed at him. It would heal, she told him, and it did. Later, after she breezed through the job interview, and the woman shook her hand and said she would be a 'wonderful fit' in the company, she wondered if the woman would have felt the same way had she walked into that office wearing her thick, kinky, God-given halo of hair, the Afro.

She did not tell her parents how she got the job; her father said, 'I have no doubt that you will excel. America creates opportunities for people to thrive. Nigeria can indeed learn a lot from them,' while her mother began to sing when Ifemelu said that, in a few years, she could become an American citizen.

Understanding America for the Non-American Black: What Do WASPs Aspire To?

Professor Hunk has a visiting professor colleague, a Jewish guy with a thick accent from the kind of European country where most people drink a glass of antisemitism at breakfast. So Professor Hunk was talking about civil rights and Jewish guy says, 'The blacks have not suffered like the Jews.' Professor Hunk replies, 'Come on, is this the oppression olympics?'

Jewish guy did not know this, but 'oppression olympics' is what smart liberal Americans say, to make you feel stupid and to make you shut up. But there IS an oppression olympics going on. American racial minorities – blacks, Hispanics, Asians, and Jews – all get shit from white folks, different kinds of shit, but shit still. Each secretly believes that it gets the worst shit. So, no, there is no United League of the Oppressed. However, all the others think they're better than blacks because, well, they're not black. Take Lili, for example, the coffee-skinned, black-haired and Spanish-speaking woman who cleaned my aunt's house in a New England town. She had a great hauteur. She was disrespectful, cleaned poorly, made demands. My aunt believed Lili didn't like working for black people. Before she finally fired her, my aunt said, 'Stupid woman, she thinks she's white.' So whiteness is the thing to aspire to. Not everyone does, of course (please, commenters, don't state the obvious) but many minorities have a conflicted longing for WASP whiteness or, more accurately, for the privileges of WASP whiteness. They probably don't really like pale skin but they certainly like walking into a store without some security dude following them. Hating Your Goy and Eating One Too, as the great Philip Roth put it. So if everyone in America aspires to be WASPs, then what do WASPs aspire to? Does anyone know?

CHAPTER 20

Ifemelu came to love Baltimore – for its scrappy charm, its streets of faded glory, its farmers' market that appeared on weekends under the bridge, bursting with green vegetables and plump fruit and virtuous souls – although never as much as her first love, Philadelphia, that city that held history in its gentle clasp. But when she arrived in Baltimore knowing she was going to live there, and not merely visiting Curt, she thought it forlorn and unlovable. The buildings were joined to one another in faded slumping rows, and on shabby corners, people were hunched in puffy jackets, black and bleak people waiting for buses, the air around them hazed in gloom. Many of the drivers outside the train station were Ethiopian or Punjabi.

Her Ethiopian taxi driver said, 'I can't place your accent. Where are you from?'

'Nigeria.'

'Nigeria? You don't look African at all.'

'Why don't I look African?'

'Because your blouse is too tight.'

'It is not too tight.'

'I thought you were from Trinidad or one of

those places.' He was looking in the rear-view with disapproval and concern. 'You have to be very careful or America will corrupt you.' When, years later, she wrote the blog post 'On the Divisions Within the Membership of Non-American Blacks in America', she wrote about the taxi driver, but she wrote of it as the experience of someone else, careful not to let on whether she was African or Caribbean, because her readers did not know which she was.

She told Curt about the taxi driver, how his sincerity had infuriated her and how she had gone to the station bathroom to see if her pink long-sleeved blouse *was* too tight. Curt laughed and laughed. It became one of the many stories he liked to tell friends. *She actually went to the bathroom to look at her blouse!* His friends were like him, sunny and wealthy people who existed on the glimmering surface of things. She liked them, and sensed that they liked her. To them, she was interesting, unusual in the way she bluntly spoke her mind. They expected certain things of her, and forgave certain things from her, because she was foreign. Once, sitting with them in a bar, she heard Curt talking to Brad, and Curt said 'blowhard'. She was struck by the word, by the irredeemable Americanness of it. Blowhard. It was a word that would never occur to her. To understand this was to realize that Curt and his friends would, on some level, never be fully knowable to her.

She got an apartment in Charles Village, a

one-bedroom with old wood floors, although she might as well have been living with Curt; most of her clothes were in his walk-in closet lined with mirrors. Now that she saw him every day, no longer just on weekends, she saw new layers of him, how difficult it was for him to be still, simply still without thinking of what next to do, how used he was to stepping out of his trousers and leaving them on the floor for days, until the cleaning woman came. Their lives were full of plans he made – Cozumel for one night, London for a long weekend – and she sometimes took a taxi on Friday evenings after work to meet him at the airport.

'Isn't this great?' he would ask her, and she would say yes, it was great. He was always thinking of what else to *do* and she told him that it was rare for her, because she had grown up not doing, but being. She added quickly, though, that she liked it all, because she did like it and she knew, too, how much he needed to hear that. In bed, he was anxious.

'Do you like that? Do you enjoy me?' he asked often. And she said yes, which was true, but she sensed that he did not always believe her, or that his belief lasted only so long before he would need to hear her affirmation again. There was something in him, lighter than ego but darker than insecurity, that needed constant buffing, polishing, waxing.

And then her hair began to fall out at the temples. She drenched it in rich, creamy conditioners, and sat under steamers until water droplets ran down her neck. Still, her hairline shifted further backwards each day.

'It's the chemicals,' Wambui told her. 'Do you know what's in a relaxer? That stuff can kill you. You need to cut your hair and go natural.'

Wambui's hair was now in short locs, which Ifemelu did not like; she thought them sparse and dull, unflattering to Wambui's pretty face.

'I don't want dreads,' she said.

'It doesn't have to be dreads. You can wear an Afro, or braids like you used to. There's a lot you can do with natural hair.'

'I can't just cut my hair,' she said.

'Relaxing your hair is like being in prison. You're caged in. Your hair rules you. You didn't go running with Curt today because you don't want to sweat out this straightness. That picture you sent me, you had your hair covered on the boat. You're always battling to make your hair do what it wasn't meant to do. If you go natural and take good care of your hair, it won't fall off like it's doing now. I can help you cut it right now. No need to think about it too much.'

Wambui was so sure, so convincing. Ifemelu found a pair of scissors. Wambui cut her hair, leaving only two inches, the new growth since her last relaxer. Ifemelu looked in the mirror. She was all big eyes and big head. At best, she looked like a boy; at worst, like an insect.

'I look so ugly I'm scared of myself.'

'You look beautiful. Your bone structure shows so well now. You're just not used to seeing yourself like this. You'll get used to it,' Wambui said.

Ifemelu was still staring at her hair. What had she done? She looked unfinished, as though the hair itself, short and stubby, was asking for attention, for something to be done to it, for *more*. After Wambui left, she went to the drugstore, Curt's baseball hat pulled over her head. She bought oils and pomades, applying one and then the other, on wet hair and then on dry hair, willing an unknown miracle to happen. Something, anything, that would make her like her hair. She thought of buying a wig, but wigs brought anxiety, the always-present possibility of flying off your head. She thought of a texturizer to loosen her hair's springy coils, stretch out the kinkiness a little, but a texturizer was really a relaxer, only milder, and she would still have to avoid the rain.

Curt told her, 'Stop stressing, babe. It's a really cool and brave look.'

'I don't want my hair to be *brave*.'

'I mean like stylish, chic.' He paused. 'You look beautiful.'

'I look like a boy.'

Curt said nothing. There was, in his expression, a veiled amusement, as though he did not see why she should be so upset but was better off not saying so.

The next day, she called in sick, and climbed back into bed.

'You didn't call in sick so we could stay a day longer in Bermuda but you call in sick because of your hair?' Curt asked, propped up by pillows, stifling laughter.

'I can't go out like this.' She was burrowing under the covers as though to hide.

'It's not as bad as you think,' he said.

'At least you finally accept that it's bad.'

Curt laughed. 'You know what I mean. Come here.'

He hugged her, kissed her, and then slid down and began to massage her feet; she liked the warm pressure, the feel of his fingers. Yet she could not relax. In the bathroom mirror, her hair had startled her, dull and shrunken from sleep, like a mop of wool sitting on her head. She reached for her phone and sent Wambui a text: *I hate my hair. I couldn't go to work today.*

Wambui's reply came minutes later: *Go online. HappilyKinkyNappy.com. It's this natural hair community. You'll find inspiration.*

She showed the text to Curt. 'What a silly name for the website.'

'I know, but it sounds like a good idea. You should check it out sometime.'

'Like now,' Ifemelu said, getting up. Curt's laptop was open on the desk. As she went to it, she noticed a change in Curt. A sudden tense quickness. His ashen, panicked move towards the laptop.

'What's wrong?' she asked.

'They mean nothing. The e-mails mean nothing.'

321

She stared at him, forcing her mind to work. He had not expected her to use his computer, because she hardly ever did. He was cheating on her. How odd, that she had never considered that. She picked up the laptop, held it tightly, but he didn't try to reach for it. He just stood and watched. The Yahoo mail page was minimized, next to a page about college basketball. She read some of the e-mails. She looked at attached photographs. The woman's e-mails – her address was SparklingPaola123 – were strongly suggestive, while Curt's were just suggestive enough to make sure she continued. *I'm going to cook you dinner in a tight red dress and sky-high heels*, she wrote, *and you just bring yourself and a bottle of wine.* Curt replied: *Red would look great on you.* The woman was about his age, but there was, in the photos she sent, an air of hard desperation, hair dyed a brassy blonde, eyes burdened by too much blue make-up, top too low-cut. It surprised Ifemelu that Curt found her attractive. His white ex-girlfriend had been fresh-faced and preppy.

'I met her in Delaware,' Curt said. 'Remember the conference thing I wanted you to come to? She started hitting on me right away. She's been after me since. She won't leave me alone. She knows I have a girlfriend.'

Ifemelu stared at one of the photos, a profile shot in black-and-white, the woman's head thrown back, her long hair flowing behind her. A woman who liked her hair and thought Curt would too.

'Nothing happened,' Curt said. 'At all. Just the

e-mails. She's really after me. I told her about you, but she just won't stop.'

She looked at him, wearing a T-shirt and shorts, so certain in his self-justifications. He was entitled in the way a child was: blindly.

'You wrote to her too,' she said.

'But that's because she wouldn't stop.'

'No, it's because you wanted to.'

'Nothing happened.'

'That is not the point.'

'I'm sorry. I know you're already upset and I hate to make it worse.'

'All your girlfriends had long flowing hair,' she said, her tone thick with accusation.

'What?'

She was being absurd, but knowing that did not make her any less so. Pictures she had seen of his ex-girlfriends goaded her, the slender Japanese with straight hair dyed red, the olive-skinned Venezuelan with corkscrew hair that fell to her shoulders, the white girl with waves and waves of russet hair. And now this woman, whose looks she did not care for, but who had long straight hair. She shut the laptop. She felt small and ugly. Curt was talking. 'I'll ask her never to contact me. This will never happen again, babe, I promise,' he said, and she thought he sounded as though it was somehow the woman's responsibility, rather than his.

She turned away, pulled Curt's baseball hat over her head, threw things in a bag and left.

★   ★   ★

323

Curt came by later, holding so many flowers she hardly saw his face when she opened the door. She would forgive him, she knew, because she believed him. Sparkling Paola was one more small adventure of his. He would not have gone further with her, but he would have kept encouraging her attention, until he was bored. Sparkling Paola was like the silver stars that his teachers pasted on the pages of his elementary school homework, sources of a shallow, fleeting pleasure.

She did not want to go out, but she did not want to be with him in the intimacy of her apartment; she still felt too raw. So she covered her hair in a headwrap and they took a walk, Curt solicitous and full of promises, walking side by side but not touching, all the way to the corner of Charles and University Parkway, and then back to her apartment.

For three days, she called in sick. Finally, she went to work, her hair a very short, overly combed and overly oiled Afro. 'You look different,' her co-workers said, all of them a little tentative.

'Does it mean anything? Like, something political?' Amy asked, Amy who had a poster of Che Guevara on her cubicle wall.

'No,' Ifemelu said.

At the cafeteria, Miss Margaret, the bosomy African American woman who presided over the counter – and, apart from two security guards, the only other black person in the company – asked,

'Why did you cut your hair, hon? Are you a lesbian?'

'No, Miss Margaret, at least not yet.'

Some years later, on the day Ifemelu resigned, she went into the cafeteria for a last lunch. 'You leaving?' Miss Margaret asked, downcast. 'Sorry, hon. They need to treat folk better around here. You think your hair was part of the problem?'

happilykinkynappy.com had a bright yellow background, message boards full of posts, thumbnail photos of black women blinking at the top. They had long trailing dreadlocks, small Afros, big Afros, twists, braids, massive raucous curls and coils. They called relaxers 'creamy crack'. They were done with pretending that their hair was what it was not, done with running from the rain and flinching from sweat. They complimented each other's photos and ended comments with 'hugs'. They complained about black magazines never having natural-haired women in their pages, about drugstore products so poisoned by mineral oil that they could not moisturize natural hair. They traded recipes. They sculpted for themselves a virtual world where their coily, kinky, nappy, woolly hair was normal. And Ifemelu fell into this world with a tumbling gratitude. Women with hair as short as hers had a name for it: TWA, Teeny Weeny Afro. She learned, from women who posted long instructions, to avoid shampoos with silicones, to use a leave-in conditioner on wet hair, to sleep in a satin scarf. She ordered products from women who made them in their kitchens and shipped them with clear instructions: BEST TO REFRIGERATE IMMEDIATELY, DOES NOT CONTAIN PRESERVATIVES. Curt would open the fridge, hold up a container labelled 'hair butter' and ask, 'Okay to spread this on my toast?' Curt thrummed with fascination about it all. He read posts on HappilyKinkyNappy.com. 'I think it's great!' he said. 'It's like this *movement* of black women.'

One day, at the farmers' market, as she stood hand in hand with Curt in front of a tray of apples, a black man walked past and muttered, 'You ever wonder why he likes you looking all jungle like that?' She stopped, unsure for a moment whether she had imagined those words, and then she looked back at the man. He walked with too much rhythm in his step, which suggested to her a certain fickleness of character. A man not worth paying any attention to. Yet his words bothered her, prised open the door for new doubts.

'Did you hear what that guy said?' she asked Curt.

'No, what did he say?'

She shook her head. 'Nothing.'

She felt dispirited and, while Curt watched a game that evening, she drove to the beauty supply store and ran her fingers through small bundles of silky straight weaves. Then she remembered a post by Jamilah1977 – *I love the sistas who love their straight weaves, but I'm never putting horse hair on my head again* – and she left the store, eager to get back and log on and post on the boards about it. She wrote: *Jamilah's words made me remember that there is nothing more beautiful than what God gave me*. Others wrote responses, posting thumbs-up signs, telling her how much they liked the photo she had put up. She had never talked about God so much. Posting on the website was like giving testimony in church; the echoing roar of approval revived her.

On an unremarkable day in early spring – the day was not bronzed with special light, nothing of any significance happened, and it was perhaps merely that time, as it often does, had transfigured her doubts – she looked in the mirror, sank her fingers into her hair, dense and spongy and glorious, and could not imagine it any other way. That simply, she fell in love with her hair.

Why Dark-Skinned Black Women – Both American and Non-American – Love Barack Obama

Many American blacks proudly say they have some 'Indian.' Which means Thank God We Are Not Full-Blooded Negroes. Which means they are not too dark. (To clarify, when white people say dark they mean Greek or Italian but when black people say dark they mean Grace Jones.) American black men like their black women

327

to have some exotic quota, like half-Chinese or splash of Cherokee. They like their women light. But beware what American blacks consider 'light.' Some of these 'light' people, in countries of Non-American Blacks, would simply be called white. (Oh, and dark American black men resent light men, for having it too easy with the ladies.)

Now, my fellow Non-American Blacks, don't get smug. Because this bullshit also exists in our Caribbean and African countries. Not as bad as with American blacks, you say? Maybe. But there nonetheless. By the way, what is it with Ethiopians thinking they are not that black? And Small Islanders eager to say their ancestry is 'mixed'? But we must not digress. So light skin is valued in the community of American blacks. But everyone pretends this is no longer so. They say the days of the paper-bag test (look this up) are gone and let's move forward. But today most of the American blacks who are successful as entertainers and as public figures, are light. Especially women. Many successful American black men have white wives. Those who deign to have black wives have light (otherwise known as high yellow) wives. And this is the reason dark women love Barack Obama. He broke the mold!

He married one of their own. He knows what the world doesn't seem to know: that dark black women totally rock. They want Obama to win because maybe finally somebody will cast a beautiful chocolate babe in a big-budget rom-com that opens in theaters all over the country, not just three artsy theaters in New York City. You see, in American pop culture, beautiful dark women are invisible. (The other group just as invisible is Asian men. But at least they get to be super smart.) In movies, dark black women get to be the fat nice mammy or the strong, sassy, sometimes scary sidekick standing by supportively. They get to dish out wisdom and attitude while the white woman finds love. But they never get to be the hot woman, beautiful and desired and all. So dark black women hope Obama will change that. Oh, and dark black women are also for cleaning up Washington and getting out of Iraq and whatnot.

CHAPTER 21

It was a Sunday morning, and Aunty Uju called, agitated and strained.

'Look at this boy! Come and see the nonsense he wants to wear to church. He has refused to wear what I brought out for him. You know that if he does not dress properly, they will find something to say about us. If they are shabby, it's not a problem, but if we are, it is another thing. This is the same way I have been telling him to tone it down at school. The other day, they said he was talking in class and he said he was talking because he had finished his work. He has to tone it down, because his own will always be seen as different, but the boy doesn't understand. Please talk to your cousin!'

Ifemelu asked Dike to take the phone to his room.

'Mom wants me to wear this really ugly shirt.' His tone was flat, dispassionate.

'I know how uncool that shirt is, Dike, but wear it for her, okay? Just to church. Just for today.'

She did know the shirt, a striped, humourless shirt that Bartholomew had bought for Dike. It was the sort of shirt Bartholomew would buy. It reminded her of his friends she had met one weekend, a Nigerian couple visiting from Maryland, their two boys sitting next to them on the sofa, both buttoned-up and stiff, caged in the airlessness of their parents' immigrant aspirations. She did not want Dike to be like them, but she understood Aunty Uju's anxieties, making her way in unfamiliar terrain as she was.

'You'll probably not see anybody you know in church,' Ifemelu said. 'And I'll talk to your mum about not making you wear it again.' She cajoled until finally Dike agreed, as long as he could wear sneakers, not the lace-ups his mother wanted.

'I'm coming up this weekend,' she told him. 'I'm bringing my boyfriend, Curt. You'll finally get to meet him.'

With Aunty Uju, Curt was solicitous and charming in that well-oiled way that slightly embarrassed Ifemelu. At dinner the other night with Wambui and some friends, Curt had reached out and refilled a wineglass here, a water glass there. Charming, was what one of the girls said later: Your boyfriend is so charming. And the thought occurred to Ifemelu that she did not like charm. Not Curt's kind, with its need to dazzle, to perform. She wished Curt were quieter and more inward. When he started conversations with people in elevators, or lavishly complimented strangers, she held her breath, certain that they could see what an attention-loving person he was. But they always

331

smiled back and responded and allowed themselves to be wooed. As Aunty Uju did. 'Curt, won't you try the soup? Ifemelu has never cooked this soup for you? Have you tried fried plantain?'

Dike watched, saying little, speaking politely and properly, even though Curt joked with him and talked sports and tried so hard to win his affection that Ifemelu feared he might do somersaults. Finally, Curt asked, 'Want to shoot some hoops?'

Dike shrugged. 'Okay.'

Aunty Uju watched them leave.

'Look at the way he behaves as if anything you touch starts smelling like perfume. He really likes you,' Aunty Uju said, and then, face wrinkling, she added, 'And even with your hair like that.'

'Aunty, *biko*, leave my hair alone,' Ifemelu said.

'It is like jute.' Aunty Uju plunged a hand into Ifemelu's Afro.

Ifemelu drew her head away. 'What if every magazine you opened and every film you watched had beautiful women with hair like jute? You would be admiring my hair now.'

Aunty Uju scoffed. 'Okay, you can speak English about it but I am just saying what is true. There is something scruffy and untidy about natural hair.' Aunty Uju paused. 'Have you read the essay your cousin wrote?'

'Yes.'

'How can he say he does not know what he is? Since when is he conflicted? And even that his name is difficult?'

332

'You should talk to him, Aunty. If that is how he feels, then that is how he feels.'

'I think he wrote that because that is the kind of thing they teach them here. Everybody is conflicted, identity this, identity that. Somebody will commit murder and say it is because his mother did not hug him when he was three years old. Or they will do something wicked and say it is a disease that they are struggling with.' Aunty Uju looked out of the window. Curt and Dike were dribbling a basketball in the backyard, and farther away was the beginning of thick woods. On Ifemelu's last visit, she had woken up to see, through the kitchen window, a pair of gracefully galloping deer.

'I am tired,' Aunty Uju said in a low voice.

'What do you mean?' Ifemelu knew, though, that it would only be more complaints about Bartholomew.

'Both of us work. Both of us come home at the same time and do you know what Bartholomew does? He just sits in the living room and turns on the TV and asks me what we are eating for dinner.' Aunty Uju scowled and Ifemelu noticed how much weight she had put on, the beginning of a double chin, the new flare of her nose. 'He wants me to give him my salary. Imagine! He said that it is how marriages are since he is the head of the family, that I should not send money home to Brother without his permission, that we should make his car payments from my salary. I want to look at private schools for Dike, with all this nonsense happening in that public school, but Bartholomew said it is too expensive. Too expensive! Meanwhile, his children went to private schools in California. He is not even bothered with all the rubbish going on in Dike's school. The other day I went there, and a teacher's assistant shouted at me across the hall. Imagine. She was so rude. I noticed she did not shout across the hall to the other parents. So I went over and told her off. These people, they make you become aggressive just to hold your dignity.' Aunty Uju shook her head. 'Bartholomew is not even bothered that Dike still calls him Uncle. I told him to encourage Dike to call him Dad but it doesn't bother him. All he wants is for me to hand over my salary to him and cook peppered gizzard for him on Saturdays while he watches European League on satellite. Why should I give him my salary? Did he pay my fees in medical school? He wants to start a business but they won't give him a loan and he says he will sue them for discrimination because his credit is not bad and he found out a man who goes to our church got a loan with much worse credit. Is it my fault that he cannot get the loan? Did anybody force him to come here? Did he not know we would be the only black people here? Did he not come here because he felt it would benefit him? Everything is money, money, money. He keeps wanting to make my work decisions for me. What does an accountant know about medicine? I just want to be comfortable. I just want to be able to pay for my child's college. I don't need to work longer hours just to accumulate money. It's not as if I am planning to buy a boat like Americans.' Aunty Uju moved away from the window and sat down at the kitchen table. 'I don't even know why I came to this place. The other day the pharmacist said my accent was incomprehensible. Imagine, I called in a medicine and she actually told me that my accent was incomprehensible. And that same day, as if somebody sent them, one patient, a useless layabout with tattoos all over his body, told me to go back to where I came from. All because I knew he was lying about being in pain and I refused to give him more pain medicine. Why do I have to take this rubbish? I blame Buhari and Babangida and Abacha, because they destroyed Nigeria.'

It was strange, how Aunty Uju often spoke about the former heads of state, invoking their names with poisoned blame, but never mentioning The General.

Curt and Dike came back into the kitchen. Dike was bright-eyed, slightly sweaty and talkative; he had, out there in the basketball space, swallowed Curt's star.

'Do you want some water, Curt?' he asked.

'Call him Uncle Curt,' Aunty Uju said.

Curt laughed. 'Or Cousin Curt. How about Coz Curt?'

'You're not my cousin,' Dike said, smiling.

335

'I would be if I married your cousin.'

'Depends on how much you are offering us!' Dike said.

They all laughed. Aunty Uju looked pleased.

'Do you want to get that drink and meet me outside, Dike?' Curt asked. 'We've got some unfinished business!'

Curt touched Ifemelu's shoulder gently, asked if she was okay, before going back outside.

'*O na-eji gi ka akwa,*' Aunty Uju said, her tone charged with admiration.

Ifemelu smiled. Curt did indeed hold her like an egg. With him, she felt breakable, precious. Later, as they left, she slipped her hand into his and squeezed; she felt proud – to be with him, and of him.

One morning, Aunty Uju woke up and went to the bathroom. Bartholomew had just brushed his teeth. Aunty Uju reached for her toothbrush and saw, inside the sink, a thick blob of toothpaste. Thick enough for a full mouth-cleaning. It sat there, far from the drain, soft and melting. It disgusted her. How exactly did a person clean their teeth and end up leaving so much toothpaste in the sink? Had he not seen it? Had he, when it fell into the sink, pressed more onto his toothbrush? Or did he just go ahead and brush anyway with an almost-dry brush? Which meant his teeth were not clean. But his teeth did not concern Aunty Uju. The blob of toothpaste left in the sink did.

On so many other mornings, she had cleaned off toothpaste, rinsed out the sink. But not this morning. This morning, she was done. She shouted his name, again and again. He asked her what was wrong. She told him the toothpaste in the sink was wrong. He looked at her and mumbled that he had been in a hurry, he was already late for work, and she told him that she, too, had work to go to, and she earned more than he did, in case he had forgotten. She was paying for his car, after all. He stormed off and went downstairs. At this point in the story, Aunty Uju paused, and Ifemelu imagined Bartholomew in his contrast-collar shirt and his trousers pulled too high up, the unflattering pleats at the front, his K-leg walk as he stormed off. Aunty Uju's voice was unusually calm over the phone.

'I've found a condo in a town called Willow. A very nice gated place near the university. Dike and I are leaving this weekend,' Aunty Uju said.

'Ahn-ahn! Aunty, so quickly?'

'I've tried. It is enough.'

'What did Dike say?'

'He said he never liked living in the woods. He didn't even say one word about Bartholomew. Willow will be so much better for him.'

Ifemelu liked the name of the town, Willow; it sounded to her like freshly squeezed beginnings.

To My Fellow Non-American Blacks: In America, You Are Black, Baby

337

Dear Non-American Black, when you make the choice to come to America, you become black. Stop arguing. Stop saying I'm Jamaican or I'm Ghanaian. America doesn't care. So what if you weren't 'black' in your country? You're in America now. We all have our moments of initiation into the Society of Former Negroes. Mine was in a class in undergrad when I was asked to give the black perspective, only I had no idea what that was. So I just made something up. And admit it – you say 'I'm not black' only because you know black is at the bottom of America's race ladder. And you want none of that. Don't deny now. What if being black had all the privileges of being white? Would you still say 'Don't call me black, I'm from Trinidad'? I didn't think so. So you're black, baby. And here's the deal with becoming black: You must show that you are offended when such words as 'watermelon' or 'tar baby' are used in jokes, even if you don't know what the hell is being talked about – and since you are a Non-American Black, the chances are that you won't know. (In undergrad a white classmate asks if I like watermelon, I say yes, and another classmate says, Oh my God that is so racist, and I'm confused. 'Wait, how?') You must nod back when a black person nods at you in a heavily white area. It is called the black nod. It is a way for black people to say 'You are not alone, I am here too.' In describing black women you admire, always use the word 'STRONG' because that is what black women are supposed to be in America. If you are a woman, please do not speak your mind as you are used to doing in your country. Because in America, strong-minded black women are SCARY. And if you are a man, be hyper-mellow, never get too excited, or somebody will worry that you're about to pull a gun. When you watch television and hear that a 'racist slur' was used, you must immediately become offended. Even though you are thinking 'But why won't they tell me exactly what was said?' Even though you would like to be able to decide for yourself how offended to be, or whether to be offended at all, you must nevertheless be very offended.

When a crime is reported, pray that it was not committed by a black person, and if it turns out to have been committed by a black person, stay well away from the crime area for weeks, or you might be stopped for fitting the profile. If a black cashier gives poor service to the non-black person in front of you, compliment that person's shoes or something, to make up for the bad service, because you're just as guilty for the cashier's crimes. If you are in an Ivy League college, and a Young Republican tells you that you got in only because of Affirmative Action, do not whip out your perfect grades from high school. Instead, gently point out that the biggest beneficiaries of Affirmative Action are white women. If you go to eat in a restaurant, please tip generously. Otherwise the next black person who comes in will get awful service, because waiters groan when they get a black table. You see, black people have a gene that makes them not tip, so please overpower that gene. If you're telling a non-black person about something racist that happened to you, make sure you are not bitter. Don't complain. Be forgiving. If possible, make it funny. Most of all, do not be angry. Black people are not supposed to be angry about racism. Otherwise you get no sympathy. This applies only for white liberals, by the way. Don't even bother telling a white conservative about anything racist that happened to you. Because the conservative will tell you that YOU are the real racist and your mouth will hang open in confusion.

CHAPTER 22

One Saturday at the mall in White Marsh, Ifemelu saw Kayode DaSilva. It was raining. She was standing inside, by the entrance, waiting for Curt to bring the car around, and Kayode almost bumped into her.

'Ifemsco!' he said.

'Oh my God. Kayode!'

They hugged, looked at each other, said all the things people said who had not seen each other in many years, both lapsing into their Nigerian voices and their Nigerian selves, louder, more heightened, adding 'o' to their sentences. He had left right after secondary school to attend university in Indiana and had graduated years ago.

'I was working in Pittsburgh but I just moved to Silver Spring to start a new job. I love Maryland. I run into Nigerians at the grocery store and in the mall, everywhere. It's like being back home. But I guess you know that already.'

'Yes,' she said, even though she did not. Her Maryland was a small, circumscribed world of Curt's American friends.

'I was planning to come and find you, by the

way.' He was looking at her, as though absorbing her details, memorizing her, for when he would tell the story of their meeting.

'Really?'

'So my guy The Zed and I were talking the other day and you came up and he said he'd heard you were living in Baltimore and since I was close by could I just find you and see that you were okay and tell him what you look like now.'

A numbness spread swiftly through her. She mumbled, 'Oh, you're still in touch?'

'Yes. We got back in touch when he moved to England last year.'

England! Obinze was in England. She had created the distance, ignoring him, changing her e-mail address and phone number, and yet she felt deeply betrayed by this news. Changes had been made in his life that she did not know about. He was in England. Only a few months ago, she and Curt had gone to England for the Glastonbury Festival, and later spent two days in London. Obinze might have been there. She might have run into him as she walked down Oxford Street.

'So what happened now? Honestly, I couldn't believe it when he said you guys were not in touch. Ahn-ahn! All of us were just waiting for the wedding invitation card o!' Kayode said.

Ifemelu shrugged. There were things scattered inside of her that she needed to gather together.

'So how have you been? How is life?' Kayode asked.

'Fine,' she said coldly. 'I'm waiting for my boyfriend to pick me up. Actually, I think that's him.'

There was, in Kayode's demeanour, a withdrawal of spirit, a pulling back of his army of warmth, because he sensed very well that she had made the choice to shut him out. She was already walking away. Over her shoulder, she said to him, 'Take care.' She was supposed to exchange phone numbers, talk for longer, behave in all the expected ways. But emotions were rioting inside her. And she found Kayode guilty for knowing about Obinze, for bringing Obinze back.

'I just ran into an old friend from Nigeria. I haven't seen him since high school,' she told Curt.

'Oh, really? That's nice. He live here?'

'In DC.'

Curt was watching her, expecting more. He would want to ask Kayode to have drinks with them, want to be friends with her friend, want to be as gracious as he always was. And this, his expectant expression, irritated her. She wanted silence. Even the radio was bothering her. What would Kayode tell Obinze? That she was dating a handsome white man in a BMW coupé, her hair an Afro, a red flower tucked behind her ear. What would Obinze make of this? What was he doing in England? A clear memory came to her, of a sunny day – the sun was always shining in her memories of him and she distrusted this – when his friend Okwudiba brought a video cassette to

343

his house, and Obinze said, 'A British film? Waste of time.' To him, only American films were worth watching. And now he was in England.

Curt was looking at her. 'Seeing him upset you?'

'No.'

'Was he like a boyfriend or something?'

'No,' she said, looking out of the window.

Later that day she would send an e-mail to Obinze's Hotmail address: *Ceiling, I don't even know how to start. I ran into Kayode today at the mall. Saying sorry for my silence sounds stupid even to me but I am so sorry and I feel so stupid. I will tell you everything that happened. I have missed you and I miss you.* And he would not reply.

'I booked the Swedish massage for you,' Curt said.

'Thank you,' she said. Then, in a lower voice, she added, to make up for her peevishness, 'You are such a sweetheart.'

'I don't want to be a sweetheart. I want to be the fucking love of your life,' Curt said with a force that startled her.

PART III

CHAPTER 23

In London, night came too soon, it hung in the morning air like a threat, and then in the afternoon a blue-grey dusk descended, and the Victorian buildings all wore a mournful air. In those first weeks, the cold startled Obinze with its weightless menace, drying his nostrils, deepening his anxieties, making him urinate too often. He would walk fast on the pavement, turned tightly into himself, hands deep in the coat his cousin had lent him, a grey wool coat whose sleeves nearly swallowed his fingers. Sometimes he would stop outside a tube station, often by a flower or a newspaper vendor, and watch the people brushing past him. They walked so quickly, these people, as though they had an urgent destination, a purpose to their lives, while he did not. His eyes would follow them, with a lost longing, and he would think: *You can work, you are legal, you are visible, and you don't even know how fortunate you are.*

It was at a tube station that he met the Angolans who would arrange his marriage, exactly two years and three days after he arrived in England; he kept count.

347

'We'll talk in the car,' one of them had said earlier over the phone. Their old-model black Mercedes was fussily maintained, the floor mats wavy from vacuuming, the leather seats shiny with polish. The two men looked alike, with thick eyebrows that almost touched, although they had told him they were just friends, and they were dressed alike, too, in leather jackets and long gold chains. Their tabletop haircuts that sat on their heads like tall hats surprised him, but perhaps it was part of their hip image, to have retro haircuts. They spoke to him with the authority of people who had done this before, and also with a slight condescension; his fate was, after all, in their hands.

'We decided on Newcastle because we know people there and London is too hot right now, too many marriages happening in London, yeah, so we don't want trouble,' one of them said. 'Everything is going to work out. Just make sure you keep a low profile, yeah? Don't attract any attention to yourself until the marriage is done. Don't fight in the pub, yeah?'

'I've never been a very good fighter,' Obinze said drily, but the Angolans did not smile.

'You have the money?' the other one asked.

Obinze handed over two hundred pounds, all in twenty-pound notes that he had taken out of the cash machine over two days. It was a deposit, to prove he was serious. Later, after he met the girl, he would pay two thousand pounds.

'The rest has to be up front, yeah? We'll use

some of it to do the running around and the rest goes to the girl. Man, you know we're not making anything from this. We usually ask for much more but we're doing this for Iloba,' the first one said.

Obinze did not believe them, even then. He met the girl, Cleotilde, a few days later, at a shopping centre, in a McDonald's whose windows looked out onto the dank entrance of a tube station across the street. He sat at a table with the Angolans, watching people hurry past, and wondering which of them was her, while the Angolans both whispered into their phones; perhaps they were arranging other marriages.

'Hello there!' she said.

She surprised him. He had expected somebody with pockmarks smothered under heavy make-up, somebody tough and knowing. But here she was, dewy and fresh, bespectacled, olive-skinned, almost childlike, smiling shyly at him and sucking a milkshake through a straw. She looked like a university freshman who was innocent or dumb, or both.

'I just wanted to know that you're sure about doing this,' he told her, and then, worried that he might frighten her away, he added, 'I'm very grateful and it won't take too much from you – in a year I'll have my papers and we'll do the divorce. But I just wanted to meet you first and make sure you are okay to do this.'

'Yes,' she said.

He watched her, expecting more. She played with her straw, shyly, not meeting his eyes, and it

349

took him a while to realize that she was reacting more to him than to the situation. She was attracted to him.

'I want to help my mum out. Things are tight at home,' she said, a trace of a non-British accent underlining her words.

'She's with us, yeah,' one of the Angolans said, impatiently, as though Obinze had dared to question what they had already told him.

'Show him your details, Cleo,' the other Angolan said.

His calling her Cleo rang false: Obinze sensed this from the way he said it, and from the way she heard it, the slight surprise on her face. It was a forced intimacy; the Angolan had never called her Cleo before. Perhaps he had never even called her anything before. Obinze wondered how the Angolans knew her. Did they have a list of young women with European Union passports who needed money? Cleotilde pushed at her hair, a mass of tight coils, and adjusted her glasses, as though first preparing herself before she presented her passport and licence. Obinze examined them. He would have thought her younger than twenty-three.

'Can I have your number?' Obinze asked.

'Just call us for anything,' the Angolans said, almost at the same time. But Obinze wrote his number on a napkin and pushed it across to her. The Angolans gave him a sly look. Later, on the phone, she told him that she had been living in

350

London for six years and was saving money to go to fashion school, even though the Angolans had told him she lived in Portugal.

'Would you like to meet?' he asked. 'It will be much easier if we try to get to know each other a little.'

'Yes,' she said without hesitation.

They ate fish and chips in a pub, a thin crust of grime on the sides of the wood table, while she talked about her love of fashion and asked him about Nigerian traditional dress. She seemed a little more mature; he noticed the shimmer on her cheeks, the more defined curl of her hair, and knew she had made an effort with her appearance.

'What will you do after you get your papers?' she asked him. 'Will you bring your girlfriend from Nigeria?'

He was touched by her obviousness. 'I don't have a girlfriend.'

'I've never been to Africa. I'd love to go.' She said 'Africa' wistfully, like an admiring foreigner, loading the word with exotic excitement. Her black Angolan father had left her white Portuguese mother when she was only three years old, she told him, and she had not seen him since, nor had she ever been to Angola. She said this with a shrug and a cynical raise of her eyebrows, as though it had never bothered her, an effort so out of character, so jarring, that it showed him just how deeply it did bother her. There were difficulties in her life that he wanted to know more about, parts of her thick shapely body that he longed to touch, but he was wary of complicating things. He would wait until after the marriage, until the business side of their relationship was finished. She seemed to understand this without their talking about it. And so as they met and talked in the following weeks, sometimes practising how they would answer questions during their immigration interview and other times just talking about football, there was, between them, the growing urgency of restrained desire. It was there in their standing close to each other, not touching, as they waited at the tube station, in their teasing each other about his support of Arsenal and her support of Manchester United, in their lingering gazes. After he had paid the Angolans two thousand pounds in cash, she told him that they had given her only five hundred pounds.

'I'm just telling you. I know you don't have any more money. I want to do this for you,' she said.

She was looking at him, her eyes liquid with things unsaid, and she made him feel whole again, made him remember how starved he was for something simple and pure. He wanted to kiss her, her upper lip pinker and shinier with lip gloss than the lower, to hold her, to tell her how deeply, irrepressibly grateful he was. She would never stir his cauldron of worries, never wave her power in his face. One Eastern European woman, Iloba had told him, had asked the Nigerian man, an hour before their court wedding, to give her a thousand pounds extra or she would walk away. In panic, the man had begun to call all his friends, to raise the money.

'Man, we gave you a good deal' was all one of the Angolans said when Obinze asked how much they had given Cleotilde, in that tone of theirs, the tone of people who knew how much they were needed. It was they, after all, who took him to a lawyer's office, a low-voiced Nigerian in a swivel chair, sliding backwards to reach a filing cabinet as he said, 'You can still get married even though your visa is expired. In fact, getting married is now your only choice.' It was they who provided water and gas bills, going back six months, with his name and a Newcastle address, they who found a man who would 'sort out' his driving licence, a man cryptically called Brown. Obinze met Brown at the train station in Barking; he stood near the gate as agreed, amid the bustle of people, looking around and waiting for his phone to ring because Brown had refused to give him a phone number.

'Are you waiting for somebody?' Brown stood there, a slight man, his winter hat pulled down to his eyebrows.

'Yes. I'm Obinze,' he said, feeling like a character in a spy novel who had to speak in silly code. Brown led him to a quiet corner, handed over an envelope, and there it was, his licence, with his photo and the genuine, slightly worn look of something owned for a year. A slight plastic card, but it weighed down his pocket. A few days later, he walked with it into a London building which, from the outside, looked like a church, steepled and grave, but inside was shabby, harried, knotted with people. Signs were scrawled on whiteboards: BIRTHS AND DEATHS THIS WAY. MARRIAGE REGISTRATION THIS WAY. Obinze, his expression carefully frozen in neutrality, handed the licence over to the registrar behind the desk.

A woman was walking towards the door, talking loudly to her companion. 'Look how crowded this place is. It's all sham marriages, all of them, now that Blunkett is after them.'

Perhaps she had come to register a death, and her words merely the lonely lashings-out of grief, but he felt the familiar tightening of panic in his chest. The registrar was examining his licence, taking too long. The seconds lengthened and curdled. *All sham marriages, all of them* rang in Obinze's head. Finally the registrar looked up and pushed across a form.

'Getting married, are we? Congratulations!' The words came out with the mechanical good cheer of frequent repetition.

'Thank you,' Obinze said, and tried to unfreeze his face.

Behind the desk, a whiteboard was propped on a wall, venues and dates of intended marriages written on it in blue; a name at the bottom caught his eye. *Okoli Okafor and Crystal Smith*. Okoli Okafor was his classmate from secondary school and university, a quiet boy who had been teased for having a surname for a first name, who later joined a vicious cult in university, and then left Nigeria during one of the long strikes. Now here he was, a ghost of a name, about to get married in England. Perhaps it was also a marriage for papers. Okoli Okafor. Everyone called him Okoli Paparazzi in university. On the day Princess Diana died, a group of students had gathered before a lecture, talking about what they had heard on the radio that morning, repeating 'paparazzi' over and over, all sounding knowing and cocksure, until, in a lull, Okoli Okafor quietly asked, 'But who exactly are the paparazzi? Are they motorcyclists?' and instantly earned himself the nickname Okoli Paparazzi.

The memory, clear as a light beam, took Obinze back to a time when he still believed the universe would bend according to his will. Melancholy descended on him as he left the building. Once, during his final year in the university, the year that people danced in the streets because General Abacha had died, his mother had said, 'One day, I will look up and all the people I know will be dead or abroad.' She had spoken wearily, as they sat in the living room, eating boiled corn and ube. He sensed, in her voice, the sadness of defeat, as though her friends who were leaving for teaching positions in Canada and America had confirmed to her a great personal failure. For a moment he felt as if he, too, had betrayed her by having his own plan: to get a postgraduate degree in America, to work in America, to live in America. It was a plan he had had for a long time. Of course he knew how unreasonable the American embassy could be – the vice chancellor, of all people, had once been refused a visa to attend a conference – but he had never doubted his plan. He would wonder, later, why he had been so sure. Perhaps it was because he had never simply wanted to go *abroad*, as many others did; some people were now going to South Africa, which amused him. It had always been America, only America. A longing nurtured and nursed over many years. The advertisement on NTA for *Andrew Checking Out*, which he had watched as a child, had given shape to his longings. 'Men, I'm checkin' out,' the character Andrew had said, staring cockily at the camera. 'No good roads, no light, no water. Men, you can't even get a bottle of soft drink!' While Andrew was checking out, General Buhari's soldiers were flogging adults in the streets, lecturers were striking for better pay, and his mother had decided that he could no longer have Fanta whenever he wanted but only on Sundays, with permission. And so, America became a place where bottles and bottles of Fanta were to be had, without permission. He would stand in front of the mirror and repeat Andrew's words: 'Men, I'm checkin' out!' Later, seeking out magazines and books and films and second-hand stories about America, his longing took on a minor mystical quality and America became where he was destined to be. He saw himself walking the streets of Harlem, discussing the merits of Mark Twain with his American friends, gazing at Mount Rushmore. Days after he graduated from university, bloated with knowledge about America, he applied for a visa at the American embassy in Lagos.

He already knew that the best interviewer was the blond-bearded man, and as he moved in the line, he hoped he would not be interviewed by the horror story, a pretty white woman famous for screaming into her microphone and insulting even grandmothers. Finally, it was his turn and the blond-bearded man said, 'Next person!' Obinze walked up and slid his forms underneath the glass. The man glanced at the forms and said, kindly, 'Sorry, you don't qualify. Next person!' Obinze was stunned. He went three more times over the next few months. Each time he was told, without a glance at his documents, 'Sorry, you don't qualify,' and each time he emerged from the air-conditioned cool of the embassy building and into the harsh sunlight, stunned and unbelieving.

'It's the terrorism fears,' his mother said. 'The Americans are now averse to foreign young men.'

She told him to find a job and try again in a year. His job applications yielded nothing. He travelled to Lagos and to Port Harcourt and to Abuja to take assessment tests, which he found easy, and he attended interviews, answering questions fluidly, but then a long empty silence would follow. Some friends were getting jobs, people who did not have his second-class upper degree and did not speak as well as he did. He wondered whether employers could smell his America-pining on his breath, or sense how obsessively he still looked at the websites of American universities. He was living with his mother, driving her car, sleeping with impressionable young students, browsing overnight at Internet cafés with all-night specials, and sometimes spending days in his room reading and avoiding his mother. He disliked her calm good cheer, how hard she tried to be positive, telling him that now President Obasanjo was in power, things were changing, the mobile phone companies and banks were growing and recruiting, even giving young people car loans. Most of the time, though, she left him alone. She did not knock on his door. She simply asked the house help, Agnes, to leave some food in the pot for him and to clear away dirty plates from his room. One day, she left him a note on the bathroom sink: *I have been invited to an academic conference in London. We should speak.* He was puzzled. When she came home from her lecture, he was in the living room waiting for her.

'Mummy, *nno*,' he said.

She acknowledged his greeting with a nod and put down her bag on the centre table. 'I'm going to put your name on my British visa application as my research assistant,' she said quietly. 'That should get you a six-month visa. You can stay with

Nicholas in London. See what you can do with your life. Maybe you can get to America from there. I know that your mind is no longer here.'

He stared at her.

'I understand this sort of thing is done nowadays,' she said, sitting down on the sofa beside him, trying to sound offhand, but he sensed her discomfort in the uncommon briskness of her words. She was from the generation of the bewildered, who did not understand what had happened to Nigeria but allowed themselves to be swept along. She was a woman who kept to herself and asked no favours, who would not lie, who would not accept even a Christmas card from her students because it might compromise her, who accounted for every single kobo spent on any committee she was on, and here she was, behaving as though truth-telling had become a luxury that they could no longer afford. It went against everything she had taught him, yet he knew that truth had indeed, in their circumstance, become a luxury. She lied for him. If anybody else had lied for him, it would not have mattered as much or even at all, but she lied for him and he got the six-month visa to the United Kingdom and he felt, even before he left, like a failure. He did not contact her for months. He did not contact her because there was nothing to tell her and he wanted to wait until he had something to tell her. He was in England for three years and spoke to her only a few times, strained conversations during which he imagined she was wondering why he had made nothing of himself. But she never asked for details; she only waited to hear what he was willing to tell. Later, when he returned home, he would feel disgusted with his own entitlement, his blindness to her, and he spent a lot of time with her, determined to make amends, to return to their former relationship, but first to attempt to map the boundaries of their estrangement.

CHAPTER 24

Everyone joked about people who went abroad to clean toilets, and so Obinze approached his first job with irony: he was indeed abroad cleaning toilets, wearing rubber gloves and carrying a pail, in an estate agent's office on the second floor of a London building. Each time he opened the swinging door of a stall, it seemed to sigh. The beautiful woman who cleaned the ladies' toilet was Ghanaian, about his age, with the shiniest dark skin he had ever seen. He sensed, in the way she spoke and carried herself, a background similar to his, a childhood cushioned by family, by regular meals, by dreams in which there was no conception of cleaning toilets in London. She ignored his friendly gestures, saying only 'Good evening' as formally as she could, but she was friendly with the white woman who cleaned the offices upstairs, and once he saw them in the deserted café, drinking tea and talking in low tones. He stood watching them for a while, a great grievance exploding in his mind. It was not that she did not want friendship, it was rather that she did not want his. Perhaps friendship in their present circumstances was impossible because she was Ghanaian and he, a Nigerian, was too close to what she was; he knew her nuances, while she was free to reinvent herself with the Polish woman, to be whoever she wanted to be.

The toilets were not bad, some urine outside the urinal, some unfinished flushing; cleaning them was much easier than it must have been for the cleaners of the campus toilets back in Nsukka, with the streaks of shit smeared on the walls that had always made him wonder why anybody would go to all that trouble. And so he was shocked, one evening, to walk into a stall and discover a mound of shit on the toilet lid, solid, tapering, centred as though it had been carefully arranged and the exact spot had been measured. It looked like a puppy curled on a mat. It was a performance. He thought about the famed repression of the English. His cousin's wife, Ojiugo, had once said, 'English people will live next to you for years but they will never greet you. It is as if they have buttoned themselves up.' There was, in this performance, something of an unbuttoning. A person who had been fired? Denied a promotion? Obinze stared at that mound of shit for a long time, feeling smaller and smaller as he did so, until it became a personal affront, a punch on his jaw. And all for three quid an hour. He took off his gloves, placed them next to the mound of shit and left the building. That evening, he received an e-mail from Ifemelu. *Ceiling, I don't even know how to start. I ran into*

Kayode today at the mall. Saying sorry for my silence sounds stupid even to me but I am so sorry and I feel so stupid. I will tell you everything that happened. I have missed you and I miss you.

He stared at the e-mail. This was what he had longed for, for so long. To hear from her. When she first stopped contacting him, he had worried himself into weeks of insomnia, roaming the house in the middle of the night, wondering what had happened to her. They had not fought, their love was as sparkling as always, their plan intact, and suddenly there was silence from her, a silence so brutal and complete. He had called and called until she changed her phone number, he had sent e-mails, he had contacted her mother, Aunty Uju, Ginika. Ginika's tone, when she said, 'Ifem needs some time, I think she has depression,' had felt like ice pressed against his body. Ifemelu was not crippled or blinded from an accident, not suddenly suffering amnesia. She was in touch with Ginika and other people but not with him. She did not *want* to keep in touch with *him*. He wrote her e-mails, asking that she at least tell him why, what had happened. Soon, his e-mails bounced back, undeliverable; she had closed the account. He missed her, a longing that tore deep into him. He resented her. He wondered endlessly what might have happened. He changed, curled more inwardly into himself. He was, by turns, inflamed by anger, twisted by confusion, withered by sadness.

And now here was her e-mail. Her tone the same,

as though she had not wounded him, left him bleeding for more than five years. Why was she writing to him now? What was there to tell her, that he cleaned toilets and had only just today encountered a curled turd? How did she know he was still alive? He could have died during their silence and she would not have known. An angry sense of betrayal overwhelmed him. He clicked Delete and Empty Trash.

His cousin Nicholas had the jowly face of a bulldog, yet still somehow managed to be very attractive, or perhaps it was not his features but his aura that appealed, the tall, broad-shouldered, striding masculinity of him. In Nsukka, he had been the most popular student on campus; his beat-up Volkswagen Beetle parked outside a beer parlour lent the drinkers there an immediate cachet. Two Big Chicks once famously fought over him in Bello Hostel, tearing each other's blouses, but he remained roguishly unattached until he met Ojiugo. She was Obinze's mother's favourite student, the only one good enough to be a research assistant, and had stopped by their house one Sunday to discuss a book. Nicholas had stopped by, too, on his weekly ritual, to eat Sunday rice. Ojiugo wore orange lipstick and ripped jeans, spoke bluntly, and smoked in public, provoking vicious gossip and dislike from other girls, not because she did these things but because she dared to without having lived abroad, or having a foreign parent, those qualities that would have made them forgive her lack of conformity. Obinze remembered how dismissive she first was of Nicholas, ignoring him while he, unused to a girl's indifference, talked more and more loudly. But in the end, they left together in his Volkswagen. They would speed around campus in that Volkswagen, Ojiugo driving and Nicholas's arm hanging from the front window, music blaring, bends taken sharply, and once with a friend lodged in the open front boot. They smoked and drank publicly together. They created glamorous myths. Once they were seen at a beer parlour, Ojiugo wearing Nicholas's large white shirt and nothing below, and Nicholas wearing a pair of jeans and nothing above. 'Things are hard, so we are sharing one outfit,' they said nonchalantly to friends.

That Nicholas had lost his youthful outrageousness did not surprise Obinze; what surprised him was the loss of even the smallest memory of it. Nicholas, husband and father, homeowner in England, spoke with a soberness so forbidding that it was almost comical. 'If you come to England with a visa that does not allow you to work,' Nicholas told him, 'the first thing to look for is not food or water, it is an NI number so you can work. Take all the jobs you can. Spend nothing. Marry an EU citizen and get your papers. Then your life can begin.' Nicholas seemed to feel that he had done his part, delivered words of wisdom, and in the following months, he hardly spoke to

Obinze at all. It was as if he was no longer the big cousin who had offered Obinze, at fifteen, a cigarette to try, who had drawn diagrams on a piece of paper to show Obinze what to do when his fingers were between a girl's legs. On weekends Nicholas walked around the house in a tense cloud of silence, nursing his worries. Only during Arsenal matches did he relax a little, a can of Stella Artois in hand, shouting 'Go, Arsenal!' with Ojiugo and their children, Nna and Nne. After the game, his face would congeal once again. He would come home from work, hug his children and Ojiugo, and ask, 'How are you? What did you people do today?' Ojiugo would list what they had done. Cello. Piano. Violin. Homework. Kumon. 'Nne is really improving her sight-reading,' she would add. Or 'Nna was careless with his Kumon and he got two wrong.' Nicholas would praise or reprimand each child, Nna who had a chubby bulldog-like face and Nne who had her mother's dark broad-faced beauty. He spoke to them only in English, careful English, as though he thought that the Igbo he shared with their mother would infect them, perhaps make them lose their precious British accents. Then he would say, 'Ojiugo, well done. I'm hungry.'

'Yes, Nicholas.'

She would serve his food, a plate on a tray taken to him in his study or in front of the TV in the kitchen. Obinze sometimes wondered if she bowed while putting it down or whether the bowing was merely in her demeanour, in the slump of her shoulders and curve of her neck. Nicholas spoke to her in the same tone as he spoke to his children. Once Obinze heard him say to her, 'You people have scattered my study. Now please leave my study, all of you.'

'Yes, Nicholas,' she said, and took the children out. 'Yes, Nicholas' was her response to almost everything he said. Sometimes, from behind Nicholas, she would catch Obinze's eye and make a funny face, inflating her cheeks into small balloons, or pushing her tongue out of the corner of her mouth. It reminded Obinze of the gaudy theatrics of Nollywood films.

'I keep thinking of how you and Nicholas were in Nsukka,' Obinze said one afternoon as he helped her cut up a chicken.

'Ahn-ahn! Do you know we used to fuck in public? We did it at the Arts Theatre. Even in the engineering building one afternoon, in a quiet corner of the corridor!' She laughed. 'Marriage changes things. But this country is not easy. I got my papers because I did postgraduate school here, but you know he only got his papers two years ago and so for so long he was living in fear, working under other people's names. That thing can do wonders to your head, *eziokwu*. It has not been easy at all for him. This job he has now is very good but he's on contract. He never knows if they will renew. He got a good offer in Ireland, you know Ireland is seriously booming now and computer programmers do well there, but he doesn't want us to move there. Education for the kids is much better here.'

Obinze selected some spice bottles from the cupboard, sprinkled them on the chicken and put the pot on the stove.

'You put nutmeg in chicken?' Ojiugo asked.

'Yes,' Obinze said. 'Don't you?'

'Me, what do I know? Whoever marries you will win a lottery, honestly. By the way, what did you say happened to you and Ifemelu? I so liked her.'

'She went to America and her eyes opened and she forgot me.'

Ojiugo laughed.

The phone rang. Because Obinze was all the time willing a call from his job agency, each time the phone did ring, a mild panic would seize his chest, and Ojiugo would say, 'Don't worry, The Zed, things will work out for you. Look at my friend Bose. Do you know she applied for asylum, was denied and went through hell before she finally got her papers? Now she owns two nurseries and has a holiday home in Spain. It will happen for you, don't worry, *rapuba*.' There was a certain vapidity to her reassurance, an automatic way of expressing goodwill, which did not require any concrete efforts on her part to help him. Sometimes he wondered, not resentfully, whether she truly wanted him to find a job, because he would no longer be able to watch the children while she popped out to Tesco to buy milk, no longer be able to make their breakfast while she supervised their practice before school, Nne on the piano or violin and Nna on the cello. There was something about those days that Obinze would come to miss, buttering toast in the weak light of morning while the sounds of music floated through the house, and sometimes, too, Ojiugo's voice, raised in praise or impatience, saying, 'Well done! Try once more!' or 'What rubbish are you doing?'

Later that afternoon, after Ojiugo brought the children home from school, she told Nna, 'Your Uncle Obinze cooked the chicken.'

'Thank you for helping Mummy, Uncle, but I don't think I'll be having any chicken.' He had his mother's playful manner.

'Look at this boy,' Ojiugo said. 'Your uncle is a better cook than I am.'

Nna rolled his eyes. 'Okay, Mummy, if you say so. Can I watch TV? Just for ten minutes?'

'Okay, ten minutes.'

It was the half-hour break after their homework and before their French tutor arrived, and Ojiugo was making jam sandwiches, carefully cutting off the crusts. Nna turned on the television, to a music performance by a man wearing many large shiny chains around his neck.

'Mummy, I've been thinking about this,' Nna said. 'I want to be a rapper.'

'You can't be a rapper, Nna.'

'But I want to, Mummy.'

'You are not going to be a rapper, sweetheart.

We did not come to London for you to become a rapper.' She turned to Obinze, stifling laughter. 'You see this boy?'

Nne came into the kitchen, a Capri-Sun in hand. 'Mummy? May I have one please?'

'Yes, Nne,' she said, and, turning to Obinze, repeated her daughter's words in an exaggerated British accent. 'Mummy, may I have one please? You see how she sounds so posh? Ha! My daughter will go places. That is why all our money is going to Brentwood School.' Ojiugo gave Nne a loud kiss on her forehead and Obinze realized, watching her idly straighten a stray braid on Nne's head, that Ojiugo was a wholly contented person. Another kiss on Nne's forehead. 'How are you feeling, Oyinneya?' she asked.

'Fine, Mummy.'

'Tomorrow, remember not to read only the line they ask you to read. Go further, okay?'

'Okay, Mummy.' Nne had the solemn demeanour of a child determined to please the adults in her life.

'You know her violin exam is tomorrow, and she struggles with sight-reading,' Ojiugo said, as though Obinze could possibly have forgotten, as though it were possible to forget when Ojiugo had been talking about it for so long. The past weekend, he had gone with Ojiugo and the children to a birthday party in an echo-filled rented hall, Indian and Nigerian children running around, while Ojiugo whispered to him about some of the children, who was clever at maths but could not spell, who was Nne's biggest rival. She knew the recent test scores of all the clever children. When she could not remember what an Indian child, Nne's close friend, had scored on a recent test, she called Nne to ask her.

'Ahn-ahn, Ojiugo, let her play,' Obinze said.

Now, Ojiugo planted a third loud kiss on Nne's forehead. 'My precious. We still have to get a dress for the party.'

'Yes, Mummy. Something red, no, burgundy.'

'Her friend is having a party, this Russian girl, they became friends because they have the same violin tutor. The first time I met the girl's mother, I think she was wearing something illegal, like the fur of an extinct animal, and she was trying to pretend that she did not have a Russian accent, being more British than the British!'

'She's nice, Mummy,' Nne said.

'I didn't say she wasn't nice, my precious,' Ojiugo said.

Nna had increased the television volume.

'Turn that down, Nna,' Ojiugo said.

'Mummy!'

'Turn down the volume right now!'

'But I can't hear anything, Mummy!'

He didn't turn down the volume and she didn't say anything else to him; instead she turned to Obinze to continue talking.

'Speaking of accents,' Obinze asked. 'Would Nna get away with that if he didn't have a foreign accent?'

'What do you mean?'

'You know last Saturday when Chika and Bose brought their children, I was just thinking that Nigerians here really forgive so much from their children because they have foreign accents. The rules are different.'

'*Mba,* it is not about accents. It is because in Nigeria, people teach their children fear instead of respect. We don't want them to fear us but that does not mean we take rubbish from them. We punish them. The boy knows I will slap him if he does any nonsense. Seriously slap him.'

'The lady doth protest too much, methinks.'

'Oh, but she'll keep her word.' Ojiugo smiled. 'You know I haven't read a book in ages. No time.'

'My mother used to say you would become a leading literary critic.'

'Yes. Before her brother's son got me pregnant.' Ojiugo paused, still smiling. 'Now it is just these children. I want Nna to go to the City of London School. And then by God's grace to Marlborough or Eton. Nne is already an academic star, and I know she'll get scholarships to all the good schools. Everything is about them now.'

'One day they will be grown and leave home and you will just be a source of embarrassment or exasperation for them and they won't take your phone calls or won't call you for weeks,' Obinze said, and as soon as he said it, he wished he had not. It was petty, it had not come out as he intended. But Ojiugo was not offended. She shrugged and said, 'Then I will just carry my bag and go and stand in front of their house.'

It puzzled him that she did not mourn all the things she could have been. Was it a quality inherent in women, or did they just learn to shield their personal regrets, to suspend their lives, subsume themselves in child care? She browsed online forums about tutoring and music and schools, and she told him what she had discovered as though she truly felt the rest of the world should be as interested as she was in how music improved the mathematics skills of nine-year-olds. Or she would spend hours on the phone talking to her friends, about which violin teacher was good and which tutorial was a waste of money.

One day, after she had rushed off to take Nna to his piano lesson, she called Obinze to say, laughing, 'Can you believe I forgot to brush my teeth?' She came home from Weight Watchers meetings to tell him how much she had lost or gained, hiding Twix bars in her handbag and then asking him, with laughter, if he wanted one. Later she joined another weight-loss programme, attended two morning meetings and came home to tell him, 'I'm not going there again. They treat you as if you have a mental problem. I said no, I don't have any internal issues, please, I just like the taste of food, and the smug woman tells me that I have something internal that I am repressing. Rubbish. These white people think that everybody has their mental problems.' She was twice the size she had been in university, and while her clothes back then had never been polished, they had the edge of a calculated style, jeans folded away from her ankles, slouchy blouses pulled off one shoulder. Now, they merely looked sloppy. Her jeans left a mound of pulpy flesh above her waist that disfigured her T-shirts, as though something alien were growing underneath.

Sometimes, her friends visited and they would sit in the kitchen talking until they all dashed off to pick up their children. In those weeks of willing the phone to ring, Obinze came to know their voices well. He could hear clearly from the tiny bedroom upstairs where he lay in bed reading.

'I met this man recently,' Chika said. 'He is nice o, but he is so bush. He grew up in Onitsha and so you can imagine what kind of bush accent he has. He mixes up *ch* and *sh*. I want to go to the chopping centre. Sit down on a sheer.'

They laughed.

'Anyway, he told me he was willing to marry me and adopt Charles. Willing! As if he was doing charity work. Willing! Imagine that. But it's not his fault, it's because we are in London. He is the kind of man I would never even look at in Nigeria, not to talk of going out with. The problem is that water never finds its different levels here in London.'

'London is a leveller. We are now all in London and we are now all the same, what nonsense,' Bose said.

'Maybe he should go and find a Jamaican woman,' Amara said. Her husband had left her for a Jamaican woman, with whom it turned out he had a secret four-year-old child, and she somehow managed to veer every conversation towards the subject of Jamaicans. 'These West Indian women are taking our men and our men are stupid enough to follow them. Next thing, they will have a baby and they don't want the men to marry them o, they just want child support. All they do is spend their money doing their hair and nails.'

'Yes,' Bose, Chika and Ojiugo all agreed. A routine, automatic agreement: Amara's emotional well-being was more important than what they actually believed.

The phone rang. Ojiugo took the call and came back to say, 'This woman who just called, she is a character. Her daughter and Nne belong to the same orchestra. I met her when Nne took her first exam. She came in her Bentley, a black woman, with a driver and everything. She asked me where we lived and when I told her, I just knew what was on her mind: how can somebody in Essex be thinking of the National Children's Orchestra? So I decided to look for trouble and I told her, My daughter goes to Brentwood, and you should have seen her face! You know people like us are not supposed to be talking about private school and music. The most we should want is a good grammar school. I just looked at the woman and I was laughing inside. Then she started telling me that music for children is very expensive. She kept telling me how expensive it is, as if she had seen my empty bank account. Imagine o! She is one of those black people who want to be the only black person in the room, so any other black person is an immediate threat to her. She just called now to tell me that she read online about an eleven-year-old girl who got grade five distinction and did not get into the National Children's Orchestra. Why would she call just to tell me that negative story?'

'Enemy of progress!' Bose said.

'Is she a Jamaican?' Amara asked.

'She is Black British. I don't know where her people came from.'

'It must be Jamaica,' Amara said.

CHAPTER 25

Sharp, the word everyone used to describe Emenike in secondary school. Sharp, full of the poisoned admiration they felt for him. Sharp Guy. Sharp Man. If exam questions leaked, Emenike knew how to get them. He knew, too, which girl had had an abortion, what property the parents of the wealthy students owned, which teachers were sleeping together. He always spoke quickly, pugnaciously, as though every conversation was an argument, the speed and force of his words suggesting authority and discouraging dissent. He knew, and he was full of an eagerness to know. Whenever Kayode returned from a London vacation, flush with relevance, Emenike would ask him about the latest music and films, and then examine his shoes and clothes. 'Is this one designer? What is the name of this one?' Emenike would ask, his eyes feral with longing. He had told everyone that his father was the igwe of his hometown, and had sent him to Lagos to live with an uncle until he turned twenty-one, to avoid the pressures of princely life. But one day, an old man arrived at school, wearing trousers with a mended patch near the knee, his face gaunt, his body bowed with the humility that poverty had forced on him. All the boys laughed after they discovered that he was really Emenike's father. The laughter was soon forgotten, perhaps because nobody had ever fully believed the prince story – Kayode, after all, always called Emenike Bush Boy behind his back. Or perhaps because they needed Emenike, who had information that nobody else did. This, the audacity of him, had drawn Obinze. Emenike was one of the few people for whom 'to read' did not mean 'to study' and so they would spend hours talking about books, bartering knowledge for knowledge and playing Scrabble. Their friendship grew. At university, when Emenike lived with him in the boys' quarters of his mother's house, people had sometimes mistaken him for a relative. 'What of your brother?' people would ask Obinze. And Obinze would say, 'He's fine,' without bothering to explain that he and Emenike were not related at all. But there were many things he did not know about Emenike, things he knew not to ask about. Emenike often left school for weeks, only vaguely saying that he had 'gone home', and he spoke endlessly of people who were 'making it' abroad. His was the coiled, urgent restlessness of a person who believed that fate had mistakenly allotted him a place below his true destiny. When he left for England during a strike in their second year, Obinze never knew how he got a visa. Still, he was pleased for him.

Emenike was ripe, bursting, with his ambition, and Obinze thought of his visa as a mercy: that ambition would finally find a release. It seemed to, quite quickly, as Emenike sent news only of progress: his postgraduate work completed, his job at the housing authority, his marriage to an Englishwoman who was a solicitor in the city.

Emenike was the first person Obinze called after he arrived in England.

'The Zed! Good to hear from you. Let me call you back, I'm just going into a managerial meeting,' Emenike said. The second time Obinze called, Emenike sounded a little harried. 'I'm at Heathrow. Georgina and I are going to Brussels for a week. I'll call you when I get back. I can't wait to catch up, man!' Emenike's e-mail response to Obinze had been similar: *So happy you are coming this way, man, can't wait to see you!* Obinze had imagined, foolishly, that Emenike would take him in, show him the way. He knew of the many stories of friends and relatives who, in the harsh glare of life abroad, became unreliable, even hostile, versions of their former selves. But what was it about the stubbornness of hope, the need to believe in your own exceptionality, that these things happened to other people whose friends were not like yours? He called other friends. Nosa, who had left right after graduation, picked him up at the tube station and drove him to a pub where other friends soon gathered. They shook hands and slapped backs and drank draught beer. They laughed about memories from school. They said little about the details of their present lives. When Obinze said he needed to get a National Insurance number, and asked, 'Guys, how I go take do?' they all shook their heads vaguely.

'Just keep your ear to the ground, man,' Chidi said.

'The thing is to come closer to central London. You're too far away from things, in Essex,' Wale said.

As Nosa drove him back to the station later, Obinze asked, 'So where do you work, guy?'

'Underground. A serious hustle, but things will get better,' Nosa said. Although Obinze knew he meant the tube, the word 'underground' made him think of doomed tunnels that fed into the earth and went on forever, ending nowhere.

'What of Mr Sharp Guy Emenike?' Nosa asked, his tone alive with malice. 'He's doing very well and he lives in Islington, with his oyinbo wife who is old enough to be his mother. He has become posh o. He doesn't talk to ordinary people any more. He can help sort you out.'

'He's been travelling a lot, we haven't yet seen,' Obinze said, hearing too clearly the limpness of his own words.

'How is your cousin Iloba?' Nosa asked. 'I saw him last year at Emeka's brother's wedding.'

Obinze had not even remembered that Iloba now lived in London; he had last seen him days before graduation. Iloba was merely from his mother's hometown, but he had been so enthusiastic about their kinship that everyone on campus assumed they were cousins. Iloba would often pull up a chair, smiling and uninvited, and join Obinze and his friends at a roadside bar, or appear at Obinze's door on Sunday afternoons when Obinze was tired from the languor of Sunday afternoons. Once, Iloba had stopped Obinze at the General Studies quad, cheerfully calling out 'Kinsman!' and then giving him a rundown of marriages and deaths of people from his mother's hometown whom he hardly knew. 'Udoakpuanyi died some weeks ago. Don't you know him? Their homestead is next to your mother's.' Obinze nodded and made appropriate sounds, humouring Iloba, because Iloba's manner was always so pleasant and oblivious, his trousers always too tight and too short, showing his bony ankles; they had earned him the nickname 'Iloba Jump Up', which soon morphed to 'Loba Jay You'.

Obinze got his phone number from Nicholas and called him.

'The Zed! Kinsman! You did not tell me you were coming to London!' Iloba said. 'How is your mother? What of your uncle, the one who married from Abagana? How is Nicholas?' Iloba sounded full of a simple happiness. There were people who were born with an inability to be tangled up in dark emotions, in complications, and Iloba was one of them. For such people, Obinze felt both admiration and boredom. When Obinze asked if

Iloba might be able to help him find a National Insurance number, he would have understood a little resentment, a little churlishness – after all, he was contacting Iloba only because he needed something – but it surprised him how sincerely eager to help Iloba was.

'I would let you use mine but I am working with it and it is risky,' Iloba said.

'Where do you work?'

'In central London. Security. It's not easy, this country is not easy, but we are managing. I like the night shifts because it gives me time to read for my course. I'm doing a master's in management at Birkbeck College.' Iloba paused. 'The Zed, don't worry, we will put our heads together. Let me ask around and let you know.'

Iloba called back two weeks later to say he had found somebody. 'His name is Vincent Obi. He is from Abia State. A friend of mine did the connection. He wants to meet you tomorrow evening.'

They met in Iloba's flat. A claustrophobic feel pervaded the flat, the concrete neighbourhood with no trees, the scarred walls of the building. Everything seemed too small, too tight.

'Nice place, Loba Jay You,' Obinze said, not because the flat was nice but because Iloba had a flat in London.

'I would have told you to come and stay with me, The Zed, but I live with two of my cousins.' Iloba placed bottles of beer and a small plate of fried chin-chin on the table. It seared a sharp homesickness in Obinze, this ritual of hospitality. He was reminded of going back to the village with his mother at Christmas, aunties offering him plates of chin-chin.

Vincent Obi was a small round man submerged in a large pair of jeans and an ungainly coat. As Obinze shook hands with him, they sized each other up. In the set of Vincent's shoulders, in the abrasiveness of his demeanour, Obinze sensed that Vincent had learned very early on, as a matter of necessity, to solve his own problems. Obinze imagined his Nigerian life: a community secondary school full of barefoot children, a polytechnic paid for with help from a number of uncles, a family of many children and a crowd of dependants in his hometown who, whenever he visited, would expect large loaves of bread and pocket money carefully distributed to each of them. Obinze saw himself through Vincent's eyes: a university staff child who grew up eating butter and now needed his help. At first Vincent affected a British accent, saying 'innit' too many times.

'This is business, innit, but I'm helping you. You can use my NI number and pay me forty per cent of what you make,' Vincent said. 'It's business, innit. If I don't get what we agree on, I will report you.'

'My brother,' Obinze said. 'That's a little too much. You know my situation. I don't have anything. Please try and come down.'

'Thirty-five per cent is the best I can do. This is

business.' He had lost his accent and now spoke Nigerian English. 'Let me tell you, there are many people in your situation.'

Iloba spoke up in Igbo. 'Vincent, my brother here is trying to save money and do his papers. Thirty-five is too much, *o rika, biko*. Please just try and help us.'

'You know that some people take half. Yes, he is in a situation but all of us are in a situation. I am helping him but this is business.' Vincent's Igbo had a rural accent. He put the National Insurance card on the table and was already writing his bank account number on a piece of paper. Iloba's mobile phone began to ring. That evening, as dusk fell, the sky muting to a pale violet, Obinze became Vincent.

CHAPTER 26

Obinze-as-Vincent informed his agency, after his experience with the curled shit on the toilet lid, that he would not be returning to that job. He scoured the newspaper job pages, made calls and hoped, until the agency offered him another job, cleaning wide passages in a detergent-packing warehouse. A Brazilian man, sallow and dark-haired, cleaned the building next to his. 'I'm Vincent,' Obinze said, when they met in the back room.

'I'm Dee.' A pause. 'No, you're not English. You can pronounce it. My real name is Duerdinhito, but the English, they cannot pronounce, so they call me Dee.'

'Duerdinhito,' Obinze repeated.

'Yes!' A delighted smile. A small bond of foreignness. They talked, while emptying their vacuum cleaners, about the 1996 Olympics, Obinze gloating about Nigeria beating Brazil and then Argentina.

'Kanu was good, I give him that,' Duerdinhito said. 'But Nigeria had luck.'

Every evening, Obinze was covered in white chemical dust. Gritty things lodged in his ears. He

385

tried not to breathe too deeply as he cleaned, wary of dangers floating in the air, until his manager told him he was being fired because of a down-sizing. The next job was a temporary replacement with a company that delivered kitchens, week after week of sitting beside white drivers who called him 'labourer', of endless construction sites full of noises and helmets, of carrying wooden planks up long stairs, unaided and unsung. In the silence with which they drove, and the tone with which they said 'labourer!', Obinze sensed the drivers' dislike. Once, when he tripped and landed on his knee, a fall so heavy that he limped back to the truck, the driver told the others at the warehouse, 'His knee is bad because he's a knee-grow!' They laughed. Their hostility rankled, but only slightly; what mattered to him was that he earned four pounds an hour, more with overtime, and when he was sent to a new delivery warehouse in West Thurrock, he worried that he might not have opportunities for overtime.

The new warehouse chief looked like the Englishman archetype Obinze carried in his mind, tall and spare, sandy-haired and blue-eyed. But he was a smiling man, and in Obinze's imagination, Englishmen were not smiling men. His name was Roy Snell. He vigorously shook Obinze's hand.

'So, Vincent, you're from Africa?' he asked, as he took Obinze around the warehouse, the size of a football field, much bigger than the last one, and alive with trucks being loaded, flattened

386

cardboard boxes being folded into a deep pit, men talking.

'Yes. I was born in Birmingham and went back to Nigeria when I was six.' It was the story he and Iloba had agreed was most convincing.

'Why did you come back? How bad are things in Nigeria?'

'I just wanted to see if I could have a better life here.'

Roy Snell nodded. He seemed like a person for whom the word 'jolly' would always be apt. 'You'll work with Nigel today, he's our youngest,' he said, gesturing towards a man with a pale doughy body, spiky dark hair and an almost cherubic face. 'I think you'll like working here, Vinny Boy!' It had taken him five minutes to go from Vincent to Vinny Boy and, in the following months, when they played table tennis during lunch break, Roy would tell the men, 'I've got to beat Vinny Boy for once!' And they would titter and repeat 'Vinny Boy'.

It amused Obinze, how keenly the men flipped through their newspapers every morning, stopping at the photo of the big-breasted woman, examining it as though it were an article of great interest, and were any different from the photo on that same page the previous day, the previous week. Their conversations, as they waited for their trucks to be loaded up, were always about cars and football and, most of all, women, each man telling stories that sounded too apocryphal and too similar to a story told the day before, the week

before, and each time they mentioned knickers –
the bird flashed her knickers – Obinze was even more
amused, because knickers were, in Nigerian
English, shorts rather than underwear, and he
imagined these nubile women in ill-fitting khaki
shorts, the kind he had worn as a junior student
in secondary school.

Roy Snell's morning greeting to him was a jab
on his belly. 'Vinny Boy! You all right? You all
right?' he would ask. He always put Obinze's name
up for the outside work that paid better, always
asked if he wanted to work weekends, which was
double time, always asked about girls. It was as if
Roy held a special affection for him, which was
both protective and kind.

'You haven't had a shag since you came to the
UK, have you, Vinny Boy? I could give you this
bird's number,' he said once.

'I have a girlfriend back home,' Obinze said.

'So what's wrong with a little shag then?'

A few men nearby laughed.

'My girlfriend has magical powers,' Obinze said.

Roy found this funnier than Obinze thought it
was. He laughed and laughed. 'She's into witchcraft, is she? All right then, no shags for you. I've
always wanted to go to Africa, Vinny Boy. I think
I'll take a holiday and go to Nigeria when you're
back there for a visit. You can show me around,
find me some Nigerian birds, Vinny Boy, but no
witchcraft!'

'Yes, I could do that.'

'Oh, I know you could! You look like you know what to do with the birds,' Roy said, with another jab at Obinze's belly.

Roy often assigned Obinze to work with Nigel, perhaps because they were the youngest men in the warehouse. That first morning, Obinze noticed that the other men, drinking coffee from paper cups and checking the board to see who would be working with whom, were laughing at Nigel. Nigel had no eyebrows; the patches of slightly pink skin where his eyebrows should have been gave his plump face an unfinished, ghostly look.

'I got pissed at the pub and my mates shaved off my eyebrows,' Nigel told Obinze, almost apologetically, as they shook hands.

'No shagging for you until you grow your eyebrows back, mate,' one of the men called out as Nigel and Obinze headed for the truck. Obinze secured the washing machines at the back, tightening the straps until they were snug, and then climbed in and studied the map to find the shortest routes to their delivery addresses. Nigel took bends sharply and muttered about how people drove these days. At a traffic light, Nigel brought out a bottle of cologne from the bag he placed at his feet, sprayed it on his neck and then offered it to Obinze.

'No thanks,' Obinze said. Nigel shrugged. Days later, he offered it again. The truck interior was dense with the scent of his cologne and Obinze would, from time to time, take deep gulps of fresh air through the open window.

'You're just new from Africa. You haven't seen the London sights, have you, mate?' Nigel asked.

'No,' Obinze said.

And so, after early deliveries in central London, Nigel would take him for a drive, showing him Buckingham Palace, the Houses of Parliament, Tower Bridge, all the while talking about his mother's arthritis, and about his girlfriend Haley's knockers. It took a while to completely understand what Nigel said, because of his accent, which was only a deeper version of the accents of the people Obinze had worked with, each word twisted and stretched until it came out of their mouths having become something else. Once Nigel said 'male' and Obinze thought he had said 'mile', and when Obinze finally understood what Nigel meant, Nigel laughed and said, 'You talk kind of posh, don't you? African posh.'

One day, months into his job, after they delivered a new fridge to an address in Kensington, Nigel said, about the elderly man who had come into the kitchen, 'He's a real gent, he is.' Nigel's tone was admiring, slightly cowed. The man had looked dishevelled and hung-over, his hair tousled, his robe open at the chest, and he had said archly, 'You do know how to put it all together,' as though he did not think they did. It amazed Obinze that, because Nigel thought the man was a 'real gent', he did not complain about the dirty kitchen, as he ordinarily would have done. And if the man had spoken with a different accent,

Nigel would have called him miserly for not giving them a tip.

They were approaching their next delivery address in South London, and Obinze had just called the homeowner to say that they were almost there, when Nigel blurted out, 'What do you say to a girl you like?'

'What do you mean?' Obinze asked.

'Truth is, I'm not really shagging Haley. I like her but I don't know how to tell her. The other day I went round her house and there was another bloke there.' Nigel paused. Obinze tried to keep his face expressionless. 'You look like you know what to say to the birds, mate,' Nigel added.

'Just tell her you like her,' Obinze said, thinking how seamlessly Nigel, at the warehouse with other men, often contributed stories of his shagging Haley, and once of shagging her friend while Haley was away on holiday. 'No games and no lines. Just say, Look, I like you and I think you're beautiful.'

Nigel gave him a wounded glance. It was as if he had convinced himself that Obinze was skilled in the art of women and expected some profundity, which Obinze wished, as he loaded the dishwasher onto a trolley and wheeled it to the door, that he had. An Indian woman opened the door, a portly, kindly housewife who offered them tea. Many people offered tea or water. Once, a sad-looking woman had offered Obinze a small pot of home-made jam, and he had hesitated, but he sensed that whatever deep unhappiness she had would be compounded if he said no, and so he had taken the jam home and it was still languishing in the fridge, unopened.

'Thank you, thank you,' the Indian woman said as Obinze and Nigel installed the new dishwasher and rolled away the old.

At the door, she gave Nigel a tip. Nigel was the only driver who split the tips down the middle with Obinze; the others pretended not to remember to share. Once, when Obinze was working with another driver, an old Jamaican woman had pushed ten pounds into his pocket when the driver was not looking. 'Thank you, brother,' she said, and it made him want to call his mother in Nsukka and tell her about it.

CHAPTER 27

A glum dusk was settling over London when Obinze walked into the bookshop café and sat down to a mocha and a blueberry scone. The soles of his feet ached pleasantly. It was not very cold; he had been sweating in Nicholas's wool coat, which now hung on the back of his chair. This was his weekly treat: to visit the bookshop, buy an overpriced caffeinated drink, read as much as he could for free, and become Obinze again. Sometimes he asked to be dropped off in central London after a delivery and he would wander about and end up in a bookshop and sink to the floor at a corner, away from the clusters of people. He read contemporary American fiction, because he hoped to find a resonance, a shaping of his longings, a sense of the America that he had imagined himself a part of. He wanted to know about day-to-day life in America, what people ate and what consumed them, what shamed them and what attracted them, but he read novel after novel and was disappointed: nothing was grave, nothing serious, nothing urgent, and most dissolved into ironic nothingness. He read American newspapers and magazines, but only skimmed the British newspapers, because there were more and more articles about immigration, and each one stoked new panic in his chest. *Schools Swamped by Asylum Seekers.* He still hadn't found someone. Last week, he had met two Nigerian men, distant friends of a friend, who said they knew an Eastern European woman, and he had paid them a hundred pounds. Now, they did not return his calls and their mobile phones went directly to voicemail. His scone was half-eaten. He did not realize how quickly the café had filled up. He was comfortable, cosy even, and absorbed in a magazine article when a woman and a little boy came up to ask if they could share his table. They were nut-coloured and dark-haired. He imagined that they were Bangladeshi or Sri Lankan.

'Of course,' he said, and shifted his pile of books and magazines, even though it had not been on the side of the table that they would use. The boy looked eight or nine years old, wearing a Mickey Mouse sweater and clutching a blue Game Boy. The woman was wearing a nose ring, a tiny glass-like thing that glittered as she moved her head this way and that. She asked if he had enough room for his magazines, if he wanted her to move her chair a little. Then she told her son, in a laughing tone that was clearly intended for Obinze, that she had never been very sure if those narrow wooden sticks next to the packets of sugar were for stirring.

'I'm not a baby!' her son said when she wanted to cut his muffin.

'I just thought it would be easier for you.'

Obinze looked up and saw that she was talking to her son but she was watching him, with something wistful in her eyes. It filled him with possibility, this chance meeting with a stranger, and the thought of the paths on which it might lead him.

The little boy had a delightful curious face. 'Do you live in London?' he asked Obinze.

'Yes,' Obinze said, but that yes did not tell his story, that he lived in London indeed but invisibly, his existence like an erased pencil sketch; each time he saw a policeman, or anyone in a uniform, anyone with the faintest scent of authority, he would fight the urge to run.

'His father passed away last year,' the woman said, in a lower voice. 'This is our first vacation in London without him. We used to do it every year before Christmas.' The woman nodded continuously as she spoke and the boy looked annoyed, as if he had not wanted Obinze to know that.

'I'm sorry,' Obinze said.

'We went to the Tate,' the boy said.

'Did you like it?' Obinze asked.

He scowled. 'It was boring.'

His mother stood up. 'We should go. We're going to see a play.' She turned to her son and added, 'You're not taking that Game Boy in, you know that.'

The boy ignored her, said 'Bye' to Obinze and turned towards the door. The mother gave Obinze a long look, even more wistful than before. Perhaps she had deeply loved her husband and this, her first awareness of feeling attraction again, was a startling revelation. He watched them leave, wondering whether to get up and ask for her contact information and yet knowing he would not. There was something about the woman that made him think of love, and, as always, Ifemelu came to his mind when he thought of love. Then, quite suddenly, a sexual urge overcame him. A tide of lust. He wanted to fuck somebody. He would text Tendai. They had met at a party Nosa took him to, and he ended up, that night, in her bed. Wise and large-hipped and Zimbabwean Tendai who had a habit of soaking in baths for too long. She stared at him in shock the first time he cleaned her flat and cooked jollof rice for her. She was so unused to being treated well by a man that she watched him endlessly, anxiously, her eyes veiled, as though holding her breath and waiting for the abuse to emerge. She knew he didn't have his papers. 'Or you would be the kind of Nigerian working in IT and driving a BMW,' she said. She had a British stay, and would have a passport in a year, and she hinted that she might be willing to help him. But he did not want the complication of marrying her for his papers; one day she would wake up and convince herself that it had never been merely for papers.

Before he left the bookshop, he sent Tendai a text: *Are you home? Was thinking of stopping by.* A freezing drizzle was falling as he walked to the tube station, tiny raindrops splattering his coat, and when he got there, he was absorbed by how many blobs of saliva were on the stairs. Why did people not wait until they left the station to spit? He sat on the stained seat of the noisy train, opposite a woman reading the evening paper. *Speak English at home, Blunkett tells immigrants.* He imagined the article she was reading. There were so many of them now published in the newspapers, and they echoed the radio and television, even the chatter of some of the men in the warehouse. The wind blowing across the British Isles was odorous with fear of asylum seekers, infecting everybody with the panic of impending doom, and so articles were written and read, simply and stridently, as though the writers lived in a world in which the present was unconnected to the past, and they had never considered this to be the normal course of history: the influx into Britain of black and brown people from countries created by Britain. Yet he understood. It had to be comforting, this denial of history. The woman closed the newspaper and looked at him. She had stringy brown hair and hard, suspicious eyes. He wondered what she was thinking. Was she wondering whether he was one of those illegal immigrants who were overcrowding an already crowded island? Later, on the train to Essex, he

397

noticed that all the people around him were Nigerians, loud conversations in Yoruba and Pidgin filled the carriage, and for a moment he saw the unfettered non-white foreignness of this scene through the suspicious eyes of the white woman on the tube. He thought again of the Sri Lankan or Bangladeshi woman and the shadow of grief from which she was only just emerging, and he thought of his mother and of Ifemelu, and the life he had imagined for himself, and the life he now had, lacquered as it was by work and reading, by panic and hope. He had never felt so lonely.

CHAPTER 28

One morning in early summer, a renewing warmth in the air, Obinze arrived at the warehouse and knew right away that something was amiss. The men avoided his eyes, an unnatural stiffness in their movements, and Nigel turned swiftly, too swiftly, towards the toilet when he saw Obinze. They knew. It had to be that they had somehow found out. They saw the headlines about asylum seekers draining the National Health Service, they knew of the hordes further crowding a crowded island, and now they knew that he was one of the damned, working with a name that was not his. Where was Roy Snell? Had he gone to call the police? Was it the police that one called? Obinze tried to remember details from the stories of people who had been caught and deported but his mind was numb. He felt naked. He wanted to turn and run but his body kept moving, against his will, towards the loading area. Then he sensed a movement behind him, quick and violent and too close, and before he could turn around, a paper hat had been pushed onto his head. It was Nigel, and with him a gathering of grinning men.

'Happy birthday, Vinny Boy!' they all said.

Obinze froze, frightened by the complete blankness of his mind. Then he realized what it was. Vincent's birthday. Roy must have told the men. Even he had not remembered to remember Vincent's date of birth.

'Oh!' was all he said, nauseous from relief.

Nigel asked him to come into the coffee room, where all the men were trooping in, and as Obinze sat with them, all of them white except for Patrick from Jamaica, passing around the muffins and Coke they had bought with their own money in honour of a birthday they believed was his, a realization brought tears to his eyes: he felt safe.

Vincent called him that evening, and Obinze was mildly surprised, because Vincent had called him only once, months ago, when he changed his bank and wanted to give him the new account number. He wondered whether to say 'Happy birthday' to Vincent, whether indeed the call was somehow related to the occasion of the birthday.

'Vincent, *kedu*?' he said.

'I want a raise.'

Had Vincent learned that from a film? Those words 'I want a raise' sounded contrived and comical. 'I want forty-five per cent. I know you are working more now.'

'Vincent, ahn-ahn. How much am I making? You know I am saving money to do this marriage thing.'

'Forty-five per cent,' Vincent said, and hung up.

Obinze decided to ignore him. He knew Vincent's

type; they would push to see how far they could go and then they would step back. If he called and tried to negotiate, it might embolden Vincent to make more demands. That he walked in every week to Vincent's bank to deposit money into his account was something Vincent would not risk losing entirely. And so when, a week later, in the morning bustle of drivers and trucks, Roy said, 'Vinny Boy, step into my office for a minute,' Obinze thought nothing of it. On Roy's desk was a newspaper, folded at the page with the photo of the big-breasted woman. Roy slowly put his cup of coffee on top of the newspaper. He seemed uncomfortable, not looking directly at Obinze.

'Somebody called yesterday. Said you're not who you say you are, that you're illegal and working with a Brit's name.' There was a pause. Obinze was stung with surprise. Roy picked up the coffee cup again. 'Why don't you just bring in your passport tomorrow and we'll clear it up, all right?'

Obinze mumbled the first words that came to him. 'Okay. I'll bring my passport tomorrow.' He walked out of the office knowing that he would never remember what he had felt moments ago. Was Roy merely asking him to bring his passport to make the dismissal easier for him, to give him an exit, or did Roy really believe that the caller had been wrong? Why would anybody call about such a thing unless it was true? Obinze had never made as much of an effort as he did the rest of the day to seem normal, to tame the rage that was engulfing him. It was not the thought of the power that Vincent had over him that infuriated him, but the recklessness with which Vincent had exercised it. He left the warehouse that evening, for the final time, wishing more than anything that he had told Nigel and Roy his real name.

Some years later in Lagos, after Chief told him to find a white man whom he could present as his General Manager, Obinze called Nigel. His mobile number had not changed.

'This is Vinny Boy.'

'Vincent! Are you all right, mate?'

'I'm fine, how are you?' Obinze said. Then, later, he said, 'Vincent is not my real name, Nigel. My name is Obinze. I have a job offer for you in Nigeria.'

CHAPTER 29

The Angolans told him how things had 'gone up', or were more 'tough', opaque words that were supposed to explain each new request for more money.

'This is not what we agreed to,' Obinze would say, or 'I don't have any extra cash right now,' and they would reply, 'Things have gone up, yeah,' in a tone that he imagined was accompanied by a shrug. A silence would follow, a wordlessness over the phone line that told him that it was his problem, not theirs. 'I'll pay it in by Friday,' he would say finally, before hanging up.

Cleotilde's gentle sympathy assuaged him. She told him, 'They've got my passport,' and he thought this vaguely sinister, almost a hostage holding.

'Otherwise we could just do this on our own,' she added. But he did not want to do it on his own, with Cleotilde. It was too important and he needed the weight of the Angolans' expertise, their experience, to make sure all went well. Nicholas had already lent him some money; he had been loath enough to ask at all, because of the judgement in Nicholas's unsmiling eyes, as though he was thinking that Obinze was soft, spoilt, and many people did not have a cousin who could lend them money. Emenike was the only other person he could ask. The last time they spoke, Emenike had told him, 'I don't know if you've seen this play in the West End, but Georgina and I have just been and we loved it,' as though Obinze, in his delivery job, saving austerely, consumed by immigration worries, would ever even think of seeing a West End play. Emenike's obliviousness had upset him, because it suggested a disregard and, even worse, an indifference to him, and to his present life. He called Emenike and said, speaking quickly, pushing the words out, that he needed five hundred pounds, which he would pay back as soon as he could find another job, and then, more slowly, he told Emenike about the Angolans, and how close he was to finally doing the marriage ceremony, but there were so many extra costs that he had not budgeted for.

'No problem. Let's meet Friday,' Emenike said.

Now, Emenike sat across from Obinze in a dimly lit restaurant, after shrugging off his jacket to reveal a tan cashmere sweater that looked faultless. He had not put on weight like most of his other friends now living abroad, didn't look different from the last time Obinze had seen him in Nsukka.

'Man, The Zed, you look well!' he said, his words aflame with dishonesty. Of course Obinze did not look well, shoulders hunched from stress, in clothes borrowed from his cousin. 'Abeg, sorry I haven't had time to see you. My work schedule is crazy and we've also been travelling a lot. I would have asked you to come and stay with us but it's not a decision I can take alone. Georgina won't understand. You know these oyinbo people don't behave like us.' His lips moved, forming something that looked like a smirk. He was making fun of his wife, but Obinze knew, from the muted awe in his tone, that it was mockery coloured by respect, mockery of what he believed, despite himself, to be inherently superior. Obinze remembered how Kayode had often said about Emenike in secondary school: He can read all the books he wants but the bush is still in his blood.

'We've just come back from America. Man, you need to go to America. No other country like it in the world. We flew to Denver and then drove to Wyoming. Georgina had just finished a really tough case, you remember I told you when I was going to Hong Kong? She was there for work and I flew over for a long weekend. So I thought we should go to America, she needed the holiday.' Emenike's phone beeped. He took it out of his pocket, glanced at it and grimaced, as though he wanted to be asked what the text was about, but Obinze did not ask. He was tired; Iloba had given him his own National Insurance card, even though it was risky for both of them to work at the same time, but all the job agencies Obinze had tried so far wanted to see a passport and not just the card. His beer tasted flat, and he wished Emenike would just give him the money. But Emenike resumed talking, gesturing, his movements fluid and sure, his manner still that of a person convinced they knew things that other people would never know. And yet there was something different in him that Obinze could not name. Emenike talked for a long time, often prefacing a story with 'The thing you have to understand about this country is this.' Obinze's mind strayed to Cleotilde. The Angolans said at least two people from her side had to come to Newcastle, to avoid any suspicion, but she had called him yesterday to suggest that she bring only one friend, so he would not have to pay for the train and hotel bills of two extra people. He had found it sweet, but he asked her to bring the two anyway; he would take no chances.

Emenike was talking about something that had happened at work. 'I had actually arrived at the meeting first, kept my files, and then I went to the loo, only to come back and for this stupid oyinbo man to tell me, Oh, I see you are keeping to African time. And you know what? I just told him off. Since then he has been sending me e-mails to go for a drink. Drink for what?' Emenike sipped his beer. It was his third and he had become looser and louder. All his stories about work had the same arc: somebody would first underestimate or belittle him, and he would then end up victorious, with the final clever word or action.

'I miss Naija. It's been so long but I just haven't had the time to travel back home. Besides, Georgina would not survive a visit to Nigeria!' Emenike said, and laughed. He had cast home as the jungle and himself as interpreter of the jungle.

'Another beer?' Emenike asked.

Obinze shook his head. A man trying to get to the table behind them brushed Emenike's jacket down from behind his chair.

'Ha, look at this man. He wants to ruin my Aquascutum. It was my last birthday present from Georgina,' Emenike said, hanging the jacket back behind his chair. Obinze did not know the brand but he knew from the stylish smirk on Emenike's face that he was supposed to be impressed.

'Sure you don't want another beer?' Emenike asked, looking around for the waitress. 'She is ignoring me. Did you notice how rude she was earlier? These Eastern Europeans just don't like serving black people.'

After the waitress had taken his order, Emenike brought out an envelope from his pocket. 'Here it is, man. I know you asked for five hundred but it's one thousand. You want to count it?'

Count it? Obinze nearly said, but the words did not leave his mouth. To be given money in the Nigerian manner was to have it pushed into your hands, fists closed, eyes averted from yours, your effusive thanks – and it had to be effusive – waved away, and you certainly did not count the money, sometimes did not even look at it until you were alone. But here was Emenike asking him to count the money. And so he did, slowly, deliberately, moving each note from one hand to the other, wondering if Emenike had hated him all those years in secondary school and university. He had not laughed at Emenike as Kayode and the other boys did, but he had not defended Emenike either. Perhaps Emenike had despised his neutrality.

'Thanks, man,' Obinze said. Of course it was a thousand pounds. Did Emenike think a fifty-pound note might have slipped out on his way to the restaurant?

'It's not a loan,' Emenike said, leaning back on his seat, smiling thinly.

'Thanks, man,' Obinze said again, and despite it all he was grateful and relieved. It had worried him, how many things he still had to pay for before the wedding, and if this was what it took, counting a cash gift while Emenike watched with power in his gaze, then so be it.

Emenike's phone rang. 'Georgina,' he said happily before he took the call. His voice was slightly raised, for Obinze's benefit. 'It's fantastic to see him again after so long.' Then, after a pause, 'Of course, darling, we should do that.'

He put his phone down and told Obinze, 'Georgina wants to come and meet us in the next half hour so we can all go to dinner. Is that okay?'

Obinze shrugged. 'I never say no to food.'

Just before Georgina arrived, Emenike told him, in a lowered tone, 'Don't mention this marriage thing to Georgina.'

He had imagined Georgina, from the way

Emenike spoke of her, as a fragile innocent, a successful lawyer who nonetheless did not truly know the evils of the world, but when she arrived, square-faced with a big square body, brown hair crisply cut, giving her an air of efficiency, he could see right away that she was frank, knowing, even world-weary. He imagined her clients instantly trusting her ability. This was a woman who would check up on the finances of charities she gave to. This was a woman who could certainly survive a visit to Nigeria. Why had Emenike portrayed her as a hapless English rose? She pressed her lips to Emenike's, then turned to shake Obinze's hand.

'Do you fancy anything in particular?' she asked Obinze, unbuttoning her brown suede coat. 'There's a nice Indian place nearby.'

'Oh, that's a bit tatty,' Emenike said. He had changed. His voice had taken on an unfamiliar modulation, his delivery slower, the temperature of his entire being much lower. 'We could go to that new place in Kensington, it's not that far.'

'I'm not sure Obinze will find it very interesting, darling,' Georgina said.

'Oh, I think he'll like it,' Emenike said. Self-satisfaction, that was the difference in him. He was married to a British woman, lived in a British home, worked at a British job, travelled on a British passport, said 'exercise' to refer to a mental rather than a physical activity. He had longed for this life, and never quite believed he would have it. Now his backbone was stiff with self-satisfaction. He was sated. In the restaurant in Kensington, a candle glowed on the table, and the blond waiter, who seemed too tall and handsome to be a waiter, served tiny bowls of what looked like green jelly.

'Our new lemon and thyme aperitif, with the compliments of the chef,' he said.

'Fantastic,' Emenike said, instantly sinking into one of the rituals of his new life: eyebrows furrowed, concentration sharp, sipping sparkling water and studying a restaurant menu. He and Georgina discussed the starters. The waiter was called to answer a question. It struck Obinze, how seriously Emenike took this initiation into the voodoo of fine dining, because when the waiter brought him what looked like three elegant bits of green weed, for which he would pay thirteen pounds, Emenike rubbed his palms together in delight. Obinze's burger was served in four pieces, arranged in a large martini glass. When Georgina's order arrived, a pile of red raw beef, an egg sunnily splayed on top of it, Obinze tried not to look at it as he ate, otherwise he might be tempted to vomit.

Emenike did most of the talking, telling Georgina about their time together at school, barely letting Obinze say anything. In the stories he told, he and Obinze were the popular rogues who always got into glamorous trouble. Obinze watched Georgina, only now becoming aware of how much older than Emenike she was. At least eight years. Her manly facial contours were softened by frequent brief

410

smiles, but they were thoughtful smiles, the smiles of a natural sceptic, and he wondered how much she believed of Emenike's stories, how much love had suspended her reason.

'We're having a dinner party tomorrow, Obinze,' Georgina said. 'You must come.'

'Yes, I forgot to mention it,' Emenike said.

'You really must come. We're having a few friends over and I think you'll enjoy meeting them,' Georgina said.

'I would love to,' Obinze said.

Their terraced home in Islington, with its short flight of well-preserved steps that led to the green front door, smelled of roasting food when Obinze arrived. Emenike let him in. 'The Zed! You're early, we're just finishing up in the kitchen. Come and stay in my study until the others come.' Emenike led him upstairs, and into the study, a clean, bright room made brighter by the white bookshelves and white curtains. The windows ate up large chunks of the walls, and Obinze imagined the room in the afternoon, flooded gloriously with light, and himself sunk in the armchair by the door, lost in a book.

'I'll come and call you in a bit,' Emenike said.

There were, on a window ledge, photos of Emenike squinting in front of the Sistine Chapel, making a peace sign at the Acropolis, standing at the Colosseum, his shirt the same nutmeg colour as the wall of the ruin. Obinze imagined him, dutiful and determined, visiting the places he was supposed to visit, thinking, as he did so, not of the things he was seeing but of the photos he would take of them and of the people who would see those photos. The people who would know that he had participated in these triumphs. On the bookshelf, Graham Greene caught his eye. He took *The Heart of the Matter* down and began to read the first chapter, suddenly nostalgic for his teenage years when his mother would reread it every few months.

Emenike came in. 'Is that Waugh?'

'No.' He showed him the book cover. 'My mother loves this book. She was always trying to get me to love her English novels.'

'Waugh is the best of them. *Brideshead* is the closest I've read to a perfect novel.'

'I think Waugh is cartoonish. I just don't get those so-called comic English novels. It's as if they can't deal with the real and deep complexity of human life and so they resort to doing this comic business. Greene is the other extreme, too morose.'

'No, man, you need to go and read Waugh again. Greene doesn't really do it for me, but the first part of *The End of the Affair* is terrific.'

'This study is the dream,' Obinze said.

Emenike shrugged. 'Do you want any books? Take anything you want.'

'Thanks, man,' Obinze said, knowing that he would not take any.

Emenike looked around, as though seeing the

study through new eyes. 'We found this desk in Edinburgh. Georgina already had some good pieces but we found some new things together.'

Obinze wondered if Emenike had so completely absorbed his own disguise that even when they were alone, he could talk about 'good furniture', as though the idea of 'good furniture' was not alien in their Nigerian world, where new things were supposed to look new. Obinze might have said something to Emenike about it but not now; too much had already shifted in their relationship. Obinze followed him downstairs. The dining table was a riot of colour, bright mismatched ceramic plates, some of them chipped at the edges, red wine goblets, deep blue napkins. In a silver bowl at the centre of the table, delicate milky flowers floated in water. Emenike made the introductions.

'This is Georgina's old friend Mark, and this is his wife, Hannah, who by the way is completing her PhD on the female orgasm, or the Israeli female orgasm.'

'Well, it isn't quite that singularly focused,' Hannah said, to general laughter, warmly shaking Obinze's hand. She had a tanned, broad-featured succouring face, the face of a person who could not abide conflict. Mark, pale-skinned and rumpled, squeezed her shoulder but did not laugh along with the others. He said 'How do you do' to Obinze in an almost formal manner.

'This is our dear friend Phillip, who is the best

413

solicitor in London, after Georgina of course,' Emenike said.

'Are all the men in Nigeria as gorgeous as you and your friend?' Phillip asked Emenike, swooning mockingly as he shook Obinze's hand.

'You'll have to come to Nigeria and see,' Emenike said, and winked, in what seemed to be a continuous flirtatiousness with Phillip.

Phillip was slender and elegant, his red silk shirt open at the neck. His mannerisms, supple gestures of his wrists, fingers swirling in the air, reminded Obinze of the boy in secondary school – his name was Hadome – who was said to pay junior students to suck his dick. Once, Emenike and two other boys had lured Hadome into the toilet and beaten him up, Hadome's eye swelling so quickly that, just before school was dismissed, it looked grotesque, like a big purple eggplant. Obinze had stood outside the toilet with other boys, boys who did not join in the beating but who laughed along, boys who taunted and goaded, boys who shouted 'Homo! Homo!'

'This is our friend Alexa. Alexa's just moved into a new place in Holland Park, after years in France, and so, lucky us, we'll be seeing much more of her. She works in music publishing. She's also a fantastic poet,' Emenike said.

'Oh, stop it,' Alexa said, and then turning to Obinze, she asked, 'So where are you from, darling?'

'Nigeria.'

'No, no, I mean in London, darling.'

'I live in Essex, actually,' he said.

'I see,' she said, as though disappointed. She was a small woman with a very pale face and tomato-red hair. 'Shall we eat, boys and girls?' She picked up one of the plates and examined it.

'I love these plates. Georgina and Emenike are never boring, are they?' Hannah said.

'We bought them from this bazaar in India,' Emenike said. 'Handmade by rural women, just so beautiful. See the detail at the edges?' He raised one of the plates.

'Sublime,' Hannah said, and looked at Obinze.

'Yes, very nice,' Obinze mumbled. Those plates, with their amateur finishing, the slight lumpiness of the edges, would never be shown in the presence of guests in Nigeria. He still was not sure whether Emenike had become a person who believed that something was beautiful because it was handmade by poor people in a foreign country, or whether he had simply learned to pretend so. Georgina poured the drinks. Emenike served the starter, crab with hard-boiled eggs. He had taken on a careful and calibrated charm. He said 'Oh dear' often. When Phillip complained about the French couple building a house next to his in Cornwall, Emenike asked, 'Are they between you and the sunset?'

Are they between you and the sunset? It would never occur to Obinze, or to anybody he had grown up with, to ask a question like that.

'So how was America?' Phillip asked.

'A fascinating place, really. We spent a few days with Hugo in Jackson, Wyoming. You met Hugo last Christmas, didn't you, Mark?'

'Yes. So what's he doing there?' Mark seemed unimpressed by the plates; he had not, like his wife, picked one up to look at it.

'It's a ski resort, but it's not pretentious. In Jackson, they say people who go to Aspen expect somebody to tie their ski boots up for them,' Georgina said.

'The thought of skiing in America makes me quite ill,' Alexa said.

'Why?' Hannah asked.

'Have they got a Disney station in the resort, with Mickey Mouse in ski gear?' Alexa asked.

'Alexa has only been to America once, when she was in school, but she loves to hate it from afar,' Georgina said.

'I've loved America from afar my whole life,' Obinze said. Alexa turned to him in slight surprise, as though she had not expected him to speak. Under the chandelier light, her red hair took on a strange, unnatural glow.

'What I've noticed being here is that many English people are in awe of America but also deeply resent it,' Obinze added.

'Perfectly true,' Phillip said, nodding at Obinze. 'Perfectly true. It's the resentment of a parent whose child has become far more beautiful and with a far more interesting life.'

'But the Americans love us Brits, they love the accent and the Queen and the double-decker,'

Emenike said. There, it had been said: the man considered himself British.

'And the great revelation Emenike had while we were there?' Georgina said, smiling. 'The difference between the American and British "bye".'

'Bye?' Alexa asked.

'Yes. He says the Brits draw it out much more, while Americans make it short.'

'That was a great revelation. It explained everything about the difference between both countries,' Emenike said, knowing that they would laugh, and they did. 'I was also thinking about the difference in approaching foreignness. Americans will smile at you and be extremely friendly but if your name is not Cory or Chad, they make no effort at saying it properly. The Brits will be surly and will be suspicious if you're too friendly but they will treat foreign names as though they are actually valid names.'

'That's interesting,' Hannah said.

Georgina said, 'It's a bit tiresome to talk about America being insular, not that we help that much, since if something major happens in America, it is the headline in Britain; something major happens here, it is on the back page in America, if at all. But I do think the most troubling thing was the garishness of the nationalism, don't you think so, darling?' Georgina turned to Emenike.

'Absolutely,' Emenike said. 'Oh, and we went to a rodeo. Hugo thought we might fancy a bit of culture.'

There was a general, tittering laughter.

'And we saw this quite unbelievable parade of little children with heavily made-up faces and then there was a lot of flag-waving and a lot of "God Bless America". I was terrified that it was the sort of place where you did not know what might happen to you if you suddenly said, "I don't like America."'

'I found America quite jingoistic, too, when I did my fellowship training there,' Mark said.

'Mark is a paediatric surgeon,' Georgina said to Obinze.

'One got the sense that people – progressive people, that is, because American conservatives come from an entirely different planet, even to this Tory – felt that they could very well criticize their country but they didn't like it at all when you did,' Mark said.

'Where were you?' Emenike asked, as if he knew America's smallest corners.

'Philadelphia. A specialty hospital called the Children's Hospital. It was quite a remarkable place and the training was very good. It might have taken me two years in England to see the rare cases that I had in a month there.'

'But you didn't stay,' Alexa said, almost triumphantly.

'I hadn't planned on staying.' Mark's face never quite dissolved into any expression.

'Speaking of which, I've just got involved with this fantastic charity that's trying to stop the UK from hiring so many African health workers,' Alexa said. 'There are simply no doctors and nurses left on that continent. It's an absolute tragedy! African doctors should stay in Africa.'

'Why shouldn't they want to practise where there is regular electricity and regular pay?' Mark asked, his tone flat. Obinze sensed that he did not like Alexa at all. 'I'm from Grimsby and I certainly don't want to work in a district hospital there.'

'But it isn't quite the same thing, is it? We're speaking of some of the world's poorest people. The doctors have a responsibility as Africans,' Alexa said. 'Life isn't fair, really. If they have the privilege of that medical degree, then it comes with a responsibility to help their people.'

'I see. I don't suppose any of us should have that responsibility for the blighted towns in the north of England?' Mark said.

Alexa's face reddened. In the sudden tense silence, the air wrinkling between them all, Georgina got up and said, 'Everyone ready for my roast lamb?'

They all praised the meat, which Obinze wished had stayed a little longer in the oven; he carefully cut around his slice, eating the sides that had greyed from cooking and leaving on his plate the bits stained with pinkish blood. Hannah led the conversation, as though to smooth the air, her voice calming, bringing up subjects they would all agree on, changing to something else if she sensed a looming disagreement. Their conversation was symphonic, voices flowing into one another, in agreement: how atrocious to treat those Chinese cockle pickers like that, how absurd, the idea of

419

fees for higher education, how preposterous that fox-hunting supporters had stormed Parliament. They laughed when Obinze said, 'I don't understand why fox hunting is such a big issue in this country. Aren't there more important things?'

'What could possibly be more important?' Mark asked drily.

'Well, it's the only way we know how to fight our class warfare,' Alexa said. 'The landed gentry and the aristocrats hunt, you see, and we liberal middle classes fume about it. We want to take their silly little toys away.'

'We certainly do,' Phillip said. 'It's monstrous.'

'Did you read about Blunkett saying he doesn't know how many immigrants there are in the country?' Alexa asked, and Obinze immediately tensed, his chest tightening.

'"Immigrant", of course, is code for Muslim,' Mark said.

'If he really wanted to know, he would go to all the construction sites in this country and do a head count,' Phillip said.

'It was quite interesting to see how this plays out in America,' Georgina said. 'They're kicking up a fuss about immigration as well. Although, of course, America has always been kinder to immigrants than Europe.'

'Well, yes, but that is because countries in Europe were based on exclusion and not, as in America, on inclusion,' Mark said.

'But it's also a different psychology, isn't it?'

Hannah said. 'European countries are surrounded by countries that are similar to one another, while America has Mexico, which is really a developing country, and so it creates a different psychology about immigration and borders.'

'But we don't have immigrants from Denmark. We have immigrants from Eastern Europe, which is our Mexico,' Alexa said.

'Except, of course, for race,' Georgina said. 'Eastern Europeans are white. Mexicans are not.'

'How did you see race in America, by the way, Emenike?' Alexa asked. 'It's an iniquitously racist country, isn't it?'

'He doesn't have to go to America for that, Alexa,' Georgina said.

'It seemed to me that in America blacks and whites work together but don't play together and here blacks and whites play together but don't work together,' Emenike said.

The others nodded thoughtfully, as though he had said something profound, but Mark said, 'I'm not sure I quite understand that.'

'I think class in this country is in the air that people breathe. Everyone knows their place. Even the people who are angry about class have somehow accepted their place,' Obinze said. 'A white boy and a black girl who grow up in the same working-class town in this country can get together and race will be secondary, but in America, even if the white boy and black girl grow up in the same neighbourhood, race would be primary.'

Alexa gave him another surprised look.

'A bit simplified but yes, that's sort of what I meant,' Emenike said, slowly, leaning back on his chair, and Obinze sensed a rebuke. He should have been quiet; this, after all, was Emenike's stage.

'But you haven't really had to deal with any racism here, have you, Emenike?' Alexa asked, and her tone implied that she already knew the answer to the question was no. 'Of course people are prejudiced, but aren't we all prejudiced?'

'Well, no,' Georgina said firmly. 'You should tell the story of the cabbie, darling.'

'Oh, that story,' Emenike said, as he got up to serve the cheese plate, murmuring something in Hannah's ear that made her smile and touch his arm. How thrilled he was, to live in Georgina's world.

'Do tell,' Hannah said.

And so Emenike did. He told the story of the taxi that he had hailed one night, on Upper Street; from afar the cab light was on but as the cab approached him, the light went off, and he assumed the driver was not on duty. After the cab passed him by, he looked back idly and saw that the cab light was back on and that, a little way up the street, it stopped for two white women.

Emenike had told Obinze this story before and he was struck now by how differently Emenike told it. He did not mention the rage he had felt standing on that street and looking at the cab. He was shaking, he had told Obinze, his hands trembling for a long time, a little frightened by his own feelings. But now, sipping the last of his red wine, flowers floating in front of him, he spoke in a tone cleansed of anger, thick only with a kind of superior amusement, while Georgina interjected to clarify: *Can you believe that?*

Alexa, flush with red wine, her eyes red below her scarlet hair, changed the subject. 'Blunkett must be sensible and make sure this country remains a refuge. People who have survived frightful wars must absolutely be allowed in!' She turned to Obinze. 'Don't you agree?'

'Yes,' he said, and felt alienation run through him like a shiver.

Alexa, and the other guests, and perhaps even Georgina, all understood the fleeing from war, from the kind of poverty that crushed human souls, but they would not understand the need to escape from the oppressive lethargy of choiceless-ness. They would not understand why people like him, who were raised well-fed and watered but mired in dissatisfaction, conditioned from birth to look towards somewhere else, eternally convinced that real lives happened in that somewhere else, were now resolved to do dangerous things, illegal things, so as to leave, none of them starving, or raped, or from burned villages, but merely hungry for choice and certainty.

CHAPTER 30

Nicholas gave Obinze a suit for the wedding. 'It's a good Italian suit,' he said. 'It's small for me so it should fit you.' The trousers were big and bunched up when Obinze tightened his belt, but the jacket, also big, shielded this unsightly pleat of cloth at his waist. Not that he minded. So focused was he on getting through the day, on finally beginning his life, that he would have swaddled his lower parts in a baby's nappy if that were required. He and Iloba met Cleotilde near the Civic Centre. She was standing under a tree with her friends, her hair pushed back with a white band, her eyes boldly lined in black; she looked like an older, sexier person. Her ivory dress was tight at her hips. He had paid for the dress. 'I haven't got any proper going-out dress,' she had said in apology when she called to tell him that she had nothing that looked convincingly bridal. She hugged him. She looked nervous, and he tried to deflect his own nervousness by thinking about them together after this, how in less than an hour, he would be free to walk with surer steps on Britain's streets, and free to kiss her.

'You have the rings?' Iloba asked her.

'Yes,' Cleotilde said.

She and Obinze had bought them the week before, plain matching cheap rings from a side-street shop, and she had looked so delighted, laughingly slipping different rings on and then off her finger, that he wondered if she wished it were a real wedding.

'Fifteen minutes to go,' Iloba said. He had appointed himself the organizer. He took pictures, his digital camera held away from his face, saying, 'Move closer! Okay, one more!' His sprightly good spirits annoyed Obinze. On the train up to Newcastle the previous day, while Obinze had spent his time looking out of the window, unable even to read, Iloba had talked and talked, until his voice became a distant murmur, perhaps because he was trying to keep Obinze from worrying too much. Now, he talked to Cleotilde's friends with an easy friendliness, about the new Chelsea coach, about *Big Brother*, as if they were all there for something ordinary and normal.

'Time to go,' Iloba said. They walked towards the Civic Centre. The afternoon was bright with sunshine. Obinze opened the door and stood aside for the others to go ahead, into the sterile hallway, where they paused to get their bearings, to be sure which way to go towards the register office. Two policemen stood behind the door, watching them with stony eyes. Obinze quieted his panic. There was nothing to worry about, nothing at all, he told himself, the Civic Centre probably had policemen present as a matter of routine; but he sensed in the sudden smallness of the hallway, the sudden thickening of doom in the air, that something was wrong, before he noticed another man approaching him, his shirtsleeves rolled up, his cheeks so red he looked as though he was wearing terrible make-up.

'Are you Obinze Maduewesi?' the red-cheeked man asked. In his hands was a sheaf of papers and Obinze could see a photocopy of his passport page.

'Yes,' Obinze said quietly, and that word, yes, was an acknowledgement to the red-cheeked immigration officer, to Iloba and to Cleotilde, and to himself that it was over.

'Your visa is expired and you are not allowed to be present in the UK,' the red-cheeked man said.

A policeman clamped handcuffs around his wrists. He felt himself watching the scene from far away, watching himself walk to the police car outside, and sink into the too-soft seat in the back. There had been so many times in the past when he had feared that this would happen, so many moments that had become one single blur of panic, and now it felt like the dull echo of an aftermath. Cleotilde had flung herself on the ground and begun to cry. She might never have visited her father's country, but he was convinced at that moment of her Africanness; how else would she be able to fling herself to the ground with that perfect dramatic flourish? He wondered if her tears were for him or for herself or for what might have been between them. She had no need to worry, though, since she was a European citizen; the policemen barely glanced at her. It was he who felt the heaviness of the handcuffs during the drive to the police station, who silently handed over his watch and his belt and his wallet, and watched the policeman take his phone and switch it off. Nicholas's large trousers were slipping down his hips.

'Your shoes too. Take off your shoes,' the policeman said.

He took off his shoes. He was led to a cell. It was small, with brown walls, and the metal bars, so thick his hand could not go around one, reminded him of the chimpanzee's cage at Nsukka's dismal, forgotten zoo. From the very high ceilings, a single bulb burned. There was an emptying, echoing vastness in that tiny cell.

'Were you aware that your visa had expired?'

'Yes,' Obinze said.

'Were you about to have a sham marriage?'

'No. Cleotilde and I have been dating for a while.'

'I can arrange for a lawyer for you, but it's obvious you'll be deported,' the immigration officer said evenly.

When the lawyer came, puffy-faced, darkened arcs under his eyes, Obinze remembered all the films in which the state lawyer is distracted and exhausted. He came with a bag but did not open it, and he sat across from Obinze, holding nothing, no file, no paper, no pen. His demeanour was pleasant and sympathetic.

'The government has a strong case and we can appeal, but to be honest it will only delay the case and you will eventually be removed from the UK,' he said, with the air of a man who had said those same words, in that same tone, more times than he wished to, or could, remember.

'I'm willing to go back to Nigeria,' Obinze said. The last shard of his dignity was like a wrapper slipping off that he was desperate to retie.

The lawyer looked surprised. 'Okay, then,' he said, and got up a little too hastily, as though grateful that his job had been made easier. Obinze watched him leave. He was going to tick on a form that his client was willing to be removed. 'Removed.' That word made Obinze feel inanimate. A thing to be removed. A thing without breath and mind. A thing.

He hated the cold heaviness of the handcuffs, the mark he imagined they left on his wrists, the glint of the interlinking circles of metal that robbed him of movement. There he was, in handcuffs, being led through the hall of Manchester Airport, and in the coolness and din of that airport, men and women and children, travellers and cleaners and security guards, watched him, wondering what evil he had done. He kept his gaze on a tall white woman hurrying ahead, hair flying behind her, knapsack hunched on her back. She would not understand his story, why he was now walking through the airport with metal clamped around his wrists, because people like her did not approach travel with anxiety about visas. She might worry about money, about a place to stay, about safety, perhaps even about visas, but never with an anxiety that wrenched at her spine.

He was led into a room, bunk beds pushed forlornly against the walls. Three men were already there. One, from Djibouti, said little, lying and staring at the ceiling as though retracing the journey of how he had ended up at a holding facility in Manchester Airport. Two were Nigerian. The younger sat up on his bed eternally cracking his fingers. The older paced the small room and would not stop talking.

'Bros, how did they get you?' he asked Obinze, with an instant familiarity that Obinze resented. Something about him reminded Obinze of Vincent. Obinze shrugged and said nothing to him; there was no need for courtesies simply because they shared a cell.

'Is there anything I could have to read, please?' Obinze asked an immigration officer when she came to lead the man from Djibouti out to see a visitor.

'Read,' she repeated, eyebrows raised.

'Yes. A book or a magazine or a newspaper,' Obinze said.

'You want to read,' she said, and on her face, a contemptuous amusement. 'Sorry. But we've got a TV room and you're allowed to go there and watch telly after lunchtime.'

In the TV room, there was a group of men, many of them Nigerians, talking loudly. The other men sat around slumped into their own sorrows, listening to the Nigerians trade their stories, sometimes laughing, sometimes self-pitying.

'Ah this na my second time. The first time I come with different passport,' one of them said.

'Na for work wey they get me o.'

'E get one guy wey they deport, him don come back get him paper. Na him wey go help me,' another said.

Obinze envied them for what they were, men who casually changed names and passports, who would plan and come back and do it over again because they had nothing to lose. He didn't have their savoir faire; he was soft, a boy who had grown up eating cornflakes and reading books, raised by a mother during a time when truth-telling was not yet a luxury. He was ashamed to be with them, among them. They did not have his shame and even this, too, he envied.

In detention, he felt raw, skinned, the outer layers of himself stripped off. His mother's voice on the phone was almost unfamiliar, a woman speaking a crisp Nigerian English, telling him, calmly, to be strong, that she would be in Lagos to receive him, and he remembered how, years ago, when General Buhari's government stopped giving essential commodities, and she no longer came home with free tins of milk, she had begun to grind soya beans at home to make milk. She said soya milk was more nutritious than cow milk and although he refused to drink the grainy fluid in the morning, he watched her do so with an uncomplaining common sense. It was what she showed now, over the phone, telling him she would come and pick him up, as though she had always nursed the possibility of this, her son in detention, waiting to be removed from a country overseas.

He thought a lot about Ifemelu, imagining what she was doing, how her life had changed. She had once told him, in university, 'You know what I admired most about you in secondary school? That you never had a problem saying "I don't know." Other boys pretended to know what they didn't know. But you just had this confidence and you could always admit that you didn't know something.' He had thought it an unusual compliment, and had cherished this image of himself, perhaps because he knew it was not entirely true. He wondered what she would think if she knew where he was now. She would be sympathetic, he was sure, but would she also, in a small way, be disappointed? He almost asked Iloba to contact her. It would not be difficult to find her; he already knew she lived in Baltimore. But he did not ask Iloba. When Iloba visited him, he talked about lawyers. They both knew that there was no point, but still Iloba talked about lawyers. He would sit across

431

from Obinze, rest his head on his hand and talk about lawyers. Obinze wondered if some of the lawyers existed only in Iloba's mind. 'I know one lawyer in London, a Ghanaian, he represented this man with no papers, the man was almost on a plane home, and the next thing we knew, the man was free. He now works in IT.' Other times, Iloba took comfort in stating what was obvious. 'If only the marriage was just done before they came,' he said. 'You know if they had come even one second after you were pronounced man and wife, they would not touch you?' Obinze nodded. He knew, and Iloba knew that he knew. On Iloba's last visit, after Obinze told him that he was being moved to Dover the next day, Iloba began to cry. 'Zed, this was not supposed to happen like this.'

'Iloba, why are you talking rubbish? Stop crying, my friend,' Obinze said, pleased to be in a position to pretend strength.

And yet when Nicholas and Ojiugo visited, he disliked how strenuously they tried to be positive, to pretend, almost, as though he was merely ill in hospital and they had come to visit him. They sat across from him, the bare cold table between them, and talked about the mundane, Ojiugo speaking a little too quickly, and Nicholas saying more in an hour than Obinze had heard him say in weeks: Nne had been accepted into the National Children's Orchestra, Nna had won yet another prize. They brought him money, novels, a bag of clothes. Nicholas had shopped for him, and most of the clothes were new and in his size. Ojiugo often asked, 'But are they treating you well? Are they treating you well?' as though the treatment was what mattered, rather than the blighted reality of it all, that he was in a holding centre, about to be deported. Nobody behaved normally. They were all under the spell of his misfortune.

'They are waiting for seats on a flight to Lagos,' Obinze said. 'They'll keep me in Dover until there's a seat available.'

Obinze had read about Dover in a newspaper. A former prison. It felt surreal, to be driven past the electronic gates, the high walls, the wires. His cell was smaller, colder, than the cell in Manchester and his cellmate, another Nigerian, told him that he was not going to allow himself to be deported. He had a hardened, fleshless face. 'I will take off my shirt and my shoes when they try to board me. I will seek asylum,' he told Obinze. 'If you take off your shirt and your shoes, they will not board you.' He repeated this often, like a mantra. From time to time he farted loudly, wordlessly, and from time to time he sank to his knees in the middle of their tiny cell, hands raised up to the heavens, and prayed. 'Father Lord, I praise your name! Nothing is too much for you! I bless your name!' His palms were deeply etched with lines. Obinze wondered what atrocities those hands had seen. He felt suffocated in that cell, let out only to exercise and to eat, food that brought to mind a bowl of boiled worms. He could not eat; he felt his body slackening, his flesh disappearing. By the day he was led into a van one early morning, a fuzz of hair, like carpet grass, had covered his entire jaw. It was not yet dawn. He was with two women and five men, all handcuffed, all bound for Nigeria, and they were marched, at Heathrow Airport, through security and immigration and onto the plane, while other passengers stared. They were seated at the very back, in the last row of seats, closest to the toilet. Obinze sat unmoving throughout the flight. He did not want his tray of food. 'No, thank you,' he said to the flight attendant.

The woman next to him said eagerly, 'Can I have his own?' She had been at Dover too. She had very dark lips and a buoyant, undefeated manner. She would, he was sure, get another passport with another name and try again.

As the plane began its descent into Lagos, a flight attendant stood above them and said loudly, 'You cannot leave. An immigration officer will come to take charge of you.' Her face tight with disgust, as though they were all criminals bringing shame on upright Nigerians like her. The plane emptied out. Obinze looked through the window, at an old jet standing in the mild late afternoon sun, until a uniformed man came walking down the aisle. His belly was large; it must have been a struggle to button up his shirt.

'Yes, yes, I have come to take charge of you! Welcome home!' he said humorously, and he

434

reminded Obinze of that Nigerian ability to laugh, to so easily reach for amusement. He had missed that. 'We laugh too much,' his mother once said. 'Maybe we should laugh less and solve our problems more.'

The uniformed man led them to an office, and handed out forms. Name. Age. Country you have come from.

'Did they treat you well?' the man asked Obinze.

'Yes,' Obinze said.

'So do you have anything for the boys?'

Obinze looked at him for a moment, his open face, his simple view of the world; deportations happened every day and the living went on living. Obinze brought from his pocket a ten-pound note, part of the money Nicholas had given him. The man took it with a smile.

Outside, it was like breathing steam; he felt light-headed. A new sadness blanketed him, the sadness of his coming days, when he would feel the world slightly off-kilter, his vision unfocused. At the cordoned-off area near Arrivals, standing apart from the other expectant people, his mother was waiting for him.

PART IV

CHAPTER 31

After Ifemelu broke up with Curt, she told Ginika, 'There was a feeling I wanted to feel that I did not feel.'

'What are you talking about? You cheated on him!' Ginika shook her head as though Ifemelu were mad. 'Ifem, honestly, sometimes I don't understand you.'

It was true, she had cheated on Curt with a younger man who lived in her apartment building in Charles Village and played in a band. But it was also true that she had longed, with Curt, to hold emotions in her hand that she never could. She had not entirely believed herself while with him – happy, handsome Curt, with his ability to twist life into the shapes he wanted. She loved him, and the spirited easy life he gave her, and yet she often fought the urge to create rough edges, to squash his sunniness, even if just a little.

'I think you are a self-sabotager,' Ginika said. 'That's why you cut off Obinze like that. And now you cheat on Curt because at some level you don't think you deserve happiness.'

'Now you are going to suggest some pills for

Self-Sabotage Disorder,' Ifemelu said. 'That's absurd.'

'So why did you do it?'

'It was a mistake. People make mistakes. People do stupid things.'

She had done it, in truth, because she was curious, but she would not tell Ginika this, because it would seem flippant; Ginika would not understand, Ginika would prefer a grave and important reason like self-sabotage. She was not even sure she liked him, Rob, who wore dirty ripped jeans, grimy boots, rumpled flannel shirts. She did not understand grunge, the idea of looking shabby because you could afford not to be shabby; it mocked true shabbiness. The way he dressed made him seem superficial to her, and yet she was curious about him, about how he would be, naked in bed with her. The sex was good the first time, she was on top of him, gliding and moaning and grasping the hair on his chest, and feeling faintly and glamorously theatrical as she did so. But the second time, after she arrived at his apartment and he pulled her into his arms, a great torpor descended on her. He was already breathing heavily, and she was extracting herself from his embrace and picking up her handbag to leave. In the elevator, she was overcome with the frightening sense that she was looking for something solid, flailing, and all she touched dissolved into nothingness. She went to Curt's apartment and told him.

'It meant nothing. It happened once and I am so sorry.'

'Stop playing,' he said, but she knew, from the unbelieving horror that was deepening the blue of his eyes, that he knew she was not playing. It took hours of sidestepping each other, of drinking tea and putting on music and checking e-mail, of Curt lying face up on the couch, still and silent, before he asked, 'Who is he?'

She told him the man's name. Rob.

'He's white?'

She was surprised that he would ask her this, and so soon. 'Yes.' She had first seen Rob months before, in the elevator, with his unkempt clothes and unwashed hair, and he had smiled at her and said, 'I see you around.' After that, whenever she saw him, he looked at her with a kind of lazy interest, as though they both knew that something would happen between them and it was only a matter of when.

'Who the fuck is he?' Curt asked.

She told him that he lived on the floor above hers, that they said hello to each other and nothing else until that evening when she saw him coming back from the liquor store and he asked if she'd like to have a drink with him and she did a stupid, impulsive thing.

'You gave him what he wanted,' Curt said. The planes of his face were hardening. It was an odd thing for Curt to say, the sort of thing Aunty Uju, who thought of sex as something a woman gave a man at a loss to herself, would say.

In a sudden giddy fit of recklessness, she corrected Curt. 'I took what I wanted. If I gave him anything, then it was incidental.'

'Listen to yourself, just fucking listen to yourself!' Curt's voice had hoarsened. 'How could you do this to me? I was so good to you.'

He was already looking at their relationship through the lens of the past tense. It puzzled her, the ability of romantic love to mutate, how quickly a loved one could become a stranger. Where did the love go? Perhaps real love was familial, somehow linked to blood, since love for children did not die as romantic love did.

'You won't forgive me,' she said, a half question.

'Bitch,' he said.

He wielded the word like a knife; it came out of his mouth sharp with loathing. To hear Curt say 'bitch' so coldly felt surreal, and tears gathered in her eyes, knowing that she had turned him into a man who could say 'bitch' so coldly, and wishing he was a man who would not have said 'bitch' no matter what. Alone in her apartment, she cried and cried, crumpled on her living room rug that was so rarely used it still smelled of the store. Her relationship with Curt was what she wanted, a crested wave in her life, and yet she had taken an axe and hacked at it. Why had she destroyed it? She imagined her mother saying it was the devil. She wished she believed in the devil, in a being outside of yourself that invaded your mind and caused you to destroy that which you cared about.

She spent weeks calling Curt, waiting in front of his building until he came out, saying over and over how sorry she was, how much she wanted to work through things. On the day she woke up and finally accepted that Curt would not return her calls, would not open the door of his apartment no matter how hard she knocked, she went alone to their favourite bar downtown. The bartender, the one who knew them, gave her a gentle smile, a sympathy smile. She smiled back and ordered another mojito, thinking that perhaps the bartender was better suited for Curt, with her brown hair blow-dried to satin, her thin arms and tight black clothes and her ability always to be seamlessly, harmlessly chatty. She would also be seamlessly, harmlessly faithful; if she had a man like Curt, she would not be interested in a curiosity copulation with a stranger who played unharmonious music. Ifemelu stared into her glass. There was something wrong with her. She did not know what it was but there was something wrong with her. A hunger, a restlessness. An incomplete knowledge of herself. The sense of something farther away, beyond her reach. She got up and left a big tip on the counter. For a long time afterwards, her memory of the end with Curt was this: speeding down Charles Street in a taxi, a little drunk and a little relieved and a little lonely, with a Punjabi driver who was proudly telling her that his children did better than American children at school.

★   ★   ★

443

Some years later, at a dinner party in Manhattan, a day after Barack Obama became the Democratic Party's candidate for President of the United States, surrounded by guests, all fervent Obama supporters who were dewy-eyed with wine and victory, a balding white man said, 'Obama will end racism in this country,' and a large-hipped, stylish poet from Haiti agreed, nodding, her Afro bigger than Ifemelu's, and said she had dated a white man for three years in California and race was never an issue for them.

'That's a lie,' Ifemelu said to her.

'What?' the woman asked, as though she could not have heard properly.

'It's a lie,' Ifemelu repeated.

The woman's eyes bulged. 'You're telling me what my own experience was?'

Even though Ifemelu by then understood that people like the woman said what they said to keep others comfortable, and to show they appreciated How Far We Have Come; even though she was by then happily ensconced in a circle of Blaine's friends, one of whom was the woman's new boyfriend, and even though she should have left it alone, she did not. She could not. The words had, once again, overtaken her; they overpowered her throat, and tumbled out.

'The only reason you say that race was not an issue is because you wish it was not. We all wish it was not. But it's a lie. I came from a country where race was not an issue; I did not think of myself as black and I only became black when I came to America. When you are black in America and you fall in love with a white person, race doesn't matter when you're alone together because it's just you and your love. But the minute you step outside, race matters. But we don't talk about it. We don't even tell our white partners the small things that piss us off and the things we wish they understood better, because we're worried they will say we're overreacting, or we're being too sensitive. And we don't want them to say, Look how far we've come, just forty years ago it would have been illegal for us to even be a couple blah blah blah, because you know what we're thinking when they say that? We're thinking why the fuck should it ever have been illegal anyway? But we don't say any of this stuff. We let it pile up inside our heads and when we come to nice liberal dinners like this, we say that race doesn't matter because that's what we're supposed to say, to keep our nice liberal friends comfortable. It's true. I speak from experience.'

The host, a Frenchwoman, glanced at her American husband, a slyly pleased smile on her face; the most unforgettable dinner parties happened when guests said unexpected, and potentially offensive, things.

The poet shook her head and said to the host, 'I'd love to take some of that wonderful dip home if you have any left,' and looked at the others as though she could not believe they were actually

445

listening to Ifemelu. But they were, all of them hushed, their eyes on Ifemelu as though she was about to give up a salacious secret that would both titillate and implicate them. Ifemelu had been drinking too much white wine; from time to time she had a swimming sensation in her head, and she would later send apology e-mails to the host and the poet. But everyone was watching her, even Blaine, whose expression she could not, for once, read clearly. And so she began to talk about Curt.

It was not that they avoided race, she and Curt. They talked about it in the slippery way that admitted nothing and engaged nothing and ended with the word 'crazy', like a curious nugget to be examined and then put aside. Or as jokes that left her with a small and numb discomfort that she never admitted to him. And it was not that Curt pretended that being black and being white were the same in America; he knew they were not. It was, instead, that she did not understand how he grasped one thing but was completely tone-deaf about another similar thing, how he could easily make one imaginative leap, but be crippled in the face of another. Before his cousin Ashleigh's wedding, for example, he dropped her off at a small spa near his childhood home, to get her eyebrows shaped. Ifemelu walked in and smiled at the Asian woman behind the counter.

'Hi. I'd like to get my eyebrows waxed.'

'We don't do curly,' the woman said.

'You don't do curly?'

'No. Sorry.'

Ifemelu gave the woman a long look; it was not worth an argument. If they did not do curly, then they did not do curly, whatever curly was. She called Curt and asked him to turn around and come back for her because the salon did not do curly. Curt walked in, his blue eyes bluer, and said he wanted to talk to the manager right away. 'You are going to fucking do my girlfriend's eyebrows or I'll shut down this fucking place. You don't deserve to have a licence.'

The woman transformed into a smiling, solicitous coquette. 'I'm so sorry, it was a misunderstanding,' she said. Yes, they could do the eyebrows. Ifemelu did not want to, worried that the woman might scald her, rip her skin off, pinch her, but Curt was too outraged on her behalf, his anger smouldering in the closed air of the spa, and so she sat, tensely, as the woman waxed her eyebrows.

As they drove back, Curt asked, 'How is the hair of your eyebrows curly anyway? And how is that hard to fucking wax?'

'Maybe they've never done a black woman's eyebrows and so they think it's different, because our hair *is* different, after all, but I guess now she knows the eyebrows are not that different.'

Curt scoffed, reaching across to take her hand, his palm warm. At the cocktail reception, he kept his fingers meshed with hers. Young females in tiny dresses, their breaths and bellies sucked in, trooped across to say hello to him and to flirt, asking if he remembered them, Ashleigh's friend from high school, Ashleigh's room-mate in college. When Curt said, 'This is my girlfriend, Ifemelu,' they looked at her with surprise, a surprise that some of them shielded and some of them did not, and in their expressions was the question 'Why her?' It amused Ifemelu. She had seen that look before, on the faces of white women, strangers on the street, who would see her hand clasped in Curt's and instantly cloud their faces with that look. The look of people confronting a great tribal loss. It was not merely because Curt was white, it was the kind of white he was, the untamed golden hair and handsome face, the athlete's body, the sunny charm and the smell, around him, of money. If he were fat, older, poor, plain, eccentric, or dread-locked, then it would be less remarkable, and the guardians of the tribe would be mollified. And it did not help that although she might be a pretty black girl, she was not the kind of black that they could, with an effort, imagine him with: she was not light-skinned, she was not biracial. At that party, as Curt held on to her hand, kissed her often, introduced her to everyone, her amusement curdled into exhaustion. The looks had begun to pierce her skin. She was tired even of Curt's protection, tired of needing protection.

Curt leaned in and whispered, 'That one, the one with the bad spray tan? She can't even see her fucking boyfriend's been checking you out since we walked in here.'

448

So he had noticed, and understood, the 'Why her?' looks. It surprised her. Sometimes, in the middle of floating on his bubbly exuberance, he would have a flash of intuition, of surprising perception, and she would wonder if there were other more primal things she was missing about him. Such as when he told his mother, who had glanced at the Sunday newspaper and mumbled that some people were still looking for reasons to complain even though America was now colour-blind, 'Come on, Mother. What if ten people who look like Ifemelu suddenly walked in here to eat? You realize our fellow diners will be less than pleased?'

'Maybe,' his mother said, noncommittal, and shot an eyebrow-raise of accusation at Ifemelu, as though to say she knew very well who had turned her son into a pathetic race warrior. Ifemelu smiled a small, victorious smile.

And yet. Once, they visited his aunt, Claire, in Vermont, a woman who had an organic farm and walked around barefoot and talked about how connected to the earth it made her feel. Did Ifemelu have such an experience in Nigeria? she asked, and looked disappointed when Ifemelu said her mother would slap her if she ever stepped outside without shoes. Claire talked, throughout the visit, about her Kenyan safari, about Mandela's grace, about her adoration for Harry Belafonte, and Ifemelu worried that she would lapse into Ebonics or Swahili. As they left her rambling house, Ifemelu said, 'I bet she's an interesting woman if she'd just be herself. I don't need her to over-assure me that she likes black people.'

And Curt said it was not about race, it was just that his aunt was hyper-aware of difference, any difference.

'She would have done the exact same thing if I had turned up with a blonde Russian,' he said.

Of course his aunt would not have done the same thing with a blonde Russian. A blonde Russian was white, and his aunt would not feel the need to prove that she liked people who looked like the blonde Russian. But Ifemelu did not tell Curt this because she wished it were obvious to him.

When they walked into a restaurant with linen-covered tables, and the host looked at them and asked Curt, 'Table for one?' Curt hastily told her the host did not mean it 'like that'. And she wanted to ask him, 'How else could the host have meant it?' When the strawberry-haired owner of the bed-and-breakfast in Montreal refused to acknowledge her as they checked in, a steadfast refusal, smiling and looking only at Curt, she wanted to tell Curt how slighted she felt, worse because she was unsure whether the woman disliked black people or liked Curt. But she did not, because he would tell her she was overreacting or tired or both. There were, simply, times that he saw and times that he was unable to see. She knew that she should tell him these thoughts, that not telling him cast a shadow over them both. Still, she chose silence. Until the day they argued about her magazine. He had picked up a copy of *Essence* from the pile on her coffee table, on a rare morning that they spent in her apartment, the air still thick with the aroma of the omelettes she had made.

'This magazine's kind of racially skewed,' he said.

'What?'

'Come on. Only black women featured?'

'You're serious,' she said.

He looked puzzled. 'Yeah.'

'We're going to the bookstore.'

'What?'

'I need to show you something. Don't ask.'

'Okay,' he said, unsure what this new adventure was but eager, with that childlike delight of his, to participate.

She drove to the bookstore in the Inner Harbor, took down copies of the different women's magazines from the display shelf and led the way to the café.

'Do you want a latte?' he asked.

'Yes, thanks.'

After they settled down on the chairs, paper cups in front of them, she said, 'Let's start with the covers.' She spread the magazines on the table, some on top of the others. 'Look, all of them are white women. This one is supposed to be Hispanic, we know this because they wrote two Spanish words here, but she looks exactly like this white woman, no difference in her skin tone and hair and features. Now, I'm going to flip through, page by page, and you tell me how many black women you see.'

'Babe, come on,' Curt said, amused, leaning back, paper cup to his lips.

'Just humour me,' she said.

And so he counted. 'Three black women,' he said, finally. 'Or maybe four. *She* could be black.'

'So three black women in maybe two thousand pages of women's magazines, and all of them are biracial or racially ambiguous, so they could also be Indian or Puerto Rican or something. Not one of them is dark. Not one of them looks like me, so I can't get clues for make-up from these magazines. Look, this article tells you to pinch your cheeks for colour because all their readers are supposed to have cheeks you can pinch for colour. This tells you about different hair products for *everyone* – and "everyone" means blondes, brunettes and redheads. I am none of those. And this tells you about the best conditioners – for straight, wavy and curly. No kinky. See what they mean by curly? My hair could never do that. This tells you about matching your eye colour and eyeshadow – blue, green and hazel eyes. But my eyes are black so I can't know what shadow works for me. This says that this pink lipstick is universal, but they mean universal if you are white because I would look like a golliwog if I tried that shade of pink. Oh, look, here is some progress. An advertisement for foundation. There are seven different shades for white skin and one generic chocolate shade, but that is progress. Now, let's talk about what is racially skewed. Do you see why a magazine like *Essence* even exists?'

'Okay, babe, okay, I didn't mean for it to be such a big deal,' he said.

That evening, Ifemelu wrote a long e-mail to Wambui about the bookstore, the magazines, the things she didn't tell Curt, things unsaid and unfinished. It was a long e-mail, digging, questioning, unearthing. Wambui replied to say, 'This is so raw and true. More people should read this. You should start a blog.'

Blogs were new, unfamiliar to her. But telling Wambui what happened was not satisfying enough; she longed for other listeners, and she longed to hear the stories of others. How many other people chose silence? How many other people had become black in America? How many had felt as though their world was wrapped in gauze? She broke up with Curt a few weeks after that, and she signed on to WordPress, and her blog was born. She would later change the name, but at first she called it *Raceteenth or Curious Observations by a Non-American Black on the Subject of Blackness in America*. Her first post was a better-punctuated version of the e-mail she had sent to Wambui. She referred to Curt as 'The Hot White Ex'. A few hours later, she checked her blog stats. Nine people had read it. Panicked, she took down the post. The next day, she put it up again, modified and edited, ending with words she still so easily remembered. She recited those words now, at the dinner table of the French and American couple, while the Haitian poet stared, arms folded.

> The simplest solution to the problem of race in America? Romantic love. Not friendship. Not the kind of safe, shallow love where the objective is that both people remain comfortable. But real deep romantic love, the kind that twists you and wrings you out and makes you breathe through the nostrils of your beloved. And because that real deep romantic love is so rare, and because American society is set up to make it even rarer between American Black and American White, the problem of race in America will never be solved.

'Oh! What a wonderful story!' the French host said, her palm placed dramatically on her chest, looking around the table, as though to seek a response. But everyone else remained silent, their eyes averted and unsure.

A Michelle Obama Shout-Out Plus Hair as Race Metaphor

White Girlfriend and I are Michelle Obama groupies. So the other day I say to her – I wonder if Michelle Obama has a weave, her hair looks fuller today, and all that heat every day must damage it. And she says – you mean her hair doesn't grow like that? So is it me or is that the perfect metaphor for race in America right there? Hair. Ever notice makeover shows on TV, how the black woman has natural hair (coarse, coily, kinky, or curly) in the ugly 'before' picture, and in the pretty 'after' picture, somebody's taken a hot piece of metal and singed her hair straight? Some black women, AB and NAB, would rather run naked in the street than come out in public with their natural hair. Because, you see, it's not professional, sophisticated, what-ever, it's just not damn normal. (Please, commenters, don't tell me it's the same as a white woman who doesn't color her hair.) When you DO have natural Negro hair, people think you 'did' something to your hair. Actually, the folk with the Afros and dreads are the ones who haven't 'done' anything to their hair. You should be asking Beyoncé what she's done. (We all love Bey but how about she show us, just once, what her hair looks like when it grows from her scalp?) I have natural kinky hair. Worn in cornrows, Afros, braids. No, it's not polit-ical. No, I am not an artist or poet or singer. Not an earth mother either. I just don't want relaxers in my hair – there are enough sources of cancer in my life as it is. (By the way, can we ban Afro wigs at Halloween? Afro is not costume, for God's sake.) Imagine if Michelle Obama got tired of all the heat and decided to go natural and appeared on TV with lots of woolly hair, or tight spirally curls. (There is no knowing what her texture will be. It is not unusual for a black woman to have three different textures on her head.) She would totally rock but poor Obama would certainly lose the independent vote, even the undecided Democrat vote.

UPDATE: ZoraNeale22, who's transitioning, asked me to post my regimen. Pure shea butter as a leave-in conditioner works for many naturals. Not for me, though. Anything with lots of shea butter leaves my hair grayish and dryish. And dry is my hair's biggest problem. I wash once a week with a silicone-free hydrating shampoo. I use a hydrating conditioner. I do not towel-dry my hair. I leave it wet, divide it in sections, and apply a creamy leave-in product (present favorite is Qhemet Biologics, other preferred brands are Oyin Handmade, Shea Moisture, Bask Beauty, and Darcy's Botanicals). Then I put my hair in three or four big cornrows, and knot my satin scarf around my head (satin is good, it preserves moisture. Cotton is bad, it soaks up moisture). I go to sleep. The next morning, I take out the cornrows and voilà, a lovely fluffy 'fro! Key is to add product while hair is wet. And I never, ever comb my hair when it's dry. I comb only when wet, or damp, or totally drenched in a creamy moisturizer. This plait-while-wet regimen can even work for our Seriously Curly White Girlfriends who are tired of flatirons and keratin treatments. Any AB and NAB naturals out there who want to share their regimen?

CHAPTER 32

For weeks, Ifemelu stumbled around, trying to remember the person she was before Curt. Their life together had happened to her, she would not have been able to imagine it if she had tried, and so, surely, she could return to what was before. But before was a slate-toned blur and she no longer knew who she had been then, what she had enjoyed, disliked, wanted. Her job bored her: she did the same bland things, writing press releases, editing press releases, copy-editing press releases, her movements rote and numbing. Perhaps it had always been so and she had not noticed, because she was blinded by the brightness of Curt. Her apartment felt like a stranger's home. On weekends, she went to Willow. Aunty Uju's condo was in a cluster of stucco buildings, the neighbourhood carefully landscaped, boulders placed at corners, and in the evenings, friendly people walked their handsome dogs. Aunty Uju had taken on a new light-heartedness; she wore a tiny anklet in the summer, a hopeful flash of gold on her leg. She had joined African Doctors for Africa, volunteering her time on two-week medical missions, and on her trip to Sudan, she met Kweku, a divorced Ghanaian doctor. 'He treats me like a princess. Just like Curt treated you,' she told Ifemelu.

'I'm trying to forget him, Aunty. Stop talking about him!'

'Sorry,' Aunty Uju said, not looking sorry at all. She had told Ifemelu to do everything to save the relationship, because she would not find another man who would love her as Curt had. When Ifemelu told Dike that she had broken up with Curt, he said, 'He was pretty cool, Coz. Are you going to be okay?'

'Yes, of course.'

Perhaps he sensed otherwise, and knew of the slight unsteadiness of her spirit; most nights she lay in bed and cried, berating herself for what she had destroyed, then telling herself that she had no reason to be crying, and crying all the same. Dike brought up a tray to her room, on which he had placed a banana and a can of peanuts.

'Snack time!' he said, with a teasing grin; he still did not understand why anybody would want to eat both together. While Ifemelu ate, he sat on the bed and told her about school. He was playing basketball now, his grades had improved, he liked a girl called Autumn.

'You're really settling in here.'

'Yeah,' he said, and his smile reminded her of what it used to be in Brooklyn, open, unguarded.

'Remember the character Goku in my Japanese anime?' he asked.

'Yes.'

'You kind of look like Goku with your Afro,' Dike said, laughing.

Kweku knocked and waited for her to say 'Come in' before he poked his head in. 'Dike, are you ready?' he asked.

'Yes, Uncle.' Dike got up. 'Let's roll!'

'We're going to the community centre, would you like to join us?' Kweku asked Ifemelu, tentatively, almost formally; he, too, knew she was suffering from a break-up. He was small and bespectacled, a gentleman and a gentle man; Ifemelu liked him because he liked Dike.

'No, thank you,' Ifemelu said. He lived in a house not far away, but some of his shirts were in Aunty Uju's closet, and Ifemelu had seen a face wash for men in Aunty Uju's bathroom, and cartons of organic yogurt in the fridge, which she knew Aunty Uju did not eat. He looked at Aunty Uju with translucent eyes, those of a man who wanted the world to know how much he loved. It reminded Ifemelu of Curt, and made her feel, again, a wistful sadness.

Her mother heard something in her voice over the phone. 'Are you sick? Did anything happen?'

'I'm fine. Just work,' she said.

Her father, too, asked why she sounded different and if all was well. She told him that all was well, that she was spending much of her time after work blogging; she was about to explain this new pastime of hers, but he said, 'I'm fairly familiar with the concept. We have been undergoing a rigorous computer literacy training in the office.'

'They have confirmed your father's application. He can take his leave when my school vacates,' her mother said. 'So we should apply for our visa quickly.'

Ifemelu had long dreamed of, and talked about, when they would be able to visit her. She could afford it now, and her mother wanted it now, but she wished it could be another time. She wanted to see them, but the thought of their visit exhausted her. She was not sure she would be able to be their daughter, the person they remembered.

'Mummy, things are very busy at work now.'

'Ahn-ahn. Are we coming to disturb your work?'

And so she sent them invitation letters, bank statements, a copy of her green card. The American embassy was better now; the staff was still rude, her father said, but you no longer had to fight and shove outside to get in line. They were given six-month visas. They came for three weeks. They seemed like strangers. They looked the same, but the dignity she remembered was gone, and left instead something small, a provincial eagerness. Her father marvelled at the industrial carpeting in the hallway of her apartment building; her mother hoarded faux-leather handbags at Kmart, paper napkins from the mall food court, even plastic shopping bags. They both posed for photos in front of JC Penney, asking Ifemelu to make sure she got the entire sign of the store. She watched them with a sneer, and for this she felt guilty; she had guarded their memories so preciously and yet, finally seeing them, she watched them with a sneer.

'I do not understand Americans. They say "job" and you think they have said "jab",' her father declared, spelling both words. 'One finds the British manner of speaking much preferable.'

Before they left, her mother asked her quietly, 'Do you have a friend?' She said 'friend' in English; the tame word parents used because they could not desecrate their tongues with 'boyfriend', even though it was exactly what they meant: somebody romantic, a marriage prospect.

'No,' Ifemelu said. 'I have been very busy with work.'

'Work is good, Ifem. But you should also keep your eyes open. Remember that a woman is like a flower. Our time passes quickly.'

Before, she might have laughed dismissively, and told her mother that she did not at all feel like a flower, but now she was too tired, it felt too much of an effort. On the day they left for Nigeria, she collapsed onto her bed, crying uncontrollably, and thinking: What is wrong with me? She was relieved that her parents had gone, and she felt guilty for feeling relief. After work, she wandered around the centre of Baltimore, aimlessly, interested in nothing. Was this what the novelists meant by ennui? On a slow Wednesday afternoon, she handed in her resignation. She had not planned to resign, but it suddenly seemed to be what she had to do, and so she typed the letter on her computer and took it to her manager's office.

'You were making such progress. Is there anything we can do to make you change your mind?' her manager asked, very surprised.

'It's personal, family reasons,' Ifemelu said vaguely. 'I really appreciate all the opportunities you've given me.'

So What's the Deal?

They tell us race is an invention, that there is more genetic variation between two black people than there is between a black person and a white person. Then they tell us black people have a worse kind of breast cancer and get more fibroids. And white folk get cystic fibrosis and osteoporosis. So what's the deal, doctors in the house? Is race an invention or not?

CHAPTER 33

The blog had unveiled itself and shed its milk teeth; by turns, it surprised her, pleased her, left her behind. Its readers increased, by the thousands from all over the world, so quickly that she resisted checking the stats, reluctant to know how many new people had clicked to read her that day, because it frightened her. And it exhilarated her. When she saw her posts reposted on another site, she flushed with accomplishment, and yet she had not imagined any of this, had never nursed any firm ambition. E-mails came from readers who wanted to support the blog. Support. That word made the blog even more apart from her, a separate thing that could thrive or not, sometimes without her and sometimes with her. So she put up a link to her PayPal account. Credits appeared, many small and one so large that when she saw it, she let out an unfamiliar sound, a blend of a gasp and a scream. It began to appear every month, anonymously, as regular as a pay cheque, and each time it did, she felt abashed, as though she had picked up something valuable on the street and kept it for herself. She wondered if it was from Curt, just as she wondered if he followed the blog, and what he thought of being referred to as The Hot White Ex. It was a half-hearted wondering; she missed what could have been, but she no longer missed him.

She checked her blog e-mail too often, like a child eagerly tearing open a present she is not sure she wants, and read mail from people asking for a drink, telling her she was a racist, giving her ideas to blog about. A fellow blogger who made hair butters first suggested advertising and, for a token fee, Ifemelu put up the image of a bounteous-haired woman on the top right side of the blog page; clicking on it led to the hair butter website. Another reader offered more money for a blinking graphic that showed, first, a long-necked model in a tight dress, then the same model in a floppy hat. Clicking on the image led to an online boutique. Soon there were e-mails about advertising Pantene shampoos and Covergirl make-up. Then an e-mail from the director of multicultural life at a prep school in Connecticut, so formal she imagined it typed on hand-cut paper with a silver crest, asking if she would speak to the students on diversity. Another e-mail came from a corporation in Pennsylvania, less formally written, telling her a local professor had identified her as a provocative race blogger and asking if she would lead their annual diversity workshop. An editor from *Baltimore Living* e-mailed to say that they wanted to include her in a Ten People to Watch feature; she was photographed next to her laptop, her face doused in shadow, under the caption 'The Blogger'. Her readers tripled. More invitations came. To receive phone calls, she wore her most serious pair of trousers, her most muted shade of lipstick, and she spoke sitting upright at her desk, legs crossed, her voice measured and sure. Yet a part of her always stiffened with apprehension, expecting the person on the other end to realize that she was play-acting this professional, this negotiator of terms, to see that she was, in fact, an unemployed person who wore a rumpled nightshirt all day, to call her 'Fraud!' and hang up. But more invitations came. Hotel and travel were covered and the fees varied. Once she said, on an impulse, that she wanted twice what she had been offered the previous week, and was shocked when the man calling from Delaware said, 'Yeah, we could do that.'

Most of the people who attended her first diversity talk, in a small company in Ohio, wore sneakers. They were all white. Her presentation was titled 'How to talk about race with colleagues of other races', but who, she wondered, would they be talking to, since they were all white? Perhaps the janitor was black.

'I'm no expert so don't quote me,' she started, and they laughed, warm encouraging laughter, and she told herself that this would go well, she need not have worried about talking to a roomful of strangers in the middle of Ohio. (She had read,

466

with mild worry, that openly sundown towns still existed here.) 'The first step to honest communication about race is to realize that you cannot equate all racisms,' she said, and then launched into her carefully prepared speech. When, at the end, she said, 'Thank you,' pleased with the fluidness of her delivery, the faces around her were frozen. The leaden clapping deflated her. Afterwards, she was left only with the director of human resources, drinking oversweet iced tea in the conference room, and talking about soccer, which he knew Nigeria played well, as though keen to discuss anything but the talk she had just given. That evening she received an e-mail: *YOUR TALK WAS BALONEY. YOU ARE A RACIST. YOU SHOULD BE GRATEFUL WE LET YOU INTO THIS COUNTRY.*

That e-mail, written in all capital letters, was a revelation. The point of diversity workshops, or multicultural talks, was not to inspire any real change but to leave people feeling good about themselves. They did not want the content of her ideas; they merely wanted the gesture of her presence. They had not read her blog but they had heard that she was a 'leading blogger' about race. And so, in the following weeks, as she gave more talks at companies and schools, she began to say what they wanted to hear, none of which she would ever write on her blog, because she knew that the people who read her blog were not the same people who attended her diversity workshops. During her

467

talks, she said: 'America has made great progress for which we should be very proud.' In her blog she wrote: *Racism should never have happened and so you don't get a cookie for reducing it.* Still more invitations came. She hired a student intern, a Haitian American, her hair worn in elegant twists, who was nimble on the Internet, looking up whatever information Ifemelu needed, and deleting inappropriate comments almost as soon as they were posted.

Ifemelu bought a small condominium. She had been startled, when she first saw the listing in the real estate section of the paper, to realize she could afford the down payment in cash. Signing her name above the word 'homeowner' had left her with a frightening sense of being grown-up, and also with a small astonishment, that this was possible because of her blog. She converted one of the two bedrooms into a study and wrote there, standing often by the window to look down at her new Roland Park neighbourhood, the restored row homes shielded by old trees. It surprised her, which blog posts got attention and which were hardly clicked on. Her post about trying to date online, 'What's Love Got to Do with It?' continued to draw comments, like something sticky, after many months.

So, still a bit sad about the break-up with The Hot White Ex, not into the bar scene, and so I signed up for online dating. And

I looked at lots of profiles. So here's the thing. In that category where you choose the ethnicity you are interested in? White men tick white women, and the braver ones tick Asian and Hispanic. Hispanic men tick white and Hispanic. Black men are the only men likely to tick 'all', but some don't even tick Black. They tick White, Asian, Hispanic. I wasn't feeling the love. But what's love got to do with all that ticking, anyway? You could walk into a grocery store and bump into someone and fall in love and that someone would not be the race you tick online. So after browsing, I cancelled my membership, thankfully still on trial, got a refund, and will be walking around blindly in the grocery store instead.

Comments came from people with similar stories and people saying she was wrong, from men asking her to put up a photo of herself, from black women sharing success stories of online dating, from people angry and from people thrilled. Some comments amused her, because they were wildly unconnected to the subject of the post. *Oh fuck off*, one wrote. *Black people get everything easy. You can't get anything in this country unless you're black. Black women are even allowed to weigh more.* Her recurring post 'Mish Mash Friday', a jumble of thoughts, drew the most clicks and comments each week. Sometimes she wrote some posts expecting ugly responses, her stomach tight with dread and excitement, but they would draw only tepid comments. Now that she was asked to speak at round-tables and panels, on public radio and community radio, always identified simply as The Blogger, she felt subsumed by her blog. She had become her blog. There were times, lying awake at night, when her growing discomforts crawled out from the crevices, and the blog's many readers became, in her mind, a judgemental angry mob waiting for her, biding their time until they could attack her, unmask her.

Open Thread: For All the Zipped-Up Negroes

This is for the Zipped-Up Negroes, the upwardly mobile American and Non-American Blacks who don't talk about Life Experiences That Have to Do Exclusively with Being Black. Because they want to keep everyone comfortable. Tell your story here. Unzip yourself. This is a safe space.

CHAPTER 34

Her blog brought Blaine back into her life. At the Blogging While Brown convention in Washington, DC, during the meet-and-greet on the first day, the hotel foyer crowded with people saying hello to others in nervously over-bright voices, she had been talking to a make-up blogger, a thin Mexican American woman wearing neon eyeshadow, when she looked up and felt herself still and quake, because standing a few delicate feet from her, in a small circle of people, was Blaine. He was unchanged, except for the black-framed glasses. Just as she remembered him on the train: tall and easy-limbed. The make-up blogger was talking about beauty companies always sending free stuff to *Bellachicana*, and the ethics of it, and Ifemelu was nodding, but was truly alert only to the presence of Blaine, and to him easing himself away from his circle, and moving towards her.

'Hi!' he said, peering at her name tag. 'So you're the Non-American Black? I love your blog.'

'Thank you,' she said. He didn't remember her. But why should he? It had been so long since the meeting on the train, and neither of them knew

471

then what the word 'blog' meant. It would amuse him to know how much she had idealized him, how he had become a person made not of flesh but of little crystals of perfection, the American man she would never have. He turned to say hello to the make-up blogger and she saw, from his name tag, that he wrote a blog about the 'intersection of academia and popular culture'.

He turned back to her. 'So are your mall visits in Connecticut still going okay? Because I still grow my own cotton.'

For a moment, her breath stalled, and then she laughed, a dizzying, exhilarating laugh, because her life had become a charmed film in which people found each other again. 'You remember!'

'I've been watching you from the other end of the room. I couldn't believe it when I saw you.'

'Oh my God, what has it been, like ten years?'

'About that. Eight?'

'You never called me back,' she said.

'I was in a relationship. It was troubled even then, but it lasted much longer than it should have.' He paused, with an expression that she would come to know well, a virtuous narrowing of his eyes that announced the high-mindedness of their owner.

E-mails and phone calls between Baltimore and New Haven followed, playful comments posted on each other's blogs, heavy flirting during late-night calls, until the day in winter when he came to her door, his hands sunk into the pockets of his tin-coloured peacoat and his collar sprinkled with snow like magic dust. She was cooking coconut rice, her apartment thick with spices, a bottle of cheap merlot on her counter, and Nina Simone playing loudly on her CD. The song 'Don't Let Me Be Misunderstood' guided them, only minutes after he arrived, across the bridge from flirting friends to lovers. Afterwards, he propped himself up on his elbow to watch her. There was something fluid, almost epicene, about his lean body, and it made her remember that he had told her he did yoga. Perhaps he could stand on his head, twist himself into unlikely permutations. When she mixed the rice, now cold, in the coconut sauce, she told him that cooking bored her, and that she had bought all these spices only the day before, and had cooked because he was visiting. She had imagined them both with ginger on their lips, yellow curry licked off her body, bay leaves crushed beneath them, but instead they had been so responsible, kissing in the living room and then her leading him to her bedroom.

'We should have done things more improbably,' she said.

He laughed. 'I like cooking, so there will be many opportunities for the improbable.' But she knew that he was not the sort of person to do things improbably. Not with his slipping on of the condom with such slow and clinical concentration. Later, when she came to know of the letters he wrote to Congress about Darfur, the teenagers he tutored at the high school on Dixwell, the shelter he volunteered at, she thought of him as a person who did not have a normal spine but had, instead, a firm reed of goodness.

It was as if because of their train meeting years ago, they could bypass several steps, ignore several unknowns, and slide into an immediate intimacy. After his first visit, she went back to New Haven with him. There were weeks that winter, cold and sunny weeks, when New Haven seemed lit from within, frosted snow clinging on shrubs, a festive quality to a world that seemed inhabited fully only by her and Blaine. They would walk to the falafel place on Howe Street for hummus, and sit in a dark corner talking for hours, and finally emerge, tongues smarting with garlic. Or she would meet him at the library after his class, where they sat in the café, drinking chocolate that was too rich, eating croissants that were too grainily whole wheat, his clutch of books on the table. He cooked organic vegetables and grains whose names she could not pronounce – bulgur, quinoa – and he swiftly cleaned up as he cooked, a splatter of tomato sauce wiped up as soon as it appeared, a spill of water immediately dabbed at. He frightened her, telling her about the chemicals that were sprayed on crops, the chemicals fed to chickens to make them grow quickly, and the chemicals used to give fruits perfect skin. Why did she think people were dying of cancer? And so before she ate an apple, she scrubbed it at the sink, even though Blaine only bought organic fruit. He told her which grains had protein, which vegetables had carotene, which fruits were too sugary. He knew about everything; she was intimidated by this and proud of this and slightly repelled by this. Little domesticities with him, in his apartment on the twentieth floor of a high-rise near the campus, became gravid with meaning – the way he watched her moisturize with cocoa butter after an evening shower, the whooshing sound his dishwasher made when it started – and she imagined a cot in the bedroom, a baby inside it, and Blaine carefully blending organic fruits for the baby. He would be a perfect father, this man of careful disciplines.

'I can't eat tempeh, I don't understand how you like it,' she told him.

'I don't like it.'

'Then why eat it?'

'It's good for me.'

He ran every morning and flossed every night. It seemed so American to her, flossing, that mechanical sliding of a string between teeth, in-elegant and functional. 'You should floss every day,' Blaine told her. And she began to floss, as she began to do other things that he did – going to the gym, eating more protein than carbohydrates – and she did them with a kind of grateful content-ment, because they improved her. He was like a salutary tonic; with him, she could only inhabit a higher level of goodness.

★   ★   ★

His best friend, Araminta, came up to visit him, and hugged Ifemelu warmly, as though they had met previously. 'Blaine hasn't really dated since he broke up with Paula. And now, he's with a sister, and a chocolate sister at that. We're making progress!' Araminta said.

'Mint, stop it,' Blaine said, but he was smiling. That his best friend was a woman, an architect with a long straight weave who wore high heels and tight jeans and coloured contact lenses, said something about Blaine that Ifemelu liked.

'Blaine and I grew up together. In high school, we were the only black kids in our class. All our friends wanted us to date, you know how they think the two black kids just have to be together, but he so wasn't my type,' Araminta said.

'You wish,' Blaine said.

'Ifemelu, can I just say how happy I am that you're not an academic? Have you heard his friends talk? Nothing is just what it is. Everything has to mean something else. It's ridiculous. The other day Marcia was talking about how black women are fat because their bodies are sites of anti-slavery resistance. Yes, that's true, if burgers and sodas are anti-slavery resistance.'

'Anybody can see through that whole anti-intellectual pose thing, Miss Drinks at Harvard Club,' Blaine said.

'Come on. A good education isn't the same thing as making the whole damn world something to be explained! Even Shan makes fun of you guys. She

476

does a great imitation of you and Grace: *canon formation and topography of the spatial and historical consciousness.*' Araminta turned to Ifemelu. 'You haven't met his sister Shan?'

'No.'

Later, when Blaine was in the bedroom, Araminta said, 'Shan's an interesting character. Don't take her too seriously when you meet her.'

'What do you mean?'

'She's great, she's very seductive, but if you think she slights you or anything like that, it's not you, it's just the way she is.' And then she said, in a lower voice, 'Blaine's a really good guy, a really good guy.'

'I know.' Ifemelu sensed, in Araminta's words, something that was either a warning or a plea.

Blaine asked her to move in after a month, but it took a year before she did, even though by then she was spending most of her time in New Haven, and had a Yale gym pass as a professor's partner, and wrote her blogs from his apartment, at a desk he had placed for her near the bedroom window. At first, thrilled by his interest, graced by his intelligence, she let him read her blog posts before she put them up. She did not ask for his edits, but slowly she began to make changes, to add and remove, because of what he said. Then she began to resent it. Her posts sounded too academic, too much like him. She had written a post about inner cities – 'Why Are the Dankest, Drabbest Parts of American Cities Full of American Blacks?' – and he told her to include details about government policy and redistricting. She did, but after rereading it, she took down the post.

'I don't want to explain, I want to observe,' she said.

'Remember people are not reading you as entertainment, they're reading you as cultural commentary. That's a real responsibility. There are kids writing college essays about your blog,' he said. 'I'm not saying you have to be academic or boring. Keep your style but add more depth.'

'It has enough depth,' she said, irritated, but with the niggling thought that he was right.

'You're being lazy, Ifem.'

He used that word, 'lazy', often, for his students who did not hand in work on time, black celebrities who were not politically active, ideas that did not match his own. Sometimes she felt like his apprentice; when they wandered through museums, he would linger at abstract paintings, which bored her, and she would drift to the bold sculptures or the naturalistic paintings, and sense in his tight smile his disappointment that she had not yet learned enough from him. When he played selections from his complete John Coltrane, he would watch her as she listened, waiting for a rapture he was sure would glaze over her, and then at the end, when she remained untransported, he would quickly avert his eyes. She blogged about two novels she loved, by Ann Petry and Gayl Jones, and Blaine said, 'They don't push the boundaries.' He spoke gently, as though he did not want to upset her, but it still had to be said. His positions were firm, so thought-through and fully realized in his own mind that he sometimes seemed surprised that she, too, had not arrived at them herself. She felt a step removed from the things he believed, and the things he knew, and she was eager to play catch-up, fascinated by his sense of rightness. Once, as they walked down Elm Street, on their way to get a sandwich, they saw the plump black woman who was a fixture on campus: always standing near the coffee shop, a woollen hat squashed on her head, offering single plastic red roses to passers-by and asking 'You got any change?' Two students were talking to her, and then one of them gave her a cappuccino in a tall paper cup. The woman looked thrilled; she threw her head back and drank from the cup.

'That's so disgusting,' Blaine said, as they walked past.

'I know,' Ifemelu said, although she did not quite understand why he felt so strongly about the homeless woman and her cappuccino gift. Weeks before, an older white woman standing in line behind them at the grocery store had said, 'Your hair is so beautiful, can I touch it?' and Ifemelu said yes. The woman sank her fingers into her Afro. She sensed Blaine tense, saw the pulsing at his temples. 'How could you let her do that?' he asked afterwards. 'Why not? How else will she know what hair like mine feels like? She probably doesn't know any black people.'

'And so you have to be her guinea pig?' Blaine asked. He expected her to feel what she did not know how to feel. There were things that existed for him that she could not penetrate. With his close friends, she often felt vaguely lost. They were youngish and well-dressed and righteous, their sentences filled with 'sort of', and 'the ways in which'; they gathered at a bar every Thursday, and sometimes one of them had a dinner party, where Ifemelu mostly listened, saying little, looking at them in wonder: were they serious, these people who were so enraged about imported vegetables that ripened in trucks? They wanted to stop child labour in Africa. They would not buy clothes made by underpaid workers in Asia. They looked at the world with an impractical, luminous earnestness that moved her, but never convinced her. Surrounded by them, Blaine hummed with references unfamiliar to her, and he would seem far away, as though he belonged to them, and when he finally looked at her, his eyes warm and loving, she felt something like relief.

She told her parents about Blaine, that she was leaving Baltimore and moving to New Haven to live with him. She could have lied, invented a new job, or simply said she wanted to move. 'His name is Blaine,' she said. 'He's an American.'

She heard the symbolism in her own words, travelling thousands of miles to Nigeria, and she knew what her parents would understand. She and

Blaine had not talked about marriage, but the ground beneath her feet felt firm. She wanted her parents to know of him, and of how good he was. She used that word in describing him: 'good'.

'An American Negro?' her father asked, sounding baffled.

Ifemelu burst out laughing. 'Daddy, nobody says Negro any more.'

'But why a Negro? Is there a substantive scarcity of Nigerians there?'

She ignored him, still laughing, and asked him to give her mother the phone. Ignoring him, even telling him that she was moving in with a man to whom she was not married, was something she could do only because she lived in America. Rules had shifted, fallen into the cracks of distance and foreignness.

Her mother asked, 'Is he a Christian?'

'No. He is a devil-worshipper.'

'Blood of Jesus!' her mother shrieked.

'Mummy, yes, he is a Christian,' she said.

'Then no problem,' her mother said. 'When will he come to introduce himself? You can plan it so that we do everything at the same time – door-knocking, bride price and wine-carrying – it will cut costs and that way he does not have to keep coming and going. America is far . . .'

'Mummy, please, we are taking things slowly for now.'

After Ifemelu hung up, still amused, she decided to change the title of her blog to *Raceteenth or*

Various Observations About American Blacks (Those Formerly Known as Negroes) by a Non-American Black.

Job Vacancy in America – National Arbiter in Chief of 'Who Is Racist'

In America, racism exists but racists are all gone. Racists belong to the past. Racists are the thin-lipped mean white people in the movies about the civil rights era. Here's the thing: the manifestation of racism has changed but the language has not. So if you haven't lynched somebody then you can't be called a racist. If you're not a bloodsucking monster, then you can't be called a racist. Somebody has to be able to say that racists are not monsters. They are people with loving families, regular folk who pay taxes. Somebody needs to get the job of deciding who is racist and who isn't. Or maybe it's time to just scrap the word 'racist.' Find something new. Like Racial Disorder Syndrome. And we could have different categories for sufferers of this syndrome: mild, medium, and acute.

CHAPTER 35

Ifemelu woke up one night to go to the bathroom, and heard Blaine in the living room, talking on the phone, his tone gentle and solacing. 'I'm sorry, did I wake you? That was my sister, Shan,' he said when he came back to bed. 'She's back in New York, from France. Her first book is about to be published and she's having a small meltdown about it.' He paused. 'Another small meltdown. Shan has lots of meltdowns. Will you go down to the city this weekend with me to see her?'

'Sure. What does she do again?'

'What doesn't Shan do? She used to work at a hedge fund. Then she left and travelled all over the world and did a bit of journalism. She met this Haitian guy and moved to Paris to live with him. Then he got sick and died. It happened very quickly. She stayed for a while, and even after she decided to move back to the States, she kept the flat in Paris. She's been with this new guy, Ovidio, for about a year now. He's the first real relationship she's had since Jerry died. Pretty decent cat. He's away this week, on assignment in California, so Shan's alone. She likes to have these gatherings, she calls them salons. She has an amazing group of friends, mostly artists and writers, and they get together at her place and have really good conversations.' He paused. 'She's a really special person.'

When Shan walked into a room, all the air disappeared. She did not breathe deeply; she did not need to: the air simply floated towards her, drawn by her natural authority, until there was nothing left for others. Ifemelu imagined Blaine's airless childhood, running after Shan to impress her, to remind her of his existence. Even now, as an adult, he was still the little brother full of desperate love, trying to win an approval that he feared he never would. They arrived at Shan's apartment early in the afternoon, and Blaine stopped to chat with the doorman, as he had chatted with their taxi driver from Penn Station, in that unforced manner that he had, forming alliances with janitors, with cleaning staff, with bus drivers. He knew how much they made and how many hours they worked; he knew they didn't have health insurance.

'Hey, Jorge, how's it going?' Blaine pronounced it the Spanish way: *Hor-hay.*

'Pretty good. How are your students over at Yale?' the doorman asked, looking pleased to see him and pleased that he taught at Yale.

'Driving me crazy as usual,' Blaine said. Then he pointed at the woman standing by the elevator with her back to them, cradling a pink yoga mat. 'Oh, there's Shan.' Shan was tiny and beautiful, with an oval face and high cheekbones, an imperious face.

'Hey!' she said, and hugged Blaine. She did not look once at Ifemelu. 'I'm so glad I went to my Pilates class. It leaves you if you leave it. Did you go running today?'

'Yep.'

'I just talked to David again. He says he'll send me alternative covers this evening. Finally they seem to be hearing me.' She rolled her eyes. The elevator's doors slid open and she led the way in, still talking to Blaine, who now seemed uncomfortable, as though he was waiting for a moment to make introductions, a moment that Shan was not willing to give.

'The marketing director called me this morning. She had that really unbearable politeness that is worse than any insult, you know? And so she tells me how booksellers love the cover already and blah blah blah. It's ridiculous,' Shan said.

'It's the herd instinct of corporate publishing. They do what everyone else does,' Blaine said.

The elevator stopped at her floor, and she turned to Ifemelu. 'Oh, sorry, I'm so stressed,' she said. 'It's nice to meet you. Blaine won't stop talking about you.' She looked at Ifemelu, a frank sizing-up that was not shy to be a frank sizing-up. 'You're very pretty.'

'*You're* very pretty,' Ifemelu said, surprising

herself, because those were not the words she would have ordinarily said, but she felt already co-opted by Shan; Shan's compliment had made her strangely happy. Shan is special, Blaine had said, and Ifemelu understood now what he meant. Shan had the air of a person who was somehow *chosen*. The gods had placed a wand on her. If she did ordinary things, they became enigmatic.

'Do you like the room?' Shan asked Ifemelu, with a sweep of her hand, taking in the dramatic furnishing: a red rug, a blue sofa, an orange sofa, a green armchair.

'I know it's supposed to mean something but I don't get it.'

Shan laughed, short sounds that seemed cut off prematurely, as though more were supposed to follow but did not, and because she merely laughed, not saying anything, Ifemelu added, 'It's interesting.'

'Yes, *interesting*.' Shan stood by the dining table and raised her leg onto it, leaning over to grasp her foot in her hand. Her body was a collection of graceful small curves, her buttocks, her breasts, her calves, and there was in her movement the entitlement of the chosen; she could stretch her leg on her dining table whenever she wanted, even with a guest in her apartment.

'Blaine introduced me to *Raceteenth*. It's a great blog,' she said.

'Thank you,' Ifemelu said.

'I have a Nigerian friend who is a writer. Do you know Kelechi Garuba?'

'I've read his work.'

'We talked about your blog the other day and he said he was sure the Non-American Black was a Caribbean because Africans don't care about race. He'll be shocked when he meets you!' Shan paused to exchange the leg on the table, leaning in to grasp her foot.

'He's always fretting about how his books don't do well. I've told him he needs to write terrible things about his own people if he wants to do well. He needs to say Africans alone are to blame for African problems, and Europeans have helped Africa more than they've hurt Africa, and he'll be famous and people will say he's so *honest*!'

Ifemelu laughed.

'Interesting picture,' she said, gesturing to a photo on a side table, of Shan holding two bottles of champagne high above her head, surrounded by tattered, smiling, brown children in what looked like a Latin American slum, shacks with patched-up tin walls behind her. 'I mean interesting literally.'

'Ovidio didn't want it displayed but I insisted. It's supposed to be ironic, obviously.'

Ifemelu imagined the insisting, a simple sentence, which would not need to be repeated and which would have Ovidio scrambling.

'So do you go home to Nigeria often?' Shan asked.

'No. Actually I haven't been home since I came to the States.'

'Why?'

'At first I couldn't afford to. Then I had work and just never seemed to make the time.'

Shan was facing her now, her arms stretched out and pushed back like wings.

'Nigerians call us *acata*, right? And it means wild animal?'

'I don't know that it means wild animal, I really don't know what it means, and I don't use it.' Ifemelu found herself almost stammering. It was true and yet in the directness of Shan's gaze, she felt guilty. Shan dripped power, a subtle and devastating kind.

Blaine emerged from the kitchen with two tall glasses of a reddish liquid.

'Virgin cocktails!' Shan said, with a childish delight, as she took a glass from Blaine.

'Pomegranate, sparkling water and a bit of cranberry,' Blaine said, giving Ifemelu the other glass. 'So when are you going to have the next salon, Shan? I was telling Ifemelu about them.'

When Blaine had told Ifemelu about Shan calling her gatherings 'salons', he had underlined the word with mockery, but now he said it with an earnestly French pronunciation: *sa-lon*.

'Oh, soon, I guess.' Shan shrugged, fond and offhand, sipped from her glass and then leaned sideways in a stretch, like a tree bent by wind.

Shan's cell phone rang. 'Where did I put that phone? It's probably David.'

The phone was on the table. 'Oh, it's Luc. I'll call him back later.'

'Who's Luc?' Blaine asked, coming out of the kitchen.

'This French guy, rich guy. It's funny, I met him at the airport for fuck's sake. I tell him I have a boyfriend and he goes "Then I will admire from afar and bide my time." He actually said "bide".' Shan sipped her drink. 'It's nice how in Europe, white men look at you like a woman, not a black woman. Now I don't want to date them, hell no, I just want to know the possibility is there.'

Blaine was nodding, agreeing. If anybody else had said what Shan did, he would instantly comb through the words in search of nuance, and he would disagree with their sweep, their simplicity. Ifemelu had once told him, as they watched a news item about a celebrity divorce, that she did not understand the unbending, unambiguous honesties that Americans required in relationships. 'What do you mean?' he asked her, and she heard a looming disagreement in his voice; he, too, believed in unbending, unambiguous honesties.

'It's different for me and I think it's because I'm from the Third World,' she said. 'To be a child of the Third World is to be aware of the many different constituencies you have and how honesty and truth must always depend on context.' She had felt clever to have thought of this explanation but Blaine shook his head even before she finished speaking and said, 'That is so lazy, to use the Third World like that.'

Now he was nodding as Shan said, 'Europeans

are just not as conservative and uptight about relationships as Americans are. In Europe the white men are thinking "I just want a hot woman." In America the white men are thinking "I won't touch a black woman but I could maybe do Halle Berry." '

'That's funny,' Blaine said.

'Of course, there's the niche of white men in this country who will only date black women, but that's a kind of fetish and it's nasty,' Shan said, and then turned her glowing gaze on Ifemelu.

Ifemelu was almost reluctant to disagree; it was strange, how much she wanted Shan to like her. 'Actually my experience has been the opposite. I get a lot more interest from white men than from African American men.'

'Really?' Shan paused. 'I guess it's your exotic credential, that whole Authentic African thing.'

It stung her, the rub of Shan's dismissal, and then it became a prickly resentment directed at Blaine, because she wished he would not agree so heartily with his sister.

Shan's phone rang again. 'Oh, that had better be David!' She took the phone into the bedroom.

'David is her editor. They want to put this sexualized image, a black torso, on her cover and she's fighting it,' Blaine said.

'Really.' Ifemelu sipped her drink and flipped through an art magazine, still irritated with him.

'Are you okay?' he asked.

'I'm fine.'

Shan was back. Blaine looked at her. 'All okay?'

She nodded. 'They're not using it. Everyone seems to be on the same page now.'

'That's great,' Blaine said.

'You should be my guest blogger for a couple of days when your book comes out,' Ifemelu said. 'You would be amazing. I would love to have you.'

Shan raised her eyebrows, an expression Ifemelu could not read, and she feared that she had been too gushing.

'Yes, I guess I could,' Shan said.

Obama Can Win Only If He Remains the Magic Negro

His pastor is scary because it means maybe Obama is not the Magic Negro after all. By the way, the pastor is pretty melodramatic, but have you been to an old school American Black church? Pure theater. But this guy's basic point is true: that American Blacks (certainly those his age) know an America different from American Whites; they know a harsher, uglier America. But you're not supposed to say that, because in America everything is fine and everyone is the same. So now that the pastor's said it, maybe Obama thinks so too, and if Obama thinks so then he isn't the Magic Negro and only a Magic Negro can win an American election. And what's a Magic Negro, you ask? The black man who is eternally wise and kind. He never reacts under great suffering, never gets angry, is never threatening. He always forgives all kinds of racist shit. He teaches the white person how to break down the sad but understandable prejudice in his heart. You see this man in many films. And Obama is straight from central casting.

CHAPTER 36

It was a surprise birthday party in Hamden, for Marcia, Blaine's friend.

'Happy birthday, Marcia!' Ifemelu said in a chorus with the other friends, standing beside Blaine. Her tongue a little heavy in her mouth, her excitement a little forced. She had been with Blaine for more than a year, but she did not quite belong with his friends.

'You bastard!' Marcia said to her husband, Benny, laughing, tears in her eyes.

Marcia and Benny both taught history, they came from the South and they even looked alike, with their smallish bodies and honey complexions and long locs grazing their necks. They wore their love like a heavy perfume, exuding a transparent commitment, touching each other, referring to each other. Watching them, Ifemelu imagined this life for her and Blaine, in a small house on a quiet street, batiks hung on the walls, African sculptures glowering in corners, and both of them existing in a steady hum of happiness.

Benny was pouring drinks. Marcia was walking around, still stunned, looking into the trays of

493

catered food spread on the dining table, and then up at the mass of balloons bobbing against the ceiling. 'When did you do all this, baby? I was just gone an hour!'

She hugged everyone, while wiping the tears from her eyes. Before she hugged Ifemelu, a wrinkle of worry flickered on her face, and Ifemelu knew that Marcia had forgotten her name. '*So* good to see you again, thank you for coming,' she said, with an extra dose of sincerity, the 'so' emphasized, as though to make up for forgetting Ifemelu's name.

'Chile!' she said to Blaine, who hugged her and lifted her slightly off the floor, both of them laughing.

'You're lighter than you were on your last birthday!' Blaine said.

'And she looks younger every day!' Paula, Blaine's ex-girlfriend, said.

'Marcia, are you going to bottle your secret?' a woman whom Ifemelu did not know asked, her bleached hair bouffant like a platinum helmet.

'Her secret is good sex,' Grace said seriously, a Korean American woman who taught African American studies, tiny and slender, always in stylishly loose-fitting clothes, so that she seemed to float in a swish of silks. 'I'm that rare thing, a Christian left-wing nut,' she had told Ifemelu when they first met.

'Did you hear that, Benny?' Marcia asked. 'Our secret is good sex.'

'That's right!' Benny said, and winked at her. 'Hey, anybody see Barack Obama's announcement this morning?'

'Yes, it's been on the news all day,' Paula said. She was short and blonde, with a clear pinkish complexion, outdoorsy and healthy, that made Ifemelu wonder if she rode horses.

'I don't even have a television,' Grace said, with a self-mocking sigh. 'I only recently sold out and got a cell phone.'

'They'll replay it,' Benny said.

'Let's eat!' It was Stirling, the wealthy one, who Blaine told her came from Boston old money; he and his father had been legacy students at Harvard. He was left-leaning and well-meaning, crippled by his acknowledgement of his own many privileges. He never allowed himself to have an opinion. 'Yes, I see what you mean,' he said often.

The food was eaten with a lot of praise and wine, the fried chicken, the greens, the pies. Ifemelu took tiny portions, pleased she had snacked on some nuts before they left; she did not like soul food.

'I haven't had corn bread this good in years,' Nathan said, seated beside her. He was a literature professor, neurotic and blinky behind his glasses, who Blaine once said was the only person at Yale that he trusted completely. Nathan had told her, some months earlier, in a voice filled with hauteur, that he did not read any fiction published after 1930. 'It all went downhill after the thirties,' he said.

She had told Blaine about it later, and there was an impatience in her tone, almost an accusation, as she added that academics were not intellectuals; they were not curious, they built their stolid tents of specialized knowledge and stayed securely in them.

Blaine said, 'Oh, Nathan just has his issues. It's not about being an academic.' A new defensiveness had begun to creep into Blaine's tone when they talked about his friends, perhaps because he sensed her discomfort with them. When she attended a talk with him, he would make sure to say it could have been better, or that the first ten minutes were boring, as though to pre-empt her own criticisms. The last talk they had attended was his ex-girlfriend Paula's, at a college in Middletown, Paula standing in front of the classroom, in a dark-green wrap dress and boots, sounding fluid and convinced, provoking and charming her audience at the same time; the young pretty political scientist who would certainly get tenure. She had glanced often at Blaine, like a student at a professor, gauging her performance from his expression. As she spoke, Blaine nodded continuously, and once even sighed aloud as though her words had brought to him a familiar and exquisite epiphany. They had remained good friends, Paula and Blaine, had kept in the same circle after she cheated on him with a woman also named Paula, and now called Pee to distinguish them from each other. 'Our relationship had been in trouble for a while. She said she was just experimenting with Pee but I could tell it was much more, and I was right because they're still together,' Blaine told Ifemelu, and it all seemed to her to be too tame, too civil. Even Paula's friendliness towards her seemed too scrubbed clean.

'How about we ditch him and go and have one drink?' Paula had said to Ifemelu that evening after her talk, her cheeks flushed from the excitement and relief of having done well.

'I'm exhausted,' Ifemelu had said.

Blaine said, 'And I need to prep for class tomorrow. Let's do something this weekend, okay?' And he hugged her goodbye.

'It wasn't too bad, was it?' Blaine asked Ifemelu on their drive back to New Haven.

'I was sure you were going to have an orgasm,' she said, and Blaine laughed. She had thought, watching Paula speak, that Paula was comfortable with Blaine's rhythms in a way that she was not, and she thought so now, as she watched Paula eat her third helping of collard greens, sitting next to her girlfriend Pee and laughing at something Marcia had said.

The woman with the helmetlike hair was eating her collard greens with her fingers.

'We humans are not supposed to eat with utensils,' she said.

Michael, seated beside Ifemelu, snorted loudly. 'Why don't you just go on and live in a cave?' he asked, and they all laughed, but Ifemelu was not sure he had been joking. He had no patience for fey talk. She liked him, cornrows running down the length of his scalp, and his expression always wry, scornful of sentimentality. 'Michael's a good cat but he tries so hard to keep it real that he can seem full of negativity,' Blaine had said when she first met Michael. Michael had been in prison for a carjacking when he was nineteen and he was fond of saying 'Some black folk don't appreciate education until after they go to prison.' He was a photographer on a fellowship and the first time Ifemelu saw his photographs, in black-and-white, in dances of shadow, their delicacy and vulnerability had surprised her. She had expected grittier imagery. Now one of those photographs hung on the wall in Blaine's apartment, opposite her writing desk.

From across the table, Paula asked, 'Did I tell you I'm having my students read your blog, Ifemelu? It's interesting how safe their thinking is and I want to push them out of their comfort zone. I loved the last post, "Friendly Tips for the American Non-Black: How to React to an American Black Talking About Blackness."'

'That is funny!' Marcia said. 'I'd love to read that.'

Paula brought out her phone and fiddled with it and then began to read aloud.

Dear American Non-Black, if an American Black person is telling you about an experience about being black, please do not

498

eagerly bring up examples from your own life. Don't say 'It's just like when I . . .' You have suffered. Everyone in the world has suffered. But you have not suffered precisely because you are an American Black. Don't be quick to find alternative explanations for what happened. Don't say 'Oh, it's not really race, it's class. Oh, it's not race, it's gender. Oh, it's not race, it's the cookie monster.' You see, American Blacks actually don't WANT it to be race. They would rather not have racist shit happen. So maybe when they say something is about race, it's maybe because it actually is? Don't say 'I'm color-blind,' because if you are color-blind, then you need to see a doctor and it means that when a black man is shown on TV as a crime suspect in your neighborhood, all you see is a blurry purplish-grayish-creamish figure. Don't say 'We're tired of talking about race' or 'The only race is the human race.' American Blacks, too, are tired of talking about race. They wish they didn't have to. But shit keeps happening. Don't preface your response with 'One of my best friends is black' because it makes no difference and nobody cares and you can have a black best friend and still do racist shit and it's probably not true anyway, the 'best' part, not the 'friend' part. Don't say your grandfather was Mexican so you can't be racist (please click here for more on There Is No United League of the Oppressed). Don't bring up your Irish great-grandparents' suffering. Of course they got a lot of shit from established America. So did the Italians. So did the Eastern Europeans. But there was a hierarchy. A hundred years ago, the white ethnics hated being hated, but it was sort of tolerable because at least black people were below them on the ladder. Don't say your grandfather was a serf in Russia when slavery happened because what matters is you are American now and being American means you take the whole shebang, America's assets and America's debts, and Jim Crow is a big-ass debt. Don't say it's just like antisemitism. It's not. In the hatred of Jews, there is also the possibility of envy – they are so clever, these Jews, they control everything, these Jews – and one must concede that a certain respect, however grudging, accompanies envy. In the hatred of American Blacks, there is no possibility of envy – they are so lazy, these blacks, they are so unintelligent, these blacks.

Don't say 'Oh, racism is over, slavery was so long ago.' We are talking about problems from the 1960s, not the 1860s. If you

500

meet an elderly American black man from Alabama, he probably remembers when he had to step off the curb because a white person was walking past. I bought a dress from a vintage shop on eBay the other day, made in 1960, in perfect shape, and I wear it a lot. When the original owner wore it, black Americans could not vote because they were black. (And maybe the original owner was one of those women, in the famous sepia photographs, standing by in hordes outside schools shouting 'Ape!' at young black children because they did not want them to go to school with their young white children. Where are those women now? Do they sleep well? Do they think about shouting 'Ape'?) Finally, don't put on a Let's Be Fair tone and say 'But black people are racist too.' Because of course we're all prejudiced (I can't even stand some of my blood relatives, grasping, selfish folks), but racism is about the power of a group and in America it's white folks who have that power. How? Well, white folks don't get treated like shit in upper-class African American communities and white folks don't get denied bank loans or mortgages precisely because they are white and black juries don't give white criminals worse sentences than black criminals for the same crime and black police officers don't stop white folk for driving while white and black companies don't choose not to hire somebody because their name sounds white and black teachers don't tell white kids that they're not smart enough to be doctors and black politicians don't try some tricks to reduce the voting power of white folks through gerrymandering and advertising agencies don't say they can't use white models to advertise glamorous products because they are not considered 'aspirational' by the 'mainstream.'

So after this listing of don'ts, what's the do? I'm not sure. Try listening, maybe. Hear what is being said. And remember that it's not about you. American Blacks are not telling you that you are to blame. They are just telling you what is. If you don't understand, ask questions. If you're uncomfortable about asking questions, say you are uncomfortable about asking questions and then ask anyway. It's easy to tell when a question is coming from a good place. Then listen some more. Sometimes people just want to feel heard. Here's to possibilities of friendship and connection and understanding.

Marcia said, 'I love the part about the dress!'
'It's cringe-funny,' Nathan said.
'So you must be raking in the speaking fees from that blog,' Michael said.

'Only most of it goes to my hungry relatives back in Nigeria,' Ifemelu said.

'It must be good to have that,' he said.

'To have what?'

'To know where you're from. Ancestors going way back, that kind of thing.'

'Well,' she said. 'Yes.'

He looked at her, with an expression that made her uncomfortable, because she was not sure what his eyes held, and then he looked away.

Blaine was telling Marcia's friend with the helmetlike hair, 'We need to get over that myth. There was nothing Judaeo-Christian about American history. Nobody liked Catholics and Jews. It's Anglo-Protestant values, not Judaeo-Christian values. Even Maryland very quickly stopped being so Catholic-friendly.' He stopped abruptly and brought his phone out of his pocket and got up. 'Excuse me, folks,' he said, and then in a lower voice to Ifemelu, 'It's Shan. I'll be right back,' and walked into the kitchen to take the call.

Benny turned on the TV and they watched Barack Obama, a thin man in a black coat that looked a size too big, his demeanour slightly uncertain. As he spoke, puffs of cloudy steam left his mouth, like smoke, in the cold air. *'And that is why, in the shadow of the Old State Capitol, where Lincoln once called on a divided house to stand together, where common hopes and common dreams still live, I stand before you today to announce my candidacy for president of the United States of America.'*

'I can't believe they've talked him into this. The guy has potential, but he needs to grow first. He needs some heft. He'll ruin it for black people because he won't come close and a black person won't be able to run for the next fifty years in this country,' Grace said.

'He just makes me feel good!' Marcia said, laughing. 'I love that, the idea of building a more hopeful America.'

'I think he stands a chance,' Benny said.

'Oh, he can't win. They'd shoot his ass first,' Michael said.

'It's so refreshing to see a politician who gets nuance,' Paula said.

'Yes,' Pee said. She had overly toned arms, thin and bulging with muscles, a pixie haircut and an air of intense anxiety; she was the sort of person whose love would suffocate. 'He sounds so smart, so articulate.'

'*You* sound like my mother,' Paula said in the barbed tone of a private fight being continued, words meaning other things. 'Why is it so remarkable that he's articulate?'

'Are we hormonal, Pauly?' Marcia asked.

'She is!' Pee said. 'Did you see she's eaten all the fried chicken?'

Paula ignored Pee, and, as though in defiance, reached out to have another slice of pumpkin pie.

'What do you think of Obama, Ifemelu?' Marcia asked, and Ifemelu guessed that Benny or Grace had whispered her name in Marcia's ear, and now Marcia was eager to unleash her new knowledge.

'I like Hillary Clinton,' Ifemelu said. 'I don't really know anything about this Obama guy.'

Blaine came back into the room. 'What did I miss?'

'Shan okay?' Ifemelu asked. Blaine nodded.

'It doesn't matter what anybody thinks of Obama. The real question is whether white people are ready for a black president,' Nathan said.

'I'm ready for a black president. But I don't think the nation is,' Pee said.

'Seriously, have you been talking to my mom?' Paula asked her. 'She said the exact same thing. If you're ready for a black president, then who exactly is this vague country that isn't ready? People say that when they can't say that *they* are not ready. And even the idea of being ready is ridiculous.'

Ifemelu borrowed those words months later, in a blog post written during the final, frenzied lap of the presidential campaign: 'Even the Idea of Being Ready Is Ridiculous.' *Does nobody see how absurd it is to ask people if they are ready for a black president? Are you ready for Mickey Mouse to be president? How about Kermit the Frog? And Rudolph the Red-Nosed Reindeer?*

'My family has impeccable liberal credentials, we've ticked all the right boxes,' Paula said, lips turned down in irony, twirling the stem of her empty wineglass. 'But my parents were always quick to tell their friends that Blaine was at Yale. As if they were saying he's one of the few good ones.'

'You're being too hard on them, Pauly,' Blaine said.

'No, really, didn't you think so?' she asked. 'Remember that awful Thanksgiving at my parents' house?'

'You mean how I wanted mac and cheese?'

Paula laughed. 'No, that's not what I mean.' But she did not say what she meant and so the memory was left unaired, wrapped in their shared privacy.

Back in Blaine's apartment, Ifemelu told him, 'I was jealous.'

It *was* jealousy, the twinge of unease, the unsettledness in her stomach. Paula had the air of a real ideologue; she could, Ifemelu imagined, slip easily into anarchy, stand at the forefront of protests, defying the clubs of policemen and the taunts of unbelievers. To sense this about Paula was to feel wanting, compared to her.

'There's nothing to be jealous about, Ifem,' Blaine said.

'The fried chicken you eat is not the fried chicken I eat, but it's the fried chicken that Paula eats.'

'What?'

'For you and Paula, fried chicken is battered. For me, fried chicken has no batter. I just thought about how you both have a lot in common.'

'We have fried chicken in common? Do you realize how loaded fried chicken is as a metaphor here?' Blaine was laughing, a gentle, affectionate laugh. 'Your jealousy is kind of sweet, but there is no chance at all of anything going on.'

She knew there was nothing going on. Blaine would not cheat on her. He was too sinewy with goodness. Fidelity came easily to him; he did not turn to glance at pretty women on the street because it did not occur to him. But she was jealous of the emotional remnants that existed between him and Paula, and by the thought that Paula was like him, good like him.

Traveling While Black

A friend of a friend, a cool AB with tons of money, is writing a book called Traveling While Black. Not just black, he says, but recognizably black because there's all kinds of black and no offense but he doesn't mean those black folk who look Puerto Rican or Brazilian or whatever, he means recognizably black. Because the world treats you differently. So here's what he says: 'I got the idea for the book in Egypt. So I get to Cairo and this Egyptian Arab guy calls me a black barbarian. I'm like, hey, this is supposed to be Africa! So I started thinking about other parts of the world and what it would be like to travel there if you're black. I'm as black as they get. White folk in the South today would

507

look at me and think there goes a big black buck. They tell you in the guidebooks what to expect if you're gay or if you're a woman. Hell, they need to do it for if you're recognizably black. Let traveling black folk know what the deal is. It's not like anybody is going to shoot you but it's great to know where to expect that people will stare at you. In the German Black Forest, it's pretty hostile staring. In Tokyo and Istanbul, everyone was cool and indifferent. In Shanghai the staring was intense, in Delhi it was nasty. I thought, "Hey, aren't we kind of in this together? You know, people of color and all?" I'd been reading that Brazil is the race mecca and I go to Rio and nobody looks like me in the nice restaurants and the nice hotels. People act funny when I'm walking to the first-class line at the airport. Kind of nice funny, like you're making a mistake, you can't look like that and fly first class. I go to Mexico and they're staring at me. It's not hostile at all, but it just makes you know you stick out, kind of like they like you but you're still King Kong.' And at this point my Professor Hunk says, 'Latin America as a whole has a really complicated relationship with blackness, which is overshadowed by that whole "we are all mestizo" story that they tell themselves. Mexico isn't as bad as places like Guatemala and Peru, where the white privilege is so much more overt, but then those countries have a much more sizable black population.' And then another friend says, 'Native blacks are always treated worse than non-native blacks everywhere in the world. My friend who was born and raised in France of Togolese parents pretends to be Anglophone when she goes shopping in Paris, because the shop attendants are nicer to black people who don't speak French. Just like American Blacks get a lot of respect in African countries.' Thoughts? Please post your own Traveling Tales.

CHAPTER 37

It seemed to Ifemelu as though she had glanced away for a moment, and looked back to find Dike transformed; her little cousin was gone, and in his place a boy who did not look like a boy, six feet tall with lean muscles, playing basketball for Willow High School, and dating the nimble blonde girl Page, who wore tiny skirts and Converse sneakers. Once, when Ifemelu asked, 'So how are things going with Page?' Dike replied, 'We're not yet having sex, if that's what you want to know.'

In the evenings, six or seven friends converged in his room, all of them white except for Min, the tall Chinese boy whose parents taught at the university. They played computer games and watched videos on YouTube, needling and jousting, all of them enclosed in a sparkling arc of careless youth, and at their centre was Dike. They all laughed at Dike's jokes, and looked to him for agreement, and in a delicate, unspoken way, they let him make their collective decisions: ordering pizza, going down to the community centre to play Ping-Pong. With them, Dike changed; he took on a swagger in his voice and in his gait, his shoulders squared, as though in a high-gear performance, and sprinkled his speech with 'ain't' and 'y'all'.

'Why do you talk like that with your friends, Dike?' Ifemelu asked.

'Yo, Coz, how you gonna treat me like that?' he said, with an exaggerated funny face that made her laugh.

Ifemelu imagined him in college; he would be a perfect student guide, leading a pack of would-be students and their parents, showing them the wonderful things about the campus and making sure to add one thing he personally disliked, all the time being relentlessly funny and bright and bouncy, and the girls would have instant crushes on him, the boys would be envious of his panache, and the parents would wish their kids were like him.

Shan wore a sparkly gold top, her breasts unbound, swinging as she moved. She flirted with everyone, touching an arm, hugging too closely, lingering over a cheek kiss. Her compliments were clotted with an extravagance that made them seem insincere, yet her friends smiled and bloomed under them. It did not matter what was said; it mattered that it was Shan who said it. Her first time at Shan's salon, and Ifemelu was nervous. There was no need to be, it was a mere gathering of friends, but still she was nervous. She had agonized about what to wear, tried on and discarded nine outfits before she decided on a teal dress that made her waist look small.

'Hey!' Shan said, when Blaine and Ifemelu arrived, exchanging hugs.

'Is Grace coming?' she asked Blaine.

'Yes. She's taking the later train.'

'Great. I haven't seen her in ages.' Shan lowered her voice and said to Ifemelu, 'I heard Grace steals her students' research.'

'What?'

'Grace. I heard she steals her students' research. Did you know that?'

'No,' Ifemelu said. She found it strange, Shan telling her this about Blaine's friend, and yet it made her feel special, admitted into Shan's intimate cave of gossip. Then, suddenly ashamed that she had not been strong enough in her defence of Grace, whom she liked, she said, 'I don't think that's true at all.'

But Shan's attention was already elsewhere.

'I want you to meet the sexiest man in New York, Omar,' Shan said, introducing Ifemelu to a man as tall as a basketball player, whose hairline was too perfectly shaped, a sharp curve sweeping his forehead, sharp angles dipping near his ears. When Ifemelu reached out to shake his hand, he bowed slightly, hand on his chest, and smiled.

'Omar doesn't touch women to whom he is not related,' Shan said. 'Which is very sexy, no?' And she tilted her head to look up suggestively at Omar.

'This is the beautiful and utterly original Maribelle, and her girlfriend Joan, who is just as beautiful. They make me feel bad!' Shan said, while Maribelle and Joan giggled, smallish white women in dark-framed oversize glasses. They both wore short dresses, one in red polka-dot, the other lace-fringed, with the slightly faded, slightly ill-fitting look of vintage-shop finds. It was, in some ways, costume. They ticked the boxes of a certain kind of enlightened, educated middle-classness, the love of dresses that were more interesting than pretty, the love of the eclectic, the love of what they were supposed to love. Ifemelu imagined them when they travelled: they would collect unusual things and fill their homes with them, unpolished evidence of their polish.

'Here's Bill!' Shan said, hugging the muscular dark man in a fedora. 'Bill is a writer but unlike the rest of us, he has oodles of money.' Shan was almost cooing. 'Bill has this great idea for a travel book called *Traveling While Black.*'

'I'd love to hear about it,' Ashanti said.

'By the way, Ashanti, girl, I adore your hair,' Shan said.

'Thank you!' Ashanti said. She was a vision in cowries: they rattled from her wrists, were strung through her curled dreadlocks, and looped around her neck. She said 'motherland' and 'Yoruba religion' often, glancing at Ifemelu as though for confirmation, and it was a parody of Africa that Ifemelu felt uncomfortable about and then felt bad for feeling so uncomfortable.

'You finally have a book cover you like?' Ashanti asked Shan.

' "Like" is a strong word,' Shan said. 'So, everyone, this book is a memoir, right? It's about tons of stuff, growing up in this all-white town, being the only black kid in my prep school, my mom's passing, all that stuff. My editor reads the manuscript and says, "I understand that race is important here but we have to make sure the book transcends race, so that it's not just about race." And I'm thinking, But why do I have to transcend race? You know, like race is a brew best served mild, tempered with other liquids, otherwise white folk can't swallow it.'

'That's funny,' Blaine said.

'He kept flagging the dialogue in the manuscript and writing on the margins: "Do people actually say this?" And I'm thinking, Hey, how many black people do you know? I mean know as equals, as friends. I don't mean the receptionist in the office and maybe the one black couple whose kid goes to your kid's school and you say hi to. I mean really know know. None. So how are you telling me how black people talk?'

'Not his fault. There aren't enough middle-class black folks to go around,' Bill said. 'Lots of liberal white folks are looking for black friends. It's almost as hard as finding an egg donor who is a tall blonde eighteen-year-old at Harvard.'

They all laughed.

'I wrote this scene about something that happened in grad school, about a Gambian woman I knew. She loved to eat baking chocolate. She always had a pack of baking chocolate in her bag. Anyway, she lived in London and she was in love with this white English guy and he was leaving his wife for her. So we were at a bar and she was telling a few of us about it, me and this other girl, and this guy Peter. Short guy from Wisconsin. And you know what Peter said to her? He said, "His wife must feel worse knowing you're black." He said it like it was pretty obvious. Not that the wife would feel bad about another woman, period, but that she would feel bad because the woman was black. So I put it in the book and my editor wants to change it because he says it's not *subtle*. Like life is always fucking subtle. And then I write about my mom being bitter at work, because she felt she'd hit a ceiling and they wouldn't let her get further because she was black, and my editor says, "Can we have more nuance? Did your mom have a bad rapport with someone at work, maybe? Or had she already been diagnosed with cancer?" He thinks we should complicate it, so it's not race alone. And I say, But it *was* race. She was bitter because she thought if everything was the same, except for her race, she would have been made vice-president. And she talked about it a lot until she died. But somehow my mom's experience is suddenly unnuanced. "Nuance" means keep people comfortable so everyone is free to think of themselves as *individuals* and everyone got where they are because of their *achievement*.'

'Maybe you should turn it into a novel,' Maribelle said.

'Are you kidding me?' Shan asked, slightly drunk, slightly dramatic, and now sitting yoga-style on the floor. 'You can't write an honest novel about race in this country. If you write about how people are really affected by race, it'll be too *obvious*. Black writers who do literary fiction in this country, all three of them, not the ten thousand who write those bullshit ghetto books with the bright covers, have two choices: they can do precious or they can do pretentious. When you do neither, nobody knows what to do with you. So if you're going to write about race, you have to make sure it's so lyrical and subtle that the reader who doesn't read between the lines won't even know it's about race. You know, a Proustian meditation, all watery and fuzzy, that at the end just leaves you feeling watery and fuzzy.'

'Or just find a white writer. White writers can be blunt about race and get all activist because their anger isn't threatening,' Grace said.

'What about this recent book, *Monk Memoirs*?' Mirabelle said.

'It's a cowardly, dishonest book. Have you read it?' Shan asked.

'I read a review,' Mirabelle said.

'That's the problem. You read more about books than you read actual books.'

Maribelle blushed. She would, Ifemelu sensed, take this quietly only from Shan.

'We are very ideological about fiction in this country. If a character is not familiar, then that character becomes unbelievable,' Shan said. 'You can't even read American fiction to get a sense of how actual life is lived these days. You read American fiction to learn about dysfunctional white folk doing things that are weird to normal white folks.'

Everyone laughed. Shan looked delighted, like a little girl showing off her singing to her parents' eminent friends.

'The world just doesn't look like this room,' Grace said.

'But it can,' Blaine said. 'We prove that the world can be like this room. It can be a safe and equal space for everyone. We just need to dismantle the walls of privilege and oppression.'

'There goes my flower child brother,' Shan said. There was more laughter.

'You should blog about this, Ifemelu,' Grace said.

'You know why Ifemelu can write that blog, by the way?' Shan said. 'Because she's African. She's writing from the outside. She doesn't really feel all the stuff she's writing about. It's all quaint and curious to her. So she can write it and get all these accolades and get invited to give talks. If she were African American, she'd just be labelled angry and shunned.'

The room was, for a moment, swollen in silence.

'I think that's fair enough,' Ifemelu said, disliking Shan, and herself, too, for bending to Shan's spell. It was true that race was not embroidered in the fabric of her history; it had not been etched on

517

her soul. Still, she wished Shan had said this to her when they were alone, instead of saying it now, so jubilantly, in front of friends, and leaving Ifemelu with an embittered knot, like bereavement, in her chest.

'A lot of this is relatively recent. Black and pan-African identities were actually strong in the early nineteenth century. The Cold War forced people to choose, and it was either you became an internationalist, which of course meant communist to Americans, or you became a part of American capitalism, which was the choice the African American elite made,' Blaine said, as though in Ifemelu's defence, but she thought it too abstract, too limp, too late.

Shan glanced at Ifemelu and smiled and in that smile was the possibility of great cruelty. When, months later, Ifemelu had the fight with Blaine, she wondered if Shan had fuelled his anger, an anger she never fully understood.

Is Obama Anything but Black?

So lots of folk – mostly non-black – say Obama's not black, he's biracial, multi-racial, black-and-white, anything but just black. Because his mother was white. But race is not biology; race is sociology. Race is not genotype; race is phenotype. Race matters because of racism. And racism is absurd because it's about how you look.

518

Not about the blood you have. It's about the shade of your skin and the shape of your nose and the kink of your hair. Booker T. Washington and Frederick Douglass had white fathers. Imagine them saying they were not black.

Imagine Obama, skin the color of a toasted almond, hair kinky, saying to a census worker – I'm kind of white. Sure you are, she'll say. Many American Blacks have a white person in their ancestry, because white slave owners liked to go a-raping in the slave quarters at night. But if you come out looking dark, that's it. (So if you are that blond, blue-eyed woman who says 'My grandfather was Native American and I get discrimination too' when black folk are talking about shit, please stop it already.) In America, you don't get to decide what race you are. It is decided for you. Barack Obama, looking as he does, would have had to sit in the back of the bus fifty years ago. If a random black guy commits a crime today, Barack Obama could be stopped and questioned for fitting the profile. And what would that profile be? 'Black Man.'

CHAPTER 38

Blaine did not like Boubacar, and perhaps this mattered or perhaps it did not matter in the story of their fight, but Blaine did not like Boubacar and her day began with visiting Boubacar's class. She and Blaine had met Boubacar at a university-hosted dinner party in his honour, a sable-skinned Senegalese professor who had just moved to the US to teach at Yale. He was blistering in his intelligence and blistering in his self-regard. He sat at the head of the table, drinking red wine and talking drily of French presidents whom he had met, of the French universities that had offered him jobs.

'I came to America because I want to choose my own master,' he said. 'If I must have a master, then better America than France. But I will never eat a cookie or go to McDonald's. How barbaric!'

Ifemelu was charmed and amused by him. She liked his accent, his English drenched in Wolof and French.

'I thought he was great,' she told Blaine later.

'It's interesting how he says ordinary things and thinks they are pretty deep,' Blaine said.

'He has a bit of an ego, but so did everyone at that table,' Ifemelu said. 'Aren't you Yale people supposed to, before you get hired?'

Blaine did not laugh, as he ordinarily would have. She sensed, in his reaction, a territorial dislike that was foreign to his nature; it surprised her. He would put on a bad French accent and mimic Boubacar. ' "Francophone Africans break for coffee, Anglophone Africans break for tea. It is impossible to get real café au lait in this country!" '

Perhaps he resented how easily she had drifted to Boubacar that day, after desserts were served, as though to a person who spoke the same silent language as she did. She had teased Boubacar about Francophone Africans, how battered their minds were by the French and how thin-skinned they had become, too aware of European slights, and yet too enamoured of Europeanness. Boubacar laughed, a familial laugh; he would not laugh like that with an American, he would be cutting if an American dared say the same thing. Perhaps Blaine resented this mutuality, something primally African from which he felt excluded. But her feelings for Boubacar were fraternal, free of desire. They met often for tea in Atticus Bookstore and talked – or she listened since he did most of the talking – about West African politics and family and home and she left, always, with the feeling of having been fortified.

By the time Boubacar told her about the new humanities fellowship at Princeton, she had begun to gaze at her past. A restlessness had taken hold of her. Her doubts about her blog had grown.

'You must apply. It would be perfect for you,' he said.

'I'm not an academic. I don't even have a graduate degree.'

'The current fellow is a jazz musician, very brilliant, but he has only a high school diploma. They want people who are doing new things, pushing boundaries. You must apply, and please use me as a reference. We need to get into these places, you know. It is the only way to change the conversation.'

She was touched, sitting across from him in a café and feeling between them the warm affinities of something shared.

Boubacar had often invited her to visit his class, a seminar on contemporary African issues. 'You might find something to blog about,' he said. And so, on the day that began the story of her fight with Blaine, she visited Boubacar's class. She sat at the back, by the window. Outside, the leaves were falling from grand old trees, people with scarf-bundled necks hurried along the sidewalk holding paper cups, the women, particularly the Asian women, pretty in slender skirts and high-heeled boots. Boubacar's students all had laptops open in front of them, the screens bright with e-mail pages, Google searches, celebrity photos. From time to time they would open a Word file and type a few words from Boubacar. Their jackets were hung behind their chairs and their body language, slouching, slightly impatient, said this: We already know the answers. After class they would go to the café in the library and buy a sandwich with zhou from North Africa, or a curry from India, and on their way to another class, a student group would give them condoms and lollipops, and in the evening they would attend tea in a master's house where a Latin American president or a Nobel laureate would answer their questions as though they mattered.

'Your students were all browsing the Internet,' she told Boubacar as they walked back to his office.

'They do not doubt their presence here, these students. They believe they should be here, they have earned it and they are paying for it. *Au fond*, they have bought us all. It is the key to America's greatness, this hubris,' Boubacar said, a black felt beret on his head, his hands sunk into his jacket pockets. 'That is why they do not understand that they should be grateful to have me stand before them.'

They had just arrived at his office when there was a knock on the half-open door.

'Come in,' Boubacar said.

Kavanagh came in. Ifemelu had met him a few times, an assistant professor of history who had lived in Congo as a child. He was curly-haired and foul-humoured, and seemed better suited for covering dangerous wars in far-flung countries than for teaching history to undergraduates. He stood at the door and told Boubacar that he was leaving

523

on a sabbatical and the department was ordering sandwiches the next day as a going-away lunch for him, and he had been told they were fancy sandwiches with such things as alfalfa sprouts.

'If I am bored enough, I will stop by,' Boubacar said.

'You should come,' Kavanagh said to Ifemelu. 'Really.'

'I'll come,' she said. 'Free lunch is always a good idea.'

As she left Boubacar's office, Blaine sent her a text: *Did you hear about Mr White at the library?*

Her first thought was that Mr White had died; she did not feel any great sadness, and for this she felt guilty. Mr White was a security guard at the library who sat at the exit and checked the back flap of each book, a rheumy-eyed man with skin so dark it had an undertone of blueberries. She was so used to seeing him seated, a face and a torso, that the first time she saw him walking, his gait saddened her: his shoulders stooped, as though burdened by lingering losses. Blaine had befriended him years ago, and sometimes during his break, Blaine would stand outside talking to him. 'He's a history book,' Blaine told her. She had met Mr White a few times. 'Does she have a sister?' Mr White would ask Blaine, gesturing to her. Or he would say 'You look tired, my man. Somebody keep you up late?' in a way Ifemelu thought inappropriate. Whenever they shook hands, Mr White squeezed her fingers, a gesture thick with suggestion, and she would pull her hand free and avoid his eyes until they left. There was, in that handshake, a claiming, a leering, and for this she had always harboured a small dislike, but she had never told Blaine because she was also sorry about her dislike. Mr White was, after all, an old black man beaten down by life and she wished she could overlook the liberties he took.

'Funny how I've never heard you speak Ebonics before,' she told Blaine, the first time she heard him talking to Mr White. His syntax was different, his cadences more rhythmic.

'I guess I've become too used to my White People Are Watching Us voice,' he said. 'And you know, younger black folk don't really do code-switching any more. The middle-class kids can't speak Ebonics and the inner-city kids speak only Ebonics and they don't have the fluidity that my generation has.'

'I'm going to blog about that.'

'I knew you would say that.'

She sent Blaine a text back: *No, what happened? Is Mr White okay? Are you done? Want to get a sandwich?*

Blaine called her and asked her to wait for him on the corner of Whitney, and soon she saw him walking towards her, a quick-moving trim figure in a grey sweater.

'Hey,' he said, and kissed her.

'You smell nice,' she said, and he kissed her again.

'You survived Boubacar's class? Even though

there were no proper croissants or pain au chocolat?'

'Stop it. What happened to Mr White?'

As they walked hand in hand to the bagel sandwich store, he told her how Mr White's friend, a black man, came by yesterday evening and the two stood outside the library. Mr White gave his friend his car keys, because the friend wanted to borrow his car, and the friend gave Mr White some money, which Mr White had lent him earlier. A white library employee, watching them, assumed that the two black men were dealing drugs and called a supervisor. The supervisor called the police. The police came and led Mr White away to be questioned.

'Oh my God,' Ifemelu said. 'Is he okay?'

'Yes. He's back at his desk.' Blaine paused. 'I think he expects this sort of thing to happen.'

'That's the actual tragedy,' Ifemelu said, and realized she was using Blaine's own words; sometimes she heard in her voice the echo of his. The actual tragedy of Emmett Till, he had told her once, was not the murder of a black child for whistling at a white woman but that some black people thought: But why did you whistle?

'I talked to him for a bit. He just shrugged the whole thing off and said it wasn't a big deal and instead he wanted to talk about his daughter, who he's really worried about. She's talking about dropping out of high school. So I'm going to step in and tutor her. I'm going to meet her Monday.'

'Blaine, that's the seventh kid you'll be tutoring,'

she said. 'Are you going to tutor the whole of inner-city New Haven?'

It was windy and he was squinting, cars driving past them on Whitney Avenue, and he turned to glance at her with narrowed eyes.

'I wish I could,' he said quietly.

'I just want to see more of you,' she said, and slipped an arm around his waist.

'The university's response is total bullshit. A simple mistake that wasn't racial at all? Really? I'm thinking of organizing a protest tomorrow, get people to come out and say this is not okay. Not in our backyard.'

He had already decided, she could tell, he was not merely thinking about it. He sat down at a table by the door while she went up to the counter to order, seamlessly ordering for him, because she was so used to him, to what he liked. When she came back with a plastic tray – her turkey sandwich and his veggie wrap lying beside two bags of baked unsalted chips – his head was bent to his phone. By evening, he had made calls and sent e-mails and texts and the news had been passed on, and his phone jingled and rang and beeped, with responses from people saying they were on board. A student called to ask him for suggestions about what to write on placards; another student was contacting the local TV stations.

The next morning, before he left for class, Blaine said, 'I'm teaching back to back so I'll see you at the library? Text me when you're on your way.'

They had not discussed it, he had simply assumed that she would be there, and so she said, 'Okay.'

But she did not go. And she did not forget. Blaine might have been more forgiving if she had simply forgotten, if she had been so submerged in reading or blogging that the protest had slipped from her mind. But she did not forget. She merely preferred to go to Kavanagh's going-away lunch instead of standing in front of the university library holding a placard. Blaine would not mind too much, she told herself. If she felt any discomfort, she was not conscious of it until she was seated in a class-room with Kavanagh and Boubacar and other professors, sipping a bottle of cranberry juice, listening to a young woman talk about her upcoming tenure review, when Blaine's texts flooded her phone. *Where are you? You okay? Great turnout, looking for you. Shan just surprised me and turned up! You okay?* She left early and went back to the apartment and, lying in bed, sent Blaine a text to say she was so sorry, she was just up from a nap that had gone on too long. *Okay. On my way home.*

He walked in and wrapped her in his arms, with a force and an excitement that had come through the door with him.

'I missed you. I really wanted you to be there. I was so happy Shan came,' he said, a little emotional, as though it had been a personal triumph of his. 'It was like a mini-America. Black kids and white kids and Asian kids and Hispanic

528

kids. Mr White's daughter was there, taking pictures of his photos on the placard, and I felt as if that finally gave him some real dignity back.'

'That's lovely,' she said.

'Shan says hello. She's getting on the train back now.'

It would have been easy for Blaine to find out, perhaps a casual mention from someone who had been at the lunch, but she never knew exactly how he did. He came back the next day and looked at her, a glare like silver in his eyes, and said, 'You lied.' It was said with a kind of horror that baffled her, as though he had never considered it possible that she could lie. She wanted to say, 'Blaine, people lie.' But she said, 'I'm sorry.'

'Why?' He was looking at her as though she had reached in and torn away his innocence, and for a moment she hated him, this man who ate her apple cores and turned even that into something of a moral act.

'I don't know why, Blaine. I just didn't feel up to it. I didn't think you would mind too much.'

'You just didn't feel up to it?'

'I'm sorry. I should have told you about the lunch.'

'How is this lunch suddenly so important? You hardly even know this Boubacar's colleague!' he said, incredulous. 'You know, it's not just about writing a blog, you have to live like you believe it. That blog is a game that you don't really take seriously, it's like choosing an *interesting* elective evening class to complete your credits.' She recognized, in his tone, a subtle accusation, not merely about her laziness, her lack of zeal and conviction, but also about her Africanness; she was not sufficiently furious because she was African, not African American.

'It's unfair of you to say that,' she said. But he had turned away from her, icy, silent.

'Why won't you talk to me?' she asked. 'I don't understand why this matters so much.'

'How can you not understand? It's the principle of it,' he said, and at that moment, he became a stranger to her.

'I'm really sorry,' she said.

He had walked into the bathroom and shut the door.

She felt withered in his wordless rage. How could principle, an abstract thing floating in the air, wedge itself so solidly between them, and turn Blaine into somebody else? She wished it were an uncivil emotion, a passion like jealousy or betrayal.

She called Araminta. 'I feel like the confused wife calling her sister-in-law to explain her husband to her,' she said.

'In high school, I remember there was some fund-raiser, and they put out a table with cookies and whatever, and you were supposed to put some money in the jar and take a cookie, and you know, I'm feeling rebellious so I just take a cookie and don't put any money in, and Blaine was furious with me. I remember thinking, Hey, it's just a

530

cookie. But I think for him it was the principle of it. He can be ridiculously high-minded sometimes. Give him a day or two, he'll get over this.'

But a day passed, then two, and Blaine remained caged in his frozen silence. On the third day of his not saying a single word to her, she packed a small bag and left. She could not go back to Baltimore – her condo was rented out and her furniture in storage – and so she went to Willow.

What Academics Mean by White Privilege, or Yes It Sucks to Be Poor and White but Try Being Poor and Non-White

So this guy said to Professor Hunk, 'White privilege is nonsense. How can I be privileged? I grew up fucking poor in West Virginia. I'm an Appalachian hick. My family is on welfare.' Right. But privilege is always relative to something else. Now imagine someone like him, as poor and as fucked up, and then make that person black. If both are caught for drug possession, say, the white guy is more likely to be sent to treatment and the black guy is more likely to be sent to jail. Everything else the same except for race. Check the stats. The Appalachian hick guy is fucked up, which is not cool, but if he were black, he'd be fucked up plus. He also said to Professor

531

Hunk: Why must we always talk about race anyway? Can't we just be human beings? And Professor Hunk replied – that is exactly what white privilege is, that you can say that. Race doesn't really exist for you because it has never been a barrier. Black folks don't have that choice. The black guy on the street in New York doesn't want to think about race, until he tries to hail a cab, and he doesn't want to think about race when he's driving his Mercedes under the speed limit, until a cop pulls him over. So Appalachian hick guy doesn't have class privilege but he sure as hell has race privilege. What do you think? Weigh in, readers, and share your experiences, especially if you are non-black.

PS – Professor Hunk just suggested I post this, a test for White Privilege, copyright a pretty cool woman called Peggy McIntosh. If you answer mostly no, then congratulations, you have white privilege. What's the point of this you ask? Seriously? I have no idea. I guess it's just good to know. So you can gloat from time to time, lift you up when you're depressed, that sort of thing. So here goes:

When you want to join a prestigious social club, do you wonder if your race will make it difficult for you to join?

When you go shopping alone at a nice

store, do you worry that you will be followed or harassed?

When you turn on mainstream TV or open a mainstream newspaper, do you expect to find mostly people of another race?

Do you worry that your children will not have books and school materials that are about people of their own race?

When you apply for a bank loan, do you worry that, because of your race, you might be seen as financially unreliable?

If you swear, or dress shabbily, do you think that people might say this is because of the bad morals or the poverty or the illiteracy of your race?

If you do well in a situation, do you expect to be called a credit to your race? Or to be described as 'different' from the majority of your race?

If you criticize the government, do you worry that you might be seen as a cultural outsider? Or that you might be asked to 'go back to X,' X being somewhere not in America?

If you receive poor service in a nice store and ask to see 'the person in charge,' do you expect that this person will be a person of another race?

If a traffic cop pulls you over, do you wonder if it is because of your race?

If you take a job with an Affirmative Action employer, do you worry that your co-workers will think you are unqualified and were hired only because of your race?

If you want to move to a nice neighborhood, do you worry that you might not be welcome because of your race?

If you need legal or medical help, do you worry that your race might work against you?

When you use the 'nude' color of underwear and Band-Aids, do you already know that it will not match your skin?

CHAPTER 39

Aunty Uju had taken up yoga. She was on her hands and knees, back arched high, on a bright blue mat on the basement floor, while Ifemelu lay on the couch, eating a chocolate bar and watching her.

'How many of those things have you eaten? And since when do you eat regular chocolate? I thought you and Blaine eat only organic, fair trade.'

'I bought them at the train station.'

'Them? How many?'

'Ten.'

'Ahn-ahn! Ten!'

Ifemelu shrugged. She had already eaten them all, but she would not tell Aunty Uju that. It had given her pleasure, buying chocolate bars from the news-stand, cheap bars filled with sugar and chemicals and other genetically modified ghastly things.

'Oh, so because you are quarrelling with Blaine, you are now eating the chocolate he doesn't like?' Aunty Uju laughed.

Dike came downstairs and looked at his mother, her arms now up in the air, warrior position. 'Mom, you look ridiculous.'

535

'Didn't your friend say that your mother was hot, the other day? This is why.'

Dike shook his head. 'Coz, I need to show you something on YouTube, this hilarious video.'

Ifemelu got up.

'Has Dike told you about the computer incident at school?' Aunty Uju asked.

'No, what?' Ifemelu asked.

'The principal called me on Monday to say that Dike hacked into the school's computer network on Saturday. This is a boy who was with me all day on Saturday. We went to Hartford to visit Ozavisa. We were there the whole day and the boy did not go near a computer. When I asked why they thought it was him, they said they got information. Imagine, you just wake up and blame my son. The boy is not even good with computers. I thought we had left them behind in that bush town. Kweku wants us to lodge a formal complaint, but I don't think it's worth the time. They have now said they no longer suspect him.'

'I don't even know *how* to hack,' Dike said drily.

'Why would they do this sort of rubbish?' Ifemelu asked.

'You have to blame the black kid first,' he said, and laughed.

Later, he told her how his friends would say, 'Hey, Dike, got some weed?' and how funny it was. He told her about the pastor at church, a white woman, who had said hello to all the other kids but when she came to him, she said, 'What's up, bro?' 'I feel like I have vegetables instead of ears, like large broccoli sticking out of my head,' he said, laughing. 'So of course it had to be me that hacked into the school network.'

'Those people in your school are fools,' Ifemelu said.

'So funny how you say that word, Coz, *fools*.' He paused and then repeated her words, 'Those people in your school are fools,' in a good mimicry of a Nigerian accent. She told him the story of the Nigerian pastor who, while giving a sermon in a church in America, said something about a beach but because of his accent, his parishioners thought he had said 'bitch' and they wrote to his bishop to complain. Dike laughed and laughed. It became one of their stock jokes. 'Hey, Coz, I just want to spend a summer day at the bitch,' he would say.

For nine days, Blaine did not take her calls. Finally he answered the phone, his voice muffled.

'Can I come this weekend so we can cook coconut rice? I'll do the cooking,' she said. Before he said 'Okay,' she sensed an intake of breath and she wondered if he was surprised that she dared to suggest coconut rice.

She watched Blaine cutting the onions, watched his long fingers and recalled them on her body, tracing lines on her collarbone, and on the darkened skin below her navel. He looked up and asked if the slices were a good size and she said, 'The onion is fine,' and thought how he had always known the right size for onions, slicing them so precisely, how he had always steamed the rice although she was going to do it now. He broke the coconut against the sink and let the water out before he began to nudge the white meat off the shell with a knife. Her hands shook as she poured rice into the boiling water and, as she watched the narrow basmati grains begin to swell, she wondered if they were failing at this, their reconciliatory meal. She checked the chicken on the stove. The spices wafted up when she opened the pot – ginger and curry and bay leaves – and she told him, unnecessarily, that it looked good.

'I didn't over-spice it like you do,' he said. She felt a momentary anger and wanted to say that it was unfair of him to hold out forgiveness like this but instead she asked if he thought she should add some water. He kept grating the coconuts and said nothing. She watched the coconut crumble into white dust; it saddened her to think that it would never be a whole coconut again, and she reached out and held Blaine from the back, wrapped her arms around his chest, felt the warmth through his sweatshirt, but he eased away and said he had to finish before the rice got too soft. She walked across the living room to look out of the window, at the clock tower, high and regal, imposing itself on the other buildings of the Yale campus below, and saw the first snow flurries swirling through the late evening air, as though flung from above, and she remembered her first winter with him, when everything had seemed burnished and unendingly new.

Understanding America for the Non-American Black: A Few Explanations of What Things Really Mean

1. Of all their tribalisms, Americans are most uncomfortable with race. If you are having a conversation with an American, and you want to discuss something racial that you find interesting, and the American says, 'Oh, it's simplistic to say it's race, racism is so complex,' it means they just want you to shut up already. Because of course racism is complex. Many abolition-ists wanted to free the slaves but didn't want black people living nearby. Lots of folk today don't mind a black nanny or black limo driver. But they sure as hell mind a black boss. What is simplistic is saying 'It's so complex.' But shut up anyway, especially if you need a job/favor from the American in question.

2. Diversity means different things to different folks. If a white person is saying a neighborhood is diverse, they mean nine percent black people. (The minute it gets to ten percent black people, the white folks

539

move out.) If a black person says diverse neighborhood, they are thinking forty percent black.

3. Sometimes they say 'culture' when they mean race. They say a film is 'mainstream' when they mean 'white folks like it or made it.' When they say 'urban' it means black and poor and possibly dangerous and potentially exciting. 'Racially charged' means we are uncomfortable saying 'racist.'

CHAPTER 40

They did not fight again until the relationship ended, but in the time of Blaine's stoniness, when Ifemelu burrowed into herself and ate whole chocolate bars, her feelings for him changed. She still admired him, his moral fibre, his life of clean lines, but now it was admiration for a person separate from her, a person far away. And her body had changed. In bed, she did not turn to him full of a raw wanting as she used to do, and when he reached for her, her first instinct was to roll away. They kissed often, but always with her lips firmly pursed; she did not want his tongue in her mouth. Their union was leached of passion, but there was a new passion, outside of themselves, that united them in an intimacy they had never had before, an unfixed, unspoken, intuitive intimacy: Barack Obama. They agreed, without any prodding, without the shadows of obligation or compromise, on Barack Obama.

At first, even though she wished America would elect a black man as president, she thought it impossible, and she could not imagine Obama as president of the United States; he seemed too slight, too skinny, a man who would be blown away by the wind. Hillary Clinton was sturdier. Ifemelu liked to watch Clinton on television, in her square trouser suits, her face a mask of resolve, her prettiness disguised, because that was the only way to convince the world that she was able. Ifemelu liked her. She wished her victory, willed good fortune her way, until the morning she picked up Barack Obama's book, *Dreams from My Father*, which Blaine had just finished and left lying on the bookshelf, some of its pages folded in. She examined the photographs on the cover, the young Kenyan woman staring befuddled at the camera, arms enclosing her son, and the young American man, jaunty of manner, holding his daughter to his chest. Ifemelu would later remember the moment she decided to read the book. Just to see. She might not have read it if Blaine had recommended it, because she more and more avoided the books he liked. But he had not recommended it, he had merely left it on the shelf, next to a pile of other books he had finished but meant to go back to. She read *Dreams from My Father* in a day and a half, sitting up on the couch, Nina Simone playing on Blaine's iPod speaker. She was absorbed and moved by the man she met in those pages, an enquiring and intelligent man, a kind man, a man so utterly, helplessly, winningly humane. He reminded her of Obinze's expression for people he liked. *Obi ocha*. A clean heart. She believed Barack Obama. When Blaine came home, she sat

542

at the dining table, watching him chop fresh basil in the kitchen, and said, 'If only the man who wrote this book could be the president of America.'

Blaine's knife stopped moving. He looked up, eyes lit, as though he had not dared hope she would believe the same thing that he believed, and she felt between them the first pulse of a shared passion. They clutched each other in front of the television when Barack Obama won the Iowa caucuses. The first battle, and he had won. Their hope was radiating, exploding into possibility: Obama could actually win this thing. And then, as though choreographed, they began to worry. They worried that something would derail him, crash his fast-moving train. Every morning, Ifemelu woke up and checked to make sure that Obama was still alive. That no scandal had emerged, no story dug up from his past. She would turn on her computer, her breath still, her heart frantic in her chest, and then, reassured that he was alive, she would read the latest news about him, quickly and greedily, seeking information and reassurance, multiple windows minimized at the bottom of the screen. Sometimes, in chat rooms, she wilted as she read the posts about Obama, and she would get up and move away from her computer, as though the laptop itself were the enemy, and stand by the window to hide her tears even from herself. *How can a monkey be president? Somebody do us a favor and put a bullet in this guy. Send him back to the African jungle. A black man will never be in the white house, dude, it's called the white house for a reason.* She tried to imagine the people who wrote those posts, under monikers like SuburbanMom231 and NormanRockwellRocks, sitting at their desks, a cup of coffee beside them, and their children about to come home on the school bus in a glow of innocence. The chat rooms made her blog feel inconsequential, a comedy of manners, a mild satire about a world that was anything but mild. She did not blog about the vileness that seemed to have multiplied each morning she logged on, more chat rooms springing up, more vitriol flourishing, because to do so would be to spread the words of people who abhorred not the man that Barack Obama was, but the idea of him as president. She blogged, instead, about his policy positions, in a recurring post titled 'This Is Why Obama Will Do It Better', often adding links to his website, and she blogged, too, about Michelle Obama. She gloried in the off-beat dryness of Michelle Obama's humour, the confidence in her long-limbed carriage, and then she mourned when Michelle Obama was clamped, flattened, made to sound tepidly wholesome in interviews. Still, there was, in Michelle Obama's overly arched eyebrows and in her belt worn higher on her waist than tradition would care for, a glint of her old self. It was this that drew Ifemelu, the absence of apology, the promise of honesty.

'If she married Obama then he can't be that

bad,' she joked often with Blaine, and Blaine would say, 'True that, true that.'

She got an e-mail from a princeton.edu address and before she read it, her hands shook from excitement. The first word she saw was 'pleased'. She had received the research fellowship. The pay was good, the requirements easy: she was expected to live in Princeton and use the library and give a public talk at the end of the year. It seemed too good to be true, an entry into a hallowed American kingdom. She and Blaine took the train to Princeton to look for an apartment, and she was struck by the town itself, the greenness, the peace and grace of it. 'I got into Princeton for undergrad,' Blaine told her. 'It was almost bucolic then. I visited and thought it was beautiful but I just couldn't see myself actually going there.'

Ifemelu knew what he meant, even now that it had changed and become, in Blaine's words, when they walked past the rows of shiny stores, 'aggressively consumer capitalist'. She felt admiration and disorientation. She liked her apartment, off Nassau Street; the bedroom window looked out to a grove of trees, and she walked the empty room thinking of a new beginning for herself, without Blaine, and yet unsure if this was truly the new beginning she wanted.

'I'm not moving here until after the election,' she said.

Blaine nodded before she finished speaking; of

course she would not move until they had seen Barack Obama through to his victory. He became a volunteer for the Obama campaign and she absorbed all of his stories about the doors he knocked on and the people behind them. One day he came home and told her about an old black woman, face shrivelled like a prune, who stood holding on to her door as though she might fall otherwise, and told him, 'I didn't think this would happen even in my grandbaby's lifetime.'

Ifemelu blogged about this story, describing the silver streaks in the woman's grey hair, the fingers quivering from Parkinson's, as though she herself had been there with Blaine. All of his friends were Obama supporters, except for Michael, who always wore a Hillary Clinton pin on his breast, and at their gatherings, Ifemelu no longer felt excluded. Even that nebulous unease when she was around Paula, part churlishness and part insecurity, had melted away. They gathered at bars and apartments, discussing details of the campaign, mocking the silliness of the news stories. Will Hispanics vote for a black man? Can he bowl? Is he patriotic?

'Isn't it funny how they say "blacks want Obama" and "women want Hillary", but what about black women?' Paula said.

'When they say "women", they automatically mean "white women", of course,' Grace said.

'What I don't understand is how anybody can say that Obama is benefiting because he's a black man,' Paula said.

'It's complicated, but he is, and also to the extent that Clinton is benefiting because she's a white woman,' Nathan said, leaning forward and blinking even more quickly. 'If Clinton were a black woman, her star would not shine so brightly. If Obama were a white man, his star might or might not shine so brightly, because some white men have become president who had no business being president, but that doesn't change the fact that Obama doesn't have a lot of experience and people are excited by the idea of a black candidate who has a real chance.'

'Although if he wins, he will no longer be black, just as Oprah is no longer black, she's Oprah,' Grace said. 'So she can go where black people are loathed and be fine. He'll no longer be black, he'll just be Obama.'

'To the extent that Obama is benefiting, and that idea of benefiting is very problematic, by the way, but to the extent that he is, it's not because he's black, it's because he's a different kind of black,' Blaine said. 'If Obama didn't have a white mother and wasn't raised by white grandparents and didn't have Kenya and Indonesia and Hawaii and all of the stories that make him somehow a bit like everyone, if he was just a plain black guy from Georgia, it would be different. America will have made real progress when an ordinary black guy from Georgia becomes president, a black guy who got a C average in college.'

'I agree,' Nathan said. And it struck Ifemelu

anew, how much everyone agreed. Their friends, like her and Blaine, were believers. True believers.

On the day Barack Obama became the nominee of the Democratic Party, Ifemelu and Blaine made love, for the first time in weeks, and Obama was there with them, like an unspoken prayer, a third emotional presence. She and Blaine drove hours to hear him speak, holding hands in a thick crowd, raising placards, CHANGE written on them in a bold white print. A black man nearby had hoisted his son onto his shoulders, and the son was laughing, his mouth full of milky teeth, one missing from the upper row. The father was looking up, and Ifemelu knew that he was stunned by his own faith, stunned to find himself believing in things he did not think he ever would. When the crowd exploded in applause, clapping and whistling, the man could not clap, because he was holding his son's legs, and so he just smiled and smiled, his face suddenly young with joyfulness. Ifemelu watched him, and the other people around them, all glowing with a strange phosphorescence, all treading a single line of unbroken emotion. They believed. They truly believed. It often came to her as a sweet shock, the knowledge that there were so many people in the world who felt exactly as she and Blaine did about Barack Obama.

On some days their faith soared. On other days, they despaired.

'This is not good,' Blaine muttered as they went

back and forth between different television channels, each showing the footage of Barack Obama's pastor giving a sermon, and his words 'God Damn America' seared their way into Ifemelu's dreams.

She first read, on the Internet, the breaking news that Barack Obama would give a speech on race, in response to the footage of his pastor, and she sent a text to Blaine, who was teaching a class. His reply was simple: *Yes!* Later, watching the speech, seated between Blaine and Grace on their living room couch, Ifemelu wondered what Obama was truly thinking and what he would feel as he lay in bed that night, when all was quiet and empty. She imagined him, the boy who knew his grandmother was afraid of black men, now a man telling that story to the world to redeem himself. She felt a small sadness at this thought. As Obama spoke, compassionate and cadenced, American flags fluttering behind him, Blaine shifted, sighed, leaned back on the couch. Finally, Blaine said, 'It's immoral to equate black grievance and white fear like this. It's just *immoral.*'

'This speech was not done to open up a conversation about race but actually to close it. He can win only if he avoids race. We all know that,' Grace said. 'But the important thing is to get him into office first. The guy's gotta do what he's gotta do. At least now this pastor business is closed.'

Ifemelu, too, felt pragmatic about the speech,

but Blaine took it personally. His faith cracked, and for a few days he lacked his bounce, coming back from his morning run without his usual sweaty high, walking around heavy-footed. It was Shan who unknowingly pulled him out of his slump.

'I have to go to the city for a few days to be with Shan,' he told Ifemelu. 'Ovidio just called me. She's not functioning.'

'She is not functioning?'

'A nervous breakdown. I dislike that expression, it has a very old wives' tale vibe to it. But that's what Ovidio called it. She's been in bed for days. She's not eating. She won't stop crying.'

Ifemelu felt a flash of irritation; even this, it seemed to her, was yet another way for Shan to demand attention.

'She's had a really hard time,' Blaine said. 'The book not getting any attention and all.'

'I know,' Ifemelu said, and yet she could feel no real sympathy, which frightened her. Perhaps it was because she held Shan responsible, at some level, for the fight with Blaine, for not wielding her power over Blaine to let him know he was overreacting.

'She'll be fine,' Ifemelu said. 'She's a strong person.'

Blaine looked at her with surprise. 'Shan is one of the most fragile people in the world. She's not strong, she's never been. But she's special.'

The last time Ifemelu had seen Shan, about a

month ago, Shan had said, 'I just knew you and Blaine would get back together.' Hers was the tone of a person talking about a beloved sibling who had returned to psychedelic drugs.

'Isn't Obama exciting?' Ifemelu had asked, hoping that this would, at least, be something she and Shan could talk about without an underlying prick of pins.

'Oh, I'm not following this election,' Shan had said dismissively.

'Have you read his book?' Ifemelu asked.

'No.' Shan shrugged. 'It would be good if somebody read *my* book.'

Ifemelu swallowed her words. *It's not about you. For once, it's not about you.*

'You should read *Dreams from My Father*. The other books are campaign documents,' Ifemelu said. 'He's the real deal.'

But Shan was not interested. She was talking about a panel she had done the week before, at a writers' festival. 'So they ask me who my favourite writers are. Of course I know they expected mostly black writers and no way am I going to tell them that Robert Hayden is the love of my life, which he is. So I didn't mention anybody black or remotely of colour or politically inclined or alive. And so I name, with insouciant aplomb, Turgenev and Trollope and Goethe, but so as not to be too indebted to dead white males because that would be a little too unoriginal, I added Selma Lagerlöf. And suddenly they don't know what to ask me, because I'd thrown the script out the window.'

'That's so funny,' Blaine said.

On the eve of Election Day, Ifemelu lay sleepless in bed.

'You awake?' Blaine asked her.

'Yes.'

They held each other in the dark, saying nothing, their breathing regular until finally they drifted into a state of half sleep and half wakefulness. In the morning, they went to the high school; Blaine wanted to be one of the first to vote. Ifemelu watched the people already there, in line, waiting for the door to open, and she willed them all to vote for Obama. It felt to her like a bereavement, that she could not vote. Her application for citizenship had been approved but the oath-taking was still weeks away. She spent a restless morning, checking all the news sites, and when Blaine came back from class he asked her to turn off the computer and television so they could take a break, breathe deeply, eat the risotto he had made. They had barely finished eating before Ifemelu turned her computer back on. Just to make sure Barack Obama was alive and well. Blaine made virgin cocktails for their friends. Araminta arrived first, straight from the train station, holding two phones, checking for updates on both. Then Grace arrived, in her swishy silks, a golden scarf at her neck, saying, 'Oh my God, I can't breathe for nervousness!' Michael came with a bottle of prosecco. 'I wish my mama was alive to see this day no matter what happens,' he said. Paula and Pee and Nathan arrived together, and soon they were all seated, on the couch and the dining chairs, eyes on the television, sipping tea and Blaine's virgin cocktails and repeating the same things they had said before. *If he wins Indiana and Pennsylvania, then that's it. It's looking good in Florida. The news from Iowa is conflicting.*

'There's a huge black voter turnout in Virginia, so it's looking good,' Ifemelu said.

'Virginia is unlikely,' Nathan said.

'He doesn't need Virginia,' Grace said, and then she screamed. 'Oh my God, Pennsylvania!'

A graphic had flashed on the television screen, a photo of Barack Obama. He had won the states of Pennsylvania and Ohio.

'I don't see how McCain can do this now,' Nathan said.

Paula was sitting next to Ifemelu a short while later when the flash of graphics appeared on the screen: Barack Obama had won the state of Virginia.

'Oh my God,' Paula said. Her hand trembling at her mouth. Blaine was sitting straight and still, staring at the television, and then came the deep voice of Keith Olbermann, whom Ifemelu had watched so obsessively on MSNBC in the past months, the voice of a searing, sparkling liberal rage; now that voice was saying 'Barack Obama is projected to be the next president of the United States of America.'

Blaine was crying, holding Araminta, who was crying, and then holding Ifemelu, squeezing her too tight, and Pee was hugging Michael and Grace was hugging Nathan and Paula was hugging Araminta and Ifemelu was hugging Grace and the living room became an altar of disbelieving joy.

Her phone beeped with a text from Dike.

I can't believe it. My president is black like me. She read the text a few times, her eyes filling with tears.

On television, Barack Obama and Michelle Obama and their two young daughters were walking onto a stage. They were carried by the wind, bathed in incandescent light, victorious and smiling.

'Young and old, rich and poor, Democrat and Republican, black, white, Hispanic, Asian, Native American, gay, straight, disabled and not disabled, Americans have sent a message to the world that we have never been just a collection of red states and blue states. We have been and always will be the United States of America.'

Barack Obama's voice rose and fell, his face solemn, and around him the large and resplendent crowd of the hopeful. Ifemelu watched, mesmerized. And there was, at that moment, nothing that was more beautiful to her than America.

Understanding America for the Non-American Black: Thoughts on the Special White Friend

One great gift for the Zipped-Up Negro is The White Friend Who Gets It. Sadly, this is not as common as one would wish, but some are lucky to have that white friend who you don't need to explain shit to. By all means, put this friend to work. Such friends not only get it, but also have great bullshit-detectors and so they totally understand that they can say stuff that you can't. So there is, in much of America, a stealthy little notion lying in the hearts of many: that white people earned their place at jobs and school while black people got in because they were black. But in fact, since the beginning of America, white people have been getting jobs because they are white. Many whites with the same qualifications but Negro skin would not have the jobs they have. But don't ever say this publicly. Let your white friend say it. If you make the mistake of saying this, you will be accused of a curiosity called 'playing the race card.' Nobody quite knows what this means.

When my father was in school in my NAB country, many American Blacks could not vote or go to good schools. The reason? Their skin color. Skin color alone was the problem. Today, many Americans say that skin color cannot be part of the solution. Otherwise it is referred to as a curiosity called 'reverse racism.' Have your white friend point out how the American Black deal is kind of like you've been unjustly imprisoned for many years, then all of a sudden you're set free, but you get no bus fare. And, by the way, you and the guy who imprisoned you are now automatically equal. If the 'slavery was so long ago' thing comes up, have your white friend say that lots of white folks are still inheriting money that their families made a hundred years ago. So if that legacy lives, why not the legacy of slavery? And have your white friend say how funny it is, that American pollsters ask white and black people if racism is over. White people in general say it is over and black people in general say it is not. Funny indeed. More suggestions for what you should have your white friend say? Please post away. And here's to all the white friends who get it.

CHAPTER 41

Aisha pulled out her phone from her pocket and then slipped it back with a frustrated sigh.

'I don't know why Chijioke not call to come,' she said.

Ifemelu said nothing. She and Aisha were alone in the salon; Halima had just left. Ifemelu was tired and her back throbbed and the salon had begun to nauseate her, with its stuffy air and rotting ceiling. Why couldn't these African women keep their salon clean and ventilated? Her hair was almost finished, only a small section, like a rabbit's tail, was left at the front of her head. She was eager to leave.

'How you get your papers?' Aisha asked.

'What?'

'How you get your papers?'

Ifemelu was startled into silence. A sacrilege, that question; immigrants did not ask other immigrants how they got their papers, did not burrow into those layered, private places; it was sufficient simply to admire that the papers had been got, a legal status acquired.

'Me, I try an American when I come, to marry. But he bring many problems, no job, and every day he say give me money, money, money,' Aisha said, shaking her head. 'How you get your own?'

Suddenly, Ifemelu's irritation dissolved, and in its place, a gossamered sense of kinship grew, because Aisha would not have asked if she were not an African, and in this new bond, she saw yet another augury of her return home.

'I got mine from work,' she said. 'The company I worked for sponsored my green card.'

'Oh,' Aisha said, as though she had just realized that Ifemelu belonged to a group of people whose green cards simply fell from the sky. People like her could not, of course, get theirs from an employer.

'Chijioke get his papers with lottery,' Aisha said. She slowly, almost lovingly, combed the section of hair she was about to twist.

'What happened to your hand?' Ifemelu asked.

Aisha shrugged. 'I don't know. It just come and after it go.'

'My aunt is a doctor. I'll take a picture of your arm and ask her what she thinks,' Ifemelu said.

'Thank you.'

Aisha finished a twist in silence.

'My father die, I don't go,' she said.

'What?'

'Last year. My father die and I don't go. Because of papers. But maybe, if Chijioke marry me, when my mother die, I can go. She is sick now. But I send her money.'

For a moment, Ifemelu did not know what to say. Aisha's wan tone, her expressionless face, magnified her tragedy.

'Sorry, Aisha,' she said.

'I don't know why Chijioke not come. So you talk to him.'

'Don't worry, Aisha. It will be okay.'

Then, just as suddenly as she had spoken, Aisha began to cry. Her eyes melted, her mouth caved and a terrifying thing happened to her face: it collapsed into despair. She kept twisting Ifemelu's hair, her hand movements unchanged, while her face, as though it did not belong to her body, continued to crumple, tears running from her eyes, her chest heaving.

'Where does Chijioke work?' Ifemelu asked. 'I will go there and talk to him.'

Aisha stared at her, the tears still sliding down her cheeks.

'I will go and talk to Chijioke tomorrow,' Ifemelu repeated. 'Just tell me where he works and what time he goes on break.'

What was she doing? She should get up and leave, and not be dragged further into Aisha's morass, but she could not get up and leave. She was about to go back home to Nigeria, and she would see her parents, and she could come back to America if she wished, and here was Aisha, hoping but not really believing that she would ever see her mother again. She would talk to this Chijioke. It was the least she could do.

She brushed the hair from her clothes and gave Aisha a thin roll of dollars. Aisha spread it out on her palm, counting briskly, and Ifemelu wondered how much would go to Mariama and how much to Aisha. She waited for Aisha to put the money into her pocket before she gave her the tip. Aisha took the single twenty-dollar bill, her eyes now dried of tears, her face back to its expressionlessness. 'Thank you.'

The room was dense with awkwardness, and Ifemelu, as though to dilute it, once again examined her hair in the mirror, patting it lightly as she turned this way and that.

'I will go and see Chijioke tomorrow and I'll call you,' Ifemelu said. She brushed at her clothes for any stray bits of hair and looked around to make sure she had taken everything.

'Thank you.' Aisha moved towards Ifemelu, as though to embrace her, then stopped, hesitant. Ifemelu gripped her shoulder gently before turning to the door.

On the train, she wondered just how she would persuade a man who didn't seem keen to marry to do so. Her head was aching and the hair at her temples, even though Aisha had not twisted too tightly, still caused a tugging discomfort, a disturbance of her neck and nerves. She longed to get home and have a long, cold shower, put her hair up in a satin bonnet, and lie down on her couch with her laptop. The train had just stopped at Princeton station when her phone rang. She stopped on the platform to fumble in her bag for it and, at first, because Aunty Uju was incoherent, talking and sobbing at the same time, Ifemelu thought she said that Dike was dead. But what Aunty Uju was saying was *o nwuchagokwa, Dike anwuchagokwa.* Dike had nearly died.

'He took an overdose of pills and went down to the basement and lay down on the couch there!' Aunty Uju said, her voice cracked with her own disbelief. 'I never go to the basement when I come back. I only do my yoga in the morning. It was God that told me to go down today to defrost the meat in the freezer. It was God! I saw him lying there looking so sweaty, sweat all over his body, and immediately I panicked. I said these people have given my son drugs.'

Ifemelu was shaking. A train whooshed past and she pressed her finger into her other ear to hear Aunty Uju's voice better. Aunty Uju was saying 'signs of liver toxicity' and Ifemelu felt choked by those words, *liver toxicity*, by her confusion, by the sudden darkening of the air.

'Ifem?' Aunty Uju asked. 'Are you there?'

'Yes.' The word had travelled up a long tunnel. 'What happened? What exactly happened, Aunty? What are you saying?'

'He swallowed a whole bottle of Tylenol. He is in the ICU now and he will be fine. God was not ready for him to die, that is all,' Aunty Uju said.

The sound of her nose-blowing was loud over the phone. 'Do you know he also took anti-nausea so that the medicine would stay in his stomach? God was not ready for him to die.'

'I am coming tomorrow,' Ifemelu said. She stood on the platform for a long time, and wondered what she had been doing while Dike was swallowing a bottle of pills.

PART V

CHAPTER 42

Obinze checked his BlackBerry often, too often, even when he got up at night to go to the toilet, and although he mocked himself, he could not stop checking. Four days, four whole days, passed before she replied. This dampened him. She was never coy, and she would have ordinarily replied much sooner. She might be busy, he told himself, although he knew very well how convenient and unconvincing a reason 'busy' was. Or she might have changed and become the kind of woman who waited four whole days so that she would not seem too eager, a thought that dampened him even more. Her e-mail was warm, but too short, telling him she was excited and nervous about leaving her life and moving back home, but there were no specifics. When was she moving back exactly? And what was it that was so difficult to leave behind? He Googled the black American again, hoping perhaps to find a blog post about a break-up, but the blog only had links to academic papers. One of them was on early hip-hop music as political activism – how American, to study hip-hop as a viable subject – and he read it hoping it would be silly, but it was interesting enough for him to read all the way to the end and this soured his stomach. The black American had become, absurdly, a rival. He tried Facebook. Kosi was active on Facebook, she put up photos and kept in touch with people, but he had deleted his account a while ago. He had at first been excited by Facebook, ghosts of old friends suddenly morphing to life with wives and husbands and children, and photos trailed by comments. But he began to be appalled by the air of unreality, the careful manipulation of images to create a parallel life, pictures that people had taken with Facebook in mind, placing in the background the things of which they were proud. Now, he reactivated his account to search for Ifemelu, but she did not have a Facebook profile. Perhaps she was as unenchanted with Facebook as he was. This pleased him vaguely, another example of how similar they were. Her black American was on Facebook, but his profile was visible only to his friends, and for a crazed moment, Obinze considered sending him a friend request, just to see if he had posted pictures of Ifemelu. He wanted to wait a few days before replying to her but he found himself that night in his study writing her a long e-mail about the death of his mother. *I never thought that she would die until she died. Does this make sense?* He had discovered that grief did not dim with time; it was instead a volatile state of being. Sometimes the pain was as abrupt as it was on the day her house help called him sobbing to say she was lying unbreathing on her bed; other times, he forgot that she had died and would make cursory plans about flying to the east to see her. She had looked askance at his new wealth, as though she did not understand a world in which a person could make so much so easily. After he bought her a new car as a surprise, she told him her old car was perfectly fine, the Peugeot 505 she had been driving since he was in secondary school. He had the car delivered to her house, a small Honda that she would not think too ostentatious, but each time he visited, he saw it parked in the garage, coated in a translucent haze of dust. He remembered very clearly his last conversation with her over the phone, three days before she died, her growing despondence with her job and with life on the campus.

'Nobody publishes in international journals,' she had said. 'Nobody goes to conferences. It's like a shallow muddy pond that we are all wallowing in.'

He wrote this in his e-mail to Ifemelu, how his mother's sadness with her job had also made him sad. He was careful not to be too heavy-handed, writing about how the church in his hometown had made him pay many dues before her funeral, and how the caterers had stolen meat at the burial, wrapping chunks of beef in fresh banana leaves and throwing them across the compound wall to their accomplices, and how his relatives had become preoccupied with the stolen meat. Voices

567

were raised, accusations flung back and forth, and an aunt had said, 'Those caterers must return every last bit of the stolen goods!' Stolen goods. His mother would have been amused about meat being a stolen good, and even by her funeral ending up a brawl about stolen meat. Why, he wrote to Ifemelu, do our funerals become so quickly about other things that are not about the person who died? Why do the villagers wait for a death before they proceed to avenge past wrongs, those real and those imagined, and why do they dig deep to the bone in their bid to get their pound of flesh?

Ifemelu's reply came an hour later, a rush of heartbroken words. *I am crying as I write this. Do you know how often I wished that she was my mother? She was the only adult – except for Aunty Uju – who treated me like a person with an opinion that mattered. You were so fortunate to be raised by her. She was everything I wanted to be. I am so sorry, Ceiling. I can imagine how ripped apart you must have felt and still sometimes feel. I am in Massachusetts with Aunty Uju and Dike and I am going through something right now that gives me a sense of that kind of pain, but only a small sense. Please give me a number so I can call – if it's okay.*

Her e-mail made him happy. Seeing his mother through her eyes made him happy. And it emboldened him. He wondered what pain she was referring to and hoped that it was the break-up with the black American, although he did not want the relationship to have mattered so much to her that the break-up would throw her into a kind of mourning. He tried to imagine how changed she would be now, how Americanized, especially after being in a relationship with an American. There was a manic optimism that he noticed in many of the people who had moved back from America in the past few years, a head-bobbing, ever-smiling, over-enthusiastic kind of manic optimism that bored him, because it was like a cartoon, without texture or depth. He hoped she had not become like that. He could not imagine that she would have. She had asked for his number. She could not feel so strongly about his mother if she did not still have feelings for him. So he wrote to her again, giving her all of his phone numbers, his three mobile phones, his office phone and his home landline. He ended his e-mail with these words: *It's strange how I have felt, with every major event that has occurred in my life, that you were the only person who would understand.* He felt giddy, but after he clicked Send, regrets assailed him. It had been too much too soon. He should not have written something so heavy. He checked his BlackBerry obsessively, day after day, and by the tenth day he realized she would not write back.

He composed a few e-mails apologizing to her, but he did not send them because it felt awkward apologizing for something he could not name. He never consciously decided to write her the long, detailed e-mails that followed. His claim, that he had missed her at every major event in his life, was grandiose, he knew, but it was not entirely false. Of course there were stretches of time when he had not actively thought about her, when he was submerged in his early excitement with Kosi, in his new child, in a new contract, but she had never been absent. He had held her always clasped in the palm of his mind. Even through her silence, and his confused bitterness.

He began to write to her about his time in England, hoping she would reply and then later looking forward to the writing itself. He had never told himself his own story, never allowed himself to reflect on it, because he was too disoriented by his deportation and then by the suddenness of his new life in Lagos. Writing to her also became a way of writing to himself. He had nothing to lose. Even if she was reading his e-mails with the black American and laughing at his stupidity, he did not mind.

Finally, she replied.

> Ceiling, sorry for the silence. Dike attempted suicide. I didn't want to tell you earlier (and I don't know why). He's doing much better, but it has been traumatic and it's affected me more than I thought it would (you know, 'attempted' doesn't mean it happened, but I've spent days crying, thinking about what might have happened). I'm sorry I didn't

call to give you my condolences about your mother. I had planned to, and appreciated your giving me your phone number, but I took Dike to his psychiatrist appointment that day and afterwards, I just couldn't get myself to do anything. I felt as if I had been felled by something. Aunty Uju tells me I have depression. You know America has a way of turning everything into an illness that needs medicine. I'm not taking medicines, just spending a lot of time with Dike, watching a lot of terrible films with vampires and spaceships. I have loved your e-mails about England and they have been so good for me, in so many ways, and I cannot thank you enough for writing them. I hope I will have a chance to fill you in on my own life – whenever that is. I've just finished a fellowship at Princeton and for years I wrote an anonymous blog about race, which then became how I made my living, and you can read the archives here. I've postponed my return home. I'll be in touch. Take care and hope all is well with you and your family.

Dike had tried to kill himself. It was impossible to comprehend. His memory of Dike was of a toddler, a white puff of Pampers at his waist, running around in the house in Dolphin Estate. Now he was a teenager who had tried to kill himself. Obinze's first thought was that he wanted to go to Ifemelu, right away. He wanted to buy a ticket and get on a plane to America and be with her, console her, help Dike, make everything right. Then he laughed at his own absurdity.

'Darling, you're not paying attention,' Kosi said to him.

'Sorry, omalicha,' he said.

'No work thoughts for now.'

'Okay, sorry. What were you saying?'

They were in the car, on their way to a nursery-primary school in Ikoyi, visiting during the open day as guests of Jonathan and Isioma, Kosi's friends from church, whose son went there. Kosi had arranged it all, their second school visit, to help them decide where Buchi would go.

Obinze had spent time with them only once, when Kosi invited them to dinner. He thought Isioma interesting; the few things she allowed herself to say were thoughtful, but she often remained silent, shrinking herself, pretending not to be as intelligent as she was, to salve Jonathan's ego, while Jonathan, a bank CEO whose photos were always in the newspapers, dominated the evening with long-winded stories about his dealings with estate agents in Switzerland, the Nigerian governors he had advised and the various companies he had saved from collapse.

He introduced Obinze and Kosi to the school headmistress, a small round Englishwoman, saying, 'Obinze and Kosi are our very close friends. I think their daughter might be joining us next year.'

'Many high-level expatriates bring their children here,' the headmistress said, her tone pride-tinged, and Obinze wondered if this was something she said routinely. She had probably said it often enough to know how well it worked, how much it impressed Nigerians.

Isioma was asking why their son was not yet doing much of mathematics and English.

'Our approach is more conceptual. We like the children to explore their environment during the first year,' the headmistress said.

'But it should not be mutually exclusive. They can also start to learn some maths and English,' Isioma said. Then, with an amusement that did not try to shield its underlying seriousness, she added, 'My niece goes to a school on the mainland and at age six she could spell "onomatopoeia"!'

The headmistress smiled tightly; she did not, her smile said, think it worthwhile to address the processes of lesser schools. Later, they sat in a large hall and watched the children's production of a Christmas play, about a Nigerian family who find an orphan on their doorstep on Christmas Day. Halfway through the play, a teacher turned on a fan that blew small bits of white cotton wool around the stage. Snow. It was snowing in the play.

'Why do they have snow falling? Are they teaching children that a Christmas is not a real Christmas unless snow falls like it does abroad?' Isioma said.

Jonathan said, 'Ahn-ahn, what is wrong with that? It's just a play!'

'It's just a play, but I also see what Isioma is saying,' Kosi said, and then turned to Obinze. 'Darling?'

Obinze said, 'The little girl that played the angel was very good.'

In the car, Kosi said, 'Your mind is not here.'

He read all the archives of *Raceteenth or Various Observations About American Blacks (Those Formerly Known as Negroes) by a Non-American Black*. The blog posts astonished him, they seemed so American and so alien, the irreverent voice with its slanginess, its mix of high and low language, and he could not imagine her writing them. He cringed reading her references to her boyfriends – The Hot White Ex, Professor Hunk. He read 'Just This Evening' a few times, because it was the most personal post she had written about the black American, and he searched for clues and subtleties, about what kind of man he was, what kind of relationship they had.

So in NYC, Professor Hunk was stopped by the police. They thought he had drugs. American Blacks and American Whites use drugs at the same rate (look this up), but say the word 'drugs' and see what image comes to everyone's mind. Professor Hunk is upset. He says he's an Ivy League professor and he knows the deal, and he wonders what it would feel like if he were some poor kid from the inner city. I feel bad for my baby. When we first met, he told me how he wanted to get straight As in high school because of a white teacher who told him to 'focus on getting a basketball scholarship, black people are physically inclined and white people are intellectually inclined, it's not good or bad, just different' (and this teacher went to Columbia, just sayin'). So he spent four years proving her wrong. I couldn't identify with this: wanting to do well to prove a point. But I felt bad then too. So off to make him some tea. And administer some TLC.

Because he had last known her when she knew little of the things she blogged about, he felt a sense of loss, as though she had become a person he would no longer recognize.

PART VI

CHAPTER 43

For the first few days, Ifemelu slept on the floor in Dike's room. *It did not happen. It did not happen.* She told herself this often, and yet endless, elliptical thoughts of what could have happened churned in her head. His bed, this room, would have been empty forever. Somewhere inside her, a gash would have ruptured that would never seal itself back. She imagined him taking the pills. Tylenol, mere Tylenol; he had read on the Internet that an overdose could kill you. What was he thinking? Did he think of her? After he came home from the hospital, his stomach pumped, his liver monitored, she searched his face, his gestures, his words, for a sign, for proof that it had really almost happened. He looked no different from before; there were no shadows under his eyes, no funereal air about him. She made him the kind of jollof rice he liked, flecked with bits of red and green peppers, and as he ate, fork moving from the plate to his mouth, saying, 'This is pretty good,' as he always had in the past, she felt her tears and her questions gathering. Why? Why had he done it? What was on his mind? She did not ask him because the therapist had said that it was best not to ask him anything yet. The days passed. She clung to him, wary of letting go and wary, also, of suffocating him. She was sleepless at first, refusing the small blue pill Aunty Uju offered her, and she would lie awake at night, thinking and turning, her mind held hostage by thoughts of what could have been, until she fell, finally, into a drained sleep. On some days, she woke up scarred with blame for Aunty Uju.

'Do you remember when Dike was telling you something and he said "we black folk" and you told him "you are not black"?' she asked Aunty Uju, her voice low because Dike was still asleep upstairs. They were in the kitchen of the condo, in the soft flare of morning light, and Aunty Uju, dressed for work, was standing by the sink and eating yogurt, scooping from a plastic cup.

'Yes, I remember.'

'You should not have done that.'

'You know what I meant. I didn't want him to start behaving like these people and thinking that everything that happens to him is because he's black.'

'You told him what he wasn't but you didn't tell him what he was.'

'What are you saying?' Aunty Uju pressed the lever with her foot, the trash can slid out and she threw in the empty yogurt cup. She had switched to part-time work so that she could spend some time with Dike, and drive him to his therapist appointments herself.

'You never reassured him.'

'Ifemelu, his suicide attempt was from depression,' Aunty Uju said gently, quietly. 'It is a clinical disease. Many teenagers suffer from it.'

'Do people just wake up and become depressed?'

'Yes, they do.'

'Not in Dike's case.'

'Three of my patients have attempted suicide, all of them white teenagers. One succeeded,' Aunty Uju said, her tone pacifying and sad, as it had been since Dike came home from the hospital.

'His depression is because of his experience, Aunty!' Ifemelu said, her voice rising, and then she was sobbing, apologizing to Aunty Uju, her own guilt spreading and sullying her. Dike would not have swallowed those pills if she had been more diligent, more awake. She had crouched too easily behind laughter, she had failed to till the emotional soil of Dike's jokes. It was true that he laughed, and that his laughter convinced with its sound and its light, but it might have been a shield, and underneath, there might have been a growing pea plant of trauma.

Now, in the shrill, silent aftermath of his suicide attempt, she wondered how much they had masked with all that laughter. She should have worried more. She watched him carefully. She guarded him. She did not want his friends to visit, although the therapist said it was fine if he wanted them to. Even Page, who had burst out crying a few days ago when she was alone with Ifemelu, saying, 'I just can't believe he didn't reach out to me.' She was a child, well-meaning and simple, and yet Ifemelu felt a wave of resentment towards her, for thinking that Dike should have reached out to her. Kweku came back from his medical mission in Nigeria, and he spent time with Dike, watching television with him, bringing calm and normalcy back.

The weeks passed. Ifemelu stopped panicking when Dike stayed a little too long in the bathroom. His birthday was days away and she asked what he would like, her tears again gathering, because she imagined his birthday passing not as the day he turned seventeen but as the day he would have turned seventeen.

'How about we go to Miami?' he said, half joking, but she took him to Miami and they spent two days in a hotel, ordering burgers at the thatch-covered bar by the pool, talking about everything but the suicide attempt.

'This is the life,' he said, lying with his face to the sun. 'That blog of yours was a great thing, had you swimming in the dough and all. Now you've closed it, we won't be able to do more of this stuff!'

'I wasn't swimming, kind of just splattering,' she said, looking at him, her handsome cousin, and the curl of wet hair on his chest made her sad, because it implied his new, tender adulthood, and she wished he would remain a child; if he remained a child then he would not have taken pills and lain on the basement couch with the certainty that he would never wake up again.

'I love you, Dike. We love you, you know that?'

'I know,' he said. 'Coz, you should go.'

'Go where?'

'Back to Nigeria, like you were planning to. I'm going to be okay, I promise.'

'Maybe you could come and visit me,' she said.

After a pause, he said, 'Yeah.'

PART VII

CHAPTER 44

At first, Lagos assaulted her; the sun-dazed haste, the yellow buses full of squashed limbs, the sweating hawkers racing after cars, the advertisements on hulking billboards (others scrawled on walls – PLUMBER CALL 080177777) and the heaps of rubbish that rose on the roadsides like a taunt. Commerce thrummed too defiantly. And the air was dense with exaggeration, conversations full of over-protestations. One morning, a man's body lay on Awolowo Road. Another morning, The Island flooded and cars became gasping boats. Here, she felt, anything could happen, a ripe tomato could burst out of solid stone. And so she had the dizzying sensation of falling, falling into the new person she had become, falling into the strange familiar. Had it always been like this or had it changed so much in her absence? When she left home, only the wealthy had mobile phones, all the numbers started with 090, and girls wanted to date 090 men. Now, her hair braider had a mobile phone, the plantain seller tending a blackened grill had a mobile phone. She had grown up knowing all the bus stops and the side streets, understanding the cryptic codes of conductors and the body language of street hawkers. Now, she struggled to grasp the unspoken. When had shopkeepers become so rude? Had buildings in Lagos always had this patina of decay? And when did it become a city of people quick to beg and too enamoured of free things?

'Americanah!' Ranyinudo teased her often. 'You are looking at things with American eyes. But the problem is that you are not even a real Americanah. At least if you had an American accent we would tolerate your complaining!'

Ranyinudo picked her up from the airport, standing by the Arrivals exit in a billowy brides-maid's dress, her blusher too red on her cheeks like bruises, the green satin flowers in her hair now askew. Ifemelu was struck by how arresting, how attractive, she was. No longer a ropy mass of gangly arms and gangly legs, but now a big, firm, curvy woman, exulting in her weight and height, and it made her imposing, a presence that drew the eyes.

'Ranyi!' Ifemelu said. 'I know my coming back is a big deal but I didn't know it was big enough for a ball gown.'

'Idiot. I came straight from the wedding. I didn't want to risk the traffic of going home first to change.'

They hugged, holding each other close. Ranyinudo smelled of a floral perfume and exhaust fumes and sweat; she smelled of Nigeria.

'You look amazing, Ranyi,' Ifemelu said. 'I mean, underneath all that war paint. Your pictures didn't even show you well.'

'Ifemsco, see you, beautiful babe, even after a long flight,' she said, laughing, dismissing the compliment, playing at her old role of the girl who was not the pretty one. Her looks had changed but the excitable, slightly reckless air about her had not. Unchanged, too, was the eternal gurgle in her voice, laughter just beneath the surface, ready to break free, to erupt. She drove fast, braking sharply and glancing often at the BlackBerry on her lap; whenever the traffic stilled, she picked it up and typed swiftly.

'Ranyi, you should text and drive only when you are alone so that you kill only yourself,' Ifemelu said.

'Haba! I don't text and drive o. I text when I'm not driving,' she said. 'This wedding was something else, the best wedding I've been to. I wonder if you'll remember the bride. She was Funke's very good friend in secondary school. Ijeoma, very yellow girl. She went to Holy Child but she used to come to our WAEC lesson with Funke. We became friends in university. If you see her now, eh, she's a serious babe. Her husband has major money. Her engagement ring is bigger than Zuma Rock.'

Ifemelu stared out of the window, half listening, thinking how unpretty Lagos was, roads infested with potholes, houses springing up unplanned like

589

weeds. Of her jumble of feelings, she recognized only confusion.

'Lime and peach,' Ranyinudo said.

'What?'

'The wedding colours. Lime and peach. The hall decoration was so nice and the cake was just beautiful. Look, I took some pictures. I'm going to put this one up on Facebook.' Ranyinudo gave Ifemelu her BlackBerry. Ifemelu held on to it so that Ranyinudo would focus on her driving.

'And I met someone o. He saw me when I was waiting outside for the mass to end. It was so hot, my foundation was melting on my face and I know I looked like a zombie, but he still came to talk to me! That's a good sign. I think this one is serious husband material. Did I tell you my mother was saying novenas to end my relationship when I was dating Ibrahim? At least she will not have a heart attack with this one. His name is Ndudi. Cool name, *abi*? You can't get more Igbo than that. And you should have seen his watch! He's into oil. His business card has Nigerian and international offices.'

'Why were you waiting outside during mass?'

'All the bridesmaids had to wait outside because our dresses were indecent.' Ranyinudo rolled 'indecent' around her tongue and chuckled. 'It happens all the time, especially in Catholic churches. We even had cover-ups but the priest said they were too lacy, so we just waited outside until the mass ended. But thank God for that or I would not have met this guy!'

Ifemelu looked at Ranyinudo's dress, its thin straps, its pleated neckline that showed no cleavage. Before she left, were bridesmaids banished from church services because their dresses had spaghetti straps? She did not think so, but she was no longer sure. She was no longer sure what was new in Lagos and what was new in herself. Ranyinudo parked on a street in Lekki, which was bare reclaimed land when Ifemelu left, but now a cavalcade of large houses encircled by high walls.

'My flat is the smallest, so I don't have parking space inside,' Ranyinudo said. 'The other tenants park inside, but you should see all the shouting that happens in the morning when somebody does not move their car out of the way, and somebody else is late for work!'

Ifemelu climbed out of the car and into the loud, discordant drone of generators, too many generators; the sound pierced the soft middle of her ears and throbbed in her head.

'No light for the past week,' Ranyinudo said, shouting to be heard above the generators.

The gateman had hurried over to help with the suitcases.

'Welcome back, Aunty,' he said to Ifemelu.

He had not merely said 'welcome' but 'welcome back', as though he somehow knew that she was truly back. She thanked him, and in the grey of the evening darkness, the air burdened with smells, she ached with an almost unbearable emotion that she could not name. It was nostalgic and

591

melancholy, a beautiful sadness for the things she had missed and the things she would never know. Later, sitting on the couch in Ranyinudo's small stylish living room, her feet sunk into the too-soft carpet, the flat-screen TV perched on the opposite wall, Ifemelu looked unbelievingly at herself. She had done it. She had come back. She turned the TV on and searched for the Nigerian channels. On NTA, the first lady, blue scarf wrapped around her face, was addressing a rally of women, and crawling across the screen were the words 'The First Lady is Empowering Women with Mosquito Nets'.

'I can't remember the last time I watched that stupid station,' Ranyinudo said. 'They lie for the government but they can't even lie well.'

'So which Nigerian channel do you watch?'

'I don't even really watch any o. I watch Style and E! Sometimes CNN and BBC.' Ranyinudo had changed into shorts and a T-shirt. 'I have a girl who comes and cooks and cleans for me, but I made this stew myself because you were coming, so you must eat it o. What will you drink? I have malt and orange juice.'

'Malt! I'm going to drink all the malt in Nigeria. I used to buy it from a Hispanic supermarket in Baltimore, but it was not the same thing.'

'I ate really nice ofada rice at the wedding, I'm not hungry,' Ranyinudo said. But, after she served Ifemelu's food on a dinner plate, she ate some rice and chicken stew from a plastic bowl, perched on the arm of the couch, while they gossiped about old friends: Priye was an event planner and had recently gone big time after being introduced to the governor's wife. Tochi had lost her job at a bank after the last bank crisis, but she had married a wealthy lawyer and had a baby.

'Tochi used to tell me how much people had in their accounts,' Ranyinudo said. 'Remember that guy Mekkus Parara who was dying for Ginika? Remember how he always had smelly yellow patches under his arms? He has major money now, but it is dirty money. You know, all these guys who do fraud in London and America, then run back to Nigeria with the money and build mighty houses in Victoria Garden City. Tochi told me that he never came to the bank himself. He used to send his boys with Ghana Must Go bags to carry ten million today, twenty million tomorrow. Me, I never wanted to work in a bank. The problem with working in a bank is that if you don't get a good branch with high-net customers, you are finished. You will spend all your time attending to useless traders. Tochi was lucky with her job and she worked in a good branch and she met her husband there. Do you want another malt?'

Ranyinudo got up. There was a luxurious, womanly slowness to her gait, a lift, a roll, a toggle of her buttocks with each step. A Nigerian walk. A walk, too, that hinted at excess, as though it spoke of something in need of toning down. Ifemelu took the cold bottle of malt from Ranyinudo and wondered if this would have been her life if she had not left, if she would be like Ranyinudo, working for an advertising company, living in a one-bedroom flat whose rent her salary could not pay, attending a Pentecostal church where she was an usher, and dating a married chief executive who bought her business-class tickets to London. Ranyinudo showed Ifemelu his photographs on her phone. In one, he was bare-chested with the slight swell of a middle-aged belly, reclining on Ranyinudo's bed, smiling the bashful smile of a man just sated from sex. In another, he was looking down in a close-up shot, his face a blurred and mysterious silhouette. There was something attractive, even distinguished, about his grey-speckled hair.

'Is it me or does he look like a tortoise?' Ifemelu said.

'It's you. But Ifem, seriously, Don is a good man o. Not like many of these useless Lagos men running around town.'

'Ranyi, you told me it was just a passing thing. But two years is not a passing thing. I worry about you.'

'I have feelings for him, I won't deny it, but I want to marry and he knows that. I used to think maybe I should have a child for him but look at Uche Okafor, remember her from Nsukka? She had a child for the managing director of Hale Bank and the man told her to go to hell, that he is not the father, and now she is left with raising a child alone. *Na wa.*'

Ranyinudo was looking at the photograph on

her phone with a faint, fond smile. Earlier, on the drive back from the airport, she had said, as she slowed down to sink into, and then climb out of, a large pothole, 'I really want Don to change this car. He has been promising for the past three months. I need a jeep. Do you see how terrible the roads are?' And Ifemelu felt something between fascination and longing for Ranyinudo's life. A life in which she waved a hand and things fell from the sky, things that she quite simply expected should fall from the sky.

At midnight, Ranyinudo turned off her generator and opened the windows. 'I have been running this generator for one straight week, can you imagine? The light situation has not been this bad in a long time.'

The coolness dissipated quickly. Warm, humid air gagged the room, and soon Ifemelu was tossing in the wetness of her own sweat. A painful throbbing had started behind her eyes and a mosquito was buzzing nearby and she felt suddenly, guiltily grateful that she had a blue American passport in her bag. It shielded her from choicelessness. She could always leave; she did not have to stay.

'What kind of humidity is this?' she said. She was on Ranyinudo's bed, and Ranyinudo was on a mattress on the floor. 'I can't breathe.'

'I can't breathe,' Ranyinudo mimicked, her voice laughter-filled. 'Haba! Americanah!'

CHAPTER 45

Ifemelu had found the listing on *Nigerian Jobs Online* – 'features editor for leading women's monthly magazine'. She edited her résumé, invented past experience as a staff writer on a women's magazine ('folded due to bankruptcy' in parentheses), and days after she sent it off by courier, the publisher of *Zoe* called from Lagos. There was, about the mature, friendly voice on the other end of the line, a vague air of inappropriateness. 'Oh, call me Aunty Onenu,' she said cheerfully when Ifemelu asked who was speaking. Before she offered Ifemelu the job, she said, tone hushed in confidence, 'My husband did not support me when I started this, because he thought men would chase me if I went to seek advertising.' Ifemelu sensed that the magazine was a hobby for Aunty Onenu, a hobby that meant something, but still a hobby. Not a passion. Not something that consumed her. And when she met Aunty Onenu, she felt this more strongly: here was a woman easy to like but difficult to take seriously.

Ifemelu went with Ranyinudo to Aunty Onenu's home in Ikoyi. They sat on leather sofas that felt cold to the touch, and talked in low voices, until Aunty Onenu appeared. A slim, smiling, well-preserved woman, wearing leggings, a large T-shirt and an overly youthful weave, the wavy hair trailing all the way to her back.

'My new features editor has come from America!' she said, hugging Ifemelu. It was difficult to tell her age, anything between fifty and sixty-five, but it was easy to tell that she had not been born with her light complexion, its sheen was too waxy and her knuckles were dark, as though those folds of skin had valiantly resisted her bleaching cream.

'I wanted you to come around before you start on Monday so I can welcome you personally,' Aunty Onenu said.

'Thank you.' Ifemelu thought the home visit unprofessional and odd, but this was a small magazine, and this was Nigeria, where boundaries were blurred, where work blended into life, and bosses were called Mummy. Besides, she already imagined taking over the running of *Zoe*, turning it into a vibrant, relevant companion for Nigerian women, and – who knew – perhaps one day buying out Aunty Onenu. And she would not welcome new recruits in her home.

'You are a pretty girl,' Aunty Onenu said, nodding, as though being pretty were needed for the job and she had worried that Ifemelu might not be. 'I liked how you sounded on the phone. I am sure with you on board our circulation will soon surpass *Glass*. You know we are a much younger publication but already catching up to them!'

A steward in white, a grave, elderly man, emerged to ask what they would drink.

'Aunty Onenu, I've been reading back issues of both *Glass* and *Zoe*, and I have some ideas about what we can do differently,' Ifemelu said, after the steward left to get their orange juice.

'You are a real American! Ready to get to work, a no-nonsense person! Very good. First of all, tell me how you think we compare to *Glass*?'

Ifemelu had thought both magazines vapid, but *Glass* was better edited, the page colours did not bleed as badly as they did in *Zoe*, and it was more visible in traffic; whenever Ranyinudo's car slowed, there was a hawker pressing a copy of *Glass* against her window. But because she could already see Aunty Onenu's obsession with the competition, so nakedly personal, she said, 'It's about the same, but I think we can do better. We need to cut down the profile interviews and do just one a month and profile a woman who has actually achieved something real on her own. We need more personal columns, and we should introduce a rotating guest column, and do more health and money, have a stronger online presence, and stop lifting foreign magazine pieces. Most of your readers can't go into the market and buy broccoli because we don't have it in Nigeria, so why does this month's *Zoe* have a recipe for cream of broccoli soup?'

'Yes, yes,' Aunty Onenu said, slowly. She seemed

astonished. Then, as though recovering herself, she said, 'Very good. We'll discuss all this on Monday.'

In the car, Ranyinudo said, 'Talking to your new boss like that, ha! If you had not come from America, she would have fired you immediately.'

'I wonder what the story is between her and the *Glass* publisher.'

'I read in one of the tabloids that they hate each other. I am sure it is man trouble, what else? Women, eh! I think Aunty Onenu started *Zoe* just to compete with *Glass*. As far as I'm concerned, she's not a publisher, she's just a rich woman who decided to start a magazine, and tomorrow she might close it and start a spa.'

'And what an ugly house,' Ifemelu said. It was monstrous, with two alabaster angels guarding the gate, and a dome-shaped fountain sputtering in the front yard.

'Ugly *kwa*? What are you talking about? The house is beautiful!'

'Not to me,' Ifemelu said, and yet she had once found houses like that beautiful. But here she was now, disliking it with the haughty confidence of a person who recognized kitsch.

'Her generator is as big as my flat and it is completely noiseless!' Ranyinudo said. 'Did you notice the generator house on the side of the gate?'

Ifemelu had not noticed. And it piqued her. This was what a true Lagosian should have noticed: the generator house, the generator size.

On Kingsway Road, she thought she saw Obinze

drive past in a low-slung black Mercedes and she sat up, straining and peering, but, slowed at a traffic jam, she saw that the man looked nothing like him. There were other imagined glimpses of Obinze over the next weeks, people she knew were not him but could have been: the straight-backed figure in a suit walking into Aunty Onenu's office, the man in the back of a car with tinted windows, his face bent to a phone, the figure behind her in the supermarket line. She even imagined, when she first went to meet her landlord, that she would walk in and discover Obinze sitting there. The estate agent had told her that the landlord preferred expatriate renters. 'But he relaxed when I told him you came from America,' he added. The landlord was an elderly man in a brown caftan and matching trousers; he had the weathered skin and wounded air of one who had endured much at the hands of others.

'I do not rent to Igbo people,' he said softly, startling her. Were such things now said so easily? Had they been said so easily and had she merely forgotten? 'That is my policy since one Igbo man destroyed my house at Yaba. But you look like a responsible somebody.'

'Yes, I am responsible,' she said, and feigned a simpering smile. The other flats she liked were too expensive. Even though pipes poked out under the kitchen sink and the toilet was lopsided and the bathroom tiles shoddily laid, this was the best she could afford. She liked the airiness of the living room, with its large windows, and the narrow flight of stairs that led to a tiny verandah charmed her, but, most of all, it was in Ikoyi. And she wanted to live in Ikoyi. Growing up, Ikoyi had reeked of gentility, a faraway gentility that she could not touch: the people who lived in Ikoyi had faces free of pimples and drivers designated 'the children's driver'. The first day she saw the flat, she stood on the verandah and looked across at the compound next door, a grand colonial house, now yellowed from decay, the grounds swallowed in foliage, grass and shrubs climbing atop one another. On the roof of the house, a part of which had collapsed and sunk in, she saw a movement, a turquoise splash of feathers. It was a peacock. The estate agent told her that an army officer had lived there during General Abacha's regime; now the house was tied up in court. And she imagined the people who had lived there fifteen years ago while she, in a little flat on the crowded mainland, longed for their spacious, serene lives.

She wrote the cheque for two years' rent. This was why people took bribes and asked for bribes; how else could anyone honestly pay two years' rent in advance? She planned to fill her verandah with white lilies in clay pots, and decorate her living room in pastels, but first, she had to find an electrician to install air conditioners, a painter to redo the oily walls, and somebody to lay new tiles in the kitchen and bathroom. The estate agent brought a man who did tiles. It took him a week and, when the estate agent called her to say that the work was done, she went eagerly to the flat. In the bathroom, she stared in disbelief. The tile edges were rough, tiny spaces gaping at the corners. One tile had an ugly crack across the middle. It looked like something done by an impatient child.

'What is this nonsense? Look at how rough this is! One tile is broken! This is even worse than the old tiles! How can you be happy with this useless work?' she asked the man.

He shrugged; he clearly thought she was making unnecessary trouble. 'I am happy with the work, Aunty.'

'You want me to pay you?'

A small smile. 'Ah, Aunty, but I have finish the work.'

The estate agent intervened. 'Don't worry, ma, he will repair the broken one.'

The tile man looked reluctant. 'But I have finish the work. The problem is the tile is breaking very easily. It is the quality of tile.'

'You have finished? You do this rubbish job and say you have finished?' Her anger was growing, her voice rising and hardening. 'I will not pay you what we agreed, no way, because you have not done what we agreed.'

The tile man was staring at her, eyes narrowed.

'And if you want trouble, trust me, you will get it,' Ifemelu said. 'The first thing I will do is call the commissioner of police and they will lock you up in Alagbon Close!' She was screaming now.

'Do you know who I am? You don't know who I am, that is why you can do this kind of rubbish work for me!'

The man looked cowed. She had surprised herself. Where had that come from, the false bravado, the easy resort to threats? A memory came to her, undiminished after so many years, of the day Aunty Uju's General died, how Aunty Uju had threatened his relatives. 'No, don't go, just stay there,' she had said to them. 'Stay there while I go and call my boys from the army barracks.'

The estate agent said, 'Aunty, don't worry, he will do the work again.'

Later, Ranyinudo told her, 'You are no longer behaving like an Americanah!' and despite herself, Ifemelu felt pleased to hear this.

'The problem is that we no longer have artisans in this country,' Ranyinudo said. 'Ghanaians are better. My boss is building a house and he is using only Ghanaians to do his finishing. Nigerians will do rubbish for you. They do not take their time to finish things properly. It's terrible. But Ifem, you should have called Obinze. He would have sorted everything out for you. This is what he does, after all. He must have all kinds of contacts. You should have called him before you even started looking for a flat. He could have given you reduced rent in one of his properties, even a free flat *sef*. I don't know what you are waiting for before you call him.'

Ifemelu shook her head. Ranyinudo, for whom

men existed only as sources of things. She could not imagine calling Obinze to ask him for reduced rent in one of his properties. Still, she did not know why she had not called him at all. She had thought of it many times, often bringing out her phone to scroll to his number, and yet she had not called. He still sent e-mails, saying he hoped she was fine, or he hoped Dike was doing better, and she replied to a few, always briefly, replies he would assume were sent from America.

CHAPTER 46

She spent weekends with her parents, in the old flat, happy simply to sit and look at the walls that had witnessed her childhood; only when she began to eat her mother's stew, an oil layer floating on top of the pureed tomatoes, did she realize how much she had missed it. The neighbours stopped by to greet her, the daughter back from America. Many of them were new and unfamiliar, but she felt a sentimental fondness for them, because they reminded her of the others she had known, Mama Bomboy downstairs who had once pulled her ear when she was in primary school and said, 'You do not greet your elders,' Oga Tony upstairs who smoked on his verandah, the trader next door who called her, for reasons she never knew, 'champion'.

'They are just coming to see if you will give them anything,' her mother said, in a whisper, as if the neighbours who had all left might overhear. 'They all expected me to buy something for them when we went to America, so I went to the market and bought small-small bottles of perfume and told them it was from America!'

Her parents liked to talk about their visit to Baltimore, her mother about the sales, her father about how he could not understand the news because Americans now used expressions like 'divvy up' and 'nuke' in serious news.

'It is the final infantilization and informalization of America! It portends the end of the American empire, and they are killing themselves from within!' he pronounced.

Ifemelu humoured them, listening to their observations and memories, and hoped that neither of them would bring up Blaine; she had told them a work issue had delayed his visit.

She did not have to lie to her old friends about Blaine, but she did, telling them she was in a serious relationship and he would join her in Lagos soon. It surprised her how quickly, during reunions with old friends, the subject of marriage came up, a waspish tone in the voices of the unmarried, a smugness in those of the married. Ifemelu wanted to talk about the past, about the teachers they had mocked and the boys they had liked, but marriage was always the preferred topic – whose husband was a dog, who was on a desperate prowl, posting too many dressed-up pictures of herself on Facebook, whose man had disappointed her after four years and left her to marry a small girl he could control. (When Ifemelu told Ranyinudo that she had run into an old classmate, Vivian, at the bank, Ranyinudo's first question was 'Is she married?') And so she used Blaine as armour. If they knew of Blaine, then the married friends would not tell her 'Don't worry, your own will come, just pray about it,' and the unmarried friends would not assume that she was a member of the self-pity party of the single. There was, also, a strained nostalgia in those reunions, some in Ranyinudo's flat, some in hers, some in restaurants, because she struggled to find, in these adult women, some remnants from her past that were often no longer there.

Tochi was unrecognizable now, so fat that even her nose had changed shape, her double chin hanging below her face like a bread roll. She came to Ifemelu's flat with her baby in one hand, her BlackBerry in the other and a house help trailing behind, holding a canvas bag full of bottles and bibs. 'Madam America' was Tochi's greeting, and then she spoke, for the rest of her visit, in defensive spurts, as though she had come determined to battle Ifemelu's Americanness.

'I buy only British clothes for my baby because American ones fade after one wash,' she said. 'My husband wanted us to move to America but I refused, because the education system is so bad. An international agency rated it the lowest in the developed countries, you know.'

Tochi had always been perceptive and thoughtful; it was Tochi who had intervened with calm reason whenever Ifemelu and Ranyinudo argued in secondary school. In Tochi's changed persona, in her need to defend against imagined slights,

Ifemelu saw a great personal unhappiness. And so she appeased Tochi, putting America down, talking only about the things she, too, disliked about America, exaggerating her non-American accent, until the conversation became an enervating charade. Finally Tochi's baby vomited, a yellowish liquid that the house help hastily wiped, and Tochi said, 'We should go, baby wants to sleep.' Ifemelu, relieved, watched her leave. People changed, sometimes they changed too much.

Priye had not changed so much as hardened, her personality coated in chrome. She arrived at Ranyinudo's flat with a pile of newspapers, full of photographs of the big wedding she had just planned. Ifemelu imagined how people would talk about Priye. She is doing well, they would say, she is really doing well.

'My phone has not stopped ringing since last week!' Priye said triumphantly, pushing back the auburn straight weave that fell across one eye; each time she raised a hand to push back the hair, which invariably fell back again across her eye since it had been sewn in to do so, Ifemelu was distracted by the brittle pink colour of her nails. Priye had the sure, slightly sinister manner of someone who could get other people to do what she wanted. And she glittered – her yellow-gold earrings, the metal studs on her designer bag, the sparkly bronze lipstick.

'It was a very successful wedding: we had seven governors in attendance, seven!' she said.

'And none of them knew the couple, I'm sure,' Ifemelu said drily.

Priye gestured, a shrug, an upward flick of her palm, to show how irrelevant that was.

'Since when has the success of weddings been measured by how many governors attend?' Ifemelu asked.

'It shows you're connected. It shows prestige. Do you know how powerful governors in this country are? Executive power is not a small thing,' Priye said.

'Me, I want as many governors as possible to come to my own wedding o. It shows levels, serious levels,' Ranyinudo said. She was studying the photographs, turning the newspaper pages slowly. 'Priye, you heard Mosope is getting married in two weeks?'

'Yes. She approached me, but their budget was too small for me. That girl never understood the first rule of life in this Lagos. You do not marry the man you love. You marry the man who can best maintain you.'

'Amen!' Ranyinudo said, laughing. 'But sometimes one man can be both o. This is the season of weddings. When will it be my turn, Father Lord?' She glanced upwards, raised her hands as though in prayer.

'I've told Ranyinudo that I'll do her wedding at no commission,' Priye said to Ifemelu. 'And I'll do yours too, Ifem.'

'Thank you, but I think Blaine will prefer a

governor-free event,' Ifemelu said, and they all laughed. 'We'll probably do something small on a beach.'

Sometimes she believed her own lies. She could see it now, she and Blaine wearing white on a beach in the Caribbean, surrounded by a few friends, running to a makeshift altar of sand and flowers, and Shan watching and hoping one of them would trip and fall.

CHAPTER 47

Onikan was the old Lagos, a slice of the past, a temple to the faded splendour of the colonial years; Ifemelu remembered how houses here had sagged, unpainted and untended, and mould crept up the walls, and gate hinges rusted and atrophied. But developers were renovating and dismantling now, and on the ground floor of a newly refurbished three-storey building, heavy glass doors opened into a reception area painted a terracotta orange, where a pleasant-faced receptionist, Esther, sat, and behind her loomed giant words in silver: ZOE MAGAZINE. Esther was full of small ambitions. Ifemelu imagined her combing through the piles of second-hand shoes and clothes in the side stalls of Tejuosho market, finding the best pieces and then haggling tirelessly with the trader. She wore neatly pressed clothes and scuffed but carefully polished high heels, read books like *Praying Your Way to Prosperity*, and was superior with the drivers and ingratiating with the editors. 'This your earring is very fine, ma,' she said to Ifemelu. 'If you ever want to throw it away, please give it to me to help you throw it

611

away.' And she ceaselessly invited Ifemelu to her church.

'Will you come this Sunday, ma? My pastor is a powerful man of God. So many people have testimonies of miracles that have happened in their lives because of him.'

'Why do you think I need to come to your church, Esther?'

'You will like it, ma. It is a spirit-filled church.'

At first, the 'ma' had made Ifemelu uncomfortable, Esther was at least five years older than she was, but status, of course, surpassed age: she was the features editor, with a car and a driver and the spirit of America hanging over her head, and even Esther expected her to play the madam. And so she did, complimenting Esther and joking with Esther, but always in that manner that was both playful and patronizing, and sometimes giving Esther things, an old handbag, an old watch. Just as she did with her driver, Ayo. She complained about his speeding, threatened to fire him for being late again, asked him to repeat her instructions to make sure he had understood. Yet she always heard the unnatural high pitch of her voice when she said these things, unable fully to convince even herself of her own madamness.

Aunty Onenu liked to say, 'Most of my staff are foreign graduates while that woman at *Glass* hires riff-raff who cannot punctuate sentences!' Ifemelu imagined her saying this at a dinner party, 'most of my staff' making the magazine sound like a large, busy operation, although it was an editorial staff of three, an administrative staff of four, and only Ifemelu and Doris, the editor, had foreign degrees. Doris, thin and hollow-eyed, a vegetarian who announced that she was a vegetarian as soon as she possibly could, spoke with a teenage American accent that made her sentences sound like questions, except for when she was speaking to her mother on the phone; then her English took on a flat, stolid Nigerianness. Her long sisterlocks were sun-bleached a coppery tone, and she dressed unusually – white socks and brogues, men's shirts tucked into pedal pushers – which she considered original, and which everyone in the office forgave her for because she had come back from abroad. She wore no make-up except for bright-red lipstick, and it gave her face a certain shock value, that slash of crimson, which was probably her intent, but her unadorned skin tended towards ashy grey and Ifemelu's first urge, when they met, was to suggest a good moisturizer.

'You went to Wellson in Philly? I went to Temple?' Doris said, as though to establish right away that they were members of the same superior club. 'You're going to be sharing this office with me and Zemaye. She's the assistant editor, and she's out on assignment until this afternoon, or maybe longer? She always stays as long as she wants.'

Ifemelu caught the malice. It was not subtle; Doris had meant for it to be caught.

'I thought you could, like, just spend this week

getting used to things? See what we do? And then next week you can start some assignments?' Doris said.

'Okay,' Ifemelu said.

The office itself, a large room with four desks, on each of which sat a computer, looked bare and untested, as though it was everybody's first day at work. Ifemelu was not sure what would make it look otherwise, perhaps pictures of family on the desks, or just more things, more files and papers and staplers, proof of its being inhabited.

'I had a great job in New York, but I decided to move back and settle down here?' Doris said. 'Like, family pressure to settle down and stuff, you know? Like I'm the only daughter? When I first got back one of my aunts looked at me and said, "I can get you a job at a good bank, but you have to cut off that dada hair."' She shook her head from side to side in mockery as she mimicked a Nigerian accent. 'I swear to God this city is full of banks that just want you to be reasonably attractive in a kind of predictable way and you have a job in customer service? Anyway, I took this job because I'm interested in the magazine business? And this is like a good place to meet people, because of all the events we get to go to, you know?' Doris sounded as if she and Ifemelu somehow shared the same plot, the same view of the world. Ifemelu felt a small resentment at this, the arrogance of Doris's certainty that she, too, would of course feel the same way as Doris.

Just before lunchtime, into the office walked a woman in a tight pencil skirt and patent shoes high as stilts, her straightened hair sleekly pulled back. She was not pretty, her facial features created no harmony, but she carried herself as though she was. Nubile. She made Ifemelu think of that word, with her shapely slenderness, her tiny waist and the unexpected high curves of her breasts.

'Hi. You're Ifemelu, right? Welcome to *Zoe*. I'm Zemaye.' She shook Ifemelu's hand, her face carefully neutral.

'Hi, Zemaye. It's nice to meet you. You have a lovely name,' Ifemelu said.

'Thank you.' She was used to hearing it. 'I hope you don't like cold rooms.'

'Cold rooms?'

'Yes. Doris likes to put the AC on too high and I have to wear a sweater in the office, but now that you are here sharing the office, maybe we can vote,' Zemaye said, settling down at her desk.

'What are you talking about? Since when do you have to wear a sweater in the office?' Doris asked.

Zemaye raised her eyebrows and pulled out a thick shawl from her drawer.

'It's the humidity that's just so crazy?' Doris said, turning to Ifemelu, expecting agreement. 'I felt like I couldn't breathe when I first came back?'

Zemaye, too, turned to Ifemelu. 'I am a Delta girl, home-made, born and bred. So I did not grow up with air conditioners and I can breathe without a room being cold.' She spoke in an impassive

615

tone, and everything she said was delivered evenly, never rising or falling.

'Well, I don't know about cold?' Doris said. 'Most offices in Lagos have air conditioners?'

'Not turned to the lowest temperature,' Zemaye said.

'You've never said anything about it?'

'I tell you all the time, Doris.'

'I mean that it actually prevents you from working?'

'It's cold, full stop,' Zemaye said.

Their mutual dislike was a smouldering, stalking leopard in the room.

'I don't like cold,' Ifemelu said. 'I think I would freeze if the AC was turned on to the lowest.'

Doris blinked. She looked not merely betrayed but surprised that she had been betrayed. 'Well, okay, we can turn it off and on throughout the day? I have a hard time breathing without the AC and the windows are so damn small?'

'Okay,' Ifemelu said.

Zemaye said nothing; she had turned to her computer, as though indifferent to this small victory, and Ifemelu felt unaccountably disappointed. She had taken sides, after all, boldly standing with Zemaye, and yet Zemaye remained expressionless, hard to read. Ifemelu wondered what her story was. Zemaye intrigued her.

Later, Doris and Zemaye were looking over photographs spread out on Doris's table, of a portly woman wearing tight ruffled clothes, when

Zemaye said, 'Excuse me, I'm pressed,' and hurried to the door, her supple movements making Ifemelu want to lose weight. Doris's eyes followed her too.

'Don't you just hate it how people say "I'm pressed" or "I want to ease myself" when they want to go to the bathroom?' Doris asked.

Ifemelu laughed. 'I know!'

'I guess "bathroom" is very American. But there's "toilet", "restroom", "the ladies".'

'I never liked "the ladies". I like "toilet".'

'Me too!' Doris said. 'And don't you just hate it when people here use "on" as a verb? On the light!'

'You know what I can't stand? When people say "take" instead of "drink". "I will take wine. I don't take beer."'

'Oh God, I know!'

They were laughing when Zemaye came back in, and she looked at Ifemelu with her eerily neutral expression and said, 'You people must be discussing the next Been-To meeting.'

'What's that?' Ifemelu asked.

'Doris talks about them all the time, but she can't invite me because it is only for people who have come from abroad.' If there was mockery in Zemaye's tone, and there had to be, she kept it under her flat delivery.

'Oh, please. "Been-To" is like so outdated? This is not 1960,' Doris said. Then to Ifemelu, she said, 'I was actually going to tell you about it. It's called

617

the Nigerpolitan Club and it's just a bunch of people who have recently moved back, some from England, but mostly from the US? Really low-key, just like sharing experiences and networking? I bet you'll know some of the people. You should totally come?'

'Yes, I'd like to.'

Doris got up and took her handbag. 'I have to go to Aunty Onenu's house.'

After she left, the room was silent, Zemaye typing at her computer, Ifemelu browsing the Internet, and wondering what Zemaye was thinking.

Finally, Zemaye said, 'So you were a famous race blogger in America. When Aunty Onenu told us, I didn't understand.'

'What do you mean?'

'Why race?'

'I discovered race in America and it fascinated me.'

'Hmm,' Zemaye murmured, as though she thought this, discovering race, an exotic and self-indulgent phenomenon. 'Aunty Onenu said your boyfriend is a black American and he is coming soon?'

Ifemelu was surprised. Aunty Onenu had asked about her personal life, with a casualness that was also insistent, and she had told her the false story of Blaine, thinking that her boss had no business with her personal life anyway, and now it seemed that personal life had been shared with other staff. Perhaps she was being too American about it, fixating on privacy for its own sake. What did it really matter if Zemaye knew of Blaine?

'Yes. He should be here by next month,' she said.

'Why is it only black people that are criminals over there?'

Ifemelu opened her mouth and closed it. Here she was, famous race blogger, and she was lost for words.

'I love *Cops*. It is because of that show that I have DSTV,' Zemaye said. 'And all the criminals are black people.'

'It's like saying every Nigerian is a 419,' Ifemelu said finally. She sounded too limp, too insufficient.

'But it is true, all of us have small 419 in our blood!' Zemaye smiled with what seemed to be, for the first time, a real amusement in her eyes. Then she added, 'Sorry o. I did not mean that your boyfriend is a criminal. I was just asking.'

CHAPTER 48

Ifemelu asked Ranyinudo to come with her and Doris to the Nigerpolitan meeting.

'I don't have energy for you returnees, please,' Ranyinudo said. 'Besides, Ndudi is finally back from all his travelling up and down and we're going out.'

'Good luck choosing a man over your friend, you witch.'

'Yes o. Are you the person that will marry me? Meanwhile I told Don I am going out with you, so make sure you don't go anywhere that he might go.' Ranyinudo was laughing. She was still seeing Don, waiting to make sure that Ndudi was 'serious' before she stopped, and she hoped, too, that Don would get her the new car before then.

The Nigerpolitan Club meeting: a small cluster of people drinking champagne in paper cups, at the poolside of a home in Osborne Estate, chic people, all dripping with savoir faire, each nursing a self-styled quirkiness – a ginger-coloured Afro, a T-shirt with a graphic of Thomas Sankara, oversize handmade earrings that hung like pieces of modern art. Their voices burred with foreign accents. *You can't find a decent smoothie in this city! Oh my God, were you at that conference? What this country needs is an active civil society.* Ifemelu knew some of them. She chatted with Bisola and Yagazie, both of whom had natural hair, worn in a twist-out, a halo of spirals framing their faces. They talked about hair salons here, where the hairdressers struggled and fumbled to comb natural hair, as though it were an alien eruption, as though their own hair was not the same way before it was defeated by chemicals.

'The salon girls are always like, "Aunty, you don't want to relax your hair?" It's ridiculous that Africans don't value our natural hair in Africa,' Yagazie said.

'I know,' Ifemelu said, and she caught the righteousness in her voice, in all their voices. They were the sanctified, the returnees, back home with an extra gleaming layer. Ikenna joined them, a lawyer who had lived outside Philadelphia and whom she had met at a Blogging While Brown convention. And Fred joined them too. He had introduced himself to Ifemelu earlier, a pudgy, well-groomed man. 'I lived in Boston until last year,' he said, in a falsely low-key way, because 'Boston' was code for Harvard (otherwise he would say MIT or Tufts or anywhere else), just as another woman said, 'I was in New Haven,' in that coy manner that pretended not to be coy, which meant that she had been at Yale. Other people joined them, all encircled by a familiarity, because they could reach so easily for the same references. Soon they were

621

laughing and listing the things they missed about America.

'Low-fat soya milk, NPR, fast Internet,' Ifemelu said.

'Good customer service, good customer service, good customer service,' Bisola said. 'Folks here behave as if they are doing you a favour by serving you. The high-end places are okay, not great, but the regular restaurants? Forget it. The other day I asked a waiter if I could get boiled yam with a different sauce than was on the menu and he just looked at me and said no. Hilarious.'

'But the American customer service can be so annoying. Someone hovering around and bothering you all the time. *Are you still working on that?* Since when did eating become work?' Yagazie said.

'I miss a decent vegetarian place?' Doris said, and then talked about her new house help who could not make a simple sandwich, about how she had ordered a vegetarian spring roll at a restaurant in Victoria Island, bit in and tasted chicken, and the waiter, when summoned, just smiled and said, 'Maybe they put chicken today.' There was laughter. Fred said a good vegetarian place would open soon, now that there was so much new investment in the country; somebody would figure out that there was a vegetarian market to cater to.

'A vegetarian restaurant? Impossible. There are only four vegetarians in this country, including Doris,' Bisola said.

'You're not vegetarian, are you?' Fred asked

Ifemelu. He just wanted to talk to her. She had looked up from time to time to find his eyes on her.

'No,' she said.

'Oh, there's this new place that opened on Akin Adesola,' Bisola said. 'The brunch is really good. They have the kinds of things we can eat. We should go next Sunday.'

They have the kinds of things we can eat. An unease crept up on Ifemelu. She was comfortable here, and she wished she were not. She wished, too, that she was not so interested in this new restaurant, did not perk up, imagining fresh green salads and steamed still-firm vegetables. She loved eating all the things she had missed while away, jollof rice cooked with a lot of oil, fried plantains, boiled yams, but she longed, also, for the other things she had become used to in America, even quinoa, Blaine's specialty, made with feta and tomatoes. This was what she hoped she had not become but feared that she had: a 'they have the kinds of things we can eat' kind of person.

Fred was talking about Nollywood, speaking a little too loudly. 'Nollywood is really public theatre, and if you understand it like that, then it is more tolerable. It's for public consumption, even mass participation, not the kind of individual experience that film is.' He was looking at her, soliciting her agreement with his eyes: they were not supposed to watch Nollywood, people like them, and if they did, then only as amusing anthropology.

623

'I like Nollywood,' Ifemelu said, even though she, too, thought Nollywood was more theatre than film. The urge to be contrarian was strong. If she set herself apart, perhaps she would be less of the person she feared she had become. 'Nollywood may be melodramatic, but life in Nigeria is very melodramatic.'

'Really?' the New Haven woman said, squeezing her paper cup in her hand, as though she thought it a great oddity, that a person at this gathering would like Nollywood. 'It is so offensive to my intelligence. I mean, the products are just bad. What does it say about us?'

'But Hollywood makes equally bad movies. They just make them with better lighting,' Ifemelu said.

Fred laughed, too heartily, to let her know he was on her side.

'It's not just about the technical stuff,' the New Haven woman said. 'The industry is regressive. I mean, the portrayal of women? The films are more misogynistic than the society.'

Ifemelu saw a man across the pool whose wide shoulders reminded her of Obinze. But he was too tall to be Obinze. She wondered what Obinze would make of a gathering like this. Would he even come? He had been deported from England, after all, so perhaps he would not consider himself a returnee like them.

'Hey, come back,' Fred said, moving closer to her, claiming personal space. 'Your mind isn't here.'

She smiled thinly. 'It is now.'

Fred knew things. He had the confidence of a person who knew practical things. He probably had a Harvard MBA and used words like 'capacity' and 'value' in conversation. He would not dream in imagery, but in facts and figures.

'There's a concert tomorrow at MUSON. Do you like classical music?' he asked.

'No.' She had not expected that he would, either.

'Are you willing to like classical music?'

'Willing to like something, it's a strange idea,' she said, now curious about him, vaguely interested in him. They talked. Fred mentioned Stravinsky and Strauss, Vermeer and Van Dyck, making unnecessary references, quoting too often, his spirits attuned across the Atlantic, too transparent in his performance, too eager to show how much he knew of the Western world. Ifemelu listened with a wide internal yawn. She had been wrong about him. He was not the MBA type who thought the world was a business. He was an impresario, well oiled and well practised, the sort of man who did a good American accent and a good British accent, who knew what to say to foreigners, how to make foreigners comfortable, and who could easily get foreign grants for dubious projects. She wondered what he was like beneath that practised layer.

'So will you come for this drinks thing?' he asked.

'I'm exhausted,' she said. 'I think I'll head home. But call me.'

CHAPTER 49

The speedboat was gliding on foaming water, past beaches of ivory sand, and trees a bursting, well-fed green. Ifemelu was laughing. She caught herself in mid-laughter, and looked at her present, an orange life jacket strapped around her, a ship in the greying distance, her friends in their sunglasses, on their way to Priye's friend's beach house, where they would grill meat and race barefoot. She thought: I'm really home. I'm home. She no longer sent Ranyinudo texts about what to do – *Should I buy meat in Shoprite or send Iyabo to the market? Where should I buy hangers?* Now she awoke to the sound of the peacocks, and got out of bed, with the shape of her day familiar and her routines unthinking. She had signed up at a gym, but had gone only twice, because after work she preferred to meet her friends, and even though she always planned not to eat, she ended up eating a club sandwich and drinking one or two Chapmans, and then she would decide to postpone the gym. Her clothes felt even tighter now. Somewhere, in a faraway part of her mind, she wanted to lose weight before she saw Obinze again. She had not called him; she would wait until she was back to her slender self.

At work, she felt an encroaching restlessness. *Zoe* stifled her. It was like wearing a scratchy sweater in the cold: she longed to yank it off, but was afraid of what would happen if she did. She thought often of starting a blog, writing about what she cared about, building it up slowly, and finally publishing her own magazine. But it was nebulous, too much of an unknown. Having this job, now that she was home, made her feel anchored. At first, she had enjoyed doing the features, interviewing society women in their homes, observing their lives and relearning old subtleties. But she soon became bored and she would sit through the interviews, half listening and half present. Each time she walked into their cemented compounds, she longed for sand in which to curl her toes. A servant or child would let her in, seat her in a living room of leather and marble that brought to mind a clean airport in a wealthy country. Then Madam would appear, warm and good-humoured, offering her a drink, sometimes food, before settling on a sofa to talk. All of them, the madams she interviewed, boasted about what they owned and where they or their children had been and what they had done, and then they capped their boasts with God. *We thank God. It is God that did it. God is faithful.* Ifemelu thought, as she left, that she could write the features without doing the interviews.

She could, also, cover events without attending them. How common that word was in Lagos, and how popular: event. It could be a product rebranding, a fashion show, an album launch. Aunty Onenu always insisted that an editor go with the photographer. 'Please make sure you mingle,' Aunty Onenu said. 'If they are not advertising with us yet, we want them to start; if they have started, we want them to increase!' To Ifemelu, Aunty Onenu said 'mingle' with great emphasis, as though this were something she thought Ifemelu did not do well. Perhaps Aunty Onenu was right. At those events, in halls aflame with balloons, rolls of silky cloth draped in corners, chairs covered in gauze and too many ushers walking around, their faces gaudily bright with make-up, Ifemelu disliked talking to strangers about *Zoe*. She would spend her time exchanging texts with Ranyinudo or Priye or Zemaye, bored, waiting until when it would not be impolite to leave. There were always two or three meandering speeches, and all of them seemed written by the same verbose, insincere person. The wealthy and the famous were recognized – 'We wish to recognize in our presence the former governor of . . .' Bottles were uncorked, juice cartons folded open, samosas and chicken satays served. Once, at an event she attended with Zemaye, the launch of a new beverage brand, she thought she saw Obinze walk past. She turned. It was not him, but it very well could have been. She imagined him attending events like this, in halls like this, with his wife by his side. Ranyinudo had told her that his wife, when she was a student, was voted the most beautiful girl at the University of Lagos, and in Ifemelu's imagination, she looked like Bianca Onoh, that beauty icon of her teenage years, high-cheekboned and almond-eyed. And when Ranyinudo mentioned his wife's name, Kosisochukwu, an uncommon name, Ifemelu imagined Obinze's mother asking her to translate it. The thought of Obinze's mother and Obinze's wife deciding which translation was better – God's Will or As It Pleases God – felt like a betrayal. That memory, of Obinze's mother saying 'translate it' all those years ago, seemed even more precious now that she had passed away.

As Ifemelu was leaving the event, she saw Don. 'Ifemelu,' he said. It took her a moment to recognize him. Ranyinudo had introduced them one afternoon, months ago, when Don dropped by Ranyinudo's flat on his way to his club, wearing tennis whites, and Ifemelu had left almost immediately, to give them privacy. He looked dapper in a navy suit, his grey-sprinkled hair burnished.

'Good evening,' she said.

'You're looking well, very well,' he said, taking in her low-cut cocktail dress.

'Thank you.'

'You don't ask about me.' As though there was

a reason for her to ask about him. He gave her his card. 'Call me, make sure you call me, eh. Let's talk. Take care.'

He was not interested in her, not particularly; he was simply a big man in Lagos, she attractive and alone, and by the laws of their universe, he had to make a pass, even if a half-hearted pass, even if he was already dating her friend, and he expected, of course, that she would not tell her friend. She slipped his card into her bag and, back home, tore it into tiny bits which she watched float in the toilet water for a while before flushing. She was, strangely, angry with him. His action said something about her friendship with Ranyinudo that she disliked. She called Ranyinudo, and was about to tell her what happened, when Ranyinudo said, 'Ifem, I'm so depressed.' And so Ifemelu merely listened. It was about Ndudi. 'He's such a *child*,' Ranyinudo said. 'If you say something he doesn't like, he will stop talking and start humming. Seriously humming, loud humming. How does a grown man behave so immaturely?'

It was monday morning. Ifemelu was reading *Postbourgie*, her favourite American blog. Zemaye was looking through a stash of glossy photographs. Doris was staring at her computer screen, cradling in her palms a mug that said I ♥ FLORIDA. On her desk, next to her computer, was a tin of loose-leaf tea.

'Ifemelu, I think this feature is too snarky?'

'Your editorial feedback is priceless,' Ifemelu said.

'What does "snarky" mean? Please explain to some of us who did not go to school in America,' Zemaye said.

Doris ignored her completely.

'I just don't think Aunty Onenu will want us to run this?'

'Convince her, you're her editor,' Ifemelu said. 'We need to get this magazine going.'

Doris shrugged and got up. 'We'll talk about it at the meeting?'

'I am so sleepy,' Zemaye said. 'I'm going to send Esther to make Nescafé before I fall asleep in the meeting.'

'Instant coffee is just awful?' Doris said. 'I'm so glad I'm not much of a coffee drinker or I would just die.'

'What is wrong with Nescafé?' Zemaye said.

'It shouldn't even be called coffee?' Doris said. 'It's like beyond bad.'

Zemaye yawned and stretched. 'Me, I like it. Coffee is coffee.'

Later, as they walked into Aunty Onenu's office, Doris ahead, wearing a loose-fitting blue pinafore and black square-heeled mary janes, Zemaye asked Ifemelu, 'Why does Doris wear rubbish to work? She looks like she is cracking a joke with her clothes.'

They sat around the oval conference table in

Aunty Onenu's large office. Aunty Onenu's weave was longer and more incongruous than the last, high and coiffed in front, with waves of hair floating to her back. She sipped from a bottle of diet Sprite and said she liked Doris's piece 'Marrying Your Best Friend'.

'Very good and inspirational,' she said.

'Ah, but Aunty Onenu, women should not marry their best friend because there is no sexual chemistry,' Zemaye said.

Aunty Onenu gave Zemaye the look given to the crazy student whom one could not take seriously, then she shuffled her papers and said she did not like Ifemelu's profile of Mrs Funmi King.

'Why did you say "she never looks at her steward when she speaks to him"?' Aunty Onenu asked.

'Because she didn't,' Ifemelu said.

'But it makes her sound wicked,' Aunty Onenu said.

'I think it's an interesting detail,' Ifemelu said.

'I agree with Aunty Onenu,' Doris said. 'Interesting or not, it is judgemental?'

'The idea of interviewing someone and writing a profile is judgemental,' Ifemelu said. 'It's not about the subject. It's about what the interviewer makes of the subject.'

Aunty Onenu shook her head. Doris shook her head.

'Why do we have to play it so safe?' Ifemelu asked.

Doris said, with false humour, 'This isn't your

632

American race blog where you provoked every-body, Ifemelu. This is like a wholesome women's magazine?'

'Yes, it is!' Aunty Onenu said.

'But Aunty Onenu, we will never beat *Glass* if we continue like this,' Ifemelu said.

Aunty Onenu's eyes widened.

'*Glass* is doing exactly what we are doing,' Doris said quickly.

Esther came in to tell Aunty Onenu that her daughter had arrived.

Esther's black high heels were shaky, and as she walked past, Ifemelu worried that the shoes would collapse and sprain Esther's ankles. Earlier in the morning, Esther had told Ifemelu, 'Aunty, your hair is jaga-jaga,' with a kind of sad honesty, about what Ifemelu considered an attractive twist-out style.

'Ehn, she is already here?' Aunty Onenu said. 'Girls, please finish the meeting. I am taking my daughter to shop for a dress and I have an after-noon meeting with our distributors.'

Ifemelu was tired, bored. She thought, again, of starting a blog. Her phone was vibrating, Ranyinudo calling, and ordinarily she would have waited until the meeting was over to call her back. But she said, 'Sorry, I have to take this, international call,' and hurried out. Ranyinudo was complaining about Don. 'He said I am not the sweet girl I used to be. That I've changed. Meanwhile, I know he has bought the jeep for me and has even cleared it at the port, but now he doesn't want to give it to me.'

Ifemelu thought about the expression 'sweet girl'. Sweet girl meant that, for a long time, Don had moulded Ranyinudo into a malleable shape, or that she had allowed him to think he had.

'What about Ndudi?'

Ranyinudo sighed loudly. 'We haven't talked since Sunday. Today he will forget to call me. Tomorrow he will be too busy. And so I told him that it's not acceptable. Why should I be making all the effort? Now he is sulking. He can never initiate a conversation like an adult, or agree that he did something wrong.'

Later, back in the office, Esther came in to say that a Mr Tolu wanted to see Zemaye.

'Is that the photographer you did the tailors article with?' Doris asked.

'Yes. He's late. He has been dodging my calls for days,' Zemaye said.

Doris said, 'You need to handle that and make sure I have the images by tomorrow afternoon? I need everything to get to the printer before three? I don't want a repeat of the printer's delay, especially now that *Glass* is printing in South Africa?'

'Okay.' Zemaye shook her mouse. 'The server is so slow today. I just need to send this thing. Esther, tell him to wait.'

'Yes, ma.'

'You are feeling better, Esther?' Doris asked.

'Yes, ma, Thank you, ma.' Esther curtsied,

Yoruba-style. She had been standing by the door as though waiting to be dismissed, listening in on the conversation. 'I am taking the medicine for typhoid.'

'You have typhoid?' Ifemelu asked.

'Didn't you notice how she looked on Monday? I gave her some money and told her to go to the hospital, not to a chemist?' Doris said.

Ifemelu wished that *she* had noticed that Esther was unwell.

'Sorry, Esther,' Ifemelu said.

'Thank you, ma.'

'Esther, sorry o,' Zemaye said. 'I saw her dull face, but I thought she was just fasting. You know she's always fasting. She will fast and fast until God gives her a husband.'

Esther giggled.

'I remember I had this really bad case of typhoid when I was in secondary school,' Ifemelu said. 'It was terrible, and it turned out I was taking an antibiotic that wasn't strong enough. What are you taking, Esther?'

'Medicine, ma.'

'What antibiotic did they give you?'

'I don't know.'

'You don't know the name?'

'Let me bring them, ma.'

Esther came back with transparent packets of pills, on which instructions, but no names, were written in a crabbed handwriting in blue ink. *Two to be taken morning and night. One to be taken three times daily.*

'We should write about this, Doris. We should have a health column with useful practical information. Somebody should let the health minister know that ordinary Nigerians go to see a doctor and the doctor gives them unnamed medicines. This can kill you. How will anybody know what you have already taken, or what you shouldn't take if you're already taking something else?'

'Ahn-ahn, but that one is a small problem: they do it so that you don't buy the medicine from someone else,' Zemaye said. 'But what about fake drugs? Go to the market and see what they are selling.'

'Okay, let's all calm down? No need to go all activist? We're not doing investigative journalism here?' Doris said.

Ifemelu began then to visualize her new blog, a blue-and-white design, and, on the masthead, an aerial shot of a Lagos scene. Nothing familiar, not a traffic clog of yellow rusted buses or a waterlogged slum of zinc shacks. Perhaps the abandoned house next to her flat would do. She would take the photo herself, in the haunted light of early evening, and hope to catch the male peacock in flight. The blog posts would be in a stark, readable font. An article about health care, using Esther's story, with pictures of the packets of nameless medicine. A piece about the Nigerpolitan Club. A fashion article about clothes that women could actually afford. Posts about people helping others, but nothing like the *Zoe* stories that always featured a wealthy person, hugging children at a motherless babies' home, with bags of rice and tins of powdered milk propped in the background.

'But, Esther, you have to stop all that fasting o,' Zemaye said. 'You know, some months Esther will give her whole salary to her church, they call it "sowing a seed", then she will come and ask me to give her three hundred naira for transport.'

'But, ma, it is just small help. You are equal to the task,' Esther said, smiling.

'Last week she was fasting with a handkerchief,' Zemaye continued. 'She kept it on her desk all day. She said somebody in her church got promoted after fasting with the handkerchief.'

'Is that what that handkerchief on her table was about?' Ifemelu asked.

'But I believe miracles totally work? I know my aunt was cured of cancer in her church?' Doris said.

'With a magic handkerchief, *abi*?' Zemaye scoffed.

'You don't believe, ma? But it is true.' Esther was enjoying the camaraderie, reluctant to return to her desk.

'So you want a promotion, Esther? Which means you want my job?' Zemaye asked.

'No, ma! All of us will be promoted in Jesus' name!' Esther said.

They were all laughing.

'Has Esther told you what spirit you have, Ifemelu?' Zemaye asked, walking to the door. 'When I first started working here, she kept

637

inviting me to her church and then one day she told me there would be a special prayer service for people with the spirit of seductiveness. People like me.'

'That's not like entirely far-fetched?' Doris said and smirked.

'What is my spirit, Esther?' Ifemelu asked.

Esther shook her head, smiling, and left the office.

Ifemelu turned to her computer. The title for the blog had just come to her. *The Small Redemptions of Lagos.*

'I wonder who Zemaye is dating?' Doris said.

'She told me she doesn't have a boyfriend.'

'Have you seen her car? Her salary can't pay for the light in that car? It's not like her family is rich or anything. I've been working with her almost a year now and I don't know what she like really does?'

'Maybe she goes home and changes her clothes and becomes an armed robber at night,' Ifemelu said.

'Whatever,' Doris said.

'We should do a piece about churches,' Ifemelu said. 'Like Esther's church.'

'That's not a good fit for *Zoe*?'

'It makes no sense that Aunty Onenu likes to run three profiles of these boring women who have achieved nothing and have nothing to say. Or the younger women with zero talent who have decided that they are fashion designers.'

'You know they pay Aunty Onenu, right?' Doris asked.

'They pay her?' Ifemelu stared. 'No, I didn't know. And you know I didn't know.'

'Well, they do. Most of them. You have to realize a lot of things happen in this country like that?'

Ifemelu got up to gather her things. 'I never know where you stand or if you stand on anything at all.'

'And you are such a judgemental bitch?' Doris screamed, her eyes bulging. Ifemelu, alarmed by the suddenness of the change, thought that perhaps Doris was, underneath her retro affectations, one of those women who could transform when provoked, and tear off their clothes and fight in the street.

'You sit there and judge everyone,' Doris was saying. 'Who do you think you are? Why do you think this magazine should be about you? It isn't yours. Aunty Onenu has told you what she wants her magazine to be and it's either you do it or you shouldn't be working here?'

'You need to get yourself a moisturizer and stop scaring people with that nasty red lipstick,' Ifemelu said. 'And you need to get a life, and stop thinking that sucking up to Aunty Onenu and helping her publish a god-awful magazine will open doors for you, because it won't.'

She left the office feeling common, shamed, by what had just happened. Perhaps this was a sign, to quit now and start her blog.

639

On her way out, Esther said, her voice earnest and low, 'Ma? I think you have the spirit of husband-repelling. You are too hard, ma, you will not find a husband. But my pastor can destroy that spirit.'

CHAPTER 50

Dike was seeing a therapist three times a week. Ifemelu called him every other day, and sometimes he spoke about his session, and other times he did not, but always he wanted to hear about her new life. She told him about her flat, and how she had a driver who drove her to work, and how she was seeing her old friends, and how, on Sundays, she loved to drive herself because the roads were empty; Lagos became a gentler version of itself, and the people in their bright church clothes looked, from far away, like flowers in the wind.

'You would like Lagos, I think,' she said, and he, eagerly, surprisingly, said, 'Can I come visit you, Coz?'

Aunty Uju was reluctant at first. 'Lagos? Is it safe? You know what he has been through. I don't think he can handle it.'

'But he asked to come, Aunty.'

'He asked to come? Since when has he known what is good for him? Is he not the same person who wanted to make me childless?'

But Aunty Uju bought Dike's ticket and now

here they were, she and Dike in her car, crawling through the crush of traffic in Oshodi, Dike looking wide-eyed out of the window. 'Oh my God, Coz, I've never seen so many black people in the same place!' he said.

They stopped at a fast-food place, where he ordered a hamburger. 'Is this horse meat, Coz? Because it isn't a hamburger.' Afterwards, he would eat only jollof rice and fried plantain.

It was auspicious, his arrival, a day after she put up her blog and a week after she resigned. Aunty Onenu did not seem surprised by her resignation, nor did she try to make her stay. 'Come and give me a hug, my dear,' was all she said, smiling vacuously, while Ifemelu's pride soured. But Ifemelu was full of sanguine expectations for *The Small Redemptions of Lagos*, with a dreamy photograph of an abandoned colonial house on its masthead. Her first post was a short interview with Priye, with photographs from weddings Priye had planned. Ifemelu thought most of the décor fussy and overdone, but the post received enthusiastic comments, especially about the décor. *Fantastic decoration. Madam Priye, I hope you will do my own wedding. Great work, carry go.* Zemaye had written, under a pseudonym, a piece about body language and sex, 'Can You Tell If Two People Are Doing It Just by Looking at Them Together?' That, too, drew many comments. But the most comments, by far, were for Ifemelu's piece about the Nigerpolitan Club.

Lagos has never been, will never be, and has never aspired to be like New York, or anywhere else for that matter. Lagos has always been undisputably itself, but you would not know this at the meeting of the Nigerpolitan Club, a group of young returnees who gather every week to moan about the many ways that Lagos is not like New York as though Lagos had ever been close to being like New York. Full disclosure: I am one of them. Most of us have come back to make money in Nigeria, to start businesses, to seek government contracts and contacts. Others have come with dreams in their pockets and a hunger to change the country, but we spend all our time complaining about Nigeria, and even though our complaints are legitimate, I imagine myself as an outsider saying: Go back where you came from! If your cook cannot make the perfect panini, it is not because he is stupid. It is because Nigeria is not a nation of sandwich-eating people and his last oga did not eat bread in the afternoon. So he needs training and practice. And Nigeria is not a nation of people with food allergies, not a nation of picky eaters for whom food is about distinctions and separations. It is a nation of people who eat beef and chicken and cow skin and intestines and dried fish in a single bowl of soup, and it is called assorted, and so get over yourselves and realize that the way of life here is just that, assorted.

The first commenter wrote: *Rubbish post. Who cares?* The second wrote: *Thank God somebody is finally talking about this. Na wa for arrogance of Nigerian returnees. My cousin came back after six years in America and the other morning she came with me to the nursery school at Unilag where I was dropping off my niece and, near the gate, she saw students standing in line for the bus and she said, 'Wow, people actually stand in line here!'* Another early commenter wrote: *Why should Nigerians who school abroad have a choice of where to get posted for their national youth service? Nigerians who school in Nigeria are randomly posted so why shouldn't Nigerians who school abroad be treated the same way?* That comment sparked more responses than the original post had. By the sixth day, the blog had one thousand unique visitors.

Ifemelu moderated the comments, deleting anything obscene, revelling in the liveliness of it all, in the sense of herself at the surging forefront of something vibrant. She wrote a long post about the expensive lifestyles of some young women in Lagos, and a day after she put it up, Ranyinudo called her, furious, her breathing heavy over the phone.

'Ifem, how can you do this kind of thing? Anyone who knows me will know it's me!'

'That's not true, Ranyi. Your story is so common.'

'What are you saying? It is so obviously me! Look at this!' Ranyinudo paused and then began to read aloud.

> There are many young women in Lagos with Unknown Sources of Wealth. They live lives they can't afford. They have only ever traveled business class to Europe but have jobs that can't even afford them a regular flight ticket. One of them is my friend, a beautiful, brilliant woman who works in advertising. She lives on The Island and is dating a big man banker. I worry that she will end up like many women in Lagos who define their lives by men they can never truly have, crippled by their culture of dependence, with desperation in their eyes and designer handbags on their wrists.

'Ranyi, honestly, nobody will know it's you. All the comments so far have been from people saying that they identify. So many women lose themselves in relationships like that. What I really had in mind was Aunty Uju and The General. That relationship destroyed her. She became a different person because of The General and she couldn't do anything for herself and when he died, she lost herself.'

'And who are you to pass judgement? How is it

different from you and the rich white guy in America? Would you have your US citizenship today if not for him? How did you get your job in America? You need to stop this nonsense. Stop feeling so superior!'

Ranyinudo hung up on her. For a long time, Ifemelu stared at the silent phone, shaken. Then she took down the post and drove over to Ranyinudo's place.

'Ranyi, I'm sorry. Please don't be angry,' she said.

Ranyinudo gave her a long look.

'You're right,' Ifemelu said. 'It's easy to be judgemental. But it was not personal, and it was not coming from a bad place. Please, *biko*. I will never invade your privacy like that again.'

Ranyinudo shook her head. 'Ifemelunamma, your problem is emotional frustration. Go and find Obinze, please.'

Ifemelu laughed. It was what she least expected to hear.

'I have to lose weight first,' she said.

'You're just afraid.'

Before Ifemelu left, they sat on the couch and drank malt and watched the latest celebrity news on E!.

Dike volunteered to moderate the blog comments, so that she could take a break.

'Oh my God, Coz, people take this stuff really personal!' he said. Sometimes he laughed aloud

646

on reading a comment. Other times, he asked her what unfamiliar expressions meant. *What's 'shine your eye'?* The first time the power went off after he arrived, the buzzing, whirring, piping sounds of her UPS startled him. 'Oh my God, is that like a fire alarm?' he asked.

'No, that's just something that makes sure my TV doesn't get destroyed by crazy power cuts.'

'*That's* crazy,' Dike said, but only days later he was going to the back of the flat to turn on the generator himself when the power went off. Ranyinudo brought her cousins to meet him, girls who were close to his age, skinny jeans clinging to their slender hips, their budding breasts outlined in tight T-shirts. 'Dike, you must marry one of them o,' Ranyinudo said. 'We need fine children in our family.' 'Ranyi!' her cousins said, abashed, hiding their shyness. They liked Dike. It was so easy to like him, with his charm and his humour and the vulnerability openly lurking underneath. On Facebook, he posted a picture Ifemelu had taken of him standing on the verandah with Ranyinudo's cousins, and he captioned it: *No lions yet to eat me, folks.*

'I wish I spoke Igbo,' he told her after they had spent an evening with her parents.

'But you understand perfectly,' she said.

'I just wish I spoke.'

'You can still learn,' she said, suddenly feeling desperate, unsure how much this mattered to him, thinking again of him lying on the couch in the basement, drenched in sweat. She wondered if she should say more or not.

'Yes, I guess so,' he said, and shrugged, as though to say it was already too late.

Some days before he left, he asked her, 'What was my father really like?'

'He loved you.'

'Did you like him?'

She did not want to lie to him. 'I don't know. He was a big man in a military government and that does something to you and the way you relate to people. I was worried for your mum because I thought she deserved better. But she loved him, she really did, and he loved you. He used to carry you with such tenderness.'

'I can't believe Mom hid from me for so long that she was his mistress.'

'She was protecting you,' Ifemelu said.

'Can we go see the house in Dolphin Estate?'

'Yes.'

She drove him to Dolphin Estate, astounded by how much it had declined. The paint was peeling on buildings, the streets pitted with potholes, and the whole estate resigned to its own shabbiness. 'It was so much nicer then,' she told him. He stood looking at the house for a while, until the gateman said, 'Yes? Any problem?' and they got back into the car.

'Can I drive, Coz?' he asked.

'Are you sure?'

He nodded. She came out of the driver's seat

and went around to his. He drove them home, hesitating slightly before he merged onto Osborne Road, and then easing into traffic with more confidence. She knew it meant something to him that she could not name. That night, when the power went off, her generator would not come on, and she suspected that her driver, Ayo, had been sold diesel spiked with kerosene. Dike complained about the heat, about mosquitoes biting him. She opened the windows, made him take off his shirt, and they lay side by side in bed talking, desultory talking, and she reached out and touched his forehead and left her hand there until she heard the gentle even breathing of his sleep.

In the morning, the sky was overcast with slate-grey clouds, the air thick with rains foreboding. From nearby a clutch of birds screeched and flew away. The rain would come down, a sea unleashed from the sky, and DSTV images would get grainy, phone networks would clog, the roads would flood and traffic would gnarl. She stood with Dike on the verandah as the early droplets came down.

'I kind of like it here,' he told her.

She wanted to say, 'You can live with me. There are good private schools here that you could go to,' but she did not.

She took him to the airport, and stayed watching until he went past security, waved and turned the corner. Back home, she heard the hollowness in her steps as she walked from bedroom to living room to verandah and then back again. Later,

Ranyinudo told her, 'I don't understand how a fine boy like Dike would want to kill himself. A boy living in America with everything. How can? That is very foreign behaviour.'

'Foreign behaviour? What the fuck are you talking about? Foreign behaviour? Have you read *Things Fall Apart*?' Ifemelu asked, wishing she had not told Ranyinudo about Dike. She was angrier with Ranyinudo than she had ever been, yet she knew that Ranyinudo meant well, and had said what many other Nigerians would say, which was why she had not told anyone else about Dike's suicide attempt, since she came back.

CHAPTER 51

It had terrified her, the first time she came to the bank, to walk past the armed security guard, and into the beeping door, where she stood in the enclosure, sealed and airless like a standing coffin, until the light changed to green. Had banks always had this ostentatious security? Before she left America, she had wired some money to Nigeria, and Bank of America had made her speak to three different people, each one telling her that Nigeria was a high-risk country; if anything happened to her money, they would not be responsible. Did she understand? The last woman she spoke to made her repeat herself. *Ma'am, I'm sorry, I didn't hear you. I need to know that you understand that Nigeria is a high-risk country.* 'I understand!' she said. They read her caveat after caveat, and she began to fear for her money, snaking its way through the air to Nigeria, and she worried even more when she came to the bank and saw the gaudy garlands of security at the entrance. But the money was safely in her account. And now, as she walked into the bank, she saw Obinze at the customer service section. He was standing with his back to her and she knew, from the height and the shape of the head, that it was him. She stopped, sick with apprehension, hoping he would not turn just yet until she had gathered her nerves. Then he turned and it was not Obinze. Her throat felt tight. Her head was filled with ghosts. Back in her car, she turned on the air conditioner and decided to call him, to free herself of the ghosts. His phone rang and rang. He was a big man now; he would not, of course, pick up a call from an unknown number. She sent a text: *Ceiling, it's me.* Her phone rang almost immediately.

'Hello? Ifem?' That voice she had not heard in so long, and it sounded both changed and unchanged.

'Ceiling! How are you?'

'You're back.'

'Yes.' Her hands were trembling. She should have sent an e-mail first. She should be chatty, ask about his wife and child, tell him that she had in fact been back for a while.

'So,' Obinze said, dragging the word. 'How are you? Where are you? When can I see you?'

'What about now?' The recklessness that often emerged when she felt nervous had pushed out those words, but perhaps it was best to see him right away and get it over with. She wished she had dressed up a bit more, maybe worn her favourite wrap dress, with its slimming cut, but her knee-length skirt was not too bad, and her high heels always made her feel confident, and her Afro was, thankfully, not yet too shrunken from the humidity.

There was a pause on Obinze's end – something hesitant? – which made her regret her rashness.

'I'm actually running a bit late for a meeting,' she added quickly. 'But I just wanted to say hi and we can meet up soon . . .'

'Ifem, where are you?'

She told him she was on her way to Jazzhole to buy a book, and would be there in a few minutes. Half an hour later, she was standing in front of the bookshop when a black Range Rover pulled in and Obinze got out from the back.

There was a moment, a caving of the blue sky, an inertia of stillness, when neither of them knew what to do, he walking towards her, she standing there squinting, and then he was upon her and they hugged. She thumped him on the back, once, twice, to make it a chummy-chummy hug, a platonic and safe chummy-chummy hug, but he pulled her ever so slightly close to him, and held her for a moment too long, as though to say he was not being chummy-chummy.

'Obinze Maduewesi! Long time! Look at you, you haven't changed!' She was flustered, and the new shrillness in her voice annoyed her. He was looking at her, an open unabashed looking, and she would not hold his gaze. Her fingers were shaking of their own accord, which was bad enough, she did not need to stare into his eyes, both of them standing there, in the hot sun, in the fumes of traffic from Awolowo Road.

'It's so good to see you, Ifem,' he said. He was calm. She had forgotten what a calm person he was. There was still, in his bearing, a trace of his teenage history: the one who didn't try too hard, the one the girls wanted and the boys wanted to be.

'You're bald,' she said.

He laughed and touched his head. 'Yes. Mostly by choice.'

He had filled out, from the slight boy of their university days to a fleshier, more muscled man, and perhaps because he had filled out, he seemed shorter than she remembered. In her high heels, she was taller than he was. She had not forgotten, but merely remembered anew, how understated his manner was, his plain dark jeans, his leather slippers, the way he walked into the bookshop with no need to dominate it.

'Let's sit down,' he said.

The bookshop was dimly cool, its air moody and eclectic, books, CDs and magazines spread out on low shelves. A man standing near the entrance nodded at them in welcome, while adjusting the large headphones around his head. They sat opposite each other in the tiny café at the back and ordered fruit juice. Obinze put his two phones on the table; they lit up often, ringing in silent mode, and he would glance at them and then away. He worked out, she could tell from the firmness of his chest, across which stretched the double front pockets of his fitted shirt.

'You've been back for a while,' he said. He was watching her again, and she remembered how she had often felt as if he could see her mind, knew things about her that she might not consciously know.

'Yes,' she said.

'So what did you come to buy?'

'What?'

'The book you wanted to buy.'

'Actually I just wanted to meet you here. I thought if it turns out that seeing you again is something I'd like to remember, then I want to remember it in Jazzhole.'

'I want to remember it in Jazzhole,' he repeated, smiling as though only she could have come up with that expression. 'You haven't stopped being honest, Ifem. Thank God.'

'I already think I'm going to want to remember this.' Her nervousness was melting away; they had raced past the requisite moments of awkwardness.

'Do you need to be anywhere right now?' he asked. 'Can you stay a while?'

'Yes.'

He switched off both his phones. A rare declaration, in a city like Lagos for a man like him, that she had his absolute attention. 'How is Dike? How is Aunty Uju?'

'They're fine. He's doing well now. He actually came to visit me here. He only just left.'

The waitress served tall cups of mango-orange juice.

'What has surprised you the most about being back?' he asked.

'Everything, honestly. I started wondering if something was wrong with me.'

'Oh, it's normal,' he said, and she remembered how he had always been quick to reassure her, to make her feel better. 'I was away for a much shorter time, obviously, but I was very surprised when I came back. I kept thinking that things should have waited for me but they hadn't.'

'I'd forgotten that Lagos is so expensive. I can't believe how much money the Nigerian wealthy spend.'

'Most of them are thieves or beggars.'

She laughed. 'Thieves or beggars.'

'It's true. And they don't just spend a lot, they expect to spend a lot. I met this guy the other day, and he was telling me how he started his satellite-dish business about twenty years ago. This was when satellite dishes were still new in the country and so he was bringing in something most people didn't know about. He put his business plan together, and came up with a good price that would fetch him a good profit. Another friend of his, who was already a businessman and was going to invest in the business, took a look at the price and asked him to double it. Otherwise, he said, the Nigerian wealthy would not buy. He doubled it and it worked.'

'Crazy,' she said. 'Maybe it's always been this way and we didn't know, because we couldn't know. It's as if we are looking at an adult Nigeria that we didn't know about.'

'Yes.' He liked that she had said 'we', she could tell, and she liked that 'we' had slipped so easily out of her.

'It's such a transactional city,' she said. 'Depressingly transactional. Even relationships, they're all transactional.'

'Some relationships.'

'Yes, some,' she agreed. They were telling each other something that neither could yet articulate. Because she felt the nervousness creeping up her fingers again, she turned to humour. 'And there is a certain bombast in the way we speak that I had also forgotten. I started feeling truly at home again when I started being bombastic!'

Obinze laughed. She liked his quiet laugh. 'When I came back, I was shocked at how quickly my friends had all become fat, with big beer bellies. I thought: What is happening? Then I realized that they were the new middle class that our democracy created. They had jobs and they could afford to drink a lot more beer and to eat out, and you know eating out for us here is chicken and chips, and so they got fat.'

Ifemelu's stomach clenched. 'Well, if you look carefully you'll notice it's not only your friends.'

657

'Oh, no, Ifem, you're not fat. You're being very American about that. What Americans consider fat can just be normal. You need to see my guys to know what I am talking about. Remember Uche Okoye? Even Okwudiba? They can't even button their shirts now.' Obinze paused. 'You put on some weight and it suits you. *I maka.*'

She felt shy, a pleasant shyness, hearing him say she was beautiful.

'You used to tease me about not having an ass,' she said.

'I take my words back. At the door, I waited for you to go ahead for a reason.'

They laughed and then, laughter tapering off, were silent, smiling at each other in the strangeness of their intimacy. She remembered how, as she got up naked from his mattress on the floor in Nsukka, he would look up and say, 'I was going to say shake it but there's nothing to shake,' and she would playfully kick him in the shin. The clarity of that memory, the sudden stab of longing it brought, left her unsteady.

'But talk of being surprised, Ceiling,' she said. 'Look at you. Big Man with your Range Rover. Having money must have really changed things.'

'Yes, I guess it has.'

'Oh, come on,' she said. 'How?'

'People treat you differently. I don't just mean strangers. Friends too. Even my cousin Nneoma. Suddenly you're getting all of this sucking-up from people because they think you expect it, all this exaggerated politeness, exaggerated praise, even exaggerated respect that you haven't earned at all, and it's so fake and so garish, it's like a bad over-coloured painting, but sometimes you start believing a little bit of it yourself and sometimes you see yourself differently. One day I went to a wedding in my hometown, and the MC was doing a lot of silly praise-singing when I came in and I realized I was walking differently. I didn't *want* to walk differently but I was.'

'What, like a swagger?' she teased. 'Show me the walk!'

'You'll have to sing my praises first.' He sipped his drink. 'Nigerians can be so obsequious. We are a confident people but we are so obsequious. It's not difficult for us to be insincere.'

'We have confidence but no dignity.'

'Yes.' He looked at her, recognition in his eyes. 'And if you keep getting that overdone sucking-up, it makes you paranoid. You don't know if anything is honest or true any more. And then people become paranoid for you, but in a different way. My relatives are always telling me: Be careful where you eat. Even here in Lagos my friends tell me to watch what I eat. Don't eat in a woman's house because she'll put something in your food.'

'And do you?'

'Do I what?'

'Watch what you eat?'

'I wouldn't in your house.' A pause. He was

659

being openly flirtatious and she was unsure what to say.

'But no,' he continued. 'I like to think that if I wanted to eat in somebody's house, it would be a person who would not think of slipping jazz into my food.'

'It all seems really desperate.'

'One of the things I've learned is that everybody in this country has the mentality of scarcity. We imagine that even the things that are not scarce are scarce. And it breeds a kind of desperation in everybody. Even the wealthy.'

'The wealthy like you, that is,' she quipped.

He paused. He often paused before he spoke. She thought this exquisite; it was as though he had such regard for his listener that he wanted his words strung together in the best possible way. 'I like to think I don't have that desperation. I sometimes feel as if the money I have isn't really mine, as if I'm holding it for someone else for a while. After I bought my property in Dubai, it was my first property outside Nigeria, I felt almost frightened and when I told Okwudiba how I felt, he said I was crazy and I should stop behaving as if life is one of the novels I read. He was so impressed by what I owned, and I just felt as if my life had become this layer of pretension after pretension and I started to get sentimental about the past. I would think about when I was staying with Okwudiba in his first small flat in Surulere and how we would heat the iron on the stove when NEPA took light.

And how his neighbour downstairs used to shout "Praise the Lord!" whenever the light came back and how even for me there was something so beautiful about the light coming back, when it's out of your control because you don't have a generator. But it's a silly sort of romance, because of course I don't want to go back to that life.'

She looked away, worried that the crush of emotions she had felt while he was speaking would now converge on her face. 'Of course you don't. You like your life,' she said.

'I live my life.'

'Oh, how mysterious we are.'

'What about you, famous race blogger, Princeton fellow, how have you changed?' he asked, smiling, leaning towards her with his elbows on the table.

'When I was babysitting in undergrad, one day I heard myself telling the kid I was babysitting "You're such a trouper!" Is there another word more American than "trouper"?'

Obinze was laughing.

'That's when I thought, yes, I may have changed a little,' she said.

'You don't have an American accent.'

'I made an effort not to.'

'I was surprised when I read the archives of your blog. It didn't sound like you.'

'I really don't think I've changed that much, though.'

'Oh, you've changed,' he said with a certitude that she instinctively disliked.

'How?'

'I don't know. You're more self-aware. Maybe more guarded.'

'You sound like a disappointed uncle.'

'No.' Another one of his pauses, but this time he seemed to be holding back. 'But your blog also made me proud. I thought: She's gone, she's learned and she's conquered.'

Again, she felt shy. 'I don't know about conquering.'

'Your aesthetics changed too,' he said.

'What do you mean?'

'Did you cure your own meats in America?'

'What?'

'I read a piece about this new movement among the American privileged classes. Where people want to drink milk straight from the cow and that sort of thing. I thought maybe you're into that, now that you wear a flower in your hair.'

She burst out laughing.

'But really, tell me how you've changed.' His tone was teasing, yet she tensed slightly at his question; it seemed too close to her vulnerable, soft core. And so she said, in a breezy voice, 'My taste, I guess. I can't believe how much I find ugly now. I can't stand most of the houses in this city. I'm now a person who has learned to admire exposed wooden rafters.' She rolled her eyes and he smiled at her self-mockery, a smile that seemed to her like a prize that she wanted to win over and over again.

'It's really a kind of snobbery,' she added.

'It's snobbery, not a kind,' he said. 'I used to have that about books. Secretly feeling that your taste is superior.'

'The problem is I'm not always secret about it.'

He laughed. 'Oh, we know that.'

'You said you used to? What happened?'

'What happened was that I grew up.'

'Ouch,' she said.

He said nothing; the slight sardonic raise of his eyebrows said that she, too, would have to grow up.

'What are you reading these days?' she asked. 'I'm sure you've read every American novel ever published.'

'I've been reading a lot more non-fiction, history and biographies. About everything, not just America.'

'What, you fell out of love?'

'I realized I could buy America, and it lost its shine. When all I had was my passion for America, they didn't give me a visa, but with my new bank account, getting a visa was very easy. I've visited a few times. I was looking into buying property in Miami.'

She felt a pang; he had visited America and she had not known.

'So what did you finally make of your dream country?'

'I remember when you first went to Manhattan and you wrote to me and said "It's wonderful but it's not heaven." I thought of that when I took my first cab ride in Manhattan.'

She remembered writing that, too, not long before she stopped contacting him, before she pushed him behind many walls. 'The best thing about America is that it gives you space. I like that. I like that you buy into the dream, it's a lie but you buy into it and that's all that matters.'

He looked down at his glass, uninterested in her philosophizing, and she wondered if what she had seen in his eyes was resentment, if he, too, was remembering how she had so completely shut him out. When he asked, 'Are you still friends with your old friends?' she thought it a question about whom else she had shut out all these years. She wondered whether to bring it up herself, whether to wait for him to. She should bring it up, she owed him that, but a wordless fear had seized her, a fear of breaking delicate things.

'With Ranyinudo, yes. And Priye. The others are now people who used to be my friends. Kind of like you and Emenike. You know, when I read your e-mails, I wasn't surprised that Emenike turned out like that. There was always something about him.'

He shook his head and finished his drink; he had earlier put the straw aside, sipping from the glass.

'Once I was with him in London and he was mocking this guy he worked with, a Nigerian guy, for not knowing how to pronounce F-e-a-t-h-e-r-s-t-o-n-e-h-a-u-g-h. He pronounced it phonetically like the guy had, which was obviously the wrong way, and he didn't say it the right way. I didn't know how to pronounce it either and he knew I didn't know, and there were these horrible minutes when he pretended we were both laughing at the guy. When of course we weren't. He was laughing at *me too.* I remember it as the moment when I realized he just had never been my friend.'

'He's an asshole,' she said.

'Asshole. Very American word.'

'Is it?'

He half raised his eyebrows as though there was no need to state the obvious. 'Emenike didn't contact me at all after I was deported. Then, last year, after somebody must have told him I was now in the game, he started calling me.' Obinze said 'in the game' in a voice thick with mockery. 'He kept asking if there were any deals we could do together, that kind of nonsense. And one day I told him I really preferred his condescension, and he hasn't called me since.'

'What of Kayode?'

'We're in touch. He has a child with an American woman.'

Obinze looked at his watch and picked up his phones. 'I hate to go but I have to.'

'Yes, me too.' She wanted to prolong this moment, sitting amid the scent of books, discovering Obinze again. Before they got into their separate cars, they hugged, both murmuring, 'So good to see you,' and she imagined his driver and her driver watching them curiously.

'I'll call you tomorrow,' he said, but she had hardly settled into the car when her phone beeped with a new text message from him. *Are you free to have lunch tomorrow?* She was free. It was a Saturday and she should ask why he would not be with his wife and child, and she should initiate a conversation about what they were doing exactly, but they had a history, a connection thick as twine, and it did not have to mean that they were doing anything, or that a conversation was necessary, and so she opened the door when he rang the bell and he came in and admired the flowers on her verandah, the white lilies that rose from the pots like swans.

'I spent the morning reading *The Small Redemptions of Lagos*. Scouring it, actually,' he said.

She felt pleased. 'What did you think?'

'I liked the Nigerpolitan Club post. A little self-righteous, though.'

'I'm not sure how to take that.'

'As truth,' he said, with that half-raising of an eyebrow that had to be a new quirk; she did not remember him doing it in the past. 'But it's a fantastic blog. It's brave and intelligent. I love the layout.' There he was again, reassuring her.

She pointed at the compound next door. 'Do you recognize that?'

'Ah! Yes.'

'I thought it would be just perfect for the blog.

Such a beautiful house and in this kind of magnificent ruin. Plus peacocks on the roof.'

'It looks a little like a courthouse. I'm always fascinated by these old houses and the stories they carry.' He tugged at the thin metal railing of her verandah, as though to check how durable it was, how safe, and she liked that he did that. 'Somebody is going to snap it up soon, tear it down, and put up a gleaming block of overpriced luxury flats.'

'Somebody like you.'

'When I started in real estate, I considered renovating old houses instead of tearing them down, but it didn't make sense. Nigerians don't buy houses because they're old. A renovated two-hundred-year-old mill granary, you know, the kind of thing Europeans like. It doesn't work here at all. But of course it makes sense because we are Third Worlders and Third Worlders are forward-looking, we like things to be new, because our best is still ahead, while in the West their best is already past and so they have to make a fetish of that past.'

'Is it me or are you now given to delivering little lectures?' she asked.

'It's just refreshing to have an intelligent person to talk to.'

She looked away, wondering if this was a reference to his wife, and disliking him for it.

'Your blog already has such a following,' he said.

'I have big plans for it. I'd like to travel through Nigeria and post dispatches from each state, with pictures and human stories, but I have to do things slowly first, establish it, make some money from advertising.'

'You need investors.'

'I don't want your money,' she said, a little sharply, keeping her eyes levelly on the sunken roof of the abandoned house. She was irritated by his comment about an intelligent person because it was, it had to be, about his wife, and she wanted to ask why he was telling her that. Why had he married a woman who was not intelligent only to turn around and tell her that his wife was not intelligent?

'Look at the peacock, Ifem,' he said, gently, as though he sensed her irritation.

They watched the peacock walk out of the shadow of a tree, then its lugubrious flight up to its favourite perch on the roof, where it stood and surveyed the decayed kingdom below.

'How many are there?' he asked.

'One male and two females. I've been hoping to see the male do its mating dance but I never have. They wake me up in the morning with their cries. Have you heard them? Almost like a child that doesn't want to do something.'

The peacock's slender neck moved this way and that, and then, as though it had heard her, it cawed, its beak parted wide, the sounds pouring out of its throat.

'You were right about the sound,' he said, moving closer to her. 'Something of a child about it. The compound reminds me of a property I have in Enugu. An old house. It was built before the war, and I bought it to tear it down, but then I decided to keep it. It's very gracious and restful, big verandahs and old frangipani trees in the back. I'm redoing the interior completely, so it will be very modern inside, but the outside has its old look. Don't laugh, but when I saw it, it reminded me of poetry.'

There was a boyishness in the way he said 'Don't laugh' that made her smile at him, half making fun of him, half letting him know she liked the idea of a house that had reminded him of poetry.

'I imagine one day when I run away from it all, I'll go and live there,' he said.

'People really do become eccentric when they become rich.'

'Or maybe we all have eccentricity in us, we just don't have the money to show it? I'd love to take you to see the house.'

She murmured something, a vague acquiescence.

His phone had been ringing for a while, an endless, dull buzzing in his pocket. Finally he brought it out, glanced at it and said, 'Sorry, I have to take this.' She nodded and went inside, wondering if it was his wife.

From the living room, she heard snatches of his voice, raised, lowered and then raised again, speaking Igbo, and when he came inside, there was a tightening in his jaw.

'Everything okay?' she asked.

'It's a boy from my hometown. I pay his school fees but he now has a mad sense of entitlement and this morning he sent me a text telling me he needs a mobile phone and could I send it to him by Friday. A fifteen-year-old boy. The gall of it. And then he starts calling me. So I've just told him off and I've told him his scholarship is off, too, just to scare some sense into his head.'

'Is he related to you?'

'No.'

She waited, expecting more.

'Ifem, I do what rich people are supposed to do. I pay school fees for a hundred students in my village and my mum's village.' He spoke with an awkward indifference; this was not a subject that he cared to talk about. He was standing by her bookshelf. 'What a beautiful living room.'

'Thank you.'

'You shipped all your books back?'

'Most of them.'

'Ah. Derek Walcott.'

'I love him. I finally get some poetry.'

'I see Graham Greene.'

'I started reading him because of your mother. I love *The Heart of the Matter*.'

'I tried reading it after she died. I wanted to love it. I thought maybe if I could just love it . . .' He touched the book, his voice trailing away.

His wistfulness moved her. 'It's real literature, the kind of human story people will read in two hundred years,' she said.

'You sound just like my mother,' he said.

He felt familiar and unfamiliar at the same time. Through the parted curtains, a crescent of light fell across the living room. They were standing by the bookshelf and she was telling him about the first time she finally read *The Heart of the Matter*, and he was listening, in that intense manner of his, as though swallowing her words like a drink. They were standing by the bookshelf and laughing about how often his mother had tried to get him to read the book. And then they were standing by the bookshelf and kissing. A gentle kiss at first, lips pressed to lips, then their tongues were touching and she felt boneless against him. He pulled away first.

'I don't have condoms,' she said, brazen, deliberately brazen.

'I didn't know we needed condoms to have lunch.'

She hit him playfully. Her entire body was invaded by millions of uncertainties. She did not want to look at his face. 'I have a girl who cleans and cooks so I have a lot of stew in my freezer and jollof rice in my fridge. We can have lunch here. Would you like something to drink?' She turned towards the kitchen.

'What happened in America?' he asked. 'Why did you just cut off contact?'

Ifemelu kept walking to the kitchen.

'Why did you just cut off contact?' he repeated quietly. 'Please tell me what happened.'

Before she sat opposite him at her small dining table and told him about the corrupt-eyed tennis coach in Ardmore, Pennsylvania, she poured them both some mango juice from a carton. She told him small details about the man's office that were still fresh in her mind, the stacks of sports magazines, the smell of damp, but when she got to the part where he took her to his room, she said, simply, 'I took off my clothes and did what he asked me to do. I couldn't believe that I got wet. I hated him. I hated myself. I really hated myself. I felt like I had, I don't know, betrayed myself.' She paused. 'And you.'

For many long minutes, he said nothing, his eyes downcast, as though absorbing the story.

'I don't really think about it much,' she added. 'I remember it, but I don't dwell on it, I don't let myself dwell on it. It's so strange now to actually talk about it. It seems a stupid reason to throw away what we had, but that's why, and as more time passed, I just didn't know how to go about fixing it.'

He was still silent. She stared at the framed caricature of Dike that hung on her wall, Dike's ears comically pointed, and wondered what Obinze was feeling.

Finally, he said, 'I can't imagine how bad you must have felt, and how alone. You should have told me. I so wish you had told me.'

She heard his words like a melody and she felt herself breathing unevenly, gulping at the air.

She would not cry, it was ridiculous to cry after so long, but her eyes were filling with tears and there was a boulder in her chest and a stinging in her throat. The tears felt itchy. She made no sound. He took her hand in his, both clasped on the table, and between them silence grew, an ancient silence that they both knew. She was inside this silence and she was safe.

CHAPTER 52

'Let's go and play table tennis. I belong to this small private club in Victoria Island,' he said.

'I haven't played in ages.'

She remembered how she had always wanted to beat him, even though he was the school champion, and how he would tell her, teasingly, 'Try more strategy and less force. Passion never wins any game, never mind what they say.' He said something similar now: 'Excuses don't win a game. You should try strategy.'

He had driven himself. In the car, he turned the engine on, and the music came on too. Bracket's 'Yori Yori'.

'Oh, I love this song,' she said.

He increased the volume and they sang along; there was an exuberance to the song, its rhythmic joyfulness, so free of artifice, that filled the air with lightness.

'Ahn-ahn! How long have you been back and you can already sing this so well?' he asked.

'First thing I did was brush up on all the contemporary music. It's so exciting, all the new music.'

'It is. Now clubs play Nigerian music.'

She would remember this moment, sitting beside Obinze in his Range Rover, stalled in traffic, listening to 'Yori Yori' – *Your love dey make my heart do yori yori. Nobody can love you the way I do* – beside them a shiny Honda, the latest model, and in front of them an ancient Datsun that looked a hundred years old.

After a few games of table tennis, all of which he won, all the time playfully taunting her, they had lunch in the small restaurant, where they were alone except for a woman reading newspapers at the bar. The manager, a round man who was almost bursting out of his ill-fitting black jacket, came over to their table often to say, 'I hope everything is fine, sah. It is very good to see you again, sah. How is work, sah.'

Ifemelu leaned in and asked Obinze, 'Is there a point at which you gag?'

'The man wouldn't come by so often if he didn't think I was being neglected. You're addicted to that phone.'

'Sorry. I was just checking the blog.' She felt relaxed and happy. 'You know, you should write for me.'

'Me?'

'Yes, I'll give you an assignment. How about the perils of being young and good-looking and rich?'

'I would be happy to write on a subject with which I can personally identify.'

'How about security? I want to do something on security. Have you had any experience on Third

675

Mainland Bridge? Somebody was telling me about leaving a club late and going back to the mainland and their car tyre burst on the bridge and they just kept going, because it's so dangerous to stop on the bridge.'

'Ifem, I live in Lekki, and I don't go clubbing. Not any more.'

'Okay.' She glanced at her phone again. 'I just want to have new, vibrant content often.'

'You're distracted.'

'Do you know Tunde Razaq?'

'Who doesn't? Why?'

'I want to interview him. I want to start this weekly feature of "Lagos from an Insider", and I want to start with the most interesting people.'

'What's interesting about him? That he is a Lagos playboy living off his father's money, said money accumulated from a diesel importation monopoly that they have because of their contact with the president?'

'He's also a music producer, and apparently a champion at chess. My friend Zemaye knows him and he's just written to her to say he will do the interview only if I let him buy me dinner.'

'He's probably seen a picture of you somewhere.' Obinze stood up and pushed back his chair with a force that surprised her. 'The guy is a dog.'

'Be nice,' she said, amused; his jealousy pleased her. He played 'Yori Yori' again on the drive back to her flat, and she swayed and danced with her arms, much to his amusement.

'I thought your Chapman was non-alcoholic,' he said. 'I want to play another song. It makes me think of you.'

Obiwon's 'Obi Mu O' started and she sat still and silent as the words filled the car: *This is that feeling that I've never felt . . . and I'm not gonna let it die.* When the male and female voices sang in Igbo, Obinze sang along with them, glancing away from the road to look at her, as though he was telling her that this was really their conversation, he calling her beautiful, she calling him beautiful, both calling each other their true friends. *Nwanyi oma, nwoke oma, omalicha nwa, ezigbo oyi m o.*

When he dropped her off, he leaned across to kiss her cheek, hesitant to come too close or to hold her, as though afraid of being defeated by their attraction. 'Can I see you tomorrow?' he asked, and she said yes. They went to a Brazilian restaurant by the lagoon, where the waiter brought skewer after skewer stacked with meat and seafood, until Ifemelu told him that she was about to be sick. The next day, he asked if she would have dinner with him, and he took her to an Italian restaurant, whose overpriced food she found bland, and the bow-tied waiters, doleful and slow-moving, filled her with faint sorrow.

They drove past Obalende on the way back, tables and stalls lining the bustling road, orange flames flickering from the hawkers' lamps.

Ifemelu said, 'Let's stop and buy fried plantain!'

Obinze found a spot farther ahead, in front of

a beer parlour, and he eased the car in. He greeted the men seated on benches drinking, his manner easy and warm, and they hailed him, 'Chief! Carry go! Your car is safe!'

The fried plantain hawker tried to persuade Ifemelu to buy fried sweet potatoes as well.

'No, only plantain.'

'What about akara, aunty? I make am now. Very fresh.'

'Okay,' Ifemelu said. 'Put four.'

'Why are you buying akara that you don't want?' Obinze asked, amused.

'Because this is real enterprise. She's selling what she makes. She's not selling her location or the source of her oil or the name of the person that ground the beans. She's simply selling what she makes.'

Back in the car, she opened the oily plastic bag of plantains, slid a small, perfectly fried yellow slice into her mouth. 'This is so much better than that thing drenched in butter that I could hardly finish at the restaurant. And you know we can't get food poisoning because the frying kills the germs,' she added.

He was watching her, smiling, and she suspected that she was talking too much. This memory, too, she would store, of Obalende at night, lit as it was by a hundred small lights, the raised voices of drunk men nearby, and the sway of a large madam's hips, walking past the car.

⋆　　⋆　　⋆

678

He asked if he could take her to lunch and she suggested a new casual place she had heard of, where she ordered a chicken sandwich and then complained about the man smoking in the corner. 'How very American, complaining about smoke,' Obinze said, and she could not tell whether he meant it as a rebuke or not.

'The sandwich comes with chips?' Ifemelu asked the waiter.

'Yes, madam.'

'Do you have real potatoes?'

'Madam?'

'Are your potatoes the frozen imported ones, or do you cut and fry your potatoes?'

The waiter looked offended. 'It is the imported frozen ones.'

As the waiter walked away, Ifemelu said, 'Those frozen things taste horrible.'

'He can't believe you're actually asking for real potatoes,' Obinze said drily. 'Real potatoes are backward for him. Remember this is our newly middle-class world. We haven't completed the first cycle of prosperity, before going back to the beginning again, to drink milk from the cow's udder.'

Each time he dropped her off, he kissed her on the cheek, both of them leaning towards each other, and then pulling back so that she could say 'Bye' and climb out of his car. On the fifth day, as he drove into her compound, she asked, 'Do you have condoms in your pocket?'

He said nothing for a while. 'No, I don't have condoms in my pocket.'

'Well, I bought a pack some days ago.'

'Ifem, why are you saying this?'

'You're married with a child and we are hot for each other. Who are we kidding with this chaste dating business? So we might as well get it over with.'

'You are hiding behind sarcasm,' he said.

'Oh, how very lofty of you.' She was angry. It was barely a week since she first saw him but already she was angry, furious that he would drop her off and go home to his other life, his real life, and that she could not visualize the details of that life, did not know what kind of bed he slept in, what kind of plate he ate from. She had, since she began to gaze at her past, imagined a relationship with him, but only in faded images and faint lines. Now, faced with the reality of him, and of the silver ring on his finger, she was frightened of becoming used to him, of drowning. Or perhaps she was already drowned, and her fear came from that knowledge.

'Why didn't you call me when you came back?' he asked.

'I don't know. I wanted to settle down first.'

'I hoped I would help you settle down.'

She said nothing.

'Are you still with Blaine?'

'What does it matter, married man, you?' she said, with an irony that sounded far too caustic; she wanted to be cool, distant, in control.

'Can I come in for a bit? To talk?'

'No, I need to do some research for the blog.'

'Please, Ifem.'

She sighed. 'Okay.'

In her flat, he sat on the couch while she sat on her armchair, as far from him as possible. She had a sudden bilious terror about whatever it was he was going to say, which she did not want to hear, and so she said, wildly, 'Zemaye wants to write a tongue-in-cheek guide for men who want to cheat. She said her boyfriend was unreachable the other day and when he finally turned up, he told her that his phone had fallen into water. She said it's the oldest story in the book, phone fell into water. I thought that was funny. I've never heard that before. So number one on her guide is never say your phone fell into water.'

'This doesn't feel like cheating to me,' he said quietly.

'Does your wife know you're here?' She was taunting him. 'I wonder how many men say that when they cheat, that it doesn't feel like cheating. I mean, would they actually ever say that it felt like cheating?'

He got up, his movements deliberate, and at first she thought he was coming closer to her, or perhaps wanted the toilet, but he walked to the front door, opened it and left. She stared at the door. She sat still for a long time, and then she got up and paced, unable to focus, wondering whether to call him, debating with herself. She decided not to call him; she resented his behaviour, his silence, his pretence. When her doorbell rang minutes later, a part of her was reluctant to open the door.

She let him in. They sat side by side on her couch.

'I'm sorry I left like that,' he said. 'I just haven't been myself since you came back and I didn't like the way you talked as if what we have is common. It isn't. And I think you know that. I think you were saying that to hurt me but mostly because *you* feel confused. I know it must be difficult for you, how we've seen each other and talked about so much but still avoided so much.'

'You're speaking in code,' she said.

He looked stressed, tight-jawed, and she longed to kiss him. It was true that he was intelligent and sure of himself, but there was an innocence about him, too, a confidence without ego, a throwback to another time and place, which she found endearing.

'I haven't said anything because sometimes I am just so happy being with you that I don't want to spoil it,' he said. 'And also because I want to have something to say first, before I say anything.'

'I touch myself thinking of you,' she said.

He stared at her, thrown slightly off balance.

'We're not single people who are courting, Ceiling,' she said. 'We can't deny the attraction between us and maybe we should have a conversation about that.'

682

'You know this isn't about sex,' he said. 'This has never been about sex.'

'I know,' she said, and took his hand. There was, between them, a weightless, seamless desire. She leaned in and kissed him, and at first he was slow in his response, and then he was pulling up her blouse, pushing down her bra cups to free her breasts. She remembered clearly the firmness of his embrace, and yet there was, also, a newness to their union; their bodies remembered and did not remember. She touched the scar on his chest, remembering it again. She had always thought the expression 'making love' a little maudlin; 'having sex' felt truer and 'fucking' was more arousing, but lying next to him afterwards, both of them smiling, sometimes laughing, her body suffused with peace, she thought how apt it was, that expression 'making love'. There was an awakening even in her nails, in those parts of her body that had always been numb. She wanted to tell him, 'There is no week that passed that I did not think of you.' But was that true? Of course there were weeks during which he was folded under layers of her life, but it *felt* true.

She propped herself up and said, 'I always saw the ceiling with other men.'

He smiled a long, slow smile. 'You know what I have felt for so long? As if I was waiting to be happy.'

He got up to go to the bathroom. She found it so attractive, his shortness, his solid firm shortness.

She saw, in his shortness, a groundedness; he could weather anything, he would not easily be swayed. He came back and she said she was hungry and he found oranges in her fridge, and peeled them, and they ate the oranges, sitting up next to each other, and then they lay entwined, naked, in a full circle of completeness, and she fell asleep and did not know when he left. She woke up to a dark, overcast rainy morning. Her phone was ringing. It was Obinze.

'How are you?' he asked.

'Groggy. Not sure what happened yesterday. Did you seduce me?'

'I'm glad your door has a dead bolt. I would have hated to wake you up to lock the door.'

'So you did seduce me.'

He laughed. 'Can I come to you?'

She liked the way he said 'Can I come to you?'

'Yes. It's raining crazily.'

'Really? It's not raining here. I'm in Lekki.'

She found this foolishly exciting, that it was raining where she was and it was not raining where he was, only minutes from her, and so she waited, with impatience, with a charged delight, until they could both see the rain together.

CHAPTER 53

And so began her heady days full of cliché: she felt fully alive, her heart beat faster when he arrived at her door, and she viewed each morning like the unwrapping of a gift. She would laugh, or cross her legs or slightly sway her hips, with a heightened awareness of herself. Her nightshirt smelled of his cologne, a muted citrus and wood scent, because she left it unwashed for as long as she could, and she delayed in wiping off a spill of hand cream he had left on her sink, and after they made love, she left untouched the indentation on the pillow, the soft groove where his head had lain, as though to preserve his essence until the next time. They often stood on her verandah and watched the peacocks on the roof of the abandoned house, from time to time slipping their hands into each other's, and she would think of the next time, and the next, that they would do this together. This was love, to be eager for tomorrow. Had she felt this way as a teenager? The emotions seemed absurd. She fretted when he did not respond to her text right away. Her mind was darkened with jealousy about his past. 'You are the great love of my life,' he told her, and she believed him, but still she was jealous of those women whom he had loved even if fleetingly, those women who had carved out space in his thoughts. She was jealous even of the women who liked him, imagining how much attention he got here in Lagos, good-looking as he was, and now also wealthy. The first time she introduced him to Zemaye, lissome Zemaye in her tight skirt and platform heels, she stifled her discomfort, because she saw in Zemaye's alert appreciative eyes the eyes of all the hungry women in Lagos. It was a jealousy of her imagination, he did nothing to aid it; he was present and transparent in his devotion. She marvelled at what an intense, careful listener he was. He remembered everything she told him. She had never had this before, to be listened to, to be truly heard, and so he became newly precious; each time he said bye at the end of a telephone call, she felt a sinking panic. It was truly absurd. Their teenage love had been less melodramatic. Or perhaps it was because the circumstances were different, and looming over them now was the marriage he never talked about. Sometimes he said, 'I can't come on Sunday until mid-afternoon,' or 'I have to leave early today,' all of which she knew were about his wife, but they did not talk further about it. He did not try to, and she did not want to, or she told herself that she did not want to. It surprised her, that he took her out openly, to lunch and to dinner, to his private club where the waiter called her 'madam', perhaps assuming she was his wife; that he stayed with her until past midnight and never showered after they made love; that he went home wearing her touch and her smell on his skin. He was determined to give their relationship as much dignity as he could, to pretend that he was not hiding even though he, of course, was. Once he said cryptically, as they lay entwined on her bed in the undecided light of late evening, 'I can stay the night, I would like to stay.' She said a quick no and nothing else. She did not want to get used to waking up beside him, did not permit herself to think of why he could stay this night. And so his marriage hung above them, unspoken, unprobed, until one evening when she did not feel like eating out. He said eagerly, 'You have spaghetti and onions. Let me cook for you.'

'As long as it doesn't give me a stomach ache.'

He laughed. 'I miss cooking. I can't cook at home.' And, in that instant, his wife became a dark spectral presence in the room. It was palpable and menacing in a way it had never been when he said, 'I can't come on Sunday until mid-afternoon,' or 'I have to leave early today.' She turned away from him, and flipped open her laptop to check on the blog. A furnace had lit itself deep inside her. He sensed it, too, the sudden import of his words, because he came and stood beside her.

'Kosi never liked the idea of my cooking. She has really basic, mainstream ideas of what a wife should be and she thought my wanting to cook was an indictment of her, which I found silly. So I stopped, just to have peace. I make omelettes but that's it and we both pretend as if my onugbu soup isn't better than hers. There's a lot of pretending in my marriage, Ifem.' He paused. 'I married her when I was feeling vulnerable; I had a lot of upheaval in my life at the time.'

She said, her back turned to him, 'Obinze, please just cook the spaghetti.'

'I feel a great responsibility for Kosi and that is all I feel. And I want you to know that.' He gently turned her around to face him, holding her shoulders, and he looked as if there were other things he wanted to say, but expected her to help him say them, and for this she felt the flare of a new resentment. She turned back to her laptop, choked with the urge to destroy, to slash and burn.

'I'm having dinner with Tunde Razaq tomorrow,' she said.

'Why?'

'Because I want to.'

'You said the other day that you wouldn't.'

'What happens when you go home and climb into bed with your wife? What happens?' she asked, and felt herself wanting to cry. Something had cracked and spoilt between them.

'I think you should go,' she said.

'No.'

'Obinze, please just go.'

He refused to leave, and later she felt grateful that he had not left. He cooked spaghetti and she

688

pushed it around her plate, her throat parched, her appetite gone.

'I'm never going to ask you for anything. I'm a grown woman and I knew your situation when I got into this,' she said.

'Please don't say that,' he said. 'It scares me. It makes me feel dispensable.'

'It's not about you.'

'I know. I know it's the only way you can feel a little dignity in this.'

She looked at him and even his reasonableness began to irritate her.

'I love you, Ifem. We love each other,' he said.

There were tears in his eyes. She began to cry, too, a helpless crying, and they held each other. Later, they lay in bed together, and the air was so still and noiseless that the gurgling sound from his stomach seemed loud.

'Was that my stomach or yours?' he asked, teasing.

'Of course it was yours.'

'Remember the first time we made love? You had just been standing on me. I loved you standing on me.'

'I can't stand on you now. I'm too fat. You would die.'

'Stop it.'

Finally, he got up and pulled on his trousers, his movements slow and reluctant. 'I can't come tomorrow, Ifem. I have to take my daughter—'

She cut him short. 'It's okay.'

'I'm going to Abuja on Friday,' he said.

'Yes, you said.' She was trying to push away the sense of a coming abandonment; it would overwhelm her as soon as he left and she heard the click of the door closing.

'Come with me,' he said.

'What?'

'Come with me to Abuja. I just have two meetings and we can stay the weekend. It'll be good for us to be in a different place, to talk. And you've never been to Abuja. I can book separate hotel rooms if you want me to. Say yes. Please.'

'Yes,' she said.

She had not permitted herself to do so earlier, but after he left, she looked at Kosi's photographs on Facebook. Kosi's beauty was startling, those cheekbones, that flawless skin, those perfect womanly curves. When she saw one photo taken at an unflattering angle, she examined it for a while and found in it a small and wicked pleasure.

She was at the hair salon when he sent her a text: *I'm sorry Ifem but I think I should probably go alone to Abuja. I need some time to think things through. I love you.* She stared at the text and, fingers shaking, she wrote him back a two-word text: *Fucking coward.* Then she turned to the hair braider. 'You are going to blow-dry my hair with that brush? You must be joking. Can't you people think?'

The hair braider looked puzzled. 'Aunty, sorry o, but that is what I use before in your hair.'

By the time Ifemelu drove into her compound, Obinze's Range Rover was parked in front of her flat. He followed her upstairs.

'Ifem, please, I want you to understand. I think it has been a little too fast, everything between us, and I want to take some time to put things in perspective.'

'A little too fast,' she repeated. 'How unoriginal. Not like you at all.'

'You are the woman I love. Nothing can change that. But I feel this sense of responsibility about what I need to do.'

She flinched from him, the hoarseness of his voice, the nebulous and easy meaninglessness of his words. What did 'responsibility about what I need to do' mean? Did it mean that he wanted to continue seeing her but had to stay married? Did it mean that he could no longer continue seeing her? He communicated clearly when he wanted to, but now here he was, hiding behind watery words.

'What are you saying?' she asked him. 'What are you trying to tell me?'

When he remained silent, she said, 'Go to hell.'

She walked into her bedroom and locked the door. From her bedroom window, she watched his Range Rover until it disappeared down the bend in the road.

CHAPTER 54

Abuja had far-flung horizons, wide roads, order; to come from Lagos was to be stunned here by sequence and space. The air smelled of power; here everyone sized everyone else up, wondering how much of a 'somebody' each was. It smelled of money, easy money, easily exchanged money. It dripped, too, of sex. Obinze's friend Chidi said he didn't chase women in Abuja because he didn't want to step on a minister's or senator's toes. Every attractive young woman here became mysteriously suspect. Abuja was more conservative than Lagos, Chidi said, because it was more Muslim than Lagos, and at parties women didn't wear revealing clothing, yet you could buy and sell sex so much more easily here. It was in Abuja that Obinze had come close to cheating on Kosi, not with any of the flashy girls in coloured contact lenses and tumbling hair weaves who endlessly propositioned him, but with a middle-aged woman in a caftan who sat next to him at the hotel bar, and said, 'I know you are bored.' She looked hungry for recklessness, perhaps a repressed, frustrated wife who had broken free on this one night.

For a moment, lust, a quaking raw lust, overcame him, but he thought about how much more bored he would be afterwards, how keen to get her out of his hotel room, and it all seemed too much of an effort.

She would end up with one of the many men in Abuja who lived idle, oily lives in hotels and part-time homes, grovelling and courting connected people so as to get a contract or to be paid for a contract. On Obinze's last trip to Abuja, one such man, whom he hardly knew, had looked for a while at two young women at the other end of the bar and then asked him casually, 'Do you have a spare condom?' and he had baulked.

Now, sitting at a white-covered table in Protea Asokoro, waiting for Edusco, the businessman who wanted to buy his land, he imagined Ifemelu next to him, and wondered what she would make of Abuja. She would dislike it, the soullessness of it, or perhaps not. She was not easy to predict. Once, at dinner in a restaurant in Victoria Island, sombre waiters hovering around, she had seemed distant, her eyes on the wall behind him, and he had worried that she was upset about something. 'What are you thinking?' he asked.

'I am thinking of how all the paintings in Lagos always look crooked, never hung straight,' she said. He laughed, and thought how, with her, he was as he had never been with another woman: amused, alert, alive. Later, as they left the restaurant, he had watched as she briskly sidestepped the puddles of water in the potholes by the gate and felt a desire to smooth all the roads in Lagos, for her.

His mind was overwrought: one minute he thought it was the right decision not to have come to Abuja with her, because he needed to think things through, and the next he was filled with self-reproach. He might have pushed her away. He had called her many times, sent texts asking if they could talk, but she had ignored him, which was perhaps for the better because he did not know what he would say if they did talk.

Edusco had arrived. A loud voice bellowing from the restaurant foyer as he spoke on the phone. Obinze did not know him well – they had done business only once before, introduced by a mutual friend – but Obinze admired men like him, men who did not know any Big Man, who had no connections, and had made their money in a way that did not defy the simple logic of capitalism. Edusco had only a primary school education before he began to apprentice for traders; he had started off with one stall in Onitsha and now owned the second-largest transport company in the country. He walked into the restaurant, bold-stepped and big-bellied, speaking his terrible English loudly; it did not occur to him to doubt himself.

Later, as they discussed the price of the land, Edusco said, 'Look, my brother. You won't sell it at that price, nobody will buy. *Ife esika kita.* The recession is biting everybody.'

694

'Bros, bring up your hand a little, this is land in Maitama we are talking about, not land in your village,' Obinze said.

'Your stomach is full. What else do you want? You see, this is the problem with you Igbo people. You don't do brother-brother. That is why I like Yoruba people, they look out for one another. Do you know that the other day I went to the Inland Revenue office near my house and one man there, an Igbo man, I saw his name and spoke to him in Igbo and he did not even answer me! A Hausa man will speak Hausa to his fellow Hausa man. A Yoruba man will see a Yoruba person anywhere and speak Yoruba. But an Igbo man will speak English to an Igbo man. I am even surprised that you are speaking Igbo to me.'

'It's true,' Obinze said. 'It's sad, it's the legacy of being a defeated people. We lost the Biafran war and learned to be ashamed.'

'It is just selfishness!' Edusco said, uninterested in Obinze's intellectualizing. 'The Yoruba man is there helping his brother, but you Igbo people? *I ga-asikwa*. Look at you now quoting me this price.'

'Okay, Edusco, why don't I give you the land for free? Let me go and bring the title and give it to you now.'

Edusco laughed. Edusco liked him, he could tell; he imagined Edusco talking about him in a gathering of other self-made Igbo men, men who were brash and striving, who juggled huge businesses and supported vast extended families. *Obinze ma ife,* he imagined Edusco saying. *Obinze is not like some of these useless small boys with money. This one is not stupid.*

Obinze looked at his almost-empty bottle of Gulder. It was strange how lost of lustre everything was without Ifemelu; even the taste of his favourite beer was different. He should have brought her with him to Abuja. It was stupid to claim that he needed time to think things over when all he was doing was hiding from a truth he already knew. She had called him a coward, and there was indeed a cowardliness in his fear of disorder, of disrupting what he did not even want: his life with Kosi, that second skin that had never quite fitted him snugly.

'Okay, Edusco,' Obinze said, suddenly feeling drained. 'I am not going to eat the land if I don't sell it.'

Edusco looked startled. 'You mean you agree to my price?'

'Yes,' Obinze said.

After Edusco left, Obinze called Ifemelu over and over but she did not answer. Perhaps her ringer was switched off, and she was eating at her dining table, wearing that pink T-shirt she wore so often, with the small hole at the neck, and HEARTBREAKER CAFÉ written across the front; her nipples, when they got hard, would punctuate those words like inverted commas. Thinking of her pink T-shirt aroused him. Or perhaps she was reading in bed, her abada wrapper spread over her like a blanket, wearing plain black boyshorts and nothing else.

All her underwear was plain black boyshorts; girly underwear amused her. Once, he had picked up those boyshorts from the floor where he had flung them after rolling them down her legs, and looked at the milky crust on the crotch, and she laughed and said, 'Ah, you want to smell it? I've never understood that whole business of smelling underwear.' Or perhaps she was on her laptop, working on the blog. Or out with Ranyinudo. Or on the phone with Dike. Or perhaps with some man in her living room, telling him about Graham Greene. A queasiness roiled in him at the thought of her with anybody else. Of course she would not be with anyone else, not so soon. Still, there was that unpredictable stubbornness in her; she might do it to hurt him. When she told him, that first day, 'I always saw the ceiling with other men,' he wondered how many there had been. He wanted to ask her, but he did not, because he feared she would tell him the truth and he feared he would forever be tormented by it. She knew, of course, that he loved her but he wondered if she knew how it consumed him, how each day was infected by her, affected by her; and how she wielded power over even his sleep. 'Kimberly adores her husband, and her husband adores himself. She should leave him but she never will,' she said once, about the woman she had worked for in America, the woman with *obi ocha*. Ifemelu's words had been light, free of shadow, and yet he heard in them the sting of other meanings.

When she told him about her American life, he listened with a keenness close to desperation. He wanted to be a part of everything she had done, be familiar with every emotion she had felt. Once she had told him, 'The thing about cross-cultural relationships is that you spend so much time explaining. My ex-boyfriends and I spent a lot of time explaining. I sometimes wondered whether we would even have anything at all to say to each other if we were from the same place,' and it pleased him to hear that, because it gave his relationship with her a depth, a lack of trifling novelty. They were from the same place and they still had a lot to say to each other.

They were talking about American politics once when she said, 'I like America. It's really the only place else where I could live apart from here. But one day a bunch of Blaine's friends and I were talking about kids and I realized that if I ever have children, I don't want them to have American childhoods. I don't want them to say "Hi" to adults, I want them to say "Good morning" and "Good afternoon." I don't want them to mumble "Good" when somebody says "How are you?" to them. Or to raise five fingers when asked how old they are. I want them to say "I'm fine, thank you" and "I'm five years old." I don't want a child who feeds on praise and expects a star for effort and talks back to adults in the name of self-expression. Is that terribly conservative? Blaine's friends said it was and for them, "conservative" is the worst insult you can get.'

He had laughed, wishing he had been there with the 'bunch of friends', and he wanted that imaginary child to be his, that conservative child with good manners. He told her, 'The child will turn eighteen and paint her hair purple,' and she said, 'Yes, but by then I would have kicked her out of the house.'

At the Abuja airport on his way back to Lagos, he thought of going to the international wing instead, buying a ticket to somewhere improbable, like Malabo. Then he felt a passing self-disgust because he would not, of course, do it; he would instead do what he was expected to do. He was boarding his Lagos flight when Kosi called.

'Is the flight on time? Remember we are taking Nigel out for his birthday,' she said.

'Of course I remember.'

A pause from her end. He had snapped.

'I'm sorry,' he said. 'I have a funny headache.'

'Darling, *ndo*. I know you're tired,' she said. 'See you soon.'

He hung up and thought about the day their baby, slippery, curly-haired Buchi, was born at the Woodlands Hospital in Houston, how Kosi had turned to him while he was still fiddling with his latex gloves and said, with something like apology, 'Darling, we'll have a boy next time.' He had recoiled. He realized then that she did not know him. She did not know him at all. She did not know he was indifferent about the gender of their child. And he felt a gentle contempt towards her,

699

for wanting a boy because they were supposed to want a boy, and for being able to say, fresh from birthing their first child, those words 'we'll have a boy next time'. Perhaps he should have talked more with her, about the baby they were expecting and about everything else, because although they exchanged pleasant sounds and were good friends and shared comfortable silences, they did not really talk. But he had never tried, because he knew that the questions he asked of life were entirely different from hers.

He knew this from the beginning, had sensed it in their first conversation after a friend introduced them at a wedding. She was wearing a satin bridesmaid's dress in fuchsia, cut low to show a cleavage he could not stop looking at, and somebody was making a speech, describing the bride as 'a woman of virtue' and Kosi nodded eagerly and whispered to him, 'She is a true woman of virtue.' It surprised him, that she could use the word 'virtue' without the slightest irony, as was done in the badly written articles in the women's section of the weekend newspapers. *The minister's wife is a homely woman of virtue.* Still, he had wanted her, chased her with a lavish single-mindedness. He had never seen a woman with such a perfect incline to her cheekbones that made her entire face seem so alive, so architectural, lifting when she smiled. He was also newly rich and newly disoriented: one week he was broke and squatting in his cousin's flat and the next he had millions of naira in his bank account. Kosi became a touchstone of realness. If he could be with her, so extraordinarily beautiful and yet so ordinary, predictable and domestic and dedicated, then perhaps his life would start to seem believably his. She moved into his house from the flat she shared with a friend and arranged her perfume bottles on his dresser, citrusy scents that he came to associate with home, and she sat in the BMW beside him as though it had always been his car, and she casually suggested trips abroad as though he had always been able to travel, and when they showered together, she scrubbed him with a rough sponge, even between his toes, until he felt reborn. Until he owned his new life. She did not share his interests – she was a literal person who did not read, she was content rather than curious about the world – but he felt grateful to her, fortunate to be with her. Then she told him her relatives were asking what his intentions were. 'They just keep asking,' she said and stressed the 'they', to exclude herself from the marriage clamour. He recognized, and disliked, her manipulation. Still, he married her. They were living together anyway, and he was not unhappy, and he imagined that she would, with time, gain a certain heft. She had not, after four years, except physically, in a way that he thought made her look even more beautiful, fresher, with fuller hips and breasts, like a well-watered houseplant.

It amused Obinze, that Nigel had decided to move to Nigeria, instead of simply visiting whenever

Obinze needed to present his white General Manager. The money was good, Nigel could now live the kind of life in Essex that he would never have imagined before, but he wanted to live in Lagos, at least for a while. And so Obinze's gleeful waiting commenced, for Nigel to weary of pepper soup and nightclubs and drinking at the shacks in Kuramo Beach. But Nigel was staying put, in his flat in Ikoyi, with a live-in house help and his dog. He no longer said, 'Lagos has so much flavour,' and he complained more about the traffic and he had finally stopped moping about his last girlfriend, a girl from Benue with a pretty face and dissembling manner, who had left him for a wealthy Lebanese businessman.

'The bloke's completely bald,' Nigel had told Obinze.

'The problem with you, my friend, is you love too easily and too much. Anybody could see the girl was a fake, looking for the next bigger thing,' Obinze told him.

'Don't say "bigger thing" like that, mate!' Nigel said.

Now he had met Ulrike, a lean, angular-faced woman with the body of a young man, who worked at an embassy and seemed determined to sulk her way through her Nigerian posting. At dinner, she wiped her cutlery with the napkin before she began eating.

'You don't do that in your country, do you?' Obinze asked coldly. Nigel darted a startled glance at him.

702

'Actually I do,' Ulrike said, squarely meeting his gaze.

Kosi patted his thigh under the table, as though to calm him down, which irritated him. Nigel, too, was irritating him, suddenly talking about the town houses Obinze was planning to build, how exciting the new architect's design was. A timid attempt to end Obinze's conversation with Ulrike.

'Fantastic plan inside, made me think of some of those pictures of fancy lofts in New York,' Nigel said.

'Nigel, I'm not using that plan. An open kitchen plan will never work for Nigerians and we are targeting Nigerians because we are selling, not renting. Open kitchen plans are for expats and expats don't buy property here.' He had already told Nigel many times that Nigerian cooking was not cosmetic, with all that pounding. It was sweaty and spicy and Nigerians preferred to present the final product, not the process.

'No more work talk!' Kosi said brightly. 'Ulrike, have you tried any Nigerian food?'

Obinze got up abruptly and went into the bathroom. He called Ifemelu and felt himself getting enraged when she still did not pick up. He blamed her. He blamed her for making him a person who was not entirely in control of what he was feeling.

Nigel came into the bathroom. 'What's wrong, mate?' Nigel's cheeks were bright red, as they always were when he drank. Obinze stood by the sink holding his phone, that drained lassitude spreading over him again. He wanted to tell Nigel, Nigel was perhaps the only friend he fully trusted, but Nigel fancied Kosi. 'She's all woman, mate,' Nigel had said to him once, and he saw in Nigel's eyes the tender and crushed longing of a man for that which was forever unattainable. Nigel would listen to him, but Nigel would not understand.

'Sorry, I shouldn't have been rude to Ulrike,' Obinze said. 'I'm just tired. I think I'm coming down with malaria.'

That night, Kosi sidled close to him, in offering. It was not a statement of desire, her caressing his chest and reaching down to take his penis in her hand, but a votive offering. A few months ago, she had said she wanted to start seriously 'trying for our son'. She did not say 'trying for our second child', she said 'trying for our son', and it was the kind of thing she learned in her church. *There is power in the spoken word. Claim your miracle.* He remembered how, months into trying to get pregnant the first time, she began to say with sulky righteousness, 'All my friends who lived very rough lives are pregnant.'

After Buchi was born, he had agreed to a thanksgiving service at Kosi's church, a crowded hall full of lavishly dressed people, people who were Kosi's friends, Kosi's kind. And he had thought of them as a sea of simple brutes, clapping, swaying simple brutes, all of them accepting and pliant before the pastor in his designer suit.

'What's wrong, darling?' Kosi asked, when he remained limp in her hand. 'Are you feeling well?'

'Just tired.'

Her hair was covered in a black hair net, her face coated in a cream that smelled of peppermint, which he had always liked. He turned away from her. He had been turning away since the day he first kissed Ifemelu. He should not compare, but he did. Ifemelu demanded of him. 'No, don't come yet, I'll kill you if you come,' she would say, or 'No, baby, don't move,' then she would dig into his chest and move at her own rhythm, and when finally she arched her back and let out a sharp cry, he felt accomplished to have satisfied her. She expected to be satisfied, but Kosi did not. Kosi always met his touch with complaisance, and sometimes he would imagine her pastor telling her that a wife should have sex with her husband, even if she didn't feel like it, otherwise the husband would find solace in a Jezebel.

'I hope you're not getting sick,' she said.

'I'm okay.' Ordinarily he would hold her, slowly rub her back until she fell asleep. But he could not get himself to do so now. So many times in the past weeks he had started to tell her about Ifemelu but had stopped. What would he say? It would sound like something from a silly film. *I am in love with another woman. There's someone else. I'm leaving you.* That these were words that anybody could say seriously, outside a film and outside the pages of a book, seemed odd. Kosi was wrapping her arms around him. He eased away and mumbled something about his stomach being upset and went into the toilet. She had put a new potpourri, a mix of dried leaves and seeds in a purple bowl, on the cover of the toilet tank. The too-strong lavender scent choked him. He emptied the bowl into the toilet and then instantly felt remorseful. She had meant well. She did not know that the too-strong scent of lavender would be unappealing to him, after all.

The first time he saw Ifemelu at Jazzhole, he had come home and told Kosi, 'Ifemelu is in town. I had a drink with her,' and Kosi had said, 'Oh, your girlfriend in university,' with an indifference so indifferent that he did not entirely trust it.

Why had he told her? Perhaps because he had sensed even then the force of what he felt, and he wanted to prepare her, to tell her in stages. But how could she not see that he had changed? How could she not see it on his face? In how much time he spent alone in his study, and in how often he went out, how late he stayed? He had hoped, selfishly, that it might alienate her, provoke her. But she always nodded, glib and accepting nods, when he told her he had been at the club. Or at Okwudiba's. Once he said that he was still chasing the difficult deal with the new Arab owners of Megatel, and he had said 'the deal' casually, as if she already knew about it, and she made vague, encouraging sounds. But he was not even involved at all with Megatel.

★   ★   ★

706

The next morning, he woke up unrested, his mind furred with a great sadness. Kosi was already up and bathed, sitting in front of her dressing table, which was full of creams and potions so carefully arranged that he sometimes imagined putting his hands under the table and overturning it, just to see how all those bottles would fare.

'You haven't made me eggs in a while, The Zed,' she said, coming over to kiss him when she saw that he was awake. And so he made her eggs, and played with Buchi in the living room downstairs, and after Buchi fell asleep, he read the newspapers, all the time his head furred with that sadness. Ifemelu was still not taking his calls. He went upstairs to the bedroom. Kosi was cleaning out a closet. A pile of shoes, high heels sticking up, lay on the floor. He stood by the door and said quietly, 'I'm not happy, Kosi. I love somebody else. I want a divorce. I will make sure you and Buchi lack nothing.'

'What?' She turned from the mirror to look at him blankly.

'I'm not happy.' It was not how he had planned to say it, but he had not even planned what to say. 'I'm in love with somebody. I will make sure . . .'

She raised her hand, her open palm facing him, to make him stop talking. Say no more, her hand said. Say no more. And it irked him that she did not want to know more. Her palm was pale, almost diaphanous, and he could see the greenish criss-cross of her veins. She lowered her hand. Then, slowly, she sank to her knees. It was an easy descent for her, sinking to her knees, because she did that often when she prayed, in the TV room upstairs, with the house help and nanny and whoever else was staying with them. 'Buchi, shh,' she would say in between the words of prayer, while Buchi would continue her toddler talk, but at the end Buchi always squeaked in a high piping voice, 'Amen!' When Buchi said 'Amen!' with that delight, that gusto, Obinze feared she would grow up to be a woman who, with that word 'amen', would squash the questions she wanted to ask of the world. And now Kosi was sinking to her knees before him and he did not want to comprehend what she was doing.

'Obinze, this is a family,' Kosi said. 'We have a child. She needs you. I need you. We have to keep this family together.'

She was kneeling and begging him not to leave and he wished she would be furious instead.

'Kosi, I love another woman. I hate to hurt you like this and . . .'

'It's not about another woman, Obinze,' Kosi said, rising to her feet, her voice steeling, her eyes hardening. 'It's about keeping this family together! You took a vow before God. I took a vow before God. I am a good wife. We have a marriage. Do you think you can just destroy this family because your old girlfriend came into town? Do you know what it means to be a responsible father? You have a responsibility to that child downstairs! What you do today can ruin her life and make her damaged until the day she dies! And all because your old girlfriend came back from America? Because you have had acrobatic sex that reminded you of your time in university?'

Obinze backed away. So she knew. He left and went into his study and locked the door. He loathed Kosi, for knowing all this time and pretending she didn't know, and for the sludge of humiliation it left in his stomach. He had been keeping a secret that was not even a secret. A multilayered guilt weighed him down, guilt not only for wanting to leave Kosi, but for having married her at all. He could not first marry her, knowing very well that he should not have done so, and now, with a child, want to leave her. She was determined to remain married and it was the least he owed her, to remain married. Panic lanced through him at the thought of remaining married; without Ifemelu, the future loomed as an endless, joyless tedium. Then he told himself that he was being silly and dramatic. He had to think of his daughter. Yet as he sat on his chair and swivelled to look for a book on the shelf, he felt himself already in flight.

Because he had retreated to his study, and slept on the couch there, because they had said nothing else to each other, he thought Kosi would not want to go to his friend Ahmed's child's christening party the next day. But in the morning Kosi laid out, on their bed, her blue lace long skirt, his blue Senegalese caftan, and in between, Buchi's flouncy blue velvet dress. She had never done that before, laid out colour-coordinated outfits for them all. Downstairs, he saw that she had made pancakes, the thick ones he liked, set out on the breakfast table. Buchi had spilled some Ovaltine on her table mat.

'Hezekiah has been calling me,' Kosi said musingly, about his cousin in Awka, who called only when he wanted money. 'He sent a text to say he can't reach you. I don't know why he pretends not to know that you ignore his calls.'

It was an odd thing for her to say, talking about Hezekiah's pretence while immersed in pretence herself; she was putting cubes of fresh pineapple on his plate, as if the previous night had never happened.

'But you should do something for him, no matter how small, otherwise he will not leave you alone,' she said.

'Do something for him' meant give him money and Obinze, all of a sudden, hated that tendency of Igbo people to resort to euphemism whenever they spoke of money, to indirect references, to gesturing instead of pointing. Find something for this person. Do something for that person. It riled him. It seemed cowardly, especially for a people who otherwise were blisteringly direct. *Fucking coward*, Ifemelu had called him. There was something cowardly even in his texting and calling her,

710

knowing she would not respond; he could have gone over to her flat and knocked on her door, even if only to have her ask him to leave. And there was something cowardly in his not telling Kosi again that he wanted a divorce, in his leaning back into the ease of Kosi's denial. Kosi took a piece of pineapple from his plate and ate it. She was unfaltering, single-minded, calm.

'Hold Daddy's hand,' she told Buchi as they walked into Ahmed's festive compound that afternoon. She wanted to will normalcy back.

She wanted to will a good marriage into being. She was carrying a present wrapped in silver paper, for Ahmed's baby. In the car, she had told him what it was, but already he had forgotten. Canopies and buffet tables dotted the massive compound, which was green and landscaped, with the promise of a swimming pool in the back. A live band was playing. Two clowns were running around. Children dancing and shrieking.

'They are using the same band we used for Buchi's party,' Kosi whispered. She had wanted a big party to celebrate Buchi's birth, and he had floated through that day, a bubble of air between him and the party. When the MC said 'the new father', he had been strangely startled to realize that the MC meant him, that he was really the new father. A father.

Ahmed's wife, Sike, was hugging him, tugging Buchi's cheeks, people milling about, laughter thick in the air's clasp. They admired the new baby,

asleep in the crook of her bespectacled grandmother's arms. And it struck Obinze that, a few
years ago, they were attending weddings, now it
was christenings and soon it would be funerals.
They would die. They would all die after trudging
through lives in which they were neither happy
nor unhappy. He tried to shake off the morose
shadow that was enveloping him. Kosi took Buchi
over to the cluster of women and children near
the living room entrance; there was some sort of
game being played in a circle, at the centre
of which was a red-lipped clown. Obinze watched
his daughter – her ungainly walk, the blue band,
speckled with silk flowers, that sat on her head of
thick hair, the way she looked up imploringly at
Kosi, her expression reminding him of his mother.
He could not bear the thought of Buchi growing
up to resent him, to lack something that he should
have been for her. But it wasn't whether or not he
left Kosi that should matter, it was how often
he saw Buchi. He would live in Lagos, after all,
and he would make sure he saw her as often
as he could. Many people grew up without fathers.
He himself had, although he had always had the
consoling spirit of his father, idealized, frozen in
joyful childhood memories. Since Ifemelu came
back, he found himself seeking stories of men who
had left their marriages, and willing the stories to
end well, the children more contented with separated parents than with married unhappy parents.
But most of the stories were of resentful children

712

who were bitter about divorce, children who had wanted even unhappy parents to remain together. Once, at his club, he had perked up as a young man talked to some friends about his own parents' divorce, how he had felt relieved by it, because their unhappiness had been heavy. 'Their marriage just blocked the blessings in our life, and the worst part is that they didn't even fight.'

Obinze, from the other end of the bar, had said, 'Good!' drawing strange looks from everyone.

He was still watching Kosi and Buchi talk to the red-lipped clown, when Okwudiba arrived. 'The Zed!'

They hugged, thumped backs.

'How was China?' Obinze asked.

'These Chinese people, ehn. Very wily people. You know the previous idiots in my project had signed a lot of nonsense deals with the Chinese. We wanted to review some of the agreements but these Chinese, fifty of them will come to a meeting and bring papers and just tell you "Sign here, sign here!" They will wear you down with negotiation until they have your money and also your wallet.' Okwudiba laughed. 'Come, let's go upstairs. I hear that Ahmed packed bottles of Dom Pérignon there.'

Upstairs, in what seemed to be a dining room, the heavy burgundy drapes were drawn, shutting out the daylight, and a bright elaborate chandelier, like a wedding cake made of crystals, hung down from the middle of the ceiling. Men were seated around the large oak table, which was crowded with bottles of wine and liquor, with dishes of rice and meat and salads. Ahmed was in and out, giving instructions to the server, listening in on conversations and adding a line or two.

'The wealthy don't really care about tribe. But the lower you go, the more tribe matters,' Ahmed was saying when Obinze and Okwudiba came in. Obinze liked Ahmed's sardonic nature. Ahmed had leased strategic rooftops in Lagos just as the mobile phone companies were coming in, and now he sublet the rooftops for their base stations and made what he wryly referred to as the only clean easy money in the country.

Obinze shook hands with the men, most of whom he knew, and asked the server, a young woman who had placed a wineglass in front of him, if he could have a Coke instead. Alcohol would sink him deeper into his marsh. He listened to the conversation around him, the joking, the needling, the telling and retelling. Then they began, as he knew they invariably would, to criticize the government – money stolen, contracts uncompleted, infrastructure left to rot.

'Look, it's very hard to be a clean public official in this country. Everything is set up for you to steal. And the worst part is, people want you to steal. Your relatives want you to steal, your friends want you to steal,' Olu said. He was thin and slouchy, with the easy boastfulness that came with his inherited wealth, his famous surname.

Once, he had apparently been offered a ministerial position and had responded, according to the urban legend, 'But I can't live in Abuja, there's no water, I can't survive without my boats.' Olu had just divorced his wife, Morenike, Kosi's friend from university. He had often badgered Morenike, who was only slightly overweight, about losing weight, about keeping him interested by keeping herself fit. During their divorce, she discovered a cache of pornographic pictures on the home computer, all of obese women, arms and bellies in rolls of fat, and she had concluded, and Kosi agreed, that Olu had a spiritual problem.

'Why does everything have to be a spiritual problem? The man just has a fetish,' Obinze had told Kosi. Now, he sometimes found himself looking at Olu with curious amusement; you could never tell with people.

'The problem is not that public officials steal, the problem is that they steal too much,' Okwudiba said. 'Look at all these governors. They leave their state and come to Lagos to buy up all the land and they will not touch it until they leave office. That is why nobody can afford to buy land these days.'

'It's true! Land speculators are just spoiling prices for everybody. And the speculators are guys in government. We have serious problems in this country,' Ahmed said.

'But it's not just Nigeria. There are land speculators everywhere in the world,' Eze said. Eze was the wealthiest man in the room, an owner of oil wells, and as many of the Nigerian wealthy were, he was free of angst, an obliviously happy man. He collected art and he told everyone that he collected art. It reminded Obinze of his mother's friend Aunty Chinelo, a professor of literature who had come back from a short stay at Harvard and told his mother over dinner at their dining table, 'The problem is we have a very backward bourgeoisie in this country. They have money but they need to become sophisticated. They need to learn about wine.' And his mother had replied, mildly, 'There are many different ways to be poor in the world but increasingly there seems to be one single way to be rich.' Later, after Aunty Chinelo left, his mother said, 'How silly. Why should they learn about wine?' It had struck Obinze – they need to learn about wine – and, in a way, it had disappointed him, too, because he had always liked Aunty Chinelo. He imagined that somebody had told Eze something similar – you need to collect art, you need to learn about art – and so the man had gone after art with the zeal of an invented interest. Every time Obinze saw Eze, and heard him talk fumblingly about his collection, he was tempted to tell Eze to give it all away and free himself.

'Land prices are no problem for people like you, Eze,' Okwudiba said.

Eze laughed, a laugh of preening agreement. He had taken off his red blazer and hung it on his

716

chair. He teetered, in the name of style, on dandyism; he always wore primary colours, and his belt buckles were always large and prominent, like buck-teeth.

From the other end of the table, Mekkus was saying, 'Do you know that my driver said he passed WAEC, but the other day I told him to write a list and he cannot write at all! He cannot spell "boy" and "cat"! Wonderful!'

'Speaking of drivers, my friend was telling me the other day that his driver is an economic homosexual, that the man follows men who give him money, meanwhile he has a wife and children at home,' Ahmed said.

'Economic homosexual!' somebody repeated, to loud general laughter. Charlie Bombay seemed particularly amused. He had a rough scarred face, the kind of man who would be most himself in the middle of a pack of loud men, eating peppery meat, drinking beer and watching Arsenal.

'The Zed! You are really quiet today,' Okwudiba said, now on his fifth glass of champagne. '*Aru adikwa?*'

Obinze shrugged. 'I'm fine. Just tired.'

'But The Zed is always quiet,' Mekkus said. 'He is a gentleman. Is it because he came here to sit with us? The man reads poems and Shakespeare. Correct Englishman.' Mekkus laughed loudly at his own non-joke. At university, he had been brilliant with electronics, he fixed CD players that were considered lost causes, and his was the first personal computer Obinze had ever seen. He graduated and went to America, then came back a short while afterwards, very furtive and very wealthy from what many said was a massive credit card fraud. His house was studded with CCTV cameras; his security men had automatic guns. And now, at the merest mention of America in a conversation, he would say, 'You know I can never enter America after the deal I did there,' as though to take the sting from the whispers that trailed him.

'Yes, The Zed is a serious gentleman,' Ahmed said. 'Can you imagine Sike was asking me whether I know anybody like The Zed that I can introduce to her sister? I said, Ahn-ahn, you are not looking for somebody like me to marry your sister and instead you are looking for somebody like The Zed, imagine o!'

'No, The Zed is not quiet because he is a gentleman,' Charlie Bombay said, in his slow manner, his thick Igbo accent adding extra syllables to his words, halfway through a bottle of cognac that he had put territorially in front of himself. 'It is because he doesn't want anybody to know how much money he has!'

They laughed. Obinze had always imagined that Charlie Bombay was a wife beater. There was no reason for him to; he knew nothing of Charlie Bombay's personal life, had never even seen his wife. Still, every time he saw Charlie Bombay, he imagined him beating his wife with a thick leather belt. He seemed full of violence, this swaggering, powerful man, this godfather who had paid for his state governor's campaign and now had a monopoly on almost every business in that state.

'Don't mind The Zed, he thinks we don't know that he owns half the land in Lekki,' Eze said.

Obinze produced an obligatory chuckle. He brought out his phone and quickly sent Ifemelu a text: *Please talk to me.*

'We haven't met, I'm Dapo,' the man sitting on the other side of Okwudiba said, reaching across to shake Obinze's hand enthusiastically, as though Obinze had just sprung into existence. Obinze enclosed his hand in a half-hearted shake. Charlie Bombay had mentioned his wealth, and suddenly he was interesting to Dapo.

'Are you into oil too?' Dapo asked.

'No,' Obinze said shortly. He had heard snatches of Dapo's conversation earlier, his work in oil consulting, his children in London. Dapo was probably one of those who installed their wife and children in England and then came back to Nigeria to chase money.

'I was just saying that the Nigerians who keep complaining about the oil companies don't understand that this economy will collapse without them,' Dapo said.

'You must be very confused if you think the oil companies are doing us a favour,' Obinze said. Okwudiba gave him an astonished look; the coldness of his tone was out of character. 'The

Nigerian government basically finances the oil industry with cash calls, and the big oils are planning to withdraw from onshore operations anyway. They want to leave that to the Chinese and focus on offshore operations only. It's like a parallel economy; they keep offshore, only invest in high-tech equipment, pump up oil from thousands of kilometres deep. No local crew. Oil workers flown in from Houston and Scotland. So, no, they are not doing us a favour.'

'Yes!' Mekkus said. 'And they are all common riff-raff. All those underwater plumbers and deep-sea divers and people who know how to repair maintenance robots underwater. Common riff-raff, all of them. You see them in the British Airways lounge. They have been on the rig for one month with no alcohol and by the time they get to the airport they are already stinking drunk and they make fools of themselves on the flight. My cousin used to be a flight attendant and she said that it got to a point that the airlines had to make these men sign agreements about drinking, otherwise they wouldn't let them fly.'

'But The Zed doesn't fly British Airways, so he wouldn't know,' Ahmed said. He had once laughed at Obinze's refusal to fly British Airways, because it was, after all, what the big boys flew.

'When I was a regular man in economy, British Airways treated me like shit from a bad diarrhoea,' Obinze said.

The men laughed. Obinze was hoping his phone

would vibrate, and chafing under his hope. He got up.

'I need to find the toilet.'

'It's just straight down,' Mekkus said.

Okwudiba followed him out.

'I'm going home,' Obinze said. 'Let me find Kosi and Buchi.'

'The Zed, *o gini*? What is it? Is it just tiredness?'

They were standing by the curving staircase, hemmed by an ornate balustrade.

'You know Ifemelu is back,' Obinze said, and just saying her name warmed him.

'I know.' Okwudiba meant that he knew more.

'It's serious. I want to marry her.'

'Ahn-ahn, have you become a Muslim without telling us?'

'Okwu, I'm not joking. I should never have married Kosi. I knew it even then.'

Okwudiba took a deep breath and exhaled, as though to brush aside the alcohol. 'Look, The Zed, many of us didn't marry the woman we truly loved. We married the woman that was around when we were ready to marry. So forget this thing. You can keep seeing her, but no need for this kind of white-people behaviour. If your wife has a child for somebody else or if you beat her, that is a reason for divorce. But to get up and say you have no problem with your wife but you are leaving for another woman? *Haba*. We don't behave like that, please.'

Kosi and Buchi were standing at the bottom of the stairs. Buchi was crying. 'She fell,' Kosi said. 'She said Daddy must carry her.'

Obinze began to descend the stairs. 'Buch-Buch! What happened?' Before he got to her, she already had her arms outstretched, waiting for him.

CHAPTER 55

O ne day, Ifemelu saw the male peacock dance, its feathers fanned out in a giant halo. The female stood by pecking at something on the ground and then, after a while, it walked away, indifferent to the male's great flare of feathers. The male seemed suddenly to totter, perhaps from the weight of its feathers or from the weight of rejection. Ifemelu took a picture for her blog. She wondered what Obinze would think of it; she remembered how he had asked if she had ever seen the male dance. Memories of him so easily invaded her mind; she would, in the middle of a meeting at an advertising agency, remember Obinze pulling out an ingrown hair on her chin with tweezers, her face up on a pillow, and him very close and very keen in examination. Each memory stunned her with its blinding luminosity. Each brought with it a sense of unassailable loss, a great burden hurtling towards her, and she wished she could duck, lower herself so that it would bypass her, so that she would save herself. Love was a kind of grief. This was what the novelists meant by suffering.

She had often thought it a little silly, the idea of suffering for love, but now she understood. She carefully avoided the street in Victoria Island where his club was, and she no longer shopped at the Palms and she imagined him, too, avoiding her part of Ikoyi, keeping away from Jazzhole. She had not run into him anywhere.

At first she played 'Yori Yori' and 'Obi Mu O' endlessly and then she stopped, because the songs brought to her memories a finality, as though they were dirges. She was wounded by the half-heartedness in his texting and calling, the limpness of his efforts. He loved her, she knew, but he lacked a certain strength; his backbone was softened by duty. When she put up the post, written after a visit to Ranyinudo's office, about the government's demolishing of hawkers' shacks, an anonymous commenter wrote, *This is like poetry*. And she knew it was him. She just knew.

> It is morning. A truck, a government truck, stops near the tall office building, beside the hawkers' shacks, and men spill out, men hitting and destroying and leveling and trampling. They destroy the shacks, reduce them to flat pieces of wood. They are doing their job, wearing 'demolish' like crisp business suits. They themselves eat in shacks like these, and if all the shacks like these disappeared in Lagos, they will go lunchless, unable to afford anything

else. But they are smashing, trampling, hitting. One of them slaps a woman, because she does not grab her pot and her wares and run. She stands there and tries to talk to them. Later, her face is burning from the slap as she watches her biscuits buried in dust. Her eyes trace a line towards the bleak sky. She does not know yet what she will do but she will do something, she will regroup and recoup and go somewhere else and sell her beans and rice and spaghetti cooked to a near mush, her Coke and sweets and biscuits.

It is evening. Outside the tall office building, daylight is fading and the staff buses are waiting. Women walk up to them, wearing flat slippers and telling slow stories of no consequence. Their high-heeled shoes are in their bags. From one woman's unzipped bag, a heel sticks out like a dull dagger. The men walk more quickly to the buses. They walk under a cluster of trees which, only hours ago, housed the livelihoods of food hawkers. There, drivers and messengers bought their lunch. But now the shacks are gone. They are erased, and nothing is left, not a stray biscuit wrapper, not a bottle that once held water, nothing to suggest that they were once there.

Ranyinudo urged her, often, to go out more, to date. 'Obinze always felt a little too cool with himself anyway,' Ranyinudo said, and although Ifemelu knew Ranyinudo was only trying to make her feel better, it still startled her, that everyone else did not think Obinze as near-perfect as she did.

She wrote her blog posts wondering what he would make of them. She wrote of a fashion show she had attended, how the model had twirled around in an ankara skirt, a vibrant swish of blues and greens, looking like a haughty butterfly. She wrote of the woman at the street corner in Victoria Island who joyously said, 'Fine Aunty!' when Ifemelu stopped to buy apples and oranges. She wrote about the views from her bedroom window: a white egret drooped on the compound wall, exhausted from heat; the gateman helping a hawker raise her tray to her head, an act so full of grace that she stood watching long after the hawker had walked away. She wrote about the announcers on radio stations, with their accents so fake and so funny. She wrote about the tendency of Nigerian women to give advice, sincere advice dense with sanctimony. She wrote about the waterlogged neighbourhood crammed with zinc houses, their roofs like squashed hats, and of the young women who lived there, fashionable and savvy in tight jeans, their lives speckled stubbornly with hope: they wanted to open hair salons, to go to university. They believed their turn would come. *We are just one step away from this life in a slum, all of us who live air-conditioned middle-class lives,* she wrote, and wondered if Obinze would agree. The pain of his absence did not decrease with time; it seemed instead to sink in deeper each day, to rouse in her even clearer memories. Still, she was at peace: to be home, to be writing her blog, to have discovered Lagos again. She had, finally, spun herself fully into being.

She was reaching back to her past. She called Blaine to say hello, to tell him she had always thought he was too good, too pure, for her, and he was stilted over the phone, as though resentful of her call, but at the end he said, 'I'm glad you called.' She called Curt and he sounded upbeat, thrilled to hear from her, and she imagined getting back together, being in a relationship free of depth and pain.

'Was it you, those large amounts of money I used to get for the blog?' she asked.

'No,' he said, and she wasn't sure whether to believe him or not. 'So you still blogging?'

'Yes.'

'About race?'

'No, just about life. Race doesn't really work here. I feel like I got off the plane in Lagos and stopped being black.'

'I bet.'

She had forgotten how very American he sounded.

'It's not been the same with anybody else,' he said. She liked hearing that. He called her late at night, Nigerian time, and they talked about what they used to do together. The memories seemed burnished now. He made vague references to visiting her in Lagos and she made vague sounds of assent.

One evening, while she was walking into Terra Kulture to see a play with Ranyinudo and Zemaye, she ran into Fred. They all sat in the restaurant afterwards, drinking smoothies.

'Nice guy,' Ranyinudo whispered to Ifemelu.

At first Fred talked, as before, about music and art, his spirit knotted up with the need to impress.

'I'd like to know what you're like when you're not performing,' Ifemelu said.

He laughed. 'If you go out with me you'll know.'

There was a silence, Ranyinudo and Zemaye looking at Ifemelu expectantly, and it amused her.

'I'll go out with you,' she said.

He took her to a nightclub, and when she said she was bored by the too-loud music and the smoke and the barely clothed bodies of strangers too close to hers, he told her sheepishly that he, too, disliked nightclubs; he had assumed she liked them. They watched films together in her flat, and then in his house in Oniru, where arch paintings hung on his wall. It surprised her that they liked the same films. His cook, an elegant man from Cotonou, made a groundnut stew that she loved. Fred played the guitar for her, and sang, his voice husky, and told her how his dream was to be a lead singer in a folksy band. He was attractive, the kind of attractiveness that grew on you. She liked him. He reached out often to push his glasses up, a small push with his finger, and she thought this endearing. As they lay naked on her bed, all pleasant and all warm, she wished it were different. If only she could feel what she wanted to feel.

And then, on a languorous Sunday evening, seven months since she had last seen him, there Obinze was, at the door of her flat. She stared at him.

'Ifem,' he said.

It was such a surprise to see him, his shaved-bald head and the beautiful gentleness of his face. His eyes were urgent, intense, and she could see the up-down chest movement of his heavy breathing. He was holding a long sheet of paper dense with writing. 'I've written this for you. It's what I would like to know if I were you. Where my mind has been. I've written everything.'

He was holding out the paper, his chest still heaving, and she stood there not reaching out for the paper.

'I know we could accept the things we can't be for each other, and even turn it into the poetic tragedy of our lives. Or we could act. I want to act. I want this to happen. Kosi is a good woman and my marriage was a kind of floating-along contentment but I should never have married her. I always knew that something was missing. I want to raise Buchi, I want to see her every day. But I've been pretending all these months and one day she'll be old enough to know I'm pretending. I moved out of the house today. I'll stay in my flat in Parkview for now and I hope to see Buchi every day if I can. I know it's taken me too long and I know you're moving on and I completely understand if you are ambivalent and need time.'

He paused, shifted. 'Ifem, I'm chasing you. I'm going to chase you until you give this a chance.'

For a long time she stared at him. He was saying what she wanted to hear and yet she stared at him.

'Ceiling,' she said, finally. 'Come in.'

TRIPLE

&

ON WINGS OF EAGLES

Ken Follett was only twenty-seven when he wrote the award-winning novel *Eye of the Needle*, which became an international bestseller. He has since written several equally successful novels including, most recently, *Whiteout*. He is also the author of the non-fiction bestseller, *On Wings of Eagles*. He lives with his family in London and Hertfordshire.

Visit the Ken Follett web site at http://www.ken-follett.com

KEN FOLLETT

TRIPLE
&
ON WINGS
OF EAGLES

PAN BOOKS

Triple first published 1979 by Macdonald General Books.
First published in paperback 1980 by Macdonald Futura.
First published by Pan Books 1998.
On Wings of Eagles first published 1983 by William Collins Sons.
First published in paperback 1984 by Corgi.
First published by Pan Books 1998.

This omnibus first published 2005 by Pan Books
an imprint of Pan Macmillan Ltd
Pan Macmillan, 20 New Wharf Road, London N1 9RR
Basingstoke and Oxford
Associated companies throughout the world
www.panmacmillan.com

ISBN 0 330 44368 2

A CIP catalogue record for this book is available from
the British Library.

Printed and bound in Great Britain by
Mackays of Chatham plc, Chatham, Kent

TRIPLE

It must be appreciated that the only difficult part of making a fission bomb of some sort is the preparation of a supply of fissionable material of adequate purity; the design of the bomb itself is relatively easy . . .

— Encyclopedia Americana

To Al Zuckerman

PROLOGUE

T HERE WAS a time, just once, when they were all
together.

They met many years ago, when they were young,
before all *this* happened; but the meeting cast shadows
far across the decades.

It was the first Sunday in November, 1947, to be exact;
and each of them met all the others – indeed, for a few
minutes they were all in one room. Some of them
immediately forgot the faces they saw and the names
they heard spoken in formal introductions. Some of
them actually forgot the whole day; and when it became
so important, twenty-one years later, they had to pretend
to remember; to stare at blurred photographs and
murmur 'Ah, yes, of course,' in a knowing way.

This early meeting is a coincidence, but not a very
startling one. They were mostly young and able; they
were destined to have power, to take decisions, and to
make changes, each in their different ways, in their
different countries; and those people often meet in
their youth at places like Oxford University. Furthermore, when all this happened, those who were not
involved initially were sucked into it just because they
had met the others at Oxford.

However, it did not seem like an historic meeting at the time. It was just another sherry party in a place where there were too many sherry parties (and, under-graduates would add, not enough sherry). It was an uneventful occasion. Well, almost.

Al Cortone knocked and waited in the hall for a dead man to open the door.

The suspicion that his friend was dead had grown to a conviction in the past three years. First, Cortone had heard that Nat Dickstein had been taken prisoner. Towards the end of the war, stories began to circulate about what was happening to Jews in the Nazi camps. Then, at the end, the grim truth came out.

On the other side of the door, a ghost scraped a chair on the floor and padded across the room.

Cortone felt suddenly nervous. What if Dickstein were disabled, deformed? Suppose he had become unhinged? Cortone had never known how to deal with cripples or crazy men. He and Dickstein had become very close, just for a few days back in 1943; but what was Dickstein like now?

The door opened, and Cortone said, 'Hi, Nat.'

Dickstein stared at him, then his face split in a wide grin and he came out with one of his ridiculous Cockney phrases: 'Gawd, stone the crows!'

Cortone grinned back, relieved. They shook hands, and slapped each other on the back, and let rip some soldierly language just for the hell of it; then they went inside.

Dickstein's home was one high-ceilinged room of an old house in a run-down part of the city. There was a single bed, neatly made up in army fashion; a heavy old wardrobe of dark wood with a matching dresser; and a table piled with books in front of a small window. Cortone thought the room looked bare. If he had to live here he would put some personal stuff all around to make the place look like his own: photographs of his family, souvenirs of Niagara and Miami Beach, his high school football trophy.

Dickstein said, 'What I want to know is, how did you find me?'

'I'll tell you, it wasn't easy.' Cortone took off his uniform jacket and laid it on the narrow bed. 'It took me most of yesterday.' He eyed the only easy chair in the room. Both arms tilted sideways at odd angles, a spring poked through the faded chrysanthemums of the fabric, and one missing foot had been replaced with a copy of Plato's *Theaetetus*. 'Can human beings sit on that?'

'Not above the rank of sergeant. But—'

'They aren't human anyway.'

They both laughed: it was an old joke. Dickstein brought a bentwood chair from the table and straddled it. He looked his friend up and down for a moment and said, 'You're getting fat.'

Cortone patted the slight swell of his stomach. 'We live well in Frankfurt – you really missed out, getting demobilized.' He leaned forward and lowered his voice, as if what he was saying was somewhat confidential. 'I have made a *fortune*. Jewellery, china, antiques all bought for cigarettes and soap. The Germans are starving. And – best of all – the girls will do anything for a Tootsie Roll.' He sat back, waiting for a laugh, but Dickstein just stared at him straight-faced. Disconcerted, Cortone changed the subject. 'One thing you ain't, is fat.'

At first he had been so relieved to see Dickstein still in one piece and grinning the same grin that he had not looked at him closely. Now he realized that his friend was worse than thin: he looked wasted. Nat Dickstein had always been short and slight, but now he seemed all bones. The dead-white skin, and the large brown eyes behind the plastic-rimmed spectacles, accentuated the effect. Between the top of his sock and the cuff of his trouser-leg a few inches of pale shin showed like matchwood. Four years ago Dickstein had been brown, stringy, as hard as the leather soles of his British Army boots. When Cortone talked about his English buddy, as he often did, he would say, 'The toughest, meanest bastard fighting soldier that ever saved my goddamn life, and I ain't shittin' you.'

'Fat? No,' Dickstein said. 'This country is still on iron rations, mate. But we manage.'

'You've known worse.'

Dickstein smiled. 'And eaten it.'

'You got took prisoner.'

'At La Molina.'

'How the hell did they tie you down?'

'Easy.' Dickstein shrugged. 'A bullet broke my leg and I passed out. When I came round I was in a German truck.'

Cortone looked at Dickstein's legs. 'It mended okay?'

'I was lucky. There was a medic in my truck on the POW train – he set the bone.'

Cortone nodded. 'And then the camp...' He thought maybe he should not ask, but he wanted to know.

Dickstein looked away. 'It was all right until they found out I'm Jewish. Do you want a cup of tea? I can't afford whisky.'

'No.' Cortone wished he had kept his mouth shut. 'Anyway, I don't drink whisky in the morning anymore. Life doesn't seem as short as it used to.'

Dickstein's eyes swivelled back toward Cortone. 'They decided to find out how many times they could break a leg in the same place and mend it again.'

'Jesus.' Cortone's voice was a whisper.

'That was the best part,' Dickstein said in a flat monotone. He looked away again.

Cortone said, 'Bastards.' He could not think of anything else to say. There was a strange expression on Dickstein's face; something Cortone had not seen before, something – he realized after a moment – that was very like fear. It was odd. After all, it was over now, wasn't it? 'Well, hell, at least we won, didn't we?' He punched Dickstein's shoulder.

Dickstein grinned. 'We did. Now, what are you doing in England? And how did you find me?'

'I managed to get a stopover in London on my way back to Buffalo. I went to the War Office...' Cortone hesitated. He had gone to the War Office to find out how and when Dickstein died. 'They gave me an address in Stepney,' he continued. 'When I got there,

7

there was only one house left standing in the whole street. In this house, underneath an inch of dust, I find this old man.'

'Tommy Coster.'

'Right. Well, after I drink nineteen cups of weak tea and listen to the story of his life, he sends me to another house around the corner, where I find your mother, drink more weak tea and hear the story of her life. By the time I get your address it's too late to catch the last train to Oxford, so I wait until the morning, and here I am. I only have a few hours – my ship sails tomorrow.'

'You've got your discharge?'

'In three weeks, two days and ninety-four minutes.'

'What are you going to do, back home?'

'Run the family business. I've discovered, in the last couple of years, that I am a terrific businessman.'

'What business is your family in? You never told me.'

'Trucking,' Cortone said shortly. 'And you? What is this with Oxford University, for Christ's sake? What are you studying?'

'Hebrew Literature.'

'You're kidding.'

'I could write Hebrew before I went to school, didn't I ever tell you? My grandfather was a real scholar. He lived in one smelly room over a pie shop in the Mile End Road. I went there every Saturday and Sunday, since before I can remember. I never complained – I loved it. Anyway, what else would I study?'

Cortone shrugged. 'I don't know, atomic physics maybe, or business management. Why study at all?'

'To become happy, clever and rich.'

Cortone shook his head. 'Weird as ever. Lots of girls here?'

'Very few. Besides, I'm busy.'

He thought Dickstein was blushing. 'Liar. You're in love, you fool. I can tell. Who is she?'

'Well, to be honest . . .' Dickstein was embarrassed. 'She's out of reach. A professor's wife. Exotic, intelligent, the most beautiful woman I've ever seen.'

Cortone made a dubious face. 'It's not promising, Nat.'

'I know, but still . . .' Dickstein stood up. 'You'll see what I mean.'

'I get to meet her?'

'Professor Ashford is giving a sherry party. I'm invited. I was just leaving when you got here.' Dickstein put on his jacket.

'A sherry party in Oxford,' Cortone said. 'Wait till they hear about this in Buffalo!'

It was a cold, bright morning. Pale sunshine washed the cream-coloured stone of the city's old buildings. They walked in comfortable silence, hands in pockets, shoulders hunched against the biting November wind which whistled through the streets. Cortone kept muttering, 'Dreaming spires. Fuck.'

There were very few people about, but after they had walked a mile or so Dickstein pointed across the road to a tall man with a college scarf wound around his neck. 'There's the Russian,' he said. He called, 'Hey, Rostov!'

The Russian looked up, waved, and crossed to their side of the street. He had an army haircut, and was too long and thin for his mass-produced suit. Cortone was beginning to think everyone was thin in this country.

Dickstein said, 'Rostov's at Balliol, same college as me. David Rostov, meet Alan Cortone. Al and I were together in Italy for a while. Going to Ashford's house, Rostov?'

The Russian nodded solemnly. 'Anything for a free drink.'

Cortone said, 'You interested in Hebrew Literature too?'

Rostov said, 'No, I'm here to study bourgeois economics.'

Dickstein laughed loudly. Cortone did not see the joke. Dickstein explained, 'Rostov is from Smolensk. He's a member of the CPSU – the Communist Party of the Soviet Union.' Cortone still did not see the joke.

'I thought nobody was allowed to leave Russia,' Cortone said.

Rostov went into a long and involved explanation which had to do with his father's having been a diplomat in Japan when the war broke out. He had an earnest expression which occasionally gave way to a sly smile. Although his English was imperfect, he managed to give Cortone the impression that he was condescending. Cortone turned off, and began to think about how you could love a man as if he was your own brother, fighting side by side with him, and then he could go off and study Hebrew Literature and you would realize you never really knew him at all.

Eventually Rostov said to Dickstein, 'Have you decided yet, about going to Palestine?'

Cortone said, 'Palestine? What for?'

Dickstein looked troubled. 'I haven't decided.'

'You should go,' said Rostov. 'The Jewish National Home will help to break up the last remnants of the British Empire in the Middle East.'

'Is that the Party line?' Dickstein asked with a faint smile.

'Yes,' Rostov said seriously. 'You're a socialist—'

'Of sorts.'

'—and it is important that the new State should be socialist.'

Cortone was incredulous. 'The Arabs are murdering you people out there. Jeez, Nat, you only just escaped from the Germans!'

'I haven't decided,' Dickstein repeated. He shook his head irritably. 'I don't know what to do.' It seemed he did not want to talk about it.

They were walking briskly. Cortone's face was freezing, but he was perspiring beneath his winter uniform. The other two began to discuss a scandal: a man called Mosley – the name meant nothing to Cortone – had been persuaded to enter Oxford in a van and make a speech at the Martyr's Memorial. Mosley was a Fascist, he gathered a moment later. Rostov was arguing that the incident proved how social democracy was closer to Fascism than Communism. Dickstein claimed the undergraduates who organized the event were just trying to be 'shocking'.

Cortone listened and watched the two men. They

were an odd couple: tall Rostov, his scarf like a striped bandage, taking long strides, his too-short trousers flapping like flags; and diminutive Dickstein with big eyes and round spectacles, wearing a demob suit, looking like a skeleton in a hurry. Cortone was no academic, but he figured he could smell out bullshit in any language, and he knew that neither of them was saying what he believed: Rostov was parroting some kind of official dogma, and Dickstein's brittle unconcern masked a different, deeper attitude. When Dickstein laughed about Mosley, he sounded like a child laughing after a nightmare. They both argued cleverly but without emotion: it was like a fencing match with blunted swords.

Eventually Dickstein seemed to realize that Cortone was being left out of the discussion and began to talk about their host. 'Stephen Ashford is a bit eccentric, but a remarkable man,' he said. 'He spent most of his life in the Middle East. Made a small fortune and lost it, by all accounts. He used to do crazy things, like crossing the Arabian Desert on a camel.'

'That might be the least crazy way to cross it,' Cortone said.

Rostov said, 'Ashford has a Lebanese wife.'

Cortone looked at Dickstein. 'She's—'

'She's younger than he is,' Dickstein said hastily. 'He brought her back to England just before the war and became Professor of Semitic Literature here. If he gives you Marsala instead of sherry it means you've overstayed your welcome.'

'People know the difference?' Cortone said.

'This is his house.'

Cortone was half expecting a Moorish villa, but the Ashford home was imitation Tudor, painted white with green woodwork. The garden in front was a jungle of shrubs. The three young men walked up a brick pathway to the house. The front door was open. They entered a small, square hall. Somewhere in the house several people laughed: the party had started. A pair of double doors opened and the most beautiful woman in the world came out.

Cortone was transfixed. He stood and stared as she came across the carpet to welcome them. He heard Dickstein say, 'This is my friend Alan Cortone,' and suddenly he was touching her long brown hand, warm and dry and fine-boned, and he never wanted to let go.

She turned away and led them into the drawing room. Dickstein touched Cortone's arm and grinned: he had known what was going on in his friend's mind.

Cortone recovered his composure sufficiently to say, 'Wow.'

Small glasses of sherry were lined up with military precision on a little table. She handed one to Cortone, smiled, and said, 'I'm Eila Ashford, by the way.'

Cortone took in the details as she handed out the drinks. She was completely unadorned: there was no make-up on her astonishing face, her black hair was straight, and she wore a white dress and sandals – yet the effect was almost like nakedness, and Cortone was embarrassed at the animal thoughts that rushed through his mind as he looked at her.

He forced himself to turn away and study his

surroundings. The room had the unfinished elegance of a place where people are living slightly beyond their means. The rich Persian carpet was bordered by a strip of peeling grey linoleum; someone had been mending the radio, and its innards were all over a kidney table; there were a couple of bright rectangles on the wallpaper where pictures had been taken down; and some of the sherry glasses did not quite match the set. There were about a dozen people in the room.

An Arab wearing a beautiful pearl-grey Western suit was standing at the fireplace, looking at a wooden carving on the mantelpiece. Eila Ashford called him over. 'I want you to meet Yasif Hassan, a friend of my family from home,' she said. 'He's at Worcester College.'

Hassan said, 'I know Dickstein.' He shook hands all around.

Cortone thought he was fairly handsome, for a nigger, and haughty, the way they were when they made some money and got invited to white homes.

Rostov asked him, 'You're from Lebanon?'

'Palestine.'

'Ah!' Rostov became animated. 'And what do you think of the United Nations partition plan?'

'Irrelevant,' the Arab said languidly. 'The British must leave, and my country will have a democratic government.'

'But then the Jews will be in a minority,' Rostov argued.

'They are in a minority in England. Should they be given Surrey as a national home?'

14

'Surrey has never been theirs. Palestine was, once.'

Hassan shrugged elegantly. 'It was – when the Welsh had England, the English had Germany, and the Norman French lived in Scandinavia.' He turned to Dickstein. 'You have a sense of justice – what do you think?'

Dickstein took off his glasses. 'Never mind justice. I want a place to call my own.'

'Even if you have to steal mine?' Hassan said.

'You can have the rest of the Middle East.'

'I don't want it.'

Rostov said, 'This discussion proves the necessity for partition.'

Eila Ashford offered a box of cigarettes. Cortone took one, and lit hers. While the others argued about Palestine, Eila asked Cortone, 'Have you known Dickstein long?'

'We met in 1943,' Cortone said. He watched her brown lips close around the cigarette. She even smoked beautifully. Delicately, she picked a fragment of tobacco from the tip of her tongue.

'I'm terribly curious about him,' she said.

'Why?'

'Everyone is. He's only a boy, and yet he seems so old. Then again, he's obviously a Cockney, but he's not in the least intimidated by all these upper-class Englishmen. But he'll talk about anything except himself.'

Cortone nodded. 'I'm finding out that I don't really know him, either.'

'My husband says he's a brilliant student.'

'He saved my life.'

15

'Good Lord.' She looked at him more closely, as if she were wondering whether he was just being melodramatic. She seemed to decide in his favour. 'I'd like to hear about it.'

A middle-aged man in baggy corduroy trousers touched her shoulder and said, 'How is everything, my dear?'

'Fine,' she said. 'Mr Cortone, this is my husband, Professor Ashford.'

Cortone said, 'How are you.' Ashford was a balding man in ill-fitting clothes. Cortone had been expecting Lawrence of Arabia. He thought: Maybe Nat has a chance after all.

Eila said, 'Mr Cortone was telling me how Nat Dickstein saved his life.'

'Really!' Ashford said.

'It's not a long story,' Cortone said. He glanced over at Dickstein, now deep in conversation with Hassan and Rostov; and noted how the three men displayed their attitudes by the way they stood: Rostov with his feet apart, wagging a finger like a teacher, sure in his dogma; Hassan leaning against a bookcase, one hand in his pocket, smoking, pretending that the international debate about the future of his country was of merely academic interest; Dickstein with arms folded tightly, shoulders hunched, head bowed in concentration, his stance giving the lie to the dispassionate character of his remarks. Cortone heard *The British promised Palestine to the Jews,* and the reply, *Beware the gifts of a thief.* He turned back to the Ashfords and began to tell them the story.

'It was in Sicily, near a place called Ragusa, a hill town,' he said. 'I'd taken a T-force around the outskirts. To the north of the town we came on a German tank in a little hollow, on the edge of a clump of trees. The tank looked abandoned but I put a grenade into it to make sure. As we drove past there was a shot – only one – and a German with a machine gun fell out of a tree. He'd been hiding up there, ready to pick us off as we passed. It was Nat Dickstein who shot him.'

Eila's eyes sparkled with something like excitement, but her husband had gone white. Obviously the professor had no stomach for tales of life and death. Cortone thought: If that upsets you, pop, I hope Dickstein never tells you any of *his* stories.

'The British had come around the town from the other side,' Cortone went on. 'Nat had seen the tank, like I did, and smelled a trap. He had spotted the sniper and was waiting to see if there were any more when we turned up. If he hadn't been so damn smart I'd be dead.'

The other two were silent for a moment. Ashford said, 'It's not long ago, but we forget so fast.'

Eila remembered her other guests. 'I want to talk to you some more before you go,' she said to Cortone. She went across the room to where Hassan was trying to open a pair of doors that gave on to the garden.

Ashford brushed nervously at the wispy hair behind his ears. 'The public hears about the big battles, but I suppose the soldier remembers those little personal incidents.'

Cortone nodded, thinking that Ashford clearly had

17

no conception of what war was like, and wondering if the professor's youth had really been as adventurous as Dickstein claimed. 'Later, I took him to meet my cousins – the family comes from Sicily. We had pasta and wine, and they made a hero of Nat. We were together only for a few days, but we were like brothers, you know?'

'Indeed.'

'When I heard he was taken prisoner, I figured I'd never see him again.'

'Do you know what happened to him?' Ashford said. 'He doesn't say much . . .'

Cortone shrugged. 'He survived the camps.'

'He was fortunate.'

'Was he?'

Ashford looked at Cortone for a moment, confused, then turned away and looked around the room. After a moment he said, 'This is not a very typical Oxford gathering, you know. Dickstein, Rostov and Hassan are somewhat unusual students. You should meet Toby – he's the archetypal undergraduate.' He caught the eye of a red-faced youth in a tweed suit and a very wide paisley tie. 'Toby, come and meet Dickstein's comrade-in-arms – Mr Cortone.'

Toby shook hands and said abruptly, 'Any chance of a tip from the stable? Will Dickstein win?'

'Win what?' Cortone said.

Ashford explained, 'Dickstein and Rostov are to play a chess match – they're both supposed to be terribly good. Toby thinks you might have inside information – he probably wants to bet on the outcome.'

Cortone said, 'I thought chess was an old man's game.'

Toby said, 'Ah!' rather loudly, and emptied his glass. He and Ashford seemed nonplussed by Cortone's remark. A little girl, four or five years old, came in from the garden carrying an elderly grey cat. Ashford introduced her with the coy pride of a man who has become a father in middle age.

'This is Suza,' he said.

The girl said, 'And this is Hezekiah.'

She had her mother's skin and hair; she too would be beautiful. Cortone wondered whether she was really Ashford's daughter. There was nothing of him in her looks. She held out the cat's paw, and Cortone obligingly shook it and said, 'How are you, Hezekiah?'

Suza went over to Dickstein. 'Good morning, Nat. Would you like to stroke Hezekiah?'

'She's very cute,' Cortone said to Ashford. 'I have to talk to Nat. Would you excuse me?' He went over to Dickstein, who was kneeling down and stroking the cat.

Nat and Suza seemed to be pals. He told her, 'This is my friend Alan.'

'We've met,' she said, and fluttered her eyelashes. Cortone thought: She learned that from her mother.

'We were in the war together,' Dickstein continued.

Suza looked directly at Cortone. 'Did you kill people?'

He hesitated. 'Sure.'

'Do you feel bad about it?'

'Not too bad. They were wicked people.'

'Nat feels bad about it. That's why he doesn't like to talk about it too much.'

The kid had got more out of Dickstein than all the grown-ups put together.

The cat jumped out of Suza's arms with surprising agility. She chased after it. Dickstein stood up.

'I wouldn't say Mrs Ashford is out of reach,' Cortone said quietly.

'Wouldn't you?' Dickstein said.

'She can't be more than twenty-five. He's at least twenty years older, and I'll bet he's no pistol. If they got married before the war, she must have been around seventeen at the time. And they don't seem affectionate.'

'I wish I could believe you,' Dickstein said. He was not as interested as he should have been. 'Come and see the garden.'

They went through the French doors. The sun was stronger, and the bitter cold had gone from the air. The garden stretched in a green-and-brown wilderness down to the edge of the river. They walked away from the house.

Dickstein said, 'You don't much like this crowd.'

'The war's over,' Cortone said. 'You and me, we live in different worlds now. All this – professors, chess matches, sherry parties . . . I might as well be on Mars. My life is doing deals, fighting off the competition, making a few bucks. I was fixing to offer you a job in my business, but I guess I'd be wasting my time.'

'Alan . . .'

'Listen, what the hell. We'll probably lose touch now

– I'm not much of a letter writer. But I won't forget that I owe you my life. One of these days you might want to call in the debt. You know where to find me.'

Dickstein opened his mouth to speak, then they heard the voices.

'Oh . . . no, not here, not now . . .' It was a woman.

'Yes!' A man.

Dickstein and Cortone were standing beside a thick box hedge which cut off a corner of the garden: someone had begun to plant a maze and never finished the job. A few steps from where they were a gap opened, then the hedge turned a right angle and ran along the river bank. The voices came clearly from the other side of the foliage.

The woman spoke again, low and throaty. 'Don't, damn you, or I'll scream.'

Dickstein and Cortone stepped through the gap.

Cortone would never forget what he saw there. He stared at the two people and then, appalled, he glanced at Dickstein. Dickstein's face was grey with shock, and he looked ill; his mouth dropped open as he gazed in horror and despair. Cortone looked back at the couple.

The woman was Eila Ashford. The skirt of her dress was around her waist, her face was flushed with pleasure, and she was kissing Yasif Hassan.

CHAPTER ONE

T HE PUBLIC-ADDRESS system at Cairo airport made a noise like a doorbell, and then the arrival of the Alitalia flight from Milan was announced in Arabic, Italian, French and English. Towfik el-Masiri left his table in the buffet and made his way out to the observation deck. He put on his sunglasses to look over the shimmering concrete apron. The Caravelle was already down and taxiing.

Towfik was there because of a cable. It had come that morning from his 'uncle' in Rome, and it had been in code. Any business could use a code for international telegrams, provided it first lodged the key to the code with the post office. Such codes were used more and more to save money – by reducing common phrases to single words – than to keep secrets. Towfik's uncle's cable, transcribed according to the registered code book, gave details of his late aunt's will. However, Towfik had another key, and the message he read was:

OBSERVE AND FOLLOW PROFESSOR FRIEDRICH SCHULZ ARRIVING CAIRO FROM MILAN WEDNESDAY 28 FEBRUARY 1968 FOR SEVERAL DAYS. AGE 51 HEIGHT 180 CM WEIGHT 150

POUNDS HAIR WHITE EYES BLUE NATIONALITY
AUSTRIAN COMPANIONS WIFE ONLY.

The passengers began to file out of the aircraft, and
Towfik spotted his man almost immediately. There was
only one tall, lean white-haired man on the flight. He
was wearing a light blue suit, a white shirt and a tie,
and carrying a plastic shopping bag from a duty-free
store and a camera. His wife was much shorter, and
wore a fashionable mini-dress and a blonde wig. As they
crossed the airfield they looked about them and sniffed
the warm, dry desert air the way most people did the
first time they landed in North Africa.

The passengers disappeared into the arrivals hall.
Towfik waited on the observation deck until the baggage came off the plane, then he went inside and
mingled with the small crowd of people waiting just
beyond the customs barrier.

He did a lot of waiting. That was something they did
not teach you – how to wait. You learned to handle
guns, memorize maps, break open safes and kill people
with your bare hands, all in the first six months of the
training course; but there were no lectures in patience,
no exercises for sore feet, no seminars on tedium. And
it was beginning to seem like *There is something wrong
here* beginning to seem *Lookout lookout* beginning to—

There was another agent in the crowd.

Towfik's subconscious hit the fire alarm while he was
thinking about patience. The people in the little crowd,
waiting for relatives and friends and business acquaint-

ances off the Milan plane, were impatient. They smoked, shifted their weight from one foot to the other, craned their necks and fidgeted. There was a middle-class family with four children, two men in the traditional striped cotton *galabiya* robes, a businessman in a dark suit, a young white woman, a chauffeur with a sign saying FORD MOTOR COMPANY, and—

And a patient man.

Like Towfik, he had dark skin and short hair and wore a European-style suit. At first glance he seemed to be with the middle-class family – just as Towfik would seem, to a casual observer, to be with the businessman in the dark suit. The other agent stood nonchalantly, with his hands behind his back, facing the exit from the baggage hall, looking unobtrusive. There was a streak of paler skin alongside his nose, like an old scar. He touched it, once, in what might have been a nervous gesture, then put his hand behind his back again.

The question was, had he spotted Towfik?

Towfik turned to the businessman beside him and said, 'I never understand why this has to take so long.' He smiled, and spoke quietly, so that the businessman leaned closer to hear him and smiled back; and the pair of them looked like acquaintances having a casual conversation.

The businessman said, 'The formalities take longer than the flight.'

Towfik stole another glance at the other agent. The man stood in the same position, watching the exit. He had not attempted any camouflage. Did that mean that he had not spotted Towfik? Or was it just that he had second-guessed Towfik, by deciding that a piece of camouflage would give him away?

The passengers began to emerge, and Towfik realized there was nothing he could do, either way. He hoped the people the agent was meeting would come out before Professor Schulz.

It was not to be. Schulz and his wife were among the first little knot of passengers to come through.

The other agent approached them and shook hands.

Of course, of course.

The agent was there to meet Schulz.

Towfik watched while the agent summoned porters and ushered the Schulzes away; then he went out by a different exit to his car. Before getting in he took off his jacket and tie and put on sunglasses and a white cotton cap. Now he would not be easily recognizable as the man who had been waiting at the meeting point.

He figured the agent would have parked in a no-waiting zone right outside the main entrance, so he drove that way. He was right. He saw the porters loading the Schulz baggage into the boot of a five-year-old grey Mercedes. He drove on.

He steered his dirty Renault on to the main highway which ran from Heliopolis, where the airport was, to Cairo. He drove at 60 kph and kept to the slow lane. The grey Mercedes passed him two or three minutes later, and he accelerated to keep it within sight. He memorized its number, as it was always useful to be able to recognize the opposition's cars.

The sky began to cloud over. As he sped down the straight, palm-lined highway, Towfik considered what he had found out so far. The cable had told him nothing about Schulz except what the man looked like and the fact that he was an Austrian professor. The meeting at the airport meant a great deal, though. It had been a kind of clandestine VIP treatment. Towfik had the agent figured for a local: everything pointed to that – his clothes, his car, his style of waiting. That meant Schulz was probably here by invitation of the government, but either he or the people he had come to see wanted the visit kept secret.

It was not much. What was Schulz professor *of*? He could be a banker, arms manufacturer, rocketry expert or cotton buyer. He might even be with Al Fatah, but Towfik could not quite see the man as a resurrected Nazi. Still, anything was possible.

Certainly Tel Aviv did not think Schulz was important: if they had, they would not have used Towfik, who was young and inexperienced, for this surveillance. It was even possible that the whole thing was yet another training exercise.

They entered Cairo on the Shari Ramses, and Towfik closed the gap between his car and the Mercedes until there was only one vehicle between them. The grey car turned right on to the Corniche al-Nil, then crossed the river by the 26 July Bridge and entered the Zamalek district of Gezira island.

There was less traffic in the wealthy, dull suburb, and Towfik became edgy about being spotted by the agent at the wheel of the Mercedes. However, two minutes later the other car turned into a residential street near the Officers' Club and stopped outside an apartment block with a jacaranda tree in the garden. Towfik immediately took a right turn and was out of sight before the doors of the other car could open. He parked, jumped out, and walked back to the corner. He was in time to see the agent and the Schulzes disappear into the building followed by a caretaker in *galabiya* struggling with their luggage.

Towfik looked up and down the street. There was nowhere a man could convincingly idle. He returned to his car, backed it around the corner and parked between two other cars on the same side of the road as the Mercedes.

Half an hour later the agent came out alone, got into his car, and drove off.

Towfik settled down to wait.

It went on for two days, then it broke.

Until then the Schulzes behaved like tourists, and seemed to enjoy it. On the first evening they had dinner in a nightclub and watched a troupe of belly-dancers. Next day they did the Pyramids and the Sphinx, with lunch at Groppi's and dinner at the Nile Hilton. In the morning on the third day they got up early and took a taxi to the mosque of Ibn Tulun.

Towfik left his car near the Gayer-Anderson Museum and followed them. They took a perfunctory look around the mosque and headed east on the Shari al-Salibah. They were dawdling, looking at fountains and buildings, peering into dark tiny shops, watching *baladi* women buy onions and peppers and camel's feet at street stalls.

They stopped at a crossroads and went into a tea-shop. Towfik crossed the street to the *sebeel*, a domed fountain behind windows of iron lace, and studied the baroque relief around its walls. He moved on up the street, still within sight of the tea-shop, and spent some time buying four misshapen giant tomatoes from a white-capped stallholder whose feet were bare.

The Schulzes came out of the tea-shop and turned north, following Towfik, into the street market. Here it was easier for Towfik to idle, sometimes ahead of them and sometimes behind. Frau Schulz bought slippers and a gold bangle, and paid too much for a sprig of mint from a half-naked child. Towfik got far enough in front of them to drink a small cup of strong, un-sweetened Turkish coffee under the awning of a café called Nasif's.

They left the street market and entered a covered *souq* specializing in saddlery. Schulz glanced at his wristwatch and spoke to his wife – giving Towfik the first faint tremor of anxiety – and then they walked a little faster until they emerged at Bab Zuweyla, the gateway to the original walled city.

For a few moments the Schulzes were obscured from Towfik's view by a donkey pulling a cart loaded with Ali-Baba jars, their mouths stoppered with crumpled paper. When the cart passed, Towfik saw that Schulz was saying goodbye to his wife and getting into an oldish grey Mercedes.

Towfik cursed under his breath.

The car door slammed and it pulled away. Frau Schulz waved. Towfik read the licence plate – it was the car he had followed from Heliopolis – and saw it go west, then turn left into the Shari Port Said.

Forgetting Frau Schulz, he turned around and broke into a run.

They had been walking for about an hour, but they had covered only a mile. Towfik sprinted through the saddlery *souq* and the street market, dodging around the stalls and bumping into robed men and women in black, dropping his bag of tomatoes in a collision with a Nubian sweeper, until he reached the museum and his car.

He dropped into the driver's seat, breathing hard and grimacing at the pain in his side. He started the engine and pulled away on an interception course for the Shari Port Said.

The traffic was light, so when he hit the main road he guessed he must be behind the Mercedes. He continued southwest, over the island of Roda and the Giza Bridge onto the Giza Road.

Schulz had not been deliberately trying to shake a tail, Towfik decided. Had the professor been a pro he would have lost Towfik decisively and finally. No, he had simply been taking a morning walk through the market before meeting someone at a landmark. But Towfik was sure that the meeting place, and the walk beforehand, had been suggested by the agent.

They might have gone anywhere, but it seemed likely they were leaving the city – otherwise Schulz could simply have taken a taxi at Bab Zuweyla – and this was the major road westward. Towfik drove very fast. Soon there was nothing in front of him but the arrow-straight grey road, and nothing either side but yellow sand and blue sky.

He reached the Pyramids without catching the Mercedes. Here the road forked, leading north to Alexandria or south to Faiyum. From where the Mercedes had picked up Schulz, this would have been an unlikely, roundabout route to Alexandria; so Towfik plumped for Faiyum.

When at last he saw the other car it was behind him, coming up very fast. Before it reached him it turned right off the main road. Towfik braked to a halt and reversed the Renault to the turnoff. The other car was already a mile ahead on the side road. He followed.

This was dangerous, now. The road probably went deep into the Western Desert, perhaps all the way to the oil field at Qattara. It seemed little used, and a strong wind might obscure it under a layer of sand. The agent in the Mercedes was sure to realize he was being followed. If he were a good agent, the sight of the Renault might even trigger memories of the journey from Heliopolis.

This was where the training broke down, and all the careful camouflage and tricks of the trade became useless; and you had to simply get on someone's tail and stick with him whether he saw you or not, because the whole point was to find out where he was going, and if you could not manage that you were no use at all.

So he threw caution to the desert wind and followed; and still he lost them.

The Mercedes was a faster car, and better designed for the narrow, bumpy road, and within a few minutes it was out of sight. Towfik followed the road, hoping he might catch them when they stopped or at least come across something that might be their destination.

Sixty kilometres on, deep in the desert and beginning to worry about getting petrol, he reached a tiny oasis village at a crossroads. A few scrawny animals grazed in sparse vegetation around a muddy pool. A jar of fava beans and three Fanta cans on a makeshift table outside a hut signified the local café. Towfik got out of the car and spoke to an old man watering a bony buffalo.

'Have you seen a grey Mercedes?'

The peasant stared at him blankly, as if he were speaking a foreign language.

'Have you seen a grey car?'

The old man brushed a large black fly off his forehead and nodded, once.

'When?'

'Today.'

That was probably as precise an answer as he could hope for. 'Which way did it go?'

The old man pointed west, into the desert.

Towfik said, 'Where can I get petrol?'

The man pointed east, toward Cairo.

Towfik gave him a coin and returned to the car. He started the engine and looked again at the petrol gauge. He had enough fuel to get back to Cairo, just; if he went farther west he would run out on the return journey.

He had done all he could, he decided. Wearily, he turned the Renault around and headed back toward the city.

Towfik did not like his work. When it was dull he was bored, and when it was exciting he was frightened. But they had told him that there was important, dangerous work to be done in Cairo, and that he had the qualities necessary to be a good spy, and that there were not enough Egyptian Jews in Israel for them to be able just to go out and find another one with all the qualities if he said no; so, of course, he had agreed. It was not out of idealism that he risked his life for his country. It was more like self-interest: the destruction of Israel would mean his own destruction; in fighting for Israel he was fighting for himself; he risked his life to save his life. It was the logical thing to do. Still, he looked forward to the time – in five years? Ten? Twenty? – when he would be too old for field work, and they would bring him home and sit him behind a desk, and he could find a nice Jewish girl and marry her and settle down to enjoy the land he had fought for.

Meanwhile, having lost Professor Schulz, he was following the wife.

She continued to see the sights, escorted now by a young Arab who had presumably been laid on by the Egyptians to take care of her while her husband was away. In the evening the Arab took her to an Egyptian restaurant for dinner, brought her home, and kissed her cheek under the jacaranda tree in the garden.

The next morning Towfik went to the main post office and sent a coded cable to his uncle in Rome:

SCHULZ MET AT AIRPORT BY SUSPECTED LOCAL AGENT. SPENT TWO DAYS SIGHTSEEING. PICKED UP BY AFORESAID AGENT AND DRIVEN DIRECTION QATTARA. SURVEILLANCE ABORTED. NOW WATCHING WIFE.

He was back in Zamalek at nine A.M. At eleven-thirty he saw Frau Schulz on a balcony, drinking coffee, and was able to figure out which of the apartments was the Schulzes'.

By lunchtime the interior of the Renault had become very hot. Towfik ate an apple and drank tepid beer from a bottle.

Professor Schulz arrived late in the afternoon, in the same grey Mercedes. He looked tired and a little rumpled, like a middle-aged man who had travelled too far. He left the car and went into the building without looking back. After dropping him, the agent drove past the Renault and looked straight at Towfik for an instant. There was nothing Towfik could do about it.

Where had Schulz been? It had taken him most of a day to get there, Towfik speculated; he had spent a night, a full day and a second night there; and it had taken most of today to get back. Qattara was only one of several possibilities: the desert road went all the way to Matruh on the Mediterranean coast; there was a turnoff to Karkur Tohl in the far south; with a change of car and a desert guide they could even have gone to a rendezvous on the border with Libya.

At nine P.M. the Schulzes came out again. The professor looked refreshed. They were dressed for dinner. They walked a short distance and hailed a taxi.

Towfik made a decision. He did not follow them.

He got out of the car and entered the garden of the building. He stepped on to the dusty lawn and found a vantage point behind a bush from where he could see into the hall through the open front door. The Nubian caretaker was sitting on a low wooden bench, picking his nose.

Towfik waited.

Twenty minutes later the man left his bench and disappeared into the back of the building.

Towfik hurried through the hall and ran, soft-footed, up the staircase.

He had three Yale-type skeleton keys, but none of them fitted the lock of apartment three. In the end he got the door open with a piece of bendy plastic broken off a college set-square.

He entered the apartment and closed the door behind him.

It was now quite dark outside. A little light from a streetlamp came through the unshaded windows. Towfik drew a small flashlight from his trousers pocket, but he did not switch it on yet.

The apartment was large and airy, with white-painted walls and English-colonial furniture. It had the sparse, chilly look of a place where nobody actually lived.

There was a big drawing room, a dining room, three bedrooms and a kitchen. After a quick general survey Towfik started snooping in earnest.

The two smaller bedrooms were bare. In the larger one, Towfik went rapidly through all the drawers and cupboards. A wardrobe held the rather gaudy dresses of a woman past her prime: bright prints, sequinned gowns, turquoise and orange and pink. The labels were American. Schulz was an Austrian national, the cable had said, but perhaps he lived in the USA. Towfik had never heard him speak.

On the bedside table were a guide to Cairo in English, a copy of *Vogue* and a reprinted lecture on isotopes.

So Schulz was a scientist.

Towfik glanced through the lecture. Most of it was over his head. Schulz must be a top chemist or physicist, he thought. If he was here to work on weaponry, Tel Aviv would want to know.

There were no personal papers – Schulz evidently had his passport and wallet in his pocket. The airline labels had been removed from the matching set of tan suitcases.

On a low table in the drawing room, two empty glasses smelled of gin: they had had a cocktail before going out.

In the bathroom Towfik found the clothes Schulz had worn into the desert. There was a lot of sand in the shoes, and on the trouser cuffs he found small dusty grey smears which might have been cement. In the breast pocket of the rumpled jacket was a blue plastic container, about one-and-a-half inches square, very slender. It contained a light-tight envelope of the kind used to protect photographic film.

Towfik pocketed the plastic box.

The airline labels from the luggage were in a waste basket in the little hall. The Schulzes' address was in Boston, Massachusetts, which probably meant that the professor taught at Harvard, MIT or one of the many lesser universities in the area. Towfik did some rapid arithmetic. Schulz would have been in his twenties during World War Two: he could easily be one of the German rocketry experts who went to the USA after the war.

Or not. You did not have to be a Nazi to work for the Arabs.

Nazi or not, Schulz was a cheapskate: his soap, toothpaste and after-shave were all taken from airlines and hotels.

On the floor beside a rattan chair, near the table with the empty cocktail glasses, lay a lined foolscap notepad, its top sheet blank. There was a pencil lying on the pad. Perhaps Schulz had been making notes on his trip while he sipped his gin sling. Towfik searched the apartment for sheets torn from the pad.

He found them on the balcony, burned to cinders in a large glass ashtray.

The night was cool. Later in the year the air would be warm and fragrant with the blossom of the jacaranda tree in the garden below. The city traffic snored in the distance. It reminded Towfik of his father's apartment in Jerusalem. He wondered how long it would be before he saw Jerusalem again.

He had done all he could here. He would look again at that foolscap pad, to see whether Schulz's pencil had pressed hard enough to leave an impression on the next page. He turned away from the parapet and crossed the balcony to the French windows leading back into the drawing room.

He had his hand on the door when he heard the voices.

Towfik froze.

'I'm sorry, honey, I just couldn't face another over-done steak.'

'We could have eaten something, for God's sake.'

The Schulzes were back.

Towfik rapidly reviewed his progress through the rooms: bedrooms, bathroom, drawing room, kitchen ... he had replaced everything he had touched, except the little plastic box. He had to keep that anyway. Schulz would have to assume he had lost it.

If Towfik could get away unseen now, they might never know he had been there.

He bellied over the parapet and hung at full length by his fingertips. It was too dark for him to see the ground. He dropped, landed lightly and strolled away.

It had been his first burglary, and he felt pleased. It had gone as smoothly as a training exercise, even to the early return of the occupant and sudden exit of spy by prearranged emergency route. He grinned in the dark. He might yet live to see that desk job.

He got into his car, started the engine and switched on the lights.

Two men emerged from the shadows and stood on either side of the Renault.

Who . . . ?

He did not pause to figure out what was going on. He rammed the gearshift into first and pulled away. The two men hastily stepped aside.

They had made no attempt to stop him. So why had they been there? To make sure he stayed in the car . . . ?

He jammed on the brakes and looked into the back seat, and then he knew, with unbearable sadness, that he would never see Jerusalem again.

A tall Arab in a dark suit was smiling at him over the snout of a small handgun.

'Drive on,' the man said in Arabic, 'but not quite so fast, please.'

Q: What is your name?
A: Towfik el-Masiri.
Q: Describe yourself.
A: Age twenty-six, five-foot-nine, one hundred and eighty pounds, brown eyes, black hair, Semitic features, light brown skin.
Q: Who do you work for?
A: I am a student.
Q: What day is today?
A: Saturday.
Q: What is your nationality?
A: Egyptian.

Q: What is twenty minus seven?

A: Thirteen.

The above questions are designed to facilitate fine calibration of the lie detector.

Q: You work for the CIA.

A: No. (TRUE)

Q: The Germans?

A: No. (TRUE)

Q: Israel, then.

A: No. (FALSE)

Q: You really are a student?

A: Yes. (FALSE)

Q: Tell me about your studies.

A: I'm doing chemistry at Cairo University. (TRUE) I'm interested in polymers. (TRUE) I want to be a petrochemical engineer. (FALSE)

Q: What are polymers?

A: Complex organic compounds with long-chain molecules – the commonest is polythene. (TRUE)

Q: What is your name?

A: I told you, Towfik el-Masiri. (FALSE)

Q: The pads attached to your head and chest measure your pulse, heartbeat, breathing and perspiration. When you tell untruths, your metabolism betrays you – you breathe faster, sweat more, and so on. This machine, which was given to us by our Russian friends, tells me when you are lying. Besides, I happen to know that Towfik el-Masiri is dead. Who are you?

A: (no reply)

Q: The wire taped to the tip of your penis is part of a

different machine. It is connected to this button here. When I press the button—

A: (scream)

Q: —an electric current passes through the wire and gives you a shock. We have put your feet in a bucket of water to improve the efficiency of the apparatus. What is your name?

A: Avram Ambache.

The electrical apparatus interferes with the functioning of the lie detector.

Q: Have a cigarette.

A: Thank you.

Q: Believe it or not, I hate this work. The trouble is, people who like it are never any good at it – you need sensitivity, you know. I'm a sensitive person ... I hate to see people suffer. Don't you?

A: (no reply)

Q: You're now trying to think of ways to resist me. Please don't bother. There is no defence against modern techniques of ... interviewing. What is your name?

A: Avram Ambache. (TRUE)

Q: Who is your control?

A: I don't know what you mean. (FALSE)

Q: Is it Bosch?

A: No, Friedman. (READING INDETERMINATE)

Q: It is Bosch.

A: Yes. (FALSE)

Q: No, it's not Bosch. It's Krantz.

A: Okay, it's Krantz – whatever you say. (TRUE)

Q: How do you make contact?

A: I have a radio. (FALSE)

Q: You're not telling me the truth.

A: (scream)

Q: How do you make contact?

A: A dead-letter box in the *faubourg*.

Q: You are thinking that when you are in pain, the lie detector will not function properly, and that there is therefore safety in torture. You are only partly right. This is a very sophisticated machine, and I spent many months learning to use it properly. After I have given you a shock, it takes only a few moments to readjust the machine to your faster metabolism; and then I can once more tell when you are lying. How do you make contact?

A: A dead-letter – (scream)

Q: Ali! He's kicked his feet free – these convulsions are very strong. Tie him again, before he comes round. Pick up that bucket and put more water in it.

(pause)

Right, he's waking, get out. Can you hear me, Towfik?

A: (indistinct)

Q: What is your name?

A: (no reply)

Q: A little jab to help you—

A: (scream)

Q: —to think.

A: Avram Ambache.

Q: What day is today?

A: Saturday.

Q: What did we give you for breakfast?

A: Fava beans.

Q: What is twenty minus seven?

A: Thirteen.

Q: What is your profession?

A: I'm a student. No don't please and a spy yes I'm a spy don't touch the button please oh god oh god—

Q: How do you make contact?

A: Coded cables.

Q: Have a cigarette. Here . . . oh, you don't seem to be able to hold it between your lips – let me help . . . there.

A: Thank you.

Q: Just try to be calm. Remember, as long as you're telling the truth, there will be no pain.
(pause)
Are you feeling better?

A: Yes.

Q: So am I. Now then, tell me about Professor Schulz. Why were you following him?

A: I was ordered to. (TRUE)

Q: By Tel Aviv?

A: Yes. (TRUE)

Q: Who in Tel Aviv?

A: I don't know. (READING INDETERMINATE)

Q: But you can guess.

A: Bosch. (READING INDETERMINATE)

Q: Or Krantz?

A: Perhaps. (TRUE)

Q: Krantz is a good man. Dependable. How's his wife?

A: Very well, I—(scream)

Q: His wife died in 1958. Why do you make me hurt you? What did Schulz do?

A: Went sightseeing for two days, then disappeared into the desert in a grey Mercedes.

Q: And you burglarized his apartment.

A: Yes. (TRUE)

Q: What did you learn?

A: He is a scientist. (TRUE)

Q: Anything else?

A: American. (TRUE) That's all. (TRUE)

Q: Who was your instructor in training?

A: Ertl. (READING INDETERMINATE)

Q: That wasn't his real name, though.

A: I don't know. (FALSE) No! Not the button let me think it was just a minute I think somebody said his real name was Manner. (TRUE)

Q: Oh, Manner. Shame. He's the old-fashioned type. He still believes you can train agents to resist interrogation. It's his fault you're suffering so much, you know. What about your colleagues? Who trained with you?

A: I never knew their real names. (FALSE)

Q: Didn't you?

A: (scream)

Q: Real names.

A: Not all of them—

Q: Tell me the ones you did know.

A: (no reply)
(scream)

The prisoner fainted.
(pause)

44

Q: What is your name?

A: Uh . . . Towfik. (scream)

Q: What did you have for breakfast?

A: Don't know.

Q: What is twenty minus seven?

A: Twenty-seven.

Q: What did you tell Krantz about Professor Schulz?

A: Sightseeing . . . Western Desert . . . surveillance aborted . . .

Q: Who did you train with?

A: (no reply)

Q: Who did you train with?

A: (scream)

Q: Who did you train with?

A: Yea, though I walk through the valley of the shadow of death—

Q: Who did you train with?

A: (scream)

The prisoner died.

When Kawash asked for a meeting, Pierre Borg went. There was no discussion about times and places: Kawash sent a message giving the rendezvous, and Borg made sure to be there. Kawash was the best double agent Borg had ever had, and that was that.

The head of the Mossad stood at one end of the northbound Bakerloo Line platform in Oxford Circus underground station, reading an advertisement for a course of lectures in Theosophy, waiting for Kawash. He had no idea why the Arab had chosen London for this meeting; no idea what he told his masters he was doing in the city; no idea, even, why Kawash was a traitor. But this man had helped the Israelis win two wars and avoid a third, and Borg needed him.

Borg glanced along the platform, looking for a high brown head with a large, thin nose. He had an idea he knew what Kawash wanted to talk about. He hoped his idea was right.

Borg was very worried about the Schulz affair. It had started out as a piece of routine surveillance, just the right kind of assignment for his newest, rawest agent in Cairo: a high-powered American physicist on vacation in Europe decides to take a trip to Egypt. The first warning sign came when Towfik lost Schulz. At that point Borg had stepped up activity on the project. A freelance journalist in Milan who occasionally made inquiries for German Intelligence had established that Schulz's air ticket to Cairo had been paid for by the wife of an Egyptian diplomat in Rome. Then the CIA had routinely passed to the Mossad a set of satellite photographs of the area around Qattara which seemed to show signs of construction work – and Borg had remembered that Schulz had been heading in the direction of Qattara when Towfik lost him.

Something was going on, and he did not know what, and that worried him.

He was always worried. If it was not the Egyptians, it was the Syrians; if it was not the Syrians it was the Fedayeen; if it was not his enemies it was his friends and the question of how long they would continue to be his friends. He had a worrying job. His mother had once said, 'Job, *nothing* – you were *born* worrying, like your poor father – if you were a *gardener* you would worry about your job.' She might have been right, but all the same, paranoia was the only rational frame of mind for a spymaster.

Now Towfik had broken contact, and that was the most worrying sign of all.

Maybe Kawash would have some answers.

A train thundered in. Borg was not waiting for a train. He began to read the credits on a movie poster. Half the names were Jewish. Maybe I should have been a movie producer, he thought.

The train pulled out, and a shadow fell over Borg. He looked up into the calm face of Kawash.

The Arab said, 'Thank you for coming.' He always said that.

Borg ignored it: he never knew how to respond to thanks. He said, 'What's new?'

'I had to pick up one of your youngsters in Cairo on Friday.'

'You *had* to?'

'Military Intelligence were bodyguarding a VIP, and they spotted the kid tailing them. Military don't have operational personnel in the city, so they asked my department to pick him up. It was an official request.'

'God *damn*,' Borg said feelingly. 'What happened to him?'

'I had to do it by the book,' Kawash said. He looked very sad. 'The boy was interrogated and killed. His name was Avram Ambache, but he worked as Towfik el-Masiri.'

Borg frowned. 'He told you his real name?'

'He's dead, Pierre.'

Borg shook his head irritably: Kawash always wanted to linger over personal aspects. 'Why did he tell you his name?'

'We're using the Russian equipment – the electric shock and the lie detector together. You're not training them to cope with it.'

Borg gave a short laugh. 'If we told them about it, we'd never get any fucking recruits. What else did he give away?'

'Nothing we didn't know. He would have, but I killed him first.'

'*You* killed him?'

'I conducted the interrogation, in order to make sure he did not say anything important. All these interviews are taped now, and the transcripts filed. We're learning from the Russians.' The sadness deepened in the brown eyes. 'Why – would you prefer that I should have someone else kill your boys?'

Borg stared at him, then looked away. Once again he had to steer the conversation away from the sentimental. 'What did the boy discover about Schulz?'

'An agent took the professor into the Western Desert.'

'Sure, but what for?'

'I don't know.'

'You must know, you're in Egyptian Intelligence!' Borg controlled his irritation. Let the man do things at his own pace, he told himself; whatever information he's got, he'll tell.

'I don't know what they're doing out there, because they've set up a special group to handle it,' Kawash said. 'My department isn't informed.'

'Any idea why?'

The Arab shrugged. 'I'd say they don't want the Russians to know about it. These days Moscow gets everything that goes through us.'

Borg let his disappointment show. 'Is that all Towfik could manage?'

Suddenly there was anger in the soft voice of the Arab. 'The kid died for you,' he said.

'I'll thank him in heaven. Did he die in vain?'

'He took this from Schulz's apartment.' Kawash drew a hand from inside his coat and showed Borg a small, square box of blue plastic.

Borg took the box. 'How do you know where he got it?'

'It has Schulz's fingerprints on it. And we arrested Towfik right after he broke into the apartment.'

Borg opened the box and fingered the light-proof envelope. It was unsealed. He took out the photographic negative.

The Arab said, 'We opened the envelope and developed the film. It's blank.'

With a deep sense of satisfaction, Borg reassembled the box and put it into his pocket. Now it all made sense; now he understood; now he knew what he had to do. A train came in. 'You want to catch this one?' he said.

Kawash frowned slightly, nodded assent, and moved to the edge of the platform as the train stopped and the doors opened. He boarded, and stood just inside. He said, 'I don't know what on earth the box is.'

Borg thought, You don't like me, but I think you're just great. He smiled thinly at the Arab as the doors of the underground train began to slide shut. 'I do,' he said.

CHAPTER TWO

THE AMERICAN girl was quite taken with Nat
Dickstein.

They worked side by side in a dusty vineyard, weeding and hoeing, with a light breeze blowing over them from the Sea of Galilee. Dickstein had taken off his shirt and worked in shorts and sandals, with the contempt for the sun which only the city-born possess.

He was a thin man, small-boned, with narrow shoulders, a shallow chest, and knobby elbows and knees. Karen would watch him when she stopped for a break – which she did often, although he never seemed to need a rest. Stringy muscles moved like knotted rope under his brown, scarred skin. She was a sensual woman, and she wanted to touch those scars with her fingers and ask him how he got them.

Sometimes he would look up and catch her staring, and he would grin, unembarrassed, and carry on working. His face was regular and anonymous in repose. He had dark eyes behind cheap round spectacles of the kind which Karen's generation liked because John Lennon wore them. His hair was dark, too, and short: Karen would have liked him to grow it. When he grinned that lopsided grin, he looked younger; though at any time it was hard to say just how old he might be. He had the strength and energy of a young man, but she had seen the concentration camp tattoo under his wristwatch, so he could not be much less than forty, she thought.

He had arrived at the kibbutz shortly after Karen, in the summer of 1967. She had come, with her deodorants and her contraceptive pills, looking for a place where she could live out hippy ideals without getting stoned twenty-four hours a day. He had been brought here in an ambulance. She assumed he had been wounded in the Six-Day War, and the other kibbutzniks agreed, vaguely, that it was something like that.

His welcome had been very different from hers. Karen's reception had been friendly but wary: in her philosophy they saw their own, with dangerous additions. Nat Dickstein returned like a long-lost son. They clustered around him, fed him soup and came away from his wounds with tears in their eyes.

If Dickstein was their son, Esther was their mother. She was the oldest member of the kibbutz. Karen had said, 'She looks like Golda Meir's mother,' and one of the others had said, 'I think she's Golda's *father*,' and they all laughed affectionately. She used a walking stick, and stomped about the village giving unsolicited advice, most of it very wise. She had stood guard outside Dickstein's sickroom chasing away noisy children, waving her stick and threatening beatings which even the children knew would never be administered.

Dickstein had recovered very quickly. Within a few days he was sitting out in the sun, peeling vegetables for the kitchen and telling vulgar jokes to the older children. Two weeks later he was working in the fields, and soon he was labouring harder than all but the youngest men.

His past was vague, but Esther had told Karen the story of his arrival in Israel in 1948, during the War of Independence.

Nineteen forty-eight was part of the recent past for Esther. She had been a young woman in London in the first two decades of the century, and had been an activist in half a dozen radical left-wing causes from suffragism to pacifism before emigrating to Palestine; but her memory went back further, to pogroms in Russia which she recalled vaguely in monstrous night-mare images. She had sat under a fig tree in the heat of the day, varnishing a chair she had made with her own gnarled hands, and talked about Dickstein like a clever but mischievous schoolboy.

'There were eight or nine of them, some from the university, some working men from the East End. If they ever had any money, they'd spent it before they got to France. They hitched a ride on a truck to Paris, then jumped a freight train to Marseilles. From there, it seems, they walked most of the way to Italy. Then they stole a huge car, a German Army staff car, a Mercedes, and drove all the way to the toe of Italy.' Esther's face was creased in smiles, and Karen thought: She would love to have been there with them.

'Dickstein had been to Sicily in the war, and it seems he knew the Mafia there. They had all the guns left over from the war. Dickstein wanted guns for Israel, but he had no money. He persuaded the Sicilians to sell a boatload of submachine guns to an Arab purchaser, and then to tell the Jews where the pickup would take place. They knew what he was up to, and they loved it. The deal was done, the Sicilians got their money, and then Dickstein and his friend stole the boat with its cargo and sailed to Israel!'

Karen had laughed aloud, there under the fig tree, and a grazing goat looked up at her balefully.

'Wait,' said Esther, 'you haven't heard the end of it. Some of the university boys had done a bit of rowing, and one of the other lot was a docker, but that was all the experience they had of the sea, and here they were sailing a five-thousand-ton cargo vessel on their own. They figured out a little navigation from first principles: the ship had charts and a compass. Dickstein had looked up in a book how to start the ship, but he says the book did not tell how to stop it. So they steamed into Haifa, yelling and waving and throwing their hats into the air, just like it was a varsity rag – and ploughed straight into the dock.

'They were forgiven instantly, of course – the guns were more precious than gold, literally. And that's when they started to call Dickstein "The Pirate".'

He did not look much like a pirate, working in the vineyard in his baggy shorts and his spectacles, Karen thought. All the same, he was attractive. She wanted to seduce him, but she could not figure out how. He obviously liked her, and she had taken care to let him know she was available. But he never made a move.

Perhaps he felt she was too young and innocent. Or maybe he was not interested in women.

His voice broke into her thoughts. 'I think we've finished.'

She looked at the sun: it was time to go. 'You've done twice as much as me.'

'I'm used to the work. I've been here, on and off, for twenty years. The body gets into the habit.'

They walked back toward the village as the sky turned purple and yellow. Karen said, 'What else do you do – when you're not here?'

'Oh . . . poison wells, kidnap Christian children.'

Karen laughed.

Dickstein said, 'How does this life compare with California?'

'This is a wonderful place,' she told him. 'I think there's a lot of work still to be done before the women are genuinely equal.'

'That seems to be the big topic at the moment.'

'You never have much to say about it.'

'Listen, I think you're right; but it's better for people to take their freedom rather than be given it.'

Karen said, 'That sounds like a good excuse for doing nothing.'

Dickstein laughed.

As they entered the village they passed a young man on a pony, carrying a rifle, on his way to patrol the borders of the settlement. Dickstein called out, 'Be careful, Yisrael.' The shelling from the Golan Heights had stopped, of course, and the children no longer had to sleep underground; but the kibbutz kept up the patrols. Dickstein had been one of those in favour of maintaining vigilance.

'I'm going to read to Mottie,' Dickstein said.

'Can I come?'

'Why not?' Dickstein looked at his watch. 'We've just got time to wash. Come to my room in five minutes.'

They parted, and Karen went into the showers. A kibbutz was the best place to be an orphan, she thought as she took off her clothes. Mottie's parents were both dead – the father blown up in the attack on the Golan Heights during the last war, the mother killed a year earlier in a shootout with Fedayeen. Both had been close friends of Dickstein. It was a tragedy for the child, of course; but he still slept in the same bed, ate in the same room, and had almost one hundred other adults to love and care for him – he was not foisted on to unwilling aunts or ageing grandparents or, worst of all, an orphanage. And he had Dickstein.

When she had washed off the dust Karen put on clean clothes and went to Dickstein's room. Mottie was already there, sitting on Dickstein's lap, sucking his thumb and listening to *Treasure Island* in Hebrew. Dickstein was the only person Karen had ever met who spoke Hebrew with a Cockney accent. His speech was even more strange now, because he was doing different voices for the characters in the story: a high-pitched boy's voice for Jim, a deep snarl for Long John Silver, and a half whisper for the mad Ben Gunn. Karen sat and watched the two of them in the yellow electric light, thinking how boyish Dickstein appeared, and how grown-up the child was.

When the chapter was finished they took Mottie to his dormitory, kissed him goodnight, and went into the dining room. Karen thought: If we continue to go about together like this, everyone will think we're lovers already.

They sat with Esther. After dinner she told them a story, and there was a young woman's twinkle in her eye. 'When I first went to Jerusalem, they used to say that if you owned a feather pillow, you could buy a house.'

Dickstein willingly took the bait. 'How was that?'

'You could sell a good feather pillow for a pound. With that pound you could join a loan society, which entitled you to borrow ten pounds. Then you found a plot of land. The owner of the land would take ten pounds deposit and the rest in promissory notes. Now you were a landowner. You went to a builder and said, "Build a house for yourself on this plot of land. All I want is a small flat for myself and my family."'

They all laughed. Dickstein looked toward the door. Karen followed his glance and saw a stranger, a stocky man in his forties with a coarse, fleshy face. Dickstein got up and went to him.

Esther said to Karen, 'Don't break your heart, child. That one is not made to be a husband.'

Karen looked at Esther, then back at the doorway. Dickstein had gone. A few moments later she heard the sound of a car starting up and driving away.

Esther put her old hand on Karen's young one, and squeezed.

Karen never saw Dickstein again.

Nat Dickstein and Pierre Borg sat in the back seat of a big black Citroën. Borg's bodyguard was driving, with his machine pistol lying on the front seat beside him. They travelled through the darkness with nothing ahead but the cone of light from the headlamps. Nat Dickstein was afraid.

He had never come to see himself the way others did, as a competent, indeed brilliant, agent who had proved his ability to survive just about anything. Later, when the game was on and he was living by his wits, grappling at close quarters with strategy and problems and personalities, there would be no room in his mind for fear; but now, when Borg was about to brief him, he had no plans to make, no forecasts to refine, no characters to assess. He knew only that he had to turn his back on peace and simple hard work, the land and the sunshine and caring for growing things; and that ahead of him there were terrible risks and great danger, lies and pain and bloodshed and, perhaps, his death. So he sat in the corner of the seat, his arms and legs crossed tightly, watching Borg's dimly lit face, while fear of the unknown knotted and writhed in his stomach and made him nauseous.

In the faint, shifting light, Borg looked like the giant in a fairy story. He had heavy features: thick lips, broad cheeks, and protruding eyes shadowed by thick brows.

As a child he had been told he was ugly, and so he had grown into an ugly man. When he was uneasy – like now – his hands went continually to his face, covering his mouth, rubbing his nose, scratching his forehead, in a subconscious attempt to hide his unsightliness. Once, in a relaxed moment, Dickstein had asked him, 'Why do you yell at everybody?' and he had replied, 'Because they're all so fucking handsome.'

They never knew what language to use when they spoke. Borg was French-Canadian originally, and found Hebrew a struggle. Dickstein's Hebrew was good and his French only passable. Usually they settled for English.

Dickstein had worked under Borg for ten years, and still he did not like the man. He felt he understood Borg's troubled, unhappy nature; and he respected his professionalism and his obsessional devotion to Israeli Intelligence; but in Dickstein's book this was not enough cause to like a person. When Borg lied to him, there were always good sound reasons, but Dickstein resented the lie no less.

He retaliated by playing Borg's tactics back against him. He would refuse to say where he was going, or he would lie about it. He never checked in on schedule while he was in the field: he simply called or sent messages with peremptory demands. And he would sometimes conceal from Borg part or all of his game plan. This prevented Borg from interfering with schemes of his own, and it was also more secure – for what Borg knew, he might be obliged to tell to politicians, and what they knew might find its way to the opposition. Dickstein knew the strength of his position – he was responsible for many of the triumphs which had distinguished Borg's career – and he played it for all it was worth.

The Citroën roared through the Arab town of Nazareth – deserted now, presumably under curfew – and went on into the night, heading for Tel Aviv. Borg lit a thin cigar and began to speak.

'After the Six-Day War, one of the bright boys in the Ministry of Defence wrote a paper entitled "The Inevitable Destruction of Israel." The argument went like this. During the War of Independence, we bought arms from Czechoslovakia. When the Soviet bloc began to take the Arab side, we turned to France, and later West Germany. Germany called off all deals as soon as the Arabs found out. France imposed an embargo after the Six-Day War. Both Britain and the United States have consistently refused to supply us with arms. We are losing our sources one by one.

'Suppose we are able to make up those losses, by continually finding new suppliers and by building our own munitions industry: even then, the fact remains that Israel must be the loser in a Middle East arms race. The oil countries will be richer than us throughout the foreseeable future. Our defence budget is already a terrible burden on the national economy whereas our enemies have nothing better to spend their billions on. When they have ten thousand tanks, we'll need six thousand; when they have twenty thousand tanks, we'll need twelve thousand; and so on. Simply by doubling their arms expenditure every year, they will be able to cripple our national economy without firing a shot.

'Finally, the recent history of the Middle East shows a pattern of limited wars about once a decade. The logic of this pattern is against us. The Arabs can afford to lose a war from time to time. We can't: our first defeat will be our last war.

'Conclusion: the survival of Israel depends on our breaking out of the vicious spiral our enemies have prescribed for us.'

Dickstein nodded. 'It's not a novel line of thought. It's the usual argument for "peace at any price." I should think the bright boy got fired from the Ministry of Defence for that paper.'

'Wrong both times. He went on to say, "We must inflict, or have the power to inflict, permanent and crippling damage to the next Arab army that crosses our borders. We must have nuclear weapons."'

Dickstein was very still for a moment; then he let out his breath in a long whistle. It was one of those devastating ideas that seems completely obvious as soon as it has been said. It would change everything. He was silent for a while, digesting the implications. His mind teemed with questions. Was it technically feasible? Would the Americans help? Would the Israeli Cabinet approve it? Would the Arabs retaliate with their own bomb? What he said was, 'Bright boy in the Ministry, hell. That was Moshe Dayan's paper.'

'No comment,' said Borg.

'Did the Cabinet adopt it?'

'There has been a long debate. Certain elder statesmen argued that they had not come this far to see the Middle East wiped out in a nuclear holocaust. But the opposition faction relied mainly on the argument that if we have a bomb, the Arabs will get one too, and we will be back at square one. As it turned out, that was their big mistake.' Borg reached into his pocket and took out a small plastic box. He handed it to Dickstein.

Dickstein switched on the interior light and examined the box. It was about an inch and a half square, thin, and blue in colour. It opened to reveal a small envelope made of heavy light-proof paper. 'What's this?' he said.

Borg said, 'A physicist named Friedrich Schulz visited Cairo in February. He is Austrian but he works in the United States. He was apparently on holiday in Europe, but his plane ticket to Egypt was paid for by the Egyptian government.

'I had him followed, but he gave our boy the slip and disappeared into the Western Desert for forty-eight hours. We know from CIA satellite pictures that there is a major construction project going on in that part of the desert. When Schulz came back, he had that in his pocket. It's a personnel dosimeter. The envelope, which is light-tight, contains a piece of ordinary photographic film. You carry the box in your pocket, or pinned to your lapel or trouser belt. If you're exposed to radiation, the film will show fogging when it's developed. Dosimeters are carried, as a matter of routine, by everyone who visits or works in a nuclear power station.'

Dickstein switched off the light and gave the box back to Borg. 'You're telling me the Arabs are already making atom bombs,' he said softly.

'That's right.' Borg spoke unnecessarily loudly.

'So the Cabinet gave Dayan the go-ahead to make a bomb of his own.'

'In principle, yes.'

'How so?'

'There are some practical difficulties. The mechanics of the business are simple – the actual clockwork of the bomb, so to speak. Anyone who can make a conventional bomb can make a nuclear bomb. The problem is getting hold of the explosive material, plutonium. You get plutonium out of an atomic reactor. It's a by-product. Now, we have a reactor, at Dimona in the Negev Desert. Did you know that?'

'Yes.'

'It's our worst-kept secret. However, we don't have the equipment for extracting the plutonium from the spent fuel. We could build a reprocessing plant, but the problem is that we have no uranium *of our own* to put through the reactor.'

'Wait a minute.' Dickstein frowned. 'We must have uranium, to fuel the reactor for normal use.'

'Correct. We get it from France, and it's supplied to us on condition we return the spent fuel to them for reprocessing, so they get the plutonium.'

'Other suppliers?'

'Would impose the same condition – it's part of all the nuclear non-proliferation treaties.'

Dickstein said, 'But the people at Dimona could siphon off some of the spent fuel without anyone noticing.'

'No. Given the quantity of uranium originally supplied, it's possible to calculate precisely how much plutonium comes out the other end. And they weigh it very carefully – it's expensive stuff.'

'So the problem is to get hold of some uranium.'

'Right.'

'And the solution?'

'The solution is, you're going to steal it.'

Dickstein looked out of the window. The moon came out, revealing a flock of sheep huddled in a corner of a field, watched by an Arab shepherd with a staff: a Biblical scene. So this was the game: stolen uranium for the land of milk and honey. Last time it had been the murder of a terrorist leader in Damascus; the time before, blackmailing a wealthy Arab in Monte Carlo to stop him funding the Fedayeen.

Dickstein's feelings had been pushed into the background while Borg talked about politics and Schulz and nuclear reactors. Now he was reminded that this involved *him*; and the fear came back, and with it a memory. After his father died the family had been desperately poor, and when creditors called, Nat had been sent to the door to say mummy was out. At the age of thirteen, he had found it unbearably humiliating, because the creditors knew he was lying, and he knew they knew, and they would look at him with a mixture of contempt and pity which pierced him to the quick.

He would never forget that feeling – and it came back, like a reminder from his unconscious, when somebody like Borg said something like, 'Little Nathaniel, go steal some uranium for your motherland.'

To his mother he had always said, 'Do I have to?' And now he said to Pierre Borg, 'If we're going to steal it anyway, why not buy it and simply refuse to send it back for reprocessing?'

'Because that way, everyone would know what we're up to.'

'So?'

'Reprocessing takes time – many months. During that time two things could happen: one, the Egyptians would hurry their programme; and two, the Americans would pressure us not to build the bomb.'

'Oh!' It was worse. 'So you want me to steal this stuff without anyone knowing that it's us.'

'More than that.' Borg's voice was harsh and throaty. 'Nobody must even know it's been stolen. It must look as if the stuff has just been lost. I want the owners, and the international agencies, to be so embarrassed about the stuff disappearing that they will hush it up. Then, when they discover they've been robbed, they will be compromised by their own cover-up.'

'It's bound to come out eventually.'

'Not before we've got our bomb.'

They had reached the coast road from Haifa to Tel Aviv, and as the car butted through the night Dickstein could see, over to the right, occasional glimpses of the Mediterranean, glinting like jewellery in the moonlight.

When he spoke he was surprised at the note of weary resignation in his voice. 'How much uranium do we need?'

'They want twelve bombs. In the yellowcake form – that's the uranium ore – it would mean about a hundred tons.'

'I won't be able to slip it into my pocket, then.' Dickstein frowned. 'What would all that cost if we bought it?'

'Something over one million US dollars.'

'And you think the losers will just hush it up?'

'If it's done right.'

'How?'

'That's your job, Pirate.'

'I'm not so sure it's possible,' Dickstein said.

'It's got to be. I told the Prime Minister we could pull it off. I laid my career on the line, Nat.'

'Don't talk to me about your bleeding career.'

Borg lit another cigar – a nervous reaction to Dickstein's scorn. Dickstein opened his window an inch to let the smoke out. His sudden hostility had nothing to do with Borg's clumsy personal appeal: that was typical of the man's inability to understand how people felt toward him. What had unnerved Dickstein was a sudden vision of mushroom clouds over Jerusalem and Cairo, of cotton fields by the Nile and vineyards beside the Sea of Galilee blighted by fallout, the Middle East wasted by fire, its children deformed for generations.

He said, 'I still think peace is an alternative.'

Borg shrugged. 'I wouldn't know. I don't get involved in politics.'

'Bullshit. '

Borg sighed. 'Look, if they have a bomb, we have to have one too, don't we?'

'If that was all there was to it, we could just hold a press conference, announce that the Egyptians are making a bomb, and let the rest of the world stop them. I think our people want the bomb anyway. I think they're glad of the excuse.'

'And maybe they're right!' Borg said. 'We can't go on fighting a war every few years – one of these days we might lose one.'

'We could make peace.'

Borg snorted. 'You're so fucking naive.'

'If we gave way on a few things – the Occupied Territories, the Law of Return, equal rights for Arabs in Israel—'

'The Arabs have equal rights.'

Dickstein smiled mirthlessly. 'You're so fucking naive.'

'Listen!' Borg made an effort at self-control. Dickstein understood his anger: it was a reaction he had in common with many Israelis. They thought that if these liberal ideas should ever take hold, they would be the thin edge of the wedge, and concession would follow concession until the land was handed back to the Arabs on a plate – and that prospect struck at the very roots of their identity. 'Listen,' Borg said again. 'Maybe we should sell our birthright for a mess of potage. But this is the real world, and the people of this country won't vote for peace-at-any-price; and in your heart you know that the Arabs aren't in any great hurry for peace either. So, in the real world, we still have to fight them; and if we're going to fight them we'd better win; and if we're to be sure of winning, you'd better steal us some uranium.'

Dickstein said, 'The thing I dislike most about you is, you're usually right.'

Borg wound down his window and threw away the stub of his cigar. It made a trail of sparks on the road, like a firecracker. The lights of Tel Aviv became visible ahead: they were almost there.

Borg said, 'You know, with most of my people I don't feel obliged to argue politics every time I give them an assignment. They just take orders, like operatives are supposed to.'

'I don't believe you,' Dickstein said. 'This is a nation of idealists, or it's nothing.'

'Maybe.'

'I once knew a man called Wolfgang. He used to say, "I just take orders." Then he used to break my leg.'

'Yeah,' Borg said. 'You told me.'

When a company hires an accountant to keep the books, the first thing he does is announce that he has so much work to do on the overall direction of the company's financial policy that he needs to hire a junior accountant to keep the books. Something similar happens with spies. A country sets up an intelligence service to find out how many tanks its neighbour has and where they are kept, and before you can say MI5 the intelligence service announces that it is so busy spying on subversive elements at home that a separate service is needed to deal with military intelligence.

So it was in Egypt in 1955. The country's fledgling intelligence service was divided into two directorates. Military Intelligence had the job of counting Israel's tanks; General Investigations had all the glamour.

The man in charge of both these directorates was called the Director of General Intelligence, just to be confusing; and he was supposed – in theory – to report to the Minister of the Interior. But another thing that always happens to spy departments is that the Head of State tries to take them over. There are two reasons for this. One is that the spies are continually hatching lunatic schemes of murder, blackmail and invasion which can be terribly embarrassing if they ever get off the ground, so Presidents and Prime Ministers like to keep a personal eye on such departments. The other reason is that intelligence services are a source of power, especially in unstable countries, and the Head of State wants that power for himself.

So the Director of General Intelligence in Cairo always, in practice, reported either to the President or to the Minister of State at the Presidency.

Kawash, the tall Arab who interrogated and killed Towfik and subsequently gave the personnel dosimeter to Pierre Borg, worked in the Directorate of General Investigations, the glamorous civilian half of the service. He was an intelligent and dignified man of great integrity, but he was also deeply religious – to the point of mysticism. His was the solid, powerful kind of mysticism which could support the most unlikely – not to say bizarre – beliefs about the real world. He adhered to a brand of Christianity which held that the return of the Jews to the Promised Land was ordained in the Bible, and was a portent of the end of the world. To work against the return was therefore a sin; to work for it, a holy task. This was why Kawash was a double agent.

The work was all he had. His faith had led him into the secret life, and there he had gradually cut himself off from friends, neighbors, and – with exceptions – family. He had no personal ambitions except to go to heaven. He lived ascetically, his only earthly pleasure being to score points in the espionage game. He was a lot like Pierre Borg, with this difference: Kawash was happy.

At present, though, he was troubled. So far he was losing points in the affair which had begun with Professor Schulz, and this depressed him. The problem was that the Qattara project was being run not by General Investigations but by the other half of the intelligence effort – Military Intelligence. However, Kawash had fasted and meditated, and in the long watches of the night he had developed a scheme for penetrating the secret project.

He had a second cousin, Assam, who worked in the office of the Director of General Intelligence – the body which coordinated Military Intelligence and General Investigations. Assam was more senior than Kawash, but Kawash was smarter.

The two cousins sat in the back room of a small, dirty coffee house near the Sherif Pasha in the heat of the day, drinking lukewarm lime cordial and blowing tobacco smoke at the flies. They looked alike in their lightweight suits and Nasser moustaches. Kawash wanted to use Assam to find out about Qattara. He had devised a plausible line of approach which he thought Assam would go for, but he knew he had to put the matter very delicately in order to win Assam's support. He appeared his usual imperturbable self, despite the anxiety he felt inside.

He began by seeming to be very direct. 'My cousin, do you know what is happening at Qattara?'

A rather furtive look came over Assam's handsome face. 'If you don't know, I can't tell you.'

Kawash shook his head, as if Assam had misunderstood him. 'I don't want you to reveal secrets. Besides, I can guess what the project is.' This was a lie. 'What bothers me is that Maraji has control of it.'

'Why?'

'For your sake. I'm thinking of your career.'

'I'm not worried—'

'Then you should be. Maraji wants your job, you must know that.'

The café proprietor brought a dish of olives and two flat loaves of pita bread. Kawash was silent until he went out. He watched Assam as the man's natural insecurity fed on the lie about Maraji.

Kawash continued, 'Maraji is reporting directly to the Minister, I gather.'

'I see all the documents, though,' Assam said defensively.

'You don't know what he is saying privately to the Minister. He is in a very strong position.'

Assam frowned. 'How did you find out about the project, anyway?'

Kawash leaned back against the cool concrete wall. 'One of Maraji's men was doing a bodyguarding job in Cairo and realized he was being followed. The tail was an Israeli agent called Towfik. Maraji doesn't have any field men in the city, so the bodyguard's request for action was passed to me. I picked Towfik up.'

Assam snorted with disgust. 'Bad enough to let himself be followed. Worse to call the wrong department for help. This is terrible.'

'Perhaps we can do something about it, my cousin.'

Assam scratched his nose with a hand heavy with rings. 'Go on.'

'Tell the Director about Towfik. Say that Maraji, for all his considerable talents, makes mistakes in picking his men, because he is young and inexperienced by comparison with someone such as yourself. Insist that you should have charge of personnel for the Qattara project. Then put a man loyal to us into a job there.'

Assam nodded slowly. 'I see.'

The taste of success was in Kawash's mouth. He leaned forward. 'The Director will be grateful to you for having discovered this area of slackness in a top-security matter. And you will be able to keep track of everything Maraji does.'

'This is a very good plan,' Assam said. 'I will speak to the Director today. I'm grateful to you, cousin.'

Kawash had one more thing to say – the most important thing – and he wanted to say it at the best possible moment. It would wait a few minutes, he decided. He stood up and said, 'Haven't you always been my patron?'

They went arm-in-arm out into the heat of the city. Assam said, 'And I will find a suitable man immediately.'

'Ah, yes,' Kawash said, as if that reminded him of another small detail. 'I have a man who would be ideal. He is intelligent, resourceful, and very discreet – and the son of my late wife's brother.'

Assam's eyes narrowed. 'So he would report to you, too.'

Kawash looked hurt. 'If this is too much for me to ask . . .' He spread his hands in a gesture of resignation.

'No,' Assam said. 'We have always helped one another.'

They reached the corner where they parted company. Kawash struggled to keep his feeling of triumph from showing in his face. 'I will send the man to see you. You will find him completely reliable.'

'So be it,' said Assam.

Pierre Borg had known Nat Dickstein for twenty years. Back in 1948 Borg had been sure the boy was not agent material, despite that stroke with the boatload of rifles. He had been thin, pale, awkward, unprepossessing. But it had not been Borg's decision, and they had given Dickstein a trial. Borg had rapidly come to acknowledge that the kid might not look much but he was smart as shit. He also had an odd charm that Borg never understood. Some of the women in the Mossad were crazy about him – while others, like Borg, failed to see the attraction. Dickstein showed no interest either way – his dossier said, 'Sex life: none.'

Over the years Dickstein had grown in skill and confidence, and now Borg would rely on him more than any other agent. Indeed, if Dickstein had been more personally ambitious he could have had the job Borg now held.

Nevertheless, Borg did not see how Dickstein could fulfil his brief. The result of the policy debate over nuclear weapons had been one of those asinine political compromises which bedevilled the work of all civil servants: they had agreed to steal the uranium only if it could be done in such a way that nobody would know, at least for many years, that Israel had been the thief. Borg had fought the decision – he had been all for a sudden, swift piece of buccaneering and to hell with the consequences. A more judicious view had prevailed in the Cabinet; but it was Borg and his team who had to put the decision into effect.

There were other men in the Mossad who could carry out a prescribed scheme as well as Dickstein – Mike, the head of Special Operations, was one, and Borg himself was another. But there was nobody else to whom Borg could say, as he had said to Dickstein: This is the problem – go solve it.

The two men spent a day in a Mossad safe house in the town of Ramat Gan, just outside Tel Aviv. Security-vetted Mossad employees made coffee, served meals, and patrolled the garden with revolvers under their jackets. In the morning Dickstein saw a young physics teacher from the Weizmann Institute at Rehovot. The scientist had long hair and a flowered tie, and he explained the chemistry of uranium, the nature of radioactivity and the working of an atomic pile with limpid clarity and endless patience. After lunch Dickstein talked to an administrator from Dimona about uranium mines, enrichment plants, fuel fabrication works, storage and transport; about safety rules and international regulations; and about the International Atomic Energy Agency, the US Atomic Energy Commission, the United Kingdom Atomic Energy Authority and Euratom.

In the evening Borg and Dickstein had dinner together. Borg was on a halfhearted diet, as usual: he ate no bread with his skewered lamb and salad, but he drank most of the bottle of red Israeli wine. His excuse was that he was calming his nerves so that he would not reveal his anxiety to Dickstein.

After dinner he gave Dickstein three keys. 'There are spare identities for you in safety-deposit boxes in London, Brussels and Zurich,' he said. 'Passports, driving licences, cash and a weapon in each. If you have to switch, leave the old documents in the box.'

Dickstein nodded. 'Do I report to you or Mike?'

Borg thought: You never report anyway, you bastard. He said, 'To me, please. Whenever possible, call me direct and use the jargon. If you can't reach me, contact any embassy and use the code for a meeting – I'll try to get to you, wherever you are. As a last resort, send coded letters via the diplomatic bags.'

Dickstein nodded expressionlessly: all this was routine. Borg stared at him, trying to read his mind. How did *he* feel? Did he think he could do it? Did he have any ideas? Did he plan to go through the motions of trying it and then report that it was impossible? Was he really convinced the bomb was the right thing for Israel?

Borg could have asked, but he would have got no answers.

Dickstein said, 'Presumably there's a deadline.'

'Yes, but we don't know what it is.' Borg began to pick onions out of the remains of the salad. 'We must have our bomb before the Egyptians get theirs. That means your uranium has to go on stream in the reactor before the Egyptian reactor goes operational. After that point, everything is chemistry – there's nothing either side can do to hurry subatomic particles. The first to start will be the first to finish.'

'We need an agent in Qattara,' Dickstein said.

'I'm working on it.'

Dickstein nodded. 'We must have a very good man in Cairo.'

This was not what Borg wanted to talk about. 'What are you trying to do, pump me for information?' he said crossly.

'Thinking aloud.'

There was silence for a few moments. Borg crunched some more onions. At last he said, 'I've told you what I want, but I've left to you all the decisions about how to get it.'

'Yes, you have, haven't you.' Dickstein stood up. 'I think I'll go to bed.'

'Have you got any idea where you're going to start?'

Dickstein said, 'Yes, I have. Goodnight.'

CHAPTER THREE

NAT DICKSTEIN never got used to being a secret agent. It was the continual deceit that bothered him. He was always lying to people, hiding, pretending to be someone he was not, surreptitiously following people and showing false documents to officials at airports. He never ceased to worry about being found out. He had a daytime nightmare in which he was surrounded suddenly by policemen who shouted, 'You're a spy! You're a spy!' and took him off to prison where they broke his leg.

He was uneasy now. He was at the Jean-Monnet building in Luxembourg, on the Kirchberg Plateau across a narrow river valley from the hilltop city. He sat in the entrance to the offices of the Euratom Safeguards Directorate, memorizing the faces of the employees as they arrived at work. He was waiting to see a press officer called Pfaffer but he had intentionally come much too early. He was looking for weakness. The disadvantage of this ploy was that all the staff got to see his face, too; but he had no time for subtle precautions.

Pfaffer turned out to be an untidy young man with an expression of disapproval and a battered brown briefcase. Dickstein followed him into an equally untidy office and accepted his offer of coffee. They spoke French. Dickstein was accredited to the Paris office of an obscure journal called *Science International.* He told Pfaffer that it was his ambition to get a job on *Scientific American.*

Pfaffer asked him, 'Exactly what are you writing about at the moment?'

'The article is called "MUF".' Dickstein explained in English, 'Material Unaccounted For.' He went on, 'In the United States radioactive fuel is continually getting lost. Here in Europe, I'm told, there's an international system for keeping track of all such material.'

'Correct,' Pfaffer said. 'The member countries hand over control of fissile substances to Euratom. We have, first of all, a complete list of civilian establishments where stocks are held – from mines through preparation and fabrication plants, stores, and reactors, to reprocessing plants.'

'You said civilian establishments.'

'Yes. The military are outside our scope.'

'Go on.' Dickstein was relieved to get Pfaffer talking before the press officer had a chance to realize how limited was Dickstein's knowledge of these subjects.

'As an example,' Pfaffer continued, 'take a factory making fuel elements from ordinary yellowcake. The raw material coming into the factory is weighed and analyzed by Euratom inspectors. Their findings are programmed into the Euratom computer and checked against the information from the inspectors at the dispatching installation – in this case, probably a uranium mine. If there is a discrepancy between the quantity that left the dispatching installation and the quantity that arrived at the factory, the computer will say so. Similar measurements are made of the material leaving the factory – quantity and quality. These figures will in turn be checked against information supplied by inspectors at the premises where the fuel is to be used – a nuclear power station, probably. In addition, all waste at the factory is weighed and analyzed.

'This process of inspection and double-checking is carried on up to and including the final disposal of radioactive wastes. Finally, stocktaking is done at least twice a year at the factory.'

'I see.' Dickstein looked impressed and felt desperately discouraged. No doubt Pfaffer was exaggerating the efficiency of the system – but even if they made half the checks they were supposed to, how could anyone spirit away one hundred tons of yellowcake without their computer noticing? To keep Pfaffer talking, he said, 'So, at any given moment, your computer knows the location of every scrap of uranium in Europe.'

'Within the member countries – France, Germany, Italy, Belgium, the Netherlands and Luxembourg. And it's not just uranium, it's all radioactive material.'

'What about details of transportation?'

'All have to be approved by us.'

Dickstein closed his notebook. 'It sounds like a good system. Can I see it in operation?'

'That wouldn't be up to us. You'd have to contact the atomic energy authority in the member country and ask permission to visit an installation. Some of them do guided tours.'

'Can you let me have a list of phone numbers?'

'Certainly.' Pfaffer stood up and opened a filing cabinet.

Dickstein had solved one problem only to be confronted with another. He had wanted to know where he could go to find out the location of stockpiles of radioactive material, and he now had the answer: Euratom's computer. But all the uranium the computer knew about was subject to the rigorous monitoring system, and therefore extremely difficult to steal. Sitting in the untidy little office, watching the smug Herr Pfaffer rummage through his old press releases, Dickstein thought: If only you knew what's in my mind, little bureaucrat, you'd have a blue fit; and he suppressed a grin and felt a little more cheerful.

Pfaffer handed him a cyclostyled leaflet. Dickstein folded it and put it in his pocket. He said, 'Thank you for your help.'

Pfaffer said, 'Where are you staying?'

'The Alfa, opposite the railway station.'

Pfaffer saw him to the door. 'Enjoy Luxembourg.'

'I'll do my best,' Dickstein said, and shook his hand.

The memory thing was a trick. Dickstein had picked it up as a small child, sitting with his grandfather in a smelly room over a pie shop in the Mile End Road, struggling to recognize the strange characters of the Hebrew alphabet. The idea was to isolate one unique feature of the shape to be remembered and ignore everything else. Dickstein had done that with the faces of the Euratom staff.

He waited outside the Jean-Monnet building in the late afternoon, watching people leave for home. Some of them interested him more than others. Secretaries, messengers and coffee-makers were no use to him, nor were senior administrators. He wanted the people in between: computer programmers, office managers, heads of small departments, personal assistants and assistant chiefs. He had given names to the likeliest ones, names which reminded him of their memorable feature: Diamante, Stiffcollar, Tony Curtis, No-nose, Snowhead, Zapata, Fatbum.

Diamante was a plump woman in her late thirties without a wedding ring. Her name came from the crystal glitter on the rims of her spectacles. Dickstein followed her to the car park, where she squeezed herself into the driving seat of a white Fiat 500. Dickstein's rented Peugeot was parked nearby.

She cross the Pont-Adolphe, driving badly but slowly, and went about fifteen kilometers southeast, finishing up at a small village called Mondorf-les-Bains. She parked in the cobbled yard of a square Luxembourgeois house with a nail-studded door. She let herself in with a key.

The village was a tourist attraction, with thermal springs. Dickstein slung a camera around his neck and wandered about, passing Diamante's house several times. On one pass he saw, through a window, Diamante serving a meal to an old woman.

The baby Fiat stayed outside the house until after midnight, when Dickstein left.

She had been a poor choice. She was a spinster living with her elderly mother, neither rich nor poor – the house was probably the mother's – and apparently without vices. If Dickstein had been a different kind of man he might have seduced her, but otherwise there was no way to get at her.

He went back to his hotel disappointed and frustrated – unreasonably so, for he had made the best guess he could on the information he had. Nevertheless he felt he had spent a day skirting the problem and he was impatient to get to grips with it so he could stop worrying vaguely and start worrying specifically.

He spent three more days getting nowhere. He drew blanks with Zapata, Fatbum and Tony Curtis.

But Stiffcollar was perfect.

He was about Dickstein's age, a slim, elegant man in a dark blue suit, plain blue tie, and white shirt with starched collar. His dark hair, a little longer than was usual for a man of his age, was greying over the ears. He wore handmade shoes.

He walked from the office across the Alzette River and uphill into the old town. He went down a narrow cobbled street and entered an old terraced house. Two minutes later a light went on in an attic window.

Dickstein hung around for two hours.

When Stiffcollar came out he was wearing close-fitting light trousers and an orange scarf around his neck. His hair was combed forward, making him look younger, and his walk was jaunty.

Dickstein followed him to the Rue Dicks, where he ducked into an unlit doorway and disappeared. Dickstein stopped outside. The door was open but there was nothing to indicate what might be inside. A bare flight of stairs went down. After a moment, Dickstein heard faint music.

Two young men in matching yellow jeans passed him and went in. One of them grinned back at him and said, 'Yes, this is the place.' Dickstein followed them down the stairs.

It was an ordinary-looking nightclub with tables and chairs, a few booths, a small dance floor and a jazz trio in a corner. Dickstein paid an entrance fee and sat at a booth, within sight of Stiffcollar. He ordered beer.

He had already guessed why the place had such a discreet air, and now, as he looked around, his theory was confirmed: it was a homosexual club. It was the first club of this kind he had been to, and he was mildly surprised to find it so unexceptionable. A few of the men wore light make-up, there were a couple of outrageous queens camping it up by the bar, and a very pretty girl was holding hands with an older woman in trousers; but most of the customers were dressed normally by the standards of peacock Europe, and there was no one in drag.

Stiffcollar was sitting close to a fair-haired man in a maroon double-breasted jacket. Dickstein had no feelings about homosexuals as such. He was not offended when people supposed, wrongly, that he might be homosexual because he was a bachelor in his early forties. To him, Stiffcollar was just a man who worked at Euratom and had a guilty secret.

He listened to the music and drank his beer. A waiter came across and said, 'Are you on your own, dear?'

Dickstein shook his head. 'I'm waiting for my friend.'

A guitarist replaced the trio and began to sing vulgar folk songs in German. Dickstein missed most of the jokes, but the rest of the audience roared with laughter. After that several couples danced.

Dickstein saw Stiffcollar put his hand on his companion's knee. He got up and walked across to their booth.

'Hello,' he said cheerfully, 'didn't I see you at the Euratom office the other day?'

Stiffcollar went white. 'I don't know . . .'

Dickstein stuck out his hand. 'Ed Rodgers,' he said, giving the name he had used with Pfaffer. 'I'm a journalist.'

Stiffcollar muttered, 'How do you do.' He was shaken, but he had the presence of mind not to give his name.

'I've got to rush away,' Dickstein said. 'It was nice to see you.'

'Goodbye, then.'

Dickstein turned away and went out of the club. He had done all that was necessary, for now: Stiffcollar knew that his secret was out, and he was frightened.

Dickstein walked towards his hotel, feeling grubby and ashamed.

He was followed from the Rue Dicks.

The tail was not a professional, and made no attempt at camouflage. He stayed fifteen or twenty steps behind, his leather shoes making a regular slap-slap on the pavement. Dickstein pretended not to notice. Crossing the road, he got a look at the tail: a large youth, long hair, worn brown leather jacket.

Moments later another youth stepped out of the shadows and stood squarely in front of Dickstein, blocking the pavement. Dickstein stood still and waited, thinking: What the hell is this? He could not imagine who could be tailing him already, nor why anyone who wanted him tailed would use clumsy amateurs from off the streets.

The blade of a knife glinted in the street light. The tail came up behind.

The youth in front said, 'All right, nancy-boy, give us your wallet.'

Dickstein was deeply relieved. They were just thieves who assumed that anyone coming out of that nightclub would be easy game.

'Don't hit me,' Dickstein said, 'I'll give you my money.' He took out his wallet.

'The wallet,' the youth said.

Dickstein did not want to fight them; but, while he could get more cash easily, he would be greatly inconvenienced if he lost all his papers and credit cards. He removed the notes from the wallet and offered them. 'I need my papers. Just take the money, and I won't report this.'

The boy in front snatched the notes.

The one behind said, 'Get the credit cards.'

The one in front was the weaker. Dickstein looked squarely at him and said, 'Why don't you quit while you're ahead, sonny?' Then he walked forward, passing the youth on the outside of the pavement.

Leather shoes beat a brief tattoo as the other rushed Dickstein, and then there was only one way for the encounter to end.

Dickstein spun about, grabbed the boy's foot as he aimed a kick, pulled and twisted, and broke the boy's ankle. The kid shouted with pain and fell down.

The one with the knife came at Dickstein then. He danced back, kicked the boy's shin, danced back, and kicked again. The boy lunged with the knife. Dickstein dodged and kicked him a third time in exactly the same place. There was a noise like a bone snapping, and the boy fell down.

Dickstein stood for a moment looking at the two injured muggers. He felt like a parent whose children had pushed him until he was obliged to strike them. He thought: Why did you make me do it? They *were* children: about seventeen, he guessed. They were vicious – they preyed on homosexuals; but that was exactly what Dickstein had been doing this night.

He walked away. It was an evening to forget. He decided to leave town in the morning.

When Dickstein was working he stayed in his hotel room as much as possible to avoid being seen. He might have been a heavy drinker, except it was unwise to drink during an operation – alcohol blunted the sharp edge of his vigilance – and at other times he felt no need of it. He spent a lot of time looking out of windows or sitting in front of a flickering television screen. He did not walk around the streets, did not sit in hotel bars, did not even eat in hotel restaurants – he always used room service. But there were limits to the precautions a man could take: he could not be invisible. In the lobby of the Alfa Hotel in Luxembourg he bumped into someone who knew him.

He was standing at the desk, checking out. He had looked over the bill and presented a credit card in the name of Ed Rodgers, and he was waiting to sign the American Express slip when a voice behind him said in English, 'My God! It's Nat Dickstein, isn't it?'

It was the moment he dreaded. Like every agent who used cover identities, he lived in constant fear of accidentally coming up against someone from his distant past who could unmask him. It was the nightmare of the policemen who shouted. 'You're a spy!' and it was the debt-collector saying, 'But your mother *is* in, I just saw her, through the window, hiding under the kitchen table.'

Like every agent he had been trained for this moment. The rule was simple: *Whoever it is, you don't know him.* They made you practise in the school. They would say, 'Today you are Chaim Meyerson, engineering student,' and so on; and you would have to walk around and do your work and be Chaim Meyerson; and then, late in the afternoon, they would arrange for you to bump into your cousin, or your old college professor, or a rabbi who knew your whole family. The first time, you always smiled and said 'Hello,' and talked about old times for a while, and then that evening your tutor told you that you were dead. Eventually you learned to look old friends straight in the eye and say, 'Who the hell are you?'

Dickstein's training came into play now. He looked first at the desk clerk, who was at that moment checking him out in the name of Ed Rodgers. The clerk did not react: presumably either he did not understand, or he had not heard, or he did not care.

A hand tapped Dickstein's shoulder. He started an apologetic smile and turned around, saying in French, 'I'm afraid you've got the wrong—'

The skirt of her dress was around her waist, her face was flushed with pleasure, and she was kissing Yasif Hassan.

'It *is* you!' said Yasif Hassan.

And then, because of the dreadful impact of the memory of that morning in Oxford twenty years ago, Dickstein lost control for an instant, and his training deserted him, and he made the biggest mistake of his career. He stared in shock, and he said, 'Christ. Hassan.'

Hassan smiled, and stuck out his hand, and said, 'How long . . . it must be . . . more than twenty years!'

Dickstein shook the proffered hand mechanically, conscious that he had blundered, and tried to pull himself together. 'It must be,' he muttered. 'What are you doing here?'

'I live here. You?'

'I'm just leaving.' Dickstein decided the only thing to do was get out, fast, before he did himself any more harm. The clerk handed him the credit-card form and he scribbled 'Ed Rodgers' on it. He looked at his wristwatch. 'Damn, I've got to catch this plane.'

'My car's outside,' Hassan said. 'I'll take you to the airport. We *must* talk.'

'I've ordered a taxi . . .'

Hassan spoke to the desk clerk. 'Cancel that cab – give this to the driver for his trouble.' He handed over some coins.

Dickstein said, 'I really am in a rush.'

'Come on, then!' Hassan picked up Dickstein's case and went outside.

Feeling helpless, foolish and incompetent, Dickstein followed.

They got into a battered two-seater English sports car. Dickstein studied Hassan as he steered the car out of a no-waiting zone and into the traffic. The Arab had changed, and it was not just age. The grey streaks in his moustache, the thickening of his waist, his deeper voice – these were to be expected. But something else was different. Hassan had always seemed to Dickstein to be

89

the archetypal aristocrat. He had been slow-moving, dispassionate and faintly bored when everyone else was young and excitable. Now his hauteur seemed to have gone. He was like his car: somewhat the worse for wear, with a rather hurried air. Still, Dickstein had sometimes wondered how much of his upper-class appearance was cultivated.

Resigning himself to the consequences of his error, Dickstein tried to find out the extent of the damage. He asked Hassan, 'You live here now?'

'My bank has its European headquarters here.'

So, maybe he's still rich, Dickstein thought. 'Which bank is that?'

'The Cedar Bank of Lebanon.'

'Why Luxembourg?'

'It's a considerable financial centre,' Hassan replied. 'The European Investment Bank is here, and they have an international stock exchange. But what about you?'

'I live in Israel. My kibbutz makes wine – I'm sniffing at the possibilities of European distribution.'

'Taking coals to Newcastle.'

'I'm beginning to think so.'

'Perhaps I can help you, if you're coming back. I have a lot of contacts here. I could set up some appointments for you.'

'Thank you. I'm going to take you up on that offer.' If the worst came to the worst, Dickstein thought, he could always keep the appointments and sell some wine.

Hassan said, 'So, now your home is in Palestine and

my home is in Europe.' His smile was forced, Dickstein thought.

'How is the bank doing?' Dickstein asked, wondering whether 'my bank' had meant 'the bank I own' or 'the bank I manage' or 'the bank I work for'.

'Oh, remarkably well.'

They seemed not to have much more to say to each other. Dickstein would have liked to ask what had happened to Hassan's family in Palestine, how his affair with Eila Ashford had ended, and why he was driving a sports car; but he was afraid the answers might be painful, either for Hassan or for himself.

Hassan asked, 'Are you married?'

'No. You?'

'No.'

'How odd,' Dickstein said.

Hassan smiled. 'We're not the type to take on responsibilities, you and I.'

'Oh, I've got responsibilities,' Dickstein said, think-ing of the orphan Mottie who had not yet finished *Treasure Island.*

'But you have a roving eye, eh?' Hassan said with a wink.

'As I recall, you were the ladies' man,' Dickstein said uncomfortably.

'Ah, those were the days.'

Dickstein tried not to think about Eila. They reached the airport, and Hassan stopped the car.

Dickstein said, 'Thank you for the lift.'

Hassan swivelled around in the bucket seat. He

stared at Dickstein. 'I can't get over this,' he said. 'You actually look younger than you did in 1947.'

Dickstein shook his hand. 'I'm sorry to be in such a rush.' He got out of the car.

'Don't forget – call me next time you're here,' Hassan said.

'Goodbye.' Dickstein closed the car door and walked into the airport.

Then, at last, he allowed himself to remember.

The four people in the chilly garden were still for one long heartbeat. Then Hassan's hands moved on Eila's body. Instantly Dickstein and Cortone moved away, through the gap in the hedge and out of sight. The lovers never saw them.

They walked toward the house. When they were well out of earshot Cortone said, 'Jesus, that was hot stuff.'

'Let's not talk about it,' Dickstein said. He felt like a man who, looking backward over his shoulder, has walked into a lamp-post: there was pain and rage, and nobody to blame but himself.

Fortunately the party was breaking up. They left without speaking to the cuckold, Professor Ashford, who was in a corner deep in conversation with a graduate student. They went to the George for lunch. Dickstein ate very little but drank some beer.

Cortone said, 'Listen, Nat, I don't know why you're getting so down in the mouth about it. I mean, it just goes to show she's available, right?'

'Yes,' Dickstein said, but he did not mean it.

The bill came to more than ten shillings. Cortone paid it. Dickstein walked him to the railway station. They shook hands solemnly, and Cortone got on the train.

Dickstein walked in the park for several hours, hardly noticing the cold, trying to sort out his feelings. He failed. He knew he was not envious of Hassan, or disillusioned with Eila, nor disappointed in his hopes, for he had never been hopeful. He was shattered, and he had no words to say why. He wished he had somebody to whom he could talk about it.

Soon after this he went to Palestine, although not just because of Eila.

In the next twenty-one years he never had a woman; but that, too, was not entirely because of Eila.

Yasif Hassan drove away from Luxembourg airport in a black rage. He could picture, as clearly as if it were yesterday, the young Dickstein: a pale Jew in a cheap suit, thin as a girl, always standing slightly hunched as if he expected to be flogged, staring with adolescent longing at the ripe body of Eila Ashford, arguing doggedly that his people would have Palestine whether the Arabs consented or not. Hassan had thought him ridiculous, a child. Now Dickstein lived in Israel, and grew grapes to make wine: he had found a home, and Hassan had lost one.

Hassan was no longer rich. He had never been fabulously wealthy, even by Levantine standards, but he had always had fine food, expensive clothes and the best education, and he had consciously adopted the manners of Arab aristocracy. His grandfather had been a successful doctor who set up his elder son in medicine and his younger son in business. The younger, Hassan's father, bought and sold textiles in Palestine, Lebanon and Transjordan. The business prospered under British rule, and Zionist immigration swelled the market. By 1947 the family had shops all over the Levant and owned their native village near Nazareth.

The 1948 war ruined them.

When the State of Israel was declared and the Arab armies attacked, the Hassan family made the fatal mistake of packing their bags and fleeing to Syria. They never came back. The warehouse in Jerusalem burned down; the shops were destroyed or taken over by Jews; and the family lands became 'administered' by the Israeli government. Hassan had heard that the village was now a kibbutz.

Hassan's father had lived ever since in a United Nations refugee camp. The last positive thing he had done was to write a letter of introduction for Yasif to his Lebanese bankers. Yasif had a university degree and spoke excellent English: the bank gave him a job.

He applied to the Israeli government for compensation under the 1953 Land Acquisition Act, and was refused.

He visited his family in the camp only once, but what he saw there stayed with him for the rest of his life. They lived in a hut made of boards and shared the communal toilets. They got no special treatment: they were just one among thousands of families without a home, a purpose or a hope. To see his father who had been a clever, decisive man ruling a large business with a firm hand, reduced now to queuing for food and wasting his life playing backgammon, made Yasif want to throw bombs at school buses.

The women fetched water and cleaned house much as always, but the men shuffled around in secondhand clothes, waiting for nothing, their bodies getting flabby while their minds grew dull. Teenagers strutted and squabbled and fought with knives, for there was nothing ahead of them but the prospect of their lives shrivelling to nothing in the baking heat of the sun.

The camp smelled of sewage and despair. Hassan never returned to visit, although he continued to write to his mother. He had escaped the trap, and if he was deserting his father, well, his father had helped him do it, so it must have been what he wanted.

He was a modest success as a bank clerk. He had intelligence and integrity, but his upbringing did not fit him for careful, calculating work involving much shuffling of memoranda and keeping of records in triplicate. Besides, his heart was elsewhere.

He never ceased bitterly to resent what had been taken from him. He carried his hatred through life like a secret burden. Whatever his logical mind might tell him, his soul said he had abandoned his father in time of need, and the guilt fed his hatred of Israel. Each year he expected the Arab armies to destroy the Zionist invaders, and each time they failed he grew more wretched and more angry.

In 1957 he began to work for Egyptian Intelligence.

He was not a very important agent, but as the bank expanded its European business he began to pick up the occasional titbit, both in the office and from general banking gossip. Sometimes Cairo would ask him for specific information about the finances of an arms manufacturer, a Jewish philanthropist, or an Arab millionaire; and if Hassan did not have the details in his bank's files he could often get them from friends and business contacts. He also had a general brief to keep an eye on Israeli businessmen in Europe, in case they were agents; and that was why he had approached Nat Dickstein and pretended to be friendly.

Hassan thought Dickstein's story was probably true. In his shabby suit, with the same round spectacles and the same inconspicuous air, he looked exactly like an underpaid salesman with a product he could not promote. However, there was that odd business in the Rue Dicks the previous night: two youths, known to the police as petty thieves, had been found in the gutter savagely disabled. Hassan had got all the details from a contact on the city police force. Clearly they had picked on the wrong sort of victim. Their injuries were professional: the man who had inflicted them had to be a soldier, a policeman, a bodyguard . . . or an agent. After an incident like that, any Israeli who flew out in a hurry the next morning was worth checking up on.

Hassan drove back to the Alfa Hotel and spoke to the desk clerk. 'I was here an hour ago when one of your guests was checking out,' he said. 'Do you remember?'

'I think so, sir.'

Hassan gave him two hundred Luxembourg francs. 'Would you tell me what name he was registered under?'

'Certainly, sir.' The clerk consulted a file. 'Edward Rodgers, from *Science International* magazine.'

'Not Nathaniel Dickstein?'

The clerk shook his head patiently.

'Would you just see whether you had a Nathaniel Dickstein, from Israel, registered at all?'

'Certainly.' The clerk took several minutes to look through a wad of papers. Hassan's excitement rose. If Dickstein had registered under a false name, then he was not a wine salesman – so what else could he be but an Israeli agent? Finally the clerk closed his file and looked up. 'Definitely not, sir.'

'Thank you.' Hassan left. He was jubilant as he drove back to his office: he had used his wits and discovered something important. As soon as he got to his desk he composed a message.

SUSPECTED ISRAELI AGENT SEEN HERE. NAT DICKSTEIN ALIAS ED RODGERS. FIVE FOOT SIX, SMALL BUILD, DARK HAIR, BROWN EYES, AGE ABOUT 40.

He encoded the message, added an extra code word at its top and sent it by telex to the bank's Egyptian headquarters. It would never get there: the extra code word instructed the Cairo post office to reroute the telex to the Directorate of General Investigations.

Sending the message was an anticlimax, of course. There would be no reaction, no thanks from the other end. Hassan had nothing to do but get on with his bank work, and try not to daydream.

Then Cairo called him on the phone.

It had never happened before. Sometimes they sent him cables, telexes, and even letters, all in code, of course. Once or twice he had met with people from Arab embassies and been given verbal instructions. But they had never phoned. His report must have caused more of a stir than he had anticipated.

The caller wanted to know more about Dickstein. 'I want to confirm the identity of the customer referred to in your message,' he said. 'Did he wear round spectacles?'

'Yes.'

'Did he speak English with a Cockney accent? Would you recognize such an accent?'

'Yes, and yes.'

'Did he have a number tattooed on his forearm?'

'I didn't see it today, but I know he has it . . . I was at Oxford University with him, years ago. I'm quite sure it is him.'

'You *know* him?' There was astonishment in the voice from Cairo. 'Is this information on your file?'

'No, I've never—'

'Then it should be,' the man said angrily. 'How long have you been with us?'

'Since 1957.'

'That explains it . . . those were the old days. Okay, now listen. This man is a very important . . . client. We want you to stay with him twenty-four hours a day, do you understand?'

'I can't,' Hassan said miserably. 'He left town.'

'Where did he go?'

'I dropped him at the airport, I don't know where he went.'

'Then find out. Phone the airlines, ask which flight he was on, and call me back in fifteen minutes.'

'I'll do my best—'

'I'm not interested in your best,' said the voice from Cairo. 'I want his destination, and I want it before he gets there. Just be sure you call me in fifteen minutes. Now that we've contacted him, *we must not lose him again.*'

'I'll get on to it right away,' said Hassan, but the line was dead before he could finish the sentence.

He cradled the phone. True, he had got no thanks from Cairo; but this was better. Suddenly he was important, his work was urgent, they were depending on him. He had a chance to do something for the Arab cause, a chance to strike back at last.

He picked up the phone again and started calling the airlines.

CHAPTER FOUR

NAT DICKSTEIN chose to visit a nuclear power station in France simply because French was the only European language he spoke passably well, except for English, but England was not part of Euratom. He travelled to the power station in a bus with an assorted party of students and tourists. The countryside slipping past the windows was a dusty southern green, more like Galilee than Essex, which had been 'the country' to Dickstein as a boy. He had travelled the world since, getting on planes as casually as any jetsetter, but he could remember the time when his horizons had been Park Lane in the west and Southend-on-Sea in the east. He could also remember how suddenly those horizons had receded, when he began to try to think of himself as a man, after his bar mitzvah and the death of his father. Other boys of his age saw themselves getting jobs on the docks or in printing plants, marrying local girls, finding houses within a quarter of a mile of their parents' homes and settling down; their ambitions were to breed a champion greyhound, to see West Ham win the Cup Final, to buy a motor car. Young Nat thought he might go to California or Rhodesia or Hong Kong and become a brain surgeon or an archaeologist or a millionaire. It was partly that he was cleverer than most of his contemporaries; partly that to them foreign languages were alien, mysterious, a school subject like algebra rather than a way of talking; but mainly the difference had to do with being Jewish. Dickstein's boyhood chess partner, Harry Chieseman, was brainy and forceful and quick-witted, but he saw himself as a working-class Londoner and believed he would always be one. Dickstein knew – although he could not remember anyone actually telling him this – that wherever they were born, Jews were able to find their way into the greatest universities, to start new industries like motion pictures, to become the most successful bankers and lawyers and manufacturers; and if they could not do it in the country where they were born, they would move somewhere else and try again. It was curious, Dickstein thought as he recollected his boyhood, that a people who had been persecuted for centuries should be so convinced of their ability to achieve anything they set their minds to. Like, when they needed nuclear bombs, they went out and got them.

The tradition was a comfort, but it gave him no help with the ways and means.

The power station loomed in the distance. As the bus got closer, Dickstein realized that the reactor was going to be bigger than he had imagined. It occupied a ten-storey building. Somehow he had imagined the thing fitting into a small room.

The external security was on an industrial, rather than military, level. The premises were surrounded by one high fence, not electrified. Dickstein looked into the gatehouse while the tour guide went through the formalities: the guards had only two closed-circuit television screens. Dickstein thought: I could get fifty men inside the compound in broad daylight without the guards noticing anything amiss. It was a bad sign, he decided glumly: it meant they had other reasons to be confident.

He left the bus with the rest of the party and walked across the tar-macadamed parking lot to the reception building. The place had been laid out with a view to the public image of nuclear energy: there were well-kept lawns and flower beds and lots of newly planted trees; everything was clean and natural, white-painted and smokeless. Looking back toward the gatehouse, Dickstein saw a grey Opel pull up on the road. One of the two men in it got out and spoke to the security guards, who appeared to give directions. Inside the car, something glinted briefly in the sun.

Dickstein followed the tour party into the lounge. There in a glass case was a rugby football trophy won by the power station's team. An aerial photograph of the establishment hung on the wall. Dickstein stood in front of it, imprinting its details on his mind, idly figuring out how he would raid the place while the back of his mind worried about the grey Opel.

They were led around the power station by four hostesses in smart uniforms. Dickstein was not interested in the massive turbines, the space-age control room with its banks of dials and switches, or the water-intake system designed to save the fish and return them to the river. He wondered if the men in the Opel had been following him, and if so, why.

He was enormously interested in the delivery bay. He asked the hostess, 'How does the fuel arrive?'

'On trucks,' she said archly. Some of the party giggled nervously at the thought of uranium running around the countryside on trucks. 'It's not dangerous,' she went on as soon as she had got the expected laugh. 'It isn't even radioactive until it is fed into the atomic pile. It is taken off the truck straight into the elevator and up to the fuel store on the seventh floor. From there, everything is automatic.'

'What about checking the quantity and quality of the consignment?' Dickstein said.

'This is done at the fuel fabrication plant. The consignment is sealed there, and only the seals are checked here.'

'Thank you.' Dickstein nodded, pleased. The system was not quite as rigorous as Mr Pfaffer of Euratom had claimed. One or two schemes began to take vague shape in Dickstein's mind.

They saw the reactor loading machine in operation. Worked entirely by remote control, it took the fuel element from the store to the reactor, lifted the concrete lid of a fuel channel, removed the spent element, inserted the new one, closed the lid and dumped the used element into a water-filled shaft which led to the cooling ponds.

The hostess, speaking perfect Parisian French in an oddly seductive voice, said, 'The reactor has three thousand fuel channels, each channel containing eight fuel rods. The rods last four to seven years. The loading machine renews five channels in each operation.'

They went on to see the cooling ponds. Under twenty feet of water the spent fuel elements were loaded into pannets, then – cool, but still highly radioactive – they were locked into fifty-ton lead flasks, two hundred elements to a flask, for transport by road and rail to a reprocessing plant.

As the hostesses served coffee and pastries in the lounge Dickstein considered what he had learned. It had occurred to him that, since plutonium was ultimately what was wanted, he might steal used fuel. Now he knew why nobody had suggested it. It would be easy enough to hijack the truck – he could do it single-handed – but how would he sneak a fifty-ton lead flask out of the country and take it to Israel without anyone noticing?

Stealing uranium from inside the power station was no more promising an idea. Sure, the security was flimsy – the very fact that he had been permitted to make this reconnaissance, and had even been given a guided tour, showed that. But fuel inside the station was locked into an automatic, remote-controlled system. The only way it could come out was by going right through the nuclear process and emerging in the cooling ponds; and then he was back with the problem of sneaking a huge flask of radioactive material through some European port.

There had to be a way of breaking into the fuel store, Dickstein supposed; then you could manhandle the stuff into the elevator, take it down, put it on a truck and drive away; but that would involve holding some or all of the station personnel at gunpoint for some time, and his brief was to do this thing surreptitiously.

A hostess offered to refill his cup, and he accepted. Trust the French to give you good coffee. A young engineer began a talk on nuclear safety. He wore unpressed trousers and a baggy sweater. Scientists and technicians all had a look about them, Dickstein had observed: their clothes were old, mismatched and comfortable, and if many of them wore beards, it was usually a sign of indifference rather than vanity. He thought it was because in their work, force of personality generally counted for nothing, brains for everything, so there was no point in trying to make a good visual impression. But perhaps that was a romantic view of science.

He did not pay attention to the lecture. The physicist from the Weizmann Institute had been much more concise. 'There is no such thing as a safe level of radiation,' he had said. 'Such talk makes you think of radiation like water in a pool: if it's four feet high you're safe, if it's eight feet high you drown. But in fact radiation levels are much more like speed limits on the highway – thirty miles per hour is safer than eighty, but not as safe as twenty, and the only way to be completely safe is not to get in the car.'

Dickstein turned his mind back to the problem of stealing uranium. It was the requirement of *secrecy* that defeated every plan he dreamed. Maybe the whole thing was doomed to failure. After all, impossible is impossible, he thought. No, it was too soon to say that. He went back to first principles.

He would have to take a consignment in transit: that much was clear from what he had seen today. Now, the fuel elements were not checked at this end, they were fed straight into the system. He could hijack a truck, take the uranium out of the fuel elements, close them up again, reseal the consignment and bribe or frighten the truck driver to deliver the empty shells. The dud elements would gradually find their way into the reactor, five at a time, over a period of months. Eventually the reactor's output would fall marginally. There would be an investigation. Tests would be done. Perhaps no conclusions would be reached before the empty elements ran out and new, genuine fuel elements went in, causing output to rise again. Maybe no one would understand what had happened until the duds were reprocessed and the plutonium recovered was too little, by which time – four to seven years later – the trail to Tel Aviv would have gone cold.

But they might find out sooner. And there was still the problem of getting the stuff out of the country.

Still, he had the outline of one possible scheme, and he felt a bit more cheerful.

The lecture ended. There were a few desultory questions, then the party trooped back to the bus. Dickstein sat at the back. A middle-aged woman said to him, 'That was my seat,' and he stared at her stonily until she went away.

Driving back from the power station, Dickstein kept looking out of the rear window. After about a mile the grey Opel pulled out of a turnoff and followed the bus. Dickstein's cheerfulness vanished.

He had been spotted. It had happened either here or in Luxembourg, probably Luxembourg. The spotter might have been Yasif Hassan – no reason why he should not be an agent – or someone else. They must be following him out of general curiosity because there was no way – was there? – that they could know what he was up to. All he had to do was lose them.

He spent a day in and around the town near the nuclear power station, travelling by bus and taxi, driving a rented car, and walking. By the end of the day he had identified the three vehicles – the grey Opel, a dirty little flatbed truck, and a German Ford – and five of the men in the surveillance team. The men looked vaguely Arabic, but in this part of France many of the criminals were North African: somebody might have hired local help. The size of the team explained why he had not sniffed the surveillance earlier. They had been able continually to switch cars and personnel. The trip to the power station, a long there-and-back journey on a country road with very little traffic, explained why the team had finally blown themselves.

The next day he drove out of town and on to the autoroute. The Ford followed him for a few miles, then the grey Opel took over. There were two men in each car. There would be two more in the flatbed truck, plus one at his hotel.

The Opel was still with him when he found a

pedestrian bridge over the road in a place where there were no turnoffs from the highway for four or five miles in either direction. Dickstein pulled over to the shoulder, stopped the car, got out and lifted the hood. He looked inside for a few minutes. The grey Opel disappeared up ahead, and the Ford went by a minute later. The Ford would wait at the next turnoff, and the Opel would come back on the opposite side of the road to see what he was doing. That was what the textbook prescribed for this situation.

Dickstein hoped these people would follow the book, otherwise his scheme would not work.

He took a collapsible warning triangle from the trunk of the car and stood it behind the offside rear wheel.

The Opel went by on the opposite side of the highway.

They were following the book.

Dickstein began to walk.

When he got off the highway he caught the first bus he saw and rode it until it came to a town. On the journey he spotted each of the three surveillance vehicles at different times. He allowed himself to feel a little premature triumph: they were going for it.

He took a taxi from the town and got out close to his car but on the wrong side of the highway. The Opel went by, then the Ford pulled off the road a couple of hundred yards behind him.

Dickstein began to run.

He was in good condition after his months of out-door work in the kibbutz. He sprinted to the pedestrian bridge, ran across it and raced along the shoulder on the other side of the road. Breathing hard and sweating, he reached his abandoned car in under three minutes.

One of the men from the Ford had got out and started to follow him. The man now realized he had been taken in. The Ford moved off. The man ran back and jumped into it as it gathered speed and swung into the slow lane.

Dickstein got into his car. The surveillance vehicles were now on the wrong side of the highway and would have to go all the way to the next junction before they could cross over and come after him. At sixty miles per hour the round trip would take them ten minutes, which meant he had at least five minutes start on them. They would not catch him.

He pulled away, heading for Paris, humming a musical chant that came from the football terraces of West Ham: 'Easy, easy, eeeezeee.'

There was a godalmighty panic in Moscow when they heard about the Arab atom bomb.

The Foreign Ministry panicked because they had not heard of it earlier, the KGB panicked because they had not heard about it first, and the Party Secretary's office panicked because the last thing they wanted was another who's-to-blame row between the Foreign Ministry and the KGB; the previous one had made life hell in the Kremlin for eleven months.

Fortunately, the way the Egyptians chose to make

their revelation allowed for a certain amount of covering of rears. The Egyptians wanted to make the point that they were not diplomatically obliged to tell their allies about this secret project, and the technical help they were asking for was not crucial to its success. Their attitude was 'Oh, by the way, we're building this nuclear reactor in order to get some plutonium to make atom bombs to blow Israel off the face of the earth, so would you like to give us a hand, or not?' The message, trimmed and decorated with ambassadorial niceties, was delivered, in the manner of an afterthought, at the end of a routine meeting between the Egyptian Ambassador in Moscow and the deputy chief of the Middle East desk at the Foreign Ministry.

The deputy chief who received the message considered very carefully what he should do with the information. His first duty, naturally, was to pass the news to his chief, who would then tell the Secretary. However, the credit for the news would go to his chief, who would also not miss the opportunity for scoring points off the KGB. Was there a way for the deputy chief to gain some advantage to himself out of the affair?

He knew that the best way to get on in the Kremlin was to put the KGB under some obligation to yourself. He was now in a position to do the boys a big favour. If he warned them of the Egyptian Ambassador's message, they would have a little time to get ready to pretend they knew all about the Arab atom bomb and were about to reveal the news themselves.

He put on his coat, thinking to go out and phone

his acquaintance in the KGB from a phone booth in case his own phone were tapped – then he realized how silly that would be, for he was going to call the KGB, and it was they who tapped people's phones anyway; so he took off his coat and used his office phone.

The KGB desk man he talked to was equally expert at working the system. In the new KGB building on the Moscow ring road, he kicked up a huge fuss. First he called his boss's secretary and asked for an urgent meeting in fifteen minutes. He carefully avoided speaking to the boss himself. He fired off half a dozen more noisy phone calls, and sent secretaries and messengers scurrying about the building to take memos and collect files. But his master stroke was the agenda. It so happened that the agenda for the next meeting of the Middle East political committee had been typed the previous day and was at this moment being run off on a duplicating machine. He got the agenda back and at the top of the list added a new item: 'Recent Developments in Egyptian Armaments – Special Report,' followed by his own name in brackets. Next he ordered the new agenda to be duplicated, still bearing the previous day's date, and sent around to the interested departments that afternoon by hand.

Then when he had made certain that half Moscow would associate his name and no one else's with the news, he went to see his boss.

The same day a much less striking piece of news came in. As part of the routine exchange of information between Egyptian Intelligence and the KGB, Cairo sent notice that an Israeli agent named Nat Dickstein had been spotted in Luxembourg and was now under surveillance. Because of the circumstances, the report got less attention than it deserved. There was only one man in the KGB who entertained the mildest suspicion that the two items might be connected.

His name was David Rostov.

David Rostov's father had been a minor diplomat whose career was stunted by a lack of connections, particularly secret service connections. Knowing this, the son, with the remorseless logic which was to characterize his decisions all his life, joined what was then called the NKVD, later to become the KGB.

He had already been an agent when he went to Oxford. In those idealistic times, when Russia had just won the war and the extent of the Stalin purge was not comprehended, the great English universities had been ripe recruiting-grounds for Soviet Intelligence. Rostov had picked a couple of winners, one of whom was still sending secrets from London in 1968. Nat Dickstein had been one of his failures.

Young Dickstein had been some kind of socialist, Rostov remembered, and his personality was suited to espionage: he was withdrawn, intense and mistrustful. He had brains, too. Rostov recalled debating the Middle East with him, and with Professor Ashford and Yasif Hassan, in the green-and-white house by the river. And the Rostov–Dickstein chess match had been a hard-fought affair.

But Dickstein did not have the light of idealism in

his eyes. He had no evangelical spirit. He was secure in his convictions, but he had no wish to convert the rest of the world. Most of the war veterans had been like that. Rostov would lay the bait – 'Of course, if you *really* want to join the struggle for world socialism, you have to work for the Soviet Union' – and the veterans would say 'Bullshit.'

After Oxford Rostov had worked in Russian embassies in a series of European capitals – Rome, Amsterdam, Paris. He never got out of the KGB and into the diplomatic service. Over the years he came to realize that he did not have the breadth of political vision to become the great statesman his father wanted him to be. The earnestness of his youth disappeared. He still thought, on balance, that socialism was probably the political system of the future; but this credo no longer burned inside him like a passion. He believed in Communism the way most people believed in God: he would not be greatly surprised or disappointed if he turned out to be wrong, and meanwhile it made little difference to the way he lived.

In his maturity he pursued narrower ambitions with, if anything, greater energy. He became a superb technician, a master of the devious and cruel skills of the intelligence game; and – equally important in the USSR as well as the West – he learned how to manipulate the bureaucracy so as to gain maximum kudos for his triumphs.

The First Chief Directorate of the KGB was a kind of Head Office, responsible for collection and analysis of information. Most of the field agents were attached to the Second Chief Directorate, the largest department of the KGB, which was involved in subversion, sabotage, treason, economic espionage and any internal police work considered politically sensitive. The Third Chief Directorate, which had been called Smersh until that name got a lot of embarrassing publicity in the West, did counter-espionage and special operations, and it employed some of the bravest, cleverest, nastiest agents in the world.

Rostov worked in the Third, and he was one of its stars.

He held the rank of colonel. He had gained a medal for liberating a convicted agent from a British jail called Wormwood Scrubs. Over the years he had also acquired a wife, two children and a mistress. The mistress was Olga, twenty years his junior, a blonde Viking goddess from Murmansk and the most exciting woman he had ever met. He knew she would not have been his lover without the KGB privileges that came with him; all the same he thought she loved him. They were alike, and each knew the other to be coldly ambitious, and somehow that had made their passion all the more frantic. There was no passion in his marriage any more, but there were other things: affection, companionship, stability and the fact that Mariya was still the only person in the world who could make him laugh helplessly, convulsively, until he fell down. And the boys: Yuri Davidovitch, studying at Moscow State University and listening to smuggled Beatles records; and Vladimir Davidovitch, the young genius, already considered a potential world champion chess player. Vladimir had applied for a place at the prestigious Phys-Mat School No. 2, and Rostov was sure he would succeed: he deserved the place on merit, and a colonel in the KGB had a little influence too.

Rostov had risen high in the Soviet meritocracy, but he reckoned he could go a little higher. His wife no longer had to queue up in markets with the hoi polloi – she shopped at the Beryozka stores with the elite – and they had a big apartment in Moscow and a little dacha on the Baltic; but Rostov wanted a chauffeur-driven Volga limousine, a second dacha at a Black Sea resort where he could keep Olga, invitations to private showings of decadent Western movies, and treatment in the Kremlin Clinic when old age began to creep up on him.

His career was at a crossroads. He was fifty this year. He spent about half his time behind a desk in Moscow, the other half in the field with his own small team of operatives. He was already older than any other agent still working abroad. From here he would go in one of two directions. If he slowed up, and allowed his past victories to be forgotten, he would end his career lecturing to would-be agents at KGB school No. 311 in Novosibirsk, Siberia. If he continued to score spectacular points in the intelligence game, he would be promoted to a totally administrative job, get appointed to one or two committees, and begin a challenging – but safe – career in the organization of the Soviet Union's intelligence effort – and *then* he would get the Volga limousine and the Black Sea dacha.

Sometime in the next two or three years he would

need to pull off another great coup. When the news about Nat Dickstein came in, he wondered for a while whether this might be his chance.

He had watched Dickstein's career with the nostalgic fascination of a mathematics teacher whose brightest pupil has decided to go to art school. While still at Oxford he had heard stories about the stolen boatload of guns, and as a result had himself initiated Dickstein's KGB file. Over the years additions had been made to the file by himself and others, based on occasional sightings, rumours, guesswork and good old-fashioned espionage. The file made it clear that Dickstein was now one of the most formidable agents in the Mossad. If Rostov could bring home his head on a platter, the future would be assured.

But Rostov was a careful operator. When he was able to pick his targets, he picked easy ones. He was no death-or-glory man: quite the reverse. One of his more important talents was the ability to become invisible when chancy assignments were being handed out. A contest between himself and Dickstein would be uncomfortably even.

He would read with interest any further reports from Cairo on what Nat Dickstein was doing in Luxembourg; but he would take care not to get involved.

He had not come this far by sticking his neck out.

The forum for discussion of the Arab bomb was the Middle East political committee. It could have been any one of eleven or twelve Kremlin committees, for the same factions were represented on all the interested committees, and they would have said the same things; and the result would have been the same, because this issue was big enough to override factional considerations.

The committee had nineteen members, but two were abroad, one was ill and one had been run over by a truck on the day of the meeting. It made no difference. Only three people counted: one from the Foreign Ministry, one KGB man and one man who represented the Party Secretary. Among the supernumeraries were David Rostov's boss, who collected all the committee memberships he could just on general principles, and Rostov himself, acting as aide. (It was by signs such as this that Rostov knew he was being considered for the next promotion.)

The KGB was against the Arab bomb, because the KGB's power was clandestine and the bomb would shift decisions into the overt sphere and out of the range of KGB activity. For that very reason the Foreign Ministry was in favour – the bomb would give them more work and more influence. The Party Secretary was against, because if the Arabs were to win decisively in the Middle East, how then would the USSR retain a foothold there?

The discussion opened with the reading of the KGB report 'Recent Developments in Egyptian Armaments'. Rostov could imagine exactly how the one fact in the report had been spun out with a little background gleaned from a phone call to Cairo, a good deal of guesswork and much bullshit, into a screed which took twenty minutes to read. He had done that kind of thing himself more than once.

A Foreign Ministry underling then stated, at some length, his interpretation of Soviet policy in the Middle East. Whatever the motives of the Zionist settlers, he said, it was clear that Israel had survived only because of the support it had received from Western capitalism; and capitalism's purpose had been to build a Middle East outpost from which to keep an eye on its oil interests. Any doubts about this analysis had been swept away by the Anglo-Franco-Israeli attack on Egypt in 1956. Soviet policy was to support the Arabs in their natural hostility to this rump of colonialism. Now, he said, although it might have been imprudent – in terms of global politics – for the USSR to *initiate* Arab nuclear armament, nevertheless once such armament had commenced it was a straightforward extension of Soviet policy to *support* it. The man talked for ever.

Everyone was so bored by this interminable statement of the obvious that the discussion thereafter became quite informal: so much so, in fact, that Rostov's boss said, 'Yes, but, shit, we can't give atom bombs to those fucking lunatics.'

'I agree,' said the Party Secretary's man, who was also chairman of the committee. 'If they have the bomb, they'll use it. That will force the Americans to attack the Arabs, with or without nukes – I'd say with. Then the Soviet Union has only two options: let down its allies, or start World War Three.'

'Another Cuba,' someone muttered.

The man from the Foreign Ministry said, 'The answer to that might be a treaty with the Americans under which both sides agree that in no circumstances will they use nuclear weapons in the Middle East.' If he could get started on a project like that, his job would be safe for twenty-five years.

The KGB man said, 'Then if the Arabs dropped the bomb, would that count as our breaking the treaty?'

A woman in a white apron entered, pulling a trolley of tea, and the committee took a break. In the interval the Party Secretary's man stood by the trolley with a cup in his hand and a mouth full of fruitcake and told a joke. 'It seems there was a captain in the KGB whose stupid son had great difficulty understanding the concepts of the Party, the Motherland, the Unions and the People. The captain told the boy to think of his father as the Party, his mother as the Motherland, his grandmother as the Unions and himself as the People. Still the boy did not understand. In a rage the father locked the boy in a wardrobe in the parental bedroom. That night the boy was still in the wardrobe when the father began to make love to the mother. The boy, watching through the wardrobe keyhole, said, "Now I understand! The Party rapes the Motherland while the Unions sleep and the People have to stand and suffer!"'

Everybody roared with laughter. The tea-lady shook her head in mock disgust. Rostov had heard the joke before.

When the committee went reluctantly back to work, it was the Party Secretary's man who asked the crucial question. 'If we refuse to give the Egyptians the technical help they're asking for, will they still be able to build the bomb?'

The KGB man who had presented the report said, 'There is not enough information to give a definite answer, sir. However, I have taken background briefing from one of our scientists on this point, and it seems that to build a crude nuclear bomb is actually no more difficult, technically, than to build a conventional bomb.'

The Foreign Ministry man said, 'I think we must assume that they will be able to build it without our help, if perhaps more slowly.'

'I can do my own guessing,' the chairman said sharply.

'Of course,' said the Foreign Ministry man, chastened.

The KGB man continued, 'Their only serious problem would be to obtain a supply of plutonium. Whether they have one or not, we simply do not know.'

David Rostov took in all this with great interest. In his opinion there was only one decision the committee could possibly take. The chairman now confirmed his view.

'My reading of the situation is as follows,' he began. 'If we help the Egyptians build their bomb, we continue and strengthen our existing Middle East policy, we improve our influence in Cairo, and we are in a position to exert some control over the bomb. If we refuse to help, we estrange ourselves from the Arabs, and we possibly leave a situation in which they still have a bomb but we have no control over it.'

The Foreign Ministry man said, 'In other words, if they're going to have a bomb anyway, there had better be a Russian finger on the trigger.'

The chairman threw him a look of irritation, and continued, 'We might, then, recommend to the Secretariat as follows: the Egyptians should be given technical help with their nuclear reactor project, such help always to be structured with a view to Soviet personnel gaining ultimate control of the weaponry.'

Rostov permitted himself the ghost of a satisfied smile: it was the conclusion he had expected.

The Foreign Ministry man said, 'So move.'

The KGB man said, 'Seconded.'

'All in favour?'

They were all in favour.

The committee proceeded to the next item on the agenda.

It was not until after the meeting that Rostov was struck by this thought: if the Egyptians were in fact *not* able to build their bomb unaided – for lack of uranium, for instance – then they had done a very expert job of bluffing the Russians into giving them the help they needed.

Rostov liked his family, in small doses. The advantage of his kind of job was that by the time he got bored with them – and it *was* boring, living with children – he was off on another trip abroad, and by the time he came back he was missing them enough to put up with them for a few more months. He was fond of Yuri, the elder boy, despite his cheap music and contentious views about dissident poets; but Vladimir, the younger, was the apple of his eye. As a baby Vladimir had been so pretty that people thought he was a girl. From the start Rostov had taught the boy games of logic, spoken to him in complex sentences, discussed with him the geography of distant countries, the mechanics of engines, and the workings of radios, flowers, water taps and political parties. He had come to the top of every class he was put into – although now, Rostov thought, he might find his equals at Phys-Mat No. 2.

Rostov knew he was trying to instil in his son some of the ambitions he himself had failed to fulfil. Fortunately this meshed with the boy's own inclinations: he knew he was clever, he liked being clever, and he wanted to be a Great Man. The only thing he balked at was the work he had to do for the Young Communist League: he thought this was a waste of time. Rostov had often said, 'Perhaps it is a waste of time, but you will never get anywhere in any field of endeavour unless you also make progress in the Party. If you want to change the system, you'll have to get to the top and change it from within.' Vladimir accepted this and went to the Young Communist League meetings: he had inherited his father's unbending logic.

Driving home through the rush-hour traffic, Rostov looked forward to a dull, pleasant evening at home. The four of them would have dinner together, then watch a television serial about heroic Russian spies outwitting the CIA. He would have a glass of vodka before bed.

Rostov parked in the road outside his home. His building was occupied by senior bureaucrats, about half of whom had small Russian-built cars like his, but there were no garages. The apartments were spacious by Moscow standards: Yuri and Vladimir had a bedroom each, and nobody had to sleep in the living room.

There was a row going on when he entered his home. He heard Mariya's voice raised in anger, the sound of something breaking, and a shout; then he heard Yuri call his mother a foul name. Rostov flung open the kitchen door and stood there, briefcase still in hand, face as black as thunder.

Mariya and Yuri confronted one another across the kitchen table: she was in a rare rage and close to hysterical tears, he was full of ugly adolescent resentment. Between them was Yuri's guitar, broken at the neck. Mariya has smashed it, Rostov thought instantly; then, a moment later: but this is not what the row is about.

They both appealed to him immediately.

'She broke my guitar!' Yuri said.

Mariya said, 'He has brought disgrace upon the family with this decadent music.'

Then Yuri again called his mother the same foul name.

Rostov dropped his briefcase, stepped forward and slapped the boy's face.

Yuri rocked backward with the force of the blow, and his cheeks reddened with pain and humiliation. The son was as tall as his father, and broader: Rostov had not struck him like this since the boy became a man. Yuri struck back immediately, his fist shooting out: if the blow had connected it would have knocked Rostov cold. Rostov moved quickly aside with the instincts of many years' training and, as gently as possible, threw Yuri to the floor.

'Leave the house,' he said quietly. 'Come back when you're ready to apologize to your mother.'

Yuri scrambled to his feet. 'Never!' he shouted. He went out, slamming the door.

Rostov took off his hat and coat and sat down at the kitchen table. He removed the broken guitar and set it carefully on the floor. Mariya poured tea and gave it to him: his hand was shaking as he took the cup. Finally he said, 'What was that all about?'

'Vladimir failed the exam.'

'Vladimir? What has that to do with Yuri's guitar? What exam did he fail?'

'For the Phys-Mat. He was rejected.'

Rostov stared at her dumbly.

Mariya said, 'I was so upset, and Yuri laughed – he is a little jealous, you know, of his younger brother – and then Yuri started playing this Western music, and I thought it could not be that Vladimir is not clever enough, it must be that his family has not enough influence, perhaps we are considered unreliable because of Yuri and his opinions and his music; I know this is foolish, but I broke his guitar in the heat of the moment.'

Rostov was no longer listening. Vladimir rejected? Impossible. The boy was smarter than his teachers, much too smart for ordinary schools, they could not handle him. The school for exceptionally gifted children was the Phys-Mat. Besides, the boy had said the examination was not difficult, he thought he had scored one hundred per cent, and he *always* knew how he had done in examinations.

'Where's Vladimir?' Rostov asked his wife.

'In his room.'

Rostov went along the corridor and knocked at the bedroom door. There was no answer. He went in. Vladimir was sitting on the bed, staring at the wall, his face red and streaked with tears.

Rostov said, 'What did you score in that exam?'

Vladimir looked up at his father, his face a mask of childish incomprehension. 'One hundred per cent,' he said. He handed over a sheaf of papers. 'I remember the questions. I remember my answers. I've checked them all twice: no mistakes. And I left the examination room five minutes before the time was up.'

Rostov turned to leave.

'Don't you *believe* me?'

'Yes, of course I do,' Rostov told him. He went into the living room, where the phone was. He called the school. The head teacher was still at work.

'Vladimir got full marks in that test,' Rostov said.

The head teacher spoke soothingly. 'I'm sorry, Comrade Colonel. Many very talented youngsters apply for places here—'

'Did they all get one hundred per cent in the exam?'

'I'm afraid I can't divulge—'

'You know who I am,' Rostov said bluntly. 'You know I can find out.'

'Comrade Colonel, I like you and I want to have your son in my school. Please don't make trouble for yourself by creating a storm about this. If your son would apply again in one year's time, he would have an excellent chance of gaining a place.'

People did not warn KGB officers against making trouble for themselves. Rostov began to understand. 'But he *did* score full marks.'

'Several applicants scored full marks in the written paper—'

'Thank you,' Rostov said. He hung up.

The living room was dark, but he did not put the lights on. He sat in his armchair, thinking. The head teacher could easily have told him that all the applicants had scored full marks; but lies did not come easily to people on the spur of the moment, evasions were easier. However, to question the results would create trouble for Rostov.

So. Strings had been pulled. Less talented youngsters had gained places because their fathers had used more influence. Rostov refused to be angry. Don't get mad at the system, he told himself: use it.

He had some strings of his own to pull.

He picked up the phone and called his boss, Feliks Vorontsov, at home. Feliks sounded a little odd, but Rostov ignored it. 'Listen, Feliks, my son has been turned down for the Phys-Mat.'

'I'm sorry to hear that,' Vorontsov said. 'Still, not everybody can get in.'

It was not the expected response. Now Rostov paid

attention to Vorontsov's tone of voice. 'What makes you say that?'

'My son was accepted.'

Rostov was silent for a moment. He had not known that Feliks's son had even applied. The boy was smart, but not half as clever as Vladimir. Rostov pulled himself together. 'Then let me be the first to congratulate you.'

'Thank you,' Feliks said awkwardly. 'What did you call about, though?'

'Oh ... look, I won't interrupt your celebration. It will keep until morning.'

'All right. Goodbye.'

Rostov hung up and put the phone gently down on the floor. If the son of some bureaucrat or politico had got into the school because of string-pulling, Rostov could have fought it: everyone's file had something nasty in it. The only kind of person he could not fight was a more senior KGB man. There was no way he could overturn this year's awards of places.

So, Vladimir would apply again next year. But the same thing could happen again. Somehow, by this time next year, he had to get into a position where the Vorontsovs of this world could not nudge him aside. Next year he would handle the whole thing differently. He would call on the head teacher's KGB file, for a start. He would get the complete list of applicants and work on any who might be a threat. He would have phones tapped and mail opened to find out who was putting on the pressure.

But first he had to get into a position of strength.

And now he realized that his complacency about his career so far had been erroneous. If they could do this to him, his star must be fading fast.

That coup which he was so casually scheduling for some time in the next two or three years had to be brought forward.

He sat in the dark living room, planning his first moves.

Mariya came in after a while and sat beside him, not speaking. She brought him food on a tray and asked him if he wanted to watch TV. He shook his head and put the food aside. A little later, she went quietly to bed.

Yuri came in at midnight, a little drunk. He entered the living room and switched on the light. He was surprised to see his father sitting there. He took a frightened step back.

Rostov stood up and looked at his elder son, remembering the growing pains of his own teenage years, the misdirected anger, the clear, narrow vision of right and wrong, the quick humiliations and the slow acquisition of knowledge. 'Yuri,' he said, 'I want to apologize for hitting you.'

Yuri burst into tears.

Rostov put an arm around his broad shoulders and led him toward his room. 'We were both wrong, you and I,' he continued. 'Your mother, too. I'm going away again soon, I'll try to bring back a new guitar.'

He wanted to kiss his son, but they had got like Westerners, afraid to kiss. Gently, he pushed him into the bedroom and closed the door on him.

Going back to the living room, he realized that in the last few minutes his plans had hardened into shape in his mind. He sat in the armchair again, this time with a soft pencil and a sheet of paper, and began to draft a memorandum.

To: Chairman, Committee for State Security
From: Acting Chief, European Desk
Copy: Chief, European Desk
Date: 24 May 1968

Comrade Andropov:

My department chief, Feliks Vorontsov, is absent today and I feel that the following matters are too urgent to await his return.

An agent in Luxembourg has reported the sighting there of the Israeli operative Nathaniel ('Nat') David Jonathan Dickstein, alias Edward ('Ed') Rodgers, known as The Pirate.

Dickstein was born in Stepney, East London, in 1925, the son of a shopkeeper. The father died in 1938, the mother in 1951. Dickstein joined the British Army in 1943, fought in Italy, was promoted sergeant and taken prisoner at La Molina. After the war he went to Oxford University to read Semitic Languages. In 1948 he left Oxford without graduating and emigrated to Palestine, where he began almost immediately to work for the Mossad.

At first he was involved in stealing and secretly buying arms for the Zionist state. In the Fifties he mounted an operation against an Egyptian-supported group of Palestinian freedom fighters based in the Gaza Strip, and was personally responsible for the booby-trap bomb which killed Commander Aly. In the late Fifties and early Sixties he was a leading member of the assassination team which hunted escaped Nazis. He directed the terrorist effort against German rocket scientists working for Egypt in 1963–4.

On his file the entry under 'Weaknesses' reads: 'None known.' He appears to have no family, either in Palestine or elsewhere. He is not interested in alcohol, narcotics or gambling. He has no known romantic liaisons, and there is on his file a speculation that he may be sexually frozen as a result of being the subject of medical experiments conducted by Nazi scientists.

I, personally, knew Dickstein intimately in the formative years 1947–8, when we were both at Oxford University. I played chess with him. I initiated his file. I have followed his subsequent career with special interest. He now appears to be operating in the territory which has been my speciality for twenty years. I doubt if there is anyone among the 110,000 employees of your committee who is as well qualified as I am to oppose this formidable Zionist operative.

I therefore recommend that you assign me to discover what Dickstein's mission is and, if appropriate, to stop him.

(Signed)
David Rostov.

To: Acting Chief, European Desk
From: Chairman, Committee for State Security
Copy: Chief, European Desk
Date: 24 May 1968

Comrade Rostov:

Your recommendation is approved.

(Signed)

Yuri Andropov.

To: Chairman, Committee for State Security
From: Chief, European Desk
Copy: Deputy Chief, European Desk
Date: 26 May 1968

Comrade Andropov:

I refer to the exchange of memoranda which took place between yourself and my deputy, David Rostov, during my recent short absence on State business in Novosibirsk.

Naturally I agree wholeheartedly with Comrade Rostov's concern and your approval thereof, although I feel there was no good reason for his haste.

As a field agent Rostov does not, of course, see things in quite the same broad perspective as his superiors, and there is one aspect of the situation which he failed to bring to your attention.

The current investigation of Dickstein was initiated by our Egyptian allies, and indeed at this moment remains exclusively their undertaking. For political reasons I would not recommend that we brush them aside without a second thought, as Rostov seems to think we can. At most, we should offer them our cooperation.

Needless to say, this latter undertaking, involving as it would international liaison between intelligence services, ought to be handled at chief-of-desk level rather than deputy-chief level.

(Signed)
Feliks Vorontsov.

To: Chief, European Desk
From: Office of the Chairman, Committee for
         State Security
Copy: Deputy Chief, European Desk
Date: 28 May 1968

Comrade Vorontsov:

Comrade Andropov has asked me to deal with your memorandum of 26 May.

He agrees that the political implications of Rostov's scheme must be taken into account, but he is unwilling to leave the initiative in Egyptian hands while we merely 'cooperate'. I have now spoken with our allies in Cairo and they have agreed that Rostov should command the team investigating Dickstein on condition that one of their agents serves as a full member of the team.

(Signed)
Maksim Bykov, personal assistant to the Chairman.

(pencilled addendum)

Feliks: Don't bother me with this again until you've got a result. And keep an eye on Rostov – he wants your job, and unless you shape up I'm going to give it to him. Yuri.

To:	Deputy Chief, European Desk
From:	Office of the Chairman, Committee for State Security
Copy:	Chief, European Desk
Date:	29 May 1968

Comrade Rostov:

Cairo has now nominated the agent to serve with your team in the Dickstein investigation. He is in fact the agent who first spotted Dickstein in Luxembourg. His name is Yasif Hassan.

(Signed)

Maksim Bykov, personal assistant to the Chairman.

When he gave lectures at the training school, Pierre Borg would say, 'Call in. Always call in. Not just when you need something, but every day if possible. We need to know what you're doing – and we may have vital information for you.' Then the trainees went into the bar and heard that Nat Dickstein's motto was: 'Never call in for less than $100,000.'

Borg was angry with Dickstein. Anger came easily to him, especially when he did not know what was happening. Fortunately anger rarely interfered with his judgment. He was angry with Kawash, too. He could understand why Kawash had wanted to meet in Rome – the Egyptians had a big team here, so it was easy for Kawash to find an excuse to visit – but there was no reason why they should meet in a goddamn bathhouse.

Borg got angry by sitting in his office in Tel Aviv, wondering and worrying about Dickstein and Kawash and the others, waiting for messages, until he began to think they would not call because they did not like him; and so he got mad and broke pencils and fired his secretary.

A bathhouse in Rome, for God's sake – the place was bound to be full of queers. Also, Borg did not like his body. He slept in pyjamas, never went swimming, never tried on clothes in shops, never went naked except to take a quick shower in the morning. Now he stood in the steam-room, wearing around his waist the largest towel he could find, conscious that he was white except for his face and hands, his flesh softly plump, with a pelt of greying hair across his shoulders.

He saw Kawash. The Arab's body was lean and dark brown, with very little hair. Their eyes met across the steamroom and, like secret lovers, they went side by side, not looking at one another, into a private room with a bed.

Borg was relieved to get out of public view and impatient to hear Kawash's news. The Arab switched on the machine that made the bed vibrate: its hum would swamp a listening device, if there were one. The two men stood close together and spoke in low voices.

Embarrassed, Borg turned his body so that he was facing away from Kawash and had to speak over his shoulder.

'I've got a man into Qattara,' Kawash said.

'*Formidable*,' Borg said, pronouncing it the French way in his great relief. 'Your department isn't even involved in the project. '

'I have a cousin in Military Intelligence.'

'Well done. Who is the man in Qattara?'

'Saman Hussein, one of yours.'

'Good, good, *good*. What did he find?'

'The construction work is finished. They've built the reactor housing, plus an administration block, staff quarters, and an airstrip. They're much farther ahead than anyone imagined.'

'What about the reactor itself? That's what counts.'

'They're working on it now. It's hard to say how long it will take – there's a certain amount of precision work.'

'Are they going to be able to manage that?' Borg wondered. 'I mean, all those complex control systems . . .'

'The controls don't need to be sophisticated, I understand. You slow the speed of the nuclear reaction simply by pushing metal rods into the atomic pile. Anyway, there's been another development. Saman found the place crawling with Russians.'

Borg said, 'Oh, fuck.'

'So now I guess they'll have all the fancy electronics they need.'

Borg sat on the chair, forgetting the bathhouse and the vibrating bed and his soft white body. 'This is bad news,' he said.

'There's worse. Dickstein is blown.'

Borg stared at Kawash, thunderstruck. 'Blown?' he said as if he did not know what the word meant. 'Blown?'

'Yes.'

Borg felt furious and despairing by turns. After a moment he said, 'How did he manage that ... the prick?'

'He was recognized by an agent of ours in Luxembourg.'

'What was he doing there?'

'*You* should know.'

'Skip it.'

'Apparently it was just a chance meeting. The agent is called Yasif Hassan. He's small fry – works for a Lebanese bank and keeps an eye on visiting Israelis. Of course, our people recognized the name Dickstein—'

'He's using his real name?' Borg said incredulously. It got worse and worse.

'I don't think so,' Kawash said. 'This Hassan knew him from way back.'

Borg shook his head slowly. 'You wouldn't think we were the Chosen People, with our luck.'

'We put Dickstein under surveillance and informed Moscow,' Kawash continued. 'He lost the surveillance team quite quickly, of course, but Moscow is putting together a big effort to find him again.'

Borg put his chin in his hand and stared without

seeing at the erotic frieze on the tiled wall. It was as if there were a world-wide conspiracy to frustrate Israeli policy in general and his plans in particular. He wanted to give it all up and go back to Quebec; he wanted to hit Dickstein over the head with a blunt instrument; he wanted to wipe that imperturbable look off Kawash's handsome face.

He made a gesture of throwing something away. 'Great,' he said. 'The Egyptians are well ahead with their reactor; the Russians are helping them; Dickstein is blown; and the KGB has put a team on him. We could lose this race, do you realize that? Then they'll have a nuclear bomb and we won't. And do you think they will use it?' He had Kawash by the shoulders now, shaking him. 'They're your people, you tell me, will they drop the bomb on Israel? You bet your ass they will!'

'Stop shouting,' Kawash said calmly. He detached Borg's hands from his shoulders. 'There's a long road ahead before one side or the other has won.'

'Yeah.' Borg turned away.

'You'll have to contact Dickstein and warn him,' Kawash said. 'Where is he now?'

'Fucked if I know,' said Pierre Borg.

CHAPTER FIVE

T HE ONLY completely innocent person whose life was ruined by the spies during the affair of the yellowcake was the Euratom official whom Dickstein named Stiffcollar.

After losing the surveillance team in France Dickstein returned to Luxembourg by road, guessing they would have set a twenty-four-hours-a-day watch for him at Luxembourg airport. And, since they had the number of his rented car, he stopped off in Paris to turn it in and hire another from a different company.

On his first evening in Luxembourg he went to the discreet nightclub in the Rue Dicks and sat alone, sipping beer, waiting for Stiffcollar to come in. But it was the fair-haired friend who arrived first. He was a younger man, perhaps twenty-five or thirty, broad-shouldered and in good shape underneath his maroon double-breasted jacket. He walked across to the booth they had occupied last time. He was graceful, like a dancer: Dickstein thought he might be the goalkeeper on a soccer team. The booth was vacant. If the couple met here every night it was probably kept for them.

The fair-haired man ordered a drink and looked at his watch. He did not see Dickstein observing him.

Stiffcollar entered a few minutes later. He wore a red V-necked sweater and a white shirt with a button-down collar. As before, he went straight to the table where his friend sat waiting. They greeted each other with a double handshake. They seemed happy. Dickstein prepared to shatter their world.

He called a waiter. 'Please take a bottle of champagne to that table, for the man in the red sweater. And bring me another beer.'

The waiter brought his beer first, then took the champagne in a bucket of ice to Stiffcollar's table. Dickstein saw the waiter point him out to the couple as the donor of the champagne. When they looked at him, he raised his beer glass in a toast, and smiled. Stiffcollar recognized him and looked worried.

Dickstein left his table and went to the cloakroom. He washed his face, killing time. After a couple of minutes Stiffcollar's friend came in. The young man combed his hair, waiting for a third man to leave the room. Then he spoke to Dickstein.

'My friend wants you to leave him alone.'

Dickstein gave a nasty smile. 'Let him tell me so himself.'

'You're a journalist, aren't you? What if your editor were to hear that you come to places like this?'

'I'm freelance.'

The young man came closer. He was five inches taller than Dickstein and at least thirty pounds heavier. 'You're to leave us alone,' he said.

'No.'

'Why are you doing this? What do you want?'

'I'm not interested in you, pretty boy. You'd better go home while I talk to your friend.'

'Damn you,' the young man said, and he grabbed the lapels of Dickstein's jacket in one large hand. He drew back his other arm and made a fist. He never landed the punch.

With his fingers Dickstein poked the young man in the eyes. The blond head jerked back and to the side reflexively. Dickstein stepped inside the swinging arm and hit him in the belly, very hard. The breath rattled out of him and he doubled over, turning away. Dickstein punched him once again, very precisely, on the bridge of the nose. Something snapped, and blood spurted. The young man collapsed on the tiled floor.

It was enough.

Dickstein went out quickly, straightening his tie and smoothing his hair on the way. In the club the cabaret had begun and the German guitarist was singing a song about a gay policeman. Dickstein paid his bill and left. As he went he saw Stiffcollar, looking worried, making his way to the cloakroom.

On the street it was a mild summer night, but Dickstein was shivering. He walked a little way, then went into a bar and ordered brandy. It was a noisy, smoky place with a television set on the counter. Dickstein carried his drink to a corner table and sat facing the wall.

The fight in the cloakroom would not be reported to the police. It would look like a quarrel over a lover, and neither Stiffcollar nor the club management would want to bring that sort of thing to official notice.

Stiffcollar would take his friend to a doctor, saying he had walked into a door.

Dickstein drank the brandy and stopped shivering. There was, he thought, no way to be a spy without doing things like this. And there was no way to be a nation, in this world, without having spies. And without a nation Nat Dickstein could not feel safe.

It did not seem possible to live honourably. Even if he gave up this profession, others would become spies and do evil on his behalf, and that was almost as bad. You had to be bad to live. Dickstein recalled that a Nazi camp doctor called Wolfgang had said much the same.

He had long ago decided that life was not about right and wrong, but about winning and losing. Still there were times when that philosophy gave him no consolation.

He left the bar and went into the street, heading for Stiffcollar's home. He had to press his advantage while the man was demoralized. He reached the narrow cobbled street within a few minutes and stood guard opposite the old terraced house. There was no light in the attic window.

The night became cooler as he waited. He began to pace up and down. European weather was dismal. At this time of year Israel would be glorious: long sunny days and warm nights, hard physical work by day and companionship and laughter in the evenings. Dickstein wished he could go home.

At last Stiffcollar and his friend returned. The friend's head was wrapped in bandages, and he was obviously having trouble seeing: he walked with one hand on Stiffcollar's arm, like a blind man. They stopped outside the house while Stiffcollar fumbled for a key. Dickstein crossed the road and approached them. They had their backs to him, and his shoes made no noise.

Stiffcollar opened the door, turned to help his friend, and saw Dickstein. He jumped with shock. 'Oh, God!'

The friend said, 'What is it? What is it?'

'It's him.'

Dickstein said, 'I have to talk to you.'

'Call the police,' said the friend.

Stiffcollar took his friend's arm and began to lead him through the door. Dickstein put out a hand and stopped them. 'You'll have to let me in,' he said. 'Otherwise I'll create a scene in the street.'

Stiffcollar said, 'He'll make our lives miserable until he gets what he wants.'

'But what does he want?'

'I'll tell you in a minute,' Dickstein said. He walked into the house ahead of them and started up the stairs.

After a moment's hesitation, they followed.

The three men climbed the stairs to the top. Stiffcollar unlocked the door of the attic flat, and they went in. Dickstein looked around. It was bigger than he imagined, and very elegantly decorated with period furniture, striped wallpaper, and many plants and pictures. Stiffcollar put his friend in a chair, then took a cigarette from a box, lit it with a table lighter and put it in his friend's mouth. They sat close together, waiting for Dickstein to speak.

'I'm a journalist,' Dickstein began.

Stiffcollar interrupted, 'Journalists interview people, they don't beat them up.'

'I didn't beat him up. I hit him twice.'

'Why?'

'He attacked me, didn't he tell you?'

'I don't believe you,' said Stiffcollar.

'How much time would you like to spend arguing about it?'

'None.'

'Good. I want a story about Euratom. A good story – my career needs it. Now then, one possibility is the prevalence of homosexuals in positions of responsibility within the organization.'

'You're a lousy bastard,' said Stiffcollar's friend.

'Quite so,' Dickstein said. 'However, I'll drop the story if I get a better one.'

Stiffcollar ran a hand across his grey-tipped hair, and Dickstein noticed that he wore clear nail polish. 'I think I understand this,' he said.

'What? What do you understand?' said his friend.

'He wants information.'

'That's right,' said Dickstein. Stiffcollar was looking relieved. Now was the time to be a little friendly, to come across as a human being, to let them think that things might not be so bad after all. Dickstein got up. There was whisky in a decanter on a highly polished side table. He poured small shots into three glasses as he said, 'Look, you're vulnerable and I've picked on you, and I expect you to hate me for that; but I'm not going to pretend that I hate you. I'm a bastard and I'm using you, and that's all there is to it. Except that I'm drinking your booze as well.' He handed them drinks and sat down again.

There was a pause, then Stiffcollar said, 'What is it that you want to know?'

'Well, now.' Dickstein took the tiniest sip of whisky: he hated the taste. 'Euratom keeps records of all movements of fissionable materials into, out of and within the member countries, right?'

'Yes.'

'To be more precise: before anyone can move an ounce of uranium from A to B he has to ask your permission.'

'Yes.'

'Complete records are kept of all permits given.'

'The records are on a computer.'

'I know. If asked, the computer would print out a list of all future uranium shipments for which permission has been given.'

'It does, regularly. A list is circulated once a month within the office.'

'Splendid,' said Dickstein. 'All I want is that list.'

There was a long silence. Stiffcollar drank some whisky. Dickstein left his alone: the two beers and one large brandy he had already drunk this evening were more than he normally took in a fortnight.

The friend said, 'What do you want the list *for*?'

'I'm going to check all the shipments in a given month. I expect to be able to prove that what people do in reality bears little or no relation to what they tell Euratom.'

Stiffcollar said, 'I don't believe you.'

The man was not stupid, Dickstein thought. He shrugged. 'What do you think I want it for?'

'I don't know. You're not a journalist. Nothing you've said has been true.'

'It makes no difference, does it?' Dickstein said. 'Believe what you like. You've no choice but to give me the list.'

'I have,' Stiffcollar said. 'I'm going to resign the job.'

'If you do,' Dickstein said slowly, 'I will beat your friend to a pulp.'

'We'll go to the police!' the friend said.

'I would go away,' Dickstein said. 'Perhaps for a year. But I would come back. And I'd find you. And I will very nearly kill you. Your face will be unrecognizable.'

Stiffcollar stared at Dickstein. 'What *are* you?'

'It really doesn't matter what I am, does it? You know I can do what I threaten.'

'Yes,' Stiffcollar said. He buried his face in his hands.

Dickstein let the silence build. Stiffcollar was cornered, helpless. There was only one thing he could do, and he was now realizing this. Dickstein let him take his time. It was several moments before Dickstein spoke.

'The printout will be bulky,' he said gently.

Stiffcollar nodded without looking up.

'Is your briefcase checked as you leave the office?'

He shook his head.

'Are the printouts supposed to be kept under lock and key?'

'No. 'Stiffcollar gathered his wits with a visible effort. 'No,' he said wearily, 'this information is not classified. It's merely confidential, not to be made public.'

'Good. Now, you'll need tomorrow to think about the details – which copy of the printout to take, exactly what you'll tell your secretary, and so on. The day after tomorrow you will bring the printout home. You'll find a note from me waiting for you. The note will tell you how to deliver the document to me.' Dickstein smiled. 'After that, you'll probably never see me again. '

Stiffcollar said, 'By God, I hope so.'

Dickstein stood up. 'You'd rather not be bothered by phone calls for a while,' he said. He found the telephone and pulled the cord out of the wall. He went to the door and opened it.

The friend looked at the disconnected wire. His eyes seemed to be recovering. He said, 'Are you afraid he'll change his mind?'

Dickstein said, 'You're the one who should be afraid of that.' He went out, closing the door softly behind him.

Life is not a popularity contest, especially in the KGB. David Rostov was now very unpopular with his boss and with all those in the section who were loyal to his boss. Feliks Vorontsov was boiling with anger at the way he had been bypassed: from now on he would do anything he could to destroy Rostov.

Rostov had anticipated this. He did not regret his decision to go for broke on the Dickstein affair. On the contrary, he was rather glad. He was already planning the finely stitched, stylishly cut dark blue English suit he would buy when he got his pass for Section 100 on the third floor of the GUM department store in Moscow.

What he did regret was leaving a loophole for Vorontsov. He should have thought of the Egyptians and their reaction. That was the trouble with the Arabs, they were so clumsy and useless that you tended to ignore them as a force in the intelligence world. Fortunately Yuri Andropov, head of the KGB and confidant of Leonid Brezhnev, had seen what Feliks Vorontsov was trying to do, namely win back control of the Dickstein project; and he had not permitted it.

So the only consequence of Rostov's error was that he would be forced to work with the wretched Arabs.

That was bad enough. Rostov had his own little team, Nik Bunin and Pyotr Tyrin, and they worked well together. And Cairo was as leaky as a sieve: half the stuff that went through them got back to Tel Aviv.

The fact that the Arab in question was Yasif Hassan might or might not help.

Rostov remembered Hassan very clearly: a rich kid, indolent and haughty, smart enough but with no drive, shallow politics, and too many clothes. His wealthy father had got him into Oxford, not his brains; and

Rostov resented that more now than he had then. Still, knowing the man should make it easier to control him. Rostov planned to start by making it clear Hassan was essentially superfluous, and was on the team for purely political reasons. He would need to be very clever about what he told Hassan and what he kept secret: say too little, and Cairo would bitch to Moscow; too much, and Tel Aviv would be able to frustrate his every move.

It was damned awkward, and he had only himself to blame for it.

He was uneasy about the whole affair by the time he reached Luxembourg. He had flown in from Athens, having changed identities twice and planes three times since Moscow. He took this little precaution because, if you came direct from Russia, the local intelligence people sometimes made a note of your arrival and kept an eye on you, and that could be a nuisance.

There was nobody to meet him at the airport, of course. He took a taxi to his hotel.

He had told Cairo he would be using the name David Roberts. When he checked into the hotel under that name, the desk clerk gave him a message. He opened the envelope as he went up in the lift with the porter. It said simply 'Room 179.'

He tipped the porter, picked up the room phone and dialled 179. A voice said, 'Hello?'

'I'm in 142. Give me ten minutes, then come here for a conference.'

'Fine. Listen, is that—'

'Shut up!' Rostov snapped. 'No names. Ten minutes.'

'Of course, I'm sorry, I—'

Rostov hung up. What kind of idiots was Cairo hiring now? The kind that used your real name over the hotel phone system, obviously. It was going to be even worse than he had feared.

There was a time when he would have been over-professional, and turned out the lights and sat watching the doorway with a gun in his hand until the other man arrived, in case of a trap. Nowadays he considered that sort of behaviour to be obsessive and left it to the actors in the television shows. Elaborate personal precautions were not his style, not any more. He did not even carry a gun, in case customs officials searched his luggage at airports. But there were precautions and precautions, weapons and weapons: he did have one or two KGB gadgets subtly concealed – including an electric tooth-brush that gave out a hum calculated to jam listening devices, a miniature Polaroid camera, and a bootlace garrotte.

He unpacked his small case quickly. There was very little in it: a safety razor, the toothbrush, two American-made wash-and-wear shirts and a change of underwear. He made himself a drink from the room bar – Scotch whisky was one of the perks of working abroad. After exactly ten minutes there was a knock on the door. Rostov opened it, and Yasif Hassan came in.

Hassan smiled broadly. 'How are you?'

'How do you do,' said Rostov, and shook his hand.

'It's twenty years . . . how have you been?'

'Busy.'

'That we should meet again, after so long, and because of Dickstein!'

'Yes. Sit down. Let's talk about Dickstein.' Rostov sat, and Hassan followed suit. 'Bring me up to date,' Rostov continued. 'You spotted Dickstein, then your people picked him up again at Nice airport. What happened next?'

'He went on a guided tour of a nuclear power station, then shook off the tail,' Hassan said. 'So we've lost him again.'

Rostov gave a grunt of disgust. 'We'll have to do better than that.'

Hassan smiled – a salesman's smile, Rostov thought – and said, 'If he wasn't the sort of agent who is bound to spot a tail and lose it, we wouldn't be so concerned about him, would we?'

Rostov ignored that. 'Was he using a car?'

'Yes. He hired a Peugeot.'

'Okay. What do you know about his movements before that, when he was here in Luxembourg?'

Hassan spoke briskly, adopting Rostov's businesslike air. 'He stayed at the Alfa Hotel for a week under the name Ed Rodgers. He gave as his address the Paris bureau of a magazine called *Science International*. There is such a magazine; they do have a Paris address, but it's only a forwarding address for mail; they do use a freelance called Ed Rodgers, but they haven't heard from him for over a year.'

Rostov nodded. 'As you may know, that is a typical Mossad cover story. Nice and tight. Anything else?'

'Yes. The night before he left there was an incident in the Rue Dicks. Two men were found quite savagely beaten. It had the look of a professional job – neatly broken bones, you know the kind of thing. The police aren't doing anything about it: the men were known thieves, thought to have been lying in wait close to a homosexual nightclub.'

'Robbing the queers as they come out?'

'That's the general idea. Anyway, there's nothing to connect Dickstein with the incident, except that he is capable of it and he was here at the time.'

'That's enough for a strong presumption,' Rostov said. 'Do you think Dickstein is a homosexual?'

'It's possible, but Cairo says there's nothing like that in his file, so he must have been very discreet about it all these years.'

'And therefore too discreet to go to queer clubs while he's on assignment. Your argument is self-defeating, isn't it?'

A trace of anger showed in Hassan's face. 'So what do you think?' he said defensively.

'My guess is that he had an informant who is queer.' He stood up and began to pace the room. He felt he had made the right start with Hassan, but enough was enough: no point in making the man surly. It was time to ease up a little. 'Let's speculate for a moment. Why would he want to look around a nuclear power station?'

Hassan said, 'The Israelis have been on bad terms

with the French since the Six-Day War. De Gaulle cut off the supply of arms. Maybe the Mossad plans some retaliation: like blowing up the reactor?'

Rostov shook his head. 'Even the Israelis aren't that irresponsible. Besides, why then would Dickstein be in Luxembourg?'

'Who knows?'

Rostov sat down again. 'What is there, here in Luxembourg? What makes it an important place? Why is your bank here, for example?'

'It's an important European capital. My bank is here because the European Investment Bank is here. But there are also several Common Market institutions – in fact, there's a European Centre over on the Ritchberg.'

'Which institutions?'

'The Secretariat of the European Parliament, the Council of Ministers, and the Court of Justice. Oh, and Euratom.'

Rostov stared at Hassan. 'Euratom?'

'It's short for the European Atomic Energy Community, but everybody—'

'I know what it is,' Rostov said. 'Don't you see the connection? He comes to Luxembourg, where Euratom has its headquarters, then he goes to visit a nuclear reactor.'

Hassan shrugged. 'An interesting hypothesis. What's that you're drinking?'

'Whisky. Help yourself. As I recall, the French helped the Israelis build their nuclear reactor. Now they've probably cut off their aid. Dickstein may be after scientific secrets.'

Hassan poured himself a drink and sat down again. 'How shall we operate, you and I? My orders are to cooperate with you.'

'My team is arriving this evening,' Rostov said. He was thinking: Cooperate, hell – you'll follow my orders. He said, 'I always use the same two men – Nik Bunin and Pyotr Tyrin. We operate very well together. They know how I like things done. I want you to work with them, do what they say – you'll learn a lot, they're very good agents.'

'And my people . . .'

'We won't need them much longer,' Rostov said briskly. 'A small team is best. Now, our first job is to make sure we see Dickstein if and when he comes back to Luxembourg.'

'I've got a man at the airport twenty-four hours a day.'

'He'll have thought of that, he won't fly in. We must cover some other spots. He might go to Euratom . . .'

'The Jean-Monnet building, yes.'

'We can cover the Alfa Hotel by bribing the desk clerk, but he won't go back there. And the nightclub in the Rue Dicks. Now, then, you said he hired a car.'

'Yes, in France.'

'He'll have dumped it by now – he knows that you know the number. I want you to call the rental company and find out where it was left – that may tell us what direction he's travelling in.'

'Very well.'

'Moscow has put his photograph on the wire, so our people will be looking out for him in every capital city in the world.' Rostov finished his drink. 'We'll catch him. One way or another.'

'Do you really think so?' Hassan asked.

'I've played chess with him, I know how his mind works. His opening moves are routine, predictable; then suddenly he does something completely un-expected, usually something highly risky. You just have to wait for him to stick out his neck – then you chop his head off.'

Hassan said, 'As I recall, you lost that chess match.'

Rostov gave a wolfish grin. 'Yes, but this is real life,' he said.

There are two kinds of shadow: pavement artists and bulldogs. Pavement artists regard the business of shadowing people as a skill of the highest order, comparable with acting or cellular biophysics or poetry. They are perfectionists, capable of being almost invis-ible. They have wardrobes of unobtrusive clothes, they practise blank expressions in front of their mirrors, they know dozens of tricks with shop doorways and bus queues, policemen and children, spectacles and shop-ping bags and hedges. They despise the bulldogs, who think that shadowing someone is the same as following him, and trail the mark the way a dog follows its master.

Nik Bunin was a bulldog. He was a young thug, the type of man who always becomes either a policeman or a criminal, depending on his luck. Luck had brought Nik into the KGB: his brother, back in Georgia, was a dope dealer, running hashish from Tbilisi to Moscow

University (where it was consumed by – among others – Rostov's son Yuri). Nik was officially a chauffeur, unofficially a bodyguard, and even more unofficially a full-time professional ruffian.

It was Nik who spotted The Pirate.

Nik was a little under six feet tall, and very broad. He wore a leather jacket across his wide shoulders. He had short blond hair and watery green eyes, and he was embarrassed about the fact that at the age of twenty-five he still did not need to shave every day.

At the nightclub in the Rue Dicks they thought he was cute as hell.

He came in at seven-thirty, soon after the club opened, and sat in the same corner all night, drinking iced vodka with lugubrious relish, just watching. Somebody asked him to dance, and he told the man to piss off in bad French. When he turned up the second night they wondered if he was a jilted lover lying in wait for a showdown with his ex. He had about him the air of what the gays called rough trade, what with those shoulders and the leather jacket and his dour expression.

Nik knew nothing of these undercurrents. He had been shown a photograph of a man and told to go to a club and look out for the man; so he memorized the face, then went to the club and looked. It made little difference to him whether the place was a whorehouse or a cathedral. He liked occasionally to get the chance to beat people up, but otherwise all he asked was regular pay and two days off every week to devote to his enthusiasms, which were vodka and colouring books.

When Nat Dickstein came into the nightclub, Nik felt no sense of excitement. When he did well, Rostov always assumed it was because he had scrupulously obeyed precise orders, and he was generally right. Nik watched the mark sit down alone, order a drink, get served and sip his beer. It looked like he, too, was waiting.

Nik went to the phone in the lobby and called the hotel. Rostov answered.

'This is Nik. The mark just came in.'

'Good!' said Rostov. 'What's he doing?'

'Waiting.'

'Good. Alone?'

'Yes.'

'Stay with him and call me if he does anything.'

'Sure.'

'I'm sending Pyotr down. He'll wait outside. If the mark leaves the club you follow him, doubling with Pyotr. The Arab will be with you in a car, well back. It's a ... wait a minute ... it's a green Volkswagen hatchback.'

'Okay.'

'Get back to him now.'

Nik hung up and returned to his table, not looking at Dickstein as he crossed the club.

A few minutes later a well-dressed, good-looking man of about forty came into the club. He looked around, then walked past Dickstein's table and went to the bar. Nik saw Dickstein pick up a piece of paper from the table and put it in his pocket. It was all very discreet:

only someone who was carefully observing Dickstein would know anything had happened.

Nik went to the phone again.

'A queer came in and gave him something – it looked like a ticket,' he told Rostov.

'Like a theatre ticket, maybe?'

'Don't know.'

'Did they speak?'

'No, the queer just dropped the ticket on the table as he went by. They didn't even look at each other.'

'All right. Stay with it. Pyotr should be outside by now.'

'Wait,' Nik said. 'The mark just came into the lobby. Hold on ... he's going to the desk ... he's handed over the ticket, that's what it was, it was a cloakroom ticket.'

'Stay on the line, tell me what happens.' Rostov's voice was deadly calm.

'The guy behind the counter is giving him a brief-case. He leaves a tip ...'

'It's a delivery. Good.'

'The mark is leaving the club.'

'Follow him.'

'Shall I snatch the briefcase?'

'No, I don't want us to show ourselves until we know what he's doing, just find out where he goes, and stay low. Go!'

Nik hung up. He gave the cloakroom attendant some notes, saying: 'I have to rush, this will cover my bill.' Then he went up the staircase after Nat Dickstein.

Out on the street it was a bright summer evening, and there were plenty of people making their way to restaurants and cinemas or just strolling. Nik looked left and right, then saw the mark on the opposite side of the road, fifty yards away. He crossed over and followed.

Dickstein was walking quickly, looking straight ahead, carrying the briefcase under his arm. Nik plodded after him for a couple of blocks. During this time, if Dickstein looked back he would see some distance behind him a man who had also been in the nightclub, and he would begin to wonder if he were being shadowed. Then Pyotr came alongside Nik, touched his arm, and went on ahead. Nik dropped back to a position from which he could see Pyotr but not Dickstein. If Dickstein looked again now, he would not see Nik and he would not recognize Pyotr. It was very difficult for the mark to sniff this kind of surveillance; but of course, the longer the distance for which the mark was shadowed, the more men were needed to keep up the regular switches.

After another half mile the green Volkswagen pulled to the kerb beside Nik. Yasif Hassan leaned across from the driving seat and opened the door. 'New orders,' he said. 'Jump in.'

Nik got into the car and Hassan steered back toward the nightclub in the Rue Dicks.

'You did very well,' Hassan said.

Nik ignored this.

'We want you to go back to the club, pick out the delivery man and follow him home,' Hassan said.

'Colonel Rostov said this?'

'Yes.'

'Okay.'

Hassan stopped the car close to the club. Nik went in. He stood in the doorway, looking carefully all about the club.

The delivery man had gone.

The computer printout ran to more than one hundred pages. Dickstein's heart sank as he flicked through the prized sheets of paper he had worked so hard to get. None of it made sense.

He returned to the first page and looked again. There were a lot of jumbled numbers and letters. Could it be in code? No – this printout was used every day by the ordinary office workers of Euratom, so it had to be fairly easily comprehensible.

Dickstein concentrated. He saw 'U234'. He knew that to be an isotope of uranium. Another group of letters and numbers was 'I80KG' – one hundred and eighty kilograms. 'I7F68' would be a date, the seventeenth of February this year. Gradually the lines of computer-alphabet letters and numbers began to yield up their meanings: he found place-names from various European countries, words such as TRAIN and TRUCK with distances affixed next to them, and names with suffixes 'SA' or 'INC', indicating companies. Eventually the layout of the entries became clear: the first line gave the quantity and type of material, the second line the name and address of the sender, and so on.

His spirits lifted. He read on with growing comprehension and a sense of achievement. About sixty consignments were listed in the printout. There seemed to be three main types: large quantities of crude uranium ore coming from mines in South Africa, Canada and France to European refineries; fuel elements – oxides, uranium metal or enriched mixtures – moving from fabrication plants to reactors; and spent fuel from reactors going for reprocessing and disposal. There were a few non-standard shipments, mostly of plutonium and transuranium elements extracted from spent fuel and sent to laboratories in universities and research institutes.

Dickstein's head ached and his eyes were bleary by the time he found what he was looking for. On the very last page there was one shipment headed 'NON-NUCLEAR.'

He had been briefly told, by the Rehovot physicist with the flowered tie, about the non-nuclear uses of uranium and its compounds in photography, in dyeing, as colouring agents for glass and ceramics and as industrial catalysts. Of course the stuff always had the potential for fission no matter how mundane and innocent its use, so the Euratom regulations still applied. However, Dickstein thought it likely that in ordinary industrial chemistry the security would be less strict.

The entry on the last page referred to two hundred tons of yellowcake, or crude uranium oxide. It was in Belgium, at a metal refinery in the countryside near the Dutch border, a site licenced for storage of fissionable material. The refinery was owned by the Société Générale de la Chimie, a mining conglomerate with head-quarters in Brussels. SGC had sold the yellowcake to a German concern called F.A. Pedler of Wiesbaden. Pedler planned to use it for 'manufacture of uranium compounds, especially uranium carbide, in commercial quantities.' Dickstein recalled that the carbide was a catalyst for the production of synthetic ammonia.

However, it seemed that Pedler were not going to work the uranium themselves, at least not initially. Dickstein's interest sharpened as he read that they had not applied for their own works in Wiesbaden to be licenced, but instead for permission to ship the yellow-cake to Genoa by sea. There it was to undergo 'non-nuclear processing' by a company called Angeluzzi e Bianco.

By sea! The implications struck Dickstein instantly: the load would be passed through a European port by someone else.

He read on. Transport would be by railway from SGC's refinery to the docks at Antwerp. There the yellowcake would be loaded on to the motor vessel *Coparelli* for shipment to Genoa. The short journey from the Italian port to the Angeluzzi e Bianco works would be made by road.

For the trip the yellowcake – looking like sand but yellower – would be packed into five hundred and sixty 200-litre oil drums with heavily sealed lids. The train would require eleven cars, the ship would carry no other cargo for this voyage, and the Italians would use six trucks for the last leg of the journey.

It was the sea journey that excited Dickstein: through

the English Channel, across the Bay of Biscay, down the Atlantic coast of Spain, through the Strait of Gibraltar and across one thousand miles of the Mediterranean.

A lot could go wrong in that distance.

Journeys on land were straightforward, controlled: a train left at noon one day and-arrived at eight-thirty the following morning; a truck travelled on roads that always carried other traffic including police cars; a plane was continually in contact with someone or other on the ground. But the sea was unpredictable, with its own laws – a trip could take ten days or twenty, there might be storms and collisions and engine trouble, unscheduled ports of call and sudden changes of direction. Hijack a plane and the whole world would see it on television an hour later; hijack a ship and no one would know about it for days, weeks, perhaps for ever.

The sea was the inevitable choice for The Pirate.

Dickstein thought on, with growing enthusiasm and a sense that the solution to his problem was within his reach. Hijack the *Coparelli* . . . then what? Transfer the cargo to the hold of the pirate ship. The *Coparelli* would probably have its own derricks. But transferring a cargo at sea could be chancy. Dickstein looked on the print-out for the proposed date of the voyage. November. That was bad. There might be storms – even the Mediterranean could blow up a gale in November. What, then? Take over the *Coparelli* and sail her to Haifa? It would be hard to dock a stolen ship secretly, even in top-security Israel.

Dickstein glanced at his wristwatch. It was past midnight. He began to undress for bed. He needed to know more about the *Coparelli*: her tonnage, how many crew, present whereabouts, who owned her, and if possible her layout. Tomorrow he would go to London. You could find out anything about ships at Lloyd's of London.

There was something else he needed to know: who was following him around Europe? There had been a big team in France. Tonight as he left the nightclub in the Rue Dicks a thuggish face had been behind him. He had suspected a tail, but the face had disappeared – coincidence, or another big team? It rather depended on whether Hassan was in the game. He could make inquiries about that, too, in England.

He wondered how to travel. If somebody had picked up his scent tonight he ought to take some precautions tomorrow. Even if the thuggish face were nobody, Dickstein had to make sure he was not spotted at Luxembourg airport.

He picked up the phone and dialled the desk. When the clerk answered, he said, 'Wake me at six-thirty, please.'

'Very good, sir.'

He hung up and got into bed. At last he had a definite target: the *Coparelli*. He did not yet have a plan, but he knew in outline what had to be done. Whatever other difficulties came up, the combination of a non-nuclear consignment and a sea journey was irresistible.

He turned out the light and closed his eyes, thinking: What a good day.

*

David Rostov had always been a condescending bastard, and he had not improved with age, thought Yasif Hassan. 'What you probably don't realize . . .' he would say with a patronizing smile; and, 'We won't need your people much longer – a small team is better;' and, 'You can tag along in the car and keep out of sight;' and now, 'Man the phone while I go to the Embassy.'

Hassan had been prepared to work under Rostov's orders as one of the team, but it seemed his status was lower than that. It was, to say the least, insulting to be considered inferior to a man like Nik Bunin.

The trouble was, Rostov had some justification. It was not that the Russians were smarter than the Arabs; but the KGB was undoubtedly a larger, richer, more powerful and more professional organization than Egyptian Intelligence.

Hassan had no choice but to suffer Rostov's attitude, justified or not. Cairo was delighted to have the KGB hunting one of the Arab world's greatest enemies. If Hassan were to complain, he rather than Rostov would be taken off the case.

Rostov might remember, thought Hassan, that it was the Arabs who had first spotted Dickstein; there would be no investigation at all had it not been for my original discovery.

All the same, he wanted to win Rostov's respect; to have the Russian confide in him, discuss developments, ask his opinion. He would have to prove to Rostov that he was a competent and professional agent, easily the equal of Nik Bunin and Pyotr Tyrin.

The phone rang. Hassan picked it up hastily. 'Hello?'

'Is the other one there?' It was Tyrin's voice.

'He's out. What's happening?'

Tyrin hesitated. 'When will he be back?'

'I don't know,' Hassan lied. 'Give me your report.'

'Okay. The client got off the train at Zurich.'

'Zurich? Go on.'

'He took a taxi to a bank, entered and went down into the vault. This particular bank has safe-deposit boxes. He came out carrying a briefcase.'

'And then?'

'He went to a car dealer on the outskirts of the city and bought a used E-type Jaguar, paying with cash he had in the case.'

'I see.' Hassan thought he knew what was coming next.

'He drove out of Zurich in the car, got onto the E17 autobahn and increased his speed to one hundred and forty miles per hour.'

'And you lost him,' said Hassan, feeling gratification and anxiety in equal parts.

'We had a taxi and an embassy Mercedes.'

Hassan was visualizing the road map of Europe. 'He could be headed for anywhere in France, Spain, Germany, Scandinavia . . . unless he doubles back, in which case Italy, Austria . . . He's vanished, then. All right – come back to base.' He hung up before Tyrin could question his authority.

So, he thought, the great KGB is not invincible after

all. Much as he liked to see them fall on their collective face, his malicious pleasure was overshadowed by the fear that they had lost Dickstein permanently.

He was still thinking about what they ought to do next when Rostov came back.

'Anything?' the Russian asked.

'Your people lost Dickstein,' Hassan said, suppressing a smile.

Rostov's face darkened. 'How?'

Hassan told him.

Rostov asked, 'So what are they doing now?'

'I suggested they might come back here. I guess they're on their way.'

Rostov grunted.

Hassan said, 'I've been thinking about what we should do next.'

'We've got to find Dickstein again.' Rostov was fiddling with something in his suitcase, and his replies were distracted.

'Yes, but apart from that.'

Rostov turned around. 'Get to the point.'

'I think we should pick up the delivery man and ask him what he passed to Dickstein.'

Rostov stood still, considering. 'Yes,' he said thoughtfully. Hassan was delighted.

'We'll have to find him . . .'

'That shouldn't be impossible,' Rostov said. 'If we keep watch on the nightclub, the airport, the Alfa Hotel and the Jean-Monnet building for a few days . . .'

Hassan watched Rostov, studying his tall thin figure, and his impassive, unreadable face with its high forehead and close-cropped greying hair. I'm right, Hassan thought, and he's got to admit it.

'You're right,' Rostov said. 'I should have thought of that.'

Hassan felt a glow of pride, and thought: maybe he's not such a bastard after all.

CHAPTER SIX

T HE CITY of Oxford had not changed as much as the people. The city was predictably different: it was bigger, the cars and shops were more numerous and more garish, and the streets were more crowded. But the predominant characteristic of the place was still the cream-coloured stone of the college buildings, with the occasional glimpse, through an arch, of the startling green turf of a deserted quadrangle. Dickstein noticed also the curious pale English light, such a contrast with the brassy glare of Israeli sunshine: of course it had always been there, but as a native he had never seen it. However, the students seemed a totally new breed. In the Middle East and all over Europe Dickstein had seen men with hair growing over their ears, with orange and pink neckerchiefs, with bell-bottom trousers and high-heeled shoes; and he had not been expecting people to be dressed as they were in 1948, in tweed jackets and corduroy trousers, with Oxford shirts and Paisley ties from Hall's. All the same he was not prepared for this. Many of them were barefoot in the streets, or wore peculiar open sandals without socks. Men and women had trousers which seemed to Dickstein to be vulgarly tight-fitting. After observing several women whose breasts wobbled freely inside loose, colourful shirts, he concluded that brassieres were out of fashion. There was a great deal of blue denim – not just jeans but shirts, jackets, skirts and even coats. And the hair! It was this that really shocked him. The men grew it not just over their ears but sometimes halfway down their backs. He saw two chaps with pigtails. Others, male and female, grew it upward and outward in great masses of curls so that they always looked as if they were peering through a hole in a hedge. This apparently being insufficiently outrageous for some, they had added Jesus beards, Mexican moustaches, or swooping side-whiskers. They might have been men from Mars.

He walked through the city centre, marvelling, and headed out. It was twenty years since he had followed this route, but he remembered the way. Little things about his college days came back to him: the discovery of Louis Armstrong's astonishing cornet-playing; the way he had been secretly self-conscious about his Cock-ney accent; wondering why everyone but he liked so much to get drunk; borrowing books faster than he could read them so that the pile on the table in his room always grew higher.

He wondered whether the years had changed him. Not much, he thought. Then he had been a frightened man looking for a fortress: now he had Israel for a fortress, but instead of hiding there he had to come out and fight to defend it. Then as now he had been a lukewarm socialist, knowing that society was unjust, not sure how it might be changed for the better. Growing older, he had gained skills but not wisdom. In fact, it seemed to him that he knew more and understood less.

He was somewhat happier now, he decided. He knew who he was and what he had to do; he had figured out what life was about and discovered that he could cope with it; although his attitudes were much the same as they had been in 1948, he was now more sure of them. However, the young Dickstein had hoped for certain other kinds of happiness which, in the event, had not come his way; indeed, the possibility had receded as the years passed. This place reminded him uncomfortably of all that. This house, especially.

He stood outside, looking at it. It had not changed at all: the paintwork was still green and white, the garden still a jungle in the front. He opened the gate, walked up the path to the door, and knocked.

This was not the efficient way to do it. Ashford might have moved away, or died, or simply gone on holiday. Dickstein should perhaps have called the university to check. However, if the inquiry was to be casual and discreet it was necessary to risk wasting a little time. Besides, he had rather liked the idea of seeing the old place again after so many years.

The door opened and the woman said, 'Yes?'

Dickstein went cold with shock. His mouth dropped open. He staggered slightly, and put a hand against the wall to steady himself. His face creased into a frown of astonishment.

It was she, and she was still twenty-five years old.

In a voice full of incredulity, Dickstein said, 'Elia . . . ?'

She stared at the odd little man on the doorstep. He looked like a don, with his round spectacles and his old grey suit and his bristly short hair. There had been nothing wrong with him when she opened the door, but as soon as he set eyes on her he had turned quite grey.

This kind of thing had happened to her once before, walking down the High Street. A delightful old gentleman had stared at her, doffed his hat, stopped her and said, 'I say, I know we haven't been introduced but . . .'

This was obviously the same phenomenon, so she said, 'I'm not Eila. I'm Suza.'

'Suza!' said the stranger.

'They say I look exactly like my mother did when she was my age. You obviously knew her. Will you come in?'

The man stayed where he was. He seemed to be recovering from the surprise, although he was still pale. 'I'm Nat Dickstein,' he said with a little smile.

'How do you do,' Suza said. 'Won't you—' Then she realized what he had said. It was her turn to be surprised. 'Mister Dickstein!' she said, her voice rising almost to a squeal. She threw her arms around his neck and kissed him.

'You remembered,' he said when she let go. He looked pleased and embarrassed.

'Of course!' she said. 'You used to pet Hezekiah. You

were the only one who could understand what he was saying.'

He gave that little smile again. 'Hezekiah the cat . . . I'd forgotten.'

'Well, come in!'

He stepped past her into the house, and she closed the door. Taking his arm, she led him across the square hall. 'This is wonderful,' she said. 'Come into the kitchen, I've been messing about trying to make a cake.'

She gave him a stool. He sat down and looked about slowly, giving little nods of recognition at the old kitchen table, the fireplace, the view through the window.

'Let's have some coffee,' Suza said. 'Or would you prefer tea?'

'Coffee, please. Thank you.'

'I expect you want to see daddy. He's teaching this morning, but he'll be back soon for lunch.' She poured coffee beans into a hand-operated grinder.

'And your mother?'

'She died fourteen years ago. Cancer.' Suza looked at him, expecting the automatic 'I'm sorry.' The words did not come, but the thought showed on his face. Somehow she liked him more for that. She ground the beans. The noise filled the silence.

When she had finished, Dickstein said, 'Professor Ashford is still teaching . . . I was just trying to work out his age.'

'Sixty-five,' she said. 'He doesn't do a lot.' Sixty-five sounded ancient but daddy didn't seem old, she thought fondly: his mind was still sharp as a knife. She wondered what Dickstein did for a living. 'Didn't you emigrate to Palestine?' she asked him.

'Israel. I live on a kibbutz. I grow grapes and make wine.'

Israel. In this house it was always called Palestine. How would daddy react to this old friend who now stood for everything daddy stood against? She knew the answer: it would make no difference, for daddy's politics were theoretical, not practical. She wondered why Dickstein had come. 'Are you on holiday?'

'Business. We now think the wine is good enough to export to Europe.'

'That's very good. And you're selling it?'

'Looking out the possibilities. Tell me about yourself. I'll bet you're not a university professor.'

The remark annoyed her a little, and she knew she was blushing faintly just below her ears: she did not want this man to think she was not clever enough to be a don. 'What makes you say that?' she said coolly.

'You're so . . . warm.' Dickstein looked away, as if he immediately regretted the choice of word. 'Anyway, too young.'

She had misjudged him. He had not been condescending. 'I have my father's ear for languages, but not his academic turn of mind, so I'm an air hostess,' she said, and wondered if it were true that she did not have an academic mind, whether she really was not clever enough to be a don. She poured boiling water into a filter, and the smell of coffee filled the room. She did not know what to say next. She glanced up at Dickstein and discovered that he was openly gazing at her, deep in thought. His eyes were large and dark brown. Suddenly she felt shy – which was most unusual. She told him so.

'Shy?' he said. 'That's because I've been staring at you as if you were a painting, or something. I'm trying to get used to the fact that you're not Eila, you're the little girl with the old grey cat.'

'Hezekiah died, it must have been soon after you left.'

'There's a lot that's changed.'

'Were you great friends with my parents?'

'I was one of your father's students. I admired your mother from a distance. Eila . . .' Again he looked away, as if to pretend that it was someone else speaking. 'She wasn't just beautiful – she was *striking*.'

Suza looked into his face. She thought: You loved her. The thought came unbidden; it was intuitive; she immediately suspected it might be wrong. However, it would explain the severity of his reaction on the doorstep when he saw her. She said, 'My mother was the original hippy – did you know that?'

'I don't know what you mean.'

'She wanted to be free. She rebelled against the restrictions put on Arab women, even though she came from an affluent, liberal home. She married my father to get out of the Middle East. Of course she found that Western society had its own ways of repressing women – so she proceeded to break most of the rules.' As she spoke Suza remembered how she had realized, while she was becoming a woman and beginning to understand passion, that her mother was promiscuous. She had been shocked, she was sure, but somehow she could not recall the feeling.

'That makes her a hippy?' Dickstein said.

'Hippies believe in free love.'

'I see.'

And from his reaction to *that* she knew that her mother had not loved Nat Dickstein. For no reason at all this made her sad. 'Tell me about your parents,' she said. She was talking to him as if they were the same age.

'Only if you pour the coffee.'

She laughed. 'I was forgetting.'

'My father was a cobbler,' Dickstein began. 'He was good at mending boots but he wasn't much of a businessman. Still, the Thirties were good years for cobblers in the East End of London. People couldn't afford new boots, so they had their old ones mended year after year. We were never rich, but we had a little more money than most of the people around us. And, of course, there was some pressure on my father from his family to expand the business, open a second shop, employ other men.'

Suza passed him his coffee. 'Milk, sugar?'

'Sugar, no milk. Thank you.'

'Do go on.' It was a different world, one she knew nothing about: it had never occurred to her that a shoe repairer would do well in a depression.

'The leather dealers thought my father was a tartar – they could never sell him anything but the best. If there was a second-rate hide they would say, "Don't bother giving that to Dickstein, he'll send it straight back." So I was told, anyway.' He gave that little smile again.

'Is he still alive?' Suza asked.

'He died before the war.'

'What happened?'

'Well. The Thirties were the Fascist years in London. They used to hold open-air meetings every night. The speakers would tell them how Jews the world over were sucking the blood of working people. The speakers, the organizers, were respectable middle-class men, but the crowds were unemployed ruffians. After the meetings they would march through the streets, breaking windows and roughing-up passersby. Our house was a perfect target for them. We were Jews; my father was a shopkeeper and therefore a bloodsucker; and, true to their propaganda, we were slightly better off than the people around us.'

He stopped, staring into space. Suza waited for him to go on. As he told this story, he seemed to huddle – crossing his legs tightly, wrapping his arms around his body, hunching his back. Sitting there on the kitchen stool, in his ill-fitting suit of clerical grey, with his elbows and knees and shoulders pointing at all angles, he looked like a bundle of sticks in a bag.

'We lived over the shop. Every damn night I used to lie awake, waiting for them to go past. I was blind terrified, mainly because I knew my father was so frightened. Sometimes they did nothing, just went by. Usually they shouted out slogans. Often, often they broke the windows. A couple of times they got into the shop and smashed it up. I thought they were going to come up the stairs. I put my head under the pillow, crying, and cursed God for making me Jewish.'

'Didn't the police do anything?'

'What they could. If they were around they stopped it. But they had a lot to do in those days. The Communists were the only people who would help us fight back, and my father didn't want their help. All the political parties were against the Fascists, of course – but it was the Reds who gave out pickaxe handles and crowbars and built barricades. I tried to join the Party but they wouldn't have me – too young.'

'And your father?'

'He just sort of lost heart. After the shop was wrecked the second time there was no money to fix it. It seemed he didn't have the energy to start again somewhere else. He went on the dole, and just kind of wasted. He died in 1938.'

'And you?'

'Grew up fast. Joined the army as soon as I looked old enough. Got taken prisoner early. Came to Oxford after the war, then dropped out and went to Israel.'

'Have you got a family out there?'

'The whole kibbutz is my family ... but I never married.'

'Because of my mother?'

'Perhaps. Partly. You're very direct.'

She felt the glow of a faint blush below her ears again: it had been a very intimate question to ask someone who was practically a stranger. Yet it had come quite naturally. She said, 'I'm sorry.'

'Don't apologize,' Dickstein said. 'I rarely talk like this. Actually, this whole trip is, I don't know, full of the past. There's a word for it. Redolent.'

'That means smelling of death.'

Dickstein shrugged.

There was a silence. I like this man a lot, Suza thought. I like his conversation and his silences, his big eyes and his old suit and his memories. I hope he'll stay a while.

She picked up the coffee cups and opened the dishwasher. A spoon slid off a saucer and bounced under the large old freezer. She said, 'Damn.'

Dickstein got down on his knees and peered underneath.

'It's there for ever, now,' Suza said. 'That thing is too heavy to move.'

Dickstein lifted one end of the freezer with his right hand and reached underneath it with his left. He lowered the end of the freezer, stood up and handed the spoon to Suza.

She stared at him. 'What are you – Captain America? That thing is *heavy*.'

'I work in the fields. How do you know about Captain America? He was the rage in my boyhood.'

'He's the rage now. The art in those comics is fantastic.'

'Well, stone the crows,' he said. 'We had to read them in secret because they were trash. Now they're art. Quite right, too.'

She smiled. 'Do you really work in the fields?' He looked like a clerk, not a field hand.

'Of course.'

'A wine salesman who actually gets dirt under his fingernails in the vineyard. That's unusual.'

'Not in Israel. We're a little ... obsessive, I suppose ... about the soil.'

Suza looked at her watch and was surprised to see how late it was. 'Daddy should be home any minute. You'll eat with us, won't you? I'm afraid it's only a sandwich.'

'That would be lovely.'

She sliced a French loaf and began to make salad. Dickstein offered to wash lettuce, and she gave him an apron. After a while she caught him watching her again, smiling. 'What are you thinking?'

'I was remembering something that would embarrass you,' he said.

'Tell me anyway.'

'I was here one evening, around six,' he began. 'Your mother was out. I had come to borrow a book from your father. You were in your bath. Your father got a phone call from France, I can't remember why. While he was talking you began to cry. I went upstairs, took you out of the bath, dried you and put you into your nightdress. You must have been four or five years old.'

Suza laughed. She had a sudden vision of Dickstein in a steamy bathroom, reaching down and effortlessly lifting her out of a hot bath full of soap bubbles. In the vision she was not a child but a grown woman with wet breasts and foam between her thighs, and his hands were strong and sure as he drew her against his chest. Then the kitchen door opened and her father came in, and the dream vanished, leaving only a sense of intrigue and a trace of guilt.

Nat Dickstein thought Professor Ashford had aged well. He was now bald except for a monkish fringe of white hair. He had put on a little weight and his movements were slower, but he still had the spark of intellectual curiosity in his eyes.

Suza said, 'A surprise guest, daddy.'

Ashford looked at him and, without hesitation, said, 'Young Dickstein! Well, I'm blessed! My dear fellow.'

Dickstein shook his hand. The grip was firm. 'How are you, professor?'

'In the pink, dear boy, especially when my daughter's here to look after me. You remember Suza?'

'We've spent the morning reminiscing,' Dickstein said.

'I see she's put you in an apron already. That's fast, even for her. I've told her she'll never get a husband this way. Take it off, dear boy, and come and have a drink.'

With a rueful grin at Suza, Dickstein did as he was told and followed Ashford into the drawing room.

'Sherry?' Ashford asked.

'Thank you, a small one.' Dickstein suddenly remembered he was here for a purpose. He had to get information out of Ashford without the old man realizing it. He had been, as it were, off-duty, for a couple of hours, and now he had to turn his mind back to work. But softly, softly, he thought.

Ashford handed him a small glass of pale sherry. 'Now tell me, what have you been up to all these years?'

Dickstein sipped the sherry. It was very dry, the way they liked it at Oxford. He told the professor the story he had given to Hassan and to Suza, about finding export markets for Israeli wine. Ashford asked informed questions. Were young people leaving the kibbutzim for the cities? Had time and prosperity eroded the communalist ideas of the kibbutzniks? Did European Jews mix and intermarry with African and Levantine Jews? Dickstein's answers were yes, no, and not much. Ashford courteously avoided the question of their opposing views on the political morality of Israel, but nevertheless there was, underlying his detached inquiries about Israeli problems, a detectable trace of eagerness for bad news.

Suza called them to the kitchen for lunch before Dickstein had an opportunity to ask his own questions. Her French sandwiches were vast and delicious. She had opened a bottle of red wine to go with them. Dickstein could see why Ashford had put on weight.

Over coffee Dickstein said, 'I ran into a contemporary of mine a couple of weeks ago – in Luxembourg, of all places.'

Ashford said, 'Yasif Hassan?'

'How did you know?'

'We've kept in touch. I know he lives in Luxembourg.'

'Have you seen him much?' Dickstein asked, thinking: Softly, softly.

'Several times, over the years.' Ashford paused. 'It

needs to be said, Dickstein, that the wars which have given you everything took everything away from him. His family lost all their money and went into a refugee camp. He's understandably bitter about Israel.'

Dickstein nodded. He was now almost certain that Hassan was in the game. 'I had very little time with him – I was on my way to catch a plane. How is he otherwise?'

Ashford frowned. 'I find him a bit ... *distrait*,' he finished, unable to find the right English word. 'Sudden errands he has to run, cancelled appointments, odd phone calls at all times, mysterious absences. Perhaps it's the behaviour of a dispossessed aristocrat.'

'Perhaps,' Dickstein said. In fact it was the typical behaviour of an agent, and he was now one hundred per cent sure that the meeting with Hassan had blown him. He said, 'Do you see anyone else from my year?'

'Only old Toby. He's on the Conservative Front Bench now.'

'Perfect!' Dickstein said delightedly. 'He always did talk like an Opposition spokesman – pompous and defensive at the same time. I'm glad he's found his niche.'

Suza said, 'More coffee, Nat?'

'No, thank you.' He stood up. 'I'll help you clear away, then I must get back to London. I'm so glad I dropped in on you.'

'Daddy will clear up,' Suza said. She grinned. 'We have an agreement. '

'I'm afraid it is so,' Ashford confessed. 'She won't be anybody's drudge, least of all mine.' The remark surprised Dickstein because it was so obviously untrue. Perhaps Suza didn't wait on him hand and foot, but she seemed to look after him the way a working wife would.

'I'll walk into town with you,' Suza said. 'Let me get my coat.'

Ashford shook Dickstein's hand. 'A real pleasure to see you, dear boy, a real pleasure.'

Suza came back wearing a velvet jacket. Ashford saw them to the door and waved, smiling.

As they walked along the street Dickstein talked just to have an excuse to keep looking at her. The jacket matched her black velvet trousers, and she wore a loose cream-coloured shirt that looked like silk. Like her mother, she knew how to dress to make the most of her shining dark hair and perfect tan skin. Dickstein gave her his arm, feeling rather old-fashioned, just to have her touching him. There was no doubt that she had the same physical magnetism as her mother: there was that something about her which filled men with the desire to possess her, a desire not so much like lust as greed; the need to *own* such a beautiful object, so that it would never be taken away. Dickstein was old enough now to know how false such desires were, and to know that Eila Ashford would not have made him happy. But the daughter seemed to have something the mother had lacked, and that was warmth. Dickstein was sorry he would never see Suza again. Given time, he might . . .

Well. It was not to be.

When they reached the station he asked her, 'Do you ever go to London?'

'Of course,' she said. 'I'm going tomorrow.'
'What for?'
'To have dinner with you,' she said.

When Suza's mother died, her father was wonderful.

She was eleven years of age: old enough to understand death, but too young to cope with it. Daddy had been calm and comforting. He had known when to leave her to weep alone and when to make her dress up and go out to lunch. Quite unembarrassed, he had talked to her about menstruation and gone with her cheerfully to buy new brassieres. He gave her a new role in life: she became the woman of the house, giving instructions to the cleaner, writing the laundry list, handing out sherry on Sunday mornings. At the age of fourteen she was in charge of the household finances. She took care of her father better than Eila ever had. She would throw away worn shirts and replace them with identical new ones without daddy ever knowing. She learned that it was possible to be alive and secure and loved even without a mother.

Daddy gave her a role, just as he had her mother; and, like her mother, she had rebelled against the role while continuing to play it.

He wanted her to stay at Oxford, to be first an undergraduate, then a graduate student, then a teacher. It would have meant that she was always around to take care of him. She said she was not smart enough, with an uneasy feeling that this was an excuse for something else, and took a job that obliged her to be away from home and unable to look after daddy for weeks at a time. High in the air and thousands of miles from Oxford, she served drinks and meals to middle-aged men, and wondered if she really had changed anything.

Walking home from the railway station. she thought about the groove she was in and whether she would ever get out of it.

She was at the end of a love affair which, like the rest of her life, had wearily followed a familiar pattern. Julian was in his late thirties, a philosophy lecturer specializing in the pre-Socratic Greeks: brilliant, dedicated and helpless. He took drugs for everything – cannabis to make love, amphetamine to work, Mogadon to sleep. He was divorced, without children. At first she had found him interesting, charming and sexy. When they were in bed he liked her to get on top. He took her to fringe theatres in London and bizarre student parties. But it all wore off: she realized that he wasn't really very interested in sex, that he took her out because she looked good on his arm, that he liked her company just because she was so impressed by his intellect. One day she found herself ironing his clothes while he took a tutorial; and then it was as good as over.

Sometimes she went to bed with men her own age or younger, mostly because she was consumed with lust for their bodies. She was usually disappointed and they all bored her eventually.

She was already regretting the impulse which had led her to make a date with Nat Dickstein. He was depressingly true to type: a generation older than she and patently in need of care and attention. Worst of all, he had been in love with her mother. At first sight he was a father-figure like all the rest.

But he was different in some ways, she told herself. He was a farmer, not an academic – he would probably be the least well-read person she had ever dated. He had gone to Palestine instead of sitting in Oxford coffee shops talking about it. He could pick up one end of the freezer with his right hand. In the time they had spent together he had more than once surprised her by not conforming to her expectations.

Maybe Nat Dickstein will break the pattern, she thought.

And maybe I'm kidding myself, again.

Nat Dickstein called the Israeli Embassy from a phone booth at Paddington Station. When he got through he asked for the Commercial Credit Office. There was no such department: this was a code for the Mossad message centre. He was answered by a young man with a Hebrew accent. This pleased Dickstein, for it was good to know there were people for whom Hebrew was a native tongue and not a dead language. He knew the conversation would automatically be tape-recorded, so he went straight into his message: 'Rush to Bill. Sale jeopardized by presence of opposition team. Henry.' He hung up without waiting for an acknowledgment.

He walked to his hotel from the station, thinking about Suza Ashford. He was to meet her at Paddington tomorrow evening. She would spend the night at the flat of a friend. Dickstein did not really know where to begin – he could not remember ever taking a woman out to dinner just for pleasure. As a teenager he had been too poor; after the war he had been too nervous and awkward; as he grew older he somehow never got into the habit. There had been dinners with colleagues, of course, and with kibbutzniks after shopping expeditions in Nazareth; but to take a woman, just the two of you, for nothing more than the pleasure of each other's company . . .

What did you do? You were supposed to pick her up in your car, wearing your dinner jacket, and give her a box of chocolates tied with a big ribbon. Dickstein was meeting Suza at the railway station, and he had neither car nor dinner jacket. Where would he take her? He did not know any posh restaurants in Israel, let alone England.

Walking alone through Hyde Park, he smiled broadly. This was a laughable situation for a man of forty-three to be in. She knew he was no sophisticate, and obviously she did not care, for she had invited herself to dinner. She would also know the restaurants and what to order. It was hardly a matter of life and death. Whatever happened, he was going to enjoy it.

There was now a hiatus in his work. Having discovered that he was blown, he could do nothing until he had talked to Pierre Borg and Borg had decided whether or not to abort. That evening he went to see a French film called *Un Homme et Une Femme*. It was a simple love story, beautifully told, with an insistent

Latin-American tune on the soundtrack. He left before the movie was halfway through, because the story made him want to cry; but the tune ran through his mind all night.

In the morning he went to a phone booth in the street near his hotel and phoned the Embassy again. When he got through to the message centre he said, 'This is Henry. Any reply?'

The voice said, 'Go to ninety-three thousand and confer tomorrow.'

Dickstein said, 'Reply: conference agenda at airport information.'

Pierre Borg would be flying in at nine-thirty tomorrow.

The four men sat in the car with the patience of spies, silent and watchful, as the day darkened.

Pyotr Tyrin was at the wheel, a stocky middle-aged man in a raincoat, drumming his fingernails on the dashboard, making a noise like pigeons' feet on a roof. Yasif Hassan sat beside him. David Rostov and Nik Bunin were in the back.

Nik had found the delivery man on the third day, the day he spent watching the Jean-Monnet building on the Kirchberg. He had reported a positive identification. 'He doesn't look quite so much of a nancy-boy in his office suit, but I'm quite sure it's him. I should say he must work here.'

'I should have guessed,' Rostov had said. 'If Dickstein is after secrets his informants won't be from the airport or the Alfa Hotel. I should have sent Nik to Euratom first.'

He was addressing Pyotr Tyrin, but Hassan heard and said, 'You can't think of everything.'

'Yes, I can,' Rostov told him.

He had instructed Hassan to get hold of a large dark car. The American Buick they now sat in was a little conspicuous, but it was black and roomy. Nik had followed the Euratom man home, and now the four spies waited in the cobbled street close to the old terraced house.

Rostov hated this cloak-and-dagger stuff. It was so old-fashioned. It belonged to the Twenties and Thirties, to places like Vienna and Istanbul and Beirut, not to western Europe in 1968. It was just *dangerous* to snatch a civilian off the street, bundle him into a car, and beat him until he gave you information. You might be seen by passersby who were not afraid to go to the police and tell what they had observed. Rostov liked things to be straightforward and clear-cut and predictable, and he preferred to use his brains rather than his fists. But this delivery man had gained in importance with each day that Dickstein failed to surface. Rostov had to know what he had delivered to Dickstein, and he had to know today.

Pyotr Tyrin said, 'I wish he would come out.'

'We're in no hurry,' Rostov said. It was not true, but he did not want the team to get edgy and impatient and make mistakes. To relieve the tension he continued speaking. 'Dickstein did this, of course. He did what we've done and what we're doing. He watched the

Jean-Monnet building, he followed this man home, and he waited here in the street. The man came out and went to the homosexual club, and then Dickstein knew the man's weakness and used it to turn him into an informant.'

Nik said, 'He hasn't been at the club the past two nights.'

Rostov said, 'He's discovered that everything has its price, especially love.'

'Love?' Nik said with scorn in his voice.

Rostov did not reply.

The darkness thickened and the street lights came on. The air coming through the open car window tasted faintly damp: Rostov saw a swirl or two of mist around the lights. The vapour came from the river. A fog would be too much to hope for in June.

Tyrin said, 'What's this?'

A fair-haired man in a double-breasted jacket was walking briskly along the street toward them.

'Quiet, now,' Rostov said.

The man stopped at the house they were watching. He rang a doorbell.

Hassan put a hand on the door handle.

Rostov hissed: 'Not yet.'

A net curtain was briefly drawn aside in the attic window.

The fair-haired man waited, tapping his foot.

Hassan said, 'The lover, perhaps?'

'For God's sake shut up,' Rostov told him.

After a minute the front door opened and the fair-haired man stepped inside. Rostov got a glimpse of the person who had opened up: it was the delivery man. The door closed and their chance was gone.

'Too quick,' Rostov said. 'Damn it.'

Tyrin began to drum his fingers again, and Nik scratched himself. Hassan gave an exasperated sigh, as if he had known all along that it was foolish to wait. Rostov decided that it was time to bring him down a peg or two.

Nothing happened for an hour.

Tyrin said, 'They're spending an evening indoors.'

'If they've had a brush with Dickstein they're probably afraid to go out at night,' Rostov said.

Nik asked, 'Do we go in?'

'There's a problem,' Rostov answered. 'From the window they can see who's at the door. I guess they won't open up for strangers.'

'The lover might stay the night,' Tyrin said.

'Quite.'

Nik said, 'We'll just have to bust in.'

Rostov ignored him. Nik always wanted to bust in, but he would not start any rough stuff until he was told to. Rostov was thinking that they might now have to snatch two people, which was more tricky and more dangerous. 'Have we got any firearms?' he said.

Tyrin opened the glove box in front of him and drew out a pistol.

'Good,' Rostov said. 'So long as you don't fire it.'

'It's not loaded,' Tyrin said. He stuffed the gun into his raincoat pocket.

Hassan said, 'If the lover stays the night do we take them in the morning?'

'Certainly not,' Rostov said. 'We can't do this sort of thing in broad daylight.'

'What, then?'

'I haven't decided.'

He thought about it until midnight, and then the problem solved itself.

Rostov was watching the doorway through half-closed eyes. He saw the first movement of the door as it began to open. He said: 'Now.'

Nik was first out of the car. Tyrin was next. Hassan took a moment to realize what was happening, then he followed suit.

The two men were saying goodnight, the younger one on the pavement, the older just inside the door wearing a robe. The older one, the delivery man, reached out and gave his lover's arm a farewell squeeze. They both looked up, alarmed, as Nik and Tyrin burst out of the car and came at them.

'Don't move, be silent,' Tyrin said softly in French, showing them the gun.

Rostov noticed that Nik's sound tactical instinct had led him to stand beside and slightly behind the younger man.

The older one said, 'Oh, my God, no, no more please.'

'Get in the car,' Tyrin said.

The younger man said, 'Why can't you fuckers leave us alone?'

Watching and listening from the back seat of the car, Rostov thought: This is the moment they decide whether to come quietly or make trouble. He glanced quickly up and down the darkened street. It was empty.

Nik, sensing that the younger man was thinking of disobedience, seized both his arms just below the shoulders and held him tightly.

'Don't hurt him, I'll go,' said the older man. He stepped out of the house.

His friend said, 'The hell you will!'

Rostov thought: *Damn*.

The younger man struggled in Nik's grip, then tried to stamp on Nik's foot. Nik stepped back a pace and hit the boy in the kidney with his right fist.

'No, Pierre!' the older one said, too loud.

Tyrin jumped him and put a big hand over the man's mouth. He struggled, got his head free, and shouted 'Help!' before Tyrin gagged him again.

Pierre had fallen to one knee and was groaning.

Rostov leaned across the back seat of the car and called through the open window, 'Let's *go*!'

Tyrin lifted the older man off his feet and carried him bodily across the pavement toward the car. Pierre suddenly recovered from Nik's punch and sprinted away. Hassan stuck out a leg and tripped him. The boy went sprawling on to the cobbled road.

Rostov saw a light go on in an upstairs window at a neighbouring house. If the fracas continued much longer they would all get arrested.

Tyrin bundled the delivery man into the back of the car. Rostov grabbed hold of him and said to Tyrin: 'I've got him. Start the car. Quick.'

Nik had picked up the younger one and was carrying him to the car. Tyrin got into the driver's seat and Hassan opened the other door. Rostov said, 'Hassan, shut the door of the house, idiot!'

Nik pushed the young man into the car next to his friend, then got into the back seat so that the two captives were between Rostov and himself. Hassan closed the door of the house and jumped into the front passenger seat of the car. Tyrin gunned the car away from the kerb.

Rostov said in English, 'Jesus Christ almighty, what a fuck-up.'

Pierre was still groaning. The older prisoner said, 'We haven't done anything to hurt you.'

'Haven't you?' Rostov replied. 'Three nights ago, at the club in the Rue Dicks, you delivered a briefcase to an Englishman.'

'Ed Rodgers?'

'That's not his name,' Rostov said.

'Are you the police?'

'Not exactly.' Rostov would let the man believe what he wanted to. 'I'm not interested in collecting evidence, building a case, and bringing you to a trial. I'm interested in what was in that briefcase.'

There was a silence. Tyrin spoke over his shoulder. 'Want me to head out of town, look for a quiet spot?'

'Wait,' Rostov said.

The older man said, 'I'll tell you.'

'Just drive around town,' Rostov told Tyrin. He looked at the Euratom man. 'So tell me.'

194

'It was a Euratom computer printout.'

'And the information on it?'

'Details of licenced shipments of fissionable materials.'

'Fissionable? You mean nuclear stuff?'

'Yellowcake, uranium metal, nuclear waste, plutonium . . .'

Rostov sat back in the seat and looked out of the window at the lights of the city going by. His blood raced with excitement: Dickstein's operation was becoming visible. Licenced shipments of fissionable materials . . . the Israelis wanted nuclear fuel. Dickstein would be looking for one of two things on that list – either a holder of uranium who might be prepared to sell some on the black market, or a consignment of uranium he might be able to steal.

As for what they would *do* with the stuff once they got it . . .

The Euratom man interrupted his thoughts. 'Will you let us go home now?'

Rostov said, 'I'll have to have a copy of that printout.'

'I can't take another one, the disappearance of the first was suspicious enough!'

'I'm afraid you'll have to,' Rostov said. 'But if you like, you can take it back to the office after we've photographed it.'

'Oh, God,' the man groaned.

'You've got no choice.'

'All right.'

'Head back to the house,' Rostov told Tyrin. To the

Euratom man he said, 'Bring the printout home tomorrow night. Someone will come to your house during the evening to photograph it.'

The big car moved through the streets of the city. Rostov felt the snatch had not been such a disaster after all. Nik Bunin said to Pierre, 'Stop looking at me.'

They reached the cobbled street. Tyrin stopped the car. 'Okay,' Rostov said. 'Let the older man out. His friend stays with us.'

The Euratom man yelped as if hurt. 'Why?'

'In case you're tempted to break down and confess everything to your bosses tomorrow. Young Pierre will be our hostage. Get out.' Nik opened the door and let the man out. He stood on the pavement for a moment. Nik got back in and Tyrin drove off.

Hassan said, 'Will he be all right? Will he do it?'

'He'll work for us until he gets his friend back,' Rostov said.

'And then?'

Rostov said nothing. He was thinking that it would probably be prudent to kill them both.

This is Suza's nightmare.

It is evening at the green-and-white house by the river. She is alone. She takes a bath, lying for a long time in the hot scented water. Afterwards she goes into the master bedroom, sits in front of the three-sided mirror, and dusts herself with powder from an onyx box that belonged to her mother.

She opens the wardrobe, expecting to find her

mother's clothes moth-eaten, falling away from the hangers in dun-coloured tatters, transparent with age; but it is not so: they are all clean and new and perfect, except for a faint odour of mothballs. She chooses a nightgown, white as a shroud, and puts it on. She gets into the bed.

She lies still for a long time, waiting for Nat Dickstein to come to his Eila. The evening becomes night. The river whispers. The door opens. The man stands at the foot of the bed and takes off his clothes. He lies on top of her, and her panic begins like the first small spark of a conflagration as she realizes that it is not Nat Dickstein but her father; and that she is, of course, long dead: and as the nightgown crumbles to dust and her hair falls out and her flesh withers and the skin of her face dries and shrinks baring the teeth and the skull and she becomes, even as the man thrusts at her, a skeleton, so she screams and screams and screams and wakes up, and she lies perspiring and shivering and frightened, wondering why nobody comes rushing in to ask what is wrong, until she realizes with relief that even the screams were dreamed; and consoled, she wonders vaguely about the meaning of the dream while she drifts back into sleep.

In the morning she is her usual cheerful self, except perhaps for a small imprecise darkness, like a smudge of cloud in the sky of her mood, not remembering the dream at all, only aware that there was once something that troubled her, not worrying any more, though, because, after all, dreaming is instead of worrying.

CHAPTER SEVEN

'N AT DICKSTEIN is going to steal some uranium,' said Yasif Hassan.

David Rostov nodded agreement. His mind was elsewhere. He was trying to figure out how to get rid of Yasif Hassan.

They were walking through the valley at the foot of the crag which was the old city of Luxembourg. Here, on the banks of the Petrusse River, were lawns and ornamental trees and footpaths. Hassan was saying, 'They've got a nuclear reactor at a place called Dimona in the Negev Desert. The French helped them build it, and presumably supplied them with fuel for it. Since the Six-Day War, de Gaulle has cut off their supplies of guns, so perhaps he's cut off the uranium as well.'

This much was obvious, Rostov thought, so it was best to allay Hassan's suspicions by agreeing vehemently. 'It would be a completely characteristic Mossad move to just go out and steal the uranium they need,' he said. 'That's exactly how those people think. They have this backs-to-the-wall mentality which enables them to ignore the niceties of international diplomacy.'

Rostov was able to guess a little farther than Hassan – which was why he was at once so elated and so anxious to get the Arab out of the way for a while. Rostov knew about the Egyptian nuclear project at Qattara: Hassan almost certainly did not – why should they tell such secrets to an agent in Luxembourg?

However, because Cairo was so leaky it was likely the Israelis also knew about the Egyptian bomb. And what would they do about it? Build their own – for which they needed, in the Euratom man's phrase, 'fissionable material'. Rostov thought Dickstein was going to try to get some uranium for an Israeli atom bomb. But Hassan would not be able to reach that conclusion, not yet; and Rostov was not going to help him, for he did not want Tel Aviv to discover how close he was.

When the printout arrived that night it would take him farther still. For it was the list from which Dickstein would probably choose his target. Rostov did not want Hassan to have that information, either.

David Rostov's blood was up. He felt the way he did in a chess game at the moment when three or four of the opponent's moves began to form a pattern and he could see from where the attack would come and how he would have to turn it into a rout. He had not forgotten the reasons why he had entered into battle with Dickstein – that other conflict inside the KGB between himself and Feliks Vorontsov, with Yuri Andropov as umpire and a place at the Phys-Mat School as the prize – but that receded to the back of his mind. What moved him now, what kept him tense and alert and sharpened the edge of his ruthlessness, was the thrill of the chase and the scent of the quarry in his nostrils.

Hassan stood in his way. Eager, amateur, touchy, bungling Hassan, reporting back to Cairo, was at this moment a more dangerous enemy than Dickstein himself. For all his faults, he was not stupid – indeed, Rostov thought, he had a sly intelligence that was typically Levantine, inherited no doubt from his capitalist father. He would know that Rostov wanted him out of the way. Therefore Rostov would have to give him a real job to do.

They passed beneath the Pont Adolphe, and Rostov stopped to look back, admiring the view through the arch of the bridge. It reminded him of Oxford, and then, suddenly, he knew what to do about Hassan.

Rostov said, 'Dickstein knows someone has been following him, and presumably he's connected that fact with his meeting with you.'

'You think so?' Hassan said.

'Well, look. He goes on an assignment, he bumps into an Arab who knows his real name and suddenly he's tailed.'

'He's sure to speculate, but he doesn't *know*.'

'You're right.' Looking at Hassan's face, Rostov realized that the Arab just loved him to say *You're right*. Rostov thought: He doesn't like me, but he wants my approval – wants it badly. He's a proud man – I can use that. 'Dickstein has to check,' Rostov went on. 'Now, are you on file in Tel Aviv?'

Hassan shrugged, with a hint of his old aristocratic nonchalance. 'Who knows?'

'How often have you had face-to-face contacts with other agents – Americans, British, Israelis?'

'Never,' Hassan said. 'I'm too careful.'

Rostov almost laughed out loud. The truth was that Hassan was too insignificant an agent to have come to the notice of the major intelligence services, and had never done anything important enough to have met other spies. 'If you're not on file,' Rostov said, 'Dickstein has to talk to your friends. Have you any acquaintances in common?'

'No. I haven't seen him since college. Anyway, he could learn nothing from my friends. They know nothing of my secret life. I don't go around telling people—'

'No, no,' Rostov said, suppressing his impatience. 'But all Dickstein would have to do is ask casual questions about your general behaviour to see whether it conforms to the pattern of clandestine work – for example, do you have mysterious phone calls, sudden absences, friends whom you don't introduce around . . . Now, is there anybody from Oxford whom you still see?'

'None of the students.' Hassan's tone had become defensive, and Rostov knew he was about to get what he wanted 'I've kept in touch with some of the faculty, on and off: Professor Ashford, in particular – once or twice he has put me in touch with people who are prepared to give money to our cause.'

'Dickstein knew Ashford, if I remember rightly.'

'Of course. Ashford had the chair of Semitic Languages, which was what both Dickstein and I read.'

'There. All Dickstein has to do is call on Ashford and mention your name in passing. Ashford will tell him what you're doing and how you behave. Then Dickstein will know you're an agent.'

'It's a bit hit-and-miss,' Hassan said dubiously.

'Not at all,' Rostov said brightly, although Hassan was right. 'It's a standard technique. I've done it myself. It works.'

'And if he has contacted Ashford . . .'

'We have a chance of picking up his trail again. So I want you to go to Oxford.'

'Oh!' Hassan had not seen where the conversation was leading, and now was boxed in. 'Dickstein might have just called on the phone . . .'

'He might, but that kind of inquiry is easier to make in person. Then you can say you were in town and just dropped by to talk about old times . . . It's hard to be that casual on the international telephone. For the same reasons, you must go there rather than call.'

'I suppose you're right,' Hassan said reluctantly. 'I was planning to make a report to Cairo as soon as we've read the printout . . .'

That was exactly what Rostov was trying to avoid. 'Good idea,' he said. 'But the report will look so much better if you can also say that you have picked up Dickstein's trail again.'

Hassan stood staring at the view, peering into the distance as if he was trying to see Oxford. 'Let's go back,' he said abruptly. 'I've walked far enough.'

It was time to be chummy. Rostov put an arm around Hassan's shoulders. 'You Europeans are soft.'

'Don't try to tell me the KGB have a tough life in Moscow.'

'Want to hear a Russian joke?' Rostov said as they climbed the side of the valley toward the road. 'Brezhnev was telling his old mother how well he had done. He showed her his apartment – huge, with Western furniture, dishwasher, freezer, servants, everything. She didn't say a word. He took her to his dacha on the Black Sea – a big villa with a swimming pool, private beach, more servants. Still she wasn't impressed. He took her to his hunting lodge in his Zil limousine, showed off the beautiful grounds, the guns, the dogs. Finally he said, "Mother, mother, why don't you say something? Aren't you proud?" So she said, "It's wonderful, Leonid. But what will you do if the Communists come back?"'

Rostov roared with laughter at his own story, but Hassan only smiled.

'You don't think it's funny?' Rostov said.

'Not very,' Hassan told him. 'It's guilt that makes you laugh at that joke. I don't feel guilty, so I don't find it funny.'

Rostov shrugged, thinking: Thank you Yasif Hassan, Islam's answer to Sigmund Freud. They reached the road and stood there for a while, watching the cars speed by as Hassan caught his breath. Rostov said, 'Oh, listen, there's something I've always wanted to ask you. Did you really screw Ashford's wife?'

'Only four or five times a week,' Hassan said, and he laughed, loudly.

Rostov said, 'Who feels guilty now?'

*

He arrived at the station early, and the train was late, so he had to wait for a whole hour. It was the only time in his life he read *Newsweek* from cover to cover. She came through the ticket barrier at a half-run, smiling broadly. Just like yesterday, she threw her arms around him and kissed him; but this time the kiss was longer. He had vaguely expected to see her in a long dress and a mink wrap, like a banker's wife on a night out at the 61 Club in Tel Aviv; but of course Suza belonged to another country and another generation, and she wore high boots which disappeared under the hem of her below-the-knee skirt, with a silk shirt under an embroidered waistcoat such as a matador might wear. Her face was not made up. Her hands were empty: no coat, no handbag, no overnight case. They stood still, smiling at each other, for a moment. Dickstein, not quite sure what to do, gave her his arm as he had the day before, and that seemed to please her. They walked to the taxi stand.

As they got into the cab Dickstein said, 'Where do you want to go?'

'You haven't booked?'

I should have reserved a table, he thought. He said, 'I don't know London restaurants.'

'Kings Road,' Suza said to the driver.

As the cab pulled away she looked at Dickstein and said, 'Hello, Nathaniel.'

Nobody ever called him Nathaniel. He liked it.

The Chelsea restaurant she chose was small, dim and trendy. As they walked to a table Dickstein thought he

saw one or two familiar faces, and his stomach tightened as he strove to place them; then he realized they
were pop singers he had seen in magazines, and he
relaxed again. He was glad his reflexes still worked like
this in spite of the atypical way he was spending his
time this evening. He was also pleased that the other
diners in the place were of all ages, for he had been a
little afraid he might be the oldest man in sight.

They sat down, and Dickstein said, 'Do you bring all
your young men here?'

Suza gave him a cold smile. 'That's the first witless
thing you've said.'

'I stand corrected.' He wanted to kick himself.

She said, 'What do you like to eat?' and the moment
passed.

'At home I eat a lot of plain, wholesome, communal
food. When I'm away I live in hotels, where I get junk
tricked out as haute cuisine. What I like is the kind of
food you don't get in either sort of place: roast leg of
lamb, steak and kidney pudding, Lancashire hot-pot.'

'What I like about you,' she grinned, 'is that you
have no idea whatsoever about what is trendy and what
isn't; and furthermore you don't give a damn.'

He touched his lapels. 'You don't like the suit?'

'I love it,' she said. 'It must have been out-of-date
when you bought it.'

He decided on roast beef from the trolley, and she
had some kind of sautéed liver which she ate with
enormous relish. He ordered a bottle of Burgundy: a
more delicate wine would not have gone well with the

liver. His knowledge of wine was the only polite accomplishment he possessed. Still, he let her drink most of it: his appetites were small.

She told him about the time she took LSD. 'It was quite unforgettable. I could feel my whole body, inside and out. I could hear my heart. My skin felt wonderful when I touched it. And the colours, of everything . . . Still, the question is, did the drug show me amazing things, or did it just make me amazed? Is it a new way of seeing the world, or does it merely synthesize the sensations you would have if you really saw the world in a new way?'

'You didn't need more of it, afterwards?' he asked.

She shook her head. 'I don't relish losing control of myself to that extent. But I'm glad I know what it's like.'

'That's what I hate about getting drunk – the loss of self-possession. Although I'm sure it's not in the same league. At any rate, the couple of times I've been drunk I haven't felt I've found the key to the universe.'

She made a dismissing gesture with her hand. It was a long, slender hand, just like Eila's; and suddenly Dickstein remembered Eila making exactly the same graceful gesture. Suza said, 'I don't believe in drugs as the solution to the world's problems.'

'What do you believe in, Suza?'

She hesitated, looking at him, smiling faintly. 'I believe that all you need is love.' Her tone was a little defensive, as if she anticipated scorn.

'That philosophy is more likely to appeal to a swinging Londoner than an embattled Israeli.'

'I guess there's no point in trying to convert you.'

'I should be so lucky.'

She looked into his eyes. 'You never know your luck.'

He looked down at the menu and said, 'It's got to be strawberries.'

Suddenly, she said, 'Tell me who you love, Nathaniel.'

'An old woman, a child and a ghost,' he said immediately, for he had been asking himself the same question. 'The old woman is called Esther, and she remembers the pogroms in Czarist Russia. The child is a boy called Mottie. He likes *Treasure Island.* His father died in the Six-Day War.'

'And the ghost?'

'You will have some strawberries?'

'Yes, please.'

'Cream?'

'No, thanks. You're not going to tell me about the ghost, are you?'

'As soon as I know, you'll know.'

It was June, and the strawberries were perfect. Dickstein said, 'Now tell me who you love.'

'Well,' she said, and then she thought for a minute. 'Well . . .' She put down her spoon. 'Oh, shit, Nathaniel, I think I love you.'

Her first thought was: What the *hell* has got into me? Why did I say that?

Then she thought: I don't care, it's true.

And finally: But *why* do I love him?

She did not know why, but she knew when. There

had been two occasions when she had been able to look inside him and see the real Dickstein: once when he spoke about the London Fascists in the Thirties, and once when he mentioned the boy whose father had been killed in the Six-Day War. Both times he had dropped his mask. She had expected to see a small, frightened man, cowering in a corner. In fact, he had appeared to be strong, confident and determined. At those moments she could sense his strength as if it were a powerful scent. It made her feel a little dizzy.

The man was weird, intriguing and powerful. She wanted to get close to him, to understand his mind, to know his secret thoughts. She wanted to touch his bony body, and feel his strong hands grasping her, and look into his sad brown eyes when he cried out in passion. She wanted his love.

It had never been like this for her before.

Nat Dickstein knew it was all wrong.

Suza had formed an attachment to him when she was five years old and he was a kind grown-up who knew how to talk to children and cats. Now he was exploiting that childhood affection.

He had loved Eila, who had died. There was something unhealthy about his relationship with her look-alike daughter.

He was not just a Jew, but an Israeli; not just an Israeli, but a Mossad agent. He of all people could not love a girl who was half Arab.

Whenever a beautiful girl falls in love with a spy, the

spy is obliged to ask himself which enemy intelligence service she might be working for.

Over the years, each time a woman had become fond of Dickstein, he had found reasons like these for being cool to her, and sooner or later she had understood and gone away disappointed; and the fact that Suza had outmanoeuvred his subconscious by being too quick for his defences was just another reason to be suspicious.

It was all wrong.

But Dickstein did not care.

They took a taxi to the flat where she planned to stay the night. She invited him in – her friends, the owners of the flat, were away on holiday – and they went to bed together; and that was when their problems began.

At first Suza thought he was going to be too eagerly passionate when, standing in the little hallway, he gripped her arms and kissed her roughly, and when he groaned, 'Oh, God,' as she took his hands and placed them on her breasts. There flashed through her mind the cynical thought: I've seen this act before, he is so overcome by my beauty that he practically rapes me, and five minutes after getting into bed he is fast asleep and snoring. Then she pulled away from his kiss and looked into his soft, big, brown eyes, and she thought: Whatever happens, it won't be an act.

She led him into the little single bedroom at the back of the flat, overlooking the courtyard. She stayed here so often that it was regarded as her room; indeed some of her clothes were in the wardrobe and the drawers. She sat on the edge of the single bed and took off her shoes. Dickstein stood in the doorway, watching. She looked up at him and smiled. 'Undress,' she said.

He turned out the light.

She was intrigued: it ran through her like the first tingle of a cannabis high. What was he really like? He was a Cockney, but an Israeli; he was a middle-aged schoolboy; a thin man as strong as a horse; a little gauche and nervous superficially, but confident and oddly powerful underneath. What did a man like *that* do in bed?

She got in beneath the sheet, curiously touched that he wanted to make love in the dark. He got in beside her and kissed her, gently this time. She ran her hands over his hard, bony body, and opened her mouth to his kisses. After a momentary hesitation, he responded; and she guessed he had not kissed like that before, or at least not for a long time.

He touched her tenderly now, with his fingertips, exploring, and he said 'Oh!' with a sense of wonder in his voice when he found her nipple taut. His caresses had none of the facile expertise so familiar to her from previous affairs: he was like . . . well, he was like a virgin. The thought made her smile in the darkness.

'Your breasts are beautiful,' he said.

'So are yours,' she said, touching them.

The magic began to work, and she became immersed in sensation: the roughness of his skin, the hair on his legs, the faint masculine smell of him. Then, suddenly, she sensed a change in him. There was no apparent reason for it, and for a moment she wondered if she might be imagining it, for he continued to caress her; but she knew that now it was mechanical, he was thinking of something else, she had lost him.

She was about to speak of it when he withdrew his hands and said, 'It's not working. I can't do it.'

She felt panic, and fought it down. She was frightened, not for herself – *You've known enough stiff pricks in your time, girl, not to mention a few limp ones* – but for him, for his reaction, in case he should be defeated or ashamed and—

She put both arms around him and held him tightly, saying, 'Whatever you do, please don't go away.'

'I won't.'

She wanted to put the light on, to see his face, but it seemed like the wrong thing to do right now. She pressed her cheek against his chest. 'Have you got a wife somewhere?'

'No.'

She put out her tongue and tasted his skin. 'I just think you might feel guilty about something. Like, me being half an Arab?'

'I don't think so.'

'Or, me being Eila Ashford's daughter? You loved her, didn't you?'

'How did you know?'

'From the way you talked about her.'

'Oh. Well, I don't think I feel guilty about that, but I could be wrong, doctor.'

'Mmm.' He was coming out of his shell. She kissed his chest. 'Will you tell me something?'

'I expect so.'

'When did you last have sex?'

'Nineteen forty-four.'

'You're kidding!' she said, genuinely astonished.

'That's the first witless thing you've said.'

'I . . . you're right, I'm sorry.' She hesitated. 'But why?'

He sighed. 'I can't . . . I'm not able to talk about it.'

'But you *must*.' She reached out to the bedside lamp and turned on the light. Dickstein closed his eyes against the glare. Suza propped herself up on one elbow. 'Listen,' she said, 'there are no rules. We're grown-ups, we're naked in bed, and this is nineteen sixty-eight: nothing is wrong, it's whatever turns you on.'

'There isn't anything.' His eyes were still closed.

'And there are no secrets. If you're frightened or disgusted or inflamed, you can say so, and you must. I've never said "I love you" before tonight, Nat. Speak to me, please.'

There was a long silence. He lay still, impassive, eyes closed. At last he began to talk.

'I didn't know where I was – still don't. I was taken there in a cattle truck, and in those days I couldn't tell one country from another by the landscape. It was a special camp, a medical research centre. The prisoners were selected from other camps. We were all young, healthy and Jewish.

'Conditions were better than in the first camp I was at. We had food, blankets, cigarettes; there was no thieving, no fighting. At first I thought I had struck lucky. There were lots of tests – blood, urine, blow into this tube, catch this ball, read the letters on the card. It was like being in a hospital. Then the experiments began.

'To this day I don't know whether there was any real scientific curiosity behind it. I mean, if somebody did those things with animals, I could see that it might be, you know, quite interesting, quite revealing. On the other hand, the doctors must have been insane. I don't know.'

He stopped, and swallowed. It was becoming more difficult for him to speak calmly. Suza whispered, 'You must tell me what happened – everything. '

He was pale, and his voice was very low. Still he kept his eyes shut. 'They took me to this laboratory. The guards who escorted me kept winking and nudging and telling me I was *glücklich* – lucky. It was a big room with a low ceiling and very bright lights. There were six or seven of them there, with a movie camera. In the middle of the room was a low bed with a mattress on it, no sheets. There was a woman on the mattress. They told me to fuck her. She was naked, and shivering – she was a prisoner too. She whispered to me, "You save my life and I'll save yours." And then we did it. But that was only the beginning.'

Suza ran her hand over his loins and found his penis taut. *Now* she understood. She stroked him, gently at first, and waited for him to go on – for she knew that now he would tell all of the story.

'After that they did variations on the experiment. Every day for months, there was something. Drugs, sometimes. An old woman. A man, once. Intercourse in different positions – standing up, sitting, everything. Oral sex, anal sex, masturbation, group sex. If you didn't perform, you were flogged or shot. That's why the story never came out after the war, do you see? Because all the survivors were guilty.'

Suza stroked him harder. She was certain, without knowing why, that this was the right thing to do. 'Tell me. All of it.'

He was breathing faster. His eyes opened and he stared up at the blank white ceiling, seeing another place and another time. 'At the end ... the most shameful of all ... she was a nun. At first I thought they were lying to me, they had just dressed her up, but then she started praying, in French. She had no legs ... they had amputated her, just to observe the effect on me ... it was horrible, and I ... and I ...'

Then he jerked, and Suza bent and closed her mouth over his penis, and he said, 'Oh, no, no, no!' in rhythm with his spasms, and then it was all over and he wept.

She kissed his tears, and told him it was all right, over and over again. Slowly he calmed down, and eventually he seemed to sleep for a few minutes. She lay there watching his face as the tension seeped away and he became peaceful. Then he opened his eyes and said, 'Why did you do that?'

'Well.' At the time she had not understood exactly why, but now she thought she did. 'I could have given you a lecture,' she said. 'I could have told you that there is nothing to be ashamed of; that everybody has grisly fantasies, that women dream of being flogged and men have visions of flogging them; that you can buy, here in London, pornographic books about sex with amputees, including full-colour pictures. I could have told you that many men would have been able to summon up enough bestiality to perform in that Nazi laboratory. I could have argued with you, but it wouldn't have made any difference. I had to show you. Besides—' She smiled ruefully. 'Besides, I have a dark side, too.'

He touched her cheek, then leaned forward and kissed her lips. 'Where did you get this wisdom, child?'

'It isn't wisdom, it's love.'

Then he held her very tightly and kissed her and called her darling and after a while they made love, very simply, hardly speaking, without confessions or dark fantasies or bizarre lusts, giving and taking pleasure with the familiarity of an old couple who know each other very well; and afterwards they went to sleep full of peace and joy.

David Rostov was bitterly disappointed with the Euratom printout. After he and Pyotr Tyrin had spent hours getting it doped out, it became clear that the list of consignments was very long. They could not possibly cover every target. The only way they could discover which one would be hit was to pick up Dickstein's trail again.

Yasif Hassan's mission to Oxford thereupon assumed much greater importance.

They waited for the Arab to call. At ten o'clock Nik Bunin, who enjoyed sleep the way other people enjoy sunbathing, went to bed. Tyrin stuck it out until midnight, then he too retired. Rostov's phone finally rang at one A.M. He jumped as if frightened, grabbed the phone, then waited a few moments before speaking in order to compose himself.

'Yes?'

Hassan's voice came three hundred miles along the international telephone cables. 'I did it. The man was here. Two days ago.'

Rostov clenched a fist in suppressed excitement. 'Jesus. What a piece of luck.'

'What now?'

Rostov considered. 'Now, he knows that we know.'

'Yes. Shall I come back to base?'

'I don't think so. Did the professor say how long the man plans to be in England?'

'No. I asked the question directly. The professor didn't know: the man didn't tell him.'

'He wouldn't.' Rostov frowned, calculating. 'First thing the man has to do now is report that he's blown. That means he has to contact his London office.'

'Perhaps he already has.'

'Yes, but he may want a meeting. This man takes precautions, and precautions take time. All right, leave it with me. I'll be in London later today. Where are you now?'

'I'm still in Oxford. I came straight here off the plane. I can't get back to London until the morning.'

'All right. Check into the Hilton and I'll contact you there around lunchtime.'

'Check. *A bientôt.*'

'Wait.'

'Still here.'

'Don't do anything on your own initiative, now. Wait until I get there. You've done well, don't screw it up.'

Hassan hung up.

Rostov sat still for a moment, wondering whether Hassan was planning some piece of foolishness or simply resented being told to be a good boy. The latter, he decided. Anyway, there was no damage he could do over the next few hours.

Rostov turned his mind back to Dickstein. The man would not give them a second chance to pick up his trail. Rostov had to move fast and he had to move now. He put on his jacket, left the hotel and took a taxi to the Russian Embassy.

He had to wait some time, and identify himself to four different people, before they would let him in in the middle of the night. The duty operator stood at attention when Rostov entered the communications room. Rostov said, 'Sit down. There's work to do. Get the London office first.'

The operator picked up the scrambler phone and began to call the Russian Embassy in London. Rostov took off his jacket and rolled up his sleeves.

The operator said, 'Comrade Colonel David Rostov

will speak to the most senior security officer there.' He motioned Rostov to pick up the extension.

'Colonel Petrov.' It was the voice of a middle-aged soldier.

'Petrov, I need some help,' Rostov said without preamble. 'An Israeli agent named Nat Dickstein is believed to be in England.'

'Yes, we've had his picture sent to us in the diplomatic pouch – but we weren't notified he was thought to be here.'

'Listen. I think he may contact his embassy. I want you to put all known Israeli legals in London under surveillance from dawn today.'

'Hang on, Rostov,' said Petrov with a half laugh. 'That's a lot of manpower.'

'Don't be stupid. You've got hundreds of men, the Israelis only have a dozen or two.'

'Sorry, Rostov, I can't mount an operation like that on your say-so.'

Rostov wanted to get the man by the throat. 'This is urgent!'

'Let me have the proper documentation, and I'm at your disposal.'

'By then he'll be somewhere else!'

'Not my fault, comrade.'

Rostov slammed the phone down, furious, and said, 'Bloody Russians! Never do anything without six sets of authorization. Get Moscow, tell them to find Feliks Vorontsov and patch him through to me wherever he is.'

The operator got busy. Rostov drummed his fingers

on the desk impatiently. Petrov was probably an old soldier close to retirement, with no ambition for anything but his pension. There were too many men like that in the KGB.

A few minutes later the sleepy voice of Rostov's boss, Feliks, came on the line. 'Yes, who is it?'

'David Rostov. I'm in Luxembourg. I need some backing. I think The Pirate is about to contact the Israeli Embassy in London and I want their legals watched.'

'So call London.'

'I did. They want authorization.'

'Then apply for it.'

'For God's sake, Feliks, I'm applying for it now!'

'There's nothing I can do at this time of night. Call me in the morning.'

'What is this? Surely you can—' Suddenly Rostov realized what was happening. He controlled himself with an effort. 'All right, Feliks. In the morning.'

'Goodbye.'

'Feliks—'

'Yes?'

'I'll remember this.'

The line went dead.

'Where next?' the operator asked.

Rostov frowned. 'Keep the Moscow line open. Give me a minute to think.' He might have guessed he would get no help from Feliks. The old fool wanted him to fail on this mission, to prove that he, Feliks, should have been given control of it in the first place. It was even possible that Feliks was pally with Petrov in

London and had unofficially told Petrov not to cooperate.

There was only one thing for Rostov to do. It was a dangerous course of action and might well get him pulled off the case – in fact it could even be what Feliks was hoping for. But he could not complain if the stakes were high, for it was he who had raised them.

He thought for a minute or two about exactly how he should do it. Then he said, 'Tell Moscow to put me through to Yuri Andropov's apartment at number twenty-six Kutuzov Prospekt.' The operator raised his eyebrows – it was probably the first and last time he would be instructed to get the head of the KGB on the phone – but he said nothing. Rostov waited, fidgeting. 'I bet it isn't like this working for the CIA,' he muttered.

The operator gave him the sign, and he picked up the phone. A voice said, 'Yes?'

Rostov raised his voice and barked: 'Your name and rank!'

'Major Pyotr Eduardovitch Scherbitsky.'

'This is Colonel Rostov. I want to speak to Andropov. It's an emergency, and if he isn't on this phone within one hundred and twenty seconds you'll spend the rest of your life building dams in Bratsk, do I make myself clear?'

'Yes, colonel. Please hold the line.'

A moment later Rostov heard the deep, confident voice of Yuri Andropov, one of the most powerful men in the world. 'You certainly managed to panic young Eduardovitch, David.'

'I had no alternative, sir.'

'All right, let's have it. It had better be good.'

'The Mossad are after uranium.'

'Good God.'

'I think The Pirate is in England. He may contact his embassy. I want surveillance on the Israelis there, but an old fool called Petrov in London is giving me the runaround.'

'I'll talk to him now, before I go back to bed.'

'Thank you, sir.'

'And, David?'

'Yes?'

'It was worth waking me up – but only just.'

There was a click as Andropov hung up. Rostov laughed as the tension drained out of him, and he thought: Let them do their worst – Dickstein, Hassan, Feliks – I can handle them.

'Success?' the operator asked with a smile.

'Yes,' Rostov said. 'Our system is inefficient and cumbersome and corrupt, but in the end, you know, we get what we want.'

CHAPTER EIGHT

IT WAS quite a wrench for Dickstein to leave Suza in the morning and go back to work.

He was still ... well, stunned ... at eleven A.M., sitting in the window of a restaurant in the Fulham Road waiting for Pierre Borg to show. He had left a message with airport information at Heathrow telling Borg to go to a café opposite the one where Dickstein now sat. He thought he was likely to stay stunned for a long time, maybe permanently.

He had awakened at six o'clock, and suffered a moment of panic wondering where he was. Then he saw Suza's long brown hand lying on the pillow beside his head, curled up like a small animal sleeping, and the night had come flooding back, and he could hardly believe his good fortune. He thought he should not wake her, but suddenly he could not keep his hands off her body. She opened her eyes at his touch, and they made love playfully, smiling at one another, laughing sometimes, and looking into each other's eyes at the moment of climax. Then they fooled around in the kitchen, half-dressed, making the coffee too weak and burning the toast.

Dickstein wanted to stay there for ever.

Suza had picked up his undershirt with a cry of horror. 'What's this?'

'My undershirt.'

'Undershirt? I forbid you to wear undershirts. They're old-fashioned and unhygienic and they'll get in the way when I want to feel your nipples.'

Her expression was so lecherous that he burst out laughing. 'All right,' he said. 'I won't wear them.'

'Good.' She opened the window and threw the undershirt out into the street, and he laughed all over again.

He said, 'But you mustn't wear trousers.'

'Why not?'

It was his turn to leer.

'But all my trousers have flies.'

'No good,' he said. 'No room to manoeuvre.'

And like that.

They acted as if they had just invented sex. The only faintly unhappy moment came when she looked at his scars and asked how he got them. 'We've had three wars since I went to Israel,' he said. It was the truth, but not the whole truth.

'What made you go to Israel?'

'Safety.'

'But it's just the opposite of *safe* there.'

'It's a different kind of safety.' He said this dismissively, not wanting to explain it, then he changed his mind, for he wanted her to know all about him. 'There had to be a place where nobody could say, "You're different, you're not a human being, you're a Jew," where nobody could break my windows or experiment on my body just because I'm Jewish. You see . . .' She had been looking at him with that clear-eyed, frank gaze of hers, and he had struggled to tell her the whole truth, without evasions, without trying to make it look better than it was. 'It didn't matter to me whether we chose Palestine or Uganda or Manhattan Island – wherever it was, I would have said, "That place is *mine*," and I would have fought tooth and nail to keep it. That's why I never try to argue the moral rights and wrongs of the establishment of Israel. Justice and fair play never entered into it. After the war . . . well, the suggestion that the concept of fair play had any role in international politics seemed like a sick joke to me. I'm not pretending this is an admirable attitude, I'm just telling you how it is for me. Any other place Jews live – New York, Paris, Toronto – no matter how good it is, how assimilated they are, they never know how long it's going to last, how soon will come the next crisis that can conveniently be blamed on them. In Israel I know that whatever happens, I won't be a victim of *that*. So, with that problem out of the way, we can get on and deal with the realities that are part of everyone's life: planting and reaping, buying and selling, fighting and dying. That's why I went, I think . . . Maybe I didn't see it all so clearly back then – in fact, I've never put it into words like this – but that's how I felt, anyway.'

After a moment Suza said, 'My father holds the opinion that Israel itself is now a racist society.'

'That's what the youngsters say. They've got a point. If . . .'

She looked at him, waiting.

'If you and I had a child, they would refuse to classify him as Jewish. He would be a second-class citizen. But I don't think that sort of thing will last for ever. At the moment the religious zealots are powerful in the government: it's inevitable, Zionism was a religious movement. As the nation matures that will fade away. The race laws are already controversial. We're fighting them, and we'll win in the end.'

She came to him and put her head on his shoulder, and they held each other in silence. He knew that she did not care about Israeli politics: it was the mention of a son that had moved her.

Sitting in the restaurant window, remembering, he knew that he wanted Suza in his life always, and he wondered what he would do if she refused to go to his country. Which would he give up, Israel or Suza? He did not know.

He watched the street. It was typical June weather: raining steadily and quite cold. The familiar red buses and black cabs swished up and down, butting through the rain, splashing in the puddles on the road. A country of his own, a woman of his own: maybe he could have both.

I should be so lucky.

A cab drew up outside the café opposite, and Dickstein tensed, leaning closer to his window and peering through the rain. He recognized the bulky figure of Pierre Borg, in a dark short raincoat and a trilby hat, climbing out of the cab. He did not recognize the second man, who got out and paid the driver. The two men went into the café. Dickstein looked up and down the road.

A grey Mark II Jaguar had stopped on a double yellow line fifty yards from the café. Now it reversed and backed into a side street, parking on the corner within sight of the café. The passenger got out and walked toward the café.

Dickstein left his table and went to the phone booth in the restaurant entrance. He could still see the café opposite. He dialled its number.

'Yes?'

'Let me speak to Bill, please.'

'Bill? Don't know him.'

'Would you just ask, please?'

'Sure. Hey, anybody here called Bill?' A pause. 'Yes, he's coming.'

After a moment Dickstein heard Borg's voice. 'Yes?'

'Who's the face with you?'

'Head of London Station. Do you think we can trust him?'

Dickstein ignored the sarcasm. 'One of you picked up a shadow. Two men in a grey Jaguar.'

'We saw them.'

'Lose them.'

'Of course. Listen, you know this town – what's the best way?'

'Send the Head of Station back to the Embassy in a cab. That should lose the Jaguar. Wait ten minutes, then take a taxi to . . .'

Dickstein hesitated, trying to think of a quiet street not too far away. 'To Redcliffe Street. I'll meet you there.'

'Okay.'

Dickstein looked across the road. 'Your tail is just going into your café.' He hung up.

He went back to his window seat and watched. The other man came out of the café, opened an umbrella, and stood at the kerb looking for a cab. The tail had either recognized Borg at the airport or had been following the Head of Station for some other reason. It did not make any difference. A taxi pulled up. When it left, the grey Jaguar came out of the side street and followed. Dickstein left the restaurant and hailed a cab for himself. Taxi drivers do well out of spies, he thought.

He told the cabbie to go to Redcliffe Street and wait. After eleven minutes another taxi entered the street and Borg got out. 'Flash your lights,' Dickstein said. 'That's the man I'm meeting.' Borg saw the lights and waved acknowledgment. As he was paying, a third taxi entered the street and stopped. Borg spotted it.

The shadow in the third taxi was waiting to see what happened. Borg realized this, and began to walk away from his cab. Dickstein told his driver not to flash his lights again.

Borg walked past them. The tail got out of his taxi, paid the driver and walked after Borg. When the tail's cab had gone Borg turned, came back to Dickstein's cab, and got in. Dickstein said, 'Okay, let's go.' They pulled away, leaving the tail on the pavement looking for another taxi. It was a quiet street: he would not find one for five or ten minutes.

Borg said, 'Slick.'

'Easy,' Dickstein replied.

The driver said, 'What was all that about, then?'

'Don't worry,' Dickstein told him. 'We're secret agents.'

The cabbie laughed. 'Where to now – Ml5?'

'The Science Museum.'

Dickstein sat back in his seat. He smiled at Borg. 'Well, Bill, you old fart, how the hell are you?'

Borg frowned at him. 'What have you got to be so fucking cheerful about?'

They did not speak again in the cab, and Dickstein realized he had not prepared himself sufficiently for this meeting. He should have decided in advance what he wanted from Borg and how he was going to get it.

He thought: What *do* I want? The answer came up out of the back of his mind and hit him like a slap. I want to give Israel the bomb – and then I want to go home.

He turned away from Borg. Rain streaked the cab window like tears. He was suddenly glad they could not speak because of the driver. On the pavement were three coatless hippies, soaking wet, their faces and hands upturned to enjoy the rain. *If I could do this, if I could finish this assignment, I could rest.*

The thought made him unaccountably happy. He looked at Borg and smiled. Borg turned his face to the window.

They reached the museum and went inside. They stood in front of a reconstructed dinosaur. Borg said, 'I'm thinking of taking you off this assignment.'

Dickstein nodded, suppressing his alarm, thinking fast. Hassan must be reporting to Cairo, and Borg's man in Cairo must be getting the reports and passing them to Tel Aviv. 'I've discovered I'm blown,' he told Borg.

'I knew that weeks ago,' Borg said. 'If you'd keep in touch you'd be up-to-date on these things.'

'If I kept in touch I'd be blown more often.'

Borg grunted and walked on. He took out a cigar, and Dickstein said, 'No smoking in here.' Borg put the cigar away.

'Blown is nothing,' Dickstein said. 'It's happened to me half a dozen times. What counts is how much they know.'

'You were fingered by this Hassan, who knows you from years back. He's working with the Russians now.'

'But what do they *know?*'

'You've been in Luxembourg and France.'

'That's not much.'

'I realize it's not much. I know you've been in Luxembourg and France too, and *I* have no idea what you did there.'

'So you'll leave me in,' Dickstein said, and looked hard at Borg.

'That depends. What *have* you been doing?'

'Well.' Dickstein continued looking at Borg. The man had become fidgety, not knowing what to do with his hands now that he could not smoke. The bright lights on the displays illuminated his bad complexion: his troubled face was like a gravel parking lot. Dickstein needed to judge very carefully how much he told Borg: enough to give the impression that a great deal had been achieved; not so much that Borg would think he could get another man to operate Dickstein's plan . . . 'I've picked a consignment of uranium for us to steal,' he began. 'It's going by ship from Antwerp to Genoa in November. I'm going to hijack the ship.'

'Shit!' Borg seemed both pleased and afraid at the audacity of the idea. He said, 'How the hell will you keep that secret?'

'I'm working on that.' Dickstein decided to tell Borg just a tantalizing little bit more. 'I have to visit Lloyd's, here in London. I'm hoping the ship will turn out to be one of a series of identical vessels – I'm told most ships are built that way. If I can buy an identical vessel, I can switch the two somewhere in the Mediterranean.'

Borg rubbed his hand across his close-cropped hair twice, then pulled at his ear. 'I don't see . . .'

'I haven't figured out the details yet, but I'm sure this is the only way to do the thing clandestinely.'

'So get on and figure out the details.'

'But you're thinking of pulling me out.'

'Yeah . . .' Borg tilted his head from one side to the other, a gesture of indecision. 'If I put an experienced man in to replace you, he may be spotted too.'

'And if you put in an unknown he won't be experienced.'

'Plus, I'm really not sure there is anyone, experienced or otherwise, who can pull this off apart from you. And there is something else you don't know.'

They stopped in front of a model of a nuclear reactor.

'Well?' Dickstein said.

'We've had a report from Qattara. The Russians are helping them now. We're in a hurry, Dickstein. I can't afford delay, and changes of plan cause delay.'

'Will November be soon enough?'

Borg considered. 'Just,' he said. He seemed to come to a decision. 'All right, I'm leaving you in. You'll have to take evasive action.'

Dickstein grinned broadly and slapped Borg on the back. 'You're a pal, Pierre. Don't you worry now. I'll run rings around them.'

Borg frowned. 'Just what is it with you? You can't stop grinning.'

'It's seeing you that does it. Your face is like a tonic. Your sunny disposition is infectious. When you smile, Pierre, the whole world smiles with you.'

'You're crazy, you prick,' said Borg.

Pierre Borg was vulgar, insensitive, malicious, and boring, but he was not stupid. 'He may be a bastard,' people would say, 'but he's a clever bastard.' By the time they parted company he knew that something important had changed in Nat Dickstein's life.

He thought about it, walking back to the Israeli Embassy at No. 2 Palace Green in Kensington. In the twenty years since they had first met, Dickstein had hardly changed. It was still only rarely that the force of the man showed through. He had always been quiet and withdrawn; he continued to look like an out-of-work bank clerk; and, except for occasional flashes of rather cynical wit, he was still dour.

Until today.

At first he had been his usual self – brief to the point of rudeness. But toward the end he had come on like the stereotyped chirpy Cockney sparrow in a Hollywood movie.

Borg had to know why.

He would tolerate a lot from his agents. Provided they were efficient, they could be neurotic, or aggressive, or sadistic, or insubordinate – so long as he knew about it. He could make allowances for faults: but he could not allow for unknown factors. He would be unsure of his hold over Dickstein until he had figured out the cause of the change. That was all. He had no objection in principle to one of his agents acquiring a sunny disposition.

He came within sight of the embassy. He would put Dickstein under surveillance, he decided. It would take two cars and three teams of men working in eight-hour shifts. The Head of London Station would complain. The hell with *him*.

The need to know why Dickstein's disposition had changed was only one reason Borg had decided not to pull him out. The other reason was more important. Dickstein had half a plan; another man might not be able to complete it. Dickstein had a mind for this sort of thing. Once Dickstein had figured it all out, *then* somebody else could take over. Borg had decided to take him off the assignment at the first opportunity. Dickstein would be furious: he would consider he had been shafted.

The hell with him, too.

Major Pyotr Alekseivitch Tyrin did not actually like Rostov. He did not like any of his superiors: in his view, you had to be a rat to get promoted above the rank of major in the KGB. Still, he had a sort of awestruck affection for his clever, helpful boss. Tyrin had considerable skills, particularly with electronics, but he could not manipulate people. He was a major only because he was on Rostov's incredibly successful team.

Abba Allon. High Street exit. Fifty-two, or nine? Where are you, fifty-two?

Fifty-two. We're close. We'll take him. What does he look like?

Plastic raincoat, green hat, moustache.

As a friend Rostov was not much; but he was a lot worse as an enemy. This Colonel Petrov in London had discovered that. He had tried to mess around with Rostov and had been surprised by a middle-of-the-night phone call from the head of the KGB, Yuri Andropov himself. The people in the London Embassy said Petrov had looked like a ghost when he hung up. Since then Rostov could have anything he wanted: if he sneezed five agents rushed out to buy handkerchiefs.

Okay, this is Ruth Davisson, and she's going . . . north . . .

Nineteen, we can take her—

Relax, nineteen. False alarm. It's a secretary who looks like her.

Rostov had commandeered all Petrov's best pavement artists and most of his cars. The area around the Israeli Embassy in London was crawling with agents – someone had said, 'There are more Reds here than in the Kremlin Clinic' – but it was hard to spot them. They were in cars, vans, minicabs, trucks and one vehicle that looked remarkably like an unmarked Metropolitan Police bus. There were more on foot, some in public buildings and others walking the streets and the footpaths of the park. There was even one inside the Embassy, asking in dreadfully broken English what he had to do to emigrate to Israel.

The Embassy was ideally suited for this kind of exercise. It was in a little diplomatic ghetto on the edge of Kensington Gardens. So many of the lovely old houses belonged to foreign legations that it was known as Embassy Row. Indeed, the Soviet Embassy was close by in Kensington Palace Gardens. The little group of streets formed a private estate, and you had to tell a policeman your business before you could get in.

Nineteen, this time it is Ruth Davisson ... nineteen, do you hear me?

Nineteen here, yes.

Are you still on the north side?

Yes. And we know what she looks like.

None of the agents was actually in sight of the Israeli Embassy. Only one member of the team could see the door – Rostov, who was a half mile away, on the twentieth floor of a hotel, watching through a powerful Zeiss telescope mounted on a tripod. Several high buildings in the West End of London had clear views across the park to Embassy Row. Indeed, certain suites in certain hotels fetched inordinately high prices because of rumours that from them you could see into Princess Margaret's backyard at the neighbouring palace, which gave its name to Palace Green and Kensington Palace Gardens.

Rostov was in one of those suites, and he had a radio transmitter as well as the telescope. Each of his sidewalk squads had a walkie-talkie. Petrov spoke to his men in fast Russian, using confusing codewords, and the wavelength on which he transmitted and on which the men replied was changed every five minutes according to a computer program built into all the sets. The system was working very well, Tyrin thought – he had invented it – except that somewhere in the cycle everyone was subjected to five minutes of BBC Radio One.

Eight, move up to the north side.

Understood.

If the Israelis had been in Belgravia, the home of the more senior embassies, Rostov's job would have been more difficult. There were almost no shops, cafés or public offices in Belgravia – nowhere for agents to make themselves unobtrusive; and because the whole district was quiet, wealthy and stuffed with ambassadors it was easy for the police to keep an eye open for suspicious activities. Any of the standard surveillance ploys – telephone repair van, road crew with striped tent – would have drawn a crowd of bobbies in minutes.

By contrast the area around the little oasis of Embassy Row was Kensington, a major shopping area with several colleges and four museums.

Tyrin himself was in a pub in Kensington Church Street. The resident KGB men had told him that the pub was frequented by detectives from 'Special Branch' – the rather coy name for Scotland Yard's political police. The four youngish men in rather sharp suits drinking whisky at the bar were probably detectives. They did not know Tyrin, and would not have been much interested in him if they had. Indeed, if Tyrin were to approach them and say, 'By the way, the KGB is tailing every Israeli legal in London at the moment,' they would probably say, 'What, again?' and order another round of drinks.

In any event Tyrin knew he was not a man to attract second glances. He was small and rather rotund, with a big nose and a drinker's veined face. He wore a grey raincoat over a green sweater. The rain had removed the last memory of a crease from his charcoal flannel trousers. He sat in a corner with a glass of English beer and a small bag of potato chips. The radio in his shirt pocket was connected by a fine, flesh-coloured wire to the plug – it looked like a hearing aid – in his left ear. His left side was to the wall. He could talk to Rostov by pretending to fumble in the inside pocket of his raincoat, turning his face away from the room and muttering into the perforated metal disc on the top edge of the radio.

He was watching the detectives drink whisky and thinking that the Special Branch must have better expense accounts than its Russian equivalent: he was allowed one pint of beer per hour, the potato crisps he had to buy himself. At one time agents in England had even been obliged to buy beer in half pints, until the accounts department had been told that in many pubs a man who drank halves was as peculiar as a Russian who took his vodka in sips instead of gulps.

Thirteen, pick up a green Volvo, two men, High Street.

Understood.

And one on foot ... I think that's Yigael Meier ... Twenty?

Tyrin was 'Twenty.' He turned his face into his shoulder and said, 'Yes. Describe him.'

Tall, grey hair, umbrella, belted coat. High Street gate.

Tyrin said, 'I'm on my way.' He drained his glass and left the pub.

It was raining. Tyrin took a collapsible umbrella from his raincoat pocket and opened it. The wet pavements were crowded with shoppers. At the traffic lights he spotted the green Volvo and, three cars behind it, 'Thirteen' in an Austin.

Another car. Five, this one's yours. Blue Volkswagen Beetle.

Understood.

Tyrin reached Palace Gate, looked up Palace Avenue, saw a man fitting the description heading toward him, and walked on without pausing. When he had calculated that the man had had time to reach the street he stood at the kerb, as if about to cross, and looked up and down. The mark emerged from Palace Avenue and turned west, away from Tyrin.

Tyrin followed.

Along High Street tailing was made easier by the crowds. Then they turned south into a maze of side streets, and Tyrin became a bit nervous; but the Israeli did not seem to be watching for a shadow. He simply butted ahead through the rain, a tall, bent figure under an umbrella, walking fast, intent on his destination.

He did not go far. He turned into a small modern hotel just off the Cromwell Road. Tyrin walked past the entrance and, glancing through the glass door, saw the mark step into a phone booth in the lobby. A little farther along the road Tyrin passed the green Volvo, and concluded that the Israeli and his colleagues in the Volvo were staking out the hotel.

He crossed the road and came back on the opposite side, just in case the mark were to come out again immediately. He looked for the blue Volkswagen Beetle and did not see it, but he was quite sure it would be close by.

He spoke into his shirt pocket. 'This is Twenty. Meier and the green Volvo have staked out the Jacobean Hotel.'

Confirmed, Twenty. Five and Thirteen have the Israeli cars covered. Where is Meier?

'In the lobby.' Tyrin looked up and down and saw the Austin which was following the green Volvo.

Stay with him.

'Understood.' Tyrin now had a difficult decision to make. If he went straight into the hotel Meier might spot him, but if he took the time to find the back entrance Meier might go away in the meanwhile.

He decided to chance the back entrance, on the

grounds that he was supported by two cars which could cover for a few minutes if the worst happened. Beside the hotel there was a narrow alley for delivery vans. Tyrin walked along it and came to an unlocked fire exit in the blank side wall of the building. He went in and found himself in a concrete stairwell, obviously built to be used only as a fire escape. As he climbed the stairs he collapsed his umbrella, put it in his raincoat pocket and took off the raincoat. He folded it and left it in a little bundle on the first half landing, where he could quickly pick it up if he needed to make a fast exit. He went to the second floor and took the elevator down to the lobby. When he emerged in his sweater and trousers he looked like a guest at the hotel.

The Israeli was still in the phone booth.

Tyrin went up to the glass door at the front of the lobby, looked out, checked his wristwatch and returned to the waiting area to sit down as if he were meeting someone. It did not seem to be his lucky day. The object of the whole exercise was to find Nat Dickstein. He was known to be in England, and it was hoped that he would have a meeting with one of the legals. The Russians were following the legals in order to witness that meeting and pick up Dickstein's trail. The Israeli team at this hotel was clearly not involved in a meeting. They were staking out someone, presumably with a view to tailing him as soon as he showed, and that someone was not likely to be one of their own agents. Tyrin could only hope that what they *were* doing would at least turn out to be of some interest.

He watched the mark come out of the phone booth

and walk off in the direction of the bar. He wondered if the lobby could be observed from the bar. Apparently not, because the mark came back a few minutes later with a drink in his hand, then sat down across from Tyrin and picked up a newspaper.

The mark did not have time to drink his beer.

The elevator doors hissed open, and out walked Nat Dickstein.

Tyrin was so surprised that he made the mistake of staring straight at Dickstein for several seconds. Dickstein caught his eye, and nodded politely. Tyrin smiled weakly and looked at his watch. It occurred to him – more in hope than conviction – that staring was such a bad mistake that Dickstein might take it as proof that Tyrin was *not* an agent.

There was no time for reflection. Moving quickly with – Tyrin thought – something of a spring in his step, Dickstein crossed to the counter and dropped a room key, then proceeded quickly out into the street. The Israeli tail, Meier, put his newspaper on the table and followed. When the plate-glass door closed behind Meier, Tyrin got up, thinking: I'm an agent following an agent following an agent. Well, at least we keep each other in employment.

He went into the elevator and pressed the button for the first floor. He spoke into his radio. 'This is Twenty. I have Pirate.' There was no reply – the walls of the building were blocking his transmission. He got out of the elevator at the first floor and ran down the fire stairs, picking up his raincoat at the half landing. As soon as he was outside he tried the radio again. 'This is Twenty, I have the Pirate.'

All right, Twenty. Thirteen has him too.

Tyrin saw the mark crossing Cromwell Road. 'I'm following Meier,' he said into his radio.

Five and Twenty, both of you listen to me. Do not follow. Have you got that – Five?

Yes.

Twenty?

Tyrin said, 'Understood.' He stopped walking and stood on the corner watching Meier and Dickstein disappear in the direction of Chelsea.

Twenty, go back into the hotel. Get his room number. Book a room close to his. Call me on the telephone as soon as it's done.

'Understood.' Tyrin turned back, rehearsing his dialogue: Excuse me, the fellow that just walked out of here, short man with glasses, I think I know him but he got into a cab before I could catch up with him . . . his name is John but we all used to call him Jack, what room . . . ? As it turned out, none of that was necessary. Dickstein's key was still on the desk. Tyrin memorized the number.

The desk clerk came over. 'Can I help you?'

'I'd like a room,' Tyrin said.

He kissed her, and he was like a man who has been thirsty all day. He savoured the smell of her skin and the soft motions of her lips. He touched her face and said, 'This, this, this is what I need.' They stared into each other's eyes, and the truth between them was like nakedness. He thought: I can do anything I want. The idea ran through his mind again and again like an incantation, a magic spell. He touched her body greedily. He stood face to face with her in the little blue-and-yellow kitchen, looking into her eyes while he fingered the secret places of her body. Her red mouth opened a fraction and he felt her breath coming faster and hot on his face; he inhaled deeply so as to breathe the air from her. He thought: If I can do anything I want, so can she; and, as if she had read his mind, she opened his shirt, and bent to his chest, and took his nipple between her teeth, and sucked. The sudden, astonishing pleasure of it made him gasp aloud. He held her head gently in his hands and rocked to and fro a little to intensify the sensation. He thought: Anything I want! He reached behind her, lifted her skirt, and feasted his eyes on the white panties clinging to her curves and contrasting with the brown skin of her long legs. His right hand stroked her face and gripped her shoulder and weighed her breasts; his left hand moved over her hips and inside her panties and between her legs; and everything felt so good, so good, that he wished he had four hands to feel her with, six. Then, suddenly, he wanted to see her face, so he gripped her shoulders and made her stand upright, saying, 'I want to look at you.' Her eyes filled with tears, and he knew that these were signs not of sadness but of intense pleasure. Again they stared into each other's eyes, and this time it was not just truth between them but raw emotion gushing from one to another in rivers, in torrents. Then he knelt at her feet like a supplicant. First he laid his head on her thighs, feeling the heat of her body through her clothing. Then he reached beneath her skirt with both hands, found the waist of her panties, and drew them down slowly, holding the shoes on her feet as she stepped out. He got up from the floor. They were still standing on the spot where they had kissed when he had first come into the room. Just there, standing up, they began to make love. He watched her face. She looked peaceful, and her eyes were half closed. He wanted to do this, moving slowly, for a long time: but his body would not wait. He was compelled to thrust harder and faster. He felt himself losing his balance, so he put both arms around her, lifted her an inch off the floor, and without withdrawing from her body moved two paces so that her back was against the wall. She pulled his shirt out of his waistband and dug her fingers into the hard muscles of his back. He linked his hands beneath her buttocks and took her weight. She lifted her legs high, her thighs gripping his hips, her ankles crossed behind his back, and, incredibly, he seemed to penetrate even deeper inside her. He felt he was being wound up like a clockwork motor, and everything she did, every look on her face, tightened the spring. He watched her through a haze of lust. There came into her eyes an expression of something like panic; a wild, wide-eyed animal emotion; and it pushed him over the edge, so that he knew that it was coming, the beautiful thing was going to happen now, and he wanted to tell her, so he said, 'Suza, here it comes,' and she said, 'Oh, and me,' and she dug her nails into the skin of his back and drew them down his spine in a long sharp tear which went through him like an electric shock and he felt the earthquake in her body just as his own erupted and he was still looking at her and he saw her mouth open wide, wide as she drew breath and the peak of delight overtook them both and she *screamed*.

'We follow the Israelis and the Israelis follow Dickstein. All it needs is for Dickstein to start following us and we can all go around in a circle for the rest of the day,' Rostov said. He strode down the hotel corridor. Tyrin hurried beside him, his short plump legs almost running to keep up.

Tyrin said, 'I was wondering what, exactly, was your thinking in abandoning the surveillance as soon as we saw him?'

'It's obvious,' Rostov said irritably; then he reminded himself that Tyrin's loyalty was valuable, and he decided to explain. 'Dickstein has been under surveillance a great deal during the last few weeks. Each time he has eventually spotted us and thrown us off. Now a certain amount of surveillance is inevitable for someone who has been in the game as long as Dickstein. But on a particular operation, the more he is followed the more likely he is to abandon what he's doing and hand it over to someone else – and we might not know who. All too often the information we gain by following someone is cancelled out because they discover that we're following them and therefore they know that we've got the information in question. This way – by abandoning the surveillance as we have done today – we know where he is but he doesn't know we know.'

'I see,' said Tyrin.

'He'll spot those Israelis in no time at all,' Rostov added. 'He must be hypersensitive by now.'

'Why do you suppose they're following their own man?'

'I really can't understand that.' Rostov frowned, thinking aloud. 'I'm sure Dickstein met Borg this morning – which would explain why Borg threw off his tail with that taxi manoeuvre. It's possible Borg pulled Dickstein out and now he's simply checking that Dickstein really does come out, and doesn't try to carry on unofficially.' He shook his head, a gesture of frustration. 'That doesn't convince me. But the alternative is that Borg doesn't trust Dickstein any more, and I find that unlikely, too. Careful, now.'

They were at the door to Dickstein's hotel room. Tyrin took out a small, powerful flashlight and shone it around the edges of the door. 'No telltales,' he said.

Rostov nodded, waiting. This was Tyrin's province. The little round man was the best general technician in the KGB, in Rostov's opinion. He watched as Tyrin took from his pocket a skeleton key, one of a large collection of such keys that he had. By trying several on the door of his own room here, he had already established which one fitted the locks of the Jacobean Hotel. He opened Dickstein's door slowly and stayed outside, looking in.

'No booby traps,' he said after a minute.

He stepped inside and Rostov followed, closing the door. This part of the game gave Rostov no pleasure at all. He liked to watch, to speculate, to plot: burglary was not his style. He felt exposed and vulnerable. If a maid should come in now, or the hotel manager, or even Dickstein who might evade the sentry in the lobby ... it would be so undignified, so humiliating. 'Let's make it fast,' he said.

The room was laid out according to the standard plan: the door opened into a little passage with the bathroom on one side and the wardrobe opposite. Beyond the bathroom the room was square, with the single bed against one wall and the television set against the other. There was a large window in the exterior wall opposite the door.

Tyrin picked up the phone and began to unscrew the mouthpiece. Rostov stood at the foot of the bed, looking around, trying to get an impression of the man who was staying in this room. There was not much to go on. The room had been cleaned and the bed made. On the bedside table were a book of chess problems and an evening newspaper. There were no signs of tobacco or alcohol. The wastepaper basket was empty. A small black vinyl suitcase on a stool contained clean underwear and one clean shirt. Rostov muttered, 'The man travels with one spare shirt!' The drawers of the dresser were empty. Rostov looked into the bathroom. He saw a toothbrush, a rechargeable electric shaver with spare plugs for different kinds of electrical outlets, and – the only personal touch – a pack of indigestion tablets.

Rostov went back into the bedroom, where Tyrin was reassembling the telephone. 'It's done.'

'Put one behind the headboard,' Rostov said.

Tyrin was taping a bug to the wall behind the bed when the phone rang.

If Dickstein returned the sentry in the lobby was to call Dickstein's room on the house phone, let it ring twice, then hang up.

It rang a second time. Rostov and Tyrin stood still, silent, waiting.

It rang again.

They relaxed.

It stopped after the seventh ring.

Rostov said, 'I wish he had a car for us to bug.'

'I've got a shirt button.'

'What?'

'A bug like a shirt button.'

'I didn't know such things existed.'

'It's new.'

'Got a needle? And thread?'

'Of course.'

'Then go ahead.'

Tyrin went to Dickstein's case and without taking the shirt out snipped off the second button, carefully removing all the loose thread. With a few swift strokes he sewed on the new button. His pudgy hands were surprisingly dexterous.

Rostov watched but his thoughts were elsewhere. He wanted desperately to do more to ensure that he would hear what Dickstein said and did. The Israeli might find the bugs in the phone and the headboard; he would not wear the bugged shirt all the time. Rostov liked to be sure of things, and Dickstein was maddeningly slippery: there was nowhere you could hook on to him. Rostov had harboured a faint hope that somewhere in this room there would be a photograph of someone Dickstein loved.

'There.' Tyrin showed him his handiwork. The shirt was plain white nylon with the commonest sort of white button. The new one was indistinguishable from the others.

'Good,' Rostov said. 'Close the case.'

Tyrin did so. 'Anything else?'

'Take another quick look around for telltales. I can't believe Dickstein would go out without taking any precautions at all.'

They searched again, quickly, silently, their movements practised and economical, showing no signs of the haste they both felt. There were dozens of ways of planting telltales. A hair lightly stuck across the crack of the door was the most simple; a scrap of paper jammed against the back of a drawer would fall out when the drawer was opened; a lump of sugar under a thick carpet would be silently crushed by a footstep; a penny behind the lining of a suitcase lid would slide from front to back if the case were opened . . .

They found nothing.

Rostov said, 'All Israelis are paranoid. Why should he be different?'

'Maybe he's been pulled out.'

Rostov grunted. 'Why else would he suddenly get careless?'

'He could have fallen in love,' Tyrin suggested.

Rostov laughed. 'Sure,' he said. 'And Joe Stalin could have been canonized by the Vatican. Let's get out of here.'

He went out, and Tyrin followed, closing the door softly behind him.

So it was a woman.

Pierre Borg was shocked, amazed, mystified, intrigued and deeply worried.

Dickstein *never* had women.

Borg sat on a park bench under an umbrella. He had been unable to think in the Embassy, with phones ringing and people asking him questions all the time, so he had come out here, despite the weather. The rain blew across the empty park in sheets, and every now and then a drop would land on the tip of his cigar and he would have to relight it.

It was the tension in Dickstein that made the man so fierce. The last thing Borg wanted was for him to learn how to relax.

The pavement artists had followed Dickstein to a small apartment house in Chelsea where he had met a woman. 'It's a sexual relationship,' one of them had said. 'I heard her orgasm.' The caretaker of the building had been interviewed, but he knew nothing about the woman except that she was a close friend of the people who owned the apartment.

The obvious conclusion was that Dickstein owned the flat (and had bribed the caretaker to lie); that he used it as a rendezvous; that he met someone from the opposition, a woman; that they made love and he told her secrets.

Borg might have bought that idea if he had found out about the woman some other way. But if Dickstein had suddenly become a traitor he would not have allowed Borg to become suspicious. He was too clever. He would have covered his tracks. He would not have led the pavement artists straight to the flat without once looking over his shoulder. His behaviour had innocence written all over it. He had met with Borg, looking like the cat that got at the cream, either not knowing or not caring that his mood was all over his face. When Borg asked what was going on, Dickstein made jokes. Borg was bound to have him tailed. Hours later Dickstein was screwing some girl who liked it so much you could hear her out in the fucking *street*. The whole thing was so damn naïve it had to be true.

All right, then. Some woman had found a way to get past Dickstein's defences and seduce him. Dickstein was reacting like a teenager because he never had a teenage. The important question was, who was she?

The Russians had files, too, and they ought to have assumed, like Borg, that Dickstein was invulnerable to a sexual approach. But maybe they thought it was worth a try. And maybe they were right.

Once again, Borg's instinct was to pull Dickstein out immediately. And once again, he hesitated. If it had been any project other than this one, any agent other than Dickstein, he would have known what to do. But Dickstein was the only man who could solve this problem. Borg had no option but to stick to his original scheme: wait until Dickstein had fully conceived his plan, then pull him out.

He could at least have the London Station investigate the woman and find out all they could about her.

Meanwhile he would just have to hope that if she were an agent Dickstein would have the sense not to tell her anything.

It would be a dangerous time, but there was no more Borg could do.

His cigar went out, but he hardly noticed. The park was completely deserted now. Borg sat on his bench, his body uncharacteristically still, holding the umbrella over his head, looking like a statue, worrying himself to death.

The fun was over, Dickstein told himself: it was time to get back to work.

Entering his hotel room at ten o'clock in the morning, he realized that – incredibly – he had left no telltales. For the first time in twenty years as an agent, he had simply forgotten to take elementary precautions. He stood in the doorway, looking around, thinking about the shattering effect that she had had on him. Leaving her and going back to work was like climbing into a familiar car which has been garaged for a year: he had to let the old habits, the old instincts, the old paranoia seep back into his mind.

He went into the bathroom and ran a tub. He now had a kind of emotional breathing-space. Suza was going back to work today. She was with BOAC, and this tour of duty would take her all the way around the world. She expected to be back in twenty-one days, but it might be longer. He had no idea where he might be in three weeks' time; which meant he did not know when he would see her again. But see her again he would, if he lived.

Everything looked different now, past and future. The last twenty years of his life seemed dull, despite the fact that he had shot people and been shot at, travelled all over the world, disguised himself and deceived people and pulled off outrageous, clandestine coups. It all seemed trivial.

Sitting in the tub he wondered what he would do with the rest of his life. He had decided he would not be a spy any more – but what would he be? It seemed all possibilities were open to him. He could stand for election to the Knesset, or start his own business, or simply stay on the kibbutz and make the best wine in Israel. Would he marry Suza? If he did, would they live in Israel? He found the uncertainty delicious, like wondering what you would be given for your birthday.

If I live, he thought. Suddenly there was even more at stake. He was afraid to die. Until now death had been something to avoid with all skill only because it constituted, so to speak, a losing move in the game. Now he wanted desperately to live: to sleep with Suza again, to make a home with her, to learn all about her, her idiosyncrasies and her habits and her secrets, the books she liked and what she thought about Beethoven and whether she snored.

It would be terrible to lose his life so soon after she had saved it.

He got out of the bath, rubbed himself dry and dressed. The way to keep his life was to win this fight.

His next move was a phone call. He considered the hotel phone, decided to start being extra careful here and now, and went out to find a call box.

The weather had changed. Yesterday had emptied the sky of rain, and now it was pleasantly sunny and warm. He passed the phone booth nearest to the hotel and went on to the next one: extra careful. He looked up Lloyd's of London in the directory and dialled their number.

'Lloyd's, good morning.'

'I need some information about a ship.'

'That's Lloyd's of London Press – I'll put you through.'

While he waited Dickstein looked out of the windows of the phone booth at the London traffic, and wondered whether Lloyd's would give him what he wanted. He hoped so – he could not think where else to go for the information. He tapped his foot nervously.

'Lloyd's of London Press.'

'Good morning, I'd like some information about a ship.'

'What sort of information?' the voice said, with – Dickstein thought – a trace of suspicion.

'I want to know whether she was built as part of a series; and if so, the names of her sister ships, who owns them, and their present locations. Plus plans, if possible.'

'I'm afraid I can't help you there.'

Dickstein's heart sank. 'Why not?'

'We don't keep plans, that's Lloyd's Register, and they only give them out to owners.'

'But the other information? The sister ships?'

'Can't help you there either.'

Dickstein wanted to get the man by the throat. 'Then who can?'

'We're the only people who have such information.'

'And you keep it secret?'

'We don't give it out over the phone.'

'Wait a minute, you mean you can't help me *over the phone*.'

'That's right.'

'But you can if I write or call personally.'

'Um . . . yes, this inquiry shouldn't take too long, so you could call personally.'

'Give me the address.' He wrote it down. 'And you could get these details while I wait?'

'I think so.'

'All right. I'll give you the name of the ship now, and you should have all the information ready by the time I get there. Her name is *Coparelli*.' He spelled it.

'And your name?'

'Ed Rodgers.'

'The company?'

'*Science International*.'

'Will you want us to bill the company?'

'No, I'll pay by personal cheque.'

'So long as you have some identification.'

'Of course. I'll be there in an hour. Goodbye.'

Dickstein hung up and left the phone booth, thinking: Thank God for that. He crossed the road to a café and ordered coffee and a sandwich.

He had lied to Borg, of course: he knew exactly how he would hijack the *Coparelli*. He would buy one of the sister ships – if there were such – and take his team on to meet the *Coparelli* at sea. After the hijack, instead of the dicey business of transferring the cargo from one ship to another offshore, he would sink his own ship and transfer its papers to the *Coparelli*. He would also paint out the *Coparelli*'s name and over it put the name of the sunken sister ship. And then he would sail what would appear to be his own ship into Haifa.

This was good, but it was still only the rudiments of a plan. What would he do about the crew of the *Coparelli*? How would the apparent loss of the *Coparelli* be explained? How would he avoid an international inquiry into the loss at sea of tons of uranium ore?

The more he thought about it, the bigger this last problem seemed. There would be a major search for any large ship which was thought to have sunk. With uranium aboard, the search would attract publicity and consequently be even more thorough. And what if the searchers found not the *Coparelli* but the sister ship which was supposed to belong to Dickstein?

He chewed over the problem for a while without coming up with any answers. There were still too many unknowns in the equation. Either the sandwich or the problem had stuck in his stomach: he took an indigestion tablet.

He turned his mind to evading the opposition. Had

he covered his tracks well enough? Only Borg could know of his plans. Even if his hotel room were bugged – even if the phone booth nearest the hotel were bugged – still nobody else could know of his interest in the *Coparelli*. He had been extra careful.

He sipped his coffee; then another customer, on his way out of the café, jogged Dickstein's elbow and made him spill coffee all down the front of his clean shirt.

'*Coparelli*,' said David Rostov excitedly. 'Where have I heard of a ship called the *Coparelli*?'

Yasif Hassan said, 'It's familiar to me, too.'

'Let me see that computer printout.'

They were in the back of a listening van parked near the Jacobean Hotel. The van, which belonged to the KGB, was dark blue, without markings, and very dirty. Powerful radio equipment occupied most of the space inside, but there was a small compartment behind the front seats where Rostov and Hassan could squeeze in. Pyotr Tyrin was at the wheel. Large speakers above their heads were giving out an undertone of distant conversation and the occasional clink of crockery. A moment ago there had been an incomprehensible exchange, with someone apologizing for something and Dickstein saying it was all right, it had been an accident. Nothing distinct had been said since then.

Rostov's pleasure at being able to listen to Dickstein's conversation was marred only by the fact that Hassan was listening too. Hassan had become self-confident since his triumph in discovering that Dickstein was in

England: now he thought he was a professional spy like everyone else. He had insisted on being in on every detail of the London operation, threatening to complain to Cairo if he were excluded. Rostov had considered calling his bluff, but that would have meant another head-on collision with Feliks Vorontsov, and Rostov did not want to go over Feliks's head to Andropov again so soon after the last time. So he had settled on an alternative: he would allow Hassan to come along, and caution him against reporting anything to Cairo.

Hassan, who had been reading the printout, passed it across to Rostov. While the Russian was looking through the sheets, the sound from the speakers changed to street noises for a minute or two, followed by more dialogue.

Where to, guv?

Dickstein's voice: *Lime Street.*

Rostov looked up and spoke to Tyrin. 'That'll be Lloyd's, the address he was given over the phone. Let's go there.'

Tyrin started the van and moved off, heading east toward the City district. Rostov returned to the printout.

Hassan said pessimistically, 'Lloyd's will probably give him a written report.'

Tyrin said, 'The bug is working very well . . . so far.' He was driving with one hand and biting the fingernails of the other.

Rostov found what he was looking for. 'Here it is!' he said. 'The *Coparelli.* Good, good, good!' He thumped his knee in enthusiasm.

Hassan said, 'Show me.'

Rostov hesitated momentarily, realized there was no way he could get out of it, and smiled at Hassan as he pointed to the last page. 'Under NON-NUCLEAR. Two hundred tons of yellowcake to go from Antwerp to Genoa aboard the motor vessel *Coparelli*.'

'That's *it*, then,' said Hassan. 'That's Dickstein's target.'

'But if you report this to Cairo, Dickstein will probably switch to a different target. Hassan—'

Hassan's colour deepened with anger. 'You've said all that once,' he said coldly.

'Okay,' Rostov said. He thought: Damn it, you have to be a diplomat too. He said, 'Now we know what he's going to steal, and who he's going to steal it from. I call that some progress.'

'We don't know when, where, or how,' Hassan said.

Rostov nodded. 'All this business about sister ships must have something to do with it.' He pulled his nose. 'But I don't see how.'

Two and sixpence, please, guv.

Keep the change.

'Find somewhere to park, Tyrin,' said Rostov.

'That's not so easy around here,' Tyrin complained.

'If you can't find a space, just stop. Nobody cares if you get a parking ticket,' Rostov said impatiently.

Good morning. My name's Ed Rodgers.

Ah, yes. Just a moment, please . . .

Your report has just been typed, Mr Rodgers. And here's the bill.

You're very efficient.

Hassan said, 'It *is* a written report.'

Thank you very much.

Goodbye, Mr Rodgers.

'He's not very chatty, is he?' said Tyrin.

Rostov said, 'Good agents never are. You might bear that in mind.'

'Yes, sir.'

Hassan said, 'Damn. Now we won't know the answers to his questions.'

'Makes no difference,' Rostov told him. 'It's just occurred to me.' He smiled. 'We know the questions. All we have to do is ask the same questions ourselves and we get the answers he got. Listen, he's on the street again. Go around the block, Tyrin, let's try to spot him.'

The van moved off, but before it had completed a circuit of the block the street noises faded again.

Can I help you, sir?

'He's gone into a shop,' Hassan said.

Rostov looked at Hassan. When he forgot about his pride, the Arab was as thrilled as a schoolboy about all this – the van, the bugs, the tailing. Maybe he would keep his mouth shut, if only so that he could continue to play spies with the Russians.

I need a new shirt.

'Oh, no!' said Tyrin.

I can see that, sir. What is it?

Coffee.

It should have been sponged right away, sir. It will be very difficult to get the stain out now. Did you want a similar shirt?

Yes. Plain white nylon, button cuffs, collar size fourteen and a half.

Here we are. This one is thirty-two and sixpence.

That's fine.

Tyrin said, 'I'll bet he charges it to expenses.'

Thank you. Would you like to put it on now, perhaps?

Yes, please.

The fitting room is just through here.

Footsteps, then a brief silence.

Would you like a bag for the old one, sir?

Perhaps you'd throw it away for me.

'That button cost two thousand roubles!' Tyrin said.

Certainly, sir.

'That's it,' Hassan said. 'We won't get any more now.'

'Two thousand rubles!' Tyrin said again.

Rostov said, 'I think we got our money's worth.'

'Where are we heading?' Tyrin asked.

'Back to the Embassy,' Rostov told him. 'I want to stretch my legs. I can't feel the left one at all. Damn, but we've done a good morning's work.'

As Tyrin drove west, Hassan said thoughtfully, 'We need to find out where the *Coparelli* is right now.'

'The squirrels can do that,' Rostov said.

'Squirrels?'

'Desk workers in Moscow Centre. They sit on their behinds all day, never doing anything more risky than crossing Granovsky Street in the rush hour, and get paid more than agents in the field.' Rostov decided to use the opportunity to further Hassan's education. 'Remember, an agent should never spend time acquiring information that is public knowledge. Anything in books, reports and files can be found by the squirrels. Since a squirrel is cheaper to run than an agent – not because of salaries but because of support work – the Committee always prefers a squirrel to do a given job of work if he can. Always use the squirrels. Nobody will think you're being lazy.'

Hassan smiled nonchalantly, an echo of his old, languid self. 'Dickstein doesn't work that way.'

'The Israelis have a completely different approach. Besides, I suspect Dickstein isn't a team man.'

'How long will the squirrels take to get us the *Coparelli*'s location?'

'Maybe a day. I'll put in the inquiry as soon as we get to the Embassy.'

Tyrin spoke over his shoulder. 'Can you put through a fast requisition at the same time?'

'What do you need?'

'Six more shirt buttons.'

'Six?'

'If they're like the last lot, five won't work.'

Hassan laughed. 'Is this Communist efficiency?'

'There's nothing wrong with Communist efficiency,' Rostov told him. 'It's Russian efficiency we suffer from.'

The van entered Embassy Row and was waved on by the duty policeman. Hassan asked, 'What do we do when we've located the *Coparelli*?'

'Obviously,' said Rostov, 'we put a man aboard.'

CHAPTER NINE

THE DON had had a bad day.

It had started at breakfast with the news that some of his people had been busted in the night. The police had stopped and searched a truck containing two thousand five hundred pairs of fur-lined bedroom slippers and five kilos of adulterated heroin. The load, on its way from Canada to New York City, had been hit at Albany. The smack was confiscated and the driver and co-driver jailed.

The stuff did not belong to the don. However, the team that did the run paid dues to him, and in return expected protection. They would want him to get the men out of jail and get the heroin back. It was close to impossible. He might have been able to do it if the bust had involved only the state police; but if only the state police had been involved, the bust would not have happened.

And that was just the start. His eldest son had wired from Harvard for more money, having gambled away the whole of his next semester's allowance weeks before classes started. He had spent the morning finding out why his chain of restaurants was losing money, and the afternoon explaining to his mistress why he could not take her to Europe this year. Finally his doctor told him he had gonorrhoea, again.

He looked in his dressing-room mirror, adjusting his bow tie, and said to himself, 'What a shitty day.'

It had turned out that the New York City police had been behind the bust: they had passed the tip to the state police in order to avoid trouble with the city Mafia. The city police could have ignored the tip, of course: the fact that they did not was a sign that the tip had originated with someone important, perhaps the Drug Enforcement Agency of the Treasury Department. The don had assigned lawyers to the jailed drivers, sent people to visit their families, and opened negotiations to buy back the heroin from the police.

He put on his jacket. He liked to change for dinner; he always had. He did not know what to do about his son Johnny. Why wasn't he home for the summer? College boys were supposed to come home for the summer. The don had thought of sending somebody to see Johnny; but then the boy would think his father was only worried about the money. It looked like he would have to go himself.

The phone rang, and the don picked it up. 'Yes.'

'Gate here, sir. I got an Englishman asking for you, won't give his name.'

'So send him anyway,' said the don, still thinking about Johnny.

'He said to tell you he's a friend from Oxford University.'

'I don't know anybody . . . wait a minute. What's he look like?'

'Little guy with glasses, looks like a bum.'

'No kidding!' The don's face broke into a smile. 'Bring him in – and put out the red carpet!'

It had been a year for seeing old friends and observing how they had changed; but Al Cortone's appearance was the most startling yet. The increase in weight which had just begun when he returned from Frankfurt seemed to have continued steadily through the years, and now he weighed at least two hundred and fifty pounds. There was a look of sensuality about his puffy face that had been only hinted at in 1947 and totally absent during the war. And he was completely bald. Dickstein thought this was unusual among Italians.

Dickstein could remember, as clearly as if it were yesterday, the occasion when he had put Cortone under an obligation. In those days he had been learning about the psychology of a cornered animal. When there is no longer any possibility of running away, you realize how fiercely you can fight. Landed in a strange country, separated from his unit, advancing across unknown terrain with his rifle in his hand, Dickstein had drawn on reserves of patience, cunning and ruthlessness he did not know he had. He had lain for half an hour in that thicket, watching the abandoned tank which he *knew* – without understanding how – was the bait in a trap. He had spotted the one sniper and was looking for another when the Americans came roaring up. That made it safe for Dickstein to shoot – if there were another sniper, he would fire at the obvious target, the

Americans, rather than search the bushes for the source of the shot.

So, with no thought for anything but his own survival, Dickstein had saved Al Cortone's life.

Cortone had been even more new to the war than Dickstein, and learning just as fast. They were both streetwise kids applying old principles to new terrain. For a while they fought together, and cursed and laughed and talked about women together. When the island was taken, they had sneaked off during the buildup for the next push and visited Cortone's Sicilian cousins.

Those cousins were the focus of Dickstein's interest now.

They had helped him once before, in 1948. There had been profit for them in that deal, so Dickstein had gone straight to them with the plan. This project was different: he wanted a favour and he could offer no percentage. Consequently he had to go to Al and call in the twenty-four-year-old debt.

He was not at all sure it would work. Cortone was rich now. The house was large – in England it would have been called a mansion – with beautiful grounds inside a high wall and guards at the gate. There were three cars in the gravel drive, and Dickstein had lost count of the servants. A rich and comfortable middle-aged American might not be in a hurry to get involved in Mediterranean political shenanigans, even for the sake of a man who had saved his life.

Cortone seemed very pleased to see him, which was a good start. They slapped each other on the back, just

as they had on that November Sunday in 1947, and
kept saying, 'How the hell are you?' to each other.

Cortone looked Dickstein up and down. 'You're the
same! I lost all my hair and gained a hundred pounds,
and you haven't even turned grey. What have you been
up to?'

'I went to Israel. I'm sort of a farmer. You?'

'Doing business, you know? Come on, let's eat and
talk.'

The meal was a strange affair. Mrs Cortone sat at the
foot of the table without speaking or being spoken to
throughout. Two ill-mannered boys wolfed their food
and left early with a roar of sports-car exhaust. Cortone
ate large quantities of the heavy Italian food and drank
several glasses of California red wine. But the most
intriguing character was a well-dressed, shark-faced
man who behaved sometimes like a friend, sometimes
like an adviser and sometimes like a servant: once
Cortone called him a counsellor. No business was talked
about during dinner. Instead they told war stories –
Cortone told most of them. He also told the story of
Dickstein's 1948 coup against the Arabs: he had heard
it from his cousins and had been as delighted as they.
The tale had become embroidered in the retelling.

Dickstein decided that Cortone was genuinely glad
to see him. Maybe the man was bored. He should be, if
he ate dinner every night with a silent wife, two surly
boys and a shark-faced counsellor. Dickstein did all he
could to keep the bonhomie going: he wanted Cortone
in a good mood when he asked his favour.

Afterwards Cortone and Dickstein sat in leather

armchairs in a den and a butler brought brandy and cigars. Dickstein refused both.

'You used to be a hell of a drinker,' Cortone said.

'It was a hell of a war,' Dickstein replied. The butler left the room. Dickstein watched Cortone sip brandy and pull on the cigar, and thought that the man ate, drank and smoked joylessly, as though he thought that if he did these things long enough he would eventually acquire the taste. Recalling the sheer fun the two of them had had with the Sicilian cousins, Dickstein wondered whether there were any real people left in Cortone's life.

Suddenly Cortone laughed out loud. 'I remember every minute of that day in Oxford. Hey, did you ever make it with that professor's wife, the Ay-rab?'

'No.' Dickstein barely smiled. 'She's dead, now.'

'I'm sorry.'

'A strange thing happened. I went back there, to that house by the river, and met her daughter . . . She looks just like Eila used to.'

'No kidding. And . . .' Cortone leered. 'And you made it with the daughter – I don't believe it!'

Dickstein nodded. 'We made it in more ways than one. I want to marry her. I plan to ask her next time I see her.'

'Will she say yes?'

'I'm not sure. I think so. I'm older than she is.'

'Age doesn't matter. You could put on a little weight, though. A woman likes to have something to get hold of.'

The conversation was annoying Dickstein, and now

he realized why: Cortone was set on keeping it trivial. It might have been the habit of years of being close-mouthed; it might have been that so much of his 'family business' was criminal business and he did not want Dickstein to know it (but Dickstein had already guessed); or there might have been something else he was afraid of revealing, some secret disappoint-ment he could not share: anyhow, the open, garrulous, excitable young man had long since disappeared inside this fat man. Dickstein longed to say, Tell me what gives you joy, and who you love, and how your life runs on.

Instead he said, 'Do you remember what you said to me in Oxford?'

'Sure. I told you I owe you a debt, you saved my life.' Cortone inhaled on his cigar.

At least that had not changed. 'I'm here to ask for your help.'

'Go ahead and ask.'

'Mind if I put the radio on?'

Cortone smiled. 'This place is swept for bugs about once a week.'

'Good,' said Dickstein, but he put the radio on all the same. 'Cards on the table, Al. I work for Israeli Intelligence.'

Cortone's eyes widened. 'I should have guessed.'

'I'm running an operation in the Mediterranean in November. It's . . .' Dickstein wondered how much he needed to tell, and decided very little. 'It's something that could mean the end of the wars in the Middle

East.' He paused, remembering a phrase Cortone had used habitually. 'And I ain't shittin' you.'

Cortone laughed. 'If you were going to shit me, I figure you would have been here sooner than twenty years.'

'It's important that the operation should not be traceable back to Israel. I need a base from which to work. I need a big house on the coast with a landing for small boats and an anchorage not too far offshore for a big ship. While I'm there – a couple of weeks, maybe more – I need to be protected from inquiring police and other nosy officials. I can think of only one place where I could get all that, and only one person who could get it for me.'

Cortone nodded. 'I know a place – a derelict house in Sicily. It's not exactly plush, kid ... no heat, no phone – but it could fill the bill.'

Dickstein smiled broadly. 'That's terrific,' he said. 'That's what I came to ask for.'

'You're kidding,' said Cortone. 'That's *all*?'

To: Head of Mossad
From: Head of London Station
Date: 29 July 1968

   Suza Ashford is almost certainly an agent of an Arab intelligence service.

   She was born in Oxford, England, 17 June 1944, the only child of Mr (now Professor) Stephen Ashford (born Guildford, England, 1908) and Eila

Zuabi (born Tripoli, Lebanon, 1925). The mother, who died in 1954, was a full-blooded Arab. The father is what is known in England as an 'Arabist'; he spent most of the first forty years of his life in the Middle East and was an explorer, entrepreneur and linguist. He now teaches Semitic Languages at Oxford University, where he is well known for his moderately pro-Arab views.

Therefore, although Suza Ashford is strictly speaking a U.K. national, her loyalties may be assumed to lie with the Arab cause.

She works as an air hostess for BOAC on intercontinental routes, travelling frequently to Tehran, Singapore and Zurich, among other places. Consequently, she has numerous opportunities to make clandestine contacts with Arab diplomatic staff.

She is a strikingly beautiful young woman (see attached photograph – which, however, does not do her justice, according to the field agent on this case). She is promiscuous, but not unusually so by the standards of her profession nor by those of her generation in London. To be specific: for her to have sexual relations with a man for the purpose of obtaining information might be an unpleasant experience but not a traumatic one.

Finally – and this is the clincher – Yasif Hassan, the agent who spotted Dickstein in Luxembourg, studied under her father, Professor Ashford, at the same time as Dickstein, and has remained in occasional contact with Ashford in the intervening years. He may have visited Ashford – a man answering his description certainly *did* visit – about the time Dickstein's affair with Suza Ashford began.

I recommend that surveillance be continued.

(Signed)

Robert Jakes

To: Head of London Station
From: Head of Mossad
Date: 30 July 1968

With all that against her, I cannot understand why you do not recommend we kill her.

(Signed)

Pierre Borg

To: Head of Mossad
From: Head of London Station
Date: 31 July 1968

I do not recommend eliminating Suza Ashford for the following reasons:

1. The evidence against her is strong but circumstantial.

2. From what I know of Dickstein, I doubt very much that he has given her any information, even if he is romantically involved.

3. If we eliminate her the other side will begin looking for another way to get at Dickstein. Better the devil we know.

4. We may be able to use her to feed false information to the other side.

5. I do not like to kill on the basis of circumstantial evidence. We are not barbarians. We are Jews.

6. If we kill a woman Dickstein loves, I think he will kill you, me and everyone else involved.

(Signed)
Robert Jakes

To: Head of London Station
From: Head of Mossad
Date: 1 August 1968
    Do it your way.

(Signed)
Pierre Borg

POSTSCRIPT (marked Personal):

Your point 5 is very noble and touching, but remarks like that won't get you promoted in this man's army. – P.B.

She was a small, old, ugly, dirty, cantankerous bitch.

Rust bloomed like a skin rash in great orange blotches all over her hull. If there had ever been any paint on her upperworks it had long ago been peeled away and blasted off and dissolved by the wind and the rain and the sea. Her starboard gunwale had been badly buckled just aft of the prow in an old collision, and nobody had ever bothered to straighten it out. Her funnel bore a layer of grime ten years thick. Her deck was scored and dented and stained; and although it was swabbed often, it was never swabbed thoroughly, so that there were traces of past cargoes – grains of corn, splinters of timber, bits of rotting vegetation and fragments of sacking – hidden behind lifeboats and under coils of rope and inside cracks and joints and holes. On a warm day she smelled foul.

She was some 2,500 tons, 200 feet long and a little over 30 feet broad. There was a tall radio mast in her blunt prow. Most of her deck was taken up by two large hatches opening into the main cargo holds. There were three cranes on deck: one forward of the hatches, one aft and one in between. The wheelhouse, officers' cabins, galley and crew's quarters were in the stern, clustered around the funnel. She had a single screw driven by a six-cylinder diesel engine theoretically capable of developing 2,450 b.h.p. and maintaining a service speed of thirteen knots.

Fully loaded, she would pitch badly. In ballast she would yaw like the very devil. Either way she would troll through seventy degrees of arc at the slightest provocation. The quarters were cramped and poorly ventilated, the galley was often flooded and the engine room had been designed by Hieronymus Bosch.

She was crewed by thirty-one officers and men, not one of whom had a good word to say for her.

The only passengers were a colony of cockroaches in the galley, a few mice and several hundred rats.

Nobody loved her, and her name was *Coparelli*.

CHAPTER TEN

NAT DICKENSTEIN went to New York to become a shipping tycoon. It took him all morning.

He looked in the Manhattan phone book and selected a lawyer with an address on the lower East Side. Instead of calling on the phone he went there personally, and was satisfied when he saw that the lawyer's office was one room over a Chinese restaurant. The lawyer's name was Mr Chung.

Dickstein and Chung took a cab to the Park Avenue offices of Liberian Corporation Services Inc., a company set up to assist people who wanted to register a Liberian corporation but had no intention of ever going within three thousand miles of Liberia. Dickstein was not asked for references, and he did not have to establish that he was honest or solvent or sane. For a fee of five hundred dollars – which Dickstein paid in cash – they registered the Savile Shipping Corporation of Liberia. The fact that at this stage Dickstein did not own so much as a rowboat was of no interest to anyone.

The company's headquarters was listed as No. 80 Broad Street, Monrovia, Liberia; and its directors were P. Satia, E.K. Nugba and J.D. Boyd, all residents of

Liberia. This was also the headquarters address of most Liberian corporations, and the address of the Liberian Trust Company. Satia, Nugba and Boyd were founding directors of many such corporations; indeed this was the way they made their living. They were also employees of the Liberian Trust Company.

Mr Chung asked for fifty dollars and cab fare. Dickstein paid him in cash and told him to take the bus.

So, without so much as giving an address, Dickstein had created a fully legitimate shipping company which could not be traced back either to him or to the Mossad.

Satia, Nugba and Boyd resigned twenty-four hours later, as was the custom; and that same day the notary public of Montserrado County, Liberia, stamped an affidavit which said that total control of the Savile Shipping Corporation now lay in the hands of one Andre Papagopolous.

By that time Dickstein was riding the bus from Zurich airport into town, on his way to meet Papagopolous for lunch.

When he had time to reflect on it, even he was shaken by the complexity of his plan, the number of pieces that had to be made to fit into the jigsaw puzzle, the number of people who had to be persuaded, bribed or coerced into performing their parts. He had been successful so far, first with Stiffcollar and then with Al Cortone, not to mention Lloyd's of London and Liberian Corporation Services, Inc., but how long could it go on?

Papagopolous was in some ways the greatest challenge: a man as elusive, as powerful, and as free of weakness as Dickstein himself.

He had been born in 1912 in a village that during his boyhood was variously Turkish, Bulgarian and Greek. His father was a fisherman. In his teenage he graduated from fishing to other kinds of maritime work, mostly smuggling. After World War Two he turned up in Ethiopia, buying for knock-down prices the piles of surplus military supplies which had suddenly become worthless when the war ended. He bought rifles, handguns, machine guns, anti-tank guns, and ammunition for all of these. He then contacted the Jewish Agency in Cairo and sold the arms at an enormous profit to the underground Israeli Army. He arranged shipping – and here his smuggling background was invaluable – and delivered the goods to Palestine. Then he asked if they wanted more.

This was how he had met Nat Dickstein.

He soon moved on, to Farouk's Cairo and then to Switzerland. His Israeli deals had marked a transition from totally illegal business to dealings which were at worst shady and at best pristine. Now he called himself a ship broker and that was most, though by no means all, of his business.

He had no address. He could be reached via half a dozen telephone numbers all over the world, but he was never *there* – always, somebody took a message and Papagopolous called you back. Many people knew him and trusted him, especially in the shipping business, for he never let anyone down; but this trust was based on reputation, not personal contact. He lived well but quietly, and Nat Dickstein was one of the few people in the world who knew of his single vice, which was that he liked to go to bed with lots of girls – but *lots*: like, ten or twelve. He had no sense of humour.

Dickstein got off the bus at the railway station, where Papagopolous was waiting for him on the pavement. He was a big man, olive-skinned with thin dark hair combed over a growing bald patch. On a bright summer day in Zurich he wore a navy-blue suit, pale blue shirt and dark blue striped tie. He had small dark eyes.

They shook hands. Dickstein said, 'How's business?'

'Up and down.' Papagopolous smiled. 'Mostly up.'

They walked through the clean, tidy streets, looking like a managing director and his accountant. Dickstein inhaled the cold air. 'I like this town,' he said.

'I've booked a table at the Veltliner Keller in the old city,' Papagopolous said. 'I know you don't care about food, but I do.'

Dickstein said, 'You've been to the Pelikanstrasse?'

'Yes.'

'Good.' The Zurich office of Liberian Corporation Services, Inc., was in the Pelikanstrasse. Dickstein had asked Papagopolous to go there to register himself as president and chief executive of Savile Shipping. For this he would receive ten thousand U.S. dollars, paid out of Mossad's account in a Swiss bank to Papagopolous's account in the same branch of the same bank – a transaction very difficult for anyone to uncover.

Papagopolous said, 'But I didn't promise to do anything else. You may have wasted your money.'

'I'm sure I didn't.'

They reached the restaurant. Dickstein had expected that Papagopolous would be known there, but there was no sign of recognition from the head waiter, and Dickstein thought: Of course, he's not known anywhere.

They ordered food and wine. Dickstein noted with regret that the domestic Swiss white wine was still better than the Israeli.

While they ate, Dickstein explained Papagopolous's duties as president of Savile Shipping.

'One: buy a small, fast ship, a thousand or fifteen hundred tons, small crew. Register her in Liberia.' This would involve another visit to the Pelikanstrasse and a fee of about a dollar per ton. 'For the purchase, take your percentage as a broker. Do some business with the ship, and take your broker's percentage on that. I don't care what the ship does so long as she completes a voyage by docking in Haifa on or before October 7. Dismiss the crew at Haifa. Do you want to take notes?'

Papagopolous smiled. 'I think not.'

The implication was not lost on Dickstein. Papagopolous was listening, but he had not yet agreed to do the job. Dickstein continued. 'Two: buy any one of the ships on this list.' He handed over a single sheet of paper bearing the names of the four sister ships of the *Coparelli*, with their owners and last known locations – the information he had got from Lloyd's. 'Offer whatever price is necessary: I must have one of them. Take your broker's percentage. Deliver her to Haifa by October 7. Dismiss the crew.'

Papagopolous was eating chocolate mousse, his smooth face imperturbable. He put down his spoon and put on gold-rimmed glasses to read the list. He folded the sheet of paper in half and set it on the table without comment.

Dickstein handed him another sheet of paper. 'Three: buy this ship – the *Coparelli*. But you must buy her at exactly the right time. She sails from Antwerp on Sunday, November 17. We must buy her *after* she sails but *before* she passes through the Strait of Gibraltar.'

Papapopolous looked dubious. 'Well . . .'

'Wait, let me give you the rest of it. Four: early in 1969 you sell ship No. 1, the little one, and ship No. 3, the *Coparelli*. You get from me a certificate showing that ship No. 2 has been sold for scrap. You send that certificate to Lloyd's. You wind up Savile Shipping.' Dickstein smiled and sipped his coffee.

'What you want to do is make a ship disappear without a trace.'

Dickstein nodded. Papagopolous was as sharp as a knife.

'As you must realize,' Papagopolous went on, 'all this is straightforward except for the purchase of the *Coparelli* while she is at sea. The normal procedure for the sale of a ship is as follows: negotiations take place, a price is agreed, and the documents are drawn up. The ship goes into dry dock for inspection. When she has been pronounced satisfactory the documents are signed, the money is paid and the new owner takes her out of dry dock. Buying a ship while she is sailing is most irregular.'

'But not impossible.'

'No, not impossible.'

Dickstein watched him. He became thoughtful, his gaze distant: he was grappling with the problem. It was a good sign.

Papagopolous said, 'We would have to open negotiations, agree on the price and have the inspection arranged for a date after her November voyage. Then, when she has sailed, we say that the purchaser needs to spend the money immediately, perhaps for tax reasons. The buyer would then take out insurance against any major repairs which might prove necessary after the inspection, but this is not the seller's concern. He is concerned about his reputation as a shipper. He will want cast-iron guarantees that his cargo will be delivered by the new owner of the *Coparelli.* '

'Would he accept a guarantee based on your personal reputation?'

'Of course. But why would I give such a guarantee?'

Dickstein looked him in the eye. 'I can promise you that the owner of the cargo will not complain.'

Papagopolous made an open-handed gesture. 'It is obvious that you are perpetrating some kind of a swindle here. You need me as a respectable front. That I can do. But you also want me to lay my reputation on the line and take your word that it will not suffer?'

'Yes. Listen. Let me ask you one thing. You trusted the Israelis once before, remember?'

'Of course.'

'Did you ever regret it?'

Papagopolous smiled, remembering the old days. 'It was the best decision I ever made.'

'So, will you trust us again?' Dickstein held his breath.

'I had less to lose in those days. I was ... thirty-five. We used to have a lot of fun. This is the most intriguing offer I've had in twenty years. What the hell, I'll do it.'

Dickstein extended his hand across the restaurant table. Papagopolous shook it.

A waitress brought a little bowl of Swiss chocolates for them to eat with their coffee. Papagopolous took one, Dickstein refused.

'Details,' Dickstein said. 'Open an account for Savile Shipping at your bank here. The Embassy will put funds in as they are required. You report to me simply by leaving a written message at the bank. The note will be picked up by someone from the Embassy. If we need to meet and talk, we use the usual phone numbers.'

'Agreed.'

'I'm glad we're doing business together again.'

Papagopolous was thoughtful. 'Ship No. 2 is a sister ship of the *Coparelli*,' he mused. 'I think I can guess what you're up to. There's one thing I'd like to know, although I'm sure you won't tell me. What the hell kind of cargo will the *Coparelli* be carrying – uranium?'

Pyotr Tyrin looked gloomily at the *Coparelli* and said, 'She's a grubby old ship.'

Rostov did not reply. They were sitting in a rented

Ford on a quay at Cardiff docks. The squirrels at Moscow Centre had informed them that the *Coparelli* would make port there today, and they were now watching her tie up. She was to unload a cargo of Swedish timber and take on a mixture of small machinery and cotton goods: it would take her some days.

'At least the mess decks aren't in the foc'sle,' Tyrin muttered, more or less to himself.

'She's not *that* old,' Rostov said.

Tyrin was surprised Rostov knew what he was talking about. Rostov continually surprised him with odd bits of knowledge.

From the rear seat of the car Nik Bunin said, 'Is that the front or the back of the boat?'

Rostov and Tyrin looked at one another and grinned at Nik's ignorance. 'The back,' Tyrin said. 'We call it the stern.'

It was raining. The Welsh rain was even more persistent and monotonous than the English, and colder. Pyotr Tyrin was unhappy. It so happened that he had done two years in the Soviet Navy. That, plus the fact that he was the radio and electronics expert, made him the obvious choice as the man to be planted aboard the *Coparelli*. He did not want to go back to sea. In truth, the main reason he had applied to join the KGB was to get out of the navy. He hated the damp and the cold and the food and the discipline. Besides, he had a warm, comfortable wife in an apartment in Moscow, and he missed her.

Of course, there was no question of his saying no to Rostov.

'We'll get you on as radio operator, but you must take your own equipment as a fallback,' Rostov said.

Tyrin wondered how this was to be managed. His approach would have been to find the ship's radio man, knock him on the head, throw him in the water, and board the ship to say, 'I hear you need a new radio operator.' No doubt Rostov would be able to come up with something a little more subtle: that was why he was a colonel.

The activity on deck had died down, and the *Coparelli*'s engines were quiet. Five or six sailors came across the gangplank in a bunch, laughing and shouting, and headed for the town. Rostov said, 'See which pub they go to, Nik.' Bunin got out of the car and followed the sailors.

Tyrin watched him go. He was depressed by the scene: the figures crossing the wet concrete quay with their raincoat collars turned up; the sounds of tugs hooting and men shouting nautical instructions and chains winding and unwinding; the stacks of pallets; the bare cranes like sentries; the smell of engine oil and the ship's ropes and salt spray. It all made him think of the Moscow flat, the chair in front of the paraffin heater, salt fish and black bread, beer and vodka in the refrigerator, and an evening of television.

He was unable to share Rostov's irrepressible cheerfulness about the way the operation was going. Once again they had no idea where Dickstein was – even though they had not exactly lost him, they had deliberately let him go. It had been Rostov's decision: he was afraid of getting too close to Dickstein, of scaring the man off. 'We'll follow the *Coparelli*, and Dickstein will come to us,' Rostov had said. Yasif Hassan had argued with him, but Rostov had won. Tyrin, who had no contribution to make to such strategic discussions, thought Rostov was correct, but also thought he had no reason to be so confident.

'Your first job is to befriend the crew,' Rostov said. interrupting Tyrin's thoughts. 'You're a radio operator. You suffered a minor accident aboard your last ship, the *Christmas Rose* – you broke your arm – and you were discharged here in Cardiff to convalesce. You got an excellent compensation payment from the owners. You are spending the money and having a good time while it lasts. You say vaguely that you'll look for another job when your money runs out. You must discover two things: the identity of the radio man, and the antici- pated date and time of departure of the ship.'

'Fine,' said Tyrin, though it was far from fine. Just *how* was he to 'befriend' these people? He was not much of an actor, in his view. Would he have to play the part of a hearty hail-fellow-well-met? Suppose the crew of this ship thought him a bore, a lonely man trying to attach himself to a jolly group? What if they just plain did not like him?

Unconsciously he squared his broad shoulders. Either he would do it, or there would be some reason why it could not be done. All he could promise was to try his best.

Bunin came back across the quay. Rostov said, 'Get in the back, let Nik drive.' Tyrin got out and held the door for Nik. The young man's face was streaming with rain. He started the car. Tyrin got in.

As the car pulled away Rostov turned around to speak to Tyrin in the back seat. 'Here's a hundred pounds,' he said, and handed over a roll of banknotes. 'Don't spend it too carefully.'

Bunin stopped the car opposite a small dockland pub on a corner. A sign outside, flapping gently in the wind, read, 'Brains Beers'. A smoky yellow light glowed behind the frosted-glass windows. There were worse places to be on a day like this, Tyrin thought.

'What nationality are the crew?' he said suddenly.

'Swedish,' Bunin said.

Tyrin's false papers made him out to be Austrian. 'What language should I use with them?'

'All Swedes speak English,' Rostov told him. There was a moment of silence. Rostov said, 'Any more questions? I want to go back to Hassan before he gets up to any mischief.'

'No more questions.' Tyrin opened the car door.

Rostov said, 'Speak to me when you get back to the hotel tonight – no matter how late.'

'Sure.'

'Good luck.'

Tyrin slammed the car door and crossed the road to the pub. As he reached the entrance someone came out, and the warm smell of beer and tobacco engulfed Tyrin for a moment. He went inside.

It was a poky little place, with hard wooden benches around the walls and plastic tables nailed to the floor.

Four of the sailors were playing darts in the corner and a fifth was at the bar calling out encouragement to them.

The barman nodded to Tyrin. 'Good morning,' Tyrin said. 'A pint of lager, a large whisky and a ham sandwich.'

The sailor at the bar turned around and nodded pleasantly. Tyrin smiled. 'Have you just made port?'

'Yes. The *Coparelli*,' the sailor replied.

'*Christmas Rose*,' Tyrin said. 'She left me behind.'

'You're lucky.'

'I broke my arm.'

'So?' said the Swedish sailor with a grin. 'You can drink with the other one.'

'I like that,' Tyrin said. 'Let me buy you a drink. What will it be?'

Two days later they were still drinking. There were changes in the composition of the group as some sailors went on duty and others came ashore; and there was a short period between four A.M. and opening time when there was nowhere in the city, legal or illegal, where one could buy a drink; but otherwise life was one long pub crawl. Tyrin had forgotten how sailors could drink. He was dreading the hangover. He was glad, however, that he had not got into a situation where he felt obliged to go with prostitutes: the Swedes were interested in women, but not in whores. Tyrin would never have been able to convince his wife that he had caught venereal disease in the service of Mother Russia. The Swedes' other vice was gambling. Tyrin had lost about fifty pounds of KGB money at poker. He was so well in with the crew of the *Coparelli* that the previous night he had been invited aboard at two A.M. He had fallen asleep on the mess deck and they had left him there until eight bells.

Tonight would not be like that. The *Coparelli* was to sail on the morning tide, and all officers and men had to be aboard by midnight. It was now ten past eleven. The landlord of the pub was moving about the room collecting glasses and emptying ashtrays. Tyrin was playing dominoes with Lars, the radio operator. They had abandoned the proper game and were now competing to see who could stand the most blocks in a line without knocking the lot down. Lars was very drunk, but Tyrin was pretending. He was also very frightened about what he had to do in a few minutes' time.

The landlord called out, 'Time, gentlemen, please! Thank you very much.'

Tyrin knocked his dominoes down, and laughed. Lars said, 'You see – I am smaller alcoholic than you.'

The other crew were leaving. Tyrin and Lars stood up. Tyrin put his arm around Lars' shoulders and together they staggered out into the street.

The night air was cool and damp. Tyrin shivered. From now on he had to stay very close to Lars. I hope Nik gets his timing right, he thought. I hope the car doesn't break down. And then: I hope to Christ Lars doesn't get killed.

He began talking, asking questions about Lars' home and family. He kept the two of them a few yards behind the main group of sailors.

They passed a blonde woman in a microskirt. She touched her left breast. 'Hello, boys, fancy a cuddle?'

Not tonight, sweetheart, Tyrin thought, and kept walking. He must not let Lars stop and chat. Timing, it was the timing. Nik, where are you?

There. They approached a dark blue Ford Capri 2000 parked at the roadside with its lights out. As the interior light flashed on and off Tyrin glimpsed the face of the man at the wheel: it was Nik Bunin. Tyrin took a flat white cap from his pocket and put it on, the signal that Bunin was to go ahead. When the sailors had passed on the car started up and moved away in the opposite direction.

Not long now.

Lars said, 'I have a fiancée.'

Oh, no, don't start that.

Lars giggled. 'She has . . . hot pants.'

'Are you going to marry her?' Tyrin was peering ahead intently, listening, talking only to keep Lars close.

Lars leered. 'What for?'

'Is she faithful?'

'Better be or I slit her throat.'

'I thought Swedish people believed in free love.' Tyrin was saying anything that came into his head.

'Free love, yes. But she better be faithful.'

'I see.'

'I can explain . . .'

Come on, Nik. Get it over with . . .

One of the sailors in the group stopped to urinate in the gutter. The others stood around making ribald remarks and laughing. Tyrin wished the man would hurry up – the timing, the timing – but he seemed as if he would go on for ever.

At last he finished, and they all walked on.

Tyrin heard a car.

He tensed. Lars said, 'What's matter?'

'Nothing.' Tyrin saw the headlights. The car was moving steadily toward them in the middle of the road. The sailors moved on to the pavement to get out of its way. It wasn't right, it shouldn't be like this, it wouldn't work this way! Suddenly Tyrin was confused and panic-stricken – then he saw the outline of the car more clearly as it passed beneath a street light, and he realized it was not the one he was waiting for, it was a patrolling police car. It went harmlessly by.

The end of the street opened into a wide, empty square, badly paved. There was no traffic about. The sailors headed straight across the middle of the square.

Now.

Come on.

They were halfway across.

Come *on*!

A car came tearing around a corner and into the square, headlights blazing. Tyrin tightened his grip on Lars' shoulder. The car was veering wildly.

'Drunk driver,' Lars said thickly.

It was a Ford Capri. It swung toward the bunch of sailors in front. They stopped laughing and scattered out of its way, shouting curses. The car turned away,

289

then screeched around and accelerated straight for Tyrin and Lars.

'Look out!' Tyrin yelled.

When the car was almost on top of them he pulled Lars to one side, jerking the man off balance, and threw himself sideways. There was a stomach-turning thud, followed by a scream and crash of breaking glass. The car went by.

It's done, Tyrin thought.

He scrambled to his feet and looked for Lars.

The sailor lay on the road a few feet away. Blood glistened in the lamplight.

Lars groaned.

He's alive, Tyrin thought; thank God.

The car braked. One of its headlights had gone out – the one that had hit Lars, he presumed. It coasted, as if the driver were hesitating. Then it gathered speed and, one-eyed, it disappeared into the night.

Tyrin bent over Lars. The other sailors gathered around, speaking Swedish. Tyrin touched Lars' leg. He yelled out in pain.

'I think his leg is broken,' Tyrin said. *Thank God that's all.*

Lights were going on in some of the buildings around the square. One of the officers said something, and a rating ran off toward a house presumably to call for an ambulance. There was more rapid dialogue and another went off in the direction of the dock.

Lars was bleeding, but not too heavily. The officer bent over him. He would not allow anyone to touch his leg.

The ambulance arrived within minutes, but it seemed forever to Tyrin: he had never killed a man, and he did not want to.

They put Lars on a stretcher. The officer got into the ambulance, and turned to speak to Tyrin. 'You had better come.'

'Yes.'

'You saved his life, I think.'

'Oh.'

He got into the ambulance with the officer.

They sped through the wet streets, the flashing blue light on the roof casting an unpleasant glow over the buildings. Tyrin sat in the back, unable to look at Lars or the officer, unwilling to look out of the windows like a tourist, not knowing where to direct his eyes. He had done many unkind things in the service of his country and Colonel Rostov – he had taped the conversations of lovers for blackmail, he had shown terrorists how to make bombs, he had helped capture people who would later be tortured – but he had never been forced to ride in the ambulance with his victim. He did not like it.

They arrived at the hospital. The ambulance men carried the stretcher inside. Tyrin and the officer were shown where to wait. And, suddenly, the rush was over. They had nothing to do but worry. Tyrin was astonished to look at the plain electric clock on the hospital wall and see that it was not yet midnight. It seemed hours since they had left the pub.

After a long wait a doctor came out. 'He's broken his leg and lost some blood,' he said. He seemed very tired. 'He's got a lot of alcohol in him, which doesn't help. But he's young, strong and healthy. His leg will mend and he should be fit again in a few weeks.'

Relief flooded Tyrin. He realized he was shaking.

The officer said, 'Our ship sails in the morning.'

'He won't be on it,' the doctor said. 'Is your captain on his way here?'

'I sent for him.'

'Fine.' The doctor turned and left.

The captain arrived at the same time as the police. He spoke to the officer in Swedish while a young sergeant took down Tyrin's vague description of the car.

Afterwards the captain approached Tyrin. 'I believe you saved Lars from a much worse accident.'

Tyrin wished people would stop saying that. 'I tried to pull him out of the way, but he fell. He was very drunk.'

'Horst here says you are between ships.'

'Yes, sir.'

'You are a fully qualified radio operator?'

'Yes, sir.'

'I need a replacement for poor Lars. Would you like to sail with us in the morning?'

Pierre Borg said, 'I'm pulling you out.'

Dickstein whitened. He stared at his boss.

Borg said, 'I want you to come back to Tel Aviv and run the operation from the office.'

Dickstein said, 'You go and fuck yourself.'

They stood beside the lake at Zurich. It was crowded with boats, their multicoloured sails flapping prettily in the Swiss sunshine. Borg said, 'No arguments, Nat.'

'No arguments, *Pierre*. I won't be pulled out. Finish.'

'I'm ordering you.'

'And I'm telling you to fuck yourself.'

'Look.' Borg took a deep breath. 'Your plan is complete. The only flaw in it is that you've been compromised: the opposition knows you're working, and they're trying to find you and screw up whatever it is you're doing. You can still run the project – all you have to do is hide your face.'

'No,' Dickstein said. 'This isn't the kind of project where you can sit in an office and push all the buttons to make it go. It's too complex, there are too many variables. I have to be in the field myself to make instant decisions.' Dickstein stopped himself talking and began to think: *Why* do I want to do it myself? Am I really the only man in Israel who can pull this off? Is it just that I want the glory?

Borg voiced his thoughts. 'Don't try to be a hero, Nat. You're too smart for that. You're a professional: you follow orders.'

Dickstein shook his head. 'You should know better than to take that line with me. Remember how Jews feel about people who always follow orders?'

'All right, so you were in a concentration camp – that doesn't give you the right to do whatever the hell you like for the rest of your life!'

Dickstein made a deprecatory gesture. 'You can stop me. You can withdraw support. But you also won't get your uranium, because I'm not going to tell anyone else how it can be done.'

Borg stared at him. 'You bastard, you mean it.'

Dickstein watched Borg's expression. He had once had the embarrassing experience of seeing Borg have a row with his teenage son Dan. The boy had stood there, sullenly confident, while Borg tried to explain that going on peace marches was disloyal to father, mother, country and God, until Borg had strangled himself with his own inarticulate rage. Dan, like Dickstein, had learned how to refuse to be bullied, and Borg would never quite know how to handle people who could not be bullied.

The script now called for Borg to go red in the face and begin to yell. Suddenly Dickstein realized that this was not going to happen. Borg was remaining calm.

Borg smiled slyly and said, 'I believe you're fucking one of the other side's agents.'

Dickstein stopped breathing. He felt as if he had been hit from behind with a sledgehammer. This was the last thing he had been expecting. He was filled with irrational guilt, like a boy caught masturbating: shame, embarrassment, and the sense of something spoiled. Suza was private, in a compartment separate from the rest of his life, and now Borg was dragging her out and holding her up to public view: Just *look* at what Nat was doing!

'No,' Dickstein said tonelessly.

'I'll give you the headlines,' Borg said. 'She's Arab, her father's politics are pro-Arab, she travels all over the world in her cover job to have opportunity for contacts, and the agent Yasif Hassan, who spotted you in Luxembourg, is a friend of the family.'

Dickstein turned to face Borg, standing too close, gazing fiercely into Borg's eyes, his guilt turning to resentment. 'That's all?'

'All? What the fuck do you mean, *all*? You'd shoot people on that much evidence!'

'Not people I know.'

'Has she got any information out of you?'

Dickstein shouted, 'No!'

'You're getting angry because you know you've made a mistake.'

Dickstein turned away and looked across the lake, struggling to make himself calm: rage was Borg's act, not his. After a long pause he said, 'Yes, I'm angry because I've made a mistake. I should have told you about her; not the other way around. I understand how it must seem to you—'

'Seem? You mean you don't believe she's an agent?'

'Have you checked through Cairo?'

Borg gave a false little laugh. 'You talk as if Cairo was my intelligence service. I can't just call and ask them to look her up in their files while I hold the line.'

'But you've got a very good double agent in Egyptian Intelligence.'

'How can he be good? Everybody seems to know about him.'

'Stop playing games. Since the Six-Day War even the newspapers say you have good doubles in Egypt. The point is, you haven't checked her.'

Borg held up both hands, palms outward, in a

gesture of appeasement. 'Okay, I'm going to check her with Cairo. It will take a little time. Meanwhile, you're going to write a report giving all details of your scheme and I'm going to put other agents on the job.'

Dickstein thought of Al Cortone and Andre Papagopolous: neither of them would do what he had agreed to do for anyone other than Dickstein. 'It won't work, Pierre,' he said quietly. 'You've got to have the uranium, and I'm the only one who can get it for you.'

'And if Cairo confirms her to be an agent?'

'I'm confident the answer will be negative.'

'But if it's not?'

'You'll kill her, I suppose.'

'Oh, no.' Borg pointed a finger at Dickstein's nose, and when he spoke there was real, deep-down malice in his voice. 'Oh, no, I won't, Dickstein. If she's an agent, *you* will kill her.'

With deliberate slowness, Dickstein took hold of Borg's wrist and removed the pointing finger from in front of his face. There was only the faintest perceptible tremor in his voice as he said, 'Yes, Pierre. I will kill her.'

CHAPTER ELEVEN

I N THE bar at Heathrow Airport David Rostov ordered another round of drinks and decided to take a gamble on Yasif Hassan. The problem, still, was how to stop Hassan telling all he knew to an Israeli double agent in Cairo. Rostov and Hassan were both going back for interim debriefing so a decision had to be made now. Rostov was going to let Hassan know everything, then appeal to his professionalism – such as it was. The alternative was to provoke him, and just now he needed him as an ally, not a suspicious antagonist.

'Look at this,' Rostov said, and he showed Hassan a decoded message.

To: Colonel David Rostov *via* London Residency
From: Moscow Centre
Date: 3 September 1968

Comrade Colonel:
    We refer to your signal g/35–21a, requesting further information concerning each of four ships named in our signal r/35–21.
    The motor vessel *Stromberg*, 2500 tons, Dutch

ownership and registration, has recently changed hands. She was purchased for DM 1,500,000 by one Andre Papagopolous, a ship broker, on behalf of the Savile Shipping Corporation of Liberia.

Savile Shipping was incorporated on 6 August this year at the New York office of Liberian Corporation Services Inc., with a share capital of five hundred dollars. The shareholders are Mr Lee Chung, a New York lawyer, and a Mr Robert Roberts, whose address is care of Mr Chung's office. The three directors were provided in the usual way by Liberian Corporation Services, and they resigned the day after the company was set up, again in the usual way. The aforementioned Papagopolous took over as president and chief executive.

Savile Shipping has also bought the motor vessel *Gil Hamilton*, 1500 tons, for £80,000.

Our people in New York have interviewed Chung. He says that 'Mr Roberts' came into his office from the street, gave no address and paid his fee in cash. He appeared to be an Englishman. The detailed description is on file here, but it is not very helpful.

Papagopolous is known to us. He is a wealthy international businessman of indeterminate nationality. Shipbroking is his principal activity. He is believed to operate close to the fringes of the law. We have no address for him. There is considerable material in his file, but much of it is speculative. He is believed to have done business with Israeli

Intelligence in 1948. Nevertheless, he has no known political affiliation.

We continue to gather information on all the ships in the list.

– Moscow Centre.

Hassan gave the sheet of paper back to Rostov. 'How do they get hold of all this stuff?'

Rostov began tearing the signal into shreds. 'It's all on file somewhere or other. The sale of the *Stromberg* would have been notified to Lloyd's of London. Someone from our consulate in Liberia would have got the details on Savile Shipping from public records in Monrovia. Our New York people got Chung's address out of the phone book, and Papagopolous was on file in Moscow. None of it is secret, except the Papagopolous file. The trick is knowing where to go to ask the questions. The squirrels specialize in that trick. It's all they do.'

Rostov put the shreds of paper into a large glass ashtray and set fire to them. 'Your people should have squirrels,' he added.

'I expect we're working on it.'

'Suggest it yourself. It won't do you any harm. You might even get the job of setting it up. That could help your career.'

Hassan nodded. 'Perhaps I will.'

Fresh drinks arrived: vodka for Rostov, gin for Hassan. Rostov was pleased that Hassan was responding well to his friendly overtures. He examined the cinders in the ashtray to make sure the signal had burned completely.

Hassan said, 'You're assuming Dickstein is behind the Savile Shipping Corporation.'

'Yes.'

'So what will we do about the *Stromberg*?'

'Well . . .' Rostov emptied his glass and set it on the table. 'My guess is he wants the *Stromberg* so he can get an exact layout of the sister ship *Coparelli*.'

'It will be an expensive blueprint.'

'He can sell the ship again. However, he may also use the *Stromberg* in the hijack of the *Coparelli* – I don't quite see how, just yet.'

'Will you put a man aboard the *Stromberg*, like Tyrin on the *Coparelli*?'

'No point. Dickstein is sure to get rid of the old crew and fill the ship with Israeli sailors. I'll have to think of something else.'

'Do we know where the *Stromberg* is now?'

'I've asked the squirrels. They'll have an answer by the time I get to Moscow.'

Hassan's flight was called. He stood up. 'We meet in Luxembourg?'

'I'm not sure. I'll let you know. Listen, there's something I've got to say. Sit down again.'

Hassan sat down.

'When we started to work together on Dickstein I was very hostile to you. I regret that now, I'm apologizing; but I must tell you there was a reason for it. You see, Cairo isn't secure. It's certain there are double agents in the Egyptian Intelligence apparatus. What I was concerned about – and still am – is that everything you report to your superiors will get back, via a double agent, to Tel Aviv; and then Dickstein will know how close we are and will take evasive action.'

'I appreciate your frankness.'

Appreciate, Rostov thought: He loves it. 'However, you are now completely in the picture, and what we must discuss is how to prevent the information you have in your possession getting back to Tel Aviv.'

Hassan nodded. 'What do you suggest?'

'Well. You'll have to tell what we've found out, of course, but I want you to be as vague as possible about the details. Don't give names, times, places. When you're pushed, complain about me, say I've refused to let you share all the information. Don't talk to anyone except the people you're obliged to report to. In particular, tell nobody about Savile Shipping, the *Stromberg*, or the *Coparelli*. As for Pyotr Tyrin being aboard the *Coparelli* – try to forget it.'

Hassan looked worried. 'What's left to tell?'

'Plenty. Dickstein, Euratom, uranium, the meeting with Pierre Borg . . . you'll be a hero in Cairo if you tell half the story.'

Hassan was not convinced. 'I'll be as frank as you. If I do this your way, my report will not be as impressive as yours.'

Rostov gave a wry smile. 'Is that unfair?'

'No,' Hassan conceded, 'you deserve most of the credit.'

'Besides, nobody but the two of us will know how different the reports are. And you're going to get all the credit you need in the end.'

'All right,' Hassan said. 'I'll be vague.'

'Good.' Rostov waved his hand for a waiter. 'You've got a little time, have a quick one before you go.' He settled back in his chair and crossed his legs. He was satisfied: Hassan would do as he had been told. 'I'm looking forward to getting home.'

'Any plans?'

'I'll try to take a few days on the coast with Mariya and the boys. We've a dacha in the Riga Bay.'

'Sounds nice.'

'It's pleasant there – but not as warm as where you're going, of course. Where will you head for – Alexandria?'

The last call for Hassan's flight came over the public address system, and the Arab stood up. 'No such luck,' he said. 'I expect to spend the whole time stuck in filthy Cairo.'

And Rostov had the peculiar feeling that Yasif Hassan was lying.

Franz Albrecht Pedler's life was ruined when Germany lost the war. At the age of fifty, a career officer in the Wehrmacht, he was suddenly homeless, penniless and unemployed. And, like millions of other Germans, he started again.

He became a salesman for a French dye manufacturer: small commission, no salary. In 1946 there were few customers, but by 1951 German industry was rebuilding and when at last things began to look up Pedler was in a good position to take advantage of the new opportunities. He opened an office in Wiesbaden, a rail junction on the right bank of the Rhine that promised to develop into an industrial centre. His product list grew, and so did his tally of customers: soon he was selling soaps as well as dyes, and he gained entry to the U.S. bases, which at the time administered that part of occupied Germany. He had learned, during the hard years, to be an opportunist: if a U.S. Army procurement officer wanted disinfectant in pint bottles, Pedler would buy disinfectant in ten-gallon drums, pour the stuff from the drums into secondhand bottles in a rented barn, put on a label saying 'F. A. Pedler's Special Disinfectant' and resell at a fat profit.

From buying in bulk and repackaging it was not a very big step to buying ingredients and manufacturing. The first barrel of F. A. Pedler's Special Industrial Cleanser – never called simply 'soap' – was mixed in the same rented barn and sold to the U.S. Air Force for use by aircraft maintenance engineers. The company never looked back.

In the late Fifties Pedler read a book about chemical warfare and went on to win a big defence contract to supply a range of solutions designed to neutralize various kinds of chemical weapon.

F. A. Pedler had become a military supplier, small but secure and profitable. The rented barn had grown into a small complex of single-storey buildings. Franz married again – his first wife had been killed in the

1944 bombing – and fathered a child. But he was still an opportunist at heart, and when he heard about a small mountain of uranium ore going cheap, he smelled a profit.

The uranium belonged to a Belgian company called Société Générale de la Chimie. Chimie was one of the corporations which ran Belgium's African colony, the Belgian Congo, a country rich in minerals. After the 1960 pullout Chimie stayed on; but, knowing that those who did not walk out would eventually be thrown out, the company expended all its efforts to ship home as much raw material as it could before the gates slammed shut. Between 1960 and 1965 it accumulated a large stockpile of yellowcake at its refinery near the Dutch border. Sadly for Chimie, a nuclear test ban treaty was ratified in the meantime, and when Chimie was finally thrown out of the Congo there were few buyers for uranium. The yellowcake sat in a silo, tying up scarce capital.

F. A. Pedler did not actually use very much uranium in the manufacture of their dyes. However, Franz loved a gamble of this sort: the price was low, he could make a little money by having the stuff refined, and if the uranium market improved – as it was likely to sooner or later – he would make a big capital profit. So he bought some.

Nat Dickstein liked Pedler right away. The German was a sprightly seventy-three-year-old who still had all his hair and the twinkle in his eye. They met on a Saturday. Pedler wore a loud sports jacket and fawn trousers, spoke good English with an American accent and gave Dickstein a glass of Sekt, the local champagne.

They were wary of each other at first. After all, they had fought on opposite sides in a war which had been cruel to them both. But Dickstein had always believed that the enemy was not Germany but Fascism, and he was nervous only that Pedler might be uneasy. It seemed the same was true of Pedler.

Dickstein had called from his hotel in Wiesbaden to make an appointment. His call had been awaited eagerly. The local Israeli consul had alerted Pedler that Mr Dickstein, a senior army procurement officer with a large shopping list, was on his way. Pedler had suggested a short tour of the factory on Saturday morning, when it would be empty, followed by lunch at his home.

If Dickstein had been genuine he would have been put off by the tour: the factory was no gleaming model of German efficiency, but a straggling collection of old huts and cluttered yards with a pervasive bad smell.

After sitting up half the night with a textbook on chemical engineering Dickstein was ready with a handful of intelligent questions about agitators and baffles, materials-handling and quality-control and packaging. He relied upon the language problem to camouflage any errors. It seemed to be working.

The situation was peculiar. Dickstein had to play the role of a buyer and be dubious and noncommittal while the seller wooed him, whereas in reality he was hoping to seduce Pedler into a relationship the German would be unable or unwilling to sever. It was Pedler's uranium he wanted, but he was not going to ask for it, now or ever. Instead he would try to manoeuvre Pedler into a position where he was dependent upon Dickstein for his livelihood.

After the factory tour Pedler drove him in a new Mercedes from the works to a wide chalet-style house on a hillside. They sat in front of a big window and sipped their Sekt while Frau Pedler – a pretty, cheerful woman in her forties – busied herself in the kitchen. Bringing a potential customer home to lunch on the weekend was a somewhat Jewish way of doing business, Dickstein mused, and he wondered if Pedler had thought of that.

The window overlooked the valley. Down below, the river was wide and slow, with a narrow road running alongside it. Small grey houses with white shutters clustered in small groups along the banks, and the vineyards sloped upward to the Pedlers' house and beyond it to the treeline. If I were going to live in a cold country, Dickstein thought, this would do nicely.

'Well, what do you think?' said Pedler.

'About the view, or the factory?''

Pedler smiled and shrugged. 'Both.'

'The view is magnificent. The factory is smaller than I expected.'

Pedler lit a cigarette. He was a heavy smoker – he was lucky to have lived so long. 'Small?'

'Perhaps I should explain what I'm looking for.'

'Please.'

Dickstein launched into his story. 'Right now the Army buys cleaning materials from a variety of suppliers: detergents from one, ordinary soap from another, solvents for machinery from someone else and so on. We're trying to cut costs, and perhaps we can do this by taking our entire business in this area to one manufacturer.'

Pedler's eyes widened. 'That is . . .' He fumbled for a phrase '. . . a tall order.'

'I'm afraid it may be too tall for you,' Dickstein said, thinking: Don't say yes!

'Not necessarily. The only reason we haven't got that kind of bulk manufacturing capacity is simply that we've never had this scale of business. We certainly have the managerial and technical knowhow, and with a large firm order we could get finance to expand . . . it all depends on the figures, really.'

Dickstein picked up his briefcase from beside his chair and opened it. 'Here are the specifications for the products,' he said, handing Pedler a list. 'Plus the quantities required and the time scale. You'll want time to consult with your directors and do your sums—'

'I'm the boss,' Pedler said with a smile. 'I don't have to consult anybody. Give me tomorrow to work on the figures, and Monday to see the bank. On Tuesday I'll call and give you prices.'

'I was told you were a good man to work with,' Dickstein said.

'There are some advantages to being a small company.'

Frau Pedler came in from the kitchen and said, 'Lunch is ready.'

My darling Suza.

I have never written a love letter before. I don't think I ever called anyone darling until now. I must tell you, it feels very good.

I am alone in a strange town on a cold Sunday afternoon. The town is quite pretty, with lots of parks, in fact I'm sitting in one of them now, writing to you with a leaky ballpoint pen and some vile green stationery, the only kind I could get. My bench is beneath a curious kind of pagoda with a circular dome and Greek columns all around in a circle – like a folly, or the kind of summer house you might find in an English country garden designed by a Victorian eccentric. In front of me is a flat lawn dotted with poplar trees, and in the distance I can hear a brass band playing something by Edward Elgar. The park is full of people with children and footballs and dogs.

I don't know why I'm telling you all this. What I really want to say is I love you and I want to spend the rest of my life with you. I knew that a couple of days after we met. I hesitated to tell you, not because I wasn't sure, but . . .

Well, if you want to know the truth, I thought it might scare you off. I know you love me, but I also know that you are twenty-five, that love comes easily to you (I'm the opposite way), and that love which comes easily may go easily. So I thought: Softly,

softly, give her a chance to get to like you before you ask her to say 'For ever.' Now that we've been apart for so many weeks I'm no longer capable of such deviousness, I just have to tell you how it is with me. For ever is what I want, and you might as well know it now.

I'm a changed man. I know that sounds trite, but when it happens to you it isn't trite at all, it's just the opposite. Life looks different to me now, in several ways – some of which you know about, others I'll tell you one day. Even this is different, this being alone in a strange place with nothing to do until Monday. Not that I mind it, particularly. But before, I wouldn't even have thought of it as something I might like or dislike. Before, there was nothing I'd prefer to do. Now there is always something I'd rather do, and you're the person I'd rather do it to. I mean *with*, not to. Well, either, or both. I'm going to have to get off that subject, it's making me fidget.

I'll be gone from here in a couple of days, don't know where I'm going next, don't know – and this is the worst part – don't even know when I'll see you again. But when I do, believe me, I'm not going to let you out of my sight for ten or fifteen years.

None of this sounds how it's supposed to sound. I want to tell you how I feel, and I can't put it into words. I want you to know what it's like for me to picture your face many times every day, to see a slender girl with black hair and hope, against all reason, that somehow she might be you, to imagine all the time what you might say about a view, a newspaper article, a small man with a large dog, a pretty dress; I want you to know how, when I get into bed alone, I just ache with the need to touch you.

I love you so much.

N.

Franz Pedler's secretary phoned Nat Dickstein at his hotel on Tuesday morning and made a date for lunch.

They went to a modest restaurant in the Wilhelmstrasse and ordered beer instead of wine: this was to be a working session. Dickstein controlled his impatience – Pedler, not he, was supposed to do the wooing.

Pedler said, 'Well, I think we can accommodate you.'

Dickstein wanted to shout 'Hooray!' but he kept his face impassive.

Pedler continued: 'The prices, which I'll give you in a moment, are conditional. We need a five-year contract. We will guarantee prices for the first twelve months; after that they may be varied in accordance with an index of world prices of certain raw materials. And there's a cancellation penalty amounting to ten per cent of the value of one year's supply.'

Dickstein wanted to say, 'Done!' and shake hands on the deal, but he reminded himself to continue to play his part. 'Ten per cent is stiff.'

'It's not excessive,' Pedler argued. 'It certainly would not recompense us for our losses if you did cancel. But it must be large enough to deter you from cancelling except under very compelling circumstances.'

'I see that. But we may suggest a smaller percentage.'

Pedler shrugged. 'Everything is negotiable. Here are the prices.'

Dickstein studied the list, then said, 'This is close to what we're looking for.'

'Does that mean we have a deal?'

Dickstein thought: Yes, yes! But he said, 'No, it means that I think we can do business.'

Pedler beamed. 'In that case,' he said, 'let's have a real drink. Waiter!'

When the drinks came Pedler raised his glass in a toast. 'To many years of business together.'

'I'll drink to that,' Dickstein said. As he raised his glass he was thinking: How about that – I did it again!

Life at sea was uncomfortable, but it was not as bad as Pyotr Tyrin had expected. In the Soviet Navy, ships had been run on the principles of unremitting hard work, harsh discipline and bad food. The *Coparelli* was very different. The captain, Eriksen, asked only for safety and good seamanship, and even there his standards were not remarkably high. The deck was swabbed occasionally, but nothing was ever polished or painted. The food was quite good, and Tyrin had the advantage of sharing a cabin with the cook. In theory Tyrin could be called upon at any hour of the day or night to send radio signals, but in practice all the traffic occurred during the normal working day so he even got his eight hours sleep every night. It was a comfortable regimen, and Pyotr Tyrin was concerned about comfort.

Sadly, the ship was the opposite of comfortable. She was a bitch. As soon as they rounded Cape Wrath and left The Minch and the North Sea she began to pitch and roll like a toy yacht in a gale. Tyrin felt terribly seasick, and had to conceal it since he was supposed to be a sailor. Fortunately this occurred while the cook was busy in the galley and Tyrin was not needed in the radio room, so he was able to lie flat on his back in his bunk until the worst was over.

The quarters were poorly ventilated and inadequately heated, so immediately it got a little damp above, the mess decks were full of wet clothing hanging up to dry and making the atmosphere worse.

Tyrin's radio gear was in his sea-bag, well protected by polythene and canvas and some sweaters. However, he could not set it up and operate it in his cabin, where the cook or anyone else might walk in. He had already made routine radio contact with Moscow on the ship's radio, during a quiet – but nonetheless tense – moment when nobody was listening; but he needed something safer and more reliable.

Tyrin was a nest-building man. Whereas Rostov would move from embassy to hotel room to safe house without noticing his environment, Tyrin liked to have a base, a place where he could feel comfortable and familiar and secure. On static surveillance, the kind of assignment he preferred, he would always find a large easy chair to place in front of the window, and would sit at the telescope for hours, perfectly content with his bag of sandwiches, his bottle of soda and his thoughts. Here on the *Coparelli*, he had found a place to nest.

Exploring the ship in daylight, he had discovered a little labyrinth of stores up in the bow beyond the for'ard hatch. The naval architect had put them there merely to fill a space between the hold and the prow. The main store was entered by a semiconcealed door down a flight of steps. It contained some tools, several drums of grease for the cranes and – inexplicably – a rusty old lawnmower. Several smaller rooms opened off the main one: some containing ropes, bits of machinery and decaying cardboard boxes of nuts and bolts; others empty but for insects. Tyrin had never seen anyone enter the area – stuff that was used was stored aft, where it was needed.

He chose a moment when darkness was falling and most of the crew and officers were at supper. He went to his cabin, picked up his sea-bag and climbed the companionway to the deck. He took a flashlight from a locker below the bridge but did not yet switch it on.

The almanac said there was a moon, but it did not show through the thick clouds. Tyrin made his way stealthily for'ard holding on to the gunwale, where his silhouette would be less likely to show against the off-white deck. There was some light from the bridge and the wheelhouse, but the duty officers would be watching the surrounding sea, not the deck.

Cold spray fell on him, and as the *Coparelli* executed her notorious roll he had to grab the rail with both hands to avoid being swept overboard. At times she shipped water – not much, but enough to soak into Tyrin's sea boots and freeze his feet. He hoped fervently that he would never find out what she was like in a real gale.

He was miserably wet and shivering when he reached the bow and entered the little disused store. He closed the door behind him, switched on his flashlight and made his way through the assorted junk to one of the small rooms off the main store. He closed that door behind him too. He took off his oilskin, rubbed his hands on his sweater to dry and warm them some, then opened his bag. He put the transmitter in a corner, lashed it to the bulkhead with a wire tied through rings in the deck, and wedged it with a cardboard box.

He was wearing rubber soles, but he put on rubber gloves as an additional precaution for the next task. The cables to the ship's radio mast ran through a pipe along the deckhead above him. With a small hacksaw pilfered from the engine room Tyrin cut away a six-inch section of the pipe, exposing the cables. He took a tap from the power cable to the power input of the transmitter, then connected the aerial socket of his radio with the signal wire from the mast.

He switched on the radio and called Moscow.

His outgoing signals would not interfere with the ship's radio because he was the radio operator and it was unlikely that anyone else would attempt to send on the ship's equipment. However, while he was using his own radio, incoming signals would not reach the ship's radio room; and he would not hear them either since his set would be tuned to another frequency. He could have wired everything so that both radios would receive at the same time, but then Moscow's replies to him would be received by the ship's radio, and somebody might notice ... Well, there was nothing very suspicious about a small ship taking a few minutes to pick up signals. Tyrin would take care to use his radio only at times when no traffic was expected for the ship.

When he reached Moscow he made: *Checking secondary transmitter.*

They acknowledged, then made: *Stand by for signal from Rostov.* All this was in a standard KGB code.

Tyrin made: *Standing by, but hurry.*

The message came: *Keep your head down until something happens. Rostov.*

Tyrin made: *Understood. Over and out.* Without waiting for their sign-off he disconnected his wires and restored the ship's cables to normal. The business of twisting and untwisting bare wires, even with insulated pliers, was time-consuming and not very safe. He had some quick-release connectors amongst his equipment in the ship's radio room: he would pocket a few and bring them here next time to speed up the process.

He was well satisfied with his evening's work. He had made his nest, he had opened his lines of communication, and he had remained undiscovered. All he had to do now was sit tight: and sitting tight was what he liked to do.

He decided to drag in another cardboard box to put in front of the radio and conceal it from a casual glance. He opened the door and shone his flashlight into the main store – and got a shock.

He had company.

The overhead light was on, casting restless shadows

with its yellow glow. In the centre of the storeroom, sitting against a grease drum with his legs stretched out before him, was a young sailor. He looked up, just as startled as Tyrin and – Tyrin realized from his face – just as guilty.

Tyrin recognized him. His name was Ravlo. He was about nineteen years old, with pale blond hair and a thin white face. He had not joined in the pub-crawls in Cardiff, yet he often looked hung over, with dark discs under his eyes and a distracted air.

Tyrin said, 'What are you doing here?' And then he saw.

Ravlo had rolled up his left sleeve past the elbow. On the deck between his legs was a phial, a watch-glass and a small waterproof bag. In his right hand was a hypodermic syringe, with which he was about to inject himself.

Tyrin frowned. 'Are you diabetic?'

Ravlo's face twisted and he gave a dry, humourless laugh.

'An addict,' Tyrin said, understanding. He did not know much about drugs, but he knew that what Ravlo was doing could get him discharged at the next port of call. He began to relax a little. This could be handled.

Ravlo was looking past him, into the smaller store. Tyrin looked back and saw that the radio was clearly visible. The two men stared at one another, each understanding that the other was doing something he needed to hide.

Tyrin said, 'I will keep your secret, and you will keep mine.'

Ravlo gave the twisted smile and the dry, humourless laugh again: then he looked away from Tyrin, down at his arm, and he stuck the needle into his flesh.

The exchange between the *Coparelli* and Moscow was picked up and recorded by a U.S. Naval Intelligence listening station. Since it was in standard KGB code, they were able to decipher it. But all it told them was that someone aboard a ship – they did not know which ship – was checking his secondary transmitter, and somebody called Rostov – the name was not on any of their files – wanted him to keep his head down. Nobody could make any sense of it, so they opened a file titled 'Rostov' and put the signal in the file and forgot about it.

CHAPTER TWELVE

WHEN HE had finished his interim debriefing in Cairo, Hassan asked permission to go to Syria to visit his parents in the refugee camp. He was given four days. He took a plane to Damascus and a taxi to the camp.

He did not visit his parents.

He made certain inquiries at the camp, and one of the refugees took him, by means of a series of buses, to Dara, across the Jordanian border, and all the way to Amman. From there another man took him on another bus to the Jordan River.

On the night of the second day he crossed the river, guided by two men who carried submachine guns. By now Hassan was wearing Arab robes and a headdress like them, but he did not ask for a gun. They were young men, their soft adolescent faces just taking on lines of weariness and cruelty, like recruits in a new army. They moved across the Jordan valley in confident silence, directing Hassan with a touch or a whisper: they seemed to have made the journey many times. At one point all three of them lay flat behind a stand of cactus while lights and soldiers' voices passed a quarter of a mile away.

Hassan felt helpless – and something more. At first he thought that the feeling was due to his being so completely in the hands of these boys, his life dependent on their knowledge and courage. But later, when they had left him and he was alone on a country road trying to get a lift, he realized that this journey was a kind of regression. For years now he had been a European banker, living in Luxembourg with his car and his refrigerator and his television set. Now, suddenly, he was walking in sandals along the dusty Palestine roads of his youth: no car, no jet; an Arab again, a peasant, a second-class citizen in the country of his birth. None of his reflexes would work here – it was not possible to solve a problem by picking up a phone or pulling out a credit card or calling a cab. He felt like a child, a pauper and a fugitive all at the same time.

He walked five miles without seeing a vehicle, then a fruit truck passed him, its engine coughing unhealthily and pouring smoke, and pulled up a few yards ahead. Hassan ran after it.

'To Nablus?' he shouted.

'Jump in.'

The driver was a heavy man whose forearms bulged with muscle as he heaved the truck around bends at top speed. He smoked all the time. He must have been certain there would not be another vehicle in the way all night, driving as he did on the crown of the road and never using the brake. Hassan could have used some sleep, but the driver wanted to talk. He told Hassan that the Jews were good rulers, business had prospered since they occupied Jordan, but of course the land must be free one day. Half of what he said was insincere, no doubt; but Hassan could not tell which half.

They entered Nablus in the cool Samaritan dawn, with a red sun rising behind the hillside and the town still asleep. The truck roared into the market square and stopped. Hassan said goodbye to the driver.

He walked slowly through the empty streets as the sun began to take away the chill of the night. He savoured the clean air and the low white buildings, enjoying every detail, basking in the glow of nostalgia for his boyhood: he was in Palestine, he was home.

He had precise directions to a house with no number in a street with no name. It was in a poor quarter, where the little stone houses were crowded too close together and nobody swept the streets. A goat was tethered outside, and he wondered briefly what it ate, for there was no grass. The door was unlocked.

He hesitated a moment outside, fighting down the excitement in his belly. He had been away too long – now he was back in the Land. He had waited too many years for this opportunity to strike a blow in revenge for what they had done to his father. He had suffered exile, he had endured with patience, he had nursed his hatred enough, perhaps too much.

He went in.

There were four or five people asleep on the floor. One of them, a woman, opened her eyes, saw him and sat up instantly, her hand under the pillow reaching for what might have been a gun.

'What do you want?'

Hassan spoke the name of the man who commanded the Fedayeen.

Mahmoud had lived not far from Yasif Hassan when they were both boys in the late Thirties, but they had never met, or if they had neither remembered it. After the European war, when Yasif went to England to study, Mahmoud tended sheep with his brothers, his father, his uncles and his grandfather. Their lives would have continued to go in quite different directions but for the 1948 war. Mahmoud's father, like Yasif's, made the decision to pack up and flee. The two sons – Yasif was a few years older than Mahmoud – met at the refugee camp. Mahmoud's reaction to the ceasefire was even stronger than Yasif's, which was paradoxical, for Yasif had lost more. But Mahmoud was possessed by a great rage that would allow him to do nothing other than fight for the liberation of his homeland. Until then he had been oblivious of politics, thinking it had nothing to do with shepherds; now he set out to understand it. Before he could do that, he had to teach himself to read.

They met again in the Fifties, in Gaza. By then Mahmoud had blossomed, if that was the right word for something so fierce. He had read Clausewitz on war and Plato's *Republic*, *Das Kapital* and *Mein Kampf*, Keynes and Mao and Galbraith and Gandhi, history and biography, classical novels and modern plays. He spoke good English and bad Russian and a smattering of Cantonese. He was directing a small cadre of terrorists on forays into Israel, bombing and shooting and stealing and then returning to disappear into the Gaza camps like rats into a garbage dump. The terrorists were getting money, weapons and intelligence from Cairo: Hassan was, briefly, part of the intelligence backup, and when they met again Yasif told Mahmoud where his ultimate loyalty lay – not with Cairo, not even with the pan-Arab cause, but with Palestine.

Yasif had been ready to abandon everything there and then – his job at the bank, his home in Luxembourg, his role in Egyptian Intelligence – and join the freedom fighters. But Mahmoud had said no, and the habit of command was already fitting him like a tailored coat. In a few years, he said – for he took a long view – they would have all the guerrillas they wanted, but they would still need friends in high places, European connections, and secret intelligence.

They had met once more, in Cairo, and set up lines of communication which bypassed the Egyptians. With the Intelligence Establishment Hassan had cultivated a deceptive image: he pretended to be a little less perceptive than he was. At first Yasif sent over much the same kind of stuff he was giving to Cairo, principally the names of loyal Arabs who were stashing away fortunes in Europe and could therefore be touched for funds. Recently he had been of more immediate practical value as the Palestinian movement began to operate in Europe. He had booked hotels and flights, rented cars and houses, stockpiled weapons and transferred funds.

He was not the kind of man to use a gun. He knew this and was faintly ashamed of it, so he was all the more proud to be so useful in other, non-violent but nonetheless practical, ways.

The results of his work had begun to explode in Rome that year. Yasif believed in Mahmoud's programme of European terrorism. He was convinced that the Arab armies, even with Russian support, could never defeat the Jews, for this allowed the Jews to think of themselves as a beleaguered people defending their homes against foreign soldiers, and that gave them strength. The truth was, in Yasif's view, that the Palestine Arabs were defending their home against invading Zionists. There were still more Arab Palestinians than Jewish Israelis. counting the exiles in the camps; and it was *they*, not a rabble of soldiers from Cairo and Damascus, who would liberate the homeland. But first they had to believe in the Fedayeen. Acts such as the Rome airport affair would convince them that the Fedayeen had international resources. And when the people believed in the Fedayeen, the people would be the Fedayeen, and then they would be unstoppable.

The Rome airport affair was trivial, a peccadillo, by comparison with what Hassan had in mind.

It was an outrageous, mind-boggling scheme that would put the Fedayeen on the front pages of the world's newspapers for weeks and prove that they were a powerful international force, not a bunch of ragged refugees. Hassan hoped desperately that Mahmoud would accept it.

Yasif Hassan had come to propose that the Fedayeen should hijack a holocaust.

They embraced like brothers, kissing cheeks, then stood back to look at one another.

'You smell like a whore,' said Mahmoud.

'You smell like a goatherd,' said Hassan. They laughed and embraced again.

Mahmoud was a big man, a fraction taller than Hassan and much broader; and he *looked* big, the way he held his head and walked and spoke. He did smell, too: a sour familiar smell that came from living very close to many people in a place that lacked the modern inventions of hot baths and sanitation and garbage disposal. It was three days since Hassan had used after-shave and talcum powder, but he still smelled like a scented woman to Mahmoud.

The house had two rooms: the one Hassan had entered, and behind that another, where Mahmoud slept on the floor with two other men. There was no upper storey. Cooking was done in a yard at the back, and the nearest water supply was one hundred yards away. The woman lit a fire and began to make a porridge of crushed beans. While they waited for it, Hassan told Mahmoud his story.

'Three months ago in Luxembourg I met a man I had known at Oxford, a Jew called Dickstein. It turns out he is a big Mossad operative. Since then I have been watching him, with the help of the Russians, in particular a KGB man named Rostov. We have discovered that Dickstein plans to steal a shipload of uranium so the Zionists will be able to make atom bombs.'

At first Mahmoud refused to believe this. He cross-questioned Hassan: how good was the information, what exactly was the evidence, who might be lying, what mistakes might have been made? Then, as Hassan's answers made more and more sense, the truth began to sink in, and Mahmoud became very grave.

'This is not only a threat to the Palestinian cause. These bombs could ravage the whole of the Middle East.'

It was like him, Hassan thought, to see the big picture.

'What do you and this Russian propose to do?' Mahmoud asked.

'The plan is to stop Dickstein and expose the Israeli plot, showing the Zionists to be lawless adventurers. We haven't worked out the details yet. But I have an alternative proposal.' He paused, trying to form the right phrases, then blurted it out. 'I think the Fedayeen should hijack the ship before Dickstein gets there.'

Mahmoud stared blankly at him for a long moment.

Hassan thought: Say something, for God's sake! Mahmoud began to shake his head from side to side slowly, then his mouth widened in a smile, and at last he began to laugh, beginning with a small chuckle and finishing up giving a huge, body-shaking bellow that brought the rest of the household around to see what was happening.

Hassan ventured, 'But what do you think?'

Mahmoud sighed. 'It's wonderful,' he said. 'I don't see how we can do it, but it's a wonderful idea.'

Then he started asking questions.

He asked questions all through breakfast and for most of the morning: the quantity of uranium, the names of the ships involved, how the yellowcake was converted into nuclear explosive, places and dates and people. They talked in the back room, just the two of them for most of the time, but occasionally Mahmoud would call someone in and tell him to listen while Hassan repeated some particular point.

About midday he summoned two men who seemed to be his lieutenants. With them listening, he again went over the points he thought crucial.

'The *Coparelli* is an ordinary merchant ship with a regular crew?'

'Yes.'

'She will be sailing through the Mediterranean to Genoa.'

'Yes.'

'What does this yellowcake weigh?'

'Two hundred tons.'

'And it is packed in drums.'

'Five hundred and sixty of them.'

'Its market price?'

'Two million American dollars.'

'And it is used to make nuclear bombs.'

'Yes. Well, it is the raw material.'

'Is the conversion to the explosive form an expensive or difficult process?'

'Not if you've got a nuclear reactor. Otherwise, yes.'

Mahmoud nodded to the two lieutenants. 'Go and tell this to the others.'

In the afternoon, when the sun was past its zenith and it was cool enough to go out, Mahmoud and Yasif walked over the hills outside the town. Yasif was desperate to know what Mahmoud really thought of his plan, but Mahmoud refused to talk about uranium. So Yasif spoke about David Rostov and said that he admired the Russian's professionalism despite the difficulties he had made for him.

'It is well to admire the Russians,' Mahmoud said, 'so long as we do not trust them. Their heart is not in our cause. There are three reasons why they take our side. The least important is that we cause trouble for the West, and anything that is bad for the West is good for the Russians. Then there is their image. The underdeveloped nations identify with us rather than with the Zionists, so by supporting us the Russians gain credit with the Third World – and remember, in the contest between the United States and the Soviet Union the Third World has all the floating voters. But the most important reason – the only *really* important reason – is oil. The Arabs have oil.'

They passed a boy tending a small flock of bony sheep. The boy was playing a flute. Yasif remembered that Mahmoud had once been a shepherd boy who could neither read nor write.

'Do you understand how important oil is?' Mahmoud said. 'Hitler lost the European war because of oil.'

'No.'

'Listen. The Russians defeated Hitler. They were bound to. Hitler knew this: he knew about Napoleon, he knew nobody could conquer Russia. So why did he try? He was running out of oil. There is oil in Georgia, in the Caucasian oilfields. Hitler had to have the Caucasus. But you cannot hold the Caucasus secure unless you have Volgograd, which was then called Stalingrad, the place where the tide turned against Hitler. Oil. That's what our struggle is about, whether we like it or not, do you realize that? If it were not for oil, nobody but us would care about a few Arabs and Jews fighting over a dusty little country like ours.'

Mahmoud was magnetic when he talked. His strong, clear voice rolled out short phrases, simple explanations, statements that sounded like devastating basic truths: Hassan suspected he said these same things often to his troops. In the back of his mind he remembered the sophisticated ways in which politics were discussed in places like Luxembourg and Oxford, and it seemed to him now that for all their mountains of information those people knew less than Mahmoud. He knew, too, that international politics were complicated: that there was more than oil behind these things, yet at bottom he believed Mahmoud was right.

They sat in the shade of a fig tree. The smooth, dun-coloured landscape stretched all around them, empty. The sky glared hot and blue, cloudless from one horizon to the other. Mahmoud uncorked a water bottle and gave it to Hassan, who drank the tepid liquid and handed it back. Then he asked Mahmoud whether he wanted to rule Palestine after the Zionists were beaten back.

'I have killed many people,' Mahmoud said. 'At first I did it with my own hands, with a knife or a gun or a bomb. Now I kill by devising plans and giving orders, but I kill them still. We know this is a sin, but I cannot repent. I have no remorse, Yasif. Even if we make a mistake, and we kill children and Arabs instead of soldiers and Zionists, still I think only, "This is bad for our reputation," not, "This is bad for my soul." There is blood on my hands, and I will not wash it off. I will not try. There is a story called *The Picture of Dorian Gray*. It is about a man who leads an evil and debilitating life, the kind of life that should make him look old, give him lines on his face and bags under his eyes, a destroyed liver and venereal disease. Still, he does not suffer. Indeed, as the years go by he seems to stay young, as if he had found the elixir of life. But in a locked room in his house there is a painting of him, and it is the picture that ages, and takes on the ravages of evil living and terrible disease. Do you know the story? It is English.'

'I saw the movie,' said Yasif.

'I read it when I was in Moscow. I would like to see that film. Do you remember how it ended?'

'Oh, yes. Dorian Gray destroyed the painting, and then all the disease and damage fell on him in an instant, and he died.'

'Yes.' Mahmoud put the stopper back in the bottle,

and looked out over the brown hillsides with unseeing eyes. Then he said, 'When Palestine is free, my picture will be destroyed.'

After that they sat in silence for a while. Eventually, without speaking, they stood up and began to walk back to the town.

Several men came to the little house in Nablus that evening at dusk, just before curfew. Hassan did not know who they were exactly: they might have been the local leaders of the movement, or an assorted group of people whose judgment Mahmoud respected, or a permanent council of war that stayed close to Mahmoud but did not actually live with him. Hassan could see the logic in the last alternative, for if they all lived together, they could all be destroyed together.

The woman gave them bread and fish and watery wine, and Mahmoud told them of Hassan's scheme. Mahmoud had thought it through more thoroughly than Hassan. He proposed that they hijack the *Coparelli* before Dickstein got there, then ambush the Israelis as they came aboard. Expecting only an ordinary crew and halfhearted resistance, Dickstein's group would be wiped out. Then the Fedayeen would take the *Coparelli* to a North African port and invite the world to come aboard and see the bodies of the Zionist criminals. The cargo would be offered to its owners for a ransom of half its market price – one million U.S. dollars.

There was a long debate. Clearly a faction of the

movement was already nervous about Mahmoud's policy of taking the war into Europe, and saw the proposed hijack as a further extension of the same strategy. They suggested that the Fedayeen could achieve most of what they wanted simply by calling a press conference in Beirut or Damascus and revealing the Israeli plot to the international press. Hassan was convinced that was not enough: accusations were cheap, and it was not the lawlessness of Israel that had to be demonstrated, it was the power of the Fedayeen.

They spoke as equals, and Mahmoud seemed to listen to each with the same attention. Hassan sat quietly, hearing the low, calm voices of these people who looked like peasants and spoke like senators. He was at once hopeful and fearful that they would adopt his plan: hopeful because it would be the fulfilment of twenty years of vengeful dreams; fearful because it would mean he would have to do things more difficult, violent and risky than the work he had been involved in so far.

In the end he could not stand it any longer and he went outside and squatted in the mean yard, smelling the night and the dying fire. A little later there was a chorus of quiet voices from inside, like voting.

Mahmoud came out and sat beside Hassan. 'I have sent for a car.'

'Oh?'

'We must go to Damascus. Tonight. There is a lot to do. It will be our biggest operation. We must start work immediately.'

'It is decided, then.'

'Yes. The Fedayeen will hijack the ship and steal the uranium.'

'So be it,' said Yasif Hassan.

David Rostov had always liked his family in small doses, and as he got older the doses got smaller. The first day of his holiday was fine. He made breakfast, they walked along the beach, and in the afternoon Vladimir, the young genius, played chess against Rostov, Mariya, and Yuri simultaneously, and won all three games. They took hours over supper, catching up on all the news and drinking a little wine. The second day was similar, but they enjoyed it less; and by the third day the novelty of each other's company had worn off. Vladimir remembered he was supposed to be a prodigy and stuck his nose back into his books; Yuri began to play degenerate Western music on the record player and argued with his father about dissident poets; and Mariya fled into the kitchen of the dacha and stopped putting make-up on her face.

So when the message came to say that Nik Bunin was back from Rotterdam and had successfully bugged the *Stromberg*, Rostov used that as an excuse to return to Moscow.

Nik reported that the *Stromberg* had been in dry dock for the usual inspection prior to completion of the sale to Savile Shipping. A number of small repairs were in progress, and without difficulty Nik had got on board, posing as an electrician, and planted a powerful radio beacon in the prow of the ship. On leaving he had been questioned by the dock foreman, who did not have any electrical work on his schedule for that day; and Nik had pointed out that if the work had not been requested, no doubt it would not have to be paid for.

From that moment, whenever the ship's power was on – which was all the time she was at sea and most of the time she was in dock – the beacon would send out a signal every thirty minutes until the ship sank or was broken up for scrap. For the rest of her life, wherever in the world she was, Moscow would be able to locate her within an hour.

Rostov listened to Nik, then sent him home. He had plans for the evening. It was a long time since he had seen Olga, and he was impatient to see what she would do with the battery-operated vibrator he had brought her as a present from London.

In Israeli Naval Intelligence there was a young captain named Dieter Koch who had trained as a ship's engineer. When the *Coparelli* sailed from Antwerp with her cargo of yellowcake Koch had to be aboard.

Nat Dickstein reached Antwerp with only the vaguest idea of how this was to be achieved. From his hotel room he phoned the local representative of the company that owned the *Coparelli*.

When I die, he thought as he waited for the connection, they will bury me from a hotel room.

A girl answered the phone. Dickstein said briskly, 'This is Pierre Beaudaire, give me the director.'

'Hold on, please.'

A man's voice, 'Yes?'

'Good morning, this is Pierre Beaudaire from the Beaudaire Crew List.' Dickstein was making it up as he went along.

'Never heard of you.'

'That's why I'm calling you. You see, we're contemplating opening an office in Antwerp, and I'm wondering whether you would be willing to try us.'

'I doubt it, but you can write to me and—'

'Are you completely satisfied with your present crew agency?'

'They could be worse. Look here—'

'One more question and I won't trouble you further. May I ask whom you use at the moment?'

'Cohen's. Now, I haven't any more time—'

'I understand. Thank you for your patience. Goodbye.'

Cohen's! That was a piece of luck. Perhaps I will be able to do this bit without brutality, Dickstein thought as he put down the phone. Cohen! It was unexpected – docks and shipping were not typical Jewish business. Well, sometimes you got lucky.

He looked up Cohen's crew agency in the phone book, memorized the address, put on his coat, left the hotel and hailed a cab. Cohen had a little two-room office above a sailor's bar in the red-light district of the city. It was not yet midday, and the night people were still asleep – the whores and thieves, musicians and strippers and waiters and bouncers, the people who made the place come to life in the evening. Now it might have been any run-down business district, grey and cold in the morning, and none too clean.

Dickstein went up a staircase to a first-floor door, knocked and went in. A middle-aged secretary presided over a small reception room furnished with filing cabinets and orange plastic chairs.

'I'd like to see Mr Cohen,' Dickstein told her.

She looked him over and seemed to think he did not appear to be a sailor. 'Are you wanting a ship?' she said doubtfully.

'No,' he said. 'I'm from Israel.'

'Oh.' She hesitated. She had dark hair and deep-set, shadowed eyes, and she wore a wedding ring. Dickstein wondered if she might be Mrs Cohen. She got up and went through a door behind her desk into the inner office. She was wearing a pants suit, and from behind she looked her age.

A minute later she reappeared and ushered him into Cohen's office. Cohen stood up, shook hands and said without preamble, 'I give to the cause every year. In the war I gave twenty thousand guilders, I can show you the cheque. This is some new appeal? There is another war?'

'I'm not here to raise money, Mr Cohen,' Dickstein said with a smile. Mrs Cohen had left the door open: Dickstein closed it. 'Can I sit down?'

'If you don't want money, sit down, have some coffee, stay all day,' said Cohen, and he laughed.

Dickstein sat. Cohen was a short man in spectacles, bald and clean-shaven, and looked to be about fifty years old. He wore a brown check suit that was not very new. He had a good little business here, Dickstein guessed, but he was no millionaire.

Dickstein said, 'Were you here in World War II?'

Cohen nodded. 'I was a young man. I went into the country and worked on a farm where nobody knew me, nobody knew I was Jewish. I was lucky.'

'Do you think it will happen again?'

'Yes. It's happened all through history, why should it stop now? It will happen again – but not in my lifetime. It's all right here. I don't want to go to Israel.'

'Okay. I work for the government of Israel. We would like you to do something for us.'

Cohen shrugged. 'So?'

'In a few weeks' time, one of your clients will call you with an urgent request. They will want an engineer officer for a ship called *Coparelli*. We would like you to send them a man supplied by us. His name is Koch, and he is an Israeli, but he will be using a different name and false papers. However, he *is* a ship's engineer – your clients will not be dissatisfied.'

Dickstein waited for Cohen to say something. You're a nice man, he thought; a decent Jewish businessman, smart and hardworking and a little frayed at the edges; don't make me get tough with you.

Cohen said, 'You're not going to tell me why the government of Israel wants this man Koch aboard the *Coparelli*?'

'No.'

There was a silence.

'You carry any identification?'

'No.'

The secretary came in without knocking and gave them coffee. Dickstein got hostile vibrations from her. Cohen used the interruption to gather his thoughts. When she had gone out he said, 'I would have to be *meshugenah* to do this.'

'Why?'

'You come in off the street saying you represent the government of Israel, yet you have no identification, you don't even tell me your name. You ask me to take part in something that is obviously underhanded and probably criminal; you will not tell me what it is that you're trying to do. Even if I believe your story, I don't know that I would approve of the Israelis doing what you want to do.'

Dickstein sighed, thinking of the alternatives: blackmail him, kidnap his wife, take over his office on the crucial day . . . He said, 'Is there anything I can do to convince you?'

'I would need a personal request from the Prime Minister of Israel before I would do this thing.'

Dickstein stood up to leave, then he thought: Why not? Why the hell not? It was a wild idea, they would think he was crazy . . . but it would work, it would serve the purpose . . . He grinned as he thought it through. Pierre Borg would have apoplexy.

He said to Cohen, 'All right.'

'What do you mean, "all right"?'

'Put on your coat. We'll go to Jerusalem.'

'Now?'

'Are you busy?'

'Are you serious?'

'I told you it's important.' Dickstein pointed to the phone on the desk. 'Call your wife.'

'She's just outside.'

Dickstein went to the door and opened it. 'Mrs Cohen?'

'Yes.'

'Would you come in here, please?'

She hurried in, looking worried. 'What is it, Josef?' she asked her husband.

'This man wants me to go to Jerusalem with him.'

'When?'

'Now.'

'You mean this week?'

Dickstein said, 'I mean this morning, Mrs Cohen. I must tell you that all this is highly confidential. I've asked your husband to do something for the Israeli government. Naturally he wants to be certain that it is the government that is asking this favour and not some criminal. So I'm going to take him there to convince him.'

She said, 'Don't get involved, Josef—'

Cohen shrugged. 'I'm Jewish, I'm involved already. Mind the shop.'

'You don't know anything about this man!'

'So I'm going to find out.'

'I don't like it.'

'There's no danger,' Cohen told her. 'We'll take a scheduled flight, we'll go to Jerusalem. I'll see the Prime Minister and we'll come back.'

'The Prime Minister!' Dickstein realized how proud

338

she would be if her husband met the Prime Minister of Israel. He said, 'This has to be secret. Mrs Cohen. Please tell people your husband has gone to Rotterdam on business. He will be back tomorrow.'

She stared at the two of them. 'My Josef meets the Prime Minister, and I can't tell Rachel Rothstein?'

Then Dickstein knew it was going to be all right.

Cohen took his coat from a hook and put it on. Mrs Cohen kissed him, then put her arms around him.

'It's all right,' he told her. 'This is very sudden and strange, but it's all right.'

She nodded dumbly and let him go.

They took a cab to the airport. Dickstein's sense of delight grew as they travelled. The scheme had an air of mischief about it, he felt a bit like a schoolboy, this was a terrific prank. He kept grinning, and had to turn his face away so that Cohen would not see.

Pierre Borg would go through the *roof*.

Dickstein bought two round-trip tickets to Tel Aviv, paying with his credit card. They had to take a connecting flight to Paris. Before they took off he called the embassy in Paris and arranged for someone to meet them in the transit lounge.

In Paris he gave the man from the embassy a message to send to Borg, explaining what was required. The diplomat was a Mossad man, and treated Dickstein with deference. Cohen was allowed to listen to the conversation, and when the man had gone back to the embassy he said, 'We could go back. I'm convinced already.'

'Oh, no,' Dickstein said. 'Now that we've come this far I want to be sure of you.'

On the plane Cohen said, 'You must be an important man in Israel.'

'No. But what I'm doing is important.'

Cohen wanted to know how to behave, how to address the Prime Minister. Dickstein told him, 'I don't know, I've never met him. Shake hands and call him by his name.'

Cohen smiled. He was beginning to share Dickstein's feeling of mischievousness.

Pierre Borg met them at Lod Airport with a car to take them to Jerusalem. He smiled and shook hands with Cohen, but he was seething underneath. As they walked to the car he muttered to Dickstein, 'You better have a fucking good reason for all this.'

'I have.'

They were with Cohen all the while, so Borg did not have an opportunity to cross-examine Dickstein. They went straight to the Prime Minister's residence in Jerusalem. Dickstein and Cohen waited in an anteroom while Borg explained to the Prime Minister what was required and why.

A couple of minutes later they were admitted. 'This is Nat Dickstein, sir,' Borg said.

They shook hands, and the Prime Minister said, 'We haven't met before, but I've heard of you, Mr Dickstein.'

Borg said, 'And this is Mr Josef Cohen of Antwerp.'

'Mr Cohen.' The Prime Minister smiled. 'You're a very cautious man. You should be a politician. Well, now . . . please do this thing for us. It is very important, and you will come to no harm from it.'

Cohen was bedazzled. 'Yes, sir, of course I will do this, I'm sorry to have caused so much trouble . . .'

'Not at all. You did the right thing.' He shook Cohen's hand again. 'Thank you for coming. Goodbye.'

Borg was less polite on the way back to the airport. He sat silent in the front seat of the car, smoking a cigar and fidgeting. At the airport he managed to get Dickstein alone for a minute. 'If you ever pull a stunt like this again . . .'

'It was necessary,' Dickstein said. 'It took less than a minute. Why not?'

'Why not, is because half my fucking department has been working all day to fix that minute. Why didn't you just point a gun at the man's head or something?'

'Because we're not barbarians,' Dickstein said.

'So people keep telling me.'

'They do? That's a bad sign.'

'Why?'

'Because you shouldn't need to be told.'

Then their flight was called. Boarding the plane with Cohen, Dickstein reflected that his relationship with Borg was in ruins. They had always talked like this, with bantering insults, but until now there had been an undertone of . . . perhaps not affection, but at least respect. Now that had vanished. Borg was genuinely hostile. Dickstein's refusal to be pulled out was a piece of basic defiance which could not be tolerated. If Dickstein had wanted to continue in the Mossad, he would have had to fight Borg for the job of director –

there was no longer sufficient room for both men in the organization. But there would be no contest now, for Dickstein was going to resign.

Flying back to Europe through the night, Cohen drank some gin and went to sleep. Dickstein ran over in his mind the work he had done in the past five months. Back in May he had started out with no real idea of how he was going to steal the uranium Israel needed. He had taken the problems as they came up, and found a solution to each one: how to locate uranium, which uranium to steal, how to hijack a ship, how to camouflage the Israeli involvement in the theft, how to prevent the disappearance of the uranium being reported to the authorities, how to placate the owners of the stuff. If he had sat down at the beginning and tried to dream up the whole scheme he could never have foreseen all the complications.

He had had some good luck and some bad. The fact that the owners of the *Coparelli* used a Jewish crew agency in Antwerp was a piece of luck; so was the existence of a consignment of uranium for non-nuclear purposes, and one going by sea. The bad luck mainly consisted of the accidental meeting with Yasif Hassan.

Hassan, the fly in the ointment. Dickstein was reasonably certain he had shaken off the opposition when he flew to Buffalo to see Cortone, and that they had not picked up his trail again since. But that did not mean they had dropped the case.

It would be useful to know how much they had found out before they lost him.

Dickstein could not see Suza again until the whole

affair was over, and Hassan was to blame for that too. If he were to go to Oxford, Hassan was sure to pick up the trail somehow.

The plane began its descent. Dickstein fastened his seat belt. It was all done now, the scheme in place, the preparations made. The cards had been dealt. He knew what was in his hand, and he knew some of his opponents' cards, and they knew some of his. All that remained was to play out the game, and no one could foretell the outcome. He wished he could see the future more clearly, he wished his plan were less complicated, he wished he did not have to risk his life once more, and he wished the game would start so that he could stop wishing and start doing things.

Cohen was awake. 'Did I dream all that?' he said.

'No.' Dickstein smiled. There was one more unpleasant duty he had to perform: he had to scare Cohen half to death. 'I told you this was important, and secret.'

'Of course, I understand.'

'You don't understand. If you talk about this to anyone other than your wife, we will take drastic action.'

'Is that a threat? What are you saying?'

'I'm saying, if you don't keep your mouth shut, we will kill your wife.'

Cohen stared, and went pale. After a moment he turned away and looked out of the window at the airport coming up to meet them.

CHAPTER THIRTEEN

MOSCOW'S HOTEL Rossiya was the largest hotel in Europe. It had 5,738 beds, ten miles of corridors, and no air-conditioning.

Yasif Hassan slept very badly there.

It was simple to say, 'The Fedayeen should hijack the ship before Dickstein gets there,' but the more he thought about it, the more terrified he was.

The Palestine Liberation Organization in 1968 was not the tightly-knit political entity it pretended to be. It was not even a loose federation of individual groups working together. It was more like a club for people with a common interest: it represented its members, but it did not control them. The individual guerrilla groups could speak with one voice through the PLO, but they did not and could not act as one. So when Mahmoud said the Fedayeen would do something, he spoke only for his own group. Furthermore, in this case it would be unwise even to ask for PLO cooperation. The organization was given money, facilities and a home by the Egyptians, but it had also been infiltrated by them: if you wanted to keep something secret from the Arab establishment, you had to keep it secret from the PLO. Of course, after the coup, when the world's press came to look over the captured ship with its atomic cargo, the Egyptians would know and would probably suspect that the Fedayeen had deliberately thwarted them, but Mahmoud would play innocent and the Egyptians would be obliged to join in the general acclamation of the Fedayeen for frustrating an Israeli act of aggression.

Anyway, Mahmoud believed he did not need the help of the others. His group had the best connections outside Palestine, the best European set-up, and plenty of money. He was now in Benghazi arranging to borrow a ship while his international team was gathered up from various parts of the world.

But the most crucial task devolved on Hassan: if the Fedayeen were to get to the *Coparelli* before the Israelis, he would have to establish exactly when and where Dickstein's hijack was to take place. For that, he needed the KGB.

He felt terribly uneasy around Rostov now. Until his visit to Mahmoud he had been able to tell himself he was working for two organizations with a common objective. Now he was indisputably a double agent, merely pretending to work with the Egyptians and the KGB while he sabotaged their plans. He felt different – he felt a traitor, in a way – and he was afraid that Rostov would observe the difference in him.

When Hassan had flown in to Moscow Rostov himself had been uneasy. He had said there was not enough room in his apartment for Hassan to stay, although Hassan knew the rest of the family were away on holiday. It seemed Rostov was hiding something.

Hassan suspected he was seeing some woman and did not want his colleague getting in the way.

After his restless night at the Hotel Rossiya, Hassan met Rostov at the KGB building on the Moscow ring road, in the office of Rostov's boss, Feliks Vorontsov. There were undercurrents there too. The two men were having an argument when Hassan entered the room, and although they broke it off immediately the air was stiff with unspoken hostility. Hassan, however, was too busy with his own clandestine moves to pay much attention to theirs.

He sat down. 'Have there been any developments?'

Rostov and Vorontsov looked at one another. Rostov shrugged. Vorontsov said, 'The *Stromberg* has been fitted with a very powerful radio beacon. She's out of dry dock now and heading south across the Bay of Biscay. The assumption would be that she is going to Haifa to take on a crew of Mossad agents. I think we can all be quite satisfied with our intelligence-gathering work. The project now falls into the sphere of positive action. Our task becomes prescriptive rather than descriptive, as it were.'

'They all talk like this in Moscow Centre,' Rostov said irreverently. Vorontsov glared at him.

Hassan said, 'What action?'

'Rostov here is going to Odessa to board a Polish merchant ship called the *Karla*,' Vorontsov said. 'She's an ordinary cargo vessel superficially, but she's very fast and has certain extra equipment – we use her quite often.'

Rostov was staring up at the ceiling, an expression of

mild distaste on his face. Hassan guessed that Rostov wanted to keep some of these details from the Egyptians: perhaps that was what he and Vorontsov had been arguing about.

Vorontsov went on, 'Your job is to get an Egyptian vessel and make contact with the *Karla* in the Mediterranean.'

'And then?' Hassan said.

'We wait for Tyrin, aboard the *Coparelli*, to tell us when the Israeli hijack takes place. He will also tell us whether the uranium is transferred from the *Coparelli* to the *Stromberg*, or simply left aboard the *Coparelli* to be taken to Haifa and unloaded.'

'And then?' Hassan persisted.

Vorontsov began to speak, but Rostov forestalled him. 'I want you to tell Cairo a cover story,' he said to Hassan. 'I want your people to think that we don't know about the *Coparelli*, we just know the Israelis are planning something in the Mediterranean and we are still trying to discover what.'

Hassan nodded, keeping his face impassive. He had to know what the plan was, and Rostov did not want to tell him! He said, 'Yes, I'll tell them that – if you tell me the actual plan.'

Rostov looked at Voronstov and shrugged. Vorontsov said, 'After the hijack the *Karla* will set a course for Dickstein's ship, whichever one carries the uranium. The *Karla* will collide with that ship.'

'Collide!'

'Your ship will witness the collision, report it, and observe that the crew of the vessel are Israelis and their cargo is uranium. You will report these facts too. There will be an international inquiry into the collision. The presence of both Israelis and stolen uranium on the ship will be established beyond doubt. Meanwhile the uranium will be returned to its rightful owners and the Israelis will be covered with opprobrium.'

'The Israelis will fight,' Hassan said.

Rostov said, 'So much the better, with your ship there to see them attack us and help us beat them off.'

'It's a good plan,' said Vorontsov. 'It's simple. All they have to do is crash – the rest follows automatically.'

'Yes, it's a good plan,' Hassan said. It fitted in perfectly with the Fedayeen plan. Unlike Dickstein, Hassan knew that Tyrin was aboard the *Coparelli*. After the Fedayeen had hijacked the *Coparelli* and ambushed the Israelis, they could throw Tyrin and his radio into the sea, then Rostov would have no way of locating them.

But Hassan needed to know when and where Dickstein intended to carry out his hijack so that the Fedayeen could be sure of getting there first.

Vorontsov's office was hot. Hassan went to the window and looked down at the traffic on the Moscow ring road. 'We need to know exactly when and where Dickstein will hijack the *Coparelli*,' he said.

'Why?' Rostov asked, making a gesture with both arms spread, palms upward. 'We have Tyrin aboard the *Coparelli* and a beacon on the *Stromberg*. We know where both of them are at all times. We need only to stay close and move in when the time comes.'

'My ship has to be in the right area at the crucial time.'

'Then follow the *Stromberg*, staying just over the horizon – you can pick up her radio signal. Or keep in touch with me on the *Karla*. Or both.'

'Suppose the beacon fails, or Tyrin is discovered?'

Rostov said, 'The risk of that must be weighed against the danger of tipping our hand if we start following Dickstein around again – assuming we could find him.'

'He has a point, though,' Vorontsov said.

It was Rostov's turn to glare.

Hassan unbuttoned his collar. 'May I open a window?'

'They don't open,' said Vorontsov.

'Haven't you people heard of air-conditioning?'

'In Moscow?'

Hassan turned and spoke to Rostov. 'Think about it. I want to be perfectly sure we nail these people.'

'I've thought about it,' Rostov said. 'We're as sure as we can be. Go back to Cairo, organize that ship and stay in touch with me.'

You patronizing bastard, Hassan thought. He turned to Vorontsov. 'I cannot, in all honesty, tell my people I'm happy with the plan unless we can eliminate that remaining uncertainty.'

Vorontsov said, 'I agree with Hassan.'

'Well, I don't,' said Rostov. 'And the plan as it stands has already been approved by Andropov.'

Until now Hassan had thought he was going to have his way, since Vorontsov was on his side and Vorontsov was Rostov's boss. But the mention of the Chairman of the KGB seemed to constitute a winning move in this game: Vorontsov was almost cowed by it, and once again Hassan had to conceal his desperation.

Vorontsov said, 'The plan can be changed.'

'Only with Andropov's approval,' Rostov said. 'And you won't get my support for the change.'

Vorontsov's lips were compressed into a thin line. He hates Rostov, thought Hassan; and so do I.

Vorontsov said, 'Very well, then.'

In all his time in the intelligence business Hassan had been part of a professional team – Egyptian Intelligence, the KGB, even the Fedayeen. There had been other people, experienced and decisive people, to give him orders and guidance and to take ultimate responsibility. Now, as he left the KGB building to return to his hotel, he realized he was on his own.

Alone, he had to find a remarkably elusive and clever man and discover his most closely guarded secret.

For several days he was in a panic. He returned to Cairo, told them Rostov's cover story, and organized the Egyptian ship Rostov had requested. The problem stayed in front of his mind like a sheer cliff he could not begin to climb until he saw at least part of the route to the top. Unconsciously he searched back in his personal history for attitudes and approaches which would enable him to tackle such a task, to act independently.

He had to go a long way back.

Once upon a time Yasif Hassan had been a different

kind of man. He had been a wealthy, almost aristocratic young Arab with the world at his feet. He had gone about with the attitude that he could do more or less anything – and thinking had made it so. He had gone to study in England, an alien country, without a qualm; and he had entered its society without caring or even wondering what people thought of him.

There had been times, even then, when he had to learn; but he did that easily too. Once a fellow under-graduate, a Viscount something-or-other, had invited him down to the country to play polo. Hassan had never played polo. He had asked the rules and watched the others play for a while, noticing how they held the mallets, how they hit the ball, how they passed it and why; then he had joined in. He was clumsy with the mallet but he could ride like the wind: he played passably well, he thoroughly enjoyed the game, and his team won.

Now, in 1968, he said to himself: I can do anything, but whom shall I emulate?

The answer, of course, was David Rostov.

Rostov was independent, confident, capable. bril-liant. He could find Dickstein, even when it seemed he was stumped, clueless, up a blind alley. He had done it twice. Hassan recalled:

Question: Why is Dickstein in Luxembourg?

Well, what do we know about Luxembourg? What is there here?

There is the stock exchange, the banks, the Council of Europe, Euratom –

Euratom!

Question: Dickstein has disappeared – where might he have gone?

Don't know.

But who do we know that he knows?

Only Professor Ashford in Oxford—

Oxford!

Rostov's approach was to search out bits of information – *any* information, no matter how trivial – in order to get on the target. The trouble was, they seemed to have used all the bits of information they had.

So I'll get some more, Hassan thought; I can do anything.

He racked his brains for all that he could remember from the time they had been at Oxford together. Dickstein had been in the war, he played chess, his clothes were shabby –

He had a mother.

But she had died.

Hassan had never met any brothers or sisters, no relatives of any sort. It was all such a long time ago, and they had not been very close even then.

There was, however, someone else who might know a little more about Dickstein: Professor Ashford.

So, in desperation, Yasif Hassan went back to Oxford.

All the way – in the plane from Cairo, the taxi from London airport to Paddington Station, the train to Oxford and the taxi to the little green-and-white house by the river – he wondered about Ashford. The truth was, he despised the professor. In his youth perhaps he had been an adventurer, but he had become a weak old man, a political dilettante, an academic who could not even hold his wife. One could not respect an old cuckold – and the fact that the English did not think like that only increased Hassan's contempt.

He worried that Ashford's weakness, together with some kind of loyalty to Dickstein as one who had been a friend and a student, might make him balk at getting involved.

He wondered whether to play up to the fact that Dickstein was Jewish. He knew from his time at Oxford that the most enduring anti-Semitism in England was that of the upper classes: the London clubs that still blackballed Jews were in the West End, not the East End. But Ashford was an exception there. He loved the Middle East, and his pro-Arab stance was ethical, not racial, in motivation. No: that approach would be a mistake.

In the end he decided to play it straight; to tell Ashford why he wanted to find Dickstein, and hope that Ashford would agree to help for the same reasons.

When they had shaken hands and poured sherry, they sat down in the garden and Ashford said, 'What brings you back to England so soon?'

Hassan told the truth. 'I'm chasing Nat Dickstein.'

They were sitting by the river in the little corner of the garden that was cut off by the hedge, where Hassan had kissed the beautiful Eila so many years ago. The corner was sheltered from the October wind, and there was a little autumn sunshine to warm them.

Ashford was guarded, wary, his face expressionless. 'I think you'd better tell me what's going on.'

Hassan observed that during the summer the professor had actually yielded a little to fashion. He had cultivated side-whiskers and allowed his monkish fringe of hair to grow long, and was wearing denim jeans with a wide leather belt beneath his old tweed jacket.

'I'll tell you,' Hassan said, with an awful feeling that Rostov would have been more subtle than this, 'but I must have your word that it will go no farther.'

'Agreed.'

'Dickstein is an Israeli spy.'

Ashford's eyes narrowed, but he said nothing.

Hassan plunged on. 'The Zionists are planning to make nuclear bombs but they have no plutonium. They need a secret supply of uranium to feed to their reactor to make plutonium. Dickstein's job is to steal that uranium – and my job is to find him and stop him. I want you to help me.'

Ashford stared into his sherry, then drained the glass at a gulp. 'There are two questions at issue here,' he said, and Hassan realized that Ashford was going to treat this as an intellectual problem, the characteristic defence of the frightened academic. 'One is whether or not I *can* help; the other, whether or not I *should*. The latter is prior, I think; morally, anyway.'

Hassan thought: I'd like to pick you up by the scruff

of the neck and shake you. Maybe I can do that, at least figuratively. He said, 'Of course you *should*. You believe in our cause.'

'It's not so simple. I'm asked to interfere in a contest between two people, both of whom are my friends.'

'But only one of them is in the right.'

'So I should help the one who is in the right – and betray the one who is in the wrong?'

'Of course.'

'There isn't any "of course" about it . . . What will you do, if and when you find Dickstein?'

'I'm with Egyptian Intelligence, professor. But my loyalty – and, I believe, yours – lies with Palestine.'

Ashford refused to take the bait. 'Go on,' he said noncommittally.

'I have to find out exactly when and where Dickstein plans to steal this uranium.' Hassan hesitated. 'The Fedayeen will get there before Dickstein and steal it for themselves.'

Ashford's eyes glittered. 'My God,' he said. 'How marvellous.'

He's almost there, Hassan thought. He's frightened, but he's excited too. 'It's easy for you to be loyal to Palestine, here in Oxford, giving lectures, going to meetings. Things are a little more difficult for those of us who are out there fighting for the country. I'm here to ask you to do something concrete about your politics, to decide whether your ideals mean anything or not. This is where you and I find out whether the Arab cause is anything more to you than a romantic concept. This is the test, professor.'

Ashford said, 'Perhaps you're right.'

And Hassan thought: I've got you.

Suza had decided to tell her father that she was in love with Nat Dickstein.

At first she had not been sure of it herself, not really. The few days they had spent together in London had been wild and happy and loving, but afterwards she had realized that those feelings could be transient. She had resolved to make no resolutions. She would carry on normally and see how things turned out.

Something had happened in Singapore to change her mind. Two of the cabin stewards on the trip were gay, and used only one of the two hotel rooms allotted to them; so the crew could use the other room for a party. At the party the pilot had made a pass at Suza. He was a quiet, smiling blond man with delicate bones and a delightfully wacky sense of humour. The steward-esses all agreed he was a piece of ass. Normally Suza would have got into bed with him without thinking twice. But she had said no, astonishing the whole crew. Thinking about it later, she decided that she no longer wanted to get laid. She had just gone off the whole idea. All she wanted was Nathaniel. It was like . . . it was a bit like five years ago when the second Beatles album came out, and she had gone through her pile of records by Elvis and Roy Orbison and the Everly Brothers and realized that she did not want to play them, they held no more enchantment for her, the old familiar tunes had been heard once too often, and now she wanted music of a higher order. Well, it was a bit like that, but more so.

Dickstein's letter had been the clincher. It had been written God knew where and posted at Orly Airport, Paris. In his small neat handwriting with its incongruously curly loops on the *g* and *y* he had poured out his heart in a manner that was all the more devastating because it came from a normally taciturn man. She had cried over that letter.

She wished she could think of a way to explain all that to her father.

She knew that he disapproved of Israelis. Dickstein was an old student, and her father had been genuinely pleased to see him and prepared to overlook the fact that the old student was on the enemy side. But now she planned to make Dickstein a permanent part of her life, a member of the family. His letter said, 'For ever is what I want,' and Suza could hardly wait to tell him, 'Oh, yes; me, too.'

She thought both sides were in the wrong in the Middle East. The plight of the refugees was unjust and pitiful, but she thought they ought to set about making themselves new homes – it was not easy, but it was easier than war, and she despised the theatrical heroics which so many Arab men found irresistible. On the other hand, it was clear that the whole damn mess was originally the fault of the Zionists, who had taken over a country that belonged to other people. Such a cynical view had no appeal for her father, who saw Right on one side and Wrong on the other, and the beautiful ghost of his wife on the side of Right.

It would be hard for him. She had long ago scotched his dreams of walking up the aisle with his daughter beside him in a white wedding dress; but he still talked occasionally of her settling down and giving him a granddaughter. The idea that this grandchild might be Israeli would come as a terrible blow.

Still, that was the price of being a parent, Suza thought as she entered the house. She called, 'Daddy, I'm home,' as she took off her coat and put down her airline bag. There was no reply, but his briefcase was in the hall: he must be in the garden. She put the kettle on and walked out of the kitchen and down toward the river, still searching in her mind for the right words with which to tell him her news. Maybe she should begin by talking about her trip, and gradually work around—

She heard voices as she approached the hedge.

'And what will you do with him?' It was her father's voice.

Suza stopped, wondering whether she ought to interrupt or not.

'Just follow him,' said another voice, a strange one. 'Dickstein must not be killed until afterwards, of course.'

She put her hand over her mouth to stifle a gasp of horror. Then, terrified, she turned around and ran, soft-footed, back to the house.

'Well, now,' said Professor Ashford, 'following what we might call the Rostov Method, let us recall everything we know about Nat Dickstein.'

Do it any way you want, Hassan thought, but for God's sake come up with *something*.

Ashford went on: 'He was born in the East End of London. His father died when he was a boy. What about the mother?'

'She's dead, too, according to our files.'

'Ah. Well, he went into the army midway through the war – 1943, I think it was. Anyway he was in time to be part of the attack on Sicily. He was taken prisoner soon afterwards, about halfway up the leg of Italy, I can't remember the place. It was rumoured – you'll remember this, I'm sure – that he had a particularly bad time in the concentration camps, being Jewish. After the war he came here. He—'

'Sicily,' Hassan interrupted.

'Yes?'

'Sicily is mentioned in his file. He is supposed to have been involved in the theft of a boatload of guns. Our people had bought the guns from a gang of criminals in Sicily.'

'If we are to believe what we read in the newspapers,' said Ashford, 'there is only one gang of criminals in Sicily.'

Hassan added, 'Our people suspected that the hijackers had bribed the Sicilians for a tip-off.'

'Wasn't it Sicily where he saved that man's life?'

Hassan wondered what Ashford was talking about. He controlled his impatience, thinking: Let him ramble – that's the whole idea. 'He saved someone's life?'

'The American. Don't you remember? I've never forgotten it. Dickstein brought the man here. A rather brutish G.I. He told me the whole story, right here at this house. Now we're getting somewhere. You must have met the man, you were here that day, don't you remember?'

'I can't say I do,' Hassan muttered. He was embarrassed . . . he had probably been in the kitchen feeling Eila up.

'It was . . . unsettling,' Ashford said. He stared at the slowly moving water as his mind went back twenty years, and his face was shadowed by sadness for a moment, as if he were remembering his wife. Then he said, 'Here we all were, a gathering of academics and students, probably discussing atonal music or existentialism while we sipped our sherry, when in came a big soldier and started talking about snipers and tanks and blood and death. It cast a real chill: that's why I recall it so clearly. He said his family originated in Sicily, and his cousins had fêted Dickstein after the life-saving incident. Did you say a Sicilian gang had tipped off Dickstein about the boatload of guns?'

'It's possible, that's all.'

'Perhaps he didn't have to bribe them.'

Hassan shook his head. This was information, the kind of trivial information Rostov always seemed to make something of – but how was he going to use it? 'I don't see what use all this is going to be to us,' he said. 'How could Dickstein's ancient hijack be connected with the Mafia?'

'The Mafia,' said Ashford. 'That's the word I was looking for. And the man's name was Cortone – Tony Cortone – no, Al Cortone, from Buffalo. I told you, I remember every detail.'

'But the connection?' Hassan said impatiently.

Ashford shrugged. 'Simply this. Once before Dickstein used his connection with Cortone to call on the Sicilian Mafia for help with an act of piracy in the Mediterranean. People repeat their youth, you know: he may do the same thing again.'

Hassan began to see: and, as enlightenment dawned, so did hope. It was a long shot, a guess, but it made sense, the chance was real, maybe he could catch up with Dickstein again.

Ashford looked pleased with himself. 'It's a nice piece of speculative reasoning – I wish I could publish it, with footnotes.'

'I wonder,' said Hassan longingly. 'I wonder.'

'It's getting cool, let's go into the house.'

As they walked up the garden Hassan thought fleetingly that he had not learned to be like Rostov; he had merely found in Ashford a substitute. Perhaps his former proud independence had gone for ever. There was something unmanly about it. He wondered if the other Fedayeen felt the same way, and if that was why they were so bloodthirsty.

Ashford said, 'The trouble is, I don't suppose Cortone will tell you anything, whatever he knows.'

'Would he tell you?'

'Why should he? He'll hardly remember me. Now, if Eila were alive, she could have gone to see him and told him some story . . .'

'Well . . .' Hassan wished Eila would stay out of the conversation. 'I'll have to try myself.'

They entered the house. Stepping into the kitchen,

361

they saw Suza; and then they looked at each other and knew they had found the answer.

By the time the two men came into the house Suza had almost convinced herself that she had been mistaken when, in the garden, she thought she heard them talk about killing Nat Dickstein. It was simply unreal: the garden, the river, the autumn sunshine, a professor and his guest ... murder had no place there, the whole idea was fantastic, like a polar bear in the Sahara Desert. Besides, there was a very good psychological explanation for her mistake: she had been planning to tell her father that she loved Dickstein, and she had been afraid of his reaction – Freud could probably have predicted that at that point she might well imagine her father plotting to kill her lover.

Because she nearly believed this reasoning, she was able to smile brightly at them and say, 'Who wants coffee? I've just made some.'

Her father kissed her cheek. 'I didn't realize you were back, my dear.'

'I just arrived, I was thinking of coming out to look for you.' Why am I telling these lies?

'You don't know Yasif Hassan – he was one of my students when you were very small.'

Hassan kissed her hand and stared at her the way people always did when they had known Eila. 'You're every bit as beautiful as your mother,' he said, and his voice was not flirtatious at all, not even flattering: it sounded amazed.

Her father said, 'Yasif was here a few months ago, shortly after a contemporary of his visited us – Nat Dickstein. You met Dickstein, I think, but you were away by the time Yasif came.'

'Was there any connec-connection?' she asked, and silently cursed her voice for cracking on the last word.

The two men looked at one another, and her father said, 'Matter of fact, there was.'

And then she knew it was true, she had not misheard, they really were going to kill the only man she had ever loved. She felt dangerously close to tears, and turned away from them to fiddle with cups and saucers.

'I want to ask you to do something, my dear,' said her father. 'Something very important, for the sake of your mother's memory. Sit down.'

No more, she thought; this can't get worse, please.

She took a deep breath, turned around, and sat down facing him.

He said, 'I want you to help Yasif here to find Nat Dickstein.'

From that moment she hated her father. She knew then suddenly, instantly, that his love for her was fraudulent, that he had never seen her as a person, that he used her as he had used her mother. Never again would she take care of him, serve him; never again would she worry about how he felt, whether he was lonely, what he needed . . . She realized, in the same flash of insight and hatred, that her mother had reached this same point with him, at some time; and that she would now do what Eila had done, and despise him.

Ashford continued, 'There is a man in America who may know where Dickstein is. I want you to go there with Yasif and ask this man.'

She said nothing. Hassan took her blankness for incomprehension, and began to explain. 'You see, this Dickstein is an Israeli agent, working against our people. We must stop him. Cortone – the man in Buffalo – may be helping him, and if he is he will not help us. But he will remember your mother, and so he may cooperate with you. You could tell him that you and Dickstein are lovers.'

'Ha-hah!' Suza's laugh was faintly hysterical, and she hoped they would assume the wrong reasons for it. She controlled herself, and managed to become numb, to keep her body still and her face expressionless, while they told her about the yellowcake, and the man aboard the *Coparelli*, and the radio beacon on the *Stromberg*, and about Mahmoud and his hijack plan, and how much it would all mean for the Palestine liberation movement; and at the end she was numb, she no longer had to pretend.

Finally her father said, 'So, my dear, will you help? Will you do it?'

With an effort of self-control that astonished her, she gave them a bright air-hostess smile, got up from her stool, and said, 'It's a lot to take in in one go, isn't it? I'll think about it while I'm in the bath.'

And she went out.

*

364

It all sank in, gradually, as she lay in the hot water with a locked door between her and them.

So this was the thing that Nathaniel had to do before he could see her again: steal a ship. And then, he had said, he would not let her out of his sight for ten or fifteen years . . . Perhaps that meant he could give up this work.

But, of course, none of his plans was going to succeed, because his enemies knew all about them. This Russian planned to ram Nat's ship, and Hassan planned to steal the ship first and ambush Nat. Either way Dickstein was in danger; either way they wanted to destroy him. Suza could warn him.

If only she knew where he was.

How little those men downstairs knew about her! Hassan simply assumed, just like an Arab male chauvinist pig, that she would do as she was told. Her father assumed she would take the Palestinian side, because he did and he was the brains of the family. He had never known what was in his daughter's mind: for that matter, he had been the same with his wife. Eila had always been able to deceive him: he never suspected that she might not be what she seemed.

When Suza realized what she had to do, she was terrified all over again.

There was, after all, a way she might find Nathaniel and warn him.

'Find Nat' was what *they* wanted her to do.

She knew she could deceive them, for they already assumed she was on their side, when she was not.

So she could do what they wanted. She could find Nat – and then she could warn him.

Would she be making things worse? To find him herself, she had to lead them to him.

But even if Hassan did not find him, Nat was in danger from the Russian.

And if he was forewarned, he could escape both dangers.

Perhaps, too, she could get rid of Hassan somehow, before she actually reached Nat.

What was the alternative? To wait, to go on as if nothing had happened, to hope for a phone call that might never come ... It was, she realized, partly her need to see Dickstein again that made her think like this, partly the thought that after the hijack he might be dead, that this might be her last chance. But there were good reasons, too: by doing nothing she might help frustrate Hassan's scheme, but that still left the Russians and their scheme.

Her decision was made. She would pretend to work with Hassan so that she could find Nathaniel.

She was peculiarly happy. She was trapped, but she felt free; she was obeying her father, yet she felt that at last she was defying him; for better or worse, she was committed to Nathaniel.

She was also very, very frightened.

She got out of the bath, dried herself, dressed, and went downstairs to tell them the good news.

*

At four A.M. on November 16, 1968, the *Coparelli* hove to at Vlissingen, on the Dutch coast, and took on board a port pilot to guide her through the channel of the Westerschelde to Antwerp. Four hours later, at the entrance to the harbour, she took on another pilot to negotiate her passage through the docks. From the main harbour she went through Royers Lock, along the Suez Canal, under the Siberia Bridge and into Kattendijk Dock, where she tied up at her berth.

Nat Dickstein was watching.

When he saw her sweep slowly in, and read the name *Coparelli* on her side, and thought of the drums of yellowcake that would soon fill her belly, he was overcome by a most peculiar feeling, like the one he had when he looked at Suza's naked body . . . yes, almost like lust.

He looked away from berth No. 42 to the railway line, which ran almost to the edge of the quay. There was a train on the line now, consisting of eleven cars and an engine. Ten of the cars carried fifty-one 200-litre drums with sealed lids and the word PLUMBAT stencilled on the side; the eleventh car had only fifty drums. He was so close to those drums, to that uranium; he could stroll over and touch the railway cars – he already had done this once, earlier in the morning, and had thought: Wouldn't it be terrific just to raid this place with choppers and a bunch of Israeli commandos and simply *steal* the stuff.

The *Coparelli* was scheduled for a fast turnaround. The port authorities had been convinced that the yellowcake could be handled safely, but all the same they did not want the stuff hanging about their harbour one minute longer than necessary. There was a crane standing by ready to load the drums on to the ship.

Nevertheless, there were formalities to be completed before loading could begin.

The first person Dickstein saw boarding the ship was an official from the shipping company. He had to give the pilots their *pourboire* and secure from the captain a crew list for the harbour police.

The second person aboard was Josef Cohen. He was here for the sake of customer relations: he would give the captain a bottle of whisky and sit down for a drink with him and the shipping company official. He also had a wad of tickets for free entry and one drink at the best nightclub in town, which he would give to the captain for the officers. And he would discover the name of the ship's engineer. Dickstein had suggested he do this by asking to see the crew list, then counting out one ticket for each officer on the list.

Whatever way he had decided to do it, he had been successful: as he left the ship and crossed the quay to return to his office he passed Dickstein and muttered, 'The engineer's name is Sarne,' without breaking stride.

It was not until afternoon that the crane went into action and the dockers began loading the drums into the three holds of the *Coparelli*. The drums had to be moved one at a time, and inside the ship each drum had to be secured with wedges of wood. As expected, the loading was not completed that day.

In the evening Dickstein went to the best nightclub in town. Sitting at the bar, close to the telephone, was a quite astonishing woman of about thirty, with black hair and a long, aristocratic face possessed of a faintly haughty expression. She wore an elegant black dress which made the most of her sensational legs and her high, round breasts. Dickstein gave her an almost imperceptible nod but did not speak to her.

He sat in a corner, nursing a glass of beer, hoping the sailors would come. Surely they would. Did sailors ever refuse a free drink?

Yes.

The club began to fill up. The woman in the black dress was propositioned a couple of times but refused both men, thereby establishing that she was not a hooker. At nine o'clock Dickstein went out to the lobby and phoned Cohen. By previous arrangement, Cohen had called the captain of the *Coparelli* on a pretext. He now told Dickstein what he had discovered: that all but two of the officers were using their free tickets. The exceptions were the captain himself, who was busy with paperwork, and the radio operator – a new man they had taken on in Cardiff after Lars broke his leg – who had a head cold.

Dickstein then dialled the number of the club he was in. He asked to speak to Mr Sarne, who, he understood, would be found in the bar. While he waited he could hear a barman calling out Sarne's name: it came to him two ways, one directly from the bar, the other through several miles of telephone cable. Eventually he heard, over the phone, a voice say, 'Yes? Hello? This is Sarne. Is anybody there? Hello?'

Dickstein hung up and walked quickly back into the bar. He looked over to where the bar phone was. The woman in the black dress was speaking to a tall, suntanned blond man in his thirties whom Dickstein had seen on the quay earlier that day. So this was Sarne.

The woman smiled at Sarne. It was a nice smile, a smile to make any man look twice: it was warm and red-lipped, showing even, white teeth, and it was accompanied by a certain languid half-closing of the eyes, which was very sexy and looked not at all as though it had been rehearsed a thousand times in front of a mirror.

Dickstein watched, spellbound. He had very little idea how this sort of thing worked, how men picked up women and women picked up men, and he understood even less how a woman could pick up a man while letting the man believe *he* was doing the picking up.

Sarne had his own charm, it seemed. He gave her his smile, a grin with something wickedly boyish in it that made him look ten years younger. He said something to her, and she smiled again. He hesitated, like a man who wants to talk some more but cannot think of anything to say; then, to Dickstein's horror, he turned away to go.

The woman was equal to this: Dickstein need not have worried. She touched the sleeve of Sarne's blazer, and he turned back to her. A cigarette had suddenly appeared in her hand. Sarne slapped his pockets for matches. Apparently he did not smoke. Dickstein groaned inwardly. The woman took a lighter from the evening bag on the bar in front of her and handed it to him. He lit her cigarette.

Dickstein could not go away, or watch from a distance; he would have a nervous breakdown. He had to listen. He pushed his way through the bar and stood behind Sarne, who was facing the woman. Dickstein ordered another beer.

The woman's voice was warm and inviting, Dickstein knew already, but now she was really using it. Some women had bedroom eyes, she had a bedroom voice.

Sarne was saying, 'This kind of thing is always happening to me.'

'The phone call?' the woman said.

Sarne nodded. 'Woman trouble. I hate women. All my life, women have caused me pain and suffering. I wish I were a homosexual.'

Dickstein was astonished. What was he saying? Did he mean it? Was he trying to give her the brush-off?

She said, 'Why don't you become one?'

'I don't fancy men.'

'Be a monk.'

'Well, you see, I have this other problem, this insatiable sexual appetite. I have to get laid, all the time, often several times a night. It's a great problem to me. Would you like a fresh drink?'

Ah. It was a line of chat. How did he think it up? Dickstein supposed that sailors did this sort of thing all the time, they had it down to a fine art.

It went on that way. Dickstein had to admire the way the woman led Sarne by the nose while letting him think he was making the running. She told him she was stopping over in Antwerp just for the night, and let him know she had a room in a good hotel. Before long he said they should have champagne, but the champagne sold in the club was very poor stuff, not like they might be able to get somewhere else; at a hotel, say; her hotel, for example.

They left when the floor show started. Dickstein was pleased: so far, so good. He watched a line of girls kicking their legs for ten minutes, then he went out.

He took a cab to the hotel and went up to the room. He stood close to the communicating door which led through to the next room. He heard the woman giggle and Sarne say something in a low voice.

Dickstein sat on the bed and checked the cylinder of gas. He turned the tap on and off quickly, and got a sharp whiff of sweetness from the face mask. It had no effect on him. He wondered how much you had to breathe before it worked. He had not had time to try out the stuff properly.

The noises from the next room became louder, and Dickstein began to feel embarrassed. He wondered how conscientious Sarne was. Would he want to go back to his ship as soon as he had finished with the woman? That would be awkward. It would mean a fight in the hotel corridor – unprofessional, risky.

Dickstein waited – tense, embarrassed. anxious. The woman was good at her trade. She knew Dickstein wanted Sarne to sleep afterwards, and she was trying to tire him. It seemed to take for ever.

It was past two A.M. when she knocked on the

communicating door. The code was three slow knocks to say he was asleep, six fast knocks to say he was leaving.

She knocked three times, slowly.

Dickstein opened the door. Carrying the gas cylinder in one hand and the face mask in the other, he walked softly into the next room.

Sarne lay flat on his back, naked, his blond hair mussed, his mouth wide open, his eyes closed. His body looked fit and strong. Dickstein went close and listened to his breathing. He breathed in, then all the way out – then, just as he began to inhale again, Dickstein turned on the tap and clapped the mask over the sleeping man's nose and mouth.

Sarne's eyes opened wide. Dickstein held the mask on more firmly. Half a breath: incomprehension in Sarne's eyes. The breath turned into a gasp, and Sarne moved his head, failed to weaken Dickstein's grip, and began to thrash about. Dickstein leaned on the sailor's chest with an elbow, thinking: For God's sake, this is too slow!

Sarne breathed out. The confusion in his eyes had turned to fear and panic. He gasped again, about to increase his struggles. Dickstein thought of calling the woman to help hold him down. But the second inhalation defeated its purpose: the struggles were perceptibly weaker; the eyelids fluttered and closed; and by the time he exhaled the second breath, he was asleep.

It had taken about three seconds. Dickstein relaxed. Sarne would probably never remember it. He gave him a little more of the gas to make sure, then he stood up.

He looked at the woman. She was wearing shoes.

stockings, and garters; nothing else. She looked ravishing. She caught his gaze, and opened her arms, offering herself: at your service, sir. Dickstein shook his head with a regretful smile that was only partly disingenuous.

He sat in the chair beside the bed and watched her dress: skimpy panties, soft brassiere, jewellery, dress, coat, bag. She came to him, and he gave her eight thousand Dutch guilders. She kissed his cheek, then she kissed the banknotes. She went out without speaking.

Dickstein went to the window. A few minutes later he saw the headlights of her sports car as it went past the front of the hotel, heading back to Amsterdam.

He sat down to wait, again. After a while he began to feel sleepy. He went into the next room and ordered coffee from room service.

In the morning Cohen phoned to say the first officer of the *Coparelli* was searching the bars, brothels and flophouses of Antwerp for his engineer.

At twelve-thirty Cohen phoned again. The captain had called him to say that all the cargo was now loaded and he was without an engineer officer. Cohen had said, 'Captain, it's your lucky day.'

At two-thirty Cohen called to say he had seen Dieter Koch aboard the *Coparelli* with his kitbag over his shoulder.

Dickstein gave Sarne a little more gas each time he showed signs of waking. He administered the last dose at six A.M. the following day, then he paid the bill for the two rooms and left.

*

When Sarne finally woke up he found that the woman he had slept with had gone without saying goodbye. He also found he was massively, ravenously hungry.

During the course of the morning he discovered that he had been asleep not for one night, as he had imagined, but for two nights and the day in between.

He had an insistent feeling in the back of his mind that there was something remarkable he had forgotten, but he never found out what had happened to him during that lost twenty-four hours.

Meanwhile, on Sunday, November 17, 1968, the *Coparelli* had sailed.

CHAPTER FOURTEEN

WHAT SUZA should have done was phone any Israeli embassy and give them a message for Nat Dickstein.

This thought occurred to her an hour after she had told her father that she would help Hassan. She was packing a case at the time, and she immediately picked up the phone in her bedroom to call Inquiries for the number. But her father came in and asked her whom she was calling. She said the airport, and he said he would take care of that.

Thereafter she constantly looked for an opportunity to make a clandestine call, but there was none. Hassan was with her every minute. They drove to the airport, caught the plane, changed at Kennedy for a flight to Buffalo, and went straight to Cortone's house.

During the journey she came to loathe Yasif Hassan. He made endless vague boasts about his work for the Fedayeen; he smiled oilily and put his hand on her knee; he hinted that he and Eila had been more than friends, and that he would like to be more than friends with Suza. She told him that Palestine would not be free until its women were free; and that Arab men had to learn the difference between being manly and being porcine. That shut him up.

They had some trouble discovering Cortone's address – Suza half hoped they would fail – but in the end they found a taxi driver who knew the house. Suza was dropped off; Hassan would wait for her half a mile down the road.

The house was large, surrounded by a high wall, with guards at the gate. Suza said she wanted to see Cortone, that she was a friend of Nat Dickstein.

She had given a lot of thought to what she should say to Cortone: should she tell him all or only part of the truth? Suppose he knew, or could find out, where Dickstein was: why should he tell her? She would say Dickstein was in danger, she had to find him and warn him. What reason did Cortone have to believe her? She would charm him – she knew how to do that with men his age – but he would still be suspicious.

She wanted to explain to Cortone the complete picture: that she was looking for Nat to warn him, but she was also being used by his enemies to lead them to him, that Hassan was half a mile down the road in a taxi waiting for her. But then he would certainly never tell her anything.

She found it very difficult to think clearly about all this. There were so many deceits and double deceits involved. And she wanted so badly to see Nathaniel's face and speak to him herself.

She still had not decided what to say when the guard opened the gate for her, then led her up the gravel drive to the house. It was a beautiful place, but rather overripe, as if a decorator had furnished it lavishly then the owners had added a lot of expensive junk of their own choosing. There seemed to be a lot of servants. One of them led Suza upstairs, telling her that Mr Cortone was having late breakfast in his bedroom.

When she walked in Cortone was sitting at a small table, digging into eggs and homefries. He was a fat man, completely bald. Suza had no memory of him from the time he had visited Oxford, but he must have looked very different then.

He glanced at her, then stood upright with a look of terror on his face and shouted: 'You should be old!' and then his breakfast went down the wrong way and he began to cough and splutter.

The servant grabbed Suza from behind, pinning her arms in a painful grip; then let her go and went to pound Cortone on the back. 'What did you do?' he yelled at her. 'What did you do, for Christ's sake?'

In a peculiar way this farce helped calm her a little. She could not be terrified of a man who had been so terrified of her. She rode the wave of confidence, sat down at his table and poured herself coffee. When Cortone stopped coughing she said, 'She was my mother.'

'My God,' Cortone said. He gave a last cough, then waved the servant away and sat down again 'You're so like her, hell, you scared me half to death.' He screwed up his eyes, remembering. 'Would you have been about four or five years old, back in, um, 1947?'

'That's right.'

'Hell, I remember you, you had a ribbon in your hair. And now you and Nat are an item.'

She said, 'So he has been here.' Her heart leaped with joy.

'Maybe,' Cortone said. His friendliness vanished. She realized he would not be easy to manipulate.

She said, 'I want to know where he is.'

'And I want to know who sent you here.'

'Nobody sent me.' Suza collected her thoughts, struggling to hide her tension. 'I guessed he might have come to you for help with this . . . project he's working on. The thing is, the Arabs know about it, and they'll kill him, and I have to warn him . . . Please, if you know where he is, please help me.'

She was suddenly close to tears, but Cortone was unmoved. 'Helping you is easy,' he said. 'Trusting you is the hard part.' He unwrapped a cigar and lit it, taking his time. Suza watched in an agony of impatience. He looked away from her and spoke almost to himself. 'You know, there was a time when I'd just see something I wanted and I'd grab it. It's not so simple any more. Now I've got all these complications. I got to make choices, and none of them are what I really want. I don't know whether it's the way things are now or if it's me.'

He turned again and faced her. 'I owe Dickstein my life. Now I have a chance to save his, if you're telling the truth. This is a debt of honour. I have to pay it myself, in person. So what do I do?' He paused.

Suza held her breath.

'Dickstein is in a wreck of a house somewhere on the Mediterranean. It's a ruin, hasn't been lived in for years, so there's no phone there. I could send a message, but I couldn't be sure it would get there, and like I said, I have to do this myself, in person.'

He drew on the cigar. 'I could tell you where to go look for him, but you just might pass the information on to the wrong people. I won't take that risk.'

'What, then?' Suza said in a high-pitched voice. 'We have to help him!'

'I know that,' Cortone said imperturbably. 'So I'm going there myself.'

'Oh!' Suza was taken by surprise: it was a possibility she had never considered.

'And what about you?' he went on. 'I'm not going to tell you where I'm headed, but you could still have people follow me. I need to keep you real close from now on. Let's face it, you could be playing it both ways. So I'm taking you with me.'

She stared at him. Tension drained out of her in a flood, she slumped in her chair. 'Oh, thank you,' she said. Then, at last, she cried.

They flew first class. Cortone always did. After the meal Suza left him to go to the toilet. She looked through the curtain into economy, hoping against hope, but she was disappointed: there was Hassan's wary brown face staring at her over the rows of headrests.

She looked into the galley and spoke to the chief

steward in a confiding voice. She had a problem, she said. She needed to contact her boyfriend but she couldn't get away from her Italian father, who wanted her to wear iron knickers until she was twenty-one. Would he phone the Israeli consulate in Rome and leave a message for a Nathaniel Dickstein? Just say, Hassan has told me everything, and he and I are coming to see you. She gave him money for the phone call, far too much, it was a way of tipping him. He wrote the message down and promised.

She went back to Cortone. Bad news, she said. One of the Arabs was back there in economy. He must be following us.

Cortone cursed, then told her never mind, the man would just have to be taken care of later.

Suza thought: Oh, God, what have I done?

From the big house on the clifftop Dickstein went down a long zigzag flight of steps cut into the rock to the beach. He splashed through the shallows to a waiting motorboat, jumped in and nodded to the man at the wheel.

The engine roared and the boat surged through the waves out to sea. The sun had just set. In the last faint light the clouds were massing above, obscuring the stars as soon as they appeared. Dickstein was deep in thought, racking his brains for things he had not done, precautions he might yet take, loopholes he still had time to close. He went over his plan again and again in his mind, like a man who has learned by heart an important speech he must make but still wishes it were better.

The high shadow of the *Stromberg* loomed ahead, and the boatman brought the little vessel around in a foamy arc to stop alongside, where a rope ladder dangled in the water. Dickstein scrambled up the ladder and on to the deck.

The ship's master shook his hand and introduced himself. Like all the officers aboard the *Stromberg*, he was borrowed from the Israeli Navy.

They took a turn around the deck. Dickstein said, 'Any problems, captain?'

'She's not a good ship,' the captain said. 'She's slow, clumsy and old. But we've got her in good shape.'

From what Dickstein could see in the twilight the *Stromberg* was in better condition than her sister ship the *Coparelli* had been in Antwerp. She was clean, and everything on deck looked squared away, shipshape.

They went up to the bridge, looked over the powerful equipment in the radio room, then went down to the mess, where the crew were finishing dinner. Unlike the officers, the ordinary seamen were all Mossad agents, most with a little experience of the sea. Dickstein had worked with some of them before. They were all, he observed, at least ten years younger than he. They were bright-eyed, well-built, dressed in a peculiar assortment of denims and homemade sweaters: all tough, humorous, well-trained men.

Dickstein took a cup of coffee and sat at one of the tables. He outranked all these men by a long way, but there was not much bull in the Israeli armed forces, and even less in the Mossad. The four men at the table nodded and said hello. Ish, a gloomy Palestine-born Israeli with a dark complexion, said, 'The weather's changing.'

'Don't say that. I was planning to get a tan on this cruise.' The speaker was a lanky ash-blond New Yorker named Feinberg, a deceptively pretty-faced man with eyelashes women envied. Calling this assignment a 'cruise' was already a standing joke. In his briefing earlier in the day Dickstein had said the *Coparelli* would be almost deserted when they hijacked it. 'Soon after she passes through the Strait of Gibraltar,' he had told them, 'her engines will break down. The damage will be such that it can't be repaired at sea. The captain cables the owners to that effect – and we are now the owners. By an apparently lucky coincidence, another of our ships will be close by. She's the *Gil Hamilton*, now moored across the bay here. She will go to the *Coparelli* and take off the whole crew except for the engineer. Then she's out of the picture: she'll go to her next port of call, where the crew of the *Coparelli* will be let off and given their train fares home.'

They had had the day to think about the briefing, and Dickstein was expecting questions. Now Levi Abbas, a short, solid man 'built like a tank and about as handsome,' Feinberg had said, asked Dickstein, 'You didn't tell us how come you're so sure the *Coparelli* will break down when you want her to.'

'Ah.' Dickstein sipped his coffee. 'Do you know Dieter Koch, in naval intelligence?'

Feinberg knew him.

'He's the *Coparelli*'s engineer.'

Abbas nodded. 'Which is also how come we know we'll be able to repair the *Coparelli*. We know what's going to go wrong.'

'Right.'

Abbas went on. 'We paint out the name *Coparelli*, rename her *Stromberg*, switch log books, scuttle the old *Stromberg* and sail the *Coparelli*, now called the *Stromberg*, to Haifa with the cargo. But why not transfer the cargo from one ship to the other at sea? We have cranes.'

'That was my original idea,' Dickstein said. 'It was too risky. I couldn't guarantee it would be possible, especially in bad weather.'

'We could still do it if the good weather holds.'

'Yes, but now that we have identical sister ships it will be easier to switch names than cargoes.'

Ish said lugubriously, 'Anyway, the good weather won't hold.'

The fourth man at the table was Porush, a crewcut youngster with a chest like a barrel of ale, who happened to be married to Abbas's sister. He said, 'If it's going to be so easy, what are all of us tough guys doing here?'

Dickstein said, 'I've been running around the world for the past six months setting up this thing. Once or twice I've bumped into people from the other side – inevitably. I don't *think* they know what we're about to do ... but if they do, we may find out just how tough we are.'

One of the officers came in with a piece of paper

and approached Dickstein. 'Signal from Tel Aviv, sir. The *Coparelli* just passed Gibraltar.'

'That's it,' said Dickstein, standing up. 'We sail in the morning.'

Suza Ashford and Al Cortone changed planes in Rome and arrived in Sicily early in the morning. Two of Cortone's cousins were at the airport to meet him. There was a long argument between them: not acrimonious, but nevertheless loudly excitable. Suza could not follow the rapid dialect properly, but she gathered the cousins wanted to accompany Cortone and he was insisting that this was something he had to do alone because it was a debt of honour.

Cortone seemed to win the argument. They left the airport, without the cousins, in a big white Fiat. Suza drove. Cortone directed her on to the coast road. For the hundredth time she played over in her mind the reunion scene with Nathaniel: she saw his slight, angular body; he looked up; he recognized her and his face split in a smile of joy; she ran to him; they threw their arms around each other; he squeezed her so hard it hurt; she said, 'Oh, I love you,' and kissed his cheek, his nose, his mouth. But she was guilty and frightened too, and there was another scene she played less often in which he stared at her stony-faced and said, 'What the hell do you think you're doing here?'

It was a little like the time she had behaved badly on Christmas Eve, and her mother got angry and told her Santa Claus would put stones in her Christmas stocking instead of toys and candy. She had not known whether to believe this or not, and she had lain awake, alternately wishing for and dreading the morning.

She glanced across at Cortone in the seat beside her. The transatlantic journey tired him. Suza found it difficult to think of him as being the same age as Nat, he was so fat and bald and ... well, he had an air of weary depravity that might have been amusing but in fact was merely elderly.

The island was pretty when the sun came out. Suza looked at the scenery, trying to distract herself so that the time would pass more quickly. The road twisted along the edge of the sea from town to town, and on her right-hand side there were views of rocky beaches and the sparkling Mediterranean.

Cortone lit a cigar. 'I used to do this kind of thing a lot when I was young,' he said. 'Get on a plane, go somewhere with a pretty girl, drive around, see places. Not any more. I've been stuck in Buffalo for years, it seems like. That's the thing with business – you get rich, but there's always something to worry about. So you never go places, you have people come to you, bring you stuff. You get too lazy to have fun.'

'You chose it,' Suza said. She felt more sympathy for Cortone than she showed: he was a man who had worked hard for all the wrong things.

'I chose it,' Cortone admitted. 'Young people have no mercy.' He gave a rare half smile and puffed on his cigar.

For the third time Suza saw the same blue car in her

rearview mirror. 'We're being followed,' she said, trying to keep her voice calm and normal.

'The Arab?'

'Must be.' She could not see the face behind the windshield. 'What will we do? You said you'd handle it.'

'I will.'

He was silent. Expecting him to say more, Suza glanced across at him. He was loading a pistol with ugly brown-black bullets. She gasped: she had never seen a real-life gun.

Cortone looked up at her, then ahead. 'Christ, watch the goddamn road!'

She looked ahead, and braked hard for a sharp bend. 'Where did you get that thing?' she said.

'From my cousin.'

Suza felt more and more as if she were in a nightmare. She had not slept in a bed for four days. From the moment when she had heard her father talking so calmly about killing Nathaniel she had been running: fleeing from the awful truth about Hassan and her father, to the safety of Dickstein's wiry arms; and, as in a nightmare, the destination seemed to recede as fast as she ran.

'Why don't you tell me where we're going?' she asked Cortone.

'I guess I can, now. Nat asked me for the loan of a house with a mooring and protection from snooping police. We're going to that house.'

Suza's heart beat faster. 'How far?'

'Couple of miles.'

A minute later Cortone said, 'We'll get there, don't rush, we don't want to die on the way.'

She realized she had unconsciously put her foot down. She eased off the accelerator but she could not slow her thoughts. Any minute now, to see him and touch his face, to kiss him hello, to feel his hands on her shoulders—

'Turn in there, on the right.'

She drove through an open gateway and along a short gravel drive overgrown with weeds to a large ruined villa of white stone. When she pulled up in front of the pillared portico she expected Nathaniel to come running out to greet her.

There were no signs of life on this side of the house.

They got out of the car and climbed the broken stone staircase to the front entrance. The great wooden door was closed but not locked. Suza opened it and they went in.

There was a great hall with a floor of smashed marble. The ceiling sagged and the walls were blotched with damp. In the centre of the hall was a great fallen chandelier sprawled on the floor like a dead eagle.

Cortone called out, 'Hello, anybody here?'

There was no reply.

Suza thought: It's a big place, he must be here, it's just that he can't hear, maybe he's out in the garden.

They crossed the hall, skirting the chandelier. They entered a cavernous bare drawing room, their footsteps echoing loudly, and went out through the glassless french doors at the back of the building.

A short garden ran down to the edge of the cliff. They walked that far and saw a long stairway cut into the rock zigzagging down to the sea.

There was no one in sight.

He's not here, Suza thought; this time, Santa really did leave me stones.

'Look.' Cortone was pointing out to sea with one fat hand. Suza looked, and saw two vessels: a ship and a motorboat. The motorboat was coming toward them fast, jumping the waves and slicing the water with its sharp prow: there was one man in it. The ship was sailing out of the bay, leaving a broad wake.

'Looks like we just missed them,' Cortone said.

Suza ran down the steps, shouting and waving insanely, trying to attract the attention of the people on the ship, knowing it was impossible, they were too far away. She slipped on the stones and fell heavily on her bottom. She began to cry.

Cortone ran down after her, his heavy body jerking on the steps. 'It's no good,' he said. He pulled her to her feet.

'The motorboat,' she said desperately. 'Maybe we can take the motorboat and catch up with the ship—'

'No way. By the time the boat gets here the ship will be too far away, much too far, and going faster than the boat can.'

He led her back up the steps. She had run a long way down, and the climb back taxed him heavily. Suza hardly noticed: she was full of misery.

Her mind was a blank as they walked up the slope of the garden and back into the house.

'Have to sit down,' Cortone said as they crossed the drawing room.

Suza looked at him. He was breathing hard, and his face was grey and covered with perspiration. Suddenly she realized it had all been too much for his overweight body. For a moment she forgot her own awful disappointment. 'The stairs,' she said.

They went into the ruined hall. She led Cortone to the wide curving staircase and sat him on the second step. He went down heavily. He closed his eyes and rested his head on the wall beside him.

'Listen,' he said, 'you can call ships . . . or send them a wire . . . we can still reach him . . .'

'Sit quietly for a minute,' she said. 'Don't talk.'

'Ask my cousins – who's there?'

Suza spun around. There had been a clink of chandelier shards, and now she saw what had caused it.

Yasif Hassan walked toward them across the hall.

Suddenly, with a massive effort, Cortone stood up.

Hassan stopped.

Cortone's breath was coming in ragged gulps. He fumbled in his pocket.

Suza said, 'No—'

Cortone pulled out the gun.

Hassan was rooted to the spot, frozen.

Suza screamed. Cortone staggered, the gun in his hand weaving about in the air.

Cortone pulled the trigger. The gun went off twice, with a huge, deafening double bang. The shots went wild. Cortone sank to the ground, his face as dark as death. The gun fell from his fingers and hit the cracked marble floor.

Yasif Hassan threw up.

Suza knelt beside Cortone.

He opened his eyes. 'Listen,' he said hoarsely.

Hassan said, 'Leave him, let's go.'

Suza turned her head to face him. At the top of her voice she shouted, 'Just fuck *off*.' Then she turned back to Cortone.

'I've killed a lot of men,' Cortone said. Suza bent closer to hear. 'Eleven men. I killed myself ... I fornicated with a lot of women ...' His voice trailed off, his eyes closed, and then he made a huge effort to speak again. 'All my goddamn life I been a thief and a bully. But I died for my friend, right? This counts for something, it has to, doesn't it?'

'Yes,' she said. 'This really counts for something.'

'Okay,' he said.

Then he died.

Suza had never seen a man die. It was awful. Suddenly there was nothing there, nothing but a body; the person had vanished. She thought: No wonder death makes us cry. She realized her own face was streaked with tears. I didn't even like him, she thought, until just now.

Hassan said, 'You did very well, now let's get out of here.'

Suza did not understand. I did well? she thought. And then she understood. Hassan did not know she had told Cortone an Arab had been following them. As far as Hassan was concerned she had done just what he wanted her to: she had led him here. Now she must try to keep up the pretence that she was on his side until she could find a way to contact Nat.

I can't lie and cheat any more, I can't, it's too much, I'm tired, she thought.

Then: You can phone a ship, or at least send a cable, Cortone said.

She could still warn Nat.

Oh, God, when can I sleep?

She stood up. 'What are we waiting for?'

They went out through the high derelict entrance. 'We'll take my car,' Hassan told her.

She thought of trying to run away from him then, but it was a foolish idea. He would let her go soon. She had done what he'd asked, hadn't she? Now he would send her home.

She got into the car.

'Wait,' Hassan said. He ran to Cortone's car, took out the keys, and threw them into the bushes. He got into his own car. 'So the man in the motorboat can't follow,' he explained.

As they drove off he said, 'I'm disappointed in your attitude. That man was helping our enemies. You should rejoice, not weep, when an enemy dies.'

She covered her eyes with her hand. 'He was helping his friend.'

Hassan patted her knee. 'You've done well, I shouldn't criticize you. You got the information I wanted.'

She looked at him. 'Did I?'

'Sure. That big ship we saw leaving the bay – that

was the *Stromberg*. I know her time of departure and her maximum speed, so now I can figure out the earliest possible moment at which she could meet up with the *Coparelli*. And I can have my men there a day earlier.' He patted her knee again, this time letting his hand rest on her thigh.

'Don't touch me,' she said.

He took his hand away.

She closed her eyes and tried to think. She had achieved the worst possible outcome by what she had done: she had led Hassan to Sicily but she'd failed to warn Nat. She must find out how to send a telegram to a ship, and do it as soon as she and Hassan parted company. There was only one other chance – the airplane steward who had promised to call the Israeli consulate in Rome.

She said, 'Oh, God, I'll be glad to get back to Oxford.'

'Oxford?' Hassan laughed. 'Not yet. You'll have to stay with me until the operation is over.'

She thought: Dear God, I can't stand it. 'But I'm so tired,' she said.

'We'll rest soon. I couldn't let you go. Security, you know. Anyway, you wouldn't want to miss seeing the dead body of Nat Dickstein.'

At the Alitalia desk in the airport three men approached Yasif Hassan. Two of them were young and thuggish, the third was a tall sharp-faced man in his fifties.

393

The older man said to Hassan, 'You damn fool, you deserve to be shot.'

Hassan looked up at him, and Suza saw naked fear in his eyes as he said, 'Rostov!'

Suza thought: Oh God, what now?

Rostov took hold of Hassan's arm. It seemed for a moment that Hassan would resist, and jerk his arm away. The two young thugs moved closer. Suza and Hassan were enclosed. Rostov led Hassan away from the ticket desk. One of the thugs took Suza's arm and they followed.

They went into a quiet corner. Rostov was obviously blazing with fury but kept his voice low. 'You might have blown the whole thing if you hadn't been a few minutes late.'

'I don't know what you mean,' Hassan said desperately.

'You think I don't know you've been running around the world looking for Dickstein? You think I can't have you followed just like any other bloody imbecile? I've been getting hourly reports on your movements ever since you left Cairo. And what made you think you could trust her?' He jerked a thumb at Suza.

'She led me here.'

'Yes, but you didn't know that then.'

Suza stood still, silent and frightened. She was hopelessly confused. The multiple shocks of the morning – missing Nat, watching Cortone die, now this – had paralyzed her ability to think. Keeping the lies straight had been difficult enough when she had been deceiving Hassan and telling Cortone a truth that Hassan thought was a lie. Now there was this Rostov, to whom Hassan was lying, and she could not even begin to think about whether what she said to Rostov should be the truth or another, different lie.

Hassan was saying, 'How did you get here?'

'On the *Karla*, of course. We were only forty or fifty miles off Sicily when I got the report that you had landed here. I also obtained permission from Cairo to order you to return there immediately and directly.'

'I still think I did the right thing,' said Hassan.

'Get out of my sight.'

Hassan walked away. Suza began to follow him but Rostov said, 'Not you.' He took her arm and began to walk.

She went with him, thinking: What do I do now?

'I know you've proved your loyalty to us, Miss Ashford, but in the middle of a project like this we can't allow newly recruited people simply to go home. On the other hand I have no people here in Sicily other than those I need with me on the ship, so I can't have you escorted somewhere else. I'm afraid you're going to have to come aboard the *Karla* with me until this business is over. I hope you don't mind. Do you know, you look exactly like your mother.'

They had walked out of the airport to a waiting car. Rostov opened the door for her. Now was the time she should run: after this it might be too late. She hesitated. One of the thugs stood beside her. His jacket fell open slightly and she saw the butt of his gun. She remembered the awful bang Cortone's gun had made in the ruined villa, and how she had screamed; and suddenly she was afraid to die, to become a lump of clay like poor fat Cortone; she was terrified of that gun and that bang and the bullet entering her body, and she began to shake.

'What is it?' Rostov said.

'Al Cortone died.'

'We know,' Rostov said. 'Get in the car.'

Suza got in the car.

Pierre Borg drove out of Athens and parked his car at one end of a stretch of beach where occasional lovers strolled. He got out and walked along the shoreline until he met Kawash coming the other way. They stood side by side, looking out to sea, wavelets lapping sleepily at their feet. Borg could see the handsome face of the tall Arab double agent by starlight. Kawash was not his usual confident self.

'Thank you for coming,' Kawash said.

Borg did not know why he was being thanked. If anyone should say thank you, it was he. And then he realized that Kawash had been making precisely that point. The man did everything with subtlety, including insults.

'The Russians suspect there is a leak out of Cairo,' Kawash said. 'They are playing their cards very close to their collective Communist chest, so to speak.' Kawash smiled thinly. Borg did not see the joke. 'Even when Yasif Hassan came back to Cairo for debriefing we didn't learn much – and *I* didn't get all the information Hassan gave.'

Borg belched loudly: he had eaten a big Greek dinner. 'Don't waste time with excuses, please. Just tell me what you do know.'

'All right,' Kawash said mildly. 'They know that Dickstein is to steal some uranium.'

'You told me that last time.'

'I don't think they know any of the details. Their intention is to let it happen, then expose it afterwards. They've put a couple of ships into the Mediterranean, but they don't know where to send them.'

A plastic bottle floated in on the tide and landed at Borg's feet. He kicked it back into the water. 'What about Suza Ashford?'

'Definitely working for the Arab side. Listen. There was an argument between Rostov and Hassan. Hassan wanted to find out exactly where Dickstein was, and Rostov thought it was unnecessary.'

'Bad news. Go on.'

'Afterwards Hassan went out on a limb. He got the Ashford girl to help him look for Dickstein. They went to a place called Buffalo, in the U.S., and met a gangster called Cortone who took them to Sicily. They missed Dickstein, but only just: they saw the *Stromberg* leave. Hassan is in considerable trouble over this. He has been ordered back to Cairo but he hasn't turned up yet.'

'But the girl led them to where Dickstein had been?'

'Exactly.'

'Jesus Christ, this is bad.' Borg thought of the message that had arrived in the Rome consulate for Nat Dickstein from his 'girl friend'. He told Kawash about it. 'Hassan has told me everything and he and I are coming to see you.' What the hell did it mean? Was it intended to warn Dickstein, or to delay him, or to confuse him? Or was it a double bluff – an attempt to make him think she was being coerced into leading Hassan to him?

'A double bluff, I should say,' Kawash said. 'She knew her role in this would eventually be exposed, so she tried for a longer lease on Dickstein's trust. You won't pass the message on ... '

'Of course not.' Borg's mind turned to another tack. 'If they went to Sicily they know about the *Stromberg*. What conclusions can they draw from that?'

'That the *Stromberg* will be used in the uranium theft?'

'Exactly. Now, if I were Rostov, I'd follow the *Stromberg*, let the hijack take place, then attack. Damn, damn, damn. I think this will have to be called off.' He dug the toe of his shoe into the soft sand. 'What's the situation at Qattara?'

'I was saving the worst news until last. All tests have been completed satisfactorily. The Russians are supplying uranium. The reactor goes on stream three weeks from today.'

Borg stared out to sea, and he was more wretched, pessimistic and depressed than he had ever been in the whole of his unhappy life. 'You know what this fucking means don't you? It means we can't call it off. It means I can't stop Dickstein. It means that Dickstein is Israel's last chance.'

Kawash was silent. After a moment Borg looked at

him. The Arab's eyes were closed. 'What are you doing?' Borg said.

The silence went on for a few moments. Finally Kawash opened his eyes, looked at Borg, and gave his polite little half smile. 'Praying,' he said.

TEL AVIV TO MV STROMBERG
PERSONAL BORG TO DICKSTEIN EYES ONLY
MUST BE DECODED BY THE ADDRESSEE
BEGINS SUZA ASHFORD CONFIRMED ARAB AGENT STOP SHE PERSUADED CORTONE TO TAKE HER AND HASSAN TO SICILY STOP THEY ARRIVED AFTER YOU LEFT STOP CORTONE NOW DEAD STOP THIS AND OTHER DATA INDICATES STRONG POSSIBILITY YOU WILL BE ATTACKED AT SEA STOP NO FURTHER ACTION WE CAN TAKE AT THIS END STOP YOU FUCKED IT UP ALL ON YOUR OWN NOW GET OUT OF IT ALONE ENDS

The clouds which had been massing over the western Mediterranean for the previous few days finally burst that night, drenching the *Stromberg* with rain. A brisk wind blew up, and the shortcomings of the ship's design became apparent as she began to roll and yaw in the burgeoning waves.

Nat Dickstein did not notice the weather.

He sat alone in his little cabin, at the table which was screwed to the bulkhead, a pencil in hand and a pad, a codebook and a signal in front of him, transcribing Borg's message word by crucifying word.

He read it over and over again, and finally sat staring at the blank steel wall in front of him.

It was pointless to speculate about why she might have done this, to invent far-fetched hypotheses that Hassan had coerced or blackmailed her, to imagine that she had acted from mistaken beliefs or confused motives: Borg had said she was a spy, and he had been right. She had been a spy all along. That was why she had made love to him.

She had a big future in the intelligence business, that girl.

Dickstein put his face in his hands and pressed his eyeballs with his fingertips, but still he could see her, naked except for her high-heeled shoes, leaning against the cupboard in the kitchen of that little flat, reading the morning paper while she waited for a kettle to boil.

The worst of it was, he loved her still. Before he met her he had been a cripple, an emotional amputee with an empty sleeve hanging where he should have had love; and she had performed a miracle, making him whole again. Now she had betrayed him, taking away what she had given, and he would be more handicapped than ever. He had written her a love letter. Dear God, he thought, what did she do when she read that letter? Did she laugh? Did she show it to Yasif Hassan and say, 'See how I've got him hooked?'

If you took a blind man, and gave him back his sight, and then, after a day made him blind again during the night while he was sleeping, this was how he would feel when he woke up.

He had told Borg he would kill Suza if she were an

agent, but now he knew that he had been lying. He could never hurt her, no matter what she did.

It was late. Most of the crew were asleep except for those taking watches. He left the cabin and went up on deck without seeing anyone. Walking from the hatch to the gunwale he got soaked to the skin, but he did not notice. He stood at the rail, looking into the darkness, unable to see where the black sea ended and the black sky began, letting the rain stream across his face like tears.

He would never kill Suza, but Yasif Hassan was a different matter.

If ever a man had an enemy, he had one in Hassan. He had loved Eila, only to see her in a sensual embrace with Hassan. Now he had fallen in love with Suza, only to find that she had already been seduced by the same old rival. And Hassan had also used Suza in his campaign to take away Dickstein's homeland.

Oh, yes, he would kill Yasif Hassan, and he would do it with his bare hands if he could. And the others. The thought brought him up out of the depths of despair in a fury: he wanted to hear bones snap, he wanted to see bodies crumple, he wanted the smell of fear and gunfire, he wanted death all around him.

Borg thought they would be attacked at sea. Dickstein stood gripping the rail as the ship sawed through the unquiet sea; the wind rose momentarily and lashed his face with cold, hard rain; and he thought, So be it; and then he opened his mouth and shouted into the wind: 'Let them come – let the bastards come!'

CHAPTER FIFTEEN

HASSAN DID not go back to Cairo, then or ever.

Exultation filled him as his plane took off from Palermo. It had been close, but he had outwitted Rostov again! He could hardly believe it when Rostov had said, 'Get out of my sight.' He had felt sure he would be forced to board the *Karla* and consequently miss the hijack by the Fedayeen. But Rostov completely believed that Hassan was merely over-enthusiastic, impulsive, and inexperienced. It had never occurred to him that Hassan might be a traitor. But then, why should it? Hassan was the representative of Egyptian Intelligence on the team and he was an Arab. If Rostov had toyed with suspicions about his loyalty, he might have considered whether he was working for the Israelis, for they were the opposition – the Palestinians, if they entered the picture at all, could be assumed to be on the Arab side.

It was wonderful. Clever, arrogant, patronizing Colonel Rostov and the might of the notorious KGB had been fooled by a lousy Palestinian refugee, a man they thought was a nobody.

But it was not over yet. He still had to join forces with the Fedayeen.

The flight from Palermo took him to Rome, where he tried to get a plane to Annaba or Constantine, both near the Algerian coast. The nearest the airlines could offer was Algiers or Tunis. He went to Tunis.

There he found a young taxi driver with a newish Renault and thrust in front of the man's face more money in American dollars than he normally earned in a year. The taxi took him across the hundred-mile breadth of Tunisia, over the border into Algeria, and dropped him off at a fishing village with a small natural harbour. One of the Fedayeen was waiting for him. Hassan found him on the beach, sitting under a propped-up dinghy, sheltering from the rain and playing backgammon with a fisherman. The three men got into the fisherman's boat and cast off.

The sea was rough as they headed out in the last of the day. Hassan, no seaman, worried that the little motorboat would capsize, but the fisherman grinned cheerfully through it all.

The trip took them less than a half hour. As they approached the looming hulk of the ship, Hassan felt again the rising sense of triumph. A ship . . . they had a *ship*.

He clambered up on to the deck while the man who had met him paid off the fisherman. Mahmoud was waiting for him on deck. They embraced, and Hassan said, 'We should weigh anchor immediately – things are moving very fast now.'

'Come to the bridge with me.'

Hassan followed Mahmoud forward. The ship was a small coaster of about one thousand tons, quite new and in good condition. She was sleek, with most of her accommodations below deck. There was a hatch for one hold. She had been designed to carry small loads quickly and to manoeuvre in local North African ports.

They stood on the foredeck for a moment, looking about.

'She's just what we need,' Hassan said joyfully.

'I have renamed her the *Nablus*,' Mahmoud told him. 'She is the first ship of the Palestine Navy.'

Hassan felt tears start to his eyes.

They climbed the ladder. Mahmoud said, 'I got her from a Libyan businessman who wanted to save his soul.'

The bridge was compact and tidy. There was only one serious lack: radar. Many of these small coastal vessels still managed without it, and there had been no time to buy the equipment and fit it.

Mahmoud introduced the captain, also a Libyan – the businessman had provided a crew as well as a ship; none of the Fedayeen were sailors. The captain gave orders to weigh anchor and start engines.

The three men bent over a chart as Hassan told what he had learned in Sicily. 'The *Stromberg* left the south coast of Sicily at midday today. The *Coparelli* was due to pass through the Strait of Gibraltar late last night, heading for Genoa. They are sister ships, with the same top speed, so the earliest they can meet is twelve hours east of the midpoint between Sicily and Gibraltar.'

The captain made some calculations and looked at

another chart. 'They will meet south-east of the island of Minorca.'

'We should intercept the *Coparelli* no less than eight hours earlier.'

The captain ran his finger back along the trade route. 'That would put her just south of the island of Ibiza at dusk tomorrow.'

'Can we make it?'

'Yes, with a little time to spare, unless there is a storm.'

'Will there be a storm?'

'Sometime in the next few days, yes. But not tomorrow, I think.'

'Good. Where is the radio operator?'

'Here. This is Yaacov.'

Hassan turned to see a small, smiling man with tobacco-stained teeth and told him, 'There is a Russian aboard the *Coparelli*, a man called Tyrin, who will be sending signals to a Polish ship, the *Karla*. You must listen on this wavelength.' He wrote it down. 'Also, there is a radio beacon on the *Stromberg* that sends a simple thirty-second tone every half hour. If we listen for that every time we will be sure the *Stromberg* is not outrunning us.'

The captain was giving a course. Down on the deck the first officer had the hands making ready. Mahmoud was speaking to one of the Fedayeen about an arms inspection. The radio operator began to question Hassan about the *Stromberg*'s beacon. Hassan was not really listening. He was thinking: Whatever happens, it will be glorious.

The ship's engines roared, the deck tilted, the prow broke water and they were on their way.

Dieter Koch, the new engineer officer of the *Coparelli*, lay in his bunk in the middle of the night thinking: but what do I say if somebody sees me?

What he had to do now was simple. He had to get up, go to the aft engineering store, take out the spare oil pump and get rid of it. It was almost certain he could do this without being seen, for his cabin was close to the store, most of the crew were asleep, and those that were awake were on the bridge and in the engine room and likely to stay there. But 'almost certain' was not enough in an operation of this importance. If anyone should suspect, now or later, what he was really up to . . .

He put on a sweater, trousers, sea boots and an oilskin. The thing had to be done, and it had to be done now. He pocketed the key to the store, opened his cabin door and went out. As he made his way along the gangway he thought: I'll say I couldn't sleep so I'm checking the stores.

He unlocked the door to the store, turned on the light, went in and closed it behind him. Engineering spares were racked and shelved all around him – gaskets, valves, plugs, cable, bolts, filters . . . given a cylinder block, you could build a whole engine out of these parts.

He found the spare oil pump in a box on a high shelf. He lifted it down – it was not bulky but it was heavy – and then spent five minutes double-checking that there was not a second spare oil pump.

Now for the difficult part.

. . . I couldn't sleep, sir, so I was checking the spares. Very good, everything in order? Yes, sir. And what's that you've got under your arm? A bottle of whisky, sir. A cake my mother sent me. The spare oil pump, sir, I'm going to throw it overboard . . .

He opened the storeroom door and looked out.

Nobody.

He killed the light, went out, closed the door behind him and locked it. He walked along the gangway and out on deck.

Nobody.

It was still raining. He could see only a few yards, which was good, because it meant others could see only that far.

He crossed the deck to the gunwale, leaned over the rail, dropped the oil pump into the sea, turned, and bumped into someone.

A cake my mother sent me, it was so dry . . .

'Who's that?' a voice said in accented English.

'Engineer. You?' As Koch spoke, the other man turned so that his profile was visible in the deck light, and Koch recognized the rotund figure and big-nosed face of the radio operator.

'I couldn't sleep,' the radio operator said. 'I was . . . getting some air.'

He's as embarrassed as I am, Koch thought. I wonder why?

'Lousy night,' Koch said. 'I'm going in.'

'Goodnight.'

Koch went inside and made his way to his cabin. Strange fellow, that radio operator. He was not one of the regular crew. He had been taken on in Cardiff after the original radioman broke his leg. Like Koch, he was something of an outsider here. A good thing he had bumped into him rather than one of the others.

Inside his cabin he took off his wet outer clothes and lay on his bunk. He knew he would not sleep. His plan for tomorrow was all worked out, there was no point in going over it again, so he tried to think of other things: of his mother, who made the best potato kugel in the world; of his fiancée, who gave the best head in the world; of his mad father now in an institution in Tel Aviv; of the magnificent tapedeck he would buy with his back pay after this assignment; of his fine apartment in Haifa; of the children he would have, and how they would grow up in an Israel safe from war.

He got up two hours later. He went aft to the galley for some coffee. The cook's apprentice was there, standing in a couple of inches of water, frying bacon for the crew.

'Lousy weather,' Koch said.

'It will get worse.'

Koch drank his coffee, then refilled the mug and a second one and took them up to the bridge. The first officer was there. 'Good morning,' Koch said.

'Not really,' said the first officer, looking out into a curtain of rain.

'Coffee?'

'Good of you. Thank you.'

Koch handed him the mug. 'Where are we?'

'Here.' The officer showed him their position on a chart. 'Dead on schedule, in spite of the weather.'

Koch nodded. That meant he had to stop the ship in fifteen minutes. 'See you later,' he said. He left the bridge and went below to the engine room.

His number two was there, looking quite fresh, as if he had taken a good long nap during his night's duty. 'How's the oil pressure?' Koch asked him.

'Steady.'

'It was going up and down a bit yesterday.'

'Well, there was no sign of trouble in the night,' the number two said. He was a little too firm about it, as if he was afraid of being accused of sleeping while the gauge oscillated.

'Good,' Koch said. 'Perhaps it's repaired itself.' He put his mug down on a level cowling, then picked it up quickly as the ship rolled. 'Wake Larsen on your way to bed.'

'Right.'

'Sleep well.'

The number two left, and Koch drank down his coffee and went to work.

The oil pressure gauge was located in a bank of dials aft of the engine. The dials were set into a thin metal casing, painted matt black and secured by four self-tapping screws. Using a large screwdriver, Koch removed the four screws and pulled the casing away. Behind it was a mass of many-coloured wires leading to the different gauges. Koch swapped his large screwdriver for a small electrical one with an insulated handle. With a few turns he disconnected one of the wires to the oil pressure gauge. He wrapped a couple of inches of insulating tape around the bare end of the wire, then taped it to the back of the dial so that only a close inspection would reveal that it was not connected to the terminal. Then he replaced the casing and secured it with the four screws.

When Larsen came in he was topping up the transmission fluid.

'Can I do that, sir?' Larsen said. He was a donkeyman greaser, and lubrication was his province.

'I've done it now,' Koch said. He replaced the filler cap and stowed the can in a locker.

Larsen rubbed his eyes and lit a cigarette. He looked over the dials, did a double take and said, 'Sir! Oil pressure zero!'

'Zero?'

'Yes!'

'Stop engines!'

'Aye, aye, sir.'

Without oil, friction between the engine's metal parts would cause a very rapid build-up of heat until the metal melted, the parts fused and the engines stopped, never to go again. So dangerous was the sudden absence of oil pressure that Larsen might well have stopped the engines on his own initiative, without asking Koch.

Everyone on the ship heard the engine die and felt the *Coparelli* lose way; even those dayworkers who were still asleep in their bunks heard it through their dreams and woke up. Before the engine was completely still the first officer's voice came down the pipe. 'Bridge! What's going on below?'

Koch spoke into the voice-pipe. 'Sudden loss of oil pressure.'

'Any idea why?'

'Not yet.'

'Keep me posted.'

'Aye, aye, sir.'

Koch turned to Larsen. 'We're going to drop the sump,' he said. Larsen picked up a toolbox and followed Koch down a half deck to where they could get at the engine from underneath. Koch told him, 'If the main bearings or the big end bearings were worn the drop in oil pressure would have been gradual. A sudden drop means a failure in the oil supply. There's plenty of oil in the system – I checked earlier – and there are no signs of leaks. So there's probably a blockage.'

Koch released the sump with a power spanner and the two of them lowered it to the deck. They checked the sump strainer, the full flow filter, the filter relief valve and the main relief valve without finding any obstructions.

'If there's no blockage, the fault must be in the pump,' Koch said. 'Break out the spare oil pump.'

'That will be in the store on the main deck,' Larsen said.

Koch handed him the key, and Larsen went above.

Now Koch had to work very quickly. He took the casing off the oil pump, exposing two broad-toothed meshing gear wheels. He took the spanner off the power drill and fitted a bit, then attacked the cogs of the gear wheels with the drill, chipping and breaking them until they were all but useless. He put down the drill, picked up a crowbar and a hammer, and forced the bar in between the two wheels, prising them apart until he heard something give with a loud, dull crack. Finally he took out of his pocket a small nut made of toughened steel, battered and chipped. He had brought it with him when he had boarded the ship. He dropped the nut into the sump.

Done.

Larsen came back.

Koch realized he had not taken the bit off the power drill: when Larsen left there had been a spanner attachment on the tool. Don't look at the drill! he thought.

Larsen said, 'The pump isn't there, sir.'

Koch fished the nut out of the sump. 'Look at this,' he said, distracting Larsen's eye from the incriminating power drill. 'This is the cause of the trouble.' He showed Larsen the ruined gear wheels of the oil pump. 'The nut must have been dropped in the last time the filters were changed. It got into the pump and it's been going round and round in those gear wheels ever since. I'm surprised we didn't hear the noise, even over the sound of the engine. Anyway, the oil pump is beyond repair, so you'll have to find that spare. Get a few hands to help you look for it.'

Larsen went out. Koch took the bit off the power drill and put back the spanner attachment. He ran up the steps to the main engine room to remove the other piece of incriminating evidence. Working at top speed in case someone else should come in, he removed the casing on the gauges and reconnected the oil pressure gauge. Now it would genuinely read zero. He replaced the casing and threw away the insulating tape.

It was finished. Now to pull the wool over the captain's eyes.

As soon as the search party admitted defeat Koch went up to the bridge. He told the captain, 'A mechanic must have dropped a nut into the oil sump last time the engine was serviced, sir.' He showed the captain the nut. 'At some point – maybe while the ship was pitching so steeply – the nut got into the oil pump. After that it was just a matter of time. The nut went around in the gear wheels until it had totally ruined them. I'm afraid we can't make gear wheels like that on board. The ship should carry a spare oil pump, but it doesn't.'

The captain was furious. 'There will be hell to pay when I find out who's responsible for this.'

'It's the engineer's job to check the spares, but as you know, sir, I came on board at the last minute.'

'That means it's Sarne's fault.'

'There may be an explanation—'

'Indeed. Such as he spent too much time chasing Belgian whores to look after his engine. Can we limp along?'

'Absolutely not, sir. We wouldn't move half a cable before she seized.'

'Damnation. Where's that radio operator?'

The first officer said, 'I'll find him, sir,' and went out.

'You're certain you can't put something together?' the captain asked Koch.

'I'm afraid you can't make an oil pump out of spare parts and string. That's why we have to carry a spare pump.'

The first officer came back with the radio operator. The captain said, 'Where the devil have you been?'

The radio operator was the rotund, big-nosed man Koch had bumped into on the deck during the night. He looked hurt. 'I was helping to search the for'ard store for the oil pump, sir, then I went to wash my hands.' He glanced at Koch, but there was no hint of suspicion in his look: Koch was not sure how much he had seen during that little confrontation on the deck, but if he had made any connection between a missing spare and a package thrown overboard by the engineer, he wasn't saying.

'All right,' the captain said. 'Make a signal to the owners: Report engine breakdown at ... What's our exact position, number one?'

The first officer gave the radio operator the position.

The captain continued: 'Require new oil pump or tow to port. Please instruct.'

Koch's shoulders slumped a little. He had done it.

Eventually the reply came from the owners: COPA-RELLI SOLD TO SAVILE SHIPPING OF ZURICH. YOUR MESSAGED PASSED TO NEW OWNERS. STAND BY FOR THEIR INSTRUCTIONS.

Almost immediately afterward there was a signal from Savile Shipping: OUR VESSEL GIL HAMILTON IN YOUR WATERS. SHE WILL COME ALONGSIDE AT APPROXI-

MATELY NOON. PREPARE TO DISEMBARK ALL CREW
EXCEPT ENGINEER. GIL HAMILTON WILL TAKE CREW TO
MARSEILLES. ENGINEER WILL AWAIT NEW OIL PUMP.
PAPAGOPOLOUS.

The exchange of signals was heard sixty miles away by
Solly Weinberg, the master of the *Gil Hamilton* and a
commander in the Israeli Navy. He muttered, 'Right on
schedule. Well done, Koch.' He set a course for the
Coparelli and ordered full speed ahead.

It was *not* heard by Yasif Hassan and Mahmoud aboard
the *Nablus* 150 miles away. They were in the captain's
cabin, bent over a sketch plan Hassan had drawn of the
Coparelli, and they were deciding exactly how they
would board her and take over. Hassan had instructed
the *Nablus*'s radio operator to listen out on two wave-
lengths: the one on which the *Stromberg*'s radio beacon
broadcast and the one Tyrin was using for his clandestine signals from the *Coparelli* to Rostov aboard
the *Karla*. Because the messages were sent on the
Coparelli's regular wavelength, the *Nablus* did not
pick them up. It would be some time before the
Fedayeen realized they were hijacking an almost abandoned ship.

The exchange was heard 200 miles away on the bridge
of the *Stromberg*. When the *Coparelli* acknowledged the

signal from Papagopolous, the officers on the bridge cheered and clapped. Nat Dickstein, leaning against a bulkhead with a mug of black coffee in his hand, staring ahead at the rain and the heaving sea, did not cheer. His body was hunched and tense, his face stiff, his brown eyes slitted behind the plastic spectacles. One of the others noticed his silence and made a remark about getting over the first big hurdle. Dickstein's muttered reply was uncharacteristically peppered with the strongest of obscenities. The cheerful officer turned away, and later in the mess observed that Dickstein looked like the kind of man who would stick a knife in you if you stepped on his toe.

And it was heard by David Rostov and Suza Ashford 300 miles away aboard the *Karla*.

Suza had been in a daze as she walked across the gangplank from the Sicilian quayside on to the Polish vessel. She had hardly noticed what was happening as Rostov showed her to her cabin – an officer's room with its own head – and said he hoped she would be comfortable. She sat on the bed. She was still there, in the same position, an hour later when a sailor brought some cold food on a tray and set it down on her table without speaking. She did not eat it. When it got dark she began to shiver, so she got into the bed and lay there with her eyes wide open, staring at nothing, still shivering.

Eventually she had slept – fitfully at first, with strange

meaningless nightmares, but in the end deeply. Dawn woke her.

She lay still, feeling the motion of the ship and looking blankly at the cabin around her; and then she realized where she was. It was like waking up and remembering the blind terror of a nightmare, except that instead of thinking: Oh, thank God it was a dream, she realized it was all true and it was still going on.

She felt horribly guilty. She had been fooling herself, she could see that now. She had convinced herself that she had to find Nat to warn him, no matter the risk: but the truth was she would have reached for any excuse to go and see him. The disastrous consequences of what she had done followed naturally from the confusion of her motives. It was true that Nat had been in danger; but he was in worse danger now, and it was Suza's fault.

She thought of that, and she thought of how she was at sea in a Polish ship commanded by Nat's enemies and surrounded by Russian thugs, and she closed her eyes tightly and pushed her head under the pillow and fought the hysteria that bubbled up in her throat.

And then she began to feel angry, and that was what saved her sanity.

She thought of her father, and how he wanted to use her to further his political ideas, and she felt angry with him. She thought of Hassan, manipulating her father, putting his hand on her knee, and she wished she had slapped his face while she had the chance. Finally she thought of Rostov, with his hard, intelligent face and his cold smile, and how he intended to ram Nat's ship and kill him, and she got mad as hell.

Dickstein was her man. He was funny, and he was strong, and he was oddly vulnerable, and he wrote love letters and stole ships, and he was the only man she had ever loved like *this*; and she was not going to lose him.

She was in the enemy camp, a prisoner, but only from *her* point of view. They thought she was on their side; they trusted her. Perhaps she would have a chance to throw a wrench in their works. She must look for it. She would move about the ship, concealing her fear, talking to her enemies, consolidating her position in their confidence, pretending to share their ambitions and concerns, until she saw her opportunity.

The thought made her tremble. Then she told herself: If I don't do this, I lose him; and if I lose him I don't want to live.

She got out of bed. She took off the clothes she had slept in, washed and put on clean sweater and pants from her suitcase. She sat at the small nailed-down table and ate some of the sausage and cheese that had been left there the day before. She brushed her hair and, just to boost her morale a little, put on a trace of make-up.

She tried her cabin door. It was not locked.

She went out.

She walked along a gangway and followed the smell of food to the galley. She went in and looked swiftly about.

Rostov sat alone, eating eggs slowly with a fork. He

looked up and saw her. Suddenly his face seemed icily evil, his narrow mouth hard, his eyes without emotion. Suza hesitated, then forced herself to walk toward him. Reaching his table, she leaned briefly on a chair, for her legs felt weak.

Rostov said, 'Sit down.'

She dropped into the chair.

'How did you sleep?'

She was breathing too quickly, as if she had been walking very fast. 'Fine,' she said. Her voice shook.

His sharp, sceptical eyes seemed to bore into her brain. 'You seem upset.' He spoke evenly, without sympathy or hostility.

'I . . .' Words seemed to stick in her throat, choking her. 'Yesterday . . . was confusing.' It was true, anyway: it was easy to say this. 'I never saw someone die.'

'Ah.' At last a hint of human feeling showed in Rostov's expression: perhaps he remembered the first time he watched a man die. He reached for a coffee pot and poured her a cup. 'You're very young,' he said. 'You can't be much older than my first son.'

Suza sipped at the hot coffee gratefully, hoping he would go on talking in this fashion – it would help her to calm down.

'Your son?' she said.

'Yuri Davidovitch, he's twenty.'

'What does he do?'

Rostov's smile was not as chilly as before. 'Unfortunately he spends most of his time listening to decadent music. He doesn't study as hard as he should. Not like his brother.'

Suza's breathing was slowing to normal, and her hand no longer shook when she picked up her cup. She knew that this man was no less dangerous just because he had a family; but he *seemed* less frightening when he talked like this. 'And your other son?' she asked. 'The younger one?'

Rostov nodded. 'Vladimir.' Now he was not frightening at all: he was staring over Suza's shoulder with a fond, indulgent expression on his face. 'He's very gifted. He will be a great mathematician if he gets the right schooling.'

'That shouldn't be a problem,' she said, watching him. 'Soviet education is the best in the world.'

It seemed like a safe thing to say, but must have had some special significance for him, because the faraway look disappeared and his face turned hard and cold again. 'No,' he said. 'It shouldn't be a problem.' He continued eating his eggs.

Suza thought urgently: He was becoming friendly, I mustn't lose him now. She cast about desperately for something to say. What did they have in common, what could they talk about? Then she was inspired. 'I wish I could remember you from when you were at Oxford.'

'You were very small.' He poured himself some coffee. 'Everyone remembers your mother. She was easily the most beautiful woman around. And you're exactly like her.'

That's better, Suza thought. She asked him, 'What did you study?'

'Economics.'

'Not an exact science in those days, I imagine.'

'And not much better today.'

Suza put on a faintly solemn expression. 'We speak of bourgeois economics, of course.'

'Of course.' Rostov looked at her as if he could not tell whether she were serious or not. He seemed to decide she was.

An officer came into the galley and spoke to him in Russian. Rostov looked at Suza regretfully. 'I must go up to the bridge.'

She had to go with him. She forced herself to speak calmly. 'May I come?'

He hesitated. Suza thought: He *should* let me. He's enjoyed talking to me, he believes I'm on his side, and if I learn any secrets how could he imagine I could use them, stuck here on a KGB ship?

Rostov said: 'Why not?'

He walked away. Suza followed.

Up in the radio room Rostov smiled as he read through the messages and translated them for Suza's benefit. He seemed delighted with Dickstein's ingenuity. 'The man is smart as hell,' he said.

'What's Savile Shipping?' Suza asked.

'A front for Israeli Intelligence. Dickstein is eliminating all the people who have reason to be interested in what happens to the uranium. The shipping company isn't interested because they no longer own the ship. Now he's taking off the captain and crew. No doubt he has some kind of hold over the people who actually own the uranium. It's a beautiful scheme.'

This was what Suza wanted. Rostov was talking to her like a colleague, she was at the centre of events; she must be able to find a way to foul things up for him. She said, 'I suppose the breakdown was rigged?'

'Yes. Now Dickstein can take over the ship without firing a shot.'

Suza thought fast. When she 'betrayed' Dickstein she had proved her loyalty to the Arab side. Now the Arab side had split into two camps: in one were Rostov, the KGB and Egyptian Intelligence; in the other Hassan and the Fedayeen. Now Suza could prove her loyalty to Rostov's side by betraying Hassan.

She said, as casually as she possibly could, 'And so can Yasif Hassan, of course.'

'What?'

'Hassan can also take over the *Coparelli* without firing a shot.'

Rostov stared at her. The blood seemed to drain from his thin face. Suza was shocked to see him suddenly lose all his poise and confidence. He said, 'Hassan intends to hijack the *Coparelli?*'

Suza pretended to be shocked. 'Are you telling me that you didn't *know?*'

'But who? Not the Egyptians, surely!'

'The Fedayeen. Hassan said this was *your* plan.'

Rostov banged the bulkhead with his fist, looking very uncool and Russian for a moment. 'Hassan is a liar and a traitor!'

This was Suza's chance, she knew. She thought: Give me strength. She said: 'Maybe we can stop him . . .'

Rostov looked at her. 'What's his plan?'

'To hijack the *Coparelli* before Dickstein gets there, then ambush the Israeli team, and sail to . . . he didn't tell me exactly, somewhere in North Africa. What was your plan?'

'To ram the ship after Dickstein had stolen the uranium—'

'Can't we still do that?'

'No. We're too far away, we'd never catch them.'

Suza knew that if she did not do the next bit exactly right, both she and Dickstein would die. She crossed her arms to stop the shaking. She said, 'Then there is only one thing we can do.'

Rostov looked up at her. 'There is?'

'We must warn Dickstein of the Fedayeen ambush so that he can take back the *Coparelli*.'

There. She had said it. She watched Rostov's face. He must swallow it, it was logical, it was the right thing for him to do!

Rostov was thinking hard. He said, 'Warn Dickstein so that he can take the *Coparelli* back from the Fedayeen. Then he can proceed according to his plan and we can proceed according to ours.'

'Yes!' said Suza. 'That's the only way! Isn't it? Isn't it?'

FROM: SAVILE SHIPPING, ZURICH

TO: ANGELUZZI E BIANCO, GENOA

YOUR YELLOWCAKE CONSIGNMENT FROM F.A. PEDLER INDEFINITELY DELAYED DUE TO ENGINE TROUBLE AT SEA. WILL ADVISE SOONEST OF NEW DELIVERY DATES. PAPAGOPOLOUS.

*

As the *Gil Hamilton* came into view, Pyotr Tyrin cornered Ravlo, the addict, in the 'tweendecks of the *Coparelli*. Tyrin acted with a confidence he did not feel. He adopted a bullying manner and grabbed hold of Ravlo's sweater. Tyrin was a bulky man, and Ravlo was somewhat wasted. Tyrin said, 'Listen, you're going to do something for me.'

'Sure, anything you say.'

Tyrin hesitated. It would be risky. Still, there was no alternative. 'I need to stay on board ship when the rest of you go on the *Gil Hamilton*. If I'm missed, you will say that you have seen me go over.'

'Right, okay, sure.'

'If I'm discovered, and I have to board the *Gil Hamilton*, you can be sure I'll tell them your secret.'

'I'll do everything I can.'

'You'd better.'

Tyrin let him go. He was not reassured: a man like that would promise you anything, but when it came to the crunch he might fall to pieces.

All hands were summoned on deck for the changeover. The sea was too rough for the *Gil Hamilton* to come alongside, so she sent a launch. Everyone had to wear lifebelts for the crossing. The officers and crew of the *Coparelli* stood quietly in the pouring rain while they were counted, then the first sailor went over the side and down the ladder, jumped into the well of the launch.

The boat would be too small to take the whole crew – they would have to go over in two or three detachments, Tyrin realized. While everyone's attention was on the first men to go over the rail, Tyrin whispered to Ravlo, 'Try and be last to go.'

'All right.'

The two of them edged out to the back of the crowd on deck. The officers were peering over the side at the launch. The men were standing, waiting, facing toward the *Gil Hamilton*.

Tyrin slipped back behind a bulkhead.

He was two steps from a lifeboat whose cover he had loosened earlier. The stem of the boat could be seen from the deck amidships, where the sailors were standing, but the stern could not. Tyrin moved to the stern, lifted the cover, got in and from inside put the cover back in place.

He thought: If I'm discovered now I've had it.

He was a big man, and the life jacket made him bigger. With some difficulty he crawled the length of the boat to a position from which he could see the deck through an eyelet in the tarpaulin. Now it was up to Ravlo.

He watched as a second detachment of men went down the ladder to the launch, then heard the first officer say, 'Where's that radio operator?'

Tyrin looked for Ravlo and located him. Speak. damn you!

Ravlo hesitated. 'He went over with the first lot, sir.'

Good boy!

'Are you sure?'

'Yes, sir. I saw him.'

The officer nodded and said something about not being able to tell one from another in this filthy rain.

The captain called to Koch, and the two men stood talking in the lee of a bulkhead, close to Tyrin's hiding place. The captain said, 'I've never heard of Savile Shipping, have you?'

'No, sir.'

'This is all wrong, selling a ship while she's at sea, then leaving the engineer in charge of her and taking the captain off.'

'Yes, sir. I imagine they're not seafaring people, these new owners.'

'They're surely not, or they'd know better. Probably accountants.' There was a pause. 'You could refuse to stay alone, of course, then I would have to stay with you. I'd back you up afterwards.'

'I'm afraid I'd lose my ticket.'

'Right, I shouldn't have suggested it. Well, good luck.'

'Thank you, sir.'

The third group of seamen had boarded the launch. The first officer was at the top of the ladder waiting for the captain, who was still muttering about accountants as he turned around, crossed the deck and followed the first officer over the side.

Tyrin turned his attention to Koch, who now thought he was the only man aboard the *Coparelli*. The engineer watched the launch go across to the *Gil Hamilton*, then climbed the ladder to the bridge.

Tyrin cursed aloud. He wanted Koch to go below so

that he could get to the for'ard store and radio to the *Karla*. He watched the bridge, and saw Koch's face appear from time to time behind the glass. If Koch stayed there, Tyrin would have to wait until dark before he could contact Rostov and report.

It looked very much as if Koch planned to remain on the bridge all day.

Tyrin settled down for a long wait.

When the *Nablus* reached the point south of Ibiza where Hassan expected to encounter the *Coparelli*, there was not a single ship in sight.

They circled the point in a widening spiral while Hassan scanned the desolate rainswept horizon through binoculars.

Mahmoud said, 'You have made a mistake.'

'Not necessarily.' Hassan was determined he would not appear panicked. 'This was just the earliest point at which we could meet her. She doesn't have to travel at top speed.'

'Why should she be delayed?'

Hassan shrugged, seeming less worried than he was. 'Perhaps the engine isn't running well. Perhaps they've had worse weather than we have. A lot of reasons.'

'What do you suggest, then?'

Mahmoud was also very uneasy, Hassan realized. On this ship he was not in control, only Hassan could make the decisions. 'We travel south-west, backing along the *Coparelli*'s route. We must meet her sooner or later.'

'Give the order to the captain,' Mahmoud said, and

went below to his troops, leaving Hassan on the bridge with the captain.

Mahmoud burned with the irrational anger of tension. So did his troops, Hassan had observed. They had been expecting a fight at midday, and now they had to wait, dawdling about in the crew quarters and the galley, cleaning weapons, playing cards, and bragging about past battles. They were hyped up for combat, and inclined to play dangerous knife-throwing games to prove their courage to each other and to themselves. One of them had quarrelled with two seamen over an imaginary insult, and had cut them both about the face with a broken glass before the fight was broken up. Now the crew were staying well away from the Fedayeen.

Hassan wondered how he would handle them if he were Mahmoud. He had thought along these lines a lot recently. Mahmoud was still the commander, but he was the one who had done all the important work: discovered Dickstein, brought the news of his plan, conceived the counter-hijack, and established the *Stromberg*'s whereabouts. He was beginning to wonder what would be his position in the movement when all this was over.

Clearly, Mahmoud was wondering the same thing.

Well. If there was to be a power struggle between the two of them, it would have to wait. First they had to hijack the *Coparelli* and ambush Dickstein. Hassan felt a little nauseous when he thought about that. It was all very well for the battle-hardened men below to convince themselves they looked forward to a fight, but

Hassan had never been in war, never even had a gun pointed at him except by Cortone in the ruined villa. He was afraid, and he was even more afraid of disgracing himself by showing his fear, by turning and running away, by throwing up as he had done in the villa. But he also felt excited, for if they won – if they won!

There was a false alarm at four-thirty in the afternoon when they sighted another ship coming toward them, but after examining her through binoculars Hassan announced she was not the *Coparelli*, and as she passed they were able to read the name on her side: *Gil Hamilton*.

As daylight began to fade Hassan became worried. In this weather, even with navigation lights, two ships could pass within half a mile of one another at night without seeing each other. And there had been not a sound out of the *Coparelli*'s secret radio all afternoon, although Yaacov had reported that Rostov was trying to raise Tyrin. To be certain that the *Coparelli* did not pass the *Nablus* in the night they would have to go about and spend the night travelling toward Genoa at the *Coparelli*'s speed, then resume searching in the morning. But by that time the *Stromberg* would be close by and the Fedayeen might lose the chance of springing a trap on Dickstein.

Hassan was about to explain this to Mahmoud – who had just returned to the bridge – when a single white light winked on in the distance.

'She's at anchor,' said the captain.

'How can you tell?' Mahmoud asked.

'That's what a single white light means.'

Hassan said, 'That would explain why she wasn't off Ibiza when we expected her. If that's the *Coparelli*, you should prepare to board.'

'I agree,' said Mahmoud, and went off to tell his men.

'Turn out your navigation lights,' Hassan told the captain.

As the *Nablus* closed with the other ship, night fell.

'I'm almost certain that's the *Coparelli*,' Hassan said.

The captain lowered his binoculars. 'She has three cranes on deck, and all her upperworks are aft of the hatches.'

'Your eyesight is better than mine,' Hassan said. 'She's the *Coparelli*.'

He went below to the galley, where Mahmoud was addressing his troops. Mahmoud looked at him as he stepped inside. Hassan nodded. 'This is it.'

Mahmoud turned back to his men. 'We do not expect much resistance. The ship is crewed by ordinary seamen, and there is no reason for them to be armed. We go in two boats, one to attack the port side and one the starboard. On board our first task is to take the bridge and prevent the crew from using the radio. Next we round up the crew on deck.' He paused and turned to Hassan. 'Tell the captain to get as close as possible to the *Coparelli* and then stop engines.'

Hassan turned. Suddenly he was errand boy again: Mahmoud was demonstrating that he was still the battle leader. Hassan felt the humiliation bring a rush of blood to his cheeks.

'Yasif.'

He turned back.

'Your weapon.' Mahmoud threw him a gun. Hassan caught it. It was a small pistol, almost a toy, the kind of gun a woman might carry in her handbag. The Fedayeen roared with laughter.

Hassan thought: I can play these games too. He found what looked like the safety catch and released it. He pointed the gun at the floor and pulled the trigger. The report was very loud. He emptied the gun into the deck.

There was a silence.

Hassan said, 'I thought I saw a mouse.' He threw the gun back to Mahmoud.

The Fedayeen laughed even louder.

Hassan went out. He went back up to the bridge, passed the message to the captain, and returned to the deck. It was very dark now. For a time all that could be seen of the *Coparelli* was its light. Then, as he strained his eyes, a silhouette of solid black became distinguishable against the wash of dark grey.

The Fedayeen, quiet now, had emerged from the galley and stood on deck with the crew. The *Nablus*'s engines died. The crew lowered the boats.

Hassan and his Fedayeen went over the side.

Hassan was in the same boat as Mahmoud. The little launch bobbed on the waves, which now seemed immense. They approached the sheer side of the *Coparelli*. There was no sign of activity on the ship. Surely, Hassan thought, the officer on watch must hear the

431

sound of two engines approaching? But no alarms sounded, no lights flooded the deck, no one shouted orders or came to the rail.

Mahmoud was first up the ladder.

By the time Hassan reached the *Coparelli*'s deck the other team was swarming over the starboard gunwale.

Men poured down the companionways and up the ladders. Still there was no sign of the *Coparelli*'s crew. Hassan had a dreadful premonition that something had gone terribly wrong.

He followed Mahmoud up to the bridge. Two of the men were already there. Hassan asked, 'Did they have time to use the radio?'

'Who?' Mahmoud said.

They went back down to the deck. Slowly the men were emerging from the bowels of the boat, looking puzzled, their cold guns in their hands.

Mahmoud said: 'The wreck of the *Marie Celeste*.'

Two men came across the deck with a frightened looking sailor between them.

Hassan spoke to the sailor in English. 'What's happened here?'

The sailor replied in some other language.

Hassan had a sudden terrifying thought. 'Let's check the hold,' he said to Mahmoud.

They found a companionway leading below and went down into the hold. Hassan found a light switch and turned it on.

The hold was full of large oil drums, sealed and secured with wooden wedges. The drums had the word PLUMBAT stencilled on their sides.

'That's it,' said Hassan. 'That's the uranium.'

They looked at the drums, then at each other. For a moment all rivalry was forgotten.

'We did it,' said Hassan. 'By God, we did it.'

As darkness fell Tyrin had watched the engineer go forward to switch on the white light. Coming back, he had not gone up to the bridge but had walked farther aft and entered the galley. He was going to get something to eat. Tyrin was hungry too. He would give his arm for a plate of salted herring and a loaf of brown bread. Sitting cramped in his lifeboat all afternoon, waiting for Koch to move, he had had nothing to think about but his hunger, and he had tortured himself with thoughts of caviar, smoked salmon, marinated mushrooms and most of all brown bread.

Not yet, Pyotr, he told himself.

As soon as Koch had disappeared from sight, Tyrin got out of the lifeboat, his muscles protesting as he stretched, and hurried along the deck to the for'ard store.

He had shifted the boxes and junk in the main store so that they concealed the entrance to his small radio room. Now he had to get down on hands and knees, pull away one box, and crawl through a little tunnel to get in.

The set was repeating a short two-letter signal. Tyrin checked the code book and found it meant he was to switch to another wavelength before acknowledging. He set the radio to transmit and followed his instructions.

Rostov immediately replied. CHANGE OF PLAN. HASSAN WILL ATTACK COPARELLI.

Tyrin frowned in puzzlement, and made: REPEAT PLEASE.

HASSAN IS A TRAITOR, FEDAYEEN WILL ATTACK COPARELLI.

Tyrin said aloud: 'Jesus, what's going on?' The *Coparelli* was *here*, he was on it . . . Why would Hassan . . . for the uranium, of course.

Rostov was still signalling. HASSAN PLANS TO AMBUSH DICKSTEIN. FOR OUR PLAN TO PROCEED WE MUST WARN DICKSTEIN OF THE AMBUSH.

Tyrin frowned as he decoded this, then his face cleared as he understood. 'Then we'll be back to square one,' he said to himself. 'That's clever. But what do I do?'

He made: HOW?

YOU WILL CALL STROMBERG ON COPARELLI'S REGULAR WAVELENGTH AND SEND FOLLOWING MESSAGE PRECISELY REPEAT PRECISELY. QUOTE COPARELLI TO STROMBERG I AM BOARDED ARABS I THINK. WATCH UNQUOTE.

Tyrin nodded. Dickstein would think that Koch had time to get a few words off before the Arabs killed him. Forewarned, Dickstein should be able to take the *Coparelli*. Then Rostov's *Karla* could collide with Dickstein's ship as planned. Tyrin thought: But what about me?

He made: UNDERSTOOD. He heard a distant bump, as if something had hit the ship's hull. At first he ignored it, then he remembered there was nobody

434

aboard but him and Koch. He went to the door of the for'ard store and looked out.

The Fedayeen had arrived.

He closed the door and hurried back to his transmitter. He made: HASSAN IS HERE.

Rostov replied, SIGNAL DICKSTEIN NOW.

WHAT DO I DO THEN?

HIDE.

Thanks very much, Tyrin thought. He signed off and tuned to the regular wavelength to signal the *Stromberg*.

The morbid thought occurred to him that he might never eat salted herring again.

'I've heard of being armed to the teeth, but this is ridiculous,' said Nat Dickstein, and they all laughed.

The message from the *Coparelli* had altered his mood. At first he had been shocked. How had the opposition managed to learn so much of his plan that they had been able to hijack the *Coparelli* first? Somewhere he must have made terrible errors of judgment. Suza . . .? But there was no point now in castigating himself. There was a fight ahead. His black depression vanished. The tension was still there, coiled tight inside him like a steel spring, but now he could ride it and use it, now he had something to do with it.

The twelve men in the mess room of the *Stromberg* sensed the change in Dickstein and they caught his eagerness for the battle, although they knew some of them would die soon.

Armed to the teeth they were. Each had an Uzi 9-mm

435

submachine gun, a reliable, compact firearm weighing nine pounds when loaded with the 25-round magazine and only an inch over two feet long with its metal stock extended. They had three spare magazines each. Each man had a 9-mm Luger in a belt holster – the pistol would take the same cartridges as the machine gun – and a clip of four grenades on the opposite side of his belt. Almost certainly, they all had extra weapons of their own choice: knives, blackjacks, bayonets, knuckle-dusters and others more exotic, carried superstitiously, more like lucky charms than fighting implements.

Dickstein knew their mood, knew they had caught it from him. He had felt it before with men before a fight. They were afraid, and – paradoxically – the fear made them eager to get started, for the waiting was the worst part, the battle itself was anaesthetic, and afterwards you had either survived or you were dead and did not care any more.

Dickstein had figured his battle plan in detail and briefed them. The *Coparelli* was designed like a miniature tanker, with holds forward and amidships, the main superstructure on the afterdeck, and a secondary superstructure in the stern. The main superstructure contained the bridge, the officers' quarters and the mess; below it were crew's quarters. The stern superstructure contained the galley, below that stores, and below these the engine room. The two superstructures were separate above deck, but below deck they were connected by gangways.

They were to go over in three teams. Abbas's would

attack the bows. The other two, led by Bader and Gibli, would go up the port and starboard ladders at the stern.

The two stern teams were detailed to go below and work forward, flushing out the enemy amidships where they could be mown down by Abbas and his men from the prow. The strategy was likely to leave a pocket of resistance at the bridge, so Dickstein planned to take the bridge himself.

The attack would be by night; otherwise they would never get aboard – they would be picked off as they came over the rails. That left the problem of how to avoid shooting at one another as well as the enemy. For this he provided a recognition signal, the word *Aliyah*, and the attack plan was designed so that they were not expected to confront one another until the very end.

Now they were waiting.

They sat in a loose circle in the galley of the *Stromberg*, identical to the galley of the *Coparelli* where they would soon be fighting and dying. Dickstein was speaking to Abbas: 'From the bows you'll control the foredeck, an open field of fire. Deploy your men behind cover and stay there. When the enemy on deck reveal their positions, pick them off. Your main problem is going to be hailing fire from the bridge.'

Slumped in his chair, Abbas looked even more like a tank than usual. Dickstein was glad Abbas was on his side. 'And we hold our fire at first.'

Dickstein nodded. 'Yes. You've a good chance of getting aboard unseen. No point in shooting until you know the rest of us have arrived.'

Abbas nodded. 'I see Porush is on my team. You know he's my brother-in-law.'

'Yes. I also know he's the only married man here. I thought you might want to take care of him.'

'Thanks.'

Feinberg looked up from the knife he was cleaning. The lanky New Yorker was not grinning for once. 'How do you figure these Arabs?'

Dickstein shook his head. 'They could be regular army or Fedayeen.'

Feinberg grinned. 'Let's hope they're regular army – we make faces, they surrender.'

It was a lousy joke, but they all laughed anyway.

Ish, always pessimistic, sitting with his feet on a table and his eyes closed, said, 'Going over the rail will be the worst part. We'll be naked as babes.'

Dickstein said, 'Remember that they believe we're expecting to take over a deserted boat. Their ambush is supposed to be a big surprise for us. They're looking for an easy victory – but we're prepared. And it will be dark—'

The door opened and the captain came in. 'We've sighted the *Coparelli*.'

Dickstein stood up. 'Let's go. Good luck, and don't take any prisoners.'

CHAPTER SIXTEEN

THE THREE boats pulled away from the *Stromberg* in the last few minutes before dawn.

Within seconds the ship behind them was invisible. She had no navigation lights, and deck lights and cabin lamps had been extinguished, even below the waterline, to ensure that no light escaped to warn the *Coparelli*.

The weather had worsened during the night. The captain of the *Stromberg* said it was still not bad enough to be called a storm, but the rain was torrential, the wind strong enough to blow a steel bucket clattering along the deck, the waves so high that now Dickstein was obliged to cling tightly to his bench seat in the well of the motorboat.

For a while they were in limbo, with nothing visible ahead or behind. Dickstein could not even see the faces of the four men in the boat with him. Feinberg broke the silence: 'I still say we should have postponed this fishing trip until tomorrow.'

Whistling past the graveyard.

Dickstein was as superstitious as the rest: underneath his oilskin and his life jacket he wore his father's old striped waistcoat with a smashed fob watch in the pocket over his heart. The watch had once stopped a German bullet.

Dickstein was thinking logically, but in a way he knew he had gone a little crazy. His affair with Suza, and her betrayal, had turned him upside down: his old values and motivations had been jolted, and the new ones he had acquired with her had turned to dust in his hands. He still cared for some things: he wanted to win this battle, he wanted Israel to have the uranium, and he wanted to kill Yasif Hassan; the one thing he did not care about was himself. He had no fear, suddenly, of bullets and pain and death. Suza had betrayed him, and he had no burning desire to live a long life with that in his past. So long as Israel got its bomb, Esther would die peacefully, Mottie would finish *Treasure Island*, and Yigael would look after the grapes.

He gripped the barrel of the machine gun beneath his oilskin.

They crested a wave and suddenly, there in the next trough, was the *Coparelli*.

Switching from forward to reverse several times in rapid succession, Levi Abbas edged his boat closer to the bows of the *Coparelli*. The white light above them enabled him to see quite clearly, while the outward-curving hull shielded his boat from the sight of anyone on deck or on the bridge. When the boat was close enough to the ladder Abbas took a rope and tied it around his waist under the oilskin. He hesitated a moment, then shucked off the oilskin, unwrapped his gun and slung the gun over his neck. He stood with one foot in the boat and one on the gunwale, waited for his moment, and jumped.

He hit the ladder with both feet and both hands. He untied the rope around his waist and secured it to a rung of the ladder. He went up the ladder almost to the top, then stopped. They should go over the rail as close together as possible.

He looked back down. Sharrett and Sapir were already on the ladder below him. As he looked, Porush made his jump, landed awkwardly and missed his grip, and for a moment Abbas's breath caught in his throat; but Porush slipped down only one rung before he manged to hook an arm around the side of the ladder and arrest his descent.

Abbas waited for Porush to come up close behind Sapir, then he went over the rail. He landed softly on all fours and crouched low beside the gunwale. The others followed swiftly: one, two, three. The white light was above them and they were very exposed.

Abbas looked about. Sharrett was the smallest and he could wriggle like a snake. Abbas touched his shoulder and pointed across the deck. 'Take cover on the port side.'

Sharret bellied across two yards of open deck, then he was partly concealed by the raised edge of the for'ard hatch. He inched forward.

Abbas looked up and down the deck. At any moment they could be spotted; they would know nothing until a hail of bullets tore into them. Quick, quick! Up in the stem was the winding gear for the anchor, with a large pile of slack chain. 'Sapir.' Abbas pointed, and Sapir crawled along the deck to the position.

'I like the crane,' Porush said.

Abbas looked at the derrick towering over them, dominating the whole of the foredeck. The control cabin was some ten feet above deck level. It would be a dangerous position, but it made good tactical sense. 'Go,' he said.

Porush crawled forward, following Sharrett's route. Watching, Abbas thought: He's got a fat ass – my sister feeds him too well. Porush gained the foot of the crane and began to climb the ladder. Abbas held his breath – if one of the enemy should happen to look this way now, while Porush was on the ladder – then he reached the cabin.

Behind Abbas, in the prow, was a companion head over a short flight of steps leading down to a door. The area was not big enough to be called a fo'c'sle, and there was almost certainly no proper accommodation in there – it was simply a for'ard store. He crawled to it, crouched at the foot of the steps in the little well, and gently cracked the door. It was dark inside. He closed the door and turned around, resting his gun on the head of the steps, satisfied that he was alone.

There was very little light at the stern end, and Dickstein's boat had to get very close to the *Coparelli*'s starboard ladder. Gibli, the team leader, found it difficult to keep the boat in position. Dickstein found a boathook in the well of the launch and used it to hold the boat steady, pulling toward the *Coparelli* when the sea tried to part them and pushing away when the boat and the ship threatened to collide broadside.

Gibli, who was ex-army, insisted on adhering to the Israeli tradition that the officers lead their men from in front, not from behind: he had to go first. He always wore a hat to conceal his receding hairline, and now he sported a beret. He crouched at the edge of the boat while it slid down a wave: then, in the trough when boat and ship moved closer together, he jumped. He landed well and moved upward.

On the edge, waiting for his moment, Feinberg said, 'Now, then – I count to three, then open my parachute, right?' Then he jumped.

Katzen went next, then Raoul Dovrat. Dickstein dropped the boathook and followed. On the ladder, he leaned back and looked up through the streaming rain to see Gibli reach the level of the gunwale then swing one leg over the rail.

Dickstein looked back over his shoulder and saw a faint band of lighter grey in the distant sky, the first sign of dawn.

Then there was a sudden shocking burst of machine-gun fire and a shout.

Dickstein looked up again to see Gibli falling slowly backward off the top of the ladder. His beret came off and was whipped away by the wind, disappearing into the darkness. Gibli fell down, down past Dickstein and into the sea.

Dickstein shouted, 'Go, go, go!'

Feinberg flew over the rail. He would hit the deck

rolling, Dickstein knew, then – yes, there was the sound of his gun as he gave covering fire for the others—

And Katzen was over and there were four, five, many guns crackling, and Dickstein was scampering up the ladder and pulling the pin from a grenade with his teeth and hurling it up and over the rail some thirty yards forward, where it would cause a diversion without injuring any of his men already on deck, and then Dovrat was over the rail and Dickstein saw him hit the deck rolling, gain his feet, dive for cover behind the stern superstructure and Dickstein yelled, 'Here I come you fuckers' and went over in a high-jumper's roll, landed on hands and knees, bent double under a sheet of covering fire and scampered to the stern.

'Where are they?' he yelled.

Feinberg stopped shooting to answer him. 'In the galley,' he said, jerking a thumb toward the bulkhead beside them. 'In the lifeboats, and in the doorways amidships.'

'All right.' Dickstein got to his feet. 'We hold this position until Bader's group makes the deck. When you hear them open fire, move. Dovrat and Katzen, hit the galley door and head below. Feinberg, cover them, then work your way forward along this edge of the deck. I'll make for the first lifeboat. Meantime give them something to distract their attention from the port stern ladder and Bader's team. Fire at will.'

Hassan and Mahmoud were interrogating the sailor when the shooting started. They were in the chartroom, aft of the bridge. The sailor would speak only German, but Hassan spoke German. His story was that the *Coparelli* had broken down and the crew had been taken off, leaving him to wait in the ship until a spare part arrived. He knew nothing of uranium or hijacks or Dickstein. Hassan did not believe him, for – as he pointed out to Mahmoud – if Dickstein could arrange for the ship to break down, he could surely arrange for one of his own men to be left aboard it. The sailor was tied to a chair, and now Mahmoud was cutting off his fingers one by one in an attempt to make him tell a different story.

They heard one quick burst of firing, then a silence, then a second burst followed by a barrage. Mahmoud sheathed his knife and went down the stairs which led from the chartroom to the officers' quarters.

Hassan tried to assess the situation. The Fedayeen were grouped in three places – the lifeboats, the galley and the main amidships superstructure. From where he was Hassan could see both port and starboard sides of the deck, and if he went forward from the chartroom to the bridge he could see the foredeck. Most of the Israelis seemed to have boarded the ship at the stern. The Fedayeen, both those immediately below Hassan and those in the lifeboats at either side, were firing toward the stern. There was no firing from the galley, which must mean the Israelis had taken it. They must have gone below, but they had left two men on deck, one on either side, to guard their rear.

Mahmoud's ambush had failed, then. The Israelis were supposed to be mown down as they came over the rail. In fact they had succeeded in reaching cover, and now the battle was even.

The fighting on deck was stalemated, with both sides shooting at each other from good cover. That was the Israelis' intention, Hassan assumed: to keep the opposition busy on deck while they made their progress below. They would attack the Fedayeen stronghold, the amidships superstructure, from below, after making their way the length of the 'tweendecks gangways.

Where was the best place to be? Right where he was, Hassan decided. To reach him the Israelis had to fight their way along the 'tweendecks, then up through the officers' quarters, then up again to the bridge and chartroom. It was a tough position to take.

There was a huge explosion from the bridge. The heavy door separating bridge and chartroom rattled, sagged on its hinges and fell slowly inward. Hassan looked through.

A grenade had landed in the bridge. The bodies of three Fedayeen were spread across the bulkheads. All the glass of the bridge was smashed. The grenade must have come from the foredeck, which meant that there was another group of Israelis in the prow. As if to confirm his supposition, a burst of gunfire came from the for'ard crane.

Hassan picked up a submachine gun from the floor, rested it on the window frame, and began to shoot back.

*

Levi Abbas watched Porush's grenade sail through the air and into the bridge, then saw the explosion shatter what remained of the glass. The guns from that quarter were briefly silenced, and then a new one started up. For a minute Abbas could not figure out what the new gun was shooting at, for none of the bullets landed near him. He looked at either side. Sapir and Sharrett were both shooting at the bridge, and neither seemed to be under fire. Abbas looked up at the crane. Porush – it was Porush who was under fire. There was a burst from the cabin of the crane as Porush fired back.

The shooting from the bridge was amateurish, wild and inaccurate – the man was just spraying bullets. But he had a good position. He was high, and well protected by the walls of the bridge. He would hit something sooner or later. Abbas took out a grenade and lobbed it, but it fell short. Only Porush was close enough to throw into the bridge, and he had used all his grenades – only the fourth had landed on target.

Abbas fired again, then looked up at the control cabin of the crane. As he looked, he saw Porush come toppling backward out of the control cabin, turn over in the air, and fall like a dead weight to the deck.

Abbas thought: And how will I tell my sister?

The gunman in the bridge stopped firing, then resumed with a burst in Sharrett's direction. Unlike Abbas and Sapir, Sharrett had very little cover: he was squeezed between a capstan and the gunwale. Abbas and Sapir both shot at the bridge. The unseen sniper was improving: bullets stitched a seam in the deck toward Sharrett's capstan; then Sharrett screamed, jumped sideways, and jerked as if electrocuted while more bullets thudded into his body, until at last he lay still and the screaming stopped.

The situation was bad. Abbas's team was supposed to command the foredeck, but at the moment the man on the bridge was doing that. Abbas had to take him out.

He threw another grenade. It landed short of the bridge and exploded; the flash might dazzle the sniper for a second or two. When the bang came Abbas was on his feet and running for the crane, the crash of Sapir's covering fire in his ears. He made the foot of the ladder and started firing before the sniper on the bridge saw him. Then bullets were clanging on the girders all around him. It seemed to take him an age to climb each step. Some lunatic part of his mind began to count the steps: seven-eight-nine-ten—

He was hit by a ricochet. The bullet entered his thigh just below the hip bone. It did not kill him, but the shock of it seemed to paralyze the muscles in the lower half of his body. His feet slipped from the rungs of the ladder. He had a moment of confused panic as he discovered that his legs would not work. Instinctively he grabbed for the ladder with his hands, but he missed and fell. He turned partly over and landed awkwardly, breaking his neck; and he died.

The door to the for'ard store opened slightly and a wide-eyed, frightened Russian face looked out; but nobody saw it, and it went back inside; and the door closed.

As Katzen and Dovrat rushed the galley, Dickstein took advantage of Feinberg's covering fire to move forward. He ran, bent double, past the point at which they had boarded the ship and past the galley door, to throw himself behind the first of the lifeboats, one that had already been grenaded. From there, in the faint but increasing light, he could make out the lines of the amidships superstructure, shaped like a flight of three steps rising forward. At the main deck level was the officers' mess, the officers' dayroom, the sick bay and a passenger cabin used as a dry store. On the next level up were officers' cabins, heads, and the captain's quarters. On the top deck was the bridge with adjoining chartroom and radio booth.

Most of the enemy would now be at deck level in the mess and the dayroom. He could bypass them by climbing a ladder alongside the funnel to the walkway around the second deck, but the only way to the bridge was through the second deck. He would have to take out any soldiers in the cabins on his own.

He looked back. Feinberg had retreated behind the galley, perhaps to reload. He waited until Feinberg started shooting again, then got to his feet. Firing wildly from the hip, he broke from behind the lifeboat and dashed across the afterdeck to the ladder. Without breaking stride, he jumped on to the fourth rung and

scrambled up, conscious that for a few seconds he made
an easy target, hearing a clutch of bullets rattle on the
funnel beside him, until he reached the level of the
upper deck and flung himself across the walkway to
fetch up, breathing hard and shaking with effort, lying
against the door to the officers' quarters.

'Stone the bloody crows,' he muttered.

He reloaded his gun. He put his back to the door
and slowly slid upright to a porthole in the door at eye
level. He risked a look. He saw a passage with three
doors on either side and, at the far end, ladders going
down to the mess and up to the chartroom. He knew
that the bridge could be reached by either of two
outside ladders leading up from the main deck as well
as by way of the chartroom. However, the Arabs still
controlled that part of the deck and could cover the
outside ladders; therefore the only way to the bridge
was this way.

He opened the door and stepped in. He crept along
the passage to the first cabin door, opened it, and threw
in a grenade. He saw one of the enemy begin to turn
around, and closed the door. He heard the grenade
explode in the small space. He ran to the next door on
the same side, opened it, and threw in another grenade.
It exploded into empty space.

There was one more door on this side, and he had
no more grenades.

He ran to the door, threw it open, and went in
firing. There was one man here. He had been firing
through the porthole, but now he was easing his gun

out of the hole and turning around. Dickstein's burst of bullets sliced him in half.

Dickstein turned and faced the open door, waiting. The door of the opposite cabin flew open and Dickstein shot down the man behind it.

Dickstein stepped into the gangway, firing blind. There were two more cabins to account for. The door of the nearer one opened as Dickstein was spraying it, and a body fell out.

One to go. Dickstein watched. The door opened a crack, then closed again. Dickstein ran down the gangway, and kicked open the door, sprayed the cabin. There was no return fire. He stepped inside: the occupant had been hit by a ricochet and lay bleeding on the bunk.

Dickstein was seized with a kind of mad exultation: he had taken the entire deck on his own.

Next, the bridge. He ran forward along the gangway. At the far end the companionway led up to the chartroom and down to the officers' mess. He stepped on to the ladder, looked up, and threw himself down and away as the snout of a gun poked down at him and began to fire.

His grenades were gone. The man in the chartroom was impregnable to gunfire. He could stay behind the edge of the companionhead and fire blind down the ladder. Dickstein had to get on the ladder, for he wanted to go up.

He went into one of the forward cabins to overlook the deck and try to assess the situation. He was appalled when he saw what had happened on the foredeck: only one of the four men of Abbas's team was still firing, and Dickstein could just make out three bodies. Two or three guns seemed to be firing from the bridge at the remaining Israeli, trapping him behind a stack of anchor chain.

Dickstein looked to the side. Feinberg was still well aft – he had not managed to progress forward. And there was still no sign of the men who had gone below.

The Fedayeen were well entrenched in the mess below him. From their superior position they were able to keep at bay the men on deck and the men in the 'tweendecks below them. The only way to take the mess would be to attack it from all sides at once – including from above. But that meant taking the bridge first. And the bridge was impregnable.

Dickstein ran back along the gangway and out of the aft door. It was still pouring with rain, but there was a dim cold light in the sky. He could make out Feinberg on one side and Dovrat on the other. He called out their names until he caught their attention, then pointed at the galley. He jumped from the walkway to the afterdeck, raced across it, and dived into the galley.

They had got his meaning. A moment later they followed him in. Dickstein said, 'We have to take the mess.'

'I don't see how,' said Feinberg.

'Shut up and I'll tell you. We rush it from all sides at once: port, starboard, below and above. First we have to take the bridge. I'm going to do that. When I get there I'll sound the foghorn. That will be the signal. I want you both to go below and tell the men there.'

452

'How will you reach the bridge?' Feinberg said.

Dickstein said, 'Over the roof.'

On the bridge, Yasif Hassan had been joined by Mahmoud and two more of his Fedayeen, who took up firing positions while the leaders sat on the floor and conferred.

'They can't win,' Mahmoud said. 'From here we control too much deck. They can't attack the mess from below, because the companionway is easy to dominate from above. They can't attack from the sides or the front because we can fire down on them from here. They can't attack from above because we control the down companion. We just keep shooting until they surrender.'

Hassan said, 'One of them tried to take this companion a few minutes ago. I stopped him.'

'You were on your own up here?'

'Yes.'

He put his hands on Hassan's shoulders. 'You are now one of the Fedayeen,' he said.

Hassan voiced the thought that was on both their minds. 'After this?'

Mahmoud nodded. 'Equal partners.'

They clasped hands.

Hassan repeated, 'Equal partners.'

Mahmoud said, 'And now, I think they will try for that companionway again – it's their only hope.'

'I'll cover it from the chartroom,' Hassan said.

They both stood up; then a stray bullet from the

foredeck came in through the glassless windows and entered Mahmoud's brain, and he died instantly.

And Hassan was the leader of the Fedayeen.

Lying on his belly, arms and legs spread wide for traction, Dickstein inched his way across the roof. It was curved, and totally without handholds, and it was slick with rain. As the *Coparelli* heaved and shifted in the waves, the roof tilted forward, backward, and from side to side. All Dickstein could do was press himself to the metal and try to slow his slide.

At the forward end of the roof was a navigation light. When he reached that he would be safe, for he could hold on to it. His progress toward it was painfully slow. He got within a foot of it, then the ship rolled to port and he slid away. It was a long roll, and it took him all the way to the edge of the roof. For a moment he hung with one arm and a leg over a thirty-foot drop to the deck. The ship rolled a little more, the rest of his leg went over and he tried to dig the fingernails of his right hand into the painted metal of the roof.

There was an agonizing pause.

The *Coparelli* rolled back.

Dickstein let himself go with the roll, sliding faster and faster toward the navigation light.

But the ship pitched up, the roof tilted backward, and he slid in a long curve, missing the light by a yard. Once again he pressed his hands and feet into the metal, trying to slow himself down; once again he went all the way to the edge; once again he hung over the drop to the deck; but this time it was his right arm which dangled over the edge, and his machine gun slipped off his right shoulder and fell into a lifeboat.

She rolled back and pitched forward, and Dickstein found himself sliding with increasing speed toward the navigation light. This time he reached it. He grabbed with both hands. The light was about a foot from the forward edge of the roof. Immediately below the edge were the front windows of the bridge. their glass smashed out long ago, and two gun barrels poking out through them.

Dickstein held on to the light, but he could not stop his slide. His body swung about in a wide sweep, heading for the edge. He saw that the front of the roof, unlike the sides, had a narrow steel gutter to take away the rain from the glass below. As his body swung over the edge he released his grip on the navigation light, let himself slide forward with the pitch of the ship, grabbed the steel gutter with his fingertips, and swung his legs down and in. He came flying through the broken windows feet first to land in the middle of the bridge. He bent his knees to take the shock of landing, then straightened up. His submachine gun had been lost and he had no time to draw his pistol or his knife. There were two Arabs on the bridge, one on either side of him, both holding machine guns and firing down on to the deck. As Dickstein straightened up they began to turn toward him, their faces a picture of amazement.

Dickstein was fractionally nearer the one on the port side. He lashed out with a kick which, more by luck than by judgment, landed on the point of the man's elbow, momentarily paralyzing his gun arm. Then Dickstein jumped for the other man. His machine gun was swinging toward Dickstein just a split second too late: Dickstein got inside its swing. He brought up his right hand in the most vicious two-stroke blow he knew: the heel of his hand hit the point of the Arab's chin, snapping his head back for the second stroke as Dickstein's hand, fingers stiffened for a karate chop, came down hard into the exposed flesh of the soft throat.

Before the man could fall Dickstein grabbed him by the jacket and swung him around between himself and the other Arab. The other man was bringing up his gun. Dickstein lifted the dead man and hurled him across the bridge as the machine gun opened up. The dead body took the bullets and crashed into the other Arab, who lost his balance, went backward out through the open doorway and fell to the deck below.

There was a third man in the chartroom, guarding the companionway leading down. In the three seconds during which Dickstein had been on the bridge the man had stood up and turned around; and now Dickstein recognized Yasif Hassan.

Dickstein dropped to a crouch, stuck out a leg, kicked at the broken door which lay on the floor between himself and Hassan. The door slid along the deck, striking Hassan's feet. It was only enough to throw him off balance, but as he spread his arms to recover his equilibrium Dickstein moved.

Until this moment Dickstein had been like a machine, reacting reflexively to everything that confronted him, letting his nervous system plan every move without conscious thought, allowing training and instinct to guide him; but now it was more than that. Now, faced with the enemy of all he had ever loved, he was possessed by blind hatred and mad rage.

It gave him added speed and power.

He took hold of Hassan's gun arm by the wrist and shoulder, and with a downward pull broke the arm over his knee. Hassan screamed and the gun dropped from his useless hand. Turning slightly, Dickstein brought his elbow back in a blow which caught Hassan just under the ear. Hassan turned away, falling. Dickstein grabbed his hair from behind, pulling the head backward; and as Hassan sagged away from him he lifted his foot high and kicked. His heel struck the back of Hassan's neck at the moment he jerked the head. There was a snap as all the tension went out of the man's muscles and his head lolled, unsupported, on his shoulders.

Dickstein let go and the body crumpled.

He stared at the harmless body with exultation ringing in his ears.

Then he saw Koch.

The engineer was tied to a chair, slumped over, pale as death but conscious. There was blood on his clothes. Dickstein drew his knife and cut the ropes that bound Koch. Then saw the man's hands.

He said, 'Christ.'

'I'll live,' Koch muttered. He did not get up from the chair.

Dickstein picked up Hassan's machine gun and

checked the magazine. It was almost full. He moved out on to the bridge and located the foghorn.

'Koch,' he said, 'can you get out of that chair?'

Koch got up, swaying unsteadily until Dickstein stepped across and supported him, leading him through to the bridge. 'See this button? I want you to count slowly to ten, then lean on it.'

Koch shook his head to clear it. 'I think I can handle it.'

'Start. Now.'

'One,' Koch said. 'Two.'

Dickstein went down the companionway and came out on the second deck, the one he had cleared himself. It was still empty, He went on down, and stopped just before the ladder emerged into the mess. He figured all the remaining Fedayeen must be here, lined against the walls, shooting out through portholes and doorways; one or two perhaps watching the companionway. There was no safe, careful way to take such a strong defensive position.

Come on, Koch!

Dickstein had intended to spend a second or two hiding in the companionway. At any moment one of the Arabs might look up it to check. If Koch had collapsed he would have to go back up there and—

The foghorn sounded.

Dickstein jumped. He was firing before he landed. There were two men close to the foot of the ladder. He shot them first. The firing from outside went into a crescendo. Dickstein turned in a rapid half circle, dropped to one knee to make a smaller target, and sprayed the Fedayeen along the walls. Suddenly there was another gun as Ish came up from below; then Feinberg was at one door, shooting; and Dovrat, wounded, came in through another door. And then, as if by signal, they all stopped shooting, and the silence was like thunder.

All the Fedayeen were dead.

Dickstein, still kneeling, bowed his head in exhaustion. After a moment he stood up and looked at his men. 'Where are the others?' he said.

Feinberg gave him a peculiar look. 'There's someone on the foredeck, Sapir I think.'

'And the rest?'

'That's it,' Feinberg said. 'All the others are dead.'

Dickstein slumped against a bulkhead. 'What a price,' he said quietly.

Looking out through the smashed porthole he saw that it was day.

CHAPTER SEVENTEEN

A YEAR earlier the BOAC jet in which Suza Ashford was serving dinner had abruptly begun to lose height for no apparent reason over the Atlantic Ocean. The pilot had switched on the seat-belt lights. Suza had walked up and down the aisle, saying, 'Just a little turbulence,' and helping people fasten their seat belts, all the time thinking: We're going to die, we're all going to die.

She felt like that now.

There had been a short message from Tyrin: *Israel is attacking* – then silence. At this moment Nathaniel was being shot at. He might be wounded, he might have been captured, he might be dead; and while Suza seethed with nervous tension she had to give the radio operator the BOAC Big Smile and say. 'It's quite a setup you've got here.'

The *Karla*'s radio operator was a big grey-haired man from Odessa. His name was Aleksandr, and he spoke passable English. 'It cost one hundred thousand dollar,' he said proudly. 'You know about radio?'

'A little ... I used to be an air hostess.' She had said 'used to be' without forethought, and now she wondered whether that life really was gone. 'I've seen the air crew using their radios. I know the basics.'

'Really, this is four radios,' Aleksandr explained. 'One picks up the *Stromberg* beacon. One listens to Tyrin on *Coparelli*. One listens to *Coparelli*'s regular wave-length. And this one wanders. Look.'

He showed her a dial whose pointer moved around slowly. 'It seeks a transmitter, stops when it finds one,' Aleksandr said.

'That's incredible. Did you invent that?'

'I am an operator, not inventor, sadly.'

'And you can broadcast on any of the sets, just by switching to TRANSMIT?'

'Yes, Morse code or speech. But of course, on this operation nobody uses speech.'

'Did you have to go through long training to become a radio operator?'

'Not long. Learning Morse is easy. But to be a ship's radioman you must know how to repair the set.' He lowered his voice. 'And to be a KGB operator, you must go to spy school.' He laughed, and Suza laughed with him, thinking: come on, Tyrin; and then her wish was granted.

The message began, Aleksandr started writing and at the same time said to Suza, 'Tyrin. Get Rostov, please.'

Suza left the bridge reluctantly; she wanted to know what was in the message. She hurried to the mess, expecting to find Rostov there drinking strong black coffee, but the room was empty. She went down another deck and made her way to his cabin. She knocked on the door.

His voice in Russian said something which might have meant come in.

She opened the door. Rostov stood there in his shorts, washing in a bowl.

'Tyrin's coming through,' Suza said. She turned to leave.

'Suza.'

She turned back. 'What would you say if I surprised you in your underwear?'

'I'd say piss off,' she said.

'Wait for me outside.'

She closed the door, thinking: That's done it.

When he came out she said, 'I'm sorry.'

He gave a tight smile. 'I should not have been so unprofessional. Let's go.'

She followed him up to the radio room, which was immediately below the bridge in what should have been the captain's cabin. Because of the mass of extra equipment, Aleksandr had explained, it was not possible to put the radio operator adjacent to the bridge, as was customary. Suza had figured out for herself that this arrangement had the additional advantage of segregating the radio from the crew when the ship carried a mixture of ordinary seamen and KGB agents.

Aleksandr had transcribed Tyrin's signal. He handed it to Rostov, who read it in English. 'Israelis have taken *Coparelli*. *Stromberg* alongside. Dickstein alive.'

Suza went limp with relief. She had to sit down. She slumped into a chair.

No one noticed. Rostov was already composing his reply to Tyrin: 'We will hit at six A.M. tomorrow.'

The tide of relief went out for Suza and she thought: Oh, God, what do I do now?

Nat Dickstein stood in silence, wearing a borrowed seaman's cap, as the captain of the *Stromberg* read the words of the service for the dead, raising his voice against the noise of wind, rain and sea. One by one the canvas-wrapped bodies were tipped over the rail into the black water: Abbas, Sharrett, Porush, Gibli, Bader, Remez, and Jabotinsky. Seven of the twelve had died. Uranium was the most costly metal in the world.

There had been another funeral earlier. Four Fedayeen had been left alive – three wounded, one who had lost his nerve and hidden – and after they had been disarmed Dickstein had allowed them to bury their dead. Theirs had been a bigger funeral – they had dropped twenty-five bodies into the sea. They had hurried through their ceremony under the watchful eyes – and guns – of three surviving Israelis, who understood that this courtesy should be extended to the enemy but did not have to like it.

Meanwhile, the *Stromberg*'s captain had brought aboard all his ship's papers. The team of fitters and joiners, which had come along in case it was necessary to alter the *Coparelli* to match the *Stromberg*, was set to work repairing the battle damage. Dickstein told them to concentrate on what was visible from the deck: the rest would have to wait until they reached port. They set about filling holes, repairing furniture, and replacing panes of glass and metal fittings with spares

cannibalized from the doomed *Stromberg*. A painter
went down a ladder to remove the name *Coparelli*
from the hull and replace it with the stencilled letters
S-T-R-O-M-B-E-R-G. When he had finished he set about
painting over the repaired bulkheads and woodwork
on deck. All the *Coparelli*'s lifeboats, damaged beyond
repair, were chopped up and thrown over the side, and
the *Stromberg*'s boats were brought over to replace them.
The new oil pump, which the *Stromberg* had carried on
Koch's instructions, was installed in the *Coparelli*'s
engine.

Work had stopped for the burial. Now, as soon as
the captain had uttered the final words, it began again.
Towards the end of the afternoon the engine rumbled
to life. Dickstein stood on the bridge with the captain
while the anchor was raised. The crew of the *Stromberg*
quickly found their way round the new ship, which was
identical to their old one. The captain set a course and
ordered full speed ahead.

It was almost over, Dickstein thought. The *Coparelli*
had disappeared: for all intents and purposes the ship
in which he now sailed was the *Stromberg*, and the
Stromberg was legally owned by Savile Shipping. Israel
had her uranium, and nobody knew how she had got
it. Everyone in the chain of operation was now taken
care of – except Pedler, still the legal owner of the
yellowcake. He was the one man who could ruin the
whole scheme if he should become either curious or
hostile. Papagopolous would be handling him right
now: Dickstein silently wished him luck.

'We're clear,' the captain said.

The explosives expert in the chartroom pulled a lever on his radio detonator, then everybody watched the empty *Stromberg*, now more than a mile away.

There was a loud, dull thud, like thunder, and the *Stromberg* seemed to sag in the middle. Her fuel tanks caught fire and the stormy evening was lit by a gout of flame reaching for the sky. Dickstein felt elation and faint anxiety at the sight of such great destruction. The *Stromberg* began to sink, slowly at first and then faster. Her stern went under; seconds later her bows followed; her funnel poked up above the water for a moment like the raised arm of a drowning man, and then she was gone.

Dickstein smiled faintly and turned away.

He heard a noise. The captain heard it too. They went to the side of the bridge and looked out, and then they understood.

Down on the deck, the men were cheering.

Franz Albrecht Pedler sat in his office on the outskirts of Wiesbaden and scratched his snowy-white head. The telegram from Angeluzzi e Bianco in Genoa, translated from the Italian by Pedler's multilingual secretary, was perfectly plain and at the same time totally incomprehensible. It said: PLEASE ADVISE SOONEST OF NEW EXPECTED DELIVERY DATE OF YELLOWCAKE.

As far as Pedler knew there was nothing wrong with the old expected delivery date, which was a couple of days away. Clearly Angeluzzi e Bianco knew something he did not. He had already wired the shippers: IS

YELLOWCAKE DELAYED? He felt a little annoyed with them. Surely they should have informed him as well as the receiving company if there was a delay. But maybe the Italians had their wires crossed. Pedler had formed the opinion during the war that you could never trust Italians to do what they were told. He had thought they might be different nowadays, but perhaps they were the same.

He stood at his window, watching the evening gather over his little cluster of factory buildings. He could almost wish he had not bought the uranium. The deal with the Israeli Army, all signed, sealed and delivered, would keep his company in profit for the rest of his life, and he no longer needed to speculate.

His secretary came in with the reply from the shippers, already translated: COPARELLI SOLD TO SAVILE SHIPPING OF ZURICH WHO NOW HAVE RESPONSIBILITY FOR YOUR CARGO. WE ASSURE YOU OF COMPLETE RELIABILITY OF PURCHASERS. There followed the phone number of Savile Shipping and the words SPEAK TO PAPAGOPOLOUS.

Pedler gave the telegram back to the secretary. 'Would you call that number in Zurich and get this Papagopolous on the line please?'

She came back a few minutes later. 'Papagopolous will call you back.'

Pedler looked at his watch. 'I suppose I'd better wait for his call. I might as well get to the bottom of this now that I've started.'

Papagopolous came through ten minutes later. Pedler said to him, 'I'm told you are now responsible for my cargo on board the *Coparelli*. I've had a cable from the Italians asking for a new delivery date – is there some delay?'

'Yes, there is,' Papagopolous said. 'You should have been informed – I'm terribly sorry.' The man spoke excellent German but it was still clear he was not a German. It was also clear he was not really terribly sorry. He went on, 'The *Coparelli*'s oil pump broke down at sea and she is becalmed. We're making arrangements to have your cargo delivered as early as possible.'

'Well, what am I to say to Angeluzzi e Bianco?'

'I have told them that I will let them know the new date just as soon as I know it myself,' Papagopolous said. 'Please leave it to me. I will keep you both informed.'

'Very well. Goodbye.'

Odd, Pedler thought as he hung up the phone. Looking out of the window, he saw that all the workers had left. The staff car parking lot was empty except for his Mercedes and his secretary's Volkswagen. What the hell, time to go home. He put on his coat. The uranium was insured. If it was lost he would get his money back. He turned out the office lights and helped his secretary on with her coat, then he got into his car and drove home to his wife.

Suza Ashford did not close her eyes all night.

Once again, Nat Dickstein's life was in danger. Once again, she was the only one who could warn him. And this time she could not deceive others into helping her.

She had to do it alone.

It was simple. She had to go to the *Karla*'s radio room, get rid of Aleksandr, and call the *Coparelli*.

I'll never do it, she thought. The ship is full of KGB. Aleksandr is a big man. I want to go to sleep. For ever. It's impossible. I can't do it.

Oh, Nathaniel.

At four A.M. she put on jeans, a sweater, boots and an oilskin. The full bottle of vodka she had taken from the mess – 'to help me sleep' – went in the inside pocket of the oilskin.

She had to know the *Karla*'s position.

She went up to the bridge. The first officer smiled at her. 'Can't sleep?' he said in English.

'The suspense is too much,' she told him. The BOAC Big Smile. Is your seat belt fastened, sir? Just a little turbulence, nothing to worry about. She asked the first officer, 'Where are we?'

He showed her their position on the map, and the estimated position of the *Coparelli*.

'What's that in numbers?' she said.

He told her the coordinates, the course, and the speed of the *Karla*. She repeated the numbers once aloud and twice more in her head, trying to burn them into her brain. 'It's fascinating,' she said brightly. 'Everyone on a ship has a special skill . . . Will we reach the *Coparelli* on time, do you think?'

'Oh, yes,' he said. 'Then – boom.'

She looked outside. It was completely black – there

were no stars and no ships' lights in sight. The weather was getting worse.

'You're shivering,' the first officer said. 'Are you cold?'

'Yes,' she said, though it was not the weather making her shiver. 'When is Colonel Rostov getting up?'

'He's to be called at five.'

'I think I'll try to get another hour's sleep.'

She went down to the radio room. Aleksandr was there. 'Couldn't you sleep, either?' she asked him.

'No. I've sent my number two to bed.'

She looked over the radio equipment. 'Aren't you listening to the *Stromberg* any more?'

'The signal stopped. Either they found the beacon, or they sank the ship. We think they sank her.'

Suza sat down and took out the bottle of vodka. She unscrewed the cap. 'Have a drink.' She handed him the bottle.

'Are you cold?'

'A little.'

'Your hand is shaking.' He took the bottle and put it to his lips, taking a long swallow. 'Ah, thank you.' He handed it back to her.

Suza drank a mouthful for courage. It was rough Russian vodka, and it burned her throat, but it had the desired effect. She screwed down the cap and waited for Aleksandr to turn his back on her.

'Tell me about life in England,' he said conversationally. 'Is it true that the poor starve while the rich get fat?'

'Not many people starve,' she said. Turn around,

469

damn it, turn *around*. I can't do this facing you. 'But there is great inequality.'

'Are there different laws for rich and poor?'

'There's a saying: "The law forbids rich and poor alike to steal bread and sleep under bridges."'

Aleksandr laughed. 'In the Soviet Union people are equal, but some have privileges. Will you live in Russia now?'

'I don't know.' Suza opened the bottle and passed it to him again.

He took a long swallow and gave it back. 'In Russia you won't have such clothes.'

The time was passing too quickly, she had to do it now. She stood up to take the bottle. Her oilskin was open down the front. Standing before him, she tilted her head back to drink from the bottle, knowing he would stare at her breasts as they jutted out. She allowed him a good look, then shifted her grip on the bottle and brought it down as hard as she could on top of his head.

There was a sickening thud as it hit him. He stared at her dazedly. She thought: You're supposed to be knocked out! His eyes would not shut. What do I do? She hesitated, then she gritted her teeth and hit him again.

His eyes closed and he slumped in the chair. Suza got hold of his feet and pulled. As he came off the chair his head hit the deck, making Suza wince, but then she thought: It's just as well, he'll stay out longer.

She dragged him to a cupboard. She was breathing fast, from fear as well as exertion. From her jeans pocket she took a long piece of baling twine she had picked up in the stern. She tied Aleksandr's feet, then turned him over and bound his hands behind his back.

She had to get him into the cupboard. She glanced at the door. Oh, God, don't let anyone come in now! She put his feet in, then straddled his unconscious body and tried to lift him. He was a heavy man. She got him half upright, but when she tried to shift him into the cupboard he slipped from her grasp. She got behind him to try again. She grasped him beneath the armpits and lifted. This way was better: she could lean his weight against her chest while she shifted her grip. She got him half upright again, then wrapped her arms around his chest and inched sideways. She had to go into the cupboard with him, let him go, then wriggle out from underneath him.

He was in a sitting position now, his feet against one side of the cupboard, his knees bent, and his back against the opposite side. She checked his bonds: still tight. But he could still shout! She looked about for something to stuff in his mouth to gag him. She could see nothing. She could not leave the room to search for something because he might come round in the meantime. The only thing that she could think of was her pantyhose.

It seemed to take her for ever to do it. She had to pull off her borrowed sea boots, take off her jeans, pull her pantyhose off, put her jeans on, get into her boots, then crumple the nylon cloth into a ball and stuff it between his slack jaws.

She could not close the cupboard door. 'Oh, God!'

she said out loud. It was Aleksandr's elbow that was in the way. His bound hands rested on the floor of the cupboard, and because of his slumped position his arms were bent outward. No matter how she pushed and shoved at the door that elbow stopped it from closing. Finally she had to get back into the cupboard with him and turn him slightly sideways so that he leaned into the corner. Now his elbow was out of the way.

She looked at him a moment longer. How long did people stay knocked out? She had no idea. She knew she should hit him again, but she was afraid of killing him. She went and got the bottle, and even lifted it over her head; but at the last moment she lost her nerve, put the bottle down, and slammed the cupboard door.

She looked at her wristwatch and gave a cry of dismay: it was ten minutes to five. The *Coparelli* would soon appear on the *Karla*'s radar screen, and Rostov would be here, and she would have lost her chance.

She sat down at the radio desk, switched the lever to TRANSMIT, selected the set that was already tuned to the *Coparelli*'s wavelength and leaned over the microphone.

'Calling *Coparelli*, come in please.'

She waited.

Nothing.

'Damn you to hell, Nat Dickstein, *speak* to me. Nathaniel!'

Nat Dickstein stood in the amidships hold of the *Coparelli*, staring at the drums of sandy metallic ore that had cost so much. They looked nothing special – just large black oil drums with the word PLUMBAT stencilled on their sides. He would have liked to open one and feel the stuff, just to know what it was like, but the lids were heavily sealed.

He felt suicidal. Instead of the elation of victory, he had only bereavement. He could not rejoice over the terrorists he had killed, he could only mourn for his own dead.

He went over the battle again, as he had been doing throughout a sleepless night. If he had told Abbas to open fire as soon as he got aboard it might have distracted the Fedayeen long enough for Gibli to get over the rail without being shot. If he had gone with three men to take out the bridge with grenades at the very start of the fight the mess might have been taken earlier and lives would have been saved. If . . . but there were a hundred things he would have done differently if he had been able to see into the future, or if he were just a wiser man.

Well, Israel would now have atom bombs to protect her for ever.

Even that thought gave him no joy. A year ago it would have thrilled him. But a year ago he had not met Suza Ashford.

He heard a noise and looked up. It sounded as if people were running around on deck. Some nautical crisis, no doubt.

Suza had changed him. She had taught him to expect more out of life than victory in battle. When he had anticipated this day, when he had thought about what it would feel like to have pulled off this tremendous coup, she had always been in his daydream, waiting for him somewhere, ready to share his triumph. But she would not be there. Nobody else would do. And there was no joy in a solitary celebration.

He had stared long enough. He climbed the ladder out of the hold, wondering what to do with the rest of his life. He emerged on deck. A rating peered at him. 'Mr Dickstein?'

'Yes. What do you want?'

'We've been searching the ship for you, sir ... It's the radio, someone is calling the *Coparelli*. We haven't answered, sir, because we're not supposed to be the *Coparelli*, are we? But she says—'

'She?'

'Yes, sir. She's coming over clear – speech, not Morse code. She sounds close. And she's upset. "Speak to me, Nathaniel," she says, stuff like that, sir.'

Dickstein grabbed the rating by his peajacket. 'Nathaniel?' he shouted. 'Did she say Nathaniel?'

'Yes, sir, I'm sorry, if—'

But Dickstein was heading for the bridge at a run.

The voice of Nat Dickstein came over the radio: 'Who is calling *Coparelli*?'

She found her voice. 'Oh, Nat, at last.'

'Suza? Is that Suza?'

'Yes, yes.'

'Where are you?'

She gathered her thoughts. 'I'm with David Rostov

474

on a Russian ship called the *Karla*. Make a note of this.'
She gave him the position, course and speed just as the
first officer had told them to her. 'That was at four-ten
this morning. Nat, this ship is going to ram yours at six
A.M.'

'Ram? Why? Oh, I see . . .'

'Nat, they'll catch me at the radio any minute, what
are we going to do, quickly—'

'Can you create a diversion of some kind at precisely
five-thirty?'

'Diversion?'

'Start a fire, shout "man overboard", anything to
keep them all very busy for a few minutes.'

'Well – I'll try—'

'Do your best. I want them all running around,
nobody quite sure what's going on or what to do – are
they all KGB?'

'Yes.'

'Okay, now—'

The door of the radio room opened – Suza flipped
the switch to TRANSMIT and Dickstein's voice was
silenced and David Rostov walked in. He said, 'Where's
Aleksandr?'

Suza tried to smile. 'He went for coffee. I'm minding
the shop.'

'The damn fool . . .' His curses switched into Russian
as he stormed out.

Suza moved the lever to RECEIVE.

Nat said, 'I heard that. You'd better make yourself
scarce until five-thirty—'

'Wait,' she shouted. 'What are you going to do?'

'Do?' he said. 'I'm coming to get you.'

'Oh,' she said. 'Oh, thank you.'

'I love you.'

As she switched off, Morse began to come through on another set. Tyrin would have heard every word of her conversation, and now he would be trying to warn Rostov. She had forgotten to tell Nat about Tyrin.

She could try to contact Nat again, but it would be very risky, and Tyrin would get his message through to Rostov in the time it took Nat's men to search the *Coparelli*, locate Tyrin and destroy his equipment. And when Tyrin's message got to Rostov, he would know Nat was coming, and he would be prepared.

She had to block that message.

She also had to get away.

She decided to wreck the radio.

How? All the wiring must be behind the panels. She would have to take a panel off. She needed a screwdriver. Quickly, quickly before Rostov gives up looking for Aleksandr! She found Aleksandr's tools in a corner and picked out a small screwdriver. She undid the screws on two corners of the panel. Impatient, she pocketed the screwdriver and forced the panel out with her hands. Inside was a mass of wires like psychedelic spaghetti. She grabbed a fistful and pulled. Nothing happened: she had pulled too many at once. She selected one, and tugged: it came out. Furiously she pulled wires until fifteen or twenty were hanging loose. Still the Morse code chattered. She poured the remains of the vodka into the innards of the radio. The Morse stopped, and every light on the panel went out.

There was a thump from inside the cupboard. Aleksandr must be coming round. Well, they would know everything as soon as they saw the radio now anyway.

She went out, closing the door behind her.

She went down the ladder and out on to the deck, trying to figure out where she could hide and what kind of diversion she could create. No point now in shouting 'man overboard' – they certainly would not believe her after what she had done to their radio and their radio operator. Let down the anchor? She would not know where to begin.

What was Rostov likely to do now? He would look for Aleksandr in the galley, the mess, and his cabin. Not finding him, he would return to the radio room, and then would start a shipwide search for her.

He was a methodical man. He would start at the prow and work backwards along the main deck, then send one party to search the upperworks and another to sweep below, deck by deck, starting at the top and working down.

What was the lowest part of the ship? The engine room. That would have to be her hiding place. She went inside and found her way to a downward companionway. She had her foot on the top rung of the ladder when she saw Rostov.

And he saw her.

She had no idea where her next words came from. 'Aleksandr's come back to the radio room. I'll be back in a moment.'

Rostov nodded grimly, and went off in the direction of the radio room.

She headed straight down through two decks and emerged into the engine room. The second engineer was on duty at night. He stared at her as she came in and approached him.

'This is the only warm place on the ship,' she said cheerfully. 'Mind if I keep you company?'

He looked mystified, and said slowly, 'I cannot . . . speak English . . . please.'

'You don't speak English?'

He shook his head.

'I'm cold,' she said, and mimed a shiver. She held her hands out toward the throbbing engine. 'Okay?'

He was more than happy to have this beautiful girl for company in his engine room. 'Okay,' he said, nodding vigorously.

He continued to stare at her, with a pleased look on his face, until it occurred to him that he should perhaps show some hospitality. He looked about, then pulled a pack of cigarettes from his pocket and offered her one.

'I don't usually, but I think I will,' she said, and took a cigarette. It had a small cardboard tube for a filter. The engineer lit it for her. She looked up at the hatch, half expecting to see Rostov. She looked at her watch. It could not be five-twenty-five already! She had no time to think. Diversion, start a diversion. Shout 'man overboard', drop the anchor, light a fire—

Light a fire.

With what?

Petrol, there must be petrol, or diesel fuel, or something, right here in the engine room.

She looked over the engine. Where did the petrol

come in? The thing was a mass of tubes and pipes. Concentrate, concentrate! She wished she had learned more about the engine of her car. Were boat engines the same? No, sometimes they used truck fuel. Which kind was this? It was supposed to be a fast ship, so perhaps it used petrol, she remembered vaguely that petrol engines were more expensive to run but faster. If it was a petrol engine it would be similar to the engine of her car. Were there cables leading to spark plugs? She had changed a spark plug once.

She stared. Yes, it was like her car. There were six plugs, with leads from them to a round cap like a distributor. Somewhere there had to be a carburettor. The petrol went through the carburettor. It was a small thing that sometimes got blocked—

The voice-pipe barked in Russian, and the engineer walked toward it to answer. His back was to Suza.

She had to do it now.

There was something about the size of a coffee tin with a lid held on by a central nut. It could be the carburettor. She stretched herself across the engine and tried to undo the nut with her fingers. It would not budge. A heavy plastic pipe led into it. She grabbed it and tugged. She could not pull it out. She remembered she had put Aleksandr's screwdriver into her oilskin pocket. She took it out and jabbed at the pipe with the sharp end. The plastic was thick and tough. She stabbed the screwdriver into it with all her might. It made a small cut in the surface of the pipe. She stuck the point of the screwdriver into the cut and worked it.

The engineer reached the voice-pipe and spoke into it in Russian.

Suza felt the screwdriver break through the plastic. She tugged it out. A spray of clear liquid jetted out of the little hole, and the air was filled with the unmistakable smell of petrol. She dropped the screwdriver and ran toward the ladder.

She heard the engineer answer yes in Russian and nod his head to a question from the voice-pipe. An order followed. The voice was angry. As she reached the foot of the ladder she looked back. The engineer's smiling face had been transformed into a mask of malice. She went up the ladder as he ran across the engine-room deck after her.

At the top of the ladder she turned around. She saw a pool of petrol spreading over the deck, and the engineer stepping on the bottom rung of the ladder. In her hand she still held the cigarette he had given her. She threw it toward the engine, aiming at the place where the petrol was squirting out of the pipe.

She did not wait to see it land. She carried on up the ladder. Her head and shoulders were emerging on to the next deck when there was a loud *whooosh*, a bright red light from below, and a wave of scorching heat. Suza screamed as her trousers caught fire and the skin of her legs burned. She jumped the last few inches of the ladder and rolled. She beat at her trousers, then struggled out of her oilskin and managed to wrap it around her legs. The fire was killed, but the pain got worse.

She wanted to collapse. She knew if she lay down she

would pass out and the pain would go, but she had to get away from the fire, and she had to be somewhere where Nat could find her. She forced herself to stand up. Her legs felt as if they were still burning. She looked down to see bits like burned paper falling off, and she wondered if they were bits of trouser or bits of leg.

She took a step.

She could walk.

She staggered along the gangway. The fire alarm began to sound all over the ship. She reached the end of the gangway and leaned on the ladder.

Up, she had to go up.

She raised one foot, placed it on the bottom rung, and began the longest climb of her life.

CHAPTER EIGHTEEN

FOR THE second time in twenty-four hours Nat Dickstein was crossing huge seas in a small boat to board a ship held by the enemy. He was dressed as before, with life jacket, oilskin, and sea boots; and armed as before with submachine gun, pistol and grenades; but this time he was alone, and he was terrified.

There had been an argument aboard the *Coparelli* about what to do after Suza's radio message. Her dialogue with Dickstein had been listened to by the captain, Feinberg, and Ish. They had seen the jubilation in Nat's face, and they had felt entitled to argue that his judgment was now distorted by personal involvement.

'It's a trap,' argued Feinberg. 'They can't catch us, so they want us to turn and fight.'

'I know Rostov,' Dickstein said hotly. 'This is exactly how his mind works: he waits for you to make a break, then he pounces. This ramming idea has his name written all over it.'

Feinberg got angry. 'This isn't a game, Dickstein.'

'Listen, Nat,' Ish said more reasonably, 'let's us carry on and be ready to fight if and when they catch us. What have we got to gain by sending a boarding party?'

'I'm not suggesting a boarding party. I'm going alone.'

'Don't be a damn fool,' Ish said. 'If you go, so do we – you can't take a ship alone.'

'Look,' Dickstein said, trying to pacify them. 'If I make it, the *Karla* will never catch this ship. If I don't, the rest of you can still fight when the *Karla* gets to you. And if the *Karla* really can't catch you, and it's a trap, then I'm the only one who falls into it. It's the best way.'

'I don't think it's the best way,' Feinberg said.

'Nor do I,' Ish said.

Dickstein smiled. 'Well, I do, and it's my life, and besides, I'm the senior officer here and it's my decision, so to hell with all of you.'

So he had dressed and armed himself, and the captain had shown him how to operate the launch's radio and how to maintain an interception course with the *Karla*, and they had lowered the launch, and he had climbed down into it and pulled away.

And he was terrified.

It was impossible for him to overcome a whole boat-load of KGB all on his own. However, he was not planning that. He would not fight with any of them if he could help it. He would get aboard, hide himself until Suza's diversion began, and then look for her; and when he had found her, he would get off the *Karla* with her and flee. He had a small magnetic mine with him that he would fix to the *Karla*'s side before boarding. Then, whether he managed to escape or not, whether the whole thing was a trap or genuine, the *Karla* would have a hole blown in her side big enough to keep her from catching the *Coparelli*.

He was sure it was not a trap. He knew she was there, he knew that somehow she had been in their power and had been forced to help them, he knew she had risked her life to save his. He knew that she loved him.

And *that* was why he was terrified.

Suddenly he wanted to live. The blood-lust was gone: he was no longer interested in killing his enemies, defeating Rostov, frustrating the schemes of the Fedayeen or outwitting Egyptian Intelligence. He wanted to find Suza, and take her home, and spend the rest of his life with her. He was afraid to die.

He concentrated on steering his boat. Finding the *Karla* at night was not easy. He could keep a steady course but he had to estimate and make allowance for how much the wind and the waves were carrying him sideways. After fifteen minutes he knew he should have reached her, but she was nowhere to be seen. He began to zigzag in a search pattern, wondering desperately how far off course he was.

He was contemplating radioing the *Coparelli* for a new fix when suddenly the *Karla* appeared out of the night alongside him. She was moving fast, faster than his launch could go, and he had to reach the ladder at her bows before she was past, and at the same time avoid a collision. He gunned the launch forward, swerved away as the *Karla* rolled toward him, then turned back, homing in, while she rolled the other way.

He had the rope tied around his waist ready. The ladder came within reach. He flipped the engine of his launch into idle, stepped on the gunwale, and jumped. The *Karla* began to pitch forward as he landed on the ladder. He clung on while her prow went down into the waves. The sea came up to his waist, up to his shoulders. He took a deep breath as his head went under. He seemed to be under water for ever. The *Karla* just kept on going down. When he felt his lungs would burst she hesitated, and at last began to come up; and that seemed to take even longer. At last he broke surface and gulped lungfuls of air. He went up the ladder a few steps, untied the rope around his waist and made it fast to the ladder, securing the boat to the *Karla* for his escape. The magnetic mine was hanging from a rope across his shoulders. He took it off and slapped it on to the *Karla*'s hull.

The uranium was safe.

He shed his oilskin and climbed up the ladder.

The sound of the launch engine was inaudible in the noise of the wind, the sea, and the *Karla*'s own engines, but something must have attracted the attention of the man who looked over the rail just as Dickstein came up level with the deck. For a moment the man stared at Dickstein, his face registering amazement. Then Dickstein reached out his hand for a pull as he climbed over the rail. Automatically, with a natural instinct to help someone trying to get aboard out of the raging sea, the other man grabbed his arm. Dickstein got one leg over the rail, used his other hand to grab the outstretched arm, and threw the other man overboard and into the sea. His cry was lost in the wind. Dickstein brought the other leg over the rail and crouched down on the deck.

It seemed nobody had seen the incident.

The *Karla* was a small ship, much smaller than the *Coparelli*. There was only one superstructure, located amidships, two decks high. There were no cranes. The foredeck had a big hatch over the for'ard hold, but there was no aft hold: the crew accommodations and the engine room must occupy all the below-deck space aft, Dickstein concluded.

He looked at his watch. It was five-twenty-five. Suza's diversion should begin any moment, if she could do it.

He began to walk along the deck. There was some light from the ship's lamps, but one of the crew would have to look twice at him before being sure he was not one of them. He took his knife out of the sheath at his belt: he did not want to use his gun unless he had to, for the noise would start a hue and cry.

As he drew level with the superstructure a door opened, throwing a wedge of yellow light on to the rain-spattered deck. He dodged around the corner, flattening himself against the for'ard bulkhead. He heard two voices speaking Russian. The door slammed, and the voices receded as the men walked aft in the rain.

In the lee of the superstructure he crossed to the port side and continued toward the stern. He stopped at the corner and, looking cautiously around it, saw the two men cross the afterdeck and speak to a third man in the stern. He was tempted to take all three out with a burst from his submachine gun – three men was probably one fifth of the opposition – but decided not to: it was too early, Suza's diversion had not yet started and he had no idea where she was.

The two men came back along the starboard deck and went inside. Dickstein walked up to the remaining man in the stern, who seemed to be on guard. The man spoke to him in Russian. Dickstein grunted something unintelligible, the man replied with a question, then Dickstein was close enough and he jumped forward and cut the man's throat.

He threw the body overboard and retraced his steps. Two dead, and still they did not know he was on board. He looked at his watch. The luminous hands showed five-thirty. It was time to go inside.

He opened a door and saw an empty gangway and a companionway leading up, presumably to the bridge. He climbed the ladder. Loud voices came from the bridge. As he emerged through the companionhead he saw three men – the captain, the first officer and the second sublieutenant, he guessed. The first officer was shouting into the voice-pipe. A strange noise was coming back. As Dickstein brought his gun level, the captain pulled a lever and an alarm began to sound all over the ship. Dickstein pulled the trigger. The loud chatter of the gun was partly smothered by the wailing klaxon of the fire alarm. The three men were killed where they stood.

Dickstein hurried back down the ladder. The alarm must mean that Suza's diversion had started. Now all he had to do was stay alive until he found her.

The companionway from the bridge met the deck at

a junction of two gangways – a lateral one, which Dickstein had used, and another running the length of the superstructure. In response to the alarm doors were opening and men emerging all down both gangways. None of them seemed to be armed: this was a fire alarm, not a call to battle stations. Dickstein decided to run a bluff, and shoot only if it failed. He proceeded briskly along the central gangway, pushing his way through the milling men, shouting, 'Get out of the way' in German. They stared at him, not knowing who he was or what he was doing, except that he seemed to be in authority and there was a fire. One or two spoke to him. He ignored them. There was a rasping order from somewhere, and the men began to move purposefully. Dickstein reached the end of the gangway and was about to go down the ladder when the officer who had given the order came into sight and pointed at him, shouting a question.

Dickstein dropped down.

On the lower deck things were better organized. The men were running in one direction, toward the stern, and a group of three hands under the supervision of an officer was breaking out fire-fighting gear. There, in a place where the gangway widened for access to hoses, Dickstein saw something which made him temporarily unhinged, and brought a red mist of hatred to his eyes.

Suza was on the floor, her back to the bulkhead. Her legs were stretched out in front of her, her trousers torn. He could see her scorched and blackened skin through the tatters. He heard Rostov's voice, shouting at her over the sound of the alarm: 'What did you tell Dickstein?'

Dickstein jumped from the ladder onto the deck. One of the hands moved in front of him. Dickstein knocked him to the deck with an elbow blow to the face, and jumped on Rostov.

Even in his rage, he realized that he could not use the gun in this confined space while Rostov was so close to Suza. Besides, he wanted to kill the man with his hands.

He grabbed Rostov's shoulder and spun him around. Rostov saw his face. 'You!' Dickstein hit him in the stomach first, a pile-driving blow that buckled him at the waist and made him gasp for air. As his head came down Dickstein brought a knee up fast and hard, snapping Rostov's chin up and breaking his jaw; then, continuing the motion, he put all his strength behind a kick into the throat that smashed Rostov's neck and drove him backward into the bulkhead.

Before Rostov had completed his fall Dickstein turned quickly around, went down on one knee to bring his machine gun off his shoulder, and with Suza behind him and to one side opened fire on three hands who appeared in the gangway.

He turned again, picking Suza up in a fireman's lift, trying not to touch her charred flesh. He had a moment to think, now. Clearly the fire was in the stern, the direction in which all the men had been running. If he went forward now he was less likely to be seen.

He ran the length of the gangway, then carried her up the ladder. He could tell by the feel of her body on his shoulder that she was still conscious. He came off the top of the ladder to the main deck level, found a door and stepped out.

There was some confusion out on deck. A man ran past him, heading for the stern; another ran off in the opposite direction. Somebody was in the prow. Down in the stern a man lay on the deck with two others bending over him; presumably he had been injured in the fire.

Dickstein ran forward to the ladder that he had used to board. He eased his gun on to his shoulder, shifted Suza a little on the other shoulder, and stepped over the rail.

Looking about the deck as he started to go down, he knew that they had seen him.

It was one thing to see a strange face on board ship, wonder who he was, and delay asking questions until later because there was a fire alarm; but it was quite another to see someone leaving the ship with a body over his shoulder.

He was not quite halfway down the ladder when they began to shoot at him.

A bullet pinged off the hull beside his head. He looked up to see three men leaning over the rail, two of them with pistols. Holding on to the ladder with his left hand, he put his right hand to his gun, pointed up and fired. His aim was hopeless but the men pulled back.

And he lost his balance.

As the prow of the ship pitched up, he swayed to the left, dropped his gun into the sea and grabbed hold of the ladder with his right hand. His right foot slipped off the rung – and then, to his horror, Suza began to slip from his left shoulder.

'Hold on to me,' he yelled at her, no longer sure whether she was conscious or not. He felt her hands clutch at his sweater, but she continued to slip away, and now her unbalanced weight was pulling him even more to the left.

'No!' he yelled.

She slipped off his shoulder and went plunging into the sea.

Dickstein turned, saw the launch, and jumped, landing with a jarring shock in the well of the boat.

He called her name into the black sea all around him, swinging from one side of the boat to the other, his desperation increasing with every second she failed to surface. And then he heard, over the noise of the wind, a scream. Turning toward the sound he saw her head just above the surface, between the side of the boat and the hull of the *Karla*.

She was out of his reach.

She screamed again.

The launch was tied to the *Karla* by the rope, most of which was piled on the deck of the boat. Dickstein cut the rope with his knife, letting go of the end that was tied to the *Karla*'s ladder and throwing the other end toward Suza.

As she reached for the rope the sea rose again and engulfed her.

Up on the deck of the *Karla* they started shooting over the rail again.

He ignored the gunfire.

Dickstein's eyes swept the sea. With the ship and the boat pitching and rolling in different directions the chances of a hit were relatively slim.

After a few seconds that seemed hours, Suza surfaced again. Dickstein threw her the rope. This time she was able to grab it. Swiftly he pulled it, bringing her closer and closer until he was able to lean over the gunwale of the launch perilously and take hold of her wrists.

He had her now, and he would never let her go.

He pulled her into the well of the launch. Up above a machine gun opened fire. Dickstein threw the launch into gear, then fell on top of Suza, covering her body with his own. The launch moved away from the *Karla*, undirected, riding the waves like a lost surfboard.

The shooting stopped. Dickstein looked back. The *Karla* was out of sight.

Gently he turned Suza over, fearing for her life. Her eyes were closed. He took the wheel of the launch, looked at the compass, and set an approximate course. He turned on the boat's radio and called the *Coparelli*. Waiting for them to come in, he lifted Suza toward him and cradled her in his arms.

A muffled thud came across the water like a distant explosion: the magnetic mine.

The *Coparelli* replied. Dickstein said, 'The *Karla* is on fire. Turn back and pick me up. Have the sick bay ready for the girl – she's badly burned.' He waited for their acknowledgment, then switched off and stared at Suza's expressionless face. 'Don't die,' he said. 'Please don't die.'

She opened her eyes and looked up at him. She opened her mouth, struggling to speak. He bent his head to her. She said, 'Is it really you?'

'It's me,' he said.

The corners of her mouth lifted in a faint smile. 'I'll make it.'

There was the sound of a tremendous explosion. The fire had reached the fuel tanks of the *Karla*. The sky was lit up for several moments by a sheet of flame, the air was filled with a roaring noise, and the rain stopped. The noise and the light died, and so did the *Karla*.

'She's gone down,' Dickstein said to Suza. He looked at her. Her eyes were closed, she was unconscious again, but she was still smiling.

EPILOGUE

NATHANIEL DICKSTEIN resigned from the Mossad, and his name passed into legend. He married Suza and took her back to the kibbutz, where they tended grapes by day and made love half the night. In his spare time he organized a political campaign to have the laws changed so that his children could be classified Jewish; or, better still, to abolish classification.

They did not have children for a while. They were prepared to wait: Suza was young, and he was in no hurry. Her burns never healed completely. Sometimes, in bed, she would say, 'My legs are horrible,' and he would kiss her knees and tell her, 'They're beautiful, they saved my life.'

When the opening of the Yom Kippur War took the Israeli armed forces by surprise, Pierre Borg was blamed for the lack of advance intelligence, and he resigned. The truth was more complicated. The fault lay with a Russian intelligence officer called David Rostov – an elderly-looking man who had to wear a neck brace every moment of his life. He had gone to Cairo and, beginning with the interrogation and death of an Israeli agent called Towfik early in 1968, he had investigated all the events of that year and concluded that Kawash was a double agent. Instead of having Kawash tried and hanged for espionage, Rostov had told the Egyptians how to feed him disinformation, which Kawash, in all innocence, duly passed on to Pierre Borg.

The result was that Nat Dickstein came out of retirement to take over Pierre Borg's job for the duration of the war. On Monday, October 8, 1973, he attended a crisis meeting of the Cabinet. After three days of war the Israelis were in deep trouble. The Egyptians had crossed the Suez Canal and pushed the Israelis back into Sinai with heavy casualties. On the other front, the Golan Heights, the Syrians were pushing forward, again with heavy losses to the Israeli side. The proposal before the Cabinet was to drop atom bombs on Cairo and Damascus. Not even the most hawkish ministers actually relished the idea; but the situation was desperate and the Americans were dragging their heels over the arms airlift which might save the day.

The meeting was coming around to accepting the idea of using nuclear weapons when Nat Dickstein made his only contribution to the discussion: 'Of course, we could *tell* the Americans that we plan to drop these bombs – on Wednesday, say – unless they start the airlift immediately . . .'

And that is exactly what they did.

The airlift turned the tide of the war, and later a similar crisis meeting took place in Cairo. Once again, nobody was in favour of nuclear war in the Middle East; once again, the politicians gathered around the table began to persuade one another that there was no alternative; and once again, the proposal was stopped by an unexpected contribution.

This time it was the military that stepped in. Knowing of the proposal that would be before the assembled presidents, they had run checks on their nuclear strike force in readiness for a positive decision; and they had found that all the plutonium in the bombs had been taken out and replaced with iron filings. It was assumed that the Russians had done this, as they had mysteriously rendered unworkable the nuclear reactor in Qattara, before being expelled from Egypt in 1972.

That night, one of the presidents talked to his wife for five minutes before falling asleep in his chair. 'It's all over,' he told her. 'Israel has won – permanently. They have the bomb, and we do not, and that single fact will determine the course of history in our region for the rest of the century.'

'What about the Palestine refugees?' his wife said.

The president shrugged and began to light his last pipe of the day. 'I remember reading a story in the London *Times* . . . this must be five years ago, I suppose. It said that the Free Wales Army had put a bomb in the police station in Cardiff.'

'Wales?' said his wife. 'Where is Wales?'

'It is a part of England, more or less.'

'I remember,' she said. 'They have coal mines and choirs.'

'That's right. Have you any idea how long ago the Anglo-Saxons conquered the Welsh?'

'None at all.'

'Nor have I, but it must be more than a thousand years ago, because the Norman French conquered the Anglo-Saxons nine hundred years ago. You see? A thousand years, and they are still bombing police stations! The Palestinians will be like the Welsh ... They can bomb Israel for a thousand years, but they will always be the losers.'

His wife looked up at him. All these years they had been together, and still he was capable of surprising her. She had thought she would never hear words like this from him.

'I will tell you something else,' he went on. 'There will have to be peace. We cannot possibly win, now, so we will have to make peace. Not now; perhaps not for five or ten years. But the time will come, and then I will have to go to Jerusalem and say, "No more war." I may even get some credit for it, when the dust settles. It is not how I planned to go down in history, but it's not such a bad way, for all that. "The man who brought peace to the Middle East." What would you say to that?'

His wife got up from her chair and came across to hold his hands. There were tears in her eyes. 'I would give thanks to God,' she said.

Franz Albrecht Pedler died in 1974. He died content. His life had seen some ups and downs – he had, after all, lived through the most ignominious period in the history of his nation – but he had survived and ended his days happily.

He had guessed what had happened to the uranium. One day early in 1969 his company had received a cheque for two million dollars, signed by A. Papagopolous, with a statement from Savile Shipping which read: 'To lost cargo.' The next day a representative of the Israeli Army had called, bringing the payment for the first shipment of cleaning materials. As he left, the army man had said, 'On the matter of your lost cargo, we would be happy if you were not to pursue any further inquiries.'

Pedler began to understand then. 'But what if Euratom asks me questions?'

'Tell them the truth,' the man said. 'The cargo was lost, and when you tried to discover what had happened to it, you found that Savile Shipping had gone out of business.'

'Have they?'

'They have.'

And that was what Pedler told Euratom. They sent an investigator to see him, and he repeated his story, which was completely true, if not truly complete. He said to the investigator, 'I suppose there will be publicity about all this soon.'

'I doubt it,' the investigator told him. 'It reflects badly on us. I don't suppose we'll broadcast the story unless we get more information.'

They did not get more information, of course; at least, not in Pedler's lifetime.

On Yom Kippur in 1974 Suza Dickstein went into labour.

In accordance with the custom of this particular

kibbutz, the baby was delivered by its father, with a midwife standing by to give advice and encouragement.

The baby was small, like both parents. As soon as its head emerged it opened its mouth and cried. Dickstein's vision became watery and blurred. He held the baby's head, checked that the cord was not around its neck, and said, 'Almost there, Suza.'

Suza gave one more heave, and the baby's shoulders were born, and after that it was all downhill. Dickstein tied the cord in two places and cut it, then again in accordance with the local custom he put the baby in the mother's arms.

'Is it all right?' she said.

'Perfect,' said the midwife.

'What is it?'

Dickstein said, 'Oh, God, I didn't even look . . . it's a boy.'

A little later Suza said, 'What shall we call him? Nathaniel?'

'I'd like to call him Towfik,' Dickstein said.

'Towfik? Isn't that an Arab name?'

'Yes.'

'Why? Why Towfik?'

'Well,' he said, 'that's a long story.'

POSTSCRIPT

From the London *Daily Telegraph* of May 7, 1977:

ISRAEL SUSPECTED OF HIJACKING SHIP WITH URANIUM
by Henry Miller in New York

Israel is believed to have been behind the disappearance from the high seas nine years ago of a uranium shipment large enough to build 30 nuclear weapons, it was disclosed yesterday.

Officials say that the incident was 'a real James Bond affair' and that although intelligence agencies in four countries investigated the mystery, it was never determined what had actually happened to the 200 tons of uranium ore that vanished . . .

– Quoted by permission of The Daily Telegraph, Ltd.

ON WINGS
OF EAGLES

I bare you on eagles' wings,
and brought you unto myself.
Exodus 19.4

CAST OF CHARACTERS

Dallas

Ross Perot, Chairman of the Board, Electronic Data
  Systems Corporation, Dallas, Texas.

Merv Stauffer, Perot's right-hand man.

T. J. Marquez, a vice-president of EDS.

Tom Walter, chief financial officer of EDS.

Mitch Hart, a former president of EDS who had good
  connections in the Democratic Party.

Tom Luce, founder of the Dallas law firm Hughes &
  Hill.

Bill Gayden, president of EDS World, a subsidiary of
  EDS.

Mort Meyerson, a vice-president of EDS.

Tehran

Paul Chiapparone, country manager, EDS Corporation
  Iran; Ruthie Chiapparone, his wife.

Bill Gaylord, Paul's deputy; Emily Gaylord, Bill's
  wife.

Lloyd Briggs, Paul's No. 3.

Rich Gallagher, Paul's administrative assistant; Cathy
  Gallagher, Rich's wife; Buffy, Cathy's poodle.

CAST OF CHARACTERS

Paul Bucha, formerly country manager of EDS
    Corporation Iran, latterly based in Paris.
Bob Young, country manager for EDS in Kuwait.
John Howell, lawyer with Hughes & Hill.
Keane Taylor, manager of the Bank Omran project.

The team

    Col Arthur D. 'Bull' Simons, in command.
    Jay Coburn, second-in-command.
    Ron Davis, point.
    Ralph Boulware, shotgun.
    Joe Poché, driver.
    Glenn Jackson, driver.
    Pat Sculley, flank.
    Jim Schwebach, flank and explosives.

The Iranians

    Abolhasan, Lloyd Briggs's deputy and the most
        senior Iranian employee.
    Majid, assistant to Jay Coburn; Fara, Majid's
        daughter.
    Rashid, Seyyed, and 'the Cycle Man': trainee systems
        engineers.
    Gholam, personnel/purchasing officer under Jay
        Coburn.
    Hosain Dadgar, examining magistrate.

At the US Embassy

    William Sullivan, Ambassador.
    Charles Naas, Minister Counselor, Sullivan's deputy.
    Lou Goelz, Consul General.

Bob Sorenson, Embassy official.
Ali Jordan, Iranian employed by the Embassy.
Barry Rosen, press attaché.

Istanbul

'Mr Fish', resourceful travel agent.
Ilsman, employee of MIT, the Turkish intelligence
    agency.
'Charlie Brown', interpreter.

Washington

Zbigniew Brzezinski, National Security Adviser.
Cyrus Vance, Secretary of State.
David Newsom, Under Secretary at the State
    Department.
Henry Precht, Head of the Iran Desk at the State
    Department.
Mark Ginsberg, White House: State Department
    liaison.
Admiral Tom Moorer, former Chairman of the Joint
    Chiefs of Staff.

ACKNOWLEDGEMENTS

Many people helped me by talking to me for hours on end, by replying to my letters, and by reading and correcting drafts of the book. For their patience, frankness, and willing co-operation I thank especially the following:

Paul and Ruthie Chiapparone, Bill and Emily Gaylord;

Jay and Liz Coburn, Joe Poché, Pat and Mary Sculley, Ralph and Mary Boulware, Jim Schwebach, Ron Davis, Glenn Jackson;

Bill Gayden, Keane Taylor, Rich and Cathy Gallagher, Paul Bucha, Lloyd Briggs, Bob Young, John Howell, 'Rashid', Toni Dvoranchik, Kathy Marketos;

T. J. Marquez, Tom Walter, Tom Luce;

Merv Stauffer, for whom nothing is too much trouble;

Margot Perot, Bette Perot;

John Carlen, Anita Melton;

Henry Kissinger, Zbigniew Brzezinski, Ramsey Clark, Bob Strauss, William Sullivan, Charles Naas, Lou Goelz, Henry Precht, John Stempel;

Dr Manuchehr Razmara;

Stanley Simons, Bruce Simons, Harry Simons;

Lt-Col Charles Krohn at the Pentagon;

ACKNOWLEDGEMENTS

Major Dick Meadows, Major-General Robert McKinnon;
Dr Walter Stewart, Dr Harold Kimmerling.

As usual, I was helped by two indefatigable researchers,
Dan Starer in New York and Caren Meyer in London.

I was also helped by the remarkable switchboard staff
at EDS headquarters in Dallas.

More than a hundred hours of taped interviews were
transcribed, mainly by Sally Walther, Claire Woodward,
Linda Huff, Cheryl Hibbitts, and Becky DeLuna.

Finally I thank Ross Perot, without whose astonishing
energy and determination not only this book, but the
adventure which is its subject, would not have been
possible.

PREFACE

This is a true story about a group of people who, accused of crimes they did not commit, decided to make their own justice.

When the adventure was over there was a court case, and they were cleared of all charges. The case is not part of my story, but because it established their innocence I have included details of the court's Findings and Judgment as an appendix to this book.

In telling the story I have taken two small liberties with the truth.

Several people are referred to by pseudonyms or nicknames, usually to protect them from the revenge of the Government of Iran. The false names are: Majid, Fara, Abolhasan, Mr Fish, Deep Throat, Rashid, the Cycle Man, Mehdi, Malek, Gholam, Seyyed and Charlie Brown. All other names are real.

Secondly, in recalling conversations which took place three or four years ago people rarely remember the exact words used; furthermore real-life conversation, with its gestures and interruptions and unfinished sentences, often makes no sense when it is written down. So the dialogue in this book is both reconstructed and edited. However, every reconstructed conversation has been shown to at least one of the participants for correction or approval.

With these two qualifications, I believe every word of what follows is true. This is not a 'fictionalization' or a 'non-fiction novel'. I have not invented anything. What you are about to read is what really happened.

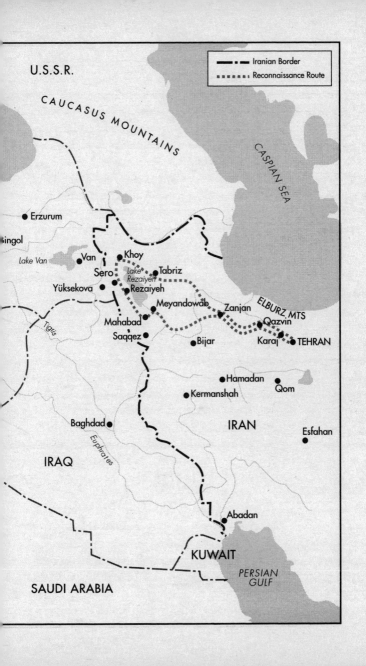

CHAPTER ONE

I

I T ALL started on 5 December 1978.

Jay Coburn, Director of Personnel for EDS Corporation Iran, sat in his office in uptown Tehran with a lot on his mind.

The office was in a three-storey concrete building known as Bucharest (because it was in an alley off Bucharest Street). Coburn was on the first floor, in a room large by American standards. It had a parquet floor, a smart wood executive desk, and a picture of the Shah on the wall. He sat with his back to the window. Through the glass door he could see into the open-plan office where his staff sat at typewriters and telephones. The glass door had curtains, but Coburn never closed them.

It was cold. It was always cold: thousands of Iranians were on strike, the city's power was intermittent, and the heating was off for several hours most days.

Coburn was a tall, broad-shouldered man, five feet eleven inches and two hundred pounds. His red-brown hair was cut businessman-short and carefully combed, with a part. Although he was only thirty-two he looked nearer to forty. On closer examination, his youth showed in his attractive, open face and ready smile; but

1

he had an air of early maturity, the look of a man who grew up too fast.

All his life he had shouldered responsibility: as a boy, working in his father's flower shop; at the age of twenty, as a helicopter pilot in Vietnam; as a young husband and father; and now, as Personnel Director, holding in his hands the safety of 131 American employees and their 220 dependents in a city where mob violence ruled the streets.

Today, like every day, he was making phone calls around Tehran trying to find out where the fighting was, where it would break out next, and what the prospects were for the next few days.

He called the US Embassy at least once a day. The Embassy had an information room which was manned twenty-four hours a day. Americans would call in from different areas of the city to report demonstrations and riots, and the Embassy would spread the news that this district or that was to be avoided. But for advance information and advice Coburn found the Embassy close to useless. At weekly briefings, which he attended faithfully, he would always be told that Americans should stay indoors as much as possible and keep away from crowds at all costs, but that the Shah was in control and evacuation was not recommended at this time. Coburn understood their problem – if the US Embassy said the Shah was tottering, the Shah would surely fall – but they were so cautious they hardly gave out any information at all.

Disenchanted with the Embassy, the American business community in Tehran had set up its own information network. The biggest US corporation in town was Bell Helicopter, whose Iran operation was run by a retired Major-General, Robert N. Mackinnon. Mackinnon had a first-class intelligence service and he shared everything. Coburn also knew a couple of intelligence officers in the US military and he called them.

Today the city was relatively quiet: there were no major demonstrations. The last outbreak of serious trouble had been three days earlier, on 2 December, the first day of the general strike, where seven hundred people had been reported killed in street fighting. According to Coburn's sources the lull could be expected to continue until 10 December, the Moslem holy day of Ashura.

Coburn was worried about Ashura. The Moslem winter holiday was not a bit like Christmas. A day of fasting and mourning for the death of the Prophet's grandson Husayn, its keynote was remorse. There would be massive street processions, during which the more devout believers would flog themselves. In that atmosphere hysteria and violence could erupt fast.

This year, Coburn feared, the violence might be directed against Americans.

A series of nasty incidents had convinced him that anti-American feeling was growing rapidly. A card had been pushed through his door saying: 'If you value your life and possessions, get out of Iran.' Friends of his had received similar postcards. Spray-can artists had painted 'Americans live here' on the wall of his house. The bus which took his children to the Tehran American School had been rocked by a crowd of demonstrators. Other

3

EDS employees had been yelled at in the streets and had their cars damaged. One scary afternoon, Iranians at the Ministry of Health and Social Welfare – EDS's biggest customer – had gone on the rampage, smashing windows and burning pictures of the Shah, while EDS executives in the building barricaded themselves inside an office until the mob went away.

In some ways the most sinister development was the change in the attitude of Coburn's landlord.

Like most Americans in Tehran, Coburn rented half of a two-family home: he and his wife lived upstairs, and the landlord's family lived on the ground floor. When the Coburns had arrived, in March of that year, the landlord had taken them under his wing. The two families had become friendly. Coburn and the landlord discussed religion: the landlord gave him an English translation of the Koran, and the landlord's daughter would read to her father out of Coburn's Bible. They all went on weekend trips to the countryside together. Scott, Coburn's seven-year-old son, played soccer in the street with the landlord's boys. One weekend the Coburns had the rare privilege of attending a Moslem wedding. It had been fascinating. Men and women had been segregated all day, so Coburn and Scott went with the men, his wife Liz and their three daughters went with the women, and Coburn never got to see the bride at all.

After the summer things had gradually changed. The weekend trips stopped. The landlord's sons were forbidden to play with Scott in the street. Eventually all contact between the two families ceased even within the confines of the house and its courtyard, and the children would be reprimanded for just speaking to Coburn's family.

The landlord had not suddenly started hating Americans. One evening he had proved that he still cared for the Coburns. There had been a shooting incident in the street: one of his sons had been out after curfew, and soldiers had fired at the boy as he ran home and scrambled over the courtyard wall. Coburn and Liz had watched the whole thing from their upstairs veranda, and Liz had been scared. The landlord had come up to tell them what had happened and reassure them that all was well. But he clearly felt that for the safety of his family he could not be *seen* to be friendly with Americans: he knew which way the wind was blowing. For Coburn it was yet another bad sign.

Now, Coburn heard on the grapevine, there was wild talk in the mosques and bazaars of a holy war against Americans beginning on Ashura. It was five days away, yet the Americans in Tehran were surprisingly calm.

Coburn remembered when the curfew had been introduced: it had not even interfered with the monthly EDS poker game. He and his fellow-gamblers had simply brought their wives and children, turned it into a slumber party, and stayed until morning. They had got used to the sound of gunfire. Most of the heavy fighting was in the older, southern sector where the bazaar was, and in the area around the University; but everyone heard shots from time to time. After the first few occasions they had become curiously indifferent to it. Whoever was speaking would pause, then continue when the shooting stopped, just as he might in the States when a jet aircraft passed overhead. It was as if they could not imagine that shots might be aimed at *them*.

Coburn was *not* blasé about gunfire. He had been shot at rather a lot during his young life. In Vietnam he had piloted both helicopter gunships, in support of ground operations, and troop/supply-carrying ships, landing and taking off in battlefields. He had killed people, and he had seen men die. In those days the Army gave an Air Medal for every twenty-five hours of combat flying: Coburn had come home with thirty-nine of them. He also got two Distinguished Flying Crosses, a Silver Star, and a bullet in his calf – the most vulnerable part of a helicopter pilot. He had learned, during that year, that he could handle himself pretty well in action, when there was so much to do and no time to be frightened. But every time he returned from a mission, when it was all over and he could think about what he had done, his knees would shake.

In a strange way he was grateful for the experience. He had grown up fast, and it had given him an edge over his contemporaries in business life. It had also given him a healthy respect for the sound of gunfire.

But most of his colleagues did not feel that way, nor did their wives. Whenever evacuation was discussed they resisted the idea. They had time, work and pride invested in EDS Corporation Iran, and they did not want to walk away from it. Their wives had turned the rented apartments into real homes, and they were making plans for Christmas. The children had their schools, their friends, their bicycles and their pets.

Surely, they were telling themselves, if we just lie low and hang on, the trouble will blow over.

Coburn had tried to persuade Liz to take the kids back to the States, not just for their safety, but because the time might come when he had to evacuate some 350 people all at once, and he would need to give that job his complete undivided attention, without being distracted by private anxiety for his own family. Liz had refused to go.

He sighed when he thought of Liz. She was funny and feisty and everyone enjoyed her company, but she was not a good corporate wife. EDS demanded a lot from its executives: if you needed to work all night to get the job done, you worked all night. Liz resented that. Back in the States, working as a recruiter, Coburn had often been away from home Monday to Friday, travelling all over the country, and she had hated it. She was happy in Tehran because he was home every night. If he was going to stay here, she said, so was she. The children liked it here too. It was the first time they had lived outside the United States, and they were intrigued by the different language, and culture of Iran. Kim, the eldest at eleven, was too full of confidence to get worried. Kristi, the eight-year-old, was somewhat anxious, but then she was the emotional one, always the quickest to over-react. Both Scott, seven, and Kelly, the baby at four, were too young to comprehend the danger.

So they stayed, like everyone else, and waited for things to get better – or worse.

Coburn's thoughts were interrupted by a tap at the

door, and Majid walked in. A short, stocky man of about fifty with a luxuriant moustache, he had once been wealthy: his tribe had owned a great deal of land and had lost it in the land reform of the sixties. Now he worked for Coburn as an administrative assistant, dealing with the Iranian bureaucracy. He spoke fluent English and was highly resourceful. Coburn liked him a lot: Majid had gone out of his way to be helpful when Coburn's family arrived in Iran.

'Come in,' Coburn said. 'Sit down. What's on your mind?'

'It's about Fara.'

Coburn nodded. Fara was Majid's daughter, and she worked with her father: her job was to make sure that all American employees always had up-to-date visas and work permits. 'Some problem?' Coburn said.

'The police asked her to take two American passports from our files *without telling anyone.*'

Coburn frowned. 'Any passports in particular?'

'Paul Chiapparone's and Bill Gaylord's.'

Paul was Coburn's boss, the head of EDS Corporation Iran. Bill was second-in-command and manager of their biggest project, the contract with the Ministry of Health. 'What the hell is going on?' Coburn said.

'Fara is in great danger,' Majid said. 'She was instructed not to tell anyone about this. She came to me for advice. Of course I had to tell you, but I'm afraid she will get into very serious trouble.'

'Wait a minute, let's back up,' Coburn said. 'How did this happen?'

'She got a telephone call this morning from the

8

Police Department, Residence Permit Bureau, American Section. They asked her to come to the office. They said it was about James Nyfeler. She thought it was routine. She arrived at the office at eleven-thirty and reported to the Head of the American Section. First he asked for Mr Nyfeler's passport and residence permit. She told him that Mr Nyfeler is no longer in Iran. Then he asked about Paul Bucha. She said that Mr Bucha also was no longer in the country.'

'Did she?'

'Yes.'

Bucha *was* in Iran, but Fara might not have known that, Coburn thought. Bucha had been resident here, had left the country, and had come back in, briefly: he was due to fly back to Paris tomorrow.

Majid continued: 'The officer then said: "I suppose the other two are gone also?" Fara saw that he had four files on his desk, and she asked which other two. He told her Mr Chiapparone and Mr Gaylord. She said she had just picked up Mr Gaylord's residence permit earlier this morning. The officer told her to get the passports and residence permits of both Mr Gaylord and Mr Chiapparone and bring them to him. She was to do it quietly, not to cause alarm.'

'What did she say?' Coburn asked.

'She told him she could not bring them today. He instructed her to bring them tomorrow morning. He told her she was officially responsible for this, and he made sure there were witnesses to these instructions.'

'This doesn't make any sense,' Coburn said.

'If they learn that Fara has disobeyed them—'

'We'll think of a way to protect her,' Coburn said. He was wondering whether Americans were obliged to surrender their passports on demand. He had done so, recently, after a minor car accident, but had later been told he did not have to. 'They didn't say why they wanted the passports?'

'They did not.'

Bucha and Nyfeler were the predecessors of Chiapparone and Gaylord. Was that a clue? Coburn did not know.

Coburn stood up. 'The first decision we have to make is what Fara is going to tell the police tomorrow morning,' he said. 'I'll talk to Paul Chiapparone and get back to you.'

On the ground floor of the building Paul Chiapparone sat in his office. He, too, had a parquet floor, an executive desk, a picture of the Shah on the wall and a lot on his mind.

Paul was thirty-nine years old, of middle height, and a little overweight, mainly because he was fond of good food. With his olive skin and thick black hair he looked very Italian. His job was to build a complete modern social security system in a primitive country. It was not easy.

In the early seventies Iran had had a rudimentary social security system which was inefficient at collecting contributions and so easy to defraud that one man could draw benefit several times over for the same illness. When the Shah decided to spend some of his twenty billion dollars a year oil revenues creating a welfare state, EDS got the contract. EDS ran Medicare and Medicaid programmes for several States in the US, but in Iran they had to start from scratch. They had to issue a social security card to each of Iran's thirty-two million people, organize payroll deductions so that wage-earners paid their contributions, and process claims for benefits. The whole system would be run by computers – EDS's speciality.

The difference between installing a data processing system in the States and doing the same job in Iran was, Paul found, like the difference between making a cake from a packet mix and making one the old-fashioned way with all the original ingredients. It was often frustrating. Iranians did not have the can-do attitude of American business executives, and seemed often to create problems instead of solving them. At EDS headquarters back in Dallas, Texas, not only were people expected to do the impossible, but it was usually due yesterday. Here in Iran everything was impossible and in any case not due until 'fardah' – usually translated 'tomorrow', in practice 'some time in the future'.

Paul had attacked the problems in the only way he knew: by hard work and determination. He was no intellectual genius. As a boy he had found school work difficult, but his Italian father, with the immigrant's typical faith in education, had pressured him to study, and he had got good grades. Sheer persistence had served him well ever since. He could remember the early days of EDS in the States, back in the sixties, when every new contract could make or break the company;

and he had helped build it into one of the most dynamic and successful corporations in the world. The Iranian operation would go the same way, he had been sure, particularly when Jay Coburn's recruitment and training programme began to deliver more Iranians capable of top management.

He had been all wrong, and he was only just beginning to understand why.

When he and his family arrived in Iran, in August 1977, the petrodollar boom was already over. The government was running out of money. That year an anti-inflation programme increased unemployment just when a bad harvest was driving yet more starving peasants into the cities. The tyrannical rule of the Shah was weakened by the human-rights policies of American President Jimmy Carter. The time was ripe for political unrest.

For a while Paul did not take much notice of local politics. He knew there were rumblings of discontent, but that was true of just about every country in the world, and the Shah seemed to have as firm a grip on the reins of power as any ruler. Like the rest of the world, Paul missed the significance of the events of the first half of 1978.

On 7 January the newspaper *Etelaat* published a scurrilous attack on an exiled clergyman called Ayatollah Khomeini, alleging, among other things, that he was homosexual. The following day, eighty miles from Tehran in the town of Qom – the principal centre of religious education in the country – outraged theology students staged a protest sit-in which was bloodily broken up by the military and the police. The confrontation escalated, and seventy people were killed in two more days of disturbances. The clergy organized a memorial procession for the dead forty days later in accordance with Islamic tradition. There was more violence during the procession, and the dead were commemorated in another memorial forty days on ... The processions continued, and grew larger and more violent, through the first six months of the year.

With hindsight, Paul could see that calling these marches 'funeral processions' had been a way to circumvent the Shah's ban on political demonstrations. But at the time he had had no idea that a massive political movement was building. Nor had anyone else.

In August this year Paul went home to the States on leave. (So did William Sullivan, the US Ambassador to Iran.) Paul loved all kinds of water sports, and he had gone to a sports fishing tournament in Ocean City, New Jersey, with his cousin Joe Porreca. His wife Ruthie and the children, Karen and Ann Marie, went to Chicago to visit Ruthie's parents. Paul was a little anxious because the Ministry of Health still had not paid EDS's bill for the month of June; but it was not the first time they had been late with a payment, and Paul had left the problem in the hands of his second-in-command, Bill Gaylord, and he was fairly confident Bill would get the money in.

While he was in the US the news from Iran was bad. Martial law was declared on 7 September, and the following day more than a hundred people were killed by soldiers during a demonstration in Jaleh Square in the heart of Tehran.

When the Chiapparone family came back to Iran the very air seemed different. For the first time Paul and Ruthie could hear shooting in the streets at night. They were alarmed: suddenly they realized that trouble for the Iranians meant trouble for *them.* There was a series of strikes. The electricity was continually being cut off, so they dined by candlelight and Paul wore his topcoat in the office to keep warm. It became more and more difficult to get money out of the banks, and Paul started a cheque-cashing service at the office for employees. When they got low on heating oil for their home Paul had to walk around the streets until he found a tanker, then bribe the driver to come to the house and deliver.

His business problems were worse. The Minister of Health and Social Welfare, Dr Sheikholeslamizadeh, had been arrested under Article 5 of martial law, which permitted a prosecutor to jail anyone without giving a reason. Also in jail was Deputy Minister Reza Neghabat, with whom Paul had worked closely. The Ministry still had not paid its June bill, nor any since, and now owed EDS more than four million dollars.

For two months Paul tried to get the money. The individuals he had dealt with previously had all gone. Their replacements usually did not return his calls. Sometimes someone would promise to look into the problem and call back. After waiting a week for the call that never came, Paul would telephone once again, to be told that the person he spoke to last week had now left the Ministry. Meetings would be arranged then cancelled. The debt mounted at the rate of $1.4 million a month.

On 14 November Paul wrote to Dr Heidargholi Emrani, the Deputy Minister in charge of the Social Security Organization, giving formal notice that if the Ministry did not pay up within a month EDS would stop work. The threat was repeated on 4 December by Paul's boss, the President of EDS World, at a personal meeting with Dr Emrani.

That was yesterday.

If EDS pulled out, the whole Iranian social security system would collapse. Yet it was becoming more and more apparent that the country was bankrupt and simply could not pay its bills. What, Paul wondered, would Dr Emrani do now?

He was still wondering when Jay Coburn walked in with the answer.

At first, however, it did not occur to Paul that the attempt to steal his passport might have been intended to keep him, and therefore EDS, in Iran.

When Coburn had given him the facts he said: 'What the hell did they do that for?'

'I don't know. Majid doesn't know, and Fara doesn't know.'

Paul looked at him. The two men had become close in the last month. For the rest of the employees Paul was putting on a brave face, but with Coburn he had been able to close the door and say OK, what do you really think?

Coburn said: 'The first question is, What do we do about Fara? She could be in trouble.'

15

'She has to give them some kind of an answer.'

'A show of co-operation?'

'She could go back and tell them that Nyfeler and Bucha are no longer resident . . .'

'She already told them.'

'She could take their exit visas as proof.'

'Yeah,' Coburn said dubiously. 'But it's you and Bill they're really interested in now.'

'She could say that the passports aren't kept in the office.'

'They may know that's not true – Fara may even have taken passports down there in the past.'

'Say senior executives don't have to keep their passports in the office.'

'That might work.'

'Any convincing story to the effect that she was physically unable to do what they asked her.'

'Good. I'll discuss it with her and Majid.' Coburn thought for a moment. 'You know, Bucha has a reservation on a flight out tomorrow. He could just go.'

'He probably should – they think he's not here anyway.'

'You could do the same.'

Paul reflected. Maybe he should get out now. What would the Iranians do then? They might just try to detain someone else. 'No,' he said. 'If we're going, I should be the last to leave.'

'Are we going?' Coburn asked.

'I don't know.' Every day for weeks they had asked each other that question. Coburn had developed an evacuation plan which could be put into effect instantly.

Paul had been hesitating, with his finger on the button. He knew that his ultimate boss, back in Dallas, wanted him to evacuate – but it meant abandoning the project on which he had worked so hard for the last sixteen months. 'I don't know,' he repeated. 'I'll call Dallas.'

That night Coburn was at home, in bed with Liz, and fast asleep when the phone rang.

He picked it up in the dark. 'Yeah?'

'This is Paul.'

'Hello.' Coburn turned on the light and looked at his wristwatch. It was 2 a.m.

'We're going to evacuate,' Paul said.

'You got it.'

Coburn cradled the phone and sat on the edge of the bed. In a way it was a relief. There would be two or three days of frantic activity, but then he would know that the people whose safety had been worrying him for so long were back in the States, out of reach of these crazy Iranians.

He ran over in his mind the plans he had made for just this moment. First he had to inform a hundred and thirty families that they would be leaving the country within the next forty-eight hours. He had divided the city into sectors, with a team leader for each sector: he would call the leaders, and it would be their job to call the families. He had drafted leaflets for the evacuees telling them where to go and what to do. He just had to fill in the blanks with dates, times and flight numbers, then have the leaflets duplicated and distributed.

17

He had picked a lively and imaginative young Iranian systems engineer, Rashid, and given him the job of taking care of the homes, cars and pets which would be left behind by the fleeing Americans and – eventually – shipping their possessions to the US. He had appointed a small logistics group to organize plane tickets and transport to the airport.

Finally, he had conducted a small-scale rehearsal of the evacuation with a few people. It had worked.

Coburn got dressed and made coffee. There was nothing he could do for the next couple of hours, but he was too anxious and impatient to sleep.

At 4 a.m. he called the half-dozen members of the logistics group, woke them, and told them to meet him at the 'Bucharest' office immediately after curfew.

Curfew began at nine each evening and ended at five in the morning. For an hour Coburn sat waiting, smoking and drinking a lot of coffee and going over his notes.

When the cuckoo clock in the hall chirped five he was at the front door, ready to go.

Outside there was a thick fog. He got into his car and headed for Bucharest, crawling along at fifteen miles per hour.

Three blocks from his house, half a dozen soldiers leaped out of the fog and stood in a semicircle in front of his car, pointing their rifles at his windscreen.

'Oh, shit,' Coburn said.

One of the soldiers was still loading his gun. He was trying to put the clip in backwards, and it would not fit.

18

He dropped it, and went down on one knee, scrabbling around on the ground looking for it. Coburn would have laughed if he had not been scared.

An officer yelled at Coburn in Farsi. Coburn lowered the window. He showed the officer his wristwatch and said: 'It's after five.'

The soldiers had a conference. The officer came back and asked Coburn for his identification.

Coburn waited anxiously. This would be the worst possible day to get arrested. Would the officer believe that Coburn's watch was right and his was wrong?

At last the soldiers got out of the road and the officer waved Coburn on.

Coburn breathed a sigh of relief and drove slowly on.

Iran was like that.

II

Coburn's logistics group went to work making plane reservations, chartering buses to take people to the airport, and photocopying handout leaflets. At 10 a.m. Coburn got the team leaders into Bucharest and started them calling the evacuees.

He got reservations for most of them on a Pan Am flight to Istanbul on Friday 8 December. The remainder – including Liz Coburn and the four children – would get a Lufthansa flight to Frankfurt that same day.

As soon as the reservations were confirmed, two top executives at EDS headquarters, Merv Stauffer and T. J.

Marquez, left Dallas for Istanbul to meet the evacuees, shepherd them to hotels, and organize the next stage of their flight back home.

During the day there was a small change in plan. Paul was still reluctant to abandon his work in Iran. He proposed that a skeleton staff of about ten senior men stay behind, to keep the office ticking over, in the hope that Iran would quiet down and EDS would eventually be able to resume working normally. Dallas agreed. Among those who volunteered to stay were Paul himself, his deputy Bill Gaylord, Jay Coburn, and most of Coburn's evacuation logistics group. Two people who stayed behind reluctantly were Carl and Vickie Commons: Vickie was nine months pregnant and would leave after her baby was born.

On Friday morning Coburn's team, their pockets full of ten thousand rial (about $140) notes for bribes, virtually took over a section of Mehrabad Airport in western Tehran. Coburn had people writing tickets behind the Pan Am counter, people at passport control, people in the departure lounge, and people running baggage handling equipment. The plane was over-booked: bribes ensured that no one from EDS was bumped off the flight.

There were two especially tense moments. An EDS wife with an Australian passport had been unable to get an exit visa because the Iranian government offices which issued exit visas were all on strike. (Her husband and children had American passports and therefore did not need exit visas.) When the husband reached the passport control desk, he handed over his passport and his children's in a stack with six or seven other passports. As the guard tried to sort them out, EDS people in the queue behind began to push forward and cause a commotion. Some of Coburn's team gathered around the desk asking loud questions and pretending to get angry about the delay. In the confusion the woman with the Australian passport walked through the departure lounge without being stopped.

Another EDS family had adopted an Iranian baby and had not yet been able to get a passport for the child. Only a few months old, the baby would fall asleep, lying face down, on its mother's forearm. Another EDS wife, Kathy Marketos – of whom it was said that she would try anything once – put the sleeping baby on her own forearm, draped her raincoat over it, and carried it out to the plane.

However, it was many hours before anyone got on to a plane. Both flights were delayed. There was no food to be bought at the airport and the evacuees were famished, so just before curfew some of Coburn's team drove around the city buying anything edible they could find. They purchased the entire contents of several *kuche* stalls – street-corner stands that sold candy, fruit and cigarettes – and they went into a Kentucky Fried Chicken and did a deal for its stock of bread rolls. Back at the airport, passing food out to EDS people in the departure lounge, they were almost mobbed by the other hungry passengers waiting for the same flights. On the way back downtown two of the team were caught and arrested for being out after curfew, but the soldier who stopped them got distracted by another car which tried to escape, and the EDS men drove off while he was shooting the other way.

The Istanbul flight left just after midnight. The Frankfurt flight took off the next day, thirty-one hours late.

Coburn and most of the team spent the night at Bucharest. They had no one to go home to.

While Coburn was running the evacuation, Paul had been trying to find out who wanted to confiscate his passport and why.

His administrative assistant, Rich Gallagher, was a young American who was good at dealing with Iranian bureaucracy. Gallagher was one of those who had volunteered to stay in Tehran. His wife Cathy had also stayed behind. She had a good job with the US military in Tehran. The Gallaghers did not want to leave. Furthermore, they had no children to worry about – just a poodle called Buffy.

The day Fara was asked to take the passports – 5 December – Gallagher visited the US Embassy with one of the people whose passports had been demanded: Paul Bucha, who no longer worked in Iran but happened to be in town on a visit.

They met with Consul General Lou Goelz. Goelz, an experienced consul in his fifties, was a portly balding man with a fringe of white hair: he would have made a good Santa Claus. With Goelz was an Iranian member of the consular staff, Ali Jordan.

Goelz advised Bucha to catch his plane. Fara had told

the police – in all innocence – that Bucha was not in Iran, and they had appeared to believe her. There was every chance that Bucha could sneak out.

Goelz also offered to hold the passports and residence permits of Paul and Bill for safekeeping. That way, if the police made a formal demand for the documents, EDS would be able to refer them to the Embassy.

Meanwhile, Ali Jordan would contact the police and try to find out what the hell was going on.

Later that day the passports and papers were delivered to the Embassy.

Next morning Bucha caught his plane and got out. Gallagher called the Embassy. Ali Jordan had talked to General Biglari of the Tehran Police Department. Biglari had said that Paul and Bill were being detained in the country and would be arrested if they tried to leave.

Gallagher asked why.

They were being held as 'material witnesses in investigation', Jordan understood.

'*What* investigation?'

Jordan did not know.

Paul was puzzled, as well as anxious, when Gallagher reported all this. He had not been involved in a road accident, had not witnessed a crime, had no connections with the CIA ... Who or what was being investigated? EDS? Or was the investigation just an excuse for keeping Paul and Bill in Iran so that they would continue to run the social security system's computers?

The police had made one concession. Ali Jordan had argued that the police were entitled to confiscate the

23

residence permits, which were the property of the Iranian Government, but not the passports, which were US Government property. General Biglari had conceded this.

Next day Gallagher and Ali Jordan went to the police station to hand the documents over to Biglari. On the way Gallagher asked Jordan whether he thought there was a chance Paul and Bill would be accused of wrongdoing.

'I doubt that very much,' said Jordan.

At the police station the General warned Jordan that the Embassy would be held responsible if Paul and Bill left the country by any means – such as a US military aircraft.

The following day – 8 December, the day of the evacuation – Lou Goelz called EDS. He had found out, through a 'source' at the Iranian Ministry of Justice, that the investigation in which Paul and Bill were supposed to be material witnesses was an investigation into corruption charges against the jailed Minister of Health, Dr Sheikholeslamizadeh.

It was something of a relief to Paul to know, at last, what the whole thing was about. He could happily tell the investigators the truth: EDS paid no bribes. He doubted whether anyone had bribed the Minister. Iranian bureaucrats were notoriously corrupt, but Dr Sheik – as Paul called him for short – seemed to come from a different mould. An orthopaedic surgeon by training, he had a perceptive mind and an impressive ability to master detail. In the Ministry of Health he had surrounded himself with a group of progressive young technocrats who found ways to cut through red tape and get things done. The EDS project was only part of his ambitious plan to bring Iranian health and welfare services up to American standards. Paul did not think Dr Sheik was lining his own pockets at the same time.

Paul had nothing to fear – if Goelz's 'source' was telling the truth. But was he? Dr Sheik had been arrested three months ago. Was it a coincidence that the Iranians had suddenly realized that Paul and Bill were material witnesses when Paul told them that EDS would leave Iran unless the Ministry paid its bills?

After the evacuation, the remaining EDS men moved into two houses and stayed there, playing poker, during 10 and 11 December, the holy days of Ashura. There was a high-stakes house and a low-stakes house. Both Paul and Coburn were at the high-stakes house. For protection they invited Coburn's 'spooks' – his two contacts in military intelligence – who carried guns. No weapons were allowed at the poker table, so the spooks had to leave their firearms in the hall.

Contrary to expectations, Ashura passed relatively peacefully: millions of Iranians attended anti-Shah demonstrations all over the country, but there was little violence.

After Ashura, Paul and Bill again considered skipping the country, but they were in for a shock. As a preliminary they asked Lou Goelz at the Embassy to give them back their passports. Goelz said that if he did that he would be obliged to inform General Biglari. That would amount to a warning to the police that Paul and Bill were trying to sneak out.

Goelz insisted that he had told EDS, when he took the passports, that this was his deal with the police; but he must have said it rather quietly because no one could remember it.

Paul was furious. *Why* had Goelz had to make *any* kind of deal with the police? He was under no obligation to tell them what he did with an American passport. It was not his job to help the police detain Paul and Bill in Iran, for God's sake! The Embassy was there to *help Americans*, wasn't it?

Couldn't Goelz renege on his stupid agreement, and return the passports quietly, perhaps informing the police a couple of days later, when Paul and Bill were safely home? Absolutely not, said Goelz. If he quarrelled with the police they would make trouble for everyone else, and Goelz had to worry about the other twelve thousand Americans still in Iran. Besides, the names of Paul and Bill were now on the 'stop list' held by the airport police: even with all their documents in order they would never get through passport control.

When the news that Paul and Bill were well and truly stuck in Iran reached Dallas, EDS and its lawyers went into high gear. Their Washington contacts were not as good as they would have been under a Republican administration, but they still had some friends. They talked to Bob Strauss, a high-powered White House troubleshooter who happened to be a Texan; Admiral Tom Moorer, a former Chairman of the Joint Chiefs of Staff, who knew many of the generals now running Iran's military government; and Richard Helms, past Director of the CIA and a former US Ambassador to

Iran. As a result of the pressure they put on the State Department, the US Ambassador in Tehran, William Sullivan, raised the case of Paul and Bill in a meeting with the Iranian Prime Minister, General Azhari.

None of this brought any results.

The thirty days which Paul had given the Iranians to pay their bill ran out, and on 16 December he wrote to Dr Emrani formally terminating the contract. But he had not given up. He asked a handful of evacuated executives to come back to Tehran, as a sign of EDS's willingness to try to resolve its problems with the Ministry. Some of the returning executives, encouraged by the peaceful Ashura, even brought their families back.

Neither the Embassy nor EDS's lawyers in Tehran had been able to find out *who* had ordered Paul and Bill to be detained. It was Majid, Fara's father, who eventually got the information out of General Biglari. The investigator was examining magistrate Hosain Dadgar, a mid-level functionary within the office of the public prosecutor, in a department which dealt with crimes by civil servants and had very broad powers. Dadgar was conducting the inquiry into Dr Sheik, the jailed former Minister of Health.

Since the Embassy could not persuade the Iranians to let Paul and Bill leave the country, and would not give back their passports quietly, could they at least arrange for this Dadgar to question Paul and Bill as soon as possible so that they could go home for Christmas? Christmas did not mean much to the Iranians, said Goelz, but New Year did, so he would try to fix a meeting before then.

27

During the second half of December the rioting started again (and the first thing the returning executives did was plan for a second evacuation). The general strike continued, and petroleum exports – the government's most important source of income – ground to a halt, reducing to zero EDS's chances of getting paid. So few Iranians turned up for work at the Ministry that there was nothing for the EDS men to do, and Paul sent half of them home to the States for Christmas.

Paul packed his bags, closed up his house, and moved into the Hilton, ready to go home at the first opportunity.

The city was thick with rumours. Jay Coburn fished up most of them in his net and brought the interesting ones to Paul. One more disquieting than most came from Bunny Fleischaker, an American girl with friends at the Ministry of Justice. Bunny had worked for EDS in the States, and she kept in touch here in Tehran although she was no longer with the company. She called Coburn to say that the Ministry of Justice planned to arrest Paul and Bill.

Paul discussed this with Coburn. It contradicted what they were hearing from the US Embassy. The Embassy's advice was surely better than Bunny Fleischaker's, they agreed. They decided to take no action.

Paul spent Christmas Day quietly, with a few colleagues, at the home of Pat Sculley, a young EDS manager who had volunteered to return to Tehran. Sculley's wife Mary had also come back and she cooked Christmas dinner. Paul missed Ruthie and the children.

Two days after Christmas the Embassy called. They had succeeded in setting up a meeting for Paul and Bill with examining magistrate Hosain Dadgar. The meeting was to take place the following morning, 28 December, at the Ministry of Health building on Eisenhower Avenue.

Bill Gaylord came into Paul's office a little after nine, carrying a cup of coffee, dressed in the EDS uniform: business suit, white shirt, quiet tie, black brogue shoes.

Like Paul, Bill was thirty-nine, of middle height, and stocky; but there the resemblance ended. Paul had dark colouring, heavy eyebrows, deep-set eyes and a big nose: in casual clothes he was often mistaken for an Iranian until he opened his mouth and spoke English with a New York accent. Bill had a flat, round face and very white skin: nobody would take him for anything but an Anglo.

They had a lot in common. Both were Catholic, although Bill was more devout. They loved good food. Both had trained as systems engineers and joined EDS in the mid-sixties, Bill in 1965 and Paul in 1966. Both had had splendid careers with EDS, but although Paul had joined a year later he was now senior to Bill. Bill knew the health care business inside out, and he was a first-class 'people manager', but he was not as pushy and dynamic as Paul. Bill was a deep thinker and a careful organizer. Paul would never have to worry about Bill making an important presentation: Bill would have prepared every word.

29

They worked together well. When Paul was hasty, Bill would make him pause and reflect. When Bill wanted to plan his way around every bump in the road, Paul would tell him just to get in and drive.

They had been acquainted in the States but had got to know one another well in the last nine months. When Bill had arrived in Tehran, last March, he had lived at the Chiapparones' house until his wife Emily and the children came over. Paul felt almost protective toward him. It was a shame that Bill had had nothing but problems here in Iran.

Bill was much more worried by the rioting and the shooting than most of the others – perhaps because he had not been here long, perhaps because he was more of a worrier by nature. He also took the passport problem more seriously than Paul. At one time he had even suggested that the two of them take a train to the north-east of Iran and cross the border into Russia, on the grounds that nobody would expect American businessmen to escape via the Soviet Union.

Bill also missed Emily and the children badly, and Paul felt somewhat responsible, because he had asked Bill to come to Iran.

Still, it was almost over. Today they would see Mr Dadgar and get their passports back. Bill had a reservation on a plane out tomorrow. Emily was planning a welcome-home party for him on New Year's Eve. Soon all this would seem like a bad dream.

Paul smiled at Bill. 'Ready to go?'

'Any time.'

'Let's get Abolhasan.' Paul picked up the phone.

Abolhasan was the most senior Iranian employee, and advised Paul on Iranian business methods. The son of a distinguished lawyer, he was married to an American woman, and spoke very good English. One of his jobs was translating EDS's contracts into Farsi. Today he would translate for Paul and Bill at their meeting with Dadgar.

He came immediately to Paul's office and the three men left. They did not take a lawyer with them. According to the Embassy, this meeting would be routine, the questioning informal. To take lawyers along would not only be pointless, but might antagonize Mr Dadgar and lead him to suspect that Paul and Bill had something to hide. Paul would have liked to have a member of the Embassy staff present, but this idea also had been turned down by Lou Goelz: it was not normal procedure to send Embassy representatives to a meeting such as this. However, Goelz had advised Paul and Bill to take with them documents establishing when they had come to Iran, what their official positions were, and the scope of their responsibilities.

As the car negotiated its way through the usual insane Tehran traffic, Paul felt depressed. He was glad to be going home, but he hated to admit failure. He had come to Iran to build up EDS's business here, and he found himself dismantling it. Whatever way you looked at it the company's first overseas venture had been a failure. It was not Paul's fault that the government of Iran had run out of money, but that was small consolation: excuses did not make profits.

They drove down the tree-lined Eisenhower Avenue,

as wide and straight as any American highway, and pulled into the courtyard of a square, ten-storey building set back from the street and guarded by soldiers with automatic rifles. This was the Social Security Organization of the Ministry of Health and Social Welfare. It was to have been the power-house of the new Iranian welfare state: here, side by side, the Iranian government and EDS had worked to build a social security system. EDS occupied the entire seventh floor. Bill's office was there.

Paul, Bill and Abolhasan showed their passes and went in. The corridors were dirty and poorly decorated, and the building was cold: the heat was off again. They were directed to the office Mr Dadgar was using.

They found him in a small room with dirty walls, sitting behind an old grey steel desk. In front of him on the desk were a notebook and a pen. Through the window Paul could see the data centre EDS was building next door.

Abolhasan introduced everyone. There was an Iranian woman sitting on a chair beside Dadgar's desk: her name was Mrs Nourbash, and she was Dadgar's interpreter.

They all sat down on dilapidated metal chairs. Tea was served. Dadgar began to speak in Farsi. His voice was soft but rather deep, and his expression was blank. Paul studied him as he waited for the translation. Dadgar was a short, stocky man in his fifties, and for some reason he made Paul think of Archie Bunker. His complexion was dark and his hair was combed forward, as if to hide the fact that it was receding. He had a moustache and glasses, and he wore a sober suit.

Dadgar finished speaking, and Abolhasan said: 'He warns you that he has the power to arrest you if he finds your answers to his questions unsatisfactory. In case you did not realize this, he says you may postpone the interview to give your lawyers time to arrange bail.'

Paul was surprised by this development, but he evaluated it fast, just like any other business decision. OK, he thought, the worst thing that can happen is that he won't believe us and he will arrest us – but we're not murderers, we'll be out on bail in twenty-four hours. Then we might be confined to the country, and we would have to meet with our attorneys and try to work things out . . . which is no worse than the situation we're in now.

He looked at Bill. 'What do you think?'

Bill shrugged. 'Goelz says this meeting is routine. The stuff about bail sounds like a formality – like reading you your rights.'

Paul nodded. 'And the last thing we want is a postponement.'

'Then let's get it over with.'

Paul turned to Mrs Nourbash. 'Please tell Mr Dadgar that neither of us has committed a crime, and neither of us has any knowledge of anyone else committing a crime, so we are confident that no charges will be made against us, and we would like to get this finished up today so that we can go home.'

Mrs Nourbash translated.

Dadgar said he wanted first to interview Paul alone. Bill should come back in an hour.

Bill left.

Bill went up to his office on the seventh floor. He picked up the phone, called Bucharest, and reached Lloyd Briggs. Briggs was number three in the hierarchy after Paul and Bill.

'Dadgar says he has the power to arrest us,' Bill told Briggs. 'We might need to put up bail. Call the Iranian attorneys and find out what that means.'

'Sure,' Briggs said. 'Where are you?'

'In my office here at the Ministry.'

'I'll get back to you.'

Bill hung up and waited. The idea of his being arrested was kind of ridiculous – despite the widespread corruption of modern Iran, EDS had never paid bribes to get contracts. But even if bribes had been paid, Bill would not have paid them: his job was to deliver the product, not to win the order.

Briggs called back within a few minutes. 'You've got nothing to worry about,' he said. 'Just last week a man accused of murder had his bail set at a million and a half rials.'

Bill did a quick calculation: that was twenty thousand dollars. EDS could probably pay that in cash. For some weeks they had been keeping large amounts of cash, both because of the bank strikes and for use during the evacuation. 'How much do we have in the office safe?'

'Around seven million rials, plus fifty thousand dollars.'

So, Bill thought, even if we are arrested we'll be able to post bail immediately. 'Thanks,' he said. 'That makes me feel a lot better.'

Downstairs, Dadgar had written down Paul's full name, date and place of birth, schools attended, experience in computers, and qualifications: and he had carefully examined the document which officially named Paul as Country Manager for Electronic Data Systems Corporation Iran. Now he asked Paul to give an account of how EDS had secured its contract with the Ministry of Health.

Paul took a deep breath. 'First, I would like to point out that I was not working in Iran at the time the contract was negotiated and signed, so I do not have first-hand knowledge of this. However, I will tell you what I understand the procedure to have been.'

Mrs Nourbash translated and Dadgar nodded.

Paul continued, speaking slowly and rather formally to help the translator. 'In 1975 an EDS executive, Paul Bucha, learned that the Ministry was looking for a data-processing company experienced in health insurance and social security work. He came to Tehran, had meetings with Ministry officials, and determined the nature and scale of the work the Ministry wanted done. He was told that the Ministry had already received proposals for the project from Louis Berger and Company, Marsh and McClennan, ISIRAN, and UNIVAC, and that a fifth proposal was on its way from Cap Gemini Sogeti. He said that EDS was the leading data-processing company in the United States and that our company specialized in exactly this kind of health care work. He offered the Ministry a free preliminary study. The offer was accepted.'

When he paused for translation, Paul noticed, Mrs Nourbash seemed to say less than he had said; and what Dadgar wrote down was shorter still. He began to speak more slowly and pause more often. 'The Ministry obviously liked EDS's proposals, because they then asked us to perform a detailed study for two hundred thousand dollars. The results of our study were presented in October 1975. The Ministry accepted our proposal and began contract negotiations. By August 1976 the contract was agreed.'

'Was everything above board?' Dadgar asked through Mrs Nourbash.

'Absolutely,' Paul said. 'It took another three months to go through the lengthy process of getting all the necessary approvals from many government departments, including the Shah's court. None of these steps was omitted. The contract went into effect at the end of the year.'

'Was the contract price exorbitant?'

'It showed a maximum expected pre-tax profit of twenty per cent, which is in line with other contracts of this magnitude, both here and in other countries.'

'And has EDS fulfilled its obligations under the contract?'

This was something on which Paul *did* have first-hand knowledge. 'Yes, we have.'

'Could you produce evidence?'

'Certainly. The contract specifies that I should meet with Ministry officials at certain intervals to review progress: those meetings have taken place and the Ministry has the minutes of the meetings on file. The contract lays down a complaints procedure for the Ministry to use if EDS fails to fulfil its obligations: that procedure has never been used.'

Mrs Nourbash translated, but Dadgar did not write anything down. He must know all this anyway, Paul thought.

He added: 'Look out of the window. There is our data centre. Go and see it. There are computers in it. Touch them. They work. They produce information. Read the printouts. They are being *used.*'

Dadgar made a brief note. Paul wondered what he was really after.

The next question was: 'What is your relationship with the Mahvi group?'

'When we first came to Iran we were told that we had to have Iranian partners in order to do business here. The Mahvi group are our partners. However, their main role is to supply us with Iranian staff. We meet with them periodically, but they have little to do with the running of our business.'

Dadgar asked why Dr Towliati, a Ministry official, was on the EDS payroll. Was this not a conflict of interest?

Here at last was a question that made sense. Paul

could see how Towliati's role could appear irregular. However, it was easily explained. 'In our contract we undertake to supply expert consultants to help the Ministry make the best use of the service we provide. Dr Towliati is such a consultant. He has a data processing background, and he is familiar with both Iranian and American business methods. He is paid by EDS, rather than by the Ministry, because Ministry salaries are too low to attract a man of his calibre. However, the Ministry is obliged to reimburse us for his salary, as laid down in the contract; so he is not *really* paid by us.'

Once again Dadgar wrote down very little. He could have got all this information from the files, Paul thought: perhaps he has.

Dadgar asked: 'But why does Dr Towliati sign invoices?'

'That's easy,' Paul replied. 'He does not, and never has. The closest he comes is this: he would inform the Minister that a certain task has been completed, where the specification of that task is too technical for verification by a layman.' Paul smiled. 'He takes his responsibility to the Ministry very seriously – he is easily our harshest critic, and he will characteristically ask a lot of tough questions before verifying completion of a task. I sometimes wish I did have him in my pocket.'

Mrs Nourbash translated. Paul was thinking: What is Dadgar after? First he asks about the contract negotiations, which happened before my time; then about the Mahvi group and Dr Towliati, as if they were sensationally important. Maybe Dadgar himself doesn't

38

know what he's looking for – maybe he's just fishing, hoping to come up with evidence of something illegal.

How long can this farce go on?

Bill was outside in the corridor, wearing his topcoat to keep out the cold. Someone had brought him a glass of tea, and he warmed his hands on it while he sipped. The building was dark as well as cold.

Dadgar had immediately struck Bill as being different from the average Iranian. He was cold, gruff and inhospitable. The Embassy had said Dadgar was 'favourably disposed' toward Bill and Paul, but that was not the impression Bill had.

Bill wondered what game Dadgar was playing. Was he trying to intimidate them, or was he seriously considering arresting them? Either way, the meeting was not turning out the way the Embassy had anticipated. Their advice, to come without lawyers or Embassy representatives, now looked mistaken: perhaps they just did not want to get involved. Anyway, Paul and Bill were on their own now. It was not going to be a pleasant day. But at the end of it they would be able to go home.

Looking out of the window, he saw that there was some excitement down on Eisenhower Avenue. Some distance along the street, dissidents were stopping cars and putting Khomeini posters on the windscreens. The soldiers guarding the Ministry building were stopping the cars and tearing the posters up. As he waited, the

soldiers became more belligerent. They broke the head-
light of a car, and the windscreen of another, as if to
teach the drivers a lesson. Then they pulled a driver out
of a car and punched him around.

The next car they picked on was a taxi, a Tehran
orange cab. It went by without stopping, not surprisingly; but the soldiers seemed angered and chased it,
firing their guns. Cab and pursuing soldiers disappeared
from Bill's sight.

After that the soldiers ended their grim game and
returned to their posts inside the walled courtyard in
front of the Ministry building. The incident, with its
queer mixture of childishness and brutality, seemed to
sum up what was going on in Iran. The country was
going down the drain. The Shah had lost control and
the rebels were determined to drive him out or kill him.
Bill felt sorry for the people in the cars, victims of
circumstance who could do nothing but hope that
things would get better. If Iranians are no longer safe,
he thought, Americans must be in even more danger.
We've got to get out of this country.

Two Iranians were hanging about in the same corridor, watching the fracas on Eisenhower. They seemed
as appalled as Bill at what they saw.

Morning turned into afternoon. Bill got more tea
and a sandwich for lunch. He wondered what was
happening in the interrogation room. He was not
surprised to be kept waiting: in Iran, 'an hour' meant
nothing more precise than 'later, maybe'. But as the day
wore on he became more uneasy. Was Paul in trouble
in there?

The Iranians stayed in the corridor all afternoon, doing nothing. Bill wondered vaguely who they were. He did not speak to them.

He wished the time would pass more quickly. He had a reservation on tomorrow's plane. Emily and the kids were in Washington, where both Emily's and Bill's parents lived. They had a big party planned for him on New Year's Eve. He could hardly wait to see them all again.

He should have left Iran weeks ago, when the fire-bombing started. One of the people whose homes had been bombed was a girl with whom he had gone to high school in Washington. She was married to a diplomat at the US Embassy. Bill had talked to them about the incident. Nobody had been hurt, luckily, but it had been very scary. I should have taken heed, and got out then, he thought.

At last Abolhasan opened the door and called: 'Bill! Come in, please.'

Bill looked at his watch. It was five o'clock. He went in.

'It's cold,' he said as he sat down.

'It's warm enough in this seat,' Paul said with a strained smile. Bill looked at Paul's face. He seemed very uncomfortable.

Dadgar drank a glass of tea and ate a sandwich before he began to question Bill. Watching him, Bill thought: this guy is trying to trap us so he won't have to let us leave the country.

The interview started. Bill gave his full name, date and place of birth, schools attended, qualifications, and

41

experience. Dadgar's face was blank as he asked the questions and wrote down the answers: he was like a machine.

Bill began to see why the interview with Paul had taken so long. Each question had to be translated from Farsi into English and each answer from English into Farsi. Mrs Nourbash did the translation, Abolhasan interrupting with clarifications and corrections.

Dadgar questioned him about EDS's performance of the Ministry contract. Bill answered at length and in detail, although the subject was both complicated and highly technical, and he was pretty sure that Mrs Nourbash could not really understand what he was saying. Anyway, no one could hope to grasp the complexities of the entire project by asking a handful of general questions. What kind of foolishness was this, he wondered? Why did Dadgar want to sit all day in a freezing cold room and ask stupid questions? It was some kind of Persian ritual, Bill decided. Dadgar needed to pad out his records, show that he had explored every avenue and protect himself in advance against possible criticism for letting them go. At the absolute worst, he might detain them in Iran a while longer. Either way, it was just a matter of time.

Both Dadgar and Mrs Nourbash seemed hostile. The interview became more like a courtroom cross-examination. Dadgar said that EDS's progress reports to the Ministry had been false, and EDS had used them to make the Ministry pay for work that had not been done. Bill pointed out that Ministry officials, who were in a position to know, had never suggested that the reports were inaccurate. If EDS had fallen down on the job, where were the complaints? Dadgar could examine the Ministry's files.

Dadgar asked about Dr Towliati, and when Bill explained Towliati's role, Mrs Nourbash – speaking before Dadgar had given her anything to translate – replied that Bill's explanation was untrue.

There were several miscellaneous questions, including a completely mystifying one: did EDS have any Greek employees? Bill said they did not, wondering what that had to do with anything. Dadgar seemed impatient. Perhaps he had hoped that Bill's answers would contradict Paul's; and now, disappointed, he was just going through the motions. His questioning became perfunctory and hurried; he did not follow up Bill's answers with further questions or requests for clarifications; and he wound up the interview after an hour.

Mrs Nourbash said: 'You will now please sign your names against each of the questions and answers in Mr Dadgar's notebook.'

'But they're in Farsi – we can't read a word of it!' Bill protested. It's a trick, he thought; we'll be signing a confession to murder or espionage or some other crime Dadgar has invented.

Abolhasan said: 'I will look over his notes and check them.'

Paul and Bill waited while Abolhasan read through the notebook. It seemed a very cursory check. He put the book down on the desk.

'I advise you to sign.'

Bill was sure he should not – but he had no choice. If he wanted to go home, he had to sign.

He looked at Paul. Paul shrugged. 'I guess we'd better do it.'

They went through the notebook in turn, writing their names beside the incomprehensible squiggles of Farsi.

When they finished, the atmosphere in the room was tense. Now, Bill thought, he has to tell us we can go home.

Dadgar shuffled his papers into a neat stack while he talked to Abolhasan in Farsi for several minutes. Then he left the room. Abolhasan turned to Paul and Bill, his face grave.

'You are being arrested,' he said.

Bill's heart sank. No plane, no Washington, no Emily, no New Year's Eve party . . .

'Bail has been set at ninety million tomans, sixty for Paul and thirty for Bill.'

'Jesus!' Paul said. 'Ninety million tomans is . . .'

Abolhasan worked it out on a scrap of paper. 'A little under thirteen million dollars.'

'You're kidding!' Bill said. 'Thirteen *million*? A murderer's bail is twenty *thousand.*'

Abolhasan said: 'He asks whether you are ready to post the bail.'

Paul laughed. 'Tell him I'm a little short now, I'm going to have to go to the bank.'

Abolhasan said nothing.

'He can't be serious,' Paul said.

'He's serious,' said Abolhasan.

Suddenly Bill was mad as hell – mad at Dadgar, mad at Lou Goelz, mad at the whole damn world. It had been a sucker trap and they had fallen right into it. Why, they had walked in here of their own free will, to keep an appointment made by the US Embassy. They had done nothing wrong and nobody had a shred of evidence against them – yet they were going to jail, and worse, an Iranian jail!

Abolhasan said: 'You are allowed one phone call each.'

Just like the cop shows on TV – one phone call then into the slammer.

Paul picked up the phone and dialled. 'Lloyd Briggs, please. This is Paul Chiapparone . . . Lloyd? I can't make dinner tonight. I'm going to jail.'

Bill thought: Paul doesn't really believe it yet.

Paul listened for a moment, then said: 'How about calling Gayden, for a start?' Bill Gayden, whose name was so similar to Bill Gaylord's, was president of EDS World and Paul's immediate boss. As soon as this news reaches Dallas, Bill thought, these Iranian jokers will see what happens when EDS really gets into gear.

Paul hung up and Bill took his turn on the phone. He dialled the US Embassy and asked for the Consul General.

'Goelz? This is Bill Gaylord. We've just been arrested, and bail has been set at thirteen million dollars.'

'How did that happen?'

Bill was infuriated by Goelz's calm measured voice. 'You arranged this meeting and you told us we could leave afterwards!'

'I'm sure, if you've done nothing wrong—'

'What do you mean *if*?' Bill shouted.

'I'll have someone down at the jail as soon as possible,' Goelz said.

Bill hung up.

The two Iranians who had been hanging about in the corridor all day came in. Bill noticed they were big and burly, and realized they must be plain-clothes policemen.

Abolhasan said: 'Dadgar said it would not be necessary to handcuff you.'

Paul said, 'Gee, thanks.'

Bill suddenly recalled the stories he had heard about the torturing of prisoners in the Shah's jails. He tried not to think about it.

Abolhasan said: 'Do you want to give me your briefcases and wallets?'

They handed them over. Paul kept back a hundred dollars.

'Do you know where the jail is?' Paul asked Abolhasan.

'You're going to a Temporary Detention Facility at the Ministry of Justice on Khayyam Street.'

'Get back to Bucharest fast and give Lloyd Briggs all the details.'

'Sure.'

One of the plain-clothes policemen held the door open, Bill looked at Paul. Paul shrugged.

They went out.

The policemen escorted them downstairs and into a little car. 'I guess we'll have to stay in jail for a couple of hours,' Paul said. 'It'll take that long for the Embassy and EDS to get people down there to bail us out.'

'They might be there already,' Bill said optimistically.

The bigger of the two policemen got behind the wheel. His colleague sat beside him in the front. They pulled out of the courtyard and into Eisenhower Avenue, driving fast. Suddenly they turned into a narrow one-way street, heading the wrong way at top speed. Bill clutched the seat in front of him. They swerved in and out, dodging the cars and buses coming the other way, other drivers honking and shaking their fists.

They headed south and slightly east. Bill thought ahead to their arrival at the jail. Would people from EDS or the Embassy be there to negotiate a reduction in the bail so that they could go home instead of to a cell? Surely the Embassy staff would be outraged at what Dadgar had done. Ambassador Sullivan would intervene to get them released at once. After all, it was iniquitous to put two Americans in an Iranian jail when no crime had been committed and then set bail at thirteen million dollars. The whole situation was ridiculous.

Except that here he was, sitting in the back of this car, silently looking out of the windows and wondering what would happen next.

As they went farther south, what he saw through the window frightened him even more.

In the north of the city, where the Americans lived and worked, riots and fighting were still an occasional

47

phenomenon, but here – Bill now realized – they must be continuous. The black hulks of burned buses smouldered in the streets. Hundreds of demonstrators were running riot, yelling and chanting, setting fires and building barricades. Young teenagers threw Molotov cocktails – bottles of gasoline with blazing rag fuses – at cars. Their targets seemed random. We might be next, Bill thought. He heard shooting, but it was dark and he could not see who was firing at whom. The driver never went at less than top speed. Every other street was blocked by a mob, a barricade or a blazing car: the driver turned around, blind to all traffic signals, and raced through side streets and back alleys at breakneck speed to circumvent the obstacles. We're not going to get there alive, Bill thought. He touched the rosary in his pocket.

It seemed to go on for ever – then, suddenly, the little car swung into a circular courtyard and pulled up. Without speaking, the burly driver got out of the car and went into the building.

The Ministry of Justice was a big place, occupying a whole city block. In darkness – the street lights were all off – Bill could make out what seemed to be a five-storey building. The driver was inside for ten or fifteen minutes. When he came out he climbed behind the wheel and drove around the block. Bill assumed he had registered his prisoners at the front desk.

At the rear of the building the car mounted the kerb and stopped on the sidewalk by a pair of steel gates set into a long, high brick wall. Somewhere over to the right, where the wall ended, there was a vague outline of a small park or garden. The driver got out. A peephole opened in one of the steel doors, and there was a short conversation in Farsi. Then the doors opened. The driver motioned Paul and Bill to get out of the car.

They walked through the doors.

Bill looked around. They were in a small courtyard. He saw ten or fifteen guards armed with automatic weapons scattered about. In front of him was a circular driveway with parked cars and trucks. To his left, up against the brick wall, was a single-storey building. On his right was another steel door.

The driver went up to the second steel door and knocked. There was another exchange in Farsi through another peephole. Then the door was opened, and Paul and Bill were ushered inside.

They were in a small reception area with a desk and a few chairs. Bill looked around. There were no lawyers, no Embassy staff, no EDS executives here to spring him from jail. We're on our own, he thought, and this is going to be dangerous.

A guard stood behind the desk with a ballpoint pen and a pile of forms. He asked a question in Farsi. Guessing, Paul said: 'Paul Chiapparone', and spelled it.

Filling out the forms took close to an hour. An English-speaking prisoner was brought from the jail to help translate. Paul and Bill gave their Tehran addresses, phone numbers, and dates of birth, and listed their possessions. Their money was taken away and they were each given two thousand rials, about thirty dollars.

They were taken into an adjoining room and told to

remove their clothes. They both stripped to their under-shorts. Their clothing and their bodies were searched. Paul was told to get dressed again, but Bill was not. It was very cold: the heat was off here, too. Naked and shivering, Bill wondered what would happen now. Obviously they were the only Americans in the jail. Everything he had ever read or heard about being in prison was awful. What would the guards do to him and Paul? What would the other prisoners do? Surely, any minute now someone would come to get him released.

'Can I put on my coat?' he asked the guard.

The guard did not understand.

'Coat,' Bill said, and mimed putting on a coat.

The guard handed him his coat.

A little later another guard came in and told him to get dressed.

They were led back into the reception area. Once again Bill looked around expectantly for lawyers or friends; once again he was disappointed.

They were taken through the reception area. Another door was opened. They went down a flight of stairs into the basement.

It was cold, dim and dirty. There were several cells, all crammed with prisoners, all of them Iranian. The stink of urine made Bill close his mouth and breathe shallowly through his nose. The guard opened the door to cell number nine. They walked in.

Sixteen unshaven faces stared at them, alive with curiosity. Paul and Bill stared back, horrified.

The cell door clanged shut behind them.

CHAPTER TWO

I

UNTIL THIS moment, life had been extremely good to Ross Perot.

On the morning of 28 December 1978 he sat at the breakfast table in his mountain cabin at Vail, Colorado, and was served breakfast by Holly, the cook.

Perched on the mountainside and half-hidden in the aspen forest, the 'log cabin' had six bedrooms, five bathrooms, a thirty-foot living room, and an après-ski recuperation room with a Jacuzzi pool in front of the fireplace. It was just a holiday home.

Ross Perot was rich.

He had started EDS with a thousand dollars, and now the shares in the company, more than half of which he still owned personally, were worth several hundred million dollars. He was the sole owner of the Petrus Oil and Gas Company which had reserves worth hundreds of millions. He also had an awful lot of Dallas real estate. It was difficult to figure out exactly how much money he had – a lot depended on just how you counted it – but it was certainly more than five hundred million dollars and probably less than a billion.

In novels, fantastically rich people were portrayed as greedy, power-mad, neurotic, hated and unhappy –

always unhappy. Perot did not read many novels. He was happy.

He did not think it was the money that made him happy. He believed in money-making, in business and profits, because that was what made America tick; and he enjoyed a few of the toys money could buy – the cabin cruiser, the speedboats, the helicopter – but rolling around in hundred-dollar bills had never been one of his daydreams. He *had* dreamed of building a successful business that would employ thousands of people; but his greatest dream-come-true was right here in front of his eyes. Running around in thermal underwear, getting ready to go skiing, was his family. Here was Ross Junior, twenty years old, and if there was a finer young man in the state of Texas, Perot had yet to meet him. Here were four – count 'em, four – daughters: Nancy, Suzanne, Carolyn and Catherine. They were all healthy, smart and lovable. Perot had sometimes told interviewers that he would measure his success in life by how his children turned out. If they grew into good citizens with a deep concern for other people, he would consider his life worthwhile. (The interviewer would say: 'Hell, I believe you, but if I put stuff like that in the article the readers will think I've been bought off!' And Perot would just say: 'I don't care. I'll tell you the truth: you write whatever you like.') And the children had turned out just exactly how he had wished, so far. Being brought up in circumstances of great wealth and privilege had not spoiled them at all. It was almost miraculous.

Running around after the children with ski-lift tickets,

wool socks and sunscreen lotion was the person responsible for this miracle, Margot Perot. She was beautiful,
loving, intelligent, classy and a perfect mother. She
could, if she had wanted to, have married a John
Kennedy, a Paul Newman, a Prince Rainier, or a Rocke-
feller. Instead she had fallen in love with Ross Perot
from Texarkana, Texas; five feet seven with a broken
nose and nothing in his pocket but hopes. All his life
Perot had believed he was lucky. Now, at the age of
forty-eight, he could look back and see that the luckiest
thing that ever happened to him was Margot.

He was a happy man with a happy family, but a
shadow had fallen over them this Christmas. Perot's
mother was dying. She had bone cancer. On Christmas
Eve she had fallen at home. It was not a heavy fall, but
because the cancer had weakened her bones, she had
broken her hip and had to be rushed to Baylor Hospital
in downtown Dallas.

Perot's sister, Bett, spent that night with their mother,
then, on Christmas Day, Perot and Margot and the five
children loaded the presents into the station wagon and
drove to the hospital. Grandmother was in such good
spirits that they all thoroughly enjoyed their day. However, she did not want to see them the following day:
she knew they had planned to go skiing, and she insisted
they go, despite her illness. Margot and the children left
for Vail on 26 December, but Perot stayed behind.

There followed a battle of wills such as Perot had
fought with his mother in childhood. Lulu May Perot
was only an inch or two over five feet, and slight, but
she was no more frail than a sergeant in the Marines.

She told him he worked hard and he needed the holiday. He replied that he did not want to leave her. Eventually the doctors intervened, and told him he was doing her no good by staying against her will. The next day he joined his family in Vail. She had won, as she always did when he was a boy.

One of their battles had been fought over a Boy Scout trip. There had been flooding in Texarkana, and the Scouts were planning to camp near the disaster area for three days and help with relief work. Young Perot was determined to go, but his mother knew that he was too young – he would only be a burden to the scoutmaster. He kept on and on at her, and she just smiled sweetly and said no.

That time he won a concession from her: he was allowed to go and help pitch tents the first day, but he had to come home in the evening. It wasn't much of a compromise. But he was quite incapable of defying her. He just had to imagine the scene when he would come home, and think of the words he would use to tell her that he had disobeyed her – and he knew he could not do it.

He was never spanked. He could not remember even being yelled at. She did not rule him by fear. With her fair hair, blue eyes, and sweet nature, she bound him – and his sister Bette – in chains of love. She would just look you in the eye and tell you what to do, and you simply could not bring yourself to make her unhappy.

Even at the age of twenty-three, when he had been around the world and come home again, she would say:

\

'Who have you got a date with tonight? Where are you going? What time will you be back?' And when he came home he would always have to kiss her goodnight. But by this time their battles were few and far between, for her principles were so deeply embedded in him that they had become his own. She now ruled the family like a constitutional monarch, wearing the trappings of power and legitimizing the decision-makers.

He had inherited more than her principles. He also had her iron will. He, too, had a way of looking people in the eye. He had married a woman who resembled his mother. Blonde and blue-eyed, Margot also had the kind of sweet nature that Lulu May had. But Margot did not dominate Perot.

Everybody's mother has to die, and Lulu May was now eighty-two, but Perot could not be stoical about it. She was still a big part of his life. She no longer gave him orders, but she did give him encouragement. She had encouraged him to start EDS, and she had been the company's book-keeper during the early years as well as a founding director. He could talk over problems with her. He had consulted her in December 1969, at the height of his campaign to publicize the plight of American prisoners-of-war in North Vietnam. He had been planning to fly to Hanoi, and his colleagues at EDS had pointed out that if he put his life in danger the price of EDS stock might fall. He was faced with a moral dilemma: did he have the right to make shareholders suffer, even for the best of causes? He had put the question to his mother. Her answer had been unhesitating.

'Let them sell their shares.' The prisoners were dying, and that was far more important than the price of EDS stock.

It was the conclusion Perot would have come to on his own. He did not really need her to tell him what to do. Without her, he would be the same man and do the same things. He was going to miss her, that was all. He was going to miss her very badly indeed.

But he was not a man to brood. He could do nothing for her today. Two years ago, when she had a stroke, he had turned Dallas upside down on a Sunday afternoon to find the best neurosurgeon in town and bring him to the hospital. He responded to a crisis with action. But if there was nothing to be done, he was able to shut the problem out of his mind, forgetting the bad news and going on with the next task. He would not now spoil his family's holiday by walking around with a mournful face. He would enter into the fun and games, and enjoy the company of his wife and children.

The phone rang, interrupting his thoughts, and he stepped into the kitchen to pick it up.

'Ross Perot,' he said.

'Ross, this is Bill Gayden.'

'Hi, Bill.' Gayden was an EDS old-timer, having joined the company in 1967. In some ways he was the typical salesman. He was a jovial man, everybody's buddy. He liked a joke, a drink, a smoke and a hand of poker. He was also a wizard financier, very good around acquisitions, mergers and deals, which was why Perot had made him president of EDS World. Gayden's sense of humour was irrepressible – he would find something funny to say in the most serious situations – but now he sounded sombre.

'Ross, we got a problem.'

It was an EDS catch-phrase: *We got a problem.* It meant bad news.

Gayden went on: 'It's Paul and Bill.'

Perot knew instantly what he was talking about. The way in which his two senior men in Iran had been prevented from leaving the country was highly sinister, and it had never been far from his mind, even while his mother lay dying. 'But they're supposed to be allowed out today.'

'They've been arrested.'

The anger began as a small, hard knot in the pit of Perot's stomach. 'Now, Bill, I was assured that they would be allowed to leave Iran as soon as this interview was over. Now I want to know how this has happened.'

'They just slung them in jail.'

'On what charges?'

'They didn't specify charges.'

'Under what law did they jail them?'

'They didn't say.'

'What are we doing to get them out?'

'Ross, they set bail at ninety million tomans. That's twelve million, seven hundred and fifty thousand dollars.'

'Twelve *million?*'

'That's right.'

'Now how the devil has this happened?'

'Ross, I've been on the phone with Lloyd Briggs for half an hour, trying to understand it, and the fact is that Lloyd doesn't understand it either.'

Perot paused. EDS executives were supposed to give him answers, not questions. Gayden knew better than to call without briefing himself as thoroughly as possible. Perot was not going to get any more out of him right now; Gayden just didn't have the information.

'Get Tom Luce into the office,' Perot said. 'Call the State Department in Washington. This takes priority over everything else. I don't want them to stay in that jail another damn minute!'

Margot pricked up her ears when she heard him say *damn*: it was most unusual for him to curse, especially in front of the children. He came in from the kitchen with his face set. His eyes were as blue as the Arctic Ocean, and as cold. She knew that look. It was not just anger: he was not the kind of man to dissipate his energy in a display of bad temper. It was a look of inflexible determination. It meant he had decided to do something and he would move heaven and earth to get it done. She had seen that determination, that strength in him, when she had first met him, at the Naval Academy in Annapolis . . . could it really be twenty-five years ago? It was the quality that cut him out from the herd, made him different from the mass of men. Oh, he had other qualities – he was smart, he was funny, he could charm the birds out of the trees – but what made him *exceptional* was his strength of will. When he got that look in his

eyes you could no more stop him than you could stop a
railway train on a downhill gradient.

'The Iranians put Paul and Bill in jail,' he said.

Margot's thoughts flew at once to their wives. She
had known them both for years. Ruthie Chiapparone
was a small, placid, smiling girl with a shock of fair hair.
She had a vulnerable look: men wanted to protect her.
She would take it hard. Emily Gaylord was tougher, at
least on the surface. A thin blonde woman, Emily was
vivacious and spirited: she would want to get on a plane
and go spring Bill from jail herself. The difference in
the two women showed in their clothes: Ruthie chose
soft fabrics and gentle outlines; Emily went in for smart
tailoring and bright colours. Emily would suffer on the
inside.

'I'm going back to Dallas,' Ross said.

'There's a blizzard out there,' said Margot, looking
out at the snowflakes swirling down the mountainside.
She knew she was wasting her breath: snow and ice
would not stop him now. She thought ahead: Ross would
not be able to sit behind a desk in Dallas for very long
while two of his men were in an Iranian jail. He's not
going to Dallas, she thought; he's going to Iran.

'I'll take the four-wheel drive,' he said. 'I can catch a
plane in Denver.'

Margot suppressed her fears and smiled brightly.
'Drive carefully, won't you,' she said.

Perot sat hunched over the wheel of the GM Suburban,
driving carefully. The road was icy. Snow built up along

the bottom edge of the windscreen, shortening the travel of the wipers. He peered at the road ahead. Denver was 106 miles from Vail. It gave him time to think.

He was still furious.

It was not just that Paul and Bill were in jail. They were in jail because they had gone to Iran, and they had gone to Iran because Perot had sent them there.

He had been worried about Iran for months. One day, after lying awake at night thinking about it, he had gone in to the office and said: 'Let's evacuate. If we're wrong, all we've lost is the price of three or four hundred plane tickets. Do it today.'

It had been one of the rare occasions on which his orders were not carried out. Everyone had dragged their feet, in Dallas and in Tehran. Not that he could blame them. He had lacked determination. If he had been firm they would have evacuated that day; but he had not, and the following day the passports had been called for.

He owed Paul and Bill a lot anyway. He felt a special debt of loyalty to the men who had gambled their careers by joining EDS when it was a struggling young company. Many times he had found the right man, interviewed him, got him interested, and offered him the job, only to find that, on talking it over with his family, the man had decided that EDS was just too small, too new, too risky.

Paul and Bill had not only taken the chance – they had worked their butts off to make sure their gamble paid. Bill had designed the basic computer system for

the administration of Medicare and Medicaid programmes which, used now in many American States,
formed the foundation of EDS's business. He had
worked long hours, spent weeks away from home, and
moved his family all over the country in those days. Paul
had been no less dedicated: when the company had too
few men and very little cash, Paul had done the work of
three systems engineers. Perot could remember the
company's first contract in New York, with Pepsico; and
Paul walking from Manhattan across the Brooklyn
Bridge in the snow, to sneak past a picket line – the
plant was on strike – and go to work.

Perot owed it to Paul and Bill to get them *out.*

He owed it to them to get the Government of the
United States to bring the whole weight of its influence
to bear on the Iranians.

America had asked for Perot's help, once; and he
had given three years of his life – and a *bunch* of money
– to the prisoners-of-war campaign. Now he was going
to ask for America's help.

His mind went back to 1969, when the Vietnam war
was at its height. Some of his friends from the Naval
Academy had been killed or captured: Bill Leftwich, a
wonderfully warm, strong, kind man, had been killed in
battle at the age of thirty-nine; Bill Lawrence was a
prisoner of the North Vietnamese. Perot found it hard
to watch his country, the greatest country in the world,
losing a war because of lack of will; and even harder to
see millions of Americans protesting, not without justification, that the war was wrong and *should* not be won.
Then, one day in 1969, he had met little Billy Singleton,

a boy who did not know whether he had a father or not. Billy's father had gone missing in Vietnam before ever seeing his son: there was no way of knowing whether he was a prisoner, or dead. It was heartbreaking.

For Perot, sentiment was not a mournful emotion but a clarion call to action.

He learned that Billy's father was not unique. There were many, perhaps hundreds, of wives and children who did not know whether their husbands and fathers had been killed or just captured. The Vietnamese, arguing that they were not bound by the rules of the Geneva Convention because the United States had never declared war, refused to release the names of their prisoners.

Worse still, many of the prisoners were dying of brutality and neglect. President Nixon was planning to 'Vietnamize' the war and disengage in three years' time, but by then, according to CIA reports, half the prisoners would have died. Even if Billy Singleton's father were alive, he might not survive to come home.

Perot wanted to do something.

EDS had good connections with the Nixon White House. Perot went to Washington and talked to Chief Foreign Policy Advisor Henry Kissinger. And Kissinger had a plan.

The Vietnamese were maintaining, at least for the purposes of propaganda, that they had no quarrel with the American people – only with the US Government. Furthermore, they were presenting themselves to the world as the little guy in a David-and-Goliath conflict. It seemed that they valued their public image. It might be possible, Kissinger thought, to embarrass them into improving their treatment of prisoners, and releasing their names, by an international campaign to publicize the sufferings of the prisoners and their families.

The campaign must be privately financed, and must *seem* to be quite unconnected with the Government, even though in reality it would be closely monitored by a team of White House and State Department people.

Perot accepted the challenge. (Perot could resist anything but a challenge. His eleventh-grade teacher, one Mrs Duck, had realized this. 'It's a shame', Mrs Duck had said, 'that you're not as smart as your friends.' Young Perot insisted he *was* as smart as his friends. 'Well, why do they make better grades than you?' It was just that they were interested in school and he was not, said Perot. 'Anybody can stand there and tell me that they *could* do something,' said Mrs Duck. 'But let's look at the record: your friends can do it and you can't.' Perot was cut to the quick. He told her that he would make straight As for the next six weeks. He made straight As, not just for six weeks, but for the rest of his high school career. The perceptive Mrs Duck had discovered the only way to manipulate Perot: challenge him.)

Accepting Kissinger's challenge, Perot went to J. Walter Thompson, the largest advertising agency in the world, and told them what he wanted to do. They offered to come up with a plan of campaign within thirty to sixty days and show some results in a year. Perot turned them down: he wanted to start today and see results tomorrow. He went back to Dallas and put together a

small team of EDS executives who began calling newspaper executives and placing simple, unsophisticated
advertisements which they wrote themselves.

And the mail came in truckloads.

For Americans who were pro-war, the treatment of
the prisoners showed that the Vietnamese really were
the bad guys; and for those who were anti-war the plight
of the prisoners was one more reason for getting out of
Vietnam. Only the most hard-line protesters resented
the campaign. In 1970 the FBI told Perot that the Viet
Cong had instructed the Black Panthers to murder him.
(At the crazy end of the sixties this had not sounded
particularly bizarre.) Perot hired body-guards. Sure
enough, a few weeks later a squad of men climbed the
fence around Perot's seventeen-acre Dallas property.
They were chased off by savage dogs. Perot's family,
including his indomitable mother, would not hear of
him giving up the campaign for the sake of their safety.

His greatest publicity stunt took place in December
1969, when he chartered two planes and tried to fly into
Hanoi with Christmas dinners for the prisoners-of-war.
Of course, he was not allowed to land; but during a slow
news period he created enormous international awareness of the problem. He spent two million dollars, but
he reckoned the publicity would have cost sixty million
to buy. And a Gallup poll he commissioned afterwards
showed that the feelings of Americans toward the North
Vietnamese were overwhelmingly negative.

During 1970 Perot used less spectacular methods.
Small communities all over the United States were

encouraged to set up their own POW campaigns. They raised funds to send people to Paris to badger the North Vietnamese delegation there. They organized telethons, and built replicas of the cages in which some of the POWs lived. They sent so many protest letters to Hanoi that the North Vietnamese postal system collapsed under the strain. Perot stumped the country, giving speeches anywhere he was invited. He met with North Vietnamese diplomats in Laos, taking with him lists of their people held in the south, mail from them, and film of their living conditions. He also took a Gallup associate with him, and together they went over the results of the poll with the North Vietnamese.

Some or all of it worked. The treatment of American POWs improved, mail and parcels began to get through to them, and the North Vietnamese started to release names. Most importantly, the prisoners heard of the campaign – from newly captured American soldiers – and the news boosted their morale enormously.

Eight years later, driving to Denver in the snow, Perot recalled another consequence of the campaign, a consequence which had then seemed no more than mildly irritating, but could now be important and valuable. Publicity for the POWs had meant, inevitably, publicity for Ross Perot. He had become nationally known. He would be remembered in the corridors of power – and especially in the Pentagon. That Washington monitoring committee had included Admiral Tom Moorer, then Chairman of the Joint Chiefs of Staff; Alexander Haig, then assistant to Kissinger and now Commander in Chief of NATO forces; William Sullivan, then a Deputy Assistant Secretary of State and now US Ambassador to Iran; and Kissinger himself.

These people would help Perot get inside the Government, find out what was happening, and promote help fast. He would call Richard Helms, who had in the past been both head of the CIA and US Ambassador in Tehran. He would call Kermit Roosevelt, son of Teddy, who had been involved in the CIA coup which put the Shah back on the throne in 1953 . . .

But what if none of this works? he thought.

It was his habit to think more than one step ahead.

What if the Carter administration could not or would not help?

Then, he thought, I'm going to break them out of jail.

How would we go about something like that? We've never done anything like it. Where would we start? Who could help us?

He thought of EDS executives Merv Stauffer and T. J. Marquez, and his secretary Sally Walther, who had been key organizers of the POW campaign: making complex arrangements half across the world by phone was meat and drink to them, but . . . a prison break? And who would staff the mission? Since 1968 EDS's recruiters had given priority to Vietnam veterans – a policy begun for patriotic reasons and continued when Perot found that the vets often made first-class businessmen – but the men who had once been lean, fit, highly-trained soldiers were now overweight, out-of-condition computer executives, more comfortable with a telephone than with a rifle. And who would plan and lead the raid?

Finding the best man for the job was Perot's speciality. Although he was one of the most successful self-made men in the history of American capitalism, he was not the world's greatest computer expert, nor the world's greatest salesman, nor even the world's greatest business administrator. He did just one thing superbly well: pick the right man, give him the resources, motivate him, then leave him alone to do the job.

Now, as he approached Denver, he asked himself: who is the world's greatest rescuer?

Then he thought of Bull Simons.

A legend in the US Army, Colonel Arthur D. 'Bull' Simons had hit the headlines in November 1970 when he and a team of commandos raided the Son Tay prison camp, twenty-three miles outside Hanoi, in an attempt to rescue American prisoners of war. The raid had been a brave and well-organized operation, but the intelligence on which all the planning was based had been faulty: the prisoners had been moved, and were no longer at Son Tay. The raid was widely regarded as a fiasco which in Perot's opinion was grossly unfair. He had been invited to meet the Son Tay Raiders, to boost their morale by telling them that here was at least one American citizen who was grateful for their bravery. He had spent a day at Fort Bragg in North Carolina – and he had met Colonel Simons.

Peering through his windscreen, Perot could picture Simons against the cloud of falling snowflakes: a big man, just under six feet tall, with the shoulders of an ox.

His white hair was cropped in a military crewcut, but his bushy eyebrows were still black. Either side of his big nose, two deep lines ran down to the corners of his mouth, giving him a permanently aggressive expression. He had a big head, big ears, a strong jaw, and the most powerful hands Perot had ever seen. The man looked as if he had been carved from a single block of granite.

After spending a day with him, Perot thought: in a world of counterfeits, he is the genuine article.

That day and in years to come Perot learned a lot about Simons. What impressed him most was the attitude of Simons's men towards their leader. He reminded Perot of Vince Lombardi, the legendary coach of the Green Bay Packers: he inspired in his men emotions ranging from fear through respect and admiration to love. He was an imposing figure and an aggressive commander – he cursed a lot, and would tell a soldier: 'Do what I say or I'll cut your bloody head off!' – but that by itself could not account for his hold on the hearts of sceptical, battle-hardened commandos. Beneath the tough exterior there was a tough interior.

Those who had served under him liked nothing better than to sit around telling Simons stories. Although he had a bull-like physique, his nickname came not from that but, according to legend, from a game played by Rangers called The Bull Pen. A pit would be dug, six feet deep, and one man would get into it. The object of the game was to find out how many men it took to throw the first man out of the pit. Simons thought the game was foolish, but was once needled into playing it. It took fifteen men to get him out, and several of them spent the night in hospital with broken fingers and noses and severe bite wounds. After that he was called 'Bull'.

Perot learned later that almost everything in this story was exaggerated. Simons played the game more than once; it generally took four men to get him out; no one ever had any broken bones. Simons was simply the kind of man about whom legends are told. He earned the loyalty of his men not by displays of bravado but by his skill as a military commander. He was a meticulous, endlessly patient planner; he was cautious (one of his catch-phrases was: 'That's a risk we don't have to take') and he took a pride in bringing all his men back from a mission alive.

In the Vietnam war Simons had run Operation White Star. He went to Laos with 107 men and organized twelve battalions of Mao tribesmen to fight the Vietnamese. One of the battalions defected to the other side, taking as prisoners some of Simons's Green Berets. Simons took a helicopter and landed inside the stockade where the defecting battalion was. On seeing Simons, the Laotian colonel stepped forward, stood at attention, and saluted. Simons told him to produce the prisoners immediately, or he would call an airstrike and destroy the entire battalion. The colonel produced the prisoners. Simons took them away, then called the airstrike anyway. Simons had come back from Laos three years later with all his 107 men. Perot had never checked out this legend – he liked it the way it was.

The second time Perot met Simons was after the war. Perot virtually took over a hotel in San Francisco and threw a weekend party for the returning prisoners-of-war to meet the Son Tay Raiders. It cost Perot a quarter of a million dollars, but it was a hell of a party. Nancy Reagan, Clint Eastwood and John Wayne came. Perot would never forget the meeting between John Wayne and Bull Simons. Wayne shook Simons's hand with tears in his eyes and said: 'You *are* the man I play in the movies.'

Before the tickertape parade, Perot asked Simons to talk to his Raiders and warn them against reacting to demonstrators. 'San Francisco has had more than its share of anti-war demonstrations,' Perot said. 'You didn't pick your Raiders for their charm. If one of them gets irritated he might just snap some poor devil's neck and regret it later.'

Simons looked at Perot. It was Perot's first experience of The Simons Look. It made you feel as if you were the biggest fool in history. It made you wish you had not spoken. It made you wish the ground would swallow you up.

'I've already talked to them,' Simons said. 'There won't be a problem.'

That weekend and later, Perot got to know Simons better, and saw other sides of his personality. Simons could be very charming, when he chose to be. He enchanted Perot's wife Margot, and the children thought he was wonderful. With his men he spoke soldiers' language, using a great deal of profanity, but he was surprisingly articulate when talking at a banquet or press conference. His college major had been journalism. Some of his tastes were simple – he read

Westerns by the boxful, and enjoyed what his sons called 'supermarket music' – but he also read a lot of non-fiction, and had a lively curiosity about all sorts of things. He could talk about antiques or history as easily as battles and weaponry.

Perot and Simons, two wilful, dominating personalities, got along by giving one another plenty of room. They did not become close friends. Perot never called Simons by his first name, Art (although Margot did). Like most people, Perot never knew what Simons was thinking unless Simons chose to tell him. Perot recalled their first meeting in Fort Bragg. Before getting up to make his speech, Perot had asked Simons's wife Lucille: 'What is Colonel Simons really like?' She had replied: 'Oh, he's just a great big teddy bear.' Perot repeated this in his speech. The Son Tay Raiders fell apart. Simons never cracked a smile.

Perot did not know whether this impenetrable man would care to rescue two EDS executives from a Persian jail. Was Simons grateful for the San Francisco party? Perhaps. After that party, Perot had financed Simons on a trip to Laos to search for MIAs – American soldiers Missing In Action – who had not come back with the prisoners-of-war. On his return from Laos, Simons had remarked to a group of EDS executives: 'Perot is a hard man to say no to.'

As he pulled into Denver airport, Perot wondered whether, six years later, Simons would still find him a hard man to say no to.

But that contingency was a long way down the line. Perot was going to try everything else first.

He went into the terminal, bought a seat on the next flight to Dallas, and found a phone. He called EDS and spoke to T.J. Marquez, one of his most senior executives, who was known as T.J. rather than Tom because there were so many Toms around EDS. 'I want you to go find my passport, and get me a visa for Iran.'

T.J. said: 'Ross, I think that's the world's worst idea.'

T.J. would argue until nightfall if you let him. 'I'm not going to debate with you,' Perot said curtly. 'I talked Paul and Bill into going over there, and I'm going to get them out.'

He hung up the phone and headed for the departure gate. All in all, it had been a rotten Christmas.

T.J. was a little wounded. An old friend of Perot's as well as a vice-president of EDS, he was not used to being talked to like the office boy. This was a persistent failing of Perot's: when he was in high gear, he trod on people's toes and never knew he had hurt them. He was a remarkable man, but he was not a saint.

II

Ruthie Chiapparone also had a rotten Christmas.

She was staying at her parents' home, an eighty-five-year-old two-storey house on the southwest side of Chicago. In the rush of the evacuation from Iran she had left behind most of the Christmas presents she had bought for her daughters Karen, eleven, and Ann Marie, five; but soon after arriving in Chicago she had gone shopping with her brother Bill and bought some more. Her family did their best to make Christmas Day happy. Her sister and three brothers visited, and there were lots more toys for Karen and Ann Marie; but everyone asked about Paul.

Ruthie needed Paul. A soft, dependent woman, five years younger than her husband – she was thirty-four – she loved him partly because she could lean on his broad shoulders and feel safe. She had always been looked after. As a child, even when her mother was out at work – supplementing the wages of Ruthie's father, a truck driver – Ruthie had two older brothers and an older sister to take care of her.

When she first met Paul he had ignored her.

She was secretary to a Colonel; Paul was working on data processing for the Army in the same building. Ruthie used to go down to the cafeteria to get coffee for the Colonel, some of her friends knew some of the young officers, she sat down to talk with a group of them, and Paul was there and he ignored her. So she ignored him for a while, then all of a sudden he asked her for a date. They dated for a year and a half and then got married.

Ruthie had not wanted to go to Iran. Unlike most of the EDS wives, who had found the prospect of moving to a new country exciting, Ruthie had been highly anxious. She had never been outside the United States – Hawaii was the farthest she had ever travelled – and the Middle East seemed a weird and frightening place. Paul took her to Iran for a week in June of 1977, hoping she would like it, but she was not reassured. Finally she agreed to go, but only because the job was so important to him.

However, she ended up liking it. The Iranians were nice to her, the American community there was close-knit and sociable, and Ruthie's serene nature enabled her to deal calmly with the daily frustrations of living in a primitive country, like the lack of supermarkets and the difficulty of getting a washing machine repaired in less than about six weeks.

Leaving had been strange. The airport had been crammed, just an unbelievable number of people in there. She had recognized many of the Americans, but most of the people were fleeing Iranians. She had thought: 'I don't want to leave like this – why are you pushing us out? What are you doing?' She had travelled with Bill Gaylord's wife Emily. They went via Copenhagen, where they spent a freezing cold night in a hotel where the windows would not close: the children had to sleep in their clothes. When she got back to the States, Ross Perot had called her and talked about the passport problem, but Ruthie had not really understood what was happening.

During that depressing Christmas Day – so unnatural to have Christmas with the children and no Daddy – Paul had called from Tehran. 'I've got a present for you,' he had said.

'Your airline ticket?' she asked hopefully.

'No. I bought you a rug.'

'That's nice.'

He had spent the day with Pat and Mary Sculley, he

told her. Someone else's wife had cooked his Christmas dinner, and he had watched someone else's children open their presents.

Two days later she heard that Paul and Bill had an appointment, the following day, to see the man who was making them stay in Iran. After the meeting they would be let go.

The meeting was today, 28 December. By midday Ruthie was wondering why nobody from Dallas had called her yet. Tehran was eight and a half hours ahead of Chicago; surely the meeting was over? By now Paul should be packing his suitcase to come home.

She called Dallas and spoke to Jim Nyfeler, an EDS man who had left Tehran last June. 'How did the meeting work out?' she asked him.

'It didn't go too well, Ruthie . . .'

'What do you mean, it didn't go too well?'

'They were arrested.'

'They were arrested? You're kidding!'

'Ruthie, Bill Gayden wants to talk to you.'

Ruthie held the line. Paul *arrested?* Why? For what? By whom?

Gayden, the president of EDS World and Paul's boss, came on the line. 'Hello, Ruthie.'

'Bill, what is all this?'

'We don't understand it,' Gayden said. 'The Embassy over there set up this meeting, and it was supposed to be routine, they weren't accused of any crime . . . Then, around six-thirty their time, Paul called Lloyd Briggs and told him they were going to jail.'

'Paul's in *jail?*'

'Ruthie, try not to worry too much. We got a bunch of lawyers working on it, we're getting the State Department on the case, and Ross is already on his way back from Colorado. We're sure we can straighten this out in a couple of days. It's just a matter of days, really.'

'All right,' said Ruthie. She was dazed. It didn't make sense. How could her husband be in jail? She said goodbye to Gayden and hung up.

What was going on out there?

The last time Emily Gaylord had seen her husband Bill, she had thrown a plate at him.

Sitting in her sister Dorothy's home in Washington, talking to Dorothy and her husband Tim about how they might help to get Bill out of jail, she could not forget that flying plate.

It had happened in their house in Tehran. One evening in early December Bill came home and said that Emily and the children were to return to the States the very next day.

Bill and Emily had four children: Vickie, fifteen; Jackie, twelve; Jenny, nine; and Chris, six. Emily agreed that they should be sent back, but she wanted to stay. She might not be able to do anything to help Bill, but at least he would have someone to talk to.

It was out of the question, said Bill. She was leaving tomorrow. Ruthie Chiapparone would be on the same plane. All the other EDS wives and children would be evacuated a day or two later.

They argued. Emily got madder and madder until finally she could no longer express her frustration in words, so she picked up a plate and hurled it at him.

He would never forget it, she was sure: it was the only time in eighteen years of marriage that she had exploded like that. She was highly strung, spirited, excitable – but not violent.

Mild, gentle Bill, it was the last thing he deserved . . .

When she first met him she was twelve, he was fourteen and she hated him. He was in love with her best friend Cookie, a strikingly attractive girl, and all he ever talked about was who Cookie was dating and whether Cookie might like to go out and was Cookie allowed to do this or that . . . Emily's sisters and brother really liked Bill. She could not get away from him, for their families belonged to the same country club and her brother played golf with Bill. It was her brother who finally talked Bill into asking Emily for a date, long after he had forgotten Cookie; and, after years of mutual indifference, they fell madly in love.

By then Bill was in college, studying aeronautical engineering 240 miles away in Blacksburg, Virginia, and coming home for vacations and occasional weekends. They could not bear to be so far apart so, although Emily was only eighteen, they decided to get married.

It was a good match. They came from similar backgrounds, affluent Washington Catholic families, and Bill's personality – sensitive, calm, logical – complemented Emily's nervous vivacity. They went through a lot together over the next eighteen years. They lost a child with brain damage, and Emily had major surgery three times. Their troubles brought them closer together.

And here was a new crisis: Bill was in jail.

Emily had not yet told her mother. Mother's brother, Emily's Uncle Gus, had died that day, and Mother was already terribly upset. Emily could not talk to her about Bill yet. But she could talk to Dorothy and Tim.

Her brother-in-law Tim Reardon was a US Attorney in the Justice Department and had very good connections. Tim's father had been an administrative assistant to President John F. Kennedy, and Tim had worked for Ted Kennedy. Tim also knew personally the Speaker of the House of Representatives, Thomas P. 'Tip' O'Neill, and Maryland Senator Charles Mathias. He was familiar with the passport problem, for Emily had told him about it as soon as she got back to Washington from Tehran, and he had discussed it with Ross Perot.

'I could write a letter to President Carter, and ask Ted Kennedy to deliver it personally,' Tim was saying.

Emily nodded. It was hard for her to concentrate. She wondered what Bill was doing right now.

Paul and Bill stood just inside Cell No 9, cold, numb, and desperate to know what would happen next.

Paul felt very vulnerable: a white American in a business suit, unable to speak more than a few words of Farsi, faced by a crowd of what looked like thugs and murderers. He suddenly remembered reading that men were frequently raped in jail, and he wondered grimly how he would cope with something like that.

Paul looked at Bill. His face was white with tension.

One of the inmates spoke to them in Farsi. Paul said: 'Does anyone here speak English?'

From another cell across the corridor a voice called: 'I speak English.'

There was a shouted conversation in rapid Farsi, then the interpreter called: 'What is your crime?'

'We haven't done anything,' Paul said.

'What are you accused of?'

'Nothing. We're just ordinary American businessmen with wives and children, and we don't know why we're in jail.'

This was translated. There was more rapid Farsi, then the interpreter said: 'The one who is talking to me, he is the boss of your cell, because he is there the longest.'

'We understand,' Paul said.

'He will tell you where to sleep.'

The tension eased as they talked. Paul took in his surroundings. The concrete walls were painted what might once have been orange but now just looked dirty. There was some kind of thin carpet or matting covering most of the concrete floor. Around the cell were six sets of bunks, stacked three high: the lowest bunk was no more than a thin mattress on the floor. The room was lit by a single dim bulb and ventilated by a grille in the wall which let in the bitterly cold night air. The cell was very crowded.

After a while a guard came down, opened the door

of Cell No 9, and motioned Paul and Bill to come out.

This is it, Paul thought; we'll be released now. Thank God I don't have to spend a night in that awful cell.

They followed the guard upstairs and into a little room. He pointed at their shoes.

They understood they were to take their shoes off.

The guard handed them each a pair of plastic slippers.

Paul realized with bitter disappointment that they were not about to be released; he *did* have to spend a night in the cell. He thought with anger of the Embassy staff: they had arranged the meeting with Dadgar, they had advised Paul against taking lawyers, they had said Dadgar was 'favourably disposed'. Ross Perot would say: 'Some people can't organize a two-car funeral.' That applied to the US Embassy. They were simply incompetent. Surely, Paul thought, after all the mistakes they have made, they ought to come here *tonight* and try to get us out?

They put on the plastic slippers and followed the guard back downstairs.

The other prisoners were getting ready for sleep, lying on the bunks and wrapping themselves in thin wool blankets. The cell boss, using sign language, showed Paul and Bill where to lie down. Bill was on the middle bunk of a stack, Paul below him with just a thin mattress between his body and the floor.

They lay down. The light stayed on, but it was so dim it hardly mattered. After a while Paul no longer noticed the smell, but he did not get used to the cold. With the concrete floor, the open vent, and no heating, it was almost like sleeping out of doors. What a terrible life criminals lead, Paul thought, having to endure conditions such as these; I'm glad I'm not a criminal. One night of this will be more than enough.

III

Ross Perot took a taxi from the Dallas/Fort Worth regional airport to EDS corporate headquarters at 7171 Forest Lane. At the EDS gate he rolled down the window to let the security guards see his face, then sat back again as the car wound along the quarter-mile driveway through the park. The site had once been a country club, and these grounds a golf course. EDS headquarters loomed ahead, a seven-storey office building, and next to it a tornado-proof blockhouse containing the vast computers with their thousands of miles of magnetic tape.

Perot paid the driver, walked into the office building, and took the elevator to the fifth floor, where he went to Gayden's corner office.

Gayden was at his desk. Gayden always managed to look untidy, despite the EDS dress code. He had taken his jacket off. His tie was loosened, the collar of his button-down shirt was open, his hair was mussed, and a cigarette dangled from the corner of his mouth. He stood up when Perot walked in.

'Ross, how's your mother?'

'She's in good spirits, thank you.'

'That's good.'

Perot sat down. 'Now, where are we on Paul and Bill?'

Gayden picked up the phone, saying: 'Lemme get T.J. in here.' He punched T. J. Marquez's number and said: 'Ross is here . . . Yeah. My office.' He hung up and said: 'He'll be right down. Uh . . . I called the State Department. The head of the Iran Desk is a man called Henry Precht. At first he wouldn't return my call. In the end I told his secretary, I said: "If he doesn't call me within twenty minutes, I'm going to call CBS and ABC and NBC and in one hour's time Ross Perot is going to give a press conference to say that we have two Americans in trouble in Iran and our country won't help them." He called back five minutes later.'

'What did he say?'

Gayden sighed. 'Ross, their basic attitude up there is that if Paul and Bill are in jail they must have done something wrong.'

'But what are they going to *do*?'

'Contact the Embassy, look into it, blah blah blah.'

'Well, we're going to have to put a firecracker under Precht's tail,' Perot said angrily. 'Now, Tom Luce is the man to do that.' Luce, an aggressive young lawyer, was the founder of the Dallas firm of Hughes & Hill, which handled most of EDS's legal business. Perot had retained him as EDS's counsel years ago, mainly because Perot could relate to a young man who, like himself, had left a big company to start his own business and was struggling to pay the bills. Hughes & Hill, like EDS, had grown rapidly. Perot had never regretted hiring Luce.

Gayden said: 'Luce is right here in the office somewhere.'

'How about Tom Walter?'

'He's here too.'

Walter, a tall Alabaman with a voice like molasses, was EDS's chief financial officer and probably the smartest man, in terms of sheer brains, in the company. Perot said: 'I want Walter to go to work on the bail. I don't want to pay it, but I will if we have to. Walter should figure out how we go about paying it. You can bet they won't take American Express.'

'Okay,' Gayden said.

A voice from behind said: 'Hi, Ross!'

Perot looked around and saw T. J. Marquez. 'Hi, Tom.' T.J. was a tall, slim man of forty with Spanish good looks: olive skin, short, curly black hair, and a big smile which showed lots of white teeth. The first employee Perot ever hired, he was living evidence that Perot had an uncanny knack of picking good men. T.J. was now a vice-president of EDS, and his personal shareholding in the company was worth millions of dollars. 'The Lord has been good to us,' T.J. would say. Perot knew that T.J.'s parents had really struggled to send him to college. Their sacrifices had been well rewarded. One of the best things about the meteoric success of EDS, for Perot, had been sharing the triumph with people like T.J.

T.J. sat down and talked fast. 'I called Claude.'

Perot nodded. Claude Chappelear was the company's in-house lawyer.

'Claude's friendly with Matthew Nimetz, counsellor to Secretary of State Vance. I thought Claude might get Nimetz to talk to Vance himself. Nimetz called personally a little later. He wants to help us. He's going to send a cable under Vance's name to the US Embassy in Tehran, telling them to get off their butts. And he's going to write a personal note to Vance about Paul and Bill.'

'Good.'

'We also called Admiral Moorer. He's up to speed on this whole thing because we consulted him about the passport problem. Moorer's going to talk to Ardeshir Zahedi. Now, Zahedi is not just the Iranian Ambassador in Washington but also the Shah's brother-in-law, and he's now back in Iran – running the country, some say. Moorer will ask Zahedi to vouch for Paul and Bill. Right now we're drafting a cable for Zahedi to send to the Ministry of Justice.'

'Who's drafting it?'

'Tom Luce.'

'Good.' Perot summed up. 'We've got the Secretary of State, the Head of the Iran Desk, the Embassy, and the Iranian Ambassador all working on the case. That's good. Now let's talk about what else we can do.'

T.J. said: 'Tom Luce and Tom Walter have an appointment with Admiral Moorer in Washington tomorrow. Moorer also suggested we call Richard Helms – he used to be Ambassador to Iran after he quit the CIA.'

'I'll call Helms,' Perot said. 'And I'll call Al Haig and

Henry Kissinger. I want you two to concentrate on getting all our people out of Iran.'

Gayden said: 'Ross, I'm not sure that's necessary—'

'I don't want a discussion, Bill,' said Perot. 'Let's get it done. Now, Lloyd Briggs has to stay there and deal with the problem – he's the boss, with Paul and Bill in jail. Everyone else comes home.'

'You can't make them come home if they don't want to,' Gayden said.

'Who'll want to stay?'

'Rich Gallagher. His wife—'

'I know. Okay, Briggs and Gallagher stay. Nobody else.' Perot stood up. 'I'll get started on those calls.'

He took the elevator to the seventh floor and walked through his secretary's office. Sally Walther was at her desk. She had been with him for years, and had been involved in the prisoners-of-war campaign and the San Francisco party. (She had come back from that weekend with a Son Tay Raider in tow, and Captain Udo Walther was now her husband.) Perot said to her: 'Call Henry Kissinger, Alexander Haig, and Richard Helms.'

He went through to his own office and sat at his desk. The office, with its panelled walls, costly carpet, and shelves of antiquarian books, looked more like a Victorian library in an English country house. He was surrounded by souvenirs and his favourite art. For the house Margot bought Impressionist paintings, but in his office Perot preferred American art: Norman Rockwell originals and the Wild West bronzes of Frederic Remington. Through the window he could see the slopes of the old golf course.

Perot did not know where Henry Kissinger might be spending the holidays: it could take Sally a while to find him. There was time to think about what to say. Kissinger was not a close friend. It would need all his salesmanship to grab Kissinger's attention and, in the space of a short phone call, win his sympathy.

The phone on his desk buzzed, and Sally called: 'Henry Kissinger for you.'

Perot picked it up. 'Ross Perot.'

'I have Henry Kissinger for you.'

Perot waited.

Kissinger had once been called the most powerful man in the world. He knew the Shah personally. But how well would he remember Ross Perot? The prisoners-of-war campaign had been big, but Kissinger's projects had been bigger: peace in the Middle East, rapprochement between the US and China, the ending of the Vietnam war . . .

'Kissinger here.' It was the familiar deep voice, its accent a curious mixture of American vowels and German consonants.

'Dr Kissinger, this is Ross Perot. I'm a businessman in Dallas, Texas, and—'

'Hell, Ross, I know who you are,' said Kissinger.

Perot's heart leaped. Kissinger's voice was warm, friendly and informal. This was great! Perot began to tell him about Paul and Bill: how they had gone voluntarily to see Dadgar, how the State Department had let them down. He assured Kissinger they were innocent, and pointed out that they had not been charged with any crime, nor had the Iranians produced an atom of evidence against them. 'These are my men, I sent them there, and I have to get them back,' he finished.

'I'll see what I can do,' Kissinger said.

Perot was exultant. 'I sure appreciate it!'

'Send me a short briefing paper with all the details.'

'We'll get it to you today.'

'I'll get back to you, Ross.'

'Thank you, sir.'

The line went dead.

Perot felt terrific. Kissinger had remembered him, had been friendly and willing to help. He wanted a briefing paper: EDS could send it today—

Perot was struck by a thought. He had no idea where Kissinger had been speaking from – it might have been London, Monte Carlo, Mexico . . .

'Sally?'

'Yes, sir?'

'Did you find out *where* Kissinger is?'

'Yes, sir.'

Kissinger was in New York, in his duplex at the exclusive River House apartment complex on East 52nd Street. From the window he could see the East River.

He remembered Ross Perot clearly. Perot was a rough diamond. He helped causes with which Kissinger was sympathetic, usually causes having to do with prisoners. In the Vietnam war Perot's campaign had been courageous, even though he had sometimes harassed Kissinger beyond the point of what was do-able. Now some of Perot's own people were prisoners.

Kissinger could readily believe that they were innocent. Iran was on the brink of civil war: justice and due process meant little over there now. He wondered whether he could help. He wanted to: it was a good cause. He was no longer in office, but he still had friends. He would call Ardeshir Zahedi, he decided, as soon as the briefing paper arrived from Dallas.

Perot felt good about the conversation with Kissinger. *Hell, Ross, I know who you are.* That was worth more than money. The only advantage of being famous was that it sometimes helped get important things done.

T.J. came in. 'I have your passport,' he said. 'It already had a visa for Iran, but Ross, I don't think you should go. All of us here can work on the problem, but you're the key man. The last thing we need is for you to be out of contact – in Tehran or just up in a plane somewhere – at the moment when we have to make a crucial decision.'

Perot had forgotten all about going to Tehran. Everything he had heard in the last hour encouraged him to think it would not be necessary. 'You might be right,' he said to T.J. 'We have so many things going in the area of negotiation – only one of them has to work. I won't go to Tehran. Yet.'

IV

Henry Precht was probably the most harassed man in Washington.

A long-serving State Department official with a bent for art and philosophy and a wacky sense of humour, he had been making American policy on Iran more or less by himself for much of 1978, while his superiors – right up to President Carter – focused on the Camp David agreement between Egypt and Israel.

Since early November, when things had really started to warm up in Iran, Precht had been working seven days a week from eight in the morning until nine at night. And those damn Texans seemed to think he had nothing else to do but talk to them on the phone.

The trouble was, the crisis in Iran was not the only power struggle Precht had to worry about. There was another fight going on, in Washington, between Secretary of State Cyrus Vance – Precht's boss – and Zbigniew Brzezinski, the President's National Security Advisor.

Vance believed, like President Carter, that American foreign policy should reflect American morality. The American people believed in freedom, justice and democracy, and they did not want to support tyrants. The Shah of Iran was a tyrant. Amnesty International had called Iran's human rights record the worst in the world, and the many reports of the Shah's systematic use of torture had been confirmed by the International Commission of Jurists. Since the CIA had put the Shah in power and the USA had kept him there, a President who talked a lot about human rights had to do something.

In January 1977 Carter had hinted that tyrants might be denied American aid. Carter was indecisive – later that year he visited Iran and lavished praise on the Shah – but Vance believed in the human-rights approach.

Zbigniew Brzezinski did not. The National Security Advisor believed in power. The Shah was an ally of the United States, and should be supported. Sure, he should be encouraged to stop torturing people – but not yet. His regime was under attack: this was no time to liberalize it.

'When would be the time?' asked the Vance faction. The Shah had been strong for most of his twenty-five years of rule, but had never shown much inclination toward moderate government. Brzezinski replied: 'Name one single moderate government in that region of the world.'

There were those in the Carter administration who thought that if America did not stand for freedom and democracy there was no point in having a foreign policy at all. But that was a somewhat extreme view, so they fell back on a pragmatic argument: the Iranian people had had enough of the Shah, and they were going to get rid of him regardless of what Washington thought.

'Rubbish,' said Brzezinski. 'Read history. Revolutions succeed when rulers make concessions, and fail when those in power crush the rebels with an iron fist. The Iranian army, four hundred thousand strong, can easily put down any revolt.'

The Vance faction – including Henry Precht – did not agree with the Brzezinski Theory of Revolutions: threatened tyrants make concessions because the rebels are strong, not the other way around, they said. More importantly, they did not believe that the Iranian army was four hundred thousand strong. Figures were hard to get, but soldiers were deserting at a rate which fluctuated around eight per cent per month, and there were whole units which would go over to the revolutionaries intact in the event of all-out civil war.

The two Washington factions were getting their information from different sources. Brzezinski was listening to Ardeshir Zahedi, the Shah's brother-in-law and the most powerful pro-Shah figure in Iran. Vance was listening to Ambassador Sullivan. Sullivan's cables were not as consistent as Washington could have wished, perhaps because the situation in Iran was sometimes confusing, but since September the general trend of his reports had been to say that the Shah was doomed.

Brzezinski said Sullivan was running around with his head cut off and could not be trusted. Vance's supporters said that Brzezinski dealt with bad news by shooting the messenger.

The upshot was that the United States did nothing. One time the State Department drafted a cable to Ambassador Sullivan, instructing him to urge the Shah to form a broad-based civilian coalition government: Brzezinski killed the cable. Another time Brzezinski phoned the Shah and assured him that he had the support of President Carter; the Shah asked for a confirming cable; the State Department did not send the cable. In their frustration both sides leaked stuff to the newspapers, so that the whole world knew that Washington's policy on Iran was paralysed by in-fighting.

With all that going on, the last thing Precht needed was a gang of Texans on his tail thinking they were the only people in the world with a problem.

Besides, he knew, he thought, exactly why EDS was in trouble. On asking whether EDS was represented by an agent in Iran, he was told: 'Yes – Mr Abolfath Mahvi.' That explained everything. Mahvi was a well known Tehran middleman, nicknamed 'the king of the five percenters' for his dealings in military contracts. Despite his high-level contacts the Shah had put him on a blacklist of people banned from doing business in Iran. *This* was why EDS was suspected of corruption.

Precht would do what he could. He would get the Embassy in Tehran to look into the case, and perhaps Ambassador Sullivan might be able to put pressure on the Iranians to release Chiapparone and Gaylord. But there was no way the United States Government was going to put all other Iranian questions on the back burner. They were attempting to support the existing regime, and this was no time to unbalance that regime further by threatening a break in diplomatic relations over two jailed businessmen, especially when there were another twelve thousand US citizens in Iran, all of whom the State Department was supposed to look after. It was unfortunate, but Chiapparone and Gaylord would just have to sweat it out.

*

Henry Precht meant well. However, early in his involvement with Paul and Bill, he – like Lou Goelz – made a
mistake which at first wrongly coloured his attitude to
the problem and later made him defensive in all his
dealings with EDS. Precht acted as if the investigation in
which Paul and Bill were supposed to be witnesses was a
legitimate judicial inquiry into allegations of corruption,
rather than a barefaced act of blackmail. Goelz, on this
assumption, decided to co-operate with General Biglari.
Precht, making the same mistake, refused to treat Paul
and Bill as criminally kidnapped Americans.

Whether Abolfath Mahvi was corrupt or not, the fact
was that he had not made a penny out of EDS's contract
with the Ministry. Indeed, EDS had got into trouble in
its early days for *refusing* to give Mahvi a piece of the
action.

It happened like this. Mahvi helped EDS get its first,
small contract in Iran, creating a document control
system for the Iranian Navy. EDS, advised that by law
they had to have a local partner, promised Mahvi a third
of the profit. When the contract was completed, two
years later, EDS duly paid Mahvi four hundred thousand
dollars.

But while the Ministry contract was being negotiated
Mahvi was on the blacklist. Nevertheless, when the deal
was about to be signed, Mahvi – who by this time was *off*
the blacklist again – demanded that the contract be
given to a joint company owned by him and EDS.

EDS refused. While Mahvi had earned his share of
the Navy contract, he had done nothing for the Ministry
deal.

Mahvi claimed that EDS's association with him had smoothed the way for the Ministry contract through the twenty-four different government bodies which had to approve it. Furthermore, he said, he had helped obtain a tax ruling favourable to EDS which was written into the contract: EDS only got the ruling because Mahvi had spent time with the Minister of Finance in Monte Carlo.

EDS had not asked for his help, and did not believe that he had given it. Furthermore, Ross Perot did not like the kind of 'help' that takes place in Monte Carlo.

EDS's Iranian attorney complained to the Prime Minister, and Mahvi was carpeted for demanding bribes. Nevertheless his influence was so great that the Ministry of Health would not sign the contract unless EDS made him happy.

EDS had a series of stormy negotiations with Mahvi. EDS still refused point blank to share profits with him. In the end there was a face-saving compromise: a joint company, acting as subcontractor to EDS, would recruit and employ all EDS's Iranian staff. In fact the joint company never made money, but that was later. At the time Mahvi accepted the compromise and the Ministry contract was signed.

So EDS had not paid bribes, and the Iranian government knew it; but Henry Precht did not, nor did Lou Goelz. Consequently their attitude to Paul and Bill was equivocal. Both men spent many hours on the case but neither gave it top priority. When EDS's combative lawyer Tom Luce talked to them as if they were idle or stupid or both, they became indignant and said they might do better if he would get off their backs.

Precht in Washington and Goelz in Tehran were the crucial, ground-level operatives dealing with the case. Neither of them was idle. Neither was incompetent. But they both made mistakes, they both became somewhat hostile to EDS, and in those vital first few days they both failed to help Paul and Bill.

CHAPTER THREE

I

A GUARD OPENED the cell door, looked around, pointed at Paul and Bill, and beckoned them.

Bill's hopes soared. Now they would be released.

They got up and followed the guard upstairs. It was good to see daylight through the windows. They went out of the door and across the courtyard to the little one-storey building beside the entrance gate. The fresh air tasted heavenly.

It had been a terrible night. Bill had lain on the thin mattress, dozing fitfully, startled by the slightest movement from the other prisoners, looking around anxiously in the dim light from the all-night bulb. He had known it was morning when a guard came with glasses of tea and rough hunks of bread for breakfast. He had not felt hungry. He had said a rosary.

Now it seemed his prayers were being answered.

Inside the one-storey building was a visiting room furnished with simple tables and chairs. Two people were waiting. Bill recognized one of them: it was Ali Jordan, the Iranian who worked with Lou Goelz at the Embassy. He shook hands and introduced his colleague, Bob Sorenson.

'We brought you some stuff,' Jordan said. 'A battery shaver – you'll have to share it – and some dungarees.'

Bill looked at Paul. Paul was staring at the two Embassy men, looking as if he were about to explode. 'Aren't you going to get us out of here?' Paul said.

'I'm afraid we can't do that.'

'God damn it, you got us in here!'

Bill sat down slowly, too depressed to be angry.

'We're very sorry this has happened,' said Jordan. 'It came as a complete surprise to us. We were told that Dadgar was favourably disposed towards you ... The Embassy is filing a very serious protest.'

'But what are you doing to get us *out?*'

'You must work through the Iranian legal system. Your attorneys—'

'Jesus Christ,' Paul said disgustedly.

Jordan said: 'We have asked them to move you to a better part of the jail.'

'Gee, thanks.'

Sorenson asked: 'Uh, is there anything else you need?'

'There's nothing I need,' Paul said. 'I'm not planning to be here very long.'

Bill said: 'I'd like to get some eye drops.'

'I'll see that you do,' Sorenson promised.

Jordan said: 'I think that's all for now . . .' He looked at the guard.

Bill stood up.

Jordan spoke in Farsi to the guard, who motioned Paul and Bill to the door.

They followed the guard back across the courtyard.

Jordan and Sorenson were low-ranking Embassy staff, Bill reflected. Why hadn't Goelz come? It seemed that the Embassy thought it was EDS's job to get them out: sending Jordan and Sorenson was a way of notifying the Iranians that the Embassy was concerned but at the same time letting Paul and Bill know that they could not expect much help from the US Government. We're a problem the Embassy wants to ignore, Bill thought angrily.

Inside the main building, the guard opened a door they had not been through before, and they went from the reception area into a corridor. On their right were three offices. On their left were windows looking out into the courtyard. They came to another door, this one made of thick steel. The guard unlocked it and ushered them through.

The first thing Bill saw was a TV set.

As he looked around he started to feel a little better. This part of the jail was more civilized than the basement. It was relatively clean and light, with grey walls and grey carpeting. The cell doors were open and the prisoners were walking around freely. Daylight came in through the windows.

They continued along a hall with two cells on the right and, on the left, what appeared to be a bathroom: Bill looked forward to a chance to get clean again after his night downstairs. Glancing through the last door on the right, he saw shelves of books. Then the guard turned left and led them down a long narrow corridor and into the last cell.

There they saw someone they knew.

It was Reza Neghabat, the Deputy Minister in charge of the Social Security Organization at the Ministry of Health. Both Paul and Bill knew him well and had worked closely with him before his arrest last September. They shook hands enthusiastically. Bill was relieved to see a familiar face, and someone who spoke English.

Neghabat was astonished. 'Why are you in here?'

Paul shrugged. 'I kind of hoped you might be able to tell us that.'

'But what are you accused of?'

'Nothing,' said Paul. 'We were interrogated yesterday by Mr Dadgar, the magistrate who's investigating your former Minister, Dr Sheik. He arrested us. No charges, no accusations. We're supposed to be "material witnesses", we understand.'

Bill looked around. On either side of the cell were paired stacks of bunks, three high, with another pair beside the window, making eighteen altogether. As in the cell downstairs, the bunks were furnished with thin foam rubber mattresses, the bottom bunk of the three being no more than a mattress on the floor, and grey wool blankets. However, here some of the prisoners seemed to have sheets as well. The window, opposite the door, looked out into a courtyard. Bill could see grass, flowers and trees, as well as parked cars belonging, presumably, to guards. He could also see the low building where they had just talked with Jordan and Sorenson.

Neghabat introduced Paul and Bill to their cellmates, who seemed friendly and a good deal less villainous than the inmates of the basement. There were several free bunks – the cell was not as crowded as the one downstairs – and Paul and Bill took beds on either side of the doorway. Bill's was the middle bunk of three, but Paul was on the floor again.

Neghabat showed them around. Next to their cell was a kitchen, with tables and chairs, where the prisoners could make tea and coffee or just sit and talk. For some reason it was called the Chatanooga Room. Beside it was a hatch in the wall at the end of the corridor: this was a commissary, Neghabat explained, where from time to time you could buy soap, towels and cigarettes.

Walking back down the long corridor, they passed their own cell – No 5 – and two more cells before emerging into the hall, which stretched away to their right. The room Bill had glanced into earlier turned out to be a combination guard's office and library, with books in English as well as Farsi. Next to it were two more cells. Opposite these cells was the bathroom, with sinks, showers and toilets. The toilets were Persian style – like a shower tray with a drain hole in the middle. Bill learned that he was not likely to get the shower he longed for: normally there was no hot water.

Beyond the steel door, Neghabat said, was a little office used by a visiting doctor and dentist. The library was always open and the TV was on all evening, although of course programmes were in Farsi. Twice a week the prisoners in this section were taken out into the courtyard to exercise by walking in a circle for half an hour. Shaving was compulsory: the guards would allow moustaches but not beards.

During the tour they met two more people they

knew. One was Dr Towliati, the Ministry data-processing consultant about whom Dadgar had questioned them. The other was Hussein Pasha, who had been Neghabat's financial man at the Social Security Organization.

Paul and Bill shaved with the electric razor brought in by Sorenson and Jordan. Then it was noon, and time for lunch. In the corridor wall was an alcove screened by a curtain. From there the prisoners took a linoleum mat, which they spread on the cell floor, and some cheap tableware. The meal was steamed rice with a little lamb, plus bread and yoghurt, and tea or Pepsi-Cola to drink. They sat cross legged on the floor to eat. For Paul and Bill, both gourmets, it was a poor lunch. However, Bill found he had an appetite: perhaps it was the cleaner surroundings.

After lunch they had more visitors: their Iranian attorneys. The lawyers did not know why they had been arrested, did not know what would happen next, and did not know what they could do to help. It was a desultory, depressing conversation. Paul and Bill had no faith in them anyway, for it was these lawyers who had advised Lloyd Briggs that the bail would not exceed twenty thousand dollars. They returned no wiser and no happier.

They spent the rest of the afternoon in the Chatanooga Room, talking to Neghabat, Towliati and Pasha. Paul described his interrogation by Dadgar in detail. Each of the Iranians was highly interested in any mention of his own name during the interrogation. Paul told Dr Towliati how his name had come up, in connection with a suggested conflict of interest. Towliati described how he, too, had been questioned by Dadgar in the same way before being thrown in jail. Paul recollected that Dadgar had asked about a memorandum written by Pasha. It had been a completely routine request for statistics, and nobody could figure out what was supposed to be special about it.

Neghabat had a theory as to why they were in jail. 'The Shah is making a scapegoat of us, to show the masses that he really is cracking down on corruption – but he picked a project where there was no corruption. There is nothing to crack down on – but if he releases us, he will look weak. If he had looked instead at the construction business he would have found an unbelievable amount of corruption . . .'

It was all very vague. Neghabat was just rationalizing. Paul and Bill wanted specifics: *who* ordered the crackdown, *why* pick on the Ministry of Health, *what* kind of corruption was supposed to have taken place, and *where* were the informants who had put the finger on the individuals who were now in jail? Neghabat was not being evasive – he simply had no answers. His vagueness was characteristically Persian: ask an Iranian what he had for breakfast and ten seconds later he would be explaining his philosophy of life.

At six o'clock they returned to their cell for supper. It was pretty grim – no more than the leftovers from lunch mashed into a dip to be spread on bread, with more tea.

After supper they watched TV. Neghabat translated the news. The Shah had asked an opposition leader, Shahpour Bakhtiar, to form a civilian government, replacing the generals who had ruled Iran since November. Neghabat explained that Shahpour was leader of the Bakhtiar tribe, and that he had always refused to have anything to do with the regime of the Shah. Nevertheless, whether Bakhtiar's government could end the turmoil would depend on the Ayatollah Khomeini.

The Shah had also denied rumours that he was leaving the country.

Bill thought this sounded encouraging. With Bakhtiar as Prime Minister the Shah would remain and ensure stability but the rebels would at last have a voice in governing their own country.

At ten o'clock the TV went off and the prisoners returned to their cells. The other inmates hung towels and pieces of cloth across their bunks to keep out the light: here, as downstairs, the bulb would shine all night. Neghabat said Paul and Bill could get their visitors to bring in sheets and towels for them.

Bill wrapped himself in the thin grey blanket and settled down to try to sleep. We're here for a while, he thought resignedly; we must make the best of it. Our fate is in the hands of others.

II

Their fate was in the hands of Ross Perot, and in the next two days all his high hopes came to nothing.

At first the news had been good. Kissinger had called back on Friday, 29 December, to say that Ardeshir Zahedi would get Paul and Bill released. First, though,

US Embassy officials had to hold two meetings: one with people from the Ministry of Justice, the other with representatives of the Shah's court.

In Tehran the American Ambassador's deputy, Minister-Counsellor Charles Naas, was personally setting up those meetings.

In Washington, Henry Precht at the State Department was also talking to Ardeshir Zahedi. Emily Gaylord's brother-in-law, Tim Reardon, had spoken to Senator Kennedy. Admiral Moorer was working his contacts with the Iranian military government. The only disappointment in Washington had been Richard Helms, the former US Ambassador to Tehran: he had said candidly that his old friends no longer had any influence.

EDS consulted three separate Iranian lawyers. One was an American who specialized in representing US corporations in Tehran. The other two were Iranians: one had good contacts in pro-Shah circles, the other was close to the dissidents. All three had agreed that the way Paul and Bill had been jailed was highly irregular and that the bail was astronomical. The American, John Westberg, had said that the highest bail he had ever heard of in Iran was a hundred thousand dollars. The implication was that the magistrate who had jailed Paul and Bill was on weak ground.

Here in Dallas, EDS's chief financial officer Tom Walter, the slow-talking Alabaman, was working on how EDS might – if necessary – go about posting bail of $12,750,000. The lawyers had advised him that bail could be in one of three forms: cash; a letter of credit drawn on an Iranian bank; or a lien on property in Iran. EDS had no property worth that much in Tehran – the computers actually belonged to the Ministry – and, with the Iranian banks on strike and the country in turmoil, it was not possible to send in thirteen million dollars in cash; so Walter was organizing a letter of credit. T. J. Marquez, whose job it was to represent EDS to the investment community, had warned Perot that it might not be legal for a public company to pay that much money in what amounted to ransom. Perot deftly sidestepped that problem: he would pay the money personally.

Perot had been optimistic that he would get Paul and Bill out of jail in *one* of the three ways – legal pressure, political pressure, or by paying the bail.

Then the bad news started coming in.

The Iranian lawyers changed their tune. In turn they reported that the case was 'political', had 'high political content', and was 'a political hot potato'. John Westberg, the American, had been asked by his Iranian partners not to handle the case because it would bring the firm into disfavour with powerful people. Evidently, Examining Magistrate Hosain Dadgar was *not* on weak ground.

Lawyer Tom Luce and financial officer Tom Walter had gone to Washington and, accompanied by Admiral Moorer, had visited the State Department. They had expected to sit down around a table with Henry Precht and formulate an aggressive campaign for the release of Paul and Bill. But Henry Precht was cool. He had shaken hands with them – he could hardly do less, when they were accompanied by a former Chairman of the Joint

Chiefs of Staff – but he had not sat down with them. He had handed them over to a subordinate. The subordinate reported that none of the State Department's efforts had achieved anything: neither Ardeshir Zahedi nor Charlie Naas had been able to get Paul and Bill released.

Tom Luce, who did not have the patience of Job, got mad as hell. It was the State Department's job to protect Americans abroad, he said, and so far all State had done was to get Paul and Bill thrown in jail! Not so, he was told; what State had done so far was above and beyond their normal duty. If Americans abroad committed crimes they were subject to foreign laws. The State Department's duties did not include springing people from jail. But, Luce argued, Paul and Bill had *not* committed a crime – they were being held hostage for thirteen million dollars! He was wasting his breath. He and Tom Walter returned to Dallas empty handed.

Late last night Perot had called the US Embassy in Tehran and asked Charles Naas why he still had not met with the officials named by Kissinger and Zahedi. The answer was simple: those officials were making themselves unavailable to Naas.

Today Perot had called Kissinger again and reported this. Kissinger was sorry: he did not think there was anything more he could do. However, he would call Zahedi and try again.

One more piece of bad news completed the picture. Tom Walter had been trying to establish, with the Iranian lawyers, the conditions under which Paul and

Bill might be released on bail. For example, would they have to promise to return to Iran for further questioning if required, or could they be interrogated outside the country? Neither, he was told: *if they were released from prison they still would not be able to leave Iran.*

Now it was New Year's Eve. For three days Perot had been living at the office, sleeping on the floor and eating cheese sandwiches. There was nobody to go home to – Margot and the children were still in Vail – and, because of the nine-and-a-half-hour time difference between Texas and Iran, important phone calls were often made in the middle of the night. He was leaving the office only to visit his mother, who was now out of hospital and recuperating at her Dallas home. Even with her he talked about Paul and Bill – she was keenly interested in the progress of events.

This evening he felt the need of hot food, and he decided to brave the weather – Dallas was suffering an ice storm – and drive a mile or so to a fish restaurant.

He left the building by the back door and got behind the wheel of his station wagon. Margot had a Jaguar, but Perot preferred nondescript cars.

He wondered just how much influence Kissinger had now, in Iran or anywhere. Zahedi and any other Iranian contacts Kissinger had might be like Richard Helms's friends – all out of the mainstream, powerless. The Shah seemed to be hanging on by the skin of his teeth.

On the other hand, that whole group might soon need friends in America, and welcome the opportunity to do Kissinger a favour.

While he was eating, Perot felt a large hand on his shoulder, and a deep voice said: 'Ross, what are you doing here, eating all by yourself on New Year's Eve?'

He turned around to see Roger Staubach, quarterback for the Dallas Cowboys, a fellow Naval Academy graduate and an old friend. 'Hi, Roger! Sit down.'

'I'm here with the family,' Staubach said. 'The heat's off in our house on account of the ice storm.'

'Well, bring them over.'

Staubach beckoned to his family, then said: 'How's Margot?'

'Fine, thank you. She's skiing with the children in Vail. I had to come back – we've got a big problem.' He proceeded to tell the Staubach family all about Paul and Bill.

He drove back to the office in good spirits. There were still a bunch of good people in the world.

He thought again of Colonel Simons. Of all the schemes he had for getting Paul and Bill out, the jailbreak was the one with the longest lead time: Simons would need a team of men, a training period, equipment ... And yet Perot still had not done anything about it. It had seemed such a distant possibility, a last resort: while negotiations had seemed promising he had blocked it out of his mind. He was still not ready to call Simons – he would wait for Kissinger to have one more try with Zahedi – but perhaps there was something he could do to prepare for Simons.

Back at EDS, he found Pat Sculley. Sculley, a West Point graduate, was a thin, boyish, restless man of thirty-one. He had been a project manager in Tehran and had come out with the 8 December evacuation. He had returned after Ashura, then come out again when Paul and Bill were arrested. His job at the moment was to make sure that the Americans remaining in Tehran – Lloyd Briggs, Rich Gallagher and his wife, Paul and Bill – had reservations on a flight out every day, just in case the prisoners should be released.

With Sculley was Jay Coburn, who had organized the evacuation and then, on 22 December, had come home to spend Christmas with his family. Coburn had been about to go back to Tehran when he got the news that Paul and Bill had been arrested, so he had stayed in Dallas and organized the second evacuation. A placid, stocky man, Coburn smiled a lot – a slow smile that began as a twinkle in his eye and often ended in a shoulder-shaking belly-laugh.

Perot liked and trusted both men. They were what he called eagles: high-flyers, who used their initiative, got the job done, gave him results not excuses. The motto of EDS's recruiters was: Eagles Don't Flock – You Have To Find Them One At A Time. One of the secrets of Perot's business success was his policy of going looking for men like this, rather than waiting and hoping they would apply for the job.

Perot said to Sculley: 'Do you think we're doing everything we need to do for Paul and Bill?'

Sculley responded without hesitation. 'No, I don't.'

Perot nodded. These young men were never afraid to speak out to the boss: that was one of the things that made them eagles. 'What do you think we ought to do?'

'We ought to break them out,' Sculley said. 'I know it sounds strange, but I really think that if we don't, they have a good chance of getting killed in there.'

Perot did not think it sounded strange: that fear had been at the back of his mind for three days. 'I'm thinking of the same thing.' He saw surprise on Sculley's face. 'I want you two to put together a list of EDS people who could help do it. We'll need men who know Tehran, have some military experience – preferably in Special Forces type action – and are one hundred per cent trustworthy and loyal.'

'We'll get on it right away,' Sculley said enthusiastically.

The phone rang and Coburn picked it up. 'Hi, Keane! Where are you . . . Hold on a minute.'

Coburn covered the mouthpiece with his hand and looked at Perot. 'Keane Taylor is in Frankfurt. If we're going to do something like this, he ought to be on the team.'

Perot nodded. Taylor, a former Marine sergeant, was another of his eagles. Six feet two and elegantly dressed, Taylor was a somewhat irritable man, which made him the ideal butt for practical jokes. Perot said: 'Tell him to go back to Tehran. But don't explain why.'

A slow smile spread across Coburn's young-old face. 'He ain't gonna like it.'

Sculley reached across the desk and switched on the speaker so they could all hear Taylor blow his cool.

Coburn said: 'Keane, Ross wants you to go back to Iran.'

'What the hell for?' Taylor demanded.

Coburn looked at Perot. Perot shook his head.

Coburn said: 'Uh, there's a lot we need to do, in terms of tidying up, administratively speaking—'

'You tell Perot I'm not going back in there for any administrative bullshit!'

Sculley started to laugh.

Coburn said: 'Keane, I have somebody else here who wants to talk to you.'

Perot said: 'Keane, this is Ross.'

'Oh. Uh, hello, Ross.'

'I'm sending you back to do *something very important.*'

'Oh.'

'Do you understand what I'm saying?'

There was a long pause, then Taylor said: 'Yes, sir.'

'Good.'

'I'm on my way.'

'What time is it there?' Perot asked.

'Seven o'clock in the morning.'

Perot looked at his own watch. It said midnight.

Nineteen seventy-nine had begun.

Taylor sat on the edge of the bed in his Frankfurt hotel room, thinking about his wife.

Mary was in Pittsburgh with the children, Mike and Dawn, staying at Taylor's brother's house. Taylor had called her from Tehran before leaving and told her he was coming home. She had been very happy to hear it. They had made plans for the future: they would return to Dallas, put the kids in school . . .

Now he had to call and tell her he would not be coming home after all.

She would be worried.

Hell, *he* was worried.

He thought about Tehran. He had not worked on the Ministry of Health project, but had been in charge of a smaller contract, to computerize the old-fashioned manual book-keeping systems of Bank Omran. One day about three weeks ago, a mob had formed outside the bank – Omran was the Shah's bank. Taylor had sent his people home. He and Glenn Jackson were the last to leave: they locked up the building and started walking north. As they turned the corner on to the main street, they walked into the mob. At that moment the army opened fire and charged down the street.

Taylor and Jackson ducked into a doorway. Someone opened the door and yelled at them to get inside. They did – but before their rescuer could lock it again four of the demonstrators forced their way in, chased by five soldiers.

Taylor and Jackson flattened themselves against the wall and watched the soldiers, with their truncheons and rifles, beat up the demonstrators. One of the rebels made a break for it. Two of his fingers were almost torn off his hand, and blood spurted all over the glass door. He got out but collapsed in the street. The soldiers dragged the other three demonstrators out. One was a bloody mess but conscious. The other two were out cold, or dead.

Taylor and Jackson stayed inside until the street was clear. The Iranian who had saved them kept saying: 'Get out while you can.'

And now, Taylor thought, I have to tell Mary that I've just agreed to go back into all that.

To do *something very important*.

Obviously it had to do with Paul and Bill; and if Perot could not talk about it on the phone, presumably it was something at least clandestine and quite possibly illegal.

In a way Taylor was glad, despite his fear of the mobs. While still in Tehran he had talked on the phone with Bill's wife, Emily Gaylord, and had promised not to leave without Bill. The orders from Dallas, that everyone but Briggs and Gallagher had to get out, had forced him to break his word. Now the orders had changed, and perhaps he could keep his promise to Emily after all.

Well, he thought, I can't walk back, so I'd better find a plane. He picked up the phone again.

Jay Coburn remembered the first time he had seen Ross Perot in action. He would never forget it as long as he lived.

It happened in 1971. Coburn had been with EDS less than two years. He was a recruiter, working in New York City. Scott was born that year at a little Catholic hospital. It was a normal birth and, at first, Scott appeared to be a normal, healthy baby.

The day after he was born, when Coburn went to visit, Liz said Scott had not been brought in for his feed that morning. At the time Coburn took no notice. A few minutes later, a woman came in and said: 'Here are the pictures of your baby.'

'I don't remember any pictures being taken,' Liz said. The woman showed her the photographs. 'No, that's not my baby.'

The woman looked confused for a moment then said: 'Oh! That's right, yours is the one that's got the problem.'

It was the first Coburn and Liz had heard of any problem.

Coburn went to see the day-old Scott, and had a terrible shock. The baby was in an oxygen tent, gasping for air, and as blue as a pair of denim jeans. The doctors were in consultation about him.

Liz became almost hysterical, and Coburn called their family doctor and asked him to come to the hospital. Then he waited.

Something wasn't stacking up right. What kind of a hospital was it where they didn't tell you your new-born baby was dying? Coburn became distraught.

He called Dallas and asked for his boss, Gary Griggs. 'Gary, I don't know why I'm calling you, but I don't know what to do.' And he explained.

'Hold the phone,' said Griggs.

A moment later there was an unfamiliar voice on the line. 'Jay?'

'Yes.'

'This is Ross Perot.'

Coburn had met Perot, two or three times, but had never worked directly for him. Coburn wondered whether Perot even remembered what he looked like: EDS had more than a thousand employees at that time.

'Hello, Ross.'

'Now, Jay, I need some information.' Perot started asking questions: what was the address of the hospital? What were the doctors' names? What was their diagnosis? As he answered, Coburn was thinking bemusedly: does Perot even know who I am?

'Hold on a minute, Jay.' There was a short silence. 'I'm going to connect you with Doctor Urschel, a close friend of mine and a leading cardiac surgeon here in Dallas.' A moment later Coburn was answering more questions from the doctor.

'Don't you do a thing,' Urschel finished. 'I'm going to talk to the doctors on that staff. You just stay by the phone so we can get back in touch with you.'

'Yes, sir,' said Coburn dazedly.

Perot came back on the line. 'Did you get all that? How's Liz doing?'

Coburn thought: how the hell does he know my wife's name? 'Not too well,' Coburn answered. 'Her doctor's here and he's given her some sedation . . .'

While Perot was soothing Coburn, Dr Urschel was animating the hospital staff. He persuaded them to move Scott to New York University Medical Centre. Minutes later Scott and Coburn were in an ambulance on the way to the city.

They got stuck in a traffic jam in the Midtown Tunnel.

Coburn got out of the ambulance, ran more than a mile to the toll gate, and persuaded an official to hold up all lanes of traffic except the one the ambulance was in.

When they reached New York University Medical

Centre there were ten or fifteen people waiting outside for them. Among them was the leading cardiovascular surgeon on the east coast, who had been flown in from Boston in the time it had taken the ambulance to reach Manhattan.

As baby Scott was rushed inside, Coburn handed over the envelope of X-rays he had brought from the other hospital. A woman doctor glanced at them. 'Where are the rest?'

'That's all,' Coburn replied.

'That's all they *took*?'

New X-rays revealed that, as well as a hole in the heart, Scott had pneumonia. When the pneumonia was treated the heart condition came under control.

And Scott survived. He turned into a soccer-playing, tree-climbing, creek-wading, thoroughly healthy little boy. And Coburn began to understand the way people felt about Ross Perot.

Perot's single-mindedness, his ability to focus narrowly on one thing and shut out distractions until he got the job done, had its disagreeable side. He could wound people. A day or two after Paul and Bill were arrested, he had walked into an office where Coburn was talking on the phone to Lloyd Briggs in Tehran. It had sounded to Perot like Coburn was giving instructions, and Perot believed strongly that people in head office should not give orders to those out there on the battlefield who knew the situation best. He had given Coburn a merciless telling-off in front of a room full of people.

Perot had other blind spots. When Coburn had worked in Recruiting, each year the company had named someone 'Recruiter of the Year'. The names of the winners were engraved on a plaque. The list went back years, and in time some of the winners left the company. When that happened Perot wanted to erase their names from the plaque. Coburn thought that was weird. So the guy left the company – so what? He had been Recruiter of the Year, one year, and why try to change history? It was almost as if Perot took it as a personal insult that someone should want to work elsewhere.

Perot's faults were of a piece with his virtues. His peculiar attitude toward people who left the company was the obverse of his intense loyalty to his employees. His occasional unfeeling harshness was just a part of the incredible energy and determination without which he would never have created EDS. Coburn found it easy to forgive Perot's shortcomings.

He had only to look at Scott.

'Mr Perot?' Sally called. 'It's Henry Kissinger.'

Perot's heart missed a beat. Could Kissinger and Zahedi have done it in the last twenty-four hours? Or was he calling to say he had failed?

'Ross Perot.'

'Hold the line for Henry Kissinger, please.'

A moment later Perot heard the familiar guttural accent. 'Hello, Ross?'

'Yes.' Perot held his breath.

'I have been assured that your men will be released tomorrow at ten a.m., Tehran time.'

Perot let out his breath in a long sigh of relief. 'Dr Kissinger, that's just about the best news I've heard since I don't know when. I can't thank you enough.'

'The details are to be finalized today by US Embassy officials and the Iranian Foreign Ministry, but this is a formality: I have been advised that your men will be released.'

'It's just great. We sure appreciate your help.'

'You're welcome.'

It was nine-thirty in the morning in Tehran, midnight in Dallas. Perot sat in his office, waiting. Most of his colleagues had gone home, to sleep in a bed for a change, happy in the knowledge that by the time they woke up Paul and Bill would be free. Perot was staying at the office to see it through to the end.

In Tehran, Lloyd Briggs was at the Bucharest office, and one of the Iranian employees was outside the jail. As soon as Paul and Bill appeared, the Iranian would call Bucharest and Briggs would call Perot.

Now that the crisis was almost over, Perot had time to wonder where he had gone wrong. One mistake occurred to him immediately. When he had decided, on 4 December, to evacuate all his staff from Iran, he had not been determined enough and he had let others drag their feet and raise objections until it was too late.

But the big mistake had been doing business in Iran in the first place. With hindsight he could see that. At the time, he had agreed with his marketing people – and with many other American businessmen – that oil-rich, stable, Western-orientated Iran presented excellent opportunities. He had not perceived the strains beneath the surface, he knew nothing about the Ayatollah Khomeini, and he had not foreseen that one day there would be a President naïve enough to try to impose American beliefs and standards on a Middle Eastern country.

He looked at his watch. It was half past midnight. Paul and Bill should be walking out of that jail right now.

Kissinger's good news had been confirmed by a phone call from David Newsom, Cy Vance's deputy at the State Department. And Paul and Bill were getting out not a moment too soon. The news from Iran had been bad again today. Bakhtiar, the Shah's new Prime Minister, had been rejected by the National Front, the party which was now seen as the moderate opposition. The Shah had announced that he might take a vacation. William Sullivan, the American Ambassador, had advised the dependents of all Americans working in Iran to go home, and the embassies of Canada and Britain had followed suit. But the strike had closed the airports, and hundreds of women and children were stranded. However, Paul and Bill would not be stranded. Perot had had good friends at the Pentagon ever since the POW campaign: Paul and Bill would be flown out on a US Air Force jet.

At one o'clock Perot called Tehran. There was no news. Well, he thought, everyone says the Iranians have no sense of time.

The irony of this whole thing was that EDS had never paid bribes, in Iran or anywhere else. Perot hated the idea of bribery. EDS's Code of Conduct was set out in a 12-page booklet given to every new employee. Perot had written it himself. 'Be aware that federal law and the laws of most states prohibit giving anything of value to a government official with the intent to influence any official act . . . Since the absence of such intent might be difficult to prove, neither money nor anything of value should be given to a federal, state or foreign government official . . . A determination that a payment or practice is not forbidden by law does not conclude the analysis . . . It is always appropriate to make further enquiry into the ethics . . . Could you do business in complete trust with someone who acts the way you do? The answer must be *YES*.' The last page of the booklet was a form which the employee had to sign, acknowledging that he had received and read the Code.

When EDS first went to Iran, Perot's puritan principles had been reinforced by the Lockheed scandal. Daniel J. Haughton, chairman of the Lockheed Aircraft Corporation, had admitted to a Senate committee that Lockheed routinely paid millions of dollars in bribes to sell its planes abroad. His testimony had been an embarrassing performance which disgusted Perot: wriggling on his seat, Haughton had told the committee that the payments were not bribes but 'kickbacks'. Subsequently the Foreign Corrupt Practices Act made it an offence under US law to pay bribes in foreign countries.

Perot had called in lawyer Tom Luce and made him personally responsible for ensuring that EDS never paid bribes. During the negotiation of the Ministry of Health contract in Iran, Luce had offended not a few EDS executives by the thoroughness and persistence with which he had cross-examined them about the propriety of their dealings.

Perot was not hungry for business. He was already making millions. He did not *need* to expand abroad. If you have to pay bribes to do business there, he had said, why, we just won't do business there.

His business principles were deeply ingrained. His ancestors were Frenchmen who came to New Orleans and set up trading posts along the Red River. His father, Gabriel Ross Perot, had been a cotton broker. The trade was seasonal, and Ross Senior had spent a lot of time with his son, often talking about business. 'There's no point in buying cotton from a farmer *once*,' he would say. 'You have to treat him fairly, earn his trust, and develop a relationship with him, so that he'll be happy to sell you his cotton year after year. *Then* you're doing business.' Bribery just did not fit in there.

At one-thirty Perot called the EDS office in Tehran again. Still there was no news. 'Call the jail, or send somebody down there,' he said. 'Find out when they're getting out.'

He was beginning to feel uneasy.

What will I do if this doesn't work out? he thought. If

I put up the bail, I'll have spent thirteen million dollars and still Paul and Bill will be forbidden to leave Iran. Other ways of getting them out using the legal system come up against the obstacle raised by the Iranian lawyers – that the case is political, which seems to mean that Paul's and Bill's innocence makes no difference. But political pressure had failed so far: neither the US Embassy in Tehran nor the State Department in Washington had been able to help; and if Kissinger should fail, that would surely be the end of all hope in that area. What then was left?

Force.

The phone rang. Perot snatched up the receiver. 'Ross Perot.'

'This is Lloyd Briggs.'

'Are they out?'

'No.'

Perot's heart sank. 'What's happening?'

'We spoke to the jail. They have no instructions to release Paul and Bill.'

Perot closed his eyes. The worst had happened. Kissinger had failed.

He sighed. 'Thank you, Lloyd.'

'What do we do next?'

'I don't know,' said Perot.

But he *did* know.

He said goodbye to Briggs and hung up the phone.

He would not admit defeat. Another of his father's principles had been: take care of the people who work for you. Perot could remember the whole family driving twelve miles on Sundays to visit an old black man who had used to mow their lawn, just to make sure that he was well and had enough to eat. Perot's father would employ people he did not need, just because they had no job. Every year the Perot family car would go to the County Fair crammed with black employees, each of whom was given a little money to spend and a Perot business card to show if anyone tried to give him a hard time. Perot could remember one who had ridden a freight train to California and, on being arrested for vagrancy, had shown Perot's father's business card. The sheriff had said: 'We don't care whose nigger you are, we're throwing you in jail.' But he had called Perot Senior, who had wired the train fare for the man to come back. 'I been to California, and I'se back,' the man said when he reached Texarkana; and Perot Senior gave him back his job.

Perot's father did not know what civil rights were: this was how you treated other human beings. Perot had not known his parents were unusual until he grew up.

His father would not leave his employees in jail. Nor would Perot.

He picked up the phone: 'Get T. J. Marquez.'

It was two in the morning, but T.J. would not be surprised: this was not the first time Perot had woken him up in the middle of the night, and it would not be the last.

A sleepy voice said: 'Hello?'

'Tom, it doesn't look good.'

'Why?'

'They haven't been released and the jail says they aren't going to be.'

'Aw, *damn*.'

'Conditions are getting worse over there – did you see the news?'

'I sure did.'

'Do you think it's time for Simons?'

'Yeah, I think it is.'

'Do you have his number?'

'No, but I can get it.'

'Call him,' said Perot.

III

Bull Simons was going crazy.

He was thinking of burning down his house.It was an old wood-frame bungalow, and it would go up like a pile of matchwood, and that would be the end of it. The place was hell to him – but it was a hell he did not want to leave, for what made it hell was the bitter-sweet memory of the time when it had been heaven.

Lucille had picked the place. She saw it advertised in a magazine, and together they had flown down from Fort Bragg, North Carolina, to look it over. At Red Bay, in a dirt-poor part of the Florida Panhandle, the ramshackle house stood in forty acres of rough timber. But there was a two-acre lake with bass in it. Lucille had loved it.

That had been in 1971. It was time for Simons to retire. He had been a colonel for ten years, and if the Son Tay Raid could not get him promoted to general, nothing would. The truth was, he did not fit in the

General's Club: he had always been a reserve officer, he had never been to a top military school such as West Point, his methods were unconventional, and he was no good at going to Washington cocktail parties and kissing ass. He knew he was a goddam fine soldier and if that was not good enough, why, Art Simons was not good enough. So he retired, and did not regret it.

He had passed the happiest years of his life here at Red Bay. All their married life he and Lucille had endured periods of separation, sometimes as much as a year without seeing one another, during his tours in Vietnam, Laos and Korea. From the moment he retired they were together all day and all night, every day of the year. Simons raised hogs. He knew nothing about farming, but he got the information he needed out of books, and built his own pens. Once the operation was under way he found there was not much to do but feed the pigs and look at them so he spent a lot of time fooling around with his collection of 150 guns, and eventually set up a little gunsmithing shop where he would repair his and his neighbours' weapons and load his own ammunition. Most days he and Lucille would wander, hand in hand, through the woods and down to the lake where they might catch a bass. In the evening, after supper, she would go to the bedroom as if she were preparing for a date, and come out later, wearing a housecoat over her nightgown and a red ribbon in her dark, dark hair, and sit on his lap . . .

Memories like these were breaking his heart.

Even the boys had seemed to grow up, at last, during those golden years. Harry, the younger, had come home one day and said: 'Dad, I've got a heroin habit and a cocaine habit and I need your help.' Simons knew little about drugs. He had smoked marijuana once, in a doctor's office in Panama, before giving his men a talk on drugs, just so that he could tell them that he knew what it was like; but all he knew about heroin was that it killed people. Still, he had been able to help Harry by keeping him busy, out in the open, building hog pens. It had taken a while. Many times Harry left the house and went into town to score dope, but he always came back, and eventually he did not go into town any more.

The episode had brought Simons and Harry together again. Simons would never be close to Bruce, his elder son; but at least he had been able to stop worrying about the boy. Boy? He was in his thirties, and just about as bull-headed as ... well, as his father. Bruce had found Jesus and was determined to bring the rest of the world to the Lord – starting with Colonel Simons. Simons had practically thrown him out. However, unlike Bruce's other youthful enthusiasms – drugs, I Ching, back-to-nature communes – Jesus had lasted, and at least Bruce had settled down to a stable way of life, as pastor of a tiny church in the frozen north-west of Canada.

Anyway, Simons was through agonizing about the boys. He had brought them up as well as he could, for better or worse, and now they were men, and had to take care of themselves. He was taking care of Lucille.

She was a tall, handsome, statuesque woman with a penchant for big hats. She looked pretty damn impressive behind the wheel of their black Cadillac. But in fact she was the reverse of formidable. She was soft, easy-going, and lovable. The daughter of two teachers, she had needed someone to make decisions for her, someone she could follow blindly and trust completely; and she had found what she needed in Art Simons. He in turn was devoted to her. By the time he retired, they had been married for thirty years, and in all that time he had never been in the least interested in another woman. Only his job, with its overseas postings, had come between them; and now that was over. He had told her: 'My retirement plans can be summed up in one word: you.'

They had seven wonderful years.

Lucille died of cancer on 16 March 1978.

And Bull Simons went to pieces.

Every man had a breaking-point, they said. Simons had thought the rule did not apply to him. Now he knew it did: Lucille's death broke him. He had killed many people, and seen more die, but he had not understood the meaning of death until now. For thirty-seven years they had been together, and now, suddenly, *she just wasn't there.*

Without her, he did not see what life was supposed to be about. There was no point in anything. He was sixty years old and he could not think of a single goddam reason for living another day. He stopped taking care of himself. He ate cold food from cans and let his hair – which had always been so short – grow long. He fed the hogs religiously at 3.45 p.m. every day, he knew perfectly well that it hardly mattered what time of day you fed a pig. He started taking in stray dogs, and soon had thirteen of them, scratching the furniture and messing on the floor.

He knew he was close to losing his mind, and only the iron self-discipline which had been part of his character for so long enabled him to retain his sanity. When he first thought of burning the place down, he knew his judgement was unbalanced, and he promised himself he would wait a year, and see how he felt then.

His brother Stanley was worried about him, he knew. Stan had tried to get him to pull himself together: had suggested he gave some lectures, had even tried to get him to join the Israeli army. Simons was Jewish by ancestry, but thought of himself as American: he did not want to go to Israel. He could not pull himself together. It was as much as he could do to live from day to day.

He did not need someone to take care of him – he had never needed that. On the contrary, he needed someone to take care of. That was what he had done all his life. He had taken care of Lucille, he had taken care of the men under his command. Nobody could rescue him from his depression, for his role in life was to rescue others. That was why he had been reconciled with Harry but not with Bruce: Harry had come to him asking to be rescued from his heroin habit, but Bruce had come offering to rescue Art Simons by bringing him to the Lord. In military operations, Simons's aim had always been to bring all his men back alive. The Son Tay Raid would have been the perfect climax to his career, if only there had been prisoners in the camp to rescue.

Paradoxically, the only way to rescue Simons was to ask him to rescue someone else.

It happened at two o'clock in the morning on 2 January 1979.

The phone woke him.

'Bull Simons?' The voice was vaguely familiar.

'Yeah.'

'This is T. J. Marquez from EDS in Dallas.'

Simons remembered: EDS, Ross Perot, the POW campaign, the San Francisco party . . . 'Hello, Tom.'

'Bull, I'm sorry to wake you.'

'It's okay. What can I do for you?'

'We have two people in jail in Iran, and it looks like we may not be able to get them out by any conventional means. Would you be willing to help us?'

Would he be *willing*? 'Hell, yes,' Simons said. 'When do we start?'

CHAPTER FOUR

I

ROSS PEROT drove out of EDS and turned left on
Forest Lane then right on Central Expressway.
He was heading for the Hilton Inn on Central and
Mockingbird. He was about to ask seven men to risk
their lives.

Sculley and Coburn had made their list. Their own
names were at the top, followed by five more.

How many American corporate chiefs in the twentieth century had asked seven employees to perpetrate a
jailbreak? Probably none.

During the night Coburn and Sculley had called
the other five, who were scattered all over the United
States, staying with friends and relations after their
hasty departure from Tehran. Each had been told only
that Perot wanted to see him in Dallas today. They
were used to midnight phone calls and sudden summon-
ses – that was Perot's style – and they had all agreed to
come.

As they arrived in Dallas they had been steered away
from EDS headquarters and sent to check in at the
Hilton Inn. Most of them should be there by now,
waiting for Perot.

He wondered what they would say when he told them

he wanted them to go back to Tehran and bust Paul and Bill out of jail.

They were good men, and loyal to him, but loyalty to an employer did not normally extend to risking your life. Some of them might feel that the whole idea of a rescue by violence was foolhardy. Others would think of their wives and children, and for their sakes refuse – quite reasonably.

I have no right to ask these men to do this, he thought. I must take care not to put any pressure on them. No salesmanship today, Perot: just straight talk. They must understand that they're free to say: no, thanks, boss; count me out.

How many of them would volunteer?'

One in five, Perot guessed.

If that were the case it would take several days to get a team together, and he might end up with people who did not know Tehran.

What if *none* volunteered?

He pulled into the car park of the Hilton Inn and switched off the engine.

Jay Coburn looked around. There were four other men in the room: Pat Sculley, Glenn Jackson, Ralph Boulware and Joe Poché. Two more were on their way: Jim Schwebach was coming from Eau Claire, Wisconsin, and Ron Davis from Columbus, Ohio.

The Dirty Dozen they were not.

In their business suits, white shirts and sober ties, with their short haircuts and clean-shaven faces and well-fed bodies, they looked like what they were: ordinary American business executives. It was hard to see them as a squad of mercenaries.

Coburn and Sculley had made separate lists but these five men had been on both. Each had worked in Tehran – most had been on Coburn's evacuation team. Each had either military experience or some relevant skill. Each was a man Coburn trusted completely.

While Sculley was calling them in the early hours of this morning Coburn had gone to the personnel files and put together a folder on each man, detailing his age, height, weight, marital status and knowledge of Tehran. As they arrived in Dallas, each of them completed another sheet recounting his military experience, military schools attended, weapons training and other special skills. The folders were for Colonel Simons, who was on his way from Red Bay. But before Simons arrived, Perot had to ask these men whether they were willing to volunteer.

For Perot's meeting with them, Coburn had taken three adjoining rooms. Only the middle room would be used: the rooms on either side had been rented as a precaution against eavesdroppers. It was all rather melodramatic.

Coburn studied the others, wondering what they were thinking. They still had not been told what this was all about, but they had probably guessed.

He could not tell what Joe Poché was thinking: nobody ever could. A short, quiet man of thirty-two, Poché kept his emotions locked away. His voice was always low and even, his face generally blank. He had spent six years in the Army, and had seen action as commander of a howitzer battery in Vietnam. He had fired just about every weapon the army possessed up to some level of proficiency, and had killed time, in Vietnam, practising with a forty-five. He had spent two years with EDS in Tehran, first designing the enrolment system – the computer program which listed the names of people eligible for health care benefit – and later as the programmer responsible for loading the files which made up the data base for the whole system. Coburn knew him to be a deliberate, logical thinker, a man who would not give his assent to any idea or plan until he had questioned it from all angles and thought out all its consequences slowly and carefully. Humour and intuition were not among his strengths: brains and patience were.

Ralph Boulware was a full five inches taller than Poché. One of the two black men on the list, he had a chubby face and small, darting eyes, and he talked very fast. He had spent nine years in the Air Force as a technician, working on the complex inboard computer and radar systems of bombers. In Tehran for only nine months, he had started as data preparation manager and had swiftly been promoted to data centre manager. Coburn knew him well and liked him a lot. In Tehran they had got drunk together. Their children had played together and their wives had become friends. Boulware loved his family, loved his friends, loved his job, loved his life. He *enjoyed living* more than anyone else Coburn could think of, with the possible exception of Ross Perot. Boulware was also a highly independent-minded son of a gun. He never had any trouble speaking out. Like many successful black men, he was a shade oversensitive, and liked to make it clear he was not to be pushed around. In Tehran over Ashura, when he had been in the high-stakes poker game with Coburn and Paul, everyone else had slept in the house for safety, as previously agreed; but Boulware had not. There had been no discussion, no announcement: Boulware just went home. A few days later he had decided that the work he was doing did not justify the risk to his safety, so he returned to the States. He was not a man to run with the pack just because it was a pack: if he thought the pack was running the wrong way he would leave it. He was the most sceptical of the group assembling at the Hilton Inn: if anyone was going to pour scorn on the idea of a jailbreak, Boulware would.

Glenn Jackson looked less like a mercenary than any of them. A mild man with spectacles, he had no military experience, but he was an enthusiastic hunter and an expert shot. He knew Tehran well, having worked there for Bell Helicopter as well as for EDS. He was such a straight, forthright, honest guy, Coburn thought, that it was hard to imagine him getting involved in the deception and violence that a jailbreak would entail. Jackson was also a Baptist – the others were Catholic, except for Poché who did not say what he was – and Baptists were famous for punching Bibles, not faces. Coburn wondered how Jackson would make out.

He had a similar concern about Pat Sculley. Sculley had a good military record – he had been five years in the army, ending up as a Ranger instructor with the rank of captain – but he had no combat experience. Aggressive and outgoing in business, he was one of EDS's brightest up-and-coming young executives. Like Coburn, Sculley was an irrepressible optimist, but whereas Coburn's attitudes had been tempered by war, Sculley was youthfully naïve. If this thing gets violent, Coburn wondered, will Sculley be hard enough to handle it?

Of the two men who had not yet arrived, one was the most qualified to take part in a jailbreak, and the other perhaps the least.

Jim Schwebach knew more about combat than he did about computers. Eleven years in the army, he had served with the 5th Special Forces Group in Vietnam, doing the kind of commando work Bull Simons specialized in, clandestine operations behind enemy lines; and he had even more medals than Coburn. Because he had spent so many years in the military he was still a low-level executive, despite his age, which was thirty-five. He had been a trainee systems engineer when he went to Tehran, but he was mature and dependable, and Coburn had made him a team leader during the evacuation. Only five feet six inches, Schwebach had the erect, chin-up posture of many short men, and the indomitable fighting spirit which is the only defence of the smallest boy in the class. No matter what the score, it could be 12–0, ninth inning and two outs, Schwebach would be up on the edge of the dugout, clawing away and trying to figure out how to get an extra hit. Coburn admired him for volunteering – out of high-principled patriotism – for extra tours in Vietnam. In battle,

Coburn thought, Schwebach would be the last guy you would want to take prisoner – if you had your druthers, you would make sure you killed the little son of a bitch before you captured him, he would make so much trouble.

However, Schwebach's feistiness was not immediately apparent. He was a very ordinary-looking fellow. In fact, you hardly noticed him. In Tehran he had lived farther south than anyone else, in a district where there were no other Americans, yet he had often walked around the streets, wearing a beat-up old field jacket, blue jeans and a knit cap, and had never been bothered. He could lose himself in a crowd of two – a talent which might be useful in a jailbreak.

The other missing man was Ron Davis. At thirty he was the youngest on the list. The son of a poor black insurance salesman, Davis had risen fast in the white world of corporate America. Few people who started, as he had, in operations ever made it to management on the customer side of the business. Perot was especially proud of Davis: 'Ron's career achievement is like a moonshot,' he would say. Davis had acquired a good knowledge of Farsi in a year and a half in Tehran, working under Keane Taylor, not on the Ministry contract but on the smaller, separate project to computerize Bank Omran, the Shah's bank. Davis was cheerful, flippant, full of jokes, a juvenile version of Richard Pryor, but without the profanity. Coburn thought he was the most sincere of the men on the list. Davis found it easy to open up and talk about his feelings and his personal life. For that reason Coburn thought of him as vulnerable. On the other hand, perhaps the ability to talk honestly about yourself to others was a sign of great inner confidence and strength.

Whatever the truth about Davis's emotional toughness, physically he was as hard as a nail. He had no military experience but he was a karate Black Belt. One time in Tehran, three men had attacked and attempted to rob him: he had beaten them all up in a few seconds. Like Schwebach's ability to be inconspicuous, Davis's karate was a talent which might become useful.

Like Coburn, all six men were in their thirties.

They were all married.

And they all had children.

The door opened and Perot walked in.

He shook hands, saying 'How are you?' and 'Good to see you!' as if he really meant it, remembering the names of their wives and children. He's *good* with people, Coburn thought.

'Schwebach and Davis didn't get here yet,' Coburn told him.

'All right,' Perot said, sitting down. 'I'll have to see them later. Send them to my office as soon as they arrive.' He paused. 'I'll tell them exactly what I'm going to tell y'all.'

He paused again, as if gathering his thoughts. Then he frowned and looked hard at them. 'I'm asking for volunteers for a project that might involve loss of life. At this stage I can't tell you what it's about, although you can probably guess. I want you to take five or ten minutes, or more, to think about it, then come back and talk to me one at a time. Think *hard*. If you choose, *for any reason,* not to get involved, you can just say so, and no one outside this room will ever know about it. If you decide to volunteer, I'll tell you more. Now go away and think.'

They all stood up and, one by one, they left the room.

I could get killed on Central Expressway, thought Joe Poché.

He knew perfectly well what the dangerous project was: they were going to get Paul and Bill out of jail.

He had suspected as much since two-thirty a.m., when he had been woken up, at his mother-in-law's house in San Antonio, by a phone call from Pat Sculley. Sculley, the world's worst liar, had said: 'Ross asked me to call you. He wants you to come to Dallas in the morning to begin work on a study in Europe.'

Poché had said; 'Pat, why in hell are you calling me at two-thirty in the morning to tell me that Ross wants me to work on a study in Europe?'

'It is kind of important. We need to know when you can be here.'

Okay, Poché thought resignedly, it's something he can't talk about on the phone. 'My first flight is probably around six or seven o'clock in the morning.'

'Fine.'

Poché had made a plane reservation then gone back to bed. As he set his alarm clock for five a.m. he said to his wife:

'I don't know what this is all about, but I wish somebody would be straight, just for once.'

In fact he had a pretty good idea what it was all about, and his suspicions had been confirmed, later in the day, when Ralph Boulware had met him at the Coit Road bus station and, instead of taking him to EDS, had driven him this hotel and refused to talk about what was going on.

Poché liked to think everything through, and he had had plenty of time to consider the idea of busting Paul and Bill out of jail. It made him glad, glad as hell. It reminded him of the old days, when there were only three thousand people in the whole of EDS, and they had talked about the Faith. It was their word for a whole bunch of attitudes and beliefs about how a company ought to deal with its employees. What it boiled down to was: EDS took care of its people. As long as you were giving your maximum effort to the company, it would stand by you through thick and thin: when you were sick, when you had personal or family problems, when you got yourself into any kind of trouble . . . It was a bit like a family. Poché felt good about that, although he did not talk about the feeling – he did not talk much about any of his feelings.

EDS had changed since those days. With ten thousand people instead of three thousand, the family atmosphere could not be so intense. Nobody talked about the Faith any more. But it was still there: this meeting proved it. And although his face was as expressionless as ever, Joe Poché was glad. Of *course* they would go in there and bust their friends out of jail. Poché was just happy to get a chance to be on the team.

Contrary to Coburn's expectation, Ralph Boulware did not pour scorn on the idea of a rescue. The sceptical, independent-minded Boulware was as hot for the idea as anyone.

He, too, had guessed what was going on, helped – like Poché – by Sculley's inability to lie convincingly.

Boulware and his family were staying with friends in Dallas. On New Year's Day Boulware had been doing nothing much, and his wife had asked him why he did not go to the office. He said there was nothing for him to do there. She did not buy that. Mary Boulware was the only person in the world who could bully Ralph, and in the end he went to the office. There he ran into Sculley.

'What's happening?' Boulware had asked.

'Oh, nothing,' Sculley said.

'What are you doing?'

'Making plane reservations, mostly.'

Sculley's mood seemed strange. Boulware knew him well – in Tehran they had ridden to work together in the mornings and his instinct told him Sculley was not telling the truth.

'Something's wrong,' Boulware said. 'What's going on?'

'There's nothing going on, Ralph!'

'What are they doing about Paul and Bill?'

'They're going through all the channels to try and

get them out. The bail is thirteen million dollars, and we have to get the money into the country—'

'Bull *shit*. The whole government system, the whole judicial system has broken down over there. There ain't no channels *left*. What are y'all going to do?'

'Look, don't worry about it.'

'You guys ain't going to try to go in and get them out, are you?'

Sculley said nothing.

'Hey, count me in,' Boulware said.

'What do you mean, count you in?'

'It's obvious you're going to try to do something.'

'What do you mean?'

'Let's don't play games any more. *Count me in.*'

'OK.'

For him it was a simple decision. Paul and Bill were his friends, and it could as easily have been Boulware in jail, in which case he would have wanted his friends to come and get him out.

There was another factor. Boulware was enormously fond of Pat Sculley. Hell, he *loved* Sculley. He also felt very protective toward him. In Boulware's opinion, Sculley really did not understand that the world was full of corruption and crime and sin: he saw what he wanted to see, a chicken in every pot, a Chevrolet on every driveway, a world of Mom and apple pie. If Sculley was going to be involved in a jailbreak, he would need Boulware to take care of him. It was an odd feeling to have about another man more or less your own age, but there it was.

That was what Boulware had thought on New Year's

Day, and he felt the same today. So he went back into the hotel room and said to Perot what he had said to Sculley: 'Count me in.'

Glenn Jackson was not afraid to die.

He knew what was going to happen after death, and he had no fears. When the Lord wanted to call him home, why, he was ready to go.

However, he was concerned about his family. They had just been evacuated from Iran, and were now staying at his mother's house in East Texas. He had not yet had time even to start looking for a place for them all to live. If he got involved in this, he was not going to have time to go off and take care of family matters: it would be left to Carolyn. All on her own, she would have to rebuild the life of the family here in the States. She would have to find a house, get Cheryl, Cindy and Glenn Junior into schools, buy or rent some furniture . . .

Carolyn was kind of a dependent person. She would not find it easy.

Plus, she was already mad at him. She had come to Dallas with him that morning, but Sculley had told him to send her home. She was not permitted to check in to the Hilton Inn with her husband. That had made her angry.

But Paul and Bill had wives and families, too. 'Thou shalt love thy neighbour as thyself.' It was in the Bible twice: Leviticus, chapter 19, verse 18; and Matthew's

Gospel, chapter 19, verse 19. Jackson thought: If I were stuck in jail in Tehran I'd sure love for somebody to do something for me.

So he volunteered.

Sculley had made his choice days ago.

Before Perot started talking about a rescue Sculley had been discussing the idea. It had first come up the day after Paul and Bill were arrested, the day Sculley flew out of Tehran with Joe Poché and Jim Schwebach. Sculley had been upset at leaving Paul and Bill behind, all the more so because Tehran had become dramatically more violent in the last few days. At Christmas two Afghanis caught stealing in the bazaar had been summarily hanged by a mob; and a taxi driver who tried to jump the queue at a gas station had been shot in the head by a soldier. What would they do to Americans, once they got started? It hardly bore thinking about.

On the plane Sculley had sat next to Jim Schwebach. They had agreed that Paul's and Bill's lives were in danger. Schwebach, who had experience in clandestine commando-type operations, had agreed with Sculley that it should be possible for a few determined Americans to rescue two men from an Iranian jail.

So Sculley had been surprised and delighted when, three days later, Perot had said: 'I've been thinking the same thing.'

Sculley had put his own name on the list.

He did not need time to think about it.

He volunteered.

Sculley had also put Coburn's name on the list – without telling Coburn.

Until this moment, happy-go-lucky Coburn, who lived from day to day, had not even thought about being on the team himself.

But Sculley had been right: Coburn wanted to go.

He thought: Liz won't like it.

He sighed. There were many things his wife did not like, these days.

She was clinging, he thought. She had not liked his being in the military, she did not like his having hobbies which took him away from her, and she did not like his working for a boss who felt free to call on him at all hours of the day or night for special tasks.

He had never lived the way she wanted, and it was probably too late to start now. If he went to Tehran to rescue Paul and Bill, Liz might hate him for it. But if he did not go, he would probably hate her for making him stay behind.

Sorry, Liz, he thought; here we go again.

Jim Schwebach arrived later in the afternoon but heard the same speech from Perot.

Schwebach had a highly developed sense of duty. (He had once wanted to be a priest, but two years in a Catholic seminary had soured him on organized religion.) He had spent eleven years in the Army, and had volunteered for repeated tours in Vietnam, out of that same sense of duty. In Asia he had seen a lot of people doing their jobs badly, and he knew he did his well. He had thought: if I walk away from this, someone else will do what I'm doing, but *he* will do it badly, and in consequence a man will lose his arm, his leg, or his life. I've been trained to do this, and I'm good at it, and I owe it to them to carry on doing it.

He felt much the same about the rescue of Paul and Bill. He was the only member of the proposed team who had actually done this sort of thing before. They needed him.

Anyway, he liked it. He was a fighter by disposition. Perhaps this was because he was five and a half feet tall. Fighting was his thing, it was where he lived. He did not hesitate to volunteer.

He couldn't wait to get started.

Ron Davis, the second black man on the list and the youngest of them all, did hesitate.

He arrived in Dallas early that evening and was taken straight to EDS Headquarters on Forest Lane. He had never met Perot, but had talked to him on the phone from Tehran during the evacuation. For a few days, during that period, they had kept a phone line open between Dallas and Tehran all day and all night. Someone had to sleep with the phone to his ear at the Tehran end, and frequently the job had fallen to Davis. One time Perot himself had come on the line.

'Ron, I know it's bad over there and we sure appreciate your staying. Now, is there anything I can do for you?'

Davis was surprised. He was only doing what his friends were doing, and he did not expect a special thank you. But he did have a special worry. 'My wife has conceived, and I haven't seen her for a while,' he told Perot. 'If you could have someone call her and tell her I'm okay and I'll be home as soon as possible, I'd appreciate it.'

Davis had been surprised to learn from Marva, later, that Perot had not had someone call her – he had called himself.

Now, meeting Perot for the first time, Davis was once again impressed. Perot shook his hand warmly and said: 'Hi, Ron, how are you?' just as if they had been friends for years.

However, listening to Perot's speech about 'loss of life', Davis had doubts. He wanted to know more about the rescue. He would be glad to help Paul and Bill, but he needed to be assured that the whole project would be well organized and professional.

Perot told him about Bull Simons, and that settled it.

Perot was just so proud of them.

Every single one had volunteered.

He sat in his office. It was dark outside. He was waiting for Simons.

Smiling Jay Coburn; boyish Pat Sculley; Joe Poché, the man of iron; Ralph Boulware, tall, black and sceptical; mild-mannered Glenn Jackson; Jim Schwebach the scrapper; Ron Davis the comedian.

Every single one!

He was grateful as well as proud, for the burden they had shouldered was more his than theirs.

One way and another it had been quite a day. Simons had agreed instantly to come and help. Paul Walker, an EDS security man who had (coincidentally) served with Simons in Laos, had jumped on a plane in the middle of the night and flown to Red Bay to take care of Simons's pigs and dogs. And seven young executives had dropped everything at a moment's notice and agreed to take off for Iran to organize a jailbreak.

They were now down the hall, in the EDS boardroom, waiting for Simons, who had checked in to the Hilton Inn and gone to dinner with T. J. Marquez and Merv Stauffer.

Perot thought about Stauffer. Stocky, bespectacled, forty years old, an economics graduate, Stauffer was Perot's right-hand-man. He could remember vividly their first meeting, when he had interviewed Stauffer. A graduate of some college in Kansas, Merv had looked right off the farm, in his cheap coat and slacks. He had been wearing white socks.

During the interview, Perot had explained, as gently as he knew how, that white socks were not appropriate clothing for a business meeting.

But the socks were the only mistake Stauffer had made. He impressed Perot as being smart, tough, organized and used to hard work.

As the years went by Perot had learned that Stauffer

had yet more useful talents. He had a wonderful mind for detail – something Perot lacked. He was completely unflappable. And he was a great diplomat. When EDS landed a contract, it often meant taking over an existing data processing department, with its staff. This could be difficult: the staff were naturally wary, touchy, and sometimes resentful. Merv Stauffer – calm, smiling, helpful, soft-spoken, gently determined – could smooth their feathers like no one else.

Since the late sixties he had been working directly with Perot. His speciality was taking a hazy, crazy idea from Perot's restless imagination, thinking it through, putting the pieces together and making it work. Occasionally he would conclude that the idea was impracticable – and when *Stauffer* said that, Perot began to think that maybe it was impracticable.

His appetite for work was enormous. Even among the workaholics on the seventh floor, Stauffer was exceptional. As well as doing whatever Perot had dreamed up in bed the previous night, he supervised Perot's real estate company and his oil company, managed Perot's investments and planned Perot's estate.

The best way to help Simons, Perot decided, would be to give him Merv Stauffer.

He wondered whether Simons had changed. It had been years since they last met. The occasion had been a banquet. Simons had told him a story.

During the Son Tay Raid, Simons's helicopter had landed in the wrong place. It was a compound very like the prison camp, but some four hundred yards distant, and it contained a barracks full of sleeping enemy soldiers. Awakened by the noise and the flares, the soldiers had begun to stumble out of the barracks, sleepy, half-dressed, carrying their weapons. Simons had stood outside the door, with a lighted cigar in his mouth. Beside him was a burly sergeant. As each man came through the door, he would see the glow of Simons's cigar, and hesitate. Simons would shoot him. The sergeant would heave the corpse aside, then they would wait for the next one.

Perot had been unable to resist the question: 'How many men did you kill?'

'Must have been seventy or eighty,' Simons had said in a matter-of-fact voice.

Simons had been a great soldier, but now he was a pig farmer. Was he still fit? He was sixty years old, and he had suffered a stroke even before Son Tay. Did he still have a sharp mind? Was he still a great leader of men?

He would want total control of the rescue, Perot was certain. The Colonel would do it his way or not at all. That suited Perot just fine: it was his way to hire the best man for the job then let him get on with it. But was Simons *still* the greatest rescuer in the world?

He heard voices in the outer office. They had arrived. He stood up, and Simons walked in with T. J. Marquez and Merv Stauffer.

'Colonel Simons, how are you?' said Perot. He never called Simons 'Bull' – he thought it was corny.

'Hello, Ross,' said Simons, shaking hands.

The handshake was firm. Simons was dressed casually, in khaki pants. His shirt collar was open, showing the muscles of his massive neck. He looked older: more lines in that aggressive face, more grey in the crewcut hair, which was also longer than Perot had ever seen it. But he seemed fit and hard. He still had the same deep, tobacco-roughened voice, with a faint but clear trace of a New York accent. He was carrying the folders Coburn had put together on the volunteers.

'Sit down,' said Perot. 'Did y'all have dinner?'

'We went to Dusty's,' said Stauffer.

Simons said: 'When was the last time this room was swept for bugs?'

Perot smiled. Simons was still sharp, as well as fit. Good. He replied: 'It's never been swept, Colonel.'

'From now on I want every room we use to be swept every day.'

Stauffer said: 'I'll see to that.'

Perot said: 'Whatever you need, Colonel, just tell Merv. Now, let's talk business for a minute. We sure appreciate you coming here to help us, and we'd like to offer you some compensation—'

'Don't even think about it,' Simons said gruffly.

'Well—'

'I don't want payment for rescuing Americans in trouble,' Simons said. 'I never got a bonus for it yet, and I don't want to start now.'

Simons was offended. The force of his displeasure filled the room. Perot backed off quickly: Simons was one of the very few people of whom he was wary.

The old warrior hasn't changed a bit, Perot thought. Good.

'The team is waiting for you in the boardroom. I see

you have the folders, but I know you'll want to make your own assessment of the men. They all know Tehran, and they all have either military experience or some skill which may be useful – but in the end the choice of the team is up to you. If for any reason you don't like these men, we'll get some more. You're in charge here.' Perot hoped Simons would not reject anyone, but he had to have the option.

Simons stood up. 'Let's go to work.'

T.J. hung back after Simons and Stauffer left. He said in a low voice: 'His wife died.'

'Lucille?' Perot had not heard. 'I'm sorry.'

'Cancer.'

'How did he take it, did you get an idea?'

T.J. nodded. 'Bad.'

As T.J. went out, Perot's twenty-year-old son, Ross Junior, walked in. It was common for Perot's children to drop by the office, but this time, when a secret meeting was in session in the boardroom, Perot wished his son had chosen another moment. Ross Junior must have seen Simons in the hall. The boy had met Simons before and knew who he was. By now, Perot thought, he's figured out that the only reason for Simons to be here is to organize a rescue.

Ross sat down and said: 'Hi, Dad. I've been by to see Grandmother.'

'Good,' Perot said. He looked fondly at his only son. Ross Junior was tall, broad-shouldered, slim, and a deal better looking than his father. Girls clustered around him like flies: the fact that he was heir to a fortune was only one of the attractions. He handled it the way he handled everything: with immaculate good manners and a maturity beyond his years.

Perot said: 'You and I need to have a clear understanding about something. I expect to live to be a hundred, but if anything should happen to me, I want you to leave college and come home and take care of your mother and your sisters.'

'I would,' Ross said. 'Don't worry.'

'And if anything should happen to your mother, I want you to live at home and raise your sisters. I know it would be hard on you, but I wouldn't want you to hire people to do it. They would need *you*, a member of the family. I'm counting on you to live at home with them and see they're properly raised—'

'Dad, that's what I would have done if you'd never brought it up.'

'Good.'

The boy got up to go. Perot walked to the door with him.

Suddenly Ross put his arm around his father and said: 'Love you, Pop.'

Perot hugged him back.

He was surprised to see tears in his son's eyes.

Ross went out.

Perot sat down. He should not have been surprised by those tears: the Perots were a close family, and Ross was a warm-hearted boy.

Perot had no specific plans to go to Tehran, but he knew that if his men were going there to risk their lives, he would not be far behind. Ross Junior had known the same thing.

The whole family would support him, Perot knew. Margot might be entitled to say 'While you're risking your life for your employees, what about us?' but she would never say it. All through the prisoners-of-war campaign, when he had gone to Vietnam and Laos, when he had tried to fly into Hanoi, when the family had been forced to live with bodyguards, they had never complained, never said 'What about us?' On the contrary, they had encouraged him to do whatever he saw to be his duty.

While he sat thinking, Nancy, his eldest daughter walked in.

'Poops!' she said. It was her pet name for her father.

'Little Nan! Come in!'

She came around the desk and sat on his lap.

Perot adored Nancy. Eighteen years old, blonde, tiny but strong, she reminded him of his mother. She was determined and hard-headed, like Perot, and she probably had as much potential to be a business executive as her brother.

'I came to say goodbye – I'm going back to Vanderbilt.'

'Did you drop by Grandmother's house?'

'I sure did.'

'Good girl.'

She was in high spirits, excited about going back to school, oblivious of the tension and the talk of death here on the seventh floor.

'How about some extra funds?' she said.

Perot smiled indulgently and took out his wallet. As usual, he was helpless to resist her.

153

She pocketed the money, hugged him, kissed his cheek, jumped off his lap, and bounced out of the room without a care in the world.

This time there were tears in Perot's eyes.

It was like a reunion, Jay Coburn thought: the old Tehran hands in the boardroom waiting for Simons, chatting about Iran and the evacuation. There was Ralph Boulware talking at ninety miles an hour; Joe Poché sitting and thinking, looking about as animated as a robot in a sulk; Glenn Jackson saying something about rifles; Jim Schwebach smiling his lopsided smile, the smile that made you think he knew something you didn't; and Pat Sculley talking about the Son Tay Raid. They all knew, now, that they were about to meet the legendary Bull Simons. Sculley, when he had been a Ranger instructor, had taught Simons's famous raid, and he knew all about the meticulous planning, the endless rehearsals, and the fact that Simons had brought back all of his fifty-nine men alive.

The door opened and a voice said: 'All stand.'

They pushed back their chairs and stood up.

Coburn looked around.

Ron Davis walked in grinning all over his black face.

'Goddam you, Davis!' said Coburn, and they all laughed as they realized they had been fooled. Davis walked around the room slapping hands and saying hello.

That was Davis: always the clown.

Coburn looked at all of them and wondered how

they would change when faced with physical danger. Combat was a funny thing, you could never predict how people would cope with it. The man you thought the bravest would crumble, and the one you expected to run scared would be solid as a rock.

Coburn would never forget what combat had done to him.

The crisis had come a couple of months after he arrived in Vietnam. He was flying support aircraft, called 'slicks' because they had no weapons systems. Six times a day he had come out of the battle zone with a full load of troops. It had been a good day: not a shot had been fired at his helicopter.

The seventh time was different.

A burst of 12.75 fire had hit the aircraft and severed the tail-rotor drive shaft.

When the main rotor of a helicopter turns, the body of the aircraft has a natural tendency to turn in the same direction. The function of the tail-rotor is to counteract this tendency. If the tail-rotor stops, the helicopter starts spinning.

Immediately after take-off, when the aircraft is only a few feet off the ground, the pilot can deal with tail-rotor loss by landing again before the spinning becomes too fast. Later, when the aircraft is at cruising height and normal flying speed, the flow of wind across the fuselage is strong enough to prevent the helicopter turning. But Coburn was at a height of 150 feet, the worst possible position, too high to land quickly but not yet travelling fast enough for the wind flow to stabilize the fuselage.

The standard procedure was a simulated engine stall.

Coburn had learned and rehearsed the routine at flying school, and he went into it instinctively, but it did not work: the aircraft was already spinning too fast.

Within seconds he was so dizzy he had no idea where he was. He was unable to do anything to cushion the crash landing. The helicopter came down on its right skid (he learned afterwards) and one of the rotor blades flexed down under the impact, slicing through the fuselage and into the head of his co-pilot, who died instantly.

Coburn smelled fuel and unstrapped himself. That was when he realized he was upside down, for he fell on his head. But he got out of the aircraft, his only injury a few compressed neck vertebrae. His crew chief also survived.

The crew had been belted in, but the seven troops in the back had not. The helicopter had no doors, and the centrifugal force of the spin had thrown them out at a height of more than a hundred feet. They were all dead.

Coburn was twenty years old at the time.

A few weeks later he took a bullet in the calf, the most vulnerable part of a helicopter pilot, who sits in an armoured seat but leaves his lower legs exposed.

He had been angry before, but now he just had the *ass*. Pissed off with being shot at, he went in to his commanding officer and demanded to be assigned to gunships so that he could kill some of those bastards down there who were trying to kill him.

His request was granted.

That was the point at which smiling Jay Coburn had

turned into a cool-headed, cold-hearted professional soldier. He made no close friends in the Army. If someone in the unit was wounded Coburn would shrug and say: 'Well, that's what he gets combat pay for.' He suspected his comrades thought he was a little sick. He did not care. He was happy flying gunships. Every time he strapped himself in he knew he was going out there to kill or be killed. Clearing out areas in advance of ground troops, knowing that women and children and innocent civilians were getting hurt, Coburn just closed his mind and opened fire.

Eleven years later, looking back, he could think: I was an animal.

Schwebach and Poché, the two quietest men in the room, would understand: they had been there too, they knew how it had been. The others did not: Sculley, Boulware, Jackson and Davis. If this rescue turns nasty, Coburn wondered again, how will they make out?

The door opened, and Simons came in.

II

The room fell silent as Simons walked to the head of the conference table.

He's a *big* son of a bitch, Coburn thought.

T. J. Marquez and Merv Stauffer came in after Simons and sat near the door.

Simons threw a black plastic suitcase into a corner, dropped into a chair, and lit a small cigar.

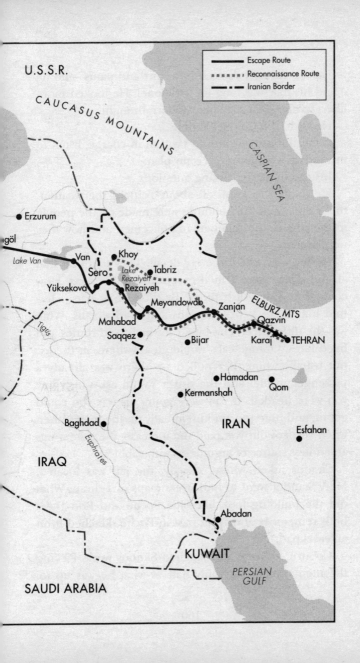

He was casually dressed in a shirt and pants – no tie – and his hair was long for a Colonel. He looked more like a farmer than a soldier, Coburn thought.

He said: 'I'm Colonel Simons.'

Coburn expected him to say, I'm in charge, listen to me and do what I say, this is my plan.

Instead he started asking questions.

He wanted to know all about Tehran: the weather, the traffic, what the buildings were made of, the people in the streets, the numbers of policemen and how they were armed.

He was interested in every detail. They told him that all the police were armed except the traffic cops. How could you distinguish them? By their white hats. They told him there were blue cabs and orange cabs. What was the difference? The blue cabs had fixed routes and fixed fares. Orange cabs would go anywhere, in theory, but usually when they pulled up there was already a passenger inside, and the driver would ask which way you were headed. If you were going his way you could get in, and note the amount already on the meter; then when you got out you paid the increase: the system was an endless source of arguments with cabbies.

Simons asked where, exactly, the jail was located. Merv Stauffer went to find street maps of Tehran. What did the building look like? Joe Poché and Ron Davis both remembered driving past it. Poché sketched it on an easel pad.

Coburn sat back and watched Simons work. Picking the men's brains was only half of what he was up to,

Coburn realized. Coburn had been an EDS recruiter for years, and he knew a good interviewing technique when he saw it. Simons was sizing up each man, watching reactions, testing for common sense. Like a recruiter, he asked a lot of open-ended questions, often following with 'Why?', giving people an opportunity to reveal themselves, to brag or bullshit or show signs of anxiety.

Coburn wondered whether Simons would flunk any of them.

At one point he said: 'Who is prepared to die doing this?'

Nobody said a word.

'Good,' said Simons. 'I wouldn't take anyone who was planning on dying.'

The discussion went on for hours. Simons broke it up soon after midnight. It was clear by then that they did not know enough about the jail to begin planning the rescue. Coburn was deputized to find out more overnight: he would make some phone calls to Tehran.

Simons said: 'Can you ask people about the jail without letting them know why you want the information?'

'I'll be discreet,' Coburn said.

Simons turned to Merv Stauffer. 'We'll need a secure place for us all to meet. Somewhere that isn't connected with EDS.'

'What about the hotel?'

'The walls are thin.'

Stauffer considered for a moment. 'Ross has a little house at Lake Grapevine, out toward DFW airport.

There won't be anyone out there swimming or fishing in this weather, that's for sure.'

Simons looked dubious.

Stauffer said: 'Why don't I drive you out there in the morning so you can look it over?'

'Okay.' Simons stood up. 'We've done all we can at this point in the game.'

They began to drift out.

As they were leaving, Simons asked Davis for a word in private.

'You ain't so goddam tough, Davis.'

Ron Davis stared at Simons in surprise.

'What makes you think you're a tough guy?' Simons said.

Davis was floored. All evening Simons had been polite, reasonable, quiet-spoken. Now he was making like he wanted to fight. What was happening?

Davis thought of his martial arts expertise, and of the three muggers he had disposed of in Tehran, but he said: 'I don't consider myself a tough guy.'

Simons acted as if he had not heard. 'Against a pistol your karate is no bloody good whatsoever.'

'I guess not—'

'This team does not need any ba-ad black bastards spoiling for a fight.'

Davis began to see what this was all about. Keep cool, he told himself. 'I did not volunteer for this because I want to fight people, Colonel, I—'

'Then why *did* you volunteer?'

162

'Because I know Paul and Bill and their wives and children and I want to help.'

Simons nodded dismissively. 'I'll see you tomorrow.'

Davis wondered whether that meant he had passed the test.

In the afternoon on the next day, 3 January 1979, they all met at Perot's weekend house on the shore of Lake Grapevine.

The two or three other houses nearby appeared empty, as Merv Stauffer had predicted. Perot's house was screened by several acres of rough woodland, and had lawns running down to the water's edge. It was a compact wood-frame building, quite small – the garage for Perot's speedboats was bigger than the house.

The door was locked and nobody had thought to bring the keys. Schwebach picked a window lock and let them in.

There was a living-room, a couple of bedrooms, a kitchen and a bathroom. The place was cheerfully decorated in blue and white, with inexpensive furniture.

The men sat around the living-room with their maps and easel pads and magic markers and cigarettes. Coburn reported. Overnight he had spoken to Majid and two or three other people in Tehran. It had been difficult, trying to get detailed information about the jail while pretending to be only mildly curious, but he thought he had succeeded.

The jail was part of the Ministry of Justice complex

which occupied a whole city block, he had learned. The jail entrance was at the rear of the block. Next to the entrance was a courtyard, separated from the street only by a twelve-foot-high fence of iron railings. This court-yard was the prisoners' exercise area. Clearly, it was also the prison's weak point.

Simons agreed.

All they had to do, then, was wait for an exercise period, get over the fence, grab Paul and Bill, bring them back over the fence, and get out of Iran.

They got down to details.

How would they get over the fence? Would they use ladders, or climb on each other's shoulders?

They would arrive in a van, they decided, and use its roof as a step. Travelling in a van rather than a car had another advantage: nobody would be able to see inside while they were driving to – and, more importantly, away from – the jail.

Joe Poché was nominated driver because he knew the streets of Tehran best.

How would they deal with the prison guards? They did not want to kill anyone. They had no quarrel with the Iranian man in the street, nor with the guards: it was not the fault of those people that Paul and Bill were unjustly imprisoned. Furthermore, if there was any killing, the subsequent hue-and-cry would be worse, making escape from Iran more hazardous.

But the prison guards would not hesitate to shoot them.

The best defence, Simons said, was a combination of surprise, shock and speed.

They would have the advantage of surprise. For a few seconds the prison guards would not understand what was happening.

Then the rescuers would have to do something to make the guards take cover. Shotgun fire would be best. A shotgun would make a big flash and a lot of noise, especially in a city street: the shock would cause the guards to react defensively instead of attacking the rescuers. That would give them a few more seconds.

With speed, those seconds might be enough.

And then they might not.

The room filled with tobacco smoke as the plan took shape. Simons sat there, chain-smoking his little cigars, listening, asking questions, guiding the discussion. This was a very democratic army, Coburn thought. As they got involved in the plan, his friends were forgetting about their wives and children, their mortgages, their lawn mowers and station wagons; forgetting, too, how outrageous was the very idea of their snatching prisoners out of a jail. Davis stopped clowning, Sculley no longer seemed boyish but became very cold and calculating. Poché wanted to talk everything to death, as usual; Boulware was sceptical, as usual.

Afternoon wore into evening. They decided the van would pull on to the pavement beside the iron railings. This sort of parking would not be in the least remarkable in Tehran, they told Simons. Simons would be sitting in the front seat, beside Poché, with a shotgun beneath his coat. He would jump out and stand in front of the van. The back door of the van would open and

Ralph Boulware would get out, also with a shotgun under his coat.

So far, nothing out of the ordinary would appear to have happened.

With Simons and Boulware ready to give covering fire, Ron Davis would get out of the van, climb on the roof, step from the roof to the top of the fence, then jump down into the courtyard. Davis was chosen for this role because he was the youngest and fittest, and the jump – a twelve-foot drop – would be hard to take.

Coburn would follow Davis over the fence. He was not in good shape, but his face was more familiar than any other to Paul and Bill, so they would know as soon as they saw him that they were being rescued.

Next, Boulware would lower a ladder into the courtyard.

Surprise might take them this far, if they were quick; but at this point the guards were sure to react. Simons and Boulware would now fire their shotguns into the air.

The prison guards would hit the dirt, the Iranian prisoners would run around in terrified confusion, and the rescuers would have gained a few more seconds.

What if there were interference from *outside* the jail, Simons asked – from police or soldiers in the street, revolutionary rioters or just public-spirited passers-by?

There would be two flanking guards, they decided; one at either end of the street. They would arrive in a car a few seconds before the van. They would be armed with handguns. Their job was simply to *stop* anyone who came to interfere with the rescue. Jim Schwebach and Pat Sculley were nominated. Coburn was sure Schwebach would not hesitate to shoot people if necessary; and Sculley, although he had never in his life shot anyone, had become so surprisingly ice-cool during the discussion that Coburn supposed he would be equally ruthless.

Glenn Jackson would drive the car: the question of Glenn the Baptist shooting people would not arise.

Meanwhile, in the confusion in the courtyard, Ron Davis would provide close cover, dealing with any nearby guards, while Coburn cut Paul and Bill out of the herd and urged them up the ladder. They would jump from the top of the fence to the roof of the van, then from there to the ground, and finally inside the van. Coburn would follow, then Davis.

'Hey, I'm taking the biggest risk of all,' said Davis. 'Hell, I'm first in and last out – maximum exposure.'

'No shit,' said Boulware. 'Next question.'

Simons would get into the front of the van, Boulware would jump in the back and close the door, and Poché would drive them away at top speed.

Jackson, in the car, would pick up the flanking guards, Schwebach and Sculley, and follow the van.

During the getaway, Boulware would be able to shoot through the back window of the van, and Simons would cover the road ahead. Any really serious pursuit would be taken care of by Sculley and Schwebach in the car.

At a prearranged spot they would dump the van and split up in several cars, then head for the air base at

Doshen Toppeh, on the outskirts of the city. A US Air Force jet would fly them out of Iran: it would be Perot's job to arrange that somehow.

At the end of the evening they had the skeleton of a workable plan.

Before they left, Simons told them not to talk about the rescue – not to their wives, *not even to each other* – outside the lake house. They should each think up a cover story to explain why they would be going out of the US in a week or so. And, he added, looking at their full ashtrays and their ample waistlines, each man should devise his own exercise programme for getting in shape.

The rescue was no longer a zany idea in Ross Perot's mind: it was real.

Jay Coburn was the only one who made a serious effort to deceive his wife.

He went back to the Hilton Inn and called Liz. 'Hi, honey.'

'Hi, Jay! Where are you?'

'I'm in Paris . . .'

Joe Poché also called his wife from the Hilton.

'Where are you?' she asked him.

'I'm in Dallas.'

'What are you doing?'

'Working at EDS, of course.'

'Joe, EDS in Dallas has been calling *me* to ask where you are!'

Poché realized that someone who was not in on the secret of the rescue team had been trying to locate him.

168

'I'm not working with those guys, I'm working directly with Ross. Somebody forgot to tell someone else, that's all.'

'What are you working on?'

'It has to do with some things that have to be done for Paul and Bill.'

'Oh . . .'

When Boulware got back to the home of the friends with whom his family was staying, his daughters, Stacy Elaine and Kecia Nicole, were asleep. His wife said: 'How was your day?'

I've been planning a jailbreak, Boulware thought. He said: 'Oh, okay.'

She looked at him strangely. 'Well, what did you do?'

'Nothing much.'

'For someone who was doing *nothing much*, you've been pretty busy. I called two or three times – they said they couldn't find you.'

'I was around. Hey, I think I'd like a beer.'

Mary Boulware was a warm, open woman to whom deceit was foreign. She was also intelligent. But she knew that Ralph had some firm ideas about the roles of husband and wife. The ideas might be old-fashioned but they worked in this marriage. If there was an area of his business life that he didn't want to tell her about, well, she wasn't about to fight him over it.

'One beer, coming up . . .'

Jim Schwebach did not try to fool his wife Rachel. She had already outguessed him. When Schwebach had got the original call from Pat Sculley, Rachel had asked: 'Who was that?'

'That was Pat Sculley in Dallas. They want me to go down there and work on a study in Europe.'

Rachel had known Jim for almost twenty years – they had started dating when he was sixteen, she eighteen – and she could read his mind. She said: 'They're going back over there to get those guys out of jail.'

Schwebach said feebly: 'Rachel, you don't understand, I'm out of that line of business, I don't do that any more.'

'That's what you're going to do . . .'

Pat Sculley could not lie successfully even to his colleagues, and with his wife he did not try. He told Mary everything.

Ross Perot told Margot everything.

And even Simons, who had no wife to pester him, broke security by telling his brother Stanley in New Jersey . . .

It proved equally impossible to keep the rescue plan from other senior executives at EDS. The first to figure it all out was Keane Taylor, the tall, irritable, well-dressed ex-Marine whom Perot had turned around in Frankfurt and sent back to Tehran.

Since that New Year's Day, when Perot had said: 'I'm sending you back to do *something very important*,' Taylor had been sure that a secret operation was being planned; and it did not take him long to figure out who was doing it.

One day, on the phone from Tehran to Dallas, he had asked for Ralph Boulware.

'Boulware's not here,' he was told.

'When will he be back?'

'We're not sure.'

Taylor, never a man to suffer fools gladly, had raised his voice. 'So, *where* has he gone?'

'We're not sure.'

'What do you *mean*, you're not sure?'

'He's on vacation.'

Taylor had known Boulware for years. It had been Taylor who gave Boulware his first management opportunity. They were drinking partners. Many times Taylor, drinking himself sober with Ralph in the early hours of the morning, had looked around and realized his was the only white face in an all-black bar. Those nights they would stagger back to whichever of their homes was nearest, and the unlucky wife who welcomed them would call the other and say: 'It's okay, they're here.'

Yes, Taylor knew Boulware; and he found it hard to believe that Ralph would go on vacation while Paul and Bill were still in jail.

Next day he asked for Pat Sculley, and got the same runaround.

Boulware *and* Sculley on vacation while Paul and Bill were in jail?'

Bullshit.

Next day he asked for Coburn.

Same story.

It was beginning to make sense: Coburn had been with Perot when Perot sent Taylor back to Tehran. Coburn, Director of Personnel, evacuation mastermind, would be the right choice to organize a secret operation.

Taylor and Rich Gallagher, the other EDS man still in Tehran, started making a list.

Boulware, Sculley, Coburn, Ron Davis, Jim Schwebach and Joe Poché were all 'on vacation'.

That group had a few things in common.

When Paul Chiapparone had first come to Tehran he found that EDS's operation there was not organized to his liking: it had been too loose, too casual, too Persian. The Ministry contract had not been running to time. Paul had brought in a number of tough, down-to-earth EDS troubleshooters and together they had knocked the business back into shape. Taylor himself had been one of Paul's tough guys. So had Bill Gaylord. And Coburn, and Sculley, and Boulware, and all the guys who were now 'on vacation'.

The other thing they had in common was that they were all members of the EDS Tehran Roman Catholic Sunday Brunch Poker School. Like Paul and Bill, like Taylor himself, they were Catholics, with the exception of Joe Poché (and of Glenn Jackson, the only rescue team member Taylor failed to spot). Each Sunday they had met at the Catholic Mission in Tehran. After the service they would all go to the house of one of them for brunch. And while the wives were cooking and the children playing, the men would get into a poker game.

There was nothing like poker for revealing a man's true character.

If, as Taylor and Gallagher now suspected, Perot had asked Coburn to put together a team of completely trustworthy men, then Coburn was sure to have picked them from the poker school.

'Vacation, my *ass*,' Taylor said to Gallagher. 'This is a rescue team.'

The rescue team returned to the lake house on the morning of 4 January and went over the whole plan again.

Simons had endless patience for detail, and he was determined to prepare for every possible snag that anyone could dream up. He was much helped by Joe Poché, whose tireless questioning – wearying though it was, to Coburn at least – was in fact highly creative, and led to numerous improvements of the rescue scenario.

First, Simons was dissatisfied with the arrangements for protecting the rescue team's flanks. The idea of Schwebach and Sculley, short but deadly, just plain *shooting* anyone who tried to interfere was crude. It would be better to have some kind of diversion, to distract any police or military types who might be nearby. Schwebach suggested setting fire to a car down the street from the jail. Simons was not sure that would be enough – he wanted to blow up a whole building. Anyway, Schwebach was given the job of designing a time bomb.

They thought of a small precaution which would shave a second or two off the time for which they would be exposed. Simons would get out of the van some distance from the jail and walk up to the fence. If all was clear he would give a hand signal for the van to approach.

Another weak element of the plan was the business

of getting out of the van and climbing on its roof. All that jumping out and scrambling up would use precious seconds. And would Paul and Bill, after weeks in prison, be fit enough to climb a ladder and jump off the roof of a van?

All sorts of solutions were canvassed – an extra ladder, a mattress on the ground, grab handles on the roof – but in the end the team came up with a simple solution: they would cut a hole in the roof of the van and get in and out through that. Another little refinement, for those who had to jump back down through the hole, was a mattress on the floor of the van to soften their landing.

The getaway journey would give them time to alter their appearances. In Tehran they planned to wear jeans and casual jackets, and they were all beginning to grow beards and moustaches to look less conspicuous there; but in the van they would carry business suits and electric shavers, and before switching to the cars they would all shave and change their clothes.

Ralph Boulware, independent as ever, did not want to wear jeans and a casual jacket beforehand. In a business suit with a white shirt and a tie he felt comfortable and able to assert himself, especially in Tehran where good western clothing labelled a man as a member of the dominant class in society. Simons calmly gave his assent: the most important thing, he said, was for everyone to feel comfortable and confident during the operation.

At the Doshen Toppeh air base, from which they

planned to leave in an Air Force jet, there were both American and Iranian planes and personnel. The Americans would of course be expecting them, but what if the Iranian sentries at the entrance gave them a hard time? They would all carry forged military identity cards, they decided. Some wives of EDS executives had worked for the military in Tehran and still had their ID cards: Merv Stauffer would get hold of one and use it as a model for the forgeries.

Throughout all this Simons was still very low-key, Coburn observed. Chain-smoking his cigars (Boulware told him: 'Don't worry about getting shot, you're going to die of cancer!') he did little more than ask questions. The plans were made in a round-table discussion, with everyone contributing, and decisions were arrived at by mutual agreement. Yet Coburn found himself coming to respect Simons more and more. The man was know-ledgeable, intelligent, painstaking and imaginative. He also had a sense of humour.

Coburn could see that the others were also beginning to get the measure of Simons. If anyone asked a dumb question, Simons would give a sharp answer. In conse-quence, they would hesitate before asking a question, and wonder what his reaction might be. In this way he was getting them to think like him.

Once on that second day at the lake house they felt the full force of his displeasure. It was, not surprisingly, young Ron Davis who angered him.

They were a humorous bunch, and Davis was the funniest. Coburn approved of that: laughter helped to ease the tension in an operation such as this. He suspected Simons felt the same. But one time Davis went too far.

Simons had a pack of cigars on the floor beside his chair, and five more packs out in the kitchen. Davis, getting to like Simons and characteristically making no secret of it, said with genuine concern: 'Colonel, you smoke too many cigars, it's bad for your health.'

By way of reply he got the Simons Look, but he ignored the warning.

A few minutes later he went into the kitchen and hid the five packs of cigars in the dishwasher.

When Simons finished the first pack he went looking for the rest and could not find them. He could not operate without tobacco. He was about to get in a car and go to a store when Davis opened the dishwasher and said: 'I have your cigars here.'

'You keep those, goddam it,' Simons growled, and he went out.

When he came back with another five packs he said to Davis: 'These are mine. Keep your goddam hands off them.'

Davis felt like a child who had been put in the corner. It was the first and last prank he played on Colonel Simons.

While the discussion went on, Jim Schwebach sat on the floor, trying to make a bomb.

To smuggle a bomb, or even just its component parts, through Iranian customs would have been dangerous – 'That's a risk we don't have to take,' Simons said – so

Schwebach had to design a device which could be assembled from ingredients readily available in Tehran.

The idea of blowing up a building was dropped: it was too ambitious and would probably kill innocent people. They would make do with a blazing car as a diversion. Schwebach knew how to make 'instant napalm' from gasoline, soap flakes and a little oil. The timer and the fuse were his two problems. In the States he would have used an electrical timer connected with a toy rocket motor; but in Tehran he would be restricted to more primitive mechanisms.

Schwebach enjoyed the challenge. He liked fooling around with anything mechanical: his hobby was an ugly-looking stripped-down '73 Oldsmobile Cutlass that went like a bullet out of a gun.

At first he experimented with an old-fashioned clockwork stove-top timer which used a striker to hit a bell. He attached a phosphorus match to the striker and substituted a piece of sandpaper for the bell, to ignite the match. The match in turn would light a mechanical fuse.

The system was unreliable, and caused great hilarity among the rest of the team, who jeered and laughed every time the match failed to ignite.

In the end Schweback settled on the oldest timing device of all: a candle.

He test-burned a candle to see how long it took to burn down one inch, then he cut another candle off at the right length for fifteen minutes.

Next he scraped the heads off several old-fashioned

phosphorus matches and ground up the inflammable material into a powder. This he packed tightly into a piece of aluminium kitchen foil. Then he stuck the foil into the base of the candle. When the candle burned all the way down, it heated the aluminium foil and the ground-up match-heads exploded. The foil was thinner at the bottom so that the explosion would travel downward.

The candle, with this primitive but reliable fuse in its base, was set into the neck of a plastic jar, about the size of a hip flask, full of jellied gasoline.

'You light the candle and walk away from it,' Schwebach told them when his design was complete. 'Fifteen minutes later you've got a nice little fire going.'

And any police, soldiers, revolutionaries or passers-by – plus, quite possibly, some of the prison guards – would have their attention fixed on a blazing automobile three hundred yards up the street while Ron Davis and Jay Coburn were jumping over the fence into the prison courtyard.

That day they moved out of the Hilton Inn. Coburn slept at the lake house, and the others checked in to the Airport Marina – which was closer to Lake Grapevine – all except Ralph Boulware, who insisted on going home to his family.

They spent the next four days training, buying equipment, practising their shooting, rehearsing the jailbreak, and further refining the plan.

Shotguns could be bought in Tehran, but the only

kind of ammunition allowed by the Shah was birdshot. However, Simons was expert at reloading ammunition, so they decided to smuggle their own shot into Iran.

The trouble with putting buckshot into birdshot slugs would be that they would get relatively few shot into the smaller slugs: the ammunition would have great penetration but little spread. They decided to use No 2 shot, which would spread wide enough to knock down more than one man at a time, but had enough penetration to smash the windscreen of a pursuing car.

In case things turned really nasty, each member of the team would also carry a Walther PPK in a holster. Merv Stauffer got Bob Snyder, head of security at EDS and a man who knew when not to ask questions, to buy the PPKs at Ray's Sporting Goods in Dallas. Schwebach had the job of figuring out how to smuggle the guns into Iran.

Stauffer inquired which US airports did *not* fluoroscope outgoing baggage: one was Kennedy.

Schwebach bought two Vuitton trunks, deeper than ordinary suitcases, with reinforced corners and hard sides. With Coburn, Davis and Jackson he went to the woodwork shop at Perot's Dallas home and experimented with ways of constructing false bottoms in the cases.

Schwebach was perfectly happy about carrying guns through Iranian customs in a false-bottom case. 'If you know how customs people work, you don't get stopped,' he said. His confidence was not shared by the rest of the team. In case he did get stopped and the guns were found, there was a fall-back plan. He would say the case was not his. He would return to the baggage claim area and there, sure enough, would be another Vuitton trunk just like the first, but full of personal belongings and containing no guns.

Once the team was in Tehran they would have to communicate with Dallas by phone. Coburn was quite sure that Iranians bugged the phone lines, so the team developed a simple code.

GR meant A, GS meant B, GT meant C, and so on through GZ which meant I; then HA meant J, HB meant K, through HR which meant Z. Numbers one through nine were IA through II: zero was IJ.

They would use the military alphabet, in which A is called Alpha, B is Bravo, C is Charlie and so on.

For speed, only key words would be coded. The sentence 'He is with EDS' would therefore become 'He is with Golf Victor Golf Uniform Hotel Kilo.'

Only three copies of the key to the code were made. Simons gave one to Merv Stauffer, who would be the team's contact here in Dallas. He gave the other two to Jay Coburn and Pat Sculley, who – though nothing was said formally – were emerging as his lieutenants.

The code would prevent an accidental leak through a casual phone tap, but – as computer men knew better than anyone – such a simple letter cipher could be broken by an expert in a few minutes. As a further precaution, therefore, certain common words had special code groups: Paul was AG, Bill was AH, the American Embassy was GC, and Tehran was AU. Perot was always referred to as The Chairman, guns were tapes, the prison was The Data Centre, Kuwait was Oil

Town, Istanbul was Resort, and the attack on the prison was Plan A. Everyone had to memorize these special code words.

If anyone were questioned about the code he was to say that it was used to abbreviate teletype messages.

The code name for the whole rescue was Operation Hotfoot. It was an acronym, dreamed up by Ron Davis: Help Our Two Friends Out of Tehran. Simons was tickled by that. 'Hotfoot has been used so many times for operations,' he said, 'and this is the first time it's ever been appropriate.'

They rehearsed the attack on the prison at least a hundred times.

In the grounds of the lake house, Schwebach and Davis nailed up a plank between two trees at a height of twelve feet, to represent the courtyard fence. Merv Stauffer brought them a van borrowed from EDS security.

Time and time again Simons walked up to the 'fence' and gave a hand signal; Poché drove the van up and stopped it at the fence; Boulware jumped out of the back; Davis got on the roof and jumped over the fence; Coburn followed; Boulware climbed on the roof and lowered the ladder into the 'courtyard'; 'Paul' and 'Bill' – played by Schwebach and Sculley, who did not need to rehearse their roles as flanking guards – came up the ladder and over the fence, followed by Coburn and then Davis; everyone scrambled into the van; and Poché drove off at top speed.

Sometimes they switched roles so that each man learned how to do everyone else's job. They prioritized tasks so that, if one of them dropped out, wounded or for any other reason, they knew automatically who would take his place. Schweback and Sculley, playing the parts of Paul and Bill, sometimes acted sick and had to be carried up the ladder and over the fence.

The advantage of physical fitness became apparent during the rehearsals. Davis could come back over the fence in a second and a half, touching the ladder twice: nobody else could do it anywhere near that fast.

One time Davis went over too fast and landed awkwardly on the frozen ground, straining his shoulder. The injury was not serious but it gave Simons an idea. Davis would travel to Tehran with his arm in a sling, carrying a bean bag for exercise. The bag would be weighted with No 2 shot.

Simons timed the rescue, from the moment the van stopped at the fence to the moment it pulled away with everyone inside. In the end, according to his stopwatch, they could do it in under thirty seconds.

They practised with the Walther PPKs at the Garland Public Shooting Range. They told the range operator that they were security men from all over the country on a course in Dallas, and they had to get their target practice in before they could go home. He did not believe them, especially after T. J. Marquez turned up looking just like a Mafia chieftain in a movie, with his black coat and black hat, and took ten Walther PPKs and five thousand rounds of ammunition out of the trunk of his black Lincoln.

After a little practice they could all shoot reasonably well except Davis. Simons suggested he try shooting lying down, since that was the position he would be in when he was in the courtyard; and he found he could do much better that way.

It was bitterly cold out in the open, and they all huddled in a little shack, trying to get warm, while they were not shooting – all except Simons, who stayed outside all day long, as if he were made of stone.

He was not made of stone: when he got into Merv Stauffer's car at the end of the day he said: 'Jesus *Christ* it's cold.'

He had begun to needle them about how soft they were. They were always talking about where they would go to eat and what they would order, he said. When *he* was hungry he would open a can. He would laugh at someone for nursing a drink: when he was thirsty he would fill a tumbler with water and drink it straight down, saying: 'I didn't pour it to look at it.' He showed them how he could shoot, one time: every bullet in the centre of the target. Once Coburn saw him with his shirt off: his physique would have been impressive on a man twenty years younger.

It was a tough-guy act, the whole performance. What was peculiar was that none of them ever laughed at it. With Simons, it was the real thing.

One evening at the lake house he showed them the best way to kill a man quickly and silently.

He had ordered – and Merv Stauffer had purchased – Gerber knives for each of them, short stabbing weapons with a narrow two-edge blade.

'It's kind of small,' said Davis, looking at his. 'Is it long enough?'

'It is unless you want to sharpen it when it comes out the other side,' Simons said.

He showed them the exact spot in the small of Glenn Jackson's back where the kidney was located. 'A single stab, right there, is lethal,' he said.

'Wouldn't he scream?' Davis asked.

'It hurts so bad he can't make a sound.'

While Simons was demonstrating Merv Stauffer had come in, and now he stood in the doorway, open-mouthed, with a McDonald's paper sack in either arm. Simons saw him and said: 'Look at this guy – he can't make a sound and nobody's stuck him yet.'

Merv laughed and started handing round the food. 'You know what the McDonald's girl said to me, in a completely empty restaurant, when I asked for thirty hamburgers and thirty orders of fries?'

'What?'

'What they always say – "Is this to eat here or to go?"'

Simons just loved working for private enterprise.

One of his biggest headaches in the Army had always been supplies. Even planning the Son Tay Raid, an operation in which the President himself was personally interested, it had seemed as if he had to fill in six requisition forms and get approval from twelve generals every time he needed a new pencil. Then, when all the paperwork was done, he would find that the items were out of stock, or there was a four month wait for delivery, or – worst of all – when the stuff came it did not work. Twenty-two per cent of the blasting caps he ordered misfired. He had tried to get night-sights for his raiders. He learned that the Army had spent seventeen years trying to develop a night-sight, but by 1970 all they had were six hand-built prototypes. Then he discovered a perfectly good British-made night-sight available from Armalite Corporation for $49.50, and that was what the Son Tay Raiders took to Vietnam.

At EDS there were no forms to be filled and no permissions to be sought, at least not for Simons: he told Merv Stauffer what he needed and Stauffer got it, usually the same day. He asked for, and got, ten Walther PPKs and ten thousand rounds of ammunition; a selection of holsters, both left-handed and right-handed, in different styles so the men could pick the kind they felt most comfortable with; shotgun ammunition reloading kits in 12-gauge, 16-gauge and 20-gauge; and cold-weather clothes for the team including coats, mittens, shirts, socks and woollen stocking caps. One day he asked for a hundred thousand dollars in cash: two hours later T. J. Marquez arrived at the lake house with the money in an envelope.

It was different from the Army in other ways. His men were not soldiers who could be bullied into submission: they were some of the brightest young corporate executives in the United States. He had realized from the start that he could not assume command. He had to earn their loyalty.

These men would obey an order if they agreed with it. If not, they would discuss it. That was fine in the boardroom but useless on the battlefield.

They were squeamish, too. The first time they talked about setting fire to a car as a diversion, someone had objected on the grounds that innocent passers-by might get hurt. Simons needled them about their Boy Scout morality, saying they were afraid of losing their merit badges, and calling them 'you Jack Armstrongs' after the too-good-to-be-true radio character who went around solving crimes and helping old ladies cross the road.

They also had a tendency to forget the seriousness of what they were doing. There was a lot of joking and a certain amount of horseplay, particularly from young Ron Davis. A measure of humour was useful in a team on a dangerous mission, but sometimes Simons had to put a stop to it and bring them back to reality with a sharp remark.

He gave them all the opportunity to back out at any time. He got Ron Davis on his own again and said: 'You're going to be the first one over the fence – don't you have some reservations about that?'

'Yeah.'

'Good thing you do, otherwise I wouldn't take you. Suppose Paul and Bill don't come right away? Suppose they figure that if they head for the fence they'll get shot? You'll be stuck there and the guards will see you. You'll be in bad trouble.'

'Yeah.'

'Me, I'm sixty years old, I've lived my life. Hell, I

don't have a thing to lose. But you're a young man – and Marva's pregnant, isn't she?'

'Yeah.'

'Are you really sure you want to do this?'

'Yeah.'

He worked on them all. There was no point in his telling *them* that his military judgement was better than theirs: they had to come to that conclusion themselves. Similarly, his tough-guy act was intended to let them know that from now on such things as keeping warm, eating, drinking, and worrying about innocent by-standers would not occupy much of their time or attention. The shooting practice and the knife lesson also had a hidden purpose: the last thing Simons wanted was any killing on this operation, but learning how to kill reminded the men that the rescue could be a life-and-death affair.

The biggest element in his psychological campaign was the endless practising of the assault on the jail. Simons was quite sure that the jail would *not* be exactly as Coburn had described it, and that the plan would have to be modified. A raid *never* went precisely accord-ing to the scenario – as he knew better than most.

The rehearsals for the Son Tay Raid had gone on for weeks. A complete replica of the prison camp had been built, out of two-by-four timbers and target cloth, at Eglin Air Base in Florida. The bloody thing had to be dismantled every morning before dawn and put up again at night, because the Russian reconnaissance satellite Cosmos 355 passed over Florida twice every twenty-four hours. But it had been a beautiful thing:

every goddam tree and ditch in the Son Tay prison camp had been reproduced in the mock up. And then, after all those rehearsals, when they did it for real one of the helicopters – the one Simons was in – had landed in the wrong place.

Simons would never forget the moment he realized the mistake. His helicopter was taking off again, having discharged the raiders. A startled Vietnamese guard emerged from a foxhole and Simons shot him in the chest. Shooting broke out, a flare went up, and Simons saw that the buildings surrounding him were not the buildings of the Son Tay camp. 'Get that fucking chopper back in here!' he yelled to his radio operator. He told a sergeant to turn on a strobe light to mark the landing zone.

He knew where they were: four hundred yards from Son Tay, in a compound marked on intelligence maps as a school. This was no school. There were enemy troops everywhere. It was a barracks, and Simons realized that his helicopter pilot's mistake had been a lucky one, for now he was able to launch a pre-emptive attack and wipe out a concentration of enemy troops who might otherwise have jeopardized the whole operation.

That was the night he stood outside a barracks and shot eighty men in their underwear.

No, an operation never went exactly according to plan. But becoming proficient at executing the scenario was only half the purpose of rehearsals anyway. The other half – and, in the case of the EDS men, the important half – was learning to work together as a team. Oh, they were already terrific as an *intellectual* team – give them each an office and a secretary and a telephone and they would computerize the world – but working together with their hands and their bodies was different. When they had started on 3 January, they would have had trouble launching a rowboat as a team. Five days later they were a machine.

And that was all that could be done here in Texas. Now they had to take a look at the real-life jail.

It was time to go to Tehran.

Simons told Stauffer he wanted to meet with Perot again.

III

While the rescue team was in training, President Carter got his last chance of preventing a bloody revolution in Iran.

And he blew it.

This is how it happened . . .

Ambassador William Sullivan went to bed content on the night of 4 January in his private apartment within the large, cool residence in the Embassy compound at the corner of Roosevelt and Takht-e-Jamshid avenues in Tehran.

Sullivan's boss, Secretary of State Cyrus Vance, had been busy with the Camp David negotiations all through November and December, but now he was back in

Washington and concentrating on Iran – and boy, did it show. Vagueness and vacillation had ended. The cables containing Sullivan's instructions had become crisp and decisive. Most importantly, the United States at last had a strategy for dealing with the crisis: they were going to talk to the Ayatollah Khomeini.

It was Sullivan's own idea. He was now sure that the Shah would soon leave Iran and Khomeini would return in triumph. His job, he believed, was to preserve America's relationship with Iran through the change of government, so that when it was all over Iran would still be a stronghold of American influence in the Middle East. The way to do that was to help the Iranian armed forces to stay intact and to continue American military aid to any new regime.

Sullivan had called Vance on the secure telephone link and told him just that. The US should send an emissary to Paris to see the Ayatollah, Sullivan had urged. Khomeini should be told that the main concern of the US was to preserve the territorial integrity of Iran and deflect Soviet influence; that the Americans did not want to see a pitched battle in Iran between the Army and the Islamic revolutionaries; and that, once the Ayatollah was in power, the US would offer him the same military assistance and arms sales it had given the Shah.

It was a bold plan. There would be those who would accuse the US of abandoning a friend. But Sullivan was sure it was time for the Americans to cut their losses with the Shah and look to the future.

To his intense satisfaction, Vance had agreed.

So had the Shah. Weary, apathetic, and no longer willing to shed blood in order to stay in power, the Shah had not even put up a show of reluctance.

Vance had nominated, as his emissary to the Ayatollah, Theodore H. Eliot, a senior diplomat who had served as economic counsellor in Tehran and spoke Farsi fluently. Sullivan was delighted with the choice.

Ted Eliot was scheduled to arrive in Paris in two days' time, on 6 January.

In one of the guest bedrooms at the ambassadorial Residence, Air Force General Robert 'Dutch' Huyser was also going to bed. Sullivan was not as enthusiastic about the Huyser Mission as he was about the Eliot Mission. Dutch Huyser, the deputy commander (under Haig) of US forces in Europe, had arrived yesterday to persuade Iranian generals to support the new Bakhtiar government in Tehran. Sullivan knew Huyser. He was a fine soldier, but no diplomat. He spoke no Farsi and he did not know Iran. But even if he had been ideally qualified his task would have been hopeless. The Bakhtiar government had failed to gain the support even of the moderates, and Shahpour Bakhtiar himself had been expelled from the centrist National Front party merely for accepting the Shah's invitation to form a government. Meanwhile the army which Huyser was trying futilely to swing to Bakhtiar continued to weaken as soldiers in their thousands deserted and joined the revolutionary mobs in the streets. The best Huyser could hope for was to hold the army together a little longer, while Eliot in Paris arranged for the peaceful return of the Ayatollah.

If it worked it would be a great achievement for Sullivan, something any diplomat could be proud of for the rest of his life: his plan would have strengthened the country *and* saved lives.

As he went to sleep, there was just one worry nagging at the back of his mind. The Eliot Mission, for which he had such high hopes, was a State Department scheme, identified in Washington with Secretary of State Vance. The Huyser Mission was the idea of Zbigniew Brzezinski, the National Security Advisor. The enmity between Vance and Brzezinski was notorious. And at this moment Brzezinski, after the summit meeting in Guadeloupe, was deep-sea fishing in the Caribbean with President Carter. As they sailed over the clear blue sea, what was Brzezinski whispering in the President's ear?

The phone woke Sullivan in the early hours of the morning. It was the duty officer, calling from the communications vault in the Embassy building just a few yards away. An urgent cable had arrived from Washington. The Ambassador might want to read it immediately.

Sullivan got out of bed and walked across the lawns to the Embassy, full of foreboding.

The cable said that the Eliot Mission was cancelled.

The decision had been taken by the President. Sullivan's comments on the change of plan were *not* invited. He was instructed to tell the Shah that the United States Government no longer intended to hold talks with the Ayatollah Khomeini.

Sullivan was heartbroken.

This was the end of America's influence in Iran. It also meant that Sullivan personally had lost his chance of distinguishing himself as Ambassador by preventing a bloody civil war.

He sent an angry message back to Vance, saying the President had made a gross mistake and should reconsider.

He went back to bed, but he could not sleep.

In the morning another cable informed him that the President's decision would stand.

Wearily, Sullivan made his way up the hill to the palace to tell the Shah.

The Shah appeared drawn and tense that morning. He and Sullivan sat down and drank the inevitable cup of tea. Then Sullivan told him that President Carter had cancelled the Eliot Mission.

The Shah was upset. 'But *why* have they cancelled it?' he said agitatedly.

'I don't know,' Sullivan replied.

'But how do they expect to influence those people if they won't even talk to them?'

'I don't know.'

'Then what does Washington intend to do now?' asked the Shah, throwing up his hands in despair.

'I don't know,' said Sullivan.

IV

'Ross, this is *idiotic*,' Tom Luce said loudly. 'You're going to destroy the company and you're going to destroy your*self*.'

Perot looked at his lawyer. They were sitting in Perot's office. The door was closed.

Luce was not the first to say this. During the week, as the news had spread through the seventh floor, several of Perot's top executives had come in to tell him that a rescue team was a foolhardy and dangerous notion, and he should drop the idea. 'Stop worrying,' Perot had told them. 'Just concentrate on what you have to do.'

Tom Luce was characteristically vociferous. Wearing an aggressive scowl and a courtroom manner, he argued his case as if a jury were listening.

'I can only advise you on the legal situation, but I'm here to tell you that this rescue can cause more problems, and *worse* problems, than you've got now. Hell, Ross, I can't make a *list* of the laws you're going to break!'

'Try,' said Perot.

'You'll have a mercenary army – which is illegal here, in Iran, and in every country the team would pass through. Anywhere they go they'd be liable to criminal penalties and you could have ten men in jail instead of two.

'But it's worse than that. Your men would be in a position much worse than soldiers in battle – international laws and the Geneva convention, which protect soldiers in uniform, would not protect the rescue team.

'If they get captured in Iran ... Ross, they'll be *shot*. If they get captured in any country that has an extradition treaty with Iran, they'll be sent back and shot. Instead of two innocent employees in jail, you could have eight *guilty* employees *dead*.

'And if that happens the families of the dead men may turn on you – understandably, because this whole thing will look *stupid*. The widows will have *huge* claims against EDS in the American courts. They could bankrupt the company. Think of the ten thousand people who would be out of a job if that happened. Think of yourself – Ross, there might even be criminal charges against you which could put *you* in jail!'

Perot said calmly: 'I appreciate your advice, Tom.'

Luce stared at him. 'I'm not getting through to you, am I?'

Perot smiled. 'Sure you are. But if you go through life worrying about all the bad things that can happen, you soon convince yourself that it's best to do nothing at all.'

The truth was that Perot knew something Luce did not.

Ross Perot was lucky.

All his life he had been lucky.

As a twelve-year-old boy he had had a paper route in the poor black district of Texarkana. The Texarkana Gazette cost twenty-five cents a week in those days, and on Sundays, when he collected the money, he would end up with forty or fifty dollars in quarters in his purse. And every Sunday, somewhere along the route, some poor man who had spent his week's wages in the bar the previous night would try to take the money from little Ross. This was why no other boy would deliver papers in that district. But Ross was never scared. He was on a horse; the attempts were never very determined; and he was lucky. He never lost his money.

He had been lucky again in getting admitted to the Naval Academy at Annapolis. Applicants had to be sponsored by a Senator or a Congressman, and of course the Perot family did not have the right contacts. Anyway, young Ross had never even *seen* the sea – the farthest he had ever travelled was to Dallas, 180 miles away. But there was a young man in Texarkana called Josh Morriss Junior who had been to Annapolis and told Ross all about it, and Ross had fallen in love with the Navy without ever seeing a ship. So he just kept writing to Senators begging for sponsorship. He succeeded – as he would many times during later life – because he was too dumb to know it was impossible.

It was not until many years later that he found out how it had happened. One day back in 1949 Senator W. Lee O'Daniel was clearing out his desk: it was the end of his term and he was not going to run again. An aide said: 'Senator, we have an unfilled appointment to the Naval Academy.'

'Does anyone want it?' the Senator said.

'Well, we've got this boy from Texarkana who's been trying for years . . .'

'Give it to him,' said the Senator.

The way Perot heard the story, his name was never actually mentioned during the conversation.

He had been lucky once again in setting up EDS when he did. As a computer salesman for IBM, he realized that his customers did not always make the best use of the machines he sold them. Data processing was a new and specialized skill. The banks were good at banking, the insurance companies were good at insurance, the manufacturers were good at manufacturing – and the computer men were good at data processing. The customer did not want the machine, he wanted the fast, cheap information it could provide. Yet, too often, the customer spent so much time creating his new data processing department and learning how to use the machine that his computer caused him trouble and expense instead of saving them. Perot's idea was to sell a total package – a complete data processing department with machinery, software and staff. The customer had only to say, in simple language, what information he needed, and EDS would give it to him. Then he could get on with what he was good at – banking, insurance or manufacturing.

IBM turned down Perot's idea. It was a good concept but the pickings would be small. Out of every dollar spent on data processing, eighty cents went into hardware – the machinery – and only twenty cents into software, which was what Perot wanted to sell. IBM did not want to chase pennies under the table.

So Perot drew a thousand dollars out of his savings and started up on his own. Over the next decade the proportions changed until software was taking seventy cents of every data processing dollar, and Perot became one of the richest self-made men in the world.

The chairman of IBM, Tom Watson, met Perot in a restaurant one day and said: 'I just want to know one thing, Ross. Did you foresee that the ratio would change?'

'No,' said Perot. 'The twenty cents looked good enough to me.'

Yes, he was lucky; but he had to give his luck room to operate. It was no good sitting in a corner being careful. You never got the chance to be lucky unless you took risks. All his life Perot had taken risks.

This one just happened to be the biggest.

Merv Stauffer walked into the office. 'Ready to go?' he said.

'Yes.'

Perot got up and the two men left the office. They went down in the elevator and got into Stauffer's car, a brand-new four-door Lincoln Versailles. Perot read the nameplate on the dashboard: 'Merv and Helen Stauffer.' The interior of the car stank of Simons's cigars.

'He's waiting for you,' Stauffer said.

'Good.'

Perot's oil company, Petrus, had offices in the next building along Forest Lane. Merv had already taken Simons there, then come for Perot. Afterwards he would take Perot back to EDS then return for Simons. The object of the exercise was secrecy: as few people as possible were to see Simons and Perot together.

In the last six days, while Simons and the rescue team had been doing their thing out at Lake Grapevine, the prospects of a legal solution to the problem of Paul and Bill had receded. Kissinger, having failed with Ardeshir Zahedi, was unable to do anything else to help. Lawyer Tom Luce had been busy calling every single one of the twenty-four Texas Congressmen, both Texas Senators, and anyone else in Washington who would take his calls; but what they all did was to call the State Department to find out what was going on, and all the calls ended up on the desk of Henry Precht.

EDS's chief financial officer Tom Walter still had not found a bank willing to post a letter of credit for $12,750,000. The difficulty, Walter had explained to Perot, was this: under American law, an individual or a corporation could renege on a letter of credit if there was proof that the letter had been signed under illegal pressure, for example blackmail or kidnapping. The banks saw the imprisonment of Paul and Bill as a straightforward piece of extortion, and they knew EDS would be able to argue, in an American court, that the letter was invalid and the money should not be paid. In theory that would not matter, for by then Paul and Bill would be home, and the American bank would simply – and quite legally – refuse to honour the letter of credit when it was presented for payment by the Iranian government. However, most American banks had large loans outstanding with Iran, and their fear was that the Iranians would retaliate by deducting $12,750,000 from what they owed. Walter was still searching for a large bank that did no business with Iran.

So, unfortunately, Operation Hotfoot was still Perot's best bet.

Perot left Stauffer in the car park and went into the oil company building.

He found Simons in the little office reserved for Perot. Simons was eating peanuts and listening to a portable radio. Perot guessed that the peanuts were his lunch and the radio was to swamp any eavesdropping devices that might be hidden in the room.

They shook hands. Perot noticed that Simons was growing a beard. 'How are things?' he said.

'They're good,' Simons answered. 'The men are beginning to pull together as a team.'

'Now,' said Perot, 'you realize you can reject any member of the team you find unsatisfactory.' A couple of days earlier Perot had proposed an addition to the team, a man who knew Tehran and had an outstanding military record, but Simons had turned him down after a short interview, saying: 'That guy believes his own bullshit.' Now Perot wondered whether Simons had found fault, during the training period, with any of the others. He went on: 'You're in charge of the rescue, and—'

'There's no need,' Simons said. 'I don't want to reject anyone.' He laughed softly. 'They're easily the most intelligent squad I've ever worked with, and that does create a problem, because they think orders are to be discussed, not obeyed. But they're learning to turn off their thinking switches when necessary. I've made it very clear to them that at some point in the game discussion ends and blind obedience is called for.'

Perot smiled. 'Then you've achieved more in six days than I have in sixteen years.'

'There's no more we can do here in Dallas,' Simons said. 'Our next step is to go to Tehran.'

Perot nodded. This might be his last chance to call off Operation Hotfoot. Once the team left Dallas, they might be out of touch and they would be out of his control. The die would be cast.

Ross, this is idiotic. You're going to destroy the company and you're going to destroy yourself.

Hell, Ross, I can't make a list of the laws you're going to break!

Instead of two innocent employees in jail, you could have eight guilty employees dead.

Well, we've got this boy from Texarkana who's been trying for years . . .

'When do you want to leave?' Perot asked Simons.

'Tomorrow.'

'Good luck,' said Perot.

CHAPTER FIVE

I

WHILE SIMONS was talking to Perot in Dallas, Pat Sculley – the world's worst liar – was in Istanbul, trying and failing to pull the wool over the eyes of a wily Turk.

Mr Fish was a travel agent who had been 'discovered' during the December evacuation by Merv Stauffer and T. J. Marquez. They had hired him to make arrangements for the evacuees' stopover in Istanbul, and he had worked miracles. He had booked them all into the Sheraton and organized buses to take them from the airport to the hotel. When they arrived there had been a meal waiting for them. They had left him to collect their baggage and clear it through customs, and it appeared outside their hotel as if by magic. Next day there had been video movies for the children and sight-seeing tours for the adults to keep everyone occupied while they waited for their flights to New York. Mr Fish achieved all this while most of the hotel staff were on strike – T.J. found out later that Mrs Fish had made the beds in the hotel rooms. Once onward flights had been reserved, Merv Stauffer had wanted to duplicate a handout sheet with instructions for everyone, but the hotel's photocopier was broken: Mr Fish got an electrician to mend it at five o'clock on a Sunday morning. Mr Fish could *make it happen*.

Simons was still worried about smuggling the Walther PPKs into Tehran, and when he heard how Mr Fish had cleared the evacuees' baggage through Turkish customs he proposed that the same man be asked to solve the problem of the guns. Sculley had left for Istanbul on 8 January.

The following day he met Mr Fish at the coffee shop in the Sheraton. Mr Fish was a big, fat man in his late forties, dressed in drab clothes. But he was shrewd: Sculley was no match for him.

Sculley told him that EDS needed help with two problems. 'One, we need an aircraft that can fly into and out of Tehran. Two, we want to get some baggage through customs without it being inspected. Naturally, we'll pay you anything reasonable for help with these problems.'

Mr Fish looked dubious. 'Why do you want to do these things?'

'Well, we've got some magnetic tapes for computer systems in Tehran,' Sculley said. 'We've got to get them in there and we can't take any chances. We don't want anyone to X-ray those tapes or do anything that could damage them, and we can't risk having them confiscated by some petty customs official.'

'And for this, you need to hire a plane and get your bags through customs unopened?'

'Yes, that's right.' Sculley could see that Mr Fish did not believe a word of it.

Mr Fish shook his head. 'No, Mr Sculley. I have been

happy to help your friends before, but I am a travel agent, not a smuggler. I will not do this.'

'What about the plane – can you get us a plane?'

Mr Fish shook his head again. 'You will have to go to Amman, Jordan. Arab Wings run charter flights from there to Tehran. That is the best suggestion I can make.'

Sculley shrugged. 'Okay.'

A few minutes later he left Mr Fish and went up to his room to call Dallas.

His first assignment as a member of the rescue team had not gone well.

When Simons got the news he decided to leave the Walther PPKs in Dallas.

He explained his thinking to Coburn. 'Let's not jeopardize the whole mission, right at the start, when we're not even sure we're going to need the handguns: that's a risk we don't have to take, not yet anyway. Let's get in the country and see what we're up against. If and when we need the guns, Schwebach will go back to Dallas and get 'em.'

The guns were put in the EDS vault, together with a tool Simons had ordered for filing off the serial numbers. (Since that was against the law it would not be done until the last possible moment.)

However, they would take the false-bottomed suitcase and do a dry run. They would also take the No 2 shot – Davis would carry it in his beanbag – and the equipment Simons needed for reloading the shot into birdshot cartridges – Simons would carry that himself.

There was now no point in going via Istanbul, so Simons sent Sculley to Paris to book hotel rooms there and try to get reservations for the team on a flight into Tehran.

The rest of the team took off from the Dallas/Fort Worth Regional Airport at 11.05 a.m. on 10 January aboard Braniff flight 341 to Miami, where they transferred to National 4 to Paris.

They met up with Sculley at Orly Airport, in the picture gallery between the restaurant and the coffee shop, the following morning.

Coburn noticed that Sculley was jumpy. Everyone was becoming infected with Simons's security-consciousness, he realized. Coming over from the States, although they had all been on the same plane, they had travelled separately, sitting apart and not acknowledging one another. In Paris Sculley had got nervous about the staff at the Orly Hilton and suspected that someone was listening to his phone calls, so Simons – who was always uneasy in hotels anyway – had decided they would talk in the picture gallery.

Sculley had failed in his second assignment, to get onward reservations from Paris to Tehran for the team. 'Half the airlines have just stopped flying to Iran, because of the political unrest and the strike at the airport,' he said. 'What flights there are, are overbooked with Iranians trying to get home. All I have is a rumour that Swissair are flying in from Zurich.'

They split into two groups. Simons, Coburn, Poché and Boulware would go to Zurich and try for the Swissair flight. Sculley, Schwebach, Davis and Jackson would stay in Paris. Simons's group flew Swissair first class to Zurich. Coburn sat next to Simons. They spent the whole of the flight eating a splendid lunch of shrimp and steak. Simons raved about how good the food was. Coburn was amused, remembering how Simons had said: 'When you're hungry, you open a can.'

At Zurich airport the reservations desk for the Tehran flight was mobbed by Iranians. The team could get only one seat on the plane. Which of them should go? Coburn, they decided. He would be the logistics man. As Director of Personnel and as evacuation mastermind he had the most complete knowledge of EDS resources in Tehran: 150 empty houses and apartments, 60 abandoned cars and jeeps, 200 Iranian employees – those who could be trusted and those who couldn't – and the food, drink and tools left behind by the evacuees. Going in first, Coburn could arrange transport, supplies and a hideout for the rest of the team.

So Coburn said goodbye to his friends and got on the plane, heading for chaos, violence and revolution.

That same day, unknown to Simons and the rescue team, Ross Perot took British Airways flight 172 from New York to London. He, too, was on his way to Tehran.

The flight from Zurich to Tehran was all too short.

Coburn spent the time anxiously running over in his mind the things he had to do. He could not make a list: Simons would not allow anything to be written down.

His first job was to get through customs with the false-bottomed case. There were no guns in it: if the case was inspected and the secret compartment discovered, Coburn was to say that it was for carrying delicate photographic equipment.

Next he had to select some abandoned houses and apartments for Simons to consider as hideouts. Then he had to find cars and make sure there was a supply of gasoline for them.

His cover story, for the benefit of Keane Taylor, Rich Gallagher and EDS's Iranian employees, was that he was arranging shipment of evacuees' personal belongings back to the States. Coburn had told Simons that Taylor ought to be let in on the secret: he would be a valuable asset to the rescue team. Simons had said he would make that decision himself, after meeting Taylor.

Coburn wondered how to hoodwink Taylor.

He was still wondering when the plane landed.

Inside the terminal, all the airport staff were in Army uniforms. That was how the airport had been kept open despite the strike, Coburn realized: the military were running it.

He picked up the suitcase with the false bottom and walked through customs. No one stopped him.

The arrivals hall was a zoo. The waiting crowds were more unruly than ever. The Army was not running the airport on military lines.

He fought his way through the crowd to the cab rank. He skirted two men who appeared to be fighting over a taxi, and took the next in line.

Riding into town, he noticed a good deal of military hardware on the road, especially near the airport. There were many more tanks about than there had been when he left. Was that a sign that the Shah was still in control? In the press the Shah was still talking as if he were in control, but then so was Bakhtiar. So, for that matter, was the Ayatollah, who had just announced the formation of a Council of the Islamic Revolution to take over the government, just as if he were already in power in Tehran instead of sitting in a villa outside Paris at the end of a telephone line. In truth, nobody was in charge; and while that hindered the negotiations for the release of Paul and Bill, it would probably help the rescue team.

The cab took him to the office they called Bucharest, where he found Keane Taylor. Taylor was in charge now, for Lloyd Briggs had gone to New York to brief EDS's lawyers in person. Taylor was sitting at Paul Chiapparone's desk, in an immaculate vested suit, just as if he were a million miles away from the nearest revolution instead of in the middle of it. He was astonished to see Coburn.

'Jay! When the hell did you get here?'

'Just arrived,' Coburn said.

'What's with the beard – you trying to get yourself fired?'

'I thought it might make me look less American here.'

'Did you ever see an Iranian with a ginger beard?'

'No,' Coburn laughed.

'So what are you here for?'

'Well, we're obviously not going to bring our people back in here in the foreseeable future, so I've come to police up everyone's personal belongings to get them shipped back to the States.'

Taylor shot him a funny look but did not comment. 'Where are you going to stay? We've all moved into the Hyatt Crown Regency, it's safer.'

'How about I use your old house?'

'Whatever you say.'

'Now, about these belongings. Do you have those envelopes everyone left, with their house keys and car keys and instructions for disposal of their household goods?'

'I sure do – I've been referring to them. Everything people don't want shipped, I've been selling – washers and dryers, refrigerators: I'm running a permanent garage sale here.'

'Can I have the envelopes?'

'Sure.'

'How's the car situation?'

'We've rounded up most of them. I've got them parked at a school, with some Iranians watching them, if they're not selling them.'

'What about gas?'

'Rich got four 55-gallon drums from the Air Force and we've got them full down in the basement.'

'I thought I smelled gas when I came in.'

'Don't strike a match down there in the dark, we'll all be blown to hell.'

'What do you do about topping up the drums?'

'We use a couple of cars as tankers – a Buick and a Chevy, with big US gas tanks. Two of our drivers spend all day waiting in gas lines. When they get filled up they come back here and we siphon the gas into the drums, then send the cars back to the filling station. Sometimes you can buy gas from the front of the line. Grab someone who's just filled up and offer him ten times the pump price for the gas in his car. There's a whole economy grown up around the gas lines.'

'What about fuel oil for the houses, for heating?'

'I've got a source, but he charges me ten times the old price. I'm spending money like a drunken sailor here.'

'I'm going to need twelve cars.'

'Twelve cars, huh, Jay?'

'That's what I said.'

'You'll have room to stash them, at my house – it's got a big walled courtyard. Would you . . . for any reason . . . like to be able to get the car refuelled without any of the Iranian employees seeing you?'

'I sure would.'

'Just bring an empty car to the Hyatt and I'll swap it for a full one.'

'How many Iranians do we still have?'

'Ten of the best, plus four drivers.'

'I'd like a list of their names.'

'Did you know Ross is on his way in?'

'Shit, no!' Coburn was astonished.

'I just got word. He's bringing Bob Young, from Kuwait, to take over this administrative stuff from me, and John Howell to work on the legal side. They want me to work with John on the negotiations and bail.'

'Is that a fact.' Coburn wondered what was on Perot's mind. 'Okay, I'm taking off for your place.'

'Jay, why don't you tell me what's up?'

'There's nothing I can tell you.'

'Screw you, Coburn. I want to know what's going down.'

'You got all I'm going to tell you.'

'Screw you again. Wait till you see what cars you get – you'll be lucky if they have a steering wheel.'

'Sorry.'

'Jay . . .'

'Yeah?'

'That's the funniest looking suitcase I've ever seen.'

'So it is, so it is.'

'I *know* what you're up to, Coburn.'

Coburn sighed. 'Let's go for a walk.'

They went out into the street, and Coburn told Taylor about the rescue team.

Next day Coburn and Taylor went to work on hideouts.

Taylor's house, No 2 Aftab Street, was ideal. Conveniently close to the Hyatt for switching cars, it was also in the Armenian section of the city, which might be less hostile to Americans if the rioting got worse. It had a working phone and a supply of heating oil. The walled courtyard was big enough to park six cars, and there was a back entrance which could be used as an escape route if a squad of police came to the front door. And the landlord did not live on the premises.

Using the street map of Tehran on the wall of Coburn's office – which had, since the evacuation, been marked with the location of every EDS home in the city – they picked three more empty houses as alternative hideouts.

During the day, as Taylor got the cars gassed up, Coburn drove them one by one from Bucharest to the houses, parking three cars at each of the four locations.

Looking again at his wall map, he tried to recall which of the wives had worked for the American military, for the families with commissary privileges always had the best food. He listed eight likely prospects. Tomorrow he would visit them and pick up canned and dried food and bottled drinks for the hideouts.

He selected a fifth apartment, but did not visit it. It was to be a safe house, a hideout for a serious emergency: no one would go there until it had to be used.

That evening, alone in Taylor's apartment, he called Dallas and asked for Merv Stauffer.

Stauffer was cheerful, as always. 'Hi Jay! How are you?'

'Fine.'

'I'm glad you called, because I have a message for you. Got a pencil?'

'Sure do.'

'Okay. Honky Keith Goofball Zero Honky Dummy—'

'Merv,' Coburn interrupted.

'Yeah?'

'What the hell are you talking about, Merv?'

'It's the code, Jay.'

'What is Honky Keith Goofball?'

'H for Honky, K for Keith—'

'Merv, H is Hotel, K is Kilo . . .'

'Oh!' said Stauffer. 'Oh, I didn't realize you were supposed to use certain particular words . . .'

Coburn started to laugh. 'Listen,' he said, 'get someone to give you the military alphabet before next time.'

Stauffer was laughing to himself. 'I sure will,' he said. 'I guess we'll have to make do with my own version this time, though.'

'Okay, off you go.'

Coburn took down the coded message, then – still using the code – he gave Stauffer his location and phone number. After hanging up, he decoded the message Stauffer had given him.

It was good news. Simons and Joe Poché were arriving in Tehran the next day.

II

By 11 January – the day Coburn arrived in Tehran and Perot flew to London – Paul and Bill had been in jail exactly two weeks.

In that time they had showered once. When the guards learned that there was hot water, they gave each cell five minutes in the showers. Modesty was forgotten as the men crowded into the cubicles for the luxury of being warm and clean for a while. They washed not only themselves but all their clothes as well.

After a week the jail had run out of bottled gas for cooking, so the food, as well as being starchy and short on vegetables, was now cold. Fortunately they were allowed to supplement the diet with oranges, apples and nuts brought in by visitors.

Most evenings the electricity was off for an hour or

two, and then the prisoners would light candles or flashlights. The jail was full of deputy Ministers, government contractors, and Tehran businessmen. Two members of the Empress's Court were in Cell No 5 with Paul and Bill. The latest arrival in their cell was Dr Siazi, who had worked at the Ministry of Health under Dr Sheik as manager of a department called Rehabilitation. Siazi was a psychiatrist, and he used his knowledge of the human mind to boost morale among his fellow prisoners. He was forever dreaming up games and diversions to enliven the dreary routine: he instituted a supper-time ritual whereby everyone in the cell had to tell a joke before they could eat. When he learned the amount of Paul's and Bill's bail he assured them they would have a visit from Farrah Fawcett Majors, whose husband was a mere Six Million Dollar Man.

Paul developed a curiously strong relationship with the 'father' of the cell, the longest resident who by tradition was cell boss. A small man in late middle age, he did what little he could to help the Americans, encouraging them to eat and bribing the guards for little extras for them. He knew only a dozen or so words of English, and Paul spoke little Farsi, but they managed halting conversations. Paul learned that he had been a prominent businessman, owning a construction company and a London hotel. Paul showed him the photographs which Taylor had brought in of Karen and Ann Marie, and the old man learned their names. For all Paul knew, he might have been as guilty as hell of whatever he was accused of; but the concern and warmth he displayed towards the foreigners was enormously heartening.

Paul was also touched by the bravery of his EDS colleagues in Tehran. Lloyd Briggs, who had now gone to New York; Rich Gallagher, who had never left; and Keane Taylor, who had come back; all risked their lives every time they drove through the riots to visit the jail. Each of them also faced the danger that Dadgar might take it into his head to seize them as additional hostages. Paul was particularly grateful when he heard that Bob Young was on his way in, for Bob's wife had a new baby, and this was an especially bad time for him to put himself in danger.

Paul had at first imagined he was going to be released any minute. Now he was telling himself he would get out any day.

One of their cellmates had been let out. He was Lucio Randone, an Italian builder employed by the construction company Condotti d'Acqua. Randone came back to visit, bringing two very large bars of Italian chocolate, and told Paul and Bill that he had talked to the Italian Ambassador in Tehran about them. The Ambassador had promised to see his American counterpart and reveal the secret of getting people out of jail.

But the biggest source of Paul's optimism was Dr Ahmad Houman, the attorney Briggs had retained to replace the Iranian lawyers who had given bad advice on the bail. Houman had visited them during their first week in jail. They had sat in the jail's reception area – not, for some reason, in the visiting room in the low building across the courtyard – and Paul had feared that this would inhibit a frank laywer-client discussion; but Houman was not intimidated by the presence of prison guards. 'Dadgar is trying to make a name for himself,' he had announced.

Could that be it? An over-enthusiastic prosecutor trying to impress his superiors – or perhaps the revolutionaries – with his anti-American diligence?'

'Dadgar's office is very powerful,' Houman went on. 'But in this case he is out on a limb. He did not have cause to arrest you, and the bail is exorbitant.'

Paul began to feel good about Houman. He seemed knowledgeable and confident. 'So what are you going to do?'

'My strategy will be to get the bail reduced.'

'How?'

'First I will talk to Dadgar. I hope I will be able to make him see how outrageous the bail is. But if he remains intransigent, I will go to his superiors in the Ministry of Justice and persuade them to order him to reduce the bail.'

'And how long do you expect that to take?'

'Perhaps a week.'

It was taking more than a week, but Houman had made progress. He had come back to the jail to report that Dadgar's superiors at the Ministry of Justice had agreed to force Dadgar to back down and reduce the bail to a sum EDS could pay easily and swiftly out of funds currently in Iran. Exuding contempt for Dadgar and confidence in himself, he announced triumphantly that everything would be finalized at a second meeting between Paul and Bill and Dadgar on 11 January.

Sure enough, that day Dadgar came to the jail in the afternoon. He wanted to see Paul alone first, as he had before. Paul was in fine spirits as the guard walked him across the courtyard. Dadgar was just an over-enthusiastic prosecutor, he thought, and now he had been slapped down by his superiors and would have to eat humble pie.

Dadgar was waiting, with the same woman translator beside him. He nodded curtly, and Paul sat down, thinking: he doesn't look very humble.

Dadgar spoke in Farsi, and Mrs Nourbash translated: 'We are here to discuss the amount of your bail.'

'Good,' said Paul.

'Mr Dadgar has received a letter on this subject from officials at the Ministry of Health and Social Welfare.'

She began to translate the letter.

The Ministry officials were demanding that bail for the two Americans should be *increased* to twenty-three million dollars – almost double – to compensate for the Ministry's losses since EDS had switched off the computers.

It dawned on Paul that he was *not* going to be released today.

The letter was a put-up job. Dadgar had neatly out-manoeuvred Dr Houman. This meeting was nothing but a charade.

It made him *mad*.

To *hell* with being polite to this bastard, he thought.

When the letter had been read he said: 'Now I have something to say, and I want you to translate every word. Is that clear?'

'Of course,' said Mrs Nourbash.

Paul spoke loudly and clearly. 'You have now held me in jail for fourteen days. I have not been taken before a court. No charges have been brought against me. You have yet to produce a single piece of evidence implicating me in any crime whatsoever. You have not even specified what crime I might be accused of. Are you proud of Iranian justice?'

To Paul's surprise, the appeal seemed to melt Dadgar's icy gaze a little. 'I am sorry,' Dadgar said, 'that you have to be the one to pay for the things your company has done wrong.'

'No, no, no,' Paul said. 'I *am* the company. I am the person responsible. If the company had done wrong I should be the one to suffer. But we have done nothing wrong. In fact we have done far in excess of what we were committed to do. EDS got this contract because we are the only company in the world capable of doing this job – creating a fully automated welfare system in an underdeveloped country of thirty million subsistence farmers. *And we have succeeded.* Our data processing system issues social security cards. It keeps a register of deposits at the bank in the Ministry's account. Every morning it produces a summary of the welfare claims made the previous day. It prints the payroll for the entire Ministry of Health and Social Welfare. It produces weekly and monthly financial reports for the Ministry.

Why don't you go to the Ministry and *look at the printouts?* No, wait a minute,' he said as Dadgar began to speak, 'I haven't finished.'

Dadgar shrugged.

Paul went on: 'There is readily available proof that EDS has fulfilled its contract. It is equally easy to establish that the Ministry has not kept its side of the deal, that is to say, it has not paid us for six months and currently owes us something in excess of ten million dollars. Now, think about the Ministry for a moment. Why hasn't it paid EDS? Because it hasn't got the money. Why not? You and I know it spent its entire budget during the first seven months of the current year and the government hasn't got the funds to top it up. There might well be a degree of incompetence in some departments. What about those people who overspent their budgets? Maybe they're looking for an excuse – someone to blame for what's gone wrong – a scapegoat. And isn't it convenient that they have EDS – a capitalist company, an American company – right in there working with them? In the current political atmosphere, people are eager to hear about the wickedness of the Americans, quick to believe that we are cheating Iran. *You* are not supposed to believe that the Americans are to blame unless there is evidence. Isn't it time you asked yourself *why* anyone should make false accusations against me and my company? *Isn't it time you started to investigate the goddam Ministry?*'

The woman translated the last sentence. Paul studied Dadgar: his expression had frozen again. He said something in Farsi.

Mrs Nourbash translated. 'He will see the other one now.'

Paul stared at her.

He had wasted his breath, he realized. He might just as well have recited nursery rhymes. Dadgar was immovable.

Paul was deeply depressed. He lay on his mattress, looking at the pictures of Karen and Ann Marie which he had stuck on the underside of the bunk above him. He missed the girls badly. Being unable to see them made him realize that in the past he had taken them for granted. Ruthie too. He looked at his watch: it was the middle of the night in the States now. Ruthie would be asleep, alone in a big bed. How good it would be to climb in beside her and hold her in his arms. He put the thought out of his mind: he was just making himself miserable with self-pity. He had no need to worry about them. They were out of Iran, out of danger, and he knew that whatever might happen, Perot would take care of them. That was the good thing about Perot. He asked a lot of you – boy, he was just about the most demanding employer you could have – but when you needed to rely on him, he was like a rock.

Paul lit a cigarette. He had a cold. He could never get warm in the jail. He felt too down to do anything. He did not want to go to the Chattanooga Room and drink tea; he did not want to watch the news in gibberish on TV; he did not want to play chess with Bill. He did not want to go to the library for a new book. He had been reading *The Thorn Birds* by Colleen McCullough. He had found it a very emotional book. It was about several generations of families, and it made him think of his own family. The central character was a priest, and Paul as a Catholic had been able to associate with that. He had read the book three times. He had also read *Hawaii* by James Mitchener, *Airport* by Arthur Hailey, and *The Guinness Book of Records*. He never wanted to read another book for the rest of his life.

Sometimes he thought about what he would do when he got out, and let his mind wander on his favourite pastimes, boating and fishing. But that could be depressing.

He could not remember a time in his adult life when he had been at a loss for something to do. He was always busy. At the office he would typically have three days' work backed up. Never, *never*, did he lie down smoking and wondering how on earth he could keep himself amused.

But the worst thing of all was the helplessness. Although he had always been an employee, going where his boss sent him and doing what he was ordered to do, nevertheless he had always known that he could at any time get on a plane and go home, or quit his job, or say no to his boss. Ultimately the decisions had been his. Now he could not make any decisions about his own life. He could not even do anything about his plight. With every other problem he had ever had, he had been able to work on it, try things, *attack* the problem. Now he just had to sit and suffer.

He realized that he had never known the meaning of freedom until he lost it.

III

The demonstration was relatively peaceful. There were several blazing cars, but otherwise no violence: the demonstrators were marching up and down carrying pictures of Khomeini and putting flowers in the turrets of tanks. The soldiers looked on passively.

The traffic was at a standstill.

It was 14 January, the day after Simons and Poché flew in. Boulware had gone back to Paris, and now he and the other four were waiting there for a flight to Tehran. Meanwhile Simons, Coburn and Poché were heading downtown to reconnoitre the jail.

After a few minutes Joe Poché turned off the car engine and sat there, silent and expressionless as usual.

By contrast Simons, sitting next to him, was animated. 'This is history being made in front of our eyes!' he said. 'Very few people get to observe first hand a revolution in progress.'

He was a history buff, Coburn had gathered, and revolutions were his speciality. Coming through the airport, on being asked what was his occupation and the purpose of his visit, he said he was a retired farmer and this was the only chance he was ever likely to get of seeing a revolution. He had been telling the truth.

Coburn was *not* thrilled to be in the middle of it. He did not enjoy sitting in a little car – they had a Renault

4 – surrounded by excitable Muslim fanatics. Despite his new-grown beard he did not look Iranian. Nor did Poché. Simons did, however: his hair was longer now, he had olive skin and a big nose, and he had grown a white beard. Give him some worry beads and stand him on a corner and nobody would suspect for a minute that he was American.

But the crowd was not interested in Americans, and eventually Coburn became confident enough to get out of the car and go into a baker's shop. He bought barbari bread: long flat loaves with a delicate crust which were baked fresh every day and cost seven rials – ten cents. Like French bread, it was delicious when new but went stale very quickly. It was usually eaten with butter or cheese. Iran was run on barbari bread and tea.

They sat watching the demonstration and chewing on the bread until, at last, the traffic began to move again. Poché followed the route he had mapped out the previous evening. Coburn wondered what they would find when they reached the jail. On Simons's orders he had kept away from downtown until now. It was too much to hope that the jail would be exactly as he had described it eleven days ago at Lake Grapevine: the team had based a very precise attack plan on quite imprecise intelligence. Just how imprecise, they would soon find out.

They reached the Ministry of Justice and drove around to Khayyam Street, the side of the block on which the jail entrance was located.

Poché drove slowly, but not too slowly, past the jail.

Simons said, 'Oh, *shit.*'

Coburn's heart sank.

The jail was radically different from the mental picture he had built up.

The entrance consisted of two steel doors fourteen feet high. On one side was a single-storey building with barbed wire along its roof. On the other side was a taller building of grey stone, five storeys high.

There were no iron railings. There was no courtyard.

Simons said: 'So where's the fucking exercise yard?'

Poché drove on, made a few turns, and came back along Khayyam Street in the opposite direction.

This time Coburn did see a little courtyard with grass and trees, separated from the street by a fence of iron railings twelve feet high; but it plainly had nothing to do with the jail, which was farther up the street. Somehow, in that telephone conversation with Majid, the exercise yard of the jail had got mixed up with this little garden.

Poché made one more pass around the block.

Simons was thinking ahead. 'We can get in there,' he said. 'But we have to know what we'll be up against once we're over the wall. Someone will have to go in and reconnoitre.'

'Who?' said Coburn.

'You,' said Simons.

Coburn walked up to the jail entrance with Rich Gallagher and Majid. Majid pressed the bell and they waited.

Coburn had become the 'outside man' of the rescue

team. He had already been seen at Bucharest by Iranian employees, so his presence in Tehran could not be kept secret. Simons and Poché would stay indoors as much as possible and keep away from EDS premises: nobody need know they were here. It would be Coburn who would go to Hyatt to see Taylor and switch cars. And it was Coburn who went inside the jail.

As he waited he ran over in his mind all the points Simons had told him to watch out for – security, numbers of guards, weaponry, layout of the place, cover, high ground; it was a long list, and Simons had a way of making you anxious to remember every detail of his instructions.

A peephole in the door opened, Majid said something in Farsi.

The door was opened and the three of them went in.

Straight ahead of him Coburn saw a courtyard with a grassed traffic circle and cars parked on the far side. Beyond the cars a building rose five storeys high over the courtyard. To his left was the one-storey building he had seen from the street, with the barbed wire on its roof. To his right was another steel door.

Coburn was wearing a long, bulky down coat – Taylor had dubbed it the Michelin Man coat – under which he could easily have concealed a shotgun, but he was not searched by the guard at the gate. I could have had eight weapons on me, he thought. That was encouraging: security was slack.

He noted that the gate guard was armed with a small pistol.

The three visitors were led into the low building on

the left. The Colonel in charge of the jail was in the visiting room, along with another Iranian. The second man, Gallagher had warned Coburn, was always present during visits, and spoke perfect English: presumably he was there to eavesdrop. Coburn had told Majid he did not want to be overheard while talking to Paul, and Majid agreed to engage the eavesdropper in conversation.

Coburn was introduced to the Colonel. In broken English, the man said he was sorry for Paul and Bill, and he hoped they would be released soon. He seemed sincere. Coburn noted that neither the Colonel nor the eavesdropper was armed.

The door opened, and Paul and Bill walked in.

They both stared at Coburn in surprise – neither of them had been forewarned that he was in town, and the beard was an additional shock.

'What the hell are you doing here?' Bill said, and smiled broadly.

Coburn shook hands warmly with both of them. Paul said: 'Boy, I can't believe you're here.'

'How's my wife?' Bill said.

'Emily's fine, so is Ruthie,' Coburn told them.

Majid started talking loudly in Farsi to the Colonel and the eavesdropper. He seemed to be telling them a complicated story with many gestures. Rich Gallagher began to speak to Bill, and Coburn sat Paul down.

Simons had decided that Coburn should question Paul about routines at the jail, and level with him about the rescue plan. Paul was picked rather than Bill because, in Coburn's opinion, Paul was likely to be the leader of the two.

'If you haven't guessed it already,' Coburn began, 'we're going to get y'all out of here by force if necessary.'

'I guessed it already,' Paul said. 'I'm not sure it's a good idea.'

'What?'

'People might get hurt.'

'Listen, Ross has retained just about the best man in the whole world for this kind of operation, and we have carte blanche—'

'I'm not sure I want it.'

'You ain't being asked for your permission, Paul.'

Paul smiled. 'Okay.'

'Now I need some information. Where do you exercise?'

'Right there in the courtyard.'

'When?'

'Thursdays.'

Today was Monday. The next exercise period would be 18 January. 'How long do you spend out there?'

'About an hour.'

'What time of day?'

'It varies.'

'Shit.' Coburn made an effort to look relaxed, to avoid lowering his voice conspicuously or glancing over his shoulder to see whether anyone might be listening: this had to look like a normal friendly visit. 'How many guards are there in this jail?'

'Around twenty.'

'All uniformed, all armed?'

'All uniformed, some armed with handguns.'

'No rifles?'

'Well ... none of the regular guards have rifles, but ... See, our cell is just across the courtyard and has a window. Well, in the morning there's a group of about twenty different guards, like an elite corps you might say. They have rifles and wear kind of shiny helmets. They have reveille right here, then I never see them for the rest of the day. I don't know where they go.'

'Try and find out.'

'I'll try.'

'Which is your cell?'

'When you go out of here, the window is more or less opposite you. If you start in the right-hand corner of the courtyard and count toward the left, it's the third window. But they close the shutters when there are visitors – so we can't see women coming in, they say.'

Coburn nodded, trying to memorize it all. 'You need to do two things,' he said. 'One: a survey of the inside of the jail, with measurements as accurate as possible. I'll come back and get the details from you so we can draw a plan. Two: get in shape. Exercise daily. You'll need to be fit.'

'Okay.'

'Now, tell me your daily routine.'

'They wake us up at six o'clock,' Paul began.

Coburn concentrated, knowing he would have to repeat all this to Simons. Nevertheless, at the back of his mind one thought nagged: if we don't know what time of day they exercise, how the hell do we know when to go over the wall?

'Visiting time is the answer,' Simons said.

'How so?' Coburn asked.

'It's the one situation when we can *predict* they will be out of the actual jail and vulnerable to a snatch, at a definite moment in time.'

Coburn nodded. The three of them were sitting in the living-room of Keane Taylor's house. It was a big room with a Persian carpet. They had drawn three chairs into the middle, around a coffee table. Beside Simons's chair, a small mountain of cigar ash was growing on the carpet. Taylor would be furious.

Coburn felt drained. Being debriefed by Simons was even more harrowing than he had anticipated. When he was sure he had told everything, Simons thought of more questions. When Coburn could not quite remember something, Simons made him think hard until he did remember. Simons drew from him information he had not consciously registered, just by asking the right questions.

'The van and the ladder – that scenario is out,' Simons said. 'Their weak point now is their loose routine. We can get two men in there as visitors, with shotguns or Walthers under their coats. Paul and Bill would be brought to that visiting area. Our two men should be able to overpower the Colonel and the eavesdropper without any trouble – and without making enough noise to alarm anyone else in the vicinity. Then . . .'

'Then what?'

'That's the problem. The four men would have to come out of the building, cross the courtyard, reach the gate, either open it or climb it, reach the street, and get in a car . . .'

'It sounds possible,' Coburn said. 'There's just one guard at the gate . . .'

'A number of things about this scenario bother me,' Simons said. 'One: the windows in the high building that overlooks the courtyard. While our men are in the courtyard, anyone looking out of any one of the windows will see them. Two: the elite guard with shiny helmets and rifles. Whatever happens, our people have to slow down at the gate. If there's just one guard with a rifle looking out of one of those high windows, he could pick off the four of them like shooting fish in a barrel.'

'We don't know the guards are in the high building.'

'We don't know they're *not*.'

'It seems like a small risk—'

'We're not going to take *any* risks we don't have to. Three: the traffic in this goddam city is a bastard. You just can't talk about jumping in a car and getting away. We could run into a demonstration fifty yards down the street. No. This snatch has got to be *quiet*. We must have *time*. What is that Colonel like, the one in charge of the place?'

'He was quite friendly,' Coburn said. 'He seemed genuinely sorry for Paul and Bill.'

'I wonder whether we can get to him. Do we know anything at all about him?'

'No.'

'Let's find out.'

'I'll put Majid on it.'

'The Colonel would have to make sure there were no guards around at visiting time. We could make it look good by tying him up, or even knocking him out . . . If he can be bribed, we can still bring this thing off.'

'I'll get on it right away,' said Coburn.

IV

On 13 January Ross Perot took off from Amman, Jordan, in a Lear jet of Arab Wings, the charter operation of Royal Jordanian Airlines. The plane headed for Tehran. In the baggage hold was a net bag containing half a dozen professional-sized videotapes, the kind used by television crews: this was Perot's 'cover'.

As the little jet flew east, the British pilot pointed out the junction of the Tigris and Euphrates rivers. A few minutes later the plane developed hydraulic trouble and had to turn back.

It had been that kind of journey.

In London he had caught up with lawyer John Howell and EDS manager Bob Young, both of whom had been trying for days to get a flight into Tehran. Eventually Young discovered that Arab Wings was flying in, and the three men had gone to Amman. Arriving there in the middle of the night had been an experience all on its own: it looked to Perot as if all the bad guys of Jordan were sleeping at the airport. They found a taxicab to take them to a hotel. John Howell's room had no bathroom: the facilities were right there beside the bed. In Perot's room the toilet was so close to the bath that he had to put his feet in the tub when he sat on the john. And like that . . .

Bob Young had thought of the videotapes 'cover'. Arab Wings regularly flew tapes into and out of Tehran for NBC TV News. Sometimes NBC would have its own man to carry the tapes; other times the pilot would take them. Today, although NBC did not know it, Perot would be their bagman. He was wearing a sports jacket, a little plaid hat and no tie. Anyone watching for Ross Perot might not look twice at the regular NBC messenger with his regular net bag.

Arab Wings had agreed to this ruse. They had also confirmed that they could take Perot out again on this NBC tape run.

Back in Amman, Perot, Howell and Young and the pilot boarded a replacement jet and took off again. As they climbed high over the desert Perot wondered whether he was the craziest man in the world or the sanest.

There were powerful reasons why he should not go to Tehran. For one thing, the mobs might consider him the ultimate symbol of bloodsucking American capitalism and string him up on the spot. More likely, Dadgar might get to know that he was in town and try to arrest him. Perot was not sure he understood Dadgar's motives in jailing Paul and Bill, but the man's mysterious purposes would surely be even better served by having Perot behind bars. Why, Dadgar could set bail at a hundred million dollars and feel confident of getting it, if the money was what he was after.

But negotiations for the release of Paul and Bill were stalled, and Perot wanted to go to Tehran to kick ass in one last attempt at a legitimate solution before Simons and the team risked their lives in an assault on the prison.

There had been times, in business, when EDS had been ready to admit defeat but had gone on to victory because Perot himself had insisted on going one more mile. This was what leadership was all about.

That was what he told himself, and it was all true, but there was another reason for his trip. He simply could not sit in Dallas, comfortable and safe, while other people risked their lives on his instructions.

He knew only too well that if he were jailed in Iran he, and his colleagues, and his company, would be in much worse trouble than they were now. Should he do the prudent thing, and stay, he had wondered, or should he follow his deepest instincts, and go? It was a moral dilemma. He had discussed it with his mother.

She knew she was dying. And she knew that, even if Perot should come back alive and well after a few days, she might no longer be there. Cancer was rapidly destroying her body, but there was nothing wrong with her mind, and her sense of right and wrong was as clear as ever. 'You don't have a choice, Ross,' she had said. 'They're your men. You sent them over there. They didn't do anything wrong. Our government won't help them. *You* are responsible for them. It's up to you to get them out. You have to go.'

So here he was, feeling that he was doing the right thing, if not the smart thing.

The Lear jet left the desert behind and climbed over the mountains of western Iran. Unlike Simons and Coburn and Poché, Perot was a stranger to physical danger. He had been too young for World War Two and too old for Vietnam, and the Korean war had finished while Ensign Perot was on his way there aboard the destroyer USS *Sigourney*. He had been shot at just once, during the prisoners-of-war campaign, landing in a jungle in Laos aboard an ancient DC3: he had heard pinging noises but had not realized the aircraft had been hit until after it landed. His most frightening experience, since the days of the Texarkana paper-route thieves, had been in another plane over Laos, when a door right next to his seat fell off. He had been asleep. When he woke up he looked for a light for a second, before realizing he was leaning out of the aircraft. Fortunately he had been strapped in.

He was not sitting next to a door today.

He looked through the window and saw, in a bowl-shaped depression in the mountains, the city of Tehran, a mud-coloured sprawl dotted with white skyscrapers. The plane began to lose height.

Okay, he thought, now we're coming down. It's time to start thinking and using your head, Perot.

As the plane landed he felt tense, wired, alert: he was pumping adrenalin.

The plane taxied to a halt. Several soldiers with machine-guns slung over their shoulders ambled casually across the tarmac.

Perot got out. The pilot opened the baggage hold and handed him the net bag of tapes.

Perot and the pilot walked across the tarmac. Howell and Young followed, carrying their suitcases.

Perot felt grateful for his inconspicuous appearance. He thought of a Norwegian friend, a tall, blond Adonis who complained of looking too impressive. 'You're lucky, Ross,' he would say. 'When you walk into a room no one notices you. When people see me they expect too much – I can't live up to their expectations.' No one would ever take *him* for a messenger boy. But Perot, with his short stature and homely face and off-the-rack clothes, could be convincing in the part.

They entered the terminal. Perot told himself that the military, which was running the airport, and the Ministry of Justice, for which Dadgar worked, were two separate government bureaucracies; and if one of them knew what the other was doing, or whom it was seeking, why, this would have to be the most efficient operation in the history of government.

He walked up to the desk and showed his passport.

It was stamped and handed back to him.

He walked on.

He was not stopped by customs.

The pilot showed him where to leave the bag of television tapes. Perot put them down, then said goodbye to the pilot.

He turned around and saw another tall, distinguished-looking friend: Keane Taylor. Perot liked Taylor.

'Hi, Ross, how did it go?' Taylor said.

'Great,' Perot said with a smile. 'They weren't looking for the ugly American.'

They walked out of the airport. Perot said: 'Are you satisfied that I didn't send you back here for any administrative bullshit?'

'I sure am,' Taylor said.

They got into Taylor's car. Howell and Young got in the back.

As they pulled away, Taylor said: 'I'm going to take an indirect route, to avoid the worst of the riots.'

Perot did not find this reassuring.

The road was lined with tall, half-finished concrete buildings with cranes on top. Work seemed to have stopped. Looking closely, Perot saw that people were living in the shells. It seemed an apt symbol of the way the Shah had tried to modernize Iran too quickly.

Taylor was talking about cars. He had stashed all EDS's cars in a school playground and hired some Iranians to guard them, but he had discovered that the Iranians were busy running a used car lot, selling the damn things.

There were long lines at every gas station, Perot noticed. He found that ironic in a country rich in oil. As well as cars, there were people in the queues, holding cans. 'What are they doing?' Perot asked. 'If they don't have cars, why do they need gas?'

'They sell it to the highest bidder,' Taylor explained. 'Or you can rent an Iranian to stand in line for you.'

They were stopped briefly at a roadblock. Driving on, they passed several burning cars. A lot of civilians were standing around with machine-guns. The scene was peaceful for a mile or two, then Perot saw more burning cars, more machine-guns, another roadblock. Such sights ought to have been frightening, but somehow they were not. It seemed to Perot that the people were just enjoying letting loose for a change, now that the Shah's iron grip was at last being relaxed. Certainly the military was doing nothing to maintain order, as far as he could see.

There was always something weird about seeing violence as a tourist. He recalled flying over Laos in a light plane and watching people fighting on the ground: he had felt tranquil, detached. He supposed that battle was like that: it might be fierce if you were in the middle of it, but five minutes away nothing was happening.

They drove into a huge circle with a monument in its centre that looked like a spaceship of the far future, towering over the traffic on four gigantic splayed legs. 'What is *that*?' said Perot.

'The Shahyad Monument,' Taylor said. 'There's a museum in the top.'

A few minutes later they pulled into the forecourt of the Hyatt Crown Regency. 'This is a new hotel,' Taylor said. 'They've just opened it, poor bastards. It's good for us, though – wonderful food, wine, music in the restaurant in the evenings ... We're living like kings in a city that's falling apart.'

They went into the lobby and took the elevator. 'You don't have to check in,' Taylor told Perot. 'Your suite is in my name. No sense in having your name written down anywhere.'

'Right.'

They got out at the eleventh floor. 'We've all got rooms along this hall,' Taylor said. He unlocked a door at the far end of the corridor.

Perot walked in, glanced around, and smiled. 'Would you look at this?' The sitting room was vast. Next to it was a large bedroom. He looked into the bathroom: it was big enough for a cocktail party.

'Is it all right?' Taylor said with a grin.

'If you'd seen the room I had last night in Amman you wouldn't bother to ask.'

Taylor left him to settle in.

Perot went to the window and looked out. His suite was at the front of the hotel, so he could look down and see the forecourt. I might hope to have a warning, he thought, if a squad of soldiers or a revolutionary mob comes for me.

But what would I do?

He decided to map an emergency escape route. He left his suite and walked up and down the corridor. There were several empty rooms with unlocked doors. At either end was an exit to a staircase. He went down the stairs to the floor below. There were more empty rooms, some without furniture or decoration: the hotel was unfinished, like so many buildings in this town.

I could take this staircase down, he thought, and if I heard them coming up I could duck back into one of the corridors and hide in an empty room. That way I could get to ground level.

He walked all the way down the stairs and explored the ground floor.

He wandered through several banqueting rooms which he supposed were unused most, if not all, of the time. There was a labyrinth of kitchens with a thousand hiding places: he particularly noticed some empty food containers big enough for a small man to climb into. From the banqueting area he could reach the health club at the back of the hotel. It was pretty fancy, with a sauna and a pool. He opened a door at the rear and found himself outside, in the hotel car park. Here he could take an EDS car and disappear into the city, or walk to the next hotel, the Evin; or just run into the forest of unfinished skyscrapers which began on the far side of the car park.

He re-entered the hotel and took the elevator. As he rode up, he resolved always to dress casually in Tehran. He had brought with him khaki pants and some chequered flannel shirts, and he also had a jogging outfit. He could not help looking American, with his pale, clean-shaven face and blue eyes and ultra-short crewcut; but, if he should find himself on the run, he could at least make sure he did not look like an *important* American, much less the multimillionaire owner of Electronic Data Systems Corporation.

He went to find Taylor's room and get a briefing. He wanted to go to the American Embassy and talk to Ambassador Sullivan; he wanted to go to the head-quarters of MAAG, the US Military Assistance and Advisory Group, and see General Huyser and General Gast; he wanted to get Taylor and John Howell hyped up to put a bomb under Dadgar's tail; he wanted to *move*, to *go*, to get this problem *solved*, to get Paul and Bill *out*, and *fast*.

He banged on Taylor's door and walked in. 'Okay, Keane,' he said. 'Bring me up to speed.'

CHAPTER SIX

I

J OHN HOWELL was born in the ninth minute of the ninth hour of the ninth day of the ninth month of 1946, his mother often said.

He was a short, small man with a bouncy walk. His fine light-brown hair was receding early, he had a slight squint, and his voice was faintly hoarse, as if he had a permanent cold. He spoke very slowly and blinked a lot.

Thirty-two years old, he was an associate in Tom Luce's Dallas law firm. Like so many of the people around Ross Perot, Howell had achieved a responsible position at a young age. His greatest asset as a lawyer was stamina: 'John wins by *outworking* the opposition,' Luce would say. Most weekends Howell would spend either Saturday or Sunday at the office, tidying up loose ends, finishing tasks that had been interrupted by the phone, and preparing for the week ahead. He would get frustrated when family activities deprived him of that sixth working day. In addition, he often worked late into the evening and missed dinner at home, which sometimes made his wife Angela unhappy.

Like Perot, Howell was born in Texarkana. Like Perot, he was short in stature and long on guts. Nevertheless, at midday on 14 January he was scared. He was about to meet Dadgar.

The previous afternoon, immediately after arriving in Tehran, Howell had met with Ahmad Houman, EDS's new local attorney. Dr Houman had advised him *not* to meet Dadgar, at least not yet: it was perfectly possible that Dadgar intended to arrest all the EDS Americans he could find, and that might include lawyers.

Howell had found Houman impressive. A big, rotund man in his sixties, well dressed by Iranian standards, he was a former President of the Iran Bar Association. Although his English was not good – French was his second language – he seemed confident and knowledgeable.

Houman's advice gelled with Howell's instinct. He always liked to prepare very thoroughly for any kind of confrontation. He believed in the old maxim of trial lawyers: never ask a question unless you already know the answer.

Houman's advice was reinforced by Bunny Fleischaker. An American girl with Iranian friends in the Ministry of Justice, Bunny had warned Jay Coburn, back in December, that Paul and Bill were going to be arrested, but at the time no one had believed her. Events had given her retrospective credibility, and she was taken seriously when, early in January, she called Rich Gallagher's home at eleven o'clock one evening.

The conversation had reminded Gallagher of the phone calls in the movie *All The President's Men*, in which nervous informants talked to the newspaper reporters

242

in improvised code. Bunny began by saying: 'D'you know who this is?'

'I think so,' Gallagher said.

'You've been told about me.'

'Yes.'

EDS's phones were bugged and the conversations were being taped, she explained. The reason she had called was to say that there was a strong chance Dadgar would arrest more EDS executives. She recommended they either leave the country or move into a hotel where there were lots of newspaper reporters. Lloyd Briggs, who as Paul's No 3 seemed the likeliest target for Dadgar, had left the country – he needed to return to the States to brief EDS's lawyers anyway. The others, Gallagher and Keane Taylor, had moved into the Hyatt.

Dadgar had not arrested any more EDS people – yet.

Howell needed no more convincing. He was going to stay out of Dadgar's way until he was sure of the ground rules.

Then, at eight-thirty this morning, Dadgar had raided Bucharest.

He had turned up with half a dozen investigators and demanded to see EDS's files. Howell, hiding in an office on another floor, had called Houman. After a quick discussion he had advised all EDS personnel to co-operate with Dadgar.

Dadgar had wanted to see Chiapparone's files. The filing cabinet in Paul's secretary's office was locked and nobody could find the key. Of course that made Dadgar all the more keen to see the files. Keane Taylor had solved the problem in characteristically direct fashion: he had got a crowbar and broken the cabinet open.

Meanwhile Howell snuck out of the building, met Dr Houman, and went to the Ministry of Justice.

That too had been scary, for he had been obliged to fight his way through an unruly crowd which was demonstrating, outside the Ministry, against the holding of political prisoners.

Howell and Houman had an appointment with Dr Kian, Dadgar's superior.

Howell told Kian that EDS was a reputable company which had done nothing wrong, and it was eager to cooperate in any investigation in order to clear its name, but it wanted to get its employees out of jail.

Kian said he had asked one of his assistants to ask Dadgar to review the case.

That sounded to Howell like nothing at all.

He told Kian he wanted to talk about a reduction in the bail.

The conversation took place in Farsi, with Houman translating. Houman said that Kian was not inflexibly opposed to a reduction in the bail. In Houman's opinion they might expect it to be halved.

Kian gave Howell a note authorizing him to visit Paul and Bill in jail.

The meeting had been just about fruitless, Howell thought afterwards, but at least Kian had not arrested him.

When he returned to Bucharest he found that Dadgar had not arrested anyone either.

His lawyer's instinct still told him not to see Dadgar; but now that instinct struggled with another side of his personality; impatience. There were times when Howell wearied of research, preparation, foresight, planning – times when he wanted to *move* on a problem instead of thinking about it. He liked to take the initiative, to have the opposition reacting to him, rather than the other way around. This inclination was reinforced by the presence in Tehran of Ross Perot, always up first in the morning, asking people what they had achieved yesterday and what tasks they intended to accomplish today, always on everyone's back. So impatience got the better of caution, and Howell decided to confront Dadgar.

This was why he was scared.

If he was unhappy, his wife was more so.

Angela Howell had not seen much of her husband in the last two months. He had spent most of November and December in Tehran, trying to persuade the Ministry to pay EDS's bill. Since getting back to the States he had been staying at EDS headquarters until all hours of the night, working on the Paul and Bill problem, when he was not dashing off to New York for meetings with Iranian lawyers there. On 31 December Howell had arrived home at breakfast-time, after working all night, at EDS, to find Angela and baby Michael, nine months old, huddled in front of a wood fire in a cold, dark house: the ice storm had caused a power failure. He had moved them into his sister's apartment and gone off to New York again.

Angela had had about as much as she could take, and

when he announced he was going to Tehran again she had been upset. 'You *know* what's going on over there,' she had said. '*Why* do you have to go back?'

The trouble was that he did not have a simple answer to that question. It was not clear just what he was going to do in Tehran. He was going to work on the problem, but he did not know how. If he had been able to say, 'Look, this is what has to be done, and it's my responsibility, and I'm the only one who can do it,' she might have understood.

'John, we're a family. I need your help to take care of all this,' she had said, meaning the ice storm, the blackouts, and the baby.

'I'm sorry. Just do the best you can. I'll try to stay in touch,' Howell had said.

They were not the kind of married couple to express their feelings by yelling at each other. On the frequent occasions when he upset her by working late, leaving her to sit alone and eat the dinner she had fixed for him, a certain coolness was the closest they came to fighting. But this was worse than missing supper: he was abandoning her and the baby just when they needed him.

They had a long talk that evening. At the end of it she was no happier, but she was at least resigned.

He had called her several times since, from London and from Tehran. She was watching the riots on the TV news and worrying about him. She would have been even more worried if she had known what he was about to do now.

He pushed domestic concerns to the back of his mind and went to find Abolhasan.

Abolhasan was EDS's senior Iranian employee. When Lloyd Briggs had departed for New York, Abolhasan had been left in charge of EDS in Iran. (Rich Gallagher, the only American still there, was not a manager.) Then Keane Taylor had returned and assumed overall charge, and Abolhasan had been offended. Taylor was no diplomat. (Bill Gayden had coined the sarcastic phrase 'Keane's Marine Corps sensitivity training'.) There had been friction. But Howell got on fine with Abolhasan, who could translate not just the Farsi language but also Persian customs and methods for his American employers.

Dadgar knew Abolhasan's father, a distinguished lawyer, and had met Abolhasan himself at the interrogation of Paul and Bill, so this morning Abolhasan had been appointed liaison man with Dadgar's investigators, and had been instructed to make sure they had everything they asked for.

Howell said to Abolhasan: 'I've decided I should meet with Dadgar. What do you think?'

'Sure,' Abolhasan said. He had an American wife and spoke English with an American accent. 'I don't think that'll be a problem.'

'Okay. Let's go.'

Abolhasan led Howell to Paul Chiapparone's conference room. Dadgar and his assistants were sitting around the big table, going through EDS's financial records. Abolhasan asked Dadgar to step into the adjoining room, Paul's office; then he introduced Howell.

Dadgar gave a businesslike handshake.

They sat around the table in the corner of the office. Dadgar did not look to Howell like a monster, just a rather weary middle-aged man who was losing his hair.

Howell began by repeating to Dadgar what he had said to Dr Kian: 'EDS is a reputable company which has done nothing wrong, and we are willing to co-operate with your investigation. However, we cannot tolerate having two senior executives in jail.'

Dadgar's answer – translated by Abolhasan – surprised him. 'If you have done nothing wrong, why have you not paid the bail?'

'There's no connection between the two,' Howell said. 'Bail is a guarantee that someone will appear for trial, not a sum to be forfeited if he is guilty. Bail is repaid as soon as the accused man appears in court, regardless of the verdict.' While Abolhasan translated, Howell wondered whether 'bail' was the correct English translation of whatever Farsi word Dadgar was using to describe the $12,750,000 he was demanding. And now Howell recalled something else that might be significant. On the day Paul and Bill were arrested, he had talked on the phone with Abolhasan, who reported that the $12,750,000 was, according to Dadgar, the total amount EDS had been paid to date by the Ministry of Health, and Dadgar's argument had been that if the contract had been corruptly awarded then EDS was not entitled to that money. (Abolhasan had not translated this remark to Paul and Bill at the time.)

In fact EDS had been paid a good deal more than thirteen million dollars, so the remark had not made much sense, and Howell had discounted it. Perhaps that had been a mistake: it might just be that Dadgar's arithmetic was wrong.

Abolhasan was translating Dadgar's reply. 'If the men are innocent, there is no reason why they should not appear for trial, so you would risk nothing by paying the bail.'

'An American corporation can't do that,' Howell said. He was not lying, but he was being deliberately deceitful. 'EDS is a publicly-traded company, and under American securities laws it can only use its money for the benefit of its shareholders. Paul and Bill are free individuals: the company cannot guarantee that they will show up for trial. Consequently we cannot spend the company's money this way.'

This was the initial negotiating position Howell had previously formulated; but as Abolhasan translated he could see it was making little impression on Dadgar.

'Their families have to put up the bail,' he went on. 'Right now they are raising money in the States, but thirteen million dollars is out of the question. Now, if the bail were lowered to a more reasonable figure, they might be able to pay it.' This was all lies, of course: Ross Perot was going to pay the bail, if he had to, and if Tom Walter could find a way to get the money into Iran.

It was Dadgar's turn to be surprised. 'Is it true that you could not force your men to appear for trial?'

'Sure it's true,' Howell said. 'What are we going to do, lock them in chains? We're not a police force. You see, you're holding *individuals* in jail for alleged crimes of a *corporation*.'

249

Dadgar's reply was: 'No, they are in jail for what they have done personally.'

'Which is?'

'They obtained money from the Ministry of Health by means of false progress reports.'

'This obviously cannot apply to Bill Gaylord, because the Ministry had paid none of the bills presented since he arrived in Tehran – so what is he accused of?'

'He falsified reports, and I will not be cross-examined by you, Mr Howell.'

Howell suddenly remembered that Dadgar could put him in jail.

Dadgar went on: 'I am conducting an investigation. When it is complete, I will either release your clients or prosecute them.'

Howell said, 'We're willing to co-operate with your investigation. In the meantime, what can we do to get Paul and Bill released?'

'Pay the bail.'

'And if they are released on bail, will they be permitted to leave Iran?'

'No.'

II

Jay Coburn walked through the double sliding glass doors into the lobby of the Sheraton. On his right was the long registration desk. To his left were the hotel shops. In the centre of the lobby was a couch.

In accordance with his instructions, he bought a

copy of *Newsweek* magazine at the news-stand. He sat on the couch, facing the doors so that he could see everyone who came in, and pretended to read the magazine.

He felt like a character in a spy movie.

The rescue plan was in a holding pattern while Majid researched the Colonel in charge of the jail. Meanwhile Coburn was doing a job for Perot.

He had an assignation with a man nicknamed Deep Throat (after the secretive character who gave 'deep background' to reporter Bob Woodward in *All The President's Men*). This Deep Throat was an American management consultant who gave seminars to foreign corporate executives on how to do business with the Iranians. Before Paul and Bill were arrested, Lloyd Briggs had engaged Deep Throat to help EDS get the Ministry to pay its bills. He had advised Briggs that EDS was in bad trouble, but for a payment of two and a half million dollars they could get the slate wiped clean. At the time EDS had scorned this advice: the government owed money to EDS, not vice versa; it was the Iranians who needed to get the slate wiped clean.

The arrest had given credibility to Deep Throat (as it had to Bunny Fleischaker) and Briggs had contacted him again. 'Well, they're mad at you now,' he had said. 'It's going to be harder than ever, but I'll see what I can do.'

He called back yesterday. He could solve the problem, he said. He demanded a face-to-face meeting with Ross Perot.

Taylor, Howell, Young and Gallagher all agreed there

was *no way* Perot was going to expose himself to such a meeting – they were horrified that Deep Throat even knew Perot was in town. So Perot asked Simons if he could send Coburn instead, and Simons consented.

Coburn had called Deep Throat and said he would be representing Perot.

'No, no,' said Deep Throat, 'it has to be Perot himself.'

'Then all deals are off,' Coburn had replied.

'Okay, okay.' Deep Throat had backed down and given Coburn instructions.

Coburn had to go to a certain phone box in the Vanak area, not far from Keane Taylor's house, at eight p.m.

At exactly eight o'clock the phone in the booth rang. Deep Throat told Coburn to go to the Sheraton, which was nearby, and sit in the lobby reading *Newsweek*. They would meet there and identify one another by a code. Deep Throat would say: 'Do you know where Pahlavi Avenue is?' It was a block away, but Coburn was to reply: 'No, I don't, I'm new in town.'

That was why he felt like a spy in a movie.

On Simons's advice he was wearing his long, bulky down coat, the one Taylor called his Michelin Man coat. The object was to find out whether Deep Throat would frisk him. If not, he would be able, at any future meetings, to wear a recording device under the coat and tape the conversation.

He flicked through the pages of *Newsweek*.

'Do you know where Pahlavi Avenue is?'

Coburn looked up to see a man of about his own

height and weight, in his early forties, with dark slicked-down hair and glasses. 'No, I don't, I'm new in town.'

Deep Throat looked around nervously. 'Let's go,' he said. 'Over there.'

Coburn got up and followed him to the back of the hotel. They stopped in a dark passage. 'I'll have to frisk you,' said Deep Throat.

Coburn raised his arms. 'What are you afraid of?'

Deep Throat gave a scornful laugh. 'You can't trust anyone. There are no rules any more in this town.' He finished his search.

'Do we go back in the lobby now?'

'No. I could be under surveillance – I can't risk being seen with you.'

'Okay. What are you offering?'

Deep Throat gave the same scornful laugh. 'You guys are in *trouble*,' he said. 'You've already messed up once, by refusing to listen to people who *know* this country.'

'How did we mess up?'

'You think this is Texas. It's not.'

'But *how* did we mess up?'

'You could have got out of this for two and a half million dollars. Now it'll cost you six.'

'What's the deal?'

'Just a minute. You let me down last time. This is going to be your last chance. This time, there's no backing out at the last minute.'

Coburn was beginning to dislike Deep Throat. The man was a wise guy. His whole manner said *You're such fools, and I know so much more than you, it's hard for me to descend to your level.*

'Who do we pay the money to?' Coburn asked.

'A numbered account in Switzerland.'

'And how do we know we'll get what we're paying for?'

Deep Throat laughed. 'Listen, the way things work in this country, you don't let go of your money until the goods are delivered. That's the way to get things done here.'

'Okay, so what's the arrangement?'

'Lloyd Briggs meets me in Switzerland and we open an escrow account and sign a letter of agreement which is lodged with the bank. The money is released from the account when Chiapparone and Gaylord get out – which will be immediately, if you'll just let me handle this.'

'Who gets the money?'

Deep Throat shook his head contemptuously.

Coburn said: 'Well, how do we know you really have a deal wired?'

'Look, I'm just passing on information from people close to the person who's causing you a problem.'

'You mean Dadgar?'

'You'll never learn, will you?'

As well as finding out what Deep Throat's proposal was, Coburn had to make a personal evaluation of the man. Well, he had made it now: Deep Throat was full of shit.

'Okay,' Coburn said. 'We'll be in touch.'

*

Keane Taylor poured a little rum into a big glass, added ice, and filled the glass with Coke. This was his regular drink.

Taylor was a big man, six feet two, 210 pounds, with a chest like a barrel. He had played football in the Marines. He took care with his clothes, favouring suits with deep plunging vests and shirts with button-down collars. He wore large gold-rimmed glasses. He was thirty-nine, and losing his hair.

The young Taylor had been a hell-raiser – a dropout from college, busted down from Sergeant in the Marines for disciplinary offences – and he still disliked close supervision. He preferred working in the World subsidiary of EDS because head office was so far away.

He was under close supervision now. After four days in Tehran Ross Perot was savage.

Taylor dreaded the evening debriefing sessions with his boss. After he and Howell had spent the day dashing around the city, fighting the traffic, the demonstrations, and the intransigence of Iranian officialdom, they would then have to explain to Perot why they had achieved precisely nothing.

To make matters worse, Perot was confined to the hotel most of the time. He had gone out only twice: once to the US Embassy and once to US Military Headquarters. Taylor had made sure no one offered him the keys to a car or any local currency, to discourage any impulse Perot might have had to take a walk. But the result was that Perot was like a caged bear, and being debriefed by him was like getting into the cage with the bear.

At least Taylor no longer had to pretend that he did not know about the rescue team. Coburn had taken him to meet Simons, and they had talked for three hours – or rather, Taylor had talked: Simons just asked questions. They had sat in the living-room of Taylor's house, with Simons dropping cigar ash on Taylor's carpet; and Taylor had told him that Iran was like an animal with its head cut off: the head – the Ministers and officials – were still trying to give orders, but the body – the Iranian people – were off doing their own thing. Consequently, political pressure would not free Paul and Bill: they would have to be bailed out or rescued. For three hours Simons had never changed the tone of his voice, never offered an opinion, never even moved from his chair.

But the Simons ice was easier to deal with than the Perot fire. Each morning Perot would knock on the door while Taylor was shaving. Taylor got up a little earlier each day, in order to be ready when Perot came, but Perot got up earlier each day too, until Taylor began to fantasize that Perot listened outside the door all night, waiting to catch him shaving. Perot would be full of ideas which had come to him during the night: new arguments for Paul's and Bill's innocence, new schemes for persuading the Iranians to release them. Taylor and John Howell – the tall and the short, like Batman and Robin – would head off in the Batmobile to the Ministry of Justice or the Ministry of Health, where officials would demolish Perot's ideas in seconds. Perot was still using a legalistic, rational, American approach, and, in

Taylor's opinion, had yet to realize that the Iranians were not playing according to those rules.

This was not all Taylor had on his mind. His wife, Mary, and the children, Mike and Dawn, were staying with his parents in Pittsburgh. Taylor's mother and father were both over eighty, both in failing health. His mother had a heart condition. Mary was having to deal with that on her own. She had not complained, but he could tell, when he talked to her on the phone, that she was not happy.

Taylor sighed. He could not cope with all the world's problems at one time. He topped up his drink, then, carrying the glass, left his room and went to Perot's suite for the evening bloodbath.

Perot paced up and down the sitting-room of his suite, waiting for the negotiating team to gather. He was doing no good here in Tehran and he knew it.

He had suffered a chilly reception at the US Embassy. He had been shown into the office of Charles Naas, the Ambassador's deputy. Naas had been gracious, but had given Perot the same old story about how EDS should work through the legal system for the release of Paul and Bill. Perot had insisted on seeing the Ambassador. He had come halfway round the world to see Sullivan, and he was not going to leave before speaking to him. Eventually Sullivan came in, shook Perot's hand, and told him he was most unwise to come to Iran. It was clear that Perot was a *problem* and Sullivan did not want any more *problems*. He talked for a while, but did not sit down, and he left as soon as he could. Perot was not used to such treatment. He was, after all, an important American, and in normal circumstances a diplomat such as Sullivan would be at least courteous, if not deferential.

Perot also met Lou Goelz, who seemed sincerely concerned about Paul and Bill but offered no concrete help.

Outside Naas's office he ran into a group of military attachés who recognized him. Since the prisoners-of-war campaign Perot had always been able to count on a warm reception from the American military. He sat down with the attachés and told them his problem. They said candidly that they could not help. 'Look, forget what you read in the paper, forget what the State Department is saying publicly,' one of them told him. 'We don't have any power here, we don't have any control – you're wasting your time in the US Embassy.'

Perot had also wasted his time at US Military Headquarters. Cathy Gallagher's boss, Colonel Keith Barlow, chief of the US Support Activity Command in Iran, had sent a bulletproof car to the Hyatt. Perot had got in with Rich Gallagher. The driver had been Iranian: Perot wondered which side he was on.

They met with Air Force General Phillip Gast, chief of the US Military Assistance Advisory Group (MAAG) in Iran, and General 'Dutch' Huyser. Perot knew Huyser slightly, and remembered him as a strong, dynamic man; but now he looked drained. Perot knew from the newspapers that Huyser was President Carter's emissary, here to persuade the Iranian military to back the doomed Bakhtiar government; and Perot guessed that Huyser had no stomach for the job.

Huyser candidly said he would like to help Paul and Bill but at the moment he had no leverage with the Iranians: he had nothing to trade. Even if they got out of jail, Huyser said, they would be in danger here. Perot told them he had that taken care of: Bull Simons was here to look after Paul and Bill once they got out. Huyser burst out laughing, and a moment later Gast saw the joke: they knew who Simons was, and they knew he would be planning more than a babysitting job.

Gast offered to supply fuel to Simons, but that was all. Warm words from the military, cold words from the Embassy; little or no real help from either. And nothing but excuses from Howell and Taylor.

Sitting in a hotel room all day was driving Perot crazy. Today Cathy Gallagher had asked him to take care of her poodle, Buffy. She made it sound like an honour – a measure of her high esteem for Perot – and he had been so surprised that he had agreed. Sitting looking at the animal, he had realized that this was a funny occupation for the leader of a major international business, and he wondered how the hell he had let himself be talked into it. He got no sympathy from Keane Taylor, who thought it was funny as hell. After a few hours Cathy had come back from the hairdresser's or wherever she had been, and had taken the dog back; but Perot's mood remained black.

There was a knock at Perot's door, and Taylor came

in, carrying his usual drink. He was followed by John Howell, Rich Gallagher and Bob Young. They all sat down.

'Now,' said Perot, 'did you tell them that we'd guarantee to produce Paul and Bill for questioning anywhere in the US or Europe, on thirty days' notice, at any time in the next two years?'

'They're not interested in that idea,' said Howell.

'What do you mean, they're not interested?'

'I'm just telling you what they said—'

'But if this is an investigation, rather than a blackmail attempt, all they need is to be sure that Paul and Bill will be available for questioning.'

'They're sure already. I guess they see no reason to make changes.'

It was maddening. There seemed no way to reason with the Iranians, no way to reach them. 'Did you suggest they release Paul and Bill into the custody of the US Embassy?'

'They turned that down, too.'

'Why?'

'They didn't say.'

'Did you ask them?'

'Ross, they don't have to give reasons. They're in charge here, and they know it.'

'But they're responsible for the safety of their prisoners.'

'It's a responsibility that doesn't seem to weigh too heavily on them.'

Taylor said: 'Ross, they're not playing to our rules.

Putting two men in jail is not a big deal to them. Paul and Bill's safety is not a big deal—'

'So what rules are they playing to? Can you tell me that?'

There was a knock on the door and Coburn walked in, wearing his Michelin Man coat and his black knit hat. Perot brightened: perhaps he would have good news. 'Did you meet with Deep Throat?'

'Sure did,' said Coburn, taking off his coat.

'All right, let's have it.'

'He says he can get Paul and Bill released for six million dollars. The money would be paid into an escrow account in Switzerland and released when Paul and Bill leave Iran.'

'Hell, that ain't bad,' said Perot. 'We get out with fifty cents on the dollar. Under US law it would even be legal – it's a ransom. What kind of guy is Deep Throat?'

'I don't trust the bastard,' said Coburn.

'Why?'

Coburn shrugged. 'I don't know, Ross . . . He's shifty, flaky . . . A bullshitter . . . I wouldn't give him sixty cents to go to the store and get me a pack of cigarettes. That's my gut feeling.'

'But, listen, what do you expect?' Perot said. 'This is bribery – pillars of the community don't get involved in this kind of thing.'

Howell said: 'You *said* it. This is bribery.' His deliberate, throaty voice was unusually passionate. 'I don't like this one bit.'

'I don't *like* it,' Perot said. 'But you've all been telling me that the Iranians aren't playing to our rules.'

'Yes, but *listen*,' Howell said fervently. 'The straw I've been clinging to all through this is that *we've done nothing wrong* – and someday, somehow, somewhere, somebody is going to recognize that, and then all this will evaporate . . . I'd *hate* to give up that straw.'

'It hasn't got us far.'

'Ross, I believe that with time and patience we will succeed. But if we get involved in bribery we no longer have a case!'

Perot turned to Coburn. 'How do we *know* Deep Throat has a deal wired with Dadgar?'

'We don't know,' Coburn said. 'His argument is, we don't pay until we get results, so what do we have to lose?'

'Everything,' Howell said. 'Never mind what is legal in the United States, this could seal our fate in Iran.'

Taylor said: 'It stinks. The whole thing stinks.'

Perot was surprised by their reactions. He, too, hated the idea of bribery, but he was prepared to compromise his principles to get Paul and Bill out of jail. The good name of EDS was precious to him, and he was loath to let it be associated with corruption, just as John Howell was; but Perot knew something Howell did not know: that Colonel Simons and the rescue team faced risks more grave than this.

Perot said: 'Our good name hasn't done Paul and Bill any good so far.'

'It's not just our good name,' Howell persisted. 'Dadgar must be pretty sure by now that we aren't guilty of corruption – but if he could catch us in a bribe situation he could still save face.'

That was a point, Perot thought. 'Could this be a trap?'

'Yes!'

It made sense. Unable to get any evidence against Paul and Bill, Dadgar pretends to Deep Throat that he can be bribed, then – when Perot falls for it – announces to the world that EDS is, after all, corrupt. Then they would all be put in jail with Paul and Bill. And, being guilty, they would stay there.

'All right,' said Perot reluctantly. 'Call Deep Throat and tell him no, thanks.'

Coburn stood up. 'Okay.'

It had been another fruitless day, Perot thought. The Iranians had him all ways. Political pressure they ignored. Bribery could make matters worse. If EDS paid the bail, Paul and Bill would still be kept in Iran.

Simons's team still looked like the best bet.

But he was not going to tell the negotiating team that.

'All right,' he said. 'We'll just try again tomorrow.'

III

Tall Keane Taylor and short John Howell, like Batman and Robin, tried again on 17 January. They drove to the Ministry of Health building on Eisenhower Avenue, taking Abolhasan as interpreter, and met Dadgar at 10 a.m. With Dadgar were officials of the Social Security Organization, the department of the Ministry which was run by EDS's computers.

Howell had decided to abandon his initial negotiating position, that EDS could not pay the bail because of American securities law. It was equally useless to demand to know the charges against Paul and Bill and what evidence there was: Dadgar could stonewall that approach by saying he was still investigating. But Howell did not have a new strategy to replace the old. He was playing poker with no cards in his hand. Perhaps Dadgar would deal him some today.

Dadgar began by explaining that the staff of the Social Security Organization wanted EDS to turn over to them what was known as the 125 Data Centre.

This small computer, Howell recalled, ran the payroll and pensions for the Social Security Organization staff. What these people wanted was to get their own wages, even while Iranians generally were not getting their social security benefits.

Keane Taylor said: 'It's not that simple. Such a turnover would be a very complex operation needing many skilled staff. Of course they are all back in the States.'

Dadgar replied: 'Then you should bring them back in.'

'I'm not that stupid,' Taylor said.

Taylor's Marine Corps sensitivity training was operating, Howell thought.

Dadgar said: 'If he speaks like that he will go to jail.'

'Just like my staff would if I brought them back to Iran,' said Taylor.

Howell broke in. 'Would you be able to give a legal

guarantee that any returning staff would not be arrested or harassed in any way?'

'I could not give a formal guarantee,' Dadgar replied. 'However, I would give my personal word of honour.'

Howell darted an anxious glance at Taylor. Taylor did not speak, but his expression said he would not give two cents for Dadgar's word of honour. 'We could certainly investigate ways of arranging the turnover,' Howell said. Dadgar had at last given him something to bargain with, even though it was not much. 'There would have to be safeguards, of course. For example, you would have to certify that the machinery was handed over to you in a good condition . . .' Howell was shadowboxing. If the data centre was handed over, there would be a price: the release of Paul and Bill.

Dadgar demolished that idea with his next sentence. 'Every day new complaints are being made about your company to my investigators, complaints which would justify increases in the bail. However, if you co-operate in the turnover of the 125 Data Centre, I can in return ignore the new complaints and refrain from increasing the bail.'

Taylor said: 'Goddam it, this is nothing but blackmail!'

Howell realized that the 125 Data Centre was a sideshow. Dadgar had raised the question, no doubt at the urging of these officials, but he did not care about it enough to offer serious concessions. So what *did* he care about?

Howell thought of Lucio Randone, the former cellmate of Paul and Bill. Randone's offer of help had been followed up by EDS manager Paul Bucha, who had gone to Italy to talk to Randone's company, Condotti d'Acqua. Bucha reported that the company had been building apartment blocks in Tehran when their Iranian financiers ran out of money. The company naturally stopped building; but many Iranians had already paid for apartments under construction. Given the present atmosphere it was not surprising that the foreigners got blamed, and Randone had been jailed as a scapegoat. The company had found a new source of finance and resumed building, and Randone had got out of jail at the same time, in a package deal arranged by an Iranian lawyer, Ali Azmayesh. Bucha also reported that the Italians kept saying: 'Remember, Iran will always be Iran, it never changes.' He took this to be a hint that a bribe was part of the package deal. Howell also knew that a traditional channel for paying a bribe was a lawyer's fee: the lawyer would do, say a thousand dollars' worth of work and pay a ten-thousand-dollar bribe, then charge his client eleven thousand dollars. This hint of corruption made Howell nervous, but despite that he had gone to see Azmayesh, who had advised him: 'EDS does not have a legal problem, it has a business problem.' If EDS could come to a business arrangement with the Ministry of Health, Dadgar would go away. Azmayesh had not mentioned bribery.

All this had started, Howell thought, as a business problem: the customer unable to pay, the supplier refusing to go on working. Might a compromise be possible, under which EDS would switch on the computers and the Ministry would pay at least some money? He decided to ask Dadgar directly.

'Would it help if EDS were to renegotiate its contract with the Ministry of Health?'

'This might be very helpful,' Dadgar answered. 'It would not be a legal solution to our problem, but it might be a practical solution. Otherwise, to waste all the work that has been done in computerizing the Ministry would be a pity.'

Interesting, thought Howell. They want a modern social security system – or their money back. Putting Paul and Bill in jail on thirteen million dollars bail was their way of giving EDS those two options – and no others. We're getting straight talk, at last.

He decided to be blunt. 'Of course, it would be out of the question to begin negotiations while Chiapparone and Gaylord are still in jail.'

Dadgar replied: 'Still, if you commit to good-faith negotiations, the Ministry will call me and the charges might be changed, the bail might be reduced, and Chiapparone and Gaylord might even be released on their personal guarantees.'

Nothing could be plainer than that, Howell thought. EDS had better go see the Minister of Health.

Since the Ministry stopped paying its bills there had been two changes of government. Dr Sheikholeslamizadeh, who was now in jail, had been replaced by a general; and then, when Bakhtiar became Prime Minister, the general had in turn been replaced by a new

Minister of Health. Who, Howell wondered, was the new guy; and what was he like?

'Mr Young, of the American company EDS, is calling you, Minister,' said the secretary.

Dr Razmara took a deep breath. 'Tell him that American businessmen may no longer pick up the phone and call Ministers of the Iranian government and expect to talk to us as if we were their employees,' he said. He raised his voice. 'Those days are over!'

Then he asked for the EDS file.

Manuchehr Razmara had been in Paris over Christmas. French-educated – he was a cardiologist – and married to a Frenchwoman, he considered France his second home, and spoke fluent French. He was also a member of the Iranian National Medical Council and a friend of Shahpour Bakhtiar, and when Bakhtiar had become Prime Minister he had called his friend Razmara in Paris and asked him to come home to be Minister of Health.

The EDS file was handed to him by Dr Emrani, the Deputy Minister in charge of social security. Emrani had survived the two changes of government: he had been here when the trouble had started.

Razmara read the file with mounting anger. The EDS project was insane. The basic contract price was forty-eight million dollars, with escalators taking it up to a possible ninety million. Razmara recalled that Iran had twelve thousand working doctors to serve a population of thirty-two million, and that there were sixty-four thousand villages without tap water; and he concluded that whoever had signed the deal with EDS were fools or traitors, or both. How could they *possibly* justify spending millions on computers when the people lacked the fundamental necessities of public health like clean water? There could only be one explanation: they had been bribed.

Well they would suffer. Emrani had prepared this dossier for the special court which prosecuted corrupt civil servants. Three people were in jail: former Minister Sheikholeslamizadeh and two of his Deputy Ministers, Reza Neghabat and Nili Arame. That was as it should be. The blame for the mess they were in should fall primarily on Iranians. However, the Americans were also culpable. American businessmen and their government had encouraged the Shah in his mad schemes, and had taken their profits: now they must suffer. Furthermore, according to the file, EDS had been spectacularly incompetent: the computers were not yet working, after two and a half years, yet the automation project had so disrupted Emrani's department that the old-fashioned systems were not working either, with the result that Emrani could not monitor his department's expenditure. This was a principal cause of the Ministry's overspending its budget, the file said.

Razmara noted that the US Embassy was protesting about the jailing of the two Americans, Chiapparone and Gaylord, because there was no evidence against them. That was typical of the Americans. Of course there was no proof: bribes were not paid by cheque. The Embassy was also concerned for the safety of the two prisoners. Razmara found this ironic. *He* was concerned for *his* safety. Each day when he went to the office he wondered whether he would come home alive.

He closed the file. He had no sympathy for EDS or its jailed executives. Even if he had wanted to have them released, he would not have been able to, he reflected. The anti-American mood of the people was rising to fever pitch. The government of which Razmara was a part, the Bakhtiar regime, had been installed by the Shah and was therefore widely suspected of being pro-American. With the country in such turmoil, any Minister who concerned himself with the welfare of a couple of greedy American capitalist lackeys would be sacked if not lynched – and quite rightly. Razmara turned his attention to more important matters.

The next day his secretary said: 'Mr Young, of the American company EDS, is here asking to see you, Minister.'

The arrogance of the Americans was infuriating. Razmara said: 'Repeat to him the message I gave you yesterday – then give him five minutes to get off the premises.'

IV

For Bill, the big problem was time.

He was different from Paul. For Paul – restless, aggressive, strong-willed, ambitious – the worst of being in jail was the helplessness. Bill was more placid by nature: he accepted that there was nothing to do but pray, so he prayed. (He did not wear his religion on his sleeve: he did his praying late at night, before going to sleep, or early in the morning before the others woke up.) What got to Bill was the excruciating slowness with which time passed. A day in the real world – a day of solving problems, making decisions, taking phone calls, and attending meetings – was no time at all: a day in jail was endless. Bill devised a formula for conversion of real time to jail time.

Real Time		Jail Time
1 Second	=	1 Minute
1 Minute	=	1 Hour
1 Hour	=	1 Day
1 Week	=	1 Month
1 Month	=	1 Year

Time took on this new dimension for Bill after two or three weeks in jail, when he realized there was going to be no quick solution to the problem. Unlike a convicted criminal, he had not been sentenced to ninety days or five years, so he could gain no comfort from scratching a calendar on the wall as a countdown to freedom. It made no difference how many days had passed: his remaining time in jail was indefinite, therefore endless.

His Persian cellmates did not seem to feel this way. It was a revealing cultural contrast: the Americans, trained to get fast results, were tortured by suspense; the Iranians were content to wait for '*fardah*', tomorrow, next week, sometime, eventually – just as they had been in business.

Nevertheless, as the Shah's grip weakened Bill thought he saw signs of desperation in some of them, and he came to mistrust them. He was careful not to tell them who was in town from Dallas or what progress was being made in the negotiations for his release: he was afraid that, clutching at straws, they would have tried to trade information to the guards.

He was becoming a well-adjusted jailbird. He learned to ignore dirt and bugs, and he got used to cold, starchy unappetizing food. He learned to live within a small, clearly defined personal boundary, the prisoner's 'turf'. He stayed active.

He found ways to fill the endless days. He read books, taught Paul chess, exercised in the hall, talked to the Iranians to get every word of the radio and TV news, and prayed. He made a minutely detailed survey of the jail, measuring the cells and the corridors and drawing plans and sketches. He kept a diary, recording every trivial event of jail life, plus everything his visitors told him and all the news. He used initials instead of names and sometimes put in invented incidents or altered versions of real incidents, so that if the diary were confiscated or read by the local authorities it would confuse them.

Like prisoners everywhere, he looked forward to visitors as eagerly as a child waiting for Christmas. The EDS people brought decent food, warm clothing, new books, and letters from home. One day Keane Taylor brought a picture of Bill's six-year-old son, Christopher, standing in front of the Christmas tree. Seeing his little boy, even in a photograph, gave Bill strength: a powerful reminder of what he had to hope for, it renewed his resolve to hang on and not despair.

Bill wrote letters to Emily and gave them to Keane, who would read them to her over the phone. Bill had known Keane for ten years, and they were quite close – they had lived together after the evacuation. Bill knew that Keane was not as insensitive as his reputation would indicate – half of that was an act – but still it was embarrassing to write 'I love you' knowing that Keane would be reading it. Bill got over the embarrassment, because he wanted very badly to tell Emily and the children how much he loved them, just in case he never got another chance to say it in person. The letters were like those written by pilots on the eve of a dangerous mission.

The most important gift brought by the visitors was news. The all-too-brief meetings in the low building across the courtyard were spent discussing the various efforts being made to get Paul and Bill out. It seemed to Bill that time was the key factor. Sooner or later, one approach or another had to work. Unfortunately, as time passed, Iran went downhill. The forces of the revolution were gaining momentum. Would EDS get Paul and Bill out before the whole country exploded?

It was increasingly dangerous for the EDS people to come to the south of the city, where the jail was. Paul and Bill never knew when the next visit would come, or whether there would be a visit. As four days went by, then five, Bill would wonder whether all the others had gone back to the United States and left him and Paul behind. Considering that the bail was impossibly high, and the streets of Tehran impossibly dangerous, might they all give up Paul and Bill as a lost cause? They might be forced, against their wills, to leave in order to save their own lives. Bill recalled the American withdrawal from Vietnam, with the last Embassy officials being lifted off the roofs by helicopter; and he could imagine the scene repeated at the US Embassy in Tehran.

He was occasionally reassured by a visit from an Embassy official. They, too, were taking a risk in coming, but they never brought any hard news about Government efforts to help Paul and Bill, and Bill came to the conclusion that the State Department was inept.

Visits from Dr Houman, their Iranian attorney, were at first highly encouraging; but then Bill realized that in typically Iranian fashion Houman was promising much and producing little. The fiasco of the meeting with Dadgar was desperately depressing. It was frightening to see how easily Dadgar out-manoeuvred Houman, and how determined Dadgar was to keep Paul and Bill jailed. Bill had not slept that night.

When he thought about the bail he found it staggering. No one had ever paid that much ransom, anywhere in the world. He recalled news stories about American businessmen kidnapped in South America and held for a million or two million dollars. (They were usually killed.) Other kidnappings, of millionaires, politicians and celebrities had involved demands for three or four million – never thirteen. No one would pay that much for Paul and Bill.

Besides, even that much money would not buy them the right to leave the country. They would probably be kept under house arrest in Tehran, while the mobs took over. Bail sometimes seemed more like a trap than a way of escape. It was a catch-22.

The whole experience was a lesson in values. Bill learned that he could do without his fine house, his cars, fancy food, and clean clothes. It was no big deal to be living in a dirty room with bugs crawling across the walls. Everything he had in life had been stripped away, and he discovered that the only thing he cared about was his family. When you got right down to it, that was all that really counted: Emily, Vicki, Jackie, Jenny and Chris.

Coburn's visit had cheered him a little. Seeing Jay in that big down coat and woollen hat, with a growth of red beard on his chin, Bill had guessed that he was not in Tehran to work through legal channels. Coburn had spent most of the visit with Paul, and if Paul had learned more, he had not passed it on to Bill. Bill was content: he would find out as soon as he needed to know.

But the day after Coburn's visit there was bad news. On 16 January the Shah left Iran.

The television set in the hall of the jail was switched on, exceptionally, in the afternoon. Paul and Bill, with all the other prisoners, watched the little ceremony in the Imperial Pavilion at Mehrabad Airport. There was the Shah, with his wife, three of his four children, his mother-in-law, and a crowd of courtiers. There, to see them off, was Prime Minister Shahpour Bakhtiar, and a crowd of generals. Bakhtiar kissed the Shah's hand, and the royal party went out to the airplane.

The Ministry people in the jail were gloomy: most of

them had been friends, of one kind or another, with the royal family or its immediate circle. Now their patrons were leaving: it meant, at the very least, that they had to resign themselves to a long stay in jail. Bill felt that the Shah had taken with him the last chance of a pro-American outcome in Iran. Now there would be more chaos and confusion, more danger to all Americans in Tehran – and less chance of a swift release for Paul and Bill.

Soon after the television showed the Shah's jet rising into the sky, Bill began to hear a background noise, like a distant crowd, from outside the jail. The noise quickly grew to a pandemonium of shouting and cheering and hooting of horns. The TV showed the source of the noise: a crowd of hundreds of thousands of Iranians was surging through the streets, yelling: '*Shah raft!*' The Shah has gone! Paul said it reminded him of the New Year's Day Parade in Philadelphia. All cars were driving with their headlights on and most were hooting continuously. Many drivers pulled their windscreen wipers forward, attached rags to them, and turned them on, so that they swayed from side to side, permanent mechanical flag-wavers. Truck-loads of jubilant youths careered around the streets celebrating, and all over the city crowds were pulling down and smashing statues of the Shah. Bill wondered what the mobs would do next. This led him to wonder what the guards and the other prisoners would do next. In the hysterical release of all this pent-up Iranian emotion, would Americans become targets?

He and Paul stayed in their cell for the rest of the day, trying to be inconspicuous. They lay on their bunks, talking desultorily. Paul smoked. Bill tried not to think about the terrifying scenes he had watched on TV, but the roar of that lawless multitude, the collective shout of revolutionary triumph, penetrated the prison walls and filled his ears, like the deafening crack and roll of nearby thunder a moment before the lightning strikes.

Two days later, on the morning of 18 January, a guard came to Cell No 5 and said something in Farsi to Reza Neghabat, the former Deputy Minister. Neghabat translated to Paul and Bill: 'You must get your things together. They are moving you.'

'Where to?' Paul asked.

'To another jail.'

Alarm bells rang in Bill's mind. What kind of jail were they going to? The kind where people were tortured and killed? Would EDS be told where they had gone, or would the two of them simply disappear? This place was not wonderful, but it was the devil they knew.

The guard spoke again, and Neghabat said: 'He tells you not to be concerned, this is for your own good.'

It was the work of minutes to put together their toothbrushes, their shared shaver, and their few spare clothes. Then they sat and waited – for three hours.

It was unnerving. Bill had got used to this jail, and – despite his occasional paranoia – basically he trusted his cellmates. He feared the change would be for the worse.

Paul asked Neghabat to try to get news of the move to EDS, maybe by bribing the Colonel in charge of the jail.

The cell father, the old man who had been so concerned for their welfare, was upset that they were leaving. He watched sadly as Paul took down the pictures of Karen and Ann Marie. Impulsively, Paul gave the photographs to the old man, who was visibly moved and thanked him profusely.

At last they were taken out into the courtyard and herded on to a minibus, along with half a dozen other prisoners from different parts of the jail. Bill looked around at the others, trying to figure out what they had in common. One was a Frenchman. Were all the foreigners being taken to a jail of their own, for their safety? But another was the burly Iranian who had been boss of the downstairs cell where they had spent their first night – a common criminal, Bill assumed.

As the bus pulled out of the courtyard, Bill spoke to the Frenchman. 'Do you know where we're going?'

'I am to be released,' the Frenchman said.

Bill's heart leaped. This was good news! Perhaps they were all to be released.

He turned his attention to the scene in the streets. It was the first time for three weeks he had seen the outside world. The government buildings all around the Ministry of Justice were damaged: the mobs really had run wild. Burned cars and broken windows were everywhere. The streets were full of soldiers and tanks but they were doing nothing, not maintaining order, not even controlling the traffic. It seemed to Bill only a matter of time before the weak Bakhtiar government would be overthrown.

What had happened to the EDS people – Taylor, Howell, Young, Gallagher and Coburn? They had not appeared at the jail since the Shah left. Had they been forced to flee, to save their own lives? Somehow Bill was sure they were still in town, still trying to get him and Paul out of jail. He began to hope that this transfer had been arranged by them. Perhaps, instead of taking the prisoners to a different jail, the bus would divert and take them to the US air base. The more he thought about it, the more he believed that everything had been arranged for their release. No doubt the American Embassy had realized, since the departure of the Shah, that Paul and Bill were in serious danger, and had at last got on the case with some real diplomatic muscle. The bus ride was a ruse, a cover story to get them out of the Ministry of Justice jail without arousing the suspicion of hostile Iranian officials such as Dadgar.

The bus was heading north. It passed through districts with which Bill was familiar, and he began to feel safer as the turbulent south of the city receded behind him.

Also, the air base was to the north.

The bus entered a wide square dominated by a huge structure like a fortress. Bill looked interestedly at the building. Its walls were about twenty-five feet high and dotted with guard towers and machine-gun emplacements. The square was full of Iranian women in chadors, the traditional black robes, all making a heck of a noise. Was this some kind of palace, or mosque? Or perhaps a military base?

The bus approached the fortress and slowed down.

Oh, *no*.

A pair of huge steel doors were set centrally in the front. To Bill's horror, the bus drove up and stopped with its nose to the gateway.

This awesome place was the new prison, the new nightmare.

The gates opened and the bus entered.

They were not going to the air base, EDS had not arranged a deal, the Embassy had not got moving, they were not going to be released.

The bus stopped again. The steel doors closed behind it and a second pair of doors opened in front. The bus passed through and stopped in a massive compound dotted with buildings. A guard said something in Farsi, and all the prisoners stood up to get off the bus.

Bill felt like a disappointed child. Life is rotten, he thought. What did I do to deserve this?

What did I do?

'Don't drive so fast,' said Simons.

Joe Poché said: 'Do I drive unsafe?'

'No, I just don't want you violating the laws.'

'What laws?'

'Just be careful.'

Coburn interrupted: 'We're there.'

Poché stopped the car.

They all looked across the heads of the weird women in black and saw the vast fortress of Gasr Prison.

'Jesus Christ,' said Simons. His deep, rough voice was tinged with awe. 'Just look at that bastard.'

They all stared at the high walls, the enormous gates, the guard towers and the machine-gun nests.

Simons said: 'That place is worse than the Alamo.'

It dawned on Coburn that their little rescue team could not attack this place, not without the help of the entire US Army. The rescue they had planned so carefully and rehearsed so many times was now completely irrelevant. There would be no modifications or improvements to the plan, no new scenarios; the whole idea was dead.

They sat in the car for a while, each with his own thoughts.

'Who are those women?' Coburn wondered aloud.

'They have relatives in the jail,' Poché explained.

Coburn could hear a peculiar noise. 'Listen,' he said. 'What *is* that?'

'The women,' said Poché. 'Wailing.'

Colonel Simons had looked up at an impregnable fortress once before.

He had been Captain Simons then, and his friends had called him Art, not Bull.

It was October 1944. Art Simons, twenty-six years old, was commander of Company B, 6th Ranger Infantry Battalion. The Americans were winning the war in the Pacific, and were about to attack the Philippine Islands.

Ahead of the invading US forces, the 6th Rangers were already there, committing sabotage and mayhem behind enemy lines.

Company B landed on Homonhon Island in the Leyte Gulf and found there were no Japanese on the island. Simons raised the Stars and Stripes on a coconut palm in front of two hundred docile natives.

That day a report came in that the Japanese garrison on nearby Suluan Island was massacring civilians. Simons requested permission to take Suluan. Permission was refused. A few days later he asked again. He was told that no ships could be spared to transport Company B across the water. Simons asked permission to use native transportation. This time he got the okay.

Simons commandeered three native sailboats and eleven canoes and appointed himself Admiral of the Fleet. He sailed at two a.m. with eighty men. A storm blew up, seven of the canoes capsized, and Simons's fleet returned to shore with most of the navy swimming.

They set off again the next day. This time they sailed by daylight, and – since Japanese planes still controlled the air – the men stripped off and concealed their uniforms and equipment in the bottoms of the boats, so that they would look like native fishermen. The ruse worked, and Company B made landfall on Suluan Island. Simons immediately reconnoitred the Japanese garrison.

That was when he looked up at an impregnable fortress.

The Japanese were garrisoned at the south end of the

island, in a lighthouse at the top of a three-hundred-foot coral cliff.

On the west side a trail led half way up the cliff to a steep flight of steps cut into the coral. The entire stairway and most of the trail were in full view of the sixty-foot lighthouse tower and three west-facing buildings on the lighthouse platform. It was a perfect defensive position: two men could have held off five hundred on that flight of coral steps.

But there was always a way.

Simons decided to attack from the east, by scaling the cliff.

The assault began at one a.m. on 2 November. Simons and fourteen men crouched at the foot of the cliff, directly below the garrison. Their faces and hands were blacked: there was a bright moon and the terrain was as open as an Iowa prairie. For silence they communicated by signals and wore their socks over their boots.

Simons gave the signal and they began to climb.

The sharp edges of the coral sliced into the flesh of their fingers and the palms of their hands. In places there were no footholds, and they had to go up climbing vines hand-over-hand. They were completely vulnerable: if one curious sentry should look over the platform, down the east side of the cliff, he would see them instantly, and could pick them off one by one: easy shooting.

They were half-way up when the silence was rent by a deafening clang. Someone's rifle stock had banged against a coral cone. They all stopped and lay still against the face of the cliff. Simons held his breath and waited for the rifle shot from above which would begin the massacre. It never came.

After ten minutes they went on.

The climb took a full hour.

Simons was first over the top. He crouched on the platform, feeling naked in the bright moonlight. No Japanese were visible but he could hear voices from one of the low buildings. He trained his rifle on the lighthouse.

The rest of the men began to reach the platform. The attack was to start as soon as they got the machine-gun set up.

Just as the gun came over the edge of the cliff, a sleepy Japanese soldier wandered into view, heading for the latrine. Simons signalled to his point guard, who shot the Japanese; and the firefight began.

Simons turned immediately to the machine-gun. He held one leg and the ammunition box while the gunner held down the other leg and fired. The astonished Japanese ran out of the buildings straight into the deadly hail of bullets.

Twenty minutes later it was all over. Some fifteen of the enemy had been killed. Simons's squad suffered two casualties, neither fatal. And the 'impregnable' fortress had been taken.

There was always a way.

CHAPTER SEVEN

I

THE AMERICAN Embassy's Volkswagen minibus threaded its way through the streets of Tehran, heading for Gasr Square. Ross Perot sat inside. It was 19 January, the day after Paul and Bill were moved, and Perot was going to visit them in the new jail.

It was a little crazy.

Everyone had gone to great lengths to hide Perot in Tehran, for fear that Dadgar – seeing a far more valuable hostage than Paul or Bill – would arrest him and throw him in jail. Yet here he was, heading for the jail of his own free will, with his own passport in his pocket for identification.

His hopes were pinned on the notorious inability of government everywhere to let its right hand know what its left was doing. The Ministry of Justice might want to arrest him, but it was the military who ran the jails, and the military had no interest in him.

Nevertheless, he was taking precautions. He would go in with a group of people – Rich Gallagher and Jay Coburn were on the bus, as well as some Embassy people who were going in to visit an American woman in the jail – and he was wearing casual clothes and carrying a cardboard box containing groceries, books and warm clothing for Paul and Bill.

Nobody at the prison would know his face. He would have to give his name as he went in, but why would a minor clerk or prison guard recognize it? His name might be on a list at the airport, at police stations or at hotels; but the prison would surely be the *last* place Dadgar would expect him to turn up.

Anyway, he was determined to take the risk. He wanted to boost Paul's and Bill's morale, and to show them that he was willing to stick out his neck for them. It would be the only achievement of his trip: his efforts to get the negotiations moving had come to nothing.

The bus entered Gasr Square and he got his first sight of the new prison. It was formidable. He could not imagine how Simons and his little rescue team could possibly break in there.

In the square were scores of people, mostly women in chadors, making a lot of noise. The bus stopped near the huge steel doors. Perot wondered about the bus driver: he was Iranian, and he knew who Perot was . . .

They all got out. Perot saw a television camera near the prison entrance.

His heart missed a beat.

It was an *American* crew.

What the hell were they doing there?

He kept his head down as he pushed his way through the crowd, carrying his cardboard box. A guard looked out of a small window set into the brick wall beside the gates. The television crew seemed to be taking no notice of him. A minute later a little door in one of the gates swung open, and the visitors stepped inside.

The door clanged shut behind them.

Perot had passed the point of no return.

He walked on, through a second pair of steel doors, into the prison compound. It was a big place, with streets between the buildings, and chickens and turkeys running around loose. He followed the others through a doorway into a reception room.

He showed his passport. The clerk pointed to a register. Perot took out his pen and signed 'H. R. Perot' more or less legibly.

The clerk handed back the passport and waved him on.

He had been right. Nobody here had heard of Ross Perot.

He walked on into a waiting room – and stopped dead.

Standing there, talking to an Iranian in general's uniform, was someone who knew perfectly well who Ross was.

It was Ramsey Clark, a Texan who had been US Attorney General under President Lyndon B. Johnson. Perot had met him several times and knew Clark's sister Mimi very well.

For a moment Perot froze. That explains the television cameras, he thought. He wondered whether he could keep out of Clark's sight. Any moment now, he thought, Ramsey will see me and say to the general: 'Lord, there's Ross Perot of EDS,' and if I look as if I'm trying to hide it will be even worse.

He made a snap decision.

He walked over to Clark, stuck out his hand, and said: 'Hello, Ramsey, what are you doing in jail?'

Clark looked down – he was six foot three – and laughed.

They shook hands.

'How's Mimi?' Perot asked before Clark had a chance to perform introductions.

The general was saying something in Farsi to an underling.

Clark said: 'Mimi's fine.'

'Well, good to see you,' Perot said, and walked on.

His mouth was dry as he went out of the waiting-room and into the prison compound with Gallagher, Coburn and the Embassy people. That had been a close shave. An Iranian in colonel's uniform joined them: he had been assigned to take care of them, Gallagher said. Perot wondered what Clark was saying to the general now . . .

Paul was sick. The cold he had caught in the first jail had recurred. He was coughing persistently and had pains in his chest. He could not get warm, in this jail or in the old one: for three whole weeks he had been cold. He had asked his EDS visitors to get him warm under-wear, but for some reason they had not brought any.

He was also miserable. He really had expected that Coburn and the rescue team would ambush the bus that brought him and Bill here from the Ministry of Justice, and when the bus had entered the impregnable Gasr Prison he had been bitterly disappointed.

General Mohari, who ran the prison, had explained to Paul and Bill that he was in charge of all the jails in Tehran, and he had arranged for their transfer to this one for their own safety. It was small consolation: being less vulnerable to the mobs, this place was also more difficult, if not impossible, for the rescue team to attack.

The Gasr Prison was part of a large military complex. On its west side was the Old Gasr Ghazar Palace, which had been turned into a police academy by the Shah's father. The prison compound had once been the palace gardens. To the north was a military hospital; to the east an army camp where helicopters took off and landed all day.

The compound itself was bounded by an inner wall twenty-five or thirty feet high, and an outer wall twelve feet high. Inside were fifteen or twenty separate buildings, including a bakery, a mosque, and six cell blocks, one reserved for women.

Paul and Bill were in Building No 8. It was a two-storey block in a courtyard surrounded by a fence of tall iron bars covered with chicken wire. The environment was not bad, for a jail. There was a fountain in the middle of the courtyard, rose bushes around the sides, and ten or fifteen pine trees. The prisoners were allowed outside during the day, and could play volley-ball or ping-pong in the courtyard. However, they could not pass through the courtyard gate, which was manned by a guard.

The ground floor of the building was a small hospital with twenty or so patients, mostly mental cases. They screamed a lot. Paul and Bill and a handful of other prisoners were on the first floor. They had a large cell, about twenty feet by thirty, which they shared with only one other prisoner, an Iranian lawyer in his fifties who spoke English and French as well as Farsi. He had shown them pictures of his villa in France. There was a TV set in the cell.

Meals were prepared by some of the prisoners – who were paid for this by the others – and eaten in a separate dining room. The food here was better than at the first jail. Extra privileges could be bought, and one of the other inmates, apparently a hugely wealthy man, had a private room and meals brought in from outside. The routine was relaxed: there were no set times for getting up and going to bed.

For all that Paul was thoroughly depressed. A measure of extra comfort meant little. What he wanted was freedom.

He was not much cheered when they were told, on the morning of 19 January, that they had visitors.

There was a visiting room on the ground floor of Building No 8, but today, without explanation, they were taken out of the building and along the street.

Paul realized they were headed for a building known as the Officers' Club, set in a small tropical garden with ducks and peacocks. As they approached the place he glanced around the compound and saw his visitors coming in the opposite direction.

He could not believe his eyes.

'My God!' he said delightedly. 'It's Ross!'

Forgetting where he was, he turned to run over to Perot: the guard jerked him back.

'Can you believe this?' he said to Bill. 'Perot's here!'

The guard hustled him through the garden. Paul kept looking back at Perot, wondering whether his eyes were deceiving him. He was led into a big circular room with banqueting tables around the outside and walls covered with small triangles of mirrored glass: it was like a small ballroom. A moment later Perot came in with Gallagher, Coburn and several other people.

Perot was grinning broadly. Paul shook his hand, then embraced him. It was an emotional moment. Paul felt the way he did when he listened to *The Star Spangled Banner*: a kind of shiver went up and down his spine. He was loved, he was cared for, he had friends, he belonged. Perot had come half across the world into the middle of a revolution just to visit him.

Perot and Bill embraced and shook hands. Bill said: 'Ross, what in the world are *you* doing here? Have you come to take us home?'

'Not quite,' Perot said. 'Not yet.'

The guards gathered at the far end of the room to drink tea. The Embassy staff who had come in with Perot sat around another table, talking to a woman prisoner.

Perot put his box on a table. 'There's some long underwear in here for you,' he said to Paul. 'We couldn't buy any, so this is mine, and I want it back, you hear?'

'Sure,' Paul grinned.

'We brought you some books as well, and groceries – peanut butter and tuna fish and juice and I don't know what.' He took a stack of envelopes from his pocket. 'And your mail.'

Paul glanced at his. There was a letter from Ruthie. Another envelope was addressed to 'Chapanoodle'. Paul smiled: that would be from his friend David Behne, whose son Tommy, unable to pronounce 'Chiapparone' had dubbed Paul 'Chapanoodle'. He pocketed the letters to read later, and said: 'How's Ruthie?'

'She's just fine. I talked to her on the phone,' Perot said. 'Now, we have assigned one man to each of your wives, to make sure everything necessary is done to take care of them. Ruthie's in Dallas now, staying with Jim and Cathy Nyfeler. She's buying a house, and Tom Walter is handling all the legal details for her.'

He turned to Bill. 'Emily has gone to visit her sister Vickie in North Carolina. She needed a break. She's been working with Tim Reardon in Washington, putting pressure on the State Department. She wrote to Rosalynn Carter – you know, as one wife to another – she's trying everything. Matter of fact, we're all trying everything . . .'

As Perot ran down the long list of people who had been asked to help – from Texas Congressmen all the way up to Henry Kissinger – Bill realized that the main purpose of Perot's visit was to boost his and Paul's morale. It was something of an anticlimax. For a moment back there, when he had seen Perot walking across the compound with the other guys, grinning all over his face, Bill had thought: here comes the rescue party – at last they've got this damn thing solved, and Perot is coming to tell us personally. He was disappointed. But he cheered up as Perot talked. With his letters from home and his box of goodies Perot was like Santa Claus; and his presence here, and the big grin on his face, symbolized a tremendous defiance of Dadgar, the mobs and everything that threatened them.

Bill was worried, now, about Emily's morale. He knew instinctively what was going on in his wife's mind. The fact that she had gone to North Carolina told him she had given up hope. It had become too much for her to keep up a façade of normality with the children at her parents' house. He knew, somehow, that she had started smoking again. That would puzzle little Chris. Emily had given up smoking when she went into hospital to have her gall bladder removed, and she had told Chris then that she had had her smoker taken out. Now he would wonder how it had got back in.

'If all this fails,' Perot was saying, 'we have another team in town who will get you out of here by other methods. You'll recognize all the members of the team except one, the leader, an older man.'

Paul said: 'I have a problem with that, Ross. Why should a bunch of guys get cut up for the sake of two?'

Bill wondered just what was being planned. Would a helicopter fly over the compound and pick them up? Would the US Army storm the walls? It was hard to imagine – but with Perot, anything could happen.

Coburn said to Paul: 'I want you to observe and

memorize all the details you can about the compound and the prison routine, just like before.'

Bill was feeling embarrassed about his moustache. He had grown it to make him look more Iranian. EDS executives were not allowed to have moustaches or beards, but he had not expected to see Perot. It was silly, he knew, but he felt uncomfortable about it. 'I apologize for this,' he said, touching his upper lip. 'I'm trying to be inconspicuous. I'll shave it off as soon as I get out of here.'

'Keep it,' Perot said with a smile. 'Let Emily and the children see it. Anyway, we're going to change the dress code. We've had the results of the employee attitude survey, and we'll probably permit moustaches, and coloured shirts too.'

Bill looked at Coburn. 'And beards?'

'No beards. Coburn has a very special excuse.'

The guards came to break up the party. Visiting time was over.

Perot said: 'We don't know whether we'll get you out quickly or slowly. Tell yourselves it will be slowly. If you get up each morning thinking "Today could be the day", you may have a lot of disappointments and become demoralized. Prepare yourselves for a long stay, and you may be pleasantly surprised. But always remember this: we *will* get you out.'

They all shook hands. Paul said: 'I really don't know how to thank you for coming, Ross.'

Perot smiled. 'Just don't leave without my underwear.'

They all walked out of the building. The EDS men

headed across the compound towards the prison gate, leaving Paul and Bill and their guards watching. As his friends disappeared, Bill was seized by a longing just to go with them.

Not today, he told himself; not today.

Perot wondered whether he would be allowed to leave.

Ramsey Clark had had a full hour to let the cat out of the bag. What had he said to the general? Would there be a reception committee waiting in the administration block at the prison entrance?

His heart beat faster as he entered the waiting room. There was no sign of the general or of Clark. He walked through and into the reception area. Nobody looked at him.

With Coburn and Gallagher close behind, he walked through the first set of doors.

Nobody stopped him.

He was going to get away with it.

He crossed the little courtyard and waited by the big gates.

The small door set in one of the gates was opened.

Perot walked out of the prison.

The TV cameras were still there.

All I need, he thought, having gotten this far, is to have the US networks show my picture . . .

He pushed his way through the crowd to the Embassy minibus and climbed aboard.

Coburn and Gallagher got on with him, but the Embassy people had lagged behind.

Perot sat on the bus, looking out of the window. The crowd in the square seemed malevolent. They were shouting in Farsi. Perot had no idea what they were saying.

He wished the Embassy people would hurry up.

'Where *are* those guys?' he said tetchily.

'They're coming,' Coburn said.

'I thought we'd all just come on out, get in the bus and *leave*.'

A minute later the prison door opened again and the Embassy people came out. They got on the bus. The driver started the engine and pulled away across the Gasr Square.

Perot relaxed.

He need not have worried quite so much. Ramsey Clark, who was there at the invitation of Iranian human-rights groups, did not have such a good memory. He had known that Perot's face was vaguely familiar, but thought he was Colonel Frank Borman, the president of Eastern Airlines.

II

Emily Gaylord sat down with her needlepoint. She was making a nude for Bill.

She was back at her parents' house in Washington, and it was another normal day of quiet desperation. She had driven Vicki to high school then returned and taken

Jackie, Jenny and Chris to elementary school. She had dropped by her sister Dorothy's place and talked for a while with her and her husband, Tim Reardon. Tim was still working through Senator Kennedy and Congressman Tip O'Neill to put pressure on the State Department.

Emily was becoming obsessed with Dadgar, the mystery man who had the power to put her husband in jail and keep him there. She wanted to confront Dadgar herself, and ask him personally why he was doing this to her. She had even asked Tim to try to get her a diplomatic passport, so she could go to Iran and just knock on Dadgar's door. Tim had said it was a pretty crazy idea, and she realized he was right; but she was desperate to do something, anything, to get Bill back.

Now she was waiting for the daily call from Dallas. It was usually Ross, T. J. Marquez or Jim Nyfeler who called. After that she would pick up the children then help them with their homework for a while. Then there was nothing ahead but the lonely night.

She had only recently told Bill's parents that he was in jail. Bill had asked her, in a letter read over the phone by Keane Taylor, not to tell them until it was absolutely necessary, because Bill's father had a history of strokes and the shock might be dangerous. But after three weeks the pretence had become impossible, so she had broken the news; and Bill's father had been angry at having been kept in the dark so long. Sometimes it was hard to know the right thing to do.

The phone rang, and she snatched it up. 'Hello?'

'Emily? This is Jim Nyfeler.'

'Hi, Jim, what's the news?'

'Just that they've been moved to another jail.'

Why was there *never* any good news?

'It's nothing to worry about,' Jim said. 'In fact, it's good. The old jail was in the south of the city, where the fighting is. This one is further north, and more secure – they'll be safer there.'

Emily lost her cool. 'But Jim,' she yelled, 'You've been telling me for three weeks that they're perfectly safe in jail, *now* you say they've been moved to a new jail and now they'll be safe!'

'Emily—'

'Come on, please don't lie to me!'

'Emily—'

'Just tell it like it is and be upfront, okay?'

'Emily, I don't think they have been in danger up till now, but the Iranians are taking a sensible precaution, okay?'

Emily felt ashamed of herself for getting mad at him. 'I'm sorry, Jim.'

'That's all right.'

They talked a little longer, then Emily hung up and went back to her needlepoint. I'm losing my grip, she thought. I'm going around in a trance, taking the kids to school, talking to Dallas, going to bed at night and getting up in the morning . . .

Visiting her sister Vickie for a few days had been a good idea, but she didn't really need a change of scene – what she needed was Bill.

It was hard to keep on hoping. She began to think about how life might be without Bill. She had an aunt who worked in Woody's department store in Washington: maybe she could get a job there. Or she could talk to her father about getting secretarial work. She wondered whether she would ever fall in love with anyone else, if Bill should die in Tehran. She thought not.

She remembered when they were first married. Bill had been at college, and they were short of money, but they had gone ahead and done it because they could not bear to be apart any longer. Later, as Bill's career began to take off, they prospered, and gradually bought better cars, bigger houses, more expensive clothes ... more *things*. How worthless those *things* were, she thought now; how little it mattered whether she was rich or poor. Bill was what she wanted, and he was all she needed. He would always be enough for her, enough to make her happy.

If he ever came back.

Karen Chiapparone said: 'Mommy, why doesn't Daddy call? He always calls when he's away.'

'He called today,' Ruthie lied. 'He's fine.'

'Why did he call when I was at school? I'd like to talk to him.'

'Honey, it's difficult to get through from Tehran, the lines are so busy, he just has to call when he can.'

'Oh.'

Karen wandered off to watch TV, and Ruthie sat down. It was getting dark outside. She was finding it increasingly difficult to lie to everyone about Paul.

That was why she had left Chicago and come to

Dallas. Living with her parents and keeping the secret from them had become impossible. Mom would say: 'Why do Ross and the fellows from EDS keep calling you?'

'They just want to make sure we're okay, you know,' Ruthie would say with a forced smile.

'That is so nice of Ross to call.'

Here in Dallas she could at least talk openly to other EDS people. Moreover, now that the Iran business was certain to be closed down, Paul would be based at EDS headquarters, at least for a while, so Dallas would be their home; and Karen and Anne Marie had to go to school.

They were all living with Jim and Cathy Nyfeler. Cathy was especially sympathetic, for her husband had been on the original list of four men whose passports Dadgar had asked for: if Jim had happened to be in Iran at the time, he would now be in jail with Paul and Bill. Stay with us, Cathy had said; it will only be for maybe a week, then Paul will be back. That had been at the beginning of January. Since then Ruthie had proposed getting an apartment of her own, but Cathy would not hear of it.

Right now Cathy was at the hairdresser's, the children were watching TV in another room, and Jim was not yet home from work, so Ruthie was alone with her thoughts.

With Cathy's help she was keeping busy and putting on a brave face. She had enrolled Karen in school and found a kindergarten for Ann Marie. She went out to lunch with Cathy and some of the other EDS wives – Mary Boulware, Liz Coburn, Mary Sculley, Marva Davis, and Toni Dvoranchik. She wrote bright optimistic letters to Paul, and listened to his bright, optimistic replies read over the phone from Tehran. She shopped and went to dinner parties.

She had killed a lot of time house-hunting. She did not know Dallas well, but she remembered Paul saying that Central Expressway was a nightmare, so she looked for houses well away from it. She had found one she liked and decided to buy it, so there would be a real home for Paul to come back to, but there were legal problems because he was not here to sign the papers: Tom Walter was trying to sort that out.

Ruthie was making it look good, but inside she was dying.

She rarely slept more than an hour at night. She kept waking up wondering whether she would ever see Paul again. She tried to think about what she would do if he did not come back. She supposed she would return to Chicago and stay with Mom and Dad for a while, but she would not want to live with them permanently. No doubt she could get some kind of a job ... But it was not the practical business of living without a man and taking care of herself that bothered her: it was the idea of being without Paul, forever. She could not imagine what life would be like if he were not there. What would she do, what would she care about, what would she want, what could possibly make her happy? She was completely dependent on him, she realized. She could not live without him.

She heard a car outside. That would be Jim, home from work: perhaps he would have some news.

A moment later he came in. 'Hi, Ruthie. Cathy not home?'

'She's at the hairdresser's. What happened today?'

'Well . . .'

She knew from his expression that he had nothing good to tell her and he was trying to find an encouraging way of saying so.

'Well, they had a meeting scheduled to talk about the bail, but the Iranians didn't turn up. Tomorrow—'

'But *why*?' Ruthie fought to keep calm. 'Why don't they turn up when they arrange these meetings?'

'You know, sometimes they're called out on strike, and sometimes people just can't move around the city because of . . . because of the demonstrations, and so on . . .'

She seemed to have been hearing reports like this for weeks. There were always delays, postponements, frustrations. 'But, Jim,' she began; then the tears started and she could not stop them. 'Jim . . .' Her throat tightened up until she could not speak. She thought: all I want is my husband! Jim stood there looking helpless and embarrassed. All the misery she had kept locked up for so long suddenly flooded out, and she could not control herself any longer. She burst into tears and ran from the room. She rushed to her bedroom, threw herself on the bed and lay there sobbing her heart out.

Liz Coburn sipped her drink. Across the table were Pat Sculley's wife, Mary, and another EDS wife who had been evacuated from Tehran, Toni Dvoranchik. The three women were at Recipes, a restaurant on Greenville Avenue, Dallas. They were drinking strawberry Daiquiris.

Toni Dvoranchik's husband was here in Dallas. Liz knew that Pat Sculley had disappeared, like Jay, in the direction of Europe. Now Mary Sculley was talking as if Pat had gone not just to Europe but to Iran.

'Is Pat in Tehran?' Liz asked.

'They're all in Tehran, I guess,' Mary said.

Liz was horrified. 'Jay in Tehran . . .' She wanted to cry. Jay had told her he was in Paris. Why couldn't he tell the truth? Pat Sculley had told Mary the truth. But Jay was different. Some men would play poker for a few hours, but Jay had to play all night and all the next day. Other men would play nine or eighteen holes of golf: Jay would play thirty-six. Lots of men had demanding jobs, but Jay had to work for EDS. Even in the Army, when the two of them had been not much more than kids, Jay had to volunteer for one of the most dangerous assignments, helicopter pilot. Now he had gone to Tehran in the middle of a revolution. Same old thing, she thought: he's gone away, he's lying to me, and he's in danger. She suddenly felt cold all over, as if she were in shock. He's not coming back, she thought numbly. He's not going to get out of there alive.

III

Perot's good spirits soon passed. He had got into the prison, defying Dadgar, and had cheered up Paul and

KEN FOLLETT

Bill; but Dadgar still held all the cards. After six days in Tehran he understood why the political pressure he had been putting on in Washington had been ineffectual: the old regime in Iran was struggling for survival and had no control. Even if he posted the bail – and a lot of problems had to be solved before that could happen – Paul and Bill would still be held in Iran. And Simons's rescue plan was now in tatters, ruined by the move to the new prison. There seemed to be no hope.

That night Perot went to see Simons.

He waited until dark, for safety. He wore his jogging suit with tennis shoes and a dark businessman's over-coat. Keane Taylor drove him.

The rescue team had moved out of Taylor's house. Taylor had now met Dadgar face-to-face, and Dadgar had started examining EDS's records: it was possible, Simons had reasoned, that Dadgar would raid Taylor's house, looking for incriminating documents. So Simons, Coburn and Poché were living in the home of Bill and Toni Dvoranchik, who were now back in Dallas. Two more of the team had made it to Tehran from Paris: Pat Sculley and Jim Schwebach, the short but deadly duo who had been flank guards in the original, now useless, rescue scenario.

In a typical Tehran arrangement, Dvoranchik's home was the ground floor of a two-storey house, with the landlord living upstairs. Taylor and the rescue team left Perot alone with Simons. Perot looked around the living-room distastefully. No doubt the place had been spotless when Toni Dvoranchik lived here, but now, inhabited by five men none of whom was very interested in housekeeping, it was dirty and run-down, and it stank of Simons's cigars.

Simons's huge frame was slumped in an armchair. His white whiskers were bushy and his hair long. He was chain-smoking, as usual; drawing heavily on his little cigar and inhaling with relish.

'You've seen the new prison,' Perot said.

'Yeah,' Simons rasped.

'What do you think?'

'The idea of taking that place with the kind of frontal attack we had in mind just isn't worth talking about.'

'That's what I figured.'

'Which leaves a number of possibilities.'

It does? thought Perot.

Simons went on: 'One. I understand there are cars parked in the prison compound. We may find a way to get Paul and Bill driven out of there in the trunk of a car. As part of that plan, or as an alternative, we may be able to bribe or blackmail this general who is in charge of the place.'

'General Mohari.'

'Right. One of your Iranian employees is getting us a rundown on the man.'

'Good.'

'Two. The negotiating team. If they can get Paul and Bill released under house arrest, or something of that kind, we can snatch the two of them. Get Taylor and those guys to concentrate on this house arrest idea. Agree to any conditions the Iranians care to name, but get 'em out of that jail. Working on the assumption that they would be confined to their homes and kept under surveillance, we're developing a new rescue scenario.'

Perot was beginning to feel better. There was an aura of confidence about this massive man. A few minutes ago Perot had felt almost helpless: now Simons was calmly listing fresh approaches to the problem, as if the move to the new jail, the bail problems, and the collapse of the legitimate government were minor snags rather than total catastrophe.

'Three,' Simons went on. 'There's a revolution going on here. Revolutions are predictable. The same things happen every damn time. You can't say *when* they'll occur, only that they *will*, sooner or later. And one of the things that always happens is, the mob storms the prisons and lets everyone out.'

Perot was intrigued. 'Is that so?'

Simons nodded. 'Those are the three possibilities. Of course, at this point in the game we can't pick one: we have to prepare for each of them. Whichever of the three happens first, we'll need a plan for getting everyone out of this goddam country just as soon as Paul and Bill are in our hands.'

'Yes.' Perot was worried about his own departure: that of Paul and Bill would be a good deal more hazardous. 'I've had promises of help from the American military—'

'Sure,' Simons said. 'I'm not saying they're insincere, but I will say they have higher priorities, and I'm not prepared to place a great deal of reliance on their promises.'

'All right.' That was a matter for Simons's judgement, and Perot was content to leave it to him. In fact, he was content to leave everything to Simons. Simons was probably the best qualified man in the world to do this job, and Perot had complete faith in him. 'What can I do?'

'Get back to the States. For one thing, you're in danger here. For another, I need you over there. Chances are, when we eventually come out, it won't be on a scheduled flight. We may not fly at all. You'll have to pick us up somewhere – it could be Iraq, Kuwait, Turkey or Afghanistan – and that will take organizing. Go home and stay ready.'

'Okay.' Perot stood up. Simons had done to him what Perot sometimes did to his staff: inspired them with the strength to go one more mile when the game seemed lost. 'I'll leave tomorrow.'

He got a reservation on British Airways flight 200, Tehran to London via Kuwait, leaving at 10.20 a.m. on 20 January, the next day.

He called Margot and asked her to meet him in London. He wanted a few days alone with her: they might not get another chance, once the rescue started to unfold.

They had had good times in London in the past. They would stay at the Savoy Hotel. (Margot liked Claridge's, but Perot did not: they turned the heat too high, and if he opened the windows he was kept awake by the roar of the all-night traffic along Brook Street.)

He and Margot would see plays and concerts, and go to Margot's favourite London nightclub, Annabel's. For a few days they would enjoy life.

If he got out of Iran.

In order to minimize the amount of time he would have to spend at the airport, he stayed at the hotel until the last minute. He called the airport to find out whether the flight would leave on time, and was told that it would.

He checked in a few minutes before ten o'clock.

Rich Gallagher, who accompanied him to the airport, went off to enquire whether the authorities were planning to give Perot a hard time. Gallagher had done this before. Together with an Iranian friend who worked for Pan Am, he walked through to passport control carrying Perot's passport. The Iranian explained that a VIP was coming through, and asked to clear the passport in advance. The official at the desk obligingly looked through the loose-leaf folder which contained the stop list and said there would be no problems for Mr Perot. Gallagher returned with the good news.

Perot remained apprehensive. If they wanted to pick him up, they might be smart enough to lie to Gallagher.

Affable Bill Gayden, the president of EDS World, was flying in to take over direction of the negotiating team. Gayden had left Dallas for Tehran once before, but had turned back in Paris on hearing about Bunny Fleischaker's warning of more arrests to come. Now he, like Perot, had decided to risk it. By chance his flight came in while Perot was waiting to leave, and they had an opportunity to talk. In his suitcase Gayden had eight

American passports belonging to EDS executives who looked vaguely like Paul or Bill.

Perot said: 'I thought you were getting forged passports for them. Couldn't you find a way?'

'Yeah, we found a way,' Gayden said. 'If you need a passport in a hurry, you can take all the documentation down to the courthouse in Dallas, then they put everything in an envelope and you carry it to New Orleans, where they issue the passport. It's just a plain government envelope sealed with scotch tape, so you could open it on the way to New Orleans, take out the photographs, replace them with photographs of Paul and Bill – which we have – re-seal the envelope, and, bingo, you've got passports for Paul and Bill in false names. But it's against the law.'

'So what did you do instead?'

'I told all the evacuees that I had to have their passports in order to get their belongings shipped over from Tehran. I got a hundred and two passports, and I picked the best eight. I bogused up a letter from someone in the States to someone here in Tehran saying: "Here are the passports you asked for us to return so you could deal with the immigration authorities," just so that I've got a piece of paper to show if I'm asked why the hell I'm carrying eight passports.'

'If Paul and Bill use those passports to cross a frontier, they'll be breaking the law anyway.'

'If we get that far, we'll break the law.'

Perot nodded. 'It makes sense.'

His flight was called. He said goodbye to Gayden and to Taylor, who had driven him to the airport and would take Gayden to the Hyatt. Then he went off to discover the truth about the stop list.

He went first through a 'Passengers Only' gate where his boarding pass was checked. He walked along a corridor to a booth where he paid a small sum as airport tax. Then, on his right, he saw a series of passport control desks.

Here the stop list was kept.

One of the desks was manned by a girl who was absorbed in a paperback book. Perot approached her. He handed over his passport and a yellow exit form. The form had his name at the top.

The girl took the yellow sheet, opened his passport, stamped it, and handed it back without looking at him. She returned to her book immediately.

Perot walked into the departure lounge.

The flight was delayed.

He sat down. He was on tenterhooks. At any moment the girl could finish her book, or just get bored with it, and start checking the stop list against the names on the yellow forms. Then, he imagined, they would come for him, the police or the military or Dadgar's investigators, and he would go to jail, and Margot would be like Ruthie and Emily, not knowing whether she would ever see her husband again.

He checked the departures board every few seconds: it just said DELAYED.

He sat on the edge of his chair for the first hour.

Then he began to feel resigned. If they were going to catch him they would, and there was nothing he could do about it. He started to read a magazine. Over the next hour he read everything in his briefcase. Then he started talking to the man sitting next to him. Perot learned that the man was an English engineer working in Iran on a project for a large British company. They chatted for a while, then swapped magazines.

In a few hours, Perot thought, I'll be in a beautiful hotel suite with Margot – or in an Iranian jail. He pushed the thought from his mind.

Lunchtime went by, and the afternoon wore on. He began to believe they were not going to come for him.

The flight was finally called at six o'clock.

Perot stood up. If they come for me now . . .

He joined the crowd and approached the departure gate. There was a security check. He was frisked and waved through.

I've almost made it, he thought as he boarded the plane. He sat between two fat people in an economy seat – it was an all-economy flight. I think I've made it.

The doors were closed and the plane began to move.

It taxied on to the runway and gathered speed.

The plane took off.

He had made it.

He had always been lucky.

His thoughts turned to Margot. She was handling this crisis the way she had handled the prisoners-of-war adventures: she understood her husband's concept of duty and she never complained. That was why he could stay focused on what he had to do, and block out negative thoughts that would excuse inaction. He was lucky to have her. He thought of all the lucky things that had happened to him: good parents, getting into the Naval Academy, meeting Margot, having such fine children, starting EDS, getting good people to work for him, brave people like the volunteers he had left behind in Iran . . .

He wondered superstitiously whether an individual had a certain limited quantity of luck in his life. He saw his luck as sand in an hour-glass, slowly but steadily running out. What happens, he thought, when it's all gone?

The plane descended towards Kuwait. He was out of Iranian airspace. He had escaped.

While the plane was refuelling he walked to the open door and stood there, breathing the fresh air and ignoring the stewardess who kept asking him to return to his seat. There was a nice breeze blowing across the tarmac, and it was a relief to get away from the fat people sitting either side of him. The stewardess eventually gave up and went to do something else. He watched the sun go down. Luck, he thought; I wonder how much I've got left?

CHAPTER EIGHT

I

THE RESCUE team in Tehran now consisted of Simons, Coburn, Poché, Sculley and Schwebach. Simons decided that Boulware, Davis and Jackson would not come to Tehran. The idea of rescuing Paul and Bill by frontal assault was now dead, so he did not need such a big team. He sent Glenn Jackson to Kuwait, to investigate that end of the southerly route out of Iran. Boulware and Davis went back to the States to await further orders.

Majid reported to Coburn that General Mohari, the man in charge of Gasr Prison, was not easily corruptible, but had two daughters at school in the United States. The team briefly discussed kidnapping the girls and forcing Mohari to help Paul and Bill escape; but they rejected the idea. (Perot hit the roof when he learned they had even *discussed* it.) The idea of sneaking Paul and Bill out in the trunk of a car was put on the back burner for a while.

For two or three days they concentrated on what they would do if Paul and Bill were released under house arrest. They went to look at the houses the two men had occupied before the arrest. The snatch would be easy unless Dadgar put Paul and Bill under surveillance. The team would use two cars, they decided. The first car would pick up Paul and Bill. The second, following at a distance, would contain Sculley and Schwebach, who would be responsible for eliminating anyone who tried to tail the first car. Once again, the deadly duo would do the killing.

The two cars would keep in touch by short-wave radio, they decided. Coburn called Merv Stauffer in Dallas and ordered the equipment. Boulware would take the radios to London: Schwebach and Sculley would go to London to meet him and pick them up. While in London, the deadly duo would try to get hold of some good maps of Iran, for use during the escape from the country, should the team have to leave by road. (No good maps of the country were to be found in Tehran, as the Jeep Club had learned in happier days: Gayden said Persian maps were at the 'turn left by the dead horse' level.)

Simons wanted also to prepare for the third possibility – that Paul and Bill would be released by a mob storming the prison. What should the team do in that eventuality? Coburn was continuously monitoring the situation in the city, calling his contacts in US military intelligence and several trustworthy Iranian employees: if the prison were overrun he would know very quickly. What then? Someone would have to look for Paul and Bill and bring them to safety. But a bunch of Americans driving into the middle of a riot would be asking for trouble: Paul and Bill would be safer mingling inconspicuously with the crowd of escaping prisoners. Simons told Coburn to speak to Paul about this possibility, next time he visited the jail, and instruct Paul to head for the Hyatt Hotel.

However, an Iranian could go looking for Paul and Bill in the riots. Simons asked Coburn to recommend an Iranian employee of EDS who was really street-smart.

Coburn thought immediately of Rashid.

He was a dark-skinned, rather good-looking twenty-three-year-old from an affluent Tehran family. He had completed EDS's training programme for systems engineers. He was intelligent and resourceful, and he had bags of charm. Coburn recalled the last time Rashid had demonstrated his talent for improvisation. Ministry of Health employees who were on partial strike had refused to key the data for the payroll system, but Rashid had got all the input together, taken it down to Bank Omran, talked someone there into keying the data, then run the program on the Ministry computer. The trouble with Rashid was that you had to keep an eye on him, because he never consulted anyone before implementing his unconventional ideas. Getting the data keyed the way he had constituted strike breaking, and might have got EDS in big trouble – indeed, when Bill had heard about it he had been more anxious than pleased. Rashid was excitable and impulsive, and his English was not so good, so he tended to dash off and do his own crazy thing without telling anyone, a tendency which made his managers nervous. But he always got away with it. He could talk his way into and out of anything. At the airport, meeting people or seeing them off, he always managed to pass through all the 'Passengers Only' barriers even though he never had a boarding card, ticket or passport to show. Coburn knew him well, and liked him enough to have brought him home for supper several times. Coburn also trusted him completely, especially since the strike, when Rashid had been one of Coburn's informants among the hostile Iranian employees.

However, Simons would not trust Rashid on Coburn's say-so. Just as he had insisted on meeting Keane Taylor before letting him in on the secret, so he would want to talk to Rashid.

So Coburn arranged a meeting.

When Rashid was eight years old he had wanted to be President of the United States.

At twenty-three he knew he could never be President, but he still wanted to go to America, and EDS was going to be his ticket. He knew he had it in him to be a great businessman. He was a student of the psychology of the human being, and it had not taken him long to understand the mentality of EDS people. They wanted results, not excuses. If you were given a task, it was always better to do a little more than was expected. If for some reason the task was difficult, or even impossible, it was best not to say so: they hated to hear people whining about problems. You never said: 'I can't do that because . . .' You always said: 'This is the progress I have made so far, and this is the problem I am working on right now . . .' It so happened that these attitudes suited Rashid perfectly. He had made himself useful to EDS, and he knew the company appreciated it.

His greatest achievement had been installing computer terminals in offices where the Iranian staff were suspicious and hostile. So great was the resistance that Pat Sculley had been able to install no more than two per month: Rashid had installed the remaining eighteen in two months. He had planned to capitalize on this. He had composed a letter to Ross Perot, who – he understood – was the head of EDS, asking to be allowed to complete his training in Dallas. He had intended to ask all the EDS managers in Tehran to sign the letter, but events had overtaken him, most of the managers had been evacuated and EDS in Iran was falling to pieces. He never mailed the letter. So he would think of something else.

He could always find a way. Everything was possible for Rashid. He could do anything. He had even got out of the army. At a time when thousands of young middle-class Iranians were spending fortunes in bribes to avoid military service, Rashid, after a few weeks in uniform, had convinced the doctors that he was incurably ill with a twitching disease. His comrades and the officers over him knew that he was in perfect health, but every time he saw the doctor he twitched uncontrollably. He went before medical boards and twitched for hours – an absolutely exhausting business, he discovered. Finally, so many doctors had certified him ill that he got his discharge papers. It was crazy, ridiculous, impossible – but doing the impossible was Rashid's normal practice.

So he *knew* that he would go to America. He did not know *how*, but careful and elaborate planning was not his style anyway. He was a spur-of-the-moment man, an improviser, an opportunist. His chance would come and he would seize it.

Mr Simons interested him. He was not like the other EDS managers. They were all in their thirties and forties, but Simons was nearer to sixty. His long hair and white whiskers and big nose seemed more Iranian than American. Finally, he did not come right out with whatever was on his mind. People like Sculley and Coburn would say: 'This is the situation and this is what I want you to do and you need to have it done by tomorrow morning . . .' Simons just said: 'Let's go for a walk.'

They strolled around the streets of Tehran. Rashid found himself talking about his family, his work at EDS, and his views on the psychology of the human being. They could hear continual shooting, and the streets were alive with people marching and chanting. Everywhere they saw the wreckage of past battles, overturned cars and burned-out buildings. 'The Marxists smash up expensive cars and the Moslems trash the liquor stores,' Rashid told Simons.

'Why is this happening?' Simons asked him.

'This is the time for Iranians to prove themselves, to accomplish their ideas, and to gain their freedom.'

They found themselves in Gasr Square, facing the prison. Rashid said: 'There are many Iranians in these jails simply because they ask for freedom.'

Simons pointed at the crowd of women in chadors. 'What are they doing?'

'Their husbands and sons are unjustly imprisoned, so they gather here, wailing and crying to the guards to let the prisoners go.'

Simons said: 'Well, I guess I feel the same about Paul and Bill as those women do about their men.'

'Yes. I, too, am very concerned about Paul and Bill.'

'But what are you doing about it?' Simons asked.

Rashid was taken aback. 'I am doing everything I can to help my American friends,' he said. He thought of the dogs and cats. One of his tasks at the moment was to care for all the pets left behind by EDS evacuees – including four dogs and twelve cats. Rashid had never had pets and did not know how to deal with large aggressive dogs. Every time he went to the apartment where the dogs were stashed to feed them, he had to hire two or three men off the streets to help him restrain the animals. Twice now he had taken them all to the airport in cages, having heard that there was a flight out which would accept them; and both times the flight had been cancelled. He thought of telling Simons about this, but somehow he knew that Simons would not be impressed.

Simons was up to something, Rashid thought, and it was not a business matter. Simons struck him as an experienced man – you could see that just by looking at his face. Rashid did not believe in experience. He believed in fast education. Revolution, not evolution. He liked the inside track, short cuts, accelerated development, superchargers. Simons was different. He was a patient man, and Rashid, analysing Simons's psychology, guessed that the patience came from a strong will. When he is ready, Rashid thought, he will let me know what he wants from me.

'Do you know anything about the French Revolution?' Simons asked.

'A little.'

'This place reminds me of the Bastille – a symbol of oppression.'

It was a good comparison, Rashid thought.

Simons went on: 'The French revolutionaries stormed the Bastille and let all the prisoners out.'

'I think the same will happen here. It's a possibility, at least.'

Simons nodded. 'If it happens, someone ought to be here to take care of Paul and Bill.'

'Yes.' That will be me, Rashid thought.

They stood together in Gasr Square, looking at the high walls and huge gates, and the wailing women in their black robes. Rashid recalled his principle: always do a little more than EDS asks of you. What if the mobs ignored Gasr Prison? Maybe he should make sure they did not. The mob was nothing but people like Rashid – young, discontented Iranian men who wanted to change their lives. He might not only join the mob – he might lead it. He might lead an attack on the prison. He, Rashid, might rescue Paul and Bill.

Nothing was impossible.

II

Coburn did not know all that was going on in Simons's mind at this point. He had not been in on Simons's conversations with Perot and Rashid, and Simons did not volunteer much information. From what Coburn did know, the three possibilities – the trunk-of-a-car-trick, the house-arrest-and-snatch routine, and the storming of the Bastille – seemed pretty vague. Furthermore, Simons was doing nothing to *make it happen*, but appeared content to sit around the Dvoranchik place discussing ever-more-detailed scenarios. Yet none of this made Coburn uneasy. He was an optimist anyway; and he – like Ross Perot – figured there was no point in second-guessing the world's greatest rescue expert.

While the three possibilities were simmering, Simons concentrated on routes out of Iran, the problem Coburn thought of as 'Getting Out of Dodge'.

Coburn looked for ways of flying Paul and Bill out. He poked around warehouses at the airport, toying with the idea of shipping Paul and Bill as freight. He talked to people at each of the airlines, trying to develop contacts. He eventually had several meetings with the chief of security at Pan Am, telling him everything except the names of Paul and Bill. They talked about getting the two fugitives on a scheduled flight wearing Pan Am cabin crew uniforms. The security chief wanted to help, but the airline's liability proved in the end to be an insuperable problem. Coburn then considered stealing a helicopter. He scouted a chopper base in the south of the city, and decided the theft was feasible. But, given the chaos of the Iranian military, he suspected the aircraft were not being properly maintained, and he knew they were short of spare parts. Then again, some of them might have contaminated fuel.

He reported all this to Simons. Simons was already uneasy about airports, and the snags uncovered by Coburn reinforced his prejudice. There were always police and military around airports; if something went wrong there was no escape – airports were designed to prevent people wandering where they should not go; at an airport you always had to put yourself in the hands of others. Furthermore, in that situation your worst enemy could be the people escaping: they needed to be *very* cool. Coburn thought Paul and Bill had the nerves to go through something like that, but there was no point telling Simons so: Simons always had to make his own assessment of a man's character, and he had never met Paul or Bill.

So, in the end, the team focused on getting out by road.

There were six ways.

To the north was the USSR, not a hospitable country. To the east were Afghanistan, equally inhospitable, and Pakistan, whose border was too far away – almost a thousand miles, mostly across desert. To the south was the Persian Gulf, with friendly Kuwait just fifty or a hundred miles across the water. That was promising. To the west was unfriendly Iraq; to the north-west, friendly Turkey.

Kuwait and Turkey were the destinations they favoured.

Simons asked Coburn to have a trustworthy Iranian employee drive south all the way to the Persian Gulf, to find out whether the road was passable and the country-side peaceful. Coburn asked the Cycle Man, so called because he zipped around Tehran on a motorcycle. A trainee systems engineer like Rashid, the Cycle Man was about twenty-five, short, and street-smart. He had learned English at school in California, and could talk with any regional American accent – Southern, Puerto Rican, anything. EDS had hired him despite his lack of a college degree because he scored remarkably high marks in aptitude tests. When EDS's Iranian employees had joined the general strike, and Paul and Coburn had called a mass meeting to discuss it with them, the Cycle Man had astonished everyone by speaking out vehemently against his colleagues and in favour of the management. He made no secret of his pro-American feelings, yet Coburn was quite sure the Cycle Man was involved with the revolutionaries. One day he had asked Keane Taylor for a car. Taylor had given him one. Next day he asked for another. Taylor obliged. The Cycle Man always used his motorcycle anyway: Taylor and Coburn were pretty sure the cars were for the revolutionaries. They did not care: it was more important that the Cycle Man became obligated to them.

So, in return for past favours, the Cycle Man drove to the Persian Gulf.

He came back a few days later and reported that anything was possible if you had enough money. You could get to the Gulf and you could buy or rent a boat.

He had no idea what would happen when you disembarked in Kuwait.

That question was answered by Glenn Jackson.

As well as being a hunter and a Baptist, Glenn Jackson was a Rocket Man. His combination of first-class mathematical brain and ability to stay calm under stress had got him into Mission Control at NASA's Manned Space-craft Centre in Houston as a flight controller. His job had been to design and operate the computer programs which calculated trajectories for in-flight manoeuvring.

Jackson's unflappability had been severely tested on Christmas Day, 1968, during the last mission he worked on, the lunar flyby. When the spacecraft came out from behind the moon, astronaut Jim Lovell had read down the list of numbers, called residuals, which told Jackson how close the craft was to its planned course. Jackson had got a fright: the numbers were way outside the acceptable limits of error. Jackson asked CAPCOM to have the astronaut read them down again, to double-check. Then he told the flight director that if those numbers were correct, the three astronauts were as good as dead: there was not enough fuel to correct such a huge divergence.

Jackson asked for Lovell to read the numbers a third time, extra carefully. They were the same. Then Lovell said: 'Oh, wait a minute, I'm reading these wrong . . .'

When the real numbers came through it turned out that the manoeuvre had been almost perfect.

All that was a long way from busting into a prison.

Still, it was beginning to look like Jackson would never get the chance to perpetrate a jailbreak. He had been cooling his heels for a week when he got instructions from Simons, via Dallas, to go to Kuwait.

He flew to Kuwait and moved into Bob Young's house. Young had gone to Tehran to help the negotiating team, and his wife Kris and her new baby were in the States on vacation. Jackson told Malloy Jones, who was Acting Country Manager in Young's absence, that he had come to help with the preliminary study EDS was doing for Kuwait's central bank. He did a little work for the benefit of his cover story, then started looking around.

He spent some time at the airport, watching the immigration officers. They were being very tough, he soon learned. Hundreds of Iranians without passports were flying in to Kuwait: they were being handcuffed and put on the next flight back. Jackson concluded that Paul and Bill could not possibly fly in to Kuwait.

Assuming they could get in by boat, would they later be allowed to *leave* without passports? Jackson went to see the American consul, saying that one of his children seemed to have lost a passport, and asking what was the procedure for replacing it. In the course of a long and rambling discussion the consul revealed that the Kuwaitis had a way of checking, when they issued an exit visa, whether the person had entered the country legally.

That was a problem, but perhaps not an insoluble one: once inside Kuwait Paul and Bill would be safe from Dadgar, and surely the US Embassy would then give them back their passports. The main question was: assuming the fugitives could reach the south of Iran and embark on a small boat, would they be able to land unnoticed in Kuwait? Jackson travelled the sixty-mile length of the Kuwait coast, from the Iraqi border in the north to the Saudi-Arabian border in the south. He spent many hours on the beaches, collecting seashells in winter. Normally, he had been told, coastal patrols were very light. But the exodus from Iran had changed everything. There were thousands of Iranians who wanted to leave the country almost as badly as Paul and Bill did, and those Iranians, like Simons, could look at a map and see the Persian Gulf to the south with friendly Kuwait just across the water. The Kuwait coastguard was wise to all this. Everywhere Jackson looked he saw, out at sea, at least one patrol boat. And they appeared to be stopping *all* small craft.

The prognosis was gloomy. Jackson called Merv Stauffer in Dallas and reported that the Kuwait exit was a no-no.

That left Turkey.

Simons had favoured Turkey all along. It involved a shorter drive than Kuwait. Furthermore Simons knew Turkey. He had served there in the fifties as part of the American military aid programme, training the Turkish Army. He even spoke a little of the language.

So he sent Ralph Boulware to Istanbul.

Ralph Boulware grew up in bars. His father, Benjamin Russell Boulware, was a tough and independent black man who had a series of small businesses: a grocery store, house property, bootlegging, but mostly bars. Ben Boulware's theory of child-raising was that if he knew where they were he knew what they were doing, so he kept his boys mostly within his sight, which meant mostly in the bar. It was not much of a childhood, and it left Ralph feeling that he had been an adult all his life.

He had realized he was different from other boys his age when he went to college and found his contemporaries getting all excited about gambling, drinking and going with women. He knew all about gamblers, drunks and whores already. He dropped out of college and joined the Air Force.

In nine years in the Air Force he had never seen action, and while he was on the whole glad about that, it had left him wondering whether he had what it took to fight in a shooting war. The rescue of Paul and Bill might give him the chance to find out, he had thought; but Simons had sent him from Paris back to Dallas. It looked like he was going to be ground crew again. Then new orders came.

They came via Merv Stauffer, Perot's right-hand man who was now Simons's link with the scattered rescue team. Stauffer went to Radio Shack and bought six five-channel two-way radios, ten rechargers, a supply of batteries, and a device for running the radios off a dashboard cigar lighter. He gave the equipment to Boulware and told him to meet Sculley and Schwebach in London before going on to Istanbul.

Stauffer also gave him forty thousand dollars in cash, for expenses, bribes, and general purposes.

The night before Boulware left, his wife started giving him a hard time about money. He had taken a thousand dollars out of the bank, without telling her, before he went to Paris – he believed in carrying cash money –

and she had subsequently discovered how little was left in their account. Boulware did not want to explain to her why he had taken the money and how he had spent it. Mary insisted that she needed money. Boulware was not too concerned about that: she was staying with good friends and he knew she would be looked after. But she didn't buy his brush-off, and – as often happened when she was really determined – he decided to make her happy. He went into the bedroom, where he had left the box containing the radios and the forty thousand dollars, and counted out five hundred. Mary came in while he was doing it, and saw what was in the box.

Boulware gave her the five hundred and said: 'Will that hold you?'

'Yes,' she said.

She looked at the box, then at her husband. 'I'm not even going to ask,' she said; and she went out.

Boulware left the next day. He met Schwebach and Sculley in London, gave them five of the six radio sets, kept one for himself, and flew on to Istanbul.

He went from the airport straight to the office of Mr Fish, the travel agent.

Mr Fish met him in an open-plan office with three or four other people sitting around.

'My name is Ralph Boulware, and I work for EDS,' Boulware began. 'I think you know my daughters, Stacy Elaine and Kecia Nicole.' The girls had played with Mr Fish's daughters during the evacuees' stopover in Istanbul.

Mr Fish was not very warm.

'I need to talk to you,' Boulware said.

'Fine, talk to me.'

Boulware looked around the room. 'I want to talk to you in private.'

'Why?'

'You'll understand when I talk to you.'

'These are my partners. There are no secrets here.'

Mr Fish was giving Boulware a hard time. Boulware could guess why. There were two reasons. First, after all that Mr Fish had done during the evacuation, Don Norsworthy had tipped him $150, which was derisory, in Boulware's opinion. ('I didn't know what to do!' Norsworthy had said. 'The man's bill was twenty-six thousand dollars. What should I have tipped him – ten per cent?')

Secondly, Pat Sculley had approached Mr Fish with a transparent tale about smuggling computer tapes into Iran. Mr Fish was neither a fool nor a criminal, Boulware guessed; and of course he had refused to have anything to do with Sculley's scheme.

Now Mr Fish thought EDS people were (a) cheapskates and (b) dangerously amateurish law-breakers.

But Mr Fish was a small businessman. Boulware understood small businessmen – his father had been one. They spoke two languages: straight talk, and cash money. Cash money would solve problem (a) and straight talk problem (b).

'Okay, let's start again,' Boulware said. 'When EDS was here you really helped those people, treated the children nice, and did a great deal for us. When they

left there was a mix-up about showing you our appreciation. We're embarrassed that this was not handled
properly and I need to settle that score.'

'It's no big deal—'

'We're sorry,' Boulware said, and he gave Mr Fish a
thousand dollars in hundred-dollar bills.

The room went very quiet.

'Well, I'm going to check in to the Sheraton,' Boulware said. 'Maybe we can talk later.'

'I'll come with you,' said Mr Fish.

He personally checked Boulware into the hotel and
ensured that he got a good room, then agreed to meet
him for dinner that night in the hotel coffee shop.

Mr Fish was a high-class hustler, Boulware thought as
he unpacked. The man had to be smart, to have what
appeared to be a very prosperous business in this dirt-
poor country. The evacuees' experience showed that he
had the enterprise to do more than issue plane tickets
and make hotel bookings. He had the right contacts to
oil the wheels of bureaucracy, judging by the way he
had got everyone's baggage through customs. He had
also helped solve the problem of the adopted Iranian
baby with no passport. EDS's mistake had been to see
that he was a hustler and overlook the fact that he was
high-class – deceived, perhaps, by his unimpressive
appearance: he was rather fat and dressed in drab
clothes. Boulware, learning from past mistakes, thought
he could handle Mr Fish.

That night over dinner Boulware told him he wanted
to go to the Iran–Turkey border to meet some people
coming out.

Mr Fish was horrified. 'You don't understand,' he said. 'That is a *terrible* place. The people are Kurds and Azerbaijanis – wild mountain men, they don't obey any government. You know how they live up there? By smuggling, robbery and murder. I personally would not dare to go there. If you, an American, go there, you will never come back. Never.'

Boulware thought he was probably exaggerating. 'I have to go there, even if it's dangerous,' he said. 'Now, can I buy a light plane?'

Mr Fish shook his head. 'It is illegal in Turkey for individuals to own airplanes.'

'A helicopter?'

'Same thing.'

'All right, can I charter a plane?'

'It is possible. Where there is no scheduled flight, you can charter.'

'Are there scheduled flights to the border area?'

'No.'

'All right.'

'However, chartering is so unusual that you will surely attract the attention of the authorities . . .'

'We have no plans to do anything illegal. All the same, we don't need the hassle of being investigated. So let's set up the option of chartering. Find out about price and availability, but hold off from making any kind of booking. Meanwhile, I want to know more about getting there by land. If you don't want to escort me, fine, but maybe you can find somebody who will.'

'I'll see what I can do.'

They met several times over the next few days. Mr

Fish's initial coolness totally disappeared, and Boulware felt they were becoming friends. Mr Fish was alert and articulate. Although he was no criminal, he would break the law if the risks and rewards were proportionate, Boulware guessed. Boulware had some sympathy with that attitude – he, too, would break the law under the right circumstances. Mr Fish was also a shrewd interrogator, and bit by bit Boulware told him the full story. Paul and Bill would probably have no passports, he admitted; but once in Turkey they would get new ones at the nearest American Consulate. Paul and Bill might have some trouble getting out of Iran, he said, and he wanted to be prepared to cross the border himself, perhaps in a light aircraft, to bring them out. None of this fazed Mr Fish as much as the idea of travelling in bandit country.

However, a few days later he introduced Boulware to a man who had relatives among the mountain bandits. Mr Fish whispered that the man was a criminal, and he certainly looked the part: he had a scar on his face and little beady eyes. He said he could guarantee Boulware safe passage to the border and back, and his relatives could even take Boulware across the border into Iran, if necessary.

Boulware called Dallas and told Merv Stauffer about the plan. Stauffer relayed the news to Coburn, in code; and Coburn told Simons. Simons vetoed it. If the man is a criminal, Simons pointed out, we can't trust him.

Boulware was annoyed. He had gone to some trouble to set it up. Did Simons imagine it was easy to get these people? And if you wanted to travel in bandit country, who else but a bandit would escort you? But Simons was the boss, and Boulware had no option but to ask Mr Fish to start all over again.

Meanwhile, Sculley and Schwebach flew in to Istanbul.

The deadly duo had been on a flight from London to Tehran via Copenhagen when the Iranians had closed their airport again, so Sculley and Schwebach joined Boulware in Istanbul. Cooped up in the hotel, waiting for something to happen, the three of them got cabin fever. Schwebach reverted to his Green Beret role and tried to make them all keep fit by running up and down the hotel stairs. Boulware did it once and then gave up. They became impatient with Simons, Coburn and Poché, who seemed to be sitting in Tehran doing nothing: why didn't those guys *make it happen*? Then Simons sent Sculley and Schwebach back to the States. They left the radios with Boulware.

When Mr Fish saw the radios he had a fit. It was highly illegal to own a radio transmitter in Turkey, he told Boulware. Even ordinary transistor radios had to be registered with the government, for fear their parts would be used to make transmitters for terrorists. 'Don't you understand how *conspicuous* you are?' he said to Boulware. 'You're running up a phone bill of a couple of thousand dollars a week, and you're paying *cash*. You don't appear to be doing business here. The maids are sure to have seen the radios and talked about it. By now you must be under surveillance. Forget your friends in Iran – *you* are going to end up in jail.'

Boulware agreed to get rid of the radios. The snag

about Simons's apparently endless patience was that further delay caused new problems. Now Sculley and Schwebach could not get back into Iran, yet still nobody had any radios. Meanwhile Simons kept saying no to things. Mr Fish pointed out that there were two border crossings from Iran to Turkey, one at Sero and the other at Barzagan. Simons had picked Sero. Barzagan was a bigger and more civilized place, Mr Fish pointed out; everyone would be a little safer there. Simons said no.

A new escort was found to take Boulware to the border. Mr Fish had a business colleague whose brother-in-law was in the Milli Istihbarat Teskilati, or MIT, the Turkish equivalent of the CIA. The name of this secret policeman was Ilsman. His credentials would secure for Boulware army protection in bandit country. Without such credentials, Mr Fish said, the ordinary citizen was in danger not only from bandits but from the Turkish army.

Mr Fish was very jumpy. On the way to meet Ilsman, he took Boulware through a whole cloak-and-dagger routine, changing cars and switching to a bus for part of the journey, as if he were trying to shake off a tail. Boulware could not see the need for all that if they were really going to visit a perfectly upright citizen who just happened to work in the intelligence community. But Boulware was a foreigner in a strange country, and he just had to go along with Mr Fish and trust the man.

They ended up at a big, run-down apartment building in an unfamiliar section of the city. The power was off – just like Tehran – so it took Mr Fish a while to find the right apartment in the dark. At first he could get no answer. His attempt to be secretive fell apart at this point, for he had to hammer on the door for what seemed like half an hour, and every other inhabitant of the building got a good look at the visitors in the meantime. Boulware just stood there feeling like a white man in Harlem. At last a woman opened up, and they went in.

It was a small, drab apartment crowded with ancient furniture and dimly lit by a couple of candles. Ilsman was a short man of about Boulware's age, thirty-five. He had not seen his feet for many years – he was *gross*. He made Boulware think of the stereotyped fat police sergeant in the movies, with a suit too small and a sweaty shirt and a wrinkled tie wrapped around the place where his neck would have been if he had had a neck.

They sat down, and the woman – Mrs Ilsman, Boulware presumed – served tea – just like Tehran! Boulware explained his problem, with Mr Fish translating. Ilsman was suspicious. He cross-questioned Boulware about the two fugitive Americans. How could Boulware be sure they were innocent? Why did they have no passports? What would they bring into Turkey? In the end he seemed convinced that Boulware was levelling with him, and he offered to get Paul and Bill from the border to Istanbul for eight thousand dollars, all in.

Boulware wondered if Ilsman was for real. Smuggling Americans into the country was a funny pastime for an intelligence agent. And if Ilsman really was MIT, who was it that Mr Fish thought might have been following him and Boulware across town?

Perhaps Ilsman was freelancing. Eight thousand dollars was a lot of money in Turkey. It was even possible that Ilsman would tell his superiors what he was doing. After all – Ilsman might figure – if Boulware's story were true no harm would be done by helping; and if Boulware were lying, the best way to find out what he was really up to might be to accompany him to the border.

Anyway, at this point Ilsman seemed to be the best Boulware could get. Boulware agreed the price, and Ilsman broke out a bottle of scotch.

While other members of the rescue team were fretting in various parts of the world, Simons and Coburn were driving the road from Tehran to the Turkish border.

Reconnaissance was a watchword with Simons, and he wanted to be familiar with every inch of his escape route before he embarked on it with Paul and Bill. How much fighting was there in that part of the country? What was the police presence? Were the roads passable in winter? Were the filling stations open?

In fact there were two routes to Sero, the border crossing he had chosen. (He preferred Sero because it was a little-used frontier post at a tiny village, so there would be few people and the border would be lightly guarded, whereas Barzagan – the alternative Mr Fish kept recommending – would be busier.) The nearest large town to Sero was Rezaiyeh. Directly across the path from Tehran to Rezaiyeh lay Lake Rezaiyeh, a hundred miles long: you had to drive around it, either to the north or to the south. The northerly route went through large towns and would have better roads. Simons therefore preferred the southerly route, provided the roads were passable. On this reconnaissance trip, he decided, they would check out both routes, the northerly going and the southerly on the return.

He decided that the best kind of car for the trip was a Range Rover. There were no dealerships or used car lots open in Tehran now, so Coburn gave the Cycle Man the job of getting hold of two Range Rovers. The Cycle Man's solution to the problem was characteristically ingenious. He had a notice printed with his telephone number and the message: 'If you would like to sell your Range Rover, call this number.' Then he went around on his motorcycle and put a copy under the windscreen wipers of every Range Rover he saw parked on the streets.

He got two vehicles for $20,000 each, and he also bought tools and spare parts for all but the most major repairs.

Simons and Coburn took two Iranians with them: Majid, and a cousin of Majid's who was a professor at an agricultural college in Rezaiyeh. The professor had come to Tehran to put his American wife and their children on a plane to the States: taking him back to Rezaiyeh was Simons's cover story for the trip.

They left Tehran early in the morning, with one of Keane Taylor's 55-gallon drums of gasoline in the back. For the first hundred miles, as far as Qazvin, there was a modern freeway. After Qazvin the road was a two-lane blacktop. The hillsides were covered with snow, but the road itself was clear. If it's like this all the way to the border, Coburn thought, we could get there in a day.

They stopped at Zanjan, two hundred miles from Tehran and the same distance from Rezaiyeh, and spoke to the local chief of police, who was related to the professor. (Coburn could never quite work out the family relationships of Iranians: they seemed to use the word 'cousin' rather loosely.) This part of the country was peaceful, the police chief said, if they were to encounter any problems it would happen in the area of Tabriz.

They drove on through the afternoon, on narrow but good country roads. After another hundred miles they entered Tabriz. There was a demonstration going on, but it was nothing like the kind of battle they had got used to in Tehran, and they even felt secure enough to take a stroll around the bazaar.

Along the way Simons had been talking to Majid and the professor. It seemed like a casual conversation, but by now Coburn was familiar with Simons's technique, and he knew that the Colonel was feeling these two out, deciding whether he could trust them. So far the prognosis seemed good, for Simons began to drop hints about the real purpose of the trip.

The professor said that the countryside around Tabriz was pro-Shah, so before they moved on Simons stuck a photograph of the Shah on the windscreen.

The first sign of trouble came a few miles north of Tabriz, where they were stopped by a roadblock. It was an amateur affair, just two tree-trunks laid across the road in such a way that cars could manoeuvre around them but could not pass through at speed. It was manned by villagers armed with axes and sticks.

Majid and the professor talked to the villagers. The professor showed his university identity card, and said that the Americans were scientists come to help him with a research project. It was clear, Coburn thought, that the rescue team would need to bring Iranians when and if they did the trip with Paul and Bill, to handle situations like this.

The villagers let them pass.

A little later, Majid stopped and waved down a car coming in the opposite direction. The professor talked to the driver of the other car for a few minutes, then reported that the next town, Khoy, was anti-Shah. Simons took down the picture of the Shah from the windscreen and replaced it with one of the Ayatollah Khomeini. From then on they would stop oncoming cars regularly and change the picture according to local politics.

On the outskirts of Khoy there was another roadblock.

Like the first one, it looked unofficial, and was manned by civilians; but this time the ragged men and boys standing behind the tree-trunks were holding guns.

Majid stopped the car and they all got out.

To Coburn's horror a teenage boy pointed a gun at him.

Coburn froze.

The gun was a 9mm Llama pistol. The boy looked about sixteen. He had probably never handled a firearm before today, Coburn thought. Amateurs with guns were *dangerous.* The boy was holding the gun so tightly that his knuckles showed white.

Coburn was scared. He had been shot at many times, in Vietnam, but what frightened him now was the possibility that he would be killed by goddam *accident.*

'Rooskie,' the boy said. 'Rooskie.'

He thinks I'm a Russian, Coburn realized.

Perhaps it was because of the bushy red beard and the little black wool cap.

'No, American,' Coburn said.

The boy kept his pistol levelled.

Coburn stared at those white knuckles and thought: I just hope the punk doesn't *sneeze.*

The villagers searched Simons, Majid and the professor. Coburn, who could not take his eyes off the kid, heard Majid say: 'They're looking for weapons.' The only weapon they had was a little knife which Coburn was wearing in a scabbard behind his back, under his shirt.

A villager began to search Coburn, and at last the kid lowered his pistol.

Coburn breathed again.

Then he wondered what would happen when they found his knife.

The search was not thorough, and the knife was not found.

The vigilantes believed the story about the scientific project. 'They apologize for searching the old man,' Majid said. The 'old man' was Simons, who was now looking just like an elderly Iranian peasant. 'We can go on,' Majid added.

340

They climbed back into the car.

Outside Khoy they turned south, looping over the top end of the lake, and drove down the western shore to the outskirts of Rezaiyeh.

The professor guided them into the town by remote roads, and they saw no roadblocks. The journey from Tehran had taken them twelve hours, and they were now an hour away from the border crossing at Sero.

That evening they all had dinner – chella kebab, the Iranian dish of rice and lamb – with the professor's landlord, who happened to be a customs official. Majid gently pumped the landlord for information, and learned that there was very little activity at the Sero frontier station.

They spent the night at the professor's house, a two-storey villa on the outskirts of the town.

In the morning Majid and the professor drove to the border and back. They reported that there were no roadblocks and the route was safe. Then Majid went into town to seek out a contact from whom he could buy firearms, and Simons and Coburn went to the border.

They found a small frontier post with only two guards. It had a customs warehouse, a weighbridge for lorries, and a guard house. The road was barred by a low chain stretched betwen a post on one side and the wall of the guard house on the other. Beyond the chain was about two hundred yards of no-man's land, then another, smaller frontier post on the Turkish side.

They got out of the car to look around. The air was pure and bitingly cold. Simons pointed across the hillside. 'See the tracks?'

Coburn followed Simons's finger. In the snow, close behind the border station, was a trail where a small caravan had crossed the border, impudently close to the guards.

Simons pointed again, this time above their heads. 'Easy to cut the guards off.' Coburn looked up and saw a single telephone wire leading down the hill from the station. A quick snip and the guards would be isolated.

The two of them walked down the hill and took a side road, no more than a dirt track, into the hills. After a mile or so they came to a small village, just a dozen or so houses made of wood or mud brick. Speaking halting Turkish, Simons asked for the chief. A middle-aged man in baggy trousers, waistcoat and headdress appeared. Coburn listened without understanding as Simons talked. Finally Simons shook the chief's hand, and they left.

'What was all that about?' Coburn asked as they walked away.

'I told him I wanted to cross the border on horseback at night with some friends.'

'What did he say?'

'He said he could arrange it.'

'How did you know the people in that particular village were smugglers?'

'Look around you,' Simons said.

Coburn looked around at the bare snow-covered slopes.

'What do you see?' Simons asked.

'Nothing.'

'Right. There is no agriculture here, no industry. How do you think these people make a living? They're *all* smugglers.'

They returned to the Range Rover and drove back into Rezaiyeh. That evening Simons explained his plan to Coburn.

Simons, Coburn, Poché, Paul and Bill would drive from Tehran to Rezaiyeh in the two Range Rovers. They would bring Majid and the professor with them as interpreters. In Rezaiyeh they would stay at the professor's house. The villa was ideal: no one else lived there, it was detached from other houses, and from there quiet roads led out of the city. Between Tehran and Rezaiyeh they would be unarmed: judging by what had happened at the roadblocks, guns would get them into trouble. However, at Rezaiyeh they would buy guns. Majid had made a contact in the city who would sell them Browning 12-gauge shotguns for six thousand dollars apiece. The same man could also get Llama pistols.

Coburn would cross the border legitimately in one of the Range Rovers and link up with Boulware, who would also have a car, on the Turkish side. Simons, Poché, Paul and Bill would cross on horseback with the smugglers. (That was why they needed the guns: in case the smugglers should decide to 'lose' them in the mountains.) On the other side they would meet Coburn and Boulware. They would all drive to the nearest American consulate and get new passports for Paul and Bill. Then they would fly to Dallas.

It was a good plan, Coburn thought; and he now saw

that Simons was right to insist on Sero rather than Barzagan, for it would be difficult to sneak across the border in a more civilized, heavily populated area.

They returned to Tehran the next day. They left late and did most of the journey by night, so as to be sure to arrive in the morning, after curfew was lifted. They took the southerly route, passing through the small town of Mahabad. The road was a single-lane dirt track through the mountains, and they had the worst possible weather: snow, ice, and high winds. Nevertheless the roads were passable, and Simons determined to use this route, rather than the northerly one, for the escape itself.

If it ever happened.

III

One evening Coburn went to the Hyatt and told Keane Taylor he needed twenty-five thousand dollars in Iranian rials by the following morning.

He didn't say why.

Taylor got twenty-five thousand dollars in hundreds from Gayden, then called a carpet dealer he knew in the south of the city and agreed an exchange rate.

Taylor's driver, Ali, was highly reluctant to take him downtown, especially after dark, but after some argument he agreed.

They went to the shop. Taylor sat down and drank tea with the carpet dealer. Two more Iranians came in: one was introduced as the man who would exchange

Taylor's money; the other was his bodyguard, and looked like a hoodlum.

Since Taylor's phone call, the carpet dealer said, the exchange rate had changed rather dramatically – in the carpet dealer's favour.

'I'm insulted!' Taylor said angrily. 'I'm not going to do business with you people!'

'This is the best exchange rate you can get,' said the carpet man.

'The hell it is!'

'It's very dangerous for you to be in this part of the city, carrying all that money.'

'I'm not alone,' Taylor said. 'I've got six people waiting for me.'

He finished his tea and stood up. He walked slowly out of the shop and jumped in the car. 'Ali, let's get out of here, fast.'

They drove north. Taylor directed Ali to another carpet dealer, an Iranian Jew with a shop near the palace. The man was just closing up when Taylor walked in.

'I need to change some dollars for rials,' Taylor said.

'Come back tomorrow,' said the man.

'No, I need them tonight.'

'How much?'

'Twenty-five thousand dollars.'

'I don't have anything like that much.'

'I've really got to have them tonight.'

'What's it for?'

'It's to do with Paul and Bill.'

345

The carpet dealer nodded. He had done business with several EDS people and he knew that Paul and Bill were in jail. 'I'll see what I can do.'

He called his brother from the back of the shop and sent him out. Then he opened his safe and took out all his rials. He and Taylor stood there counting money: the dealer counted the dollars and Taylor the rials. A few minutes later a kid came in with his hands full of rials and dumped them on the counter. He left without speaking. Taylor realized the carpet dealer was rounding up all the cash he could lay his hands on.

A young man came up on a motor scooter, parked outside, and walked in with a bag full of rials. While he was in the shop someone stole his motor scooter. The young man dropped the bag of money and ran after the thief, yelling at the top of his voice.

Taylor went on counting.

Just another business day in revolutionary Tehran.

John Howell was changing. With each day that went by he became a little less the upright American lawyer and a little more the devious Persian negotiator. In particular, he began to see bribery in a different light.

Mehdi, an Iranian accountant who had done occasional work for EDS, had explained things to him like this: 'In Iran many things are achieved by friendship. There are several ways to become Dadgar's friend. Me, I would sit outside his house every day until he talked to me. Another way for me to become his friend would be to give him two hundred thousand dollars. If you like I could arrange something like this for you.'

Howell discussed this proposal with the other members of the negotiating team. They assumed that Mehdi was offering himself as a bribe intermediary, as Deep Throat had. But this time Howell was not so quick to reject the idea of a corrupt deal for Paul's and Bill's freedom.

They decided to play along with Mehdi. They might be able to expose the deal and discredit Dadgar. Alternatively, they might decide the arrangement was solid and pay up. Either way, they wanted a clear sign from Dadgar that he was bribeable.

Howell and Keane Taylor had a series of meetings with Mehdi. The accountant was as jumpy as Deep Throat had been, and would not let the EDS people come to his office during normal working hours: he always met them early in the morning or late at night, or at his house or down back alleys. Howell kept pressing him for an unmistakable signal: Dadgar was to come to a meeting wearing odd socks, or with his tie on backwards. Mehdi would propose ambiguous signals, such as Dadgar giving the Americans a hard time. On one occasion Dadgar did give them a hard time, as Mehdi had forecast, but that might have happened anyway.

Dadgar was not the only one giving Howell a hard time. Howell was talking to Angela on the phone every four or five days, and she wanted to know when he was coming home. He did not know. Paul and Bill were naturally pressing him for hard news, but his progress was so slow and indefinite that he could not possibly give them deadlines. He found this frustrating, and when Angela started questioning him on the same point he had to suppress his irritation.

The Mehdi initiative came to nothing. Mehdi introduced Howell to a lawyer who claimed to be close to Dadgar. The lawyer did not want a bribe – just normal legal fees. EDS retained him, but at the next meeting Dadgar said: 'Nobody has any special relationship with me. If anybody tries to tell you differently, don't believe them.'

Howell was not sure what to make of all this. Had there been nothing in it right from the start? Or had EDS's caution frightened Dadgar into dropping a demand for a bribe? He would never know.

On 30 January Dadgar told Howell he was interested in Abolfath Mahvi, EDS's Iranian partner. Howell began to prepare a dossier on EDS's dealings with Mahvi.

Howell now believed that Paul and Bill were straightforward commercial hostages. Dadgar's investigation into corruption might be genuine, but he knew by now that Paul and Bill were innocent, therefore he must be holding them on orders from above. The Iranians had originally wanted either their promised computerized welfare system or their money back. Giving them their welfare system meant renegotiating the contract – but the new government was not interested in renegotiating and in any case was unlikely to stay in power long enough to consummate a deal.

If Dadgar could not be bribed, convinced of Paul's and Bill's innocence, or ordered by his superior to release them on the basis of a new contract between EDS and the Ministry, there remained to Howell only one option: pay the bail. Dr Houman's efforts to get the amount reduced had come to nothing. Howell now concentrated on ways of getting thirteen million dollars from Dallas to Tehran.

He had learned, bit by bit, that there was an EDS rescue team in Tehran. He was astonished that the head of an American corporation would set in motion something like that. He was also reassured, for if he could only get Paul and Bill out of jail, somebody else was standing by to get them out of Iran.

Liz Coburn was frantic with worry.

She sat in the car with Toni Dvoranchik and Toni's husband Bill. They were heading for the Royal Tokyo restaurant. It was on Greenville Avenue, not far from Recipes, the place where Liz and Toni had drunk Daiquiris with Mary Sculley and Mary had shattered Liz's world by saying: 'They're all in Tehran, I guess.'

Since that moment Liz had been living in constant, stark terror.

Jay was everything to her. He was Captain America, he was Superman, he was her whole life. She did not see how she could live without him. The thought of losing him scared her to death.

She called Tehran constantly but never reached him. She called Merv Stauffer every day, saying: 'When is Jay coming home? Is he all right? Will he get out alive?' Merv tried to soothe her, but he would not give her any information and so she would demand to speak to Ross Perot. Merv would tell her that was not possible. Then she would call her mother and burst into tears and pour out all her anxiety and fear and frustration over the phone.

The Dvoranchiks were kind. They were trying to take her mind off her worries.

'What did you do today?' Toni asked.

'I went shopping,' Liz said.

'Did you buy anything?'

'Yes.' Liz started to cry. 'I bought a black dress. Because Jay isn't coming home.'

During those days of waiting, Jay Coburn learned a good deal about Simons.

One day Merv Stauffer called from Dallas to say that Simons's son Harry had been on the phone, worried. Harry had called his father's house and spoken to Paul Walker, who was minding the farm. Walker had said he did not know where Simons was, and had advised Harry to call Merv Stauffer at EDS. Harry was naturally worried, Stauffer said. Simons called Harry from Tehran and reassured him.

Simons told Coburn that Harry had had some problems, but he was a good boy at heart. He spoke of his son with a kind of resigned affection. (He never mentioned Bruce, and it was not until much later that Coburn realized Simons had two sons.)

Simons talked a lot about his late wife, Lucille, and how happy the two of them had been after Simons retired. They had been very close during the last few years, Coburn gathered, and Simons seemed to regret that it had taken him so long to realize how much he loved her. 'Hold on to your mate,' he advised Coburn. 'She's the most important person in your life.'

Paradoxically, Simons's advice had the opposite effect on Coburn. He envied the companionship Simons and Lucille had had, and he wanted that for himself; but he was so sure he could never achieve it with Liz that he wondered if someone else would be his true soul-mate.

One evening Simons laughed and said: 'You know, I wouldn't do this for anyone else.'

It was a characteristically cryptic Simons remark. Sometimes, Coburn had learned, you got an explanation, sometimes you did not. This time Coburn got an explanation: Simons told him why he felt indebted to Ross Perot.

The aftermath of the Son Tay Raid had been a bitter experience for Simons. Although the raiders had not brought back any American POWs, it had been a brave try, and Simons expected the American public to see it that way. Indeed, he had argued, at a breakfast meeting with Defence Secretary Melvin Laird, in favour of releasing the news of the raid to the press. 'This is a perfectly legitimate operation,' he had told Laird. 'These are American prisoners. This is something Americans traditionally do for Americans. For Christ's sake, what is it we're afraid of here?'

He soon found out. The press and the public saw the raid as a failure and yet another intelligence foul-up. The banner headline on the front page of the next day's

Washington Post read: US RAID TO RESCUE POWS FAILS. When Senator Robert Dole introduced a resolution praising the raid and said 'Some of these men have been languishing in prison for five years,' Senator Kennedy replied. 'And they're still there!'

Simons went to the White House to receive the Distinguished Service Cross for 'extraordinary heroism' from President Nixon. The rest of the raiders were to be decorated by Defence Secretary Laird. Simons was enraged to learn that over half of his men were to get nothing more than the Army Commendation Ribbon, only slightly better than a Good Conduct Ribbon, and known to soldiers as a Green Weenie. Mad as hell, he picked up the phone and asked for the Army Chief of Staff, General Westmoreland. He got the Acting Chief, General Palmer. Simons told Palmer about the Green Weenies and said: 'General, I don't want to embarrass the Army, but one of my men is just likely to shove an Army Commendation Ribbon up Mr Laird's ass.' He got his way. Laird awarded four Distinguished Service Crosses, fifty Silver Stars, and no Green Weenies.

The POWs got a huge morale boost from the Son Tay Raid (which they heard about from incoming prisoners). An important side-effect of the raid was that the POW camps – where many prisoners had been kept permanently in solitary confinement – were closed, and all the Americans were brought in to two large prisons where there was not enough room to keep them apart. Nevertheless, the world branded the raid a failure, and Simons felt a grave injustice had been done to his men.

The disappointment rankled with him for years –

until, one weekend, Ross Perot threw a mammoth party in San Francisco, persuaded the Army to round up the Son Tay Raiders from all over the world, and introduced them to the prisoners they had tried to rescue. That weekend, Simons felt, his raiders had at last got the thanks they deserved. And Ross Perot had been responsible.

'That's why I'm here,' Simons told Coburn. 'Sure as hell, I wouldn't do this for anyone else.'

Coburn, thinking of his son Scott, knew exactly what Simons meant.

IV

On 22 January hundreds of homafars – young Air Force officers – mutinied at bases in Dezful, Hamadan, Isfahan and Mashad, and declared themselves loyal to the Ayatollah Khomeini.

The significance of the event was not apparent to National Security Adviser Zbigniew Brzezinski, who still expected the Iranian military to crush the Islamic revolution; nor to Premier Shahpour Bakhtiar, who was talking about meeting the revolutionary challenge with a minimum of force; nor to the Shah, who instead of going to the United States was hanging on in Egypt, waiting to be summoned back to save his country in its hour of need.

Among the people who did see its significance were Ambassador William Sullivan and General Abbas Gharabaghi, the Iranian Chief of Staff.

Sullivan told Washington that the idea of a pro-Shah counter-coup was moonshine, the revolution was going to succeed and the US had better start thinking about how it would live with the new order. He received a harsh reply from the White House suggesting that he was disloyal to the President. He decided to resign, but his wife talked him out of it: he had a responsibility to the thousands of Americans still in Iran, she pointed out, and he could hardly walk out on them now.

General Gharabaghi also contemplated resigning. He was in an impossible situation. He had sworn his oath of loyalty, not to the parliament or the government of Iran, but to the Shah personally; and the Shah was gone. For the time being Gharabaghi took the view that the military owed loyalty to the Constitution of 1906, but that meant little in practice. Theoretically the military ought to support the Bakhtiar government. Gharabaghi had been wondering for some weeks whether he could rely on his soldiers to follow orders and fight for Bakhtiar against the revolutionary forces. The revolt of the homafars showed that he could not. He realized – as Brzezinski did not – that the army was not a machine to be switched on and off at will, but a collection of people, sharing the aspirations, the anger and the revivalist religion of the rest of the country. The soldiers wanted a revolution as much as the civilians. Gharabaghi concluded that he could no longer control his troops, and he decided to resign.

On the day that he announced his intention to his fellow generals, Ambassador William Sullivan was summoned to Prime Minister Bakhtiar's office at six o'clock in the evening. Sullivan had heard, from US General 'Dutch' Huyser, of Gharabaghi's intended resignation, and he assumed that this was what Bakhtiar wanted to talk about.

Bakhtiar waved Sullivan to a seat, saying with an enigmatic smile: '*Nous serons trois.*' There will be three of us. Bakhtiar always spoke French with Sullivan.

A few minutes later General Gharabaghi walked in. Bakhtiar spoke of the difficulties that would be created if the general were to resign. Gharabaghi began to reply in Farsi, but Bakhtiar made him speak French. As the general talked, he toyed with what seemed to be an envelope in his pocket. Sullivan guessed it was his letter of resignation.

As the two Iranians argued in French, Bakhtiar kept turning to the American Ambassador for support. Sullivan secretly thought Gharabaghi was absolutely right to resign, but his orders from the White House were to encourage the military to support Bakhtiar, so he doggedly argued, against his own convictions, that Gharabaghi should not resign. After a discussion of half an hour, the general left without delivering his letter of resignation. Bakhtiar thanked Sullivan profusely for his help. Sullivan knew it would do no good.

On 24 January Bakhtiar closed Tehran's airport to stop Khomeini entering Iran. It was like opening an umbrella against a tidal wave. On 26 January soldiers killed fifteen pro-Khomeini protectors in street fighting in Tehran. Two days later Bakhtiar offered to go to Paris for talks with the Ayatollah. For a ruling Prime Minister to offer to visit an exiled rebel was a fantastic admission of weakness, and Khomeini saw it that way: he refused to talk unless Bakhtiar first resigned. On 29 January thirty-five people died in the fighting in Tehran and another fifty in the rest of the country. Gharabaghi, bypassing his Prime Minister, began talks with the rebels in Tehran, and gave his consent for the return of the Ayatollah. On 30 January Sullivan ordered the evacuation of all nonessential Embassy personnel and all dependents. On 1 February Khomeini came home.

His Air France jumbo jet landed at 9.15 a.m. Two million Iranians turned out to greet him. At the airport the Ayatollah made his first public statement. 'I beg God to cut off the hands of all evil foreigners and all their helpers.'

Simons saw it all on TV, then he said to Coburn: 'That's it. The people are going to do it for us. The mob will take that jail.'

CHAPTER NINE

I

AT MIDDAY on 5 February John Howell was on the point of getting Paul and Bill out of jail.

Dadgar had said that he would accept bail in one of three forms: cash, a bank guarantee, or a lien on property. Cash was out of the question. Firstly, anyone who flew into the lawless city of Tehran with $12,750,000 in a suitcase might never reach Dadgar's office alive. Secondly, Dadgar might take the money and still keep Paul and Bill, either by raising the bail or by rearresting them on some new pretext. (Tom Walter suggested using counterfeit money but nobody knew where to get it.) There had to be a *document* which gave Dadgar the money and at the same time gave Paul and Bill their freedom. In Dallas, Tom Walter had at last found a bank willing to issue a letter of credit for the bail, but Howell and Taylor were having trouble finding an Iranian bank to accept it and issue the guarantee Dadgar required. Meanwhile, Howell's boss Tom Luce thought about the third option, a lien on property, and came up with a wild and whacky idea that just might work: pledging the US Embassy in Tehran as bail for Paul and Bill.

The State Department was by now loosening up but was not quite ready to pledge its Tehran embassy as bail.

However, it was ready to give the guarantee of the United States Government. That in itself was unique: the USA standing bail for two jailed men!

First, Tom Walter in Dallas got a bank to issue a letter of credit in favour of the State Department for $12,750,000. Because this transaction took place entirely within the US it was accomplished in hours rather than days. Once the State Department in Washington had the letter, Minister Counsellor Charles Naas – Ambassador Sullivan's deputy – would deliver a diplomatic note saying that Paul and Bill, once released, would make themselves available to Dadgar for questioning, otherwise the bail would be paid by the Embassy.

Right now Dadgar was in a meeting with Lou Goelz, Consul General at the Embassy. Howell had not been invited to attend, but Abolhasan was there for EDS.

Howell had had a preliminary meeting with Goelz yesterday. Together they had gone over the terms of the guarantee, with Goelz reading the phrases in his quiet, precise voice. Goelz was changing. Two months ago Howell had found him maddeningly correct: it was Goelz who had refused to give back Paul's and Bill's passports without telling the Iranians. Now Goelz seemed ready to try the unconventional. Perhaps living in the middle of a revolution had made the old boy unbend a little.

Goelz had told Howell that the decision to release Paul and Bill would be made by Prime Minister Bakhtiar, but it must first be cleared with Dadgar. Howell was hoping Dadgar would not make trouble, for Goelz was not the type of man to bang the table and force Dadgar to back down.

There was a tap at the door and Abolhasan walked in.

Howell could tell from his face that he brought bad news.

'What happened?'

'He turned us down,' Abolhasan said.

'Why?'

'He won't accept the guarantee of the United States Government.'

'Did he give a reason?'

'There's nothing in the law that says he can accept that as bail. He has to have cash, a bank guarantee—'

'Or a lien on property, I know.' Howell felt numb. There had been so many disappointments, so many dead ends, he was no longer capable of resentment or anger. 'Did you say anything about the Prime Minister?'

'Yes. Goelz told him we would take this proposal to Bakhtiar.'

'What did Dadgar say to that?'

'He said it was typical of the Americans. They try to resolve things by bringing influence to bear at high levels, with no concern for what is happening at lower levels. He also said that if his superiors did not like the way he was handling the case, they could take him off it, and he would be very happy, because he was weary of it.'

Howell frowned. What did all this mean? He had recently concluded that what the Iranians really wanted was the money. Now they had flatly turned it down. Was this genuinely because of the technical problem that the law did not specify a government guarantee as an acceptable form of bail – or was that an excuse? Perhaps it was genuine. The EDS case had always been politically sensitive, and now that the Ayatollah had returned, Dadgar might well be terrified of doing anything that could be construed as pro-American. Bending the rules to accept an unconventional form of bail might get him into trouble. What would happen if Howell succeeded in putting up bail in the legally required form? Would Dadgar then feel he had covered his rear, and release Paul and Bill? Or would he invent another excuse?

There was only one way to find out.

The week the Ayatollah returned to Iran, Paul and Bill asked for a priest.

Paul's cold seemed to have turned to bronchitis. He had asked for the prison doctor. The doctor did not speak English, but Paul had no trouble explaining his problem: he coughed, and the doctor nodded.

Paul was given some pills which he assumed were penicillin, and a bottle of cough medicine. The taste of the medicine was strikingly familiar, and he had a sudden, vivid flashback: he saw himself as a little boy, and his mother pouring the glutinous syrup from an old-fashioned bottle on to a spoon and dosing him with it. This was exactly the same stuff. It eased his cough, but he had already done some damage to the muscles in his chest, and he suffered a sharp pain every time he breathed deeply.

He had a letter from Ruthie which he read and re-read. It was an ordinary, newsy kind of letter. Karen was in a new school, and having some trouble adjusting. This was normal: every time she changed schools, Karen would be sick to her stomach for the first couple of days. Ann Marie, Paul's younger daughter, was much more happy-go-lucky. Ruthie was still telling her mother that Paul would be home in a couple of weeks, but the story was becoming implausible for that two-week deadline had now been stretched for two months. She was buying a house, and Tom Walter was helping her with the legal processes. Whatever emotions Ruthie was going through, she did not put them in the letter.

Keane Taylor was the most frequent visitor to the jail. Each time he came, he would hand Paul a pack of cigarettes with fifty or a hundred dollars folded inside. Paul and Bill could use the money in jail to buy special privileges, such as a bath. During one visit the guard left the room for a moment, and Taylor handed over four thousand dollars.

On another visit Taylor brought Father Williams.

Williams was pastor of the Catholic Mission where, in happier times, Paul and Bill had met with the EDS Tehran Roman Catholic Sunday Brunch Poker School. Williams was eighty years old, and his superiors had given him permission to leave Tehran, because of the danger. He had preferred to stay at his post. This kind of thing was not new to him, he told Paul and Bill: he had been a missionary in China during World War Two, when the Japanese had invaded, and later, during the revolution which brought Mao-Tse Tung to power. He himself had been imprisoned, so he understood what Paul and Bill were going through.

Father Williams boosted their morale almost as much as Ross Perot had. Bill, who was more devout than Paul, felt deeply strengthened by the visit. It gave him the courage to face the unknown future. Father Williams granted them absolution for their sins before he left. Bill still did not know whether he would get out of the jail alive, but now he felt prepared to face death.

Iran exploded into revolution on Friday 9 February 1979.

In just over a week Khomeini had destroyed what was left of legitimate government. He had called on the military to mutiny and the members of parliament to resign. He had appointed a 'provisional government' despite the fact that Bakhtiar was still officially Prime Minister. His supporters, organized into revolutionary committees, had taken over responsibility for law and order and garbage collection, and had opened more than a hundred Islamic co-operative stores in Tehran. On 8 February a million people or more marched through the city in support of the Ayatollah. Street fighting went on continually between stray units of loyalist soldiers and gangs of Khomeini men.

On 9 February, at two Tehran air bases – Doshen Toppeh and Farahabad – formations of homafars and cadets gave a salute to Khomeini. This infuriated the Javadan Brigade, which had been the Shah's personal bodyguard, and they attacked both air bases. The homafars barricaded themselves in and repelled the loyalist troops, helped by crowds of armed revolutionaries milling around inside and outside the bases.

Units of both the Marxist Fedayeen and the Muslim Mujahedeen guerrillas rushed to Doshen Toppeh. The armoury was broken open and weapons were distributed indiscriminately to soldiers, guerrillas, revolutionaries, demonstrators, and passers-by.

That night at eleven o'clock the Javadan Brigade returned in force. Khomeini supporters within the military warned the Doshen Toppeh rebels that the Brigade was on its way, and the rebels counter-attacked before the Brigade reached the base. Several senior officers among the loyalists were killed early in the battle. The fighting continued all night, and spread to a large area around the base.

By noon on the following day, the battlefield had widened to include most of the city.

That day John Howell and Keane Taylor went downtown for a meeting.

Howell was convinced they would get Paul and Bill released within hours. They were all set to pay the bail.

Tom Walter had a Texas bank ready to issue a letter of credit for $12,750,000 to the New York branch of Bank Melli. The plan was that the Tehran branch of Bank Melli would then issue a bank guarantee to the Ministry of Justice, and Paul and Bill would be bailed out. It had not worked quite that way. The deputy managing director of Bank Melli, Sadr-Hashemi, had recognized – as had all the bankers – that Paul and Bill were commercial hostages, and that once they were out of jail EDS could argue in an American court that the money had been extorted and should not be paid. If that happened, Bank Melli in New York would not be able to collect on the letter of credit – but Bank Melli in Tehran would still have to pay the money to the Iranian Ministry of Justice. Sadr-Hashemi said he would change his mind only if his New York lawyers told him there was no way EDS could block payment on the letter of credit. Howell knew perfectly well that no decent American attorney would issue such an option.

Then Keane Taylor thought of Bank Omran. EDS had a contract to install an on-line computerized accounting system for Bank Omran, and Taylor's job in Tehran had been to supervise this contract, so he knew the bank's officials. He met with Farhad Bakhtiar, who was one of the top men there as well as being a relative of Prime Minister Shahpour Bakhtiar. It was clear that the Prime Minister was going to fall from power any day, and Farhad was planning to leave the country. Perhaps that was why he was less concerned than Sadr-Hashemi about the possibility that the $12,750,000 would never be paid. Anyway, for whatever reason, he had agreed to help.

Bank Omran did not have a US branch. How, then, could EDS pay the money? It was agreed that the Dallas bank would lodge its letter of credit with the Dubai branch of Bank Omran by a system called Tested Telex. Dubai would then call Tehran on the phone to confirm that the letter of credit had been received, and the

Tehran branch of Bank Omran would issue the guarantee to the Ministry of Justice.

There were delays. Everything had to be approved by the board of directors of Bank Omran, and by the bank's lawyers. Everyone who looked at the deal suggested small changes in the language. The changes, in English and Farsi, had to be communicated to Dubai and to Dallas, then a new telex had to be sent from Dallas to Dubai, tested, and approved by phone with Tehran. Because the Iranian weekend was Thursday and Friday, there were only three days in the week when both banks were open; and because Tehran was nine and a half hours ahead of Dallas there was never a time of day when both banks were open. Furthermore, the Iranian banks were on strike a good deal of the time. Consequently a two-word change could take a week to arrange.

The last people who had to approve the deal were the Iranian central bank. Getting that approval was the task Howell and Taylor had set themselves for Saturday 10 February.

The city was relatively quiet at 8.30 in the morning when they drove to Bank Omran. They met with Farhad Bakhtiar. To their surprise he said that the request for approval was already with the central bank. Howell was delighted – for once something was happening ahead of time in Iran! He left some documents with Farhad, including a signed letter of agreement, and he and Taylor drove farther downtown to the central bank.

The city was waking up now, the traffic was even more nightmarish than usual, but dangerous driving was Taylor's speciality, and he tore through the streets, cutting across lanes of traffic, U-turning in the middle of freeways, and generally beating the Iranian drivers at their own game.

At the central bank they had a long wait to see Mr Farhang, who would give approval. Eventually he stuck his head out of his office door and said the deal had already been approved and the approval notified to Bank Omran.

This was good news!

They got back into the car and headed for Bank Omran. Now they could tell that there was serious fighting in parts of the city. The noise of gunfire was continuous, and plumes of smoke rose from burning buildings. Bank Omran was opposite a hospital, and the dead and wounded were being brought in from the battle zones in cars, pick-up trucks and buses, all the vehicles having white cloths tied to their radio antennae to signify emergency, all hooting constantly. The street was jammed with people, some coming to give blood, others to visit the sick, still others to identify corpses.

They had resolved the bail problem not a moment too soon. Not only Paul and Bill, but now Howell and Taylor and all of them were in grave danger. They had to get out of Iran fast.

Howell and Taylor went into the bank and found Farhad.

'The central bank has approved the deal,' Howell told him.

'I know.'

'Is the letter of agreement all right?'

'No problems.'

'Then, if you give us the bank guarantee, we can go to the Ministry of Justice with it right away.'

'Not today.'

'*Why not?*'

'Our lawyer, Dr Emami, has reviewed the credit document and wishes to make some small changes.'

Taylor muttered: 'Jesus *Christ.*'

Farhad said: 'I have to go to Geneva for five days.'

Forever was more likely.

'My colleagues will look after you, and if you have any problems just call me in Switzerland.'

Howell suppressed his anger. Farhad knew perfectly well that things were not that simple: with him away everything would be more difficult. But nothing would be accomplished by an emotional outburst, so Howell just said: 'What are the changes?'

Farhad called in Dr Emami.

'I also need the signatures of two more directors of the bank,' Farhad said. 'I can get those at the board meeting tomorrow. And I need to check the references of the National Bank of Commerce in Dallas.'

'And how long will that take?'

'Not long. My assistants will deal with it while I am away.'

Dr Emami showed Howell the changes he proposed in the language of the credit letter. Howell was happy to agree to them, but the rewritten letter would have to go through the time-consuming process of being transmitted from Dallas to Dubai by Tested Telex and from Dubai to Tehran by telephone.

'Look,' said Howell. 'Let's try to get all this done *today*. You could check the references of the Dallas bank *now*. We could find those other two bank directors, wherever in the city they are, and get their signatures *this afternoon*. We could call Dallas, give them the language changes, and get them to send the telex now. Dubai could confirm to you *this afternoon*. You could issue the bank guarantee—'

'There is a holiday in Dubai today,' said Farhad.

'All right, Dubai can confirm tomorrow morning—'

'There is a strike tomorrow. Nobody will be here at the bank.'

'Monday, then—'

The conversation was interrupted by the sound of a siren. A secretary put her head around the door and said something in Farsi. 'There is an early curfew,' Farhad translated. 'We must all leave now.'

Howell and Taylor sat there looking at each other. Two minutes later they were alone in the office. They had failed yet again.

That evening, Simons said to Coburn: 'Tomorrow is the day.'

Coburn thought he was full of shit.

II

In the morning on Sunday 11 February the negotiating team went as usual to the EDS office they called 'Bucharest'. John Howell left, taking Abolhasan with him, for an eleven o'clock meeting with Dadgar at the Ministry of Health. The others – Keane Taylor, Bill Gayden, Bob Young and Rich Gallagher – went up on the roof to watch the city burn.

Bucharest was not a high building but it was located on a slope of the hills which rose to the north of Tehran, so from the roof they could see the city laid out like a tableau. To the south and east, where modern sky-scrapers rose out of the low-rise villas and slums, great palls of smoke billowed up into the murky air, while helicopter gunships buzzed around the fires like wasps at a barbecue. One of EDS's Iranian drivers brought a transistor radio up to the roof and tuned it to a station which had been taken over by the revolutionaries. With the help of the radio and the driver's translation they tried to identify the burning buildings.

Keane Taylor, who had abandoned his elegant vested suits for jeans and cowboy boots, went downstairs to take a phone call. It was the Cycle Man.

'You need to get out of there,' the Cycle Man told Taylor. 'Get out of the country as quickly as you can.'

'You know we can't do that,' Taylor said. 'We can't leave without Paul and Bill.'

'It's going to be very dangerous for you.'

Taylor could hear, at the other end of the line, the noise of a terrific battle. 'Where the hell are you, anyway?'

'Near the bazaar,' said the Cycle Man. 'I'm making Molotov cocktails. They brought in helicopters this morning and we just figured out how to shoot them down. We burned four tanks—'

The line went dead.

Incredible, Taylor thought as he cradled the phone. In the middle of a battle, he suddenly thinks of his American friends, and calls to warn us. Iranians will never cease to surprise me.

He went back up on the roof.

'Look at this,' Bill Gayden said to him. Gayden, the jovial president of EDS World, had also switched to off-duty clothes: nobody was even pretending to do business any more. He pointed to a column of smoke in the east. 'If that isn't the Gasr Prison burning, it's damn close.'

Taylor peered into the distance. It was hard to tell.

'Call Dadgar's office at the Ministry of Health,' Gayden told Taylor. 'Howell should be there now. Get him to ask Dadgar to release Paul and Bill to the custody of the Embassy, for their own safety. If we don't get them out they're going to burn to death.'

John Howell had hardly expected Dadgar to turn up. The city was a battlefield, and an investigation into corruption under the Shah now seemed an academic exercise. But Dadgar was there in his office, waiting for Howell. Howell wondered what the hell was driving the man. Dedication? Hatred of Americans? Fear of the incoming revolutionary government? He would probably never know.

Dadgar had asked Howell about EDS's relationship with Abolfath Mahvi, and Howell had promised a complete dossier. It seemed the information was important to Dadgar's mysterious purposes, for a few days later he had pressed Howell for the dossier, saying: 'I can

370

interrogate the people here and get the information I need,' which Howell took as a threat to arrest more EDS executives.

Howell had prepared a twelve-page dossier in English, with a covering letter in Farsi. Dadgar read the covering letter, then spoke. Abolhasan translated: 'Your company's helpfulness is laying the ground for a change in my attitude towards Chiapparone and Gaylord. Our legal code provides for such leniency towards those who supply information.'

It was farcical. They could all be killed in the next few hours, and here was Dadgar still talking about applicable provisions of the legal code.

Abolhasan began to translate the dossier aloud into Farsi. Howell knew that choosing Mahvi as an Iranian partner had not been the smartest move EDS ever made: Mahvi had got the company its first, small contract in Iran, but subsequently he had been blacklisted by the Shah and had caused trouble over the Ministry of Health contract. However, EDS had nothing to hide. Indeed, Howell's boss Tom Luce, in his eagerness to place EDS above suspicion, had filed details of the EDS–Mahvi relationship with the American Securities Exchange Commission, so that much of what was in the dossier was already public knowledge.

The phone interrupted Abolhasan's translation. Dadgar picked it up then handed it to Abolhasan, who listened for a moment then said: 'It's Keane Taylor.'

A minute later he hung up and said to Howell: 'Keane has been up on the roof at Bucharest. He says there are fires down by Gasr Prison. If the mob attacks the prison Paul and Bill could get hurt. He suggested we ask Dadgar to turn them over to the American Embassy.'

'Okay,' Howell said. 'Ask him.'

He waited while Abolhasan and Dadgar conversed in Farsi.

Finally, Abolhasan said: 'According to our laws, they have to be kept in an Iranian prison. He can't consider the US Embassy to be an Iranian prison.'

Crazier and crazier. The whole country was falling apart and Dadgar was still consulting his book of rules. Howell said: 'Ask him how he proposes to guarantee the safety of two American citizens who have not been charged with any crime.'

Dadgar's reply was: 'Don't be concerned. The worst that could happen is that the prison might be overrun.'

'And what if the mob decides to attack Americans?'

'Chiapparone will probably be safe – he could pass for Iranian.'

'Terrific,' said Howell. 'And what about Gaylord?'

Dadgar just shrugged.

Rashid left his house early that morning.

His parents, his brother and his sister planned to stay indoors all day, and they had urged him to do the same, but he would not listen. He knew it would be dangerous on the streets, but he could not hide at home while his countrymen were making history. Besides, he had not forgotten his conversation with Simons.

He was living by impulse. On Friday he had found

himself at Farahabad air base during the clash between the homafars and the loyalist Javadan Brigade. For no particular reason, he had gone into the armoury and started passing out rifles. After half an hour of that he got bored and left.

The same day he had seen a dead man for the first time. He had been at the mosque when a bus driver who had been shot by soldiers had been brought in. On impulse Rashid had uncovered the face of the corpse. A whole section of the head was destroyed, a mixture of blood and brains: it had been sickening. The incident seemed like a warning, but Rashid was in no mood to heed warnings. The streets were where things were happening, and he had to be there.

This morning the atmosphere was electric. Crowds were everywhere. Hundreds of men and boys were toting automatic rifles. Rashid, wearing a flat English cap and an open-neck shirt, mingled with them, feeling the excitement. Anything could happen today.

He was vaguely heading for Bucharest. He still had duties: he was negotiating with two shipping companies to transport the belongings of the EDS evacuees back to the States; and he had to feed the abandoned dogs and cats. The scenes on the streets changed his mind. Rumour said that the Evin Prison had been stormed last night; today it might be the turn of the Gasr Prison, where Paul and Bill were.

Rashid wished he had an automatic rifle like the others.

He passed an Army building which appeared to have been invaded by the mob. It was a six-storey block containing an armoury and a draft registration office. Rashid had a friend who worked there, Malek. It occurred to him that Malek might be in trouble. If he had come to work this morning, he would be wearing his Army uniform – and that alone might be enough to get him killed today. I could lend Malek my shirt, Rashid thought; and impulsively he went into the building.

He pushed his way through the crowd on the ground floor and found the staircase. The rest of the building seemed empty. As he climbed, he wondered whether soldiers were hiding out on the upper floors: if so, they might shoot anyone who came along. He went on regardless. He climbed to the top floor. Malek was not there; nobody was there. The Army had abandoned the place to the mob.

Rashid returned to the ground floor. The crowd had gathered around the entrance to the basement armoury, but no one was going in. Rashid pushed his way to the front and said: 'Is this door locked?'

'It might be booby-trapped,' someone said.

Rashid looked at the door. All thoughts of going to Bucharest had now left him. He wanted to go to the Gasr Prison, and he wanted to carry a gun.

'I don't think this armoury is booby-trapped,' he said, and he opened the door.

He went down the staircase.

The basement consisted of two rooms divided by an archway. The place was dimly lit by narrow strip windows high in the walls, just above street level. The floor was of black mosaic tiles. In the first room were open boxes of loaded magazines. In the second were G3 machine guns.

After a minute some of the crowd upstairs followed him down.

He grabbed three machine guns and a sack of magazines and left. As soon as he got outside the building, people jumped all over him, asking for weapons: he gave away two of the guns and some of the ammunition.

Then he walked away, heading for Gasr Square.

Some of the mob went with him.

On the way they had to pass a military garrison. A skirmish was going on there. A steel door in the high brick wall around the garrison had been smashed down, as if a tank had rolled through it, and the brickwork on either side of the entrance had crumbled. A burning car stood across the way in.

Rashid went around the car and through the entrance.

He found himself in a large compound. From where he stood, a bunch of people were shooting haphazardly at a building a couple of hundreds yards away. Rashid took cover behind a wall. The people who had followed him joined in the shooting, but he held his fire. Nobody was really aiming. They were just trying to scare the soldiers in the building. It was a funny kind of battle. Rashid had never imagined the revolution would be like this: just a disorganized crowd with guns they hardly knew how to use, wandering around on a Sunday morning, firing at walls encountering half-hearted resistance from invisible troops.

Suddenly a man near him fell dead.

It happened so quickly: Rashid did not even see him fall. At one moment the man was standing four feet away from Rashid, firing his rifle; next moment he lay on the ground with his forehead blown away.

They carried the corpse out of the compound. Someone found a jeep. They put the body in the jeep and drove off. Rashid returned to the skirmish.

Ten minutes later, for no apparent reason, a piece of wood with a white undershirt tied to its end was waved out of one of the windows in the building they had been shooting at. The soldiers had surrendered.

Just like that.

There was a sense of anticlimax.

This is my chance, Rashid thought.

It was easy to manipulate people if you understood the psychology of the human being. You just had to study the people, comprehend their situation, and figure out their needs. These people, Rashid decided, want excitement and adventure. For the first time in their lives they have guns in their hands: they need a target, and anything that symbolizes the regime of the Shah will do.

Right now they were standing around wondering where to go next.

'Listen!' Rashid shouted.

They all listened – they had nothing better to do.

'I'm going to the Gasr Prison!'

Someone cheered.

'The people in there are prisoners of the regime – if we are against the regime we should let them out!'

Several people shouted their agreement.

He started walking.

They followed him.

It's the mood they're in, he thought; they'll follow anyone who seems to know where to go.

He started with a band of twelve or fifteen men and boys, but as he walked the group grew: everyone with nowhere to go automatically joined in.

Rashid had become a revolutionary leader.

Nothing was impossible.

He stopped just before Gasr Square and addressed his army. 'The jails must be taken over by the people, just like the police stations and the garrisons; this is our responsibility. There are people in Gasr Prison who are guilty of nothing. They are just like us – our brothers, our cousins. Like us, they only want their freedom. But they were braver than us, for *they* demanded their freedom while the Shah was here, and they were thrown in jail for it. Now we shall let them out!'

They all cheered.

He remembered something Simons had said. 'The Gasr Prison is our Bastille!'

They cheered louder.

Rashid turned and ran into the square.

He took cover on the street corner opposite the huge steel entrance gates of the prison. There was a fair-sized mob in the square already, he realized; probably the prison would be stormed today with or without his help. But the important thing was to help Paul and Bill.

He raised his gun and fired in the air.

The mob in the square scattered, and the shooting began in earnest.

Once again the resistance was half-hearted. A few guards fired back from the gun towers on the walls and from the windows close to the gates. As far as Rashid could see, no one on either side was hit. Once again, the battle ended not with a bang but with a whimper: the guards simply disappeared from the walls and the shooting stopped.

Rashid waited a couple of minutes, to make sure they had gone, then he ran across the square to the prison entrance.

The gates were locked.

The mob crowded around. Someone fired a burst at the gates, trying to shoot them open. Rashid thought: he's seen too many cowboy movies. Another man produced a crowbar from somewhere, but it was impossible to force the gates open. We would need dynamite, Rashid thought.

In the brick wall beside the gates was a little barred window, through which a guard could see who was outside. Rashid smashed the glass with his gun, then started to attack the brickwork in which the bars were embedded. The man with the crowbar helped him, then three or four others crowded around, trying to loosen the bars with their hands, their gun barrels, and anything else that came to hand. Soon the bars came out and fell to the ground.

Rashid wriggled through the window.

He was inside.

Anything was possible.

He found himself in a little guardroom. There were no guards. He put his head out of the door. Nobody.

He wondered where the keys to the cell blocks were kept.

He went out of the office and past the big gates to another guardroom on the far side of the entrance. There he found a big bunch of keys.

He returned to the gates. Inset into one of them was a small door secured by a simple bar.

Rashid lifted the bar and opened the door.

The mob poured in.

Rashid stood back. He handed keys to anyone who would take them, saying, 'Open every cell – let the people go!'

They swarmed past him. His career as a revolutionary leader was over. He had achieved his objective. He, Rashid, had led the storming of the Gasr Prison!

Once again, Rashid had done the impossible.

Now he had to find Paul and Bill among the eleven thousand eight hundred inmates of the jail.

Bill woke up at six o'clock. All was quiet.

He had slept well, he realized with some surprise. He had not expected to sleep at all. The last thing he remembered was lying on his bunk listening to what sounded like a pitched battle outside. If you're tired enough, he thought, I suppose you can sleep anywhere. Soldiers sleep in foxholes. You become acclimatized. No matter how frightened you may be, in the end your body takes control and you nod off.

He said a rosary.

He washed, brushed his teeth, shaved, and dressed, then he sat looking out of the window, waiting for breakfast, wondering what EDS was planning for today.

Paul woke up around seven. He looked at Bill and said: 'Couldn't sleep?'

'Sure I slept,' Bill said. 'I've been up an hour or so.'

'I didn't sleep well. The shooting was heavy most of the night.' Paul got out of his bunk and went to the bathroom.

A few minutes later breakfast came: bread and tea. Bill opened a can of orange juice that had been brought in by Keane Taylor.

The shooting started again around eight o'clock.

The prisoners speculated about what might be going on outside, but no one had any hard information. All they could see was the helicopters darting across the skyline, apparently shooting down at rebel positions on the ground. Every time a helicopter flew over the prison Bill watched for a ladder to come dropping out of the sky into the courtyard of Building No 8. This was his regular daydream. He also fantasized about a small group of EDS people, led by Coburn and an older man, swarming over the prison wall with rope ladders; or a large force of American military arriving at the last minute, like the cavalry in the western movies, blasting a huge gap in the wall with dynamite.

He had done more than daydream. In his quiet, apparently casual way, he had inspected every inch of the building and courtyard, estimating the fastest way out under various imagined circumstances. He knew how many guards there were and how many rifles they possessed. Whatever might happen, he was ready.

It began to look as if today would be the day.

The guards were not following their normal routines. In jail everything was done by routine: a prisoner, with little else to do, observed the patterns and quickly became familiar with them. Today everything was different. The guards appeared nervous, whispering in corners, hurrying everywhere. The sounds of battle outside grew louder. With all this going on, was it *possible* that today would end like any other day? We might escape, Bill thought, or we might get killed; but surely we won't be turning off the TV and lying down on our bunks as usual tonight.

At about ten-thirty he saw most of the officers crossing the prison compound, heading north, as if they were going to a meeting. They hurried back half an hour later. The major in charge of Building No 8 went into his office. He emerged a couple of minutes later – in civilian clothes! He carried a shapeless parcel – his uniform? – out of the building. Looking through the window, Bill saw him put the parcel in the trunk of his BMW, which was parked outside the courtyard fence, then get in the car and drive away.

What did that mean? Would all the officers leave? Was that how it would happen – would Paul and Bill be able just to walk out?

Lunch came a little before noon. Paul ate but Bill was not hungry. The firing seemed very close now, and they could hear shouting and chanting from the streets.

Three of the guards in Building No 8 suddenly appeared in civilian clothes.

This *had* to be the end.

Paul and Bill went downstairs and into the courtyard. The mental patients on the ground floor all seemed to be screaming. Now the guards in the gun towers were firing into the streets outside: the prison must be under attack.

Was that good news or bad, wondered Bill. Did EDS know this was happening? Could it be part of Coburn's rescue? There had been no visitors for two days. Had they all gone home? Were they still alive?

The sentry who normally guarded the courtyard gate had gone, and the gate was open.

The gate was open!

Did the guards *want* the prisoners to leave?

Other cell blocks must have been open too, for there were now prisoners as well as guards running around the compound. Bullets whistled through the trees and ricocheted off buildings.

A slug landed at Paul's feet.

They both stared at it.

The guards in the gun towers were now firing *into* the compound.

Paul and Bill turned and ran back into Building No 8.

They stood at a window, watching the mounting chaos in the compound. It was ironic: for weeks they had thought of little else but their freedom, yet now that they could walk out, they hesitated.

'What do you think we should do?' said Paul.

'I don't know. Is it more dangerous in here or out there?'

Paul shrugged.

'Hey, there's the billionaire.' They could see the rich prisoner from Building No 8 – the one who had a private room and meals brought in from outside – crossing the compound with two of his henchmen. He had shaved off his luxuriant handlebar moustache. Instead of his mink-lined camel coat, he wore a shirt and pants: he was stripped for action, travelling light, ready to move fast. He was heading north, away from the prison gates: did that mean there was a back way out?

The guards from Building No 8, all now in civilian clothes, crossed the little courtyard and went out through the gate.

Everyone was leaving, yet still Paul and Bill hesitated.

'See that motorcycle?' said Paul.

'I see it.'

'We could leave on that. I used to ride a motorcycle.'

'How would we get it over the wall?'

'Oh, yeah.' Paul laughed at his own foolishness.

Their cellmate had found a couple of big bags and he began to pack his clothes. Bill felt the urge to take off, just to get out of here, whether or not that was part of the EDS plan. Freedom was so close. But bullets were flying around out there, and the mob attacking the jail might well be anti-American. On the other hand, if the authorities were somehow to regain control of the prison, Paul and Bill would have lost their last chance of escape . . .

'I wonder where Gayden is now, the son of a bitch,' said Paul. 'The only reason I'm here is because he sent me to Iran.'

Bill looked at Paul and realized he was only joking.

The patients from the ground-floor hospital swarmed out into the courtyard: someone must have unlocked their doors. Bill could hear a tremendous commotion, like crying, from the women's cell block on the other side of the street. There were more and more people out in the compound, flocking towards the prison entrance. Looking that way, Bill saw smoke. Paul saw it at the same moment.

Bill said: 'If they're going to burn the place . . .'

'We'd better get out.'

The fire tipped the balance: their decision was made.

Bill looked around the cell. The two of them had few possessions. Bill thought of the diary he had kept faithfully for the last forty-three days. Paul had written lists of things he would do when he got back to the States, and had figured out, on a sheet of paper, the finance on the new house Ruthie was buying. They both had precious letters from home which they had read over and over again.

Paul said: 'We're probably better off not carrying anything that shows we're Americans.'

Bill had picked up his diary. Now he dropped it again. 'You're right,' he said reluctantly.

They put on their coats: Paul had a blue London Fog raincoat and Bill an overcoat with a fur collar.

They had about two thousand dollars each, money

which Keane Taylor had brought in. Paul had some cigarettes. They took nothing else.

They went out of the building and crossed the little courtyard, then hesitated at the gate. The street was now a sea of people, like the crowd leaving a sports stadium, walking and running in one mass towards the prison gates.

Paul stuck out his hand. 'Hey, good luck, Bill.'

Bill shook his hand. 'Good luck to you.'

Probably we'll both die in the next few minutes, Bill thought, most likely from a stray bullet. I'll never see the kids grow up, he realized sadly. The thought that Emily would have to manage on her own made him angry.

Amazingly enough, he felt no fear.

They stepped through the little gate, and then there was no more time for reflection.

They were swept into the throng, like twigs dropped into a fast-flowing stream. Bill concentrated on sticking close to Paul and staying upright, not to get trampled. There was still a lot of shooting. One lone guard had stayed at his post and seemed to be firing into the crowd from his gun tower. Two or three people fell – one of them was the American woman they had seen before – but it was not clear whether they had been shot or had merely stumbled. I don't want to die yet, Bill thought; I've got plans, things I want to do with my family, in my career; this is not the time, not the place for me to die; what a rotten hand of cards I've been dealt . . .

They passed the officers' club where they had met

with Perot just three weeks ago – it seemed like years. Vengeful prisoners were smashing up the club and wrecking the officers' cars outside. Where was the sense in that? For a moment the whole scene seemed unreal, like a dream, or a nightmare.

The chaos around the main prison entrance was worse. Paul and Bill held back, and managed to detach themselves from the crowd, for fear of being crushed. Bill recalled that some of the prisoners had been here for twenty-five years: it was no wonder, after that length of time, that when they smelled freedom they went berserk.

It seemed that the prison gates must still be shut, for scores of people were trying to climb the immense exterior wall. Some were standing on cars and trucks which had been pushed up against the wall. Others were climbing trees and crawling precariously along over-hanging branches. Still more had leaned planks against the brickwork and were trying to scramble up those. A few people had reached the top of the wall by one means or another and were letting down ropes and sheets to those below, but the ropes were not long enough.

Paul and Bill stood watching, wondering what to do. They were joined by some of the other foreign prisoners from Building No 8. One of them, a New Zealander charged with drug smuggling, had a big grin all over his face as if he were enjoying the whole thing hugely. There was a kind of hysterical elation in the air, and Bill began to catch it. Somehow, he thought, we're going to get out of this mess alive.

He looked around. To the right of the gates the buildings were burning. To the left, some distance away, he saw an Iranian prisoner waving as if to say: This way! There had been some construction work on that section of the wall – a building seemed to be going up on the far side – and there was a steel door in the wall to allow access to the site. Looking more closely, Bill could see that the waving Iranian had got the steel door open.

'Hey – look over there!' said Bill.

'Let's go,' said Paul.

They ran over. Several other prisoners followed. They went through the door – and found themselves trapped in a kind of cell without doors or windows. There was a smell of new cement. Builders' tools lay around. Someone grabbed a pickaxe and swung it at the wall. The fresh concrete crumbled quickly. Two or three others joined in, hacking away with anything that came to hand. Soon the hole was big enough: they dropped their tools and crawled through.

They were now between the two prison walls. The inner wall, behind them, was the high one – twenty-five or thirty feet. The outer wall, which stood between them and freedom, was only ten or twelve feet high.

An athletic prisoner managed to get up on to the top of the wall. Another man stood at its foot and beckoned. A third prisoner went forward. The man on the ground pushed him up, the one on top pulled, and the prisoner went over the wall.

It happened very quickly then.

Paul took a run at the wall.

Bill was right behind him.

Bill's mind was a blank. He ran. He felt a push, helping him up; then a pull; then he was at the top, and he jumped.

He landed on the pavement.

He got to his feet.

Paul was right beside him.

We're free! thought Bill. We're free!

He felt like dancing.

Coburn put down the phone and said: 'That was Majid. The mob has overrun the prison.'

'Good,' said Simons. He had told Coburn, earlier that morning, to send Majid down to Gasr Square.

Simons was very cool, Coburn thought. This was it – this was the big day! Now they could get out of the apartment, get on the move, activate their plans for 'Getting Out of Dodge'. Yet Simons showed no signs of excitement.

'What do we do now?' said Coburn.

'Nothing. Majid is there, Rashid is there. If those two can't take care of Paul and Bill we sure as hell won't be able to. If Paul and Bill don't turn up by nightfall, we'll do what we discussed: you and Majid will go out on a motorcycle and search.'

'And meanwhile?'

'We stick to the plan. We sit tight. We wait.'

There was a crisis at the US Embassy.

Ambassador William Sullivan had got an emergency

call for help from General Gast, head of the Military Assistance Advisory Group. MAAG headquarters was surrounded by a mob. Tanks were drawn up outside the building and shots were being exchanged. Gast and his officers, together with most of the Iranian general staff, were in a bunker underneath the building.

Sullivan had every able-bodied man in the Embassy making phone calls, trying to find revolutionary leaders who might have the authority to call off the mob. The phone on Sullivan's desk was ringing constantly. In the middle of the crisis he got a call from Under Secretary Newsom in Washington.

Newsom was calling from the Situation Room in the White House, where Zbigniew Brzezinski was chairing a meeting on Iran. He asked for Sullivan's assessment of the current position in Tehran. Sullivan gave it to him in a few short phrases, and told him that right at that moment he was preoccupied with saving the life of the senior American military officer in Iran.

A few minutes later Sullivan got a call from an Embassy official who had succeeded in reaching Ibrahim Yazdi, a Khomeini sidekick. The official was telling Sullivan that Yazdi might help when the call was overridden and Newsom came on the line again.

Newsom said: 'The National Security Advisor has asked for your view of the possibility of a coup d'état by the Iranian military to take over from the Bakhtiar government, which is clearly faltering.'

The question was so ridiculous that Sullivan blew his cool. 'Tell Brzezinski to fuck off,' he said.

'That's not a very helpful comment,' said Newsom.

'You want it translated into Polish?' Sullivan said, and he hung up the phone.

On the roof of Bucharest, the negotiating team could see the fires spreading uptown. The noise of shooting was also coming closer to where they stood.

John Howell and Abolhasan returned from their meeting with Dadgar. 'Well?' Gayden said to Howell. 'What did that bastard say?'

'He won't let them go.'

'Bastard.'

A few minutes later they all heard a noise which sounded distinctly like a bullet whizzing by. A moment later the noise came again. They decided to get off the roof.

They went down to the offices and watched from the windows. They began to see, in the street below, boys and young men with rifles. It seemed the mob had broken into a nearby armoury. This was too close for comfort: it was time to abandon Bucharest and go to the Hyatt, which was farther uptown.

They went out and jumped into two cars, then headed up the Shahanshahi Expressway at top speed. The streets were packed, and there was a carnival atmosphere. People were leaning out of their windows yelling '*Allahar Akbar!*' God is great! Most of the traffic was headed downtown, towards the fighting. Taylor drove straight through three road blocks, but nobody minded: they were all dancing.

They reached the Hyatt and assembled in the sitting-room of the eleventh-floor corner suite which Gayden had taken over from Perot. They were joined by Rich Gallagher's wife Cathy and her white poodle Buffy.

Gayden had stocked the suite with booze from the abandoned homes of EDS evacuees, and he now had the best bar in Tehran; but no one felt much like drinking.

'What do we do next?' Gayden asked.

Nobody had any ideas.

Gayden got on the phone to Dallas, where it was now six a.m. He reached Tom Walter and told him about the fires, the fighting, and the kids on the streets with their automatic rifles.

'That's all I got to report,' he finished.

In his slow Alabama drawl, Walter said: 'Other than that a quiet day, huh?'

They discussed what they would do if the phone lines went down. Gayden said he would try to get messages through via the US military: Cathy Gallagher worked for the army and she thought she could swing it.

Keane Taylor went into the bedroom and lay down. He thought about his wife, Mary. She was in Pittsburgh, staying with his parents. Taylor's mother and father were both past eighty and in failing health. Mary had called to tell him his mother had been rushed to hospital: it was her heart. Mary wanted Taylor to come home. He had spoken to his father, who had said ambiguously: 'You know what you have to do.' It was true: Taylor knew he had to stay here. But it was not easy, not for him nor for Mary.

He was dozing on Gayden's bed when the phone

rang. He reached out on the bedside table and picked it up. 'Hello?' he said sleepily.

A breathless Iranian voice said: 'Are Paul and Bill there?'

'What?' said Taylor. 'Rashid – is that you?'

'Are Paul and Bill there?' Rashid repeated.

'No. What do you mean?'

'Okay, I'm coming, I'm coming.'

Rashid hung up.

Taylor got off the bed and went into the sitting-room. 'Rashid just called,' he told the others. 'He asked me if Paul and Bill were here.'

'What did he mean?' said Gayden. 'Where was he calling from?'

'I couldn't get anything else out of him. He was all excited, and you know how bad his English is when he gets wound up.'

'Didn't he say any more?'

'He said: "I'm coming", then he hung up.'

'Shit.' Gayden turned to Howell. 'Give me the phone.' Howell was sitting with the phone to his ear, saying nothing: they were keeping the line to Dallas open. At the other end an EDS switchboard operator was listening, waiting for someone to speak. Gayden said: 'Let me talk to Tom Walter again, please.'

As Gayden told Walter about Rashid's call, Taylor wondered what it meant. Why would Rashid imagine Paul and Bill might be at the Hyatt? They were in jail – weren't they?

A few minutes later Rashid burst into the room, dirty, smelling of gunsmoke, with clips of G3 ammunition falling out of his pockets, talking a mile a minute so that nobody could understand a word. Taylor calmed him down. Eventually he said: 'We hit the prison. Paul and Bill were gone.'

Paul and Bill stood at the foot of the prison wall and looked around.

The scene in the street reminded Paul of a New York parade. In the apartment buildings across from the jail everyone was at the windows, cheering and applauding as they watched the prisoners escape. At the street corner a vendor was selling fruit from a stall. There was gunfire not far away, but in the immediate vicinity nobody was shooting. Then, as if to remind Paul and Bill that they were not yet out of danger, a car full of revolutionaries raced by with guns sticking out of every window.

'Let's get out of here,' said Paul.

'Where do we go? The US Embassy? The French Embassy?'

'The Hyatt.'

Paul started walking, heading north. Bill walked a little behind him, with his coat collar turned up and head bent to hide his pale American face. They came to an intersection. It was deserted: no cars, no people. They started across. A shot rang out.

Both of them ducked and ran back the way they had come.

It was not going to be easy.

'How are you doing?' said Paul.

'Still alive.'

They walked back past the prison. The scene was the same: at least the authorities had not yet got organized enough to start rounding up the escapers.

Paul headed south and east through the streets, hoping to circle around until he could go north again. Everywhere there were boys, some only thirteen or fourteen, with automatic rifles. On every corner was a sandbagged bunker, as if the streets were divided up into tribal territories. Farther on they had to push their way through a crowd of yelling, chanting, almost hysterical people: Paul carefully avoided meeting people's eyes, for he did not want them to notice him, let alone speak to him – if they were to learn there were two Americans in their midst they might turn ugly.

The rioting was patchy. It was like New York, where you had only to walk a few steps and turn a corner to find the character of the district completely changed. Paul and Bill went through a quiet area for half a mile, then ran into a battle. There was a barricade of overturned cars across the road and a bunch of youngsters with rifles shooting across the barricade towards what looked like a military installation. Paul turned away quickly, fearful of being hit by a stray bullet.

Each time he tried to turn north he ran into some obstruction. They were now farther from the Hyatt than they had been when they started. They were moving south, and the fighting was always worse in the south.

They stopped outside an unfinished building. 'We could duck in there and hide until nightfall,' Paul said. 'After dark nobody will notice that you're American.'

'We might get shot for being out after curfew.'

'You think there's still a curfew?'

Bill shrugged.

'We're doing all right so far,' Paul said. 'Let's go on a little longer.'

They went on.

It was two hours – two hours of crowds and street battles and stray sniper fire – before at last they could turn north. Then the scene changed. The gunfire receded, and they found themselves in a relatively affluent area of pleasant villas. They saw a child on a bicycle, wearing a T-shirt that said something about Southern California.

Paul was tired. He had been in jail for forty-five days, and during most of that time he had been sick: he was no longer strong enough to walk for hours. 'What do you say we hitchhike?' he asked Bill.

'Let's give it a try.'

Paul stood at the roadside and waved at the next car that came along. (He remembered not to stick out his thumb the American way – this was an obscene gesture in Iran.) The car stopped. There were two Iranian men in it. Paul and Bill got in the back.

Paul decided not to mention the name of the hotel. 'We're going to Tajrish,' he said. That was a bazaar area to the north of the city.

'We can take you part of the way,' said the driver.

'Thanks.' Paul offered them cigarettes, then sat back gratefully and lit one for himself.

The Iranians dropped them off at Kurosh-e-Kabir, several miles south of Tajrish, not far from where Paul had lived. They were in a main street, with plenty of traffic and a lot more people around. Paul decided not to make himself conspicuous by hitch-hiking here.

'We could take refuge in the Catholic Mission,' Bill suggested.

Paul considered. The authorities presumably knew that Father Williams had visited them in Gasr Prison just two days ago. 'The Mission might be the first place Dadgar looks for us.'

'Maybe.'

'We should go to the Hyatt.'

'The guys may not be there any longer.'

'But there'll be phones, some way to get plane tickets . . .'

'And hot showers.'

'Right.'

They walked on.

Suddenly a voice called: 'Mr Paul! Mr Bill!'

Paul's heart stopped. He looked around. He saw a car full of people moving slowly along the road beside him. He recognized one of the passengers: it was a guard from the Gasr Prison.

The guard had changed into civilian clothes, and looked as if he had joined the revolution. His big smile seemed to say: 'Don't tell who I am, and I won't tell who you are.'

He waved, then the car gathered speed and passed on.

Paul and Bill laughed with a mixture of amusement and relief.

They turned into a quiet street, and Paul started to

hitch-hike again. He stood in the road waving while Bill stayed on the sidewalk, so that motorists might think there was only one man, an Iranian.

A young couple stopped. Paul got into the car and Bill jumped in after him.

'We're headed north,' Paul said.

The woman looked at her man.

The man said: 'We could take you to Niavron Palace.'

'Thank you.'

The car pulled away.

The scene in the streets changed again. They could hear much more gunfire, and the traffic became heavier and more frantic, with all the cars honking continually. They saw press cameramen and television crews standing on car roofs taking pictures. The mob was burning the police stations near where Bill had lived. The Iranian couple looked nervous as the car inched through the crowd: having two Americans in their car could get them into trouble in this atmosphere.

It began to get dark.

Bill leaned forward. 'Boy, it's getting a bit late,' he said. 'It sure would be nice if y'all could take us to the Hyatt Hotel. We'd be happy to, you know, thank you and give you something for taking us there.'

'Okay,' said the driver.

He did not ask how much.

They passed the Niavron Palace, the Shah's winter residence. There were tanks outside, as always, but now they had white flags attached to their antennae: they had surrendered to the revolution.

The car went on, past wrecked and burning buildings, turned back every now and again by street barricades.

At last they saw the Hyatt.

'Oh, boy,' Paul said feelingly. 'An American hotel.'

They drove into the forecourt.

Paul was so grateful that he gave the Iranian couple two hundred dollars.

The car drove off. Paul and Bill waved, then walked into the hotel.

Suddenly Paul wished he were wearing his EDS uniform of business suit and white shirt, instead of prison dungarees and a dirty raincoat.

The magnificent lobby was deserted.

They walked to the reception desk. After a moment someone came out from an office.

Paul asked for Bill Gayden's room number.

The clerk checked, then told him there was no one of that name registered.

'How about Bob Young?'

'No.'

'Rich Gallagher?'

'No.'

'Jay Coburn?'

'No.'

I've got the wrong hotel, Paul thought. How could I have made a mistake like that?

'What about John Howell?' he said, remembering the lawyer.

'Yes,' the clerk said at last, and he gave them a room number on the eleventh floor.

They went up in the elevator.

They found Howell's room and knocked. There was no answer.

'What do you think we ought to do?' Bill said.

'I'm going to check in,' said Paul. 'I'm tired. Why don't we check in, have a meal. We'll call the States, tell them we're out of jail, everything will be fine.'

'Okay.'

They walked back to the elevator.

Bit by bit, Keane Taylor got the story out of Rashid.

He had stood just inside the prison gates for about an hour. The scene was a shambles; eleven thousand people were trying to get out through a small doorway, and in the panic women and old men were getting trampled. Rashid had waited, thinking of what he would say to Paul and Bill when he saw them. After an hour the flood of people slowed to a trickle, and he concluded that most people were out. He started asking: 'Have you seen any Americans?' Someone told him that all the foreigners had been kept in Building No 8. He went there and found it empty. He searched every building in the compound. He then returned to the Hyatt by the route Paul and Bill were most likely to take. Walking and hitching rides, he had looked for them all the way. At the Hyatt he had been refused admission because he was still carrying his weapon. He gave the gun away to the nearest youngster and came in.

While he was telling his story Coburn arrived, all set

to go looking for Paul and Bill on Majid's motorcycle. He had a crash helmet with a vizor that would hide his white face.

Rashid offered to take an EDS car and drive the route between the hotel and the prison, making one more sweep there and back before Coburn risked his neck in the mobs. Taylor gave him the keys to a car. Gayden got on the phone to tell Dallas the latest news. Rashid and Taylor left the suite and walked down the corridor.

Suddenly Rashid yelled: 'I thought you were dead!' and broke into a run.

Then Taylor saw Paul and Bill.

Rashid was hugging them both, screaming: 'I couldn't find you! I couldn't find you!'

Taylor ran up and embraced Paul and Bill. 'Thank God!' he said.

Rashid ran back into Gayden's suite, yelling: 'Paul and Bill are here! Paul and Bill are here!'

An instant later Paul and Bill walked in, and all hell broke loose.

CHAPTER TEN

I

I

T WAS an unforgettable moment.

Everyone was yelling, no one was listening, and they all wanted to hug Paul and Bill at the same time.

Gayden was bellowing into the phone: 'We got the guys! We got the guys! Fantastic! They just walked in the door! Fantastic!'

Somebody yelled: 'We beat them! We beat those sonsabitches!'

'We did it!'

'In your ear, Dadgar!'

Buffy barked like a mad thing.

Paul looked around at his friends, and realized that they had stayed here in the middle of a revolution to help him, and he found he had difficulty speaking.

Gayden dropped the phone and came over to shake hands. Paul, with tears in his eyes, said: 'Gayden, I just saved you twelve and a half million dollars – I think you ought to buy me a drink.'

Gayden fixed him a stiff scotch.

Paul tasted his first alcoholic drink for six weeks.

Gayden said into the phone: 'I have somebody would like to speak to you.' He handed the phone to Paul.

Paul said: 'Hello.'

He heard the syrupy voice of Tom Walter. 'Hi, there, buddy!'

'God almighty,' said Paul, out of general exhaustion and relief.

'We were wondering where you guys were!'

'So was I, for the last three hours.'

'How d'you get to the hotel, Paul?'

Paul did not have the energy to tell Walter the whole story. 'Fortunately, Keane left me a lot of money one day.'

'Fantastic. Golly, Paul! Is Bill okay?'

'Yeah, he's a little shook up but he's all right.'

'We're *all* a little shook up. Oh, boy. Boy, it's good to hear you.'

Another voice came on the line. 'Paul? This is Mitch.' Mitch Hart was a former president of EDS. 'I figured that Italian street fighter would get out of there.'

'How's Ruthie?' said Paul.

Tom Walter answered. They must be using the telephone conference circuit, Paul guessed. 'Paul, she's great. I just talked to her a little while ago. Jean's calling her right now, she's on the other phone.'

'Kids doing all right?'

'Yeah, fine. Boy, she'll be glad to hear!'

'Okay, I'll let you talk to my other half.' Paul handed the phone to Bill.

While he had been speaking, an Iranian employee, Gholam, had arrived. He had heard about the jailbreak and had gone looking for Paul and Bill in the streets around the prison.

Jay Coburn was worried by the arrival of Gholam. For

a few minutes there, Coburn had been too full of tearful joy to think of anything else, but now he reverted to his role as Simons's lieutenant. He quietly left the suite, found another open door, went into the room, and called the Dvoranchik apartment.

Simons answered the phone.

'It's Jay. They got here.'

'Good.'

'The security is all shot to hell here. They're using the names over the phone, everybody's wandering around, we have Iranian employees walking in . . .'

'Get a couple of rooms away from the others. We'll be right there.'

'Okay.' Coburn hung up.

He went down to the reception desk and asked for a two-bedroom suite on the twelfth floor. There was no problem: the hotel had hundreds of empty rooms. He gave a false name. He was not asked for his passport.

He returned to Gayden's suite.

A few minutes later Simons walked in and said: 'Hang up the goddam phone.'

Bob Young, who was holding the line open to Dallas, put down the phone.

Joe Poché walked in behind Simons and started closing the curtains.

It was incredible. Suddenly Simons was in charge. Gayden, the president of EDS World, was the senior man there; and an hour ago he had told Tom Walter that 'The Sunshine Boys' – Simons, Coburn and Poché – seemed useless and ineffectual; yet now he deferred to Simons without even thinking about it.

'Take a look around, Joe,' Simons said to Poché. Coburn knew what this meant. The team had scouted the hotel and its grounds during their weeks of waiting, and Poché would now see whether there had been any changes.

The phone rang. John Howell answered it. 'It's Abolhasan,' he said to the others. He listened for a couple of minutes, then said: 'Hold on.' He covered the mouthpiece with his hand and spoke to Simons. 'This is an Iranian employee who translates for me at meetings with Dadgar. His father is a friend of Dadgar's. He's at his father's house, and just got a call from Dadgar.'

The room went very quiet.

'Dadgar said: "Did you know the Americans are out of jail?" Abolhasan said: "It's news to me." Dadgar said: "Get hold of EDS and tell them that if they find Chiapparone and Gaylord they are to turn them in, that I'm now willing to renegotiate the bail and it ought to be much more reasonable."'

Gayden said: 'Fuck *him.*'

'All right,' Simons said. 'Tell Abolhasan to give Dadgar a message. Say we are searching for Paul and Bill, but meanwhile we hold Dadgar personally responsible for their safety.'

Howell smiled and nodded, and began speaking to Abolhasan.

Simons turned to Gayden. 'Call the American Embassy. Yell at them a little. They got Paul and Bill thrown in jail, now the jail has been stormed and we don't know where Paul and Bill are, but we hold the Embassy responsible for their safety. Make it convincing.

There *must* be Iranian spies at the Embassy – you can bet your ass Dadgar will have the text of the message in minutes.'

Gayden went to find a phone.

Simons, Coburn and Poché, with Paul and Bill, moved to the new suite Coburn had taken on the floor above.

Coburn ordered two steak dinners for Paul and Bill. He told room service to send them to Gayden's suite: there was to be no unnecessary traffic in and out of the new rooms.

Paul took a hot bath. He had been longing for it. He had not had a bath for six weeks. He revelled in the clean white bathroom, the piping hot water, the fresh cake of soap ... He would never take such things for granted again. He washed the Gasr Prison out of his hair. There were clean clothes waiting for him: someone had retrieved his suitcase from the Hilton, where he had been staying until he was arrested.

Bill took a shower. His euphoria had gone. He had imagined that the nightmare was over when he walked into Gayden's suite, but gradually it had dawned on him that he was still in danger, there was no US Air Force jet to fly him home at twice the speed of sound. Dadgar's message via Abolhasan, the appearance of Simons, and the new security precautions – this suite, Poché closing the curtains, the shuttling of the food – all made him realize that the escape had only just begun.

All the same, he enjoyed his steak dinner.

Simons was still uneasy. The Hyatt was near the Evin Hotel where the US military stayed, the Evin Prison, and an armoury: all these were natural targets for the revolutionaries. Dadgar's phone call was also worrying. Plenty of Iranians knew that the EDS people were staying at the Hyatt: Dadgar could easily find out, and send men to search for Paul and Bill.

While Simons, Coburn and Bill were discussing this in the sitting-room of the suite, the phone rang.

Simons stared at it.

It rang again.

'Who the fuck knows we're here?' Simons said.

Coburn shrugged.

Simons picked up the phone and said: 'Hello?'

There was a pause.

'Hello?'

He hung up. 'Nobody there.'

At that moment Paul walked in in his pyjamas. Simons said: 'Change your clothes, we're going to leave.'

'Why?' Paul protested.

Simons repeated: 'Change your clothes, we're going to leave.'

Paul shrugged and went back to the bathroom.

Bill found it hard to believe. On the run again already! Somehow Dadgar was staying in authority through all the violence and chaos of the revolution. But who was working for him? The guards had fled the jails, the police stations had been burned, the army had surrendered – who was left to carry out Dadgar's orders?

The Devil and all his hordes, Bill thought.

Simons went down to Gayden's suite while Paul was dressing. He got Gayden and Taylor in a corner. 'Get all these turkeys out of here,' he said in a low voice.

'The story is, Paul and Bill are in bed for the night. You'll all come to our place tomorrow morning. Leave at seven o'clock, just as if you were going to the office. Don't pack any bags, don't check out, don't pay your hotel bill. Joe Poché will be waiting for you outside and he'll have figured out a safe route to the house. I'm taking Paul and Bill there *now* – but don't tell the others that until the morning.'

'Okay,' said Gayden.

Simons went back upstairs. Paul and Bill were ready. Coburn and Poché were waiting. The five of them walked to the elevator.

As they were going down, Simons said: 'Now, let's just walk out of here like it was the normal thing to do.'

They reached the ground floor. They walked across the vast lobby and out into the forecourt. The two Range Rovers were parked there.

As they crossed the forecourt a big dark car drew up, and four or five ragged men with machine-guns jumped out.

Coburn muttered: 'Oh, shit.'

The five Americans kept walking.

The revolutionaries ran over to the doorman.

Poché threw open the doors of the first Range Rover. Paul and Bill jumped in. Poché started the engine and pulled away fast. Simons and Coburn got into the second car and followed.

The revolutionaries went into the hotel.

Poché headed down the Vanak Highway, which passed both the Hyatt and the Hilton. They could hear constant machine-gun fire over the sound of the car engines. A mile up the road, at the intersection with Pahlavi Avenue near to the Hilton, they ran into a roadblock.

Poché pulled up. Bill looked around. He and Paul had come through this intersection a few hours earlier, with the Iranian couple who had brought them to the Hyatt; but then there had been no roadblock, just one burned-out car. Now there were several burning cars, a barricade, and a crowd of revolutionaries armed with an assortment of military firearms.

One of them approached the Range Rover, and Joe Poché rolled down the window.

'Where are you going?' the revolutionary said in perfect English.

'I'm going to my mother-in-law's house in Abbas Abad,' Poché said.

Bill thought: my God, what an idiotic story to tell.

Paul was looking away, hiding his face.

Another revolutionary came up and spoke in Farsi. The first man said: 'Do you have any cigarettes?'

'No, I don't smoke,' said Poché.

'Okay, go ahead.'

Poché drove on down the Shahanshahi Expressway.

Coburn pulled the second car forward to where the revolutionaries stood.

'Are you with them?' he was asked.

'Yes.'

'Do you have any cigarettes?'

'Yes.' Coburn took a pack out of his pocket and tried to shake out a cigarette. His hands were unsteady and he could not get one out.

Simons said: 'Jay.'

'Yes.'

'*Give him the fucking pack.*'

Coburn gave the revolutionary the whole pack, and he waved them on.

II

Ruthie Chiapparone was in bed, but awake, at the Nyfeler's house in Dallas when the phone rang.

She heard footsteps in the hall. The ringing stopped, and Jim Nyfeler's voice said: 'Hello? ... Well, she's sleeping.'

'I'm awake,' Ruthie called. She got out of bed, slipped on a robe, and went into the hall.

'It's Tom Walter's wife, Jean,' said Jim, handing her the phone.

Ruthie said: 'Hi, Jean.'

'Ruth, I have good news for you. The guys are free. They got out of jail.'

'Oh, thank God!' said Ruthie.

She had not yet begun to wonder how Paul would get out of Iran.

When Emily Gaylord got back from church her mother said: 'Tom Walter called from Dallas. I said you'd call back.'

Emily snatched up the phone, dialled EDS's number, and asked for Walter.

'Hi, Em'ly,' Walter drawled. 'Paul and Bill got out of jail.'

'Tom, that's wonderful!'

'There was a jailbreak. They're safe, and they're in good hands.'

'When are they coming home?'

'We're not sure yet, but we'll keep you posted.'

'Thank you, Tom,' said Emily. 'Thank you!'

Ross Perot was in bed with Margot. The phone woke them both. Perot reached out and picked it up. 'Yes?'

'Ross, this is Tom Walter. Paul and Bill got out of jail.'

Suddenly Perot was wide awake. He sat up. 'That's great!'

Margot said sleepily: 'They're out?'

'Yes.'

She smiled. 'Oh, good!'

Tom Walter was saying: 'The jail was overrun by the revolutionaries, and Paul and Bill walked out.'

Perot's mind was clicking into gear. 'Where are they now?'

'At the hotel.'

'That's dangerous, Tom. Is Simons there?'

'Uh, when I was talking to them he was not there.'

'Tell them to call him. Taylor knows the number. And get them out of that hotel!'

'Yes, sir.'

'Call everyone into the office right away. I'll be there in a few minutes.'

'Yes, sir.'

Perot hung up. He got out of bed, threw on some clothes, kissed Margot, and ran down the stairs. He went through the kitchen and out of the back door. A security man, surprised to see him up so early, said: 'Good morning, Mr Perot.'

'Morning.' Perot decided to take Margot's Jaguar. He jumped in and raced down the driveway to the gate.

For six weeks he had felt as if he were living inside a popcorn popper. He had been trying everything, and nothing had worked; bad news had hit him from every direction, he had made no progress. Now at last things were *moving*.

He tore along Forest Lane, running red lights and breaking the speed limit. Getting them out of jail was the easy part, he reflected; now we have to get them out of Iran. The hard part hasn't even started.

In the next few minutes the whole team gathered at EDS headquarters on Forest Lane: Tom Walter, T. J. Marquez, Merv Stauffer, Perot's secretary Sally Walther, lawyer Tom Luce, and Mitch Hart, who – though he no longer worked at EDS – had been trying to use his connections in the Democratic Party to help Paul and Bill.

Until now, communications with the negotiating team in Tehran had been organized from Bill Gayden's office on the fifth floor, while on the seventh floor Merv Stauffer was quietly handling support and communications with the illegal rescue team, talking on the phone in code. Now they all realized that Simons was the key figure in Tehran, and that whatever happened next would probably be illegal; so they moved up to Stauffer's office, which was also more private.

'I'm going to go to Washington right away,' Perot told them. 'Our best hope is still an Air Force jet out of Tehran.'

Stauffer said: 'I don't know about flights to Washington from DFW on Sundays—'

'Charter a jet,' Perot said.

Stauffer picked up the phone.

'We're going to need secretaries here twenty-four hours a day for the next few days,' Perot went on.

'I'll see to that,' said T.J.

'Now, the military has promised to help us but we can't rely on them – they may have bigger fish to fry. The likeliest alternative is for the team to drive out via Turkey. In that event, the plan is for us to meet them at the border or if necessary fly into the north-west of Iran to pull them out. We need to assemble the Turkish Rescue Team. Boulware is already in Istanbul, Schwebach, Sculley and Davis are in the States – somebody call them and have the three of them meet me in Washington. We may also need a helicopter pilot and another pilot for a small fixed-wing aircraft, in case we want to sneak into Iran. Sally, call Margot and ask her to pack me a case – I'll need casual clothes, a flashlight, all-weather boots, thermal underwear, a sleeping bag and a tent.'

'Yes, sir.' Sally left the room.

'Ross, I don't think that's a good idea,' T.J. said. 'Margot might get scared.'

Perot suppressed a sigh: it was just like T.J. to argue.

But he was right. 'Okay, I'll go home and do it myself. Come with me so we can talk while I'm packing.'

'Sure.'

Stauffer put down the phone and said: 'There's a Lear jet waiting for you at Love Field.'

'Good.'

Perot and T.J. went downstairs and got in their cars. They left EDS and turned right on Forest Lane. A few seconds later, T.J. looked at his speedo and saw that he was doing eighty – and Perot, in Margot's Jaguar, was losing him.

At Page Terminal in Washington Perot ran into two old friends: Bill Clements, Governor of Texas and former Deputy Secretary of Defence; and Clements's wife Rita.

Clements said: 'Hi, Ross! What the hell are you doing in Washington on a Sunday afternoon?'

'I'm up here on business,' said Perot.

'No, what are you doing *really*,' said Clements with a grin.

'Have you got a minute?'

Clements had a minute. The three of them sat down, and Perot told the story of Paul and Bill.

When he had finished Clements said: 'There's a guy you need to talk to. I'll write down his name.'

'How am I going to get him on a Sunday afternoon?'

'Hell, I'll get him.'

The two men walked over to a pay phone. Clements put in a coin, called the Pentagon switchboard, and identified himself. He asked to be put through to the home of one of the most senior military officers in the country. Then he said: 'I've got Ross Perot from Texas with me. He's a friend of mine and a good friend to the military, and I want you to help him.' He handed the phone to Perot and walked away.

Half an hour later Perot was in an operations room in the Pentagon basement, surrounded by computer terminals, talking to half a dozen generals.

He had never met any of them before, but he felt he was among friends: they all knew of his campaign for the American prisoners-of-war in North Vietnam.

'I want to get two men out of Tehran,' Perot told them. 'Can you fly them out?'

'No,' said one of the generals. 'We're grounded in Tehran. Our air base, Doshen Toppeh, is in the hands of the revolutionaries. General Gast is in the bunker beneath MAAG headquarters, surrounded by a mob. And we have no communications because the phone lines have been cut.'

'Okay,' said Perot. He had half-expected that answer. 'I'm going to have to do it myself.'

'It's on the other side of the world, and there's a revolution going on,' said a general. 'It won't be easy.'

Perot smiled. 'I have Bull Simons over there.'

They broke up. 'Damn it, Perot!' said one of them. 'You aren't giving the Iranians an even chance!'

'Right,' Perot grinned. 'I may have to fly in myself. Now, can you give me a list of all the airfields between Tehran and the Turkish border?'

'Sure.'

'Could you find out whether any of those airfields are obstructed?'

'We can just look at the satellite photographs.'

'Now, what about radar? Is there a way to fly in there without appearing on the Iranians' radar screens?'

'Sure. We'll get you a radar map at five hundred feet.'

'Good.'

'Anything else?'

Hell, thought Perot, this is just like going into McDonald's! 'That'll do for now,' he said.

The generals started pushing buttons.

T. J. Marquez picked up the phone. It was Perot.

'I got your pilots,' T.J. told him. 'I called Larry Joseph, who used to be head of Continental Air Services in Vientiane, Laos – he's in Washington now. He found the guys – Dick Douglas and Julian Kanauch. They'll be in Washington tomorrow.'

'That's great,' said Perot. 'Now, I've been to the Pentagon and they can't fly the guys out – they're grounded in Tehran. But I have all kinds of maps and stuff so we can fly in ourselves. Now this is what I need: a jet plane, capable of crossing the Atlantic, complete with a crew, and equipped with a single-sideband radio, like we used to have in Laos, so we can make phone calls from the plane.'

'I'll get right on it,' said T.J.

'I'm at the Madison Hotel.'

'Got it.'

T.J. started calling. He contacted two Texas charter companies: neither of them had a transatlantic jet. The second, Jet Fleet, gave him the name of Executive Aircraft out of Columbus, Ohio. They could not help, and they did not know of anyone who could.

T.J. thought of Europe. He called Carl Nilsson, an EDS executive who had been working on a proposal for Martinair. Nilsson called back and said Martinair would not fly into Iran, but had given him the name of a Swiss outfit who would. T.J. called Switzerland: that company had stopped flying into Iran as of today.

T.J. dialled the number of Harry McKillop, a Braniff vice-president who lived in Paris. McKillop was out.

T.J. called Perot and confessed failure.

Perot had an idea. He seemed to remember that Sol Rogers, the president of Texas State Optical Company down in Beaumont, had either a BAC H1 or a Boeing 727, he was not sure which. Nor did he have the phone number.

T.J. called information. The number was unlisted. He called Margot. She had the number. He called Rogers. He had sold his plane.

Rogers knew of an outfit called Omni International, in Washington, which leased planes. He gave T.J. the home phone number of the president and vice-president.

T.J. called the president. He was out.

He called the vice-president. He was in.

'Do you have a transatlantic jet?' T.J. asked.

'Sure. We have two.'

T.J. breathed a sigh of relief.

'We have a 707 and a 727,' the man went on.

'Where?'

'The 707 is at Meachem Field in Fort Worth—'

'Why, that's right here!' said T.J. 'Now tell me, does it have a single-sideband radio?'

'Sure does.'

T.J. could hardly believe his luck.

'This plane is rather luxuriously fitted out,' the vice-president said. 'It was done for a Kuwaiti prince who backed out.'

T.J. was not interested in the decor. He asked about the price. The vice-president said the president would have to make the final decision. He was out for the evening but T.J. could call him first thing in the morning.

T.J. had the plane checked out by Jeff Heller, an EDS vice-president and former Vietnam pilot, and two of Heller's friends, one an American Airlines pilot and the other a flight engineer. Heller reported that the plane seemed to be in good shape, as far as they could tell without flying it. The decor was kind of over-ripe, he said with a smile.

At seven-thirty the following morning T.J. called the president of Omni and got him out of the shower. The president had talked to his vice-president and he was sure they could do business.

'Good,' said T.J. 'Now what about crew, ground facilities, insurance—'

'We don't *charter* planes,' said the president. 'We *lease* them.'

'What's the difference?'

'It's like the difference between taking a cab and renting a car. Our planes are for rent.'

'Look, we're in the computer business, we know nothing about airlines,' said T.J. 'Even though you don't normally do it, will you make a deal with us where you supply all the extras, crew and so on? We'll pay you for it.'

'It'll be complicated. The insurance alone . . .'

'But you'll do it?'

'Yes, we'll do it.'

It *was* complicated, T.J. learned during the course of the day. The unusual nature of the deal did not appeal to the insurance companies, who also hated to be hurried. It was hard to figure out which regulations EDS needed to comply with, since they were not an airline. Omni required a deposit of sixty thousand dollars in an offshore branch of a US bank. The problems were solved by EDS executive Gary Fernandes in Washington and EDS house lawyer Claude Chappelear in Dallas: the contract, which was executed at the end of the day, was a sales demonstration lease. Omni found a crew in California and sent them to Dallas to pick up the plane and fly it on to Washington.

By midnight on Monday the plane, the crew, the extra pilots and the remnants of the rescue team were all in Washington with Ross Perot.

T.J. had worked a miracle.

That was why it took so long.

III

The negotiating team – Keane Taylor, Bill Gayden, John Howell, Bob Young and Rich Gallagher, augmented now by Rashid, Cathy Gallagher, and the dog Buffy – spent the night of Sunday 11 February at the Hyatt. They got little sleep. Close by, the mob was attacking an armoury. It seemed part of the Army had now joined the revolution, for tanks were used in the attack. Towards morning they blew a hole in the wall and got in. From dawn on, a stream of orange cabs ferried weapons from the armoury downtown, to where the fighting was still heavy.

The team kept the line to Dallas open all night: John Howell lay on the couch in Gayden's sitting-room with the phone to his ear.

In the morning Rashid left early. He was not told where the others were going – no Iranians were to know the location of the hideout.

The others packed their suitcases and left them in their rooms, just in case they should get a chance to pick them up later. This was not part of Simons's instructions, and he would certainly have disapproved, for the packed bags showed that the EDS people were no longer living here – but by morning they all felt Simons was overdoing his security precautions. They gathered in Gayden's sitting-room a few minutes after the seven o'clock deadline. The Gallaghers had several bags, and did not really look as if they were going to the office.

In the foyer they met the hotel manager. 'Where are you going?' he asked incredulously.

'To the office,' Gayden told him.

'Don't you know there's a civil war going on out there? All night long we've been feeding the revolutionaries out of our kitchens. They asked if there were any Americans here – I told them there was nobody here. You must go back upstairs and stay out of sight.'

'Life must go on,' said Gayden, and they all walked out.

Joe Poché was waiting in a Range Rover, silently fuming because they were fifteen minutes late and he had instructions from Simons to be back at seven forty-five with or without them.

As they walked to the cars, Keane Taylor saw a hotel clerk drive in and park. He went over to speak to the man. 'How are the streets?'

'Roadblocks all over the place,' said the clerk. 'There's one right here, at the end of the hotel driveway. You shouldn't go out.'

'Thank you,' said Taylor.

They all got into the cars and followed Poché's Range Rover. The guards at the gate were preoccupied, trying to jam a banana clip into a machine pistol which did not take that kind of ammunition, and they paid no attention to the three cars.

The scene outside was scary. Many of the weapons from the armoury had found their way into the hands of teenage boys who had probably never handled firearms before, and the kids were running down the hill, yelling and waving their guns, and jumping into cars to tear off along the highway, shooting into the air.

Poché headed north on Shahanshahi, following a roundabout route to avoid roadblocks. At the intersection with Pahlavi there was the remains of a barricade – burned cars and tree trunks across the road – but the people manning the roadblock were celebrating, chanting and firing into the air, and the three cars drove straight through.

As they approached the hideout they entered a relatively quiet area. They turned into a narrow street then, half a block down, they drove through gates into a walled garden with an empty swimming pool. The Dvoranchik place was the bottom half of a duplex, with the landlady living upstairs. They all went in.

During Monday, Dadgar continued to search for Paul and Bill.

Bill Gayden called Bucharest, where a skeleton staff of loyal Iranians continued to man the phones. Gayden learned that Dadgar's men had called twice, speaking to two different secretaries, and asked where they could find Mr Chiapparone and Mr Gaylord. The first secretary had said she did not know the names of any of the Americans, which was a brave lie – she had been working for EDS for four years and knew everyone. The second secretary had said: 'You will have to speak to Mr Lloyd Briggs, who is in charge of the office.'

'Where is he?'

'Out of the country.'

'Well, who is in charge of the office in his absence?'

'Mr Keane Taylor.'

'Let me speak to him.'

'He's not here right now.'

The girls, bless them, had given Dadgar's men the runaround.

Rich Gallagher was keeping in touch with his friends in the military (Cathy had a job as secretary to a Colonel). He called the Evin Hotel, where most of the military were staying, and learned that 'revolutionaries' had gone to both the Evin and the Hyatt showing photographs of two Americans for whom they were looking.

Dadgar's tenacity was almost incredible.

Simons decided they could not stay at the Dvoranchik house more than forty-eight hours.

The escape plan had been devised for five men. Now there were ten men, a woman, and a dog.

They had only two Range Rovers. An ordinary car would never take those mountain roads, especially in snow. They needed another Range Rover. Coburn called Majid and asked him to try to get one.

The dog worried Simons. Rich Gallagher was planning to carry Buffy in a knapsack. If they had to walk or ride horseback through the mountains to cross the border, a single yap could get them all killed – and Buffy barked at everything. Simons said to Coburn and Taylor: 'I want you two to lose that fucking dog.'

'Okay,' Coburn said. 'Maybe I'll offer to walk it, then just let it go.'

'No,' said Simons. 'When I say lose it, I mean permanently.'

Cathy was the biggest problem. That evening she felt ill – 'Feminine problems,' Rich said. He was hoping that a day in bed would leave her feeling stronger; but Simons was not optimistic. He fumed at the Embassy. 'There are so many ways the State Department could get someone out of the country and protect them if they wanted to,' he said. 'Put them in a case, ship them out as cargo ... if they were interested it would be a snap.'

Bill began to feel like the cause of all the trouble. 'I think it's insane for nine people to risk their lives for the sake of two,' he said. 'If Paul and I weren't here none of you would be in any danger – you could just wait here until flights out resume. Maybe Paul and I should throw ourselves on the mercy of the US Embassy.'

Simons said: 'And what if you two get out, then Dadgar decides to take other hostages?'

Anyway, Coburn thought, Simons won't let these two out of his sight now, not until they're back in the USA.

The bell at the street gate rang, and everybody froze.

'Move into the bedrooms, but quietly,' Simons said.

Coburn went to the window. The landlady still thought there were only two people living here, Coburn and Poché – she had never seen Simons – and neither she nor anyone else was supposed to know that there were now eleven people in the house.

As Coburn watched, she walked across the courtyard and opened the gate. She stood there for a few minutes, talking to someone Coburn could not see, then closed the gate and came back alone.

When he heard her door slam shut upstairs, he called 'False alarm.'

They all prepared for the journey by looting the Dvoranchik place for warm clothes. Paul thought: Toni Dvoranchik would die of embarrassment if she knew about all these men going through her drawers. They ended up with a peculiar assortment of ill-fitting hats, coats and sweaters.

After that they had nothing to do but wait: wait for Majid to find another Range Rover, wait for Cathy to get better, and wait for Perot to get the Turkish Rescue Team organized.

They watched some old football games on a Betamax video. Paul played gin with Gayden. The dog got on everybody's nerves, but Coburn decided not to slit its throat until the last minute, in case there was a change of plan and it could be saved. John Howell read *The Deep* by Peter Benchley: he had seen part of the movie on the flight over and had missed the ending because the plane landed before the movie finished, and he had never figured out who were the good guys and who were the bad guys. Simons said: 'Those who wish to drink can do so, but if we have to move fast we'll be much better without any alcohol in our systems,' but despite the warning both Gayden and Gallagher surreptitiously mixed Drambuie with their coffee. The bell rang once more, and they all went through the same routine, but again it was for the landlady.

They were all remarkably good-tempered, considering how many of them were crammed into the living-room and three bedrooms of the place. The only one to get irritable was – predictably – Keane Taylor. He and Paul cooked a big dinner for everyone, almost emptying the freezer, but by the time Taylor came in from the kitchen, the others had eaten every scrap and there was nothing for him. He cursed them all roundly for a bunch of greedy hogs, and they all laughed, the way they always did when Taylor got mad.

During the night he got mad again. He was sleeping on the floor next to Coburn, and Coburn snored. The noise was so awful that Taylor could not get to sleep. He could not even wake Coburn to tell him to stop snoring, and that made him even madder.

It was snowing in Washington that night. Ross Perot was tired and tense.

With Mitch Hart, he had spent most of the day in a last-ditch effort to persuade the Government to fly his people out of Tehran. He had seen Under Secretary David Newsom at the State Department, Thomas V. Beard at the White House, and Mark Ginsberg, a young Carter aide whose job was liaison between the White House and the State Department. They were doing their best to arrange to fly the remaining one thousand Americans out of Tehran, and they were not about to make special plans for Ross Perot.

Resigned to going to Turkey, Perot went to a sporting goods store and bought himself cold-weather clothes. The leased 707 arrived from Dallas, and Pat Sculley called from Dulles Airport to say that some mechanical problems had surfaced during the flight: the transponder and the inertial navigation system did not work properly, the number one engine was using oil at twice the normal rate, there was insufficient oxygen aboard for cabin use, there were no spare tyres, and the water tank valves were frozen solid.

While mechanics worked on the plane, Perot sat in the Madison Hotel with Mort Meyerson, a vice-president of EDS.

At EDS there was a special group of Perot associates, men such as T. J. Marquez and Merv Stauffer, to whom he turned for help with matters that were not part of the day-to-day business of computer software: schemes like the prisoners-of-war campaign, the Texas War on Drugs, and the rescue of Paul and Bill. Although Meyerson did not get involved in Perot's special projects, he was fully informed about the rescue plan and had given it his blessing: he knew Paul and Bill well, having worked alongside them in earlier years as a systems engineer. For business matters he was Perot's top man and he would soon become President of EDS. (Perot would continue to be Chairman of the Board.)

Now Perot and Meyerson talked business, reviewing each of EDS's current projects and problems. Both knew, though neither said, that the reason for the conference was that Perot might never come back from Turkey.

In some ways the two men were as different as chalk and cheese. Meyerson's grandfather was a Russian Jew who had saved for two years to buy his rail ticket from

New York to Texas. Meyerson's interests ranged from athletics to the arts: he played handball, was involved with the Dallas Symphony Orchestra and was himself a good pianist. Making fun of Perot and his 'eagles', Meyerson called his own close colleagues 'Meyerson's toads'. But in many ways he was like Perot, a creative and daring businessman whose bold ideas often scared more conventional executives in EDS. Perot had given instructions that, if something were to happen to him during the rescue, all his stock would be voted by Meyerson. EDS would continue to be run by a leader, not a bureaucrat.

While Perot discussed business and worried about the plane and fumed against the State Department, his deepest concern was for his mother. Lulu May Perot was sinking fast, and Perot wanted to be with her. If she were to die while he was in Turkey he would never see her again, and that would break his heart.

Meyerson knew what was on his mind. He broke off the business talk to say: 'Ross, why don't I go?'

'What do you mean?'

'Why don't I go to Turkey instead of you? You've done your share – you went to Iran. There's nothing you can do that I can't do in Turkey. And you want to stay with your mother.'

Perot was touched. Mort didn't have to say that, he thought. 'If you're willing . . .' He was tempted. 'That's something I'd sure want to think about. Let me think about it.'

He was not sure he had the right to let Meyerson do this instead of him. 'Let's see what the others think.' He picked up the phone, called Dallas, and reached T. J. Marquez. 'Mort's offered to go to Turkey instead of me,' he told T.J. 'What's your reaction to that?'

'It's the worst idea in the world,' T.J. said. 'You've been close to this project from the start, and you couldn't possibly tell Mort everything he needs to know in a few hours. You know Simons, you know how his mind works – Mort doesn't. Plus, Simons doesn't know Mort – and you're aware of how Simons feels about trusting people he doesn't know. Well, he *won't* trust them, that's how he feels.'

'You're right,' Perot said. 'It's not for consideration.'

He hung up. 'Mort, I sure appreciate your offer, but I'm going to Turkey.'

'Whatever you say.'

A few minutes later Meyerson left, to return to Dallas in the chartered Lear jet. Perot called EDS again and spoke to Merv Stauffer. 'Now I want you guys to work in shifts and get some sleep,' Perot said. 'I don't want to be talking to a bunch of zombies back there.'

'Yes, sir!'

Perot took his own advice and got some sleep.

The phone woke him at two a.m. It was Pat Sculley, calling from the airport: the plane's mechanical problems were fixed.

Perot got a cab to Dulles Airport. It was a hair-raising thirty-mile ride on icy roads.

The Turkish Rescue Team was now together: Perot; Pat Sculley and Jim Schwebach – the deadly duo; young Ron Davis; the crew of the 707; and the two extra pilots,

Dick Douglas and Julian 'Scratch' Kanauch. But the plane was *not* mended. It needed a spare part which was not available in Washington. Gary Fernandes – the EDS manager who had worked on the leasing contract for the plane – had a friend who was in charge of ground support for one of the airlines at New York's LaGuardia Airport: he called the friend, and the friend got out of bed, found the part, and put it on a plane for Washington. Meanwhile Perot lay down on a bench in the terminal and slept for a couple more hours.

They boarded at six a.m. Perot looked around the interior of the aircraft in amazement. It had a bedroom with a king-size bed, three bars, a sophisticated hi-fi system, a television, and an office with a phone. There were plush carpets, suede upholstery and velvet walls. 'It looks like a Persian whorehouse,' said Perot, although he had never seen a Persian whorehouse.

The plane took off. Dick Douglas and Scratch Kanauch immediately curled up and went to sleep. Perot tried to follow their example: he had sixteen hours of nothing to do in front of him. As the plane headed out across the Atlantic Ocean, he wondered again whether he was doing the right thing.

He might, after all, have left Paul and Bill to take their chances in Tehran. Nobody would have blamed him: it was the Government's job to rescue them. Indeed, the Embassy might even now be able to get them out unharmed.

On the other hand, Dadgar might pick them up and throw them in jail for twenty years – and the Embassy, on past performance, might not protect them. And what would the revolutionaries do if *they* got hold of Paul and Bill? Lynch them?

No, Perot could not leave his men to take their chances – it was not his way. Paul and Bill were *his* responsibility – he did not need his mother to tell him that. The trouble was that he was now putting more men at risk. Instead of having two people hiding in Tehran, he would now have eleven employees on the run in the wilds of north-west Iran, and another four, plus two pilots, searching for them. If things went wrong – if someone got killed – the world would see this whole thing as a foolhardy adventure by a man who thought he was still living in the Wild West. He could imagine the newspaper headlines: MILLIONAIRE TEXAN'S IRAN RESCUE BID ENDS IN DEATH . . .

Suppose we lose Coburn, he thought; what would I tell his wife? Liz might find it hard to understand why I staked the lives of seventeen men to gain the freedom of two.

He had never broken the law in his life, and now he was involved in so many major illegal activities he could not count them.

He put all that out of his mind. The decision was made. If you go through life thinking about all the bad things that can happen, you soon talk yourself into doing nothing at all. Concentrate on the problems that can be solved. The chips are on the table and the wheel is in spin. The last game has begun.

IV

On Tuesday the US Embassy announced that evacuation flights for all Americans in Tehran would leave during the coming weekend.

Simons got Coburn and Poché in one of the bedrooms of the Dvoranchik place and closed the door. 'This solves some of our problems,' he said. 'I want to split them up at this point in the game. Some can take the Embassy evacuation flight, leaving a manageable group for the overland trip.'

Coburn and Poché agreed.

'Obviously, Paul and Bill have to go overland,' Simons said. 'Two of us three have to go with them: one to escort them across the mountains and the other to cross the border legitimately and meet up with Boulware. We'll need an Iranian driver for each of the two Range Rovers. That leaves us two spare seats. Who takes them? Not Cathy – she'll be much better off on the Embassy flight.'

'Rich will want to go with her,' said Coburn.

'And that fucking dog,' Simons added.

Buffy's life is saved, Coburn thought. He was rather glad.

Simons said: 'There's Keane Taylor, John Howell, Bob Young and Bill Gayden. Here's the problem: Dadgar might pick people up at the airport, and we'll end up back where we started – with EDS men in jail. Who is at most risk?'

'Gayden,' said Coburn. 'He's President of EDS

World. As a hostage, he'd be better than Paul and Bill. In fact, when Dadgar arrested Bill Gay*lord*, we wondered whether it was a mistake, and he really wanted Bill Gay*den*, but got confused because of the similarity of the names.'

'Gayden comes out overland with Paul and Bill, then.'

'John Howell is not even employed by EDS. And he's a lawyer. He should be all right.'

'Howell goes out by air.'

'Bob Young is employed by EDS in Kuwait, not Iran. If Dadgar has a list of EDS names, Young won't be on it.'

'Young flies. Taylor drives. Now, one of us has to go on the evacuation flight with the Clean Team. Joe, that's you. You've kept a lower profile than Jay. He's been on the streets, at meetings at the Hyatt – whereas nobody knows you're here.'

'Okay,' said Poché.

'So the Clean Team is the Gallaghers, Bob Young and John Howell, led by Joe. The Dirty Team is me, Jay, Keane Taylor, Bill Gayden, Paul, Bill, and two Iranian drivers. Let's go tell 'em.'

They went into the living-room and got everyone sat down. As Simons talked, Coburn admired how he announced his decision in such a way that they all thought they were being asked for their opinions rather than being told what to do.

There was some discussion of who should be in which team – both John Howell and Bob Young would have preferred to be in the Dirty Team, feeling themselves vulnerable to arrest by Dadgar – but in the end they all reached the decision Simons had already made.

The Clean Team might as well move into the Embassy compound as soon as possible, Simons said. Gayden and Joe Poché went off to find Lou Goelz, the Consul General, and talk to him about it.

The Dirty Team would leave tomorrow morning.

Coburn had to organize the Iranian drivers. These were to have been Majid and his cousin the professor, but the professor was in Rezaiyeh and could not get to Tehran, so Coburn had to find a replacement.

He had already decided on Seyyed. Seyyed was a young Iranian systems engineer like Rashid and the Cycle Man, but from a much more wealthy family: relatives of his had been high in politics and the army under the Shah. Seyyed had been educated in England and spoke with a British accent. His great asset, from Coburn's point of view, was that he came from the north-west, so he knew the territory and he spoke Turkish.

Coburn called Seyyed and they met at Seyyed's house. Coburn told him lies. 'I need to gather intelligence on the roads between here and Khoy,' Coburn said. 'I'll need someone to drive me. Will you do it?'

'Sure,' said Seyyed.

'Meet me at ten forty-five tonight at Argentine Square.'

Seyyed agreed.

Simons had instructed Coburn to go through all this. Coburn trusted Seyyed, but of course Simons did not;

so Seyyed would not know where the team was staying until he got there, and he would not know about Paul and Bill until he saw them; and from that moment on he would not be out of Simons's sight.

When Coburn returned to the Dvoranchik place, Gayden and Poché were back from seeing Lou Goelz. They had told Goelz that a few EDS men were staying in Tehran to look for Paul and Bill, but the others wanted to leave on the first evacuation flight, and stay at the Embassy in the meantime. Goelz said that the Embassy was full, but they could stay at his house.

They all thought that was pretty damn good of Goelz. Most of them had got mad at him once or twice over the last two months, and had made it pretty clear that they blamed him and his colleagues for the arrest of Paul and Bill: it was big of him to open his house to them after all that. As everything came unglued in Iran, Goelz was becoming less of a bureaucrat and showing that his heart was in the right place.

The Clean Team and the Dirty Team shook hands and wished each other luck, not knowing who needed it most; then the Clean Team left for Goelz's house.

It was now evening. Coburn and Keane Taylor went to Majid's house to pick him up: he would spend the night at the Dvoranchik place like Seyyed. Coburn and Taylor also had to get a 55-gallon drum of fuel which Majid had been keeping for them.

When they got to the house Majid was out.

They waited, fretting. At last Majid came in. He greeted them, welcomed them to his home, called for tea, the whole shooting match. Eventually Coburn said:

'We're leaving tomorrow morning. We want you to come with us now.'

Majid asked Coburn to step into another room with him, then he said: 'I can't go with you.'

'Why not?'

'I have to kill Hoveyda.'

'What?' said Coburn incredulously. 'Who?'

'Amir Abbas Hoveyda, who used to be Prime Minister.'

'Why do you have to *kill* him?'

'It's a long story. The Shah had a land reform programme; and Hoveyda tried to take away my family's tribal lands, and we rebelled, and Hoveyda put me in jail ... I have been waiting all these years for my revenge.'

'You have to kill him right away?' said Coburn, astonished.

'I have the weapons and the opportunity. In two days' time all may be different.'

Coburn was nonplussed. He did not know what to say. It was clear Majid could not be talked around.

Coburn and Taylor manhandled the fuel drum into the back of the Range Rover, then took their leave. Majid wished them luck.

Back at the Dvoranchik place, Coburn started trying to reach the Cycle Man, hoping he would replace Majid as driver. The Cycle Man was as elusive as Coburn himself. He could normally be reached at a certain phone number – some kind of revolutionary head-quarters, Coburn suspected – just once a day. The regular time for him to drop by this place was now past

– it was late evening – but Coburn tried anyway. The Cycle Man was not there. He tried a few more phone numbers without success.

At least they had Seyyed.

At ten-thirty Coburn went out to meet Seyyed. He walked through the darkened streets to Argentine Square, a mile from the Dvoranchik place, then picked his way across a construction site and into an empty building to wait.

At eleven o'clock Seyyed had not arrived.

Simons had told Coburn to wait fifteen minutes, no longer; but Coburn decided to give Seyyed a little more time.

He waited until eleven-thirty.

Seyyed was not coming.

Coburn wondered what had happened: given Seyyed's family connections, it was quite possible he had fallen victim to the revolutionaries.

For the Dirty Team this was a disaster. Now they had *no* Iranians to go with them. How the hell will we get through all those roadblocks? wondered Coburn. What a shitty break: the professor drops out, Majid drops out, the Cycle Man can't be found, then Seyyed drops out. Shit.

He left the construction site and walked away. Suddenly he heard a car. He looked back, and saw a jeep full of armed revolutionaries swing around the Square. He ducked behind a convenient bush. They went by.

He went on, hurrying now, wondering whether the curfew was in force tonight. He was almost home when the jeep came roaring back towards him.

They saw me last time, he thought, and they've come back to pick me up.

It was very dark. They might not have spotted him yet. He turned and ran back. There was no cover on this street. The noise of the jeep became louder. At last Coburn saw some shrubbery and flung himself into it. He lay there listening to his heartbeat as the jeep came closer. Were they looking for him? Had they picked up Seyyed and tortured him, and made him confess that he had an appointment with a capitalist American pig at Argentine Square at ten forty-five . . .?

The jeep went by without stopping.

Coburn picked himself up.

He ran all the way to the Dvoranchik place.

He told Simons they now had no Iranian drivers.

Simons cursed. 'Is there another Iranian we can call?'

'Only one, Rashid.'

Simons did not want to use Rashid, Coburn knew, because Rashid had led the jailbreak, and if someone who remembered him from that should see him driving a carload of Americans there might be trouble. But Coburn could not think of anyone else.

'Okay,' said Simons. 'Call him.'

Coburn dialled Rashid's number.

He was at home.

'This is Jay Coburn. I need your help.'

'Sure.'

Coburn did not want to give the address of the hideout over the phone, in case the line was wiretapped. He recalled that Bill Dvoranchik had a slight squint. He said: 'You remember the guy with the funny eye?'

'With a funny eye? Oh, yeah—'

'Don't say his name. Remember where he used to live?'

'Sure—'

'Don't say it. That's where I am. I need you here.'

'Jay, I live miles from there and I don't know how I'm going to get across the city—'

'Just try,' Coburn said. He knew how resourceful Rashid was. Give him a task and he just hated to fail. 'You'll get here.'

'Okay.'

'Thanks.' Coburn hung up.

It was midnight.

Paul and Bill had each picked a passport from the ones Gayden had brought from the States, and Simons had made them learn the names, dates of birth, personal details, and all the visas and country stamps. The photograph in Paul's passport looked more or less like Paul, but Bill's was a problem. None of them was right, and he ended up with the passport of Larry Humphreys, a blond, rather Nordic type who really did not look like Bill.

The tension mounted as the six men discussed details of the journey they would begin within the next few hours. There was fighting in Tabriz, according to Rich Gallagher's military contacts; so they would stick to the plan of taking the low road, south of Lake Rezaiyeh, passing through Mahabad. The story they would tell, if questioned, would be as close to the truth as possible – always Simons's preference when lying. They would say they were businessmen who wanted to get home to their families, the airport was closed, and they were driving to Turkey.

In support of that story, they would carry no weapons. It was a difficult decision – they knew they might regret being unarmed and helpless in the middle of a revolution – but Simons and Coburn had found, on the reconnaissance trip, that the revolutionaries at the roadblocks always searched for weapons. Simons's instinct told him they would be better off talking their way out of trouble than trying to shoot their way out.

They also decided to leave behind the 55-gallon fuel drums, on the grounds that they made the team look too professional, too organized, for businessmen quietly driving home.

They would, however, take a lot of money. Joe Poché and the Clean Team had gone off with fifty thousand dollars, but Simons's crew still had around a quarter of a million dollars, some of it in Iranian rials, deutschmarks, sterling and gold. They packed fifty thousand dollars into kitchen baggies, weighted the bags with shot, and put them in a gas can. They hid some in a Kleenex box and more in the battery hold of a flashlight. They shared the rest out for each to conceal about his person.

At one o'clock Rashid still had not arrived. Simons sent Coburn to stand at the street gate and watch for him.

Coburn stood in the darkness, shivering, hoping Rashid would show up. They would leave tomorrow with or without him, but without him they might not get far. The villagers in the countryside would probably detain

Americans just on general principles. Rashid would be the ideal guide, despite Simons's worries: the kid had a silver tongue.

Coburn's thoughts turned to home. Liz was mad at him, that he knew. She had been giving Merv Stauffer a hard time, calling every day and asking where her husband was and what was he doing and when he was coming home.

Coburn knew he would have to make some decisions when he got home. He was not sure that he was going to spend the rest of his life with Liz; and after this episode, maybe she would begin to feel the same way. I suppose we were in love, once upon a time, he thought. Where did all that go?

He heard footsteps. A short, curly-haired figure was walking along the pavement toward him, shoulders hunched against the cold.

'Rashid!' hissed Coburn.

'Jay?'

'Boy, am I glad to see you!' Coburn took Rashid's arm. 'Let's go inside.'

They went into the living-room. Rashid said hello to everyone, smiling and blinking: he blinked a lot, especially in moments of excitement, and he had a nervous cough. Simons sat him down and explained the plan to him. Rashid blinked faster.

When he understood what was being asked of him, he became a little self-important. 'I will help you on one condition,' he said, and coughed. 'I know this country and I know this culture. You are all important people in EDS, but this is not EDS. If I lead you to the border, you must agree always to do everything I say, without question.'

Coburn held his breath. *Nobody* talked like this to Simons.

But Simons grinned. 'Anything you say, Rashid.'

A few minutes later Coburn got Simons in a corner and said quietly: 'Colonel, did you mean that about Rashid being in charge?'

'Sure,' said Simons. 'He's in charge as long as he's doing what I want.'

Coburn knew, better than Simons, how hard it was to control Rashid even when Rashid was *supposed* to be obeying orders. On the other hand, Simons was the most skilled leader of small groups Coburn had ever met. Then again, this was Rashid's country, and Simons did not speak Farsi ... The last thing they needed on this trip was a power struggle between Simons and Rashid.

Coburn got on the phone to Dallas and spoke to Merv Stauffer. Paul had encoded a description of the Dirty Team's proposed route to the border, and Coburn now gave Stauffer the coded message.

Then they discussed how they would communicate en route. It would probably be impossible to call Dallas from countryside pay phones, so they decided they would pass messages through an EDS employee in Tehran, Gholam. Gholam was not to know he was being used this way. Coburn would call Gholam once a day. If all was well he would say: 'I have a message for Jim Nyfeler. We are okay.' Once the team reached Rezaiyeh he would add: 'We are at the staging area.' Stauffer, in his turn, would simply call Gholam and ask whether there were any messages. So long as all went well, Gholam would be kept in the dark. If things went wrong, the pretence would be abandoned: Coburn would level with Gholam, tell him what the trouble was and ask him to call Dallas.

Stauffer and Coburn had become so familiar with the code that they could hold a discussion, using mostly ordinary English mixed with a few letter-groups and key code words, and be sure that anyone listening in on a wiretap would be unable to figure out what they meant.

Merv explained that Perot had contingency plans to fly into north-west Iran from Turkey to pick up the Dirty Team if necessary. Perot wanted the Range Rovers to be clearly identifiable from the air, so he proposed that each of them should have a large 'X' on its roof, either painted or made of black electrician's tape. If a vehicle had to be abandoned – because it broke down, or ran out of gas, or for any other reason – the 'X' should be changed to an 'A'.

There was another message from Perot. He had talked with Admiral Moorer, who had said that things were going to get worse and the team should get out of there. Coburn told Simons this. Simons said: 'Tell Admiral Moorer that the only water here is in the kitchen sink – I look out the window and I see no ships.' Coburn laughed, and told Stauffer: 'We understand the message.'

It was almost five a.m. There was no more time to talk. Stauffer said: 'Take care of yourself, Jay.' He sounded choked up. 'Keep your head down, y'hear?'

'I sure will.'

'Good luck.'

'Bye, Merv.'

Coburn hung up.

As dawn broke, Rashid went out in one of the Range Rovers to reconnoitre the streets. He was to find a route out of the city avoiding roadblocks. If the fighting was heavy, the team would consider postponing their departure another twenty-four hours.

At the same time Coburn left in the second Range Rover to meet with Gholam. He gave Gholam cash to cover the next payday at Bucharest, and said nothing about using Gholam to pass messages to Dallas. The object of the exercise was a pretence of normality, so that it would be a few days before the remaining Iranian employees began to suspect that their American bosses had left town.

When he got back to the Dvaranchik place, the team discussed who should go in which car. Rashid should drive the lead car, obviously. His passengers would be Simons, Bill, and Keane Taylor. In the second car would be Coburn, Paul and Gayden.

Simons said: 'Coburn, you're not to let Paul out of your sight until you're in Dallas. Taylor, the same goes for you and Bill.'

Rashid came back and said the streets were remarkably quiet.

'All right,' said Simons. 'Let's get this show on the road.'

Keane Taylor and Bill went out to fill the gas tanks of the Range Rovers from the 55-gallon drum. The fuel had to be siphoned into the cars, and the only way to start the flow was to suck the fuel through: Taylor swallowed so much gasoline that he went back into the house and vomited, and for once nobody laughed at him.

Coburn had some pep pills which he had bought, on Simons's instructions, at a Tehran drugstore. He and Simons had had no sleep for twenty-four hours straight, and now they each took a pill to keep them awake.

Paul emptied the kitchen of every kind of food that would keep: crackers, cup cakes, canned puddings and cheese. It was not very nutritious but it would fill them.

Coburn whispered to Paul: 'Make sure *we* get the cassette tapes, so we can have some music in our car.'

Bill loaded the cars with blankets, flashlights and can openers.

They were ready.

They all went outside.

As they were getting into the cars, Rashid said: 'Paul, you drive the second car, please. You are dark enough to pass for Iranian if you don't speak.'

Paul glanced at Simons. Simons gave a slight nod. Paul got behind the wheel.

They drove out of the courtyard and into the street.

CHAPTER ELEVEN

I

As the Dirty Team drove out of the Dvoranchik place, Ralph Boulware was at Istanbul Airport, waiting for Ross Perot.

Boulware had mixed feelings about Perot. Boulware had been a technician when he joined EDS. Now he was a manager. He had a fine big house in a white Dallas suburb, and an income few black Americans could ever hope for. He owed it all to EDS, and to Perot's policy of promoting talent. They didn't give you all this stuff for *nothing*, of course: they gave it for brains and hard work and good business judgement. But what they did give you for nothing was the chance to show your stuff.

On the other hand, Boulware suspected Perot wanted to own his men body and soul. That was why ex-military people got on well at EDS; they were comfortable with discipline and used to a twenty-four-hours-a-day job. Boulware was afraid that one day he might have to decide whether he was his own man or Perot's.

He admired Perot for going to Iran. For a man as rich and comfortable and protected as that to put his ass on the line the way he had . . . that took some balls. There was probably not one other Chairman of the

Board of an American corporation who would *conceive* the rescue plan, let alone participate in it.

And then again, Boulware wondered – all his life he would wonder – whether he could ever really trust a white man.

Perot's leased 707 touched down at six a.m. Boulware went on board. He took in the lush decor at a glance and then forgot about it: he was in a hurry.

He sat down with Perot. 'I'm catching a plane at six-thirty so I got to make this fast,' he said. 'You can't buy a helicopter and you can't buy a light plane.'

'Why not?'

'It's against the law. You can charter a plane, but it won't take you just anywhere you want to go – you charter for a specified trip.'

'Who says?'

'The law. Also, chartering is so unusual that you'll have the government all over you asking questions and you might not want that. Now—'

'Just a minute, Ralph, not so fast,' said Perot. He had that I'm-the-boss look in his eye. 'What if we get a helicopter from another country and bring it in?'

'I have been here a month and I have looked into all this thoroughly, and you can't rent a helicopter and you can't rent a plane, and I have to leave you now to meet Simons at the border.'

Perot backed off. 'Okay. How are you going to get there?'

'Mr Fish got us a bus to go to the border. It's on its way already – I was going with it, then I had to stay behind to brief you. I'm going to fly to Adana – that's about half way – and catch up with the bus there. I got Ilsman with me, he's the secret service guy, and another guy to translate. What time do the fellows expect to reach the border?'

'Two o'clock tomorrow afternoon,' said Perot.

'It's going to be tight. I'll see you guys later.'

He ran back to the terminal building and just made his flight.

Ilsman, the fat secret service policeman, and the interpreter – Boulware did not know his name so he called him Charlie Brown – were on board. They took off at six-thirty.

They flew east to Ankara, where they waited several hours for their connection. At midday they reached Adana, near the Biblical city of Tarsus in south central Turkey.

The bus was not there.

They waited an hour.

Boulware decided the bus was not going to come.

With Ilsman and Charlie Brown, he went to the information desk and asked about flights from Adana to Van, a town about a hundred miles from the border crossing.

There were no flights to Van from *anywhere*.

'Ask where we can charter a plane,' Boulware told Charlie.

Charlie asked.

'There are no planes for charter here.'

'Can we buy a car?'

'Cars are very scarce in this part of the country.'

'Are there no car dealers in town?'

'If there are, they won't have any cars to sell.'

'Is there *any* way to get to Van from here?'

'No.'

It was like the joke about the tourist who asks a farmer for directions to London, and the farmer replies: 'If I was going to London I wouldn't start from here.'

They wandered out of the terminal and stood beside the dusty road. There was no sidewalk: this was *really* the sticks. Boulware was frustrated. So far he had had it easier than most of the rescue team – he had not even been to Tehran. Now that it was his turn to achieve something it looked like he would fail. Boulware hated to fail.

He saw a car approaching with some kind of markings in Turkish on its side. 'Hey,' he said, 'is that a cab?'

'Yes,' said Charlie.

'Hell, let's get a cab!'

Charlie hailed the cab and they got in. Boulware said: 'Tell him we want to go to Van.'

Charlie translated.

The driver pulled away.

After a few seconds the driver asked a question. Charlie translated: 'Van, where?'

'Tell him Van, Turkey.'

The driver stopped the car.

Charlie said: 'He says: "Do you know how far it is?"'

Boulware was not sure but he knew it was half across Turkey. 'Tell him yes.'

After another exchange Charlie said: 'He won't take us.'

'Does he know anyone who will?'

The driver shrugged elaborately as he replied. Charlie said: 'He's going to take us to the cab stand so we can ask around.'

'Good.'

They drove into the town. The cab stand was just another dusty piece of road with a few cars parked, none of them new. Ilsman started talking to the drivers. Boulware and Charlie found a little shop and bought a sack of hard-boiled eggs.

When they came out, Ilsman had found a driver and negotiated a price. The driver proudly pointed out his car. Boulware looked at it in dismay. It was a Chevrolet, around fifteen years old, and it looked as if it still had the original tyres.

'He says we'll need some food,' Charlie said.

'I got some eggs.'

'Maybe we'll need more.'

Boulware went back into the shop and bought three dozen oranges.

They got into the Chevrolet and drove to a filling station. The driver bought a spare tank of fuel and put it in the trunk. 'Where we're going, there are no gas stations,' Charlie explained.

Boulware was looking at a map. The journey was about five hundred miles through mountain country. 'Listen,' he said. 'There is no way this car is going to get us to the border by two o'clock tomorrow afternoon.'

'You don't understand,' Charlie said. 'This man is a *Turkish* driver.'

'Oh, boy,' said Boulware; and he sat back in the seat and closed his eyes.

They drove out of town and headed up into the mountains of central Turkey.

The road was dirt and gravel, with enormous potholes, and in places it was not much wider than the car. It snaked over the mountainsides, with a breathtaking sheer drop at one edge. There was no guard rail to stop an incautious driver shooting over the precipice into the abyss. But the scenery was spectacular, with stunning views across the sunlit valleys, and Boulware made up his mind to go back one day, with Mary and Stacy and Kecia, and do the trip again, at leisure.

Up ahead, a truck was approaching them. The cabbie braked to a halt. Two men in uniform got out of the truck. 'Army patrol,' said Charlie Brown.

The driver wound down his window. Ilsman talked to the soldiers. Boulware did not understand what was said, but it seemed to satisfy the patrol. The cabbie drove on.

An hour or so later they were stopped by another patrol, and the same thing happened.

At nightfall they spotted a roadside restaurant and pulled in. The place was primitive and filthy dirty. 'All they have is beans and rice,' said Charlie apologetically as they sat down.

Boulware smiled. 'I been eating beans and rice all my life.'

He studied the cab driver. The man was about sixty years old, and looked tired. 'I guess I'll drive for a while,' said Boulware.

Charlie translated, and the cabbie protested vehemently.

'He says you won't be able to drive that car,' Charlie said. 'It's an American car with a very peculiar gearshift.'

'Look, I *am* American,' Boulware said. 'Tell him that lots of Americans are black. And I know how to drive a 'sixty-four Chevy with a standard shift, for Pete's sake!'

The three Turks argued about it while they ate. Finally Charlie said: 'You can drive, so long as you promise to pay for the damage if you wreck the car.'

'I promise,' said Boulware, thinking: Big deal.

He paid the bill, and they walked out to the car. It was beginning to rain.

Boulware found it impossible to make any speed, but the big car was stable, and its powerful engine took the gradients without difficulty. They were stopped a third time by an army patrol. Boulware showed his American passport, and once again Ilsman made them happy somehow. This time, Boulware noted, the soldiers were unshaven and wore somewhat ragged uniforms.

As they pulled away, llsman spoke, and Charlie said: 'Try not to stop for any more patrols.'

'Why not?'

'They might rob us.'

That's great, thought Boulware.

Near the town of Maras, a hundred miles from Adana and another four hundred from Van, the rain became heavy, making the mud-and-gravel road treacherous, and Boulware had to slow down even more.

Soon after Maras, the car died.

They all got out and lifted the hood. Boulware could see nothing wrong. The driver spoke, and Charlie translated: 'He can't understand it – he has just tuned the engine with his own hands.'

'Maybe he didn't tune it right,' said Boulware. 'Let's check a few things.'

The driver got some tools and a flashlight out of the trunk, and the four men stood around the engine in the rain, trying to find out what had gone wrong.

Eventually they discovered that the points were incorrectly set. Boulware guessed that either the rain, or the thinner mountain air, had made the fault critical. It took a while to adjust the points, but finally the engine fired. Cold and wet and tired, the four men got back into the old car and Boulware drove on.

The countryside grew more desolate as they travelled east – no towns, no houses, no livestock, nothing. The road became even worse: it reminded Boulware of a trail in a cowboy movie. Soon the rain turned to snow and the road became icy. Boulware kept glancing over the sheer drop at the side. If you go off this sucker, he said to himself, you ain't going to get hurt – you're going to *die*.

Near Bingol, half way to their destination, they climbed up out of the storm. The sky was clear and there was a bright moon, almost like daylight. Boulware could see the snow clouds and the flashing lightning in the valleys below. The mountainside was frozen white, and the road was like a bobsleigh run.

Boulware thought: man, I'm going to die up here, and nobody's even going to know it, because they don't know where I am.

Suddenly the steering wheel bucked in his hands and the car slowed: Boulware had a moment of panic, thinking he was losing control, then realized he had a flat tyre. He brought the car gently to a halt.

They all got out and the cab driver opened the trunk. He hauled out the extra fuel tank to get at the spare wheel. Boulware was freezing: the temperature had to be way below zero. The cabbie refused any help and insisted on changing the wheel himself. Boulware took off his gloves and offered them to the cabbie: the man shook his head. Pride, I guess, thought Boulware.

By the time the job was done it was four a.m. Boulware said: 'Ask him if he wants to take over the driving – I'm bushed.'

The driver agreed.

Boulware got into the back. The car pulled away. Boulware closed his eyes and tried to ignore the bumps and jerks. He wondered whether he would reach the border in time. Shit, he thought, nobody could say we didn't try.

A few seconds later he was asleep.

II

The Dirty Team blew out of Tehran like a breeze.

The city looked like a battlefield from which everyone had gone home. Statues had been pulled down, cars burned, and trees felled to make roadblocks; then the roadblocks had been cleared – the cars pushed to the kerbs, the statues smashed, the trees burned. Some of those trees had been hand-watered every day for fifty years.

But there was no fighting. They saw very few people and little traffic. Perhaps the revolution was over. Or perhaps the revolutionaries were having tea.

They drove past the airport and took the highway north, following the route Coburn and Simons had taken on their reconnaissance trip. Some of Simons's plans had come to nothing, but not this one. Still Coburn was apprehensive. What was ahead of them? Did armies rage and storm in towns and hamlets still? Or was the revolution done? Perhaps the villagers had returned to their sheep and their ploughs.

Soon the two Range Rovers were bowling along at seventy miles an hour at the foot of a mountain range. On their left was a flat plain; on their right, steep green hillsides topped by snowy mountain peaks against the blue sky. Coburn looked at the car in front and saw Taylor taking photographs through the tailgate window with his Instamatic. 'Look at Taylor,' he said.

'What does he think this is?' said Gayden. 'A package tour?'

Coburn began to feel optimistic. There had been no trouble so far: maybe the whole country was calming down. Anyway, why should the Iranians give them a hard time? What was wrong with foreigners leaving the country?

Paul and Bill had false passports and were being hunted by the authorities, that was what was wrong.

Thirty miles from Tehran, just outside the town of Karaj, they came to their first roadblock. It was manned, as they usually were, by machine-gun-toting men and boys in ragged clothes.

The lead car stopped, and Rashid jumped out even before Paul had brought the second car to a halt, making sure that he rather than the Americans would do the talking. He immediately began speaking loud and rapid Farsi, with many gestures. Paul wound down the window. From what they could understand, it seemed Rashid was not giving the agreed story: he was saying something about journalists.

After a while Rashid told them all to get out of the cars. 'They want to search us for weapons.'

Coburn, remembering how many times he had been frisked on the reconnaissance trip, had concealed his little Gerber knife in the Range Rover.

The Iranians patted them down then perfunctorily searched the cars: they did not find Coburn's knife, nor did they come across the money.

A few minutes later Rashid said: 'We can go.'

A hundred yards down the road was a filling station. They pulled in: Simons wanted to keep the fuel tanks as full as possible.

While the cars were being fuelled Taylor produced a bottle of cognac, and they all took a swig, except Simons who disapproved and Rashid whose beliefs forbade him to take alcohol. Simons was mad at Rashid. Instead of saying the group were businessmen trying to go home, Rashid had said they were journalists going to cover the fighting in Tabriz. 'Stick to the goddam story,' Simons said.

'Sure,' said Rashid.

Coburn thought Rashid would probably continue to say the first thing that came into his head at the time: that was how he operated.

A small crowd gathered at the filling station, watching the foreigners. Coburn looked at the bystanders nervously. They were not exactly hostile, but there was something vaguely menacing about their quiet surveillance.

Rashid bought a can of oil.

What now?

He took the fuel can, which contained most of the money in weighted plastic bags, out of the back of the car, and poured oil into it to conceal the money. It was not a bad idea, Coburn thought, but I would have mentioned it to Simons before doing it.

He tried to read the expressions on the faces in the crowd. Were they idly curious? Resentful? Suspicious? Malevolent? He could not tell, but he wanted to get away.

Rashid paid the bill and the two cars pulled slowly out of the filling station.

They had a clear run for the next seventy miles. The road, the new Iranian State Highway, was in good condition. It ran through a valley, alongside a single-track railroad, with snow-capped mountains above. The sun was shining.

The second roadblock was outside Qazvin.

It was an unofficial one – the guards were not in uniform – but it was bigger and more organized than the last. There were two checkpoints, one after another, and a line of cars waiting.

The two Range Rovers joined the queue.

The car in front of them was searched methodically. A guard opened the trunk and took out what looked like a rolled-up sheet. He unrolled it and found a rifle. He shouted something and waved the rifle in the air.

Other guards came running. A crowd gathered. The driver of the car was questioned. One of the guards knocked him on the ground.

Rashid pulled the car out of the line.

Coburn told Paul to follow.

'What's he doing?' Gayden said.

Rashid inched through the crowd. The people made way as the Range Rover nudged them – they were interested in the man with the rifle. Paul kept the second Range Rover right on the tail of the first. They passed the first checkpoint.

'What the fuck is he doing?' asked Gayden.

'This is asking for trouble,' said Coburn.

They approached the second checkpoint. Without stopping, Rashid yelled at the guard through the window. The guard said something in reply. Rashid accelerated. Paul followed.

Coburn breathed a sigh of relief. That was just like Rashid: he did the unexpected, on impulse, without thinking through the consequences; and somehow he always got away with it. It just made life a little tense for the people with him.

Next time they stopped, Rashid explained that he had simply told the guard the two Range Rovers had been cleared at the first checkpoint.

At the next roadblock Rashid persuaded the guards to write a pass on his windscreen in magic marker, and they were waved through another three roadblocks without being searched.

Keane Taylor was driving the lead car when, climbing a long, winding hill, they saw two heavy trucks, side by side and filling the whole width of the road, coming downhill fast toward them. Taylor swerved off the road and bumped to a halt in the ditch, and Paul followed. The trucks went by, still side by side, and everyone said what a lousy driver Taylor was.

At midday they took a break. They parked near a ski-lift and lunched on dry crackers and cup cakes. Although there was snow on the mountainsides, the sun was shining and they were not cold. Taylor got out his bottle of cognac, but it had leaked and was empty: Coburn suspected that Simons had surreptitiously loosened the cork. They drank water.

They passed through the small, neat town of Zanjan, where on the reconnaissance trip Coburn and Simons had talked to the chief of police.

Just beyond Zanjan the Iranian State Highway ended – rather abruptly. In the second car, Coburn saw Rashid's Range Rover suddenly disappear from view. Paul slammed on the brakes and they got out to look.

Where the tarmac ended, Rashid had gone down a

steep slope for about eight feet and landed nose-down in mud. Off to the right, their route continued up an unpaved mountain road.

Rashid re-started the stalled engine and put the car into four-wheel drive and reverse gear. Slowly he inched back up the bank and on to the road.

The Range Rover was covered with mud. Rashid turned on the wipers and washed the windscreen. When the mud splashes were gone, so was the pass which had been written on with magic marker. Rashid could have re-written it, but nobody had a magic marker.

They drove west, heading for the southern tip of Lake Rezaiyeh. The Range Rovers were built for tough roads, and they could still do forty miles per hour. They were climbing all the time: the temperature dropped steadily, and the countryside was covered with snow, but the road was clear. Coburn wondered whether they might even make the border tonight, instead of tomorrow as planned.

Gayden, in the back seat, leaned forward and said: 'Nobody's going to believe it was this easy. We better make up some war stories to tell when we get home.'

He spoke too soon.

As daylight faded they approached Mahabad. Its outskirts were marked by a few scattered huts, made of wood and mud-brick, along the sides of a winding road. The two Range Rovers swept around a bend and pulled up sharply: the road was blocked by a parked truck and a large but apparently disciplined crowd. The men were wearing the traditional baggy trousers, black vest, red-

and-white chequered headdress and bandolier of Kurdish tribesmen.

Rashid jumped out of the lead car and went into his act.

Coburn studied the guns of the guards, and saw both Russian and American automatic weapons.

'Everyone out of the cars,' said Rashid.

By now it was routine. One by one they were searched. This time the search was a little more thorough, and they found Keane Taylor's little switchblade knife, but they let him keep it. They did not find Coburn's knife, nor the money.

Coburn waited for Rashid to say: 'We can go.' It was taking longer than usual. Rashid argued with the Kurds for a few minutes, then said: 'We have to go and see the head man of the town.'

They got back into the cars. A Kurd with a rifle joined them in each car and directed them into the little town.

They were ordered to stop outside a small whitewashed building. One of the guards went in, came out again a minute later, and got back into the car without explanation.

They stopped again outside what was clearly a hospital. Here they picked up a passenger, a young Iranian in a suit.

Coburn wondered what the hell was going on.

Finally they drove down an alley and parked outside what looked like a small private house.

They went inside. Rashid told them to take off their shoes. Gayden had several thousand dollars in hundred-dollar bills in his shoes. As he took them off he frantically stuffed the money up into the toes of the shoes.

They were ushered into a large room furnished with nothing but a beautiful Persian carpet. Simons quietly told everyone where to sit. Leaving a space in the circle for the Iranians, he put Rashid on the right of the space. Next to Rashid was Taylor, then Coburn, then Simons himself opposite the space. On Simons's right Paul and Bill sat, back a little from the line of the circle, where they would be least conspicuous. Gayden, completing the circle, sat on Bill's right.

As Taylor sat down he saw that he had a big hole in the toe of his sock, and hundred-dollar bills were poking through the hole. He cursed under his breath and hastily pushed the money back towards his heel.

The young man in the suit followed them in. He seemed educated and spoke good English. 'You are about to meet a man who has just escaped after twenty-five years in jail,' he said.

Bill almost said: Well, how about that. I've just escaped from jail myself! – but he stopped himself just in time.

'You are to be put on trial, and this man will be your judge,' the young Iranian went on.

The words *on trial* hit Paul like a blow, and he thought: we've come all this way for nothing.

III

The Clean Team spent Wednesday at Lou Goelz's house in Tehran.

Early in the morning a call came through from Tom

Walter in Dallas. The line was poor and the conversation confused, but Joe Poché was able to tell Walter that he and the Clean Team were safe, would move into the Embassy as soon as possible, and would leave the country whenever the Embassy got the evacuation flights finally organized. Poché also reported that Cathy Callagher's condition had not improved, and she had been taken to hospital the previous evening.

John Howell called Abolhasan, who had another message from Dadgar. Dadgar was willing to negotiate a lower bail. If EDS located Paul and Bill the company should turn them in and post the lower bail. The Americans should realize that it would be hopeless for Paul and Bill to try to leave Iran by regular means and very dangerous for them to leave otherwise.

Howell took that to mean that Paul and Bill would not have been allowed to get out on an Embassy evacuation flight. He wondered again whether the Clean Team might be in more danger than the Dirty Team. Bob Young felt the same. While they were discussing it, they heard shooting. It seemed to be coming from the direction of the US Embassy.

The National Voice of Iran, a radio station broadcasting from Baku across the border in the Soviet Union, had for several days been issuing 'news' bulletins about clandestine American plans for a counter-revolution. On Wednesday the National Voice announced that the files of SAVAK, the Shah's hated secret police force, had been transferred to the US Embassy. The story was almost certainly invented, but it was highly plausible: the CIA had created SAVAK and was in close contact with it, and everyone knew that US embassies – like all embassies – were full of spies thinly disguised as diplomatic attachés. Anyway, some of the revolutionaries in Tehran believed the story, and – without consulting any of the Ayatollah's aides – decided to take action.

During the morning they entered the high buildings surrounding the Embassy compound and took up position with automatic weapons. They opened fire at ten-thirty.

Ambassador William Sullivan was in his outer office, taking a call at his secretary's desk. He was speaking to the Ayatollah's Deputy Foreign Minister. President Carter had decided to recognize the new, revolutionary government in Iran, and Sullivan was making arrangements to deliver an official Note.

When he put the phone down he turned around to see his press attaché, Barry Rosen, standing there with two American journalists. Sullivan was furious, for the White House had given specific instructions that the decision to recognize the new government was to be announced in Washington, not Tehran. Sullivan took Rosen into the inner office and chewed him out.

Rosen told him that the two journalists were there to make arrangements for the body of Joe Alex Morris, the *Los Angeles Times* correspondent who had been shot during the fighting at Doshen Toppeh. Sullivan, feeling foolish, told Rosen to ask the journalists not to reveal what they had learned in overhearing Sullivan on the phone.

Rosen went out. Sullivan's phone rang. He picked it up. There was a sudden tremendous crash of gunfire, and a hail of bullets shattered his windows.

Sullivan hit the floor.

He slithered across the room and into the next office, where he came nose to nose with his deputy, Charlie Naas, who had been holding a meeting about the evacuation flights. Sullivan had two phone numbers which he could use, in an emergency, to reach revolutionary leaders. He now told Naas to call one and the army attaché to call the other. Still lying on the floor, the two men pulled telephones off a desk and started dialling.

Sullivan took out his walkie-talkie and called for reports from the Marine units in the compound.

The machine-gun attack had been covering fire for a squad of about seventy-five revolutionaries who had come over the front wall of the Embassy compound and were now advancing on the ambassadorial residence. Fortunately most of the staff were with Sullivan in the chancery building.

Sullivan ordered the Marines to fall back, not to use their rifles, and to fire their sidearms only in self-defence.

Then he crawled out of the executive suite and into the corridor.

During the next hour, as the attackers took the residence and the cafeteria building, Sullivan got all the civilians in the chancery herded into the communications vault upstairs. When he heard the attackers breaking down the steel doors of the building, he ordered the Marines inside to join the civilians in the vault. There he made them pile their weapons in a corner, and ordered everyone to surrender as soon as possible.

Eventually Sullivan himself went into the vault, leaving the army attaché and an interpreter outside.

When the attackers reached the second floor, Sullivan opened the vault door and walked out with his hands over his head.

The others – about a hundred people – followed him.

They were herded into the waiting room of the executive suite and frisked. There was a confused dispute between two factions of Iranians, and Sullivan realized that the Ayatollah's people had sent a rescue force – presumably in response to the phone calls by Charlie Naas and the army attaché – and the rescuers had arrived on the second floor at the same time as the attackers.

Suddenly a shot came through the window.

All the Americans dropped to the floor. One of the Iranians seemed to think the shot had come from within the room, and he swung his AK-47 rifle wildly at the tangle of prisoners on the floor; then Barry Rosen, the press attaché, yelled in Farsi: 'It came from outside! It came from outside!' At that moment Sullivan found himself lying next to the two journalists who had been in his outer office. 'I hope you're getting all this down in your notebooks,' he said.

Eventually they were taken out into the courtyard,

where Ibrahim Yazdi, the Ayatollah's new Deputy Prime Minister, apologized to Sullivan for the attack.

Yazdi also gave Sullivan a personal escort, a group of students who would henceforth be responsible for the safety of the US Ambassador. The leader of the group explained to Sullivan that they were well qualified to guard him. They had studied him, and were familiar with his route, for until recently their assignment had been to assassinate him.

Late that afternoon Cathy Gallagher called from the hospital. She had been given some medication which solved her problem, at least temporarily, and she wanted to rejoin her husband and the others at Lou Goelz's house.

Joe Poché did not want any more of the Clean Team to leave the house, but he also did not want any Iranians to know where they were; so he called Gholam and asked him to pick up Cathy at the hospital and bring her to the corner of the street, where her husband would meet her.

She arrived at around seven-thirty. She was feeling better, but Gholam had told her a horrifying story. 'They shot up our hotel rooms yesterday,' she said.

Gholam had gone to the Hyatt to pay EDS's bill and pick up the suitcases they had left behind, Cathy explained. The rooms had been wrecked, there were bullet-holes everywhere, and the luggage had been slashed to ribbons.

'Just our rooms?' Howell asked.

'Yes.'

'Did he find out how it happened?'

When Gholam went to pay the bill, the hotel manager had said to him: 'Who the *hell* were those people – the CIA?' Apparently, on Monday morning, after all the EDS people left the hotel, the revolutionaries had taken it over. They had harassed all the Americans, demanding their passports, and had shown pictures of the two men whom they were seeking. The manager had not recognized the men in the photographs. Nor had anyone else.

Howell wondered what had so enraged the revolutionaries that they had smashed up the rooms. Perhaps Gayden's well-stocked bar offended their Muslim sensibilities. Also left behind in Gayden's suite were a tape recorder used for dictation, some suction microphones for taping phone conversations, and a child's walkie-talkie set. The revolutionaries might have thought this was CIA surveillance gear.

Throughout the day, vague and alarming reports of what was happening at the Embassy reached Howell and the Clean Team through Goelz's houseman, who was calling friends. But Goelz returned as the others were having dinner, and after a couple of stiff drinks he was none the worse for his experience. He had spent a good deal of time lying on his ample belly in a corridor. Next day he went back to his desk, and he came home that evening with good news: evacuation flights would start on Saturday, and the Clean Team would be on the first.

Howell thought: Dadgar may have other ideas about that.

IV

In Istanbul Ross Perot had a dreadful feeling that the whole operation was slipping out of control.

He heard, via Dallas, that the US Embassy in Tehran had been overrun by revolutionaries. He also knew, because Tom Walter had talked to Joe Poché earlier, that the Clean Team had been planning to move into the Embassy compound as soon as possible. But, after the attack on the Embassy, almost all telephone lines to Tehran had been disconnected, and the White House was monopolizing the few lines left. So Perot did not know whether the Clean Team had been in the Embassy at the time of the attack, nor did he know what kind of danger they might be in even if they were still at Goelz's house.

The loss of phone contact also meant that Merv Stauffer could not call Gholam to find out whether the Dirty Team had sent 'a message for Jim Nyfeler' saying either that they were okay or that they were in trouble. The whole seventh floor crew in Dallas was at work pulling strings to get one of the few remaining lines so they could talk to Gholam. Tom Walter had got on to A.T.&T. and spoken to Ray Johnson, who handled the EDS phone account. It was a very big account – EDS's computers in different parts of the USA talked to one another along telephone lines – and Johnson had been keen to help a major customer. He had asked whether EDS's call to Tehran was a matter of life and death. You bet it is, said Tom Walter. Johnson was trying to get them a line. At the same time, T. J. Marquez was sweet-talking an international operator, trying to persuade her to break the rules.

Perot had also lost touch with Boulware, who was supposed to meet the Dirty Team on the Turkish side of the border. Boulware had last been heard from in Adana, five hundred miles from where he was supposed to be. Perot presumed he was now on his way to the rendezvous, but there was no way of telling how far he had got or whether he would make it on time.

Perot had spent most of the day trying to get a light plane or a helicopter with which to fly into Iran. The Boeing 707 was no use for that, because Perot would need to fly low and search for the Range Rovers with 'X' or 'A' on their roofs, then land on tiny disused airfields or even on a road or in a meadow. But so far his efforts had only confirmed what Boulware had told him at six o'clock that morning: it was not going to happen.

In desperation Perot had called a friend in the Drug Enforcement Agency, and asked for the phone number of the Agency's man in Turkey, thinking that narcotics people would surely know how to get hold of light planes. The DEA man had come to the Sheraton, accompanied by another man who, Perot gathered, was with the CIA; but if they knew where to get a plane they weren't telling.

In Dallas, Merv Stauffer was calling all over Europe looking for a suitable aircraft which could be bought or rented immediately and flown in to Turkey: he, too, had failed so far.

Late in the afternoon Perot had said to Pat Sculley: 'I want to talk to the highest-ranking American in Istanbul.'

Sculley had gone off and raised a little hell at the American Consulate, and now, at ten-thirty p.m., a consul was sitting in Perot's suite at the Sheraton.

Perot was levelling with him. 'My men aren't criminals of any kind,' he said. 'They're ordinary businessmen who have wives and children worrying themselves to death back home. The Iranians kept them in jail for six weeks without bringing any charges or finding any evidence against them. Now they're free and they're trying to get out of the country. If they're caught, you can imagine how much chance they'd have of justice: none at all. The way things are in Iran now, my men may not get as far as the border. I want to go in and get them, and that's where I need your help. I have to borrow, rent or buy a small aircraft. Now can you help me?'

'No,' said the consul. 'In this country it's against the law for private individuals to have aircraft. Because it's against the law, the planes aren't here even for someone who's prepared to break the law.'

'But *you* must have aircraft.'

'The State Department has no aircraft.'

Perot despaired. Was he to sit and do *nothing* to help the Dirty Team?

The consul said: 'Mr Perot, we're here to help American citizens, and I'm going to try to get you an aircraft. I'll pull whatever strings I can. But I'll tell you now that my chance of success is close to zero.'

'Well, I appreciate it.'

The consul got up to go.

Perot said: 'It's very important that my presence in Turkey is kept secret. Right now the Iranian authorities have no idea where my men are. If they should learn that I'm here they will be able to figure out how my men are getting out, and that would be a catastrophe. So please be very discreet.'

'I understand.'

The consul left.

A few minutes later the phone rang. It was T. J. Marquez calling from Dallas.

'Perot, you're on the front page of the paper today.'

Perot's heart sank: the story was out.

T.J. said: 'The Governor just appointed you Chairman of the Drug Commission.'

Perot breathed again. 'Marquez, you *scared* me.'

T.J. laughed.

'You shouldn't do that to an old man,' Perot said. 'Boy, you really caught my attention there.'

'Wait a minute, Margot's on the other line,' said T.J. 'She just wants to wish you a happy Valentine's Day.'

Perot realized it was 14 February. He said: 'Tell her I'm completely safe, and being guarded at all times by two blondes.'

'Wait a minute, I'll tell her.' T.J. came back on the line a minute later, laughing. 'She says, isn't it interesting that you need *two* to replace her?'

Perot chuckled. He had walked into that one: he should have known better than to try to score points off Margot. 'Now, did you get through to Tehran?'

'Yes. The international operator got us a line, and we blew it on a wrong number. Then A.T.&T. got us a line and we reached Gholam.'

'And?'

'Nothing. He hasn't heard from them.'

Perot's temporary cheerfulness vanished. 'What did you ask him?'

'We just said: "Are there any messages?" and he said there weren't.'

'Damn.' Perot almost wished the Dirty Team had called to say they were in trouble, for then at least he would have known their location.

He said goodbye to T.J. and got ready for bed. He had lost the Clean Team, he had lost Boulware, and now he had lost the Dirty Team. He had failed to get hold of an aircraft in which to go looking for them. The whole operation was a mess – and there was not a thing he could do about it.

The suspense was killing him. He realized that never in his life had he experienced this much tension. He had seen men crumble under stress but he had never really been able to relate to their suffering because it had never happened to him. Stress did not upset him, normally – in fact he thrived on it. But this was different.

He broke his own rule, and allowed himself to think about all the bad things that could happen. What was at stake here was his freedom, for if this rescue were to go wrong he would end up in jail. Already he had as-sembled a mercenary army, connived at the misuse of American passports, arranged the forgery of US military identity cards, and conspired to effect an illegal border crossing. He hoped he would go to jail in the US rather than in Turkey. The worst would be if the Turks sent him to Iran to be tried for his 'crimes' there.

He lay awake on his hotel bed, worrying about the Clean Team, about the Dirty Team, about Boulware, and about himself. There was nothing he could do but endure it. In the future he would be more sympathetic to the men he put under stress. If he had a future.

V

Coburn was tense, watching Simons.

They all sat in a circle on the Persian carpet, waiting for the 'judge'. Simons had told Coburn, before they left Tehran: 'Keep your eye on me.' So far Simons had been passive, rolling with the punches, letting Rashid do the talking, allowing the team to be arrested. But there might come a moment when he changed his tactics. If he decided to start a fight, he would let Coburn know a split-second before it happened.

The judge arrived.

Aged about fifty, he wore a dark blue jacket with a light tan sweater underneath, and an open-necked shirt. He had the air of a professional man, a doctor or a lawyer. He had a .45 stuck in his belt.

Rashid recognized him. His name was Habib Bolourian, and he was a leading communist.

Bolourian sat in the space Simons had intended for him.

He said something in Farsi, and the young man in

the suit – who now took on the role of interpreter – asked for their passports.

This is it, Coburn thought; this is where we get into trouble. He will look at Bill's passport and realize it belongs to someone else.

The passports were piled up on the carpet in front of Bolourian. He looked at the top one. The interpreter began to write down details. There was some confusion about surnames and given names: Iranians often got the two mixed up, for some reason. Rashid was handing the passports to Bolourian, and Gayden was leaning over and pointing out things; and it dawned on Coburn that between the two they were making the confusion worse. Rashid was giving Bolourian the same passport more than once, and Gayden, in leaning over to point out things in a passport, was covering up the photograph. Coburn admired their nerve. In the end the passports were handed back, and it seemed to Coburn that Bill's had never actually been opened.

Bolourian began to interrogate Rashid in Farsi. Rashid seemed to be telling the official cover story, about their being ordinary American businessmen trying to go home, with some embellishments about family members on the point of death in the States.

Eventually the interpreter said in English: 'Would you tell us exactly what you're doing here?'

Rashid said: 'Well, you see—' then a guard behind him slammed in the bolt on his machine-gun and stuck the barrel into the back of Rashid's neck. Rashid fell silent. Clearly the interpreter wanted to hear what the

Americans had to say, to see whether their story matched Rashid's; the guard's action was a brutal reminder that they were in the power of violent revolutionaries.

Gayden, as the senior EDS executive there, replied to the interpreter. 'We all work for a data processing company called PARS Data Systems, or PDS,' he said. In fact PDS was the Iranian company jointly owned by EDS and Abolfath Mahvi. Gayden did not mention EDS because, as Simons had pointed out before they left Tehran, Dadgar might put out a blanket arrest order on anyone connected with EDS. 'We had a contract with Bank Omran,' Gayden went on, telling the truth but by no means the whole truth. 'We weren't getting paid, people were throwing rocks at our windows, we had no money, we missed our families, and we just wanted to go home. The airport was closed so we decided to drive.'

'That's right,' said the interpreter. 'The same thing happened to me – I wanted to fly to Europe but the airport was closed.'

We may have an ally here, Coburn thought.

Bolourian asked, and the interpreter translated: 'Did you have a contract with ISIRAN?'

Coburn was astonished. For someone who had spent twenty-five years in jail, Bolourian was remarkably well-informed. ISIRAN – Information Systems Iran – was a data processing company which had once been owned by Abolfath Mahvi and had subsequently been bought by the government. The company was widely believed to have close links with the secret police, SAVAK. Worse,

EDS *did* have a contract with ISIRAN: in partnership, the two companies had created a document control system for the Iranian Navy back in 1977.

'We have absolutely nothing to do with ISIRAN,' Gayden lied.

'Can you give us some proof of who you work for?'

That was a problem. Before leaving Tehran they had all destroyed any papers connected with EDS, under Simon's instructions. Now they all searched their pockets for anything they might have overlooked.

Keane Taylor found his health insurance card, with 'Electronic Data Systems Corp.' printed across the bottom. He handed it to the interpreter, saying: 'Electronic Data Systems is the parent company of PDS.'

Bolourian got up and left the room.

The interpreter, the armed Kurds, and the EDS men waited in silence. Coburn thought: What now?

Could Bolourian possibly know that EDS had once had a contract with ISIRAN? If so, would he jump to the conclusion that the EDS men were connected with SAVAK? Or had his question about ISIRAN been a shot in the dark? In that case had he believed their story about being ordinary businessmen trying to go home?

Opposite Coburn, on the far side of the circle, Bill was feeling strangely at peace. He had peaked out on fear during the questioning, and he was simply incapable of worrying any longer. We've tried our hardest to get out, he thought, and if they put us up against the wall right now and shoot us, so be it.

Bolourian walked back in loading a gun.

Coburn glanced at Simons: his eyes were riveted on the gun.

It was an old Ml carbine that looked like it dated from World War Two.

He can't shoot us all with that, Coburn thought.

Bolourian handed the gun to the interpreter and said something in Farsi.

Coburn gathered his muscles to spring. There would be a hell of a mess if they opened fire in this room—

The interpreter took the gun and said: 'And now you will be our guests, and drink tea.'

Bolourian wrote on a piece of paper and handed it to the interpreter. Coburn realized that Bolourian had simply issued the gun to the interpreter and given him a permit to carry it. 'Christ, I thought he was going to shoot us,' Coburn muttered.

Simons's face was expressionless.

Tea was served.

It was now dark outside. Rashid asked whether there was somewhere the Americans could spend the night. 'You will be our guests,' said the interpreter. 'I will personally look after you.' Coburn thought: For that, he needs a gun? The interpreter went on: 'In the morning, our mullah will write a note to the mullah of Rezaiyeh, asking him to let you pass.'

Coburn murmured to Simons: 'What do you think? Should we stay the night here, or go on?'

'I don't think we have a choice,' Simons said. 'When he said "guests" he was just being polite.'

They drank their tea, and the interpreter said: 'Now we will go and have dinner.'

They got up and put on their shoes. Walking out to their cars, Coburn noticed that Gayden was limping. 'What's the matter with your feet?' he said.

'Not so loud,' Gayden hissed. 'I got all the money stuffed up in the toes of my shoes and my feet are killing me.'

Coburn laughed.

They got into the cars and drove off, still accompanied by Kurdish guards and the interpreter. Gayden surreptitiously eased off his shoes and rearranged the money. They pulled into a filling station. Gayden murmured: 'If they weren't going to let us go, they wouldn't take us to gas up . . . would they?'

Coburn shrugged.

They drove to the town restaurant. The EDS men sat down, and the guards sat at tables around them, forming a rough circle and cutting them off from the townspeople.

A TV set was on, and the Ayatollah was making a speech. Paul thought: Jesus, it had to be now, when we're in trouble, that this guy comes to power. Then the interpreter told him that Khomeini was saying Americans should not be molested, but should be allowed to leave Iran unharmed, and Paul felt better.

They were served chella kebab – lamb with rice. The guards ate heartily, their rifles on the tables beside their plates.

Keane Taylor ate a little rice then put down his spoon. He had a headache: he had been sharing the driving with Rashid, and he felt as if the sun had been in his eyes all day. He was also worried, for it occurred to him that Bolourian might call Tehran during the night to check out EDS. The guards kept telling him, with gestures, to eat, but he sat and nursed a coke.

Coburn was not hungry either. He had recalled that he was supposed to phone Gholam. It was late: they would be worried sick in Dallas. But what should he tell Gholam – that they were okay, or that they were in trouble?

There was some discussion about who should pay the bill when the meal was over. The guards wanted to pay, Rashid said. The Americans were anxious not to offend by offering to pay when they were supposed to be guests, but also keen to ingratiate themselves with these people. In the end Keane Taylor paid for everyone.

As they were leaving, Coburn said to the interpreter: 'I'd sure like to call Tehran, to let our people know we're all right.'

'Okay,' said the young man.

They drove to the post office. Coburn and the interpreter went in. There was a crowd of people waiting to use the three or four phone booths. The interpreter spoke to someone behind the counter, then told Coburn: 'All the lines to Tehran are busy – it's very difficult to get through.'

'Could we come back later?'

'Okay.'

They drove out of the town in the dark. After a few minutes they stopped at a gate in a fence. The moonlight showed a distant outline of what might have been a dam.

There was a long delay while keys to the gate were

found, then they drove in. They found themselves in a small park surrounding an ornate modern two-storey building made of white granite. 'This is one of the Shah's palaces,' the interpreter explained. 'He has used it only once, when he opened the power station. Tonight we will use it.'

They went inside. The place was cosily warm. The interpreter said indignantly: 'The heating has been on for three years just in case the Shah should decide to drop by.'

They all went upstairs and looked at their quarters. There was a luxurious Royal suite with an enormous fancy bathroom, then along the corridor were smaller rooms, each containing two single beds and a bathroom, presumably for the Shah's bodyguards. Under each bed was a pair of slippers.

The Americans moved into the guards' rooms and the revolutionary Kurds took over the Shah's suite. One of them decided to take a bath: the Americans could hear him splashing about, hooting and hollering. After a while he came out. He was the biggest and burliest of them, and he had put on one of the Shah's fancy bathrobes. He came mincing down the corridor while his colleagues fell about laughing. He went up to Gayden and said in heavily-accented English: 'Complete gentleman.' Gayden broke up.

Coburn said to Simons: 'What's the routine for tomorrow?'

'They want to escort us to Rezaiyeh and hand us over to the head man there,' said Simons. 'It'll help to have them with us if we meet any more roadblocks. But when we get to Rezaiyeh, we may be able to persuade them to take us to the professor's house instead of the head man.'

Coburn nodded. 'Okay.'

Rashid looked worried. 'These are bad people,' he whispered. 'Don't trust them. We've got to get out of here.'

Coburn was not sure he trusted the Kurds, but he was quite certain there would be trouble if the Americans tried to leave now.

He noticed that one of the guards had a G3 rifle. 'Hey, that's a real neat firearm,' he said.

The guard smiled and seemed to understand.

'I've never seen one before,' Coburn said. 'How do you load it?'

'Load . . . so,' said the guard, and showed him.

They sat down and the guard explained the rifle. He spoke enough English to make himself understood with the help of gestures.

After a while Coburn realized that *he* was now holding the rifle.

He started to relax.

The others wanted to take showers, but Gayden went first and used all the hot water. Paul took a cold shower: he had sure as hell got used to cold showers lately.

They learned a little about their interpreter. He was studying in Europe and had been home on holiday when the revolution caught him and prevented his going back: that was how come he knew the airport was closed.

At midnight Coburn asked him: 'Can we try to place that call again?'

'Okay.'

One of the guards escorted Coburn back into town. They went to the post office, which was still open. However, there were no lines to Tehran.

Coburn waited until two o'clock in the morning, then gave up.

When he returned to the palace beside the dam, everyone was fast asleep.

He went to bed. At least they were all still alive. That was enough to be thankful for. Nobody knew what was between them and the border. He would worry about that tomorrow.

CHAPTER TWELVE

I

'WAKE UP, Coburn, let's move, let's go!'
Simons's gravelly voice penetrated Coburn's slumber and he opened his eyes, thinking: where am I?

In the Shah's palace at Mahabad.

Oh, shit.

He got up.

Simons was getting the Dirty Team ready to go, but there was no sign of their guards: apparently they were all still asleep. The Americans made plenty of noise, and eventually the Kurds emerged from the Royal suite.

Simons said to Rashid: 'Tell them we're in a hurry, our friends are waiting at the border for us.'

Rashid told them, then said: 'We have to wait.'

Simons did not like this. 'What for?'

'They all want to take showers.'

Keane Taylor said: 'I don't see the urgency – most of them haven't taken a shower in a year or two, you'd think they could wait another day.'

Simons contained his impatience for half an hour, then told Rashid to tell the guards again that the team had to hurry.

'We have to see the Shah's bathroom,' Rashid said.

'Goddam it, we've seen it,' said Simons. 'What's the delay?'

Everyone trooped into the Royal suite and dutifully exclaimed at the shameful luxury of an unused palace; and still the guards would not move out.

Coburn wondered what was happening. Had they changed their minds about escorting the Americans to the next town? Had Bolourian checked up on EDS during the night? Simons would not be kept here much longer...

Finally the young interpreter showed up, and it turned out the guards had been waiting for him. The plan was unchanged: a group of Kurds would go with the Americans on the next leg of their journey.

Simons said: 'We have friends in Rezaiyeh – we'd like to be taken to their house, rather than go see the head man of the town.'

'It's not safe,' said the interpreter. 'The fighting is heavy north of here – the city of Tabriz is still in the hands of the Shah's supporters. I must hand you over to people who can protect you.'

'All right, but can we leave now?'

'Sure.'

They left.

They drove into the town and were ordered to stop outside a house. The interpreter went in. They all waited. Somebody brought bread and cream cheese for breakfast. Coburn got out of his car and went to Simons's. 'What's happening now?'

'This is the mullah's house,' Rashid explained. 'He

is writing a letter to the mullah of Rezaiyeh, about us.'

It was about an hour before the interpreter came out with the promised letter.

Next they drove to the police station, and there they saw their escort vehicle: a big white ambulance with a flashing red light on top, its windows knocked out, and some kind of identification scrawled on its side in Farsi with red magic marker, presumably saying 'Mahabad Revolutionary Committee' or something similar. It was full of gun-toting Kurds.

So much for travelling inconspicuously.

At last they got on the road, the ambulance leading the way.

Simons was anxious about Dadgar. Clearly no one in Mahabad had been alerted to look out for Paul and Bill, but Rezaiyeh was a much bigger town. Simons did not know whether Dadgar's authority extended into the countryside: all he knew was that so far Dadgar had always surprised everyone by his dedication and his ability to persist through changes of government. Simons wished the team did not have to be taken before the Rezaiyeh authorities.

'We have good friends in Rezaiyeh,' he told the young interpreter. 'If you could take us to their house, we'd be very safe there.'

'Oh, no,' said the interpreter. 'If I disobey orders and you get hurt, there will be hell to pay.'

Simons gave up. It was clear they were as much prisoners as guests of the Kurds. The revolution in

Mahabad was characterized by communist discipline rather than Islamic anarchy, and the only way to get rid of the escort would be by violence. Simons was not yet ready to start a fight.

Just outside the town, the ambulance pulled off the road and stopped at a little cafe.

'Why are we stopping?' Simons said.

'Breakfast,' said the interpreter.

'We don't need breakfast,' Simons said forcefully.

'But—'

'We don't need breakfast!'

The interpreter shrugged, and shouted something to the Kurds getting out of the ambulance. They got back in and the convoy drove on.

They reached the outskirts of Rezaiyeh late in the morning.

Their way was barred by the inevitable roadblock. This one was a serious, military-style affair of parked vehicles, sandbags and barbed wire. The convoy slowed, and an armed guard waved them off the road and into the forecourt of a filling station which had been turned into a command post. The approach road was well covered by machine guns in the filling station building.

The ambulance failed to stop soon enough and ran right into the barbed-wire fence.

The two Range Rovers pulled up in an orderly fashion.

The ambulance was immediately surrounded by guards, and an argument started. Rashid and the interpreter went over to join in. The Rezaiyeh revolutionaries did not automatically assume that the Mahabad revolutionaries were on their side. The Rezaiyeh men were Azerbaijanis, not Kurds, and the argument took place in Turkish as well as Farsi.

The Kurds were being ordered to turn in their weapons, it seemed, and they were refusing angrily. The interpreter was showing the note from the Mahabad mullah. Nobody was taking much notice of Rashid, who was suddenly an outsider.

Eventually the interpreter and Rashid came back to the cars. 'We're going to take you to a hotel,' said the interpreter. 'Then I will go and see the mullah.'

The ambulance was all tangled up in the barbed-wire fence, and had to be extracted before they could go. Guards from the roadblock escorted them into the town.

It was a large town by the standards of the Iranian provinces. It had plenty of concrete and stone buildings and a few paved roads. The convoy pulled up in a main street. Distant shouting could be heard. Rashid and the interpreter went into a building – presumably a hotel – and the others waited.

Coburn felt optimistic. You didn't put prisoners into a hotel before shooting them. This was just administrative hassle.

The distant shouting grew louder, and a crowd appeared at the end of the street.

In the rear car, Coburn said: 'What the hell is this?'

The Kurds jumped out of their ambulance and surrounded the two Range Rovers, forming a wedge in front of the lead car. One of them pointed to Coburn's door and made a motion like turning a key. 'Lock the doors,' Coburn said to the others.

The crowd came closer. It was some kind of street parade, Coburn realized. At the head of the procession were a number of army officers in tattered uniforms. One of them was in tears. 'You know what I think?' said Coburn. 'The army just surrendered, and they're running the officers down Main Street.'

The vengeful crowd surged around the vehicles, jostling the Kurdish guards and looking through the windows with hostile glares. The Kurds stood their ground and tried to push the crowds away from the cars. It looked as though it would turn into a fight at any moment. 'This is getting ugly,' said Gayden. Coburn kept an eye on the car in front, wondering what Simons would do.

Coburn saw the snout of a gun aimed at the window on the driver's side. 'Paul, don't look now, but someone's pointing a gun at your head.'

'Jesus . . .'

Coburn could imagine what would happen next: the mob would start rocking the cars, then they would turn them over . . .

Then, suddenly, it ended. The defeated soldiers were the main attraction, and as they passed on the crowd followed. Coburn relaxed. Paul said: 'For a minute, there . . .'

Rashid and the interpreter came out of the hotel. Rashid said: 'They don't want to know about a bunch of Americans going into their hotel – they won't take the risk.' Coburn took that to mean that feelings were running so high in the town that the hotel could get burned by the mob for taking in foreigners. 'We have to go to revolutionary headquarters.'

They drove on. There was feverish activity in the streets: lines of pick-up trucks of all shapes and sizes were being loaded with supplies, presumably for the revolutionaries still fighting in Tabriz. The convoy stopped at what appeared to be a school. There was a huge, noisy crowd outside the courtyard, apparently waiting to get in. After an argument, the Kurds persuaded the sentry to admit the ambulance and the two Range Rovers. The crowd reacted angrily when the foreigners went in. Coburn breathed a sigh of relief as the courtyard gate closed behind him.

They got out of the cars. The courtyard was crammed with shot-up automobiles. A mullah was standing on a stack of rifle crates conducting a noisy and passionate ceremony with a crowd of men. Rashid said: 'He is swearing in fresh troops to go to Tabriz and fight for the revolution.'

The guards led the Americans towards the school building on one side of the courtyard. A man came down the steps and started yelling at them angrily, pointing at the Kurds. 'They must not go into the building armed,' Rashid translated.

Coburn could tell the Kurds were getting jumpy: to their surprise they found themselves in hostile territory. They produced the note from the Mahabad mullah. There was more argument.

Eventually Rashid said: 'You all wait here. I'm going inside to talk to the leader of the revolutionary committee.' He went up the steps and disappeared.

Paul and Gayden lit cigarettes. Paul felt scared and dejected. These people were bound to call Tehran, he felt, and find out all about him. Getting sent back to jail might be the least of his worries now. He said to Gayden: 'I really appreciate what you've done for me, but it's a shame, I think we've had it.'

Coburn was more worried about the mob outside the gate. In here, at least someone was trying to maintain order. Out there was a wolf pack. What if they persuaded some goofy guard to open the gate? It would be a lynch mob. In Tehran a fellow – an Iranian – who had done something to anger a crowd had been literally pulled apart, his arms and legs torn off by people who were just crazed, hysterical.

The guards jerked their weapons, indicating that the Americans should move to one side of the courtyard and stand against the wall. They obeyed, feeling vulnerable. Coburn looked at the wall. It had bullet holes in it. Paul had seen them too, and his face was white. 'My God,' he said. 'I think we bought the farm.'

Rashid asked himself: what will be the psychology of the leader of the revolutionary committee?

He has a million things to do, Rashid thought. He has just taken control of this town, and he has never been in power before. He must deal with the officers of the defeated army, he must round up suspected SAVAK agents and interrogate them, he must get the town running normally, he must guard against a counter-revolution, and he must send troops to fight in Tabriz.

All he wants to do, Rashid concluded, is *cross things off his list.*

He has no time or sympathy for fleeing Americans. If he must make a decision, he will simply throw us in jail for the time being, and deal with us later, at his leisure. Therefore I must make sure that he does not decide.

Rashid was shown into a schoolroom. The leader was sitting on the floor. He was a tall, strong man with the thrill of victory in his face; but he looked exhausted, confused and restless.

Rashid's escort said in Farsi: 'This man comes from Mahabad with a letter from the mullah – he has six Americans with him.'

Rashid thought of a movie he had seen in which a man got into a guarded building by flashing his driving licence instead of a pass. If you had enough confidence you could undermine people's suspicions.

'No, I come from the Tehran Revolutionary Committee,' Rashid said. 'There are five or six thousand Americans in Tehran, and we have decided to send them home. The airport is closed, so we will bring them all out this way. Obviously we must make arrangements and set up procedures for handling all these people. That is why I am here. But you have many problems to deal with – perhaps I should discuss the details with your subordinates.'

'Yes,' said the leader, and waved them away.

'I'm the deputy leader,' said Rashid's escort as they left the room. They went into another room where five or six people were drinking tea. Rashid talked to the deputy leader, loud enough for the others to hear. 'These Americans just want to get home and see their families. We're happy to get rid of them, and we want to

491

treat them right so they won't have anything against the new regime.'

'Why do you have Americans with you now?' the deputy asked.

'For a trial run. This way, you know, we find out what the problems are . . .'

'But you don't have to let them cross the border.'

'Oh, yes. They are good men who have never done any harm to our country, and they have wives and children at home – one of them has a little child dying in hospital. So the Revolutionary Committee in Tehran has instructed me to see them across the border . . .'

He kept talking. From time to time the deputy would interrupt him with a question. Who did the Americans work for? What did they have with them? How did Rashid know they were not SAVAK agents spying for the counter-revolutionaries in Tabriz? For every question Rashid had an answer, and a long one. While he was talking, he could be persuasive; whereas if he were silent the others would have time to think of objections. People came in and went out continually. The deputy left three or four times.

Eventually he came in and said: 'I have to clear this with Tehran.'

Rashid's heart sank. Of course nobody in Tehran would verify his story. But it would take forever to get a call through. 'Everything has been verified in Tehran, and there is no need to re-verify,' he said. 'But if you insist, I'll take these Americans to a hotel to wait.' He added: 'You had better send some guards with us.' The deputy would have sent the guards anyway: asking for them was a way of allaying suspicion.

'I don't know,' said the deputy.

'This is not a good place to keep them,' Rashid said. 'It could cause trouble. They might be harmed.' He held his breath. Here they were trapped. In a hotel, they would at least have the chance to make a break of the border . . .

'Okay,' said the deputy.

Rashid concealed his relief.

Paul was deeply grateful to see Rashid coming down the steps of the schoolhouse. It had been a long wait. Nobody had actually pointed guns at them, but they had got an awful lot of hostile looks.

'We can go to the hotel,' said Rashid.

The Kurds from Mahabad shook hands with them and left in their ambulance. A few moments later the Americans left in the two Range Rovers, followed by four or five armed guards in another car. They drove to the hotel. This time they all went in. There was an argument between the hotel keeper and the guards, but the guards won, and the Americans were assigned four rooms on the third floor at the back, and told to keep the curtains drawn and stay away from windows in case local snipers thought Americans inviting targets.

They gathered in one of the rooms. They could hear distant gunfire. Rashid organized lunch and ate with them: barbecued chicken, rice, bread and coke. Then he left for the school.

The guards wandered in and out of the room, carrying their rifles. One of them struck Coburn as being evil. He was young, short and muscular, with black hair and eyes like a snake. As the afternoon wore on he seemed to get bored.

One time he walked in and said: 'Carter no good.'

He looked around for a reaction.

'CIA no good,' he said. 'America no good.'

Nobody replied. He went out.

'That guy is trouble,' Simons said calmly. 'Don't anybody take the bait.'

The guard tried again a little later. 'I am very strong,' he said. 'Wrestling. Wrestle champion. I went to Russia.'

Nobody spoke.

He sat down and fiddled with his gun, as if he did not know how to load it. He appealed to Coburn. 'You know guns?'

Coburn shook his head.

The guard looked at the others. 'You know guns?'

The gun was an M1, a weapon they were all familiar with, but nobody said anything.

'You want to trade?' the guard said. 'This gun for a backpack?'

Coburn said: 'We don't have a backpack and we don't want a gun.'

The guard gave up and went into the corridor again.

Simons said: 'Where the hell is Rashid?'

II

The car hit a pothole, jolting Ralph Boulware awake. He felt tired and groggy after his short, restless sleep. He looked through the windows. It was early morning. He saw the shore of a vast lake, so big he could not see the far side.

'Where are we?' he said.

'That's Lake Van,' said Charlie Brown, the interpreter.

There were houses and villages and civilian cars: they had come out of the wild mountain country and returned to what passed for civilization in this part of the world. Boulware looked at a map. He figured they were about a hundred miles from the border.

'Hey, this is good!' he said.

He saw a filling station. They really were back in civilization. 'Let's get gas,' he said.

At the filling station they got bread and coffee. The coffee was almost as good as a shower: Boulware felt raring to go. He said to Charlie: 'Tell the old man I want to drive.'

The cabbie had been doing thirty or forty miles per hour, but Boulware pushed the ancient Chevrolet up to seventy. It looked like he had a real chance of getting to the border in time to meet Simons.

Bowling along the lakeside road, Boulware heard a muffled bang, followed by a tearing sound; then the car began to buck and bump, and there was a screech of metal on stone: he had blown a tyre.

He braked hard, cursing.

They all got out and looked at the wheel: Boulware, the elderly cabbie, Charlie Brown, and fat Ilsman. The tyre was completely shredded and the wheel deformed. And they had used the spare wheel during the night, after the last blowout.

Boulware looked more closely. The wheel nuts had been stripped: even if they could get another spare, they would not be able to remove the damaged wheel.

Boulware looked around. There was a house a way up the hill. 'Let's go there,' Boulware said. 'We can phone.'

Charlie Brown shook his head. 'No phones around here.'

Boulware was not about to give up, after all he had gone through: he was too close. 'Okay,' he said to Charlie. 'Hitch a ride back to the last town and get us another cab.'

Charlie started walking. Two cars passed him without stopping, then a truck pulled up. It had hay and a bunch of children in the back. Charlie jumped in, and the truck drove out of sight.

Boulware, Ilsman and the cabbie stood looking at the lake, eating oranges.

An hour later a small European station wagon came tearing along the road and screeched to a halt. Charlie jumped out.

Boulware gave the driver from Adana five hundred dollars then got into the new taxi with Ilsman and Charlie and drove off, leaving the Chevrolet beside the lake, looking like a beached whale.

The new driver went like the wind, and by midday they were in Van, on the eastern shore of the lake. Van was a small town, with brick buildings in the centre and mud-hut suburbs. Ilsman directed the driver to the home of a cousin of Mr Fish.

They paid their driver and went in. Ilsman got into a long discussion with Mr Fish's cousin. Boulware sat in the living room, listening but not understanding, impatient to get moving. After an hour he said to Charlie: 'Listen, let's just get another cab, we don't need the cousin.'

'It's a very bad place between here and the border,' Charlie said. 'We're foreigners, we need protection.'

Boulware forced himself to be patient.

At last Ilsman shook hands with Mr Fish's cousin and Charlie said: 'His sons will take us to the border.'

There were two sons and two cars.

They drove up into the mountains. Boulware saw no sign of the dangerous bandits against whom he was being protected: just snow-covered fields, scrawny goats, and a few ragged people living in hovels.

They were stopped by the police in the village of Yuksekova, a few miles from the border, and ordered into the little whitewashed police station. Ilsman showed his credentials and they were quickly released. Boulware was impressed. Maybe Ilsman really was with the Turkish equivalent of the CIA.

They reached the border at four o'clock on Thursday afternoon, having been on the road for twenty-four hours.

The border station was in the middle of nowhere.

The guard post consisted of two wooden buildings. There was also a post office. Boulware wondered who the hell used it. Truck drivers, perhaps. Two hundred yards away, on the Iranian side, was a bigger cluster of buildings.

There was no sign of the Dirty Team.

Boulware felt angry. He had broken his neck to get here more or less on time: where the hell was Simons?

A guard came out of one of the huts and approached him, saying: 'Are you looking for the Americans?'

Boulware was surprised. The whole thing was supposed to be top secret. It looked like security had gone all to hell. 'Yes,' he said. 'I'm looking for the Americans.'

'There's a phone call for you.'

Boulware was even more surprised. 'No kidding!' The timing was phenomenal. Who the hell knew he was here?

He followed the guard into the hut and picked up the phone. 'Yes?'

'This is the American Consulate,' said the voice. 'What's your name?'

'Uh, what is this about?' Boulware said warily.

'Look, would you just tell me what you're doing there?'

'I don't know who you are and I'm not going to tell you what I'm doing.'

'Okay, listen, I know who you are and I know what you're doing. If you have any problems, call me. Got a pencil?'

Boulware took down the number, thanked the man,

and hung up, mystified. An hour ago I didn't know I was going to be here, he thought, so how could anyone else? Least of all the American Consulate. He thought again about Ilsman. Maybe Ilsman was in touch with his bosses, the Turkish MIT, who were in touch with the CIA, who were in touch with the Consulate. Ilsman could have asked somebody to make a call for him in Van, or even at the police station in Yuksekova.

He wondered whether it was good or bad that the Consulate knew what was happening. He recalled the 'help' Paul and Bill had got from the US Embassy in Tehran: with friends in the State Department a man had no need of enemies.

He pushed the Consulate to the back of his mind. The main problem now was, where was the Dirty Team?

He went back outside and looked across no-man's-land. He decided to stroll across and talk to the Iranians. He called to Ilsman and Charlie Brown to come with him.

As he approached the Iranian side he could see that the frontier guards were not in uniform. Presumably they were revolutionaries who had taken over when the government fell.

He said to Charlie: 'Ask them if they've heard anything about some American businessmen coming out in two jeeps.'

Charlie did not need to translate the reply: the Iranians shook their heads vigorously.

An inquisitive tribesman, with a ragged headband and an ancient rifle, came up on the Iranian side. There was an exchange of some length, then Charlie said: 'This man says he knows where the Americans are and he will take you to them if you pay.'

Boulware wanted to know how much, but Ilsman did not want him to accept the offer at any price. Ilsman spoke forcefully to Charlie, and Charlie translated. 'You're wearing a leather coat and leather gloves and a fine wristwatch.'

Boulware, who was into watches, was wearing one Mary had given him when they got married. 'So?'

'With clothes like that they think you're SAVAK. They *hate* SAVAK over there.'

'I'll change my clothes. I have another coat in the car.'

'No,' Charlie said. 'You have to understand, they just want to get you over there and blow your head off.'

'All right,' Boulware said.

They walked back to the Turkish side. Since there was a post office so conveniently nearby, he decided to call Istanbul and check in with Ross Perot. He went into the post office. He had to sign his name. The call would take some time to place, the clerk told him.

Boulware went back outside. The Turkish border guards were now getting edgy, Charlie told him. Some of the Iranians had wandered back with them, and the guards did not like people milling around in no-man's-land: it was disorderly.

Boulware thought: Well, I'm doing no good here.

He said: 'Would these guys call us, if the team comes across while we're back in Yuksekova?'

Charlie asked them. The guards agreed. There was a hotel in the village, they said; they would call there.

Boulware, Ilsman, Charlie and the two sons of Mr Fish's cousin got into the two cars and drove back to Yuksekova.

There they checked into the worst hotel in the whole world. It had dirt floors. The bathroom was a hole in the ground under the stairs. All the beds were in one room. Charlie Brown ordered food, and it came wrapped in newspaper.

Boulware was not sure he had made the right decision in leaving the border station. So many things could go wrong: the guards might not phone as they had promised. He decided to accept the offer of help from the American Consulate, and ask them to seek permission for him to stay at the border station. He called the number he had been given on the hotel's single ancient wind-up telephone. He got through, but the line was bad, and both parties had trouble making themselves understood. Eventually the man at the other end said something about calling back, and hung up.

Boulware stood by the fire, fretting. After a while he lost patience, and decided to return to the border without permission.

On the way they had a flat tyre.

They all stood in the road while the sons changed the wheel. Ilsman appeared nervous. Charlie explained: 'He says this is a very dangerous place, the people are all murderers and bandits.'

Boulware was sceptical. Ilsman had agreed to do all

this for a flat fee of eight thousand dollars, and Boulware now suspected the fat man was getting ready to up his price. 'Ask him how many people were killed on this road last month,' Boulware told Charlie.

He watched Ilsman's face as he replied. Charlie translated: 'Thirty-nine.'

Ilsman looked serious. Boulware thought: shit, this guy's telling the goddam *truth*. He looked around. Mountains, snow . . . He shivered.

III

In Rezaiyeh, Rashid took one of the Range Rovers and drove from the hotel back to the school which had been turned into revolutionary headquarters.

He wondered whether the deputy leader had called Tehran. Coburn had been unable to get a line, the previous night: would the revolutionary leadership have the same problem? Rashid thought they probably would. Now, if the deputy could not get through, what would he want to do? He had only two options: hold the Americans, or let them go without checking. The man might feel foolish about letting them go without checking: he might not want Rashid to know that things were so loosely organized here. Rashid decided to act as if he assumed the call had been made and verification completed.

He went into the courtyard. The deputy leader was there, leaning against a Mercedes. Rashid started talking to him about the problem of bringing six thousand

Americans through the town on the way to the border. How many people could be accommodated overnight in Rezaiyeh? What facilities were there at the Sero border station for processing them? He emphasized that the Ayatollah Khomeini had given instructions for Americans to be well treated as they left Iran, for the new government did not want to quarrel with the USA. He got on to the subject of documentation: perhaps the Rezaiyeh committee should issue passes to the Americans authorizing them to go through Sero. He, Rashid, would certainly need such a pass today, to take these six Americans through. He suggested the deputy and he should go into the school and draft a pass.

The deputy agreed.

They went into the library.

Rashid found paper and pen and gave them to the deputy.

'What should we write?' said Rashid. 'Probably we should say, the person who carries this letter can take six Americans through Sero. No, say Barzagan or Sero, in case Sero is closed.'

The deputy wrote.

'Maybe we should say, um, "It is expected that all guards will give their best co-operation and assistance, they are fully inspected and identified, and if necessary escort them."'

The deputy wrote it down.

Then he signed his name.

Rashid said: 'Maybe we should put, "Islamic Revolution Commandant Committee."'

The deputy did so.

Rashid looked at the document. It seemed somewhat inadequate, improvised. It needed something to make it look official. He found a rubber stamp and an inking pad, and stamped the letter. Then he read what the stamp said: 'Library of the School of Religion, Rezaiyeh. Founded 1344.'

Rashid put the document in his pocket.

'We should probably print six thousand of these, so they can just be signed,' he said.

The deputy nodded.

'We can talk some more about these arrangements tomorrow,' Rashid went on. 'I'd like to go to Sero now, to discuss the problem with the border officials there.'

'Okay.'

Rashid walked away.

Nothing was impossible.

He got into the Range Rover. It was a good idea to go to the border, he decided: he could find out what the problems might be before making the trip with the Americans.

On the outskirts of Rezaiyeh was a roadblock manned by teenage boys with rifles. They gave Rashid no trouble, but he worried about how they might react to six Americans: the kids were evidently itching to use their guns.

After that the road was clear. It was a dirt road, but smooth enough, and he made good speed. He picked up a hitch-hiker and asked him about crossing the border on horseback. No problem, said the hitch-hiker. It could be done, and as it happened, his brother had horses . . .

Rashid did the forty-mile journey in a little over an hour. He pulled up at the border station in his Range Rover. The guards were suspicious of him. He showed them the pass written by the deputy leader. The guards called Rezaiyeh and – they said – spoke to the deputy, who vouched for Rashid.

He stood looking across to Turkey. It was a pleasant sight. They had all been through a lot of anguish just to walk across there. For Paul and Bill it would mean freedom, home and family. For all the EDS men it would be the end of a nightmare. For Rashid it meant something else: America.

He understood the psychology of EDS executives. They had a strong sense of obligation. If you helped them, they liked to show their appreciation, to keep the books balanced. He knew he only had to ask, and they would take him with them to the land of his dreams.

The border station was under the control of the village of Sero, just half a mile away down a mountain track. Rashid decided he would go and see the village chief, to establish a friendly relationship and smooth the way for later.

He was about to turn away when two cars drove up on the Turkish side. A tall black man in a leather coat got out of the first car and came to the chain on the edge of no-man's-land.

Rashid's heart leaped. He knew that man! He started waving and yelled: 'Ralph! Ralph Boulware! Hey, Ralph!'

IV

Thursday morning found Glenn Jackson – hunter, Baptist and Rocket Man – in the skies over Tehran in a chartered jet.

Jackson had stayed in Kuwait after reporting on the possibility of Paul and Bill coming out of Iran that way. On Sunday, the day Paul and Bill got out of jail, Simons had sent orders, via Merv Stauffer, that Jackson was to go to Amman, Jordan, and there try to charter a plane to fly into Iran.

Jackson had reached Amman on Monday and had gone to work straight away. He knew that Perot had flown into Tehran from Amman on a chartered jet of Arab Wings. He also knew that the president of Arab Wings, Akel Biltaji, had been helpful, allowing Perot to go in with NBC's television tapes as a cover. Now Jackson contacted Biltaji and asked for his help again.

He told Biltaji that EDS had two men in Iran who had to be brought out. He invented false names for Paul and Bill. Even though Tehran Airport was closed, Jackson wanted to fly in and try to land. Biltaji was willing to give it a try.

However, on Wednesday Stauffer – on Simons's instructions – changed Jackson's orders. Now his mission was to check on the Clean Team: the Dirty Team was no longer in Tehran, as far as Dallas knew.

On Thursday Jackson took off from Amman and headed east.

As they came down towards the bowl in the mountains where Tehran nestled, two aircraft took off from the city.

The planes came closer, and Jackson saw that they were fighter jets of the Iranian Air Force.

He wondered what would happen next.

His pilot's radio came to life with a burst of static. As the fighters circled, the pilot talked. Jackson could not understand the conversation, but he was glad the Iranians were talking rather than shooting.

The discussion went on. The pilot seemed to be arguing. Eventually he turned to Jackson and said: 'We have to go back. They won't let us land.'

'What will they do if we land anyway?'

'Shoot us down.'

'Okay,' said Jackson. 'We'll try again this afternoon.'

On Thursday morning in Istanbul, an English-language newspaper was delivered to Perot's suite at the Sheraton.

He picked it up and eagerly read the front-page story about yesterday's takeover of the American Embassy in Tehran. None of the Clean Team was mentioned, he was relieved to see. The only injury had been suffered by a Marine Sergeant, Kenneth Krause. However, Krause was not getting the medical attention he needed, according to the newspaper.

Perot called John Carlen, the captain of the Boeing 707, and asked him to come to the suite. He showed Carlen the newspaper and said: 'How would you feel about flying in to Tehran tonight and picking up the wounded Marine?'

Carlen, a laid-back Californian with greying hair and a tan, was very cool. 'We can do that,' he said.

Perot was surprised that Carlen did not even hesitate. He would have to fly through the mountains at night with no air traffic control to help him, and land at a closed airport. 'Don't you want to talk to the rest of the crew?' Perot asked.

'No, they'll want to do it. The people who own the airplane will go bananas.'

'Don't tell them. I'll be responsible.'

'I'll need to know exactly where that Marine is going to be,' Carlen went on. 'The Embassy will have to get him to the airport. I know a lot of people at that airport – I can talk my way out again or just take off.'

Perot thought: And the Clean Team will be the stretcher bearers.

He called Dallas and reached Sally Walther, his secretary. He asked her to patch him through to General Wilson, Commandant of the Marine Corps. He and Wilson were friends.

Wilson came on the line.

'I'm in Turkey on business,' Perot told him. 'I've just read about Sergeant Krause. I have a plane here. If the Embassy can get Krause to the airport, we will fly in tonight and pick him up and see he gets proper medical care.'

'All right,' said Wilson. 'If he's dying I want you to pick him up. If not, I won't risk your crew. I'll get back to you.'

Perot got Sally back on the line. There was more bad news. A press officer in the State Department's Iran

Task Force had talked to Robert Dudney, Washington correspondent for the *Dallas Times Herald,* and revealed that Paul and Bill were on their way out overland.

Perot cursed the State Department yet again. If Dudney published the story, and the news reached Tehran, Dadgar would surely intensify border security.

The seventh floor in Dallas blamed Perot for all this. He had levelled with the consul who had come to see him the night before, and they believed the leak started with the consul. They were now frantically trying to get the story killed, but the newspaper was making no promises.

General Wilson called back. Sergeant Krause was not dying: Perot's help was not required.

Perot forgot about Krause and concentrated on his own problems.

The consul called him. He had tried his best, but he could not help Perot buy or rent a small aircraft. It was possible to charter a plane to go from one airport to another within Turkey, but that was all.

Perot said nothing to him about the press leak.

He called in Dick Douglas and Julian 'Scratch' Kanauch, the two spare pilots he had brought specifically to fly small aircraft into Iran, and told them he had failed to find any such aircraft.

'Don't worry,' said Douglas. 'We'll get an airplane.'

'How?'

'Don't ask.'

'No, I want to know how.'

'I've operated in Eastern Turkey. I know where there are planes. If you need 'em, we'll steal 'em.'

'Have you thought this through?' said Perot.

'You think it through,' Douglas said. 'If we get shot down over Iran, what difference does it make that we stole the plane? If we don't get shot down, we can put the planes back where we got them. Even if they have a few holes in them, we'll be out of the area before anybody knows. What else is there to think about?'

'That settles it,' said Perot. 'We're going.'

He sent John Carlen and Ron Davis to the airport to file a flight plan to Van, the nearest airport to the border.

Davis called from the airport to say that the 707 could not land at Van: it was a Turkish-language-only airport, so *no* foreign planes were allowed to land except US military planes carrying interpreters.

Perot called Mr Fish and asked him to arrange to fly the team to Van. Mr Fish called back a few minutes later to say it was all fixed. He would go with the team as guide. Perot was surprised: until now Mr Fish had been adamant that he would not go to Eastern Turkey. Perhaps he had become infected by the spirit of adventure.

However, Perot himself would have to stay behind. He was the hub of the wheel: he had to stay in telephone contact with the outside world, to receive reports from Boulware, from Dallas, from the Clean Team and from the Dirty Team. If the 707 had been able to land at Van, Perot could have gone, for the plane's single-sideband radio enabled him to make phone calls all over the world; but without that radio he would be out of touch in Eastern Turkey, and there would be no link between the fugitives in Iran and the people who were coming to meet them.

So he sent Pat Sculley, Jim Schwebach, Ron Davis, Mr Fish, and the pilots Dick Douglas and Julian Kanauch to Van; and he appointed Pat Sculley leader of the Turkish Rescue Team.

When they had gone he was dead in the water again. They were just another bunch of his men off doing dangerous things in dangerous places. He could only sit and wait for news.

He spent a lot of time thinking about John Carlen and the crew of the Boeing 707. He had only known them for a few days: they were ordinary Americans. Yet Carlen had been prepared to risk his life to fly into Tehran and pick up a wounded Marine. As Simons would say: This is what Americans are supposed to do for one another. It made Perot feel pretty good, despite everything.

The phone rang.

He answered. 'Ross Perot.'

'This is Ralph Boulware.'

'Hi, Ralph, where are you?'

'I'm at the border.'

'Good!'

'I've just seen Rashid.'

Perot's heart leaped. 'Great! What did he say?'

'They're safe.'

'Thank God!'

'They're in a hotel, thirty or forty miles from the border. Rashid is just scouting the territory in advance. He's gone back now. He says they'll probably cross tomorrow, but that's just his idea, and Simons might think otherwise. If they're that close I don't see Simons waiting until morning.'

'Right. Now, Pat Sculley and Mr Fish and the rest of the guys are on their way to you. They're flying to Van, then they'll rent a bus. Now where will they find you?'

'I'm based in a village called Yuksekova, closest place to the border, at a hotel. It's the only hotel in the district.'

'I'll tell Sculley.'

'Okay.'

Perot hung up. Oh, boy, he thought; at last things were beginning to go right!

Pat Sculley's orders from Perot were to go to the border, ensure that the Dirty Team got across safely, and bring them to Istanbul. If the Dirty Team failed to reach the border, he was to go into Iran and find them, preferably in a plane stolen by Dick Douglas, or failing that by road.

Sculley and the Turkish Rescue Team took a scheduled flight from Istanbul to Ankara, where the chartered jet was waiting for them. (The charter plane would take them to Van and bring them back: it would not go anywhere they pleased. The only way of making the pilot take them into Iran would have been to hijack the plane.)

The arrival of the jet seemed to be a big event in the town of Van. Getting off the plane, they were met by a contingent of policemen who looked ready to give them a hard time. But Mr Fish went into a huddle with the police chief and came out smiling.

'Now, listen,' said Mr Fish. 'We're going to check in to the best hotel in town, but I want you to know it's not the Sheraton, so please don't complain.'

They went off in two taxis.

The hotel had a high central hall with three floors of rooms reached via galleries, so that every room door could be seen from the hall. When the Americans walked in the hall was full of Turks, drinking beer and watching a soccer match on a black and white TV, yelling and cheering. As the Turks noticed the strangers, the room quietened down until there was complete silence.

They were assigned rooms. Each bedroom had two cots and a hole in the corner, screened by a shower curtain, for a toilet. There were plank floors and white-washed walls without windows. The rooms were infested with cockroaches. On each floor was one bathroom.

Sculley and Mr Fish went to get a bus to take them all to the border. A Mercedes picked them up outside the hotel and took them to what appeared to be an electrical appliance store with a few ancient TV sets in the window. The place was closed – it was evening by now – but Mr Fish banged on the iron grille protecting the windows, and someone came out.

They went into the back and sat at a table under a single light bulb. Sculley understood none of the conversation, but by the end of it Mr Fish had negotiated a bus and a driver. They returned to the hotel in the bus.

The rest of the team were gathered in Sculley's room.

Nobody wanted to sit on these beds, let alone sleep in them. They all wanted to leave for the border immediately, but Mr Fish was hesitant. 'It's two o'clock in the morning,' he said. 'And the police are watching the hotel.'

'Does that matter?' said Sculley.

'It means more questions, more trouble.'

'Let's give it a try.'

They all trooped downstairs. The manager appeared, looking anxious, and started to question Mr Fish. Then, sure enough, two policemen came in from outside and joined in the discussion.

Mr Fish turned to Sculley and said: 'They don't want us to go.'

'Why not?'

'We look very suspicious, don't you realize that?'

'Look, is it against the law for us to go?'

'No, but—'

'Then we're going. Just tell them.'

There was more argument in Turkish, but finally the policemen and the hotel manager appeared to give in, and the team boarded the bus.

They left town. The temperature dropped rapidly as they drove up into the snow-covered hills. They all had warm coats, and blankets in their backpacks, and they needed them.

Mr Fish sat next to Sculley and said: 'This is where it gets serious. I can handle the police, because I have ties with them; but I'm worried about the bandits and the soldiers – I have no connections there.'

'What d'you want to do?'

'I believe I can talk my way out of trouble so long as none of you have guns.'

Sculley considered. Only Davis was armed anyway; and Simons had always worried that weapons could get you into trouble more readily than they could get you out of it: the Walther PPKs had never left Dallas. 'Okay,' Sculley said.

Ron Davis threw his .38 out of the window into the snow.

A little later the headlights of the bus revealed a soldier in uniform standing in the middle of the road, waving. The bus driver kept right on going, as if he intended to run the man down, but Mr Fish yelled and the driver pulled up.

Looking out of the window, Sculley saw a platoon of soldiers armed with high-powered rifles on the mountainside, and thought: If we hadn't stopped, we'd have been mown down.

A sergeant and a corporal got on the bus. They checked all the passports. Mr Fish offered them cigarettes. They stood talking to him while they smoked, then they waved and got off.

A few miles farther on, the bus was stopped again, and they went through a similar routine.

The third time, the men who got on the bus had no uniforms. Mr Fish became very jumpy. 'Act casual,' he hissed at the Americans. 'Read books, just don't look at these guys.' He talked to the Turks for something like half an hour, and when the bus was finally allowed to proceed, two of them stayed on it. 'Protection,' Mr Fish said enigmatically, and he shrugged.

Sculley was nominally in charge, but there was little he could do other than follow Mr Fish's directions. He did not know the country, nor did he speak the language: most of the time he had no idea what was going on. It was hard to have control under those circumstances. The best he could do, he figured, was to keep Mr Fish pointed in the right direction and lean on him a little when he began to lose his nerve.

At four o'clock in the morning they reached Yuksekova, the nearest village to the border station. Here, according to Mr Fish's cousin in Van, they would find Ralph Boulware.

Sculley and Mr Fish went into the hotel. It was dark as a barn and smelled like the men's room at a football stadium. They yelled for a while, and a boy appeared with a candle. Mr Fish spoke to him in Turkish, then said: 'Boulware's not here. He left hours ago. They don't know where he went.'

CHAPTER THIRTEEN

I

AT THE hotel in Rezaiyeh, Jay Coburn had that sick, helpless feeling again, the feeling he had had in Mahabad, and then in the courtyard of the schoolhouse: he had no control over his own destiny, his fate was in the hands of others – in this case, the hands of Rashid.

Where the hell was Rashid?

Coburn asked the guards if he could use the phone. They took him down to the lobby. He dialled the home of Majid's cousin, the professor, in Rezaiyeh, but there was no answer.

Without much hope he dialled Gholam's number in Tehran. To his surprise he got through.

'I have a message for Jim Nyfeler,' he said. 'We are at the staging area.'

'But where are you?' said Gholam.

'In Tehran,' Coburn lied.

'I need to see you.'

Coburn had to continue the deception. 'Okay, I'll meet you tomorrow morning.'

'Where?'

'At Bucharest.'

'Okay.'

Coburn went back upstairs. Simons took him and Keane Taylor into one of the rooms. 'If Rashid isn't back by nine o'clock, we're leaving,' Simons said.

Coburn immediately felt better.

Simons went on: 'The guards are getting bored, their vigilance is slipping. We'll either sneak past them or deal with them the other way.'

'We've only got one car,' said Coburn.

'And we're going to leave it here, to confuse them. We'll walk to the border. Hell, it's only thirty or forty miles. We can go across country: we'll avoid roadblocks by avoiding roads.'

Coburn nodded. This was what he wanted. They were taking the initiative again.

'Let's get the money together,' Simons said to Taylor. 'Ask the guards to take you down to the car. Bring the Kleenex box and the flashlight up here and take the money out of them.'

Taylor left.

'We might as well eat first,' Simons said. 'It's going to be a long walk.'

Taylor went into an empty room and spilled the money out of the Kleenex box and the flashlight on to the floor.

Suddenly the door was flung open.

Taylor's heart stopped.

He looked up and saw Gayden, grinning all over his face.

'Gotcha!' Gayden said.

Taylor was furious. 'You bastard, Gayden,' he said. 'You gave me a fucking heart attack.'

Gayden laughed like hell.

The guards took them downstairs to the dining room. The Americans sat at a big circular table, and the guards took another table across the room. Lamb and rice was served, and tea. It was a grim meal: they were all worried about what might have happened to Rashid, and how they would manage without him.

There was a TV set on, and Paul could not take his eyes off the screen. He expected at any minute to see his own face appear like a 'wanted' poster.

Where the hell was Rashid?

They were only an hour from the border, yet they were trapped, under guard, and still in danger of being sent back to Tehran and jail.

Someone said: 'Hey, look who's here!'

Rashid walked in.

He came over to their table, wearing his self-important look. 'Gentlemen,' he said, 'this is your last meal.'

They all stared at him, horrified.

'In Iran, I mean,' he added hastily. 'We can leave.'

They all cheered.

'I got a letter from the revolutionary committee,' he went on. 'I went to the border to check it out. There are a couple of roadblocks on the way, but I have arranged everything. I know where we can get horses to cross the mountains – but I don't think we need them. There are no government people at the border station – the place

519

is in the hands of the villagers. I saw the head man of the village, and it will be all right for us to cross. Also, Ralph Boulware is there. I talked to him.'

Simons stood up. 'Let's move,' he said. 'Fast.'

They left their meal half-eaten. Rashid talked to the guards, and showed them his letter from the deputy leader. Keane Taylor paid the hotel bill. Rashid had bought a stack of Khomeini posters, and he gave them to Bill to stick on the cars.

They were out of there in minutes.

Bill had done a good job with the posters. Everywhere you looked on the Range Rovers, the fierce, white-bearded face of the Ayatollah glared out at you.

They pulled away, Rashid driving the first car.

On the way out of town Rashid suddenly braked, leaned out of the window, and waved frantically at an approaching taxi.

Simons growled: 'Rashid, what the fuck are you doing?'

Without answering, Rashid jumped out of the car and ran over to the taxi.

'Jesus *Christ*,' said Simons.

Rashid talked to the cab driver for a minute, then the cab went on. Rashid explained: 'I asked him to show us a way out of town by the back street. There is one roadblock I want to avoid because it is manned by kids with rifles and I don't know what they might do. The cabbie has a fare already, but he's coming back. We'll wait.'

'We won't wait very goddamn long,' Simons said.

The cab returned in ten minutes. They followed it

through the dark, unpaved streets until they came to a main road. The cabbie turned right. Rashid followed, taking the corner fast. On the left, just a few yards away, was the roadblock he had wanted to avoid, with teenage boys firing rifles into the air. The cab and the two Range Rovers accelerated fast away from the corner, before the kids could realize that someone had sneaked past them.

Fifty yards down the road, Rashid pulled into a gas station.

Keane Taylor said to him: 'What the hell are you stopping for?'

'We've got to get gas.'

'We've got three-quarters of a tankful, plenty to jump the border on – let's get *out* of here.'

'It may be impossible to get gas in Turkey.'

Simons said: 'Rashid, let's *go.*'

Rashid jumped out of the car.

When the fuel tanks had been topped up, Rashid was still haggling with the taxi driver, offering him a hundred rials – a little more than a dollar – for guiding them out of town.

Taylor said: 'Rashid, just give him a handful of money and *let's go.*'

'He wants too much,' Rashid said.

'Oh, God,' said Taylor.

Rashid settled with the cabbie for two hundred rials and got back into the Range Rover, saying: 'He would have got suspicious if I didn't argue.'

They drove out of town. The road wound up into the mountains. The surface was good and they made rapid progress. After a while the road began to follow a ridge, with deep wooded gulleys on either side. 'There was a checkpoint around here somewhere this afternoon,' Rashid said. 'Maybe they went home.'

The headlights picked out two men standing beside the road, waving them down. There was no barrier. Rashid did not brake.

'I guess we better stop,' Simons said.

Rashid kept going right past the two men.

'I said stop!' Simons barked.

Rashid stopped.

Bill stared out through the windscreen and said: 'Would you look at that?'

A few yards ahead was a bridge over a ravine. On either side of the bridge, tribesmen were emerging from the ravine. They kept coming – thirty, forty, fifty – and they were armed to the teeth.

It looked very like an ambush. If the cars had tried to rush the checkpoint, they would have been shot full of holes.

'Thank God we stopped,' Bill said fervently.

Rashid jumped out of the car and started talking. The tribesmen put a chain across the bridge and surrounded the cars. It rapidly became clear that these were the most unfriendly people the team had yet encountered. They surrounded the cars, glaring in and hefting their rifles, while two or three of them started yelling at Rashid.

It was maddening, Bill thought, to have come so far, through so much danger and adversity, only to be stopped by a bunch of dumb farmers. Wouldn't they just like to take these two fine Range Rovers and all our money? he thought. And who would ever know?

The tribesmen got meaner. They started pushing and shoving Rashid. In a minute they'll start shooting, Bill thought.

'Do nothing,' Simons said. 'Stay in the car, let Rashid handle it.'

Bill decided Rashid needed some help. He touched his pocket rosary and started praying. He said every prayer he knew. We're in God's hands now, he thought; it will take a miracle to get us out of this mess.

In the second car, Coburn sat frozen while a tribesman outside pointed a rifle directly at his head.

Gayden, sitting behind, was seized by a wild impulse, and whispered: 'Jay! Why don't you lock the door?'

Coburn felt hysterical laughter bubble up in his throat.

Rashid felt he was on the cliff-edge of death.

These tribesmen were bandits, and they would kill you for the coat on your back: they didn't care. The revolution was nothing to them. No matter who was in power, they recognized no government, obeyed no laws. They did not even speak Farsi, the language of Iran, but Turkish.

They pushed him around, yelling at him in Turkish.

He yelled back in Farsi. He was getting nowhere. They're working themselves up to shoot us all, he thought.

He heard the sound of a car. A pair of headlights approached from the direction of Rezaiyeh. A Land Rover pulled up and three men got out. One of them was dressed in a long black overcoat. The tribesmen seemed to defer to him. He addressed Rashid. 'Let me see the passports, please.'

'Sure,' said Rashid. He led the man to the second Range Rover. Bill was in the first, and Rashid wanted the overcoat man to get bored with looking at passports before he got to Bill's. Rashid tapped on the car window, and Paul rolled it down. 'Passports.'

The man seemed to have dealt with passports before. He examined each one carefully, checking the photographs against the face of the owner. Then, in perfect English, he asked questions: 'Where were you born? Where do you live? What is your date of birth?' Fortunately, Simons had made Paul and Bill learn every piece of information contained in their false passports, so Paul was able to answer the overcoat man's questions without hesitation.

Reluctantly, Rashid led the man to the first Range Rover. Bill and Keane Taylor had changed seats, so that Bill was on the far side, away from the light. The man went through the same routine. He looked at Bill's passport last. Then he said: 'The picture is not of this man.'

'Yes, it is,' Rashid said frantically. 'He's been very sick. He's lost weight, his skin has changed colour –

don't you understand that he's dying? He has to get back to America as quickly as possible so he can have the right medical attention, and you are delaying him – do you want him to die because the Iranian people had no pity for a sick man? Is this how you uphold the honour of our country? Is—'

'They're Americans,' the man said. 'Follow me.'

He turned and went into the little brick hut beside the bridge.

Rashid followed him in. 'You have no right to stop us,' he said. 'I have been instructed by the Islamic Revolution Commandant Committee in Rezaiyeh to escort these people to the border, and to delay us is a counter-revolutionary crime against the Iranian people.' He flourished the letter written by the deputy leader and stamped with the library stamp.

The man looked at it. 'Still, that one American does not look like the picture in his passport.'

'I told you, he has been sick!' Rashid yelled. 'They have been cleared to the border by the revolutionary committee! Now get these bandits out of my way!'

'We have our own revolutionary committee,' the man said. 'You will all have to come to our headquarters.'

Rashid had no choice but to agree.

Jay Coburn watched Rashid come out of the hut with the man in the long black overcoat. Rashid looked really shaken.

'We're going to their village to be checked out,' Rashid said. 'We have to go in their cars.'

It was looking bad, Coburn thought. All the other times they had been arrested, they had been allowed to stay in the Range Rovers, which made them feel a little less like prisoners. Getting out of the cars was like losing touch with base.

Also, Rashid had never looked so frightened.

They all got into the tribesmen's vehicles, a pick-up truck and a battered little station wagon. They were driven along a dirt track through the mountains. The Range Rovers followed driven by tribesmen. The track twisted away into darkness. Well, shit, this is it, Coburn thought; nobody will ever hear from us again.

After three or four miles they came to the village. There was one brick building with a courtyard: the rest were mudbrick huts with thatched roofs. But in the courtyard were six or seven fine jeeps. Coburn said: 'Jesus, these people live by stealing cars.' Two Range Rovers would make a nice addition to their collection, he thought.

The two vehicles containing the Americans were parked in the courtyard; then the Range Rovers; then two more jeeps, blocking the exit and precluding a quick getaway.

They all got out.

The man in the overcoat said: 'You need not be afraid. We just need to talk with you a while, then you can go on.' He went into the brick building.

'He's lying!' Rashid hissed.

They were herded into the building and told to take off their shoes. The tribesmen were fascinated by Keane Taylor's cowboy boots: one of them picked up the boots

526

and inspected them, then passed them around for everyone to see.

The Americans were led into a big, bare room, with a Persian rug on the floor and bundles of rolled-up bedding pushed against the walls. It was dimly lit by some kind of lantern. They sat in a circle, surrounded by tribesmen with rifles.

On trial again, just like Mahabad, Coburn thought.

He kept an eye on Simons.

In came the biggest, ugliest mullah they had ever seen; and the interrogation began again.

Rashid did the talking, in a mixture of Farsi, Turkish and English. He produced the letter from the library again, and gave the name of the deputy leader. Someone went off to check with the committee in Rezaiyeh. Coburn wondered how they would do that: the oil lamp indicated there was no electricity here, so how could they have phones? All the passports were examined again. People kept coming in and going out.

What if they have got a phone? wondered Coburn. And what if the committee in Rezaiyeh has heard from Dadgar?

We might be better off if they *do* check us out, he thought; at least that way somebody knows we're here. At the moment we could be killed, our bodies would disappear without trace in the snow, and nobody would ever know we had been here.

A tribesman came in, handed the library letter to Rashid and spoke to the mullah.

'It's okay,' Rashid said. 'We've been cleared.'

Suddenly the whole atmosphere changed.

The ugly mullah turned into the Jolly Green Giant and shook hands with everyone. 'He welcomes you to his village,' Rashid translated. Tea was brought. Rashid said: 'We are invited to be the guests of the village for the night.'

Simons said: 'Tell him definitely no. Our friends are waiting for us at the border.'

A small boy of about ten years appeared. In an effort to cement the new friendship, Keane Taylor took out a photograph of his son, Michael, aged eleven, and showed it to the tribesmen. They got very excited, and Rashid said: 'They want to have their picture taken.'

Gayden said: 'Keane, get out your camera.'

'I'm out of film,' said Taylor.

'Keane, get out your fucking camera.'

Taylor took out his camera. In fact he had three shots left, but he had no flash, and would have needed a camera far more sophisticated than his Instamatic for taking pictures by the light of the lantern. But the tribesmen lined up, waving their rifles in the air, and Taylor had no option but to snap them.

It was incredible. Five minutes earlier those people had seemed ready to murder the Americans: now they were horsing around, hooting and hollering and having a good time.

They could probably change again just as quickly.

Taylor's sense of humour took over and he started hamming it up, making like a press photographer, telling the tribesmen to smile or move closer together so he could get them all in, 'taking' dozens of shots.

More tea was brought. Coburn groaned inwardly. He

had drunk so much tea in the last few days that he felt awash with it. He surreptitiously poured his out, making an ugly brown stain on the gorgeous rug.

Simons said to Rashid: 'Tell them we have to go.'

There was a short exchange, then Rashid said: 'We must drink tea once more.'

'No,' said Simons decisively, and he stood up. 'Let's move.' Smiling calmly, nodding and bowing to the tribesmen, Simons started giving very decisive commands in a voice which belied his courteous demeanour: 'On your feet, everybody. Get your shoes on. Come on, let's get out of here, let's *go*.'

They all got up. Every man in the tribe wanted to shake hands with every one of the visitors. Simons kept herding them towards the door. They found their shoes and put them on, still bowing and shaking hands. At last they got outside and climbed into the Range Rovers. There was a wait, while the villagers manoeuvred the two jeeps blocking the exit. At last they moved off, following the same two jeeps, along the mountain track.

They were still alive, still free, still moving.

The tribesmen took them to the bridge then said goodbye.

Rashid said: 'But aren't you going to escort us to the border?'

'No,' one of them replied. 'Our territory ends at the bridge. The other side belongs to Sero.'

The man in the long black overcoat shook hands with everyone in both Range Rovers. 'Don't forget to send us the pictures,' he said to Taylor.

'You bet,' said Taylor with a straight face.

The chain across the bridge was down. The two Range Rovers drove to the far side and accelerated up the road.

'I hope we don't have the same trouble at the next village,' said Rashid. 'I saw the head man this afternoon and arranged everything with him.'

The Range Rovers built up speed.

'Slow down,' said Simons.

'No, we must hurry.'

They were a mile or so from the border.

Simons said: 'Slow the goddam jeep down, I don't want to get killed at this point in the game.'

They were driving past what looked like a filling station. There was a little hut with a light on inside. Taylor yelled: 'Stop! Stop!'

Simons said: 'Rashid—'

In the following car, Paul honked and flashed his headlights.

Out of the corner of his eye Rashid saw two men running out from the filling station, locking-and-loading their rifles as they ran.

He stood on the brake.

The car screeched to a halt. Paul had already stopped, right by the gas station. Rashid backed up and jumped out.

The two men pointed their rifles at him.

Here we go again, he thought.

He went into his routine, but they weren't interested. One of them got into each car. Rashid climbed back into the driving seat.

'Drive on,' he was told.

A minute later they were at the foot of the hill leading to the border. They could see the lights of the frontier station up above. Rashid's captor said: 'Turn right.'

'No,' said Rashid. 'We've been cleared to the border and—'

The man raised his rifle and thumbed the safety.

Rashid stopped the car. 'Listen, I came to your village this afternoon and got permission to pass—'

'Go down there.'

They were less than half a mile from Turkey and freedom.

There were seven of the Dirty Team against two guards. It was tempting . . .

A jeep came tearing down the hill from the border station and skidded to a stop in front of the Range Rover. An excited young man jumped out, carrying a pistol, and ran over to Rashid's window.

Rashid wound down the window and said: 'I'm under orders from the Islamic Revolution Commandant Committee—'

The excited young man pointed his pistol at Rashid's head. 'Go down the track!' he screamed.

Rashid gave in.

They drove along the track. It was even narrower than the last. The village was less than a mile away. When they arrived Rashid jumped out of the car, saying: 'Stay here – I'll deal with this.'

Several men came out of the huts to see what was going on. They looked even more like bandits than the inhabitants of the last village. Rashid said loudly: 'Where is the head man?'

'Not here,' someone replied.

'Then fetch him. I spoke to him this afternoon – I am a friend of his – I have permission from him to cross the border with these Americans.'

'Why are you with Americans?' someone asked.

'I am under orders from the Islamic Revolution Commandant Committee—'

Suddenly, out of nowhere, appeared the head man of the village, to whom Rashid had spoken in the afternoon. He came up and kissed Rashid on both cheeks.

In the second Range Rover, Gayden said: 'Hey, it's looking good!'

'Thank God for that,' said Coburn. 'I couldn't drink any more tea to save my life.'

The man who had kissed Rashid came over. He was wearing a heavy Afghan coat. He leaned through the car window and shook hands with everyone.

Rashid and the two guards got back into the cars.

A few minutes later they were climbing the hill to the frontier station.

Paul, driving the second car, suddenly thought about Dadgar again. Four hours ago, in Rezaiyeh, it had seemed sensible to abandon the idea of crossing the border on horseback, avoiding the road and the station. Now he was not so sure. Dadgar might have sent pictures of Paul and Bill to every airport, seaport, and border crossing. Even if there were no government people here, the photographs might be stuck up on a wall somewhere. The Iranians seemed to be glad of any excuse to detain Americans and question them. All along, EDS had underestimated Dadgar . . .

The frontier station was brightly lit by high neon lamps. The two cars drove slowly along, past the buildings, and stopped where a chain across the road marked the limit of Iranian territory.

Rashid got out.

He spoke to the guards at the station, then came back and said: 'They don't have a key to unloose the chain.'

They all got out.

Simons said to Rashid: 'Go over to the Turkish side and see if Boulware's there.'

Rashid disappeared.

Simons lifted the chain. It would not go high enough to let a Range Rover pass underneath.

Somebody found a few planks and leaned them on the chain, to see whether the cars could be driven over the chain on the planks. Simons shook his head: it was not going to work.

He turned to Coburn. 'Is there a hacksaw in the tool kit?'

Coburn went back to the car.

Paul and Gayden lit cigarettes. Gayden said: 'You need to decide what you want to do with that passport.'

'What do you mean?'

'Under American law there's a ten-thousand-dollar fine and a jail term for using a false passport. I'll pay the fine but you'll have to serve the jail term.'

Paul considered. So far he had broken no laws. He

had shown his false passport, but only to bandits and revolutionaries who had no real right to demand passports anyway. It would be kind of nice to stay on the right side of the law.

'That's right,' said Simons. 'Once we're out of this goddam country we break no laws. I don't want to have to get you out of a Turkish jail.'

Paul gave the passport to Gayden. Bill did the same. Gayden gave the passports to Taylor, who put them down the sides of his cowboy boots.

Coburn came back with a hacksaw. Simons took it from him and started sawing the chain.

The Iranian guards rushed over and started yelling at him.

Simons stopped.

Rashid came back from the Turkish side, trailing a couple of guards and an officer. He spoke to the Iranians, then told Simons: 'You can't cut the chain. They say we must wait until morning. Also the Turks don't want us to cross tonight.'

Simons muttered to Paul: 'You may be about to get sick.'

'What do you mean?'

'If I tell you so, just get sick, okay.'

Paul saw what Simons was thinking: the Turkish guards wanted to sleep, not spend the night with a crowd of Americans, but if one of the Americans was in urgent need of hospital treatment they could hardly turn him away.

The Turks went back over to their own side.

'What do we do now?' Coburn said.

'Wait,' said Simons.

All but two of the Iranian guards went into their guardhouse: it was bitterly cold.

'Make like we're prepared to wait all night,' said Simons.

The other two guards drifted off.

'Gayden, Taylor,' Simons said. 'Go in there and offer the guards money to take care of our cars.'

'Take care of them?' Taylor said incredulously. 'They'll just steal them.'

'That's right,' said Simons. 'They'll be able to steal them if they let us go.'

Taylor and Gayden went into the guardhouse.

'This is it,' said Simons. 'Coburn, get Paul and Bill and just walk across there.'

'Let's go, you guys,' said Coburn.

Paul and Bill stepped over the chain and started walking. Coburn stayed close behind them. 'Just keep walking, regardless of anything else that might happen,' Coburn said. 'If you hear yelling, or gunfire, you run, but under no circumstances do we stop or go back.'

Simons came up behind them. 'Walk faster,' he said. 'I don't want you two getting shot out here in the bloody middle of nowhere.'

They could hear some kind of argument beginning back on the Iranian side.

Coburn said: 'Y'all don't turn round, just go.'

Back on the Iranian side, Taylor was holding out a fistful of money to two guards who were glancing first at the four men walking across the border and then at the two Range Rovers, worth at least twenty thousand dollars each . . .

Rashid was saying: 'We don't know when we'll be able to come back for these cars – it could be a long time—'

One of the guards said: 'You were all to stay here until the morning—'

'The cars are really very valuable, and they must be looked after—'

The guards looked from the cars, to the people walking across to Turkey, and back to the cars again, and they hesitated too long.

Paul and Bill reached the Turkish side and walked into the guard hut.

Bill looked at his wristwatch. It was 11.45 p.m. on Thursday, 15 February, the day after Valentine's Day. On 15 February 1960 he had slipped an engagement ring on Emily's finger. The same day six years later Jackie had been born – today was her thirteenth birthday. Bill thought: here's your present, Jackie – you still have a father.

Coburn followed them into the hut.

Paul put his arm around Coburn and said: 'Jay, you just hit a home run.'

Back on the Iranian side, the guards saw that half the Americans were already in Turkey, and they decided to quit while they were ahead and take the money and the cars.

Rashid, Gayden and Taylor walked up to the chain.

At the chain Gayden stopped. 'Go ahead,' he said. 'I want to be the last guy out of here.' And he was.

II

At the hotel in Yuksekova, they sat around a smokey pot-bellied stove: Ralph Boulware, Ilsman the fat secret agent, Charlie Brown the interpreter, and the two sons of Mr Fish's cousin. They were waiting for a call from the border station. Dinner was served: some kind of meat, maybe lamb, wrapped in newspapers.

Ilsman said he had seen someone taking photographs of Rashid and Boulware at the border. With Charlie Brown translating, Ilsman said: 'If you ever have a problem about those photographs, I can solve it.'

Boulware wondered what he meant.

Charlie said: 'He believes you are an honest man, and what you are doing is noble.'

It was kind of a sinister offer, Boulware felt; like a Mafioso telling you that you are his friend.

By midnight there was still no word either from the Dirty Team or from Pat Sculley and Mr Fish, who were supposed to be on their way here with a bus. Boulware decided to go to bed. He always drank water at bedtime. There was a pitcher of water on a table. Hell, he thought, I haven't died yet. He took a drink, and found himself swallowing something solid. Oh, God, he thought; what was that? He made himself forget about it.

He was just getting to bed when a boy called him to the phone.

It was Rashid.

'Hey, Ralph?'

'Yes.'

'We're at the border!'

'I'll be right there.'

He rounded up the others and paid the hotel bill. With the sons of Mr Fish's cousin driving, they headed down the road where – as Ilsman kept saying – thirty-nine people had been killed by bandits last month. On the way they had yet another flat tyre. The sons had to change the wheel in the dark, because the batteries in their flashlight had gone dead. Boulware did not know whether to be frightened, standing there in the road waiting. Ilsman could still be a liar, a confidence trickster. On the other hand, his credentials had protected them all. If the Turkish secret service was like Turkish hotels, hell, Ilsman could be their answer to James Bond.

The wheel was changed and the cars moved off again.

They drove through the night. It's going to be all right, Boulware thought. Paul and Bill are at the border, Sculley and Mr Fish are on their way here with a bus, Perot is in Istanbul with a plane. We're going to make it.

He reached the border. Lights were on in the guard huts. He jumped out of the car and ran inside.

A great cheer went up.

There they all were: Paul and Bill, Coburn, Simons, Taylor, Gayden and Rashid.

Boulware shook hands warmly with Paul and Bill.

They all started picking up their coats and bags. 'Hey, hey, wait a minute,' Boulware said. 'Mr Fish is on the way with a bus.' He took from his pocket a bottle of

Chivas Regal he had been saving for this moment. 'But we can all have a drink!'

They all had a celebratory drink, except Rashid who did not take alcohol. Simons got Boulware in a corner. 'All right, what's happening?'

'I talked to Ross this afternoon,' Boulware told him. 'Mr Fish is on his way here, with Sculley, Schwebach and Davis. They're in a bus. Now, we could all leave right now – the twelve of us could get into the two cars, just about – but I think we should wait for the bus. For one thing, we'll all be together, so nobody can get lost any more. For another, the road out of here is supposed to be Blood Alley, you know; bandits and such like. I don't know whether that's been exaggerated, but they keep saying it, and I'm beginning to believe it. If it's a dangerous road, we'll be safer all together. And, number three, if we go to Yuksekova and wait for Mr Fish there, we can't do anything but check into the worst hotel in the world, and attract questions and hassle from a new set of officials.'

'Okay,' Simons said reluctantly. 'We'll wait a while.'

He looked *tired*, Boulware thought; an old man who just wanted to rest. Coburn looked the same: drained, exhausted, almost broken. Boulware wondered just what they had been through to get here.

Boulware himself felt terrific, even though he had had little sleep for forty-eight hours. He thought of his endless discussions with Mr Fish about how to get to the border; of the screw-up in Adana when the bus failed to come; of the taxi ride through a blizzard in the mountains . . . And here he was, after all.

The little guardhouse was bitterly cold, and the wood burning stove did nothing but fill the room with smoke. Everyone was tired, and the whisky made them drowsy. One by one they began to fall asleep on the wooden benches and the floor.

Simons did not sleep. Rashid watched him, pacing up and down like a caged tiger, chain-smoking his plastic-tipped cigars. As dawn broke he started looking out of the window, across no-man's-land to Iran.

'There's a hundred people with rifles across there,' he said to Rashid and Boulware. 'What do you think they would do if they should happen to find out exactly who it was who slipped across the border last night?'

Boulware, too, was beginning to wonder whether he had been right to propose waiting for Mr Fish.

Rashid looked out of the window. Seeing the Range Rovers on the other side, he remembered something. 'The fuel can,' he said. 'I left the can with the money. We might need the money.'

Simons just looked at him.

On impulse, Rashid walked out of the guardhouse and started across the border.

It seemed a long way.

He thought about the psychology of the guards on the Iranian side. They have written us off, he decided. If they have any doubts about whether they did right last night, then they must have spent the last few hours making up excuses, justifying their action. By now they have convinced themselves that they did the right thing. It will take them a while to change their minds.

He reached the other side and stepped over the chain.

He went to the first Range Rover and opened the tailgate.

Two guards came running out of their hut.

Rashid lifted the can out of the car and closed the tailgate. 'We forgot the oil,' he said as he started walking back towards the chain.

'What do you need it for?' asked one of the guards suspiciously. 'You don't have the cars any more.'

'For the bus,' said Rashid as he stepped over the chain. 'The bus that's taking us to Van.'

He walked away, feeling their eyes on his back.

He did not look around until he was back inside the Turkish guardhouse.

A few minutes later they all heard the sound of a motor.

They looked out of the windows. A bus was coming down the road.

They cheered all over again.

Pat Sculley, Jim Schwebach, Ron Davis and Mr Fish stepped off the bus and came into the guardhouse.

They all shook hands.

The latest arrivals had brought another bottle of whisky, so everyone had another celebratory drink.

Mr Fish went into a huddle with Ilsman and the border guards.

Gayden put his arm around Pat Sculley and said: 'Have you noticed who's with us?' He pointed.

Sculley saw Rashid, asleep in a corner. He smiled. In Tehran he had been Rashid's manager, and then,

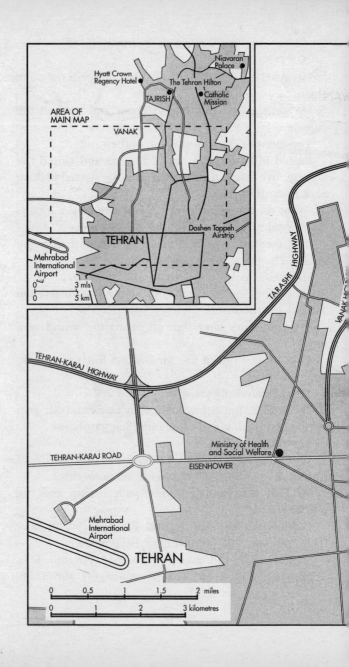

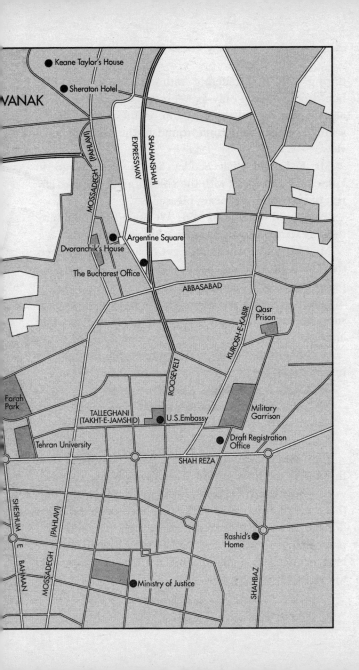

during that first meeting with Simons in the EDS boardroom – was it only six weeks ago? – he had strongly argued that Rashid should be in on the rescue. Now it seemed Simons had come round to the same point of view.

Mr Fish said: 'Pat Sculley and I have to go to Yuksekova and speak with the chief of police there. The rest of you wait here for us, please.'

'Now hold it,' Simons said. 'We waited for Boulware, then we waited for you. *Now* what are we waiting for?'

Mr Fish said: 'If we don't get clearance in advance, there will be trouble, because Paul and Bill have no passports.'

Simons turned to Boulware. 'Your guy Ilsman is supposed to have dealt with that problem,' he said angrily.

'I thought he did!' said Boulware. 'I thought he bribed them.'

'So what's happening?'

Mr Fish said: 'It's better this way.'

Simons growled: 'Make it goddam fast.'

Sculley and Mr Fish went off.

The others started a poker game. They all had thousands of dollars hidden in their shoes, and they were a little crazy. One hand Paul got a full house, with three aces in the hole; and the pot went over a thousand dollars. Keane Taylor kept raising him. Taylor had a pair of kings showing, and Paul guessed he had another king in the hole, making a full house with kings. Paul was right. He won $1,400.

A new shift of border guards arrived, including an officer who was mad as hell to find his guardhouse littered with cigarette butts, hundred-dollar bills, and poker-playing Americans, two of whom had entered the country without passports.

The morning wore on, and they all began to feel bad – too much whisky and not enough sleep. As the sun climbed in the sky, poker did not seem fun any more. Simons got jittery. Gayden started giving Boulware a hard time. Boulware wondered where Sculley and Mr Fish had got to.

Boulware was now sure he had made a mistake. They should all have left for Yuksekova as soon as he had arrived. He had made another mistake in letting Mr Fish take charge. Somehow he had lost the initiative.

At ten a.m., having been away four hours, Sculley and Mr Fish came back.

Mr Fish told the officer that they had permission to leave.

The officer said something sharp, and – as if accidentally – let his jacket fall open to reveal his pistol.

The other guards backed away from the Americans.

Mr Fish said: 'He says we leave when *he* gives permission.'

'Enough,' said Simons. He got to his feet and said something in Turkish. All the Turks looked at him in surprise: they had not realized he spoke their language.

Simons took the officer into the next room.

They came out a few minutes later. 'We can go,' said Simons.

They all went outside.

Coburn said: 'Did you bribe him, Colonel – or frighten him to death?'

Simons gave the ghost of a smile and said nothing.

Pat Sculley said: 'Want to come to Dallas, Rashid?'

For the last couple of days, Rashid reflected, they had been talking as if he would go all the way with them; but this was the first time anyone had asked him directly whether he wanted to. Now he had to make the most important decision of his life.

Want to come to Dallas, Rashid? It was a dream come true. He thought of what he was leaving behind. He had no children, no wife, not even a girlfriend – he had never been in love. But he thought of his parents, his sister and his brothers. They might need him: life was sure to be rough in Tehran for some time. Yet what help could he give them? He would be employed for a few more days, or weeks, shipping the Americans' possessions back to the States, taking care of the dogs and cats – then nothing. EDS was finished in Iran. Probably computers were finished, too, for many years. Unemployed, he would be a burden to his family, just another mouth to feed in hard times.

But in America—

In America he could continue his education. He could put his talents to work, become a success in business – especially with the help of people like Pat Sculley and Jay Coburn.

Want to come to Dallas, Rashid?

'Yes,' he said to Sculley. 'I want to go to Dallas.'

'What are you waiting for? Get on the bus!'

They all got on the bus.

Paul settled into his seat with relief. The bus pulled away, and Iran disappeared into the distance: he would probably never see the country again. There were strangers on the bus: some scruffy Turks in improvised uniforms, and two Americans who – someone mumbled – were pilots. Paul was too exhausted to inquire further. One of the Turkish guards from the border station had joined the party: presumably he was just hitching a ride.

They stopped in Yuksekova. Mr Fish told Paul and Bill: 'We have to talk to the chief of police. He has been here twenty-five years and this is the most important thing that has ever happened. But don't worry. It's all routine.'

Paul, Bill and Mr Fish got off the bus and went into the little police station. Somehow Paul was not worried. He was out of Iran, and although Turkey was not exactly a western country, at least, he felt, it was not in the throes of a revolution. Or perhaps he was just too tired to be frightened.

He and Bill were interrogated for two hours, then released.

Six more people joined the bus at Yuksekova: a woman and a child who seemed to belong to the border guard, and four very dirty men – 'Bodyguards,' said Mr Fish – who sat behind a curtain at the back of the bus.

They drove off, heading for Van where a charter plane was waiting. Paul looked out at the scenery. It was prettier than Switzerland, he thought, but incredibly poor. Huge boulders littered the road. In the fields, ragged people were treading down the snow so that their goats could get at the frozen grass beneath. There were caves with wood fences across their mouths, and it seemed that was where the people lived. They passed the ruins of a stone fortress which might have dated back to the time of the Crusades.

The bus driver seemed to think he was in a race. He drove aggressively on the winding road, apparently confident that nothing could possibly be coming the other way. A group of soldiers waved him down and he drove right past them. Mr Fish yelled at him to stop, but he yelled back and kept going.

A few miles farther on the army was waiting for them in force, probably having heard that the bus had run the last checkpoint. The soldiers stood in the road with their rifles raised, and the driver was forced to stop.

A sergeant jumped on the bus and dragged the driver off with a pistol at his head.

Now we're in trouble, Paul thought.

The scene was almost funny. The driver was not a bit cowed: he was yelling at the soldiers as loudly and as angrily as they were yelling at him.

Mr Fish, Ilsman, and some of the mystery passengers got off the bus and started talking, and eventually they squared the military. The driver was literally thrown back on the bus, but even that did not quench his spirit, and as he drove away he was still yelling out of the window and shaking his fist at the soldiers.

They reached Van late in the afternoon.

They went to the town hall, where they were handed over to the local police. The scruffy bodyguards disappeared like melting snow. The police filled in forms, then escorted them to the airstrip.

As they were boarding the plane, Ilsman was stopped by a policeman: he had a .45 pistol strapped under his arm, and it seemed that even in Turkey passengers were not allowed to take firearms on board aircraft. However, Ilsman flashed his credentials yet again and the problem went away.

Rashid was also stopped. He was carrying the fuel can with the money in it, and of course inflammable liquids were not allowed on aircraft. He told the police the can contained suntan oil for the Americans' wives, and they believed him.

They all boarded the plane. Simons and Coburn, coming down from the effects of the stay-awake pills, both stretched out and were asleep within seconds.

As the plane taxied and took off, Paul felt as elated as if it were his first plane trip. He recalled how, in jail in Tehran, he had longed to do that most ordinary thing, get on a plane and fly away. Soaring up into the clouds now gave him a feeling he had not experienced for a long time: the feeling of freedom.

III

According to the peculiar rules of Turkish air travel, the charter plane could not go where a scheduled flight was available, so they could not fly directly to Istanbul where Perot was waiting, but had to change planes in Ankara.

While they were waiting for their connection, they solved a couple of problems.

Simons, Sculley, Paul and Bill got into a taxi and asked for the American Embassy.

It was a long drive through the city. The air was brownish and had a strong smell. 'The air's bad here,' said Bill.

'High-sulphur coal,' said Simons, who had lived in Turkey in the fifties. 'They've never heard of pollution controls.'

The cab pulled up at the US Embassy. Bill looked out of the window and his heart leaped: there stood a young, handsome Marine guard in an immaculate uniform.

This was the USA.

They paid off the cab.

As they went in, Simons said to the Marine: 'Is there a motor pool here, soldier?'

'Yes, sir,' said the Marine, and gave him directions.

Paul and Bill went into the passport office. In their pockets they had passport-sized photographs of themselves which Boulware had brought from the States. They went up to the desk, and Paul said: 'We've lost our passports. We left Tehran in kind of a hurry.'

'Oh, yes,' said the clerk, as if he had been expecting them.

They had to fill in forms. One of the officials took them into a private office and told them he wanted some advice. The US Consulate in Tabriz, Iran, was under attack by revolutionaries, and the staff there might have to escape as Paul and Bill had. They told him the route they had taken and what problems they had encountered.

A few minutes later they walked out of there, each holding a sixty-day US passport. Paul looked at his and said: 'Did you ever see anything so beautiful in your whole damn life?'

Simons emptied the oil from the can and shook out the money in the weighted plastic bags. There was a hell of a mess: some of the bags had broken and there was oil all over the banknotes. Sculley started cleaning the oil off and piling the money up in ten-thousand-dollar stacks: there was $65,000 plus about the same again in Iranian rials.

While he was doing this a Marine walked in. Seeing two dishevelled, unshaven men kneeling on the floor counting out a small fortune in hundred-dollar bills, he did a double-take.

Sculley said to Simons: 'Do you think I ought to tell him, *Colonel*?'

Simons growled: 'Your buddy at the gate knows about this, soldier.'

The Marine saluted and went out.

It was eleven p.m. when they were called to board their flight to Istanbul.

They went through the final security check one by one. Sculley was just ahead of Simons. Looking back, he saw that the guard had asked to see inside the envelope Simons was carrying.

The envelope contained all the money from the fuel can.

Sculley said: 'Oh, shit.'

The soldier looked in the envelope and saw the sixty-five thousand dollars and four million rials; and all hell broke loose.

Several soldiers drew their guns, one of them called out, and officers came running.

Sculley saw Taylor, who had fifty thousand dollars in a little black bag, pushing his way through the crowd around Simons, saying: 'Excuse me, excuse me please, excuse me . . .'

Ahead of Sculley, Paul had already been cleared through the checkpoint. Sculley thrust his thirty thousand dollars into Paul's hands then turned and went back through the checkpoint.

The soldiers were taking Simons away to be interrogated. Sculley followed with Mr Fish, Ilsman, Boulware and Jim Schwebach. Simons was led into a little room. One of the officers turned, saw five people following, and said in English: 'Who are you?'

'We're all together,' Sculley said.

They sat down and Mr Fish talked to the officers. After a while he said: 'They want to see the papers which prove you brought this money into the country.'

'What papers?'

'You have to declare all the foreign currency you bring in.'

'Hell, nobody asked us!'

Boulware said: 'Mr Fish, explain to these clowns that we entered Turkey at a tiny little border station where the guards probably don't know enough to read forms and they didn't ask us to fill in any forms but we're happy to do it now.'

Mr Fish argued some more with the officers. Eventually Simons was allowed to leave, with the money; but the soldiers took down his name, passport number, and description, and the moment they landed in Istanbul Simons was arrested.

At 3 a.m. on Saturday 17 February 1979, Paul and Bill walked into Ross Perot's suite at the Istanbul Sheraton.

It was the greatest moment in Perot's life.

Emotion welled up as he embraced them both. Here they were, alive and well, after all this time, all those weeks of waiting, the impossible decisions and the awful risks. He looked at their beaming faces. The nightmare was over.

The rest of the team crowded in after them. Ron Davis was clowning, as usual. He had borrowed Perot's cold-weather clothes, and Perot had pretended to be anxious to get them back: now Davis stripped off his hat, coat and gloves, and threw them on the floor dramatically, saying: 'Here you are, Perot, here's your damned stuff!'

Then Sculley walked in and said: 'Simons got arrested at the airport.'

Perot's jubilation evaporated. 'Why?' he exclaimed in dismay.

'He was carrying a lot of money in a paper envelope and they just happened to search him.'

Perot said angrily: 'Darn it, Pat, *why* was he carrying money?'

'It was the money from the fuel can. See—'

Perot interrupted: 'After all Simons has done, why in the world did you let him take a completely unnecessary risk? Now see here. I'm taking off at noon, and if Simons isn't out of jail by then, *you* are going to stay in frigging Istanbul until he is!'

Sculley and Boulware sat down with Mr Fish. Boulware said: 'We need to get Colonel Simons out of jail.'

'Well,' said Mr Fish, 'it will take around ten days—'

'Bullshit,' said Boulware. 'Perot will not buy that. I want him out of jail *now*.'

'It's five o'clock in the morning!' Mr Fish protested.

'How much?' said Boulware.

'I don't know. Too many people know about this, in Ankara as well as Istanbul.'

'How about five thousand dollars?'

'For that, they would sell their mothers.'

'Fine,' said Boulware. 'Let's get it on.'

Mr Fish made a phone call, then said: 'My lawyer will meet us at the jail near the airport.'

Boulware and Mr Fish got into Mr Fish's battered old car, leaving Sculley to pay the hotel bill.

They drove to the jail and met the lawyer. The lawyer got into Mr Fish's car and said: 'I have a judge on the way. I've already talked to the police. Where's the money?'

Boulware said: 'The prisoner has it.'

'What do you mean?'

Boulware said: 'You go in there and bring the prisoner out, and *he* will give you the five thousand dollars.'

It was crazy, but the lawyer did it. He went into the jail and came out a few minutes later with Simons. They got into the car.

'We're not going to pay these clowns,' said Simons. 'I'll wait it out. They'll just talk themselves to death and let me go in a few days.'

Boulware said: 'Bull, please don't fight the programme. Give me the envelope.'

Simons handed over the envelope. Boulware took out five thousand dollars and gave it to the lawyer, saying: 'Here's the money. Make it happen.'

The lawyer made it happen.

Half an hour later, Boulware, Simons and Mr Fish were driven to the airport in a police car. A policeman took their passports and walked them through passport control and customs. When they came out on the tarmac, the police car was there to take them to the Boeing 707 waiting on the runway.

They boarded the plane. Simons looked around at the velvet curtains, the plush upholstery, the TV sets and the bars, and said: 'What the fuck is this?'

The crew were on board, waiting. A stewardess came up to Boulware and said: 'Would you like a drink?'

Boulware smiled.

*

The phone rang in Perot's hotel suite, and Paul happened to answer it.

A voice said: 'Hello?'

Paul said 'Hello?'

The voice said: 'Who is this?'

Paul, suspicious, said: 'Who is *this*?'

'Hey, Paul?'

Paul recognized the voice of Merv Stauffer. 'Hello, Merv!'

'Paul, I got somebody here wants to talk to you.'

There was a pause, then a woman's voice said: 'Paul?'

It was Ruthie!

'Hello, Ruthie!'

'Oh, Paul!'

'Hi! What are you doing?'

'What do you mean, what am I doing?' Ruthie said tearfully. 'I'm waiting for you!'

The phone rang. Before Emily got to it, someone picked up the extension in the children's room.

A moment later she heard a little girl scream: 'It's Dad! It's Dad!'

She rushed into the room.

All the children were jumping up and down and fighting over the phone.

Emily restrained herself for a couple of minutes, then took the phone away from them.

'Bill?'

'Hello, Emily.'

'Gee you sound good. I didn't expect you to sound . . . Oh, Bill you sound so good.'

In Dallas, Merv began to take down a message from Perot in code.

Take . . . the . . .

He was now so familiar that he could transcribe the code as he went along.

. . . . code . . . and . . .

He was puzzled, because for the last three days Perot had been giving him a hard time about the code. Perot did not have the patience to use it, and Stauffer had had to insist, saying: 'Ross, this is the way Simons wants it.' Now that the danger was past, why had Perot suddenly started to use the code?

. . . . stick . . . it . . . where . . .

Stauffer guessed what was coming, and burst out laughing.

Ron Davis called room service and ordered bacon and eggs for everyone.

While they were eating, Dallas called again. It was Stauffer. He asked for Perot.

'Ross, we just got the *Dallas Times Herald*.'

Was this to be another joke?

Stauffer went on: 'The headline on the front page says: Perot men reportedly on way out. Overland exit route from Iran indicated.'

Perot felt his blood start to boil. 'I thought we were getting that story killed!'

'Boy, Ross, we tried! The people who own or manage the paper just don't seem to be able to control the editor.'

Tom Luce came on the line, mad as hell. 'Ross, those bastards are willing to get the rescue team killed and destroy EDS and see you jailed just to be the first to print the story. We've explained the consequences to them and it just doesn't matter. Boy, when this is over we should sue them, no matter how long it takes or how much it costs—'

'Maybe,' said Perot. 'Be careful about picking a fight with people who buy ink by the barrel and paper by the ton. Now, what are the chances of this news reaching Tehran?'

'We don't know. There are plenty of Iranians in Texas, and most of them will hear about this. It's still very hard to get a phone line to Tehran, but we've managed it a couple of times, so they could too.'

'And if they do . . .'

'Then, of course, Dadgar finds out that Paul and Bill have slipped through his grasp—'

'And he could decide to take alternative hostages,' Perot said coldly. He was disgusted with the State Department for leaking the story, furious with the *Dallas Times Herald* for printing it, and maddened that there was nothing he could do about it. 'And the Clean Team is still in Tehran,' he said.

The nightmare was not over yet.

CHAPTER FOURTEEN

I

AT MIDDAY on Friday 16 February Lou Goelz called Joe Poché and told him to bring the EDS people to the US Embassy that afternoon at five o'clock. Ticketing and baggage check-in would be done at the Embassy overnight, and they could leave on a Pan Am evacuation flight on Saturday morning.

John Howell was nervous. He knew, from Abolhasan, that Dadgar was still active. He did not know what had happened to the Dirty Team. If Dadgar were to find out that Paul and Bill had gone, or if he were simply to give up on them and take a couple more hostages, the Clean Team would be arrested. And where better to make the arrests than at the airport, where everyone had to identify himself by showing his passport?

He wondered whether it was wise for them to take the first available flight: there would be a series of flights, according to Goelz. Maybe they should wait, and see what happened to the first batch of evacuees, whether there was any kind of search for EDS personnel. At least then they would know in advance what the procedures were.

But so would the Iranians. The advantage of taking the first flight was that everything would probably be confused, and the confusion might help Howell and the Clean Team slip out unnoticed.

In the end he decided the first flight was best, but he remained uneasy. Bob Young felt the same way. Although Young no longer worked for EDS in Iran – he was based in Kuwait – he had been here when the Ministry contract was first negotiated, he had met Dadgar face to face, and his name might be on some list in Dadgar's files.

Joe Poché also favoured the first flight, although he did not say much about it – he did not say much at all: Howell found him uncommunicative.

Rich and Cathy Gallagher were not sure they wanted to leave Iran. They told Poché quite firmly that, regardless of what Colonel Simons had said, Poché was not 'in charge' of them, and they had the right to make their own decision. Poché agreed, but pointed out that if they decided to take their chances here with the Iranians, they should not rely on Perot sending another rescue team in for them if they got thrown in jail. In the end the Gallaghers also decided to go on the first flight.

That afternoon they all went through their documents and destroyed everything that referred to Paul and Bill.

Poché gave each of them two thousand dollars, put five hundred dollars in his own pocket, and hid the rest of the money in his shoes, ten thousand dollars in each. He was wearing shoes borrowed from Gayden, a size too large, to accommodate the money. He also had in his pocket a million rials, which he planned to give to Lou

Goelz for Abolhasan, who would use the money to pay the remaining Iranian EDS employees their last wages.

A few minutes before five, they were saying goodbye to Goelz's houseman when the phone rang.

Poché took the call. It was Tom Walter. He said: 'We have the people. Do you understand? We have the *people*.'

'I understand,' Poché said.

They all got into the car, Cathy carrying her poodle, Buffy. Poché drove. He did not tell the others about his cryptic message from Tom Walter.

They parked in a side street near the Embassy, and left the car: it would stay there until somebody decided to steal it.

There was no relief of tension for Howell as he walked into the Embassy compound. There were at least a thousand Americans milling about, but there were also scores of armed revolutionary guards. The Embassy was supposed to be American soil, inviolate; but clearly the Iranian revolutionaries did not take any notice of such diplomatic niceties.

The Clean Team were herded into a queue.

They spent most of the night waiting in line.

They queued to fill in forms, they queued to hand in their passports, and they queued for baggage checks. All the bags were put in a huge hall, then the evacuees had to find their own bags and put the claim checks on. Then they queued to open their bags so the revolutionaries could search them. Every single piece was opened.

Howell learned that there would be two planes, both

Pan Am 747s. One would go to Frankfurt, the other to Athens. The evacuees were organized by company, but the EDS people were included with Embassy personnel who were leaving. They would be on the Frankfurt flight.

At seven o'clock on Saturday morning they were boarded on buses to go to the airport.

It was a hell of a ride.

Two or three armed revolutionaries got on each bus. As they drove out of the Embassy gates, they saw a crowd of reporters and television crews: the Iranians had decided that the flight of the humiliated Americans would be a world television event.

The bus bumped along the road to the airport. Close to Poché was a guard about fifteen years old. He stood in the aisle, swaying with the motion of the bus, his finger on the trigger of his rifle. Poché noticed that the safety catch was off.

If he stumbled . . .

The streets were full of people and traffic. Everyone seemed to know that these buses contained Americans, and their hatred was palpable. They yelled and shook their fists. A truck pulled alongside, and the driver leaned out of his window and spat on the bus.

The convoy was stopped several times. Different areas of the city seemed to be under the control of different revolutionary groups, and each group had to demonstrate its authority by stopping the buses and then giving them permission to proceed.

It took two hours to drive the six miles to the airport.

The scene there was chaotic. There were more television cameras and reporters, plus hundreds of armed men running around, some wearing scraps of uniform, some directing traffic, all of them in charge, all having a different opinion on where the buses should go.

The Americans finally got inside the terminal at 9.30.

Embassy personnel started distributing the passports they had collected during the night. Five were missing: those of Howell, Poché, Young and the Gallaghers.

After Paul and Bill had given their passports to the Embassy for safekeeping back in November, the Embassy had refused to return them without informing the police. Would they be so treacherous as to pull the same trick now?

Suddenly Poché came pushing through the crowd with five passports in his hand. 'I found them on a shelf behind a counter,' he said. 'I guess they got put there by accident.'

Bob Young saw two Americans holding photographs and scanning the crowd. To his horror, they started to approach the EDS people. They walked up to Rich and Cathy Gallagher.

Surely Dadgar would not take *Cathy* hostage?

The people smiled and said they had some of the Gallaghers' luggage.

Young relaxed.

Friends of the Gallaghers had salvaged some of the bags from the Hyatt, and had asked these two Americans to bring them to the airport and try to give them to the Gallaghers. The people had agreed, but they did not know the Gallaghers – hence the photographs.

It had been a false alarm, but if anything it increased their anxiety.

Joe Poché decided to see what he could find out. He went off and located a Pan Am ticket agent. 'I work for EDS,' Poché told the agent. 'Are the Iranians looking for anyone?'

'Yes, they're looking pretty hard for two people,' said the agent.

'Anybody else?'

'No. And the stop list is several weeks old.'

'Thanks.'

Poché went back and told the others.

The evacuees were starting to go from the check-in concourse through to the departure lounge.

Poché said: 'I suggest we split up. That way we won't look like a group, and if one or two of you get into trouble the others may still get through. I'll be last, so if anyone has to stay behind, I'll stay too.'

Bob Young looked at his suitcase and saw that it bore a luggage tag saying: 'William D. Gaylord.'

He suffered a moment of panic. If the Iranians saw that, they would think he was Bill and arrest him.

He knew how it had happened. His own suitcases had been destroyed at the Hyatt by the revolutionaries who had shot up the rooms. However, one or two cases had been left more or less undamaged, and Young had borrowed one. This was it.

He tore the luggage tag off and stuffed it into his pocket, intending to get rid of it at the first opportunity.

They all went through the 'Passengers Only' gate.

Next they had to pay the airport tax. This amused Poché: the revolutionaries must have decided that airport tax was the one good thing the Shah introduced, he thought.

The next queue was for passport control.

Howell reached the desk at noon.

The guard checked his exit documentation thoroughly, and stamped it. Next he looked at the picture in his passport, then looked hard at Howell's face. Finally he checked the name in the passport against a list he had on his desk.

Howell held his breath.

The guard handed him his passport and waved him through.

Joe Poché went through passport control last. The guard looked extra hard at him, comparing the face with the photograph, for Poché now had a red beard. But eventually he, too, was allowed through.

The Clean Team were in a jovial mood in the departure lounge: it was all over, Howell thought, now that they had come through passport control.

At two in the afternoon they began to pass through the gates. At this point there was normally a security check. This time, as well as searching for weapons, the guards were confiscating maps, photographs of Tehran, and large sums of money. None of the Clean Team lost their money, however; the guards did not look in Poché's shoes.

Outside the gates, some of the baggage was lined up on the tarmac. Passengers had to check whether any of theirs was there, and if so to open it for searching before it was loaded on to the plane. None of the Clean Team's bags had been picked out for this special treatment.

They boarded buses and were driven across the runway to where two 747s were waiting. Once again the television cameras were there.

At the foot of the ladder there was yet another passport check. Howell joined the queue of five hundred people waiting to board the Frankfurt plane. He was less worried than he had been: nobody was looking for him, it seemed.

He got on the plane and found a seat. There were several armed revolutionaries on board, both in the passenger cabin and on the flight deck. The scene became confused as people who were supposed to go to Athens realized they were on the Frankfurt plane, and vice versa. All the seats filled up, then the crew seats, and still there were people without seats.

The captain turned on the public-address system and asked for everyone's attention. The plane became quieter. 'Would passengers Paul John and William Deming please identify themselves,' he said.

Howell went cold.

John was the middle name of Paul Chiapparone.

Deming was the middle name of Bill Gaylord.

They were *still* searching for Paul and Bill.

Clearly it was not merely a question of names on a list at the airport. Dadgar was firmly in control here, and his people were relentlessly determined to find Paul and Bill.

Ten minutes later the captain came on the loudspeakers again. 'Ladies and gentlemen, we still have not located Paul John or William Deming. We have been informed that we cannot take off until these two people have been located. If anyone knows their whereabouts, will you *please* let us know.'

Will I hell, thought Howell.

Bob Young suddenly remembered the luggage tag in his pocket marked 'William D. Gaylord'. He went to the bathroom and threw it into the toilet.

The revolutionaries came down the aisle again, asking for passports. They checked each one carefully, comparing the photograph with the face of the owner.

John Howell took out a paperback book he had brought from the Dvoranchik place and tried to read it, in an effort to look unconcerned. It was *Dubai*, Robin Moore's thriller about intrigue in the Middle East. He could not concentrate on a paperback thriller: he was living a real one. Soon, he thought, Dadgar must realize that Paul and Bill are not on this plane.

And what will he do then?

He's so *determined*.

Clever, too. What a perfect way to do a passport check – on the plane, when all the passengers are in their seats and no one can hide!

But what will he do next?

He'll come aboard this damn plane himself, and walk down the aisle, looking at everyone. He won't know Rich, or Cathy, or Joe Poché, but he'll know Bob Young.

And he'll know me best of all.

*

In Dallas, T. J. Marquez got a call from Mark Ginsberg, the White House aide who had been trying to help with the problem of Paul and Bill. Ginsberg was in Washington, monitoring the situation in Tehran. He said: 'Five of your people are on a plane standing on the runway at Tehran Airport.'

'Good!' said T.J.

'It's not good. The Iranians are searching for Chiapparone and Gaylord, and they won't let the plane take off until they find the guys.'

'Oh, *hell.*'

'There's no air traffic control over Iran, so the plane has to take off before nightfall. We aren't sure what's going to happen, but there's not much time left. Your people may be taken off the plane.'

'You can't let them do that!'

'I'll keep you in touch.'

T.J. hung up. After all that Paul and Bill and the Dirty Team had been through, would EDS now end up with more of its people in a Tehran jail? It did not bear thinking about.

The time was six-thirty a.m. in Dallas, four p.m. in Tehran.

They had two hours of daylight left.

T.J. picked up the phone. 'Get me Perot.'

'Ladies and gentlemen,' said the pilot, 'Paul John and William Deming have not been located. The man in charge on the ground will now do another passport check.'

The passengers groaned.

Howell wondered who was the man in charge on the ground.

Dadgar?

It might be one of Dadgar's staff. Some of them knew Howell, some did not.

He peered along the aisle.

Someone came aboard. Howell stared. It was a man in a Pan Am uniform.

Howell relaxed.

The man went slowly down the plane, checking each of five hundred passports, doing a face-to-picture identification then examining the photographs and seals to see whether they had been tampered with.

'Ladies and gentlemen, captain speaking again. They have decided to check the baggage as it is loaded. If you hear your claim check number called would you please identify yourself.'

Cathy had all the claim checks in her handbag. As the first numbers were called, Howell saw her sorting through the checks. He tried to attract her attention, to signal her not to identify herself: it might be a trick.

More numbers were called, but nobody got up. Howell guessed everyone had decided they would rather lose their luggage than risk getting off this plane.

'Ladies and gentlemen, please identify yourselves when these numbers are called. You will not have to get off the plane, just hand over your keys so the bags can be opened for searching.'

Howell was not reassured. He watched Cathy, still

trying to catch her eye. More numbers were called, but she did not get up.

'Ladies and gentlemen, some good news. We have checked with Pan Am's European headquarters and have been given permission to take off with an overload of passengers.'

There was a ragged cheer.

Howell looked over at Joe Poché. Poché had his passport on his chest and he was sitting back with his eyes closed, apparently asleep. Joe must have ice in his veins, Howell thought.

There was sure to be a lot of pressure on Dadgar as the sun went down. It had to be obvious that Paul and Bill were not on the plane. If a thousand people were deplaned and escorted back to the Embassy, the revolutionary authorities would have to go through the whole rigmarole again tomorrow – and somebody up there was bound to say 'No way!' to that.

Howell knew that he and the rest of the Clean Team were certainly guilty of crimes now. They had connived at the escape of Paul and Bill, and whether the Iranians called that conspiracy, or being an accessory after the fact, or some other name, it had to be against the law. He went over in his mind the story they had all agreed to tell if they were arrested. They had left the Hyatt on Monday morning, they would say, and had gone to Keane Taylor's house. (Howell had wanted to tell the truth, and say the Dvoranchik place, but the others had pointed out that this might bring down trouble on the head of Dvoranchik's landlady, whereas Taylor's landlord did not live on the premises.) They had spent

Monday and Tuesday at Taylor's then had gone to Lou Goelz's house on Tuesday afternoon. From then on they would tell the truth.

The story would not protect the Clean Team: Howell knew all too well that Dadgar did not care whether his hostages were guilty or innocent.

At six o'clock the captain said: 'Ladies and gentlemen, we have permission to take off.'

The doors were slammed and the plane was moving within seconds. The passengers without seats were told by stewardesses to sit on the floor. As they taxied, Howell thought: Surely we wouldn't stop now, even if we were ordered to . . .

The 747 gathered speed along the runway and took off.

They were still in Iranian airspace. The Iranians could send up fighter jets . . .

A little later the captain said: 'Ladies and gentlemen, we have now departed Iranian airspace.'

The passengers gave a weary cheer.

We made it, Howell thought.

He picked up his paperback thriller.

Joe Poché left his seat and went to find the chief steward.

'Is there any way the pilot could get a message through to the States?' he asked.

'I don't know,' the steward said. 'Write your message, and I'll ask him.'

Poché returned to his seat and got out a paper and a pen. He wrote: *To Merv Stauffer, 7171 Forest Lane, Dallas, Texas.*

He thought for a minute about what his message should be. He recalled EDS's recruiting motto: 'Eagles don't flock – you have to find them one at a time.' He wrote:

The eagles have flown their nest.

II

Ross Perot wanted to meet up with the Clean Team before returning to the States: he was keen to get everyone together, so that he could see and touch them all and be absolutely sure they were safe and well. However, on Friday in Istanbul he could not confirm the destination of the evacuation flight which would bring the Clean Team out of Tehran. John Carlen, the laid-back pilot of the leased Boeing 707, had the answer to that problem. 'Those evacuation planes must fly up over Istanbul,' he said. 'We'll just sit on the runway until they pass overhead, then call them on radio and ask them.' In the end that was not necessary: Stauffer called on Saturday morning and told Perot the Clean Team would be on the Frankfurt plane.

Perot and the others checked out of the Sheraton at midday and went to the airport to join Boulware and Simons on the plane. They took off late in the afternoon.

When they were in the air Perot called Dallas: with the plane's single-sideband radio it was as easy as calling from New York. He reached Merv Stauffer.

'What's happening with the Clean Team?' Perot asked.

'I got a message,' said Stauffer. 'It came from the European headquarters of Pan Am. It just says: "The eagles have flown their nest".'

Perot smiled. All safe.

Perot left the flight deck and returned to the passenger cabin. His heroes looked washed out. At Istanbul Airport, he had sent Taylor into the duty-free shop to buy cigarettes, snacks and liquor, and Taylor had spent over a thousand dollars. They all had a drink to celebrate the escape of the Clean Team, but nobody was in the mood, and ten minutes later they were all sitting around on the plush upholstery with their glasses still full. Someone started a poker game, but it petered out.

The crew of the 707 included two pretty stewardesses.

Perot got them to put their arms around Taylor, then took a photograph. He threatened to show the photo to Taylor's wife, Mary, if Taylor ever gave him a hard time.

Most of them were too tired to sleep, but Gayden went back to the luxurious bedroom and lay down on the king-sized bed. Perot was a little miffed: he thought Simons, who was older and looked completely drained, should have had the bed.

But Simons was talking to one of the stewardesses, Anita Melton. She was a vivacious blonde Swedish girl in her twenties, with a zany sense of humour, a wild imagination, and a penchant for the outlandish. She was fun. Simons recognized a kindred soul, someone who did not care too much about what other people thought, an individual. He liked her. He realized that it was the first time since the death of Lucille that he had felt attracted to a woman.

He really had come back to life.

Ron Davis began to feel sleepy. The king-sized bed was big enough for two, he thought; so he went into the bedroom and lay down beside Gayden.

Gayden opened his eyes. 'Davis?' he said incredulously. 'What the hell are you doing in bed with me?'

'Don't sweat it,' said Davis. 'Now you can tell all your friends you slept with a nigger.' He closed his eyes.

As the plane approached Frankfurt, Simons recalled that he was still responsible for Paul and Bill, and his mind went back to work, extrapolating possibilities for enemy action. He asked Perot: 'Does Germany have an extradition treaty with Iran?'

'I don't know,' said Perot.

He got The Simons Look.

'I'll find out,' he added.

He called Dallas and asked for Tom Luce, the lawyer. 'Tom, does Germany have an extradition treaty with Iran?'

Luce said: 'I'm ninety-nine per cent sure they do not.'

Perot told Simons.

Simons said: 'I've seen men killed because they were ninety-nine per cent sure they were safe.'

Perot said to Luce: 'Let's get a hundred per cent sure. I'll call you again in a few minutes.'

They landed at Frankfurt and checked into a hotel within the airport complex. The German desk clerk seemed curious, and carefully noted all their passport numbers. This increased Simon's unease.

They gathered in Perot's room, and Perot called Dallas again. This time he spoke to T. J. Marquez.

T.J. said: 'I called an international lawyer in Washington, and he thinks there *is* an extradition treaty between Iran and Germany. Also he said the Germans are kind of legalistic about stuff like this, and if they got a request to pick up Paul and Bill, hell, they'd probably go right ahead and do it.'

Perot repeated all of that to Simons.

'Okay,' said Simons. 'We're not going to take any chances at this point in the game. There's a movie house with three screens down at the basement level in this airport. Paul and Bill can hide in them . . . where's Bill?'

'Gone to buy toothpaste,' someone said.

'Jay, go find him.'

Coburn went out.

Simons said: 'Paul goes in one theatre, with Jay. Bill goes in another, with Keane. Pat Sculley stands guard outside. He has a ticket so he can go in and check on the others.'

It was interesting, Perot thought, to see the switches turn and the wheels start rolling as Simons changed from an old man relaxing on a plane to a commando leader again.

Simons said: 'The entrance to the train station is down in the basement, near the movies. If there's any sign of trouble Sculley gets the four men out of the movies and they all take a subway downtown. They rent a car and drive to England. If nothing happens, we get them out of the movies when we're about to board a plane. All right, let's do it.'

Bill was down in the shopping precinct. He had changed some money and bought toothpaste, a toothbrush and a comb. He decided that a fresh new shirt would make him feel human again, so he went to change some more money. He was standing in line at the currency exchange booth when Coburn tapped him on the shoulder.

'Ross wants to see you in the hotel,' Coburn said.

'What for?'

'I can't talk about it now, you need to come on back.'

'You've got to be kidding!'

'Let's go.'

They went to Perot's room, and Perot explained to Bill what was happening. Bill could hardly believe it. He had thought for sure he was safe in modern, civilized Germany. Would he *ever* be safe? he wondered. Would Dadgar pursue him to the ends of the earth, never resting until Bill was returned to Iran or killed?

Coburn did not know whether there was any real chance of Paul and Bill getting into trouble here in Frankfurt, but he *did* know the value of Simons's elaborate precautions. Much of what Simons had planned, over the past seven weeks, had come to nothing: the attack on the first jail, the idea of snatching Paul and Bill from house arrest, the route out via Kuwait. But then some of the contingencies for which Simons planned *had* come to pass, often the most far-fetched ones: the Gasr Prison had been stormed and Rashid was there; the road to Sero, which Simons and Coburn had carefully reconnoitred, had in the end been their route out; even making Paul and Bill learn all the information on their false passports had turned out to be crucial when the man in the long black overcoat started asking questions. Coburn needed no convincing: whatever Simons said was okay with him.

They went down to the movie house. There were three films: two were porno movies and the third was *Jaws II*. Bill and Taylor got *Jaws II*. Paul and Coburn went in to see something about naked South Sea maidens.

Paul sat staring at the screen, bored and tired. The movie was in German, not that the dialogue appeared to count for much. What could be worse, he thought, than a bad X-rated movie? Suddenly he heard a loud snort. He looked at Coburn.

Coburn was fast asleep, snoring.

When John Howell and the rest of the Clean Team landed at Frankfurt, Simons had everything set up for a quick turnaround.

Ron Davis was at the arrival gate, waiting to pull the Clean Team out of the line and direct them to another gate where the Boeing 707 was parked. Ralph Boulware was watching from a distance: as soon as he saw the first member of the Clean Team arrive, he would go down to the movie theatre and tell Sculley to round up the guys inside. Jim Schwebach was in the roped-off press area, where reporters were waiting to see the American evacuees. He was sitting next to writer Pierre Salinger (who did not know how close he was to a *really* good story) and pretending to read a furniture advertisement in a German newspaper. Schwebach's job was to tail the Clean Team from one gate to the other, just to make sure no one was following them. If there was trouble, Schwebach and Davis would start a disturbance. It would not matter much if they were arrested by the Germans, for there was no reason for them to be extradited to Iran.

The plan went like clockwork. There was only one hitch: Rich and Cathy Gallagher did not want to go to Dallas. They had no friends or family there, they were not sure what their future would be, they did not know whether the dog Buffy would be allowed to enter the USA, and they did not want to get on another plane. They said goodbye and went off to make their own arrangements.

The rest of the Clean Team – John Howell, Bob Young and Joe Poché – followed Ron Davis and boarded the Boeing 707. Jim Schwebach tailed them. Ralph Boulware rounded up everyone else, and they all got on board for the flight home.

Merv Stauffer in Dallas had called Frankfurt airport and ordered food for the flight. He had asked for thirty superdeluxe meals each including fish, fowl and beef; six seafood trays with sauce, horseradish and lemon; six hors d'oeuvre trays; six sandwich trays with ham-and-cheese, roast beef, turkey and swiss cheese; six dip trays with raw vegetables and bluecheese-and-vinaigrette dip;

three cheese trays with assorted breads and crackers; four deluxe pastry trays; four fresh fruit trays; four bottles of brandy; twenty Seven-Ups and twenty ginger ales; ten club sodas and ten tonics; ten quarts of orange juice; fifty cartons of milk; four gallons of freshly brewed coffee in Thermos bottles; one hundred sets of plastic cutlery consisting of knife, fork and spoon; six dozen paper plates in two sizes; six dozen plastic glasses; six dozen Styrofoam cups; two cartons each of Kent, Marlboro, Kool and Salem Light cigarettes; and two boxes of chocolates.

There had been a mix-up, and the airport caterers had delivered the order double.

Take-off was delayed. An ice storm had dropped out of nowhere, and the Boeing 707 was last in the queue for de-icing – commercial flights had priority. Bill began to worry. The airport was going to close at midnight, and they might have to get off the plane and return to the hotel. Bill did not want to spend the night in Germany. He wanted American soil beneath his feet.

John Howell, Joe Poché and Bob Young told the story of their flight from Tehran. Both Paul and Bill were chilled to hear how implacably determined Dadgar had been to prevent their leaving the country.

At last the plane was de-iced – but its No 1 engine would not start. Pilot John Carlen traced the problem to the start valve. Engineer Ken Lenz got off the plane and held the valve open manually while Carlen started the engine.

Perot brought Rashid to the flight deck. Rashid had

never flown until yesterday, and he wanted to sit with the crew. Perot said to Carlen: 'Let's have a really spectacular take-off.'

'You got it,' said Carlen. He taxied to the runway then took off in a very steep climb.

In the passenger cabin, Gayden was laughing: he had just heard that, after six weeks in jail with all-male company, Paul had been forced to sit through an X-rated movie; and he thought it was funny as hell.

Perot popped a champagne cork and proposed a toast. 'Here's to the men who said what they were going to do, then went out and did it.'

Ralph Boulware sipped his champagne and felt a warm glow. That's right, he thought. We said what we were going to do, then we went out and did it. Right.

He had another reason to be happy. Next Monday was Kecia's birthday: she would be seven. Every time he had called Mary she had said: 'Get home in time for Kecia's birthday.' It looked like he was going to make it.

Bill began to relax at last. Now there's nothing but a plane ride between me and America and Emily and the kids, he thought. Now I'm safe.

He had imagined himself safe before: when he reached the Hyatt in Tehran, when he crossed the border into Turkey, when he took off from Van, and when he landed at Frankfurt. He had been wrong each time.

And he was wrong now.

III

Paul had always been crazy about airplanes, and now he took the opportunity to sit on the flight deck of the Boeing 707.

As the plane flew across the north of England, he realized that pilot John Carlen, engineer Ken Lenz and first officer Joe Fosnot were having trouble. On autopilot the plane was drifting, first to the left and then to the right. The compass had failed, rendering the inertial navigation system erratic.

'What does all that mean?' Paul asked.

'It means we'll have to hand-fly this thing all the way across the Atlantic,' said Carlen. 'We can do it – it's kind of exhausting, that's all.'

A few minutes later the plane became very cold, then very hot. Its pressurization system was failing.

Carlen took the plane down low.

'We can't cross the Atlantic at this height,' he told Paul.

'Why not?'

'We don't have enough fuel – an aircraft uses much more fuel at low altitudes.'

'Why can't we fly high?'

'Can't breathe up there.'

'The plane has oxygen masks.'

'But not enough oxygen to cross the Atlantic. No plane carries that much oxygen.'

Carlen and his crew fiddled with the controls for a while, then Carlen sighed and said: 'Would you get Ross up here, Paul?'

Paul fetched Perot.

Carlen said: 'Mr Perot, I think we ought to take this thing and land it as soon as we can.' He explained again why they could not cross the Atlantic with a faulty pressure system.

Paul said: 'John, I'll be forever grateful to you if we don't have to land in Germany.'

'Don't worry,' said Carlen. 'We'll head for London, Heathrow.'

Perot went back to tell the others. Carlen called London Air Traffic Control on the radio. It was one in the morning, and he was told Heathrow was closed. This is an emergency, he replied. They gave him permission to land.

Paul could hardly believe it. An emergency landing, after all he had been through!

Ken Lenz began to dump fuel to reduce the plane below its maximum landing weight.

London told Carlen there was a fog over southern England, but at the moment visibility was up to half a mile at Heathrow.

When Ken Lenz shut off the fuel dump valves, a red light that should have gone out stayed on. 'A dump chute hasn't retracted,' said Lenz.

'I can't believe this,' said Paul. He lit a cigarette.

Carlen said: 'Paul, can I have a cigarette?'

Paul stared at him. 'You told me you quit smoking ten years ago.'

'Just give me a cigarette, would you?'

Paul gave him a cigarette and said: 'Now I'm really scared.'

Paul went back into the passenger cabin. The stewardesses had everyone busy stowing trays, bottles and baggage, securing all loose objects, in preparation for landing.

Paul went into the bedroom. Simons was lying on the bed. He had shaved in cold water and there were bits of stickum tape all over his face. He was fast asleep.

Paul left him. He said to Jay Coburn: 'Does Simons know what's going on?'

'Sure does,' Coburn replied. 'He said he doesn't know how to fly a plane and there's nothing he can do so he was going to take a nap.'

Paul shook his head in amazement. How cool could you get?

He returned to the flight deck. Carlen was as laid-back as ever, his voice calm, his hands steady; but that cigarette worried Paul.

A couple of minutes later the red light went out. The dump chute had retracted.

They approached Heathrow in dense cloud and began to lose height. Paul watched the altimeter. As it dropped through six hundred feet, then five hundred feet, there was still nothing outside but swirling grey fog.

At three hundred feet it was the same. Then, suddenly, they dropped out of the cloud and there was the runway, straight ahead, lit up like a Christmas tree. Paul breathed a sigh of relief.

They touched down, and the fire engines and ambulances came screaming across the tarmac towards the plane; but it was a perfect safe landing.

*

Rashid had been hearing about Ross Perot for years. Perot was the multi-millionaire, the founder of EDS, the business wizard, the man who sat in Dallas and moved men such as Coburn and Sculley around the world like pieces on a chessboard. It had been quite an experience for Rashid to meet Mr Perot and find he was just an ordinary-looking human being, rather short and surprisingly friendly. Rashid had walked into the hotel room in Istanbul, and this little guy with the big smile and the bent nose just stuck out his hand and said: 'Hi, I'm Ross Perot,' and Rashid had shaken hands and said: 'Hi, I'm Rashid Kazemi,' just as natural as could be.

Since that moment he had felt more than ever one of the EDS team. But at Heathrow Airport he was sharply reminded that he was not.

As soon as the plane taxied to a halt, a vanload of airport police, customs men and immigration officials boarded and started asking questions. They did not like what they saw: a bunch of dirty, scruffy, smelly, unshaven men, carrying a fortune in various currencies, aboard an incredibly luxurious airplane with a Grand Caymen Islands tail number. This, they said in their British way, was highly irregular, to say the least.

However, after an hour or so of questioning, they could find no evidence that the EDS men were drug smugglers, terrorists, or members of the PLO. And as holders of US passports, the Americans needed no visas or other documentation to enter Britain. They were all admitted – except for Rashid.

Perot confronted the immigration officer. 'There's no reason why you should know who I am, but my name is Ross Perot, and if you would just check me out, maybe with the US Customs, I believe you will conclude that you can trust me. I have too much to lose by trying to smuggle an illegal immigrant into Britain. Now I will assume personal responsibility for this young man. We will be out of England in twenty-four hours. In the morning we will check with your counterparts at Gatwick Airport, and we will then get on the Braniff flight to Dallas.'

'I'm afraid we can't do that, sir,' said the official. 'This gentleman will have to stay with us until we put him on the plane.'

'If he stays, I stay,' said Perot.

Rashid was flabbergasted. Ross Perot would spend the night at the airport, or perhaps in a prison cell, rather than leave Rashid behind! It was incredible. If Pat Sculley had made such an offer, or Jay Coburn, Rashid would have been grateful but not surprised. But this was Ross Perot!

The immigration officer sighed. 'Do you know anyone in Great Britain who might vouch for you, sir?'

Perot racked his brains. Who do I know in Britain? he thought. 'I don't think – no, wait a minute.' Of course! One of Britain's greatest heroes had stayed with the Perots in Dallas a couple of times. Perot and Margot had been guests at his home in England, a place called Broadlands. 'I know Earl Mountbatten of Burma,' he said.

'I'll just have a word with my supervisor,' said the officer, and he got off the plane.

He was away a long time.

Perot said to Sculley: 'As soon as we get out of here, your job is to get us all first-class seats on that Braniff flight to Dallas in the morning.'

'Yes, sir,' said Sculley.

The immigration officer came back. 'I can give you twenty-four hours,' he said to Rashid.

Rashid looked at Perot. Oh, boy, he thought; what a guy to work for!

They checked in to the Post House hotel near the airport and Perot called Merv Stauffer in Dallas.

'Merv, we have one person here with an Iranian passport and no US visa – you know who I'm talking about.'

'Yes, sir.'

'He has saved American lives and I won't have him hassled when we get to the States.'

'Yes, sir.'

'You know who to call. Just fix it, will you?'

'Yes, sir.'

Sculley woke them all at six a.m. He had to drag Coburn out of bed. Coburn was still suffering the after-effects of Simons's stay-awake pills: ill-tempered and exhausted, he did not care whether he caught the plane or not.

Sculley had organized a bus to take them to Gatwick Airport, a good two-hour journey from Heathrow. As they went out, Keane Taylor, who was struggling with a plastic bin containing some of the dozens of bottles of liquor and cartons of cigarettes he had bought at Istanbul Airport, said: 'Hey, do any of you guys want to help me carry this stuff?'

Nobody said anything. They all got on the bus.

'Screw you, then,' said Taylor, and he gave the whole lot to the hotel doorman.

On the way to Gatwick, they heard over the bus radio that China had invaded North Vietnam. Someone said: 'That'll be our next assignment.'

'Sure,' said Simons. 'We could be dropped between the two armies. No matter which way we fired, we'd be right.'

At the airport, walking behind his men, Perot noticed other people backing away, giving them room, and he suddenly realized how terrible they all looked. Most of them had not had a good wash or a shave for days, and they were dressed in a weird assortment of ill-fitting and very dirty clothes. They probably smelled bad, too.

Perot asked for Braniff's passenger service officer. Braniff was a Dallas airline, and Perot had flown with them to London several times, so most of the staff knew him.

He asked the officer: 'Can I rent the whole of the lounge upstairs in the 747 for my party?'

The officer was staring at the men. Perot knew what he was thinking: Mr Perot's party usually consisted of a few quiet well-dressed businessmen, and now here he was with what looked like a crowd of garage mechanics who had been working on a particularly filthy engine.

The officer said: 'Uh, we can't rent you the lounge,

because of international airline regulations, sir, but I believe if your companions go up into the lounge the rest of our passengers won't disturb you too much.'

Perot saw what he meant.

As Perot boarded, he said to a stewardess: 'I want these men to have anything they want on this plane.'

Perot passed on, and the stewardess turned to her colleague, wide-eyed. 'Who the hell is *he*?'

Her colleague told her.

The movie was *Saturday Night Fever*, but the projector would not work. Boulware was disappointed: he had seen the movie before and he had been looking forward to seeing it again. Instead he sat and chewed the fat with Paul.

Most of the others went up to the lounge. Once again Simons and Coburn stretched out and went to sleep.

Half way across the Atlantic, Keane Taylor, who for the last few weeks had been carrying around anything up to a quarter of a million dollars in cash and handing it out by the fistful, suddenly took it into his head to have an accounting.

He spread a blanket on the floor of the lounge and started collecting money. One by one, the other members of the team came up, fished wads of banknotes out of their pockets, their boots, their hats and their shirtsleeves, and threw the money on the floor.

One or two other first-class passengers had come up to the lounge, despite the unsavoury appearance of Mr Perot's party; but now, when this smelly, villainous-looking crew with their beards and knit caps and dirty boots and go-to-hell coats, spread out several hundred thousand dollars on the floor and started *counting* it, the other passengers vanished.

A few minutes later a stewardess came up to the lounge and approached Perot. 'Some of the passengers are asking whether we should inform the police about your party,' she said. 'Would you come down and reassure them?'

'I'd be glad to.'

Perot went down to the first-class cabin and introduced himself to the passengers in the forward seats. Some of them had heard of him. He began to tell them what had happened to Paul and Bill.

As he talked, other passengers came up to listen. The cabin crew stopped work and stood nearby; then some of the crew from the economy cabin came along. Soon there was a whole crowd.

It began to dawn on Perot that this was a story the world would want to hear.

Upstairs, the team were playing one last trick on Keane Taylor.

While collecting the money Taylor had dropped three bundles of ten thousand dollars each, and Bill had slipped them into his own pocket.

The accounting came out wrong, of course. They all sat around on the floor, Indian fashion, suppressing their laughter, while Taylor counted it all again.

'How can I be thirty thousand dollars out?' Taylor said angrily. 'Damn it, this is all I've got! Maybe I'm not thinking clearly. What the hell is the matter with me?'

At that point Bill came up from downstairs and said: 'What's the problem, Keane?'

'God, we're thirty thousand dollars short, and I don't know what I did with all the rest of the money.'

Bill took the three stacks out of his pocket and said: 'Is this what you're looking for?'

They all laughed uproariously.

'Give me that,' Taylor said angrily. 'Damn it, Gaylord, I wish I'd left you in jail!'

They laughed all the more.

IV

The plane came down towards Dallas.

Ross Perot sat next to Rashid and told him the names of the places they were passing over. Rashid looked out of the window, at the flat brown land and the big wide roads that went straight for miles and miles. America.

Joe Poché had a good feeling. He had felt this way as captain of a rugby club in Minnesota, at the end of a long match when his side had won. The same feeling had come to him when he had returned from Vietnam. He had been part of a good team, he had survived, he had learned a lot, he had grown.

Now all he wanted to make him perfectly happy was some clean underwear.

Ron Davis was sitting next to Jay Coburn. 'Hey, Jay, what'll we do for a living, now?'

Coburn smiled. 'I don't know.'

It would be strange, Davis thought, to sit behind a desk again. He was not sure he liked the idea.

He suddenly remembered that Marva was now three

months pregnant. It would be starting to show. He wondered how she would look, with a bulging tummy.

I know what I need, he thought. I need a coke. In the can. From a machine. In a gas station. And Kentucky Fried Chicken.

Pat Sculley was thinking: no more orange cabs.

Sculley was sitting next to Jim Schwebach: they were together again, the short but deadly duo, having fired not a single shot at anyone during the whole adventure. They had been talking about what EDS could learn from the rescue. The company had projects in other Middle Eastern countries and was pushing into the Far East: should there perhaps be a permanent rescue team, a group of troubleshooters trained and fit and armed and willing to do covert operations in faraway countries? No, they decided: this had been a unique situation. Sculley realized he did not want to spend any more time in primitive countries. In Tehran he had hated the morning trial of squeezing into an orange cab with two or three grumpy people, Persian music blaring from the car radio, and the inevitable quarrel with the driver over the fare. Wherever I work next, he thought, whatever I do, I'm going to ride to the office by myself, in my own car, a big fat American automobile with air-conditioning and soft music. And when I go to the bathroom, instead of squatting over a hole in the damn floor, there will be a clean white American toilet.

As the plane touched down Perot said to him: 'Pat, you'll be last out. I want you to make sure everyone gets through the formalities and deal with any problems.'

'Sure.'

The plane taxied to a halt. The door was opened, and a woman came aboard. 'Where is the man?' she said.

'Here,' said Perot, pointing to Rashid.

Rashid was first off the plane.

Perot thought: Merv Stauffer has all *that* taken care of.

The others disembarked and went through customs.

On the other side, the first person Coburn saw was stocky, bespectacled Merv Stauffer, grinning from ear to ear. Coburn put his arms around Stauffer and hugged him. Stauffer reached into his pocket and pulled out Coburn's wedding ring.

Coburn was touched. He had left the ring with Stauffer for safekeeping. Since then, Stauffer had been the lynch-pin of the whole operation, sitting in Dallas with a phone to his ear making everything happen. Coburn had talked to him almost every day, relaying Simons's orders and demands, receiving information and advice: he knew better than anyone how important Stauffer had been, how they had all just relied on him to do whatever had to be done. Yet, with all that happening, Stauffer had remembered the wedding band.

Coburn slipped it on. He had done a lot of hard thinking about his marriage, during the empty hours in Tehran; but now all that went out of his mind, and he looked forward to seeing Liz.

Merv told him to walk out of the airport and get on a bus which was waiting outside. Coburn followed directions. On the bus he saw Margot Perot. He smiled and shook hands. Then, suddenly, the air was filled with screams of joy, and four wildly excited children threw themselves at him: Kim, Kristi, Scott and Kelly. Coburn laughed out loud and tried to hug them all at the same time.

Liz was standing behind the kids. Gently, Coburn disentangled himself. His eyes filled with tears. He put his arms around his wife, and he could not speak.

When Keane Taylor got on the bus, his wife did not recognize him. Her normally elegant husband was wearing a filthy orange ski jacket and a knitted cap. He had not shaved for a week and he had lost fifteen pounds. He stood in front of her for several seconds, until Liz Coburn said: 'Mary, aren't you going to say hello to Keane?' Then his children, Mike and Dawn, grabbed him.

Today was Taylor's birthday. He was forty-one. It was the happiest birthday of his life.

John Howell saw his wife, Angela, sitting at the front of the bus, behind the driver, with Michael, eleven months, on her lap. The baby was wearing blue jeans and a striped rugby shirt. Howell picked him up and said: 'Hi, Michael, do you remember your Daddy?'

He sat next to Angie and put his arms around her. It was kind of awkward, on the bus seat, and Howell was normally too shy for public displays of affection, but he kept right on hugging her because it felt so good.

Ralph Boulware was met by Mary and the girls, Stacy and Kecia. He picked Kecia up and said: 'Happy birthday!' Everything was as it should be, he thought as he embraced them. He had done what he was supposed to do, and the family was here, where they were supposed to be. He felt like he had proved something, if only to himself. All those years in the Air Force, tinkering with instrumentation or sitting in a plane watching bombs drop, he had never felt his courage was being tested. His relations had medals for ground fighting, but he had always had the uncomfortable feeling that he had an easy role, like the guy in the war movies who slops out the food at breakfast time before the real soldiers go off to fight. He had always wondered whether he had the right stuff. Now he thought about Turkey, and getting stuck in Adana, and driving through the blizzard in that damn sixty-four Chevy, and changing the wheel in Blood Alley with the sons of Mr Fish's cousin; and he thought about Perot's toast, to the men who said what they were going to do then went out and did it; and he knew the answer. Oh, yes. He had the right stuff.

Paul's daughters, Karen and Ann Marie, were wearing matching plaid skirts. Ann Marie, the littlest, got to him first, and he swept her up in his arms and squeezed her tight. Karen was too big to be picked up, but he hugged her just as hard. Behind them was Ruthie, his biggest little girl, all dressed in shades of honey and cream. He kissed her long and hard, then looked at her, smiling. He could not have stopped smiling if he had wanted to. He felt very mellow inside. It was the best feeling he had ever known.

Emily was looking at Bill as if she did not believe he was really there. 'Gosh,' she said lamely, 'it's good to see you again, sweetie.'

The bus went rather quiet as he kissed her. Rachel Schwebach began to cry.

Bill kissed the girls, Vicki, Jackie and Jenny, then he

looked at his son. Chris was very grown-up in a blue suit he had been given for Christmas. Bill had seen that suit before. He remembered a photograph of Chris, standing in front of the Christmas tree in his new suit; that photograph had been above Bill's bunk, in a prison cell, long ago and far away . . .

Emily kept touching him to make sure he was really there. 'You look marvellous,' she said.

Bill knew he looked absolutely terrible. He said: 'I love you.'

Ross Perot got on the bus and said: 'Is everybody here?'

'Not my Dad!' said a plaintive small voice. It was Sean Sculley.

'Don't worry,' said Perot. 'He'll be right out. He's our straight man.'

Pat Sculley had been stopped by a customs agent and asked to open his suitcase. He was carrying all the money, and of course the agent had seen it. Several more agents were summoned, and Sculley was taken into an office to be interrogated.

The agents got out some forms. Sculley began to explain, but they did not want to listen, they only wanted to fill out the form.

'Is the money yours?'

'No, it belongs to EDS.'

'Did you have it when you left the States?'

'Most of it.'

'When and how did you leave the States?'

'A week ago on a private 707.'

'Where did you go?'

'To Istanbul, then to the Iranian border.'

Another man came into the office and said: 'Are you Mr Sculley?'

'Yes.'

'I'm terribly sorry you've been troubled like this. Mr Perot is waiting for you outside.' He turned to the agents. 'You can tear up those forms.'

Sculley smiled and left. He was not in the Middle East any more. This was Dallas, where Perot was Perot.

Sculley got on the bus, and saw Mary, Sean and Jennifer. He hugged and kissed them all, then said: 'What's happening?'

'There's a little reception for you,' said Mary.

The bus started to move, but it did not go far. It stopped again a few yards away at a different gate, and they were all ushered back into the airport and led to a door marked Concorde Room.

As they walked in, a thousand people rose to their feet, cheering and clapping.

Someone had put up a huge banner reading:

JOHN HOWELL
NO. I
DADDY

Jay Coburn was overwhelmed by the size of the crowd and their reaction. What a good idea the buses had been, to give the men a chance to greet their families in private before coming in here. Who had arranged that? Stauffer, of course.

As he walked through the room towards the front, people in the crowd reached over to shake his hand, saying: Good to see you! Welcome back! He smiled and shook hands – there was David Behne, there was Dick Morrison, the faces blurred and the words melted into one big warm hello.

When Paul and Bill walked in with their wives and children, the cheering rose to a roar.

Ross Perot, standing at the front, felt tears come to his eyes. He was more tired than he had ever been in his life, but immensely satisfied. He thought of all the luck and all the coincidences that had made the rescue possible: the fact that he knew Simons, that Simons had been willing to go, that EDS had hired Vietnam veterans, that *they* had been willing to go, that the seventh floor knew how to get things achieved around the world because of their experience with the POW campaign, that T.J. had been able to rent a plane, that the mob had stormed the Gasr Prison . . .

And he thought of all the things that might have gone wrong. He recalled the proverb: success has a thousand fathers, but failure is an orphan. In a few minutes he would stand up and tell these people a little of what had happened and how Paul and Bill were brought home. But it would be hard to put into words the risks that had been taken, the awful cost if the thing had gone bad and ended in the criminal courts or worse. He remembered the day he left Tehran, and how he had superstitiously thought of his luck as sand running through an hourglass. Suddenly, he saw the hourglass again, and all the sand had run out. He grinned to himself, picked up the imaginary glass, and turned it upside down.

Simons bent down and spoke in Perot's ear. 'Remember you offered to pay me?'

Perot would never forget it. When Simons gave you that icy look, you froze. 'I sure do.'

'See this?' said Simons, inclining his head.

Paul was walking towards them, carrying Ann Marie in his arms, through the crowd of cheering friends. 'I see it,' said Perot.

Simons said: 'I just got paid.' He drew on his cigar.

At last the room quietened down, and Perot began to speak. He called Rashid over and put his arm around the young man's shoulders. 'I want you to meet a key member of the rescue team,' he said to the crowd. 'As Colonel Simons said, Rashid only weighs a hundred and forty pounds, but he has five hundred pounds of courage.'

They all laughed and clapped again. Rashid looked around. Many times, many times he had thought about going to America; but in his wildest dreams he had never imagined that his welcome would be like this!

Perot began to tell the story. Listening, Paul felt oddly humble. He was not a hero. The others were the heroes. He was privileged. He belonged with just about the finest bunch of people in the whole world.

Bill looked around the crowd and saw Ron Sperberg, a good friend and a colleague for years. Sperberg was wearing a great big cowboy hat. We're back in Texas, Bill thought. This is the heartland of the USA, the safest place in the world; they can't reach us here. This time, the nightmare is *really* over. We're back. We're safe.

We're home.

EPILOGUE

J AY AND Liz Coburn were divorced. Kristi, the second daughter, the emotional one, chose to live with her father. Coburn was made Manager of Human Resources for EDS Federal. In September 1982 he and Ross Perot Junior became the first men to fly around the world in a helicopter. The aircraft they used is now in the National Air and Space Museum in Washington, DC. It is called *Spirit of Texas*.

Paul became Comptroller of EDS and Bill became Medicaid Marketing Director in the Health Care Division.

Joe Poché, Pat Sculley, Jim Schwebach, Ron Davis and Rashid all continued to work for EDS in various parts of the world. Davis's wife Marva gave birth to a boy, Benjamin, on 18 July 1979.

Keane Taylor was made Country Manager for EDS in the Netherlands, where he was joined by Glenn Jackson. Gayden continued to be head of EDS World and therefore Taylor's boss.

John Howell was made a full partner in Tom Luce's law firm, Hughes and Hill. Angela Howell had another baby, Sarah, on 19 June 1980.

Rich Gallagher left EDS on 1 July 1979. An easterner, he had never quite felt one of the boys at EDS. Lloyd

Briggs and Paul Bucha, two more easterners, left around the same time.

Ralph Boulware also parted company with EDS.

Lulu May Perot, Ross Perot's mother, died on 3 April 1979.

Ross Perot Junior graduated from college and went to work for his father in the autumn of 1981. A year later Nancy Perot did the same. Perot himself just went on making more and more money. His real estate appreciated, his oil company found wells, and EDS won more and bigger contracts. EDS shares, priced around $18 apiece when Paul and Bill were arrested, were worth six times that four years later.

Colonel Simons died on 21 May 1979, after a series of heart attacks. In the last few weeks of his life, his constant companion was Anita Melton, the zany stewardess from the Boeing 707. They had an odd, tragic relationship: they never became lovers in the physical sense, but they were in love. They lived together in the guest cottage at Perot's Dallas house. She taught him to cook, and he started her jogging, timing her with a stopwatch. They held hands a lot. After Simons died, his son Harry and Harry's wife Shawn had a baby boy. They named him Arthur Simons, Junior.

On 4 November 1979 the US Embassy in Tehran was once again overrun by militant Iranians. This time they took hostages. Fifty-two Americans were held prisoner for more than a year. A rescue mission mounted by President Carter came to an ignominious end in the deserts of Central Iran.

But then, Carter did not have the help of Bull Simons.

APPENDIX

IN THE UNITED STATES DISTRICT COURT FOR THE NORTHERN DISTRICT OF TEXAS, DALLAS DIVISION

ELECTRONIC DATA SYSTEMS CORP. IRAN
VS.
SOCIAL SECURITY ORGANIZATION OF THE GOVERNMENT OF IRAN, THE MINISTRY OF HEALTH AND WELFARE OF THE GOVERNMENT OF IRAN, THE GOVT. OF IRAN

NO. CA3–79–218–F

(*Extracts from the Findings of Fact*)

Neither EDSCI nor anyone on its behalf procured the contract unlawfully. No evidence showed bribery of any official or employee of Defendants in order to secure the contract, nor did the evidence suggest the existence of fraud or public corruption in the procurement of the contract . . .

The price of the contract was not exorbitant; rather the evidence showed that the price was reasonable and in accordance with amounts charged by EDS to others for similar services. The price did not compare unfavourably with amounts charged by others in the health care industry for similar services . . .

The failure by SSO and the Ministry to provide written notice of non-acceptance of unpaid invoices was inexcusable and therefore constituted a breach of the contract. The assignment of Dr Towliati to SSO as Deputy Managing Director did not effect such an excuse. I do not find evidence that Dr Towliati's services influenced the process of approval for invoices, nor do I find evidence that Dr Towliati functioned improperly in his review of performance under the contract. Rather, the evidence showed that the Ministry and SSO had full and continuous opportunity to monitor EDSCI's performance. Moreover, I do not find credible evidence of trickery or that EDSCI conspired with anyone to gain wrongful approval for payment of its invoices or to deny the Defendants fair opportunity for their evaluation of EDSCI's performance under the contract . . .

EDSCI did not materially breach its performance obligations under the contract; rather, EDSCI substantially performed in accordance with the description and timing of its duties for each applicable phase up until January 16, 1978, the date of termination of the contract . . .

Recovery under the contract is not barred by Defendant's claims, unsupported by the evidence, that EDSCI procured the contract by fraud, bribery or public corruption. Specifically, the evidence did not demonstrate that EDS' relationship with the Mahvi Group was illegal. EDSCI's execution of and performance under the contract violated no Iranian law . . .

Plantiff introduced a plethora of evidence showing the fact and result of its services: testimony from those who managed and implemented the data processing systems, photographic evidence illustrating aspects of the data preparations functions developed, as well as reports jointly prepared by EDSCI and the Ministry of benefits being realized from the contract. Credible evidence failed to directly rebut this showing . . .

(*Extract from the Final Judgment*)

IT IS ORDERED, ADJUDGED and DECREED that Plaintiff Electronic Data Systems Corporation Iran have and recover of Defendants The Government of Iran, The Social Security Organization of The Government of Iran and the Ministry of Health and Welfare of The Government of Iran, jointly and severally, the sum of fifteen million, one hundred and seventy-seven thousand, four hundred and four dollars ($15,177,404), plus two million, eight hundred and twelve thousand, two hundred and fifty-one dollars ($2,812,251) as prejudgement interest, plus one million, seventy-nine thousand, eight hundred and seventy-five dollars ($1,079,875) as attorneys' fees, plus interest on all such sums at the rate of nine per cent (9%) per annum from the date hereof, plus all costs of suit herein . . .

BIBLIOGRAPHY

Beny, Roloff: *Persia, Bridge of Turquoise* London: Thames and Hudson, 1975

Carter, Jimmy: *Keeping Faith – Memoirs of a President* New York: Bantam, 1982

Forbis, William H: *Fall of the Peacock Throne* New York: Harper & Row, 1980

Ghirshman, R: *Iran* New York: Penguin, 1978

Graham, Robert: *Iran: The Illusion of Power* New York: St Martin's Press, 1980

Helms, Cynthia: *An Ambassador's Wife in Iran* New York: Dodd, Mead, 1981

Keddie, Nikki R. and Richard Tann: *Roots of Revolution* New Haven: Yale University Press, 1981

Ledeen, Michael and William Lewis: *Debacle: The American Failure in Iran* New York: Knopf, 1981

Maheu, René and Bruno Barbey: *Iran* Paris: Editions J. A., 1976

Pahlavi, Mohammed Reza: *Answer to History* New York: Stein & Day, 1980

Roosevelt, Kermit: *Countercoup: The Struggle for the Control of Iran* New York: McGraw-Hill, 1979

Schemmer, Benjamin F: *The Raid* New York: Harper & Row, 1976

Stempel, John D: *Inside the Iranian Revolution* Blooming-
    ton: Indiana University Press, 1981
Sullivan, William H: *Mission to Iran* New York: Norton,
    1981